The Arabian
Nights

THE ARABIAN NIGHTS

TALES FROM A THOUSAND AND ONE NIGHTS

*Translated, with a Preface and Notes,
by Sir Richard F. Burton*

Introduction by A. S. Byatt

THE MODERN LIBRARY

NEW YORK

2004 Modern Library Mass Market Edition

A trade paperback edition of this work was originally published by Modern Library, an imprint of The Random House Publishing Group, a division of Random House, Inc., in 2001.

LIBRARY OF CONGRESS CATALOGING-IN-PUBLICATION DATA
Arabian nights. English. Selections.
The Arabian nights: tales from a thousand and one nights / [translation and notes by] Sir Richard Francis Burton.
p.   cm.
ISBN 0-8129-7214-7
I. Burton, Richard Francis, Sir, 1821–1890. II. Title.
PJ7716.A1 B87   2001
398.22–dc21   00-47066

Modern Library website address: www.modernlibrary.com

Printed in the United States of America

2 4 6 8 9 7 5 3 1

RICHARD F. BURTON

Richard Francis Burton, the Victorian explorer, linguist, and writer best remembered today for his translation of *The Arabian Nights*, was born in Torquay, Devon, on March 19, 1821. Descended from prosperous provincial gentry, he experienced an exotic and nomadic childhood. In 1822 Burton's father, a onetime lieutenant colonel in the British army, moved the family to Beauséjour, a small château in the Loire valley. During the 1830s they wandered throughout France and Italy, returning to England for short visits. As a child Burton displayed his talent for languages, and was fluent in Greek and Latin as well as Italian and French before entering Trinity College, Oxford, in 1840 to prepare for a career in the Anglican church. He was expelled in 1842 for misbehavior and sailed to India with a commission in the Bombay Army, a military branch of the East India Company.

Burton spent the next seven years in the northern province of Sind as a field surveyor and intelligence officer, often disguising himself as a Muslim merchant. He mastered a dozen Oriental languages, including Arabic, Hindustani, and numerous other Indian languages, and absorbed everything he could about Indian culture.

In 1850 he left India for Boulogne, France, where he wrote three books about his experiences in India that endure as compelling contributions to ethnology: *Goa, and the Blue Mountains; Scinde, or, The Unhappy Valley;* and *Sindh, and the Races that Inhabit the Valley of the Indus.*

In 1853, disguised as an Afghani physician, he traveled to Medina and Mecca where he visited and sketched at great risk the sacred shrines of Islam forbidden to non-Muslims. *Personal Narrative of a Pilgrimage to El-Medinah and Mecca* (1855–1856), an encyclopedic look at the Islamic world, is widely considered his most important travelogue.

Though this book brought him acclaim in England, Burton then set off on an expedition through Ethiopia and Somaliland to the forbidden city of Harer, the citadel of Muslim learning; he was the first European to enter and leave the city without being executed. *First Footsteps in East Africa* (1856) records this adventure. Following a brief tour of duty in the Crimean War, Burton and John Speke set out from Zanzibar in 1857 in an attempt to locate the source of the Nile. *The Lake Regions of Central Africa* (1860) chronicles the two-year expedition that resulted in the discovery of Lake Tanganyika.

In 1860 he traveled across the United States to Salt Lake City. *The City of the Saints* (1861) describes the Mormon Church and offers a portrait of its leader, Brigham Young.

In 1861 Burton married Isabel Arundell, a devout Roman Catholic, and joined the British Foreign Office. Assigned to a minor consular post in Fernando Póo, a desolate island off the coast of present-day Cameroon, he studied the ethnology of native tribes and accumulated notes for four books: *Wanderings in West Africa* (1863), *Abeokuta and the Cameroons Mountains* (1863), *A Mission to Gelele, King of Dahome* (1864), and *Two Trips to Gorilla Land and the Cataracts of the Congo* (1876). While on subsequent diplomatic assignments in São Paulo, Brazil (1864–1869), and Damascus, Syria (1869–1871), he wrote *The Highlands of Brazil* (1869),

Letters from the Battle-fields of Paraguay (1870), and *Unexplored Syria* (1871).

Burton spent his final years in the quiet consulship at Trieste, Italy. Bored by official duties, he indulged in two final adventures: gold-mining expeditions to Egypt (1876–1880) and West Africa (1881–1882) that resulted in *The Gold Mines of Midian* (1878) and *To the Gold Coast for Gold* (1883). During this time he also wrote *The Kasîdah* (1880), an elegiac poem fashioned after *The Rubáiyát of Omar Khayyám*. In addition he translated Latin poems by Catullus; several works of Italian literature; and two classics of Indian erotica, the *Kama Sutra of Vatsyayana* (1883) and the *Ananga Ranga* (1885); as well as an Arabian treatise on sexuality, *The Perfumed Garden of Cheikh Nefzaoui* (1886).

In 1884 Burton began to rework and organize his translation of *The Arabian Nights*, a project undertaken in India some three decades earlier. Published in sixteen volumes over the next three years, it was both a critical and financial success. "*The Arabian Nights* is more generally loved than Shakespeare," wrote Robert Louis Stevenson. "No human face or voice greets us among [this] crowd of kings and genies, sorcerers and beggarmen. Adventure, on the most naked terms, furnishes forth the entertainment and is found enough." In 1886 Burton received a knighthood, an honor many considered long overdue, and two years later he brought out *Supplemental Nights*, a continuation of his masterpiece.

Captain Sir Richard Burton died in Trieste on October 20, 1890. Alarmed by the sexually explicit content of her husband's papers, Isabel Burton burned almost all of his notes, diaries, and manuscripts—an immeasurable loss to history. Only a handful of Burton's works appeared posthumously, notably *The Jew, the Gypsy, and El Islam* (1898) and *Wanderings in Three Continents* (1901).

CONTENTS

INTRODUCTION

A. S. Byatt

The collection of stories known as the Thousand and One Nights is in itself a symbol for infinity. The title comes from the Arabic, *Alf Layla wa Layla*, "a thousand nights and one night" and the addition of the extra "one" to the round thousand both suggests a way to mathematical infinity—you can always add one more to any number—and produces a circular, mirrorlike figure, 1001. The original collection has no one author and no one source. The stories are Indian, Persian, and Arabic, and were told in many forms many centuries before they were written down. In the tenth century a Persian collection, *Hazar Afsana* (a thousand legends), was known by Arab writers, and tales can be traced back to the *Panchatantra* (Five Books) in Sanskrit—sixth century or earlier—and the *Katha Sarit Sagara*, translated and published by C. H. Tawney (1880–1884) and republished in 1928 as *The Ocean of Story*. As Robert Irwin remarks in his indispensable *The Arabian Nights: A Companion*, quoting a mediaeval Dutch proverb, "Big fish eat little fish"—story collections tend to swallow, digest, and transmute each other. This image of container and contained in the Nights is also an infinity symbol. A character in a story invokes a character who tells a story about a character who has a story to tell. . . . Everything proliferates. The *Nights* is a maze, a web, a network, a river with infinite tributaries, a series of boxes within boxes, a bottomless pool. It turns endlessly on itself, a story about storytelling. And yet we feel it has to do with our essential nature, and not just a need for idle entertainment.

The "frame story," the tale of the angry king Shahriyar who avenged his first wife's adultery by marrying virgins and beheading them the morning after their defloration, is a deeply satisfying image of the relations between life, death, and storytelling. The wise Scheherazade saves her own life, and those of the remaining virgins of the kingdom, by telling the king (and her sister Dunyazad) a thousand and one interwoven stories, which are always unfinished at dawn—so deferring the execution daily—and enchanting. Human beings tell stories—in bars, in novels, in courtship, in genealogies—because we are finite biological creatures. We live in biological time, and we have beginnings, middles, and ends. Scheherazade keeps her own life going by telling other lives and deaths—and prolongs it long enough to bear the king three sons and extend both their lifelines into another generation. The *Nights* contain all sorts of stories, from high magic to coarse humour about farts, from jokes to disasters. Sir Richard Burton, the translator of the present selection, wrote of the magical elements: "Every man at some term or turn of his life has longed for the supernatural powers and a glimpse of Wonderland. Here he is in the midst of it. Here he sees mighty spirits summoned to work the human mite's will, however whimsical, who can transport him in an eye-twinkling whithersoever he wishes; who can ruin cities and build palaces of gold and silver, gems and jacinths. . . ." Genies are immortal beings, who can break the ineluctable rules of time and space in which humans are trapped. Scheherazade's story is the human one of birth, sex, and the fear of death. But the genes, like the genies, are potentially immortal, and carry language and the imagination from generation to generation, like the infinitely renewed, metamorphosing life of the Nights. Biology and language make stories.

One of the forms of transmutation and transmission is of course translation. The West met the Arabian Nights in the eighteenth-century French translation of Antoine Galland (1646–1715). It is, as both Irwin and Borges in his wonderful essay on the translators of the Nights point out, Galland who is responsible for the European passion for oriental Tales, and Galland whom everyone read. He worked from a manuscript now in the Bibliothèque Nationale in Paris, which is by chance the oldest extant manuscript. But he introduced tales from many other sources, oral and written, and his versions of such favourites as Aladdin and Ali Baba are the oldest extant versions—Arabic versions turn out to be translations from Galland. There are other powerful translations, both French and English. Edward William Lane's 1838–41 translation was bowdlerised to suit the sensitivities of nineteenth-century families. John Payne's 1882–84 version was printed by the Villon Society partly out of fear of prosecution for obscenity. He later worked with Burton. Joseph Charles Mardrus produced a French sixteen-volume translation in 1899 to 1904, admired by Proust and embroidered in the manner of French decadence, which was translated by Powys Mathers in 1923. Mardrus's French is spirited; his scholarship has been called in question. Husain Haddawy has recently produced a scholarly and elegant translation of parts of the Nights, but the most accessible complete translation remains Burton's extraordinary translation, eventually running to sixteen volumes with an immense apparatus of extraordinary footnotes, which appeared first in 1885 (the first ten volumes) with the supplementary volumes in 1886 to 1888.

Sir Richard Burton was one of those Victorians whose energy and achievements make any modern man quail. He lived like one of his own heroes, travelling in Goa, Equatorial Africa, Brazil, India, and the Middle East. He took part in the Crimean war. He went with J. H. Speke to find the source of the Nile and discovered Lake Tanganyika.

He disguised himself as an Afghan dervish and doctor and went on pilgrimage to the sacred cities of Mecca and Medina—a journey where unmasking would have cost him his life. He wrote books on swordsmanship and geology. According to Borges he dreamed in seventeen languages and spoke thirty-five—other sources say forty. He was an expert in erotica and his learned footnotes cover pederasty, lesbianism in harems, as well as medicine, cookery, law, and many other subjects. This life summary omits much more than it lists. He knew, and half believed, the Middle Eastern superstitious belief that no one can reach the last of the nights without falling dead. His wife, Isabel, tried to bowdlerize the Nights in his lifetime, and—"sorrowfully, reverently," according to herself—burned the manuscript of his erotic legacy, *The Scented Garden,* after his death.

Burton's style as a translator has had both admirers and detractors. Robert Irwin claims that its heavy-handedness made him want to slit his throat. He tried to invent an English version of mediaeval Arabic, drawing on Chaucer, Elizabethan English, and Sir Thomas Urquhart's 1653 translation of the first three books of Rabelais's *Gargantua and Pantagruel.* Irwin lists colorful colloquialisms that Burton took over from Urquhart—"Close-buttock game," "the two-backed beast," "springal," "shite-a-bed," "tosspot," and "looby." Burton was a great creator of new words of his own too. In the present selection a good example would be in the "Tale of the Porter and the Three Ladies," describing the "lady bright of blee, with brow beaming brilliancy, the dream of philosophy, whose eyes were fraught with Babel's gramarye and her eyebrows were arched as for archery"—which shows his delight in archaisms, alliteration, internal rhyme, and decoration all at once. But his ingenuity is often energetic and lively—"the tom-toming of the kettle-drum and tantara of trumpets and clash of cymbals" or the shepherd on page 213 whose flesh "shuddered . . . with horripilation" at the sight of an angel disguised as a tempting woman. Borges admired Burton—both in his fidelity and in his infidelity to the variegated originals—as he admired Galland and Mardrus, for remaking the Tales, as he put it, *in the wake of a literature.* (Borges's italics.) Tales are shape-shifters, self-renewing. Burton combines many readings and many writings, and something of his own fierce dynamism and elaborate intricacy.

Eastern and Western literature contain other related collections of interlinked tales—Ovid's *Metamorphoses,* Chaucer's *Canterbury Tales,* and Boccaccio's *Decameron,* whose frame story has its characters defying the Black Death by retreating to the country and telling tales. A direct descendant of the Nights is *The Saragossa Manuscript,* written by the Polish Jan Potocki between 1797 and 1815. Potocki was a Knight of Malta, a linguist and an occultist—his tales, set in Spain in 1739, are dizzily interlinked at many levels—ghouls, politics, rationalism, ghosts, necromancy, tale within tale within tale. He spent time searching vainly for a manuscript of the Nights in Morocco, and shot himself with a silver bullet made from a teapot lid in Poland. Out of such works came nineteenth-century Gothic fantasy, and the intricate, paranoid nightmare plottings of such story webs as *The Crying of Lot 49* or Lawrence Norfolk's *Lemprière's Dictionary.* Collections of tales talk to each other and borrow from each other, motifs glide from culture to culture, century to century.

—

Scheherazade's tales have lived on, like germ cells, in many literatures. In British Romantic poetry the Arabian Nights stood for the wonderful against the mundane, the imaginative against the prosaically and reductively rational. Coleridge said his mind had been "habituated to the vast" by his early reading of "Romances, & Relations of Giants & Magicians, & Genii." He used the tale of the angry and vengeful Djinn whose invisible child had been killed by a thrown date stone, as an example of pure chance or fate. Wordsworth, in the fifth book of the Prelude, describes his childhood treasure, "a little yellow, canvas-covered book, / A slender abstract of the Arabian tales" and the "promise scarcely earthly" of his discovery that there were four

large volumes of the work. Dreamers and forgers of law-
less tales, he says, confer visionary power. Earlier in Book
V he tells of a dream encounter with a strange figure on a
dromedary, who seems to be both Don Quixote and "an
Arab of the desert too," who carries a stone and a shell,
which are also "both books"—one Euclid's Elements and
the other a prophetic poem. The Arab is saving the "books"
from "the fleet waters of a drowning world"—the final
Deluge close at hand. Wordsworth has compressed two
great collections of tales in a dream pun, an Arabian Knight,
saving geometry and poetry from destruction. Again, the
Tales stand against death. And Dickens, who became the
master of serial narration and endless beginnings, comforted his lonely and miserable childhood with the Arabian Nights, living in their world, and learning their craft.

———

Various Western writers have been tempted to write the
Thousand-and-second Tale, including the American Edgar
Allan Poe and the Viennese Joseph Roth. Roth's tale of the
decadent days of the Austrian Empire, the border between
East and West, is full of furtive and voluptuous sex, sly
analysis of the operations of authorities, substitutions of
women, vanishing jewels. Poe's Scheherazade makes the
mistake of telling her ageing husband about modern marvels like steamships, radio, and telegraphs. He finds these
true tales so incredible that he concludes that she has lost
her touch and has her strangled after all. Poe is a combat-
ive and irreverent Yankee at the Persian court. John Barth,
in his "Dunyazadiad," appears in person as a balding be-
spectacled genie who tells the nervous Scheherazade the
tales she will tell because he has read them in the future
and she is his heroine—thus creating another false eternity, a circular time loop, in which storytellers hand on stories of storytellers. . . .

———

Then there are the modern oriental fabulists, Naguib
Mahfouz and Salman Rushdie, both threatened with death
for storytelling. Mahfouz's *Arabian Nights and Days* is a col-

lection of magical tales, with a political edge and a spiritual depth. His stories rework the Nights; his Shahriyar slowly learns about justice and mercy, the Angel of Death is a bric-a-brac merchant, and genies play tricks with fate. Salman Rushdie's narratives are all intertwined with the storytelling of the Nights. *Haroun and the Sea of Stories* pits a resourceful child, Haroun, against the evil Khattam-Shud who wants to drain the Ocean of the Streams of Story, which are alive, and replace it with silence and darkness. Rushdie's tale, like Scheherazade's, equates storytelling with life, but his characters and wit owe as much to Western fantasies, to *Alice in Wonderland* and the *Wizard of Oz*, as they do to the ancient Ocean of Stories or the Thousand and One Nights. Another cross-fertilization, another conversation.

———

Rushdie's Sea of Stories is "the biggest library in the universe." Jorge Luis Borges, to whom libraries, labyrinths, and books were all images of infinity, wrote in "The Garden of Forking Paths" of "that night which is at the middle of the Thousand and One Nights when Scheherazade (through a magical oversight of the copyist) begins to relate word for word the story of the Thousand and one Nights, establishing the risk of coming once again to the night when she must repeat it, and thus on to infinity." This circular tale fascinated Italo Calvino (who failed to find the episode in any translation of the Nights). Calvino's own marvellous *If on a Winter's Night a Traveler* is the endless tale of a lost Reader who keeps beginning books only to find the rest is missing, and the replacement copy turns out to be always another, quite different beginning. This novel contains a novelist, as Borges's tale contains Scheherazade within Scheherazade, who wants to write a book that will contain only the pure pleasure of anticipation of the beginning, "a book that is only an incipit," a book with no ending, perhaps like the Arabian Nights.

Marcel Proust saw himself as Scheherazade, in relation to both sex and death. He describes his Narrator's ingenious excuses for not accompanying Albertine on her little expeditions as an exercise of ingenuity greater than Scheherazade's. Albertine, however, is the one of the pair who is "insatiable for movement and life." The narrator remarks gloomily that unfortunately, whilst the "Persian storyteller" put off her death with her ingenuity, he was hastening his own. And at the end of the almost endless novel, he writes a triumphant meditation on the love of death, the sense of the presence of death, which drives him to create his great and comprehensive book, the book of his life. At one point he even personifies this presence of death as *"le sultan Sheriar"* who might or might not put a dawn end to the nocturnal writing of what could not be the Thousand and One Nights he had so loved as a child. As a child, "superstitiously attached to books I loved, as to my loves, I could not without horror imagine a work which would be different." But he has learned that one can only remake what one loves by renouncing it. "It will be a book as long as the Thousand and One Nights, but quite other." Malcolm Bowie, in his excellent *Proust Among the Stars,* comments that "the big book of death-defying stories" with which Proust's novel compares itself is not Boccaccio's *Decameron,* in which death appears as a "horrifying initial trigger to tale-telling" but the Nights, "where stories are life." "Narrate or die," for Proust's narrator as for Scheherazade is the imperative. "By mere sentences placed end on end, one's sentence is commuted for a while, and the end is postponed."

—

The Judaeo-Christian culture is founded on a linear narrative in time. It moves forward from creation through history, to redemption in the Christian case, at one point in time, and looks forward to the promised end, when time and death will cease to be. The great novels of Western culture, from *Don Quixote* to *War and Peace,* from *Moby-Dick* to *Dr. Faustus,* were constructed in the shadow of the one Book and its story. People are excited by millennial events as images of beginnings and endings. There is a difference between these great, portentous histories and the proliferation of small tales that are handed on, like gifts, like objects for delight and contemplation. Storytellers like Calvino and Scheherazade can offer readers and listeners an infinity of incipits, an illusion of inexhaustibility. Calvino's imaginary novelist sits and stares at a cartoon of Snoopy, sitting at a typewriter, with the caption "It was a dark and stormy night . . . ," the beginning of a circular shaggy dog story. Both cartoons and soap operas are versions of Scheherazade's tale-telling, worlds in which death and endings are put off indefinitely—and age too, in the case of Charlie Brown. High modernism escaped time with epiphanic visions of timeless moments, imagined infinities which have always seemed to me strained, not in the end offering any counter to fear and death. But the small artifices of elegant, well-made tales and the vulgar satisfaction of narrative curiosity do stand against death. The romantic novelist Georgette Heyer kept few fan letters, but I saw two—one from a man, who had laughed at one of her comic fops on the trolley going to a life-threatening operation, and one from a Polish woman, who had kept her fellow prisoners alive during the war by reciting, night after night, a Heyer novel she knew by heart.

———

During the bombardment of Sarajevo in 1994 a group of theater workers in Amsterdam commissioned tales, from different European writers, to be read aloud, simultaneously, in theaters in Sarajevo itself and all over Europe, every Friday until the fighting ended. This project pitted storytelling against destruction, imaginative life against real death. It may not have saved lives but it was a form of living energy. It looked back to the 1001 Nights and forward to the millennium. It was called Scheherazade 2001.

Published as "Narrate or Die: Why Scheherazade Keeps on Talking," The New York Times Magazine, *April 18, 1999.*

A. S. BYATT is a novelist and short-story writer who also has published essays and reviews, and works in radio and television. Until 1983, she taught English and American literature at University College, London. Her novels include the Booker Prize–winning *Possession*, which is available in a Modern Library clothbound edition, and the quartet *The Virgin in the Garden, Still Life, Babel Tower,* and *A Whistling Woman.* Her short-story collections include *Elementals, The Djinn in the Nightingale's Eye,* and *The Matisse Stories.*

Preface

This work, laborious as it may appear, has been to me a labour of love, an unfailing source of solace and satisfaction. During my long years of official banishment to the luxuriant and deadly deserts of Western Africa, and to the dull and dreary half-clearings of South America, it proved itself a charm, a talisman against ennui and despondency. Impossible even to open the pages without a vision starting into view; without drawing a picture from the pinacothek of the brain; without reviving a host of memories and reminiscences which are not the common property of travellers, however widely they may have travelled. From my dull and commonplace and "respectable" surroundings, the Jinn bore me at once to the land of my predilection, Arabia, a region so familiar to my mind that even at first sight, it seemed a reminiscence of some by-gone metempsychic life in the distant Past. Again I stood under the diaphanous skies, in air glorious as ether, whose every breath raises men's spirits like sparkling wine. Once more I saw the evening star hanging like a solitaire from the pure front of the western firmament; and the after-glow transfiguring and transforming, as by magic, the homely and rugged features of the scene into a fairy-land lit with a light which never shines on other soils or seas. Then would appear the woollen tents, low and black, of the true Badawin, mere dots in the boundless waste of lion-tawny clays and gazelle-brown gravels, and the camp-fire dotting like a glow-worm the village centre. Presently, sweetened by distance, would be heard the wild weird song of lads and lasses, driving or rather pelting, through the gloaming their sheep and goats; and the measured chant of the spearsmen gravely stalking behind their charge, the camels; mingled with the bleating of the flocks and the bellowing of the humpy herds; while the reremouse flitted overhead with his tiny shriek, and the rave of the jackal resounded through deepening glooms, and—most musical of music—the palm-trees answered the whispers of the night-breeze with the softest tones of falling water.

And then a shift of scene. The Shaykhs and "white-beards" of the tribe gravely take their places, sitting with outspread skirts like hillocks on the plain, as the Arabs say, around the camp-fire, whilst I reward their hospitality and secure its continuance by reading or reciting a few pages of their favourite tales. The women and children stand motionless as silhouettes outside the ring; and all are breathless with attention; they seem to drink in the words with eyes and mouths as well as with ears. The most fantastic flights of fancy, the wildest improbabilities, the most impossible of impossibilities, appear to them utterly natural, mere matters of every-day occurrence. They enter thoroughly into each phase of feeling touched upon by the author: they take a personal pride in the chivalrous nature and knightly prowess of Taj al-Mulúk; they are touched with tenderness by the self-sacrificing love of Azízah; their mouths water as they hear of heaps of untold gold given away in largess like clay; they chuckle with delight every time a Kázi or Fakír—a judge or a reverend—is scurvily entreated by some Pantagruelist of the Wilderness; and, despite their normal solemnity and impassibility, all roar with laughter, sometimes rolling upon the ground till the reader's gravity is sorely tried, at the tales of the garrulous Barber and of Ali and the Kurdish Sharper. To this magnetizing mood the sole exception is when a Badawi of superior accomplishments, who sometimes says his prayers, ejaculates a startling "Astaghfaru'llah"—I pray Allah's pardon!—for listening, not to Carlyle's "downright lies," but to light mention of the sex whose name is never heard amongst the nobility of the Desert.

Nor was it only in Arabia that the immortal Nights did me such notable service: I found the wildlings of Somaliland equally amenable to its discipline; no one was deaf to the charm and the two women-cooks of my caravan, on its way to Harar, were incontinently dubbed by my men "Shahrazad" and "Dinazad."

It may be permitted me also to note that this translation is a natural outcome of my Pilgrimage to Al-Medinah and Meccah. Arriving at Aden in the (so-called) winter of 1852, I put up with my old and dear friend, Steinhaeuser; and, when talking over Arabia and the Arabs, we at once came to the same conclusion that, while the name of this wondrous treasury of Moslem folklore is familiar to almost every English child, no general reader is aware of the valuables it contains, nor indeed will the door open to any but Arabists. Before parting we agreed to "collaborate" and produce a full, complete, unvarnished, uncastrated copy of the great original, my friend taking the prose and I the metrical part; and we corresponded upon the subject for years. But whilst I was in the Brazil, Steinhaeuser died suddenly of apoplexy at Berne in Switzerland and, after the fashion of Anglo-India, his valuable MSS. left at Aden were dispersed, and very little of his labours came into my hands.

Thus I was left alone to my work, which progressed fitfully amid a host of obstructions. At length, in the spring of 1879, the tedious process of copying began and the book commenced to take finished form. But, during the winter of 1881–82, I saw in the literary journals a notice of a new version by Mr. John Payne, well known to scholars for his prowess in English verse, especially for his translation of *The Poems of Master Francis Villon, of Paris.* Being then engaged on an expedition to the Gold Coast (for gold), which seemed likely to cover some months, I wrote to the *Athenæum* (Nov. 13, 1881) and to Mr. Payne, who was wholly unconscious that we were engaged on the same work, and freely offered him precedence and possession of the field till no longer wanted. He accepted my offer as frankly, and his priority entailed another delay lasting till the spring of 1885. These details will partly account for the lateness of my appearing, but there is yet another cause. Professional ambition suggested that literary labours, unpopular with the vulgar and the half-educated, are not likely to help a man up the ladder of promotion. But common sense presently suggested to me that, professionally speaking, I was not a success; and, at the same time, that I had no cause to be ashamed of my failure. In our day, when we live under a despotism of the lower "middle-class" Philister who can pardon anything but superiority, the prizes of competitive services are monopolized by certain "pets" of the *Médiocratie,* and prime favourites of that jealous and potent majority—the Mediocrities who know "no nonsense about merit." It is hard for an outsider to realize how perfect is the monopoly of commonplace, and to comprehend how fatal a stumbling-stone that man sets in the way of his own advancement who dares to think for himself, or who knows more or who does more than the mob of gentlemen-employés who know very little and who do even less.

Yet, however behindhand I may be, there is still ample room and verge for an English version of the *Arabian Nights' Entertainments.*

Our century of translations, popular and vernacular, from (Professor Antoine) Galland's delightful abbreviation and adaptation (A.D. 1704), in no wise represent the eastern original. The best and latest, the Rev. Mr. Foster's, which is diffuse and verbose, and Mr. G. Moir Bussey's, which is a re-correction, abound in gallicisms of style and idiom; and one and all degrade a chef-d'œuvre of the highest anthropological and ethnographical interest and importance to a mere fairy-book, a nice present for little boys.

After nearly a century had elapsed, Dr. Jonathan Scott (LL.D. H.E.I.C.'s S., Persian Secretary to the G. G. Bengal; Oriental Professor, etc., etc.), printed his *Tales, Anecdotes, and Letters, translated from the Arabic and Persian* (Cadell and Davies, London, A.D. 1800); and followed in 1811 with an edition of *The Arabian Nights' Entertainments* from the MS. of Edward Wortley Montague (in 6 vols., small 8vo, London: Longmans, etc.). This work he (and he only) describes as "Carefully revised and occasionally corrected from the Arabic." The reading public did not wholly reject it, sundry texts were founded upon the Scott version and it has been imperfectly reprinted (4 vols., 8vo, Nimmo and Bain, London, 1883). But most men, little recking what a small portion of the original they were reading, satisfied themselves with the Anglo-French epitome and metaphrase. At length in 1838, Mr. Henry Torrens, B.A., Irishman, lawyer ("of the Inner Temple") and Bengal Civilian, took a step in the right direction; and began to translate, *The Book of the Thousand Nights and One Night* (1 vol., 8vo, Calcutta: W. Thacker and Co.) from the Arabic of the Ægyptian (!) MS. edited by Mr. (afterwards Sir) William H. Macnaghten. The attempt, or rather the intention, was highly creditable; the copy was carefully moulded upon the model and offered the best example of the *verbatim et literatim* style. But the plucky author knew little of Arabic, and least of what is most wanted, the dialect of Egypt and Syria. His prose is so conscientious as to offer up spirit at the shrine of letter; and his verse, always whimsical, has at times a manner of Hibernian whoop which is comical when it should be pathetic. Lastly he printed only one volume of a series which completed would have contained nine or ten.

That amiable and devoted Arabist, the late Edward William Lane, does not score a success in his *New Translation of the Tales of a Thousand and One Nights* (London: Charles Knight and Co., 1839), of which there have been four English editions, besides American, two edited by

E. S. Poole. He chose the abbreviating Bulak Edition; and, of its two hundred tales, he has omitted about half and by far the more characteristic half: the work was intended for "the drawing-room table"; and, consequently, the work-man was compelled to avoid the "objectionable" and aught "approaching to licentiousness." He converts the Arabian Nights into the Arabian Chapters, arbitrarily changing the division and, worse still, he converts some chapters into notes. He renders poetry by prose and apologizes for not omitting it altogether: he neglects assonance and he is at once too Oriental and not Oriental enough. He had small store of Arabic at the time—Lane of the Nights is not Lane of the Dictionary—and his pages are disfigured by many childish mistakes. Worst of all, the three handsome volumes are rendered unreadable as Sale's Koran by their anglicized Latin, their sesquipedalian un-English words, and the stiff and stilted style of half a century ago when our prose was, perhaps, the worst in Europe. Their cargo of Moslem learning was most valuable to the student, but utterly out of place for readers of The Nights; re-published, as these notes have been separately (London: Chatto, 1883), they are an ethnological textbook.

Mr. John Payne has printed, for the Villon Society and for private circulation only, the first and sole complete translation of the great compendium, "comprising about four times as much matter as that of Galland, and three times as much as that of any other translator"; and I cannot but feel proud that he has honoured me with the dedication of *The Book of The Thousand Nights and One Night*. His version is most readable: his English, with a sub-flavour of the Mabinogionic archaicism, is admirable; and his style gives life and light to the nine volumes whose matter is frequently heavy enough. He succeeds admirably in the most difficult passages and he often hits upon choice and special terms and the exact vernacular equivalent of the foreign word, so happily and so picturesquely that all future trans-lators must perforce use the same expression under pain of falling far short. But the learned and versatile author bound himself to issue only five hundred copies, and "not to reproduce the work in its complete and uncastrated form." Consequently his excellent version is caviar to the general—practically unprocurable.

And here I hasten to confess that ample use has been made of the three versions above noted, the whole being blended by a *callida junctura* into a homogeneous mass. But in the presence of so many predecessors a writer is bound to show some *raison d'être* for making a fresh attempt and this I proceed to do with due reserve.

Briefly, the object of this version is to show what *The Thousand Nights and a Night* really is. Not, however, for reasons to be more fully stated in the Terminal Essay, by straining *verbum reddere verbo*, but by writing as the Arab would have written in English. On this point I am all with Saint Jerome (Pref. in Jobum) "Vel verbum e verbo, vel sensum e sensu, vel ex utroque commixtum, et medie temperatum genus translationis." My work claims to be a faithful copy of the great Eastern Saga-book, by preserving intact, not only the spirit, but even the *mécanique*, the manner and the matter. Hence, however prosy and long-drawn out be the formula, it retains the scheme of The Nights because they are a prime feature in the original. The Ráwí or reciter, to whose wits the task of supplying details is left, well knows their value: the openings carefully repeat the names of the *dramatis personæ* and thus fix them in the hearer's memory. Without the Nights no Arabian Nights! Moreover it is necessary to retain the whole apparatus: nothing more ill-advised than Dr. Jonathan Scott's strange device of garnishing The Nights with fancy head-pieces and tail-pieces or the splitting-up of Galland's narrative by merely prefixing "Nuit," etc., ending moreover, with the 234th Night: yet this has been done, apparently with the consent of the great Arabist Sylvestre de Sacy (Paris: Ernest Bourdin). Moreover, holding that the translator's glory is to add something to his native tongue, while avoiding the hideous hag-like nakedness of Torrens and the bald literalism of Lane, I have carefully Englished the picturesque turns and novel expressions of the original in all their outlandishness; for instance, when the dust-cloud raised by a tramping host is described as "walling the horizon." Hence peculiar attention has been paid to the tropes and figures which the Arabic language often packs into a single term; and I have never hesitated to coin a word when wanted, such as "she snorted and snarked," fully to represent the original. These, like many in Rabelais, are mere barbarisms unless generally adopted; in which case they become civilized and common currency.

Despite objections manifold and manifest, I have preserved the balance of sentences and the prose rhyme and rhythm which Easterns look upon as mere music. This "Saj'a," or cadence of the cooing dove, has in Arabic its special duties. It adds a sparkle to description and a point to proverb, epigram and dialogue; it corresponds with our "artful alliteration" (which in places I have substituted for it) and, generally, it defines the boundaries between the classical and the popular styles which jostle each other in The Nights. If at times it appear strained and forced, after the wont of rhymed prose, the scholar will observe that, despite the immense copiousness of assonants and consonants in Arabic, the strain is often put upon it intentionally, like the *Rims cars* of Dante and the Troubadours. This rhymed prose may be "un-English" and unpleasant, even irritating to the British ear; still I look upon it as a *sine quâ non* for a complete reproduction of the original. In the Terminal Essay I shall revert to the subject.

On the other hand when treating the versical portion, which may represent a total of ten thousand lines, I have not always bound myself by the metrical bonds of the Arabic, which are artificial in the extreme, and which in English can be made bearable only by a *tour de force*. I allude especially to the monorhyme, *Rim continuat* or *tirade monorime,* whose monotonous simplicity was preferred by the Troubadours for threnodies. It may serve well for three or four couplets but, when it extends, as in the Ghazal-canzon, to eighteen, and in the Kasidah, elegy or ode, to more, it must either satisfy itself with banal rhyme-words, when the assonants should as a rule be expressive and emphatic; or, it must display an ingenuity, a smell of the oil, which assuredly does not add to the reader's pleasure. It can perhaps be done and it should be done; but for me the task offers no attractions: I feel able to fence better in shoes than in sabots.

And now to consider one matter of special importance in the book—its *turpiloquium*. This stumbling-block is of two kinds, completely distinct. One is the simple, naïve and child-like indecency which, from Tangiers to Japan, occurs throughout general conversation of high and low in the present day. It uses, like the holy books of the Hebrews, expressions "plainly descriptive of natural situations"; and it treats in an unconventionally free and naked manner of subjects and matters which are usually, by common consent, left undescribed. As Sir William Jones observed long ago, "that anything natural can be offensively obscene never seems to have occurred to the Indians or to their legislators; a singularity (?) pervading their writings and conversation, but no proof of moral depravity." Another justly observes, *Les peuples primitifs n'y entendent pas malice: ils appellent les choses par leurs noms et ne trouvent pas condamnable ce qui est naturel.* And they are prying as children. For instance the European novelist marries off his hero and heroine and leaves them to consummate marriage in privacy; even Tom Jones has the decency to bolt the door. But the Eastern storyteller, especially this unknown "prose Shakespeare," must usher you, with a flourish, into the bridal chamber and narrate to you, with infinite gusto, everything he sees and hears. Again we must remember that grossness and indecency, in fact *les turpitudes*, are matters of time and place; what is offensive in England is not so in Egypt; what scandalizes us now would have been a tame joke *tempore Elisæ*. Withal The Nights will not be found in this matter coarser than many passages of Shakespeare, Sterne, and Swift, and their uncleanness rarely attains the perfection of Alcofribas Naiser, "divin maître et atroce cochon." The other element is absolute obscenity, sometimes, but not always, tempered by wit, humour and drollery; here we have an exaggeration of Petronius Arbiter, the handiwork of writers whose ancestry, the most religious and the most debauched of mankind, practised every abomination before the shrine of the Canopic Gods.

In accordance with my purpose of reproducing The Nights, not *virginibus puerisque,* but in as perfect a picture as my powers permit, I have carefully sought out the English equivalent of every Arabic word, however low it may be or "shocking" to ears polite; preserving, on the other hand, all possible delicacy where the indecency is not intentional; and, as a friend advises me to state, not exaggerating the vulgarities and the indecencies which, indeed, can hardly be exaggerated. For the coarseness and crassness are but the shades of a picture which would otherwise be all lights. The general tone of The Nights is exceptionally high and pure. The devotional fervour often rises to the boiling-point of fanaticism. The pathos is sweet, deep and genuine; tender, simple and true, utterly unlike much of our modern tinsel. Its life, strong, splendid and multitudinous, is everywhere flavoured with that unaffected pessimism and constitutional melancholy which strike deepest root under the brightest skies and which sigh in the face of heaven:—

> Vita quid est hominis? Viridis floriscula mortis;
> Sole Oriente oriens, sole cadente cadens.

Poetical justice is administered by the literary Kází with exemplary impartiality and severity; "denouncing evil do-ers and eulogizing deeds admirably achieved." The morale is sound and healthy; and at times we descry, through the voluptuous and libertine picture, vistas of a transcendental morality, the morality of Socrates in Plato. Subtle corruption and covert licentiousness are utterly absent; we find more real "vice" in many a short French *roman,* say *La Dame aux Camélias,* and in not a few English novels of our day than in the thousands of pages of the Arab. Here we have nothing of that most immodest modern modesty which sees covert implication where nothing is implied, and "improper" allusion when propriety is not outraged; nor do we meet with the nineteenth century refinement; innocence of the word not of the thought; morality of the tongue not of the heart, and the sincere homage paid to virtue in guise of perfect hypocrisy. It is, indeed, this unique contrast of a quaint element, childish crudities and nursery indecencies and "vain and amatorious" phrase jostling the finest and highest views of life and character, shown in the kaleidoscopic shiftings of the marvellous picture with many a "rich truth in a tale's pretence"; pointed by a rough dry humour which compares well with "wut"; the alternations of strength and weakness, of pathos and bathos, of the boldest poetry (the diction of Job) and the baldest prose (the Egyptian of to-day); the contact of religion and morality with the orgies of African Apuleius and Petronius Arbiter—at times taking away the reader's breath—and, finally, the whole dominated everywhere by that marvellous Oriental fancy, wherein the spiritual and the supernatural are as common as the material and the natural; it is this contrast, I say, which forms the chiefest charm of The Nights, which gives it the most striking originality and which makes it a perfect expositor of the medieval Moslem mind.

Explanatory notes did not enter into Mr. Payne's plan. They do with mine: I can hardly imagine The Nights being read to any profit by men of the West without commentary. My annotations avoid only one subject, parallels of European folk-lore and fabliaux which, however interesting, would overswell the bulk of a book whose specialty is anthropology. The accidents of my life, it may be said without undue presumption, my long dealings with Arabs and other Mahommedans, and my familiarity not only with their idiom but with their turn of thought, and with that racial individuality which baffles description, have given me certain advantages over the average student, however deeply he may have studied. These volumes, moreover, afford me a long-sought opportunity of noticing practices and customs which interest all mankind and which "Society" will not hear mentioned. Grote, the historian, and Thackeray, the novelist, both lamented that the *bégueulerie* of their countrymen condemned them to keep silence where publicity was required; and that they could not even claim the partial licence of a Fielding and a Smollett. Hence a score of years ago I lent my best help to the late Dr. James Hunt in founding the Anthropological Society, whose presidential chair I first occupied (pp. 2–4 *Anthropologia;* London: Balliere, Vol. I., No. 1, 1873). My motive was to supply travellers with an organ which would rescue their observations from the outer darkness of manuscript, and print their curious information on social and sexual matters out of place in the popular book intended for the Nipptisch and indeed better kept from public view. But, hardly had we begun when "Respectability," that whited sepulchre full of all uncleanness, rose up against us. "Propriety" cried us down with her brazen blatant voice, and the weak-kneed brethren fell away. Yet the organ was much wanted and is wanted still. All now known barbarous tribes in Inner Africa, America and Australia, whose instincts have not been overlaid by reason, have a ceremony which they call "making men." As soon as the boy shows proofs of puberty, he and his coevals are taken in hand by the mediciner and the Fetisheer; and, under priestly tuition, they spend months in the "bush," enduring hardships and tortures which impress the memory till they have mastered the "theorick and practick" of social and sexual relations. Amongst the civilized this fruit of the knowledge-tree must be bought at the price of the bitterest experience, and the consequences of ignorance are peculiarly cruel. Here, then, I find at last an opportunity of noticing in explanatory notes many details of the text which would escape the reader's observation, and I am confident that they will form a repertory of Eastern knowledge in its esoteric phase. The student who adds the notes of Lane (*Arabian Society,* etc., before quoted) to mine will know as much of the Moslem East and more than many Europeans who have spent half their lives in Orient lands. For facility of reference an index of anthropological notes is appended to the last volume.

The reader will kindly bear with the following technical details. Steinhaeuser and I began and ended our work with the first Bulak ("Bul.") Edition printed at the port of Cairo in A.H. 1251=A.D. 1835. But when preparing my MSS. for print I found the text incomplete, many of the stories being given in epitome and not a few ruthlessly mutilated with head or feet wanting. Like most Eastern scribes the Editor could not refrain from "improvements," which only debased the book; and his sole title to excuse is that the second Bulak Edition (4 vols. A.H. 1279=A.D. 1863), despite its being "revised and corrected by Sheik Mahommed Qotch Al-Adewi," is even worse; and the same may be said of the Cairo Edit. (4 vols. A.H. 1297=A.D. 1881). The Calcutta ("Calc.") Edition, with ten lines of Persian preface by the Editor, Ahmed al-Shirwani (A.D. 1814), was cut short at the end of the first two hundred Nights, and thus made room for Sir William Hay Macnaghten's Edition (4 vols. royal 4to) of 1839–42. This ("Mac."), as by far the least corrupt and the most complete, has been assumed for my basis with occasional reference to the Breslau Edition ("Bres.") wretchedly edited from a hideous Egyptian MS. by Dr. Maximilian Habicht (1825–43). The Bayrut Text *Alif-Leila we Leila* (4 vols. gt. 8vo, Beirut: 1881–83) is a melancholy specimen of The Nights taken entirely from the Bulak Edition by one Khalil Sarkis and converted to Christianity; beginning without Bismillah, continued with scrupulous castration and ending in ennui and disappointment. I have not used this missionary production.

As regards the transliteration of Arabic words I deliberately reject the artful and complicated system, ugly and clumsy withal, affected by scientific modern Orientalists. Nor is my sympathy with their prime object, namely to fit the Roman alphabet for supplanting all others. Those who learn languages, and many do so, by the eye as well as by the ear, well know the advantages of a special character to distinguish, for instance, Syriac from Arabic, Gujrati from Marathi. Again this Roman hand bewitched may have its use in purely scientific and literary works; but it would be wholly out of place in one whose purpose is that of the novel, to amuse rather than to instruct. Moreover the devices perplex the simple and teach nothing to the learned. Either the reader knows Arabic, in which case Greek letters, italics and "upper case," diacritical points and similar typographic oddities are, as a rule with some exceptions, unnecessary; or he does not know Arabic, when none of these expedients will be of the least use to him. Indeed it is a matter of secondary consideration what system we prefer, provided that we mostly adhere to one and the same, for the sake of a consistency which saves confusion to the reader. I have especially avoided that of Mr. Lane, adopted by Mr. Payne, for special reasons against which it was vain to protest: it represents the debased brogue of Egypt or rather of Cairo; and such a word as Kemer (ez-Zeman) would be utterly unpronounceable to a Badawi. Nor have I followed the practice of my learned friend, Reverend G. P. Badger, in mixing bars and acute accents; the former unpleasantly remind man of those hateful dactyls and spondees, and the latter should, in my humble opinion, be applied to long vowels which in Arabic double, or should double, the length of the shorts. Dr. Badger uses the acute symbol to denote accent or stress of voice; but such appoggio is unknown to those who speak with purest articulation; for instance whilst the European pronounces Mus-cat', and the Arab villager Mas'-kat; the Children of the Waste, "on whose tongues Allah descended," articulate Mas-kat. I have therefore followed the simple system adopted in my *Pilgrimage,* and have accented Arabic words only when first used, thinking it unnecessary to preserve throughout what is an eyesore to the reader and a distress to the printer. In the main I follow *Johnson on Richardson,* a work known to every Anglo-Orientalist as the old and trusty companion of his studies early and late; but even here I have made sundry deviations for reasons which will be explained in the Terminal Essay. As words are the embodiment of ideas and writing is of words, so the word is the spoken word; and we should write it as pronounced. Strictly speaking, the *e*-sound and the *o*-sound (viz. the Italian *o*-sound not the English which is peculiar to us and unknown to any other tongue) are not found in Arabic, except when the figure Imálah obliges: hence they are called "Yá al-Majhúl" and "Waw al-Majhúl" the unknown y (í) and u. But in all tongues vowel-sounds, the flesh which clothes the bones (consonants) of language, are affected by the consonants which precede and more especially which follow them, hardening and softening the articulation; and deeper sounds accompany certain letters as the sád compared with the sín. None save a defective ear would hold, as Lane does, "Maulid" (=birth-festival) "more properly pronounced 'Mo-lid.'" Yet I prefer Khokh (peach) and Jokh (broad-cloth) to Khukh and Jukh; Ohod (mount) to Uhud; Obayd (a little slave) to Ubayd; and Hosayn (a fortlet, not the p. n. Al-Husayn) to Husayn. As for the short *e* in such words as "Memlúk" for "Mamlúk" (a white slave), "Eshe" for "Asha" (supper), and "Yemen" for "Al-Yaman," I consider it a flat Egyptianism, insufferable to an ear which admires the Badawi pronunciation. Yet I prefer "Shelebi" (a dandy) from the Turkish Chelebi, to "Shalabi"; "Zebdani" (the Syrian village) to "Zabdani," and "Fes and Miknes" (by the figure Imálah) to "Fás and Miknás," our "Fez and Mequinez."

With respect to proper names and untranslated Arabic words I have rejected all system in favour of common sense. When a term is incorporated in our tongue, I refuse to follow the purist and mortify the reader by startling innovation. For instance, Aleppo, Cairo and Bassorah are preferred to Halab, Kahirah and Al-Basrah; when a word is half-naturalized, like Alcoran or Koran, Bashaw or Pasha, which the French write Pacha; and Mahomet or Mohammed (for Muhammad), the modern form is adopted because the more familiar. But I see no advantage in retaining, simply because they are the mistakes of a past generation, such words as "Roc" (for Rukh), Khalif (a pretentious blunder for Khalífah and better written Caliph) and "genie" (Jinn) a mere Gallic corruption not so terrible, however, as "a Bedouin" (=Badawi). As little too would I follow Mr. Lane in foisting upon the public such Arabisms as "Khuff" (a riding-boot), "Mikra'ah" (a palm-rod) and a host of others for which we have good English equivalents. On the other hand I would use, but use sparingly, certain Arabic exclamations, as "Bismillah" (=in the name of Allah!) and "Inshallah" (=if Allah please!), which have special applications and which have been made familiar to English ears by the genius of Fraser and Morier.

I here end these desultory but necessary details to address the reader in a few final words. He will not think lightly of my work when I repeat to him that with the aid of my annotations supplementing Lane's, the student will readily and pleasantly learn more of the Moslem's manners and customs, laws and religion than is known to the average Orientalist; and, if my labours induce him to attack the text of The Nights he will become master of much more Arabic than the ordinary Arab owns. This book is indeed a legacy which I bequeath to my fellow-countrymen in their hour of need. Over-devotion to Hindu, and especially to Sanskrit literature, has led them astray from those (so-called) "Semitic" studies, which are the more requisite for us as they teach us to deal successfully with a race more powerful than any pagans—the Moslem. Apparently England is ever forgetting that she is at present the greatest Mohammedan empire in the world. Of late years she has systematically neglected Arabism and, indeed, actively discouraged it in examinations for the Indian Civil Service, where it is incomparably more valuable than Greek and Latin. Hence, when suddenly compelled to assume the reins of government in Moslem lands, as Afghanistan in times past and Egypt at present, she fails after a fashion which scandalizes her few (very few) friends; and her crass ignorance concerning the Oriental peoples which should most interest her, exposes her to the contempt of Europe as well as of the Eastern world. When the regrettable raids of 1883–84, culminating in the miserable affairs of Tokar, Teb and Tamasi, were made upon the gallant Sudani negroids, the Bisharin outlying Sawakin, who were battling for the holy cause of liberty and religion and for escape from Turkish task-masters and Egyptian tax-gatherers, not an English official in camp, after the death of the gallant and lamented Major Morice, was capable of speaking Arabic. Now Moslems are not to be ruled by raw youths who should be at school and college instead of holding positions of trust and emolument. He who would deal with them successfully must be, firstly, honest and truthful and, secondly, familiar with and favourably inclined to their manners and customs if not to their law and religion. We may, perhaps, find it hard to restore to England those pristine virtues, that tone and temper, which made her what she is; but at any rate we (myself and a host of others) can offer her the means of dispelling her ignorance concerning the Eastern races with whom she is continually in contact.

RICHARD F. BURTON
August 15, 1885.

THE ARABIAN
NIGHTS

ALF LAYLAH WA LAYLAH.

IN THE NAME OF ALLAH,
THE COMPASSIONATING,
THE COMPASSIONATE!

PRAISE BE TO ALLAH • THE BENEFICENT KING • THE CREA-
TOR OF THE UNIVERSE • LORD OF THE THREE WORLDS •
WHO SET UP THE FIRMAMENT WITHOUT PILLARS IN ITS
STEAD • AND WHO STRETCHED OUT THE EARTH EVEN AS A
BED • AND GRACE, AND PRAYER—BLESSING BE UPON OUR
LORD MOHAMMED • LORD OF APOSTOLIC MEN • AND UPON
HIS FAMILY AND COMPANION-TRAIN • PRAYER AND BLESS-
INGS ENDURING AND GRACE WHICH UNTO THE DAY OF
DOOM SHALL REMAIN • AMEN! • O THOU OF THE THREE
WORLDS SOVEREIGN!

AND AFTERWARDS. Verily the works and words of those
gone before us have become instances and examples to
men of our modern day, that folk may view what admon-
ishing chances befel other folk and may therefrom take
warning; and that they may peruse the annals of antique
peoples and all that hath betided them, and be thereby
ruled and restrained:—Praise, therefore, be to Him who
hath made the histories of the Past an admonition unto the
Present! Now of such instances are the tales called "A
Thousand Nights and a Night," together with their far-
famed legends and wonders. Therein it is related (but
Allah is All-knowing of His hidden things and All-ruling

and All-honoured and All-giving and All-gracious and All-merciful!)[1] that, in tide of yore and in time long gone before, there was a King of the Kings of the Banu Sasan in the Islands of India and China, a Lord of armies and guards and servants and dependents.[2] He left only two sons, one in the prime of manhood and the other yet a youth, while both were Knights and Braves, albeit the elder was a doughtier horseman than the younger. So he succeeded to the empire; when he ruled the land and lorded it over his lieges with justice so exemplary that he was beloved by all the peoples of his capital and of his kingdom. His name was King Shahryar,[3] and he made his younger brother, Shah Zaman hight, King of Samarcand in Barbarian-land. These two ceased not to abide in their several realms and the law was ever carried out in their dominions; and each ruled his own kingdom, with equity and fair-dealing to his subjects, in extreme solace and enjoyment; and this condition continually endured for a score of years. But at the end of the twentieth twelvemonth the elder King yearned for a sight of his younger brother and felt that he must look upon him once more. So he took counsel with his Wazir[4] about visiting him, but the Minister, finding the project unadvisable, recommended that a letter be written and a present be sent under his charge to the younger brother with an invitation to visit the elder. Having accepted this advice the King forthwith bade prepare handsome gifts, such as horses with saddles of gem-encrusted gold; Mamelukes, or white slaves; beautiful handmaids, high-breasted virgins, and splendid stuffs and costly. He then wrote a letter to Shah Zaman expressing his warm love and great wish to see him, ending with these words, "We therefore hope of the favour and affection of the beloved brother that he will condescend to bestir himself and turn his face us-wards. Furthermore we have sent our Wazir to make all ordinance for the march, and our one and only desire is to see thee ere we die; but if thou delay or disappoint us we shall not survive the blow. Wherewith peace be upon thee!" Then King Shahryar, having sealed the missive and given it to the Wazir with the offerings aforementioned, commanded him to shorten his skirts and strain his strength and make all expedition in going and returning. "Harkening and obedience!" quoth the Minister, who fell to making ready without stay and packed up his loads and prepared all his requisites without delay. This occupied him three days, and on the dawn of the fourth he took leave of his King and marched right away, over desert and hill-way, stony waste and pleasant lea without halting by night or by day. But whenever he entered a realm whose ruler was subject to his Suzerain, where he was greeted with magnificent gifts of gold and silver and all manner of presents fair and rare, he would tarry there three days,[5] the term of the guest-rite; and, when he left on the fourth, he would be honourably escorted for a whole day's march. As soon as the Wazir drew near Shah Zaman's court in Samarcand he despatched to report his arrival one of his high officials, who presented himself before the King; and, kissing ground between his hands, delivered his message. Hereupon the King commanded sundry of his Grandees and Lords of his realm to fare forth and meet his brother's Wazir at the distance of a full day's journey; which they did, greeting him respectfully and wishing him all prosperity and forming an escort and a procession. When he entered the city he proceeded straightway to the palace, where he presented himself in the royal presence; and, after kissing ground and praying for the King's health and happiness and for victory over all his enemies, he informed him that his brother was yearning to see him, and prayed for the pleasure of a visit. He then delivered the letter which Shah Zaman took from his hand and read: it contained sundry hints and allusions which required thought; but, when the King had fully comprehended its import, he said, "I hear and I obey the commands of the beloved brother!" adding to the Wazir, "But we will not march till after the third day's hospitality." He appointed for the Minister fitting quarters of the palace; and, pitching tents for the troops, rationed them with whatever they might require of meat and drink and other necessaries. On the fourth day he made ready for wayfare and got together sumptuous presents befitting his elder brother's majesty, and stablished his chief Wazir viceroy of the land during his absence. Then he caused his tents and camels and mules to be brought forth and encamped, with their bales and loads, attendants and guards, within sight of the city, in readiness to set out next morning for his brother's capital. But when the night was half spent he bethought him that he had forgotten in his palace somewhat which he should have brought with him, so he returned privily and entered his apartments, where he found the Queen, his wife, asleep on his own carpet-bed, embracing with both arms a black cook of loathsome aspect and foul with kitchen grease and grime. When he saw this the world waxed black before his sight and he said, "If such case happen while I am yet within sight of the city what will be the doings of this damned whore during my long absence at my brother's court?" So he drew his scymitar and, cutting the two in four pieces with a single blow, left them on the carpet and returned presently to his camp without letting anyone know of what had happened. Then he gave orders for immediate departure and set out at once and began his travel; but he could not help thinking over his wife's treason and he kept ever saying to himself, "How could she do this deed by me? How could she work her own death?," till excessive grief seized him, his colour changed to yellow, his body waxed weak and he was threatened with a dangerous malady, such an one as bringeth men to die. So the Wazir shortened his stages and tarried long at the watering-stations and did his best to solace the King. Now when Shah Zaman drew near the capital of his brother he despatched vaunt-couriers and messengers of glad tidings to announce his arrival, and Shahryar came forth to meet him with his Wazirs and Emirs and Lords and Grandees of his realm; and saluted him and joyed with exceeding joy and caused the city to be decorated in his honour. When, however, the brothers met, the elder could not but see the change of complexion in the younger and questioned him of his case whereto he replied, "'Tis caused by the travails of wayfare and my case needs care, for I have suffered from the change of water and air! but Allah be praised for reuniting me with a brother so dear and so rare!" On this wise he dissembled and kept his secret, adding, "O King of the time and Caliph of the tide, only toil and moil have tinged my face yellow with bile and hath made my eyes sink deep in my head." Then the two entered the capital in all honour; and the elder brother lodged the younger in a palace overhanging the pleasure garden; and, after a time, seeing his condition still unchanged, he attributed it to his separation from his country and kingdom. So he let him wend his own ways and asked no questions of him till one day when he again said, "O my brother, I see thou art grown weaker of body and yellower of colour." "O my brother," replied Shah Zaman, "I have an internal wound:"[6] still he would not tell him what he had witnessed in his wife. Thereupon Shahryar summoned doctors and surgeons and bade them treat his brother according to the rules of art, which they did for a whole month; but their sherbets and potions naught availed, for he would dwell upon the deed of his wife, and despondency, instead of diminishing, prevailed, and leach-craft treatment utterly failed. One day his elder brother said to him, "I am going forth to hunt and course and to take my pleasure and pastime; maybe this would lighten thy heart." Shah Zaman, however, refused, saying, "O my brother, my soul yearneth for naught of this sort and I entreat thy favour to suffer me tarry quietly in this place, being wholly taken up with my malady." So King Shah Zaman passed his night in the palace and, next morning, when his brother had fared forth, he removed from his room and sat him down at one of the lattice-windows overlooking the pleasure grounds; and there he abode thinking with saddest thought over his wife's betrayal and burning sighs issued from his tortured breast. And as he continued in this case lo! a postern of the palace, which was carefully kept private, swung open and out of it came twenty slave girls surrounding his brother's wife who was wondrous fair, a model of beauty and comeliness and symmetry and perfect loveliness and who paced with the grace of a gazelle which panteth for the cooling stream. Thereupon Shah Zaman drew back from the window, but he kept the bevy in sight espying them from a place whence he could not be espied. They walked under the very lattice and advanced a little way into the garden till they came to a jetting fountain amiddlemost a great basin of water; then they stripped off their clothes and behold, ten of them were women, concubines of the King, and the other ten were white slaves. Then they all paired off, each with each: but the Queen, who was left alone, presently cried out in a loud voice, "Here to me, O my lord Saeed!" and then sprang with a drop-leap from one of the trees a big slobbering blackamoor with rolling eyes which showed the whites, a truly hideous sight.[7] He walked boldly up to her and threw his arms round her neck while she embraced him as warmly; then he bussed her and winding his legs round hers, as a button-loop clasps a button, he threw her and enjoyed her. On like wise did the other slaves with the girls till all had satisfied their passions, and they ceased not from kissing and clipping, coupling and carousing till day began to wane; when the Mamelukes rose from the damsels' bosoms and the blackamoor slave dismounted from the Queen's breast; the men resumed their disguises and all, except the negro who swarmed up the tree, entered the palace and closed the postern-door as before. Now, when Shah Zaman saw this conduct of his sister-in-law he said to himself, "By Allah, my calamity is lighter than this! My brother is a greater King among the kings than I am, yet this infamy goeth on in his very palace, and his wife is in love with that filthiest of filthy slaves. But this only showeth that they all do it[8] and that there is no woman but who cuckoldeth her husband; then the curse of Allah upon one and all and upon the fools who lean against them for support or who place the reins of conduct in their hands."

So he put away his melancholy and despondency, regret and repine, and allayed his sorrow by constantly repeating those words, adding "'Tis my conviction that no man in this world is safe from their malice!" When supper-time came they brought him the trays and he ate with voracious appetite, for he had long refrained from meat, feeling unable to touch any dish however dainty. Then he returned grateful thanks to Almighty Allah, praising Him and blessing Him, and he spent a most restful night, it having been long since he had savoured the sweet food of sleep. Next day he broke his fast heartily and began to recover health and strength, and presently regained excellent condition. His brother came back from the chase ten days after, when he rode out to meet him and they saluted each other; and when King Shahryar looked at King Shah Zaman he saw how the hue of health had returned to him, how his face had waxed ruddy and how he ate with an appetite after his late scanty diet. He wondered much and said, "O my brother, I was so anxious that thou wouldst join me in hunting and chasing, and wouldst take thy pleasure and pastime in my dominion!" He thanked him and excused himself; then the two took horse and rode into the city and, when they were seated at their ease in the palace, the food-trays were set before them and they ate their sufficiency. After the meats were removed and they had washed their hands, King Shahryar turned to his brother and said, "My mind is overcome with wonderment at thy condition. I was desirous to carry thee with me to the chase but I saw thee changed in hue, pale and wan to view, and in sore trouble of mind too. But now Alhamdolillah—glory be to God!—I see thy natural colour hath returned to thy face and that thou art again in the best of case. It was my belief that thy sickness came of severance from thy family and friends, and absence from capital and country, so I refrained from troubling thee with further questions. But now I beseech thee to expound to me the cause of thy complaint and thy change of colour, and to explain the reason of thy recovery and the return to the ruddy hue of health which I am wont to view. So speak out and hide naught!" When Shah Zaman heard this he bowed groundwards awhile his head, then raised it and said, "I will tell thee what caused my complaint and my loss of colour; but excuse my acquainting thee with the cause of its return to me and the reason of my complete recovery: indeed I pray thee not to press me for a reply." Said Shahryar, who was much surprised by these words, "Let me hear first what produced thy pallor and thy poor condition." "Know, then, O my brother," rejoined Shah Zaman, "that when thou sentest thy Wazir with the invitation to place myself between thy hands, I made ready and marched out of my city; but presently I minded me having left behind me in the palace a string of jewels intended as a gift to thee. I returned for it alone and found my wife on my carpet-bed and in the arms of a hideous black cook. So I slew the twain and came to thee, yet my thoughts brooded over this business and I lost my bloom and became weak. But excuse me if I still refuse to tell thee what was the reason of my complexion returning." Shahryar shook his head, marvelling with extreme marvel, and with the fire of wrath flaming up from his heart, he cried, "Indeed, the malice of woman is mighty!" Then he took refuge from them with Allah and said, "In very sooth, O my brother, thou hast escaped many an evil by putting thy wife to death,[9] and right excusable were thy wrath and grief for such mishap which never yet befel crowned King like thee. By Allah, had the case been mine, I would not have been satisfied without slaying a thousand women and that way madness lies! But now praise be to Allah who hath tempered to thee thy tribulation, and needs must thou acquaint me with that which so suddenly restored to thee complexion and health, and explain to me what causeth this concealment." "O King of the Age, again I pray thee excuse my so doing!" "Nay, but thou must." "I fear, O my brother, lest the recital cause thee more anger and sorrow than afflicted me." "That were but a better reason," quoth Shahryar, "for telling me the whole history, and I conjure thee by Allah not to keep back aught from me." Thereupon Shah Zaman told him all he had seen, from commencement to conclusion, ending with these words, "When I beheld thy calamity and the treason of thy wife, O my brother, and I reflected that thou art in years my senior and in sovereignty my superior, mine own sorrow was belittled by the comparison, and my mind recovered tone and temper: so throwing off melancholy and despondency, I was able to eat and drink and sleep, and thus I speedily regained health and strength. Such is the truth and the whole truth." When King Shahryar heard this he waxed wroth with exceeding wrath, and rage was like to strangle him; but presently he recovered himself and said, "O my brother, I would not give thee the lie in this matter, but I cannot credit it till I see it with mine own eyes." "An thou wouldst look upon thy calamity," quoth Shah Zaman, "rise at once and make ready again for hunting and coursing,[10] and then hide thyself with me, so shalt thou witness it and thine eyes shall verify it." "True," quoth the King; whereupon he let make proclamation of his intent to travel, and the troops and tents fared forth without the city, camping within sight, and Shahryar sallied out with them and took seat amidmost his host, bidding the slaves admit no man to him. When night came on he summoned his Wazir and said to him, "Sit thou in my stead and let none wot of my absence till the term of three days." Then the brothers disguised themselves and returned by night with all secrecy to the palace, where they passed the dark hours: and at dawn they seated themselves at the lattice overlooking the pleasure grounds, when presently the Queen and her handmaids came out as before, and passing under the windows made for the fountain. Here they stripped, ten of them being men to ten women, and the King's wife cried out, "Where art thou, O Saeed?" The hideous blackamoor dropped from the tree straightway; and, rushing into her arms without stay or delay, cried out, "I am Sa'ad al-Din Saood!"[11] The lady laughed heartily, and all fell to satisfying their lusts, and remained so occupied for a couple of hours, when the white slaves rose up from the handmaidens' breasts and the blackamoor dismounted from the Queen's bosom: then they went into the basin and, after performing the Ghusl, or complete ablution, donned their dresses and retired as they had done before. When King Shahryar saw this infamy of his wife and concubines he became as one distraught and he cried out, "Only in utter solitude can man be safe from the doings of this vile world! By Allah, life is naught but one great wrong." Presently he added, "Do not thwart me, O my brother, in what I propose;" and the other answered, "I will not." So he said, "Let us up as we are and depart forthright hence, for we have no concern with Kingship, and let us overwander Allah's earth, worshipping the Almighty till we find some one to whom the like calamity hath happened; and if we find none then will death be more welcome to us than life." So the two brothers issued from a second private postern of the palace; and they never stinted wayfaring by day and by night, until they reached a tree a-middle of a meadow hard by a spring of sweet water on the shore of the salt sea. Both drank of it and sat down to take their rest; and when an hour of the day had gone by, lo! they heard a mighty roar and uproar in the middle of the main as though the heavens were falling upon the earth; and the sea brake with waves before them, and from it towered a black pillar, which grew and grew till it rose skywards and began making for that meadow. Seeing it, they waxed fearful exceedingly and climbed to the top of the tree, which was a lofty; whence they gazed to see what might be the matter. And behold, it was a Jinni,[12] huge of height and burly of breast and bulk, broad of brow and black of blee, bearing on his head a coffer of crystal. He strode to land, wading through the deep, and coming to the tree whereupon were the two Kings, seated himself beneath it. He then set down the coffer on its bottom and out of it drew a casket, with seven padlocks of steel, which he unlocked with seven keys of steel he took from beside his thigh, and out of it a young lady to come was seen, white-skinned and of winsomest mien, of stature fine and thin,

and bright as though a moon of the fourteenth night she
had been, or the sun raining lively sheen. Even so the poet
Utayyah hath excellently said:—

> She rose like the morn as she shone through the night
> And she gilded the grove with her gracious sight:
> From her radiance the sun taketh increase when
> She unveileth and shameth the moonshine bright.
> Bow down all beings between her hands
> As she showeth charms with her veil undight.
> And she floodeth cities[13] with torrent tears
> When she flasheth her look of leven-light.

The Jinni seated her under the tree by his side and looking
at her said, "O choicest love of this heart of mine! O dame
of noblest line, whom I snatched away on thy bride night
that none might prevent me taking thy maidenhead or
tumble thee before I did, and whom none save myself hath
loved or hath enjoyed: O my sweetheart! I would lief sleep
a little while." He then laid his head upon the lady's thighs;
and, stretching out his legs which extended down to the
sea, slept and snored and snarked like the roll of thunder.
Presently she raised her head towards the tree-top and saw
the two Kings perched near the summit; then she softly
lifted off her lap the Jinni's pate which she was tired of
supporting and placed it upon the ground; then standing
upright under the tree signed to the Kings, "Come ye
down, ye two, and fear naught from this Ifrit."[14] They were
in a terrible fright when they found that she had seen them
and answered her in the same manner, "Allah upon thee[15]
and by thy modesty, O lady, excuse us from coming down!"
But she rejoined by saying, "Allah upon you both that ye
come down forthright, and if ye come not, I will rouse
upon you my husband, this Ifrit, and he shall do you to die
by the illest of deaths;" and she continued making signals
to them. So, being afraid, they came down to her and she
rose before them and said, "Stroke me a strong stroke,
without stay or delay, otherwise will I arouse and set upon

you this Ifrit who shall slay you straightway." They said to her, "O our lady, we conjure thee by Allah, let us off this work, for we are fugitives from such and in extreme dread and terror of this thy husband. How then can we do it in such a way as thou desirest?" "Leave this talk: it needs must be so;" quoth she, and she swore them by Him[16] who raised the skies on high, without prop or pillar, that, if they worked not her will, she would cause them to be slain and cast into the sea. Whereupon out of fear King Shahryar said to King Shah Zaman, "O my brother, do thou what she biddeth thee do;" but he replied, "I will not do it till thou do it before I do." And they began disputing about futtering her. Then quoth she to the twain, "How is it I see you disputing and demurring; if ye do not come forward like men and do the deed of kind ye two, I will arouse upon you the Ifrit." At this, by reason of their sore dread of the Jinni, both did by her what she bade them do; and, when they had dismounted from her, she said, "Well done!" She then took from her pocket a purse and drew out a knotted string, whereon were strung five hundred and seventy[17] seal rings, and asked. "Know ye what be these?" They answered her saying, "We know not!" Then quoth she; "These be the signets of five hundred and seventy men who have all futtered me upon the horns of this foul, this foolish, this filthy Ifrit; so give me also your two seal rings, ye pair of brothers." When they had drawn their two rings from their hands and given them to her, she said to them, "Of a truth this Ifrit bore me off on my bride-night, and put me into a casket and set the casket in a coffer and to the coffer he affixed seven strong padlocks of steel and deposited me on the deep bottom of the sea that raves, dashing and clashing with waves; and guarded me so that I might remain chaste and honest, quotha! that none save himself might have connexion with me. But I have lain under as many of my kind as I please, and this wretched Jinni wotteth not that Destiny may not be averted nor hindered by aught, and that what so woman willeth the same she fulfilleth however man nilleth. Even so saith one of them:—

Rely not on women;
Trust not to their hearts,
Whose joys and whose sorrows
Are hung to their parts!
Lying love they will swear thee
Whence guile ne'er departs:
Take Yusuf[18] for sample
'Ware sleights and 'ware smarts!
Iblis[19] ousted Adam
(See ye not?) thro' their arts.

Hearing these words they marvelled with exceeding marvel, and she went from them to the Ifrit and, taking up his head on her thigh as before, said to them softly, "Now wend your ways and bear yourselves beyond the bounds of his malice." So they fared forth saying either to other, "Allah! Allah!" and, "There be no Majesty and there be no Might save in Allah, the Glorious, the Great; and with Him we seek refuge from women's malice and sleight, for of a truth it hath no mate in might. Consider, O my brother, the ways of this marvellous lady with an Ifrit who is so much more powerful than we are. Now since there hath happened to him a greater mishap than that which befel us and which should bear us abundant consolation, so return we to our countries and capitals, and let us decide never to intermarry with womankind and presently we will show them what will be our action." Thereupon they rode back to the tents of King Shahryar, which they reached on the morning of the third day; and, having mustered the Wazirs and Emirs, the Chamberlains and high officials, he gave a robe of honour to his Viceroy and issued orders for an immediate return to the city. There he sat him upon his throne and sending for the Chief Minister, the father of the two damsels who (Inshallah!) will presently be mentioned, he said, "I command thee to take my wife and smite her to death; for she hath broken her plight and her faith." So he carried her to the place of execution and did her die. Then King Shahryar took brand in hand and repairing to the Serraglio slew all the concubines and their Mamelukes.[20] He also sware himself by a binding oath that whatever wife he married he would abate her maidenhead at night and slay her next morning to make sure of his honour; "For," said he, "there never was nor is there one chaste woman upon the face of earth." Then Shah Zaman prayed for permission to fare homewards; and he went forth equipped and escorted and travelled till he reached his own country. Meanwhile Shahryar commanded his Wazir to bring him the bride of the night that he might go in to her; so he produced a most beautiful girl, the daughter of one of the Emirs, and the King went in unto her at eventide and when morning dawned he bade his Minister strike off her head; and the Wazir did accordingly for fear of the Sultan. On this wise he continued for the space of three years; marrying a maiden every night and killing her the next morning, till folk raised an outcry against him and cursed him, praying Allah utterly to destroy him and his rule; and women made an uproar and mothers wept and parents fled with their daughters till there remained not in the city a young person fit for carnal copulation. Presently the King ordered his Chief Wazir, the same who was charged with the executions, to bring him a virgin as was his wont; and the Minister went forth and searched and found none; so he returned home in sorrow and anxiety fearing for his life from the King. Now he had two daughters, Shahrazad and Dunyazad hight,[21] of whom the elder had perused the books, annals and legends of preceding Kings, and the stories, examples and instances of by-gone men and things; indeed it was said that she had collected a thousand books of histories relating to antique races and departed rulers. She had perused the works of the poets and knew them by heart; she had studied philosophy and the sciences, arts and accomplishments; and she was pleasant and polite, wise and witty, well read and well bred. Now on that day she said to her father, "Why do I see thee thus changed and laden with cark and care? Concerning this matter quoth one of the poets:—

> Tell whoso hath sorrow
> Grief never shall last:
> E'en as joy hath no morrow
> So woe shall go past."

When the Wazir heard from his daughter these words he related to her, from first to last, all that had happened between him and the King. Thereupon said she, "By Allah, O my father, how long shall this slaughter of women endure? Shall I tell thee what is in my mind in order to save both sides from destruction?" "Say on, O my daughter," quoth he, and quoth she, "I wish thou wouldst give me in marriage to this King Shahryar; either I shall live or I shall be a ransom for the virgin daughters of Moslems and the cause of their deliverance from his hands and thine."[22] "Allah upon thee!" cried he in wrath exceeding that lacked no feeding, "O scanty of wit, expose not thy life to such peril! How durst thou address me in words so wide from wisdom and un-far from foolishness? Know that one who lacketh experience in worldly matters readily falleth into misfortune; and whoso considereth not the end keepeth not the world to friend, and the vulgar say:—I was lying at mine ease: nought but my officiousness brought me unease." "Needs must thou," she broke in, "make me a doer of this good deed, and let him kill me an he will: I shall only die a ransom for others." "O my daughter," asked he, "and how shall that profit thee when thou shalt have thrown away thy life?" and she answered, "O my father it must be, come of it what will!" The Wazir was again moved to fury and blamed and reproached her, ending with, "In very deed I fear lest the same befal thee which befel the Bull and the Ass with the Husbandman." "And what," asked she, "befel them, O my father?" Whereupon the Wazir began

THE TALE OF THE BULL[23] AND THE ASS.

Know, O my daughter, that there was once a merchant who owned much money and many men, and who was rich in cattle and camels; he had also a wife and family and he dwelt in the country, being experienced in husbandry and devoted to agriculture. Now Allah Most High had endowed him with understanding the tongues of beasts and birds of every kind, but under pain of death if he divulged the gift to any. So he kept it secret for very fear. He had in his cowhouse a Bull and an Ass each tethered in his own stall one hard by the other. As the merchant was sitting near hand one day with his servants and his children were playing about him, he heard the Bull say to the Ass, "Hail and health to thee O Father of Waking![24] for that thou enjoyest rest and good ministering; all under thee is clean-swept and fresh-sprinkled; men wait upon thee and feed thee, and thy provaunt is sifted barley and thy drink pure spring-water, while I (unhappy creature!) am led forth in the middle of the night, when they set on my neck the plough and a something called Yoke; and I tire at cleaving the earth from dawn of day till set of sun. I am forced to do more than I can and to bear all manner of ill-treatment from night to night; after which they take me back with my sides torn, my neck flayed, my legs aching and mine eyelids sored with tears. Then they shut me up in the byre and throw me beans and crushed-straw,[25] mixed with dirt and chaff; and I lie in dung and filth and foul stinks through the livelong night. But thou art ever in a place swept and sprinkled and cleansed, and thou art always lying at ease, save when it happens (and seldom enough!) that the master hath some business, when he mounts thee and rides thee to town and returns with thee forthright. So it happens that I am toiling and distrest while thou takest thine ease and thy rest; thou sleepest while I am sleepless; I hunger still while thou eatest thy fill, and I win contempt while thou winnest good will." When the Bull ceased speaking, the Ass turned towards him and said, "O Broad-o'-Brow,[26] O thou lost one! he lied not who dubbed thee Bull-head, for thou, O father of a Bull, hast neither forethought nor contrivance; thou art the simplest of simpletons,[27] and thou knowest naught of good advisers. Hast thou not heard the saying of the wise:—

> For others these hardships and labours I bear
> And theirs is the pleasure and mine is the care;
> As the bleacher who blacketh his brow in the sun
> To whiten the raiment which other men wear.[28]

But thou, O fool, art full of zeal and thou toilest and moilest before the master; and thou tearest and wearest and slayest thyself for the comfort of another. Hast thou never heard the saw that saith, None to guide and from the way go wide? Thou wendest forth at the call to dawn-prayer and thou returnest not till sundown; and through the livelong day thou endurest all manner hardships; to wit, beating and belabouring and bad language. Now hearken to me, Sir Bull! when they tie thee to thy stinking manger, thou pawest the ground with thy forehand and lashest out with thy hind hoofs and pushest with thy horns and bellowest aloud, so they deem thee contented. And when they throw thee thy fodder thou fallest on it with greed and hastenest to line thy fair fat paunch. But if thou accept my advice it will be better for thee and thou wilt lead an easier life even than mine. When thou goest a-field and they lay the thing called Yoke on thy neck, lie down and rise not again though haply they swinge thee; and, if thou rise, lie down a second time; and when they bring thee home and offer thee thy beans, fall backwards and only sniff at thy meat and withdraw thee and taste it not, and be satisfied with thy crushed straw and chaff; and on this wise feign thou art sick, and cease not doing thus for a day or two days or even three days, so shalt thou have rest from toil and moil." When the Bull heard these words he knew the Ass to be his friend and thanked him, saying, "Right is thy rede;" and prayed that all blessings might requite him, and cried, "O Father Wakener![29] thou hast made up for my failings." (Now[30] the merchant, O my daughter, understood all that passed between them.) Next day the driver took the Bull, and settling the plough on his neck,[31] made him work as wont; but the Bull began to shirk his ploughing, according to the advice of the Ass, and the ploughman drubbed him till he broke the yoke and made off; but the man caught him up and leathered him till he despaired of his life. Not the less, however, would he do nothing but stand still and drop down till the evening. Then the herd led him home and stabled him in his stall; but he drew back from his manger and neither stamped nor ramped nor butted nor bellowed as he was wont to do; whereat the man wondered. He brought him the beans and husks, but he sniffed at them and left them and lay down as far from them as he could and passed the whole night fasting. The peasant came next morning; and, seeing the manger full of beans, the crushed-straw untasted and the ox lying on his back in sorriest plight, with legs outstretched and swollen belly, he was concerned for him, and said to himself, "By Allah, he hath assuredly sickened and this is the cause why he would not plough yesterday." Then he went to the merchant and reported, "O my master, the Bull is ailing; he refused his fodder last night; nay more, he hath not tasted a scrap of it this morning." Now the merchant-farmer understood what all this meant, because he had overheard the talk between the Bull and the Ass, so quoth he, "Take that rascal donkey, and set the yoke on his neck, and bind him to the plough and make him do Bull's work." Thereupon the ploughman took the Ass, and worked him through the live-long day at the Bull's task; and, when he failed for weakness, he made him eat stick till his ribs were sore and his sides were sunken and his neck was flayed by the yoke; and when he came home in the evening he could hardly drag his limbs along, either fore-hand or hind-legs. But as for the Bull, he had passed the day lying at full length and had eaten his fodder with an excellent appetite, and he ceased not calling down blessings on the Ass for his good advice, unknowing what had come to him on his account. So when night set in and the Ass returned to the byre the Bull rose

up before him in honour, and said, "May good tidings gladden thy heart, O Father Wakener! through thee I have
rested all this day and I have eaten my meat in peace and
quiet." But the Ass returned no reply, for wrath and heart-
burning and fatigue and the beating he had gotten; and he
repented with the most grievous of repentance; and quoth
he to himself: "This cometh of my folly in giving good
counsel; as the saw saith, I was in joy and gladness, nought
save my officiousness brought me this sadness. And now I
must take thought and put a trick upon him and return him
to his place, else I die." Then he went aweary to his
manger, while the Bull thanked him and blessed him. And
even so, O my daughter, said the Wazir, thou wilt die for
lack of wits; therefore sit thee still and say naught and expose not thy life to such stress; for, by Allah, I offer thee the
best advice, which cometh of my affection and kindly solicitude for thee. "O my father," she answered, "needs must
I go up to this King and be married to him." Quoth he, "Do
not this deed;" and quoth she, "Of a truth I will:" whereat
he rejoined, "If thou be not silent and bide still, I will do
with thee even what the merchant did with his wife." "And
what did he?" asked she. Know then, answered the Wazir,
that after the return of the Ass the merchant came out on
the terrace-roof with his wife and family, for it was a
moonlit night and the moon at its full. Now the terrace
overlooked the cowhouse and presently, as he sat there
with his children playing about him, the trader heard the
Ass say to the Bull, "Tell me, O father Broad o' Brow, what
thou purposest to do to-morrow?" The Bull answered,
"What but continue to follow thy counsel, O Aliboron? Indeed it was as good as good could be and it hath given me
rest and repose; nor will I now depart from it one tittle: so,
when they bring me my meat, I will refuse it and blow out
my belly and counterfeit crank." The Ass shook his head
and said, "Beware of so doing, O Father of a Bull!" The
Bull asked, "Why," and the Ass answered, "Know that I am
about to give thee the best of counsel, for verily I heard our
owner say to the herd, If the Bull rise not from his place to

do his work this morning and if he retire from his fodder this day, make him over to the butcher that he may slaughter him and give his flesh to the poor, and fashion a bit of leather[32] from his hide. Now I fear for thee on account of this. So take my advice ere a calamity befal thee; and when they bring thee thy fodder eat it and rise up and bellow and paw the ground, or our master will assuredly slay thee: and peace be with thee!" Thereupon the Bull arose and lowed aloud and thanked the Ass, and said, "To-morrow I will readily go forth with them;" and he at once ate up all his meat and even licked the manger. (All this took place and the owner was listening to their talk.) Next morning the trader and his wife went to the Bull's crib and sat down, and the driver came and led forth the Bull who, seeing his owner, whisked his tail and brake wind, and frisked about so lustily that the merchant laughed a loud laugh and kept laughing till he fell on his back. His wife asked him, "Whereat laughest thou with such loud laughter as this?"; and he answered her, "I laughed at a secret something which I have heard and seen but cannot say lest I die my death." She returned, "Perforce thou must discover it to me, and disclose the cause of thy laughing even if thou come by thy death!" But he rejoined, "I cannot reveal what beasts and birds say in their lingo for fear I die." Then quoth she, "By Allah, thou liest! this is a mere pretext: thou laughest at none save me, and now thou wouldest hide somewhat from me. But by the Lord of the Heaven! an thou disclose not the cause I will no longer cohabit with thee: I will leave thee at once." And she sat down and cried. Whereupon quoth the merchant, "Woe betide thee! what means thy weeping? Fear Allah and leave these words and query me no more questions." "Needs must thou tell me the cause of that laugh," said she, and he replied, "Thou wottest that when I prayed Allah to vouchsafe me understanding of the tongues of beasts and birds, I made a vow never to disclose the secret to any under pain of dying on the spot." "No matter," cried she, "tell me what secret passed between the Bull and the Ass and die this very hour an thou be so minded;" and she ceased not to importune him till he was worn out and clean distraught. So at last he said, "Summon thy father and thy mother and our kith and kin and sundry of our neighbours," which she did; and he sent for the Kazi[33] and his assessors, intending to make his will and reveal to her his secret and die the death; for he loved her with love exceeding because she was his cousin, the daughter of his father's brother, and the mother of his children, and he had lived with her a life of an hundred and twenty years. Then, having assembled all the family and the folk of his neighbourhood, he said to them, "By me there hangeth a strange story, and 'tis such that if I discover the secret to any I am a dead man." Therefore quoth every one of those present to the woman, "Allah upon thee, leave this sinful obstinacy and recognise the right of this matter, lest haply thy husband and the father of thy children die." But she rejoined, "I will not turn from it till he tell me, even though he come by his death." So they ceased to urge her; and the trader rose from amongst them and repaired to an outhouse to perform the Wuzu-ablution,[34] and he purposed thereafter to return and to tell them his secret and to die. Now, daughter Shahrazad, that merchant had in his outhouses some fifty hens under one cock, and whilst making ready to farewell his folk he heard one of his many farm-dogs thus address in his own tongue the Cock, who was flapping his wings and crowing lustily and jumping from one hen's back to another and treading all in turn, saying "O Chanticleer! how mean is thy wit and how shameless is thy conduct! Be he disappointed who brought thee up?[35] Art thou not ashamed of thy doings on such a day as this?" "And what," asked the Rooster, "hath occurred this day?", when the Dog answered, "Dost thou not know that our master is this day making ready for his death? His wife is resolved that he shall disclose the secret taught to him by Allah, and the moment he so doeth he shall surely die. We dogs are all a-mourning; but thou clappest thy wings and clarionest thy loudest and treadest hen after hen. Is this an hour for pastime and pleasuring? Art thou not ashamed of thyself?"[36] "Then by Allah," quoth the Cock, "is our master a lack-wit and a man scanty of sense: if he cannot manage matters with a single wife, his life is not worth prolonging. Now I have some fifty Dame Partlets; and I please this and provoke that and starve one and stuff another; and through my good governance they are all well under my control. This our master pretendeth to wit and wisdom, and he hath but one wife, and yet knoweth not how to manage her." Asked the Dog, "What then, O Cock, should the master do to win clear of his strait?" "He should arise forthright," answered the Cock, "and take some twigs from yon mulberry-tree and give her a regular back-basting and rib-roasting till she cry:—I repent, O my lord! I will never ask thee a question as long as I live! Then let him beat her once more and soundly, and when he shall have done this he shall sleep free from care and enjoy life. But this master of ours owns neither sense nor judgment." "Now, daughter Shahrazad," continued the Wazir, "I will do to thee as did that husband to that wife." Said Shahrazad, "And what did he do?" He replied, "When the merchant heard the wise words spoken by his Cock to his Dog, he arose in haste and sought his wife's chamber, after cutting for her some mulberry-twigs and hiding them there; and then he called to her, "Come into the closet that I may tell thee the secret while no one seeth me and then die." She entered with him and he locked the door and came down upon her with so sound a beating of back and shoulders, ribs, arms and legs, saying the while, "Wilt thou ever be asking questions about what concerneth thee not?" that she was well nigh senseless. Presently she cried out, "I am of the repentant! By Allah, I will ask thee no more questions, and indeed I repent sincerely and wholesomely." Then she kissed his hand and feet and he led her out of the room submissive as a wife should be. Her parents and all the company rejoiced and sadness and mourning were changed into joy and gladness. Thus the merchant learnt family discipline from his Cock and he and his wife lived together the happiest of lives until death. And thou also, O my daughter! continued the Wazir, "Unless thou turn from this matter I will do by thee what that trader did to his wife." But she answered him with much decision, "I will never desist, O my father, nor shall this tale change my purpose. Leave such talk and tattle. I will not listen to thy words and, if thou deny me, I will marry myself to him despite the nose of thee. And first I will go up to the King myself and alone and I will say to him:—I prayed my father to wive me with thee, but he refused, being resolved to disappoint his lord, grudging the like of me to the like of thee." Her father asked, "Must this needs be?" and she answered, "Even so." Hereupon the Wazir being weary of lamenting and contending, persuading and dissuading her, all to no purpose, went up to King Shahryar and, after blessing him and kissing the ground before him, told him all about his dispute with his daughter from first to last and how he designed to bring her to him that night. The King wondered with exceeding wonder; for he had made an especial exception of the Wazir's daughter, and said to him, "O most faithful of Counsellors, how is this? Thou wottest that I have sworn by the Raiser of the Heavens that after I have gone into her this night I shall say to thee on the morrow's morning:—Take her and slay her! and, if thou slay her not, I will slay thee in her stead without fail." "Allah guide thee to glory and lengthen thy life, O King of the age," answered the Wazir, "it is she that hath so determined: all this have I told her and more; but she will not hearken to me and she persisteth in passing this coming night with the King's Majesty." So Shahryar rejoiced greatly and said, "'Tis well; go get her ready and this night bring her to me." The Wazir returned to his daughter and reported to her the command saying, "Allah make not thy father desolate by thy loss!" But Shahrazad rejoiced with exceeding joy and gat ready all she required and said to her younger sister, Dunyazad, "Note well what directions I entrust to thee! When I have gone into the King I will send for thee and when thou comest to me and seest that he hath had his carnal will of me, do thou say to me:—O my sister, an thou be not sleepy, relate to me some new story, delectable and delightsome, the better to speed our waking hours; and I will tell thee a tale which shall be our deliverance, if so Allah please, and which shall turn the King from his blood-thirsty custom." Dunyazad answered, "With love and gladness." So when it was night their father the Wazir carried Shahrazad to the King who was gladdened at the sight and asked, "Hast thou brought me my need?" and he answered, "I have." But when the King took her to his bed and fell to toying with her and wished to go in to her she wept; which made him ask, "What aileth thee?" She replied, "O King of the age, I have a younger sister and lief would I take leave of her this night before I see the dawn." So he sent at once for Dunyazad and she came and kissed the ground between his hands, when he permitted her to take her seat near the foot of the couch. Then the King arose and did away with his bride's maidenhead and the three fell asleep. But when it was midnight Shahrazad awoke and signalled to her sister Dunyazad who sat up and said, "Allah upon thee, O my sister, recite to us some new story, delightsome and delectable, wherewith to while away the waking hours of our latter night."[37] "With joy and goodly gree," answered Shahrazad, "if this pious and auspicious King permit me." "Tell on," quoth the King who chanced to be sleepless and restless and therefore was pleased with the prospect of hearing her story. So Shahrazad rejoiced; and thus, on the first night of the Thousand Nights and a Night, she began her recitations.

THE TALES OF
SHAHRAZAD

The Fisherman and the Jinni.

It hath reached me, O auspicious King, that there was a
Fisherman well stricken in years who had a wife and three
children, and withal was of poor condition. Now it was his
custom to cast his net every day four times, and no more.
On a day he went forth about noontide to the sea shore,
where he laid down his basket; and, tucking up his shirt
and plunging into the water, made a cast with his net and
waited till it settled to the bottom. Then he gathered the
cords together and haled away at it, but found it weighty;
and however much he drew it landwards, he could not pull
it up; so he carried the ends ashore and drove a stake into
the ground and made the net fast to it. Then he stripped
and dived into the water all about the net, and left not off
working hard until he had brought it up. He rejoiced
thereat and, donning his clothes, went to the net, when he
found in it a dead jackass which had torn the meshes. Now
when he saw it, he exclaimed in his grief, "There is no
Majesty, and there is no Might save in Allah the Glorious,
the Great!" Then quoth he, "This is a strange manner of
daily bread;" and he began reciting in extempore verse:—

O toiler through the glooms of night in peril and in pain
Thy toiling stint for daily bread comes not by might and
　main!
Seest thou not the fisher seek afloat upon the sea
His bread, while glimmer stars of night as set in tangled
　skein.
Anon he plungeth in despite the buffet of the waves
The while to sight the bellying net his eager glances strain;
Till joying at the night's success, a fish he bringeth home
Whose gullet by the hook of Fate was caught and cut in
　twain.
When buys that fish of him a man who spent the hours of
　night
Reckless of cold and wet and gloom in ease and comfort
　fain,
Laud to the Lord who gives to this, to that denies his wishes
And dooms one toil and catch the prey and other eat the
　fishes.[1]

Then quoth he, "Up and to it; I am sure of His beneficence,
Inshallah!" So he continued:—

> When thou art seized of Evil Fate, assume
> The noble soul's long-suffering: 'tis thy best:
> Complain not to the creature; this be 'plaint
> From one most Ruthful to the ruthlessest.

The Fisherman, when he had looked at the dead ass, got it
free of the toils and wrung out and spread his net; then he
plunged into the sea, saying, "In Allah's name!" and made a
cast and pulled at it, but it grew heavy and settled down
more firmly than the first time. Now he thought that there
were fish in it, and he made it fast, and doffing his clothes
went into the water, and dived and haled until he drew it
up upon dry land. Then found he in it a large earthern
pitcher which was full of sand and mud; and seeing this he
was greatly troubled. So he prayed pardon of Allah and,
throwing away the jar, wrung his net and cleansed it and

returned to the sea the third time to cast his net and waited till it had sunk. Then he pulled at it and found therein potsherds and broken glass. Then raising his eyes heavenwards he said, "O my God![2] verily Thou wottest that I cast not my net each day save four times;[3] the third is done and as yet Thou hast vouchsafed me nothing. So this time, O my God, deign give me my daily bread." Then, having called on Allah's name,[4] he again threw his net and waited its sinking and settling; whereupon he haled at it but could not draw it in for that it was entangled at the bottom. He cried out in his vexation "There is no Majesty and there is no Might save in Allah!" and he began reciting:—

> Fie on this wretched world, an so it be
> I must be whelmed by grief and misery:
> Tho' gladsome be man's lot when dawns the morn
> He drains the cup of woe ere eve he see:
> Yet was I one of whom the world when asked
> "Whose lot is happiest?" oft would say "'Tis he!"

Thereupon he stripped and, diving down to the net, busied himself with it till it came to land. Then he opened the meshes and found therein a cucumber-shaped jar of yellow copper,[5] evidently full of something, whose mouth was made fast with a leaden cap, stamped with the seal-ring of our Lord Sulayman son of David (Allah accept the twain!). Seeing this the Fisherman rejoiced and said, "If I sell it in the brass-bazar 'tis worth ten golden dinars." He shook it and finding it heavy continued, "Would to Heaven I knew what is herein. But I must and will open it and look to its contents and store it in my bag and sell it in the brass-market." And taking out a knife he worked at the lead till he had loosened it from the jar; then he laid the cup on the ground and shook the vase to pour out whatever might be inside. He found nothing in it; whereat he marvelled with an exceeding marvel. But presently there came forth from the jar a smoke which spired heavenwards into ether (whereat he again marvelled with mighty marvel), and which trailed along earth's surface till presently, having reached its full height, the thick vapour condensed, and became an Ifrit, huge of bulk, whose crest touched the clouds while his feet were on the ground. His head was as a dome, his hands like pitchforks, his legs long as masts and his mouth big as a cave; his teeth were like large stones, his nostrils ewers, his eyes two lamps and his look was fierce and lowering. Now when the fisherman saw the Ifrit his side muscles quivered, his teeth chattered, his spittle dried up and he became blind about what to do. Upon this the Ifrit looked at him and cried, "There is no god but *the* God, and Sulayman is the prophet of God;" presently adding, "O Apostle of Allah, slay me not; never again will I gainsay thee in word nor sin against thee in deed."[6] Quoth the Fisherman, "O Marid,[7] diddest thou say, Sulayman the Apostle of Allah; and Sulayman is dead some thousand and eight hundred years ago,[8] and we are now in the last days of the world! What is thy story, and what is thy account of thyself, and what is the cause of thy entering into this cucurbit?" Now when the Evil Spirit heard the words of the Fisherman, quoth he, "There is no god but *the* God: be of good cheer, O Fisherman!" Quoth the Fisherman, "Why biddest thou me to be of good cheer?" and he replied, "Because of thy having to die an ill death in this very hour." Said the Fisherman, "Thou deservest for thy good tidings the withdrawal of Heaven's protection, O thou distant one![9] Wherefore shouldest thou kill me and what thing have I done to deserve death, I who freed thee from the jar, and saved thee from the depths of the sea, and brought thee up on the dry land?" Replied the Ifrit, "Ask of me only what mode of death thou wilt die, and by what manner of slaughter shall I slay thee." Rejoined the Fisherman, "What is my crime and wherefore such retribution?" Quoth the Ifrit, "Hear my story, O Fisherman!" and he answered, "Say on, and be brief in thy saying, for of very sooth my life-breath is in my nostrils."[10] Thereupon quoth the Jinni, "Know, that I am one among the heretical Jann and I sinned against Sulayman, David-son (on the twain be peace!) I together with the famous Sakhr al-Jinni;[11] whereupon the Prophet sent his minister, Asaf son of Barkhiya, to seize me; and this Wazir brought me against my will and led me in bonds to him (I being downcast despite my nose) and he placed me standing before him like a suppliant. When Sulayman saw me, he took refuge with Allah and bade me embrace the True Faith and obey his behests; but I refused, so sending for this cucurbit[12] he shut me up therein, and stopped it over with lead whereon he impressed the Most High Name, and gave his orders to the Jann who carried me off, and cast me into the midmost of the ocean. There I abode an hundred years, during which I said in my heart, "Whoso shall release me, him will I enrich for ever and ever." But the full century went by and, when no one set me free, I entered upon the second five score saying, "Whoso shall release me, for him I will open the hoards of the earth." Still no one set me free and thus four hundred years passed away. Then quoth I, "Whoso shall release me, for him will I fulfil three wishes." Yet no one set me free. Thereupon I waxed wroth with exceeding wrath and said to myself, "Whoso shall release me from this time forth, him will I slay and I will give him choice of what death he will die; and now, as thou hast released me, I give thee full choice of deaths." The Fisherman, hearing the words of the Ifrit, said, "O Allah! the wonder of it that I have not come to free thee save in these days!" adding, "Spare my life, so Allah spare thine; and slay me not, lest Allah set one to slay thee." Replied the Contumacious One, "There is no help for it; die thou must; so ask by way of boon what manner of death thou wilt die." Albeit thus certified the Fisherman again addressed the Ifrit saying, "Forgive me this my death as a generous reward for having freed thee;" and the Ifrit, "Surely I would not slay thee save on account of that same release." "O Chief of the Ifrits," said the Fisherman, "I do thee good and thou requitest me with evil! in very sooth the old saw lieth not when it saith:—

> We wrought them weal, they met our weal with ill;
> Such, by my life! is every bad man's labour:
> To him who benefits unworthy wights
> Shall hap what hapt to Ummi-Amir's[13] neighbour.

Now when the Ifrit heard these words he answered, "No more of this talk, needs must I kill thee." Upon this the Fisherman said to himself, "This is a Jinni; and I am a man to whom Allah hath given a passably cunning wit, so I will now cast about to compass his destruction by my contrivance and by mine intelligence; even as he took counsel only of his malice and his forwardness."[14] He began by asking the Ifrit, "Hast thou indeed resolved to kill me?" and, receiving for all answer, "Even so," he cried, "Now in the Most Great Name, graven on the seal-ring of Sulayman the Son of David (peace be with the holy twain!), an I question thee on a certain matter wilt thou give me a true answer?" The Ifrit replied "Yea;" but, hearing mention of the Most Great Name, his wits were troubled and he said with trembling, "Ask and be brief." Quoth the Fisherman, "How didst thou fit into this bottle which would not hold thy hand; no, nor even thy foot and how came it to be large enough to contain the whole of thee?" Replied the Ifrit, "What! dost not believe that I was all there?" and the Fisherman rejoined, "Nay! I will never believe it until I see thee inside with my own eyes." The Evil Spirit on the instant shook[15] and became a vapour, which condensed, and entered the jar little and little, till all was well inside when lo! the Fisherman in hot haste took the leaden cap with the seal and stoppered therewith the mouth of the jar and called out to the Ifrit, saying, "Ask me by way of boon what death thou wilt die! By Allah, I will throw thee into the sea[16] before us and here will I build me a lodge; and whoso cometh hither I will warn him against fishing and will say:—In these waters abideth an Ifrit who giveth as a last favour a choice of deaths and fashion of slaughter to the man who saveth him!" Now when the Ifrit heard this from the Fisherman and saw himself in limbo, he was minded to escape, but this was prevented by Solomon's seal; so he knew that the Fisherman had cozened and outwitted him, and he waxed lowly and submissive and began humbly to say, "I did but jest with thee." But the other answered, "Thou liest, O vilest of the Ifrits, and meanest and filthiest!" and he set off with the bottle for the sea side; the Ifrit calling out "Nay! Nay!" and he calling out "Aye! Aye!" Thereupon the Evil Spirit softened his voice and smoothed his speech and abased himself, saying, "What wouldest thou do with me, O Fisherman?" "I will throw thee back into the sea," he answered; "where thou hast been housed and homed for a thousand and eight hundred years; and now I will leave thee therein till Judgment-day; did I not say to thee:—— Spare me and Allah shall spare thee; and slay me not lest Allah slay thee? yet thou spurnedst my supplication and hadst no intention save to deal ungraciously by me, and Allah hath now thrown thee into my hands and I am cunninger than thou." Quoth the Ifrit, "Open for me that I may bring thee weal." Quoth the Fisherman, "Thou liest, thou accursed! Nothing would satisfy thee save my death; so now I will do thee die by hurling thee into this sea." Then the Marid roared aloud and cried, "Allah upon thee, O Fisherman, don't! Spare me, and pardon my past doings; and, as I have been tyrannous, so be thou generous, for it is said among sayings that go current:——O thou who doest good to him who hath done thee evil, suffice for the ill-doer his ill-deeds, and do not deal with me as did Umamah to 'Atikah."[17] Asked the Fisherman, "And what was their case?" and the Ifrit answered, "This is not the time for story-telling and I in this prison; but set me free and I will tell thee the tale." Quoth the Fisherman, "Leave this language: there is no help but that thou be thrown back into the sea nor is there any way for thy getting out of it for ever and ever. Vainly I placed myself under thy protection,[18] and I humbled myself to thee with weeping, while thou soughtest only to slay me, who had done thee no injury deserving this at thy hands; nay, so far from injuring thee by any evil act, I worked thee nought but weal in releasing thee from that jail of thine. Now I knew thee to be an evil-doer when thou diddest to me what thou didst, and know, that when I have cast thee back into this sea, I will warn whomsoever may fish thee up of what hath befallen me with thee, and I will advise him to toss thee back again; so shalt thou abide here under these waters till the End of Time shall make an end of thee." But the Ifrit cried aloud, "Set me free; this is a noble occasion for generosity and I make covenant with thee and vow never to do thee hurt and harm; nay, I will help thee to what shall put thee out of want." The Fisherman accepted his promises on both conditions, not to trouble him as before, but on the contrary to do him service; and, after making firm the plight and swearing him a solemn oath by Allah Most Highest he opened the cucurbit. Thereupon the pillar of smoke rose up till all of it was fully out; then it thickened and once more became an Ifrit of hideous presence, who forthright administered a kick to the bottle and sent it fly-ing into the sea. The Fisherman, seeing how the cucurbit was treated and making sure of his own death, piddled in his clothes and said to himself, "This promiseth badly;" but he fortified his heart, and cried, "O Ifrit, Allah hath said:[19]—Perform your covenant; for the performance of your covenant shall be inquired into hereafter. Thou hast made a vow to me and hast sworn an oath not to play me false lest Allah play thee false, for verily he is a jealous God who respiteth the sinner, but letteth him not escape. I say to thee as said the Sage Duban to King Yunan, "Spare me so Allah may spare thee!" The Ifrit burst into laughter and stalked away, saying to the Fisherman, "Follow me;" and the man paced after him at a safe distance (for he was not assured of escape) till they had passed round the suburbs of the city. Thence they struck into the unculti-vated grounds, and crossing them descended into a broad wilderness, and lo! in the midst of it stood a mountain-tarn. The Ifrit waded in to the middle and again cried, "Follow me;" and when this was done he took his stand in the cen-tre and bade the man cast his net and catch his fish. The

Fisherman looked into the water and was much astonished to see therein vari-coloured fishes, white and red, blue and yellow; however he cast his net and, hauling it in, saw that he had netted four fishes, one of each colour. Thereat he rejoiced greatly and more when the Ifrit said to him, "Carry these to the Sultan and set them in his presence; then he will give thee what shall make thee a wealthy man; and now accept my excuse, for by Allah at this time I wot none other way of benefiting thee, inasmuch I have lain in this sea eighteen hundred years and have not seen the face of the world save within this hour. But I would not have thee fish here save once a day." The Ifrit then gave him Godspeed, saying, "Allah grant we meet again;"[20] and struck the earth with one foot, whereupon the ground clove asunder and swallowed him up. The Fisherman, much marvelling at what had happened to him with the Ifrit, took the fish and made for the city; and as soon as he reached home he filled an earthen bowl with water and therein threw the fish which began to struggle and wriggle about. Then he bore off the bowl upon his head and, repairing to the King's palace (even as the Ifrit had bidden him) laid the fish before the presence; and the King wondered with exceeding wonder at the sight, for never in his lifetime had he seen fishes like these in quality or in conformation. So he said, "Give those fish to the stranger slave-girl who now cooketh for us," meaning the bond-maiden whom the King of Roum had sent to him only three days before, so that he had not yet made trial of her talents in the dressing of meat. Thereupon the Wazir carried the fish to the cook and bade her fry them,[21] saying, "O damsel, the King sendeth this say to thee:—I have not treasured thee, O tear o' me! save for stress-time of me; approve, then, to us this day thy delicate handiwork and thy savoury cooking; for this dish of fish is a present sent to the Sultan and evidently a rarity." The Wazir, after he had carefully charged her, returned to the King, who commanded him to give the Fisherman four hundred dinars: he gave them accordingly, and the man took them to his bosom and ran off home stumbling and falling and rising again and deeming the whole thing to be a dream. However, he bought for his family all they wanted and lastly he went to his wife in huge joy and gladness. So far concerning him; but as regards the cookmaid, she took the fish and cleansed them and set them in the frying-pan, basting them with oil till one side was dressed. Then she turned them over and, behold, the kitchen wall clave asunder, and therefrom came a young lady, fair of form, oval of face, perfect in grace, with eyelids which Kohl-lines enchase.[22] Her dress was a silken head-kerchief fringed and tasseled with blue: a large ring hung from either ear; a pair of bracelets adorned her wrists; rings with bezels of priceless gems were on her fingers; and she hent in hand a long rod of rattan-cane which she thrust into the frying-pan, saying, "O fish! O fish! be ye constant to your covenant?" When the cookmaiden saw this apparition she swooned away. The young lady repeated her words a second time and a third time, and at last the fishes raised their heads from the pan, and saying in articulate speech "Yes! Yes!" began with one voice to recite:—

> Come back and so will I! Keep faith and so will I!
> And if ye fain forsake, I'll requite till quits we cry!

After this the young lady upset the frying-pan and went forth by the way she came in and the kitchen wall closed upon her. When the cookmaiden recovered from her fainting-fit, she saw the four fishes charred black as charcoal, and crying out, "His staff brake in his first bout,"[23] she again fell swooning to the ground. Whilst she was in this case the Wazir came for the fish, and looking upon her as insensible she lay, not knowing Sunday from Thursday, shoved her with his foot and said, "Bring the fish for the Sultan!" Thereupon recovering from her fainting-fit she wept and informed him of her case and all that had befallen her. The Wazir marvelled greatly and exclaiming, "This is none other than a right strange matter!" he sent after the Fisherman and said to him, "Thou, O Fisherman, must needs fetch us four fishes like those thou broughtest before." Thereupon the man repaired to the tarn and cast his net; and when he landed it, lo! four fishes were therein exactly like the first. These he at once carried to the Wazir, who went in with them to the cookmaiden and said, "Up with thee and fry these in my presence, that I may see this business." The damsel arose and cleansed the fish, and set them in the frying-pan over the fire; however they remained there but a little while ere the wall clave asunder and the young lady appeared, clad as before and holding in hand the wand which she again thrust into the frying-pan, saying, "O fish! O fish! be ye constant to your olden covenant?" And behold, the fish lifted their heads, and repeated "Yes! Yes!" and recited this couplet:

> Come back and so will I! Keep faith and so will I!
> But if ye fain forsake, I'll requite till quits we cry!

When the fishes spoke, and the young lady upset the frying-pan with her rod, and went forth by the way she came and the wall closed up, the Wazir cried out, "This is a thing not to be hidden from the King." So he went and told him what had happened, whereupon quoth the King, "There is no help for it but that I see this with mine own eyes." Then he sent for the Fisherman and commanded him to bring four other fish like the first and to take with him three men as witnesses. The Fisherman at once brought the fish: and the King, after ordering them to give him four hundred gold pieces, turned to the Wazir and said, "Up and fry me the fishes here before me!" The Minister, replying "To hear is to obey," bade bring the frying-pan, threw therein the cleansed fish and set it over the fire; when lo! the wall clave asunder, and out burst a black slave like a huge rock or a remnant of the tribe Ad[24] bearing in hand a branch of a green tree; and he cried in loud and terrible tones, "O fish! O fish! be ye all constant to your antique covenant?" whereupon the fishes lifted their heads from the frying-pan and said, "Yes! Yes! we be true to our vow;" and they again recited the couplet:

> Come back and so will I! Keep faith and so will I!
> But if ye fain forsake, I'll requite till quits we cry!

Then the huge blackamoor approached the frying-pan and upset it with the branch and went forth by the way he came in. When he vanished from their sight the King inspected the fish; and, finding them all charred black as charcoal, was utterly bewildered and said to the Wazir, "Verily this is a matter whereanent silence cannot be kept, and as for the fishes, assuredly some marvellous adventure connects with them." So he bade bring the Fisherman and asked him, saying "Fie on thee, fellow! whence come these fishes?" and he answered, "From a tarn between four heights lying behind this mountain which is in sight of thy city." Quoth the King, "How many days' march?" Quoth he, "O our lord the Sultan, a walk of half hour." The King wondered and, straightway ordering his men to march and horsemen to mount, led off the Fisherman who went before as guide, privily damning the Ifrit. They fared on till they had climbed the mountain and descended unto a great desert which they had never seen during all their lives; and the Sultan and his merry men marvelled much at the wold set in the midst of four mountains, and the tarn and its fishes of four colours, red and white, yellow and blue. The King stood fixed to the spot in wonderment and asked his troops and all present, "Hath any one among you ever seen this piece of water before now?" and all made answer, "O King of the age, never did we set eyes upon it during all our days." They also questioned the oldest inhabitants they met, men well stricken in years, but they replied, each and every, "A lakelet like this we never saw in this place." Thereupon quoth the King, "By Allah I will neither return to my capital nor sit upon the throne of my forebears till I learn the truth about this tarn and the fish therein." He then ordered his men to dismount and bivouac all around the mountain; which they did; and summoning his Wazir, a Minister of much experience, sagacious, of penetrating wit and well versed in affairs, said to him, "'Tis in my mind to do a certain thing, whereof I will inform thee; my heart telleth me to fare forth alone this night and root out the mystery of this tarn and its fishes. Do thou take thy seat at my tent-door, and say to the Emirs and Wazirs, the Nabobs and the Chamberlains, in fine to all who ask thee:—The Sultan is ill at ease, and he hath ordered me to refuse all admittance;[25] and be careful thou let none know my design." And the Wazir could not oppose him. Then the King changed his dress and ornaments and, slinging his sword over his shoulder, took a path which led up one of the mountains and marched for the rest of the night till morning dawned; nor did he cease wayfaring till the heat was too much for him. After his long walk he rested for a while, and then resumed his march and fared on through the second night till dawn, when suddenly there appeared a black point in the far distance. Hereat he rejoiced and said to himself, "Haply some one here shall acquaint me with the mystery of the tarn and its fishes." Presently, drawing near the dark object he found it a palace built of swart stone plated with iron; and, while one leaf of the gate stood wide open, the other was shut. The King's spirits rose high as he stood before the gate and rapped a light rap; but hearing no answer he knocked a second knock and a third; yet there came no sign. Then he knocked his loudest but still no answer, so he said, "Doubtless 'tis empty." Thereupon he mustered up resolution, and boldly walked through the main gate into the great hall and there cried out aloud, "Holla, ye people of the palace! I am a stranger and a wayfarer; have you aught here of victual?" He repeated his cry a second time and a third but still there came no reply; so strengthening his heart and making up his mind he stalked through the vestibule into the very middle of the palace and found no man in it. Yet it was furnished with silken stuffs gold-starred; and the hangings were let down over the door-ways. In the midst was a spa-

cious court off which set four open saloons each with its
raised daïs, saloon facing saloon; a canopy shaded the court
and in the centre was a jetting fount with four figures of
lions made of red gold, spouting from their mouths water
clear as pearls and diaphanous gems. Round about the
palace birds were let loose and over it stretched a net of
golden wire, hindering them from flying off; in brief there
was everything but human beings. The King marvelled
mightily thereat, yet felt he sad at heart for that he saw no
one to give him an account of the waste and its tarn, the
fishes, the mountains and the palace itself. Presently as he
sat between the doors in deep thought behold, there came
a voice of lament, as from a heart grief-spent, and he heard
the voice chanting these verses:—

I hid what I endured of him[26] and yet it came to light,
And nightly sleep mine eyelids fled and changed to sleepless
    night:
Oh world! Oh Fate! withhold thy hand and cease thy hurt
    and harm
Look and behold my hapless sprite in dolour and affright:
Wilt ne'er show ruth to highborn youth who lost him on
    the way
Of Love, and fell from wealth and fame to lowest basest
    wight.
Jealous of Zephyr's breath was I as on your form he breathed
But whenas Destiny descends she blindeth human sight,[27]
What shall the hapless archer do who when he fronts his foe
And bends his bow to shoot the shaft shall find his string
    undight?
When cark and care so heavy bear on youth[28] of generous
    soul
How shall he 'scape his lot and where from Fate his place of
    flight?

Now when the Sultan heard the mournful voice he sprang
to his feet; and, following the sound, found a curtain let
down over a chamber-door. He raised it and saw behind
it a young man sitting upon a couch about a cubit above

the ground; and he fair to the sight, a well shaped wight, with eloquence dight; his forehead was flower-white, his cheek rosy bright, and a mole on his cheek-breadth like an ambergris-mite; even as the poet doth indite:—

> A youth slim-waisted from whose locks and brow
> The world in blackness and in light is set.
> Throughout Creation's round no fairer show
> No rarer sight thine eye hath ever met:
> A nut-brown mole sits throned upon a cheek
> Of rosiest red beneath an eye of jet.[29]

The King rejoiced and saluted him, but he remained sitting in his caftan of silken stuff purfled with Egyptian gold and his crown studded with gems of sorts; but his face was sad with the traces of sorrow. He returned the royal salute in most courteous wise adding, "O my lord, thy dignity demandeth my rising to thee; and my sole excuse is to crave thy pardon." Quoth the King,[30] "Thou art excused, O youth; so look upon me as thy guest come hither on an especial object. I would thou acquaint me with the secrets of this tarn and its fishes and of this palace and thy loneliness therein and the cause of thy groaning and wailing." When the young man heard these words he wept with sore weeping[31] till his bosom was drenched with tears. The King marvelled and asked him, "What maketh thee weep, O young man?" and he answered, "How should I not weep, when this is my case!" Thereupon he put out his hand and raised the skirt of his garment, when lo! the lower half of him appeared stone down to his feet while from his navel to the hair of his head he was man. The King, seeing this his plight, grieved with sore grief and of his compassion cried, "Alack and well-away! in very sooth, O youth, thou heapest sorrow upon my sorrow. I was minded to ask thee the mystery of the fishes only: whereas now I am concerned to learn thy story as well as theirs. But there is no Majesty and there is no Might save in Allah, the Glorious, the Great![32] Lose no time, O youth, but tell me forthright thy whole tale." Quoth he, "Lend me thine ears, thy sight and thine insight;" and quoth the King, "All are at thy service!" Thereupon the youth began, "Right wondrous and marvellous is my case and that of these fishes; and were it graven with gravers upon the eye-corners it were a warner to whoso would be warned." "How is that?" asked the King, and the young man began to tell

THE TALE OF THE ENSORCELLED PRINCE.

Know then, O my lord, that whilome my sire was King of this city, and his name was Mahmud, entitled Lord of the Black Islands, and owner of what are now these four mountains. He ruled threescore and ten years, after which he went to the mercy of the Lord and I reigned as Sultan in his stead. I took to wife my cousin, the daughter of my paternal uncle,[33] and she loved me with such abounding love that whenever I was absent she ate not and she drank not until she saw me again. She cohabited with me for five years till a certain day when she went forth to the Hammam-bath; and I bade the cook hasten to get ready all requisites for our supper. And I entered this palace and lay down on the bed where I was wont to sleep and bade two damsels to fan my face, one sitting by my head and the other at my feet. But I was troubled and made restless by my wife's absence and could not sleep; for although my eyes were closed my mind and thoughts were wide awake. Presently I heard the slave-girl at my head say to her at my feet, "O Mas'udah, how miserable is our master and how wasted in his youth and oh! the pity of his being so betrayed by our mistress, the accursed whore!"[34] The other replied, "Yes indeed: Allah curse all faithless women and adulterous; but the like of our master, with his fair gifts, deserveth something better than this harlot who lieth abroad every night." Then quoth she who sat by my head, "Is our lord dumb or fit only for bubbling that he questioneth her not!" and quoth the other, "Fie on thee! doth our lord know her ways or doth she allow him his choice?

Nay, more, doth she not drug every night the cup she giveth him to drink before sleep-time, and put Bhang[35] into it? So he sleepeth and wotteth not whither she goeth, nor what she doeth; but we know that, after giving him the drugged wine, she donneth her richest raiment and perfumeth herself and then she fareth out from him to be away till break of day; then she cometh to him, and burneth a pastile under his nose and he awaketh from his death-like sleep." When I heard the slave-girls' words, the light became black before my sight and I thought night would never fall. Presently the daughter of my uncle came from the baths; and they set the table for us and we ate and sat together a fair half-hour quaffing our wine as was ever our wont. Then she called for the particular wine I used to drink before sleeping and reached me the cup; but, seeming to drink it according to my wont, I poured the contents into my bosom; and, lying down, let her hear that I was asleep. Then, behold, she cried, "Sleep out the night, and never wake again; by Allah, I loathe thee and I loathe thy whole body, and my soul turneth in disgust from cohabiting with thee; and I see not the moment when Allah shall snatch away thy life!" Then she rose and donned her fairest dress and perfumed her person and slung my sword over her shoulder; and, opening the gates of the palace, went her ill way. I rose and followed her as she left the palace and she threaded the streets until she came to the city gate, where she spoke words I understood not, and the padlocks dropped of themselves as if broken and the gate-leaves opened. She went forth (and I after her without her noticing aught) till she came at last to the outlying mounds[36] and a reed fence built about a round-roofed hut of mud-bricks. As she entered the door, I climbed upon the roof which commanded a view of the interior, And lo! my fair cousin had gone in to a hideous negro slave with his upper lip like the cover of a pot, and his lower like an open pot; lips which might sweep up sand from the gravel-floor of the cot. He was to boot a leper and a paralytic, lying upon a strew of sugar-cane trash and wrapped in an old blanket and the foulest rags and tatters. She kissed the earth before him, and he raised his head so as to see her and said, "Woe to thee! what call hadst thou to stay away all this time? Here have been with me sundry of the black brethren, who drank their wine and each had his young lady, and I was not content to drink because of thine absence." Then she, "O my lord, my heart's love and coolth of my eyes,[37] knowest thou not that I am married to my cousin whose very look I loathe, and hate myself when in his company? And did not I fear for thy sake, I would not let a single sun arise before making his city a ruined heap wherein raven should croak and howlet hoot, and jackal and wolf harbour and loot; nay I had removed its very stones to the back side of Mount Kaf."[38] Rejoined the slave, "Thou liest, damn thee! Now I swear an oath by the valour and honour of blackamoor men (and deem not our manliness to be the poor manliness of white men), from to-day forth if thou stay away till this hour, I will not keep company with thee nor will I glue my body with thy body. Dost play fast and loose with us, thou cracked pot, that we may satisfy thy dirty lusts, O vilest of the vile whites?" When I heard his words, and saw with my own eyes what passed between these two wretches, the world waxed dark before my face and my soul knew not in what place it was. But my wife humbly stood up weeping before and wheedling the slave, and saying, "O my beloved, and very fruit of my heart, there is none left to cheer me but thy dear self; and, if thou cast me off who shall take me in, O my beloved, O light of my eyes?" And she ceased not weeping and abasing herself to him until he deigned be reconciled with her. Then was she right glad and stood up and doffed her clothes, even to her petticoat-trousers, and said, "O my master what hast thou here for thy handmaiden to eat?" "Uncover the basin," he grumbled, "and thou shalt find at the bottom the broiled bones of some rats we dined on; pick at them, and then go to that slop-pot where thou shalt find some leavings of beer[39] which thou mayest drink." So she ate and drank and

washed her hands, and went and lay down by the side of
the slave, upon the cane-trash and crept in with him under
his foul coverlet and his rags and tatters. When I saw my
wife, my cousin, the daughter of my uncle, do this deed[40]
I clean lost my wits, and climbing down from the roof, I
entered and took the sword which she had with her and
drew it, determined to cut down the twain. I first struck at
the slave's neck and thought that the death decree had
fallen on him for he groaned a loud hissing groan, but I had
cut only the skin and flesh of the gullet and the two arter-
ies! It awoke the daughter of my uncle, so I sheathed the
sword and fared forth for the city; and, entering the palace,
lay upon my bed and slept till morning when my wife
aroused me and I saw that she had cut off her hair and had
donned mourning garments. Quoth she:—O son of my
uncle, blame me not for what I do; it hath just reached me
that my mother is dead, and my father hath been killed in
holy war, and of my brothers one hath lost his life by a
snake-sting and the other by falling down some precipice;
and I can and should do naught save weep and lament.
When I heard her words I refrained from all reproach and
said only:—Do as thou list; I certainly will not thwart thee.
She continued sorrowing, weeping and wailing one whole
year from the beginning of its circle to the end, and when
it was finished she said to me:—I wish to build me in thy
palace a tomb with a cupola, which I will set apart for my
mourning and will name the House of Lamentations.[41]
Quoth I again:—Do as thou list! Then she builded for herself a cenotaph wherein to mourn, and set on its centre a
dome under which showed a tomb like a Santon's sepulchre. Thither she carried the slave and lodged him; but he
was exceeding weak by reason of his wound, and unable to
do her love-service; he could only drink wine and from the
day of his hurt he spake not a word, yet he lived on because
his appointed hour[42] was not come. Every day, morning
and evening, my wife went to him and wept and wailed
over him and gave him wine and strong soups, and left not

off doing after this manner a second year; and I bore with
her patiently and paid no heed to her. One day, however, I
went in to her unawares; and I found her weeping and
beating her face and crying:—Why art thou absent from
my sight, O my heart's delight? Speak to me, O my life; talk
with me, O my love? When she had ended for a time her
words and her weeping I said to her:—O my cousin, let
this thy mourning suffice, for in pouring forth tears there
is little profit! Thwart me not, answered she, in aught I do,
or I will lay violent hands on myself! So I held my peace
and left her to go her own way; and she ceased not to cry
and keen and indulge her affliction for yet another year.
At the end of the third year I waxed aweary of this longsome mourning, and one day I happened to enter the
cenotaph when vexed and angry with some matter which
had thwarted me, and suddenly I heard her say:—O my
lord, I never hear thee vouchsafe a single word to me! Why
dost thou not answer me, O my master? and she began
reciting:—

> O thou tomb! O thou tomb! be his beauty set in shade?
> Hast thou darkened that countenance all-sheeny as the
>   noon?
> O thou tomb! neither earth nor yet heaven art to me
> Then how cometh it in thee are conjoined my sun and
>   moon?

When I heard such verses as these rage was heaped upon
my rage; I cried out:—Well-away! how long is this sorrow
to last? and I began repeating:—

> O thou tomb! O thou tomb! be his horrors set in blight?
> Hast thou darkened his countenance that sickeneth the soul?
> O thou tomb! neither cess-pool nor pipkin art to me
> Then how cometh it in thee are conjoined soil and coal?

When she heard my words she sprang to her feet crying:—
Fie upon thee, thou cur! all this is of thy doings; thou hast

wounded my heart's darling and thereby worked me sore woe and thou hast wasted his youth so that these three years he hath lain abed more dead than alive! In my wrath I cried:—O thou foulest of harlots and filthiest of whores ever futtered by negro slaves who are hired to have at thee![43] Yes indeed it was I who did this good deed; and snatching up my sword I drew it and made at her to cut her down. But she laughed my words and mine intent to scorn crying: To heel, hound that thou art! Alas[44] for the past which shall no more come to pass nor shall any one avail the dead to raise. Allah hath indeed now given into my hand him who did to me this thing, a deed that hath burned my heart with a fire which died not and a flame which might not be quenched! Then she stood up; and, pronouncing some words to me unintelligible, she said:—By virtue of my egromancy become thou half stone and half man; whereupon I became what thou seest, unable to rise or to sit, and neither dead nor alive. Moreover she ensorcelled the city with all its streets and garths, and she turned by her gramarye the four islands into four mountains around the tarn whereof thou questionest me; and the citizens, who were of four different faiths, Moslem, Nazarene, Jew and Magian, she transformed by her enchantments into fishes; the Moslems are the white, the Magians red, the Christians blue and the Jews yellow.[45] And every day she tortureth me and scourgeth me with an hundred stripes, each of which draweth floods of blood and cutteth the skin of my shoulders to strips; and lastly she clotheth my upper half with a hair-cloth and then throweth over them these robes.—Hereupon the young man again shed tears and began reciting:—

In patience, O my God, I endure my lot and fate;
I will bear at will of Thee whatsoever be my state:
They oppress me; they torture me; they make my life a woe
Yet haply Heaven's happiness shall compensate my strait;
Yea, straitened is my life by the bane and hate o' foes
But Mustafa and Murtaza[46] shall ope me Heaven's gate.

After this the Sultan turned towards the young Prince and said, "O youth, thou hast removed one grief only to add another grief; but now, O my friend, where is she; and where is the mausoleum wherein lieth the wounded slave?" "The slave lieth under yon dome," quoth the young man, "and she sitteth in the chamber fronting yonder door. And every day at sunrise she cometh forth, and first strippeth me, and whippeth me with an hundred strokes of the leathern scourge, and I weep and shriek; but there is no power of motion in my lower limbs to keep her off me. After ending her tormenting me she visiteth the slave, bringing him wine and boiled meats. And to-morrow at an early hour she will be here." Quoth the King, "By Allah, O youth, I will assuredly do thee a good deed which the world shall not willingly let die, and an act of derring-do which shall be chronicled long after I am dead and gone by." Then the King sat him by the side of the young Prince and talked till nightfall, when he lay down and slept; but, as soon as the false dawn[47] showed, he arose and doffing his outer garments[48] bared his blade and hastened to the place wherein lay the slave. Then was he ware of lighted candles and lamps, and the perfume of incenses and unguents; and, directed by these, he made for the slave and struck him one stroke killing him on the spot: after which he lifted him on his back and threw him into a well that was in the palace. Presently he returned and, donning the slave's gear, lay down at length within the mausoleum with the drawn sword laid close to and along his side. After an hour or so the accursed witch came; and, first going to her husband, she stripped off his clothes and, taking a whip, flogged him cruelly while he cried out, "Ah! enough for me the case I am in! take pity on me, O my cousin!" But she replied, "Didst thou take pity on me and spare the life of my true love on whom I doated?" Then she drew the cilice over his raw and bleeding skin and threw the robe upon all and went down to the slave with a goblet of wine and a bowl of meat-broth in her hands. She entered under the dome weeping and wailing, "Well-away!" and crying, "O my lord!

speak a word to me! O my master! talk awhile with me!" and began to recite these couplets:—

> How long this harshness, this unlove, shall bide?
> Suffice thee not tear-floods thou hast espied?
> Thou dost prolong our parting purposely
> And if wouldst please my foe, thou'rt satisfied!

Then she wept again and said, "O my lord! speak to me, talk with me!" The King lowered his voice and, twisting his tongue, spoke after the fashion of the blackamoors and said " 'lack! 'lack! there be no Ma'esty and there be no Might save in Allauh, the Gloriose, the Great!" Now when she heard these words she shouted for joy, and fell to the ground fainting; and when her senses returned she asked, "O my lord, can it be true that thou hast power of speech?" and the King making his voice small and faint answered, "O my cuss! dost thou deserve that I talk to thee and speak with thee?" "Why and wherefore?" rejoined she; and he replied "The why is that all the livelong day thou tormentest thy hubby; and he keeps calling on 'eaven for aid until sleep is strange to me even from evenin' till mawnin', and he prays and damns, cussing us two, me and thee, causing me disquiet and much bother: were this not so, I should long ago have got my health; and it is this which prevents my answering thee." Quoth she, "With thy leave I will release him from what spell is on him;" and quoth the King, "Release him and let's have some rest!" She cried, "To hear is to obey;" and, going from the cenotaph to the palace, she took a metal bowl and filled it with water and spake over it certain words which made the contents bubble and boil as a cauldron seetheth over the fire. With this she sprinkled her husband saying, "By virtue of the dread words I have spoken, if thou becamest thus by my spells, come forth out of that form into thine own former form." And lo and behold! the young man shook and trembled; then he rose to his feet and, rejoicing at his deliverance, cried aloud, "I testify that there is no god but *the* God, and in very truth Mohammed is His Apostle, whom Allah bless and keep!" Then she said to him, "Go forth and return not hither, for if thou do I will surely slay thee;" screaming these words in his face. So he went from between her hands; and she returned to the dome and, going down to the sepulchre, she said, "O my lord, come forth to me that I may look upon thee and thy goodliness!" The King replied in faint low words, "What[49] thing hast thou done? Thou hast rid me of the branch but not of the root." She asked, "O my darling! O my negroling! what is the root?" And he answered, "Fie on thee, O my cuss! The people of this city and of the four islands every night when it's half passed lift their heads from the tank in which thou hast turned them to fishes and cry to Heaven and call down its anger on me and thee; and this is the reason why my body's baulked from health. Go at once and set them free; then come to me and take my hand, and raise me up, for a little strength is already back in me." When she heard the King's words (and she still supposed him to be the slave) she cried joyously, "O my master, on my head and on my eyes be thy command, Bismillah!"[50] So she sprang to her feet and, full of joy and gladness, ran down to the tarn and took a little of its water in the palm of her hand and spake over it words not to be understood, and the fishes lifted their heads and stood up on the instant like men, the spell on the people of the city having been removed. What was the lake again became a crowded capital; the bazars were thronged with folk who bought and sold; each citizen was occupied with his own calling and the four hills became islands as they were whilome. Then the young woman, that wicked sorceress, returned to the King and (still thinking he was the negro) said to him, "O my love! stretch forth thy honoured hand that I may assist thee to rise." "Nearer to me," quoth the King in a faint and feigned tone. She came close as to embrace him when he took up the sword lying hid by his side and smote her across the breast, so that the point showed gleaming behind her back. Then he smote her a second time and cut her in twain and cast her to the ground in two halves. After

which he fared forth and found the young man, now freed
from the spell, awaiting him and gave him joy of his happy
release while the Prince kissed his hand with abundant
thanks. Quoth the King, "Wilt thou abide in this city or go
with me to my capital?" Quoth the youth, "O King of the
age, wottest thou not what journey is between thee and thy
city?" "Two days and a half," answered he; whereupon said
the other, "An thou be sleeping, O King, awake! Between
thee and thy city is a year's march for a well-girt walker,
and thou haddest not come hither in two days and a half
save that the city was under enchantment. And I, O King,
will never part from thee; no, not even for the twinkling of
an eye." The King rejoiced at his words and said, "Thanks
be to Allah who hath bestowed thee upon me! From this
hour thou art my son and my only son, for that in all my
life I have never been blessed with issue." Thereupon they
embraced and joyed with exceeding great joy; and, reaching the palace, the Prince who had been spell-bound informed his lords and his grandees that he was about to visit
the Holy Places as a pilgrim, and bade them get ready all
things necessary for the occasion. The preparations lasted
ten days, after which he set out with the Sultan, whose
heart burned in yearning for his city whence he had been
absent a whole twelve-month. They journeyed with an escort of Mamelukes[51] carrying all manners of precious gifts
and rarities, nor stinted they wayfaring day and night for a
full year until they approached the Sultan's capital, and
sent on messengers to announce their coming. Then the
Wazir and the whole army came out to meet him in joy
and gladness, for they had given up all hope of ever seeing their King; and the troops kissed the ground before
him and wished him joy of his safety. He entered and took
seat upon his throne and the Minister came before him
and, when acquainted with all that had befallen the young
Prince, he congratulated him on his narrow escape. When
order was restored throughout the land the King gave
largesse to many of his people, and said to the Wazir, "Hither
the Fisherman who brought us the fishes!" So he sent for

the man who had been the first cause of the city and the citizens being delivered from enchantment and, when he came into the presence, the Sultan bestowed upon him a dress of honour, and questioned him of his condition and whether he had children. The Fisherman gave him to know that he had two daughters and a son, so the King sent for them and, taking one daughter to wife, gave the other to the young Prince and made the son his head-treasurer. Furthermore he invested his Wazir with the Sultanate of the City in the Black Islands whilome belonging to the young Prince, and dispatched with him the escort of fifty armed slaves together with dresses of honour for all the Emirs and Grandees. The Wazir kissed hands and fared forth on his way; while the Sultan and the Prince abode at home in all the solace and the delight of life; and the Fisherman became the richest man of his age, and his daughters wived with the Kings, until death came to them. And yet, O King! this is not more wondrous than the story of

THE PORTER AND THE THREE
LADIES OF BAGHDAD.

Once upon a time there was a Porter in Baghdad, who was
a bachelor and who would remain unmarried. It came to
pass on a certain day, as he stood about the street leaning
idly upon his crate, behold, there stood before him an honourable woman in a mantilla of Mosul[1] silk, broidered
with gold and bordered with brocade; her walking-shoes
were also purfled with gold and her hair floated in long
plaits. She raised her face-veil[2] and, showing two black
eyes fringed with jetty lashes, whose glances were soft and
languishing and whose perfect beauty was ever blandish-
ing, she accosted the Porter and said in the suavest tones
and choicest language, "Take up thy crate and follow me."
The Porter was so dazzled he could hardly believe that he
heard her aright, but he shouldered his basket in hot haste
saying in himself, "O day of good luck! O day of Allah's
grace!" and walked after her till she stopped at the door of
a house. There she rapped, and presently came out to her
an old man, a Nazarene, to whom she gave a gold piece, receiving from him in return what she required of strained
wine clear as olive oil; and she set it safely in the hamper,

saying, "Lift and follow." Quoth the Porter, "This, by Allah, is indeed an auspicious day, a day propitious for the granting of all a man wisheth." He again hoisted up the crate and followed her; till she stopped at a fruiterer's shop and bought from him Shami[3] apples and Osmani quinces and Omani[4] peaches, and cucumbers of Nile growth, and Egyptian limes and Sultani oranges and citrons; besides Aleppine jasmine, scented myrtle berries, Damascene nenuphars, flower of privet[5] and camomile, blood-red anemones, violets, and pomegranate-bloom, eglantine and narcissus, and set the whole in the Porter's crate, saying, "Up with it." So he lifted and followed her till she stopped at a butcher's booth and said, "Cut me off ten pounds of mutton." She paid him his price and he wrapped it in a banana-leaf, whereupon she laid it in the crate and said, "Hoist, O Porter." He hoisted accordingly, and followed her as she walked on till she stopped at a grocer's, where she bought dry fruits and pistachio-kernels, Tihamah raisins, shelled almonds and all wanted for dessert, and said to the Porter, "Lift and follow me." So he up with his hamper and after her till she stayed at the confectioner's, and she bought an earthen platter, and piled it with all kinds of sweetmeats in his shop, open-worked tarts and fritters scented with musk and "soap-cakes," and lemon-loaves and melon-preserves,[6] and "Zaynab's combs," and "ladies' fingers," and "Kazi's titbits" and goodies of every description; and placed the platter in the Porter's crate. Thereupon quoth he (being a merry man), "Thou shouldest have told me, and I would have brought with me a pony or a she-camel to carry all this market-stuff." She smiled and gave him a little cuff on the nape saying, "Step out and exceed not in words, for (Allah willing!) thy wage will not be wanting." Then she stopped at a perfumer's and took from him ten sorts of waters, rose scented with musk, orange-flower, water-lily, willow-flower, violet and five others; and she also bought two loaves of sugar, a bottle for perfume-spraying, a lump of male incense, aloe-wood, ambergris and musk, with candles of Alexandria wax; and she put the whole into the basket, saying, "Up with thy crate and after me." He did so and followed until she stood before the greengrocer's, of whom she bought pickled safflower and olives, in brine and in oil; with tarragon and cream-cheese and hard Syrian cheese; and she stowed them away in the crate saying to the Porter, "Take up thy basket and follow me." He did so and went after her till she came to a fair mansion fronted by a spacious court, a tall, fine place to which columns gave strength and grace: and the gate thereof had two leaves of ebony inlaid with plates of red gold. The lady stopped at the door and, turning her face-veil sideways, knocked softly with her knuckles whilst the Porter stood behind her, thinking of naught save her beauty and loveliness. Presently the door swung back and both leaves were opened, whereupon he looked to see who had opened it; and behold, it was a lady of tall figure, some five feet high; a model of beauty and loveliness, brilliance and symmetry and perfect grace. Her forehead was flower-white; her cheeks like the anemone ruddy bright; her eyes were those of the wild heifer or the gazelle, with eyebrows like the crescent-moon which ends Sha'aban and begins Ramazan;[7] her mouth was the ring of Sulayman,[8] her lips coral-red, and her teeth like a line of strung pearls or of camomile petals. Her throat recalled the antelope's, and her breasts, like two pomegranates of even size, stood at bay as it were;[9] her body rose and fell in waves below her dress like the rolls of a piece of brocade, and her navel[10] would hold an ounce of benzoin ointment. In fine she was like her of whom the poet said:—

> On Sun and Moon of palace cast thy sight
> Enjoy her flower-like face, her fragrant light:
> Thine eyes shall never see in hair so black
> Beauty encase a brow so purely white:
> The ruddy rosy cheek proclaims her claim
> Through fail her name whose beauties we indite:
> As sways her gait I smile at hips so big
> And weep to see the waist they bear so slight.

When the Porter looked upon her his wits were waylaid, and his senses were stormed so that his crate went nigh to fall from his head, and he said to himself, "Never have I in my life seen a day more blessed than this day!" Then quoth the lady-portress to the lady-cateress, "Come in from the gate and relieve this poor man of his load." So the provisioner went in followed by the portress and the Porter and went on till they reached a spacious ground-floor hall,[11] built with admirable skill and beautified with all manner colours and carvings; with upper balconies and groined arches and galleries and cupboards and recesses whose curtains hung before them. In the midst stood a great basin full of water surrounding a fine fountain, and at the upper end on the raised daïs was a couch of juniper-wood set with gems and pearls, with a canopy like mosquito-curtains of red satin-silk looped up with pearls as big as filberts and bigger. Thereupon sat a lady bright of blee, with brow beaming brilliancy, the dream of philosophy, whose eyes were fraught with Babel's[12] gramarye and her eyebrows were arched as for archery; her breath breathed ambergris and perfumery and her lips were sugar to taste and carnelian to see. Her stature was straight as the letter I[13] and her face shamed the noon-sun's radiancy; and she was even as a galaxy, or a dome with golden marquetry or a bride displayed in choicest finery or a noble maid of Araby.[14] The[15] third lady rising from the couch stepped forward with graceful swaying gait till she reached the middle of the saloon, when she said to her sisters, "Why stand ye here? take it down from this poor man's head!" Then the cateress went and stood before him, and the portress behind him while the third helped them, and they lifted the load from the Porter's head; and, emptying it of all that was therein, set everything in its place. Lastly they gave him two gold pieces, saying, "Wend thy ways, O Porter." But he went not, for he stood looking at the ladies and admiring what uncommon beauty was theirs, and their pleasant manners and kindly dispositions (never had he seen goodlier); and he gazed wistfully at that good store of wines and sweet-scented flowers and fruits and other matters. Also he marvelled with exceeding marvel, especially to see no man in the place and delayed his going; whereupon quoth the eldest lady, "What aileth thee that goest not; haply thy wage be too little?" And, turning to her sister the cateress, she said, "Give him another dinar!" But the Porter answered, "By Allah, my lady, it is not for the wage; my hire is never more than two dirhams; but in very sooth my heart and my soul are taken up with you and your condition. I wonder to see you single with ne'er a man about you and not a soul to bear you company; and well you wot that the minaret toppleth o'er unless it stand upon four, and you want this same fourth, and women's pleasure without man is short of measure, even as the poet said:—

> Seest not we want for joy four things all told
> The harp and lute, the flute and flageolet;
> And be they companied with scents four-fold
> Rose, myrtle, anemone and violet;
> Nor please all eight an four thou wouldst withhold
> Good wine and youth and gold and pretty pet.

You be three and want a fourth who shall be a person of good sense and prudence; smart witted, and one apt to keep careful counsel." His words pleased and amused them much; and they laughed at him and said, "And who is to assure us of that? We are maidens and we fear to entrust our secret where it may not be kept, for we have read in a certain chronicle the lines of one Ibn al-Sumam:—

> Hold fast thy secret and to none unfold
> Lost is a secret when that secret's told:
> An fail thy breast thy secret to conceal
> How canst thou hope another's breast shall hold?"

When the Porter heard their words he rejoined, "By your lives! I am a man of sense and a discreet, who hath read books and perused chronicles; I reveal the fair and conceal the foul and I act as the poet adviseth:—

> None but the good a secret keep
> And good men keep it unrevealed:
> It is to me a well-shut house
> With keyless locks and door ensealed."[16]

When the maidens heard his verse and its poetical application addressed to them they said, "Thou knowest that we have laid out all our monies on this place. Now say, hast thou aught to offer us in return for entertainment? For surely we will not suffer thee to sit in our company and be our cup-companion, and gaze upon our faces so fair and so rare without paying a round sum.[17] Wottest thou not the saying:—

> Sans hope of gain
> Love's not worth a grain?"

Whereto the lady-portress added, "If thou bring anything thou art a something; if no thing, be off with thee, thou art a nothing;" but the procuratrix interposed, saying, "Nay, O my sisters, leave teasing him, for by Allah he hath not failed us this day, and had he been other he never had kept patience with me, so whatever be his shot and scot I will take it upon myself." The Porter, overjoyed, kissed the ground before her and thanked her saying, "By Allah, these monies are the first fruits this day hath given me." Hearing this they said, "Sit thee down and welcome to thee," and the eldest lady added, "By Allah, we may not suffer thee to join us save on one condition, and this it is, that no questions be asked as to what concerneth thee not, and frowardness shall be soundly flogged." Answered the Porter, "I agree to this, O my lady, on my head and my eyes be it! Lookye, I am dumb, I have no tongue." Then arose the provisioneress and tightening her girdle set the table by the fountain and put the flowers and sweet herbs in their jars, and strained the wine and ranged the flasks in row and made ready every requisite. Then sat she down, she and her sisters, placing amidst them the Porter who kept deeming himself in a dream; and she took up the wine flagon, and poured out the first cup and drank it off, and likewise a second and a third.[18] After this she filled a fourth cup which she handed to one of her sisters; and, lastly, she crowned a goblet and passed it to the Porter, saying:—

> Drink the dear draught, drink free and fain
> What healeth every grief and pain.

He took the cup in his hand and, louting low, returned his best thanks and improvised:—

> Drain not the bowl save with a trusty friend
> A man of worth whose good old blood all know:
> For wine, like wind, sucks sweetness from the sweet
> And stinks when over stench it haply blow:

Adding:—

> Drain not the bowl, save from dear hand like thine
> The cup recalls thy gifts; thou, gifts of wine.

After repeating this couplet he kissed their hands and drank and was drunk and sat swaying from side to side and pursued:—

> All drinks wherein is blood the Law unclean
> Doth hold save one, the bloodshed of the vine:
> Fill! fill! take all my wealth bequeathed or won
> Thou fawn! a willing ransome for those eyne.

Then the cateress crowned a cup and gave it to the portress, who took it from her hand and thanked her and drank. Thereupon she poured again and passed to the eldest lady who sat on the couch, and filled yet another and handed it to the Porter. He kissed the ground before them; and, after drinking and thanking them, he again began to recite:—

> Here! Here! by Allah, here!
> Cups of the sweet, the dear!
> Fill me a brimming bowl
> The Fount o' Life I speer

Then the Porter stood up before the mistress of the house and said, "O lady, I am thy slave, thy Mameluke, thy white thrall, thy very bondsman;" and he began reciting:—

> A slave of slaves there standeth at thy door
> Lauding thy generous boons and gifts galore:
> Beauty! may he come in awhile to 'joy
> Thy charms? for Love and I part nevermore!

Then the lady took the cup, and drank it off to her sisters' health, and they ceased not drinking (the Porter being in the midst of them), and dancing and laughing and reciting verses and singing ballads and ritornellos. All this time the Porter was carrying on with them, kissing, toying, biting, handling, groping, fingering; whilst one thrust a dainty morsel in his mouth, and another slapped him; and this cuffed his cheeks, and that threw sweet flowers at him; and he was in the very paradise of pleasure, as though he were sitting in the seventh sphere among the Houris[19] of Heaven. And they ceased not to be after this fashion till night began to fall. Thereupon said they to the Porter, "Bismillah,[20] O our master, up and on with those sorry old shoes of thine and turn thy face and show us the breadth of thy shoulders!" Said he, "By Allah, to part with my soul would be easier for me than departing from you: come let us join night to day, and to-morrow morning we will each wend our own way." "My life on you," said the procuratrix, "suffer him to tarry with us, that we may laugh at him: we may live out our lives and never meet with his like, for surely he is a right merry rogue and a witty."[21] So they said, "Thou must not remain with us this night save on condition that thou submit to our commands, and that whatso thou seest, thou ask no questions thereanent, nor enquire of its cause." "All right," rejoined he, and they said, "Go read the writing over the door." So he rose and went to the entrance and there found written in letters of gold wash; WHOSO SPEAKETH OF WHAT CONCERNETH HIM NOT, SHALL HEAR WHAT PLEASETH HIM NOT![22] The Porter said, "Be ye witnesses against me that I will not speak on whatso concerneth me not." Then the cateress arose, and set food before them and they ate; after which they changed their drinking-place for another, and she lighted the lamps and candles and burned ambergris and aloes-wood, and set on fresh fruit and the wine service, when they fell to carousing and talking of their lovers. And they ceased not to eat and drink and chat, nibbling dry fruits and laughing and playing tricks for the space of a full hour when lo! a knock was heard at the gate. The knocking in no wise disturbed the seance, but one of them rose and went to see what it was and presently returned, saying, "Truly our pleasure for this night is to be perfect." "How is that?" asked they; and she answered, "At the gate be three Persian Kalandars[23] with their beards and heads and eyebrows shaven; and all three blind of the left eye—which is surely a strange chance. They are foreigners from Roum-land with the mark of travel plain upon them; they have just entered Baghdad, this being their first visit to our city; and the cause of their knocking at our door is simply because they cannot find a lodging. Indeed one of them said to me:—Haply the owner of this mansion will let us have the key of his stable or some old outhouse wherein we may pass this night; for evening had surprised them and, being strangers in the land, they knew none who would give them shelter. And, O my sisters, each of them is a figure o' fun after his own fashion; and if we let them in we shall have matter to make sport of." She gave not over persuading them till they said to her, "Let them in, and make thou the usual condition

with them that they speak not of what concerneth them
not, lest they hear what pleaseth them not." So she rejoiced
and going to the door presently returned with the three
monoculars whose beards and mustachios were clean
shaven.[24] They salam'd and stood afar off by way of respect; but the three ladies rose up to them and welcomed
them and wished them joy of their safe arrival and made
them sit down. The Kalandars looked at the room and
saw that it was a pleasant place, clean swept and garnished
with flowers; and the lamps were burning and the smoke of
perfumes was spireing in air; and beside the dessert and
fruits and wine, there were three fair girls who might be
maidens; so they exclaimed with one voice, "By Allah, 'tis
good!" Then they turned to the Porter and saw that he was
a merry-faced wight, albeit he was by no means sober and
was sore after his slappings. So they thought that he was
one of themselves and said, "A mendicant like us! whether
Arab or foreigner."[25] But when the Porter heard these
words, he rose up, and fixing his eyes fiercely upon them,
said, "Sit ye here without exceeding in talk! Have you not
read what is writ over the door? surely it befitteth not fellows who come to us like paupers to wag your tongues at
us." "We crave thy pardon, O Fakir,"[26] rejoined they, "and
our heads are between thy hands." The ladies laughed con-
sumedly at the squabble; and, making peace between the
Kalandars and the Porter, seated the new guests before
meat and they ate. Then they sat together, and the portress
served them with drink; and, as the cup went round merrily, quoth the Porter to the askers, "And you, O brothers
mine, have ye no story or rare adventure to amuse us
withal?" Now the warmth of wine having mounted to their
heads they called for musical instruments; and the portress
brought them a tambourine of Mosul, and a lute of Irak,
and a Persian harp; and each mendicant took one and
tuned it; this the tambourine and those the lute and the
harp, and struck up a merry tune while the ladies sang so
lustily that there was a great noise.[27] And whilst they were

carrying on, behold, some one knocked at the gate, and the portress went to see what was the matter there. Now the cause of that knocking, O King (quoth Shahrazad) was this, the Caliph, Harun al-Rashid, had gone forth from the palace, as was his wont now and then, to solace himself in the city that night, and to see and hear what new thing was stirring; he was in merchant's gear, and he was attended by Ja'afar, his Wazir, and by Masrur his Sworder of Vengeance.[28] As they walked about the city, their way led them towards the house of the three ladies; where they heard the loud noise of musical instruments and singing and merriment; so quoth the Caliph to Ja'afar, "I long to enter this house and hear those songs and see who sing them." Quoth Ja'afar, "O Prince of the Faithful; these folk are surely drunken with wine, and I fear some mischief betide us if we get amongst them." "There is no help but that I go in there," replied the Caliph, "and I desire thee to contrive some pretext for our appearing among them." Ja'afar replied, "I hear and I obey;"[29] and knocked at the door, whereupon the portress came out and opened. Then Ja'afar came forward and kissing the ground before her said, "O my lady, we be merchants from Tiberias-town: we arrived at Baghdad ten days ago; and, alighting at the merchants' caravanserai, we sold all our merchandise. Now a certain trader invited us to an entertainment this night; so we went to his house and he set food before us and we ate: then we sat at wine and wassail with him for an hour or so when he gave us leave to depart; and we went out from him in the shadow of the night and, being strangers, we could not find our way back to our Khan. So haply of your kindness and courtesy you will suffer us to tarry with you this night, and Heaven will reward you!"[30] The portress looked upon them and seeing them dressed like merchants and men of grave looks and solid, she returned to her sisters and repeated to them Ja'afar's story; and they took compassion upon the strangers and said to her, "Let them enter." She opened the door to them, when said they to her,

"Have we thy leave to come in?" "Come in," quoth she; and the Caliph entered followed by Ja'afar and Masrur; and when the girls saw them they stood up to them in respect and made them sit down and looked to their wants, saying, "Welcome, and well come and good cheer to the guests, but with one condition!" "What is that?" asked they, and one of the ladies answered, "Speak not of what concerneth you not, lest ye hear what pleaseth you not." "Even so," said they; and sat down to their wine and drank deep. Presently the Caliph looked on the three Kalandars and, seeing them each and every blind of the left eye, wondered at the sight; then he gazed upon the girls and he was startled and he marvelled with exceeding marvel at their beauty and loveliness. They continued to carouse and to converse and said to the Caliph, "Drink!" but he replied, "I am vowed to Pilgrimage;"[31] and drew back from the wine. Thereupon the portress rose and spreading before him a table-cloth worked with gold, set thereon a porcelain bowl into which she poured willow flower water with a lump of snow and a spoonful of sugar-candy. The Caliph thanked her and said in himself, "By Allah, I will recompense her to-morrow for the kind deed she hath done." The others again addressed themselves to conversing and carousing; and, when the wine gat the better of them, the eldest lady who ruled the house rose and making obeisance to them took the cateress by the hand, and said, "Rise, O my sister and let us do what is our devoir." Both answered "Even so!" Then the portress stood up and proceeded to remove the table-service and the remnants of the banquet; and renewed the pastiles and cleared the middle of the saloon. Then she made the Kalandars sit upon a sofa at the side of the estrade, and seated the Caliph and Ja'afar and Masrur on the other side of the saloon; after which she called the Porter, and said, "How scant is thy courtesy! now thou art no stranger; nay, thou art one of the household." So he stood up and, tightening his waist-cloth, asked, "What would ye I do?" and she answered, "Stand in thy place."

Then the procuratrix rose and set in the midst of the saloon a low chair and, opening a closet, cried to the Porter, "Come help me." So he went to help her and saw two black bitches with chains round their necks; and she said to him, "Take hold of them;" and he took them and led them into the middle of the saloon. Then the lady of the house arose and tucked up her sleeves above her wrists and, seizing a scourge, said to the Porter, "Bring forward one of the bitches." He brought her forward, dragging her by the chain, while the bitch wept, and shook her head at the lady who, however, came down upon her with blows on the sconce; and the bitch howled and the lady ceased not beating her till her forearm failed her. Then, casting the scourge from her hand, she pressed the bitch to her bosom and, wiping away her tears with her hands, kissed her head. Then said she to the Porter, "Take her away and bring the second;" and, when he brought her, she did with her as she had done with the first. Now the heart of the Caliph was touched at these cruel doings; his chest straitened and he lost all patience in his desire to know why the two bitches were so beaten. He threw a wink at Ja'afar wishing him to ask, but the Minister turning towards him said by signs, "Be silent!" Then quoth the portress to the mistress of the house, "O my lady, arise and go to thy place that I in turn may do my devoir."[32] She answered, "Even so"; and, taking her seat upon the couch of juniper-wood, pargetted with gold and silver, said to the portress and cateress, "Now do ye what ye have to do." Thereupon the portress sat upon a low seat by the couch side; but the procuratrix, entering a closet, brought out of it a bag of satin with green fringes and two tassels of gold. She stood up before the lady of the house and shaking the bag drew out from it a lute which she tuned by tightening its pegs; and when it was in perfect order, she began to sing these quatrains:—

> Ye are the wish, the aim of me
> And when, O love, thy sight I see[33]

The heavenly mansion openeth;[34]
But Hell I see when lost thy sight.
From thee comes madness; nor the less
Comes highest joy, comes ecstasy:
Nor in my love for thee I fear
Or shame and blame, or hate and spite.
When Love was throned within my heart
I rent the veil of modesty;
And stints not Love to rend that veil
Garring disgrace on grace to alight;
The robe of sickness then I donned
But rent to rags was secrecy:
Wherefore my love and longing heart
Proclaim your high supremest might;
The tear-drop railing adown my cheek
Telleth my tale of ignomy:
And all the hid was seen by all
And all my riddle ree'd aright.
Heal then my malady, for thou
Art malady and remedy!
But she whose cure is in thy hand
Shall ne'er be free of bane and blight;
Burn me those eyne that radiance rain
Slay me the swords of phantasy;
How many hath the sword of Love
Laid low, their high degree despite?
Yet will I never cease to pine
Nor to oblivion will I flee.
Love is my health, my faith, my joy
Public and private, wrong or right.
O happy eyes that sight thy charms
That gaze upon thee at their gree!
Yea, of my purest wish and will
The slave of Love I'll aye be hight.

When the damsel heard this elegy in quatrains she cried
out "Alas!" "Alas!" and rent her raiment, and fell to the
ground fainting; and the Caliph saw scars of the palm-

rod[35] on her back and welts of the whip; and marvelled
with exceeding wonder. Then the portress arose and sprinkled water on her and brought her a fresh and very fine
dress and put it on her. But when the company beheld
these doings their minds were troubled, for they had no
inkling of the case nor knew the story thereof; so the
Caliph said to Ja'afar, "Didst thou not see the scars upon
the damsel's body? I cannot keep silence or be at rest till
I learn the truth of her condition and the story of this
other maiden and the secret of the two black bitches." But
Ja'afar answered, "O our lord, they made it a condition
with us that we speak not of what concerneth us not, lest
we come to hear what pleaseth us not." Then said the
portress, "By Allah, O my sister, come to me and complete
this service for me." Replied the procuratrix, "With joy and
goodly gree;" so she took the lute; and leaned it against her
breasts and swept the strings with her finger-tips, and began
singing:—

> Give back mine eyes their sleep long ravishèd
> And say me whither be my reason fled:
> I learnt that lending to thy love a place
> Sleep to mine eyelids mortal foe was made.
> They said, "We held thee righteous, who waylaid
> Thy soul?" "Go ask his glorious eyes," I said.
> I pardon all my blood he pleased to spill
> Owning his troubles drove him blood to shed.
> On my mind's mirror sun-like sheen he cast
> Whose keen reflection fire in vitals bred
> Waters of Life let Allah waste at will
> Suffice my wage those lips of dewy red:
> An thou address my love thou'lt find a cause
> For plaint and tears or ruth or lustihed.
> In water pure his form shall greet your eyne
> When fails the bowl nor need ye drink of wine.[36]

Then she quoted from the same ode:—

> I drank, but the draught of his glance, not wine;
> And his swaying gait swayed to sleep these eyne:
> 'Twas not grape-juice gript me but grasp of Past
> 'Twas not bowl o'erbowled me but gifts divine:
> His coiling curl-lets my soul ennetted
> And his cruel will all my wits outwitted.[37]

After a pause she resumed:—

> If we 'plain of absence what shall we say?
> Or if pain afflict us where wend our way?
> An I hire a truchman[38] to tell my tale
> The lovers' plaint is not told for pay:
> If I put on patience, a lover's life
> After loss of love will not last a day:
> Naught is left me now but regret, repine
> And tears flooding cheeks for ever and aye:
> O thou who the babes of these eyes[39] hast fled
> Thou art homed in heart that shall never stray;
> Would heaven I wot hast thou kept our pact
> Long as stream shall flow, to have firmest fay?
> Or hast forgotten the weeping slave
> Whom groans afflict and whom griefs waylay?
> Ah, when severance ends and we side by side
> Couch, I'll blame thy rigours and chide thy pride!

Now when the portress heard her second ode she shrieked aloud and said, "By Allah! 'tis right good!"; and laying hands on her garments tore them, as she did the first time, and fell to the ground fainting. Thereupon the procuratrix rose and brought her a second change of clothes after she had sprinkled water on her. She recovered and sat upright and said to her sister the cateress, "Onwards, and help me in my duty, for there remains but this one song." So the provisioneress again brought out the lute and began to sing these verses:—

> How long shall last, how long this rigour rife of woe
> May not suffice thee all these tears thou seest flow?

Our parting thus with purpose fell thou dost prolong
Is't not enough to glad the heart of envious foe?
Were but this lying world once true to lover-heart
He had not watched the weary night in tears of woe:
Oh pity me whom overwhelmed thy cruel will
My lord, my king, 'tis time some ruth to me thou show:
To whom reveal my wrongs, O thou who murdered me?
Sad, who of broken troth the pangs must undergo!
Increase wild love for thee and phrenzy hour by hour
And days of exile minute by so long, so slow;
O Moslems, claim *vendetta*[40] for this slave of Love
Whose sleep Love ever wastes, whose patience Love lays low:
Doth law of Love allow thee, O my wish! to lie
Lapt in another's arms and unto me cry "Go!"?
Yet in thy presence, say, what joys shall I enjoy
When he I love but works my love to overthrow?

When the portress heard the third song she cried aloud;
and, laying hands on her garments, rent them down to the
very skirt and fell to the ground fainting a third time, again
showing the scars of the scourge. Then said the three Kalandars, "Would Heaven we had never entered this house,
but had rather nighted on the mounds and heaps outside
the city! for verily our visit hath been troubled by sights
which cut to the heart." The Caliph turned to them and
asked, "Why so?" and they made answer, "Our minds are
sore troubled by this matter." Quoth the Caliph, "Are ye
not of the household?" and quoth they, "No; nor indeed
did we ever set eyes on the place till within this hour."
Hereat the Caliph marvelled and rejoined, "This man who
sitteth by you, would he not know the secret of the matter?" and so saying he winked and made signs at the Porter.
So they questioned the man but he replied, "By the All-
might of Allah, in love all are alike![41] I am the growth of
Baghdad, yet never in my born days did I darken these
doors till to-day and my companying with them was a curious matter." "By Allah," they rejoined, "we took thee for
one of them and now we see thou art one like ourselves."

Then said the Caliph, "We be seven men, and they only three women without even a fourth to help them; so let us question them of their case; and, if they answer us not, fain we will be answered by force." All of them agreed to this except Ja'afar who said,[42] "This is not my recking; let them be; for we are their guests and, as ye know, they made a compact and condition with us which we accepted and promised to keep: wherefore it is better that we be silent concerning this matter; and, as but little of the night remaineth, let each and every of us gang his own gait." Then he winked at the Caliph and whispered to him, "There is but one hour of darkness left and I can bring them before thee to-morrow, when thou canst freely question them all concerning their story." But the Caliph raised his head haughtily and cried out at him in wrath, saying, "I have no patience left for my longing to hear of them: let the Kalandars question them forthright." Quoth Ja'afar, "This is not my rede." Then words ran high and talk answered talk, and they disputed as to who should first put the question, but at last all fixed upon the Porter. And as the jangle increased the house-mistress could not but notice it and asked them, "O ye folk! on what matter are ye talking so loudly?" Then the Porter stood up respectfully before her and said, "O my lady, this company earnestly desire that thou acquaint them with the story of the two bitches and what maketh thee punish them so cruelly; and then thou fallest to weeping over them and kissing them; and lastly they want to hear the tale of thy sister and why she hath been bastinado'd with palm-sticks like a man. These are the questions they charge me to put, and peace be with thee."[43] Thereupon quoth she who was the lady of the house to the guests, "Is this true that he saith on your part?" and all replied, "Yes!" save Ja'afar who kept silence. When she heard these words she cried, "By Allah, ye have wronged us, O our guests, with grievous wronging; for when you came before us we made compact and condition with you, that whoso should speak of what concerneth him not should hear what pleaseth him not. Sufficeth ye not that we took you into our house and fed you with our best food? But the fault is not so much yours as hers who let you in." Then she tucked up her sleeves from her wrists and struck the floor thrice with her hand crying, "Come ye quickly;" and lo! a closet door opened and out of it came seven negro slaves with drawn swords in hand to whom she said, "Pinion me those praters' elbows and bind them each to each." They did her bidding and asked her, "O veiled and virtuous! is it thy high command that we strike off their heads?"; but she answered, "Leave them awhile that I question them of their condition, before their necks feel the sword." "By Allah, O my lady!" cried the Porter, "slay me not for other's sin; all these men offended and deserve the penalty of crime save myself. Now by Allah, our night had been charming had we escaped the mortification of those monocular Kalandars whose entrance into a populous city would convert it into a howling wilderness." Then he repeated these verses:—

> How fair is ruth the strong man deigns not smother!
> And fairest fair when shown to weakest brother:
> By Love's own holy tie between us twain,
> Let one not suffer for the sin of other.

When the Porter ended his verse the lady laughed despite her wrath, and came up to the party and spake thus, "Tell me who ye be, for ye have but an hour of life; and were ye not men of rank and, perhaps, notables of your tribes, you had not been so frowned and I had hastened your doom." Then said the Caliph, "Woe to thee, O Ja'afar, tell her who we are lest we be slain by mistake; and speak her fair before some horror befal us." "'Tis part of thy deserts," replied he; whereupon the Caliph cried out at him saying, "There is a time for witty words and there is a time for serious work." Then the lady accosted the three Kalandars and asked them, "Are ye brothers?"; when they answered, "No, by Allah, we be naught but Fakirs and foreigners." Then quoth she to one among them, "Wast thou born blind of one eye?"; and quoth he, "No, by Allah, 'twas a marvellous matter and a wondrous mischance which caused my eye to be torn out, and mine is a tale which, if it were written upon the eye-corners with needle-gravers, were a warner to whoso would be warned."[44] She questioned the second and third Kalandar; but all replied like the first, "By Allah, O our mistress, each one of us cometh from a different country, and we are all three the sons of Kings, sovereign Princes ruling over suzerains and capital cities." Thereupon she turned towards them and said, "Let each and every of you tell me his tale in due order and explain the cause of his coming to our place; and if his story please us let him stroke his head[45] and wend his way." The first to come forward was the Hammal, the Porter, who said, "O my lady, I am a man and a porter. This dame, the cateress, hired me to carry a load and took me first to the shop of a vintner; then to the booth of a butcher; thence to the stall of a fruiterer; thence to a grocer who also sold dry fruits; thence to a confectioner and a perfumer-cum-druggist and from him to this place where there happened to me with you what happened. Such is my story and peace be on us all!" At this the lady laughed and said, "Rub thy head and wend thy ways!"; but he cried, "By Allah, I will not stump it till I hear the stories of my companions." Then came forward one of the Monoculars and began to tell her

THE FIRST KALANDAR'S TALE.

Know, O my lady, that the cause of my beard being shorn and my eye being out-torn was as follows. My father was a King and he had a brother who was a King over another city; and it came to pass that I and my cousin, the son of my paternal uncle, were both born on one and the same day. And years and days rolled on; and, as we grew up, I used to visit my uncle every now and then and to spend a certain number of months with him. Now my cousin and I were sworn friends; for he ever entreated me with exceeding kindness; he killed for me the fattest sheep and strained the best of his wines, and we enjoyed long conversing and carousing. One day when the wine had gotten the better of us, the son of my uncle said to me, "O my cousin, I have a great service to ask of thee; and I desire that thou stay me not in whatso I desire to do!" And I replied, "With joy and goodly will." Then he made me swear the most binding oaths and left me; but after a little while he returned leading a lady veiled and richly apparelled with ornaments worth a large sum of money. Presently he turned to me (the woman being still behind him) and said, "Take this lady with thee and go before me to such a burial ground" (describing it, so that I knew the place), "and enter with her into such a sepulchre and there await my coming." The oaths I swore to him made me keep silence and suffered me not to oppose him; so I led the woman to the cemetery and both I and she took our seats in the sepulchre;⁴⁶ and hardly had we sat down when in came my uncle's son, with a bowl of water, a bag of mortar and an adze somewhat like a hoe. He went straight to the tomb in the midst of the sepulchre and, breaking it open with the adze set the stones on one side; then he fell to digging into the earth of the tomb till he came upon a large iron plate, the size of a wicket-door; and on raising it there appeared below it a staircase vaulted and winding. Then he turned to the lady and said to her, "Come now and take thy final choice!" She at once went down by the staircase and disappeared; then quoth he to me, "O son of my uncle, by way of completing thy kindness, when I shall have descended into this place, restore the trap-door to where it was, and heap back the earth upon it as it lay before; and then of thy great goodness mix this unslaked lime which is in the bag with this water which is in the bowl and, after building up the stones, plaster the outside so that none looking upon it shall say:—This is a new opening in an old tomb. For a whole year have I worked at this place whereof none knoweth but Allah, and this is the need I have of thee;" presently adding, "May Allah never bereave thy friends of thee nor make them desolate by thine absence, O son of my uncle, O my dear cousin!" And he went down the stairs and disappeared for ever. When he was lost to sight I replaced the iron plate and did all his bidding till the tomb became as it was before; and I worked almost unconsciously for my head was heated with wine. Returning to the palace of my uncle, I was told that he had gone forth a-sporting and hunting; so I slept that night without seeing him; and, when the morning dawned, I remembered the scenes of the past evening and what happened between me and my cousin; I repented of having obeyed him when penitence was of no avail. I still thought, however, that it was a dream. So I fell to asking for the son of my uncle; but there was none to answer me concerning him; and I went out to the graveyard and the sepulchres, and sought for the tomb under which he was, but could not find it; and I ceased not wandering about from sepulchre to sepulchre, and tomb to tomb, all without success till night set in. So I returned to the city, yet I could neither eat nor drink; my thoughts being engrossed with my cousin, for that I knew not what was become of him; and I grieved with exceeding grief and passed another sorrowful night, watching until the morning. Then went I a second time to the cemetery, pondering over what the son of mine uncle had done; and, sorely repenting my hearkening to him, went round among all the tombs, but could not find the tomb I sought. I mourned over the past, and remained in my mourning seven days, seeking the place and ever missing the path. Then my torture of scruples[47] grew upon me till I well-nigh went mad, and I found no way to dispel my grief save travel and return to my father. So I set out and journeyed homeward; but as I was entering my father's capital a crowd of rioters sprang upon me and pinioned me.[48] I wondered thereat with all wonderment, seeing that I was the son of the Sultan, and these men were my father's subjects and amongst them were some of my own slaves. A great fear fell upon me, and I said to my soul,[49] "Would heaven I knew what hath happened to my father!" I questioned those that bound me of the cause of their so doing, but they returned me no answer. However, after a while one of them said to me (and he had been a hired servant of our house), "Fortune hath been false to thy father; his troops betrayed him and the Wazir who slew him now reigneth in his stead and we lay in wait to seize thee by the bidding of him." I was well-nigh distraught and felt ready to faint on hearing of my father's death; when they carried me off and placed me in presence of the usurper. Now between me and him there was an olden grudge, the cause of which was this. I was fond of shooting with the stone-bow,[50] and it befel one day, as I was standing on the terrace-roof of the palace, that a bird lighted on the top of the Wazir's house when he happened to be there. I shot at the bird and missed the mark; but I hit the Wazir's eye and knocked it out as fate and fortune decreed. Now when I knocked out the Wazir's eye he could not say a single word, for that my father was King of the city; but he hated me ever after and dire was the grudge thus caused between us twain. So when I was set before him hand-bound and pinioned, he straightway gave orders for me to be beheaded. I asked, "For what crime wilt thou put me to death?"; whereupon he answered, "What crime is greater than this?" pointing the while to the place where his eye had been. Quoth I, "This I did by accident not of malice prepense;" and quoth he, "If thou didst it by accident, I will do the like by thee with intention."[51] Then cried he, "Bring him forward," and they brought me up to him, when he thrust his finger into my left eye and gouged it out; whereupon I became one-eyed as ye see me. Then he bade bind me hand and foot, and put me into a chest and said to the sworder, "Take charge of this fellow, and go off with him to the waste lands about the city; then draw thy scymitar and slay him, and leave him to feed the beasts and birds." So the headsman fared forth with me and when he was in the midst of the desert, he took me out of the chest (and I with both hands pinioned and both feet fettered) and was about to bandage my eyes before striking off my head. But I wept with exceeding weeping until I made him weep with me and, looking at him I began to recite these couplets:—

> I deemed you coat-o'-mail that should withstand
> The foeman's shafts; and you proved foeman's brand;
> I hoped your aidance in mine every chance
> Though fail my left to aid my dexter hand:
> Aloof you stand and hear the railer's gibe
> While rain their shafts on me the giber-band:
> But an ye will not guard me from my foes
> Stand clear, and succour neither these nor those!

And I also quoted:—

> I deemed my brethren mail of strongest steel;
> And so they were—from foes to fend my dart!
> I deemed their arrows surest of their aim;
> And so they were—when aiming at my heart!

When the headsman heard my lines (he had been sworder to my sire and he owed me a debt of gratitude) he cried, "O my lord, what can I do, being but a slave under orders?" presently adding, "Fly for thy life and nevermore return to this land, or they will slay thee and slay me with thee." Hardly believing in my escape, I kissed his hand and thought the loss of my eye a light matter in consideration of my escaping from being slain. I arrived at my uncle's capital; and, going in to him, told him of what had befallen my father and myself; whereat he wept with sore weeping and said, "Verily thou addest grief to my grief, and woe to my woe; for thy cousin hath been missing these many days; I wot not what hath happened to him, and none can give me news of him." And he wept till he fainted. I sorrowed and condoled with him; and he would have applied certain medicaments to my eye, but he saw that it was become as a walnut with the shell empty. Then said he, "O my son, better to lose eye and keep life!" After that I could no longer remain silent about my cousin, who was his only son and one dearly loved, so I told him all that had happened. He rejoiced with extreme joyance to hear news of his son and said, "Come now and show me the tomb;" but I replied, "By Allah, O my uncle, I know not its place, though I sought it carefully full many times, yet could not find the site." However, I and my uncle went to the graveyard and looked right and left, till at last I recognised the tomb and we both rejoiced with exceeding joy. We entered the sepulchre and loosened the earth about the grave; then, upraising the trap-door, descended some fifty steps till we came to the foot of the staircase when lo! we were stopped by a blinding smoke. Thereupon said my uncle that saying whose sayer shall never come to shame, "There is no Majesty and there is no Might, save in Allah, the Glorious, the Great!" and we advanced till we suddenly came upon a saloon, whose floor was strewed with flour and grain and provisions and all manner necessaries; and in the midst of it stood a canopy sheltering a couch. Thereupon my uncle went up to the couch and inspecting it found his son and the lady who had gone down with him into the tomb, lying in each other's embrace; but the twain had become black as charred wood; it was as if they had been cast into a pit of fire. When my uncle saw this spectacle, he spat in his son's face and said, "Thou hast thy deserts, O thou hog!52 this is thy judgment in the transitory world, and yet remaineth the judgment in the world to come, a durer and a more enduring." I marvelled at his hardness of heart, and grieving for my cousin and the lady, said, "By Allah, O my uncle, calm thy wrath: dost thou not see that all my thoughts are occupied with this misfortune, and how sorrowful I am for what hath befallen thy son, and how horrible it is that naught of him remaineth but a black heap of charcoal? And is not that enough, but thou must smite him with thy slipper?" Answered he, "O son of my brother, this youth from his boyhood was madly in love with his own sister;53 and often and often I forbade him from her, saying to myself:—They are but little ones. However, when they grew up sin befel between them; and, although I could hardly believe it, I confined him and chided him and threatened him with the severest threats; and the eunuchs and servants said to him:——Beware of so foul a thing which none before thee ever did, and which none after thee will ever do; and have a care lest thou be dishonoured and disgraced among the Kings of the day, even to the end of time. And I added:——Such a report as this will be spread abroad by caravans, and take heed not to give them cause to talk or I will assuredly curse thee and do thee to death. After that I lodged them apart and shut her up; but the accursed girl loved him with passionate love, for Satan had got the mastery of her as well as of him and made their foul sin seem fair in their sight. Now when my son saw that I separated them, he secretly built this souterrain and furnished it and transported to it victuals, even as thou seest; and, when I had gone out a-sporting, came here with his sister and hid from me. Then His righteous judgment fell upon the twain and consumed them with fire from Heaven; and verily the last judgment will deal them durer pains and more enduring!" Then he wept and I wept with him; and he looked at me and said, "Thou art my son in his stead." And I bethought me awhile of the world and of its chances, how the Wazir had slain my father and had taken his place and had put out my eye; and how my cousin had come to his death by the strangest chance: and I wept again and my uncle wept with me. Then we mounted the steps and let down the iron plate and heaped up the earth over it; and, after restoring the tomb to its former condition, we returned to the palace. But hardly had we sat down ere we heard the tom-toming of the kettle-drum and tantara of trumpets and clash of cymbals; and the rattling of warmen's lances; and the clamours of assailants and the clanking of bits and the neighing of steeds; while the world was canopied with dense dust and sand-clouds raised by the horses' hoofs.[54] We were amazed at sight and sound, knowing not what could be the matter; so we asked and were told us that the Wazir who had usurped my father's kingdom had marched his men; and that after levying his soldiery and taking a host of wild Arabs[55] into service, he had come down upon us with armies like the sands of the sea; their number none could tell and against them none could prevail. They attacked the city unawares; and the citizens, being powerless to oppose them, surrendered the place: my uncle was slain and I made for the suburbs saying to myself, "If thou fall into this villain's hands he will assuredly kill thee." On this wise all my troubles were renewed; and I pondered all that had betided my father and my uncle and I knew not what to do; for if the city people or my father's troops had recognised me they would have done their best to win favour by destroying me; and I could think of no way to escape save by shaving off my beard and my eyebrows. So I shore them off and, changing my fine clothes for a Kalandar's rags, I fared forth from my uncle's capital and made for this city, hoping that peradventure some one would assist me to the presence of the Prince of the Faithful,[56] and the Caliph who is the Viceregent of Allah upon earth. Thus have I come hither that I might tell him my tale and lay my case before him. I arrived here this very night, and was standing in doubt whither I should go, when suddenly I saw this second Kalandar; so I salam'd to him, saying:—I am a stranger! and he answered:—I too am a stranger! And as we were conversing behold, up came our companion, this third Kalandar, and saluted us saying:—I am a stranger! And we answered:—We too be strangers! Then we three walked on and together till darkness overtook us and Destiny drave us to your house. Such, then, is the cause of the shaving of my beard and mustachios and eyebrows; and the manner of my losing my left eye. They marvelled much at this tale and the Caliph said to Ja'afar, "By Allah, I have not seen nor have I heard the like of what hath happened to this Kalandar!" Quoth the lady of the house, "Rub thy head and wend thy ways;" but he replied, "I will not go, till I hear the history of the two others." Thereupon the second Kalandar came forward; and, kissing the ground, began to tell

THE SECOND KALANDAR'S TALE.

Know, O my lady, that I was not born one-eyed and mine is a strange story; an it were graven with needle-graver on the eye-corners, it were a warner to whoso would be warned. I am a King, son of a King, and was brought up like a Prince. I learned intoning the Koran according the seven schools;[57] and I read all manner books, and held disputations on their contents with the doctors and men of science; moreover I studied star-lore and the fair sayings of poets and I exercised myself in all branches of learning until I surpassed the people of my time; my skill in calligraphy exceeded that of all the scribes; and my fame was bruited abroad over all climes and cities, and all the kings learned to know my name. Amongst others the King of Hind heard of me and sent to my father to invite me to his court, with offerings and presents and rarities such as befit royalties. So my father fitted out six ships for me and my people; and we put to sea and sailed for the space of a full month till we made the land. Then we brought out the horses that were with us in the ships; and, after loading the camels with our presents for the Prince, we set forth inland. But we had marched only a little way, when behold, a dust-cloud up-flew, and grew until it walled[58] the horizon from view. After an hour or so the veil lifted and discovered beneath it fifty horsemen, ravening lions to the sight, in steel armour dight. We observed them straightly and lo! they were cutters-off of the highway, wild as wild Arabs. When they saw that we were only four and had with us but the ten camels carrying the presents, they dashed down upon us with lances at rest. We signed to them, with our fingers, as it were saying, "We be messengers of the great King of Hind, so harm us not!" but they answered on like wise, "We are not in his dominions to obey nor are we subject to his sway." Then they set upon us and slew some of my slaves and put the lave to flight; and I also fled after I had gotten a wound, a grievous hurt, whilst the Arabs were taken up with the money and the presents which were with us. I went forth unknowing whither I went, having become mean as I was mighty; and I fared on until I came to the crest of a mountain where I took shelter for the night in a cave. When day arose I set out again, nor ceased after this fashion till I arrived at a fair city and a well-filled. Now it was the season when Winter was turning away with his rime and to greet the world with his flowers came Prime, and the young blooms were springing and the streams flowed ringing, and the birds were sweetly singing, as saith the poet concerning a certain city when describing it:—

> A place secure from every thought of fear
> Safety and peace for ever lord it here:
> Its beauties seem to beautify its sons
> And as in Heaven its happy folk appear.

I was glad of my arrival for I was wearied with the way, and yellow of face for weakness and want; but my plight was pitiable and I knew not whither to betake me. So I accosted a Tailor sitting in his little shop and saluted him; he returned my salam, and bade me kindly welcome and wished me well and entreated me gently and asked me of the cause of my strangerhood. I told him all my past from first to last; and he was concerned on my account and said, "O youth, disclose not thy secret to any: the King of this city is the greatest enemy thy father hath, and there is blood-wit[59] between them and thou hast cause to fear for thy life." Then he set meat and drink before me; and I ate and drank and he with me; and we conversed freely till night-fall, when he cleared me a place in a corner of his shop and brought me a carpet and a coverlet. I tarried with him three days; at the end of which time he said to me, "Knowest thou no calling whereby to win thy living, O my son?" "I am learned in the law," I replied, "and a doctor of doctrine; an adept in art and science, a mathematician and a notable penman." He rejoined, "Thy calling is of no account in our city, where not a soul understandeth science or even writing or aught save money-making." Then said

I, "By Allah, I know nothing but what I have mentioned;" and he answered, "Gird thy middle and take thee a hatchet and a cord, and go and hew wood in the wold for thy daily bread, till Allah send thee relief; and tell none who thou art lest they slay thee." Then he bought me an axe and a rope and gave me in charge to certain woodcutters; and with these guardians I went forth into the forest, where I cut fuel-wood the whole of my day and came back in the evening bearing my bundle on my head. I sold it for half a dinar, with part of which I bought provision and laid by the rest. In such work I spent a whole year and when this was ended I went out one day, as was my wont, into the wilderness; and, wandering away from my companions, I chanced on a thickly grown lowland[60] in which there was an abundance of wood. So I entered and I found the gnarled stump of a great tree and loosened the ground about it and shovelled away the earth. Presently my hatchet rang upon a copper ring; so I cleared away the soil and behold, the ring was attached to a wooden trap-door. This I raised and there appeared beneath it a staircase. I descended the steps to the bottom and came to a door, which I opened and found myself in a noble hall strong of structure and beautifully built, where was a damsel like a pearl of great price, whose favour banished from my heart all grief and cark and care; and whose soft speech healed the soul in despair and captivated the wise and ware. Her figure measured five feet in height; her breasts were firm and upright; her cheek a very garden of delight; her colour lively bright; her face gleamed like dawn through curly tresses which gloomed like night, and above the snows of her bosom glittered teeth of a pearly white.[61] When I looked upon her I prostrated myself before Him who had created her, for the beauty and loveliness He had shaped in her, and she looked at me and said, "Art thou man or Jinni?" "I am a man," answered I, and she, "Now who brought thee to this place where I have abided five-and-twenty years without even yet seeing man in it." Quoth I (and indeed I found her words wonder-sweet, and my heart was melted to the core by them), "O my lady, my good fortune led me hither for the dispelling of my cark and care." Then I related to her all my mishap from first to last, and my case appeared to her exceeding grievous; so she wept and said, "I will tell thee my story in my turn. I am the daughter of the King Ifitamus, lord of the Islands of Abnus,[62] who married me to my cousin, the son of my paternal uncle; but on my wedding night an Ifrit named Jirjis[63] bin Rajmus, first cousin that is, mother's sister's son, of Iblis, the Foul Fiend, snatched me up and, flying away with me like a bird, set me down in this place, whither he conveyed all I needed of fine stuffs, raiment and jewels and furniture, and meat and drink and other else. Once in every ten days he comes here and lies a single night with me, and then wends his way, for he took me without the consent of his family; and he hath agreed with me that if ever I need him by night or by day, I have only to pass my hand over yonder two lines engraved upon the alcove, and he will appear to me before my fingers cease touching. Four days have now passed since he was here; and, as there remain six days before he come again, say me, wilt thou abide with me five days, and go hence the day before his coming?" I replied "Yes, and yes again! O rare, if all this be not a dream!" Hereat she was glad and, springing to her feet, seized my hand and carried me through an arched doorway to a Hammam-bath, a fair hall and richly decorate. I doffed my clothes, and she doffed hers; then we bathed and she washed me; and when this was done we left the bath, and she seated me by her side upon a high divan, and brought me sherbet scented with musk. When we felt cool after the bath, she set food before me and we ate and fell to talking; but presently she said to me, "Lay thee down and take thy rest, for surely thou must be weary." So I thanked her, my lady, and lay down and slept soundly, forgetting all that happened to me. When I awoke I found her rubbing and shampooing my feet;[64] so I again thanked her and blessed her and we sat for a while talking. Said she, "By Allah, I was sad at heart, for that I have dwelt alone underground for these five-and-twenty years; and praise be to Allah, who hath sent me some one with whom I can converse!" Then she asked, "O youth, what sayest thou to wine?" and I answered, "Do as thou wilt." Whereupon she went to a cupboard and took out a sealed flask of right old wine and set off the table with flowers and scented herbs and began to sing these lines:—

> Had we known of thy coming we fain had dispread
> The cores of our hearts or the balls of our eyes;
> Our cheeks as a carpet to greet thee had thrown
> And our eyelids had strown for thy feet to betread.

Now when she finished her verse I thanked her, for indeed love of her had gotten hold of my heart and my grief and anguish were gone. We sat at converse and carousal till nightfall, and with her I spent the night—such night never spent I in all my life! On the morrow delight followed delight till midday, by which time I had drunken wine so freely that I had lost my wits, and stood up, staggering to the right and to the left, and said "Come, O my charmer, and I will carry thee up from this underground vault and deliver thee from the spell of thy Jinni." She laughed and replied "Content thee and hold thy peace: of every ten days one is for the Ifrit and the other nine are thine." Quoth I (and in good sooth drink had got the better of me), "This very instant will I break down the alcove whereon is graven the talisman and summon the Ifrit that I may slay him, for it is a practise of mine to slay Ifrits!" When she heard my words her colour waxed wan and she said, "By Allah, do not!" and she began repeating:—

> This is a thing wherein destruction lies
> I rede thee shun it an thy wits be wise.

And these also:—

O thou who seekest severance, draw the rein
Of thy swift steed nor seek o'er much t' advance;
Ah stay! for treachery is the rule of life,
And sweets of meeting end in severance.

I heard her verse but paid no heed to her words, nay, I
raised my foot and administered to the alcove a mighty
kick and behold, the air starkened and darkened and thun-
dered and lightened; the earth trembled and quaked and
the world became invisible. At once the fumes of wine left
my head: I cried to her, "What is the matter?" and she
replied, "The Ifrit is upon us! did I not warn thee of this?
By Allah, thou hast brought ruin upon me; but fly for thy
life and go up by the way thou camest down!" So I fled up
the staircase; but, in the excess of my fear, I forgot sandals
and hatchet. And when I had mounted two steps I turned
to look for them, and lo! I saw the earth cleave asunder,
and there arose from it an Ifrit, a monster of hideousness,
who said to the damsel, "What trouble and pother be this
wherewith thou disturbest me? What mishap hath betided
thee?" "No mishap hath befallen me," she answered, "save
that my breast was straitened[65] and my heart heavy with
sadness: so I drank a little wine to broaden it and to hearten
myself; then I rose to obey a call of Nature, but the wine
had gotten into my head and I fell against the alcove."
"Thou liest, like the whore thou art!" shrieked the Ifrit;
and he looked around the hall right and left till he caught
sight of my axe and sandals and said to her, "What be
these but the belongings of some mortal who hath been
in thy society?" She answered, "I never set eyes upon them
till this moment: they must have been brought by thee
hither cleaving to thy garments." Quoth the Ifrit, "These
words are absurd; thou harlot! thou strumpet!" Then he
stripped her stark naked and, stretching her upon the floor,
bound her hands and feet to four stakes, like one crucified;[66] and set about torturing and trying to make her confess. I could not bear to stand listening to her cries and
groans; so I climbed the stair on the quake with fear; and

when I reached the top I replaced the trap-door and covered it with earth. Then repented I of what I had done with penitence exceeding; and thought of the lady and her beauty and loveliness, and the tortures she was suffering at the hands of the accursed Ifrit, after her quiet life of five-and-twenty years; and how all that had happened to her was for cause of me. I bethought me of my father and his kingly estate and how I had become a woodcutter; and how, after my time had been awhile serene, the world had again waxed turbid and troubled to me. So I wept bitterly and repeated this couplet:—

> What time Fate's tyranny shall most oppress thee
> Perpend! one day shall joy thee, one distress thee!

Then I walked till I reached the home of my friend, the Tailor, whom I found most anxiously expecting me; indeed he was, as the saying goes, on coals of fire for my account. And when he saw me he said, "All night long my heart hath been heavy, fearing for thee from wild beasts or other mischances. Now praise be to Allah for thy safety!" I thanked him for his friendly solicitude and, retiring to my corner, sat pondering and musing on what had befallen me; and I blamed and chided myself for my meddlesome folly and my frowardness in kicking the alcove. I was calling myself to account when behold, my friend, the Tailor, came to me and said, "O youth, in the shop there is an old man, a Persian,[67] who seeketh thee: he hath thy hatchet and thy sandals which he had taken to the woodcutters,[68] saying, I was going out at what time the Mu'azzin began the call to dawn-prayer, when I chanced upon these things and know not whose they are; so direct me to their owner. The woodcutters recognised thy hatchet and directed him to thee: he is sitting in my shop, so fare forth to him and thank him and take thine axe and sandals." When I heard these words I turned yellow with fear and felt stunned as by a blow; and, before I could recover myself, lo! the floor of my private room clove asunder, and out of it rose the Persian who was the Ifrit. He had tortured the lady with exceeding tortures, natheless she would not confess to him aught; so he took the hatchet and sandals and said to her, "As surely as I am Jirjis of the seed of Iblis, I will bring thee back the owner of this and these!"[69] Then he went to the woodcutters with the pretence aforesaid and, being directed to me, after waiting a while in the shop till the fact was confirmed, he suddenly snatched me up as a hawk snatcheth a mouse and flew high in air; but presently descended and plunged with me under the earth (I being aswoon the while), and lastly set me down in the subterranean palace wherein I had passed that blissful night. And there I saw the lady stripped to the skin, her limbs bound to four stakes and blood welling from her sides. At the sight my eyes ran over with tears; but the Ifrit covered her person and said, "O wanton, is not this man thy lover?" She looked upon me and replied, "I wot him not nor have I ever seen him before this hour!" Quoth the Ifrit, "What! this torture and yet no confessing;" and quoth she, "I never saw this man in my born days, and it is not lawful in Allah's sight to tell lies on him." "If thou know him not," said the Ifrit to her, "take this sword and strike off his head."[70] She hent the sword in hand and came close up to me; and I signalled to her with my eyebrows, my tears the while flowing adown my cheeks. She understood me and made answer, also by signs, "How couldest thou bring all this evil upon me?" and I rejoined after the same fashion, "This is the time for mercy and forgiveness." And the mute tongue of my case[71] spake aloud saying:—

> Mine eyes were dragomans for my tongue betied
> And told full clear the love I fain would hide:
> When last we met and tears in torrents railed
> For tongue struck dumb my glances testified:
> She signed with eye-glance while her lips were mute
> I signed with fingers and she kenned th' implied:
> Our eyebrows did all duty 'twixt us twain;
> And we being speechless Love spake loud and plain.

Then, O my mistress, the lady threw away the sword and said, "How shall I strike the neck of one I wot not, and who hath done me no evil? Such deed were not lawful in my law!" and she held her hand. Said the Ifrit, " 'Tis grievous to thee to slay thy lover; and, because he hath lain with thee, thou endurest these torments and obstinately refusest to confess. After this it is clear to me that only like loveth and pitieth like." Then he turned to me and asked me, "O man, haply thou also dost not know this woman;" whereto I answered, "And pray who may she be? assuredly I never saw her till this instant." "Then take the sword," said he, "and strike off her head and I will believe that thou wottest her not and will leave thee free to go, and will not deal hardly with thee." I replied, "That will I do;" and, taking the sword went forward sharply and raised my hand to smile. But she signed to me with her eyebrows, "Have I failed thee in aught of love; and is it thus that thou requitest me?" I understood what her looks implied and answered her with an eye-glance, "I will sacrifice my soul for thee." And the tongue of the case wrote in our hearts these lines:—

> How many a lover with his eyebrows speaketh
> To his beloved, as his passion pleadeth:
> With flashing eyne his passion he inspireth
> And well she seeth what his pleading needeth.
> How sweet the look when each on other gazeth;
> And with what swiftness and how sure it speedeth:
> And this with eyebrows all his passion writeth;
> And that with eyeballs all his passion readeth.

Then my eyes filled with tears to overflowing and I cast the sword from my hand saying, "O mighty Ifrit and hero, if a woman lacking wits and faith deem it unlawful to strike off my head, how can it be lawful for me, a man, to smite her neck whom I never saw in my whole life. I cannot do such misdeed though thou cause me drink the cup of death and perdition." Then said the Ifrit, "Ye twain show the good understanding between you; but I will let you see how such doings end." He took the sword, and struck off the lady's hands first, with four strokes, and then her feet; whilst I looked on and made sure of death and she farewelled me with her dying eyes. So the Ifrit cried at her, "Thou whorest and makest me a wittol with thine eyes;" and struck her so that her head went flying. Then turned he to me and said, "O mortal, we have it in our law that, when the wife committeth advowtry it is lawful for us to slay her. As for this damsel I snatched her away on her bride-night when she was a girl of twelve and she knew no one but myself. I used to come to her once in every ten days and lie with her the night, under the semblance of a man, a Persian; and when I was well assured that she had cuckolded me, I slew her. But as for thee I am not well satisfied that thou hast wronged me in her; nevertheless I must not let thee go unharmed; so ask a boon of me and I will grant it." Then I rejoiced, O my lady, with exceeding joy and said, "What boon shall I crave of thee?" He replied, "Ask me this boon; into what shape I shall bewitch thee; wilt thou be a dog, or an ass or an ape?" I rejoined (and indeed I had hoped that mercy might be shown me), "By Allah, spare me, that Allah spare thee for sparing a Moslem and a man who never wronged thee." And I humbled myself before him with exceeding humility, and remained standing in his presence, saying, "I am sore oppressed by circumstance." Said the Ifrit, "Lengthen not thy words! As to my slaying thee fear it not, and as to my pardoning thee hope it not; but from my bewitching thee there is no escape." Then he tore me from the ground which closed under my feet and flew with me into the firmament till I saw the earth as a large white cloud or a saucer[72] in the midst of the waters. Presently he set me down on a mountain, and taking a little dust, over which he muttered some magical words, sprinkled me therewith, saying, "Quit that shape and take thou the shape of an ape!" And on the instant I became an ape, a tailless baboon, the son of a century.[73] Now when he had left me and I saw myself in this ugly and hateful shape, I wept for myself, but resigned my soul to the tyranny of Time and Circumstance, well weeting that Fortune is fair and constant to no man. I descended the mountain and found at the foot a desert plain, long and broad, over which I travelled for the space of a month till my course brought me to the brink of the briny sea.[74] After standing there awhile, I was ware of a ship in the offing which ran before a fair wind making for the shore: I hid myself behind a rock on the beach and waited till the ship drew near, when I leaped on board. I found her full of merchants and passengers and one of them cried, "O Captain, this ill-omened brute will bring us ill-luck!" and another said, "Turn this ill-omened beast out from among us;" the Captain said, "Let us kill it!" another said, "Slay it with the sword;" a third, "Drown it;" and a fourth, "Shoot it with an arrow." But I sprang up and laid hold of the Rais's skirt,[75] and shed tears which poured down my chops. The Captain took pity on me, and said, "O merchants! this ape hath appealed to me for protection and I will protect him; henceforth he is under my charge: so let none do him aught hurt or harm, otherwise there will be bad blood between us." Then he entreated me kindly and whatsoever he said I understood and ministered to his every want and served him as a servant, albeit my tongue would not obey my wishes; so that he came to love me. The vessel sailed on, the wind being fair, for the space of fifty days; at the end of which we cast anchor under the walls of a great city wherein was a world of people, especially learned men, none could tell their number save Allah. No sooner had we arrived than we were visited by certain Mameluke-officials from the King of that city; who, after boarding us, greeted the merchants and giving them joy of safe arrival said, "Our King welcometh you, and sendeth you this roll of paper, whereupon each and every of you must write a line. For ye shall know that the King's Minister, a calligrapher of renown, is dead, and the King hath sworn a solemn oath that he will make none Wazir in his stead who cannot write as well as he could." He then gave us the scroll which measured ten cubits long by a breadth of one, and each of the merchants who knew how to write wrote a line thereon, even to the last of them; after which I stood up (still in the shape of an ape) and snatched the roll out of their hands. They feared lest I should tear it or throw it overboard; so they tried to stay me and scare me, but I signed to them that I could write, whereat all marvelled, saying, "We never yet saw an ape write." And the Captain cried, "Let him write; and if he scribble and scrabble we will kick him out and kill him; but if he write fair and scholarly I will adopt him as my son; for surely I never yet saw a more intelligent and well-mannered monkey than he. Would Heaven my real son were his match in morals and manners." I took the reed, and stretching out my paw, dipped it in ink and wrote, in the hand used for letters,[76] these two couplets:—

> Time hath recorded gifts she gave the great;
> But none recorded thine which be far higher;
> Allah ne'er orphan men by loss of thee
> Who be of Goodness mother, Bounty's sire.

And I wrote in Rayhani or larger letters elegantly curved:—[77]

> Thou hast a reed[78] of rede to every land,
> Whose driving causeth all the world to thrive;
> Nil is the Nile of Misraim by thy boons
> Who makest misery smile with fingers five.

Then I wrote in the Suls[79] character:—

> There be no writer who from Death shall fleet,
> But what his hand hath writ men shall repeat:
> Write, therefore, naught save what shall serve thee when
> Thou see't on Judgment-Day an so thou see't!

Then I wrote in the character of Naskh:[80]—

> When to sore parting Fate our love shall doom,
> To distant life by Destiny decreed,
> We cause the inkhorn's lips to 'plain our pains,
> And tongue our utterance with the talking reed.

Then I gave the scroll to the officials and, after we all had written our line, they carried it before the King. When he saw the paper no writing pleased him save my writing; and he said to the assembled courtiers, "Go seek the writer of these lines and dress him in a splendid robe of honour; then mount him on a she-mule,[81] let a band of music precede him and bring him to the presence." At these words they smiled and the King was wroth with them and cried "O accursed! I give you an order and you laugh at me?" "O King," replied they, "if we laugh 'tis not at thee and not without a cause." "And what is it?" asked he; and they answered, "O King, thou orderest us to bring to thy presence the man who wrote these lines; now the truth is that he who wrote them is not of the sons of Adam,[82] but an ape, a tailless baboon, belonging to the ship-Captain." Quoth he, "Is this true that you say?" Quoth they "Yea! by the rights of thy munificence!" The King marvelled at their words and shook with mirth and said, "I am minded to buy this ape of the Captain." Then he sent messengers to the ship with the mule, the dress, the guard and the state-drums, saying, "Not the less do you clothe him in the robe of honour and mount him on the mule and let him be surrounded by the guards and preceded by the band of music." They came to the ship and took me from the Captain and robed me in the robe of honour and, mounting me on the she-mule, carried me in state-procession through the streets; whilst the people were amazed and amused. And folk said to one another "Halloo! is our Sultan about to make an ape his Minister?"; and came all agog crowding to gaze at me, and the town was astir and turned topsy-turvy on my account. When they brought me up to the King and set me in his presence, I kissed the ground before him three times, and once before the High Chamberlain and great officers,

and he bade me be seated, and I sat respectfully on shins
and knees[83] and all who were present marvelled at my fine
manners, and the King most of all. Thereupon he ordered
the lieges to retire; and, when none remained save the
King's majesty, the Eunuch on duty and a little white slave,
he bade them set before me the table of food, containing
all manner of birds, whatever hoppeth and flieth and
treadeth in nest, such as quail and sandgrouse. Then he
signed to me to eat with him; so I rose and kissed ground
before him, then sat me down and ate with him. Presently
they set before the King choice wines in flagons of glass
and he drank: then he passed on the cup to me; and I kissed
the ground and drank and wrote on it:—

> With fire they boiled me to loose my tongue,[84]
> And pain and patience gave for fellowship:
> Hence comes it hands of men upbear me high
> And honey-dew from lips of maid I sip!

The King read my verse and said with a sigh, "Were these
gifts in a man, he would excel all the folk of his time and
age!" Then he called for the chess-board, and said, "Say,
wilt thou play with me?"; and I signed with my head, "Yes."
Then I came forward and ordered the pieces and played
with him two games, both of which I won. He was speechless with surprise; so I took the pen-case and, drawing
forth a reed, wrote on the board these two couplets:—

> Two hosts fare fighting thro' the livelong day
> Nor is their battling ever finished,
> Until, when darkness girdeth them about,
> The twain go sleeping in a single bed.[85]

The King read these lines with wonder and delight and
said to his Eunuch,[86] "O Mukbil, go to thy mistress, Sitt al-
Husn,[87] and say her, "Come, speak the King who biddeth
thee hither to take thy solace in seeing this right wondrous
ape!" So the Eunuch went out and presently returned with

the lady who, when she saw me veiled her face and said, "O my father! hast thou lost all sense of honour? How cometh it thou art pleased to send for me and show me to strange men?" "O Sitt al-Husn," said he, "no man is here save this little foot-page and the Eunuch who reared thee and I, thy father. From whom, then, dost thou veil thy face?" She answered, "This whom thou deemest an ape is a young man, a clever and polite, a wise and learned and the son of a King; but he is ensorcelled and the Ifrit Jirjaris, who is of the seed of Iblis, cast a spell upon him, after putting to death his own wife the daughter of King Ifitamus lord of the Islands of Abnus." The King marvelled at his daughter's words and, turning to me, said, "Is this true that she saith of thee?"; and I signed by a nod of my head the answer "Yea, verily;" and wept sore. Then he asked his daughter "Whence knewest thou that he is ensorcelled?"; and she answered "O my dear papa, there was with me in my childhood an old woman, a wily one and a wise and a witch to boot, and she taught me the theory of magic and its practice; and I took notes in writing and therein waxed perfect, and have committed to memory an hundred and seventy chapters of egromantic formulas, by the least of which I could transport the stones of thy city behind the Mountain Kaf and the Circumambient Main,[88] or make its site an abyss of the sea and its people fishes swimming in the midst of it." "O my daughter," said her father, "I conjure thee, by my life, disenchant this young man, that I may make him my Wazir and marry thee to him, for indeed he is an ingenious youth and a deeply learned." "With joy and goodly gree," she replied and, hending in hand an iron knife whereon was inscribed the name of Allah in Hebrew characters, she described a wide circle in the midst of the palace-hall, and therein wrote in Cufic letters mysterious names and talismans; and she uttered words and muttered charms, some of which we understood and others we understood not. Presently the world waxed dark before our sight till we thought that the sky was falling upon our heads, and lo! the Ifrit presented himself in his own shape and aspect. His hands were like many-pronged pitch-forks, his legs like the masts of great ships, and his eyes like cressets of gleaming fire. We were in terrible fear of him but the King's daughter cried at him, "No welcome to thee and no greeting, O dog!" whereupon he changed to the form of a lion and said, "O traitress, how is it thou hast broken the oath we sware that neither should contraire other!" "O accursed one," answered she, "how could there be a compact between me and the like of thee?" Then said he, "Take what thou hast brought on thyself;" and the lion opened his jaws and rushed upon her; but she was too quick for him; and, plucking a hair from her head, waved it in the air muttering over it the while; and the hair straightway became a trenchant sword-blade, wherewith she smote the lion and cut him in twain. Then the two halves flew away in air and the head changed to a scorpion and the Princess became a huge serpent and set upon the accursed scorpion, and the two fought, coiling and uncoiling, a stiff fight for an hour at least. Then the scorpion changed to a vulture and the serpent became an eagle which set upon the vulture, and hunted him for an hour's time, till he became a black tomcat, which miauled and grinned and spat. Thereupon the eagle changed into a piebald wolf and these two battled in the palace for a long time, when the cat, seeing himself overcome, changed into a worm and crept into a huge red pomegranate,[89] which lay beside the jetting fountain in the midst of the palace hall. Whereupon the pomegranate swelled to the size of a water-melon in air; and, falling upon the marble pavement of the palace, broke to pieces, and all the grains fell out and were scattered about till they covered the whole floor. Then the wolf shook himself and became a snow-white cock, which fell to picking up the grains purposing not to leave one; but by doom of destiny one seed rolled to the fountain-edge and there lay hid. The cock fell to crowing and clapping his wings and signing to us with his beak as if to ask, "Are any grains left?" But we understood not what he meant, and he cried to us with so loud a cry that we thought the palace would fall upon us. Then he ran over all the floor till he saw the grain which had rolled to the fountain edge, and rushed eagerly to pick it up when behold, it sprang into the midst of the water and became a fish and dived to the bottom of the basin. Thereupon the cock changed to a big fish, and plunged in after the other, and the two disappeared for a while and lo! we heard loud shrieks and cries of pain which made us tremble. After this the Ifrit rose out of the water, and he was as a burning flame; casting fire and smoke from his mouth and eyes and nostrils. And immediately the Princess likewise came forth from the basin and she was one live coal of flaming lowe; and these two, she and he, battled for the space of an hour, until their fires entirely compassed them about and their thick smoke filled the palace. As for us we panted for breath, being well-nigh suffocated, and we longed to plunge into the water fearing lest we be burnt up and utterly destroyed; and the King said, "There is no Majesty and there is no Might save in Allah the Glorious, the Great! Verily we are Allah's and unto Him are we returning! Would Heaven I had not urged my daughter to attempt the disenchantment of this ape-fellow, whereby I have imposed upon her the terrible task of fighting yon accursed Ifrit against whom all the Ifrits in the world could not prevail. And would Heaven we had never seen this ape, Allah never assain nor bless the day of his coming! We thought to do a good deed by him before the face of Allah,[90] and to release him from enchantment, and now we have brought this trouble and travail upon our heart." But I, O my lady, was tongue-tied and powerless to say a word to him. Suddenly, ere we were ware of aught, the Ifrit yelled out from under the flames and, coming up to us as we stood on the estrade, blew fire in our faces. The damsel overtook him and breathed blasts of fire at his face and the sparks from her and from him rained down upon us, and her sparks did us no harm, but one of his sparks alighted upon my eye and destroyed it making me a monocular ape; and another fell on the King's face scorching the lower half, burning off his beard and mustachios and causing his under teeth to fall out; while a third lighted on the Castrato's breast, killing him on the spot. So we despaired of life and made sure of death when lo! a voice repeated the saying, "Allah is most Highest! Allah is most Highest! Aidance and victory to all who the Truth believe; and disappointment and disgrace to all who the religion of Mohammed, the Moon of Faith, unbelieve." The speaker was the Princess who had burnt the Ifrit, and he was become a heap of ashes. Then she came up to us and said, "Reach me a cup of water." They brought it to her and she spoke over it words we understood not, and sprinkling me with it cried, "By virtue of the Truth, and by the Most Great name of Allah, I charge thee return to thy former shape." And behold, I shook and became a man as before, save that I had utterly lost an eye. Then she cried out, "The fire! The fire! O my dear papa an arrow from the accursed hath wounded me to the death, for I am not used to fight with the Jann; had he been a man I had slain him in the beginning. I had no trouble till the time when the pomegranate burst and the grains scattered, but I overlooked the seed wherein was the very life of the Jinni. Had I picked it up he had died on the spot, but as Fate and Fortune decreed, I saw it not; so he came upon me all unawares and there befel between him and me a sore struggle under the earth and high in air and in the water; and, as often as I opened on him a gate,[91] he opened on me another gate and a stronger, till at last he opened on me the gate of fire, and few are saved upon whom the door of fire openeth. But Destiny willed that my cunning prevail over his cunning; and I burned him to death after I vainly exhorted him to embrace the religion of Al-Islam. As for me I am a dead woman; Allah supply my place to you!" Then she called upon Heaven for help and ceased not to implore relief from the fire; when lo! a black spark shot up from her robed feet to her thighs; then it flew to her bosom and thence to her face. When it reached her face she wept and said, "I testify that there is no god but *the* God and that Mohammed is the Apostle of God!" And we looked at her and saw naught but a heap of ashes by the side of the heap that had been the Ifrit. We mourned for her and I wished I had been in her place, so had I not seen her lovely face who had worked me such weal become ashes; but there is no gainsaying the will of Allah. When the King saw his daughter's terrible death, he plucked out what was left of his beard and beat his face and rent his raiment; and I did as he did and we both wept over her. Then came in the Chamberlains and Grandees and were amazed to find two heaps of ashes and the Sultan in a fainting fit; so they stood round him till he revived and told them what had befallen his daughter from the Ifrit; whereat their grief was right grievous and the women and the slave-girls shrieked and keened,[92] and they continued their lamentations for the space of seven days. Moreover the King bade build over his daughter's ashes a vast vaulted tomb, and burn therein wax tapers and sepulchral lamps: but as for the Ifrit's ashes they scattered them on the winds, speeding them to the curse of Allah. Then the Sultan fell sick of a sickness that well-nigh brought him to his death for a month's space; and, when health returned to him and his beard grew again and he had been converted by the mercy of Allah to Al-Islam, he sent for me and said, "O youth, Fate had decreed for us the happiest of lives, safe from all the chances and changes of Time, till thou camest to us, when troubles fell upon us. Would to Heaven we had never seen thee and the foul face of thee! For we took pity on thee and thereby we have lost our all. I have on thy account first lost my daughter who to me was well worth an hundred men, secondly I have suffered that which befel me by reason of the fire and the loss of my teeth, and my Eunuch also was slain. I blame thee not, for it was out of thy power to prevent this: the doom of Allah was on thee as well as on us and thanks be to the Almighty for that my daughter delivered thee, albeit thereby she lost her own life! Go forth now, O my son, from this my city, and suffice thee what hath befallen us through thee, even although 'twas decreed for us. Go forth in peace, and if I ever see thee again I will surely slay thee." And he cried out at me. So I went forth from his presence, O my lady, weeping bitterly and hardly believing in my escape and knowing not whither I should wend. And I recalled all that had befallen me, my meeting the tailor, my love for the damsel in the palace beneath the earth, and my narrow escape from the Ifrit, even after he had determined to do me die; and how I had entered the city as an ape and was now leaving it a man once more. Then I gave thanks to Allah and said, "My eye and not my life!" and before leaving the place I entered the bath and shaved my poll and beard and mustachios and eyebrows; and cast ashes on my head and donned the coarse black woollen robe of a Kalandar. Then I journeyed through many regions and saw many a city intending for Baghdad, that I might seek audience, in the House of Peace,[93] with the Commander of the Faithful and tell him all that had befallen me. I arrived here this very night and found my brother in Allah, this first Kalandar, standing about as one perplexed; so I saluted him with "Peace be upon thee," and entered into discourse with him. Presently up came our brother, this third Kalandar, and said to us, "Peace be with you! I am a stranger;" whereto we replied, "And we too be strangers, who have come hither this blessed night." So we all three walked on together, none of us knowing the other's history, till Destiny drave us to this door and we came in to you. Such then is my story and my reason for shaving my beard and mustachios, and this is what caused the loss of my eye. Said the housemistress "Thy tale is indeed a rare; so rub thy head and wend thy ways;" but he replied, "I will not budge till I hear my companions' stories." Then came forward the third Kalandar, and said, "O illustrious lady! my history is not like that of these my comrades, but more wondrous and far more marvellous. In their case Fate and Fortune came down on them unawares; but I drew down destiny upon my own head and brought sorrow on mine own soul, and shaved my own beard and lost my own eye. Hear then

THE THIRD KALANDAR'S TALE.

Know, O my lady, that I also am a King and the son of a King and my name is Ajib son of Khazib. When my father died I succeeded him; and I ruled and did justice and dealt fairly by all my lieges. I delighted in sea trips, for my capital stood on the shore, before which the ocean stretched far and wide; and near-hand were many great islands with sconces and garrisons in the midst of the main. My fleet numbered fifty merchantmen, and as many yachts for pleasance, and an hundred and fifty sail ready fitted for holy war with the Unbelievers. It fortuned that I had a mind to enjoy myself on the islands aforesaid, so I took ship with my people in ten keel; and, carrying with me a month's victual, I set out on a twenty days' voyage. But one night a head wind struck us, and the sea rose against us with huge waves; the billows sorely buffetted us and a dense darkness settled round us. We gave ourselves up for lost and I said, "Whoso endangereth his days, e'en an he 'scape deserveth no praise." Then we prayed to Allah and besought Him; but the storm-blasts ceased not to blow against us nor the surges to strike us till morning broke, when the gale fell, the seas sank to mirrory stillness and the sun shone upon us kindly clear. Presently we made an island where we landed and cooked somewhat of food, and ate heartily and took our rest for a couple of days. Then we set out again and sailed another twenty days, the seas broadening and the land shrinking. Presently the current ran counter to us, and we found ourselves in strange waters, where the Captain had lost his reckoning, and was wholly bewildered in this sea; so said we to the look-out man,[94] "Get thee to the mast-head and keep thine eyes open." He swarmed up the mast and looked out and cried aloud, "O Rais, I espy to starboard something dark, very like a fish floating on the face of the sea, and to larboard there is a loom in the midst of the main, now black and now bright." When the Captain heard the look-out's words he dashed his turband on the deck and plucked out his beard and beat his face saying, "Good news indeed! we be all dead men; not one of us can be saved." And he fell to weeping and all of us wept for his weeping and also for our lives; and I said, "O Captain, tell us what it is the look-out saw." "O my Prince," answered he, "know that we lost our course on the night of the storm, which was followed on the morrow by a two-days' calm during which we made no way; and we have gone astray eleven days reckoning from that night, with ne'er a wind to bring us back to our true course. To-morrow by the end of the day we shall come to a mountain of black stone, hight the Magnet Mountain;[95] for thither the currents carry us willy-nilly. As soon as we are under its lea, the ship's sides will open and every nail in plank will fly out and cleave fast to the mountain; for that Almighty Allah hath gifted the loadstone with a mysterious virtue and a love for iron, by reason whereof all which is iron travelleth towards it; and on this mountain is much iron, how much none knoweth save the Most High, from the many vessels which have been lost there since the days of yore. The bright spot upon its summit is a dome of yellow laton from Andalusia, vaulted upon ten columns; and on its crown is a horseman who rideth a horse of brass and holdeth in hand a lance of laton; and there hangeth on his bosom a tablet of lead graven with names and talismans." And he presently added, "And, O King, none destroyeth folk save the rider on that steed, nor will the egromancy be dispelled till he fall from his horse."[96] Then, O my lady, the Captain wept with exceeding weeping and we all made sure of death-doom and each and every one of us farewelled his friend and charged him with his last will and testament in case he might be saved. We slept not that night and in the morning we found ourselves much nearer the Loadstone Mountain, whither the waters drave us with a violent send. When the ships were close under its lea they opened and the nails flew out and all the iron in them sought the Magnet Mountain and clove to it like a network; so that by the end of the day we were all struggling in the waves round about the mountain. Some of us were saved, but more were drowned and even those who had escaped knew not one another, so stupefied were they by the beating of the billows and the raving of the winds. As for me, O my lady, Allah (be His name exalted!) preserved my life that I might suffer whatso He willed to me of hardship, misfortune and calamity; for I scrambled upon a plank from one of the ships, and the wind and waters threw it at the feet of the Mountain. There I found a practicable path leading by steps carven out of the rock to the summit, and I called on the name of Allah Almighty[97] and breasted the ascent, clinging to the steps and notches hewn in the stone, and mounted little by little. And the Lord stilled the wind and aided me in the ascent, so that I succeeded in reaching the summit. There I found no resting-place save the dome, which I entered, joying with exceeding joy at my escape; and made the Wuzu-ablution[98] and prayed a two-bow prayer[99] of thanksgiving to God for my preservation. Then I fell asleep under the dome, and heard in my dream a mysterious Voice[100] saying, "O son of Khazib! when thou wakest from thy sleep dig under thy feet and thou shalt find a bow of brass and three leaden arrows, inscribed with talismans and characts. Take the bow and shoot the arrows at the horseman on the dome-top and free mankind from this sore calamity. When thou hast shot him he shall fall into the sea, and the horse will also drop at thy feet: then bury it in the place of the bow. This done, the main will swell and rise till it is level with the mountain-head, and there will appear on it a skiff carrying a man of laton (other than he thou shalt have shot) holding in his hand a pair of paddles. He will come to thee and do thou embark with him but beware of saying Bismillah or of otherwise naming Allah Almighty. He will row thee for a space of ten days, till he bring thee to certain Islands called the Islands of Safety, and thence thou shalt easily reach a port and find those who will convey thee to thy native land; and all this shall be fulfilled to thee so thou call not on the name of Allah." Then I started up from my sleep in joy and gladness and, hastening to do the bidding of the mysterious Voice, found the bow and arrows and shot at the horseman and tumbled him into the main, whilst the horse dropped at my feet; so I took it and buried it. Presently the sea surged up and rose till it reached the top of the mountain; nor had I long to wait ere I saw a skiff in the offing coming towards me. I gave thanks to Allah; and, when the skiff came up to me, I saw therein a man of brass with a tablet of lead on his breast inscribed with talismans and characts; and I embarked without uttering a word. The boatman rowed on with me through the first day and the second and the third, in all ten whole days, till I caught sight of the Islands of Safety; whereat I joyed with exceeding joy and for stress of gladness exclaimed, "Allah! Allah! In the name of Allah! There is no god but *the* God and Allah is Almighty."[101] Thereupon the skiff forthwith upset and cast me upon the sea; then it righted and sank deep into the depths. Now I am a fair swimmer, so I swam the whole day till nightfall, when my forearms and shoulders were numbed with fatigue and I felt like to die; so I testified to my Faith, expecting naught but death. The sea was still surging under the violence of the winds, and presently there came a billow like a hillock; and, bearing me up high in air, threw me with a long cast on dry land, that His will might be fulfilled. I crawled upon the beach and doffing my raiment wrung it out to dry and spread it in the sunshine: then I lay me down and slept the whole night. As soon as it was day, I donned my clothes and rose to look whither I should walk. Presently I came to a thicket of low trees: and, making a cast round it, found that the spot whereon I stood was an islet, a mere holm, girt on all sides by the ocean; whereupon I said to myself, "Whatso freeth me from one great calamity casteth me into a greater!" But while I was pondering my case and longing for death behold, I saw afar

off a ship making for the island; so I clomb a tree and hid
myself among the branches. Presently the ship anchored
and landed ten slaves, blackamoors, bearing iron hoes and
baskets, who walked on till they reached the middle of the
island. Here they dug deep into the ground, until they uncovered a plate of metal which they lifted, thereby opening a trap-door. After this they returned to the ship and
thence brought bread and flour, honey and fruits, clarified butter,[102] leather bottles containing liquors and many
household stuffs; also furniture, table-service and mirrors;
rugs, carpets and in fact all needed to furnish a dwelling;
and they kept going to and fro, and descending by the trap-
door, till they had transported into the dwelling all that was
in the ship. After this the slaves again went on board and
brought back with them garments as rich as may be, and in
the midst of them came an old old man, of whom very little was left, for Time had dealt hardly and harshly with
him, and all that remained of him was a bone wrapped in a
rag of blue stuff, through which the winds whistled west
and east. As saith the poet of him:—

> Time gars me tremble Ah, how sore the baulk!
> While Time in pride of strength doth ever stalk:
> Time was I walked nor ever felt I tired,
> Now am I tired albe I never walk!

And the Shaykh held by the hand a youth cast in beauty's
mould, all elegance and perfect grace; so fair that his
comeliness deserved to be proverbial; for he was as a green
bough or the tender young of the roe, ravishing every
heart with his loveliness and subduing every soul with his
coquetry and amorous ways.[103] They stinted not their
going, O my lady, till all went down by the trap-door and
did not reappear for an hour, or rather more; at the end of
which time the slaves and the old man came up without
the youth and, replacing the iron plate and carefully closing the door-slab, as it was before, they returned to the ship
and made sail and were lost to my sight. When they turned

away to depart, I came down from the tree and, going to the place I had seen them fill up, scraped off and removed the earth; and impatience possessed my soul till I had cleared the whole of it away. Then appeared the trap-door which was of wood, in shape and size like a millstone; and when I lifted it up it disclosed a winding staircase of stone. At this I marvelled and, descending the steps till I reached the last, found a fair hall, spread with various kinds of carpets and silk stuffs, wherein was a youth sitting upon a raised couch and leaning back on a round cushion with a fan in his hand and nosegays and posies of sweet scented herbs and flowers before him;[104] but he was alone and not a soul near him in the great vault. When he saw me he turned pale; but I saluted him courteously and said, "Set thy mind at ease and calm thy fears; no harm shall come near thee; I am a man like thyself and the son of a King to boot; whom the decrees of Destiny have sent to bear thee company and cheer thee in thy loneliness. But now tell me, what is thy story and what causeth thee to dwell thus in solitude under the ground?" When he was assured that I was of his kind and no Jinni, he rejoiced and his fine colour returned; and, making me draw near to him he said, "O my brother, my story is a strange story and 'tis this. My father is a merchant-jeweller possessed of great wealth, who hath white and black slaves travelling and trading on his account in ships and on camels, and trafficking with the most distant cities; but he was not blessed with a child, not even one. Now on a certain night he dreamed a dream that he should be favoured with a son, who would be short lived; so the morning dawned on my father bringing him woe and weeping. On the following night my mother conceived and my father noted down the date of her becoming pregnant.[105] Her time being fulfilled she bare me; whereat my father rejoiced and made banquets and called together the neighbours and fed the Fakirs and the poor, for that he had been blessed with issue near the end of his days. Then he assembled the astrologers and astronomers who knew the places of the planets, and the wizards and wise ones of the time, and men learned in horoscopes and nativities;[106] and they drew out my birth scheme and said to my father:—Thy son shall live to fifteen years, but in his fifteenth there is a sinister aspect; an he safely tide it over he shall attain a great age. And the cause that threateneth him with death is this. In the Sea of Peril standeth the Mountain Magnet hight; on whose summit is a horseman of yellow laton seated on a horse also of brass and bearing on his breast a tablet of lead. Fifty days after this rider shall fall from his steed thy son will die and his slayer will be he who shoots down the horseman, a Prince named Ajib son of King Khazib. My father grieved with exceeding grief to hear these words; but reared me in tenderest fashion and educated me excellently well till my fifteenth year was told. Ten days ago news came to him that the horseman had fallen into the sea and he who shot him down was named Ajib son of King Khazib. My father thereupon wept bitter tears at the need of parting with me and became like one possessed of a Jinni. However, being in mortal fear for me, he built me this place under the earth; and, stocking it with all required for the few days still remaining, he brought me hither in a ship and left me here. Ten are already past and, when the forty shall have gone by without danger to me, he will come and take me away; for he hath done all this only in fear of Prince Ajib. Such, then, is my story and the cause of my loneliness." When I heard his history I marvelled and said in my mind, "I am the Prince Ajib who hath done all this; but as Allah is with me I will surely not slay him!" So said I to him, O my lord, far from thee be this hurt and harm and then, please Allah, thou shalt not suffer cark nor care nor aught disquietude, for I will tarry with thee and serve thee as a servant, and then wend my ways; and, after having borne thee company during the forty days, I will go with thee to thy home where thou shalt give me an escort of some of thy Mamelukes with whom I may journey back to my own city; and the Almighty shall requite thee for me. He was glad to hear these words, when I rose and lighted a large wax-candle and trimmed the lamps and the three lanterns; and I set on meat and drink and sweetmeats. We ate and drank and sat talking over various matters till the greater part of the night was gone; when he lay down to rest and I covered him up and went to sleep myself. Next morning I arose and warmed a little water, then lifted him gently so as to awake him and brought him the warm water wherewith he washed his face[107] and said to me, "Heaven requite thee for me with every blessing, O youth! By Allah, if I get quit of this danger and am saved from him whose name is Ajib bin Khazib, I will make my father reward thee and send thee home healthy and wealthy; and, if I die, then my blessing be upon thee." I answered, "May the day never dawn on which evil shall betide thee; and may Allah make my last day before thy last day!" Then I set before him somewhat of food and we ate; and I got ready perfumes for fumigating the hall, wherewith he was pleased. Moreover I made him a Mankalah-cloth;[108] and we played and ate sweet-meats and we played again and took our pleasure till nightfall, when I rose and lighted the lamps, and set before him somewhat to eat, and sat telling him stories till the hours of darkness were far spent. Then he lay down to rest and I covered him up and rested also. And thus I continued to do, O my lady, for days and nights and affection for him took root in my heart and my sorrow was eased, and I said to myself, The astrologers lied[109] when they predicted that he should be slain by Ajib bin Khazib: by Allah, I will not slay him. I ceased not ministering to him and conversing and carousing with him and telling him all manner tales for thirty-nine days. On the fortieth night[110] the youth rejoiced and said, "O my brother, Alhamdolillah!—praise be to Allah—who hath preserved me from death and this is by thy blessing and the blessing of thy coming to me; and I prayed God that He restore thee to thy native land. But now, O my brother, I would thou warm me some water for the Ghusl-ablution and do thou kindly bathe me and change my clothes." I replied, "With love and gladness;" and I heated water in plenty and carrying it in to him washed his body all over, the washing of health,[111] with meal of lupins[112] and rubbed him well and changed his clothes and spread him a high bed whereon he lay down to rest, being drowsy after bathing. Then said he, "O my brother, cut me up a water-melon, and sweeten it with a little sugar-candy."[113] So I went to the store-room and bringing out a fine water-melon I found there, set it on a platter and laid it before him saying, "O my master hast thou not a knife?" "Here it is," answered he, "over my head upon the high shelf." So I got up in haste and taking the knife drew it from its sheath; but my foot slipped in stepping down and I fell heavily upon the youth holding in my hand the knife which hastened to fulfil what had been written on the Day that decided the destinies of man, and buried itself, as if planted, in the youth's heart. He died on the instant. When I saw that he was slain and knew that I had slain him, maugre myself, I cried out with an exceeding loud and bitter cry and beat my face and rent my raiment and said, "Verily we be Allah's and unto Him we be returning, O Moslems! O folk fain of Allah! there remained for this youth but one day of the forty dangerous days which the astrologers and the learned had foretold for him; and the predestined death of this beautiful one was to be at my hand. Would Heaven I had not tried to cut the watermelon. What dire misfortune is this I must bear lief or loath? What a disaster! What an affliction! O Allah mine, I implore thy pardon and declare to Thee my innocence of his death. But what God willeth let that come to pass."[114] When I was certified that I had slain him, I arose and ascending the stairs replaced the trap-door and covered it with earth as before. Then I looked out seawards and saw the ship cleaving the waters and making for the island, wherefore I was afeard and said, "The moment they come and see the youth done to death, they will know 'twas I who slew him and will slay me without respite." So I climbed up into a high tree and concealed myself among its leaves; and hardly had I done so when the ship anchored and the slaves landed with the ancient man, the youth's father, and made direct for the place and when they removed the earth they were surprised to see it soft.[115] Then they raised the trap-door and went down and found the youth lying at full length, clothed in fair new garments with a face beaming after the bath, and the knife deep in his heart. At the sight they shrieked and wept and beat their faces, loudly cursing the murderer; whilst a swoon came over the Shaykh so that the slaves deemed him dead, unable to survive his son. At last they wrapped the slain youth in his clothes and carried him up and laid him on the ground covering him with a shroud of silk. Whilst they were making for the ship the old man revived; and, gazing on his son who was stretched out, fell on the ground and strewed dust over his head and smote his face and plucked out his beard; and his weeping redoubled as he thought of his murdered son and he swooned away once more. After awhile a slave went and fetched a strip of silk whereupon they lay the old man and sat down at his head. All this took place and I was on the tree above them watching everything that came to pass; and my heart became hoary before my head waxed grey, for the hard lot which was mine, and for the distress and anguish I had undergone, and I fell to reciting:—

> "How many a joy by Allah's will hath fled
> With flight escaping sight of wisest head!
> How many a sadness shall begin the day,
> Yet grow right gladsome ere the day is sped!
> How many a weal trips on the heels of ill,
> Causing the mourner's heart with joy to thrill!"[116]

But the old man, O my lady, ceased not from his swoon till near sunset, when he came to himself and, looking upon his dead son, he recalled what had happened, and how what he had dreaded had come to pass; and he beat his face and head. Then he sobbed a single sob and his soul fled his flesh. The slaves shrieked aloud "Alas, our lord!" and show-ered dust on their heads and redoubled their weeping and wailing. Presently they carried their dead master to the ship side by side with his dead son and, having transported all the stuff from the dwelling to the vessel, set sail and disappeared from mine eyes. I descended from the tree and, raising the trap-door, went down into the underground dwelling where everything reminded me of the youth; and I looked upon the poor remains of him and began repeating these verses:—

> Their tracks I see, and pine with pain and pang
> And on deserted hearths I weep and yearn:
> And Him I pray who doomed them depart
> Some day vouchsafe the boon of safe return.[117]

Then, O my lady, I went up again by the trap-door, and every day I used to wander round about the island and every night I returned to the underground hall. Thus I lived for a month, till at last, looking at the western side of the island, I observed that every day the tide ebbed, leaving shallow water for which the flow did not compensate; and by the end of the month the sea showed dry land in that direction. At this I rejoiced making certain of my safety; so I arose and fording what little was left of the water got me to the main land, where I fell in with great heaps of loose sand in which even a camel's hoof would sink up to the knee.[118] However I emboldened my soul and wading through the sand behold, a fire shone from afar burning with a blazing light.[119] So I made for it hoping haply to find succour and broke out into these verses:—

> "Belike my Fortune may her bridle turn
> And Time bring weal although he's jealous hight;
> Forward my hopes, and further all my needs,
> And passed ills with present weals requite."

And when I drew near the fire aforesaid lo! it was a palace with gates of copper burnished red which, when the rising

sun shone thereon, gleamed and glistened from afar showing what had seemed to me a fire. I rejoiced in the sight,
and sat down over against the gate, but I was hardly settled
in my seat before there met me ten young men clothed in
sumptuous gear and all were blind of the left eye which
appeared as plucked out. They were accompanied by a
Shaykh, an old, old man, and much I marvelled at their appearance, and their all being blind in the same eye. When
they saw me, they saluted me with the Salam and asked me
of my case and my history; whereupon I related to them all
what had befallen me, and what full measure of misfortune
was mine. Marvelling at my tale they took me to the mansion, where I saw ranged round the hall ten couches each
with its blue bedding and coverlet of blue stuff[120] and
amiddlemost stood a smaller couch furnished like them
with blue and nothing else. As we entered each of the
youths took his seat on his own couch and the old man
seated himself upon the smaller one in the middle saying
to me, "O youth, sit thee down on the floor and ask not of
our case nor of the loss of our eyes." Presently he rose up
and set before each young man some meat in a charger and
drink in a large mazer, treating me in like manner; and
after that they sat questioning me concerning my adventures and what had betided me: and I kept telling them my
tale till the night was far spent. Then said the young men,
"O our Shaykh, wilt not thou set before us our ordinary?
The time is come." He replied, "With love and gladness,"
and rose and entering a closet disappeared, but presently
returned bearing on his head ten trays each covered with a
strip of blue stuff. He set a tray before each youth and,
lighting ten wax candles, he stuck one upon each tray, and
drew off the covers and lo! under them was naught but
ashes and powdered charcoal and kettle soot. Then all the
young men tucked up their sleeves to the elbows and fell a-
weeping and wailing and they blackened their faces and
smeared their clothes and buffetted their brows and beat
their breasts, continually exclaiming, "We were sitting at
our ease but our frowardness brought us unease!" They

ceased not to do thus till dawn drew nigh, when the old man rose and heated water for them; and they washed their faces, and donned other and clean clothes. Now when I saw this, O my lady, for very wonderment my senses left me and my wits went wild and heart and head were full of thought, till I forgot what had betided me and I could not keep silence feeling I fain must speak out and question them of these strangenesses; so I said to them, "How come ye to do this after we have been so open-hearted and frolicksome? Thanks be to Allah ye be all sound and sane, yet actions such as these befit none but mad men or those possessed of an evil spirit. I conjure you by all that is dearest to you, why stint ye to tell me your history, and the cause of your losing your eyes and your blackening your faces with ashes and soot?" Hereupon they turned to me and said, "O young man, hearken not to thy youthtide's suggestions and question us no questions." Then they slept and I with them and when they awoke the old man brought us somewhat of food; and, after we had eaten and the plates and goblets had been removed, they sat conversing till night-fall when the old man rose and lit the wax candles and lamps and set meat and drink before us. After we had eaten and drunken we sat conversing and carousing in companionage till the noon of night, when they said to the old man, "Bring us our ordinary, for the hour of sleep is at hand!" So he rose and brought them the trays of soot and ashes; and they did as they had done on the preceding night, nor more, nor less. I abode with them after this fashion for the space of a month during which time they used to blacken their faces with ashes every night, and to wash and change their raiment when the morn was young; and I but marvelled the more and my scruples and curiosity increased to such a point that I had to forego even food and drink. At last, I lost command of myself, for my heart was aflame with fire unquenchable and lowe unconcealable and I said, "O young men, will ye not relieve my trouble and acquaint me with the reason of thus blackening your faces and the meaning of your words:—We were sitting at our ease but our frowardness brought us unease?" Quoth they "'Twere better to keep these things secret." Still I was bewildered by their doings to the point of abstaining from eating and drinking and, at last wholly losing patience, quoth I to them, "There is no help for it: ye must acquaint me with what is the reason of these doings." They replied, "We kept our secret only for thy good: to gratify thee will bring down evil upon thee and thou wilt become a monocular even as we are." I repeated, "There is no help for it and, if ye will not, let me leave you and return to mine own people and be at rest from seeing these things, for the proverb saith:—

> Better ye 'bide and I take my leave:
> For what eye sees not heart shall never grieve."

Thereupon they said to me, "Remember, O youth, that should ill befal thee we will not again harbour thee nor suffer thee to abide amongst us;" and bringing a ram they slaughtered it and skinned it. Lastly they gave me a knife saying, "Take this skin and stretch thyself upon it and we will sew it around thee; presently there shall come to thee a certain bird, hight Rukh,[121] that will catch thee up in his pounces and tower high in air and then set thee down on a mountain. When thou feelest he is no longer flying, rip open the pelt with this blade and come out of it; the bird will be scared and will fly away and leave thee free. After this fare for half a day, and the march will place thee at a palace wondrous fair to behold, towering high in air and builded of Khalanj,[122] lign-aloes and sandalwood, plated with red gold, and studded with all manner emeralds and costly gems fit for seal-rings. Enter it and thou shalt win to thy wish for we have all entered that palace; and such is the cause of our losing our eyes and of our blackening our faces. Were we now to tell thee our stories it would take too long a time; for each and every of us lost his left eye by an adventure of his own." I rejoiced at their words and they did with me as they said; and the bird Rukh bore me off and set me down on the mountain. Then I came out of the skin and walked on till I reached the palace. The door stood open as I entered and found myself in a spacious and goodly hall, wide exceedingly, even as a horse-course; and around it were an hundred chambers with doors of sandal and aloes woods plated with red gold and furnished with silver rings by way of knockers.[123] At the head or upper end[124] of the hall I saw forty damsels, sumptuously dressed and ornamented and one and all bright as moons; none could ever tire of gazing upon them and all so lovely that the most ascetic devotee on seeing them would become their slave and obey their will. When they saw me the whole bevy came up to me and said "Welcome and well come and good cheer[125] to thee, O our lord! This whole month have we been expecting thee. Praised be Allah who hath sent us one who is worthy of us, even as we are worthy of him!" Then they made me sit down upon a high divan and said to me, "This day thou art our lord and master, and we are thy servants and thy handmaids, so order us as thou wilt." And I marvelled at their case. Presently one of them arose and set meat before me and I ate and they ate with me; whilst others warmed water and washed my hands and feet and changed my clothes, and others made ready sherbets and gave us to drink; and all gathered around me being full of joy and gladness at my coming. Then they sat down and conversed with me till night-fall, when five of them arose and laid the trays and spread them with flowers and fragrant herbs and fruits, fresh and dried, and confections in profusion. At last they brought out a fine wine-service with rich old wine; and we sat down to drink and some sang songs and others played the lute and psaltery and recorders and other instruments, and the bowl went merrily round. Hereupon such gladness possessed me that I forgot the sorrows of the world one and all and said, "This is indeed life; O sad that 'tis fleeting!" I enjoyed their company till the time came for rest; and our heads were all warm with wine, when they said, "O our lord, choose from amongst us her who shall be thy bedfellow this night and not lie with thee again till forty days be past." So I chose a girl fair of face and perfect in shape, with eyes Kohl-edged[126] by nature's hand; hair long and jet black with slightly parted teeth[127] and joining brows: 'twas as if she were some limber graceful branchlet or the slender stalk of sweet basil to amaze and to bewilder man's fancy. So I lay with her that night; none fairer I ever knew; and, when it was morning, the damsels carried me to the Hammam-bath and bathed me and robed me in fairest apparel. Then they served up food, and we ate and drank and the cup went round till nightfall when I chose from among them one fair of form and face, soft-sided and a model of grace, such an one as the poet described when he said:—

> On her fair bosom caskets twain I scanned,
> Scaled fast with musk-seals lovers to withstand;
> With arrowy glances stand on guard her eyes,
> Whose shafts would shoot who dares put forth a hand.

With her I spent a most goodly night; and, to be brief, O my mistress, I remained with them in all solace and delight of life, eating and drinking, conversing and carousing and every night lying with one or other of them. But at the head of the new year they came to me in tears and bade me farewell, weeping and crying out and clinging about me; whereat I wondered and said, "What may be the matter? verily you break my heart!" They exclaimed, "Would Heaven we had never known thee; for, though we have companied with many, yet never saw we a pleasanter than thou or a more courteous." And they wept again. "But tell me more clearly," asked I, "what causeth this weeping which maketh my gall-bladder[128] like to burst;" and they answered, "O our lord and master, it is severance which maketh us weep; and thou, and thou only, art the cause of our tears. If thou hearken to us we need never be parted and if thou hearken not we part for ever; but our hearts tell us that thou wilt not listen to our words and this is the cause of our tears and cries." "Tell me how the case standeth?" "Know, O our lord, that we are the daughters of Kings who have met here and have lived together for years; and once in every year we are perforce absent for forty days; and afterwards we return and abide here for the rest of the twelve-month eating and drinking and taking our pleasure and enjoying delights: we are about to depart according to our custom; and we fear lest after we be gone thou contraire our charge and disobey our injunctions. Here now we commit to thee the keys of the palace which containeth forty chambers and thou mayest open of these thirty and nine, but beware (and we conjure thee by Allah and by the lives of us!) lest thou open the fortieth door, for therein is that which shall separate us for ever."[129] Quoth I, "Assuredly I will not open it, if it contain the cause of severance from you." Then one among them came up to me and falling on my neck wept and recited these verses:—

> "If Time unite us after absent-while,
>   The world harsh frowning on our lot shall smile;
> And if thy semblance deign adorn mine eyes,[130]
>   I'll pardon Time past wrongs and by-gone guile."

And I recited the following:—

> "When drew she near to bid adieu with heart unstrung,
>   While care and longing on that day her bosom wrung;
> Wet pearls she wept and mine like red carnelians rolled
>   And, joined in sad *rivière*, around her neck they hung."

When I saw her weeping I said, "By Allah I will never open that fortieth door, never and no wise!" and I bade her farewell. Thereupon all departed flying away like birds; signalling with their hands farewells as they went and leaving me alone in the palace. When evening drew near I opened the door of the first chamber and entering it found myself in a place like one of the pleasaunces of Paradise. It was a garden with trees of freshest green and ripe fruits of yellow sheen; and its birds were singing clear and keen and rills ran wimpling through the fair terrene. The sight and sounds brought solace to my sprite; and I walked among the trees, and I smelt the breath of the flowers on the breeze; and heard the birdies sing their melodies hymning the One, the Almighty in sweetest litanies; and I looked upon the apple whose hue is parcel red and parcel yellow; as said the poet:—

> Apple whose hue combines in union mellow
> My fair's red cheek, her hapless lover's yellow.

Then I looked upon the pear whose taste surpasseth sherbet and sugar; and the apricot[131] whose beauty striketh the eye with admiration, as if she were a polished ruby. Then I went out of the place and locked the door as it was before. When it was the morrow I opened the second door; and entering found myself in a spacious plain set with tall date-palms and watered by a running stream whose banks were shrubbed with bushes of rose and jasmine, while privet and eglantine, oxe-eye, violet and lily, narcissus, origane and the winter gilliflower carpeted the borders; and the breath of the breeze swept over these sweet-smelling growths diffusing their delicious odours right and left, perfuming the world and filling my soul with delight. After taking my pleasure there awhile I went from it and, having closed the door as it was before, opened the third door wherein I saw a high open hall pargetted with particoloured marbles and *pietra dura* of price and other precious stones, and hung with cages of sandal-wood and eagle-wood; full of birds which made sweet music, such as the "Thousand-voiced,"[132] and the cushat, the merle, the turtle-dove and the Nubian ring-dove. My heart was filled with pleasure thereby; my grief was dispelled and I slept in that aviary till dawn. Then I unlocked the door of the fourth chamber and therein found a grand saloon with forty smaller chambers giving upon it. All their doors stood open: so I entered and found them full of pearls and jacinths and beryls and emeralds and corals and carbuncles, and all manner precious gems and jewels, such as tongue of man may not describe. My thought was stunned at the sight and I said to myself, "These be things methinks united which could not be found save in the treasuries of a King of Kings, nor could the monarchs of the world have collected the like of these!" And my heart dilated and my sorrows ceased, "For," quoth I, "now verily am I the monarch of the age, since by Allah's grace this enormous wealth is mine; and I have forty damsels under my hand nor is there any to claim them save myself." Then I gave not over opening place after place until nine and thirty days were passed and in that time I had entered every chamber except that one whose door the Princesses had charged me not to open. But my thoughts, O my mistress, ever ran on that forbidden fortieth[133] and Satan urged me to open it for my own undoing; nor had I patience to forbear, albeit there wanted of the trysting time but a single day. So I stood before the chamber aforesaid and, after a moment's hesitation, opened the door which was plated with red gold, and entered. I was met by a perfume whose like I had never before smelt; and so sharp and subtle was the odour that it made my senses drunken as with strong wine, and I fell to the ground in a fainting fit which lasted a full hour. When I came to myself I strengthened my heart and, entering, found myself in a chamber whose floor was bespread with saffron and blazing with light from branched candelabra of gold and lamps fed with costly oils, which diffused the scent of musk and ambergris. I saw there also two great censers each big as a mazer-bowl,[134] flaming with lign-aloes, nadd-perfume,[135] ambergris and honied scents; and the place was full of their fragrance. Presently, O my lady, I espied a noble steed, black as the murks of night when murkiest, standing, ready saddled and bridled (and his saddle was of red gold) before two mangers, one of clear crystal wherein was husked sesame, and the other also of crystal containing water of the rose scented with musk. When I saw this I marvelled and said to myself, "Doubtless in this animal must be some wondrous mystery;" and Satan cozened me, so I led him without the palace and mounted him; but he would not stir from his place. So I hammered his sides with my heels, but he moved not, and then I took the rein-whip[136] and struck him withal. When he felt the blow, he neighed a neigh with a sound like deafening thunder and, opening a pair of wings[137] flew up with me in the firmament of heaven far beyond the eyesight of man. After a full hour of flight he descended and alighted on a terrace roof and shaking me off his back lashed me on the face with his tail and gouged out my left eye causing it roll along my cheek. Then he flew away. I went down from the terrace and found myself again amongst the ten one-eyed youths sitting upon their ten couches with blue covers; and they cried out when they saw me, "No welcome to thee, nor aught of good cheer! We all lived of lives the happiest and we ate and drank of the best; upon brocades and cloths of gold we took our rest, and we slept with our heads on beauty's breast, but we could not await one day to gain the delights of a year!" Quoth I, "Behold I have become one like unto you and now I would have you bring me a tray full of blackness, wherewith to blacken my face, and receive me into your society." "No, by Allah," quoth they, "thou shalt not sojourn with us and now get thee hence!" So they drove me away. Finding them reject me thus I foresaw that matters would go hard with me, and I remembered the many miseries which Destiny had written upon my forehead; and I fared forth from among them heavy-hearted and tearful-eyed, repeating to myself these words, "I was sitting at mine ease but my frowardness brought me to unease." Then I shaved beard and mustachios and eyebrows, renouncing the world, and wandered in Kalandar-garb about Allah's earth; and the Almighty decreed safety for me till I arrived at Baghdad, which was on the evening of this very night. Here I met these two other Kalandars standing bewildered; so I saluted them saying, "I am a stranger!" and they answered, "And we likewise be strangers!" By the freak of Fortune we were like to like, three Kalandars and three monoculars all blind of the left eye. Such, O my lady, is the cause of the shearing of my beard and the manner of my losing an eye. Said the lady to him, "Rub thy head and wend thy ways;" but he answered, "By Allah, I will not go until I hear the stories of these others." Then the lady, turning towards the Caliph and Ja'afar and Masrur, said to them, "Do ye also give an account of yourselves, you men!" Whereupon Ja'afar stood forth and told her what he had told the portress as they were entering the house; and when she heard his story of their being merchants and Mosul-men who had outrun the watch, she said, "I grant you your lives each for each sake, and now away with you all." So they all went out and when they were in the street, quoth the Caliph to the Kalandars, "O company, whither go ye now, seeing that the morning hath not yet dawned?" Quoth they, "By Allah, O our lord, we know not where to go." "Come and pass the rest of the night with us," said the Caliph and, turning to Ja'afar, "Take them home with thee and to-morrow bring them to my presence that we may chronicle their adventures." Ja'afar did as the Caliph bade him and the Commander of the Faithful returned to his palace; but sleep gave no sign of visiting him that night and he lay awake pondering the mishaps of the three Kalandar-princes and impatient to know the history of the ladies and the two black bitches. No sooner had morning dawned than he went forth and sat upon the throne of his sovereignty; and, turning to Ja'afar, after all his Grandees and Officers of state were gathered together, he said, "Bring me the three ladies and the two bitches and the three Kalandars." So Ja'afar fared forth and brought them all before him (and the ladies were veiled); then the Minister turned to them and said in the Caliph's name, "We pardon you your maltreatment of us and your want of courtesy, in consideration of the kindness which forewent it, and for that ye knew us not: now however I would have you to know that ye stand in presence of the fifth[138] of the sons of Abbas, Harun al-Rashid, brother of Caliph Musa al-Hadi, son of Al-Mansur; son of Mohammed the brother of Al-Saffah bin Mohammed who was first of the royal house. Speak ye therefore before him the truth and the whole truth!" When the ladies heard Ja'afar's words touching the Commander of the Faithful, the eldest came forward and said, "O Prince of True Believers, my story is one which, were it graven with needle-gravers upon the eye-corners were a warner for whoso would be warned and an example for whoso can take profit from example." And she began to tell

THE ELDEST LADY'S TALE.

Verily a strange tale is mine and 'tis this:—Yon two black bitches are my eldest sisters by one mother and father; and these two others, she who beareth upon her the signs of stripes and the third our procuratrix are my sisters by another mother. When my father died, each took her share of the heritage and, after a while my mother also deceased, leaving me and my sisters-german three thousand dinars; so each daughter received her portion of a thousand dinars and I the same, albe the youngest. In due course of time my sisters married with the usual festivities and lived with their husbands, who bought merchandise with their wives' monies and set out on their travels together. Thus they threw me off. My brothers-in-law were absent with their wives five years, during which period they spent all the money they had and, becoming bankrupt, deserted my sisters in foreign parts amid stranger folk. After five years my eldest sister returned to me in beggar's gear with her clothes in rags and tatters[139] and a dirty old mantilla;[140] and truly she was in the foulest and sorriest plight. At first sight I did not know my own sister; but presently I recognised her and said "What state is this?" "O our sister," she replied, "words cannot undo the done; and the reed of Destiny hath run through what Allah decreed." Then I sent her to the bath and dressed her in a suit of mine own, and boiled for her a bouillon and brought her some good wine and said to her, "O my sister, thou art the eldest, who still standest to us in the stead of father and mother; and, as for the inheritance which came to me as to you twain, Allah hath blessed it and prospered it to me with increase; and my circumstances are easy, for I have made much money by spinning and cleaning silk; and I and you will share my wealth alike." I entreated her with all kindliness and she abode with me a whole year, during which our thoughts and fancies were always full of our other sister. Shortly after she too came home in yet fouler and sorrier plight than that of my eldest sister; and I dealt by her still more honourably than I had done by the first, and each of them had a share of my substance. After a time they said to me, "O our sister, we desire to marry again, for indeed we have not patience to drag on our days without husbands and to lead the lives of widows bewitched;" and I replied, "O eyes of me![141] ye have hitherto seen scanty weal in wedlock, for now-a-days good men and true are become rarities and curiosities; nor do I deem your projects advisable, as ye have already made trial of matrimony and have failed." But they would not accept my advice and married without my consent: nevertheless I gave them outfit and dowries out of my money; and they fared forth with their mates. In a mighty little time their husbands played them false and, taking whatever they could lay hands upon, levanted and left them in the lurch. Thereupon they came to me ashamed and in abject case and made their excuses to me, saying, "Pardon our fault and be not wroth with us;[142] for although thou art younger in years yet art thou older in wit; henceforth we will never make mention of marriage; so take us back as thy hand-maidens that we may eat our mouthful." Quoth I, "Welcome to you, O my sisters, there is naught dearer to me than you." And I took them in and redoubled my kindness to them. We ceased not to live after this loving fashion for a full year, when I resolved to sell my wares abroad and first to fit me a conveyance for Bassorah; so I equipped a large ship, and loaded her with merchandise and valuable goods for traffic, and with provaunt and all needful for a voyage, and said to my sisters, "Will ye abide at home whilst I travel, or would ye prefer to accompany me on the voyage?" "We will travel with thee," answered they, "for we cannot bear to be parted from thee." So I divided my monies into two parts, one to accompany me and the other to be left in charge of a trusty person, for, as I said to myself, Haply some accident may happen to the ship and yet we remain alive; in which case we shall find on our return what may stand us in good stead. I took my two sisters and we went a-voyaging some days and nights; but the master was careless enough to miss his course, and the ship went astray with us and entered a sea other than the sea we sought. For a time we knew naught of this; and the wind blew fair for us ten days, after which the lookout man went aloft to see about him and cried, "Good news!" Then he came down rejoicing and said, "I have seen what seemeth to be a city as 'twere a pigeon." Hereat we rejoiced and, ere an hour of the day had passed, the buildings showed plain in the offing and we asked the Captain, "What is the name of yonder city?" and he answered, "By Allah I wot not, for I never saw it before and never sailed these seas in my life: but, since our troubles have ended in safety, remains for you only to land there with your merchandise and, if you find selling profitable, sell and make your market of what is there; and if not, we will rest here two days and provision ourselves and fare away." So we entered the port and the Captain went up town and was absent awhile, after which he returned to us and said, "Arise; go up into the city and marvel at the works of Allah with His creatures and pray to be preserved from His righteous wrath!" So we landed and going up into the city, saw at the gate men hending staves in hand; but when we drew near them, behold, they had been translated[143] by the anger of

Allah and had become stones. Then we entered the city and found all who therein woned into black stones enstoned: not an inhabited house appeared to the espier, nor was there a blower of fire.[144] We were awe struck at the sight and threaded the market streets where we found the goods and gold and silver left lying in their places; and we were glad and said, "Doubtless there is some mystery in all this." Then we dispersed about the thoroughfares and each busied himself with collecting the wealth and money and rich stuffs, taking scanty heed of friend or comrade. As for myself I went up to the castle which was strongly fortified; and, entering the King's palace by its gate of red gold, found all the vaiselle of gold and silver, and the King himself seated in the midst of his Chamberlains and Nabobs and Emirs and Wazirs; all clad in raiment which confounded man's art. I drew nearer and saw him sitting on a throne incrusted and inlaid with pearls and gems; and his robes were of gold-cloth adorned with jewels of every kind, each one flashing like a star. Around him stood fifty Mamelukes, white slaves, clothed in silks of divers sorts holding their drawn swords in their hands; but when I drew near to them lo! all were black stones. My understanding was confounded at the sight, but I walked on and entered the great hall of the Harim,[145] whose walls I found hung with tapestries of gold-striped silk and spread with silken carpets embroidered with golden flowers. Here I saw the Queen lying at full length arrayed in robes purfled with fresh young[146] pearls; on her head was a diadem set with many sorts of gems each fit for a ring[147] and around her neck hung collars and necklaces. All her raiment and her ornaments were in natural state but she had been turned into a black stone by Allah's wrath. Presently I espied an open door for which I made straight and found leading to it a flight of seven steps. So I walked up and came upon a place pargetted with marble and spread and hung with gold-worked carpets and tapestry, amiddlemost of which stood a throne of juniper-wood inlaid with pearls and precious stones and set with bosses of emeralds. In the further wall was an alcove whose curtains, bestrung with pearls, were let down and I saw a light issuing therefrom; so I drew near and perceived that the light came from a precious stone as big as an ostrich-egg, set at the upper end of the alcove upon a little chryselephantine couch of ivory and gold; and this jewel, blazing like the sun, cast its rays wide and side. The couch also was spread with all manner of silken stuffs amazing the gazer with their richness and beauty. I marvelled much at all this, especially when seeing in that place candles ready lighted; and I said in my mind, "Needs must some one have lighted these candles." Then I went forth and came to the kitchen and thence to the buttery and the King's treasure-chambers; and continued to explore the palace and to pace from place to place; I forgot myself in my awe and marvel at these matters and I was drowned in thought till the night came on. Then I would have gone forth, but knowing not the gate I lost my way, so I returned to the alcove whither the lighted candles directed me and sat down upon the couch; and wrapping myself in a coverlet, after I had repeated somewhat from the Koran, I would have slept but could not, for restlessness possessed me. When night was at its noon I heard a voice chanting the Koran in sweetest accents; but the tone thereof was weak; so I rose, glad to hear the silence broken, and followed the sound until I reached a closet whose door stood ajar. Then peeping through a chink I considered the place and lo! it was an oratory wherein was a prayer-niche[148] with two wax candles burning and lamps hanging from the ceiling. In it too was spread a prayer-carpet whereupon sat a youth fair to see; and before him on its stand[149] was a copy of the Koran, from which he was reading. I marvelled to see him alone alive amongst the people of the city and entering saluted him; whereupon he raised his eyes and returned my salam. Quoth I, "Now by the Truth of what thou readest in Allah's Holy Book, I conjure thee to answer my question." He looked upon me with a smile and said, "O handmaid of Allah, first tell me the cause of thy coming hither, and I in turn will tell what hath befallen both me and the people of this city, and what was the reason of my escaping their doom." So I told him my story whereat he wondered; and I questioned him of the people of the city, when he replied, "Have patience with me for awhile, O my sister!" and, reverently closing the Holy Book, he laid it up in a satin bag. Then he seated me by his side; and I looked at him and behold, he was as the moon at its full, fair of face and rare of form, soft-sided and slight, of well-proportioned height, and cheek smoothly bright and diffusing light. I glanced at him with one glance of eyes which caused me a thousand sighs; and my heart was at once taken captive-wise; so I asked him, "O my lord and my love, tell me that whereof I questioned thee;" and he answered, "Hearing is obeying! Know, O handmaid of Allah, that this city was the capital of my father who is the King thou sawest on the throne transfigured by Allah's wrath to a black stone, and the Queen thou foundest in the alcove is my mother. They and all the people of the city were Magians who fire adored in lieu of the Omnipotent Lord[150] and were wont to swear by lowe and heat and shade and light, and the spheres revolving day and night. My father had ne'er a son till he was blest with me near the last of his days; and he reared me till I grew up and prosperity anticipated me in all things. Now it is fortuned there was with us an old woman well stricken in years, a Moslemah who, inwardly believing in Allah and His Apostle, conformed outwardly with the religion of my people; and my father placed thorough confidence in her for that he knew her to be trustworthy and virtuous; and he treated her with ever-increasing kindness believing her to be of his own belief. So when I was well-nigh grown up my father committed me to her charge saying:—Take him and educate him and teach him the rules of our faith; let him have the best instructions and cease not thy fostering care of him. So she took me and taught me the tenets of Al-Islam with the divine ordinances[151] of the Wuzu-ablution and the five daily prayers and she made me learn the Koran by rote, often repeating:—Serve none save Allah Almighty! When I had mastered this much of knowledge she said to me:—O my son, keep this matter concealed from thy sire and reveal naught to him lest he slay thee. So I hid it from him and I abode on this wise for a term of days when the old woman died, and the people of the city redoubled in their impiety[152] and arrogance and the error of their ways. One day, while they were as wont, behold, they heard a loud and terrible sound and a crier crying out with a voice like roaring thunder so every ear could hear, far and near:—O folk of this city leave ye your fire-worshipping and adore Allah the All-compassionate King! At this, fear and terror fell upon the citizens and they crowded to my father (he being King of the city) and asked him:—What is this awesome voice we have heard, for it hath confounded us with the excess of its terror?; and he answered:—Let not a voice fright you nor shake your steadfast sprite nor turn you back from the faith which is right. Their hearts inclined to his words and they ceased not to worship the fire and they persisted in rebellion for a full year from the time they heard the first voice; and on the anniversary came a second cry and a third at the head of the third year, each year once. Still they persisted in their malpractises till one day at break of dawn, judgment and the wrath of Heaven descended upon them with all suddenness, and by the visitation of Allah all were metamorphosed into black stones,[153] they and their beasts and their cattle; and none was saved save myself who at the time was engaged in my devotions. From that day to this I am in the case thou seest, constant in prayer and fasting and reading and reciting the Koran; but I am indeed grown weary by reason of my loneliness, having none to bear me company." Then said I to him (for in very sooth he had won my heart and was the lord of my life and soul), "O youth, wilt thou fare with me to Baghdad city and visit the Olema and men learned in the law and doctors of divinity and get thee increase of wisdom and understanding and theology? And know that she who standeth in thy presence will be thy handmaid, albeit she be head of her family and mistress over men and eunuchs and servants and slaves. Indeed my life was no life before it fell in with thy youth. I have here a ship laden with merchandise; and in very truth Destiny drove me to this city that I might come to the knowledge of these matters, for it was fated that we should meet." And I ceased not to persuade him and speak him fair and use every art till he consented. I slept that night at his feet and hardly knowing where I was for excess of joy. As soon as the next morning dawned (she pursued, addressing the Caliph), I arose and we entered the treasuries and took thence whatever was light in weight and great in worth; then we went down side by side from the castle to the city, where we were met by the Captain and my sisters and slaves who had been seeking for me. When they saw me they rejoiced and asked what had stayed me, and I told them all I had seen and related to them the story of the young Prince and the transformation wherewith the citizens had been justly visited. Hereat all marvelled, but when my two sisters (these two bitches, O Commander of the Faithful!) saw me by the side of my young lover they jaloused me on his account and were wroth and plotted mischief against me. We awaited a fair wind and went on board rejoicing and ready to fly for joy by reason of the goods we had gotten, but my own greatest joyance was in the youth; and we waited awhile till the wind blew fair for us and then we set sail and fared forth. Now as we sat talking, my sisters asked me, "And what wilt thou do with this handsome young man?"; and I answered, "I purpose to make him my husband!" Then I turned to him and said, "O my lord, I have that to propose to thee wherein thou must not cross me; and this it is that, when we reach Baghdad, my native city, I offer thee my life as thy handmaiden in holy matrimony, and thou shalt be to me baron and I will be femme to thee." He answered, "I hear and I obey!; thou art my lady and my mistress and whatso thou doest I will not gainsay." Then I turned to my sisters and said, "This is my gain; I content me with this youth and those who have gotten aught of my property let them keep it as their gain with my good will." "Thou sayest and doest well," answered the twain, but they imagined mischief against me. We ceased not spooning before a fair wind till we had exchanged the sea of peril for the seas of safety and, in a few days, we made Bassorah-city, whose buildings loomed clear before us as evening fell. But after we had retired to rest and were sound asleep, my two sisters arose and took me up, bed and all, and threw me into the sea: they did the same with the young Prince who, as he could not swim, sank and was drowned and Allah enrolled him in the noble army of Martyrs.[154] As for me would Heaven I had been drowned with him, but Allah deemed that I should be of the saved; so when I awoke and found myself in the sea and saw the ship making off like a flash of lightning, He threw in my way a piece of timber which I bestrided, and the waves tossed me to and fro till they cast me upon an island coast, a high land and an uninhabited. I landed and walked about the island the rest of the night and, when morning dawned, I saw a rough track barely fit for child of Adam to tread, leading to what proved a shallow ford connecting island and mainland. As soon as the sun had risen I spread my garments to dry in its rays; and ate of the fruits of the island and drank of its waters; then I set out along the foot-track and ceased not walking till I reached the mainland. Now when there remained between me and the city but a two hours' journey behold, a great serpent, the bigness of a date-palm, came fleeing towards me in all haste, gliding along now to the right then to the left till she was close upon me, whilst her tongue lolled ground-wards a span long and swept the dust as she went. She was pursued by a Dragon[155] who was not longer than two lances, and of slender build about the bulk of a spear and, although her terror lent her speed, and she kept wriggling from side to side, he overtook her and seized her by the tail, whereat her tears streamed down and her tongue was thrust out in her agony. I took pity on her and, picking up a stone and calling upon Allah for aid, threw it at the Dragon's head with such force that he died then and there; and the serpent opening a pair of wings flew into the lift and disappeared from before my eyes. I sat down marvelling over that adventure, but I was weary and, drowsiness overcoming me, I slept where I was for a while. When I awoke I found a jet-black damsel sitting at my feet shampooing them; and by her side stood two black bitches (my sisters, O Commander of the Faithful!). I was ashamed before her[156] and, sitting up, asked her, "O my sister, who and what art thou?"; and she answered, "How soon hast thou forgotten me! I am she for whom thou wroughtest a good deed and sowedest the seed of gratitude and slewest her foe; for I am the serpent whom by Allah's aidance thou didst just now deliver from the Dragon. I am a Jinniyah and he was a Jinn who hated me, and none saved my life from him save thou. As soon as thou freedest me from him I flew on the wind to the ship whence thy sisters threw thee, and removed all that was therein to thy house. Then I ordered my attendant Marids to sink the ship and I transformed thy two sisters into these black bitches; for I know all that hath passed between them and thee; but as for the youth, of a truth he is drowned." So saying she flew up with me and the bitches, and presently set us down on the terrace-roof of my house, wherein I found ready stored the whole of what property was in my ship, nor was aught of it missing. "Now (continued the serpent that was), I swear by all engraven on the seal-ring of Solomon[157] (with whom be peace!) unless thou deal to each of these bitches three hundred stripes every day I will come and imprison thee for ever under the earth." I answered, "Hearkening and obedience!"; and away she flew. But before going she again charged me saying, "I again swear by Him who made the two seas flow[158] (and this be my second oath) if thou gainsay me I will come and transform thee like thy sisters." Since then I have never failed, O Commander of the Faithful, to beat them with that number of blows till their blood flows with my tears, I pitying them the while, and well they wot that their being scourged is no fault of mine and they accept my excuses. And this is my tale and my history! The Caliph marvelled at her adventures and then signed to Ja'afar who said to the second lady, the Portress, "And thou, how camest thou by the welts and wheals upon thy body?" So she began the

TALE OF THE PORTRESS.

Know, O Commander of the Faithful, that I had a father who, after fulfilling his time, deceased and left me great store of wealth. I remained single for a short time and presently married one of the richest of his day. I abode with him a year when he also died, and my share of his property amounted to eighty thousand dinars in gold according to the holy law of inheritance.[159] Thus I became passing rich and my reputation spread far and wide, for I had made me ten changes of raiment, each worth a thousand dinars. One day as I was sitting at home, behold, there came in to me an old woman[160] with lantern jaws and cheeks sucked in, and eyes rucked up, and eyebrows scant and scald, and head bare and bald; and teeth broken by time and mauled, and back bending and necknape nodding, and face blotched, and rheum running, and hair like a snake black-and-white-speckled, in complexion a very fright, even as saith the poet of the like of her:—

> Ill-omened hag! unshriven be her sins
> Nor mercy visit her on dying bed:
> Thousand head-strongest he-mules would her guiles,
> Despite their bolting, lead with spider thread.

When the old woman entered she salamed to me and kissing the ground before me, said, "I have at home an orphan daughter and this night are her wedding and her displaying.[161] We be poor folks and strangers in this city knowing none inhabitant and we are broken-hearted. So do thou earn for thyself a recompense and a reward in Heaven by being present at her displaying and, when the ladies of this city shall hear that thou art to make act of presence, they also will present themselves; so shalt thou comfort her affliction, for she is sore bruised in spirit and she hath none to look to save Allah the Most High." Then she wept and kissed my feet reciting these couplets:—

> Thy presence bringeth us a grace
> We own before thy winsome face:
> And wert thou absent ne'er an one
> Could stand in stead or take thy place.

So pity gat hold on me and compassion and I said, "Hearing is consenting and, please Allah, I will do somewhat more for her; nor shall she be shown to her bridegroom save in my raiment and ornaments and jewelry." At this the old woman rejoiced and bowed her head to my feet and kissed them, saying, "Allah requite thee weal, and comfort thy heart even as thou has comforted mine! But, O my lady, do not trouble thyself to do me this service at this hour; be thou ready by supper-time,[162] when I will come and fetch thee." So saying she kissed my hand and went her ways. I set about stringing my pearls and donning my brocades and making my toilette, little recking what Fortune had in womb for me, when suddenly the old woman stood before me, simpering and smiling till she showed every tooth stump, and quoth she, "O my mistress, the city madams have arrived and when I apprized them that thou promisedst to be present, they were glad and they are now awaiting thee and looking eagerly for thy coming and for the honour of meeting thee." So I threw on my mantilla and, making the old crone walk before me and my handmaidens behind me, I fared till we came to a street well watered and swept neat, where the winnowing breeze blew cool and sweet. Here we were stopped by a gate arched over with a dome of marble stone firmly seated on solidest foundation, and leading to a Palace whose walls from earth rose tall and proud, and whose pinnacle was crowned by the clouds,[163] and over the doorway were writ these couplets:—

> I am the wone where Mirth shall ever smile;
> The home of Joyance through my lasting while:
> And 'mid my court a fountain jets and flows,
> Nor tears nor troubles shall that fount defile:
> The marge with royal Nu'uman's[164] bloom is dight,
> Myrtle, Narcissus-flower and Chamomile.

Arrived at the gate, before which hung a black curtain, the old woman knocked and it was opened to us; when we entered and found a vestibule spread with carpets and hung around with lamps all alight and wax candles in candelabra adorned with pendants of precious gems and noble ores. We passed on through this passage till we entered a saloon, whose like for grandeur and beauty is not to be found in this world. It was hung and carpeted with silken stuffs, and was illuminated with branches, sconces and tapers ranged in double row, an avenue abutting on the upper or noble end of the saloon, where stood a couch of juniper-wood encrusted with pearls and gems and surmounted by a baldaquin with mosquito-curtains of satin looped up with margarites. And hardly had we taken note of this when there came forth from the baldaquin a young lady and I looked, O Commander of the Faithful, upon a face and form more perfect than the moon when fullest, with a favour brighter than the dawn gleaming with saffron-hued light. The fair young girl came down from the estrade and said to me, "Welcome and well come and good cheer to my sister, the dearly-beloved, the illustrious, and a thousand greetings!" Then she recited these couplets:—

> An but the house could know who cometh 'twould rejoice,
> And kiss the very dust whereon thy foot was placed;
> And with the tongue of circumstance the walls would say,
> "Welcome and hail to one with generous gifts engraced!"

Then sat she down and said to me, "O my sister, I have a brother who hath had sight of thee at sundry wedding-feasts and festive seasons: he is a youth handsomer than I, and he hath fallen desperately in love with thee, for that bounteous Destiny hath garnered in thee all beauty and perfection; and he hath given silver to this old woman that she might visit thee; and she hath contrived on this wise to foregather us twain. He hath heard that thou art one of the nobles of thy tribe nor is he aught less in his; and, being desirous to ally his lot with thy lot, he hath practised this device to bring me in company with thee; for he is fain to marry thee after the ordinance of Allah and his Apostle; and in what is lawful and right there is no shame." When I heard these words and saw myself fairly entrapped in the house, I said, "Hearing is consenting." She was delighted at this and clapped her hands;[165] whereupon a door opened and out of it came a young man blooming in the prime of life, exquisitely dressed, a model of beauty and loveliness and symmetry and perfect grace, with gentle winning manners and eyebrows like a bended bow and shaft on cord, and eyes which bewitched all hearts with sorcery lawful in the sight of the Lord. When I looked at him my heart inclined to him and I loved him; and he sat by my side and talked with me a while, when the young lady again clapped her hands and behold, a side-door opened and out of it came the Kazi with his four assessors as witnesses; and they saluted us and, sitting down, drew up and wrote out the marriage-contract between me and the youth and retired. Then he turned to me and said, "Be our night blessed," presently adding, "O my lady, I have a condition to lay on thee." Quoth I, "O my lord, what is that?" Whereupon he arose and fetching a copy of the Holy Book presented it to me saying, "Swear hereon thou wilt never look at any other than myself nor incline thy body or thy heart to him." I swore readily enough to this and he joyed with exceeding joy and embraced me round the neck while love for him possessed my whole heart. Then they set the table[166] before us and we ate and drank till we were satisfied; but I was dying for the coming of the night. And when night did come he led me to the bride-chamber and slept with me on the bed and continued to kiss and embrace me till the morning—such a night I had never seen in my dreams. I lived with him a life of happiness and delight for a full month, at the end of which I asked his leave[167] to go on foot to the bazar and buy me certain especial stuffs and he gave me permission. So I donned my mantilla and, taking with me the old woman and a slave-girl,[168] I went to the khan of the silk-mercers, where I seated myself in the shop-front of a young merchant whom the old woman recommended, saying to me, "This youth's father died when he was a boy and left him great store of wealth: he hath by him a mighty fine[169] stock of goods and thou wilt find what thou seekest with him, for none in the bazar hath better stuffs than he." Then she said to him, "Show this lady the most costly stuffs thou hast by thee;" and he replied, "Hearkening and obedience!" Then she whispered me, "Say a civil word to him!"; but I replied, "I am pledged to address no man save my lord." And as she began to sound his praise I said sharply to her, "We want nought of thy sweet speeches; our wish is to buy of him whatsoever we need, and return home." So he brought me all I sought and I offered him his money, but he refused to take it saying, "Let it be a gift offered to my guest this day!" Then quoth I to the old woman, "If he will not take the money, give him back his stuff." "By Allah," cried he, "not a thing will I take from thee: I sell it not for gold or for silver, but I give it all as a gift for a single kiss; a kiss more precious to me than everything the shop containeth." Asked the old woman, "What will the kiss profit thee?"; and, turning to me, whispered, "O my daughter, thou hearest what this young fellow saith? What harm will it do thee if he get a kiss from thee and thou gettest what thou seekest at that price?" Replied I, "I take refuge with Allah from such action! Knowest thou not that I am bound by an oath?"[170] But she answered, "Now whist! just let him kiss thee and neither speak to him nor lean over him, so shalt thou keep thine oath and thy silver, and no harm whatever shall befal thee." And she ceased not to persuade me and importune me and make light of the matter till evil entered into my mind and I put my head in the poke[171] and, declaring I would ne'er consent, consented. So I veiled my eyes and held up the edge of my mantilla between me and the people passing and he put his mouth to my cheek under the veil. But while kissing me he bit me so hard a bite that it tore the flesh from my cheek,[172] and blood flowed fast and faintness came over me. The old woman caught me in her arms and, when I came to myself, I found the shop shut up and her sorrowing over me and saying "Thank Allah for averting which might have been worse!" Then she said to me, "Come, take heart and let us go home before the matter become public and thou be dishonoured. And when thou art safe inside the house feign sickness and lie down and cover thyself up; and I will bring thee powders and plasters to cure this bite withal, and thy wound will be healed at the latest in three days." So after a while I arose and I was in extreme distress and terror came full upon me; but I went on little by little till I reached the house when I pleaded illness and lay me down. When it was night my husband came in to me and said, "What hath befallen thee, O my darling, in this excursion of thine?"; and I replied, "I am not well: my head acheth badly." Then he lighted a candle and drew near me and looked hard at me and asked, "What is that wound I see on thy cheek and in the tenderest part too?" And I answered, "When I went out to-day with thy leave to buy stuffs, a camel laden with firewood jostled me and one of the pieces tore my veil and wounded my cheek as thou seest; for indeed the ways of this city are strait." "To-morrow," cried he, "I will go complain to the Governor, so shall he gibbet every fuel-seller in Baghdad." "Allah upon thee," said I, "burden not thy soul with such sin against any man. The fact is I was riding on an ass and it stumbled, throwing me to the ground; and my cheek lighted upon a stick or a bit of glass and got this wound." "Then," said he, "to-morrow I will go up to Ja'afar the Barmaki and tell him the story, so shall he kill every donkey-boy in Baghdad." "Wouldst thou destroy all these men because of my wound," said I, "when this which befel me was by decree of Allah and His destiny?" But he answered, "There is no help for it;" and, springing to his feet, plied me with words and pressed me till I was perplexed and frightened; and I stuttered and stammered and my speech waxed thick and I said, "This is a mere accident by decree of Allah." Then, O Commander of the Faithful, he guessed my case and said, "Thou hast been false to thine oath." He at once cried out with a loud cry, whereupon a door opened and in came seven black slaves whom he commanded to drag me from my bed and throw me down in the middle of the room. Furthermore, he ordered one of them to pinion my elbows and squat upon my head; and a second to sit upon my knees and secure my feet; and drawing his sword he gave it to a third and said, "Strike her, O Sa'ad, and cut her in twain and let each one take half and cast it into the Tigris[173] that the fish may eat her; for such is the retribution due to those who violate their vows and are unfaithful to their love." And he redoubled in wrath and recited these couplets:—

> An there be one who shares with me her love,
>   I'd strangle Love tho' life by Love were slain;
> Saying, O Soul, Death were the nobler choice,
>   For ill is Love when shared 'twixt partners twain.

Then he repeated to the slave, "Smite her, O Sa'ad!" And when the slave who was sitting upon me made sure of the command he bent down to me and said, "O my mistress, repeat the profession of Faith and bethink thee if there be any thing thou wouldst have done; for verily this is the last hour of thy life." "O good slave," said I, "wait but a little while and get off my head that I may charge thee with my last injunctions." Then I raised my head and saw the state I was in, how I had fallen from high degree into lowest disgrace; and into death after life (and such life!) and how I had brought my punishment on myself by my own sin;

whereupon the tears streamed from mine eyes and I wept with exceeding weeping. The slave drew near me, O Commander of the Faithful, and I made sure of death and, despairing of life, committed my affairs to Almighty Allah, when behold, the old woman rushed in and threw herself at my husband's feet and kissed them and wept and said, "O my son, by the rights of my fosterage and by my long service to thee, I conjure thee pardon this young lady, for indeed she hath done nothing deserving such doom. Thou art a very young man and I fear lest her death be laid at thy door; for it is said:—Whoso slayeth shall be slain. As for this wanton (since thou deemest her such) drive her out from thy doors, from thy love and from thy heart." And she ceased not to weep and importune him till he relented and said, "I pardon her, but needs must I set on her my mark which shall show upon her all her life." Then he bade the slaves drag me along the ground and lay me out at full length, after stripping me of all my clothes;[174] and when the slaves had so sat upon me that I could not move, he fetched in a rod of quince-tree and came down with it upon my body, and continued beating me on the back and sides till I lost consciousness from excess of pain, and I despaired of life. Then he commanded the slaves to take me away as soon as it was dark, together with the old woman to show them the way and throw me upon the floor of the house wherein I dwelt before my marriage. They did their lord's bidding and cast me down in my old home and went their ways. I did not revive from my swoon till dawn appeared, when I applied myself to the dressing of my wounds with ointments and other medicaments; and I medicined myself, but my sides and ribs still showed signs of the rod as thou hast seen. I lay in weakly case and confined to my bed for four months before I was able to rise and health returned to me. At the end of that time I went to the house where all this had happened and found it a ruin; the street had been pulled down endlong and rubbish-heaps rose where the building erst was; nor could

I learn how this had come about. Then I betook myself to this my sister on my father's side and found with her these two black bitches. I saluted her and told her what had betided me and the whole of my story and she said, "O my sister, who is safe from the despite of Time and secure? Thanks be to Allah who hath brought thee off safely;" and she began to say:—

> Such is the World, so bear a patient heart
> When riches leave thee and when friends depart!

Then she told me her own story, and what had happened to her with her two sisters and how matters had ended; so we abode together and the subject of marriage was never on our tongues for all these years. After a while we were joined by our other sister, the procuratrix, who goeth out every morning and buyeth all we require for the day and night; and we continued in such condition till this last night. In the morning our sister went out, as usual, to make her market and then befel us what befel from bringing the Porter into the house and admitting these three Kalandar-men. We entreated them kindly and honourably and a quarter of the night had not passed ere three grave and respectable merchants from Mosul joined us and told us their adventures. We sat talking with them but on one condition which they violated, whereupon we treated them as sorted with their breach of promise, and made them repeat the account they had given of themselves. They did our bidding and we forgave their offence; so they departed from us and this morning we were unexpectedly summoned to thy presence. And such is our story! The Caliph wondered at her words and bade the tale be recorded and chronicled and laid up in his muniment-chambers. Then he asked the eldest lady, the mistress of the house, "Knowest thou the whereabouts of the Ifritah who spelled thy sisters?"; and she answered, "O Commander of the Faithful, she gave me a ringlet of her hair saying:—Whenas thou wouldest see me, burn a couple of these hairs and I will be with thee forthright, even though I were beyond Caucasus-mountain." Quoth the Caliph, "Bring me hither the hair." So she brought it and he threw the whole lock upon the fire. As soon as the odour of the burning hair dispread itself, the palace shook and trembled, and all present heard a rumbling and rolling of thunder and a noise as of wings and lo! the Jinniyah who had been a serpent stood in the Caliph's presence. Now she was a Moslemah, so she saluted him and said, "Peace be with thee, O Vicar[175] of Allah;" whereto he replied, "And with thee also be peace and the mercy of Allah and His blessing." Then she continued, "Know that this damsel sowed for me the seed of kindness, wherefor I cannot enough requite her, in that she delivered me from death and destroyed mine enemy. Now I had seen how her sisters dealt with her and felt myself bound to avenge her on them. At first I was minded to slay them, but I feared it would be grievous to her, so I transformed them to bitches; but if thou desire their release, O Commander of the Faithful, I will release them to pleasure thee and her for I am of the Moslems." Quoth the Caliph, "Release them and after we will look into the affair of the beaten lady and consider her case carefully; and if the truth of her story be evidenced I will exact retaliation[176] from him who wronged her." Said the Ifritah, "O Commander of the Faithful, I will forthwith release them and will discover to thee the man who did that deed by this lady and wronged her and took her property, and he is the nearest of all men to thee!" So saying she took a cup of water and muttered a spell over it and uttered words there was no understanding; then she sprinkled some of the water over the faces of the two bitches, saying, "Return to your former human shape!" whereupon they were restored to their natural forms and fell to praising their Creator. Then said the Ifritah, "O Commander of the Faithful, of a truth he who scourged this lady with rods is thy son Al-Amin brother of Al-Maamun;[177] for he had heard of her beauty and loveliness and he played a lover's stratagem with her and married her according to the law and committed the crime (such as it is) of scourging her. Yet indeed he is not to be blamed for beating her, for he laid a condition on her and swore her by a solemn oath not to do a certain thing; however, she was false to her vow and he was minded to put her to death, but he feared Almighty Allah and contented himself with scourging her, as thou hast seen, and with sending her back to her own place. Such is the story of the second lady and the Lord knoweth all." When the Caliph heard these words of the Ifritah, and knew who had beaten the damsel, he marvelled with mighty marvel and said, "Praise be to Allah, the Most High, the Almighty, who hath shown His exceeding mercy towards me, enabling me to deliver these two damsels from sorcery and torture, and vouchsafing to let me know the secret of this lady's history! And now by Allah, we will do a deed which shall be recorded of us after we are no more." Then he summoned his son Al-Amin and questioned him of the story of the second lady, the portress; and he told it in the face of truth; whereupon the Caliph bade call into presence the Kazis and their witnesses and the three Kalandars and the first lady with her sisters german who had been ensorcelled; and he married the three to the three Kalandars whom he knew to be princes and sons of Kings and he appointed them chamberlains about his person, assigning to them stipends and allowances and all that they required, and lodging them in his palace at Baghdad. He returned the beaten lady to his son, Al-Amin, renewing the marriage-contract between them, and gave her great wealth and bade rebuild the house fairer than it was before. As for himself he took to wife the procuratrix and lay with her that night: and next day he set apart for her an apartment in his Serraglio, with handmaidens for her service and a fixed daily allowance. And the people marvelled at their Caliph's generosity and natural beneficence and princely wisdom; nor did he forget to send all these histories to be recorded in his annals. When Shahrazad ceased speaking Dunyazad exclaimed, "O my own sister, by Allah in very sooth this is a right pleasant tale and a delectable; never was heard the like of it, but prithee tell me now another story to while away what yet remaineth of the waking hours of this our night." She replied, "With love and gladness if the King give me leave;" and he said, "Tell thy tale and tell it quickly." So she began, in these words,

THE TALE OF THE THREE APPLES.

They relate, O King of the age and lord of the time and of these days, that the Caliph Harun al-Rashid summoned his Wazir Ja'afar one night and said to him, "I desire to go down into the city and question the common folk concerning the conduct of those charged with its governance; and those of whom they complain we will depose from office and those whom they commend we will promote." Quoth Ja'afar, "Hearkening and obedience!" So the Caliph went down with Ja'afar and Eunuch Masrur to the town and walked about the streets and markets and, as they were threading a narrow alley, they came upon a very old man with a fishing-net and crate to carry small fish on his head, and in his hands a staff; and, as he walked at a leisurely pace, he repeated these lines:—

> They say me:—Thou shinest a light to mankind
> With thy lore as the night which the Moon doth uplight!
> I answer, "A truce to your jests and your gibes;
> Without luck what is learning?—a poor-devil wight!
> If they take me to pawn with my lore in my pouch,
> With my volumes to read and my ink-case to write,

For one day's provision they never could pledge me;
As likely on Doomsday to draw bill at sight:"
How poorly, indeed, doth it fare wi' the poor,
With his pauper existence and beggarly plight:
In summer he faileth provision to find;
In winter the fire-pot's his only delight:
The street-dogs with bite and with bark to him rise,
And each losel receives him with bark and with bite:
If he lift up his voice and complain of his wrong,
None pities or heeds him, however he's right;
And when sorrows and evils like these he must brave
His happiest homestead were down in the grave.

When the Caliph heard his verses he said to Ja'afar, "See this poor man and note his verses, for surely they point to his necessities." Then he accosted him and asked, "O Shaykh, what be thine occupation?" and the poor man answered, "O my lord, I am a fisherman with a family to keep and I have been out between mid-day and this time; and not a thing hath Allah made my portion wherewithal to feed my family. I cannot even pawn myself to buy them a supper and I hate and disgust my life and I hanker after death." Quoth the Caliph, "Say me, wilt thou return with us to Tigris' bank and cast thy net on my luck, and whatsoever turneth up I will buy of thee for an hundred gold pieces?" The man rejoiced when he heard these words and said, "On my head be it! I will go back with you;" and, returning with them river-wards, made a cast and waited a while; then he hauled in the rope and dragged the net ashore and there appeared in it a chest padlocked and heavy. The Caliph examined it and lifted it finding it weighty; so he gave the fisherman two hundred dinars and sent him about his business; whilst Masrur, aided by the Caliph, carried the chest to the palace and set it down and lighted the candles. Ja'afar and Masrur then broke it open and found therein a basket of palm-leaves corded with red worsted. This they cut open and saw within it a piece of carpet which they lifted out, and under it was a woman's mantilla folded in four, which they pulled out; and at the bottom of the chest they came upon a young lady, fair as a silver ingot, slain and cut into nineteen pieces. When the Caliph looked upon her he cried, "Alas!" and tears ran down his cheeks and turning to Ja'afar he said, "O dog of Wazirs,[1] shall folk be murdered in our reign and be cast into the river to be a burden and a responsibility for us on the Day of Doom? By Allah, we must avenge this woman on her murderer and he shall be made die the worst of deaths!" And presently he added, "Now, as surely as we are descended from the Sons of Abbas,[2] if thou bring us not him who slew her, that we do her justice on him, I will hang thee at the gate of my palace, thee and forty of thy kith and kin by thy side." And the Caliph was wroth with exceeding rage. Quoth Ja'afar, "Grant me three days' delay;" and quoth the Caliph, "We grant thee this." So Ja'afar went out from before him and returned to his own house, full of sorrow and saying to himself, "How shall I find him who murdered this damsel, that I may bring him before the Caliph? If I bring other than the murderer, it will be laid to my charge by the Lord: in very sooth I wot not what to do." He kept his house three days and on the fourth day the Caliph sent one of the Chamberlains for him and, as he came into the presence, asked him, "Where is the murderer of the damsel?" to which answered Ja'afar, "O Commander of the Faithful, am I inspector of murdered folk that I should ken who killed her?" The Caliph was furious at his answer and bade hang him before the palace-gate and commanded that a crier cry through the streets of Baghdad, "Whoso would see the hanging of Ja'afar, the Barmaki, Wazir of the Caliph, with forty of the Barmecides,[3] his cousins and kinsmen, before the palace-gate, let him come and let him look!" The people flocked out from all the quarters of the city to witness the execution of Ja'afar and his kinsmen, not knowing the cause. Then they set up the gallows and made Ja'afar and the others stand underneath in readiness for execution, but whilst every eye was looking for the Caliph's signal, and the crowd wept for Ja'afar and his cousins of the Barmecides, lo and behold! a young man fair of face and neat of dress and of favour like the moon raining light, with eyes black and bright, and brow flower-white, and cheeks red as rose and young down where the beard grows, and a mole like a grain of ambergris, pushed his way through the people till he stood immediately before the Wazir and said to him, "Safety to thee from this strait, O Prince of the Emirs and Asylum of the poor! I am the man who slew the woman ye found in the chest, so hang me for her and do her justice on me!" When Ja'afar heard the youth's confession he rejoiced at his own deliverance, but grieved and sorrowed for the fair youth; and whilst they were yet talking behold, another man well stricken in years pressed forwards through the people and thrust his way amid the populace till he came to Ja'afar and the youth, whom he saluted saying, "Ho thou the Wazir and Prince sans-peer! believe not the words of this youth. Of a surety none murdered the damsel but I; take her wreak on me this moment; for, an thou do not thus, I will require it of thee before Almighty Allah." Then quoth the young man, "O Wazir, this is an old man in his dotage who wotteth not whatso he saith ever, and I am he who murdered her, so do thou avenge her on me!" Quoth the old man, "O my son, thou art young and desirest the joys of the world and I am old and weary and surfeited with the world: I will offer my life as a ransom for thee and for the Wazir and his cousins. No one murdered the damsel but I, so Allah upon thee, make haste to hang me, for no life is left in me now that hers is gone." The Wazir marvelled much at all this strangeness and, taking the young man and the old man, carried them before the Caliph, where, after kissing the ground seven times between his hands, he said, "O Commander of the Faithful, I bring thee the murderer of the damsel!" "Where is he?" asked the Caliph and Ja'afar answered, "This young man saith, I am the murderer, and this old man giving him the lie saith, I am the murderer, and behold, here are the twain standing before thee." The Caliph looked at the old man and the young man and asked, "Which of you killed the girl?" The young man replied, "No one slew her save I;" and the old man answered, "Indeed none killed her but myself." Then said the Caliph to Ja'afar, "Take the twain and hang them both;" but Ja'afar rejoined, "Since one of them was the murderer, to hang the other were mere injustice."[4] "By Him who raised the firmament and dispread the earth like a carpet," cried the youth, "I am he who slew the damsel;" and he went on to describe the manner of her murder and the basket, the mantilla and the bit of carpet, in fact all that the Caliph had found upon her. So the Caliph was certified that the young man was the murderer; whereat he wondered and asked him, "What was the cause of thy wrongfully doing this damsel to die and what made thee confess the murder without the bastinado, and what brought thee here to yield up thy life, and what made thee say Do her wreak upon me?" The youth answered, "Know, O Commander of the Faithful, that this woman was my wife and the mother of my children; also my first cousin and the daughter of my paternal uncle, this old man who is my father's own brother. When I married her she was a maid[5] and Allah blessed me with three male children by her; she loved me and served me and I saw no evil in her, for I also loved her with fondest love. Now on the first day of this month she fell ill with grievous sickness and I fetched in physicians to her; but recovery came to her little by little and, when I wished her to go to the Hammam-bath, she said:——There is a something I long for before I go to the bath and I long for it with an exceeding longing. To hear is to comply, said I. And what is it? Quoth she, I have a queasy craving for an apple, to smell it and bite a bit of it. I replied:——Hadst thou a thousand longings I would try to satisfy them! So I went on the instant into the city and sought for apples but could find none; yet, had they cost a gold piece each, would I have bought them. I was vexed at this and went home and said:——O daughter of my uncle, by Allah I can find none! She was distressed, being yet very weakly, and her weakness increased greatly on her that night and I felt anxious and alarmed on her account. As soon as morning dawned I went out again and made the round of the gardens, one by one, but found no apples anywhere. At last there met me an old gardener, of whom I asked about them and he answered:—O my son, this fruit is a rarity with us and is not now to be found save in the garden of the Commander of the Faithful at Bassorah, where the gardener keepeth it for the Caliph's eating. I returned to my house troubled by my ill-success; and my love for my wife and my affection moved me to undertake the journey. So I gat me ready and set out and travelled fifteen days and nights, going and coming, and brought her three apples which I bought from the gardener for three dinars. But when I went in to my wife and set them before her, she took no pleasure in them and let them lie by her side; for her weakness and fever had increased on her and her malady lasted without abating ten days, after which she began to recover health. So I left my house and betaking me to my shop sat there buying and selling; and about midday behold, a great ugly black slave, long as a lance and broad as a bench, passed by my shop holding in hand one of the three apples wherewith he was playing. Quoth I:—O my good slave, tell me whence thou tookest that apple, that I may get the like of it? He laughed and answered:—I got it from my mistress, for I had been absent and on my return I found her lying ill with three apples by her side, and she said to me:—My horned wittol of a husband made a journey for them to Bassorah and bought them for three dinars. So I ate and drank with her and took this one from her.[6] When I heard such words from the slave, O Commander of the Faithful, the world grew black before my face, and I arose and locked up my shop and went home beside myself for excess of rage. I looked for the apples and finding only two of the three asked my wife:—O my cousin, where is the third apple?; and raising her head languidly she answered:—I wot not, O son of my uncle, where 'tis gone! This convinced me that the slave had spoken the truth, so I took a knife and coming behind her got upon her breast without a word said and cut her throat. Then I hewed off her head and her limbs in pieces and, wrapping her in her mantilla and a rag of carpet, hurriedly sewed up the whole which I set in a chest and, locking it tight, loaded it on my he-mule and threw it into the Tigris with my own hands. So Allah upon thee, O Commander of the Faithful, make haste to hang me, as I fear lest she appeal for vengeance on Resurrection Day. For, when I had thrown her into the river and no one knew aught of it, as I went back home I found my eldest son crying and yet he knew naught of what I had done with his mother. I asked him:—What hath made thee weep, my boy?; and he answered:—I took one of the three apples which were by my mammy and went down into the lane to play with my brethren when behold, a big long black slave snatched it from my hand and said, Whence hadst thou this? Quoth I, My father travelled far for it, and brought it from Bassorah for my mother who was ill and two other apples for which he paid three ducats. He took no heed of my words and I asked for the apple a second and a third time, but he cuffed me and kicked me and went off with it. I was afraid lest my mother should swinge me on account of the apple, so for fear of her I went with my brother outside the city and stayed there till evening closed in upon us; and indeed I am in fear of her; and now by Allah, O my father, say nothing to her of this or it may add to her ailment! When I heard what my child said I knew that the slave was he who had foully slandered my wife, the daughter of my uncle, and was certified that I had slain her wrongfully. So I wept with exceeding weeping and presently this old man, my paternal uncle and her father, came in; and I told him what had happened and he sat down by my side and wept and we ceased not weeping till midnight. We have kept up mourning for her these last five days and we lamented her in the deepest sorrow for that she was unjustly done to die. This came from the gratuitous lying of the slave, the blackamoor, and this was the manner of my killing her; so I conjure thee, by the honour of thine ancestors, make haste to kill me and do her justice upon me, as there is no living for me after her!" The Caliph marvelled at his words and said, "By Allah the young man is excusable: I will hang none but the accursed slave and I will do a deed which shall comfort the ill-at-ease and suffering, and which shall please the All-glorious King." Then he turned to Ja'afar and said to him, "Bring before me this accursed slave who was the sole cause of this calamity; and, if thou bring him not before me within three days, thou shalt be slain in his stead." So Ja'afar fared forth weeping and saying, "Two deaths have already beset me, nor shall the crock come off safe from every shock.[7] In this matter craft and cunning are of no avail; but He who preserved my life the first time can preserve it a second time. By Allah, I will not leave my house during the three days of life which remain to me and let the Truth (whose perfection be praised!) do e'en as He will." So he kept his house three days, and on the fourth day he summoned the Kazis and legal witnesses and made his last will and testament, and took leave of his children weeping. Presently in came a messenger from the Caliph and said to him, "The Commander of the Faithful is in the most violent rage that can be, and he sendeth to seek thee and he sweareth that the day shall certainly not pass without thy being hanged unless the slave be forthcoming." When Ja'afar heard this he wept, and his children and slaves and all who were in the house wept with him. After he had bidden adieu to everybody except his youngest daughter, he proceeded to farewell her; for he loved this wee one, who was a beautiful child, more than all his other children; and he pressed her to his breast and kissed her and wept bitterly at parting from her; when he felt something round inside the bosom of her dress and asked her, "O my little maid, what is in thy bosom pocket?"; "O my father," she replied, "it is an apple with the name of our Lord the Caliph written upon it. Rayhan our slave brought it to me four days ago and would not let me have it till I gave him two dinars for it." When Ja'afar heard speak of the slave and the apple, he was glad and put his hand into his child's pocket[8] and drew out the apple and knew it and rejoiced saying, "O ready Dispeller of trouble!"[9] Then he bade them bring the slave and said to him, "Fie upon thee, Rayhan! whence haddest thou this apple?" "By Allah, O my master," he replied, "though a lie may get a man once off, yet may truth get him off, and well off, again and again. I did not steal this apple from thy palace nor from the gardens of the Commander of the Faithful. The fact is that five days ago, as I was walking along one of the alleys of this city, I saw some little ones at play and this apple in hand of one of them. So I snatched it from him and beat him and he cried and said, O youth this apple is my mother's and she is ill. She told my father how she longed for an apple, so he travelled to Bassorah and bought her three apples for three gold pieces, and I took one of them to play withal. He wept again, but I paid no heed to what he said and carried it off and brought it here, and my little lady bought it of me for two dinars of gold. And this is the whole story." When Ja'afar heard his words he marvelled that the murder of the damsel and all this misery should have been caused by his slave; he grieved for the relation of the slave to himself, while rejoicing over his own deliverance, and he repeated these lines:—

> If ill betide thee through thy slave,
> Make him forthright thy sacrifice:
> A many serviles thou shalt find,
> But life comes once and never twice.

Then he took the slave's hand and, leading him to the Caliph, related the story from first to last and the Caliph marvelled with extreme astonishment, and laughed till he fell on his back and ordered that the story be recorded and be made public amongst the people. But Ja'afar said, "Marvel not, O Commander of the Faithful, at this adventure, for it is not more wondrous than the History of the Wazir Nur al-Din Ali of Egypt and his brother Shams al-Din Mohammed." Quoth the Caliph, "Out with it; but what can be stranger than this story?" And Ja'afar answered, "O Commander of the Faithful, I will not tell it thee, save on condition that thou pardon my slave;" and the Caliph rejoined, "If it be indeed more wondrous than that of the three apples, I grant thee his blood, and if not I will surely slay thy slave." So Ja'afar began in these words the

Tale of Nur al-Din Ali and His Son Badr al-Din Hasan.

Know, O Commander of the Faithful, that in times of yore the land of Egypt was ruled by a Sultan endowed with justice and generosity, one who loved the pious poor and companied with the Olema and learned men; and he had a Wazir, a wise and an experienced, well versed in affairs and in the art of government. This Minister, who was a very old man, had two sons, as they were two moons; never man saw the like of them for beauty and grace, the elder called Shams al-Din Mohammed and the younger Nur al-Din Ali; but the younger excelled the elder in seemliness and pleasing semblance, so that folk heard his fame in far countries and men flocked to Egypt for the purpose of seeing him. In course of time their father, the Wazir, died and was deeply regretted and mourned by the Sultan, who sent for his two sons and, investing them with dresses of honour,[1] said to them, "Let not your hearts be troubled, for ye shall stand in your father's stead and be joint Ministers of Egypt." At this they rejoiced and kissed the ground before him and performed the ceremonial mourning[2] for their father during a full month; after which time they entered upon the Wazirate, and the power passed into their hands

as it had been in the hands of their father, each doing duty
for a week at a time. They lived under the same roof and
their word was one; and whenever the Sultan desired to
travel they took it by turns to be in attendance on him. It
fortuned one night that the Sultan purposed setting out on
a journey next morning, and the elder, whose turn it was
to accompany him, was sitting conversing with his brother
and said to him, "O my brother, it is my wish that we both
marry, I and thou, two sisters; and go in to our wives on
one and the same night." "Do, O my brother, as thou desirest," the younger replied, "for right is thy recking and
surely I will comply with thee in whatso thou sayest." So
they agreed upon this and quoth Shams al-Din, "If Allah
decree that we marry two damsels and go in to them on the
same night, and they shall conceive on their bride-nights
and bear children to us on the same day, and by Allah's will
thy wife bear thee a son and my wife bear me a daughter,
let us wed them either to other, for they will be cousins."
Quoth Nur al-Din, "O my brother, Shams al-Din, what
dower[3] wilt thou require from my son for thy daughter?"
Quoth Shams al-Din, "I will take three thousand dinars
and three pleasure gardens and three farms; and it would
not be seemly that the youth make contract for less than
this." When Nur al-Din heard such demand he said, "What
manner of dower is this thou wouldest impose upon my
son? Wottest thou not that we are brothers and both by
Allah's grace Wazirs and equal in office? It behoveth thee
to offer thy daughter to my son without marriage settlement; or, if one need be, it should represent a mere nomi-
nal value by way of show to the world: for thou knowest
that the masculine is worthier than the feminine, and my
son is a male and our memory will be preserved by him,
not by thy daughter." "But what," said Shams al-Din, "is
she to have?"; and Nur al-Din continued, "Through her we
shall not be remembered among the Emirs of the earth;
but I see thou wouldest do with me according to the
saying:—An thou wouldst bluff off a buyer, ask him high
price and higher; or as did a man who, they say, went to a

friend and asked something of him being in necessity and
was answered:—Bismillah,[4] in the name of Allah, I will do
all what thou requirest but come to-morrow! Whereupon
the other replied in this verse:—

> When he who is asked a favour saith "To-morrow,"
> The wise man wots 'tis vain to beg or borrow.

Quoth Shams al-Din, "Basta![5] I see thee fail in respect to
me by making thy son of more account than my daughter;
and 'tis plain that thine understanding is of the meanest
and that thou lackest manners. Thou remindest me of thy
partnership in the Wazirate, when I admitted thee to share
with me only in pity for thee, and not wishing to mortify
thee; and that thou mightest help me as a manner of assistant. But since thou talkest on this wise, by Allah, I will
never marry my daughter to thy son; no, not for her weight
in gold!" When Nur al-Din heard his brother's words he
waxed wroth and said, "And I too, I will never, never marry
my son to thy daughter; no, not to keep from my lips the
cup of death." Shams al-Din replied, "I would not accept
him as a husband for her, and he is not worth a paring of
her nail. Were I not about to travel I would make an example of thee; however when I return thou shalt see, and I
will show thee, how I can assert my dignity and vindicate
my honour. But Allah doeth whatso He willeth."[6] When
Nur al-Din heard this speech from his brother, he was
filled with fury and lost his wits for rage; but he hid what
he felt and held his peace; and each of the brothers passed
the night in a place far apart, wild with wrath against the
other. As soon as morning dawned the Sultan fared forth in
state and crossed over from Cairo[7] to Jizah[8] and made for
the Pyramids, accompanied by the Wazir Shams al-Din,
whose turn of duty it was, whilst his brother Nur al-Din, who
passed the night in sore rage, rose with the light and
prayed the dawn-prayer. Then he betook himself to his
treasury and, taking a small pair of saddle-bags, filled them
with gold; and he called to mind his brother's threats and

the contempt wherewith he had treated him, and he repeated these couplets:—

Travel! and thou shalt find new friends for old ones left
  behind;
Toil! for the sweets of human life by toil and moil are found:
The stay-at-home no honour wins nor aught attains but
  want;
So leave thy place of birth[9] and wander all the world around!
I've seen, and very oft I've seen, how standing water stinks,
And only flowing sweetens it and trotting makes it sound:
And were the moon for ever full and ne'er to wax or wane,
Man would not strain his watchful eyes to see its gladsome
  round:
Except the lion leave his lair he ne'er would fell his game;
Except the arrow leave the bow ne'er had it reached its
  bound:
Gold-dust is dust the while it lies untravelled in the mine,
And aloes-wood mere fuel is upon its native ground:
And gold shall win his highest worth when from his goal
  ungoal'd;
And aloes sent to foreign parts grows costlier than gold.

When he ended his verse he bade one of his pages saddle
him his Nubian mare-mule with her padded selle. Now
she was a dapple-grey,[10] with ears like reed-pens and legs
like columns and a back high and strong as a dome builded
on pillars; her saddle was of gold-cloth and her stirrups of
Indian steel, and her housing of Ispahan velvet; she had
trappings which would serve the Chosroes, and she was
like a bride adorned for her wedding night. Moreover he
bade lay on her back a piece of silk for a seat, and a prayer-
carpet under which were his saddle-bags. When this was
done he said to his pages and slaves, "I purpose going forth
apleasuring outside the city on the road to Kalyub-town,[11]
and I shall lie three nights abroad; so let none of you follow
me, for there is something straiteneth my breast." Then he
mounted the mule in haste; and, taking with him some

provaunt for the way, set out from Cairo and faced the open and uncultivated country lying around it.[12] About noontide he entered Bilbays-city,[13] where he dismounted and stayed awhile to rest himself and his mule and ate some of his victual. He bought at Bilbays all he wanted for himself and forage for his mule and then fared on the way of the waste. Towards night-fall he entered a town called Sa'adiyah[14] where he alighted and took out somewhat of his viaticum and ate; then he spread his strip of silk on the sand and set the saddle-bags under his head and slept in the open air; for he was still overcome with anger. When morning dawned he mounted and rode onward till he reached the Holy City,[15] Jerusalem, and thence he made Aleppo, where he dismounted at one of the caravanserais and abode three days to rest himself and the mule and to smell the air.[16] Then, being determined to travel afar and Allah having written safety in his fate, he set out again, wending without wotting whither he was going; and, having fallen in with certain couriers, he stinted not travelling till he had reached Bassorah-city albeit he knew not what the place was. It was dark night when he alighted at the Khan, so he spread out his prayer-carpet and took down the saddle-bags from the back of the mule and gave her with her furniture in charge of the door-keeper that he might walk her about. The man took her and did as he was bid. Now it so happened that the Wazir of Bassorah, a man shot in years, was sitting at the lattice-window of his palace opposite the Khan and he saw the porter walking the mule up and down. He was struck by her trappings of price and thought her a nice beast fit for the riding of Wazirs or even of royalties; and the more he looked the more was he perplexed till at last he said to one of his pages, "Bring hither yon doorkeeper." The page went and returned to the Wazir with the porter who kissed the ground between his hands, and the Minister asked him, "Who is the owner of yonder mule and what manner of man is he?"; and he answered, "O my lord, the owner of this mule is a comely young man of pleasant manners, withal grave and dignified, and doubtless one of the sons of the merchants." When the Wazir heard the doorkeeper's words he arose forthright; and, mounting his horse, rode to the Khan[17] and went in to Nur al-Din who, seeing the Minister making towards him, rose to his feet and advanced to meet him and saluted him. The Wazir welcomed him to Bassorah and dismounting, embraced him and made him sit down by his side and said, "O my son, whence comest thou and what dost thou seek?" "O my lord," Nur al-Din replied, "I have come from Cairo-city of which my father was whilome Wazir; but he hath been removed to the grace of Allah;" and he informed him of all that had befallen him from beginning to end, adding, "I am resolved never to return home before I have seen all the cities and countries of the world." When the Wazir heard this, he said to him, "O my son, hearken not to the voice of passion lest it cast thee into the pit; for indeed many regions be waste places and I fear for thee the turns of Time." Then he let load the saddle-bags and the silk and prayer-carpets on the mule and carried Nur al-Din to his own house, where he lodged him in a pleasant place and entreated him honourably and made much of him, for he inclined to love him with exceeding love. After a while he said to him, "O my son, here am I left a man in years and have no male children, but Allah hath blessed me with a daughter who eveneth thee in beauty; and I have rejected all her many suitors, men of rank and substance. But affection for thee hath entered into my heart; say me, then, wilt thou be to her a husband? If thou accept this, I will go up with thee to the Sultan of Bassorah[18] and will tell him that thou art my nephew, the son of my brother, and bring thee to be appointed Wazir in my place that I may keep the house for, by Allah, O my son, I am stricken in years and aweary." When Nur al-Din heard the Wazir's words, he bowed his head in modesty and said, "To hear is to obey!" At this the Wazir rejoiced and bade his servants prepare a feast and decorate the great assembly-hall, wherein they were wont to celebrate the marriages of Emirs and Grandees. Then he assembled his friends and the notables of the reign and the merchants of Bassorah and when all stood before him he said to them, "I had a brother who was Wazir in the land of Egypt, and Allah Almighty blessed him with two sons, whilst to me, as well ye wot, He hath given a daughter. My brother charged me to marry my daughter to one of his sons, whereto I assented; and, when my daughter was of age to marry, he sent me one of his sons, the young man now present, to whom I purpose marrying her, drawing up the contract and celebrating the night of unveiling with due ceremony: for he is nearer and dearer to me than a stranger and, after the wedding, if he please he shall abide with me, or if he desire to travel I will forward him and his wife to his father's home." Hereat one and all replied, "Right is thy recking;" and they looked at the bridegroom and were pleased with him. So the Wazir sent for the Kazi and legal witnesses and they wrote out the marriage contract, after which the slaves perfumed the guests with incense,[19] and served them with sherbet of sugar and sprinkled rose-water on them and all went their ways. Then the Wazir bade his servants take Nur al-Din to the Hammam-baths and sent him a suit of the best of his own especial raiment, and napkins and towelry and bowls and perfume-burners and all else that was required. And after the bath, when he came out and donned the dress, he was even as the full moon on the fourteenth night; and he mounted his mule and stayed not till he reached the Wazir's palace. There he dismounted and went in to the Minister and kissed his hands, and the Wazir bade him welcome, saying, "Arise and go in to thy wife this night, and on the morrow I will carry thee to the Sultan, and pray Allah bless thee with all manner of weal." So Nur al-Din left him and went in to his wife the Wazir's daughter. Thus far concerning him, but as regards his elder brother, Shams al-Din, he was absent with the Sultan a long time and when he returned from his journey he found not his brother; and he asked of his servants and slaves who answered, "On the day of thy departure with the Sultan, thy brother mounted his mule fully caparisoned as for state procession saying:—I am going towards Kalyub-town and I shall be absent one day or at most two days; for my breast is straitened, and let none of you follow me. Then he fared forth and from that time to this we have heard no tidings of him." Shams al-Din was greatly troubled at the sudden disappearance of his brother and grieved with exceeding grief at the loss and said to himself, "This is only because I chided and upbraided him the night before my departure with the Sultan; haply his feelings were hurt and he fared forth a-travelling; but I must send after him." Then he went in to the Sultan and acquainted him with what had happened and wrote letters and dispatches, which he sent by running footmen to his deputies in every province. But during the twenty days of his brother's absence Nur al-Din had travelled far and had reached Bassorah; so after diligent search the messengers failed to come at any news of him and returned. Thereupon Shams al-Din despaired of finding his brother and said, "Indeed I went beyond all bounds in what I said to him with reference to the marriage of our children. Would that I had not done so! This all cometh of my lack of wit and want of caution." Soon after this he sought in marriage the daughter of a Cairene merchant[20] and drew up the marriage contract and went in to her. And it so chanced that, on the very same night when Shams al-Din went in to his wife, Nur al-Din also went in to his wife the daughter of the Wazir of Bassorah; this being in accordance with the will of Almighty Allah, that He might deal the decrees of Destiny to His creatures. Furthermore, it was as the two brothers had said; for their two wives became pregnant by them on the same night and both were brought to bed on the same day; the wife of Shams al-Din, Wazir of Egypt, of a daughter, never in Cairo was seen a fairer; and the wife of Nur al-Din of a son, none more beautiful was ever seen in his time, as one of the poets said concerning the like of him:—

That jetty hair, that glossy brow,
  My slender waisted youth, of thine,
Can darkness round creation throw,
  Or make it brightly shine.
The dusky mole that faintly shows
  Upon his cheek, ah! blame it not;
The tulip-flower never blows
  Undarkened by its spot.[21]

They named the boy Badr al-Din Hasan and his grandfather, the Wazir of Bassorah, rejoiced in him and, on the
seventh day after his birth, made entertainments and spread
banquets which would befit the birth of Kings' sons and
heirs. Then he took Nur al-Din and went up with him to
the Sultan, and his son-in-law, when he came before the
presence of the King, kissed the ground between his hands
and repeated these verses, for he was ready of speech, firm
of sprite and good in heart as he was goodly in form:—

The world's best joys long be thy lot, my lord!
  And last while darkness and the dawn o'erlap:
O thou who makest, when we greet thy gifts,
  The world to dance and Time his palms to clap.[22]

Then the Sultan rose up to honour them and, thanking
Nur al-Din for his fine compliment, asked the Wazir, "Who
may be this young man?"; and the Minister answered,
"This is my brother's son," and related his tale from first to
last. Quoth the Sultan, "And how comes he to be thy
nephew and we have never heard speak of him?" Quoth
the Minister, "O our lord the Sultan, I had a brother who
was Wazir in the land of Egypt and he died, leaving two
sons, whereof the elder hath taken his father's place and
the younger, whom thou seest, came to me. I had sworn I
would not marry my daughter to any but him; so when he
came I married him to her.[23] Now he is young and I am old;
my hearing is dulled and my judgment is easily fooled;
wherefore I would solicit our lord the Sultan[24] to set him

in my stead, for he is my brother's son and my daughter's husband; and he is fit for the Wazirate, being a man of good counsel and ready contrivance." The Sultan looked at Nur al-Din and liked him, so he stablished him in office as the Wazir had requested and formally appointed him, presenting him with a splendid dress of honour and a she-mule from his private stud; and assigning to him solde, stipends and supplies. Nur al-Din kissed the Sultan's hand and went home, he and his father-in-law, joying with exceeding joy and saying, "All this followeth on the heels of the boy Hasan's birth!" Next day he presented himself before the King and, kissing the ground, began repeating:—

> Grow thy weal and thy welfare day by day:
> And thy luck prevail o'er the envier's spite;
> And ne'er cease thy days to be white as day,
> And thy foeman's day to be black as night!

The Sultan bade him be seated on the Wazir's seat, so he sat down and applied himself to the business of his office and went into the cases of the lieges and their suits, as is the wont of Ministers; while the Sultan watched him and wondered at his wit and good sense, judgment and insight. Wherefor he loved him and took him into intimacy. When the Divan was dismissed Nur al-Din returned to his house and related what had passed to his father-in-law who rejoiced. And thenceforward Nur al-Din ceased not so to administer the Wazirate that the Sultan would not be parted from him night or day; and increased his stipends and supplies till his means were ample and he became the owner of ships that made trading voyages at his command, as well as of Mamelukes and blackamoor slaves; and he laid out many estates and set up Persian wheels and planted gardens. When his son Hasan was four years of age, the old Wazir deceased, and he made for his father-in-law a sumptuous funeral ceremony ere he was laid in the dust. Then he occupied himself with the education of this son and, when the boy waxed strong and came to the age of seven, he brought him a Fakih, a doctor of law and religion, to teach him in his own house and charged him to give him a good education and instruct him in politeness and good manners. So the tutor made the boy read and retain all varieties of useful knowledge, after he had spent some years in learning the Koran by heart;[25] and he ceased not to grow in beauty and stature and symmetry. The professor brought him up in his father's palace teaching him reading, writing and cyphering, theology and belles lettres. His grandfather the old Wazir had bequeathed to him the whole of his property when he was but four years of age. Now during all the time of his earliest youth he had never left the house, till on a certain day his father, the Wazir Nur al-Din, clad him in his best clothes and, mounting him on a she-mule of the finest, went up with him to the Sultan. The King gazed at Badr al-Din Hasan and marvelled at his comeliness and loved him. As for the city-folk, when he first passed before them with his father, they marvelled at his exceeding beauty and sat down on the road expecting his return, that they might look their fill on his beauty and loveliness and symmetry and perfect grace. And they blessed him aloud as he passed and called upon Almighty Allah to bless him.[26] The Sultan entreated the lad with especial favour and said to his father, "O Wazir, thou must needs bring him daily to my presence;" whereupon he replied, "I hear and I obey." Then the Wazir returned home with his son and ceased not to carry him to court till he reached the age of twenty. At that time the Minister sickened and, sending for Badr al-Din Hasan, said to him, "Know, O my son, that the world of the Present is but a house of mortality, while that the Future is a house of eternity. I wish, before I die, to bequeath thee certain charges and do thou take heed of what I say and incline thy heart to my words." Then he gave him his last instructions as to the properest way of dealing with his neighbours and the due management of his affairs; after which he called to mind his brother and his home and his native land and wept over his separation from those he had first loved. Then he wiped away his tears and, turning to his son, said to him, "Before I proceed, O my son, to my last charges and injunctions, know that I have a brother, and thou hast an uncle, Shams al-Din hight, the Wazir of Cairo, with whom I parted, leaving him against his will. Now take thee a sheet of paper and write upon it whatso I say to thee." Badr al-Din took a fair leaf and set about doing his father's bidding and he wrote thereon a full account of what had happened to his sire first and last; the dates of his arrival at Bassorah and of his foregathering with the Wazir; of his marriage, of his going in to the Minister's daughter and of the birth of his son; brief, his life of forty years from the day of his dispute with his brother, adding the words, "And this is written at my dictation and may Almighty Allah be with him when I am gone!" Then he folded the paper and sealed it and said, "O Hasan, O my son, keep this paper with all care; for it will enable thee to establish thine origin and rank and lineage and, if anything contrary befal thee, set out for Cairo and ask for thine uncle and show him this paper and say to him that I died a stranger far from mine own people and full of yearning to see him and them." So Badr al-Din Hasan took the document and folded it; and, wrapping it up in a piece of waxed cloth, sewed it like a talisman between the inner and outer cloth of his skull-cap and wound his light turband[27] round it. And he fell to weeping over his father and at parting with him, and he but a boy. Then Nur al-Din lapsed into a swoon, the forerunner of death; but presently recovering himself he said, "O Hasan, O my son, I will now bequeath to thee five last behests. The FIRST BEHEST is, Be over-intimate with none, nor frequent any, nor be familiar with any; so shalt thou be safe from his mischief;[28] for security lieth in seclusion of thought and a certain retirement from the society of thy fellows; and I have heard it said by a poet:—

> In this world there is none thou mayst count upon
>   To befriend thy case in the nick of need:
> So live for thyself nursing hope of none
>   Such counsel I give thee: enow, take heed!

The SECOND BEHEST is, O my son: Deal harshly with none lest fortune with thee deal hardly; for the fortune of this world is one day with thee and another day against thee and all worldly goods are but a loan to be repaid. And I have heard a poet say:—

> Take thought nor haste to win the thing thou wilt;
> Have ruth on man for ruth thou may'st require:
> No hand is there but Allah's hand is higher;
> No tyrant but shall rue worse tyrant's ire!

The THIRD BEHEST is, Learn to be silent in society and let thine own faults distract thine attention from the faults of other men: for it is said:—In silence dwelleth safety, and thereon I have heard the lines that tell us:—

> Reserve's a jewel, Silence safety is;
> Whenas thou speakest many a word withhold:
> For an of Silence thou repent thee once,
> Of speech thou shalt repent times manifold.

The FOURTH BEHEST, O my son, is Beware of wine-bibbing, for wine is the head of all frowardness and a fine solvent of human wits. So shun, and again I say, shun mixing strong liquor; for I have heard a poet say:—[29]

> From wine[30] I turn and whoso wine-cups swill;
> Becoming one of those who deem it ill:
> Wine driveth man to miss salvation-way,[31]
> And opes the gateway wide to sins that kill.

The FIFTH BEHEST, O my son, is Keep thy wealth and it will keep thee; guard thy money and it will guard thee; and waste not thy substance lest haply thou come to want and must fare a-begging from the meanest of mankind. Save thy dirhams and deem them the sovereignest salve for the wounds of the world. And here again I have heard that one of the poets said:—

When fails my wealth no friend will deign befriend:
When wealth abounds all friends their friendship tender:
How many friends lent aid my wealth to spend;
But friends to lack of wealth no friendship render."

On this wise Nur al-Din ceased not to counsel his son Badr al-Din Hasan till his hour came and, sighing one sobbing sigh, his life went forth. Then the voice of mourning and keening rose high in his house and the Sultan and all the grandees grieved for him and buried him; but his son ceased not lamenting his loss for two months, during which he never mounted horse, nor attended the Divan nor presented himself before the Sultan. At last the King, being wroth with him, stablished in his stead one of his Chamberlains and made him Wazir, giving orders to seize and set seals on all Nur al-Din's houses and goods and domains. So the new Wazir went forth with a mighty posse of Chamberlains and people of the Divan, and watchmen and a host of idlers to do this and to seize Badr al-Din Hasan and carry him before the King, who would deal with him as he deemed fit. Now there was among the crowd of followers a Mameluke of the deceased Wazir who, when he had heard this order, urged his horse and rode at full speed to the house of Badr al-Din Hasan; for he could not endure to see the ruin of his old master's son. He found him sitting at the gate with head hung down and sorrowing, as was his wont, for the loss of his father; so he dismounted and kissing his hand said to him, "O my lord and son of my lord, haste ere ruin come and lay waste!" When Hasan heard this he trembled and asked, "What may be the matter?"; and the man answered, "The Sultan is angered with thee and hath issued a warrant against thee, and evil cometh hard upon my track; so flee with thy life!" At these words Hasan's heart flamed with the fire of bale, and his rose-red cheek turned pale, and he said to the Mameluke, "O my brother, is there time for me to go in and get some worldly gear which may stand me in stead during my strangerhood?" But the slave replied, "O my lord, up at once and save thyself and leave this house, while it is yet time." And he quoted these lines:—

> Escape with thy life, if oppression betide thee,
> And let the house tell of its builder's fate!
> Country for country thou'lt find, if thou seek it;
> Life for life never, early or late.
> It is strange men should dwell in the house of abjection,
> When the plain of God's earth is so wide and so great![32]

At these words of the Mameluke, Badr al-Din covered his head with the skirt of his garment and went forth on foot till he stood outside of the city, where he heard folk saying, "The Sultan hath sent his new Wazir to the house of the old Wazir, now no more, to seal his property and seize his son Badr al-Din Hasan and take him before the presence, that he may put him to death;" and all cried, "Alas for his beauty and his loveliness!" When he heard this he fled forth at hazard, knowing not whither he was going, and gave not over hurrying onwards till Destiny drove him to his father's tomb. So he entered the cemetery and, threading his way through the graves, at last he reached the sepulchre where he sat down and let fall from his head the skirt of his long robe[33] which was made of brocade with a gold-embroidered hem whereon were worked these couplets:—

> O thou whose forehead, like the radiant East,
> Tells of the stars of Heaven and bounteous dews:
> Endure thine honour to the latest day,
> And Time thy growth of glory ne'er refuse!

While he was sitting by his father's tomb behold, there came to him a Jew as he were a Shroff,[34] a money-changer, with a pair of saddle-bags containing much gold, who accosted him and kissed his hand, saying, "Whither bound, O my lord: 'tis late in the day and thou art clad but lightly and I read signs of trouble in thy face?" "I was sleeping within this very hour," answered Hasan, "when my father appeared to me and chid me for not having visited his tomb; so I awoke trembling and came hither forthright lest the day should go by without my visiting him, which would have been grievous to me." "O my lord," rejoined the Jew,[35] "thy father had many merchantmen at sea and, as some of them are now due, it is my wish to buy of thee the cargo of the first ship that cometh into port with this thousand dinars of gold." "I consent," quoth Hasan, whereupon the Jew took out a bag full of gold and counted out a thousand sequins which he gave to Hasan, the son of the Wazir, saying, "Write me a letter of sale and seal it." So Hasan took a pen and paper and wrote these words in duplicate, "The writer, Hasan Badr al-Din, son of Wazir Nur al-Din, hath sold to Isaac the Jew all the cargo of the first of his father's ships which cometh into port, for a thousand dinars, and he hath received the price in advance." And after he had taken one copy the Jew put it into his pouch and went away; but Hasan fell a-weeping as he thought of the dignity and prosperity which had erst been his and night came upon him; so he leant his head against his father's grave and sleep overcame him: Glory to Him who sleepeth not! He ceased not slumbering till the moon rose, when his head slipped from off the tomb and he lay on his back, with limbs outstretched, his face shining bright in the moonlight. Now the cemetery was haunted day and night by Jinns who were of the True Believers, and presently came out a Jinniyah who, seeing Hasan asleep, marvelled at his beauty and loveliness and cried, "Glory to God! this youth can be none other than one of the Wuldan of Paradise."[36] Then she flew firmament-wards to circle it, as was her custom, and met an Ifrit on the wing who saluted her and said to him, "Whence comest thou?" "From Cairo," he replied. "Wilt thou come with me and look upon the beauty of a youth who sleepeth in yonder burial place?" she asked, and he answered, "I will." So they flew till they lighted at the tomb and she showed him the youth and said, "Now diddest thou ever in thy born days see aught like this?" The

Ifrit looked upon him and exclaimed, "Praise be to Him that hath no equal! But, O my sister, shall I tell thee what I have seen this day?" Asked she, "What is that?" and he answered, "I have seen the counterpart of this youth in the land of Egypt. She is the daughter of the Wazir Shams al-Din and she is a model of beauty and loveliness, of fairest favour and formous form, and dight with symmetry and perfect grace. When she had reached the age of nineteen,[37] the Sultan of Egypt heard of her and, sending for the Wazir her father, said to him:—Hear me, O Wazir: it hath reached mine ear that thou hast a daughter and I wish to demand her of thee in marriage. The Wazir replied:—O our lord the Sultan, deign accept my excuses and take compassion on my sorrows, for thou knowest that my brother, who was partner with me in the Wazirate, disappeared from amongst us many years ago and we wot not where he is. Now the cause of his departure was that one night, as we were sitting together and talking of wives and children to come, we had words on the matter and he went off in high dudgeon. But I swore that I would marry my daughter to none save to the son of my brother on the day her mother gave her birth, which was nigh upon nineteen years ago. I have lately heard that my brother died at Bassorah, where he had married the daughter of the Wazir and that she bare him a son; and I will not marry my daughter but to him in honour of my brother's memory. I recorded the date of my marriage and the conception of my wife and the birth of my daughter; and from her horoscope I find that her name is conjoined with that of her cousin;[38] and there are damsels in foison for our lord the Sultan. The King, hearing his Minister's answer and refusal, waxed wroth with exceeding wrath and cried:—When the like of me asketh a girl in marriage of the like of thee, he conferreth an honour, and thou rejectest me and puttest me off with cold[39] excuses! Now, by the life of my head I will marry her to the meanest of my men in spite of the nose of thee![40] There was in the palace a horse-groom which was a Gobbo with a bunch to his breast and a hunch to his back; and the Sultan sent for him and married him to the daughter of the Wazir, lief or loath, and hath ordered a pompous marriage procession for him and that he go in to his bride this very night. I have now just flown hither from Cairo, where I left the Hunchback at the door of the Hammam-bath amidst the Sultan's white slaves who were waving lighted flambeaux about him. As for the Minister's daughter she sitteth among her nurses and tirewomen, weeping and wailing; for they have forbidden her father to come near her. Never have I seen, O my sister, more hideous being than this Hunchback[41] whilst the young lady is the likest of all folk to this young man, albeit even fairer than he." At this the Jinniyah cried at him "Thou liest! this youth is handsomer than any one of his day." The Ifrit gave her the lie again, adding, "By Allah, O my sister, the damsel I speak of is fairer than this; yet none but he deserveth her, for they resemble each other like brother and sister or at least cousins. And, well-away! how she is wasted upon that Hunchback!" Then said she, "O my brother, let us get under him and lift him up and carry him to Cairo, that we may compare him with the damsel of whom thou speakest and so determine whether of the twain is the fairer." "To hear is to obey!" replied he, "thou speakest to the point; nor is there a righter recking than this of thine, and I myself will carry him." So he raised him from the ground and flew with him like a bird soaring in upper air, the Ifritah keeping close by his side at equal speed, till he alighted with him in the city of Cairo and set him down on a stone bench and woke him up. He roused himself and finding that he was no longer at his father's tomb in Bassorah-city he looked right and left and saw that he was in a strange place; and he would have cried out; but the Ifrit gave him a cuff which persuaded him to keep silence. Then he brought him rich raiment and clothed him therein and, giving him a lighted flambeau, said, "Know that I have brought thee hither, meaning to do thee a good turn for the love of Allah: so take this torch and mingle with the people at the Hammam-door and walk on with them without stopping till thou reach the house of the wedding-festival; then go boldly forward and enter the great saloon; and fear none, but take thy stand at the right hand of the Hunchback bridegroom; and, as often as any of the nurses and tirewomen and singing-girls come up to thee,[42] put thy hand into thy pocket which thou wilt find filled with gold. Take it out and throw to them and spare not; for as often as thou thrustest fingers in pouch thou shalt find it full of coin. Give largesse by handsful and fear nothing, but set thy trust upon Him who created thee, for this is not by thine own strength but by that of Allah Almighty, that His decrees may take effect upon His creatures." When Badr al-Din Hasan heard these words from the Ifrit he said to himself, "Would Heaven I knew what all this means and what is the cause of such kindness!" However, he mingled with the people and, lighting his flambeau, moved on with the bridal procession till he came to the bath where he found the Hunchback already on horseback. Then he pushed his way in among the crowd, a veritable beauty of a man in the finest apparel, wearing tarbush[43] and turband and a long-sleeved robe purfled with gold; and, as often as the singing-women stopped for the people to give them largesse, he thrust his hand into his pocket and, finding it full of gold, took out a handful and threw it on the tambourine[44] till he had filled it with gold pieces for the music-girls and the tirewomen. The singers were amazed by his bounty and the people marvelled at his beauty and loveliness and the splendour of his dress. He ceased not to do thus till he reached the mansion of the Wazir (who was his uncle), where the Chamberlains drove back the people and forbade them to go forward; but the singing-girls and the tirewomen said, "By Allah we will not enter unless this young man enter with us, for he hath given us length o' life with his largesse and we will not display the bride unless he be present." Therewith they carried him into the bridal hall and made him sit down defying the evil glances of the hunchbacked bridegroom. The wives of the Emirs and Wazirs and Chamberlains and Courtiers all stood in double line, each holding a massy cierge ready lighted; all wore thin face-veils and the two rows right and left extended from the bride's throne[45] to the head of the hall adjoining the chamber whence she was to come forth. When the ladies saw Badr al-Din Hasan and noted his beauty and loveliness and his face that shone like the new moon, their hearts inclined to him and the singing-girls said to all that were present, "Know that this beauty crossed our hands with naught but red gold; so be not chary to do him womanly service and comply with all he says, no matter what he ask."[46] So all the women crowded round Hasan with their torches and gazed on his loveliness and envied him his beauty; and one and all would gladly have lain on his bosom an hour or rather a year. Their hearts were so troubled that they let fall their veils from before their faces and said, "Happy she who be-longeth to this youth or to whom he belongeth!"; and they called down curses on the crooked groom and on him who was the cause of his marriage to the girl-beauty; and as often as they blessed Badr al-Din Hasan they damned the Hunchback, saying, "Verily this youth and none else de-serveth our Bride: ah, well-away for such a lovely one with this hideous Quasimodo; Allah's curse light on his head and on the Sultan who commanded the marriage!" Then the singing-girls beat their tabrets and lulliloo'd with joy, announcing the appearing of the bride; and the Wazir's daughter came in surrounded by her tirewomen who had made her goodly to look upon; for they had perfumed her and incensed her and adorned her hair; and they had robed her in raiment and ornaments befitting the mighty Chos-roes Kings. The most notable part of her dress was a loose robe worn over her other garments: it was diapered in red gold with figures of wild beasts, and birds whose eyes and beaks were of gems, and claws of red rubies and green beryl; and her neck was graced with a necklace of Yamani work, worth thousands of gold pieces, whose bezels were great round jewels of sorts, the like of which was never owned by Kaysar or by Tobba King.[47] And the bride was as the full moon when at fullest on fourteenth night; and as she paced into the hall she was like one of the Houris of Heaven—praise be to Him who created her in such splendour of beauty! The ladies encompassed her as the white contains the black of the eye, they clustering like stars whilst she shone amongst them like the moon when it eats up the clouds. Now Badr al-Din Hasan of Bassorah was sitting in full gaze of the folk, when the bride came forward with her graceful swaying and swimming gait, and her hunchbacked bridegroom stood up to meet[48] and receive her: she, however, turned away from the wight and walked forward till she stood before her cousin Hasan, the son of her uncle. Whereat the people laughed. But when the wedding-guests saw her thus attracted towards Badr al-Din they made a mighty clamour and the singing-women shouted their loudest; whereupon he put his hand into his pocket and, pulling out a handful of gold, cast it into their tambourines and the girls rejoiced and said, "Could we win our wish this bride were thine!" At this he smiled and the folk came round him, flambeaux in hand like the eyeball round the pupil, while the Gobbo bridegroom was left sitting alone much like a tail-less baboon; for every time they lighted a candle for him it went out willy-nilly, so he was left in darkness and silence and looking at naught but himself.[49] When Badr al-Din Hasan saw the bridegroom sitting lonesome in the dark, and all the wedding-guests with their flambeaux and wax candles crowding about himself, he was bewildered and marvelled much; but when he looked at his cousin, the daughter of his uncle, he rejoiced and felt an inward delight: he longed to greet her and gazed intently on her face which was radiant with light and brilliancy. Then the tirewomen took off her veil and displayed her in all her seven toilettes before Hasan al-Basri, wholly neglecting the Gobbo who sat moping alone;

and, when she opened her eyes[50] she said, "O Allah make this man my goodman and deliver me from the evil of this hunchbacked groom." As soon as they had made an end of this part of the ceremony they dismissed the wedding guests who went forth, women, children and all, and none remained save Hasan and the Hunchback, whilst the tire-women led the bride into an inner room to change her garb and gear and get her ready for the bridegroom. Thereupon Quasimodo came up to Badr al-Din Hasan and said, "O my lord, thou hast cheered us this night with thy good company and overwhelmed us with thy kindness and courtesy; but now why not get thee up and go?" "Bismillah;" he answered, "In Allah's name so be it!"; and rising, he went forth by the door, where the Ifrit met him and said, "Stay in thy stead, O Badr al-Din, and when the Hunchback goes out to the closet of ease go in without losing time and seat thyself in the alcove; and when the bride comes say to her:—'Tis I am thy husband, for the King devised this trick only fearing for thee the evil eye, and he whom thou sawest is but a Syce, a groom, one of our stablemen. Then walk boldly up to her and unveil her face; for jealousy hath taken us of this matter." While Hasan was still talking with the Ifrit behold, the groom fared forth from the hall and entering the closet of ease sat down on the stool. Hardly had he done this when the Ifrit came out of the tank,[51] wherein the water was, in semblance of a mouse and squeaked out "Zeek!" Quoth the Hunchback, "What ails thee?"; and the mouse grew and grew till it became a coal-black cat and caterwauled "Meeao! Meeao!"[52] Then it grew still more and more till it became a dog and barked out "Owh! Owh!" When the bridegroom saw this he was frightened and exclaimed "Out with thee, O unlucky one!"[53] But the dog grew and swelled till it became an ass-colt that brayed and snorted in his face "Hauk! Hauk!"[54] Whereupon the Hunchback quaked and cried, "Come to my aid, O people of the house!" But behold, the ass-colt grew and became big as a buffalo and walled the way before him and spake with the voice of the sons of Adam, saying, "Woe to thee, O thou Hunchback, thou stinkard, O thou filthiest of grooms!" Hearing this the groom was seized with a colic and he sat down on the jakes in his clothes with teeth chattering and knocking together. Quoth the Ifrit, "Is the world so strait to thee thou findest none to marry save my lady-love?" But as he was silent the Ifrit continued, "Answer me or I will do thee dwell in the dust!" "By Allah," replied the Gobbo, "O King of the Buffaloes, this is no fault of mine, for they forced me to wed her; and verily I wot not that she had a lover amongst the buffaloes; but now I repent, first before Allah and then before thee." Said the Ifrit to him, "I swear to thee that if thou fare forth from this place, or thou utter a word before sunrise, I assuredly will wring thy neck. When the sun rises wend thy went and never more return to this house." So saying, the Ifrit took up the Gobbo bridegroom and set him head downwards and feet upwards in the slit of the privy,[55] and said to him, "I will leave thee here but I shall be on the look-out for thee till sunrise; and, if thou stir before then, I will seize thee by the feet and dash out thy brains against the wall: so look out for thy life!" Thus far concerning the Hunchback, but as regards Badr al-Din Hasan of Bassorah he left the Gobbo and the Ifrit jangling and wrangling and, going into the house, sat him down in the very middle of the alcove; and behold, in came the bride attended by an old woman who stood at the door and said, "O Father of Uprightness,[56] arise and take what God giveth thee." Then the old woman went away and the bride, Sitt al-Husn or the Lady of Beauty hight, entered the inner part of the alcove broken-hearted and saying in herself, "By Allah I will never yield my person to him; no, not even were he to take my life!" But as she came to the further end she saw Badr al-Hasan and she said, "Dearling! art thou still sitting here? By Allah I was wishing that thou wert my bridegroom or, at least, that thou and the hunchbacked horse-groom were part-ners in me." He replied, "O beautiful lady, how should the Syce have access to thee, and how should he share in thee with me?" "Then," quoth she, "who *is* my husband, thou or he?" "Sitt al-Husn," rejoined Hasan, "we have not done this for mere fun,[57] but only as a device to ward off the evil eye from thee; for when the tirewomen and singers and wedding guests saw thy beauty being displayed to me, they feared fascination and thy father hired the horse-groom for ten dinars and a porringer of meat to take the evil eye off us; and now he hath received his hire and gone his gait." When the Lady of Beauty heard these words she smiled and rejoiced and laughed a pleasant laugh. Then she whispered him, "By the Lord thou hast quenched a fire which tortured me and now, by Allah, O my little dark-haired darling, take me to thee and press me to thy bosom!" Then she began singing:—

> By Allah, set thy foot upon my soul;
> Since long, long years for this alone I long:
> And whisper tale of love in ear of me;
> To me 'tis sweeter than the sweetest song!
> No other youth upon my heart shall lie;
> So do it often, dear, and do it long.

Then she stripped off her outer gear and she threw open her chemise from the neck downwards and showed her person and all the rondure of her hips. When Badr al-Din saw the glorious sight his desires were roused, and he arose and doffed his clothes, and wrapping up in his bag-trousers[58] the purse of gold which he had taken from the Jew and which contained the thousand dinars, he laid it under the edge of the bedding. Then he took off his turband and set it upon the settle[59] atop of his other clothes, remaining in his skull-cap and fine shirt of blue silk laced with gold. Whereupon the Lady of Beauty drew him to her and he did likewise. Then he took her to his embrace and found her a pearl unpierced; and he abated her virginity and had joyance of her youth in his virility; and she conceived by him that very night. Then he laid his hand under her head and she did the same and they embraced and fell asleep in each other's arms, as a certain poet said of such lovers in these couplets:—

> Visit thy lover, spurn what envy told;
> No envious churl shall smile on love ensoul'd
> Merciful Allah made no fairer sight
> Than coupled lovers single couch doth hold;
> Breast pressing breast and robed in joys their own,
> With pillowed forearms cast in finest mould;
> And when heart speaks to heart with tongue of love,
> Folk who would part them hammer steel ice-cold:
> If a fair friend thou find who cleaves to thee,
> Live for that friend,[60] that friend in heart enfold.
> O ye who blame for love us lover kind
> Say, can ye minister to diseased mind?

This much concerning Badr al-Din Hasan and Sitt al-Husn his cousin; but as regards the Ifrit, as soon as he saw the twain asleep, he said to the Ifritah, "Arise; slip thee under the youth and let us carry him back to his place ere dawn overtake us; for the day is nearhand." Thereupon she came forward and, getting under him as he lay asleep, took him up clad only in his fine blue shirt, leaving the rest of his garments; and ceased not flying (and the Ifrit vying with her in flight) till the dawn advised them that it had come upon them mid-way, and the Muezzin began his call from the Minaret, "Haste ye to salvation! Haste ye to salvation!"[61] Then Allah suffered His angelic host to shoot down the Ifrit with a shooting star,[62] so he was consumed, but the Ifritah escaped and she descended with Badr al-Din at the place where the Ifrit was burnt, and did not carry him back to Bassorah, fearing lest he come to harm. Now by the order of Him who predestineth all things, they alighted at Damascus of Syria, and the Ifritah set down her burden at one of the city-gates and flew away. When day arose and the doors were opened, the folk who came forth saw a handsome youth, with no other raiment but his blue shirt of gold-embroidered silk and skull-cap,[63] lying upon the ground drowned in sleep after the hard labour of the night which had not suffered him to take his rest. So the folk looking at him said, "O her luck with whom this one spent the night! but would he had waited to don his garments." Quoth another, "A sorry lot are the sons of great families! Haply he but now came forth of the tavern on some occasion of his own and his wine flew to his head,[64] whereby he hath missed the place he was making for and strayed till he came to the gate of the city; and finding it shut lay him down and went to by-by!" As the people were bandying guesses about him suddenly the morning breeze blew upon Badr al-Din and raising his shirt to his middle showed a stomach and navel with something below it,[65] and legs and thighs clear as crystal and smooth as cream. Cried the people, "By Allah he is a pretty fellow!"; and at the cry Badr al-Din awoke and found himself lying at a city-gate with a crowd gathered around him. At this he greatly marvelled and asked, "Where am I, O good folk; and what causeth you thus to gather round me, and what have I had to do with you?"; and they answered, "We found thee lying here asleep during the call to dawn-prayer and this is all we know of the matter, but where diddest thou lie last night?"[66] "By Allah, O good people," replied he, "I lay last night in Cairo." Said somebody, "Thou hast surely been eating Hashish;"[67] and another, "He is a fool;" and a third, "He is a *citrouille*;" and a fourth asked him, "Art thou out of thy mind? thou sleepest in Cairo and thou wakest in the morning at the gate of Damascus-city!"[68] Cried he, "By Allah, my good people, one and all, I lie not to you: indeed I lay yesternight in the land of Egypt and yesternoon I was at Bassorah." Quoth one, "Well! well!"; and quoth another, "Ho! ho!"; and a third, "So! so!"; and a fourth cried, "This youth is mad, is possessed of the Jinni!" So they clapped hands at him and said to one another, "Alas, the pity of it for his youth: by Allah a madman! and madness is no respecter of persons." Then said they to him, "Collect thy wits and return to thy reason! How couldest thou be in

Bassorah yesterday and in Cairo yesternight and withal awake in Damascus this morning?" But he persisted, "Indeed I was a bridegroom in Cairo last night." "Belike thou hast been dreaming," rejoined they, "and sawest all this in thy sleep." So Hasan took thought for a while and said to them, "By Allah, this is no dream; nor vision-like doth it seem! I certainly was in Cairo where they displayed the bride before me, in presence of a third person, the Hunchback groom who was sitting hard by. By Allah, O my brother, this be no dream, and if it were a dream, where is the bag of gold I bore with me and where are my turband and my robe, and my trousers?" Then he rose and entered the city, threading its highways and by-ways and bazar-streets; and the people pressed upon him and jeered at him, crying out "Madman! madman!" till he, beside himself with rage, took refuge in a cook's shop. Now that Cook had been a trifle too clever, that is, a rogue and thief; but Allah had made him repent and turn from his evil ways and open a cookshop; and all the people of Damascus stood in fear of his boldness and his mischief. So when the crowd saw the youth enter his shop, they dispersed being afraid of him, and went their ways. The Cook looked at Badr al-Din and, noting his beauty and loveliness, fell in love with him forthright and said, "Whence comest thou, O youth? Tell me at once thy tale, for thou art become dearer to me than my soul." So Hasan recounted to him all that had befallen him from beginning to end (but in repetition there is no fruition) and the Cook said, "O my lord Badr al-Din, doubtless thou knowest that this case is wondrous and this story marvellous; therefore, O my son, hide what hath betide thee, till Allah dispel what ills be thine; and tarry with me here the meanwhile, for I have no child and I will adopt thee." Badr al-Din replied, "Be it as thou wilt, O my uncle!" Whereupon the Cook went to the bazar and bought him a fine suit of clothes and made him don it; then fared with him to the Kazi, and formally declared that he was his son. So Badr al-Din Hasan became known in Damascus-city as the Cook's son and he sat with him in the shop to take the silver, and on this wise he sojourned there for a time. Thus far concerning him; but as regards his cousin, the Lady of Beauty, when morning dawned she awoke and missed Badr al-Din Hasan from her side; but she thought that he had gone to the privy and she sat expecting him for an hour or so; when behold, entered her father Shams al-Din Mohammed, Wazir of Egypt. Now he was disconsolate by reason of what had befallen him through the Sultan, who had entreated him harshly and had married his daughter by force to the lowest of his menials and he too a lump of a groom hunch-backed withal, and he said to himself, "I will slay this daughter of mine if of her own free will she have yielded her person to this accursed carle." So he came to the door of the bride's private chamber, and said, "Ho! Sitt al-Husn." She answered him, "Here am I! here am I![69] O my lord," and came out unsteady of gait after the pains and pleasures of the night; and she kissed his hand, her face showing redoubled brightness and beauty for having lain in the arms of that gazelle, her cousin. When her father, the Wazir, saw her in such case, he asked her, "O thou accursed, art thou rejoicing because of this horse-groom?", and Sitt al-Husn smiled sweetly and answered, "By Allah, don't ridicule me: enough of what passed yesterday when folk laughed at me, and evened me with that groom-fellow who is not worthy to bring my husband's shoes or slippers; nay who is not worth the paring of my husband's nails! By the Lord, never in my life have I nighted a night so sweet as yesternight!, so don't mock by reminding me of the Gobbo." When her parent heard her words he was filled with fury, and his eyes glared and stared, so that little of them showed save the whites and he cried, "Fie upon thee! What words are these? 'Twas the hunchbacked horse-groom who passed the night with thee!" "Allah upon thee," replied the Lady of Beauty, "do not worry me about the Gobbo, Allah damn his father;[70] and leave jesting with me; for this groom was only hired for ten dinars and a por-ringer of meat and he took his wage and went his way. As for me I entered the bridal-chamber, where I found my true bridegroom sitting, after the singer-women had displayed me to him; the same who had crossed their hands with red gold, till every pauper that was present waxed wealthy; and I passed the night on the breast of my bonny man, a most lively darling, with his black eyes and joined eyebrows."[71] When her parent heard these words the light before his face became night, and he cried out at her saying, "O thou whore! What is this thou tellest me? Where be thy wits?" "O my father," she rejoined, "thou breakest my heart; enough for thee that thou hast been so hard upon me! Indeed my husband who took my virginity is but just now gone to the draughthouse and I feel that I have conceived by him."[72] The Wazir rose in much marvel and entered the privy where he found the hunchbacked horse-groom with his head in the hole and his heels in the air. At this sight he was confounded and said, "This is none other than he, the rascal Hunchback!" So he called to him, "Ho, Hunchback!" The Gobbo grunted out, *"Taghum! Taghum!"*[73] thinking it was the Ifrit spoke to him; so the Wazir shouted at him and said, "Speak out, or I'll strike off thy pate with this sword." Then quoth the Hunchback, "By Allah, O Shaykh of the Ifrits, ever since thou settest me in this place, I have not lifted my head; so Allah upon thee, take pity and entreat me kindly!" When the Wazir heard this he asked, "What is this thou sayest? I'm the bride's father and no Ifrit." "Enough for thee that thou hast well nigh done me die," answered Quasimodo; "now go thy ways before he come upon thee who hath served me thus. Could ye not marry me to any save the lady-love of buffaloes and the beloved of Ifrits? Allah curse her and curse him who married me to her and was the cause of this my case." Then said the Wazir to him, "Up and out of this place!" "Am I mad," cried the groom, "that I should go with thee without leave of the Ifrit whose last words to me were:——When the sun rises, arise and go thy gait. So hath the sun risen or no?; for I dare not budge from this place till then." Asked the Wazir, "Who brought thee hither?"; and he answered, "I came here yesternight for a call of nature and to do what none can do for me, when lo! a mouse came out of the water, and squeaked at me and swelled and waxed gross till it was big as a buffalo, and spoke to me words that entered my ears. Then he left me here and went away, Allah curse the bride and him who married me to her!" The Wazir walked up to him and lifted his head out of the cesspool hole; and he fared forth running for dear life and hardly crediting that the sun had risen; and repaired to the Sultan to whom he told all that had befallen him with the Ifrit. But the Wazir returned to the bride's private chamber, sore troubled in spirit about her, and said to her, "O my daughter, explain this strange matter to me!" Quoth she, " 'Tis simply this. The bridegroom to whom they displayed me yestereve lay with me all night, and took my virginity and I am with child by him. He is my husband and if thou believe me not, there are his turband, twisted as it was, lying on the settle and his dagger and his trousers beneath the bed with a something, I wot not what, wrapped up in them." When her father heard this he entered the private chamber and found the turband which had been left there by Badr al-Din Hasan, his brother's son, and he took it in hand and turned it over, saying, "This is the turband worn by Wazirs, save that it is of Mosul stuff."[74] So he opened it and, finding what seemed to be an amulet sewn up in the Fez, he unsewed the lining and took it out; then he lifted up the trousers wherein was the purse of the thousand gold pieces and, opening that also, found in it a written paper. This he read and it was the sale-receipt of the Jew in the name of Badr al-Din Hasan, son of Nur al-Din Ali, the Egyptian; and the thousand dinars were also there. No sooner had Shams al-Din read this than he cried out with a loud cry and fell to the ground fainting; and as soon as he revived and understood the gist of the matter he marvelled and said, "There is no god, but *the* God, whose All-might is over all things! Knowest thou, O my daughter, who it was that became the husband of thy virginity?" "No," answered she, and he said, "Verily he is the son of my brother, thy cousin, and this thousand dinars is thy dowry. Praise be to Allah! and would I wot how this matter came about!" Then opened he the amulet which was sewn up and found therein a paper in the handwriting of his deceased brother, Nur al-Din the Egyptian, father of Badr al-Din Hasan; and, when he saw the handwriting, he kissed it again and again; and he wept and wailed over his dead brother. Then he read the scroll and found in it recorded the dates of his brother's marriage with the daughter of the Wazir of Bassorah, and of his going in to her, and her conception, and the birth of Badr al-Din Hasan and all his brother's history and doings up to his dying day. So he marvelled much and shook with joy and, comparing the dates with his own marriage and going in unto his wife and the birth of his daughter, Sitt al-Husn, he found that they perfectly agreed. So he took the document and, repairing with it to the Sultan, acquainted him with what had passed, from first to last; whereat the King marvelled and commanded the case to be at once recorded.[75] The Wazir abode that day expecting to see his brother's son but he came not; and he waited a second day, a third day and so on to the seventh day, without any tidings of him. So he said, "By Allah, I will do a deed such as none hath ever done before me!"; and he took reed-pen and ink and drew upon a sheet of paper the plan of the whole house, showing whereabouts was the private chamber with the curtain in such a place and the furniture in such another and so on with all that was in the room. Then he folded up the sketch and, causing all the furniture to be collected, he took Badr al-Din's garments and the turband and Fez and robe and purse, and carried the whole to his house and locked them up, against the coming of his nephew, Badr al-Din Hasan, the son of his lost brother, with an iron padlock on which he set his seal. As for the Wazir's daughter, when her tale of months was fulfilled, she bare a son like the full moon, the image of his father in beauty and loveliness and fair proportions and perfect grace. They cut his navel string[76] and Kohl'd his eyelids to strengthen his eyes, and gave him over to the nurses and nursery governesses,[77] naming him Ajib, the Wonderful. His day was as a month and his month was as a year;[78] and, when seven years had passed over him, his grandfather sent him to school, enjoining the master to teach him Koran-reading, and to educate him well. He remained at the school four years, till he began to bully his schoolfellows and abuse them and bash them and thrash them and say, "Who among you is like me? I am the son of the Wazir of Egypt!" At last the boys came in a body to complain to the Monitor[79] of what hard usage they were wont to have from Ajib, and he said to them, "I will tell you somewhat you may do to him so that he shall leave off coming to the school, and it is this. When he enters tomorrow, sit ye down about him and say some one of you to some other:——By Allah none shall play with us at this game except he tell us the names of his mamma and papa; for he who knows not the names of his mother and his father is a bastard, a son of adultery,[80] and he shall not play with us." When morning dawned the boys came to school, Ajib being one of them, and all flocked round him saying, "We will play a game wherein none shall join save he can tell the name of his mamma and his papa." And they all cried, "By Allah, good!" Then quoth one of them, "My name is Majid and my mammy's name is Alawiyah and my daddy's Izz al-Din." Another spoke in like guise and yet a third, till Ajib's turn came, and he said, "My name is Ajib, and my mother's is Sitt al-Husn, and my father's Shams al-Din, the Wazir of Cairo." "By Allah," cried they, "the Wazir is not thy true father." Ajib answered, "The Wazir is my father in very deed." Then the boys all laughed and clapped their hands at him, saying, "He does not know who is his papa: get out from among us, for none shall play with us except he know his father's name." Thereupon they dispersed from around him and laughed him to scorn; so his breast was straitened and he well nigh choked with tears and hurt feelings. Then said the Monitor to him, "We know that the Wazir is thy grandfather, the father of thy mother, Sitt al-Husn, and not thy father. As for thy father, neither dost thou know him nor yet do we; for the Sultan married thy mother to the hunchbacked horse-groom: but the Jinni came and slept with her and thou hast no known father. Leave, then, comparing thyself too advantageously with the little ones of the school, till thou know that thou hast a lawful father; for until then thou wilt pass for a child of adultery amongst them. Seest thou not that even a huckster's son knoweth his own sire? Thy grandfather is the Wazir of Egypt; but as for thy father we wot him not and we say indeed that thou hast none. So return to thy sound senses!" When Ajib heard these insulting words from the Monitor and the school boys and understood the reproach they put upon him, he went out at once and ran to his mother, Sitt al-Husn, to complain; but he was crying so bitterly that his tears prevented his speech for a while. When she heard his sobs and saw his tears her heart burned as though with fire for him, and she said, "O my son, why dost thou weep? Allah keep the tears from thine eyes! Tell me what hath betided thee?" So he told her all that he heard from the boys and from the Monitor and ended with asking, "And who, O my mother, is my father?" She answered, "Thy father is the Wazir of Egypt;" but he said, "Do not lie to me. The Wazir is thy father, not mine! who then is my father? Except thou tell me the very truth I will kill myself with this hanger."[81] When his mother heard him speak of his father she wept, remembering her cousin and her bridal night with him and all that occurred there and then, and she repeated these couplets:—

> Love in my heart they lit and went their ways,
> And all I love to furthest lands withdrew;
> And when they left me sufferance also left,
> And when we parted Patience bade adieu:
> They fled and flying with my joys they fled,
> In very constancy my spirit flew:
> They made my eyelids flow with severance tears
> And to the parting-pang these drops are due:
> And when I long to see reunion-day,
> My groans prolonging sore for ruth I sue:

Then in my heart of hearts their shapes I trace,
And love and longing care and cark renew:
O ye, whose names cling round me like a cloak,
Whose love yet closer than a shirt I drew,
Beloved ones! how long this hard despite?
How long this severance and this coy shy flight?

Then she wailed and shrieked aloud and her son did the
like; and behold, in came the Wazir whose heart burnt
within him at the sight of their lamentations and he said,
"What makes you weep?" So the Lady of Beauty acquainted
him with what happened between her son and the school
boys; and he also wept, calling to mind his brother and
what had past between them and what had betided his
daughter and how he had failed to find out what mystery
there was in the matter. Then he rose at once and, repairing to the audience-hall, went straight to the King and told
his tale and craved his permission[82] to travel eastward to
the city of Bassorah and ask after his brother's son. Furthermore he besought the Sultan to write for him letters
patent, authorising him to seize upon Badr al-Din, his
nephew and son-in-law, wheresoever he might find him.
And he wept before the King, who had pity on him and
wrote royal autographs to his deputies in all climes[83] and
countries and cities; whereat the Wazir rejoiced and prayed
for blessings on him. Then, taking leave of his Sovereign,
he returned to his house, where he equipped himself and
his daughter and his adopted child Ajib, with all things
meet for a long march; and set out and travelled the first
day and the second and the third and so forth till he arrived
at Damascus-city. The Wazir encamped on the open space
called Al-Hasa;[84] and, after pitching tents, said to his servants, "A halt here for two days!" So they went into the city
upon their several occasions, this to sell and that to buy;
this to go to the Hammam and that to visit the Cathedral-
mosque of the Banu Umayyah, the Ommiades, whose like
is not in this world.[85] Ajib also went, with his attendant
eunuch, for solace and diversion to the city and the ser-

vant followed with a quarter-staff[86] of almond-wood so heavy that if he struck a camel therewith the beast would never rise again.[87] When the people of Damascus saw Ajib's beauty and brilliancy and perfect grace and symmetry (for he was a marvel of comeliness and winning loveliness, softer than the cool breeze of the North, sweeter than limpid waters to man in drowth, and pleasanter than the health for which sick man sueth), a mighty many followed him, whilst others ran on before and sat down on the road until he should come up, that they might gaze on him, till, as Destiny had decreed, the Eunuch stopped opposite the shop of Ajib's father, Badr al-Din Hasan. Now his beard had grown long and thick and his wits had ripened during the twelve years which had passed over him, and the Cook and ex-rogue having died, the so-called Hasan of Bassorah had succeeded to his goods and shop, for that he had been formally adopted before the Kazi and witnesses. When his son and the Eunuch stepped before him he gazed on Ajib and, seeing how very beautiful he was, his heart fluttered and throbbed, and blood drew to blood and natural affection spake out and his bowels yearned over him. He had just dressed a conserve of pomegranate grains with sugar, and Heaven-implanted love wrought within him; so he called to his son Ajib and said, "O my lord, O thou who hast gotten the mastery of my heart and my very vitals and to whom my bowels yearn; say me, wilt thou enter my house and solace my soul by eating of my meat?" Then his eyes streamed with tears which he could not stay, for he bethought him of what he had been and what he had become. When Ajib heard his father's words his heart also yearned himwards and he looked at the Eunuch and said to him, "Of a truth, O my good guard, my heart yearns to this cook; he is as one that hath a son far away from him: so let us enter and gladden his heart by tasting of his hospitality. Perchance for our so doing Allah may reunite me with my father." When the Eunuch heard these words he cried, "A fine thing this, by Allah! Shall the sons of Wazirs be seen eating in a common cook-shop? Indeed I keep off the folk from thee with this quarter-staff lest they even look upon thee; and I dare not suffer thee to enter this shop at all." When Hasan of Bassorah heard his speech he marvelled and turned to the Eunuch with the tears pouring down his cheeks; and Ajib said, "Verily my heart loves him!" But he answered, "Leave this talk, thou shalt not go in." Thereupon the father turned to the Eunuch and said, "O worthy sir, why wilt thou not gladden my soul by entering my shop? O thou who art like a chestnut, dark without but white of heart within! O thou of the like of whom a certain poet said . . ." The Eunuch burst out a-laughing and asked— "Said what? Speak out by Allah and be quick about it." So Hasan the Bassorite began reciting these couplets:—

> If not master of manners or aught but discreet
> In the household of Kings no trust could he take;
> And then for the Harem! What Eunuch[88] is he
> Whom angels would serve for his service sake.

The Eunuch marvelled and was pleased at these words, so he took Ajib by the hand and went into the cook's shop: whereupon Hasan the Bassorite ladled into a saucer some conserve of pomegranate-grains wonderfully good, dressed with almonds and sugar, saying, "You have honoured me with your company: eat then and health and happiness to you!" Thereupon Ajib said to his father, "Sit thee down and eat with us; so perchance Allah may unite us with him we long for." Quoth Hasan, "O my son, hast thou then been afflicted in thy tender years with parting from those thou lovest?" Quoth Ajib, "Even so, O nuncle mine; my heart burns for the loss of a beloved one who is none other than my father; and indeed I come forth, I and my grandfather,[89] to circle and search the world for him. Oh, the pity of it, and how I long to meet him!" Then he wept with exceeding weeping, and his father also wept seeing him weep and for his own bereavement, which recalled to him his long separation from dear friends and from his mother; and the Eunuch was moved to pity for him. Then they ate together till they were satisfied; and Ajib and the slave rose and left the shop. Hereat Hasan the Bassorite felt as though his soul had departed his body and had gone with them; for he could not lose sight of the boy during the twinkling of an eye, albeit he knew not that Ajib was his son. So he locked up his shop and hastened after them; and he walked so fast that he came up with them before they had gone out of the western gate. The Eunuch turned and asked him, "What ails thee?"; and Badr al-Din answered, "When ye went from me, meseemed my soul had gone with you; and, as I had business without the city-gate, I purposed to bear you company till my matter was ordered and so return." The Eunuch was angered and said to Ajib, "This is just what I feared! we ate that unlucky mouthful (which we are bound to respect), and here is the fellow following us from place to place; for the vulgar are ever the vulgar." Ajib, turning and seeing the Cook just behind him, was wroth and his face reddened with rage and he said to the servant, "Let him walk the highway of the Moslems; but, when we turn off it to our tents, and find that he still follows us, we will send him about his business with a flea in his ear." Then he bowed his head and walked on, the Eunuch walking behind him. But Hasan of Bassorah followed them to the plain Al-Hasa; and, as they drew near to the tents, they turned round and saw him close on their heels; so Ajib was very angry, fearing that the Eunuch might tell his grandfather what had happened. His indignation was the hotter for apprehension lest any say that after he had entered a cook-shop the cook had followed him. So he turned and looked at Hasan of Bassorah and found his eyes fixed on his own, for the father had become a body without a soul; and it seemed to Ajib that his eye was a treacherous eye or that he was some lewd fellow. So his rage redoubled and, stooping down, he took up a stone weighing half a pound and threw it at his father. It struck him on the forehead, cutting it open from eye-brow to eye-brow and causing the blood to stream down: and Hasan fell to the ground in a swoon whilst Ajib and the Eunuch made for the tents. When the father came to himself he wiped away the blood and tore off a strip from his turband and bound up his head, blaming himself the while, and saying, "I wronged the lad by shutting up my shop and following, so that he thought I was some evil-minded fellow." Then he returned to his place where he busied himself with the sale of his sweetmeats; and he yearned after his mother at Bassorah, and wept over her and broke out repeating:—

> Unjust it were to bid the World[90] be just
> And blame her not: She ne'er was made for justice:
> Take what she gives thee, leave all grief aside,
> For now to fair and then to foul her lust is.

So Hasan of Bassorah set himself steadily to sell his sweetmeats; but the Wazir, his uncle, halted in Damascus three days and then marched upon Emesa, and passing through that town he made enquiry there and at every place where he rested. Thence he fared on by way of Hamah and Aleppo and thence through Diyar Bakr and Maridin and Mosul, still enquiring, till he arrived at Bassorah-city. Here, as soon as he had secured a lodging, he presented himself before the Sultan, who entreated him with high honour and the respect due to his rank, and asked the cause of his coming. The Wazir acquainted him with his history and told him that the Minister Nur al-Din was his brother; whereupon the Sultan exclaimed, "Allah have mercy upon him!" and added, "My good Sahib!;[91] he was my Wazir for fifteen years and I loved him exceedingly. Then he died leaving a son who abode only a single month after his father's death; since which time he has disappeared and we could gain no tidings of him. But his mother, who is the daughter of my former Minister, is still among us." When the Wazir Shams al-Din heard that his nephew's mother was alive and well, he rejoiced and said, "O King, I much desire to meet her." The King on the instant gave him leave to visit her; so he betook himself to the mansion of his brother, Nur al-Din, and cast sorrowful glances on all things in and around it and kissed the threshold. Then he bethought him of his brother, Nur al-Din Ali, and how he had died in a strange land far from kith and kin and friends; and he wept and repeated these lines:—

> I wander 'mid these walls, my Layla's walls,
> And kissing this and other wall I roam:
> 'Tis not the walls or roof my heart so loves,
> But those who in this house had made their home.

Then he passed through the gate into a courtyard and found a vaulted doorway builded of hardest syenite[92] inlaid with sundry kinds of multi-coloured marble. Into this he walked and wandered about the house and, throwing many a glance around, saw the name of his brother, Nur al-Din, written in gold wash upon the walls. So he went up to the inscription and kissed it and wept and thought of how he had been separated from his brother and had now lost him for ever. Then he walked on till he came to the apartment of his brother's widow, the mother of Badr al-Din Hasan, the Egyptian. Now from the time of her son's disappearance she had never ceased weeping and wailing through the light hours and the dark; and, when the years grew longsome with her, she built for him a tomb of marble in the midst of the saloon and there used to weep for him day and night, never sleeping save thereby. When the Wazir drew near her apartment, he heard her voice and stood behind the door while she addressed the sepulchre in verse and said:—

> Answer, by Allah! Sepulchre, are all his beauties gone?
> Hath change the power to blight his charms, that Beauty's
>   paragon?
> Thou art not earth, O Sepulchre! nor art thou sky to me;
> How comes it, then, in thee I see conjoint the branch and
>   moon?

While she was bemoaning herself after this fashion, behold, the Wazir went in to her and saluted her and informed her that he was her husband's brother; and, telling her all that had passed between them, laid open before her the whole story, how her son Badr al-Din Hasan had spent a whole night with his daughter full ten years ago but had disappeared in the morning. And he ended with saying, "My daughter conceived by thy son and bare a male child who is now with me, and he is thy son and thy son's son by my daughter." When she heard the tidings that her boy, Badr al-Din, was still alive and saw her brother-in-law, she rose up to him and threw herself at his feet and kissed them. Then the Wazir sent for Ajib and his grandmother stood up and fell on his neck and wept; but Shams al-Din said to her, "This is no time for weeping; this is the time to get thee ready for travelling with us to the land of Egypt; haply Allah will reunite me and thee with thy son and my nephew." Replied she, "Hearkening and obedience;" and, rising at once, collected her baggage and treasures and her jewels, and equipped herself and her slave-girls for the march, whilst the Wazir went to take his leave of the Sultan of Bassorah, who sent by him presents and rarities for the Soldan of Egypt. Then he set out at once upon his homeward march and journeyed till he came to Damascus-city where he alighted in the usual place and pitched tents, and said to his suite, "We will halt a se'nnight here to buy presents and rare things for the Soldan." Now Ajib bethought him of the past so he said to the Eunuch, "O Laik, I want a little diversion; come, let us go down to the great bazar of Damascus,[93] and see what hath become of the cook whose sweetmeats we ate and whose head we broke, for indeed he was kind to us and we entreated him scurvily." The Eunuch answered, "Hearing is obeying!" So they went forth from the tents; and the tie of blood drew Ajib towards his father, and forthwith they passed through the gateway, Bab al-Faradis[94] hight, and entered the city and ceased not walking through the streets till they reached the cookshop, where they found Hasan of Bassorah standing at the door. It was near the time of mid-afternoon prayer[95] and it so fortuned that he had just dressed a confection of pomegranate-grains. When the twain drew near to him and Ajib saw him, his heart yearned towards him, and noticing the scar of the blow, which time had darkened on his brow, he said to him, "Peace be on thee, O man!,[96] know that my heart is with thee." But when Badr al-Din looked upon his son his vitals yearned and his heart fluttered, and he hung his head earthwards and sought to make his tongue give utterance to his words, but he could not. Then he raised his head humbly and suppliant-wise towards his boy and repeated these couplets:—

I longed for my beloved but when I saw his face,
Abashed I held my tongue and stood with downcast eye;
And hung my head in dread and would have hid my love,
But do whatso I would hidden it would not lie:
Volumes of plaints I had prepared, reproach and blame,
But when we met, no single word remembered I.

And then said he to them, "Heal my broken heart and eat of my sweetmeats; for, by Allah, I cannot look at thee but my heart flutters. Indeed I should not have followed thee the other day, but that I was beside myself." "By Allah," answered Ajib, "thou dost indeed love us! We ate in thy house a mouthful when we were here before and thou madest us repent for it, for that thou followedst us and wouldst have disgraced us; so now we will not eat aught with thee save on condition that thou make oath not to go out after us nor dog us. Otherwise we will not visit thee again during our present stay; for we shall halt a week here, whilst my grandfather buys certain presents for the King." Quoth Hasan of Bassorah, "I promise you this." So Ajib and the Eunuch entered the shop, and his father set before them a saucer-full of conserve of pomegranate-grains. Said Ajib, "Sit thee down and eat with us, so haply shall Allah dispel our sorrows." Hasan the Bassorite was joyful and sat down and ate with them; but his eyes kept gazing fixedly on Ajib's

face, for his very heart and vitals clove to him; and at last
the boy said to him, "Did I not tell thee thou art a most
noyous dotard?; so do stint thy staring in my face!" Hasan
kept putting morsels into Ajib's mouth at one time and at
another time did the same by the Eunuch and they ate till
they were satisfied and could no more. Then all rose up
and the cook poured water on their hands;[97] and, loosing a
silken waist-shawl, dried them and sprinkled them with
rose-water from a casting-bottle he had by him. Then he
went out and presently returned with a gugglet of sherbet
flavoured with rose-water, scented with musk and cooled
with snow; and he set this before them saying, "Complete
your kindness to me!" So Ajib took the gugglet and drank
and passed it to the Eunuch; and it went round till their
stomachs were full and they were surfeited with a meal
larger than their wont. Then they went away and made
haste in walking till they reached the tents, and Ajib went
in to his grandmother, who kissed him and, thinking of
her son, Badr al-Din Hasan, groaned aloud and wept. Then
she asked Ajib, "O my son! where hast thou been?"; and
he answered, "In Damascus-city;" whereupon she rose and
set before him a bit of scone and a saucer of conserve of
pomegranate-grains (which was too little sweetened), and
she said to the Eunuch, "Sit down with thy master!" Said
the servant to himself, "By Allah, we have no mind to eat: I
cannot bear the smell of bread;" but he sat down and so did
Ajib, though his stomach was full of what he had eaten already and drunken. Nevertheless he took a bit of the bread
and dipped it in the pomegranate-conserve and made shift
to eat it, but he found it too little sweetened, for he was
cloyed and surfeited, so he said, "Faugh; what be this wild-
beast stuff?"[98] "O my son," cried his grandmother, "dost
thou find fault with my cookery? I cooked this myself and
none can cook it as nicely as I can save thy father, Badr al-
Din Hasan." "By Allah, O my lady," Ajib answered, "this
dish is nasty stuff; for we saw but now in the city of Bassorah a cook who so dresseth pomegranate-grains that the
very smell openeth a way to the heart and the taste would

make a full man long to eat; and, as for this mess compared with his, 'tis not worth either much or little." When his grandmother heard his words she waxed wroth with exceeding wrath and looked at the servant and said, "Woe to thee! dost thou spoil my son,[99] and dost take him into common cookshops?" The Eunuch was frightened and denied, saying, "We did not go into the shop; we only passed by it." "By Allah," cried Ajib, "but we *did* go in and we ate till it came out of our nostrils, and the dish was better than thy dish!" Then his grandmother rose and went and told her brother-in-law, who was incensed against the Eunuch, and sending for him asked him, "Why didst thou take my son into a cookshop?"; and the Eunuch being frightened answered, "We did not go in." But Ajib said, "We *did* go inside and ate conserve of pomegranate-grains till we were full; and the cook gave us to drink of iced and sugared sherbet." At this the Wazir's indignation redoubled and he questioned the Castrato but, as he still denied, the Wazir said to him, "If thou speak sooth, sit down and eat before us." So he came forward and tried to eat, but could not and threw away the mouthful crying "O my lord! I am surfeited since yesterday." By this the Wazir was certified that he had eaten at the cook's and bade the slaves throw him[100] which they did. Then they came down on him with a rib-basting which burned him till he cried for mercy and help from Allah, saying, "O my master, beat me no more and I will tell thee the truth;" whereupon the Wazir stopped the bastinado and said, "Now speak thou sooth." Quoth the Eunuch, "Know then that we did enter the shop of a cook while he was dressing conserve of pomegranate-grains and he set some of it before us: by Allah! I never ate in my life its like, nor tasted aught nastier than this stuff which is now before us."[101] Badr al-Din Hasan's mother was angry at this and said, "Needs must thou go back to the cook and bring me a saucer of conserved pomegranate-grains from that which is in his shop and show it to thy master, that he may say which be the better and the nicer, mine or his." Said the unsexed "I will." So on the instant she gave him a saucer

and a half dinar and he returned to the shop and said to
the cook, "O Shaykh of all Cooks,[102] we have laid a wager
concerning thy cookery in my lord's house, for they have
conserve of pomegranate-grains there also; so give me this
half-dinar's worth and look to it; for I have eaten a full meal
of stick on account of thy cookery, and so do not let me eat
aught more thereof." Hasan of Bassorah laughed and answered, "By Allah, none can dress this dish as it should be
dressed save myself and my mother, and she at this time is
in a far country." Then he ladled out a saucer-full; and, finishing it off with musk and rose-water, put it in a cloth
which he sealed[103] and gave it to the Eunuch, who hastened
back with it. No sooner had Badr al-Din Hasan's mother
tasted it and perceived its fine flavour and the excellence of
the cookery, than she knew who had dressed it, and she
screamed and fell down fainting. The Wazir, sorely startled, sprinkled rose-water upon her and after a time she recovered and said, "If my son be yet of this world, none
dressed this conserve of pomegranate-grains but he; and
this Cook is my very son Badr al-Din Hasan; there is no
doubt of it nor can there be any mistake, for only I and he
knew how to prepare it and I taught him." When the Wazir
heard her words he joyed with exceeding joy and said, "Oh
the longing of me for a sight of my brother's son! I wonder
if the days will ever unite us with him! Yet it is to Almighty
Allah alone that we look for bringing about this meeting."
Then he rose without stay or delay and, going to his suite
said to them, "Be off, some fifty of you with sticks and
staves to the Cook's shop and demolish it; then pinion his
arms behind him with his own turband, saying:—It was
thou madest that foul mess of pomegranate-grains! and
drag him here perforce but without doing him a harm."
And they replied, "It is well." Then the Wazir rode off
without losing an instant to the Palace and, foregathering
with the Viceroy of Damascus, showed him the Sultan's orders. After careful perusal he kissed the letter, and placing
it upon his head said to his visitor, "Who is this offender

of thine?" Quoth the Wazir, "A man which is a cook." So the Viceroy at once sent his apparitors to the shop; which they found demolished and everything in it broken to pieces; for whilst the Wazir was riding to the palace his men had done his bidding. Then they awaited his return from the audience, and Hasan of Bassorah who was their prisoner kept saying, "I wonder what they have found in the conserve of pomegranate-grains to bring things to this pass!"[104] When the Wazir returned to them, after his visit to the Viceroy who had given him formal permission to take up his debtor and depart with him, on entering the tents he called for the Cook. They brought him forward pinioned with his turband; and, when Badr al-Din Hasan saw his uncle, he wept with exceeding weeping and said, "O my lord, what is my offence against thee?" "Art thou the man who dressed that conserve of pomegranate-grains?", asked the Wazir, and he answered "Yes! didst thou find in it aught to call for the cutting off of my head?" Quoth the Wazir, "That were the least of thy desserts!" Quoth the cook, "O my lord, wilt thou not tell me my crime and what aileth the conserve of pomegranate-grains?" "Presently," replied the Wazir and called aloud to his men, saying "Bring hither the camels." So they struck the tents and by the Wazir's orders the servants took Badr al-Din Hasan, and set him in a chest which they padlocked and put on a camel. Then they departed and stinted not journeying till nightfall, when they halted and ate some victual, and took Badr al-Din Hasan out of his chest and gave him a meal and locked him up again. They set out once more and travelled till they reached Kimrah, where they took him out of the box and brought him before the Wazir who asked him, "Art thou he who dressed that conserve of pomegranate-grains?" He answered "Yes, O my lord!"; and the Wazir said "Fetter him!" So they fettered him and returned him to the chest and fared on again till they reached Cairo and lighted at the quarter called Al-Raydaniyah.[105] Then the Wazir gave order to take Badr al-Din Hasan out of the chest and sent for a carpenter and said to him, "Make me a cross of wood[106] for this fellow!" Cried Badr al-Din Hasan "And what wilt thou do with it?"; and the Wazir replied, "I mean to crucify thee thereon, and nail thee thereto and parade thee all about the city." "And why wilt thou use me after this fashion?" "Because of thy villanous cookery of conserved pomegranate-grains; how durst thou dress it and sell it lacking pepper?" "And for that it lacked pepper wilt thou do all this to me? Is it not enough that thou hast broken my shop and smashed my gear and boxed me up in a chest and fed me only once a day?" "Too little pepper! too little pepper! this is a crime which can be expiated only upon the cross!" Then Badr al-Din Hasan marvelled and fell a-mourning for his life; whereupon the Wazir asked him, "Of what thinkest thou?"; and he answered him, "Of maggoty heads like thine;[107] for an thou had one ounce of sense thou hadst not treated me thus." Quoth the Wazir, "It is our duty to punish thee lest thou do the like again." Quoth Badr al-Din Hasan, "Of a truth my offence were over-punished by the least of what thou hast already done to me; and Allah damn all conserve of pomegranate-grains and curse the hour when I cooked it and would I had died ere this!" But the Wazir rejoined, "There is no help for it: I must crucify a man who sells conserve of pomegranate-grains lacking pepper." All this time the carpenter was shaping the wood and Badr al-Din looked on; and thus they did till night, when his uncle took him and clapped him into the chest, saying, "The thing shall be done to-morrow!" Then he waited till he knew Badr al-Din Hasan to be asleep, when he mounted; and, taking the chest up before him, entered the city and rode on to his own house, where he alighted and said to his daughter, Sitt al-Husn, "Praised be Allah who hath reunited thee with thy husband, the son of thine uncle! Up now, and order the house as it was on thy bridal night." So the servants arose and lit the candles; and the Wazir took out his plan of the nuptial chamber, and directed them what to do till they had set everything in its stead, so that whoever saw it would have no doubt but it was the very night of the marriage. Then he bade them put down Badr al-Din Hasan's turband on the settle, as he had deposited it with his own hand, and in like manner his bag-trousers and the purse which were under the mattress; and told his daughter to undress herself and go to bed in the private chamber as on her wedding-night, adding, "When the son of thine uncle comes in to thee, say to him:—Thou hast loitered while going to the privy; and call him to lie by thy side and keep him in converse till daybreak, when we will explain the whole matter to him." Then he bade take Badr al-Din Hasan out of the chest, after loosing the fetters from his feet and stripping off all that was on him save the fine shirt of blue silk in which he had slept on his wedding-night; so that he was well nigh naked and trouser-less. All this was done whilst he was sleeping on utterly unconscious. Then, by doom of Destiny, Badr al-Din Hasan turned over and awoke; and, finding himself in a lighted vestibule, said to himself, "Surely I am in the mazes of some dream." So he rose and went on a little to an inner door and looked in and lo! he was in the very chamber wherein the bride had been displayed to him; and there he saw the bridal alcove and the settle and his turband and all his clothes. When he saw this he was confounded and kept advancing with one foot, and retiring with the other, saying, "Am I sleeping or waking?" And he began rubbing his forehead and saying (for indeed he was thoroughly astounded), "By Allah, verily this is the chamber of the bride who was displayed before me! Where am I then? I was surely but now in a box!" Whilst he was talking with himself, Sitt al-Husn suddenly lifted the corner of the chamber-curtain and said, "O my lord, wilt thou not come in? Indeed thou hast loitered long in the water-closet." When he heard her words and saw her face he burst out laughing and said, "Of a truth this is a very nightmare among dreams!" Then he went in sighing, and pondered what had come to pass with him and was perplexed about his case, and his affair became yet more obscure to him when he saw his turband and bag-trousers and when, feeling the pocket, he found the purse containing the thousand gold pieces. So he stood still and muttered, "Allah is all knowing! Assuredly I am dreaming a wild waking dream!" Then said the Lady of Beauty to him, "What ails thee to look puzzled and perplexed?"; adding, "Thou wast a very different man during the first of the night!" He laughed and asked her, "How long have I been away from thee?"; and she answered him, "Allah preserve thee and His Holy Name be about thee! Thou didst but go out an hour ago for an occasion and return. Are thy wits clean gone?" When Badr al-Din Hasan heard this, he laughed,[108] and said, "Thou hast spoken truth; but, when I went out from thee, I forgot myself awhile in the draughthouse and dreamed that I was a cook at Damascus and abode there ten years; and there came to me a boy who was of the sons of the great, and with him an Eunuch." Here he passed his hand over his forehead and, feeling the scar, cried, "By Allah, O my lady, it must have been true, for he struck my forehead with a stone and cut it open from eye-brow to eye-brow; and here is the mark: so it must have been on wake." Then he added, "But perhaps I dreamt it when we fell asleep, I and thou, in each other's arms, for meseems it was as though I travelled to Damascus without tarbush and trousers and set up as a cook there." Then he was perplexed and considered for awhile, and said, "By Allah, I also fancied that I dressed a conserve of pomegranate-grains and put too little pepper in it. By Allah, I must have slept in the numerocent and have seen the whole of this in a dream; but how long was that dream!" "Allah upon thee," said Sitt al-Husn, "and what more sawest thou?" So he related all to her; and presently said, "By Allah had I not woke up they would have nailed me to a cross of wood!" "Wherefore?" asked she; and he answered, "For putting too little pepper in the conserve of pomegranate-grains, and meseemed they demolished my shop and dashed to pieces my pots and pans, destroyed all my stuff and put me in a box; then they sent for the carpenter to fashion a cross for me and would have crucified me thereon. Now Alhamdolillah! thanks be to Allah, for that all this happened to me in sleep, and not on wake." Sitt al-Husn laughed and clasped him to her bosom and he her to his: then he thought again and said, "By Allah, it could not be save while I was awake: truly I know not what to think of it." Then he lay down and all the night he was bewildered about his case, now saying, "I was dreaming!" and then saying, "I was awake!", till morning, when his uncle Shams al-Din, the Wazir, came to him and saluted him. When Badr al-Din Hasan saw him he said, "By Allah, art thou not he who bade bind my hands behind me and smash my shop and nail me to a cross on a matter of conserved pomegranate-grains because the dish lacked a sufficiency of pepper?" Whereupon the Wazir said to him, "Know, O my son, that truth hath shown it soothfast and the concealed hath been revealed![109] Thou art the son of my brother, and I did all this with thee to certify myself that thou wast indeed he who went in unto my daughter that night. I could not be sure of this, till I saw that thou knewest the chamber and thy turband and thy trousers and thy gold and the papers in thy writing and in that of thy father, my brother; for I had never seen thee afore that and knew thee not; and as to thy mother I have prevailed upon her to come with me from Bassorah." So saying, he threw himself on his nephew's breast and wept for joy; and Badr al-Din Hasan, hearing these words from his uncle, marvelled with exceeding marvel and fell on his neck and also shed tears for excess of delight. Then said the Wazir to him, "O my son, the sole cause of all this is what passed between me and thy sire;" and he told him the manner of his father wayfaring to Bassorah and all that had occurred to part them. Lastly the Wazir sent for Ajib; and when his father saw him he cried, "And this is he who struck me with the stone!" Quoth the Wazir "This is thy son!" And Badr al-Din Hasan threw himself upon his boy and began repeating:—

> Long have I wept o'er severance' ban and bane,
> Long from mine eyelids tear-rills rail and rain:
> And vowed I if Time re-union bring
> My tongue from name of "Severance" I'll restrain:
> Joy hath o'ercome me to this stress that I
> From joy's revulsion to shed tears am fain:
> Ye are so trained to tears, O eyne of me!
> You weep with pleasure as you weep with pain.

When he had ended his verse his mother came in and threw herself upon him and began reciting:—

> When we met we complained,
> Our hearts were sore wrung:
> But plaint is not pleasant
> Fro' messenger's tongue.

Then she wept and related to him what had befallen her since his departure, and he told her what he had suffered, and they thanked Allah Almighty for their reunion. Two days after his arrival the Wazir Shams al-Din went in to the Sultan and, kissing the ground between his hands, greeted him with the greeting due to Kings. The Sultan rejoiced at his return and his face brightened and, placing him hard by his side,[110] asked him to relate all he had seen in his wayfaring and whatso had betided him in his going and coming. So the Wazir told him all that had passed from first to last and the Sultan said, "Thanks be to Allah for thy victory[111] and the winning of thy wish and thy safe return to thy children and thy people! And now I needs must see the son of thy brother, Hasan of Bassorah, so bring him to the audience-hall to-morrow." Shams al-Din replied, "Thy slave shall stand in thy presence to-morrow, Inshallah, if it be God's will." Then he saluted him and, returning to his own house, informed his nephew of the Sultan's desire to see him, whereto replied Hasan, whilome the Bassorite, "The slave is obedient to the orders of his lord." And the result was that next day he accompanied his uncle, Shams al-Din, to the Divan; and, after

saluting the Sultan and doing him reverence in most ceremonious obeisance and with most courtly obsequiousness,
he began improvising these verses:—

> The first in rank to kiss the ground shall deign
> Before you, and all ends and aims attain:
> You are Honour's fount; and all that hope of you,
> Shall gain more honour than Hope hoped to gain.

The Sultan smiled and signed to him to sit down. So he
took a seat close to his uncle, Shams al-Din, and the King
asked him his name. Quoth Badr al-Din Hasan, "The
meanest of thy slaves is known as Hasan the Bassorite, who
is instant in prayer for thee day and night." The Sultan was
pleased at his words and, being minded to test his learning
and prove his good breeding, asked him, "Dost thou remember any verses in praise of the mole on the cheek?"
He answered, "I do," and began reciting:—

> When I think of my love and our parting-smart,
> My groans go forth and my tears upstart:
> He's a mole that reminds me in colour and charms
> O' the black o' the eye and the grain[112] of the heart.

The King admired and praised the two couplets and said
to him, "Quote something else; Allah bless thy sire and
may thy tongue never tire!" So he began:—

> That cheek-mole's spot they evened with a grain
> Of musk, nor did they here the simile strain:
> Nay, marvel at the face comprising all
> Beauty, nor falling short by single grain.

The King shook with pleasure[113] and said to him, "Say
more: Allah bless thy days!" So he began:—

> O you whose mole on cheek enthroned recalls
> A dot of musk upon a stone of ruby,

Grant me your favours! Be not stone at heart!
Core of my heart whose only sustenance *you* be!

Quoth the King, "Fair comparison, O Hasan![114] thou hast
spoken excellently well and hast proved thyself accomplished in every accomplishment! Now explain to me how
many meanings be there in the Arabic language[115] for
the word *Khal* or *mole*." He replied, "Allah keep the King!
Seven and fifty and some by tradition say fifty." Said the
Sultan, "Thou sayest sooth," presently adding, "Hast thou
knowledge as to the points of excellence in beauty?" "Yes,"
answered Badr al-Din Hasan, "Beauty consisteth in brightness of face, clearness of complexion, shapeliness of nose,
gentleness of eyes, sweetness of mouth, cleverness of speech,
slenderness of shape and seemliness of all attributes. But
the acme of beauty is in the hair and, indeed, al-Shihab the
Hijazi hath brought together all these items in his doggerel
verse of the metre Rajaz[116] and it is this:—

> Say thou to skin "Be soft," to face "Be fair,"
> And gaze, nor shall they blame howso thou stare:
> Fine nose in Beauty's list is high esteemed;
> Nor less an eye full, bright and debonnair:
> Eke did they well to laud the lovely lips
> (Which e'en the sleep of me will never spare);
> A winning tongue, a stature tall and straight;[117]
> A seemly union of gifts rarest rare:
> But Beauty's acme in the hair one views it;
> So hear my strain and with some few excuse it!"

The Sultan was captivated by his converse and, regarding
him as a friend, asked, "What meaning is there in the saw
Shurayh[118] is foxier than the fox?" And he answered, "Know,
O King (whom Almighty Allah keep!) that the legist Shurayh was wont, during the days of the plague, to make a
visitation to Al-Najaf; and, whenever he stood up to pray,
there came a fox which would plant himself facing him
and which, by mimicking his movements, distracted him

from his devotions. Now when this became longsome to him, one day he doffed his shirt and set it upon a cane and shook out the sleeves; then placing his turband on the top and girding its middle with a shawl, he stuck it up in the place where he used to pray. Presently up trotted the fox according to his custom and stood over against the figure, whereupon Shurayh came behind him, and took him. Hence the sayer saith, Shurayh foxier than the fox." When the Sultan heard Badr al-Din Hasan's explanation he said to his uncle, Shams al-Din, "Truly this the son of thy brother is perfect in courtly breeding and I do not think that his like can be found in Cairo." At this Hasan arose and kissed the ground before him and sat down again as a Mameluke should sit before his master. When the Sultan had thus assured himself of his courtly breeding and bearing and his knowledge of the liberal arts and belles-lettres, he joyed with exceeding joy and invested him with a splendid robe of honour and promoted him to an office whereby he might better his condition.[119] Then Badr al-Din Hasan arose and, kissing the ground before the King, wished him continuance of glory and asked leave to retire with his uncle, the Wazir Shams al-Din. The Sultan gave him leave and he issued forth and the two returned home, where food was set before them and they ate what Allah had given them. After finishing his meal Hasan repaired to the sitting-chamber of his wife, the Lady of Beauty, and told her what had past between him and the Sultan; whereupon quoth she, "He cannot fail to make thee a cup-companion and give thee largesse in excess and load thee with favours and bounties; so shalt thou, by Allah's blessing, dispread, like the greater light, the rays of thy perfection wherever thou be, on shore or on sea." Said he to her, "I purpose to recite a Kasidah, an ode, in his praise, that he may redouble in affection for me." "Thou art right in thine intent," she answered, "so gather thy wits together and weigh thy words, and I shall surely see my husband favoured with his highest favour." Thereupon Hasan shut himself up and composed these couplets on a solid base and abounding in

inner grace and copied them out in a hand-writing of the
nicest taste. They are as follows:—

Mine is a Chief who reached most haught estate,
Treading the pathways of the good and great:
His justice makes all regions safe and sure,
And against froward foes bars every gate:
Bold lion, hero, saint, e'en if you call
Seraph or Sovran[120] he with all may rate!
The poorest suppliant rich from him returns,
All words to praise him were inadequate.
He to the day of peace is saffron Morn,
And murky Night in furious warfare's bate.
Bow 'neath his gifts our necks, and by his deeds
As King of freeborn[121] souls he 'joys his state:
Allah increase for us his term of years,
And from his lot avert all risks and fears!

When he had finished transcribing the lines, he despatched
them, in charge of one of his uncle's slaves, to the Sultan,
who perused them and his fancy was pleased; so he read
them to those present and all praised them with the highest praise. Thereupon he sent for the writer to his sitting-
chamber and said to him, "Thou art from this day forth my
boon-companion and I appoint to thee a monthly solde of
a thousand dirhams, over and above that I bestowed on
thee aforetime." So Hasan rose and, kissing the ground before the King several times, prayed for the continuance of
his greatness and glory and length of life and strength.
Thus Badr al-Din Hasan the Bassorite waxed high in honour and his fame flew forth to many regions and he abode
in all comfort and solace and delight of life with his uncle
and his own folk till Death overtook him. When the Caliph
Harun al-Rashid heard this story from the mouth of his
Wazir, Ja'afar the Barmecide, he marvelled much and said,
"It behoves that these stories be written in letters of liquid
gold." Then he set the slaves at liberty and assigned to the
youth who had slain his wife such a monthly stipend as

sufficed to make his life easy; he also gave him a concubine from amongst his own slave-girls and the young man became one of his cup-companions. "Yet this story (continued Shahrazad) is in no wise stranger than the tale of Ghanim bin Ayyub, and what betided him." Quoth the King, "And what may that be?" So Shahrazad began, in these words,

Tale of Ghanim bin Ayyub,[1]
the Distraught,
the Thrall o' Love.

It hath reached me, O auspicious King, that in times of yore and in years and ages long gone before, there lived in Damascus a merchant among the merchants, a wealthy man who had a son like the moon on the night of his fulness[2] and withal sweet of speech, who was named Ghanim bin Ayyub surnamed the Distraught, the Thrall o' Love. He had also a daughter, own sister to Ghanim, who was called Fitnah, a damsel unique in beauty and loveliness. Their father died and left them abundant wealth, and amongst other things an hundred loads[3] of silks and brocades, musk-pods and mother o' pearl; and there was written on every bale, "This is of the packages intended for Baghdad," it having been his purpose to make the journey thither, when Almighty Allah took him to Himself, which was in the time of the Caliph Harun al-Rashid. After a while his son took the loads and, bidding farewell to his mother and kindred and townsfolk, went forth with a company of merchants, putting his trust in Allah Almighty, who decreed him safety, so that he arrived without let or stay at Baghdad. There he hired for himself a fair dwelling house which he furnished with carpets and cushions, curtains and hangings; and therein stored his bales and stabled his mules and camels, after which he abode a while resting. Presently the merchants and notables of Baghdad came and saluted him, after which he took a bundle containing ten pieces of costly stuffs, with the prices written on them, and carried it to the merchants' bazar, where they welcomed and saluted him and showed him all honour; and, making him dismount from his beast, seated him in the shop of the Syndic of the market, to whom he delivered the package. He opened it and drawing out the pieces of stuff, sold them for him at a profit of two dinars on every dinar of prime cost. At this Ghanim rejoiced and kept selling his silks and stuffs one after another, and ceased not to do on this wise for a full year. On the first day of the following year he went, as was his wont, to the Exchange which was in the bazar, but found the gate shut; and enquiring the reason was told, "One of the merchants is dead and all the others have gone to follow his bier,[4] and why shouldst thou not win the meed of good deeds by walking with them?"[5] He replied "Yes," and asked for the quarter where the funeral was taking place, and one directed him thereto. So he purified himself by the Wuzu-ablution[6] and repaired with the other merchants to the oratory, where they prayed over the dead, then walked before the bier to the burial-place, and Ghanim, who was a bashful man, followed them being ashamed to leave them. They presently issued from the city, and passed through the tombs until they reached the grave where they found that the deceased's kith and kin had pitched a tent over the tomb and had brought thither lamps and wax candles. So they buried the body and sat down while the readers read out and recited the Koran over the grave; and Ghanim sat with them, being overcome with bashfulness and saying to himself "I cannot well go away till they do." They tarried listening to the Koranic perlection till nightfall, when the servants set supper and sweetmeats[7] before them and they ate till they were satisfied; then they washed their hands and again took their places. But Ghanim's mind was preoccupied with his house and goods, being in fear of robbers, and he said to himself, "I am a stranger here and supposed to have money: if I pass the night abroad the thieves will steal my money-bags and my bales to boot." So when he could no longer control his fear he arose and left the assembly, having first asked leave to go about some urgent business; and following the signs of the road he soon came to the city-gate. But it was midnight and he found the doors locked and saw none going or coming nor heard aught but the hounds baying and the wolves howling. At this he exclaimed, "There is no Majesty and there is no Might save in Allah! I was in fear for my property and came back on its account, but now I find the gate shut and I am in mortal fear for my life!" Then he turned back and, looking out for a place where he could sleep till morning, presently found a Santon's tomb, a square of four walls with a date-tree in the central court and a granite gateway. The door was wide open; so he entered and would fain have slept, but sleep came not to him; and terror and a sense of desolation oppressed him, for that he was alone amidst the tombs. So he rose to his feet and, opening the door, looked out and lo! he was ware of a light afar off in the direction of the city-gate; then walking a little way towards it, he saw that it was on the road whereby he had reached the tomb. This made him fear for his life, so he hastily shut the door and climbed to the top of the date-tree where he hid himself in the heart of the fronds. The light came nearer and nearer till it was close to the tomb; then it stopped and he saw three slaves, two bearing a chest and one with a lanthorn, an adze and a basket containing some mortar. When they reached the tomb, one of those who were carrying the case said, "What aileth thee O Sawab?"; and said the other, "What is the matter O Kafur?"[8] Quoth he, "Were we not here at supper-tide and did we not leave the door open?" "Yes," replied the other, "that is true." "See," said Kafur, "now it is shut and barred." "How weak are your wits!" cried the third who bore the adze and his name was Bukhayt,[9] "know ye not that the owners of the gardens use to come out from Baghdad and tend them and, when evening closes upon them, they enter this place and shut the door, for fear lest the wicked blackmen, like ourselves, should catch them and roast 'em and eat 'em."[10] "Thou sayest sooth," said the two others, "but by Allah, however that may be, none amongst us is weaker of wits than thou." "If ye do not believe me," said Bukhayt, "let us enter the tomb and I will rouse the rat for you; for I doubt not but that, when he saw the light and us making for the place, he ran up the date-tree and hid there for fear of us." When Ghanim heard this, he said in himself, "O curstest of slaves! May Allah not have thee in His holy keeping for this thy craft and keenness of wit! There is no Majesty and there is no Might save in Allah, the Glorious, the Great! How shall I win free of these blackamoors?" Then said the two who bore the box to him of the adze, "Swarm up the wall and open the gate for us, O Bukhayt, for we are tired of carrying the chest on our necks; and when thou hast opened the gate thou shalt have one of those we catch inside, a fine fat rat which we will fry for thee after such excellent fashion that not a speck of his fat shall be lost." But Bukhayt answered, "I am afraid of somewhat which my weak wits have suggested to me: we should do better to throw the chest over the gateway; for it is our treasure." "If we throw it 'twill break," replied they; and he said, "I fear lest there be robbers within who murder folk and plunder their goods, for evening is their time of entering such places and dividing their spoil." "O thou weak o' wits," said both the bearers of the box, "how could they ever get in here!"[11] Then they set down the chest and climbing over the wall dropped inside and opened the gate, whilst the third slave (he that was called Bukhayt) stood by them holding the adze, the lanthorn and the hand-basket containing the mortar. After this they locked the gate and sat down; and presently one of them said, "O my brethren, we are wearied with walking and with lifting up and setting down the chest, and with unlocking and locking the gate; and now 'tis midnight, and we have no breath left to open a tomb and bury the box: so let us rest here two or three hours, then rise and do the job. Meanwhile each of us shall tell how he came to be castrated and all that befel him from first to last, the better to pass away our time while we take our rest." Thereupon the first, he of the lanthorn and whose name was Bukhayt, said, "I'll tell you my tale." "Say on," replied they; so he began as follows the

TALE OF THE FIRST EUNUCH, BUKHAYT.

Know, O my brothers, that when I was a little one, some five years old, I was taken home from my native country by a slave-driver who sold me to a certain Apparitor.[12] My purchaser had a daughter three years old, with whom I was brought up, and they used to make mock of me, letting me play with her and dance for her and sing to her,[13] till I reached the age of twelve and she that of ten; and even then they did not forbid me seeing her. One day I went in to her and found her sitting in an inner room, and she looked as if she had just come out of the bath which was in the house; for she was scented with essences and reek of aromatic woods, and her face shone like the circle of the moon on the fourteenth night. She began to sport with me, and I with her, till, before I knew what I did, I did away her maidenhead. When I saw this, I ran off and took refuge with one of my comrades. Presently her mother came in to her; and seeing her in this case, fainted clean away. However she managed the matter advisedly and hid it from the girl's father out of good will to me; nor did they cease to call to me and coax me, till they took me from where I was. After two months had passed by, her mother married her to a young man, a barber who used to shave her papa, and portioned and fitted her out of her own monies; whilst the father knew nothing of what had passed. On the night of consummation they cut the throat of a pigeon-poult and sprinkled the blood on her shift.[14] After a while they seized me unawares and gelded me; and, when they brought her to her bridegroom, they made me her Agha,[15] her eunuch, to walk before her wheresoever she went, whether to the bath or to her father's house. I abode with her a long time enjoying her beauty and loveliness by way of kissing and coupling with her,[16] till she died, and her husband and mother and father died also; when they seized me for the Royal Treasury as being the property of an intestate, and I found my way hither, where I became your comrade. This, then, O my brethren, is the cause of my cullions being cut off; and peace be with you! He ceased and his fellow began in these words the

TALE OF THE SECOND EUNUCH, KAFUR.

Know, O my brothers that, when beginning service as a boy of eight, I used to tell the slave-dealers regularly and exactly one lie every year, so that they fell out with one another, till at last my master lost patience with me and, carrying me down to the market, ordered the brokers to cry, "Who will buy this slave, knowing his blemish and making allowance for it?" He did so and they asked him, "Pray, what may be his blemish?" and he answered, "He telleth me one single lie every year." Now a man that was a merchant came up and said to the broker, "How much do they allow for him with his blemish?" "They allow six hundred dirhams," he replied; and said the other, "Thou shalt have twenty dirhams for thyself." So he arranged between him and the slave-dealer who took the coin from him and the broker carried me to the merchant's house and departed, after receiving his brokerage. The trader clothed me with suitable dress, and I stayed in his service the rest of my twelvemonth, until the new year began happily. It was a blessed season, plenteous in the produce of the earth, and the merchants used to feast every day at the house of some one among them, till it was my master's turn to entertain them in a flower-garden without the city. So he and the other merchants went to the garden, taking with them all that they required of provaunt and else beside, and sat eating and carousing and drinking till mid-day, when my master, having need of some matter from his home, said to me, "O slave, mount the she-mule and hie thee to the house and bring from thy mistress such and such a thing and return quickly." I obeyed his bidding and started for the house but, as I drew near it, I began to cry out and shed tears, whereupon all the people of the quarter collected, great and small; and my master's wife and daughters, hearing the noise I was making, opened the door and asked me what was the matter. Said I, "My master was sitting with his friends beneath an old wall, and it fell on one and all of them; and when I saw what had happened to them, I mounted the mule and came hither in haste to tell you." When my master's daughters and wife heard this, they screamed and rent their raiment and beat their faces, whilst the neighbours came around them. Then the wife overturned the furniture of the house, one thing upon another, and tore down the shelves and broke the windows and the lattices and smeared the walls with mud and indigo, saying to me, "Woe to thee, O Kafur! come help me to tear down these cupboards and break up these vessels and this chinaware,[17] and the rest of it." So I went to her and aided her to smash all the shelves in the house with whatever stood upon them, after which I went round about the terrace-roofs and every part of the place, spoiling all I could and leaving no china in the house unbroken till I had laid waste the whole, crying out the while "Well-away! my master!" Then my mistress fared forth bare-faced wearing a head-kerchief and naught else, and her daughters and the children sallied out with her, and said to me, "O Kafur, go thou before us and show us the place where thy master lieth dead, that we may take him from under the fallen wall and lay him on a bier and bear him to the house and give him a fine funeral." So I went forth before them crying out,

"Alack, my master!"; and they after me with faces and heads bare and all shrieking, "Alas! Alas for the man!" Now there remained none in the quarter, neither man nor woman, nor epicene, nor youth, nor maid, nor child, nor old trot, but went with us smiting their faces and weeping bitterly, and I led them leisurely through the whole city. The folk asked them what was the matter, whereupon they told them what they had heard from me, and all exclaimed, "There is no Majesty and there is no Might save in Allah!" Then said one of them, "He was a personage of conse-quence; so let us go to the Governor and tell him what hath befallen him." When they told the Governor, he rose and mounted and, taking with him labourers, with spades and baskets, went on my track, with many people behind him; and I ran on before them, howling and casting dust on my head and beating my face, followed by my mistress and her children keening for the dead. But I got ahead of them and entered the garden before them, and when my master saw me in this state, I smiting my face and saying, "Well-away! my mistress! Alas! Alas! Alas! who is left to take pity on me, now that my mistress is gone? Would I had been a sacrifice to her!", he stood aghast and his colour waxed yellow and he said to me, "What aileth thee O Kafur! What *is* the mat-ter?" "O my lord," I replied, "when thou sentest me to the house, I found that the saloon-wall had given way and had fallen like a layer upon my mistress and her children!" "And did not thy mistress escape?" "No, by Allah, O my master; not one of them was saved; the first to die was my mistress, thine elder daughter!" "And did not my younger daughter escape?"; "No, she did not!" "And what became of the mare-mule I use to ride, is she safe?" "No, by Allah, O my master, the house-walls and the stable-walls buried every living thing that was within doors, even to the sheep and geese and poultry, so that they all became a heap of flesh and the dogs and cats are eating them and not one of them is left alive." "And hath not thy master, my elder son, escaped?" "No, by Allah! not one of them was saved, and now there is naught left of house or household, nor even a sign of them: and, as for the sheep and geese and hens, the cats and dogs have devoured them." When my master heard this the light became night before his sight; his wits were dazed and he so lost command of his senses that he could not stand firm on his feet: he was as one struck with a sudden palsy and his back was like to break. Then he rent his raiment and plucked out his beard and, casting his turband from off his head, buffetted his face till the blood ran down and he cried aloud, "Alas, my children! Alas, my wife! Alas, my calamity! To whom ever befel that which hath befallen me?" The merchants, his friends, also cried aloud at his crying and wept for his weeping and tore their clothes, being moved to pity of his case; and so my master went out of the garden, smiting his face with such violence that from excess of pain he staggered like one drunken with wine. As he and the merchants came forth from the garden-gate, behold, they saw a great cloud of dust and heard a loud noise of crying and lamentation; so they looked and lo! it was the Governor with his attendants and the townsfolk, a world of people, who had come out to look on, and my master's family following them, all screaming and crying aloud and weeping exceeding sore weeping. The first to address my owner were his wife and children; and when he saw them he was confounded and laughed[18] and said to them, "How is it with all of you and what befel you in the house and what hath come to pass to you?" When they saw him they exclaimed, "Praise be to Allah for thy preservation!" and threw themselves upon him and his children hung about him crying, "Alack, our father! Thanks to Allah for thy safety, O our father!" And his wife said to him, "Art thou indeed well? Laud to Allah who hath shown us thy face in safety!" And indeed she was confounded and her reason fled when she saw him, and she asked, "O, my lord, how didst thou escape, thou and thy friends the merchants?"; and he answered her, "And how fared it with thee in the house?" Quoth they, "We were all well, whole and healthy, nor hath aught of evil befallen us in the house, save that thy slave Kafur came to us, bareheaded with torn garments and howling:—Alas, the master! Alas, the master! So we asked him:—What tidings, O Kafur? and he answered:—A wall of the garden hath fallen on my master and his friends the merchants, and they are all crushed and dead!" "By Allah," said my master, "he came to me but now howling:—Alas, my mistress! Alas, the children of the mistress!, and said:— My mistress and her children are all dead, every one of them!" Then he looked round and seeing me with my turband rent in rags round my neck, howling and weeping with exceeding weeping and throwing dust upon my head, he cried out at me. So I came to him and he said, "Woe to thee, O ill-omened slave! O whoreson knave! O thou damned breed! What mischief thou hast wrought? By Allah! I will flog thy skin from thy flesh and cut thy flesh from thy bones!" I rejoined, "By Allah, thou canst do nothing of the kind with me, O my lord, for thou boughtest me with my blemish; and there are honest men to bear witness against thee that thou didst so accepting the condition, and that thou knewest of my fault which is to tell one lie every year. Now this is only a half-lie, but by the end of the year I will tell the other half, then will the lie stand whole and complete." "O dog, son of a dog!", cried my master, "O most accursed of slaves, is this all of it but a half-lie? Verily if it be a half-lie 'tis a whole calamity! Get thee from me, thou art free in the face of Allah!" "By Allah," rejoined I, "if thou free me, I will not free thee till my year is completed and I have told thee the half-lie which is left. When this is done, go down with me to the slave-market and sell me as thou boughtest me to whoso will buy me with my blemish; but thou shalt not manumit me, for I have no handicraft whereby to gain my living;[19] and this my demand is a matter of law which the doctors have laid down in the Chapter of Emancipation."[20] While we were at these words, up came the crowd of people, and the neighbours of the quarter, men, women and children, together with the Governor and his suite offering condolence. So my master and the other merchants went to him and informed him of the adventure, and how this was but a half-lie, at which all wondered, deeming it a whole lie and a big one. And they cursed me and reviled me, while I stood laughing and grinning at them, till at last I asked, "How shall my master slay me when he bought me with this my blemish?" Then my master returned home and found his house in ruins, and it was I who had laid waste the greater part of it,[21] having broken things which were worth much money, as also had done his wife, who said to him, " 'Twas Kafur who broke the vessels and chinaware." Thereupon his rage redoubled and he struck hand upon hand exclaiming, "By Allah! in my life never saw I a whoreson like this slave; and he saith this is but a half-lie! How, then, if he had told me a whole lie? He would ruin a city, aye or even two." Then in his fury he went to the Governor, and they gave me a neat thing in the bastinado-line and made me eat stick till I was lost to the world and a fainting-fit came on me; and, whilst I was yet senseless, they brought the barber who docked me and gelded me[22] and cauterised the wound. When I revived I found myself a clean eunuch with nothing left, and my master said to me, "Even as thou hast burned my heart for the things I held dearest, so have I burnt thy heart for that of thy members whereby thou settest most store!" Then he took me and sold me at a profit, for that I was become an eunuch. And I ceased not bringing trouble upon all, wherever I was sold, and was shifted from lord to lord and from notable to notable, being sold and being bought, till I entered the palace of the Commander of the Faithful. But now my spirit is broken and my tricks are gone from me, so—alas!—are my ballocks. When the two slaves heard his history, they laughed at him and chaffed him and said, "Truly thou art skite[23] and skite-son! Thou liedest an odious lie." Then quoth they to the third slave, "Tell us thy tale." "O sons of my uncle," quoth he, "all that ye have said is idle: I will tell you the cause of my losing my testicles, and indeed I deserved to lose even more, for I undid both my mistress and my master's eldest son and heir: but my story is a long one and this is not the time to tell it; for the dawn, O my cousins, draweth near and if morning come upon us with this chest still unburied, we shall get into sore disgrace and our lives will pay for it. So up with you and open the door and, when we get back to the palace, I will tell you my story and the cause of my losing my precious stones." Then he swarmed up and dropped down from the wall inside and opened the door, so they entered and, setting down the lantern, dug between four tombs a hole as long as the chest and of the same breadth. Kafur plied the spade and Sawab removed the earth by baskets-full till they reached the depth of the stature of a man;[24] then they laid the chest in the hole and threw back the earth over it: then they went forth and shutting the door disappeared from Ghanim's eyes. When all was quiet and he felt sure that he was left alone in the place, his thought was busied about what the chest contained and he said to himself, "Would that I knew the contents of that box!" However, he waited till day broke, when morning shone and showed her sheen: whereupon he came down from the date-tree and scooped away the earth with his hands, till the box was laid bare and disengaged from the ground. Then he took a large stone and hammered at the lock till he broke it and, opening the lid, beheld a young lady, a model of beauty and loveliness, clad in the richest of garments and jewels of gold and such necklaces of precious stones that, were the Sultan's country evened with them, it would not pay their price. She had been drugged with Bhang, but her bosom, rising and falling, showed that her breath had not departed. When Ghamin saw her, he knew that some one had played her false and hocussed her; so he pulled her out of the chest and laid her on the ground with her face upwards. As soon as she smelt the breeze and the air entered her nostrils, mouth and lungs, she sneezed and choked and coughed; when there fell from out her throat a pill of Cretan Bhang, had an elephant smelt it he would have slept from night to night. Then she opened her eyes and glancing around said, in sweet voice and gracious words, "Woe to thee O wind! there is naught in thee to satisfy the thirsty, nor aught to gratify one whose thirst is satisfied! Where is Zahr al-Bostan?" But no one answered her, so she turned her and cried out, "Ho Sabihah! Shajarat al-Durr! Nur al-Huda! Najmat al-Subh! be ye awake? Shahwah, Nuzhah, Halwa, Zarifah, out on you, speak!"[25] But no one answered; so she looked all around and said, "Woe's me! have they entombed me in the tombs? O Thou who knowest what man's thought enwombs and who givest compensation on the Day of Doom, who can have brought me from amid hanging screens and curtains veiling the Harim-rooms and set me down between four tombs?" All this while Ghanim was standing by: then he said to her, "O my lady, here are neither screened rooms nor palace-Harims nor yet tombs; only the slave henceforth devoted to thy love, Ghanim bin Ayyub, sent to thee by the Omniscient One above, that all thy troubles He may remove and win for thee every wish that doth behove!" Then he held his peace. She was reassured by his words and cried, "I testify that there is no god but *the* God, and I testify that Mohammed is the Apostle of God!"; then she turned to Ghanim and, placing her hands before her face, said to him in the sweetest speech, "O blessed youth, who brought me hither? See, I am now come to myself." "O my lady," he replied, "three slave-eunuchs came here bearing this chest;" and related to her the whole of what had befallen him, and how evening having closed upon him had proved the cause of her preservation, otherwise she had died smothered.[26] Then he asked her who she was and what was her story, and she answered, "O youth, thanks be to Allah who hath cast me into the hands of the like of thee! But now rise and put me back into the box; then fare forth upon the road and hire the first camel-driver or muleteer thou findest to carry it to thy house. When I am there, all will be well and I will tell thee my tale and acquaint thee with my adventures, and great shall be thy gain by means of me." At this he rejoiced and went outside the tomb. The day was now dazzling bright and the firmament shone with light and the folk had begun to circulate; so he hired a man with a mule and, bringing him to the tomb, lifted the chest wherein he had put the damsel and set it on the mule. Her love now engrossed his heart and he fared homeward with her rejoicing, for that she was a girl worth ten thousand gold pieces and her raiment and ornaments would fetch a mint of money. When Ghanim son of Ayyub arrived with the chest at his house, he opened it and took out the young lady, who looked about her and, seeing that the place was handsome, spread with carpets and dight with cheerful colours and other deckings; and noting the stuffs up-piled and packed bales and other else than that, knew that he was a substantial merchant and a man of much money. Thereupon she uncovered her face and looked at him, and lo! he was a fair youth; so when she saw him she loved him and said, "O my lord, bring us something to eat." "On my head and mine eyes!" replied he; and, going down to the bazar, bought a roasted lamb and a dish of sweetmeats and with these dry fruits and wax candles, besides wine and whatsoever was required of drinking materials, not forgetting perfumes. With all this gear he returned to the house; and when the damsel saw him she laughed and kissed him and clasped his neck. Then she began caressing him, which made his love wax hotter till it got the mastery of his heart. They ate and drank and each had conceived the fondest affection; for indeed the two were one in age and one in loveliness; and when night came on Ghamin bin Ayyub, the Distraught, the Thrall o' Love, rose and lit the wax candles and lamps till the place blazed with light;[27] after which he produced the wine-service and spread the table. Then both sat down again, he and she, and he kept filling and giving her to drink, and she kept filling and giving him to drink, and they played and toyed and laughed and recited verses; whilst their joy increased and they clove in closer love each to each (glory be to the Uniter of Hearts!). They ceased not to carouse after this fashion till near upon dawn when drowsiness overcame them and they slept where they were, apart each from other, till the morning.[28] Then Ghanim arose and going to the market, bought all they required of meat and vegetables and wine and what not, and brought them to the house; whereupon both sat down to eat and ate their sufficiency, when he set on wine. They drank and each played with each, till their cheeks flushed red and their eyes took a darker hue and Ghanim's soul longed to kiss the girl and to lie with her and he said, "O my lady, grant me one kiss of that dear mouth: perchance 't will quench the fire of my heart." "O Ghanim," replied she, "wait till I am drunk and dead to the world; then steal a kiss of me, secretly and on such wise that I may not know thou hast kissed me." Then she rose and taking off her upper dress sat in a thin shift of fine linen and a silken head-kerchief.[29] At this passion inflamed Ghanim and he said to her, "O my lady, wilt thou not vouchsafe me what I asked of thee?" "By Allah," she replied, "that may not be thine, for there is written upon my trouser-string[30] a hard word!" Thereupon Ghanim's heart sank and desire grew on him as its object offered difficulties and his affection increased and love-fires rose hotter in his heart, while she refused herself to him saying, "Thou canst not possess me." They ceased not to make love and enjoy their wine and wassail, whilst Ghanim was drowned in the sea of love and longing; but she redoubled in coyness and cruelty till the night brought on the darkness and let fall on them the skirts of sleep. Thereupon Ghanim rose and lit the lamps and wax candles, and refreshed the room and removed the table; then he took her feet and kissed them and, finding them like fresh cream, pressed his face[31] on them and said to her, "O my lady, take pity on one thy love hath ta'en and thine eyes hath slain; for indeed I were heart-whole but for thy bane!" And he wept somewhat. "O my lord, and light of my eyes," quoth she, "by Allah, I love thee in very sooth

and I trust to thy truth, but I know that I may not be thine."
"And what is the obstacle?" asked he; when she answered,
"To-night I will tell thee my tale, that thou mayst accept
my excuse." Then she threw herself upon him and winding her arms like a necklace about his neck, kissed him and
caressed him and promised him her favours; and they
ceased not playing and laughing till love gat the firmest
hold upon both their hearts. And so it continued a whole
month, both passing the night on a single carpet-bed, but
whenever he would enjoy her, she put him off; whilst mutual love increased upon them and each could hardly abstain from other. One night, as he lay by her side, and both
were warm with wine, Ghanim passed his hand over her
breasts and stroked them; then he slipped it down to her
waist as far as her navel. She awoke and, sitting up, put
her hand to her trousers and finding them fast tied, once
more fell asleep. Presently, he again felt her and sliding his
hand down to her trouser-string, began pulling at it,
whereupon she awoke and sat upright. Ghanim also sat up
by her side and she asked him, "What dost thou want?" "I
want to lie with thee," he answered, "and that we may deal
openly and frankly with each other." Quoth she, "I must
now declare to thee my case, that thou mayst know my
quality; then will my secret be disclosed to thee and my
excuse become manifest to thee." Quoth he, "So be it!"
Thereat she opened the skirt of her shift and, taking up
her trouser-string, said to him, "O my lord, read what is
worked on the flat of this string:" so he took it in hand, and
saw these words broidered on it in gold, "I AM THINE,
AND THOU ART MINE, O COUSIN OF THE APOS-
TLE!"[32] When he read this, he withdrew his hand and said
to her, "Tell me who thou art!" "So be it," answered she;
"know that I am one of the concubines of the Commander
of the Faithful, and my name is Kut al-Kulub—the Food of
Hearts. I was brought up in his palace and, when I grew to
woman's estate, he looked on me and, noting what share of
beauty and loveliness the Creator had given me, loved me

with exceeding love, and assigned me a separate apartment, and gave me ten slave-girls to wait on me and all
these ornaments thou seest me wearing. On a certain day
he set out for one of his provinces, and the Lady Zubaydah
came to one of the slave-girls in my service and said to
her:—I have something to require of thee. What is it, O my
lady? asked she and the Caliph's wife answered:—When
thy mistress Kut al-Kulub is asleep, put this piece of Bhang
into her nostrils and drop it into her drink; and thou shalt
have of me as much money as will satisfy thee. With love
and gladness; replied the girl and took the Bhang from her,
being a glad woman because of the money and because
aforetime she had been one of Zubaydah's slaves. So she
put the Bhang in my drink, and when it was night I drank,
and the drug had no sooner settled in my stomach than I
fell to the ground, my head touching my feet, and knew
naught of my life but that I was in another world. When
her device succeeded, she bade put me in this chest, and
secretly brought in the slaves and the doorkeepers and
bribed them; and, on the night when thou wast perched
upon the date-tree, she sent the blacks to do with me as
thou sawest. So my delivery was at thy hands, and thou
broughtest me to this house and hast entreated me honourably and with thy kindest. This is my story, and I wot
not what is become of the Caliph during my absence.
Know then my condition and divulge not my case." When
Ghanim heard her words and knew that she was a concubine of the Caliph, he drew back, for awe of the Caliphate
beset him, and sat apart from her in one of the corners
of the place, blaming himself and brooding over his affair
and patiencing his heart bewildered for love of one he
could not possess. Then he wept for excess of longing, and
plained him of Fortune and her injuries, and the world and
its enmities (and praise be to Him who causeth generous
hearts to be troubled with love and the beloved, and who
endoweth not the minds of the mean and miserly with so
much of it as eveneth a grain-weight!). So he began repeating:—

The lover's heart for his beloved must meet
Sad pain, and from her charms bear sore defeat:
What is Love's taste? They asked and answered I,
Sweet is the taste but ah! 'tis bitter-sweet.

Thereupon Kut al-Kulub arose and took him to her bosom
and kissed him; for the love of him was firm fixed in her
heart, so that she disclosed to him her secret and all the
affection she felt; and, throwing her arms round Ghanim's
neck like a collar of pearls, kissed him again and yet again.
But he held off from her in awe of the Caliph. Then they
talked together a long while (and indeed both were drowned
in the sea of their mutual love); and, as the day broke, Ghanim rose and donned his clothes and going to the bazar,
as was his wont, took what the occasion required and returned home. He found her weeping; but when she saw
him she checked herself and, smiling through her tears,
said, "Thou hast desolated me, O beloved of my heart. By
Allah, this hour of absence hath been to me like a year![33] I
have explained to thee my condition in the excess of my
eager love for thee; so come now near me, and forget the
past and have thy will of me." But he interrupted her crying, "I seek refuge with Allah! This thing may never be.
How shall the dog sit in the lion's stead? What is the lord's
is unlawful to the slave!" So he withdrew from her, and sat
down on a corner of the mat. Her passion for him increased with his forbearance; so she seated herself by his
side and caroused and played with him, till the two were
flushed with wine, and she was mad for her own dishonour.
Then she sang these verses:—

The lover's heart is like to break in twain:
Till when these coy denials ah! till when?
O thou who fliest me sans fault of mine,
Gazelles are wont at times prove tame to men:
Absence, aversion, distance and disdain,
How shall young lover all these ills sustain?

Thereupon Ghanim wept and she wept at his weeping, and they ceased not drinking till nightfall, when he rose and spread two beds, each in its place. "For whom is this second bed?" asked she, and he answered her, "One is for me and the other is for thee: from this night forth we must not sleep save thus, for that which is the lord's is unlawful to the thrall." "O my master!" cried she, "let us have done with this, for all things come to pass by Fate and Fortune." But he refused, and the fire was lighted in her heart and, as her longing waxed fiercer, she clung to him and cried, "By Allah, we will not sleep save side by side!" "Allah forefend!" he replied and prevailed against her and lay apart till the morning, when love and longing redoubled on her and distraction and eager thirst of passion. They abode after this fashion three full-months, which were long and lonesome indeed, and every time she made advances to him, he would refuse himself and say, "Whatever belongeth to the master is unlawful to the man." They abode in this state a long time, and fear kept Ghanim aloof from her. So far concerning these two; but as regards the Lady Zubaydah, when, in the Caliph's absence she had done this deed by Kut al-Kulub she became perplexed, saying to herself, "What shall I tell my cousin when he comes back and asks for her? What possible answer can I make to him?" Then she called an old woman, who was about her and discovered her secret to her saying, "How shall I act seeing that Kut al-Kulub died by such untimely death?" "O my lady," quoth the old crone, "the time of the Caliph's return is near; so do thou send for a carpenter and bid him make thee a figure of wood in the form of a corpse. We will dig a grave for it midmost the palace and there bury it: then do thou build an oratory over it and set therein lighted candles and lamps, and order each and every in the palace to be clad in black.[34] Furthermore command thy handmaids and eunuchs as soon as they know of the Caliph's returning from his journey, to spread straw over the vestibule-floors and, when the Commander of the Faithful enters and asks what is the matter, let them say:—Kut al-Kulub is dead, and may Allah abundantly compensate thee for the loss of her!;[35] and, for the high esteem in which she was held of our mistress, she hath buried her in her own palace. When he hears this he will weep and it shall be grievous to him; then will he cause perlections of the Koran to be made for her and he will watch by night at her tomb. Should he say to himself:—Verily Zubaydah, the daughter of my uncle, hath compassed in her jealousy the death of Kut al-Kulub; or, if love-longing overcome him and he bid her be taken out of her tomb, fear thou not; for when they dig down and come to the image in human shape he will see it shrouded in costly grave-clothes; and, if he wish to take off the winding-sheet that he may look upon her, do thou forbid him or let some other forbid him, saying:— The sight of her nakedness is unlawful. The fear of the world to come will restrain him and he will believe that she is dead and will restore the figure to its place and thank thee for thy doings; and thus thou shalt escape, please Almighty Allah, from this slough of despond." When the Lady Zubaydah heard her words, she commended the counsel and gave her a dress of honour and a large sum of money, ordering her to do all she had said. So the old woman set about the business forthright and bade the carpenter make her the aforesaid image; and, as soon as it was finished, she brought it to the Lady Zubaydah, who shrouded it and buried it and built a sepulchre over it, wherein they lighted candles and lamps, and laid down carpets about the tomb. Moreover she put on black and she spread abroad in the Harim that Kut al-Kulub was dead. After a time the Caliph returned from his journey and went up to the palace, thinking only of Kut al-Kulub. He saw all the pages and eunuchs and handmaids habited in black, at which his heart fluttered with extreme fear; and, when he went in to the Lady Zubaydah, he found her also garbed in black. So he asked the cause of this and they gave him tidings of the death of Kut al-Kulub, whereon he fell a-swooning. As soon as he came to himself, he asked for her tomb, and the Lady Zubaydah said to him, "Know, O Prince of the Faithful, that for especial honour I have buried her in my own palace." Then he repaired in his travelling-garb[36] to the tomb that he might wail over her, and found the carpets spread and the candles and lamps lighted. When he saw this, he thanked Zubaydah for her good deed and abode perplexed, halting between belief and unbelief till at last suspicion overcame him and he gave order to open the grave and take out the body. When he saw the shroud and would have removed it to look upon her, the fear of Allah Almighty restrained him, and the old woman (taking advantage of the delay) said, "Restore her to her place." Then he sent at once for Fakirs and Koran-readers, and caused perlections to be made over her tomb and sat by the side of the grave, weeping till he fainted; and he continued to frequent the tomb and sit there for a whole month, at the end of which time it so happened one day that he entered the Serraglio, after dismissing the Emirs and Wazirs, and lay down and slept awhile; and there sat at his head a slave-girl fanning him, and at his feet a second rubbing and shampooing them. Presently he awoke and, opening his eyes, shut them again and heard the hand-maid at his head saying to her who was at his feet, "A nice business this, O Khayzaran!" and the other answered her "Well, O Kazib al-Ban?"[37] "Verily," said the first, "our lord knoweth naught of what hath happened and sitteth and watching by a tomb wherein is only a log of wood carved by the carpenter's art." "And Kut al-Kulub," quoth the other, "what hath befallen her?" She replied, "Know that the Lady Zubaydah sent a pellet of Bhang by one of the slave-women who was bribed to drug her; and when sleep overpowered her she let put her in a chest, and ordered Sawab and Kafur and Bukhayt to throw her amongst the tombs." "What dost thou say, O Kazib al-Ban?" asked Khayzaran, "is not the Lady Kut al-Kulub dead?" "Nay, by Allah!" she answered "and long may her youth be saved from death! but I have heard the Lady Zubaydah say that she is in the house of a young merchant named Ghanim bin Ayyub of Damascus, hight the Distraught, the Thrall o' Love; and she hath been with him these four months, whilst our lord is weeping and watching by night at a tomb wherein is no corpse." They kept on talking this sort of talk, and the Caliph gave ear to their words; and, by the time they had ceased speaking, he knew right well that the tomb was a feint and a fraud, and that Kut al-Kulub had been in Ghanim's house for four months. Whereupon he was angered with exceeding anger and rising up, he summoned the Emirs of his state; and his Wazir Ja'afar the Barmaki came also and kissed the ground between his hands. The Caliph said to him in fury: "Go down, O Ja'afar, with a party of armed men and ask for the house of Ghanim son of Ayyub: fall upon it and spoil it and bring him to me with my slave-girl, Kut al-Kulub, for there is no help but that I punish him!" "To hear is to obey," said Ja'afar; and setting out with the Governor and the guards and a world of people, repaired to Ghanim's house. Now about that time the youth happened to have brought back a pot of dressed meat and was about to put forth his hand to eat of it, he and Kut al-Kulub, when the lady, happening to look out saw calamity surrounding the house on every side; for the Wazir and the Governor, the night-guard and the Mamelukes with swords drawn had girt it as the white of the eye girdeth the black. At this she knew that tidings of her had reached the Caliph, her lord; and she made sure of ruin, and her colour paled and her fair features changed and her favour faded. Then she turned to Ghanim and said to him, "O my love? fly for thy life!" "What shall I do," asked he, "and whither shall I go, seeing that my money and means of maintenance are all in this house?"; and she answered, "Delay not lest thou be slain and lose life as well as wealth." "O my loved one and light of mine eyes!" he cried, "How shall I do to get away when they have surrounded the house?" Quoth she, "Fear not;" and, stripping off his fine clothes, dressed him in ragged old garments, after which she took the pot and, putting in it bits of broken bread and a saucer of meat,[38] placed the whole in a basket and setting it upon his head said, "Go out in this guise and fear not for me who wotteth right well what thing is in my hand for the Caliph."[39] So he went out amongst them, bearing the basket with its contents, and the Protector vouch-safed him His protection and he escaped the snares and perils that beset him, by the blessing of his good conscience and pure conduct. Meanwhile Ja'afar dismounted and entering the house, saw Kut al-Kulub who had dressed and decked herself in splendid raiments and ornaments and filled a chest with gold and jewellery and precious stones and rarities and what else was light to bear and of value rare. When she saw Ja'afar come in, she rose and, kissing the ground before him, said, "O my lord, the Reed hath written of old the rede which Allah decreed!"[40] "By Allah, O my lady," answered Ja'afar, "he gave me an order to seize Ghanim son of Ayyub;" and she rejoined, "O my lord, he made ready his goods and set out therewith for Damascus and I know nothing more of him; but I desire thee to take charge of this chest and deliver it to me in the Harim of the Prince of the Faithful." "Hearing and obedience," said Ja'afar, and bade his men bear it away to the head-quarters of the Caliphate together with Kut al-Kulub, commanding them to entreat her with honour as one in high esteem. They did his bidding after they had wrecked and plundered Ghanim's house. Then Ja'afar went in to the Caliph and told him all that had happened, and he ordered Kut al-Kulub to be lodged in a dark chamber and appointed an old woman to serve her, feeling convinced that Ghanim had debauched her and slept with her. Then he wrote a mandate to the Emir Mohammed bin Sulayman al-Zayni, his viceroy in Damascus, to this effect:—"The instant thou shalt receive this our letter, seize upon Ghanim bin Ayyub and send him to us." When the missive came to the viceroy, he kissed it and laid it on his head; then he let proclaim in the bazars, "Whoso is desirous to plunder, away with him

to the house of Ghanim son of Ayyub."[41] So they flocked
hither, when they found that Ghanim's mother and sister
had built him a tomb[42] in the midst of the house and sat by
it weeping for him; whereupon they seized the two without telling them the cause and, after spoiling the house,
carried them before the viceroy. He questioned them concerning Ghanim and both replied, "For a year or more we
have had no news of him." So they restored them to their
place. Thus far concerning them; but as regards Ghanim,
when he saw his wealth spoiled and his ruin utterest he
wept over himself till his heart well-nigh brake. Then he
fared on at random till the last of the day, and hunger grew
hard on him and walking wearied him. So coming to a village he entered a mosque[43] where he sat down upon a mat
and propped his back against the wall; but presently he
sank to the ground in his extremity of famine and fatigue. There he lay till dawn, his heart fluttering for want
of food; and, owing to his sweating, the lice[44] coursed over
his skin; his breath waxed fetid and his whole condition
was changed. When the villagers came to pray the dawn-
prayer, they found him prostrate, ailing, hunger-lean, yet
showing evident signs of former affluence. As soon as
prayers were over, they drew near him; and, understanding
that he was starved with hunger and cold, they gave him an
old robe with ragged sleeves and said to him, "O stranger,
whence art thou and what sickness is upon thee?" He
opened his eyes and wept but returned no answer; whereupon one of them, who saw that he was starving, brought
him a saucer of honey and two barley scones. He ate a little and they sat with him till sun-rise, when they went to
their work. He abode with them in this state for a month,
whilst sickness and weakliness grew upon him; and they
wept for him and, pitying his condition, took counsel with
one another upon his case and agreed to forward him to
the hospital in Baghdad.[45] Meanwhile behold, two beggar-
women, who were none other than Ghanim's mother and
sister,[46] came into the mosque and, when he saw them, he
gave them the bread that was at his head; and they slept by

his side that night but he knew them not. Next day the villagers brought a camel and said to the cameleer, "Set this sick man on thy beast and carry him to Baghdad and put him down at the Spital-door; so haply he may be medicined and be healed and thou shalt have thy hire."[47] "To hear is to comply," said the man. So they brought Ghanim, who was asleep, out of the mosque and set him, mat and all, on the camel; and his mother and sister came out among the crowd to gaze upon him, but they knew him not. However, after looking at him and considering him carefully they said, "Of a truth he favours our Ghanim, poor boy!; can this sick man be he?" Presently, he woke and finding himself bound with ropes on a camel's back, he began to weep and complain,[48] and the village-people saw his mother and sister weeping over him, albeit they knew him not. Then they fared forth for Baghdad, but the camelman forewent them and, setting Ghanim down at the Spital-gate, went away with his beast. The sick man lay there till dawn and, when the folk began to go about the streets, they saw him and stood gazing at him, for he had become as thin as a toothpick, till the Syndic of the bazar came up and drove them away from him, saying, "I will gain Paradise through this poor creature; for if they take him into the Hospital, they will kill him in a single day."[49] Then he made his young men carry him to his house, where they spread him a new bed with a new pillow,[50] and he said to his wife, "Tend him carefully;" and she replied, "Good! on my head be it!" Thereupon she tucked up her sleeves and warming some water, washed his hands, feet and body; after which she clothed him in a robe belonging to one of her slavegirls and made him drink a cup of wine and sprinkled rosewater over him. So he revived and complained, and the thought of his beloved Kut al-Kulub made his grief redouble. Thus far concerning him; but as regards Kut al-Kulub, when the Caliph was angered against her, he ordered her to a dark chamber where she abode eighty days, at the end of which the Caliph, happening to pass on a certain day the place where she was, heard her repeating poetry, and after she ceased reciting her verse, saying, "O my darling, O my Ghanim! how great is thy goodness and how chaste is thy nature! thou didst well by one who did ill by thee and thou guardedst his honour who garred thine become dishonour, and his Harim thou didst protect who to enslave thee and thine did elect! But thou shalt surely stand, thou and the Commander of the Faithful, before the Just Judge, and thou shalt be justified of him on the Day when the Lord (to whom be honour and glory!) shall be Kazi and the Angels of Heaven shall be witnesses!" When the Caliph heard her complaint, he knew that she had been wronged and, returning to the palace, sent Masrur the Eunuch for her. She came before him with bowed head and eyes tearful and heart sorrowful; and he said to her, "O Kut al-Kulub, I find thou accusest me of tyranny and oppression, and thou avouchest that I have done ill by one who did well by me. Who is this who hath guarded my honour while I garred his become dishonour? Who protected my Harim and whose Harim I wrecked?" "He is Ghanim son of Ayyub," replied she, "for he never approached me in wantonness or with lewd intent, I swear by thy munificence, O Commander of the Faithful!" Then said the Caliph, "There is no Majesty and there is no Might save in Allah! Ask what thou wilt of me, O Kut al-Kulub." "O Prince of the Faithful!", answered she, "I require of thee only my beloved Ghanim son of Ayyub." He did as she desired, whereupon she said, "O Lord of the Moslems, if I bring him to thy presence, wilt thou bestow me on him?"; and he replied, "If he come into my presence, I will give thee to him as the gift of the generous who revoketh not his largesse." "O Prince of True Believers," quoth she, "suffer me to go and seek him; haply Allah may unite me with him;" and quoth he, "Do even as thou wilt." So she rejoiced and, taking with her a thousand dinars in gold, went out and visited the elders of the various faiths and gave alms in Ghanim's name.[51] Next day she walked to the merchants' bazar and disclosed her object to the Syndic and gave him money, saying, "Bestow this in charity to the stranger!" On the following Friday she fared to the bazar (with other thousand dinars) and, entering the goldsmiths' and jewellers' market-street, called the Chief and presented to him a thousand dinars with these words, "Bestow this in charity to the stranger!" The Chief looked at her (and he was the Syndic who had taken in Ghanim) and said, "O my lady, wilt thou come to my house and look upon a youth, a stranger I have there and see how goodly and graceful he is?" Now the stranger was Ghanim, son of Ayyub, but the Chief had no knowledge of him and thought him to be some wandering pauper, some debtor whose wealth had been taken from him, or some lover parted from his beloved. When she heard his words her heart fluttered and her vitals[52] yearned, and she said to him, "Send with me one who shall guide me to thy house." So he sent a little lad who brought her to the house wherein was the head man's stranger-guest and she thanked him for this. When she reached the house, she went in and saluted the Syndic's wife, who rose and kissed the ground between her hands, for she knew her. Then quoth Kut al-Kulub, "Where is the sick man who is with thee?" She wept and replied, "Here is he, O my lady; by Allah, he is come of good folk and he beareth the signs of gentle breeding: you see him lying on yonder bed." So she turned and looked at him; and she saw something like him, but he was worn and wasted till he had become lean as a toothpick, so his identity was doubtful to her and she could not be certain that it was he. Yet pity for him possessed her and she wept saying, "Verily the stranger is unhappy, even though he be a prince in his own land!"; and his case was grievous to her and her heart ached for him, yet she knew him not to be Ghanim. Then she furnished him with wine and medicines and she sat awhile by his head, after which she mounted and returned to her palace and continued to visit every bazar in quest of her lover. Meanwhile Ghanim's mother and sister Fitnah arrived at Baghdad and met the Syndic, who carried them to Kut al-Kulub and said to her, "O Princess of Beneficent ladies, there came to our city this day a woman and her daughter, who are fair of favour and signs of good breeding and dignity are apparent in them, though they be dressed in hair-cloth and have each one a wallet hanging to her neck; and their eyes are tearful and their hearts are sorrowful. So I have brought them to thee that thou mayst give them refuge, and rescue them from beggary, for they are not of asker-folk and, if it please Allah, we shall enter Paradise through them." "By Allah, O my master," cried she, "thou makest me long to see them! Where are they?", adding, "Here with them to me!" So he bade the eunuch bring them in; and, when she looked on them and saw that they were both of distinguished beauty, she wept for them and said, "By Allah, these are people of condition and show plain signs of former opulence." "O my lady," said the Syndic's wife, "we love the poor and the destitute, more especially as reward in Heaven will recompense our love; and, as for these persons, haply the oppressor hath dealt hardly with them and hath plundered their property and harried their houses." Then Ghanim's mother and sister wept with sore weeping, remembering their former prosperity and contrasting it with their present poverty and miserable condition; and their thoughts dwelt upon son and brother, whilst Kut al-Kulub wept for their weeping; and they said, "We beseech Allah to reunite us with him whom we desire, and he is none other but my son named Ghanim bin Ayyub!" When Kut al-Kulub heard this, she knew them to be the mother and sister of her lover and wept till a swoon came over her. When she revived she turned to them and said, "Have no fear and sorrow not, for this day is the first of your prosperity and the last of your adversity!" When Kut al-Kulub had consoled them she bade the Syndic lead them to his house and let his wife carry them to the Hammam and dress them in handsome clothes and take care of them and honour them with all honour; and she gave him a sufficient sum of money. Next day, she mounted and, riding to his house, went in to his wife who rose up and kissed her hands and thanked her for her kindness. There she saw Ghanim's mother and sister whom the Syndic's wife had taken to the Hammam and clothed afresh, so that the traces of their former condition became manifest upon them. She sat talking with them awhile, after which she asked the wife about the sick youth who was in her house and she replied, "He is in the same state." Then said Kut al-Kulub, "Come, let us go and visit him." So she arose, she and the Chief's wife and Ghanim's mother and sister, and went in to the room where he lay and sat down near him. Presently Ghanim bin Ayyub, the Distraught, the Thrall o' Love, heard them mention the name of Kut al-Kulub; whereupon life returned to him, emaciated and withered as he was, and he raised his head from the pillow and cried aloud, "O Kut al-Kulub!" She looked at him and made certain it was he and shrieked rather than said, "Yes, O my beloved!" "Draw near to me;" said he, and she replied, "Surely thou art Ghanim bin Ayyub?"; and he rejoined "I am indeed!" Hereupon a swoon came upon her; and, as soon as Ghanim's mother and his sister Fitnah heard these words, both cried out "O our joy!" and fainted clean away. When they all recovered, Kut al-Kulub exclaimed, "Praise be to Allah who hath brought us together again and who hath reunited thee with thy mother and thy sister!" And she related to him all that had befallen her with the Caliph and said, "I have made known the truth to the Commander of the Faithful, who believed my words and was pleased with thee; and now he desireth to see thee," adding, "He hath given me to thee." Thereat he rejoiced with extreme joy, when she said, "Quit not this place till I come back" and, rising forthwith, betook herself to her palace. There she opened the chest which she had brought from Ghanim's house and, taking out some of the dinars, gave them to the Syndic saying, "Buy with this money for each of them four complete suits of the finest stuffs and twenty kerchiefs, and else beside of whatsoever they require;" after which she carried all three to the baths and had them washed and bathed and made ready for them consommés, and galangale-water and cider against their coming out. When they left the Hammam, they put on the new clothes, and she abode with them three days feeding them with chicken meats and bouillis, and making them drink sherbet of sugar candy. After three days their spirits returned; and she carried them again to the baths, and when they came out and had changed their raiment, she led them back to the Syndic's house and left them there, whilst she returned to the palace and craved permission to see the Caliph. When he ordered her to come in, she entered and, kissing the ground between his hands, told him the whole story and how her lord, Ghanim bin Ayyub, yclept the Distraught, the Thrall o' Love, and his mother and sister were now in Baghdad. When the Caliph heard this, he turned to the eunuchs and said, "Here with Ghanim to me." So Ja'afar went to fetch him; but Kut al-Kulub forewent him and told Ghanim, "The Caliph hath sent to fetch thee before him," and charged him to show readiness of tongue and firmness of heart and sweetness of speech. Then she robed him in a sumptuous dress and gave him dinars in plenty, saying, "Be lavish of largesse to the Caliph's household as thou goest in to him." Presently Ja'afar, mounted on his Nubian mule, came to fetch him; and Ghanim advanced to welcome the Wazir and, wishing him long life, kissed the ground before him. Now the star of his good fortune had risen and shone brightly; and Ja'afar took him; and they ceased not faring together, he and the Minister, till they went in to the Commander of the Faithful. When he stood in the presence, he looked at the Wazirs and Emirs and Chamberlains, and Viceroys and Grandees and Captains, and then at the Caliph. Hereupon he sweetened his speech and his eloquence and, bowing his head to the ground, broke out in these extempore couplets:—

> May that Monarch's life span a mighty span,
> Whose lavish of largesse all lieges scan:
> None other but he shall be Kaysar hight,
> Lord of lordly hall and of haught Divan:
> Kings lay their gems on his threshold-dust

As they bow and salam to the mighty man;
And his glances foil them and all recoil,
Bowing beards aground and with faces wan:
Yet they gain the profit of royal grace,
The rank and station of high soldan.
Earth's plain is scant for thy world of men,
Camp there in Kaywan's[53] Empyrean!
May the King of Kings ever hold thee dear;
Be counsel thine and right steadfast plan,
Till thy justice spread o'er the wide-spread earth
And the near and the far be of equal worth.

When he ended his improvisation the Caliph was pleased by it and marvelled at the eloquence of his tongue and the sweetness of his speech, and said to him, "Draw near to me." So he drew near and quoth the King, "Tell me thy tale and declare to me thy case." So Ghanim sat down and related to him what had befallen him in Baghdad, of his sleeping in the tomb and of his opening the chest after the three slaves had departed, and informed him, in short, of everything that had happened to him from commencement to conclusion—none of which we will repeat for interest fails in twice told tales. The Caliph was convinced that he was a true man; so he invested him with a dress of honour, and placed him near himself in token of favour, and said to him, "Acquit me of the responsibility I have incurred."[54] And Ghanim so did, saying, "O our lord the Sultan, of a truth thy slave and all things his two hands own are his master's." The Caliph was pleased at this and gave orders to set apart a palace for him and assigned to him pay and allowances, rations and donations, which amounted to something immense. So he removed thither with sister and mother; after which the Caliph, hearing that his sister Fitnah was in beauty a very "fitnah,"[55] a mere seduction, demanded her in marriage of Ghanim who replied, "She is thy handmaid as I am thy slave." The Caliph thanked him and gave him an hundred thousand dinars, then summoned the witnesses and the Kazi, and on one and the same day they wrote out the two contracts of marriage between the Caliph and Fitnah and between Ghanim bin Ayyub and Kut al-Kulub; and the two marriages were consummated on one and the same night. When it was morning, the Caliph gave orders to record the history of what had befallen Ghanim from first to last and to deposit it in the royal muniment-rooms, that those who came after him might read it and marvel at the dealings of Destiny and put their trust in Him who created the night and the day. Thereupon quoth Shahryar to Shahrazad, "I desire that thou tell me somewhat about birds," and hearing this, Shahrazad began to relate

THE TALE OF THE BIRDS AND
BEASTS AND THE CARPENTER.

Quoth she, It hath reached me, O auspicious King, that in times of yore and in ages long gone before, a peacock abode with his wife on the sea-shore. Now the place was infested with lions and all manner wild beasts, withal it abounded in trees and streams. So cock and hen were wont to roost by night upon one of the trees, being in fear of the beasts, and went forth by day questing food. And they ceased not thus to do till their fear increased on them and they searched for some place wherein to dwell other than their old dwelling-place; and in the course of their search behold, they happened on an island abounding in streams and trees. So they alighted there and ate of its fruits and drank of its waters. But whilst they were thus engaged, lo! up came to them a duck in a state of extreme terror, and stayed not faring forwards till she reached the tree whereon were perched the two peafowl, when she seemed re-assured in mind. The peacock doubted not but that she had some rare story; so he asked her of her case and the cause of her concern, whereto she answered, "I am sick for sorrow, and my horror of the son of Adam:[1] so beware, and again I say beware of the sons of Adam!" Rejoined the pea-

cock, "Fear not now that thou hast won our protection."
Cried the duck, "Alhamdolillah! glory to God, who hath
done away my cark and care by means of you being near!
For indeed I come of friendship fain with you twain." And
when she had ended her speech the peacock's wife came
down to her and said, "Well come and welcome and fair
cheer! No harm shall hurt thee: how can son of Adam
come to us and we in this isle which lieth amiddlemost of
the sea? From the land he cannot reach us neither can he
come against us from the water. So be of good cheer and
tell us what hath betided thee from the child of Adam."
Answered the duck, "Know, then, O thou peahen, that of a
truth I have dwelt all my life in this island safely and
peacefully, nor have I seen any disquieting thing, till one
night, as I was asleep, I sighted in my dream the semblance
of a son of Adam, who talked with me and I with him.
Then I heard a voice say to me:—O thou duck, beware of
the son of Adam and be not imposed on by his words nor
by that he may suggest to thee; for he aboundeth in wiles
and guiles; so beware with all wariness of his perfidy, for
again I say, he is crafty and right cunning even as singeth of
him the poet:—

> He'll offer sweetmeats with his edgèd tongue,
> And fox thee with the foxy guile of fox.

And know thou that the son of Adam circumventeth the
fishes and draweth them forth of the seas; and he shooteth
the birds with a pellet of clay,[2] and trappeth the elephant
with his craft. None is safe from his mischief and neither
bird nor beast escapeth him; and on this wise have I told
thee what I have heard concerning the son of Adam. So I
awoke, fearful and trembling, and from that hour to this my
heart hath not known gladness, for dread of the son of
Adam, lest he surprise me unawares by his wile or trap me
in his snares. By the time the end of the day overtook me,
my strength was grown weak and my spunk failed me; so,
desiring to eat and drink, I went forth walking, troubled in

spirit and with a heart ill at ease. Now when I reached yonder mountain I saw a tawny lion-whelp at the door of a cave; and sighting me he joyed in me with great joy, for my colour pleased him and my gracious shape; so he cried out to me saying:—Draw nigh unto me. I went up to him and he asked me, What is thy name, and what is thy nature? Answered I, My name is Duck, and I am of the bird-kind; and I added, But thou, why tarriest thou in this place till this time? Answered the whelp, My father the lion hath for many a day warned me against the son of Adam, and it came to pass this night that I saw in my sleep the semblance of a son of Adam. And he went on to tell me the like of that I have told you. When I heard these words, I said to him, O lion, I take asylum with thee, that thou mayest kill the son of Adam and be steadfast in resolve to his slaughter; verily I fear him for myself with extreme fear and to my fright affright is added for that thou also dreadest the son of Adam, albeit thou art Sultan of savage beasts. Then I ceased not, O my sister, to bid the young lion beware of the son of Adam and urge him to slay him, till he rose of a sudden and at once from his stead and went out and he fared on, and I after him and I noted him lashing flanks with tail. We advanced in the same order till we came to a place where the roads forked and saw a cloud of dust arise which, presently clearing away, discovered below it a run-away naked ass, now galloping and running at speed and now rolling in the dust. When the lion saw the ass, he cried out to him, and he came up to him in all humility. Then said the lion:—Harkye, crack-brain brute! What is thy kind and what be the cause of thy coming hither? He replied, O son of the Sultan! I am by kind an ass—Asinus Caballus—and the cause of my coming to this place is that I am fleeing from the son of Adam. Asked the lion-whelp, Dost thou fear then that he will kill thee? Answered the ass, Not so, O son of the Sultan, but I dread lest he put a cheat on me and mount upon me; for he hath a thing called Pack-saddle, which he setteth on my back; also a thing called Girths which he bindeth about my belly; and a thing called Crupper which he putteth under my tail, and a thing called Bit which he placeth in my mouth: and he fashioneth me a goad[3] and goadeth me with it and maketh me run more than my strength. If I stumble he curseth me, and if I bray, he revileth me;[4] and at last when I grow old and can no longer run, he putteth on me a pannel of[5] wood and delivereth me to the water-carriers, who load my back with water from the river in skins and other vessels, such as jars, and I cease not to wone in misery and abasement and fatigue till I die, when they cast me on the rubbish-heaps to the dogs. So what grief can surpass this grief and what calamities can be greater than these calamities? Now when I heard, O peahen, the ass's words, my skin shuddered, and became as gooseflesh at the son of Adam; and I said to the lion-whelp, O my lord, the ass of a verity hath excuse and his words add terror to my terror. Then quoth the young lion to the ass, Whither goest thou? Quoth he, Before sunrise I espied the son of Adam afar off, and fled from him; and now I am minded to flee forth and run without ceasing for the greatness of my fear of him, so haply I may find me a place of shelter from the perfidious son of Adam. Whilst the ass was thus discoursing with the lion-whelp, seeking the while to take leave of us and go away, behold, appeared to us another cloud of dust, whereat the ass brayed and cried out and looked hard and let fly a loud fart.[6] After a while the dust lifted and discovered a black steed finely dight with a blaze on the forehead like a dirham round and bright;[7] handsomely marked about the hoof with white and with firm strong legs pleasing to sight and he neighed with affright. This horse ceased not running till he stood before the whelp, the son of the lion who, when he saw him, marvelled and made much of him and said, What is thy kind, O majestic wild beast, and wherefore fleest thou into this desert wide and vast? He replied, O lord of wild beasts, I am a steed of the horse-kind, and the cause of my running is that I am fleeing from the son of Adam. The lion-whelp wondered at the horse's speech and cried to him:—Speak not such words for it is shame to thee, seeing that thou art tall and stout. And how cometh it that thou fearest the son of Adam, thou, with thy bulk of body and thy swiftness of running, when I, for all my littleness of stature am resolved to encounter the son of Adam and, rushing on him, eat his flesh, that I may allay the affright of this poor duck and make her dwell in peace in her own place? But now thou hast come here and thou hast wrung my heart with thy talk and turned me back from what I had resolved to do, seeing that, for all thy bulk, the son of Adam hath mastered thee and hath feared neither thy height nor thy breadth, albeit, wert thou to kick him with one hoof thou wouldst kill him, nor could he prevail against thee, but thou wouldst make him drink the cup of death. The horse laughed when he heard the whelp's words and replied, Far, far is it from my power to overcome him, O Prince. Let not my length and my breadth nor yet my bulk delude thee with respect to the son of Adam; for that he, of the excess of his guile and his wiles, fashioneth me a thing called Hobble and applieth to my four legs a pair of ropes made of palm-fibres bound with felt, and gibbeteth me by the head to a high peg, so that I being tied up remain standing and can neither sit nor lie down. And when he is minded to ride me, he bindeth on his feet a thing of iron called Stirrup[8] and layeth on my back another thing called Saddle, which he fasteneth by two Girths passed under my armpits. Then he setteth in my mouth a thing of iron he called Bit, to which he tieth a thing of leather called Rein; and, when he sitteth in the saddle on my back, he taketh the rein in his hand and guideth me with it, goading my flanks the while with the shovel-stirrups till he maketh them bleed. So do not ask, O son of our Sultan, the hardships I endure from the son of Adam. And when I grow old and lean and can no longer run swiftly, he selleth me to the miller who maketh me turn in the mill, and I cease not from turning night and day till I grow decrepit. Then he in turn vendeth me to the knacker who cutteth my throat and flayeth off my hide and plucketh out my tail, which he selleth to the sieve-maker;

and he melteth down my fat for tallow-candles. When the young lion heard the horse's words, his rage and vexation redoubled and he said, When didst thou leave the son of Adam? Replied the horse, At mid-day and he is upon my track. Whilst the whelp was thus conversing with the horse lo! there rose a cloud of dust and, presently opening out, discovered below it a furious camel gurgling and pawing the earth with his feet and never ceasing so to do till he came up with us. Now when the lion-whelp saw how big and buxom he was, he took him to be the son of Adam and was about to spring upon him when I said to him, O Prince, of a truth this is not the son of Adam, this be a camel, and he seemeth to be fleeing from the son of Adam. As I was thus conversing, O my sister, with the lion-whelp, the camel came up and saluted him; whereupon he returned the greeting and said:—What bringeth thee hither? Replied he, I came here fleeing from the son of Adam. Quoth the whelp, And thou, with thy huge frame and length and breadth, how cometh it that thou fearest the son of Adam, seeing that with one kick of thy foot thou wouldst kill him? Quoth the camel, O son of the Sultan, know that the son of Adam hath subtleties and wiles, which none can withstand nor can any prevail against him, save only Death; for he putteth into my nostrils a twine of goat's hair he calleth Nose-ring,[9] and over my head a thing he calleth Halter; then he delivereth me to the least of his little children, and the youngling draweth me along by the nose-ring, my size and strength nothwithstanding. Then they load me with the heaviest of burdens and go long journeys with me and put me to hard labour through the hours of the night and the day. When I grow old and stricken in years and disabled from working, my master keepeth me not with him, but selleth me to the knacker who cutteth my throat and vendeth my hide to the tanners and my flesh to the cooks: so do not ask the hardships I suffer from the son of Adam. When didst thou leave the son of Adam? asked the young lion; and he answered, At sundown, and I suppose that coming to my place after my departure and not finding me there, he is now in search of me: wherefore let me go, O son of the Sultan, that I may flee into the wolds and the wilds. Said the whelp, Wait awhile, O camel, till thou see how I will tear him, and give thee to eat of his flesh, whilst I craunch his bones and drink his blood. Replied the camel, O King's son, I fear for thee from the child of Adam, for he is wily and guilefull. And he began repeating these verses:—

> When the tyrant enters the lieges' land,
> Naught remains for the lieges but quick remove!

Now whilst the camel was speaking with the lion-whelp, behold, there rose a cloud of dust which, after a time, opened and showed an old man scanty of stature and lean of limb; and he bore on his shoulder a basket of carpenter's tools and on his head a branch of a tree and eight planks. He led little children by the hand and came on at a trotting pace,[10] never stopping till he drew near the whelp. When I saw him, O my sister, I fell down for excess of fear; but the young lion rose and walked forward to meet the carpenter and when he came up to him, the man smiled in his face and said to him, with a glib tongue and in courtly terms:— O King who defendeth from harm and lord of the long arm, Allah prosper thine evening and thine endeavouring and increase thy valiancy and strengthen thee! Protect me from that which hath distressed me and with its mischief hath oppressed me, for I have found no helper save only thyself. And the carpenter stood in his presence weeping and wailing and complaining. When the whelp heard his sighing and his crying he said, I will succour thee from that thou fearest. Who hath done thee wrong and what art thou, O wild beast, whose like in my life I never saw, nor ever espied one goodlier of form or more eloquent of tongue than thou? What is thy case? Replied the man, O lord of wild beasts, as to myself I am a carpenter; but as to who hath wronged me, verily he is a son of Adam, and by break of dawn after this coming night[11] he will be with thee in this place. When the lion-whelp heard these words of the carpenter, the light was changed to night before his sight and he snorted and roared with ire and his eyes cast forth sparks of fire. Then he cried out saying, By Allah, I will assuredly watch through this coming night till dawn, nor will I return to my father till I have won my will. Then he turned to the carpenter and asked, Of a truth I see thou art short of step and I would not hurt thy feelings for that I am generous of heart; yet do I deem thee unable to keep pace with the wild beasts: tell me then whither thou goest? Answered the carpenter, Know that I am on my way to thy father's Wazir, the lynx; for when he heard that the son of Adam had set foot in this country he feared greatly for himself and sent one of the wild beasts on a message for me, to make him a house wherein he should dwell, that it might shelter him and fend off his enemy from him, so not one of the sons of Adam should come at him. Accordingly I took up these planks and set forth to find him. Now when the young lion heard these words he envied the lynx and said to the carpenter, By my life there is no help for it but thou make me a house with these planks ere thou make one for Sir Lynx! When thou hast done my work, go to him and make him whatso he wisheth. The carpenter replied, O lord of wild beasts, I cannot make thee aught till I have made the lynx what he desireth: then will I return to thy service and build thee a house as a fort to ward thee from thy foe. Exclaimed the lion-whelp, By Allah, I will not let thee leave this place till thou build me a house of planks. So saying he made for the carpenter and sprang upon him, thinking to jest with him, and cuffed him with his paw, knocking the basket off his shoulder; and threw him down in a fainting fit, whereupon the young lion laughed at him and said, Woe to thee, O carpenter, of a truth thou art feeble and hast no force; so it is excusable in thee to fear the son of Adam. Now when the carpenter fell on his back, he waxed exceeding wroth; but he dissembled his wrath for fear of the whelp and sat up and smiled in his face, saying, Well, I will make for thee the house. With this he took the planks he had brought and nailed together the house, which he made in the form of a chest after the measure of the young lion. And he left the door open, for he had cut in the box a large aperture, to which he made a stout cover and bored many holes therein. Then he took out some newly wrought nails and a hammer and said to the young lion, Enter the house through this opening, that I may fit it to thy measure. Thereat the whelp rejoiced and went up to the opening, but saw that it was strait; and the carpenter said to him, Enter and crouch down on thy legs and arms! So the whelp did thus and entered the chest, but his tail remained outside. Then he would have drawn back and come out; but the carpenter said to him, Wait patiently a while till I see if there be room for thy tail with thee. The young lion did as he was bid when the carpenter twisted up his tail and, stuffing it into the chest, whipped the lid on to the opening and nailed it down; whereat the whelp cried out and said, O carpenter, what is this narrow house thou hast made me? Let me out, sirrah! But the carpenter answered, Far be it, far be it from thy thought! Repentance for past avails naught, and indeed of this place thou shalt not come out. He then laughed and resumed, Verily thou art fallen into the trap and from thy duresse there is no escape, O vilest of wild beasts! Rejoined the whelp, O my brother, what manner of words are these thou addressest to me? The carpenter replied, Know, O dog of the desert! that thou hast fallen into that which thou fearedst: Fate hath upset thee, nor shall caution set thee up. When the whelp heard these words, O my sister, he knew that this was indeed the very son of Adam, against whom he had been warned by his sire in waking state and by the mysterious Voice in sleeping while; and I also was certified that this was indeed he without doubt; wherefore great fear of him for myself seized me and I withdrew a little apart from him and waited to see what he would do with the young lion. Then I saw, O my sister, the son of Adam dig a pit in that place hard by the chest which held the whelp and, throwing the box into the hole, heap dry wood upon it and burn the young lion with fire. At this sight, O sister mine, my fear of the son of Adam redoubled and in my affright I have been these two days fleeing from him." But when the peahen heard from the duck this story, she wondered with exceeding wonder and said to her, "O my sister, here thou art safe from the son of Adam, for we are in one of the islands of the sea whither there is no way for the son of Adam; so do thou take up thine abode with us till Allah make easy thy case and our case." Quoth the duck, "I fear lest some calamity come upon me by night, for no runaway can rid him of fate by flight." Rejoined the peahen, "Abide with us, and be like unto us;" and ceased not to persuade her, till she yielded, saying, "O my sister, thou knowest how weak is my resistance; but verily had I not seen thee here, I had not remained." Said the peahen, "That which is on our foreheads[12] we must indeed fulfil, and when our doomed day draweth near, who shall deliver us? But not a soul departeth except it have accomplished its predestined livelihood and term." Now the while they talked thus, a cloud of dust appeared and approached them, at sight of which the duck shrieked aloud and ran down into the sea, crying out, "Beware! beware! though flight there is not from Fate and Lot!"[13] After awhile, the dust opened out and discovered under it an antelope; whereat the duck and the peahen were reassured and the peacock's wife said to her companion, "O my sister, this thou seest and wouldst have me beware of is an antelope, and here he is, making for us. He will do us no hurt, for the antelope feedeth upon the herbs of the earth and even as thou are of the bird-kind, so is he of the beast-kind. Be therefore of good cheer and cease care-taking; for care-taking wasteth the body." Hardly had the peahen done speaking, when the antelope came up to them, thinking to shelter him under the shade of the tree; and, sighting the peahen and the duck, saluted them and said, "I came to this island to-day and I have seen none richer in herbage nor pleasanter for habitation." Then he besought them for company and amity and, when they saw his friendly behaviour to them, they welcomed him and gladly accepted his offer. So they struck up a sincere friendship and sware thereto; and they slept in one place and they ate and drank together; nor did they cease dwelling in safety, eating and drinking their fill, till one day there came thither a ship which had strayed from her course in the sea. She cast anchor near them and the crew came forth and dispersed about the island. They soon caught sight of the three friends, antelope, peahen and duck, and made for them; whereupon the peahen flew up into the tree and thence winged her way through air; and the antelope fled into the desert, but the duck abode paralysed by fear. So they chased her till they caught her and she cried out and said, "Caution availed me naught against Fate and Lot!"; and they bore her off to the ship. Now when the peahen saw what had betided the duck, she removed from the island, saying, "I see that misfortunes lie in ambush for all. But for yonder ship, parting had not befallen between me and this duck, because she was one of the truest of friends." Then she flew off and rejoined the antelope, who saluted her and gave her joy of her safety and asked for the duck, to which she replied, "The enemy hath taken her, and I loathe the sojourn of this island after her." The antelope sorrowed with great sorrow, but dissuaded the peahen from her resolve to remove from the island. So they abode there together with him, eating and drinking, in peace and safety, except that they ceased not to mourn for the loss of the duck; and the antelope said to the peahen, "O my sister, thou seest how the folk who came forth of the ship were the cause of our severance from the duck and of her destruction; so do thou beware of them and guard thyself from them and from the wile of the son of Adam and his guile." But the peahen replied, "I am assured that nought caused her death save her neglecting to say Subhan' Allah, glory to God; indeed I often said to her:—Exclaim thou, Praised be Allah, and verily I fear for thee, because thou neglectest to laud the Almighty; for all things created by Allah glorify Him on this wise, and whoso neglecteth the formula of praise[14] him destruction waylays." When the antelope heard the peahen's words he exclaimed, "Allah make fair thy face!" and betook himself to repeating the formula of praise, and ceased not therefrom a single hour. And it is said that his form of adoration was as follows:— "Praise be the Requiter of every good and evil thing, the Lord of Majesty and of Kings the King!" And a tale is also told on this wise of

THE HERMITS.

A certain hermit worshipped on a certain mountain, whither resorted a pair of pigeons; and the worshipper was wont to make two parts of his daily bread, eating one half himself and giving the other to the pigeon pair. He also prayed for them both that they might be blest with issue: so they increased and multiplied greatly. Now they resorted only to that mountain where the hermit was, and the reason of their foregathering with the holy man was their assiduity in repeating "Praised be Allah!" for it is recounted that the pigeon[1] sayeth in praise, "Praised be the Creator of all Creatures, the Distributor of daily bread, the Builder of the heavens and Dispreader of the earths!" And that couple ceased not to dwell together in the happiest of life, they and their brood till the holy man died, when the company of the pigeons was broken up and they dispersed among the towns and villages and mountains. Now it is told that on a certain other mountain there dwelt a shepherd, a man of piety and good sense and chastity; and he had flocks of sheep which he tended, and he made his living by their milk and wool. The mountain which gave him a home abounded in trees and pasturage and also in wild beasts, but these had no power over his flocks; so he ceased not to dwell upon that highland in full security, taking no thought to the things of the world, by reason of his beatitude and his assiduity in prayer and devotion, till Allah ordained that he should fall sick with exceeding sickness. Thereupon he betook himself to a cavern in the mountain and his sheep used to go out in the morning to the pasturage and take refuge at night in the cave. But Allah Almighty, being minded to try him and prove his patience and his obedience, sent him one of His angels, who came in to him in the semblance of a fair woman and sat down before him. When the shepherd saw that woman seated before him, his flesh shuddered at her with horripilation[2] and he said to her, "O thou woman, what was it invited thee to this my retreat? I have no need of thee, nor is there aught betwixt me and thee which calleth for thy coming in to me." Quoth she, "O man, dost thou not behold my beauty and loveliness and the fragrance of my breath; and knowest thou not the need women have of men and men of women? So who shall forbid thee from me when I have chosen to be near thee and desire to enjoy thy company? Indeed, I come to thee willingly and do not withhold myself from thee, and near us there is none whom we need fear; and I wish to abide with thee as long as thou sojournest in this mountain, and be thy companion and thy true friend. I offer myself to thee, for thou needest the service of woman: and if thou have carnal connection with me and know me, thy sickness shall be turned from thee and health return to thee; and thou wilt repent thee of the past for having foresworn the company of women during the days that are now no more. In very sooth, I give thee good advice: so incline to my counsel and approach me." Quoth the shepherd, "Go out from me, O woman deceitful and perfidious! I will not incline to thee nor approach thee. I want not thy company nor wish for union with thee; he who coveteth the coming life renounceth thee, for thou seducest mankind, those of past time and those of present time. Allah the Most High lieth in wait for His servants and woe unto him who is cursed with thy company!" Answered she, "O thou that errest from the truth and wanderest from the way of reason, turn thy face to me and look upon my charms and take thy full of my nearness, as did the wise who have gone before thee. Indeed, they were richer than thou in experience and sharper of wit; withal they rejected not, as thou rejectest, the enjoyment of women; nay, they took their pleasure of them and their company even as thou renouncest them, and it did them no hurt in things temporal or things spiritual. Wherefore do thou recede from thy resolve and thou shalt praise the issue of thy case." Rejoined the shepherd, "All thou sayest I deny and abhor, and all thou offerest I reject: for thou art cunning and perfidious and there is no honesty in thee nor is there honour. How much of foulness hidest thou under thy beauty, and how many a pious man hast thou seduced from his duty and made his end penitence and perdition? Avaunt from me, O thou who devotest thyself to corrupt others!" Thereupon, he threw his goat's-hair cloak over his head that he might not see her face, and betook himself to calling upon the name of his Lord. And when the angel saw the excellence of his submission to the Divine Will, she went out from him and ascended to heaven. Now hard by the hermit's hill was a village wherein dwelt a pious man, who knew not the other's station, till one night he heard in a dream a Voice saying to him, "In such a place near to thee is a devout man: go thou to him and be at his command!" So when morning dawned he set out to wend thither, and what time the heat was grievous upon him, he came to a tree which grew beside a spring of running water. So he sat down to rest in the shadow of that tree and behold, he saw beasts and birds coming to that fount to drink; but when they caught sight of the devotee sitting there, they took fright and fled from before his face. Then said he, "There is no Majesty and there is no Might save Allah! I rest not here but to the hurt of these beasts and fowls." So he arose, blaming himself and saying, "Verily my tarrying here this day hath wronged these animals, and what excuse have I towards my Creator and the Creator of these birds and beasts for that I was the cause of their flight from their drink and their daily food and their place of pasturage? Alas for my shame before my Lord on the day when He shall avenge the hornless sheep on the sheep with horns!"[3] Then he wept for that he had driven the birds and beasts from the spring by sitting down under the tree, and he fared on till he came to the shepherd's dwelling and going in, saluted him. The shepherd returned his salutation and embraced him, weeping and saying, "What hath brought thee to this place where no man hath ever yet come to me." Quoth the other devotee, "I saw in my sleep one who described to me this thy stead and bade me repair to thee and salute thee: so I came, in obedience to the commandment." The shepherd welcomed him, rejoicing in his company and the twain abode upon that mountain, worshipping Allah with the best of worship; and they ceased not serving their Lord in the cavern and living upon the flesh and milk of their sheep, having clean put away from them riches and children and what not, till the Certain, the Inevitable became their lot. And this is the end of their story. Quoth the Sultan, "O Shahrazad, how excellent are these thy stories, and how delightsome! Hast thou more of such edifying tales?" Answered she:—"I will relate

THE TALE OF KAMAR AL-ZAMAN.

There was in times of yore and in ages long gone before a King called Shahriman,[1] who was lord of many troops and guards, and officers, and who reigned over certain islands, known as the Khalidan Islands,[2] on the borders of the land of the Persians. But he was stricken in years and his bones were wasted, without having been blessed with a son, albeit he had four wives, daughters of Kings, and threescore concubines, with each of whom he was wont to lie one night in turn.[3] This preyed upon his mind and disquieted him, so that he complained thereof to one of his Wazirs, saying, "Verily I fear lest my kingdom be lost when I die, for that I have no son to succeed me." The Minister answered, "O King, peradventure Allah shall yet bring something to pass; so rely upon the Almighty and be instant in prayer. It is also my counsel that thou spread a banquet and invite to it the poor and needy, and let them eat of thy food; and supplicate the Lord to vouchsafe thee a son; for perchance there may be among thy guests a righteous soul whose prayers find acceptance; and thereby thou shalt win thy wish." So the King rose, made the lesser ablution, and prayed a two-bow prayer,[4] then he cried upon Allah with pure intention; after which he called his chief wife to bed and lay with her forthright. By grace of God she conceived and, when her months were accomplished, she bore a male child, like the moon on the night of fulness. The King named him Kamar al-Zaman,[5] and rejoiced in him with extreme joy and bade the city be dressed out in his honour; so they decorated the streets seven days, whilst the drums beat and the messengers bore the glad tidings abroad. Then wet and dry nurses were provided for the boy and he was reared in splendour and delight, until he reached the age of fifteen. He grew up of surpassing beauty and seemlihead and symmetry, and his father loved him so dear that he could not brook to be parted from him day or night. One day he complained to a certain of his Ministers anent the excess of his love for his only child, saying, "O thou the Wazir, of a truth I fear for my son, Kamar al-Zaman, the shifts and accidents which befal man and fain would I marry him in my life-time." Answered the Wazir, "O King, know thou that marriage is one of the most honourable of mortal actions, and thou wouldst indeed do well and right to marry thy son in thy lifetime, ere thou make him Sultan." On this quoth the King, "Hither with my son Kamar al-Zaman;" so he came and bowed his head to the ground in modesty before his sire. "O Kamar al-Zaman," said King Shahriman, "of a truth I desire to marry thee and rejoice in thee during my lifetime." Replied he, "O my father, know that I have no lust to marry nor doth my soul incline to women; for that concerning their craft and perfidy I have read many books and heard much talk, even as saith the poet:—

> Now, an of women ask ye, I reply:—
> In their affairs I'm versed a doctor rare!
> When man's head grizzles and his money dwindles,
> In their affections he hath naught for share.

And another said:—

Rebel against women and so shalt thou serve Allah the
    more;
The youth who gives women the rein must forfeit all hope
    to soar.
They'll baulk him when seeking the strange device,
    Excelsior,
Tho' waste he a thousand of years in the study of science
    and lore."

And when he had ended his verses he continued, "O my father, wedlock is a thing whereto I will never consent; no,
not though I drink the cup of death." When Sultan Shahriman heard these words from his son, light became darkness in his sight and he grieved thereat with great grief;
yet, for the great love he bore him, he was unwilling to repeat his wishes and was not wroth with him, but caressed
him and spake him fair and showed him all manner of
kindness such as tendeth to induce affection. All this, and
Kamar al-Zaman increased daily in beauty and loveliness
and amorous grace; and the King bore with him for a
whole year till he became perfect in eloquence and elegant
wit. All men were ravished with his charms; and every
breeze that blew bore the tidings of his gracious favour; his
fair sight was a seduction to the loving and a garden of delight to the longing, for he was honey-sweet of speech and
the sheen of his face shamed the full moon; he was a model
of symmetry and blandishment and engaging ways; his
shape was as the willow-wand or the rattan-cane and his
cheeks might take the place of rose or red anemone. When
the year came to an end, the King called his son to him and
said, "O my son, wilt thou not hearken to me?" Whereupon
Kamar al-Zaman fell down for respect and shame before
his sire and replied, "O my father, how should I not hearken to thee, seeing that Allah commandeth me to obey
thee and not gainsay thee?" Rejoined King Shahriman, "O
my son, know that I desire to marry thee and rejoice in
thee whilst yet I live, and make thee King over my realm,
before my death." When the Prince heard his sire pro-

nounce these words he bowed his head awhile, then raised
it and said, "O my father, this is a thing which I will never
do; no, not though I drink the cup of death! I know of a
surety that the Almighty hath made obedience to thee a
duty in religion; but, Allah upon thee! press me not in this
matter of marriage, nor fancy that I will ever marry my life
long; for that I have read the books both of the ancients
and the moderns, and have come to know all the mischiefs
and miseries which have befallen them through women and
their endless artifices. And how excellent is the saying of
the poet:—

> He whom the randy motts entrap
> Shall never see deliverance!
> Though build he forts a thousand-fold,
> Whose mighty strength lead-plates enhance,[6]
> Their force shall be of no avail;
> These fortresses have not a chance!
> Women aye deal in treachery
> To far and near o'er earth's expanse;
> With fingers dipt in Henna-blood
> And locks in braids that mad the glance;
> And eyelids painted o'er with Kohl
> They gar us drink of dire mischance."

Now when King Shahriman heard these his son's words
and learnt the import of his verses and poetical quotations,
he made no answer, of his excessive love for him, but redoubled in graciousness and kindness to him. He at once
broke up the audience and, as soon as the seance was over,
he summoned his Minister and taking him apart, said to
him, "O thou the Wazir! tell me how I shall deal with my
son in the matter of marriage. Of a truth I took counsel
with thee thereon and thou didst counsel me to marry him,
before making him King. I have spoken with him of wedlock time after time and he still gainsaid me; so do thou, O
Wazir, forthright advise me what to do." Answered the
Minister, "O King, wait another year and, if after that thou

be minded to speak to him on the matter of marriage, speak not to him privily, but address him on a day of state, when all the Emirs and Wazirs are present with the whole of the army standing before thee. And when all are in crowd then send for thy son, Kamar al-Zaman, and summon him; and, when he cometh, broach to him the matter of marriage before the Wazirs and Grandees and Officers of State and Captains; for he will surely be bashful and daunted by their presence and will not dare to oppose thy will." Now when King Shahriman heard his Wazir's words, he rejoiced with exceeding joy, seeing success in the project, and bestowed on him a splendid robe of honour. Then he took patience with his son another year, whilst, with every day that passed over him, Kamar al-Zaman increased in beauty and loveliness, and elegance and perfect grace, till he was nigh twenty years old. Indeed Allah had clad him in the cloak of comeliness and had crowned him with the crown of completion: his eye-glance was more bewitching than Harut and Marut[7] and the play of his luring looks more misleading than Taghut;[8] and his cheeks shone like the dawn rosy-red and his eyelashes stormed the keen-edged blade: the whiteness of his brow resembled the moon shining bright, and the blackness of his locks was as the murky night; and his waist was more slender than the gossamer[9] and his back parts than two sand-heaps bulkier, making a Babel of the heart with their softness; but his waist complained of the weight of his hips and loins; and his charms ravished all mankind. So King Shahriman, having accepted the counsel of his Wazir, waited for another year and a great festival, a day of state when the audience hall was filled with his Emirs and Wazirs and Grandees of his reign and Officers of State and Captains of might and main. Thereupon he sent for his son Kamar al-Zaman who came, and kissing the ground before him three times, stood in presence of his sire with his hands behind his back the right grasping the left.[10] Then said the King to him, "Know O my son, that I have not sent for thee on this occasion and

summoned thee to appear before this assembly and all
these officers of estate here awaiting our orders save and
except that I may lay a commandment on thee, wherein do
thou not disobey me; and my commandment is that thou
marry, for I am minded to wed thee to a King's daughter
and rejoice in thee ere I die." When the Prince heard this
much from his royal sire, he bowed his head groundwards
awhile, then raising it towards his father and being moved
thereto at that time by youthful folly and boyish ignorance,
replied, "But for myself I will never marry; no, not though
I drink the cup of death! As for thee, thou art great in age
and small of wit: hast thou not, twice ere this day and before this occasion, questioned me of the matter of marriage,
and I refused my consent? Indeed thou dotest and are not
fit to govern a flock of sheep!" So saying Kamar al-Zaman
unclasped his hands from behind his back and tucked up
his sleeves above his elbows before his father, being in a
fit of fury; moreover, he added many words to his sire,
knowing not what he said in the trouble of his spirits. The
King was confounded and ashamed, for that this befel in
the presence of his grandees and soldier-officers assembled on a high festival and a state occasion; but presently
the majesty of Kingship took him, and he cried out at his
son and made him tremble. Then he called to the guards
standing before him and said, "Seize him!" So they came
forward and laid hands on him and, binding him, brought
him before his sire, who bade them pinion his elbows behind his back and in this guise make him stand before the
presence. And the Prince bowed down his head for fear
and apprehension, and his brow and face were beaded and
spangled with sweat; and shame and confusion troubled
him sorely. Thereupon his father abused him and reviled
him and cried, "Woe to thee, thou son of adultery and
nursling of abomination![11] How durst thou answer me on
this wise before my captains and soldiers? But hitherto
none hath chastised thee. Knowest thou not that this deed
thou hast done were a disgrace to him had it been done by

the meanest of my subjects?" And the King commanded his Mamelukes to loose his elbow-bonds and imprison him in one of the bastions of the citadel. So they took the Prince and thrust him into an old tower, wherein there was a dilapidated saloon and in its middle a ruined well, after having first swept it and cleansed its floor-flags and set therein a couch on which they laid a mattress, a leathern rug and a cushion; and then they brought a great lanthorn and a wax candle, for that place was dark, even by day. And lastly the Mamelukes led Kamar al-Zaman thither, and stationed an eunuch at the door. And when all this was done, the Prince threw himself on the couch, sad-spirited and heavy-hearted; blaming himself and repenting of his injurious conduct to his father, whenas repentance availed him naught, and saying, "Allah curse marriage and marriageables and married women, the traitresses all! Would I had hearkened to my father and accepted a wife! Had I so done it had been better for me than this jail." This is how it fared with him; but as regards King Shahriman, he remained seated on his throne all through the day until sundown; then he took the Minister apart and said to him, "Know thou, O Wazir, that thou and thou only wast the cause of all this that hath come to pass between me and my son by the advice thou wast pleased to devise; and so what dost thou counsel me to do now?" Answered he, "O King, leave thy son in limbo for the space of fifteen days: then summon him to thy presence and bid him wed; and assuredly he shall not gainsay thee again." The King accepted the Wazir's opinion and lay down to sleep that night troubled at heart concerning his son; for he loved him with dearest love because he had no other child but this; and it was his wont every night not to sleep, save after placing his arm under his son's neck. So he passed that night in trouble and unease on the Prince's account, tossing from side to side, as he were laid on coals of Artemisia-wood;[12] for he was overcome with doubts and fears and sleep visited him not all that livelong night; but his eyes ran over with tears and he began repeating:—

While slanderers slumber, longsome is my night;
Suffice thee a heart so sad in parting-plight;
I say, while night in care slow moments by,
"What! no return for thee, fair morning light?"

Such was the case with King Shahriman; but as regards Kamar al-Zaman, when the night came upon him the eunuch set the lanthorn before him and lighting the wax-candle, placed it in the candlestick; then brought him somewhat of food. The Prince ate a little and continually reproached himself for his unseemly treatment of his father, saying to himself, "O my soul, knowest thou not that a son of Adam is the hostage of his tongue, and that a man's tongue is what casteth him into deadly perils?" Then his eyes ran over with tears and he bewailed that which he had done, from anguished vitals and aching heart, repenting him with exceeding repentance of the wrong wherewith he had wronged his father. Now when he had made an end of eating, he asked for the wherewithal to wash his hands and when the Mameluke had washed them clean of the remnants of food, he arose and made the Wuzu-ablution and prayed the prayers of sundown and nightfall, conjoining them in one; after which he lay down upon his couch which was covered with a mattress of satin from al-Ma'adin town, the same on both sides and stuffed with the raw silk of Irak; and under his head was a pillow filled with ostrich-down. And when ready for sleep, he doffed his outer clothes and drew off his bag-trousers and lay down in a shirt of delicate stuff smooth as wax; and he donned a headkerchief of azure Marazi[13] cloth; and at such time and on this guise Kamar al-Zaman was like the full-orbed moon, when it riseth on its fourteenth night. Then, drawing over his head a coverlet of silk, he fell asleep with the lanthorn burning at his feet and the wax-candle over his head, and he ceased not sleeping through the first third of the night, not knowing what lurked for him in the womb of the Future, and what the Omniscient had decreed for him. Now, as Fate and Fortune would have it, both tower and saloon were old and had been many years deserted; and there was therein a Roman well inhabited by a Jinniyah of the seed of Iblis[14] the Accursed, by name Maymunah, daughter of Al-Dimiryat, a renowned King of the Jann. And as Kamar al-Zaman continued sleeping till the first third of the night, Maymunah came up out of the Roman well and made for the firmament, thinking to listen by stealth to the converse of the angels; but when she reached the mouth of the well, she saw a light shining in the tower, contrary to custom; and having dwelt there many years without seeing the like, she said to herself "Never have I witnessed aught like this"; and, marvelling much at the matter, determined that there must be some cause therefor. So she made for the light and found the eunuch sleeping within the door; and inside she saw a couch spread, whereon was a human form with the wax-candle burning at his head and the lanthorn at his feet, and she wondered to see the light and stole towards it little by little. Then she folded her wings and stood by the bed and, drawing back the coverlid, discovered Kamar al-Zaman's face. She was motionless for a full hour in admiration and wonderment; for the lustre of his visage outshone that of the candle; his face beamed like a pearl with light; his eyelids were languorous like those of the gazelle; the pupils of his eyes were intensely black and brilliant;[15] his cheeks were rosy red; his eyebrows were arched like bows and his breath exhaled a scent of musk. Now when Maymunah saw him, she pronounced the formula of praise,[16] and said, "Blessed be Allah, the best of Creators!"; for she was of the true-believing Jinn; and she stood awhile gazing on his face, exclaiming and envying the youth his beauty and loveliness. And she said in herself, "By Allah! I will do no hurt to him nor let any harm him; nay, from all of evil will I ransom him, for this fair face deserveth not but that folk should gaze upon it and for it praise the Lord. Yet how could his family find it in their hearts to leave him in such desert place where, if one of our Marids came upon him at this hour, he would assuredly slay him." Then the Ifritah

Maymunah bent over him and kissed him between the eyes, and presently drew back the sheet over his face which she covered up; and after this she spread her wings and soaring into the air, flew upwards. And after rising high from the circle of the saloon she ceased not winging her way through air and ascending skywards till she drew near the heaven of this world, the lowest of the heavens. And behold, she heard the noisy flapping of wings cleaving the welkin and, directing herself by the sound, she found when she drew near it that the noise came from an Ifrit called Dahnash. So she swooped down on him like a sparrow-hawk and, when he was aware of her and knew her to be May-munah, the daughter of the King of the Jinn, he feared her and his side-muscles quivered; and he implored her for-bearance, saying, "I conjure thee by the Most Great and August Name and by the most noble talisman graven upon the seal-ring of Solomon, entreat me kindly and harm me not!" When she heard these words her heart inclined to him and she said, "Verily, thou conjurest me, O accursed, with a mighty conjuration. Nevertheless, I will not let thee go, till thou tell me whence thou comest at this hour." He replied, "O Princess, Know that I come from the uttermost end of China-land and from among the Islands, and I will tell thee of a wonderful thing I have seen this night. If thou find my words true, let me wend my way and write me a patent under thy hand and with thy sign manual that I am thy freedman, so none of the Jinn-hosts, whether of the upper who fly or of the lower who walk the earth or of those who dive beneath the waters, do me let or hindrance." Rejoined Maymunah, "And what is it thou hast seen this night, O liar, O accursed! Tell me without leasing and think not to escape from my hand with falses, for I swear to thee by the letters graven upon the bezel of the seal-ring of Solomon David-son (on both of whom be peace!), except thy speech be true, I will pluck out thy feathers with mine own hand and strip off thy skin and break thy bones!" Quoth the Ifrit Dahnash son of Shamhurish[17] the Flyer, "I accept, O my lady, these conditions." Then he resumed, "Know, O my mistress, that I come to-night from the Islands of the Inland Sea in the parts of China, which are the realms of King Ghayur, lord of the Islands and the Seas and the Seven Palaces. There I saw a daughter of his, than whom Allah hath made none fairer in her time: I cannot picture her to thee, for my tongue would fail to describe her with her due of praise; but I will name to thee a somewhat of her charms by way of approach. Now her hair is like the nights of disunion and separation and her face like the days of union and delectation; and right well hath the poet said when picturing her:—

> She dispread the locks from her head one night,
> Showing four-fold nights into one night run;
> And she turned her visage towards the moon,
> And two moons showed at moment one.

She hath a nose like the edge of the burnished blade and cheeks like purple wine or anemones blood-red: her lips as coral and cornelian shine and the water of her mouth is sweeter than old wine; its taste would quench Hell's fiery pain. Her tongue is moved by wit of high degree and ready repartee: her breast is a seduction to all that see it (glory be to Him who fashioned it and finished it!); and joined thereto are two upper arms smooth and rounded; even as saith of her the poet Al-Walahan:[18]—

> She hath wrists which, did her bangles not contain,
> Would run from out her sleeves in silvern rain.

She hath breasts like two globes of ivory, from whose brightness the moons borrow light, and a stomach like little waves as it were a figured cloth of the finest Egyptian linen made by the Copts, with creases like folded scrolls, ending in a waist slender past all power of imagination; based upon back parts like a hillock of blown sand, that force her to sit

when she would lief stand, and awaken her, when she fain
would sleep, even as saith of her and describeth her the
poet:—

> She hath those hips conjoined by thread of waist,
> Hips that o'er me and her too tyrannise;
> My thoughts they daze whene'er I think of them,
> And weigh her down whene'er she would uprise.[19]

And those back parts are upborne by thighs smooth and
round and by a calf like a column of pearl, and all this re-
poseth upon two feet, narrow, slender and pointed like
spear-blades,[20] the handiwork of the Protector and Requiter, I wonder how, of their littleness, they can sustain
what is above them. But I cut short my praises of her
charms fearing lest I be tedious." Now when Maymunah
heard the description of that Princess and her beauty and
loveliness, she stood silent in astonishment; whereupon
Dahnash resumed, "The father of this fair maiden is a
mighty King, a fierce knight, immersed night and day in
fray and fight; for whom death hath no fright and the escape of his foe no dread, for that he is a tyrant masterful
and a conqueror irresistible, lord of troops and armies and
continents and islands, and cities and villages, and his
name is King Ghayur, Lord of the Islands and of the Seas
and of the Seven Palaces. Now he loveth his daughter, the
young maiden whom I have described to thee, with dearest love and, for affection of her, he hath heaped together
the treasures of all the kings and built her therewith seven
palaces, each of a different fashion; the first of crystal, the
second of marble, the third of China steel, the fourth of
precious stones and gems of price, the fifth of porcelain
and many-hued onyxes and ring-bezels, the sixth of silver
and the seventh of gold. And he hath filled the seven palaces
with all sorts of sumptuous furniture, rich silken carpets
and hangings and vessels of gold and silver and all manner
of gear that kings require; and hath bidden his daughter to

abide in each by turns for a certain season of the year; and her name is the Princess Budur.[21] Now when her beauty became known and her name and fame were bruited abroad in the neighbouring countries, all the kings sent to her father to demand her of him in marriage, and he consulted her on the matter, but she disliked the very word wedlock with a manner of abhorrence and said, O my father, I have no mind to marry; no, not at all; for I am a sovereign Lady and a Queen suzerain ruling over men, and I have no desire for a man who shall rule over me. And the more suits she refused, the more her suitors' eagerness increased and all the Royalties of the inner Islands of China sent presents and rarities to her father with letters asking her in marriage. So he pressed her again and again with advice on the matter of espousals; but she ever opposed to him refusals, till at last she turned upon him angrily and cried, O my father, if thou name matrimony to me once more, I will go into my chamber and take a sword and, fixing its hilt in the ground, will set its point to my waist; then will I press upon it, till it come forth from my back, and so slay myself. Now when the King heard these words, the light became darkness in his sight and his heart burned for her as with a flame of fire, because he feared lest she should kill herself; and he was filled with perplexity concerning her affair and the kings her suitors. So he said to her, If thou be determined not to marry and there be no help for it: abstain from going and coming in and out. Then he placed her in a house and shut her up in a chamber, appointing ten old women as duennas to guard her, and forbade her to go forth to the Seven Palaces; moreover, he made it appear that he was incensed against her, and sent letters to all the kings, giving them to know that she had been stricken with madness by the Jinns; and it is now a year since she hath thus been secluded." Then continued the Ifrit Dahnash, addressing the Ifritah Maymunah, "And I, O my lady, go to her every night and take my fill of feeding my sight on her face and I kiss her between the eyes: yet, of my love to her, I do her no hurt neither mount her, for that her youth is fair and her grace surpassing: every one who seeth her jealouseth himself for her. I conjure thee, therefore, O my lady, to go back with me and look on her beauty and loveliness and stature and perfection of proportion; and after, if thou wilt, chastise me or enslave me; and win to thy will, for it is thine to bid and to forbid." So saying, the Ifrit Dahnash bowed his head towards the earth and drooped his wings downwards; but Maymunah laughed at his words and spat in his face and answered, "What is this girl of whom thou pratest but a potsherd wherewith to wipe after making water?[22] Faugh! Faugh! By Allah, O accursed, I thought thou hadst some wondrous tale to tell me or some marvellous news to give me. How would it be if thou were to sight my beloved? Verily, this night I have seen a young man, whom if thou saw though but in a dream, thou wouldst be palsied with admiration and spittle would flow from thy mouth." Asked the Ifrit, "And who and what is this youth?"; and she answered, "Know, O Dahnash, that there hath befallen the young man the like of what thou tellest me befel thy mistress; for his father pressed him again and again to marry, but he refused, till at length his sire waxed wroth at being opposed and imprisoned him in the tower where I dwell: and I came up to-night and saw him." Said Dahnash, "O my lady, shew me this youth, that I may see if he be indeed handsomer than my mistress, the Princess Budur, or not; for I cannot believe that the like of her liveth in this our age." Rejoined Maymunah, "Thou liest, O accursed, O most ill-omened of Marids and vilest of Satans![23] Sure am I that the like of my beloved is not in this world. Art thou mad to fellow thy beloved with my beloved?" He said, "Allah upon thee, O my lady, go back with me and look upon my mistress, and after I will return with thee and look upon thy beloved." She answered, "It must needs be so, O accursed, for thou art a knavish devil; but I will not go with thee nor shalt thou come with me, save upon condition of a wager which is this. If the lover thou lovest and of whom thou boastest so bravely, prove handsomer than mine whom I mentioned and whom I love and of whom I boast, the bet shall be thine against me; but if my beloved prove the handsomer the bet shall be mine against thee." Quoth Dahnash the Ifrit, "O my lady, I accept this thy wager and am satisfied thereat; so come with me to the Islands." Quoth Maymunah; "No! for the abode of my beloved is nearer than the abode of thine: here it is under us; so come down with me to see my beloved and after we will go look upon thy mistress." "I hear and I obey," said Dahnash. So they descended to earth and alighted in the saloon which the tower contained; then Maymunah stationed Dahnash beside the bed and, putting out her hand, drew back the silken coverlet from Kamar al-Zaman's face, when it glittered and glistened and shimmered and shone like the rising sun. She gazed at him for a moment, then turning sharply round upon Dahnash said, "Look, O accursed, and be not the basest of madmen; I am a maid, yet my heart he hath waylaid." So Dahnash looked at the Prince and long continued gazing steadfastly on him then, shaking his head, said to Maymunah, "By Allah, O my Lady, thou art excusable; but there is yet another thing to be considered, and that is, that the estate female differeth from the male. By Allah's might, this thy beloved is the likest of all created things to my mistress in beauty and loveliness and grace and perfection; and it is as though they were both cast alike in the mould of seemlihead." Now when Maymunah heard these words, the light became darkness in her sight and she dealt him with her wing so fierce a buffet on the head as well-nigh made an end of him. Then quoth she to him, "I conjure thee, by the light of his glorious countenance, go at once, O accursed, and bring hither thy mistress whom thou lovest so fondly and foolishly, and return in haste that we may lay the twain together and look on them both as they lie asleep side by side; so shall it appear to us which be the goodlier and more beautiful of the two. Except thou obey me this very moment, O accursed, I will dart my sparks at thee with my fire and consume thee; yea, in pieces I will rend thee and into the deserts cast thee, that to stay-at-home and way-

Those eyne wherein white jostles black![128] That dearling
  dainty frame!

When Dahnash heard the poesy which Maymunah spake
in praise of her beloved, he joyed with exceeding joy and
marvelled with excessive wonderment and said, "Thou
hast celebrated thy beloved in song and thou hast indeed
done well in praise of him whom thou lovest! And there is
no help for it but that I also in my turn do my best to en-
fame my mistress, and recite somewhat in her honour."
Then the Ifrit went up to the lady Budur; and, kissing her
between the eyes, looked at Maymunah and at his beloved
Princess and recited the following verses, albeit he had no
skill in poesy:—

> Love for my fair they chide in angry way;
> Unjust for ignorance, yea unjustest they!
> Ah lavish favours on the love-mad, whom
> Taste of thy wrath and parting woe shall slay:
> In sooth for love I'm wet with railing tears,
> That rail mine eyelids blood thou mightest say:
> No marvel what I bear for love, 'tis marvel
> That any know my "me" while thou 'rt away:
> Unlawful were our union did I doubt
> Thy love, or heart incline to other May.

When Maymunah heard these lines from the Ifrit, she said,
"Thou hast done well, O Dahnash! But say thou which of
the two is the handsomer?" And he answered, "My mistress
Budur is handsomer than thy beloved!" Cried Maymunah,
"Thou liest, O accursed. Nay, my beloved is more beautiful than thine!" But Dahnash persisted, "Mine is the fairer."
And they ceased not to wrangle and challenge each other's
words till Maymunah cried out at Dahnash and would
have laid violent hands on him; but he humbled himself to
her and, softening his speech, said, "Let not the truth be
a grief to thee, and cease we this talk, for all we say is to

testify in favour of our lovers; rather let each of us with-draw the claim and seek we one who shall judge fairly be-tween us which of the two be fairer; and by his sentence we will abide." "I agree to this," answered she and smote the earth with her foot, whereupon there came out of it an Ifrit blind of an eye, hump-backed and scurvy-skinned, with eye-orbits slit up and down his face.[29] On his head were seven horns and four locks of hair fell to his heels; his hands were pitchfork-like and his legs mast-like and he had nails as the claws of a lion, and feet as the hoofs of the wild ass.[30] When that Ifrit rose out of the earth and sighted Maymunah, he kissed the ground before her and, standing with his hands clasped behind him, said, "What is thy will, O my mistress, O daughter of my King?"[31] She replied, "O Kashkash, I would have thee judge between me and this accursed Dahnash." And she made known to him the mat-ter, from first to last, whereupon the Ifrit Kashkash looked at the face of the youth and then at the face of the girl; and saw them lying asleep, embraced, each with an arm under the other's neck, alike in beauty and loveliness and equal in grace and goodliness. The Marid gazed long upon them, marvelling at their seemlihead; and, after carefully observ-ing the twain, he turned to Maymunah and Dahnash, and said to them, "By Allah, if you will have the truth, I tell you fairly the twain be equal in beauty, and loveliness and per-fect grace and goodliness, nor can I make any difference between them on account of their being man and woman. But I have another thought which is that we wake each of them in turn, without the knowledge of the other, and whichever is the more enamoured shall be held inferior in seemlihead and comeliness." Quoth Maymunah, "Right is this recking," and quoth Dahnash, "I consent to this." Then Dahnash changed himself to the form of the flea and bit Kamar al-Zaman, whereupon he started from sleep in a fright and rubbed the bitten part, his neck, and scratched it hard because of the smart. Then turning sideways, he found lying by him something whose breath was sweeter than musk and whose skin was softer than cream. Hereat marvelled he with great marvel and he sat up and looked at what lay beside him; when he saw it to be a young lady like an union pearl, or a shining sun, or a dome seen from afar on a well-built wall; for she was five feet tall, bosomed high and rosy-cheeked; even as saith of her the poet:—

> Four things which ne'er conjoin, unless it be
> To storm my vitals and to shed my blood:
> Brow white as day and tresses black as night
> Cheeks rosy red and lips which smiles o'erflood.

And when Kamar al-Zaman saw the lady Budur, daughter of King Ghayur, and her beauty and comeliness, she was sleeping clad in a shift of Venetian silk, without her petticoat-trousers, and wore on her head a kerchief embroidered with gold and set with stones of price: her ears were hung with twin earrings which shone like constellations and round her neck was a collar of union pearls, of size unique, past the competence of any King. When he saw this, his reason was confounded and natural heat began to stir in him; Allah awoke in him the desire of coition and he said to himself, "Whatso Allah willeth, that shall be, and what He willeth not shall never be!" So saying, he put out his hand and, turning her over, loosed the collar of her chemise; then arose before his sight her bosom, with its breasts like double globes of ivory; whereat his inclination for her redoubled and he desired her with exceeding hot desire. He would have awakened her but she would not awake, for Dahnash had made her sleep heavy; so he shook her and moved her, saying, "O my beloved, awake and look at me; I am Kamar al-Zaman." But she awoke not, neither moved her head; whereupon he considered her case for a long hour and said to himself, "If I guess aright, this is the damsel to whom my father would have married me and these three years past I have refused her; but Inshallah!— God willing—as soon as it is dawn, I will say to him:— Marry me to her, that I may enjoy her, nor will I let half the day pass ere I possess her and take my fill of her beauty and loveliness." Then he bent over Budur to buss her, whereat the Jinniyah Maymunah trembled and was abashed and Dahnash, the Ifrit, was like to fly for joy. But, as Kamar al-Zaman was about to kiss her upon the mouth, he was ashamed before Allah and turned away his head and averted his face, saying to his heart, "Have patience." Then he took thought awhile and said, "I will be patient; haply my father when he was wroth with me and sent me to this jail, may have brought my young lady and made her lie by my side to try me with her, and may have charged her not to be readily awakened when I would arouse her, and may have said to her:—Whatever thing Kamar al-Zaman do to thee, make me ware thereof; or belike my sire standeth hidden in some stead whence (being himself unseen) he can see all I do with this young lady; and to-morrow he will scold me and cry:—How cometh it that thou sayest, I have no mind to marry; and yet thou didst kiss and embrace yonder damsel? So I will withhold myself lest I be ashamed before my sire; and the right and proper thing to do is not to touch her at this present, nor even to look upon her, except to take from her somewhat which shall serve as a token to me and a memorial of her; that some sign endure between me and her." Then Kamar al-Zaman raised the young lady's hand and took from her little finger a seal-ring worth an immense amount of money, for that its bezel was a precious jewel and around it were graven these couplets:—

> Count not that I your promises forgot,
> Despite the length of your delinquencies:
> Be generous, O my lord, to me inclining;
> Haply your mouth and cheeks these lips may kiss:
> By Allah, ne'er will I relinquish you
> Albe you *will* transgress love's boundaries.

Then Kamar al-Zaman took the seal-ring from the little finger of Queen Budur and set it on his own; then, turning his back to her, went to sleep.[32] When Maymunah the Jinniyah saw this, she was glad and said to Dahnash and

the ring he had taken, and bussed his inner lips and hands,
nor did she leave any part of him unkissed; after which she
took him to her breast and embraced him and, laying one
of her hands under his neck and the other under his armpit, nestled close to him and fell asleep by his side. After
doing that which she did, quoth Maymunah to Dahnash,
"Sawst thou, O accursed, how proudly and coquettishly
my beloved bore himself, and how hotly and passionately
thy mistress showed herself to my dearling? There can be
no doubt that my beloved is handsomer than thine; nevertheless I pardon thee." Then she wrote him a document of
manumission and turned to Kashkash and said, "Go, help
Dahnash to take up his mistress and aid him to carry her
back to her own place, for the night waneth apace and
there is but little left of it." "I hear and I obey;" answered
Kashkash. So the two Ifrits went forward to Princess Budur
and upraising her flew away with her; then, bearing her
back to her own place, they laid her on her bed, whilst
Maymunah abode alone with Kamar al-Zaman, gazing
upon him as he slept, till the night was all but spent, when
she went her way. As soon as morning morrowed, the
Prince awoke from sleep and turned right and left, but
found not the maiden by him and said in his mind, "What
is this business? It is as if my father would incline me to
marriage with the damsel who was with me and have now
taken her away by stealth, to the intent that my desire for
wedlock may redouble." Then he called out to the eunuch
who slept at the door, saying, "Woe to thee, O damned one,
arise at once!" So the eunuch rose, bemused with sleep, and
brought him basin and ewer, whereupon Kamar al-Zaman
entered the water-closet and did his need;[37] then, coming
out made the Wuzu-ablution and prayed the dawn-prayer,
after which he sat telling on his beads the ninety-and-nine
names of Almighty Allah. Then he looked up and, seeing
the eunuch standing in service upon him, said, "Out on thee,
O Sawab! Who was it came hither and took away the young
lady from my side and I still sleeping?" Asked the eunuch,
"O my lord, what manner of young lady?" "The young lady

who lay with me last night," replied Kamar al-Zaman. The eunuch was startled at his words and said to him, "By Allah, there hath been with thee neither young lady nor other! How should young lady have come in to thee, when I was sleeping in the doorway and the door was locked? By Allah, O my lord, neither male nor female hath come in to thee!" Exclaimed the Prince, "Thou liest, O pestilent slave!: is it of thy competence also to hoodwink me and refuse to tell me what is become of the young lady who lay with me last night and decline to inform me who took her away?" Replied the eunuch (and he was affrighted at him), "By Allah, O my lord, I have seen neither young lady nor young lord!" His words only angered Kamar al-Zaman the more and he said to him, "O accursed one, my father hath indeed taught thee deceit! Come hither." So the eunuch came up to him, and the Prince took him by the collar and dashed him to the ground; whereupon he let fly a loud fart[38] and Kamar al-Zaman, kneeling upon him, kicked him and throttled him till he fainted away. Then he dragged him forth and tied him to the well-rope, and let him down like a bucket into the well and plunged him into the water, then drew him up and lowered him down again. Now it was hard winter weather, and Kamar al-Zaman ceased not to plunge the eunuch into the water and pull him up again and douse him and haul him whilst he screamed and called for help; and the Prince kept on saying "By Allah, O damned one, I will not draw thee up out of this well till thou tell me and fully acquaint me with the story of the young lady and who it was took her away, whilst I slept." Answered the eunuch, after he had seen death staring him in the face; "O my lord, let me go and I will relate to thee the truth and the whole tale." So Kamar al-Zaman pulled him up out of the well, all but dead for suffering, what with cold and the pain of dipping and dousing, drubbing and dread of drowning. He shook like cane in hurricane, his teeth were clenched as by cramp and his clothes were drenched and his body befouled and torn by the rough sides of the well: briefly he was in a sad pickle. Now when

Kamar al-Zaman saw him in this sorry plight, he was concerned for him; but, as soon as the eunuch found himself on the floor, he said to him, "O my lord, let me go and doff my clothes and wring them out and spread them in the sun to dry, and don others; after which I will return to thee forthwith and tell thee the truth of the matter." Answered the Prince, "O rascal slave! hadst thou not seen death face to face, never hadst thou confessed to fact nor told me a word; but go now and do thy will, and then come back to me at once and tell me the truth." Thereupon the eunuch went out, hardly crediting his escape, and ceased not running, stumbling and rising in his haste, till he came in to King Shahriman, whom he found sitting at talk with his Wazir of Kamar al-Zaman's case. The King was saying to the Minister, "I slept not last night, for anxiety concerning my son, Kamar al-Zaman, and indeed I fear lest some harm befal him in that old tower. What good was there in imprisoning him?" Answered the Wazir, "Have no care for him. By Allah, no harm will befal him! None at all! Leave him in prison for a month till his temper yield and his spirit be broken and he return to his senses." As the two spoke behold, up rushed the eunuch, in the aforesaid plight, making the King who was troubled at sight of him; and he cried "O our lord the Sultan! Verily, thy son's wits are fled and he hath gone mad; he hath dealt with me thus and thus, so that I am become as thou seest me, and he kept saying:—A young lady lay with me this night and stole away secretly whilst I slept. Where is she? And he insisteth on my letting him know where she is and on my telling him who took her away. But I have seen neither girl nor boy: the door was locked all through the night, for I slept before it with the key under my head, and I opened to him in the morning with my own hand." When King Shahriman heard this, he cried out, saying, "Alas, my son!"; and he was enraged with sore rage against the Wazir, who had been the cause of all this case and said to him, "Go up, bring me news of my son and see what hath befallen his mind." So the Wazir rose and, stumbling over his long skirts, in his fear of the King's wrath, hastened with the slave to the tower. Now the sun had risen and when the Minister came in to Kamar al-Zaman, he found him sitting on the couch reciting the Koran; so he saluted him and seated himself by his side, and said to him, "O my lord, this wretched eunuch brought us tidings which troubled and alarmed us and which incensed the King." Asked Kamar al-Zaman, "And what hath he told you of me to trouble my father? In good sooth he hath troubled none but me." Answered the Wazir, "He came to us in fulsome state and told us of thee a thing which Heaven forfend; and the slave added a lie which it befitteth not to repeat, Allah preserve thy youth and sound sense and tongue of eloquence, and forbid to come from thee aught of offence!" Quoth the Prince, "O Wazir, and what thing did this pestilent slave say of me?" The Minister replied, "He told us that thy wits had taken leave of thee and thou wouldst have it that a young lady lay with thee last night, and thou wast instant with him to tell thee whither she went and thou diddest torture him to that end." But when Kamar al-Zaman heard these words, he was enraged with sore rage and he said to the Wazir, "'Tis manifest to me in very deed that you people taught the eunuch to do as he did and forbade him to tell me what became of the young lady who lay with me last night. But thou, O Wazir, art cleverer than the eunuch; so do thou tell me without stay or delay, whither went the young lady who slept on my bosom last night; for it was you who sent her and bade her sleep in my embrace and we lay together till dawn; but, when I awoke, I found her not. So where is she now?" Said the Wazir, "O my lord Kamar al-Zaman, Allah's name encompass thee about! By the Almighty, we sent none to thee last night, but thou layest alone, with the door locked on thee and the eunuch sleeping behind it, nor did there come to thee young lady or any other. Regain thy reason, O my lord, and stablish thy senses and occupy not thy mind with vanities." Rejoined Kamar al-Zaman who was incensed at his words, "O Wazir, the young lady in question is my beloved, the fair one with the black eyes and rosy cheeks, whom I held in my arms all last night." So the Minister wondered at his words and asked him, "Didst thou see this damsel last night with thine own eyes on wake or in sleep?" Answered Kamar al-Zaman, "O ill-omened old man, dost thou fancy I saw her with my ears? Indeed, I saw her with my very eyes and awake, and I touched her with my hand, and I watched by her full half the night, feeding my vision on her beauty and loveliness and grace and tempting looks. But you had schooled her and charged her to speak no word to me; so she feigned sleep and I lay by her side till dawn, when I awoke and found her gone." Rejoined the Wazir, "O my lord Kamar al-Zaman, haply thou sawest this in thy sleep; it must have been a delusion of dreams or a deception caused by eating various kinds of food, or a suggestion of the accursed devils." Cried the Prince, "O pestilent old man! wilt thou too make a mock of me and tell me this was haply a delusion of dreams, when that eunuch confessed to the young lady, saying:—At once I will return to thee and tell thee all about her?" With these words, he sprang up and rushed at the Wazir and gripped hold of his beard (which was long[39]) and, after gripping it, he twisted his hand in it and haling him off the couch, threw him on the floor. It seemed to the Minister as though his soul departed his body for the violent plucking at his beard; and Kamar al-Zaman ceased not kicking the Wazir and basting his breast and ribs and cuffing him with open hand on the nape of his neck till he had well-nigh beaten him to death. Then said the old man in his mind, "Just as the eunuch-slave saved his life from this lunatic youth by telling him a lie, thus it is even fitter that I do likewise; else he will destroy me. So now for my lie to save myself, he being mad beyond a doubt." Then he turned to Kamar al-Zaman and said, "O my lord, pardon me; for indeed thy father charged me to conceal from thee this affair of the young lady; but now I am weak and weary and wounded with tunding; for I am an old man and lack strength and bottom to endure blows. Have, therefore, a little patience with me and I will tell thee all and acquaint thee with the story of the young woman." When the Prince heard this, he left off drubbing him and said, "Wherefore couldst thou not tell me the tale until after shame and blows? Rise now, unlucky old man that thou art, and tell me her story." Quoth the Wazir, "Say, dost thou ask of the young lady with the fair face and perfect form?" Quoth Kamar al-Zaman, "Even so! Tell me, O Wazir, who it was that led her to me and laid her by my side, and who was it that took her away from me by night; and let me know forthright whither she is gone, that I myself may go to her at once. If my father did this deed to me that he might try me by means of that beautiful girl, with a view to our marriage, I consent to wed her and free myself of this trouble; for he did all these dealings with me only because I refused wedlock. But now I consent and I say again, I consent to matrimony: so tell this to my father, O Wazir, and advise him to marry me to that young lady; for I will have none other and my heart loveth none save her alone. Now rise up at once and haste thee to my father and counsel him to hurry on our wedding and bring me his answer within this very hour." Rejoined the Wazir, "'Tis well!" and went forth from him, hardly believing himself out of his hands. Then he set off from the tower, walking and tripping up as he went, for excess of fright and agitation, and he ceased not hurrying till he came in to King Shahriman, who said to him as he sighted him, "O thou Wazir, what man hath brought thee to grief and whose mischief hath treated thee in way unlief; how happeneth it that I see thee dumb-foundered and coming to me thus astounded?" Replied the Wazir, "O King! I bring thee good news." "And what is it?" quoth Shahriman, and quoth the Wazir, "Know that thy son Kamar al-Zaman's wits are clean gone and that he hath become stark mad." Now when the King heard these words of the Minister, light became darkness in his sight and he said, "O Wazir, make clear to me the nature of his madness." Answered the Wazir, "O my lord, I hear and I obey." Then he told him that such and such had passed and acquainted him with all that his son had done; whereupon the King said to him, "Hear, O Wazir, the good tidings which I gave thee in return for this thy fair news of my son's insanity; and it shall be the cutting off of thy head and the forfeiture of my favour, O most ill-omened of Wazirs and foulest of Emirs! for I feel that thou hast caused my son's disorder by the wicked advice and the sinister counsel thou hast given me first and last. By Allah, if aught of mischief or madness have befallen my son I will most assuredly nail thee upon the palace-dome and make thee drain the bitterest draught of death!" Then he sprang up and, taking the Wazir with him, fared straight for the tower and entered it. And when Kamar al-Zaman saw the two, he rose to his father in haste from the couch whereon he sat and kissing his hands drew back and hung down his head and stood before him with his arms behind him, and thus remained for a full hour. Then he raised his head towards his sire; the tears gushed from his eyes and streamed down his cheeks and he began repeating:—

> "Forgive the sin 'neath which my limbs are trembling,
> For the slave seeks for mercy from his master;
> I've done a fault, which calls for free confession,
> Where shall it call for mercy, and forgiveness?"[40]

When the King heard this, he arose and embraced his son, and kissing him between the eyes, made him sit by his side on the couch; then he turned to the Wazir and, looking on him with eyes of wrath, said, "O dog of Wazirs, how didst thou say of my son such and such things and make my heart quake for him?" Then he turned to the Prince and said, "O my son, what is to-day called?" He answered, "O my father, this day is the Sabbath, and to-morrow is First day: then come Second day, Third, Fourth, Fifth day and lastly Friday."[41] Exclaimed the King, "O my son, O Kamar al-Zaman, praised be Allah for the preservation of thy reason! What is the present month called in our Arabic?" "Zu'l-Ka'adah," answered Kamar al-Zaman, "and it is followed by Zu'l-hijjah; then cometh Muharram, then Safar, then Rabi'a the First and Rabi'a the Second, the two Jamadas, Rajab, Sha'aban, Ramazan and Shawwal." At this the King rejoiced exceedingly and spat in the Wazir's face, saying, "O wicked old man, how canst thou say that my son is mad? And now none is mad but thou." Hereupon the Minister shook his head and would have spoken, but bethought himself to wait awhile and see what might next befal. Then the King said to his child, "O my son, what words be these thou saidest to the eunuch and the Wazir, declaring:—I was sleeping with a fair damsel this night?[242] What damsel is this of whom thou speakest?" Then Kamar al-Zaman laughed at his father's words and replied, "O my father, know that I can bear no more jesting; so add me not another mock or even a single word on the matter, for my temper hath waxed short by that you have done with me. And know, O my father, with assured knowledge, that I consent to marry, but on condition that thou give me to wife her who lay by my side this night; for I am certain it was thou sentest her to me and madest me in love with her and then despatchest a message to her before the dawn and tookest her away from beside me." Rejoined the King, "The name of Allah encompass thee about, O my son, and be thy wit preserved from witlessness! What thing be this young lady whom thou fanciest I sent to thee last night and then again that I sent to withdraw her from thee before dawn? By the Lord, O my son, I know nothing of this affair, and Allah upon thee, tell me if it be a delusion of dreaming or a deception caused by indisposition. For verily thou layest down to sleep last night with thy mind occupied anent marriage and troubled with the talk of it (Allah damn marriage and the hour when I spake of it and curse him who counselled it!); and without doubt or diffidence I can say that being moved in mind by the mention of wedlock thou dreamedest that a handsome young lady embraced thee and didst fancy thou sawest her when awake. But all this, O my son, is but an imbroglio of dreams." Replied Kamar al-Zaman, "Leave this talk and swear to me by Allah, the All-creator, the Omniscient; the Humbler of the tyrant Cæsars and the Destroyer of the Chosroes, that thou knowest naught of the young lady nor of her woning-place." Quoth the King, "By the Might of Allah Almighty, the God of Moses and Abraham, I know naught of all this and never even heard of it; it is assuredly a delusion of dreams thou hast seen in sleep." Then the Prince replied to his sire, "I will give thee a self-evident proof that it happened to me when on wake. Now let me ask thee, did it ever befal any man to dream that he was battling a sore battle and after to awake from sleep and find in his hand a sword-blade besmeared with blood?" Answered the King, "No, by Allah, O my son, this hath never been." Rejoined Kamar al-Zaman, "I will tell thee what happened to me and it was this. Meseemed I awoke from sleep in the middle of the past night and found a girl lying by my side, whose form was like mine and whose favour was as mine. I embraced her and turned her about with my hand and took her seal-ring, which I put on my finger, and she pulled off my ring and put it on hers. Then I went to sleep by her side, but refrained from her for shame of thee, deeming that thou hadst sent her to me, intending to tempt me with her and incline me to marriage, and suspecting thee to be hidden somewhere whence thou couldst see what I did with her. And I was ashamed even to kiss her on the mouth for thy account, thinking over this temptation to wedlock; and, when I awoke at point of day, I found no trace of her, nor could I come at any news of her, and there befel me what thou knowest of with the eunuch and with the Wazir. How then can this case have been a dream and a delusion, when the ring is a reality? Save for her ring on my finger I should indeed have deemed it a dream; but here is the ring on my little finger: look at it, O King, and see what is its worth." So saying he handed the ring to his father, who examined it and turned it over, then looked to his son and said, "Verily, there is in this ring some mighty mystery and some strange secret. What befel thee last night with the girl is indeed a hard nut to crack, and I know not how intruded upon us this intruder. None is the cause of all this pother save the Wazir; but, Allah upon thee, O my son, take patience, so haply the Lord may turn to gladness this thy grief and to thy sadness bring complete relief. And now, O my son, I am certified at this hour that thou art not mad; but thy case is a strange one which none can clear up for thee save the Almighty." Cried the Prince, "By Allah, O my father, deal kindly with me and seek out this young lady and hasten her coming to me; else I shall die of woe and of my death shall no one know." Then he betrayed the ardour of his passion; and turned towards his father and repeated these two couplets:—

> If your promise of personal call prove untrue,
> Deign in vision to grant me an interview:
> Quoth they, "How can phantom[43] appear to the sight
> Of a youth, whose sight is fordone, perdue?"

Then, after ending his poetry, Kamar al-Zaman again turned to his father, with submission and despondency, and shedding tears in flood, began repeating these lines:—

> Beware that eye-glance which hath magic might;
> Wherever turn those orbs it bars our flight:
> Nor be deceived by low sweet voice, that breeds
> A fever festering in the heart and sprite:
> So soft that silky skin, were rose to touch it
> She'd cry and teardrops rain for pain and fright:
> Did Zephyr e'en in sleep pass o'er her land,
> Scented he'd choose to dwell in scented site:
> Her necklets vie with tinkling of her belt;
> Her wrists strike either wristlet dumb with spite:
> When would her bangles buss those rings in ear,
> Upon the lover's eyne high mysteries 'light:
> I'm blamed for love of her, nor pardon claim;
> Eyes are not profiting which lack foresight:
> Heaven strip thee, blamer mine! unjust art thou;
> Before this fawn must every eye low bow.[44]

After which he said, "By Allah, O my father, I cannot endure to be parted from her even for an hour." The King smote hand upon hand and exclaimed, "There is no Majesty and there is no Might save in Allah, the Glorious, the Great! No cunning contrivance can profit us in this affair." Then he took his son by the hand and carried him to the palace, where Kamar al-Zaman lay down on the bed of languor and the King sat at his head, weeping and mourning over him and leaving him not, night or day, till at last the Wazir came in to him and said, "O King of the age and the time, how long wilt thou remain shut up with thy son and hide thyself from thy troops? Haply, the order of thy realm may be deranged, by reason of thine absence from thy Grandees and Officers of State. It behoveth the man of understanding, if he have various wounds in his body, to apply him first to medicine the most dangerous; so it is my counsel to thee that thou remove thy son from this place to the pavilion which is in the palace overlooking the sea; and shut thyself up with him there, setting apart in every week two days, Thursday and Monday, for state receptions and progresses and reviews. On these days let thine Emirs and Wazirs and Chamberlains and Viceroys and high Officials and Grandees of the realm and the rest of the levies and the lieges have access to thee and submit their affairs to thee; and do thou their needs and judge among them and give and take with them and bid and forbid. And the rest of the week thou shalt pass with thy son, Kamar al-Zaman, and cease not thus doing till Allah shall vouchsafe relief to you twain. Think not, O King, that thou art safe from the shifts of Time and the strokes of Change which come like a traveller in the night; for the wise man is ever on his guard." When the Sultan heard his Wazir's words he saw that they were right and deemed his counsel wise, and it had effect upon him for he feared lest the order of the state be deranged so he rose at once and bade transport his son from his sick room to the pavilion in the palace overlooking the sea. Now this palace was girt round by the waters and was approached by a causeway twenty cubits wide. It had windows on all sides commanding an ocean-view; its floor was paved with parti-coloured marbles and its ceiling was painted in the richest pigments and figured with gold and lapis-lazuli. They furnished it for Kamar al-Zaman with splendid upholstery, embroidered rugs and carpets of the richest silk; and they clothed the walls with choice brocades and hung curtains bespangled with gems of price. In the midst they set him a couch of juniper-wood[45] inlaid with pearls and jewels, and Kamar al-Zaman sat down thereon, but the excess of his concern and passion for the young lady had wasted his charms and emaciated his body; he could neither eat nor drink nor sleep; and he was like a man who had been sick twenty years of sore sickness. His father seated himself at his head, grieving for him with the deepest grief, and every Monday and Thursday he gave his Wazirs and Emirs and Chamberlains and Viceroys and Lords of the realm and levies and the rest of his lieges leave to come up to him in that pavilion. So they entered and did their several service and duties and abode with him till the end of the day, when they went their ways and the King returned to his son in the pavilion whom he left not night nor day; and he ceased not doing on this wise for many days and nights. Such was the case with Kamar al-Zaman, son of King Shahriman; but as regards Princess Budur, daughter of King Ghayur, Lord of the Isles and the Seven Palaces, when the two Jinns bore her up and laid her on her bed, she slept till daybreak, when she awoke and sitting upright looked right and left, but saw not the youth who had lain in her bosom. At this her vitals fluttered, her reason fled and she shrieked a loud shriek which awoke all her slave-girls and nurses and duennas. They flocked in to her; and the chief of them came forward and asked, "What aileth thee, O my lady?" Answered the Princess, "O wretched old woman, where is my beloved, the handsome youth who lay last night in my bosom? Tell me whither he is gone." Now when the duenna heard this, the light starkened in her sight and she feared from her mischief with sore affright, and said to her, "O my Lady Budur, what unseemly words are these?" Cried the Princess, "Woe to thee, pestilent crone that thou art! I ask thee again where is my beloved, the goodly youth with the shining face and the slender form, the jetty eyes and the joined eyebrows, who lay with me last night from supper-tide until near day-break?" She rejoined, "By Allah, O my lady, I have seen no young man nor any other. I conjure thee, carry not this un-seemly jest too far lest we all lose our lives; for perhaps the joke may come to thy father's ears and who shall then de-liver us from his hand?" The Princess rejoined, "In very sooth a youth lay with me last night, one of the fairest-faced of men." Exclaimed the duenna, "Heaven preserve thy reason! indeed no one lay with thee last night." There-upon the Princess looked at her hand and, finding Kamar al-Zaman's seal-ring on her finger instead of her own, said to her, "Woe to thee, thou accursed! thou traitress! wilt thou lie to me and tell me that none lay with me last night and swear to me a falsehood in the name of the Lord?" Replied the duenna, "By Allah, I do not lie to thee nor have I sworn falsely." Then the Princess was incensed by her words and, drawing a sword she had by her, she smote the old woman with it and slew her;[46] whereupon the eunuch and the waiting-women and the concubines cried out at her, and ran to her father and, without stay or delay, ac-quainted him with her case. So the King went to her, and asked her, "O my daughter, what aileth thee?"; and she an-swered, "O my father, where is the youth who lay with me last night?" Then her reason fled from her head and she cast her eyes right and left and rent her raiment even to the skirt. When her sire saw this, he bade the women lay hands on her; so they seized her and manacled her, then putting a chain of iron about her neck, made her fast to one of the palace-windows and there left her.[47] Thus far concerning Princess Budur; but as regards her father, King Ghayur, the world was straitened upon him when he saw what had befallen his daughter, for that he loved her and her case was not a little grievous to him. So he summoned on it the doctors and astrologers and men skilled in talisman-writing and said to them, "Whoso healeth my daughter of what ill she hath, I will marry him to her and give him half of my kingdom; but whoso cometh to her and cureth her not, I will strike off his head and hang it over her palace-gate." Accordingly, all who went in to her, but failed to heal her, he beheaded and hung their heads over the palace-gates, till he had beheaded on her account forty doctors and crucified forty astrologers; wherefor the general held aloof from her, all the physicians having failed to medicine her malady; and her case was a puzzle to the men of science and the adepts in cabalistic characters. And as her longing and passion redoubled and love and distraction were sore upon her, she poured forth tears and repeated these couplets:—

My fondness, O my moon, for thee my foeman is,
And to thy comradeship the nights my thought compel:
In gloom I bide with fire that flames below my ribs,
Whose lowe I make comparison with heat of Hell:
I'm plagued with sorest stress of pine and ecstasy;
Nor clearest noontide can that horrid pain dispel.

And when the lady Budur ceased repeating her poetry, she wept till her eyes waxed sore and her cheeks changed form and hue, and in this condition she continued three years. Now she had a foster-brother, by name Marzawan,[48] who was travelling in far lands and absent from her the whole of this time. He loved her with an exceeding love, passing the love of brothers; so when he came back he went in to his mother and asked for his sister, the Princess Budur. She answered him, "O my son, thy sister hath been smitten with madness and hath passed these three years with a chain of iron about her neck; and all the physicians and men of science have failed of healing her." When Marzawan heard these words he said, "I must needs go in to her; peradventure I may discover what she hath, and be able to medicine her;" and his mother replied, "Needs must thou visit her, but wait till to-morrow, that I may contrive some thing to suit thy case." Then she went a-foot to the palace of the Lady Budur and, accosting the eunuch in charge of the gates, made him a present and said to him, "I have a daughter, who was brought up with thy mistress and since then I married her; and, when that befel the Princess which befel her, she became troubled and sore concerned, and I desire of thy favour that my daughter may go in to her for an hour and look on her; and then return whence she came, so shall none know of it." Quoth the eunuch, "This may not be except by night, after the King hath visited his child and gone away; then come thou and thy daughter." So she kissed the eunuch's hand and, returning home, waited till the morrow at nightfall; and when it was time she arose and sought her son Marzawan and attired him in woman's apparel; then, taking his hand in hers, led him towards the palace, and ceased not walking with him till she came upon the eunuch after the Sultan had ended his visit to the Princess. Now when the eunuch saw her, he rose to her, and said, "Enter, but do not prolong thy stay!" So they went in and Marzawan beheld the Lady Budur in the aforesaid plight, he saluted her, after his mother had doffed his woman's garb: then he took out of their satchel books he had brought with him; and, lighting a wax candle, he began to recite certain conjurations. Thereupon the Princess looked at him and recognising him, said, "O my brother, thou hast been absent on thy travels, and thy news have been cut off from us." He replied, "True! but Allah hath brought me back safe and sound, I am now minded to set out again nor hath aught delayed me but the news I hear of thee; wherefore my heart burned for thee and I came to thee, so haply I may free thee of thy malady." She rejoined, "O my brother, thinkest thou it is madness aileth me?" "Yes," answered he, and she said, "Not so, by Allah!" Then she let Marzawan know that she was love-daft and he said, "Tell me concerning thy tale and what befel thee: haply there may be in my hand something which shall be a means of deliverance for thee." Quoth she, "O my brother, hear my story which is this. One night I awoke from sleep, in the last third of the night[49] and, sitting up, saw by my side the handsomest of youths that be, and tongue faileth to describe him, for he was as a willow-wand or an Indian rattan-cane. So methought it was my father who had done on this wise in order thereby to try me, for that he had consulted me concerning wedlock, when the Kings sought me of him to wife, and I had refused. It was this thought withheld me from arousing him, for I feared that, if I did aught or embraced him, he would per-adventure inform my father of my doings. But in the morning, I found on my finger his seal-ring, in place of my own which he had taken. And, O my brother, my heart was seized with love of him at first sight; and, for the violence of my passion and longing, I have never savoured the taste of sleep and have no occupation save weeping alway and repeating verses night and day. And this, O my brother, is my story and the cause of my madness." Then she poured forth tears and presently continued, "See then, O my brother, how thou mayest aid me in mine affliction." So Marzawan bowed his head groundwards awhile, wondering and not knowing what to do, then he raised it and said to her, "All thou hast spoken to me I hold to be true, though the case of the young man pass my understanding: but I will go round about all lands and will seek for what may heal thee; haply Allah shall appoint thy healing to be at my hand. Meanwhile, take patience and be not disqui-eted." Thereupon Marzawan farewelled her, praying that she might be constant and returned to his mother's house, where he passed the night. And when the morrow dawned, having equipped himself for his journey, he fared forth and ceased not faring from city to city and from island to island for a whole month, till he came to a town named Al-Tayrab.[50] Here he went about scenting news of the towns-folk, so haply he might light on a cure for the Princess's malady, for in every capital he entered or passed by, it was reported that Queen Budur, daughter of King Ghayur, had lost her wits. But arriving at Al-Tayrab city, he heard that Kamar al-Zaman, son of King Shahriman, was fallen sick and afflicted with melancholy madness. So Marzawan asked the name of the Prince's capital and they said to him, "It is on the Islands of Khalidan and it lieth distant from our city a whole month's journey by sea, but by land it is six months' march." So he went down to the sea in a ship which was bound for the Khalidan Isles, and she sailed with a favouring breeze for a whole month, till they came in sight of the capital; and there remained for them but to make the land when, behold, there came out on them a tempestuous wind which carried away the masts and rent the canvas, so that the sails fell into the sea and the ship capsized, with all on board, and each sought his own safety; and as for Marzawan the set of the sea carried him under the King's palace, wherein was Kamar al-Zaman. And by the decree of destiny it so happened that this was the day on which King Shahriman gave audience to his Grandees and high officers, and he was sitting, with his son's head on his lap, whilst an eunuch fanned away the flies; and the Prince had not spoken neither had he eaten nor drunk for two days, and he was grown thinner than a spindle.[51] Now the Wazir was standing respectfully a-foot near the latticed window giving on the sea and, raising his eyes, saw Marzawan being beaten by the billows and at his last gasp; whereupon his heart was moved to pity for him, so he drew near to the King and moving his head towards him said, "I crave thy leave, O King, to go down to the court of the pavilion and open the water-gate that I may rescue a man who is at the point of drowning in the sea and bring him forth of danger into deliverance; peradventure, on this account Allah may free thy son from what he hath!" The King replied, "O thou Wazir, enough is that which hath befallen my son through thee and on thine account. Haply, if thou rescue this drowning man, he will come to know our affairs, and look on my son who is in this state and exult over me; but I swear by Allah, that if this half-drowned wretch come hither and learn our condition and look upon my son and then fare forth and speak of our secrets to any, I will assuredly strike off thy head before his; for thou, O my Minister, art the cause of all that hath betided us, first and last. Now do as thou wilt." Thereupon the Wazir sprang up and, opening the private postern which gave upon the sea, descended to the causeway; then walked on twenty steps and came to the water where he saw Marzawan nigh unto death. So he put out his hand to him and, catching him by his hair, drew him ashore in a state of insensibility, with belly full of water and eyes half out of his head. The Wazir waited till he came to himself, when he pulled off his wet clothes and clad him in a fresh suit, covering his head with one of his servants' turbands; after which he said to him, "Know that I have been the means of saving thee from drowning: do not thou requite me by causing my death and thine own." Asked Marzawan, "And how so?"; and the Wazir answered, "Thou art at this hour about to go up and pass among Emirs and Wazirs, all of them silent and none speaking, because of Kamar al-Zaman, the son of the Sultan." Now when Marzawan heard the name of Kamar al-Zaman, he knew that this was he whom he had heard spoken of in sundry cities and of whom he came in search, but he feigned ignorance and asked the Wazir, "And who is Kamar al-Zaman?" Answered the Minister, "He is the son of Sultan Shahriman and he is sore sick and lieth strown on his couch restless alway, eating not nor drinking neither sleeping night or day; indeed he is nigh upon death and we have lost hope of his living and are certain that he is dying. Beware lest thou look too long on him, or thou look on any place other than that where thou settest thy feet: else thou art a lost man, and I also." He replied, "Allah upon thee, O Wazir, I implore thee, of thy favour, acquaint me touching this youth thou describest, what is the cause of the condition in which he is." The Wazir replied, "I know none, save that, three years ago, his father required him to wed, but he refused; whereat the King was wroth and imprisoned him. And when he awoke on the morrow, he fancied that during the night he had been roused from sleep and had seen by his side a young lady of passing loveliness, whose charms tongue can never express; and he assured us that he had plucked off her seal-ring from her finger and had put it on his own and that she had done likewise; but we know not the secret of all this business. So by Allah, O my son, when thou comest up with me into the palace, look not on the Prince, but go thy way; for the Sultan's heart is full of wrath against me." So said Marzawan to himself, "By Allah; this is the one I sought!" Then he followed the Wazir up to the palace, where the Minister seated himself at the Prince's feet; but Marzawan found forsooth nothing to do but go up to Kamar al-Zaman and stand before him at gaze. Upon this the Wazir died of affright in his skin, and kept looking at Marzawan and signalling him to wend his way; but he feigned not to see him and gave not over gazing upon Kamar al-Zaman, till he was well assured that it was indeed he whom he was seeking, and cried, "Exalted be Allah, Who hath made his shape even as her shape and his complexion as her complexion and his cheek as her cheek!" Upon this Kamar al-Zaman opened his eyes and gave earnest ear to his speech, and he sighed and, turning his tongue in his mouth, said to his sire, "O my father, let this youth come and sit by my side." Now when the King heard these words from his son, he rejoiced with exceeding joy, though at the first his heart had been set against Marzawan and he had determined that the stranger's head needs must be stricken off: but when he heard Kamar al-Zaman speak, his anger left him and he arose and drawing Marzawan to him, seated him by his son and turning to him said, "Praised be Allah for thy safety!" He replied, "Allah preserve thee! and preserve thy son to thee!" and called down blessings on the King. Then the King asked, "From what country art thou?"; and he answered, "From the Islands of the Inland Sea, the kingdom of King Ghayur,

Lord of the Isles and the Seas and the Seven Palaces."
Quoth King Shahriman, "Maybe thy coming shall be blessed
to my son and Allah vouchsafe to heal what is in him."
Quoth Marzawan, "Inshallah, naught shall be save what
shall be well!" Then turning to Kamar al-Zaman, he said to
him in his ear unheard of the King and his court, "O my
lord! be of good cheer, and hearten thy heart and let thine
eyes be cool and clear and, with respect to her for whose
sake thou art thus, ask not of her case on thine account.
But thou keptest thy secret and fellest sick, while she told
her secret and they said she had gone mad; so she is now in
prison, with an iron chain about her neck, in most piteous
plight; but, Allah willing, the healing of both of you shall
come from my hand." Now when Kamar al-Zaman heard
these words, his life returned to him and he took heart and
felt a thrill of joy and signed to his father to help him sit
up; and the King was like to fly for gladness and rose
hastily and lifted him up. Presently, of his fear for his son,
he shook the kerchief of dismissal;[52] and all the Emirs and
Wazirs withdrew; then he set two pillows for his son to
lean upon, after which he bade them perfume the palace
with saffron and decorate the city, saying to Marzawan,
"By Allah, O my son, of a truth thine aspect be a lucky and
a blessed!" And he made as much of him as he might
and called for food, and when they brought it, Marzawan
came up to the Prince and said, "Rise, eat with me." So he
obeyed him and ate with him, and all the while the King
invoked blessings on Marzawan and said, "How auspicious
is thy coming, O my son!" And when the father saw his
boy eat, his joy and gladness redoubled, and he went out
and told the Prince's mother and all the household. Then
he spread throughout the palace the good news of the
Prince's recovery and the King commanded the decoration of the city and it was a day of high festival. Marzawan
passed that night with Kamar al-Zaman, and the King also
slept with them in joy and delight of his son's recovery.
And when the next morning dawned, and the King had
gone away and the two young men were left alone, Kamar

al-Zaman told his story from beginning to end to Marzawan who said, "In very sooth I know her with whom thou didst foregather; her name is the Princess Budur and she is daughter to King Ghayur." Then he related to him all that had passed with the Princess from first to last and acquainted him with the excessive love she bore him, saying, "All that befel thee with thy father hath befallen her with hers, and thou art without doubt her beloved, even as she is thine; so brace up thy resolution and take heart, for I will bring thee to her and unite you both anon and deal with you even as saith the poet:—

> Albe to lover adverse be his love,
> And show aversion howso may he care;
> Yet will I manage that their persons[53] meet,
> E'en as the pivot of a scissor-pair."

And he ceased not to comfort and solace and encourage Kamar al-Zaman and urge him to eat and drink till he ate food and drank wine, and life returned to him and he was saved from his ill case; and Marzawan cheered him and diverted him with talk and songs and stories, and in good time he became free of his disorder and stood up and sought to go to the Hammam.[54] So Marzawan took him by the hand and both went to the bath, where they washed their bodies and made them clean. And his father in his joy at this event freed the prisoners and presented splendid dresses to his grandees and bestowed large alm-gifts upon the poor and bade decorate the city seven days. Then quoth Marzawan to Kamar al-Zaman, "Know, O my lord, that I came not from the Lady Budur save for this purpose, and the object of my journey was to deliver her from her present case; and it remaineth for us only to devise how we may get to her, since thy father cannot brook the thought of parting from thee. So it is my counsel that to-morrow thou ask his leave to go abroad hunting. Then do thou take with thee a pair of saddle-bags full of money and mount a swift steed, and lead a spare horse, and I will do the like, and say to thy sire:—I have a mind to divert myself with hunting the desert and to see the open country and there to pass one night. Suffer not any servant to follow us, for as soon as we reach the open country, we will go our ways." Kamar al-Zaman rejoiced in this plan with great joy and cried, "It is good." Then he stiffened his back and, going in to his father, sought his leave and spoke as he had been taught, and the King consented to his going forth a-hunting and said, "O my son, blessed be the day that restoreth thee to health! I will not gainsay thee in this; but pass not more than one night in the desert and return to me on the morrow; for thou knowest that life is not good to me without thee, and indeed I can hardly believe thee to be wholly recovered from what thou hadst,[55] because thou art to me as he of whom quoth the poet:—

> Albe by me I had through day and night
> Solomon's carpet and the Chosroes' might,
> Both were in value less than wing of gnat,
> Unless these eyne could hold thee aye in sight."[56]

Then the King equipped his son Kamar al-Zaman and Marzawan for the excursion, bidding make ready for them four horses, together with a dromedary to carry the money and a camel to bear the water and belly-timber; and Kamar al-Zaman forbade any of his attendants to follow him. His father farewelled him and pressed him to his breast and kissed him, saying, "I ask thee in the name of Allah, be not absent from me more than one night, wherein sleep will be unlawful to me, for I am even as saith the poet:—

> Thou present, in the Heaven of heavens I dwell;
> Bearing thine absence is of hells my Hell:
> Pledged be for thee my soul! If love for thee
> Be crime, my crime is of the fellest fell.
> Does love-lowe burn thy heart as burns it mine,
> Doomed night and day Gehenna-fire to smell?"

Answered Kamar al-Zaman, "O my father, Inshallah, I will lie abroad but one night!" Then he took leave of him, and he and Marzawan mounted and leading the spare horses, the dromedary with the money and the camel with the water and victual, turned their faces towards the open country; and they travelled from the first of the day till nightfall, when they halted and ate and drank and fed their beasts and rested awhile; after which they again took horse and ceased not journeying for three days, and on the fourth they came to a spacious tract wherein was a thicket. They alighted in it and Marzawan, taking the camel and one of the horses, slaughtered them and cut off their flesh and stripped their bones. Then he doffed from Kamar al-Zaman his shirt and trousers which he smeared with the horse's blood and he took the Prince's coat which he tore to shreds and befouled with gore; and he cast them down in the fork of the road. Then they ate and drank and mounting set forward again; and, when Kamar al-Zaman asked why this was done, and said, "What is this, O my brother, and how shall it profit us?"; Marzawan replied, "Know that thy father, when we have outstayed the second night after the night for which we had his leave, and yet we return not, will mount and follow in our track till he come hither; and, when he happeneth upon this blood which I have spilt and he seeth thy shirt and trousers rent and gore-fouled, he will fancy that some accident befel thee from bandits or wild-beasts; so he will give up hope of thee and return to his city, and by this device we shall win our wishes." Quoth Kamar al-Zaman, "By Allah, this be indeed a rare device! Thou hast done right well."⁵⁷ Then the two fared on days and nights and all that while Kamar al-Zaman did naught but complain when he found himself alone, and he ceased not weeping till they drew near their journey's end, when Marzawan said to him, "Look! these be King Ghayur's Islands;" whereat Kamar al-Zaman joyed with exceeding joy and thanked him for what he had done, and kissed him between the eyes and strained him to his bosom. And after reaching the Islands and entering the city they took up their lodging in a khan, where they rested three days from the fatigues of their wayfare; after which Marzawan carried Kamar al-Zaman to the bath and, clothing him in merchant's gear, provided him with a geomantic tablet of gold,[58] with a set of astrological instruments and with an astrolabe of silver, plated with gold. Then he said to him, "Arise, O my lord, and take thy stand under the walls of the King's palace and cry out:—I am the ready Reckoner; I am the Scrivener; I am he who weeteth the Sought and the Seeker; I am the finished man of Science; I am the Astrologer accomplished in experience! Where then is he that seeketh? As soon as the King heareth this, he will send after thee and carry thee in to his daughter the Princess Budur, thy lover; but when about going in to her do thou say to him:—Grant me three days' delay, and if she recover, give her to me to wife; and if not, deal with me as thou dealest with those who forewent me. He will assuredly agree to this, so as soon as thou art alone with her, discover thyself to her; and when she seeth thee, she will recover strength and her madness will cease from her and she will be made whole in one night. Then do thou give her to eat and drink, and her father, rejoicing in her recovery, will marry thee to her and share his kingdom with thee; for he hath imposed on himself this condition and so peace be upon thee." Now when Kamar al-Zaman heard these words he exclaimed, "May I never lack thy benefits!", and, taking the set of instruments aforesaid, sallied forth from the caravanserai in the dress of his order. He walked on till he stood under the walls of King Ghayur's palace, where he began to cry out, saying, "I am the Scribe, I am the ready Reckoner, I am he who knoweth the Sought and the Seeker; I am he who openeth the Volume and summeth up the Sums;[59] who Dreams can expound whereby the sought is found! Where then is the seeker?" Now when the city people heard this, they flocked to him, for it was long since they had seen Scribe or Astrologer, and they stood round him and, looking upon him, they saw one in the prime of beauty and grace and perfect elegance, and they marvelled at his loveliness, and his fine stature and symmetry. Presently one of them accosted him and said, "Allah upon thee, O thou fair and young, with the eloquent tongue! incur not this affray; nor throw thy life away in thine ambition to marry the Princess Budur. Only cast thine eyes upon yonder heads hung up; all their owners have lost their lives in this same venture." Yet Kamar al-Zaman paid no heed to them, but cried out at the top of his voice, saying, "I am the Doctor, the Scrivener! I am the Astrologer, the Calculator!" And all the townsfolk forbade him from this, but he regarded them not at all, saying in his mind, "None knoweth desire save whoso suffereth it." Then he began again to cry his loudest, shouting, "I am the Scrivener, I am the Astrologer!" Thereupon all the townsfolk were wroth with him and said to him, "Thou art nothing but an imbecile, silly, self-willed lad! Have pity on thine own youth and tender years and beauty and loveliness." But he cried all the more, "I am the Astrologer, I am the Calculator! Is there any one that seeketh?" As he was thus crying and the people forbidding him, behold, King Ghayur heard his voice and the clamour of the lieges and said to his Wazir, "Go down and bring me yon Astrologer." So the Wazir went down in haste, and taking Kamar al-Zaman from the midst of the crowd led him up to the King; and when in the presence he kissed the ground and began versifying:—

> Eight glories meet, all, all conjoined in thee,
> Whereby may Fortune aye thy servant be:
> Lere, lordliness, grace, generosity;
> Plain words, deep meaning, honour, victory!

When the King looked upon him, he seated him by his side and said to him, "By Allah, O my son, an thou be not an astrologer, venture not thy life nor comply with my condition; for I have bound myself that whoso goeth in to my daughter and healeth her not of that which hath befallen her I will strike off his head; but whoso healeth her him I will marry to her. So let not thy beauty and loveliness delude thee: for, by Allah! and again, by Allah! if thou cure her not, I will assuredly cut off thy head." And Kamar al-Zaman replied, "This is thy right; and I consent, for I wot of this ere came I hither." Then King Ghayur took the Kazis to witness against him and delivered him to the eunuch, saying, "Carry this one to the Lady Budur." So the eunuch took him by the hand and led him along the passage; but Kamar al-Zaman outstripped him and pushed on before, whilst the eunuch ran after him, saying, "Woe to thee! Hasten not to thine own ruin: never yet saw I astrologer so eager for his proper destruction; but thou weetest not what calamities are before thee." Then the eunuch stationed Kamar al-Zaman behind the curtain of the Princess's door and the Prince said to him, "Which of the two ways will please thee more; treat and cure thy lady from here or go in and heal her within the curtain?" The eunuch marvelled at his words and answered, "An thou heal her from here it were better proof of thy skill." Upon this Kamar al-Zaman sat down behind the curtain and, taking out ink-case, pen and paper, wrote the following: "This is the writ of one whom passion swayeth. * and whom longing waylayeth * and wakeful misery slayeth. * one who despaireth of living * and looketh for naught but dying * with whose mourning heart * nor comforter nor helper taketh part * One whose sleepless eyes * none succoureth from anxieties * whose day is passed in fire * and his night in torturing desire * whose body is wasted for much emaciation * and no messenger from his beloved bringeth him consolation." And beneath his lines he wrote these cadenced sentences, "The heart's pain is removed * by union with the beloved * and whomso his lover paineth * only Allah assaineth! * If we or you have wrought deceit * may the deceiver win defeat! * There is naught goodlier than a lover who keeps faith * with the beloved who works him scathe." Then, by way of subscription, he wrote, "From the distracted and despairing man * whom love and longing trepan * from the lover under passion's ban * the prisoner of transport and distraction * from this Kamar al-Zaman * son of Shahriman * to the peerless one * of the fair Houris the pearl-union * to the Lady Budur * daughter of King Al-Ghayur * Know thou that by night I am sleepless * and by day in distress * consumed with increasing wasting and pain * and longing and love unfain * abounding in sighs * with tear-flooded eyes * by passion captive ta'en * of Desire the slain * with heart seared by the parting of us twain * the debtor of longing-bane, of sickness cup-companion * I am the sleepless one, who never closeth eye * the slave of love, whose tears run never dry * for the fire of my heart is still burning * and never hidden is the flame of my yearning." Then on the margin Kamar al-Zaman wrote this admired verse:—

> Salam from graces hoarded by my Lord
> To her, who holds my heart and soul in hoard!

And at the end he added this other verse:—

> I've sent the ring from off thy finger bore
> I when we met, now deign my ring restore!

Then Kamar al-Zaman set the Lady Budur's ring inside the letter and sealed it and gave it to the eunuch, who took it and went in with it to his mistress; and, when the Lady Budur opened it, she found therein her own very ring. Then she read the paper and when she understood its purport and knew that it was from her beloved, and that he in person stood behind the curtain, her reason began to fly and her breast swelled for joy and rose high; and she repeated these couplets:—

Long, long have I bewailed the sev'rance of our loves,
With tears that from my lids streamed down like burning
  rain;
And vowed that, if the days deign reunite us two,
My lips should never speak of severance again:
Joy hath o'erwhelmed me so that, for the very stress
Of that which gladdens me to weeping I am fain.
Tears are become to you a habit, O my eyes,
So that ye weep as well for gladness as for pain.[60]

And having finished her verse, the Lady Budur stood up forthwith and, firmly setting her feet to the wall, strained with all her might upon the collar of iron, till she brake it from her neck and snapped the chains. Then going forth from behind the curtain she threw herself on Kamar al-Zaman and kissed him on the mouth, like a pigeon feeding its young.[61] And she embraced him with all the stress of her love and longing and said to him, "O my lord, do I wake or sleep and hath the Almighty indeed vouchsafed us reunion after disunion? Laud be to Allah who hath our loves repaired, even after we despaired!" Now when the eunuch saw her in this case, he went off running to King Ghayur and, kissing the ground before him, said, "O my lord, know that this Astrologer is indeed the Shaykh of all astrologers, who are fools to him, all of them; for verily he hath cured thy daughter while standing behind the curtain and without going in to her." Quoth the King, "Look well to it, is this news true?" Answered the Eunuch, "O my lord, rise and come and see for thyself how she hath found strength to break the iron chains and is come forth to the Astrologer, kissing and embracing him." Thereupon the King arose and went in to his daughter who, when she saw him, stood up in haste and covered her head.[62] Thereupon the King was so transported for joy at her recovery that he felt like to fly and kissed her between the eyes, for he loved her with dearest love; then, turning to Kamar al-Zaman, he asked him who he was, and said, "What countryman art thou?" So the Prince told him his name and rank, and informed him that he was the son of King Shahriman, and presently related to him the whole story from beginning to end; and acquainted him with what happened between himself and the Lady Budur; and how he had taken her seal-ring from her finger and had placed it on his own; whereat Ghayur marvelled and said, "Verily your story deserveth in books to be chronicled, and when you are dead and gone age after age be read." Then he summoned Kazis and witnesses forthright and married the Lady Budur to Prince Kamar al-Zaman; after which he bade decorate the city seven days long. So they spread the tables with all manner of meats, whilst the drums beat and the criers announced the glad tidings, and all the troops donned their richest clothes; and they illuminated the city and held high festival. Then Kamar al-Zaman went in to the Lady Budur and the King rejoiced in her recovery and in her marriage; and praised Allah for that He had made her to fall in love with a goodly youth of the sons of Kings. So they unveiled her and displayed the bride before the bridegroom; and both were the living likeness of each other in beauty and comeliness and grace and love-allurement. Then Kamar al-Zaman lay with her that night and took his will of her, whilst she in like manner fulfilled her desire of him and enjoyed his charms and grace; and they slept in each other's arms till the morning. On the morrow, the King made a wedding-feast to which he gathered all comers from the Islands of the Inner and Outer Seas, and he spread the tables with choicest viands nor ceased the banquetting for a whole month. Now when Kamar al-Zaman had thus fulfilled his will and attained his inmost desire, and whenas he had tarried awhile with the Princess Budur, he bethought him of his father, King Shahriman, and saw him in a dream, saying, "O my son, is it thus thou dealest with me?" and reciting in the vision these two couplets:—

Indeed to watch the darkness-moon he blighted me,
And to star-gaze through longsome night he plighted me:
Easy, my heart! for haply he'll unite with thee;
And patience, Sprite! with whatso ills he dight to thee.

Now after seeing his father in the dream and hearing his reproaches, Kamar al-Zaman awoke in the morning, afflicted and troubled, whereupon the Lady Budur questioned him and he told her what he had seen. Thereupon she and he went in to her sire and, telling him what had passed, besought his leave to travel. He gave the Prince the permission he sought; but the Princess said, "O my father, I cannot bear to be parted from him." Quoth Ghayur, her sire, "Then go thou with him," and gave her leave to be absent a whole twelve-month and afterwards to visit him in every year once; so she kissed his hand and Kamar al-Zaman did the like. Thereupon King Ghayur proceeded to equip his daughter and her bridegroom for the journey, and furnished them with outfit and appointments for the march; and brought out of his stables horses marked with his own brand, blood-dromedaries[63] which can journey ten days without water, and prepared a litter for his daughter, besides loading mules and camels with victual; moreover, he gave them slaves and eunuchs to serve them and all manner of travelling gear; and on the day of departure, when King Ghayur took leave of Kamar al-Zaman, he bestowed on him ten splendid suits of cloth of gold embroidered with stones of price, together with ten riding horses and ten she-camels, and a treasury of money;[64] and he charged him to love and cherish his daughter the Lady Budur. Then the King accompanied them to the farthest limits of his Islands where, going in to his daughter Budur in the litter, he kissed her and strained her to his bosom, weeping and repeating:—

> O thou who wooest Severance, easy fare!
> For love-embrace belongs to lover-friend:
> Fare softly! Fortune's nature falsehood is,
> And parting shall love's every meeting end.

Then leaving his daughter, he went to her husband and bade him farewell and kissed him; after which he parted from them and, giving the order for the march he returned to his capital with his troops. The Prince and Princess and their suite fared on without stopping through the first day and the second and the third and the fourth; nor did they cease faring for a whole month till they came to a spacious champaign, abounding in pasturage, where they pitched their tents; and they ate and drank and rested, and the Princess Budur lay down to sleep. Presently, Kamar al-Zaman went in to her and found her lying asleep clad in a shift of apricot-coloured silk that showed all and everything; and on her head was a coif of gold-cloth embroidered with pearls and jewels. The breeze raised her shift which laid bare her navel and showed her breasts and displayed a stomach whiter than snow, each one of whose dimples would contain an ounce of benzoin-ointment.[65] At this sight, his love and longing redoubled, and he began reciting:—

> An were it asked me when by hell-fire burnt,
>   When flames of heart my vitals hold and hem,
> "Which wouldst thou chose, say wouldst thou rather them,
>   Or drink sweet cooling draught?" I'd answer, "Them!"

Then he put his hand to the band of her petticoat-trousers and drew it and loosed it, for his soul lusted after her, when he saw a jewel, red as dye-wood, made fast to the band. He untied it and examined it and, seeing two lines of writing graven thereon, in a character not to be read, marvelled and said in his mind, "Were not this bezel something to her very dear she had not bound it to her trousers-band nor hidden it in the most privy and precious place about her person, that she might not be parted from it. Would I knew what she doth with this and what is the secret that is in it." So saying, he took it and went outside the tent to look at it in the light, and the while he was holding it behold, a bird swooped down on him and, snatching the same from his hand, flew off with it and then lighted on the ground. Thereupon Kamar al-Zaman fearing to lose the jewel, ran after the bird; but it flew on before him, keeping just out of his reach, and ceased not to draw him on from dale to dale and from hill to hill, till the night starkened and the firmament darkened, when it roosted on a high tree. So Kamar al-Zaman stopped under the tree confounded in thought and faint for famine and fatigue, and giving himself up for lost, would have turned back, but knew not the way whereby he came, for that darkness had overtaken him. Then he exclaimed, "There is no Majesty and there is no Might save in Allah, the Glorious, the Great!"; and laying him down under the tree (whereon was the bird) slept till the morning, when he awoke and saw the bird also wake up and fly away. He arose and walked after it, and it flew on little by little before him, after the measure of his faring; at which he smiled and said, "By Allah, a strange thing! Yesterday, this bird flew before me as fast as I could run, and to-day, knowing that I have awoke tired and cannot run, he flieth after the measure of my faring. By Allah, this is wonderful! But I must needs follow this bird whether it lead me to death or to life; and I will go wherever it goeth, for at all events it will not abide save in some inhabited land."[66] So he continued to follow the bird which roosted every night upon a tree; and he ceased not pursuing it for a space of ten days, feeding on the fruits of the earth and drinking of its waters. At the end of this time, he came in sight of an inhabited city, whereupon the bird darted off like the glance of the eye and, entering the town, disappeared from Kamar al-Zaman, who knew not what it meant or whither it was gone; so he marvelled at this and exclaimed, "Praise be to Allah who hath brought me in safety to this city!" Then he sat down by a stream and washed his hands and feet and face and rested awhile; and, recalling his late easy and pleasant life of union with his beloved and contrasting it with his present plight of trouble and fatigue and distress and strangerhood and famine and severance, the tears streamed from his eyes. And as soon as he had taken his rest, he rose and walked on little by little, till he entered the city[67] not knowing whither he should wend. He crossed the city from end to end, entering by the land-gate, and ceased not faring on till he came out at the sea-gate, for the city stood on the sea-shore. Yet he met not a single one of its citizens. And after issuing from the land-gate he fared forwards and ceased not faring till he found himself among the orchards and gardens of the place; and, passing among the trees presently came to a garden and stopped before its door; whereupon the keeper came out to him and saluted him. The Prince returned his greeting and the gardener bade him welcome, saying, "Praised be Allah that thou hast come off safe from the dwellers of this city! Quick, come into the garth, ere any of the townfolk see thee." Thereupon Kamar al-Zaman entered that garden, wondering in mind, and asked the keeper, "What may be the history of the people of this city and who may they be?" The other answered, "Know that the people of this city are all Magians: but Allah upon thee, tell me how thou camest to this city and what caused thy coming to our capital." Accordingly Kamar al-Zaman told the gardener all that had befallen him from beginning to end, whereat he marvelled with great marvel and said, "Know, O my son, that the cities of Al-Islam lie far from us; and between us and them is a four months' voyage by sea and a whole twelve months' journey by land. We have a ship which saileth every year with merchandise to the nearest Moslem country and which entereth the seas of the Ebony Islands and thence maketh the Khalidan Islands, the dominions of King Shahriman." Thereupon Kamar al-Zaman considered awhile and concluded that he could not do better than abide in the garden with the gardener and become his assistant, receiving for pay one fourth of the produce. So he said to him, "Wilt thou take me into thy service, to help thee in this garden?" Answered the gardener, "To hear is to consent;" and began teaching him to lead the water to the roots of the trees. So Kamar al-Zaman abode with him, watering the trees and hoeing up the weeds and wearing a short blue frock which reached to his knees. And he wept floods of tears; for he had no rest day or night, by reason of his strangerhood and he ceased not to repeat verses upon his beloved. Such was the case with Kamar al-Zaman; but as regards his wife, the Lady Budur, when she awoke she sought her husband and found him not: then she saw her petticoat-trousers undone, for the band had been loosed and the bezel lost, whereupon she said to herself, "By Allah, this is strange! Where is my husband? It would seem as if he had taken the talisman and gone away, knowing not the secret which is in it. Would to Heaven I knew whither can he have wended! But it must needs have been some extraordinary matter that drew him away, for he cannot brook to leave me a moment. Allah curse the stone and damn its hour!" Then she considered awhile and said in her mind, "If I go out and tell the varlets and let them learn that my husband is lost, they will lust after me: there is no help for it but that I use stratagem." So she rose and donned some of her husband's clothes and riding-boots, and a turband like his, drawing one corner of it across her face for a mouth-veil.[68] Then, setting a slave-girl in her litter, she went forth from the tent and called to the pages who brought her Kamar al-Zaman's steed; and she mounted and bade them load the beasts and resume the march. So they bound on the burdens and departed; and she concealed her trick, none doubting but she was Kamar al-Zaman, for she favoured him in face and form; nor did she cease journeying, she and her suite, days and nights, till they came in sight of a city overlooking the Salt Sea, where they pitched their tents without the walls and halted to rest. The Princess asked the name of the town and was told, "It is called the City of Ebony; its King is named Armanus, and he hath a daughter Hayat al-Nufus[69] hight." When the Lady Budur halted within sight of the Ebony City to take her rest, King Armanus sent a messenger, to learn what King it was who had encamped without his capital; so the messenger, coming to the tents, made enquiry anent their King, and was told that she was a King's son who had lost the way being bound for the Khalidan Islands; whereupon he returned to King Armanus with the tidings; and, when the King heard them, he straight-way rode out with the lords of his land to greet the stranger on arrival. As he drew near the tents the Lady Budur came to meet him on foot, whereupon the King alighted and they saluted each other. Then he took her to the city and, bringing her up to the palace, bade them spread the tables and trays of food and commanded them to transport her company and baggage to the guest-house. So they abode there three days; at the end of which time the King came in to the Lady Budur. Now she had that day gone to the Hammam and her face shone as the moon at its full, a seduction to the world and a rending of the veil of shame to mankind; and Armanus found her clad in a suit of silk, embroidered with gold and jewels; so he said to her, "O my son, know that I am a very old man, decrepit withal, and Allah hath blessed me with no child save one daughter, who resembleth thee in beauty and grace; and I am now waxed unfit for the conduct of the state. She is thine, O my son; and, if this my land please thee and thou be willing to abide and make thy home here, I will marry thee to her and give thee my kingdom and so be at rest." When Princess Budur heard this, she bowed her head and her forehead sweated for shame, and she said to herself, "How shall I do, and I a woman? If I refuse and depart from him, I cannot be safe but that haply he send after me troops to slay me; and if I consent, belike I shall be put to shame. I have lost my beloved Kamar al-Zaman and know not what is become of him; nor can I escape from this scrape save by holding my peace and consenting and abiding here, till Allah bring about what is to be." So she raised her head and made submission to King Armanus, saying, "Hearkening and obedience!"; whereat he rejoiced and bade the herald make proclamation throughout the Ebony Islands to hold high festival and decorate the houses. Then he assembled his Chamberlains and Nabobs, and Emirs and Wazirs and his officers of state and the Kazis of the city; and, formally abdicating his Sultanate, endowed Budur therewith and invested her in all the vestments of royalty. The Emirs and Grandees went in to her and did her homage, nothing doubting but that she was a young man, and all who looked on her bepissed their bag trousers, for the excess of her beauty and loveliness. Then, after the Lady Budur had been made Sultan and the drums had been beaten in announcement of the glad event, and she had been ceremoniously enthroned, King Armanus proceeded to equip his daughter Hayat al-Nufus for marriage, and in a few days, they brought the Lady Budur in to her, when they seemed as it were two moons risen at one time or two suns in conjunction. So they entered the bridal-chamber and the doors were shut and the curtains let down upon them, after the attendants had lighted the wax candles and spread for them the carpet-bed. When Budur found herself alone with the Princess Hayat al-Nufus, she called to mind her beloved Kamar al-Zaman and grief was sore upon her. She sat down beside the Princess Hayat al-Nufus and kissed her on the mouth; after which rising abruptly, she made the minor ablution and betook herself to her devotions; nor did she leave praying till Hayat al-Nufus fell asleep, when she slipt into bed and lay with her back to her till morning. And when day had broke the King and Queen came in to their daughter and asked her how she did, whereupon she told them what she had seen, and repeated to them the verses she had heard. Thus far concerning Hayat al-Nufus and her father; but as regards Queen Budur she went forth and seated herself upon the royal throne and all the Emirs and Captains and Officers of state came up to her and wished her joy of the kingship, kissing the earth before her and calling down blessings upon her. And she accosted them with smiling face and clad them in robes of honour, augmenting the fiefs of the high officials and giving largesse to the levies; wherefore all the people loved her and offered up prayers for the long endurance of her reign, doubting not but that she was a man. And she ceased not sitting all day in the hall of audience, bidding and forbidding; dispensing justice, releasing prisoners and remitting the customs-dues, till nightfall, when she withdrew to the apartment prepared for her. Here she found Hayat al-Nufus seated; so she sat down by her side and, clapping her on the back, coaxed and caressed her and kissed her between the eyes. Then Queen Budur stood up and wiped away her tears and, making the lesser ablution,[70] applied her to pray: nor did she give over praying till drowsiness overcame the Lady Hayat al-Nufus and she slept, whereupon the Lady Budur came and lay by her till the morning. At daybreak, she arose and prayed the dawn-prayer; and presently seated herself on the royal throne and passed the day in ordering and counter-ordering and giving laws and administering justice. This is how it fared with her; but as regards King Armanus he went in to his daughter and asked her how she did; so she told him all that had befallen her and repeated to him the verses which Queen Budur had recited, adding, "O my father, never saw I one more abounding in sound sense and modesty than my husband, save that he doth nothing but weep and sigh." He answered, "O my daughter, have patience with him yet this third night, and if he go not in unto thee and do away with thy maidenhead, we shall know how to proceed with him and oust him from the throne and banish him the country." And on this wise he agreed with his daughter what course he would take and night came on, Queen Budur arose from the throne of her kingdom and betaking herself to the palace, entered the apartment prepared for her. There she found the wax candles lighted and the Princess Hayat al-Nufus seated and awaiting her; whereupon she bethought her of her husband and what had betided them both of sorrow and severance in so short a space; she wept and sighed and groaned groan upon groan, and would have risen to pray, but, lo and behold! Hayat al-Nufus caught her by the skirt and clung to her saying, "O my lord, art thou not ashamed before my father, after all his favour, to neglect me at such a time as this?" When Queen Budur heard her words, she sat down in the same place and said, "O my beloved, what is this thou sayest?" She replied, "What I say is that I never saw any so proud of himself as thou. Is every fair one so disdainful? I say not this to incline thee to me; I say it only of my fear for thee from King Armanus; because he purposeth, unless thou go in unto me this very night, and do away my maidenhead, to strip thee of the kingship on the morrow and banish thee his kingdom; and peradventure his excessive anger may lead him to slay thee. But I, O my lord, have ruth on thee and give thee fair warning; and it is thy right to reck."[71] Now when Queen Budur heard her speak these words, she bowed her head groundwards awhile in sore perplexity and said in herself, "If I refuse I'm lost; and if I obey I'm shamed. But I am now Queen of all the Ebony Islands and they are under my rule, nor shall I ever again meet my Kamar al-Zaman save in this place; for there is no way for him to his native land but through the Ebony Islands. Verily, I know not what to do in my present case, but I commit my care to Allah who directeth all for the best, for I am no man that I should arise and go to this virgin girl." Then quoth Queen Budur to Hayat al-Nufus, "O my beloved, that I have neglected thee and abstained from thee is in my own despite." And she told her her whole story from beginning to end and showed her person to her, saying, "I conjure thee by Allah to keep my counsel, for I have concealed my case only that Allah may reunite me with my beloved Kamar al-Zaman and then come what may." The Princess heard her with extreme wonderment and was moved to pity and prayed Allah to reunite her with her beloved, saying, "Fear nothing, O my sister; but have patience till Allah bring to pass that which must come to pass:" and she began repeating:—

> None but the men of worth a secret keep;
> With worthy men a secret's hidden deep;
> As in a room, so secrets lie with me,
> Whose door is sealed, lock shot and lost the key.[72]

And when Hayat al-Nufus had ended her verses, she said, "O my sister, verily the breasts of the noble and brave are of secrets the grave; and I will not discover thine." Then they toyed and embraced and kissed and slept till near the Mu'ezzin's call to dawn-prayer, when Hayat al-Nufus arose and took a pigeon-poult,[73] and cut its throat over her smock and besmeared herself with its blood. Then she pulled off her petticoat-trousers and cried aloud, whereupon her people hastened to her and raised the usual lullilooing and outcries of joy and gladness. Presently her mother came in to her and asked her how she did and busied herself about her and abode with her till evening; whilst the Lady Budur arose with the dawn, and repaired to the bath and, after washing herself pure, proceeded to the hall of audience, where she sat down on her throne and dispensed justice among the folk. Now when King Armanus heard the loud cries of joy, he asked what was the matter and was informed of the consummation of his daughter's marriage; whereat he rejoiced and his breast swelled with gladness and he made a great marriage-feast whereof the merry-making lasted a long time. Such was their case: but as regards King Shahriman it was on this wise. After his son had fared forth to the chase accompanied by Marzawan, as before related, he tarried patiently awaiting their return at nightfall; but when his son did not appear, he passed a sleepless night and the dark hours were longsome upon him; his restlessness was excessive, his excitement grew upon him and he thought the morning would never dawn. And when day broke he sat expecting his son and waited till noon, but he came not; whereat his heart forebode separation and was fired with fears for Kamar al-Zaman; and he cried, "Alas! my son!" and he wept till his clothes were drenched with tears, and repeated with a beating heart:—

> Love's votaries I ceased not to oppose,
> Till doomed to taste Love's bitter and Love's sweet:
> I drained his rigour-cup to very dregs,
> Self-humbled at its slaves' and freemen's feet:
> Fortune had sworn to part the loves of us;
> She kept her word how truly, well I weet!

And when he ended his verse, he wiped away his tears and bade his troops make ready for a march and prepare for a long expedition. So they all mounted and set forth, headed by the Sultan, whose heart burnt with grief and was fired with anxiety for his son Kamar al-Zaman; and they advanced by forced marches. Now the King divided his host into six divisions, a right wing and a left wing, a vanguard and a rear-guard;[74] and bade them rendezvous for the morrow at the cross-roads. Accordingly they separated and scoured the country all the rest of that day till night, and they marched through the night and at noon of the ensuing day they joined company at the place where four roads met. But they knew not which the Prince followed, till they saw the sign of torn clothes and sighted shreds of flesh and beheld blood still sprinkled by the way and they noted every piece of the clothes and fragment of mangled flesh scattered on all sides. Now when King Shahriman saw this, he cried from his heart-core a loud cry, saying, "Alas, my son!"; and buffetted his face and pluckt his beard and rent his raiment, doubting not but his son was dead. Then he gave himself up to excessive weeping and wailing, and the troops also wept for his weeping, all being assured that Prince Kamar al-Zaman had perished. They threw dust on their heads, and the night surprised them shedding tears and lamenting till they were like to die. Then King Shahriman returned with the troops to his capital, giving up his son for lost, and deeming that wild beasts or banditti had set upon him and torn him to pieces; and made proclamation that all in the Khalidan Islands should don black in mourning for him. Moreover, he built, in his memory, a pavilion, naming it House of Lamentations; and on Mondays and Thursdays he devoted himself to the business of the state and ordering the affairs of his levies and lieges; and the rest of the week he was wont to spend in the House of Lamentations, mourning for his son and bewailing him with elegiac verses.[75] Such was the case with King Shahriman; but as regards Queen Budur daughter of King

Ghayur, she abode as ruler in the Ebony Islands, whilst the folk would point to her with their fingers, and say, "Yonder is the son-in-law of King Armanus." And every night she lay with Hayat al-Nufus, to whom she lamented her desolate state and longing for her husband Kamar al-Zaman, weeping and describing to her his beauty and loveliness, and yearning to enjoy him though but in a dream: And at times she would repeat:—

> Well Allah wots that since my severance from thee,
>   I wept till forced to borrow tears at usury:
> "Patience!" my blamer cried, "Heartsease right soon shalt see!"
>   Quoth I, "Say, blamer, where may home of Patience be?"

This is how it fared with Queen Budur; but as regards Kamar al-Zaman, he abode with the gardener in the garden for no short time, weeping night and day and repeating verses bewailing the past time of enjoyment and delight; whilst the gardener kept comforting him and assuring him that the ship would set sail for the land of the Moslems at the end of the year. And in this condition he continued till one day he saw the folk crowding together and wondered at this; but the gardener came in to him and said, "O my son, give over work for this day nor lead water to the trees; for it is a festival day, whereon folk visit one another. So take thy rest and only keep thine eye on the garden, whilst I go look after the ship for thee; for yet but a little while and I send thee to the land of the Moslems." Upon this, he went forth from the garden leaving to himself Kamar al-Zaman, who fell to musing upon his case till his heart was like to break and the tears streamed from his eyes. So he wept with excessive weeping till he swooned away and, when he recovered, he rose and walked about the garden, pondering what Time had done with him and bewailing the long endurance of his estrangement and separation from those he loved. As he was thus absorbed in melancholy thought, his foot stumbled and he fell on his face, his forehead striking against the projecting root of a tree; and the blow cut it open and his blood ran down and mingled with his tears. Then he rose and, wiping away the blood, dried his tears and bound his brow with a piece of rag; then continued his walk about the garden engrossed by sad reverie. Presently, he looked up at a tree and saw two birds quarrelling thereon, and one of them rose up and smote the other with its beak on the neck and severed from its body its head, wherewith it flew away, whilst the slain bird fell to the ground before Kamar al-Zaman. As it lay, behold, two great birds swooped down upon it alighting, one at the head and the other at the tail, and both drooped their wings and bowed their bills over it and, extending their necks towards it, wept. Kamar al-Zaman also wept when seeing the birds thus bewail their mate, and called to mind his wife and father. Then he looked at the twain and saw them dig a grave and therein bury the slain bird; after which they flew away far into the firmament and disappeared for a while; but presently they returned with the murtherer-bird and, alighting on the grave of the murthered, stamped on the slayer till they had done him to death. Then they rent his belly and tearing out his entrails, poured the blood on the grave of the slain:[76] moreover, they stripped off his skin and tare his flesh in pieces and, pulling out the rest of the bowels, scattered them hither and thither. All this while Kamar al-Zaman was watching them wonderingly; but presently, chancing to look at the place where the two birds had slain the third, he saw therein something gleaming. So he drew near to it and noted that it was the crop of the dead bird. Whereupon he took it and opened it and found the talisman which had been the cause of his separation from his wife. But when he saw it and knew it, he fell to the ground a-fainting for joy; and, when he revived, he said "Praised be Allah! This is a foretaste of good and a presage of reunion with my beloved." Then he examined the jewel and passed it over his eyes;[77] after which he bound it to his forearm, rejoicing in coming weal, and walked about till nightfall awaiting the gardener's return; and when he came not, he lay down and slept in his wonted place. At daybreak he rose to his work and, girding his middle with a cord of palm-fibre, took hatchet and basket and walked down the length of the garden, till he came to a carob-tree and struck the axe into its roots. The blow rang and resounded; so he cleared away the soil from the place and discovered a trap-door and raised it and found a winding stair, which he descended and came to an ancient vault of the time of Ad and Thamud,[78] hewn out of the rock. Round the vault stood many brazen vessels of the bigness of a great oil-jar which he found full of gleaming red gold: whereupon he said to himself, "Verily sorrow is gone and solace is come!" Then he mounted from the souterrain to the garden and, replacing the trap-door as it was before, busied himself in conducting water to the trees till the last of the day, when the gardener came back and said to him, "O my son, rejoice at the good tidings of a speedy return to thy native land: the merchants are ready equipped for the voyage and the ship in three days' time will set sail for the City of Ebony, which is the first of the cities of the Moslems; and after making it, thou must travel by land a six months' march till thou come to the Islands of Khalidan, the dominions of King Shahriman." At this Kamar al-Zaman rejoiced and began repeating:—

Part not from one whose wont is not to part from you;
Nor with your cruel taunts an innocent mortify:
Another so long-parted had ta'en heart from you,
And had his whole condition changed,—but not so I.

Then he kissed the gardener's hand and said, "O my father, even as thou hast brought me glad tidings, so I also have great good news for thee," and told him anent his discovery of the vault; whereat the gardener rejoiced and said, "O my son, fourscore years have I dwelt in this garden and

have never hit on aught; whilst thou, who hast not sojourned with me a year, hast discovered this thing; wherefore it is Heaven's gift to thee, which shall end thy crosses
and aid thee to rejoin thy folk and foregather with her thou
lovest." Quoth Kamar al-Zaman, "There is no help but it
must be shared between me and thee." Then he carried
him to the underground-chamber and showed him the
gold, which was in twenty jars: he took ten and the gardener ten, and the old man said to him, "O my son, fill thyself leather bottles[79] with the sparrow-olives[80] which grow
in this garden, for they are not found except in our land;
and the merchants carry them to all parts. Lay the gold in
the bottles and strew it over with olives: then stop them
and cover them and take them with thee in the ship." So
Kamar al-Zaman arose without stay or delay and took fifty
leather bottles and stored in each somewhat of the gold,
and closed each one after placing a layer of olives over the
gold; and at the bottom of one of the bottles he laid the talisman. Then sat he down to talk with the gardener, confident of speedy reunion with his own people and saying to
himself, "When I come to the Ebony Islands I will journey
thence to my father's country and enquire for my beloved
Budur. Would to Heaven I knew whether she returned to
her own land or journeyed on to my father's country or
whether there befel her any accident by the way." Then,
while he awaited the end of the term of days, he told the
gardener the tale of the birds and what had passed between
them; whereat the hearer wondered; and they both lay
down and slept till the morning. The gardener awoke sick
and abode thus two days; but on the third day, his sickness
increased on him, till they despaired of his life and Kamar
al-Zaman grieved with sore grief for him. Meanwhile behold, the Master and his crew came and enquired for the
gardener; and, when Kamar al-Zaman told them that he
was sick, they asked, "Where be the youth who is minded
to go with us to the Ebony Islands?" "He is your servant
and he standeth before you!" answered the Prince and bade
them carry the bottles of olives to the ship; so they trans-

ported them, saying, "Make haste, thou, for the wind is fair;" and he replied, "I hear and obey." Then he carried his provaunt on board and, returning to bid the gardener farewell, found him in the agonies of death; so he sat down at his head and closed his eyes, and his soul departed his body; whereupon he laid him out and committed him to the earth unto the mercy of Allah Almighty. Then he made for the ship but found that she had already weighed anchor and set sail; nor did she cease to cleave the seas till she disappeared from his sight. So he went back to whence he came heavy-hearted with whirling head; and neither would he address a soul nor return a reply; and reaching the garden and sitting down in cark and care he threw dust on his head and buffetted his cheeks. But anon he rented the place of its owner and hired a man to help him in irrigating the trees. Moreover, he repaired the trap-door and he went to the underground chamber and bringing the rest of the gold to grass, stowed it in other fifty bottles which he filled up with a layer of olives. Then he enquired of the ship and they told him that it sailed but once a year; at which his trouble of mind redoubled and he cried sore for that which had betided him, above all for the loss of the Princess Budur's talisman, and spent his nights and days weeping and repeating verses. Such was his case; but as regards the ship she sailed with a favouring wind till she reached the Ebony Islands. Now by decree of destiny, Queen Budur was sitting at a lattice-window overlooking the sea and saw the galley cast anchor upon the strand. At this sight, her heart throbbed and she took horse with the Chamberlains and Nabobs and, riding down to the shore, halted by the ship, whilst the sailors broke bulk and bore the bales to the storehouses; after which she called the captain to her presence and asked what he had with him. He answered "O King, I have with me in this ship aromatic drugs and cosmetics and healing powders and ointments and plasters and precious metals and rich stuffs and rugs of Yemen leather, not to be borne of mule or camel, and all manner of ottars and spices and perfumes, civet and ambergris and camphor and Sumatra aloes-wood, and tamarinds[81] and sparrow-olives to boot, such as are rare to find in this country." When she heard talk of sparrow-olives her heart longed for them and she said to the ship-master, "How much of olives hast thou?" He replied, "Fifty bottles full, but their owner is not with us; so the King shall take what he will of them." Quoth she, "Bring them ashore, that I may see them." Thereupon he called to the sailors, who brought her the fifty bottles; and she opened one and, looking at the olives, said to the captain, "I will take the whole fifty and pay you their value, whatso it be." He answered, "By Allah, O my lord, they have no value in our country; moreover their shipper tarried behind us, and he is a poor man." Asked she, "And what are they worth here?" and he answered "A thousand dirhams." "I will take them at a thousand," she said and bade them carry the fifty bottles to the palace. When it was night, she called for a bottle of olives and opened it, there being none in the room but herself and the Princess Hayat al-Nufus. Then, placing a dish before her she turned into it the contents of the jar, when there fell out into the dish with the olives a heap of red gold; and she said to the Lady Hayat al-Nufus, "This is naught but gold!" So she sent for the rest of the bottles and found them all full of precious metal and scarce enough olives to fill a single jar. Moreover, she sought among the gold and found therein the talisman, which she took and examined and behold, it was that which Kamar al-Zaman had taken from off the band of her petticoat trousers. Thereupon she cried out for joy and slipped down in a swoon; and when she recovered she said to herself, "Verily, this talisman was the cause of my separation from my beloved Kamar al-Zaman; but now it is an omen of good." Then she showed it to Hayat al-Nufus and said to her, "This was the cause of disunion and now, please Allah, it shall be the cause of reunion." As soon as day dawned she seated herself on the royal throne and sent for the ship-master, who came into the presence and kissed the ground before

her. Quoth she, "Where didst thou leave the owner of
these olives?" Quoth he, "O King of the age, we left him
in the land of the Magians and he is a gardener there." She
rejoined, "Except thou bring him to me, thou knowest
not the harm which awaiteth thee and thy ship." Then she
bade them seal up the magazines of the merchants and said
to them, "Verily the owner of these olives hath borrowed of
me and I have a claim upon him for debt and, unless ye
bring him to me, I will without fail do you all die and seize
your goods." So they went to the captain and promised him
the hire of the ship, if he would go and return a second
time, saying, "Deliver us from this masterful tyrant." Accordingly the skipper embarked and set sail and Allah decreed him a prosperous voyage, till he came to the Island
of the Magians and, landing by night, went up to the garden. Now the night was long upon Kamar al-Zaman, and
he sat, bethinking him of his beloved, and bewailing what
had befallen him and versifying:—

> A night whose stars refused to run their course,
> A night of those which never seem outworn:
> Like Resurrection-day, of longsome length[82]
> To him that watched and waited for the morn.

Now at this moment, the captain knocked at the garden
gate, and Kamar al-Zaman opened and went out to him,
whereupon the crew seized him and went down with him
on board the ship and set sail forthright; and they ceased
not voyaging days and nights, whilst Kamar al-Zaman
knew not why they dealt thus with him; but when he questioned them they replied, "Thou hast offended against the
Lord of the Ebony Islands, the son-in-law of King Armanus, and thou hast stolen his monies, miserable that
thou art!" Said he, "By Allah! I never entered that country
nor do I know where it is!" However, they fared on with
him, till they made the Ebony Islands and landing, carried
him up to the Lady Budur, who knew him at sight and said,

"Leave him with the eunuchs, that they take him to the bath." Then she relieved the merchants of the embargo and gave the captain a robe of honour worth ten thousand pieces of gold; and, after returning to the palace, she went in that night to the Princess Hayat al-Nufus and told her what had passed, saying, "Keep thou my counsel, till I accomplish my purpose, and do a deed which shall be recorded and shall be read by Kings and commoners after we be dead and gone." And when she gave orders that they bear Kamar al-Zaman to the bath, they did so and clad him in a royal habit so that, when he came forth, he resembled a willow-bough or a star which shamed the greater and lesser light[83] and its glow, and his life and soul returned to his frame. Then he repaired to the palace and went in to the Princess Budur; and when she saw him she schooled her heart to patience, till she should have accomplished her purpose; and she bestowed on him Mamelukes and eunuchs, camels and mules. Moreover, she gave him a treasury of money and she ceased not advancing him from dignity to dignity, till she made him Lord High Treasurer and committed to his charge all the treasures of the state; and she admitted him to familiar favour and acquainted the Emirs with his rank and dignity. And all loved him, for Queen Budur did not cease day by day to increase his allowances. As for Kamar al-Zaman, he was at a loss anent the reason of her thus honouring him; and he gave gifts and largesse out of the abundance of the wealth; and he devoted himself to the service of King Armanus; so that the King and all the Emirs and people, great and small, adored him and were wont to swear by his life. Nevertheless, he ever marvelled at the honour and favour shown him by Queen Budur and said to himself, "By Allah, there needs must be a reason for this affection! Peradventure, this King favoureth me not with these immoderate favours save for some ill purpose and, therefore, there is no help but that I crave leave of him to depart his realm." So he went in to Queen Budur and said to her, "O King, thou hast overwhelmed me with favours, but it will fulfil the measure of thy bounties if thou take from me all thou hast been pleased to bestow upon me, and permit me to depart." She smiled and asked, "What maketh thee seek to depart and plunge into new perils, whenas thou art in the enjoyment of the highest favour and greatest prosperity?" Answered Kamar al-Zaman, "O King, verily this favour, if there be no reason for it, is indeed a wonder of wonders, more by token that thou hast advanced me to dignities such as befit men of age and experience, albeit I am as it were a young child." And Queen Budur rejoined, "The reason is that I love thee for thine exceeding loveliness and thy surpassing beauty; and if thou wilt but grant me my desire of thy body, I will advance thee yet farther in honour and favour and largesse; and I will make thee Wazir, for all thy tender age, even as the folk made me Sultan over them and I no older than thou; so that nowadays there is nothing strange when children take the head and by Allah, he was a gifted man who said:—

> It seems as though of Lot's tribe were our days,
> And crave with love to advance the young in years."[84]

When Kamar al-Zaman heard these words, he was abashed and his cheeks flushed till they seemed a-flame; and he said, "I need not these favours which lead to the commission of sin; I will live poor in wealth but wealthy in virtue and honour." Quoth she, "I am not to be duped by thy scruples, arising from prudery and coquettish ways." Now when Kamar al-Zaman heard these words, he said, "O King, I have not the habit of these doings, nor have I strength to bear these heavy burthens for which elder than I have proved unable; then how will it be with my tender age?" But she smiled at his speech and retorted, "Indeed, it is a matter right marvellous how error springeth from the disorder of man's intendiment! Since thou art a boy, why standest thou in fear of sin or the doing of things forbidden, seeing that thou art not yet come to years of canonical responsibility; and the offences of a child incur neither punishment nor reproof? Verily, thou hast committed thyself to a quibble for the sake of contention, and it is thy duty to bow before a proposal of fruition, so henceforward cease from denial and coyness, for the commandment of Allah is a decree fore-ordained:[85] indeed, I have more reason than thou to fear falling and by sin to be misled." When Kamar al-Zaman heard these words, the light became darkness in his sight and he said, "O King, thou hast in thy household fair women and female slaves, who have not their like in this age: shall not these suffice thee without me? Do thy will with them and let me go!" She replied, "Thou sayest sooth, but it is not with them that one who loveth thee can heal himself of torment and can abate his fever; for, when tastes and inclinations are corrupted by vice, they hear and obey other than good advice." When Kamar al-Zaman heard these words, and was certified that there was no escaping compliance with what willed she, he said, "O King of the age, if thou must needs have it so, make convenant with me that thou wilt do this thing with me but once, though it avail not to correct thy depraved appetite; and that thou wilt never again require this thing of me to the end of time; so perchance shall Allah purge me of the sin." She replied, "I promise thee this same, hoping that Allah of His favour will relent towards us and blot out our mortal offence; for the girdle of heaven's forgiveness is not indeed so strait, but it may compass us around and absolve us of the excess of our heinous sins and bring us to the light of salvation out of the darkness of error; and indeed excellently well saith the poet:—

> Of evil thing the folk suspect us twain;
> And to this thought their hearts and souls are bent:
> Come, dear! let's justify and free their souls
> That wrong us; one good bout and then—repent!"[86]

Thereupon she made with him an agreement and a covenant and swore a solemn oath by Him who is Self-existent, that this thing should befal betwixt them but once and never again for all time, and that the desire of him was driving her to death and perdition. So he rose up with her, on this condition, and went with her to her own boudoir, that she might quench the lowe of her lust, saying, "There is no Majesty, and there is no Might save in Allah, the Glorious, the Great! This is the fated decree of the All-powerful, the All-wise!"; and he doffed his bag-trousers, shamefull and abashed, with the tears running from his eyes for stress of affright. Thereat she smiled and making him mount upon a couch with her, said to him, "After this night, thou shalt see naught that will offend thee." Then she turned to him bussing and bosoming him and he found her thighs cooler than cream and softer than silk, so he said to her, "O King, I cannot find that thou art like other men; what then moved thee to do this deed?" Then loudly laughed Queen Budur till she fell on her back,[87] and said, "O my dearling, how quickly thou hast forgotten the nights we have lain together!" Then she made herself known to him, and he knew her for his wife, the Lady Budur, daughter of King al-Ghayur, Lord of the Isles and the Seas. So he embraced her and she embraced him and that hour was such as maketh a man to forget his father and his mother. Then Queen Budur told Kamar al-Zaman all that had befallen her from beginning to end and he did likewise; after which he began to upbraid her, saying, "What moved thee to deal with me as thou hast done this night?" She replied, "Pardon me! for I did this by way of jest, and that pleasure and gladness might be increased." And when dawned the morn and day arose with its sheen and shone, she sent to King Armanus, sire of the Lady Hayat al-Nufus, and acquainted him with the truth of the case and that she was wife to Kamar al-Zaman. Moreover, she told him their tale and the cause of their separation, and how his daughter was a virgin, pure as when she was born. He marvelled at their story with exceeding marvel and bade them chronicle it in letters of gold. Then he turned to Kamar al-Zaman and said,

"O King's son, art thou minded to become my son-in-law by marrying my daughter?" Replied he, "I must consult the Queen Budur, as she hath a claim upon me for benefits without stint." And when he took counsel with her, she said, "Right is thy recking; marry her and I will be her handmaid; for I am her debtor for kindness and favour and good offices, and obligations manifold, especially as we are here in her place and as the King her father hath whelmed us with benefits."[88] Now when he saw that she inclined to this and was not jealous of Hayat al-Nufus, he agreed with her upon this matter and told King Armanus what she had said; whereat he rejoiced with great joy. Then he went out and, seating himself upon his chair of estate, assembled all the Wazirs, Emirs, Chamberlains and Grandees, to whom he related the whole story of Kamar al-Zaman and his wife, Queen Budur, from first to last; and acquainted them with his desire to marry his daughter Hayat al-Nufus to the Prince and make him King in the stead of Queen Budur. Whereupon said they all, "Since he is the husband of Queen Budur, who hath been our King till now, whilst we deemed her son-in-law to King Armanus, we are all content to have him to Sultan over us; and we will be his servants, nor will we swerve from his allegiance." So Armanus rejoiced hereat and, summoning Kazis and witnesses and the chief officers of state, bade draw up the contract of marriage between Kamar al-Zaman and his daughter, the Princess Hayat al-Nufus. Then he held high festival, giving sumptuous marriage-feasts and bestowing costly dresses of honour upon all the Emirs and Captains of the host; moreover he distributed alms to the poor and needy and set free all the prisoners. The whole world rejoiced in the coming of Kamar al-Zaman to the throne, blessing him and wishing him endurance of glory and prosperity, renown and felicity; and, as soon as he became King, he remitted the customs-dues and released all men who remained in gaol. Thus he abode a long while, ordering himself worthily towards his lieges; and he lived with his two wives in peace, happiness, constancy and content, lying the night with each of them in turn, till there overtook them the Destroyer of delights and the Sunderer of societies, and Allah knoweth all things!—And there is a story of

HATIM OF THE TRIBE OF TAYY.

It is told of Hatim of the tribe of Tayy,[1] that when he died, they buried him on the top of a mountain and set over his grave two troughs hewn out of two rocks and stone girls with dishevelled hair. At the foot of the hill was a stream of running water, and when wayfarers camped there, they heard loud crying and keening in the night, from dark till daybreak; but when they arose in the morning, they found nothing but the girls carved in stone. Now when Zu 'l-Kura'a,[2] King of Himyar, going forth of his tribe, came to that valley, he halted to pass the night there and, when he drew near the mountain, he heard the keening and said, "What lamenting is that on yonder hill?" They answered him, saying, "Verily this be the tomb of Hatim al-Tayyi over which are two troughs of stone and stone figures of girls with dishevelled hair; and all who camp in this place by night hear this crying and keening." So he said jestingly, "O Hatim of Tayy! we are thy guests this night, and we are lank with hunger." Then sleep overcame him, but presently he awoke in affright and cried out, saying, "Help, O Arabs! Look to my beast!" So they came to him, and finding his she-camel struggling and struck down, they stabbed her in the throat and roasted her flesh and ate. Then they asked him what had happened and he said, "When I closed my eyes, I saw in my sleep Hatim of Tayy who came to me sword in hand and cried:—Thou comest to us and we have nothing by us. Then he smote my she-camel with his sword, and she had surely died even though ye had not come to her and slaughtered her."[3] Now when morning dawned the King mounted the beast of one of his companions and, taking the owner up behind him, set out and fared on till midday, when they saw a man coming towards them, mounted on a camel and leading another, and said to him, "Who art thou?" He answered, "I am Adi,[4] son of Hatim of Tayy; where is Zu 'l-Kura'a, Emir of Himyar?" Replied they, "This is he;" and he said to the prince, "Take this she-camel in place of thy beast which my father slaughtered for thee." Asked Zu 'l-Kura'a, "Who told thee of this?" and Adi answered, "My father appeared to me in a dream last night and said to me:—Harkye, Adi; Zu 'l-Kura'a, King of Himyar, sought the guest-rite of me and I, having naught to give him, slaughtered his she-camel, that he might eat: so do thou carry him a she-camel to ride, for I have nothing." And Zu 'l-Kura'a took her, marvelling at the generosity of Hatim of Tayy alive and dead. And amongst instances of generosity is

THE TALE OF MA'AN SON OF ZAIDAH AND THE BADAWI.

Now Ma'an bin Zaidah went forth one day to the chase with his company, and they came upon a herd of gazelles; so they separated in pursuit and Ma'an was left alone to chase one of them. When he had made prize of it he alighted and slaughtered it; and as he was thus engaged, he espied a person[1] coming forth out of the desert on an ass. So he remounted and riding up to the new-comer, saluted him and asked him, "Whence comest thou?" Quoth he, "I come from the land of Kuza'ah, where we have had a two years' dearth; but this year it was a season of plenty and I sowed early cucumbers.[2] They came up before their time, so I gathered what seemed the best of them and set out to carry them to the Emir Ma'an bin Zaidah, because of his well-known beneficence and notorious munificence." Asked Ma'an, "How much dost thou hope to get of him?"; and the Badawi answered, "A thousand dinars." Quoth the Emir, "What if he say this is too much?" Said the Badawi, "Then I will ask five hundred dinars." "And if he say, Too much?"

"Then three hundred!" "And if he say yet, Too much?" "Then two hundred!" "And if he say yet, Too much?" "Then one hundred!" "And if he say yet, Too much?" "Then, fifty!" "And if he say yet, Too much?" "Then thirty!" "And if he say still, Too much?" asked Ma'an bin Zaidah. Answered the Badawi, "I will make my ass set his four feet in his Honour's home[3] and return to my people, disappointed and empty-handed." So Ma'an laughed at him and urged his steed till he came up with his suite and returned to his place, when he said to his chamberlain, "An there come to thee a man with cucumbers and riding on an ass admit him to me." Presently up came the Badawi and was admitted to Ma'an's presence; but knew not the Emir for the man he had met in the desert, by reason of the gravity and majesty of his semblance and the multitude of his eunuchs and attendants, for he was seated on his chair of estate with his officers ranged in lines before him and on either side. So he saluted him and Ma'an said to him "What bringeth thee, O brother of the Arabs?" Answered the Badawi, "I hoped in the Emir, and have brought him curly cucumbers out of season." Asked Ma'an, "And how much dost thou expect of us?" "A thousand dinars," answered the Badawi. "This is far too much," quoth Ma'an. Quoth he, "Five hundred." "Too much!" "Then three hundred." "Too much!" "Two hundred." "Too much!" "One hundred." "Too much!" "Fifty." "Too much!" At last the Badawi came down to thirty dinars; but Ma'an still replied, "Too much!" So the Badawi cried, "By Allah, the man who met me in the desert brought me bad luck! But I will not go lower than thirty dinars." The Emir laughed and said nothing; whereupon the wild Arab knew that it was he whom he had met and said, "O my lord, except thou bring the thirty dinars, see ye, there is the ass tied ready at the door and here sits Ma'an, his honour, at home." So Ma'an laughed, till he fell on his back; and, calling his steward, said to him, "Give him a thousand dinars and five hundred and three hundred and two hundred and one hundred and fifty and thirty;

and leave the ass tied up where he is." So the Arab to his amazement, received two thousand one hundred and eighty dinars, and Allah have mercy on them both and on all generous men! And I have also heard, O auspicious King, a tale of

THE CITY OF MANY-COLUMNED

IRAM AND ABDULLAH SON OF

ABI KILABAH.[1]

It is related that Abdullah bin Abi Kilabah went forth in
quest of a she-camel which had strayed from him; and, as
he was wandering in the deserts of Al-Yaman and the district of Saba,[2] behold, he came upon a great city girt by a
vast castle around which were palaces and pavilions that
rose high into middle air. He made for the place thinking
to find there folk of whom he might ask concerning his
she-camel; but, when he reached it, he found it desolate,
without a living soul in it. So (quoth he) I alighted and,
hobbling my dromedary, and composing my mind, entered
into the city. Now when I came to the castle, I found it had
two vast gates (never in the world was seen their like for
size and height) inlaid with all manner jewels and jacinths,
white and red, yellow and green. Beholding this I marvelled with great marvel and thought the case mighty
wondrous; then entering the citadel in a flutter of fear and
dazed with surprise and affright, I found it long and wide
about equalling Al-Medinah[3] in point of size; and therein
were lofty palaces laid out in pavilions all built of gold and
silver and inlaid with many-coloured jewels and jacinths
and chrysolites and pearls. And the door-leaves in the

pavilions were like those of the castle for beauty; and their floors were strewn with great pearls and balls, no smaller than hazel-nuts, of musk and ambergris and saffron. Now when I came within the heart of the city and saw therein no created beings of the Sons of Adam I was near swooning and dying for fear. Moreover, I looked down from the great roofs of the pavilion-chambers and their balconies and saw rivers running under them; and in the main streets were fruit-laden trees and tall palms; and the manner of their building was one brick of gold and one of silver. So I said to myself, "Doubtless this is the Paradise promised for the world to come." Then I loaded me with the jewels of its gravel and the musk of its dust as much as I could carry and returned to my own country, where I told the folk what I had seen. After a time the news reached Mu'awiyah, son of Abu Sufyan, who was then Caliph in Al-Hijaz; so he wrote to his lieutenant in San'a of Al-Yaman to send for the teller of the story and question him of the truth of the case. Accordingly the lieutenant summoned me and questioned me of my adventure and of all appertaining to it; and I told him what I had seen, whereupon he despatched me to Mu'awiyah, before whom I repeated the story of the strange sights; but he would not credit it. So I brought out to him some of the pearls and balls of musk and ambergris and saffron, in which latter there was still some sweet savour; but the pearls were grown yellow and had lost pearly colour. Now Mu'awiyah wondered at this and, sending for Ka'ab al-Ahbar[4] said to him, "O Ka'ab, I have sent for thee to ascertain the truth of a certain matter and hope that thou wilt be able to certify me thereof." Asked Ka'ab, "What is it, O Commander of the Faithful?"; and Mu'awiyah answered, "Wottest thou of any city founded by man which is builded of gold and silver, the pillars whereof are of chrysolite and rubies and its gravel pearls and balls of musk and ambergris and saffron?" He replied, "Yes, O Commander of the Faithful, this is 'Iram with pillars decked and dight, the like of which was never made in the lands,'⁵ and the builder was Shaddad son of Ad the Greater."⁶ Quoth the Caliph, "Tell us something of its history," and Ka'ab said:—Ad the Greater had two sons, Shadid and Shaddad who, when their father died, ruled conjointly in his stead, and there was no King of the Kings of the earth but was subject to them. After awhile Shadid died and his brother Shaddad reigned over the earth alone. Now he was fond of reading in antique books; and, happening upon the description of the world to come and of Paradise, with its pavilions and galleries and trees and fruits and so forth, his soul moved him to build the like thereof in this world, after the fashion aforesaid. Now under his hand were an hundred thousand Kings, each ruling over an hundred thousand chiefs, commanding each an hundred thousand warriors; so he called these all before him and said to them, "I find in ancient books and annals a description of Paradise, as it is to be in the next world, and I desire to build me its like in this world. Go ye forth therefore to the goodliest tract on earth and the most spacious and build me there a city of gold and silver, whose gravel shall be chrysolite and rubies and pearls; and for support of its vaults make pillars of jasper. Fill it with palaces, whereon ye shall set galleries and balconies and plant its lanes and thoroughfares with all manner trees bearing yellow-ripe fruits and make rivers to run through it in channels of gold and silver." Whereat said one and all, "How are we able to do this thing thou hast commanded, and whence shall we get the chrysolites and rubies and pearls whereof thou speakest?" Quoth he, "What! weet ye not that the Kings of the world are subject to me and under my hand and that none therein dare gainsay my word?" Answered they, "Yes, we know that." Whereupon the King rejoined, "Fare ye then to the mines of chrysolites and rubies and pearls and gold and silver and collect their produce and gather together all of value that is in the world and spare no pains and leave naught; and take also for me such of these things as be in men's hands and let nothing escape you: be diligent and beware of disobedience." And thereupon he wrote letters to all the Kings of the world and bade them gather together whatso of these things was in their subjects' hands, and get them to the mines of precious stones and metals, and bring forth all that was therein, even from the abysses of the seas. This they accomplished in the space of 20 years, for the number of rulers then reigning over the earth was three hundred and sixty Kings; and Shaddad presently assembled from all lands and countries architects and engineers and men of art and labourers and handicraftsmen, who dispersed over the world and explored all the wastes and wolds and tracts and holds. At last they came to an uninhabited spot, a vast and fair open plain clear of sand-hills and mountains, with founts flushing and rivers rushing, and they said, "This is the manner of place the King commanded us to seek and ordered us to find." So they busied themselves in building the city even as bade them Shaddad, King of the whole earth in its length and breadth; leading the fountains in channels and laying the foundations after the prescribed fashion. Moreover, all the Kings of earth's several reigns sent thither jewels and precious stones and pearls large and small and carnelian and refined gold and virgin silver upon camels by land, and in great ships over the waters, and there came to the builders' hands of all these materials so great a quantity as may neither be told nor counted nor conceived. So they laboured at the work three hundred years; and, when they had brought it to end, they went to King Shaddad and acquainted him therewith. Then said he, "Depart and make thereon an impregnable castle, rising and towering high in air, and build around it a thousand pavilions, each upon a thousand columns of chrysolite and ruby and vaulted with gold, that in each pavilion a Wazir may dwell." So they returned forthwith and did this in other twenty years; after which they again presented themselves before King Shaddad and informed him of the accomplishment of his will. Then he commanded his Wa-

zirs, who were a thousand in number, and his Chief Officers and such of his troops and others as he put trust in,
to prepare for departure and removal to Many-Columned
Iram, in the suite and at the stirrup of Shaddad, son of Ad,
King of the world; and he bade also such as he would of his
women and his Harim and of his handmaids and eunuchs
make them ready for the journey. They spent twenty years
in preparing for departure, at the end of which time Shaddad set out with his host, rejoicing in the attainment of his
desire till there remained but one day's journey between
him and Iram of the Pillars. Then Allah sent down on him
and on the stubborn unbelievers with him a mighty rushing sound from the Heavens of His power, which destroyed
them all with its vehement clamour, and neither Shaddad
nor any of his company set eyes on the city.[7] Moreover,
Allah blotted out the road which led to the city, and it
stands in its stead unchanged until the Resurrection Day
and the Hour of Judgment. So Mu'awiyah wondered greatly
at Ka'ab al-Ahbar's story and said to him, "Hath any mortal ever made his way to that city?" He replied, "Yes; one of
the companions of Mohammed (on whom be blessing and
peace!) reached it, doubtless and forsure after the same
fashion as this man here seated." And (quoth Al-Sha'abi[8])
it is related, on the authority of learned men of Himyar in
Al-Yaman that Shaddad, when destroyed with all his host
by the sound, was succeeded in his Kingship by his son
Shaddad the Less, whom he left viceregent in Hazramaut
and Saba, when he and his marched upon Many-columned
Iram. Now as soon as he heard of his father's death on the
road, he caused his body to be brought back from the
desert to Hazramaut[9] and bade them hew him out a tomb
in a cave, where he laid the body on a throne of gold and
threw over the corpse three-score and ten robes of cloth
of gold, purfled with precious stones. Lastly at his sire's
head he set up a tablet of gold whereon were graven these
verses:—

Take warning O proud,
And in length o' life vain!
I'm Shaddad son of Ad,
Of the forts castellain;
Lord of pillars and power,
Lord of tried might and main,
Whom all earth-sons obeyed
For my mischief and bane;
And who held East and West
In mine awfullest reign.
He preached me salvation
Whom God did assain,[10]
But we crossed him and asked
"Can no refuge be ta'en?"
When a Cry on us cried
From th' horizon plain,
And we fell on the field
Like the harvested grain,
And the Fixt Day await
We, in earth's bosom lain!

Al-Sa'alibi also relateth:—It chanced that two men once entered this cave and found steps at its upper end; so they descended and came to an underground chamber, an hundred cubits long by forty wide and an hundred high. In the midst stood a throne of gold, whereon lay a man of huge bulk, filling the whole length and breadth of the throne. He was covered with jewels and raiment gold-and-silver-wrought, and at his head was a tablet of gold bearing an inscription. So they took the tablet and carried it off, together with as many bars of gold and silver and so forth as they could bear away. And men also relate the tale of

THE SWEEP AND
THE NOBLE LADY.

During the season of the Meccan pilgrimage, whilst the people were making circuit about the Holy House and the place of compassing was crowded, behold, a man laid hold of the covering of the Ka'abah[1] and cried out, from the bottom of his heart, saying, "I beseech thee, O Allah, that she may once again be wroth with her husband and that I may know her!" A company of the pilgrims heard him and seized him and carried him to the Emir of the pilgrims, after a sufficiency of blows; and, said they, "O Emir, we found this fellow in the Holy Places, saying thus and thus." So the Emir commanded to hang him; but he cried, "O Emir, I conjure thee, by the virtue of the Apostle (whom Allah bless and preserve!), hear my story and then do with me as thou wilt." Quoth the Emir, "Tell thy tale forthright." Know then, O Emir, quoth the man, that I am a sweep who works in the sheep-slaughterhouses and carries off the blood and the offal to the rubbish-heaps outside the gates. And it came to pass as I went along one day with my ass loaded, I saw the people running away and one of them said to me, "Enter this alley, lest haply they slay thee." Quoth I, "What aileth the folk running away?" and one of the eunuchs, who were passing, said to me, "This is the Harim[2] of one of the notables and her eunuchs drive the people out of her way and beat them all, without respect to persons." So I turned aside with the donkey and stood still awaiting the dispersal of the crowd; and I saw a number of eunuchs with staves in their hands, followed by nigh thirty women slaves, and amongst them a lady as she were a willow-wand or a thirsty gazelle, perfect in beauty and grace and amorous languor, and all were attending upon her. Now when she came to the mouth of the passage where I stood, she turned right and left and, calling one of the Castratos, whispered in his ear; and behold, he came up to me and laid hold of me, whilst another eunuch took my ass and made off with it. And when the spectators fled, the first eunuch bound me with a rope and dragged me after him till I knew not what to do; and the people followed us and cried out, saying, "This is not allowed of Allah! What hath this poor scavenger done that he should be bound with ropes?" and praying the eunuchs, "Have pity on him and let him go, so Allah have pity on you!" And I the while said in my mind, "Doubtless the eunuchry seized me, because their mistress smelt the stink of the offal and it sickened her. Belike she is with child or ailing; but there is no Majesty and there is no Might save in Allah, the Glorious, the Great!" So I continued walking on behind them, till they stopped at the door of a great house; and, entering before me, brought me into a big hall—I know not how I shall describe its magnificence—furnished with the finest furniture. And the women also entered the hall; and I bound and held by the eunuch and saying to myself, "Doubtless they will torture me here till I die and none know of my death." However, after a while, they carried me into a neat bath-room leading out of the hall; and as I sat there, behold, in came three slave-girls who seated themselves round me and said to me, "Strip off thy rags and tatters." So I pulled off my threadbare clothes and one of them fell a-rubbing my legs and feet whilst another scrubbed my head and a third shampooed my body. When they had made an end of washing me, they brought me a parcel of clothes and said to me, "Put these on"; and I answered, "By Allah, I know not how!" So they came up to me and dressed me, laughing together at me the while; after which they brought casting-bottles full of rose-water, and sprinkled me therewith. Then I went out with them into another saloon; by Allah, I know not how to praise its splendour for the wealth of paintings and furniture therein; and entering it, I saw a person seated on a couch of Indian rattan, with ivory feet and before her a number of damsels. When she saw me she rose to me and called me; so I went up to her and she seated me by her side. Then she bade her slave-girls bring food, and they brought all manner of rich meats, such as I never saw in all my life; I do not even know the names of the dishes, much less their nature. So I ate my fill and when the dishes had been taken away and we had washed our hands, she called for fruits which came without stay or delay and ordered me eat of them; and when we had ended eating she bade one of the waiting-women bring the wine furniture. So they set on flagons of divers kinds of wine and burned perfumes in all the censers, what while a damsel like the moon rose and served us with wine to the sound of the smitten strings; and I drank, and the lady drank, till we were seized with wine and the whole time I doubted not but that all this was an illusion of sleep. Presently, she signed to one of the damsels to spread us a bed in such a place, which being done, she rose and took me by the hand and led me thither, and lay down and I lay with her till the morning, and as often as I pressed her to my breast I smelt the delicious fragrance of musk and other perfumes that exaled from her and could not think otherwise but that I was in Paradise or in the vain phantasies of a dream. Now when it was day, she asked me where I lodged and I told her, "In such a place;" whereupon she gave me leave to depart, handing to me a kerchief worked with gold and silver and containing somewhat tied in it, and took leave of me, saying, "Go to the bath with this." I rejoiced and said to myself, "If there be but five coppers here, it will buy me this day my morning meal." Then I left her, as though I were leaving Paradise, and returned to my poor crib where I opened the kerchief and found in it fifty miskals of gold. So I buried them in the ground and, buying two farthings' worth of bread and "kitchen,"[3] seated me at the door and broke my fast; after which I sat pondering my case and continued so doing till the time of afternoon-prayer, when lo! a slave-girl accosted me saying, "My mistress calleth for thee." I followed her to the house aforesaid and, after asking permission, she carried me into the lady, before whom I kissed the ground, and she commanded me to sit and called for meat and wine as on the previous day; after which I again lay with her all night. On the morrow, she gave me a second kerchief, with other fifty dinars therein, and I took it and going home, buried this also. In such pleasant condition I continued eight days running, going in to her at the hour of afternoon-prayer and leaving her at daybreak; but, on the eighth night, as I lay with her, behold, one of her slave-girls came running in and said to me, "Arise, go up into yonder closet." So I rose and went into the closet, which was over the gate, and presently I heard a great clamour and tramp of horse; and, looking out of the window which gave on the street in front of the house, I saw a young man as he were the rising moon on the night of fulness come riding up attended by a number of servants and soldiers who were about him on foot. He alighted at the door and entering the saloon found the lady seated on the couch; so he kissed the ground between her hands then came up to her and kissed her hands; but she would not speak to him. However, he continued patiently to humble himself, and soothe her and speak her fair, till he made his peace with her, and they lay together that night. Now when her husband had made his peace with the young lady, he lay with her that night; and next morning, the soldiers came for him and he mounted and rode away; whereupon she drew near to me and said, "Sawst thou yonder man?" I answered, "Yes;" and she said, "He is my husband, and I will tell thee what befel me with him. It came to pass one day that we were sitting, he and I, in the garden within the house, and behold, he rose from my side and was absent a long while, till I grew tired of waiting and said to myself:— Most like, he is in the privy. So I arose and went to the water-closet, but not finding him there, went down to the kitchen, where I saw a slave-girl; and when I enquired for him, she showed him to me lying with one of the cook-maids. Hereupon, I swore a great oath that I assuredly would do adultery with the foulest and filthiest man in Baghdad; and the day the eunuch laid hands on thee, I had been four days going round about the city in quest of one who should answer to this description, but found none fouler nor filthier than thy good self. So I took thee and there passed between us that which Allah fore-ordained to us; and now I am quit of my oath." Then she added, "If, however, my husband return yet again to the cookmaid and lie with her, I will restore thee to thy lost place in my favours." Now when I heard these words from her lips, what while she pierced my heart with the shafts of her glances, my tears streamed forth, till my eyelids were chafed sore with weeping. Then she made them give me other fifty dinars (making in all four hundred gold pieces I had of her) and bade me depart. So I went out from her and came hither, that I might pray Allah (extolled and exalted be He!) to make her husband return to the cookmaid, that haply I might be again admitted to her favours. When the Emir of the pilgrims heard the man's story, he set him free and said to the bystanders, "Allah upon you, pray for him, for indeed he is excusable." And men also tell the tale of

ALI THE PERSIAN.

It is said that the Caliph Harun al-Rashid, being restless
one night, sent for his Wazir and said to him, "O Ja'afar, I
am sore wakeful and heavy-hearted this night, and I desire
of thee what may solace my spirit and cause my breast to
broaden with amusement." Quoth Ja'afar, "O Commander
of the Faithful, I have a friend, by name Ali the Persian,
who hath store of tales and pleasant stories, such as lighten
the heart and make care depart." Quoth the Caliph, "Fetch
him to me," and quoth Ja'afar, "Hearkening and obedience;" and, going out from before him, sent to seek Ali the
Persian and when he came said to him, "Answer the summons of the Commander of the Faithful." "To hear is to
obey," answered Ali, and at once followed the Wazir into
the presence of the Caliph who bade him be seated and
said to him, "O Ali, my heart is heavy within me this night
and it hath come to my ear that thou hast great store of
tales and anecdotes; so I desire of thee that thou let me
hear what will relieve my despondency and brighten my
melancholy." Said he, "O Commander of the Faithful, shall
I tell thee what I have seen with my eyes or what I have
heard with my ears?" He replied, "An thou have seen aught

worth the telling, let me hear that." Replied Ali:—Hearkening and obedience. Know thou, O Commander of the Faithful, that some years ago I left this my native city of Baghdad on a journey, having with me a lad who carried a light leathern bag. Presently we came to a certain city, where, as I was buying and selling behold, a rascally Kurd fell on me and seized my wallet perforce, saying, "This is my bag, and all which is in it is my property." Thereupon, I cried aloud "Ho Moslems,¹ one and all, deliver me from the hand of the vilest of oppressors!" But the folk said "Come, both of you, to the Kazi and abide ye by his judgment with joint consent." So I agreed to submit myself to such decision and we both presented ourselves before the Kazi, who said, "What bringeth you hither and what is your case and your quarrel?" Quoth I, "We are men at difference, who appeal to thee and make complaint and submit ourselves to thy judgment." Asked the Kazi, "Which of you is the complainant?"; so the Kurd came forward² and said, "Allah preserve our lord the Kazi! Verily, this bag is my bag and all that is in it is my swag. It was lost from me and I found it with this man mine enemy." The Kazi asked, "When didst thou lose it?"; and the Kurd answered, "But yesterday, and I passed a sleepless night by reason of its loss." "An it be thy bag," quoth the Kazi, "tell me what is in it." Quoth the Kurd, "There were in my bag two silver styles for eye-powder and antimony for the eyes and a kerchief for the hands, wherein I had laid two gilt cups and two candlesticks. Moreover it contained two tents and two platters and two spoons and a cushion and two leather rugs and two ewers and a brass tray and two basins and a cooking-pot and two water-jars and a ladle and a sacking-needle and a she-cat and two bitches and a wooden trencher and two sacks and two saddles and a gown and two fur pelisses and a cow and two calves and a she-goat and two sheep and an ewe and two lambs and two green pavilions and a camel and two she-camels and a lioness and two lions and a she-bear and two jackals and a mattrass and two sofas and an upper chamber and two saloons and a portico and two sitting-rooms and a kitchen with two doors and a company of Kurds who will bear witness that the bag is my bag." Then said the Kazi to me, "And thou, sirrah, what sayest thou?" So I came forward, O Commander of the Faithful (and indeed the Kurd's speech had bewildered me), and said, "Allah advance our lord the Kazi! Verily, there was naught in this my wallet, save a little ruined tenement and another without a door and a dog-house and a boys' school and youths playing dice and tents and tent-ropes and the cities of Bassorah and Baghdad and the palace of Shaddad bin Ad and an ironsmith's forge and a fishing-net and cudgels and pickets and girls and boys and a thousand pimps who will testify that the bag is my bag." Now when the Kurd heard my words, he wept and wailed and said, "O my lord the Kazi, this my bag is known and what is in it is a matter of renown; for in this bag there be castles and citadels and cranes and beasts of prey and men playing chess and draughts. Furthermore, in this my bag is a brood-mare and two colts and a stallion and two blood-steeds and two long lances; and it containeth eke a lion and two hares and a city and two villages and a whore and two sharking panders and an hermaphrodite and two gallows-birds and a blind man and two wights with good sight and a limping cripple and two lameters and a Christian ecclesiastic and two deacons and a patriarch and two monks and a Kazi and two assessors, who will be evidence that the bag is my bag." Quoth the Kazi to me, "And what sayst thou, O Ali?" So, O Commander of the Faithful, being filled with rage, I came forward and said, "Allah keep our lord the Kazi! I had in this my wallet a coat of mail and a broad-sword and armouries and a thousand fighting arms and a sheep-fold with its pasturage and a thousand barking dogs and gardens and vines and flowers and sweet smelling herbs and figs and apples and statues and pictures and flagons and goblets and fair-faced slave-girls and singing-women and marriage-feasts and tumult and clamour and great tracts of land and brothers of success, which were robbers, and a company of daybreak-raiders with swords and spears and bows and arrows and true friends and dear ones and intimates and comrades and men imprisoned for punishment and cup-companions and a drum and flutes and flags and banners and boys and girls and brides (in all their wedding bravery), and singing-girls and five Abyssinian women and three Hindi maidens and four damsels of Al-Medinah and a score of Greek girls and eighty Kurdish dames and seventy Georgian ladies and Tigris and Euphrates and a fowling net and a flint and steel and many-columned Iram and a thousand rogues and pimps and horse-courses and stables and mosques and baths and a builder and a carpenter and a plank and a nail and a black slave with his flageolet and a captain and a caravan-leader and towns and cities and an hundred thousand dinars and Cufa and Anbar[3] and twenty chests full of stuffs and twenty store-houses for victual and Gaza and Askalon and from Damietta to Al-Sawan;[4] and the palace of Kisra Anushirwan and the kingdom of Solomon and from Wadi Nu'uman to the land of Khorasan and Balkh and Ispahan and from India to the Sudan. Therein also (may Allah prolong the life of our lord the Kazi!) are doublets and cloths and a thousand sharp razors to shave off the Kazi's beard, except he fear my resentment and adjudge the bag to be my bag." Now when the Kazi heard what I and the Kurd avouched, he was confounded and said, "I see ye twain be none other than two pestilent fellows, atheistical villains who make sport of Kazis and magistrates and stand not in fear of reproach. Never did tongue tell nor ear hear aught more extraordinary than that which we pretend. By Allah, from China to Shajarat Umm Ghaylan, nor from Fars to Sudan nor from Wadi Nu'uman to Khorasan, was ever heard the like of what ye avouch or credited the like of what ye affirm. Say, fellows, be this bag a bottomless sea or the Day of Resurrection that shall gather together the just and unjust?" Then the Kazi bade them open the bag; so I opened it and behold, there was in it bread and a lemon and cheese and olives. So I threw the bag down before the Kurd and ganged my gait. Now when the Caliph heard this tale from Ali the Persian, he laughed till he fell on his back and made him a handsome present.[5] And men also relate a tale of

THE MAN WHO STOLE
THE DISH OF GOLD
WHEREIN THE DOG ATE.

Some time erst there was a man, who had accumulated debts, and his case was straitened upon him, so that he left his people and family and went forth in distraction; and he ceased not wandering on at random till he came after a time to a city tall of walls and firm of foundations. He entered it in a state of despondency and despair, harried by hunger and worn with the weariness of his way. As he passed through one of the main streets, he saw a company of the great going along; so he followed them till they reached a house like to a royal palace. He entered with them, and they stayed not faring forwards till they came in presence of a person seated at the upper end of a saloon, a man of the most dignified and majestic aspect, surrounded by pages and eunuchs, as he were of the sons of the Wazirs. When he saw the visitors, he rose to greet them and received them with honour; but the poor man aforesaid was confounded at his own boldness, when beholding the goodliness of the place and the crowd of servants and attendants; so drawing back, in perplexity and fear for his life sat down apart in a place afar off, where none should see him. Now it chanced that whilst he was sitting, behold, in came a man with four sporting-dogs, whereon were various kinds of raw silk and brocade[1] and wearing round their necks collars of gold with chains of silver, and tied up each dog in a place set privy for him; after which he went out and presently returned with four dishes of gold, full of rich meats, which he set severally before the dogs, one for each. Then he went away and left them, whilst the poor man began to eye the food, for stress of hunger, and longed to go up to one of the dogs and eat with him; but fear of them withheld him. Presently, one of the dogs looked at him and Allah Almighty inspired the dog with a knowledge of his case; so he drew back from the platter and signed to the man, who came and ate till he was filled. Then he would have withdrawn, but the dog again signed to him to take for himself the dish and what food was left in it, and pushed it towards him with his forepaw. So the man took the dish and leaving the house, went his way, and none followed him. Then he journeyed to another city where he sold the dish and buying with the price a stock-in-trade, returned to his own town. There he sold his goods and paid his debts; and he throve and became affluent and rose to perfect prosperity. He abode in his own land; but after some years had passed he said to himself, "Needs must I repair to the city of the owner of the dish, and, carry him a fit and handsome present and pay him the money-value of that which his dog bestowed upon me." So he took the price of the dish and a suitable gift; and, setting out, journeyed day and night, till he came to that city; he entered it and sought the place where the man lived; but he found there naught save ruins mouldering in row and croak of crow, and house and home desolate and all conditions in changed state. At this, his heart and soul were troubled, and he repeated the saying of him who saith:—

> Void are the private rooms of treasury:
> As void were hearts of fear and piety:
> Changed is the Wady nor are its gazelles
> Those fawns, nor sand-hills those I wont to see.

Now when the man saw these mouldering ruins and witnessed what the hand of time had manifestly done with the place, leaving but traces of the substantial things that erewhiles had been, a little reflection made it needless for him to enquire of the case; so he turned away. Presently, seeing a wretched man, in a plight which made him shudder and feel goose-skin, and which would have moved the very rock to ruth, he said to him, "Ho thou! What have time and fortune done with the lord of this place? Where are his lovely faces, his shining full moons and splendid stars; and what is the cause of the ruin that is come upon his abode, so that nothing save the walls thereof remain?" Quoth the other, "He is the miserable thou seest mourning that which hath left him naked. But knowest thou not the words of the Apostle (whom Allah bless and keep!), wherein is a lesson to him who will learn by it and a warning to whoso will be warned thereby and guided in the right way, 'Verily it is the way of Allah Almighty to raise up nothing of this world, except He cast it down again?'[2] If thou question of the cause of this accident, indeed it is no wonder, considering the chances and changes of Fortune. I was the lord of this place and I built it and founded it and owned it; and I was the proud possessor of its full moons lucent and its circumstance resplendent and its damsels radiant and its garniture magnificent, but Time turned and did away from me wealth and servants and took from me what it had lent (not given); and brought upon me calamities which it held in store hidden. But there must needs be some reason for this thy question: so tell it me and leave wondering." Thereupon, the man who had waxed wealthy being sore concerned, told him the whole story, and added, "I have brought thee a present, such as souls desire, and the price of thy dish of gold which I took; for it was the cause of my affluence after poverty, and of the replenishment of my dwelling-place, after desolation, and of the dispersion of my trouble and straitness." But the man shook his head, and weeping and groaning and complaining of his lot answered, "Ho thou! methinks thou art mad;

for this is not the way of a man of sense. How should a dog of mine make generous gift to thee of a dish of gold and I meanly take back the price of what a dog gave? This were indeed a strange thing! Were I in extremest unease and misery, by Allah, I would not accept of thee aught; no, not the worth of a nail-paring! So return whence thou camest in health and safety."[3] Whereupon the merchant kissed his feet and taking leave of him, returned whence he came, praising him and reciting this couplet:—

Men and dogs together are all gone by;
So peace be with all of them! dogs and men!

And Allah is All-knowing! Again men tell the tale of

THE RUINED MAN
WHO BECAME RICH AGAIN
THROUGH A DREAM.[1]

There lived once in Baghdad a wealthy man and made of money, who lost all his substance and became so destitute that he could earn his living only by hard labour. One night he lay down to sleep, dejected and heavy hearted, and saw in a dream a Speaker[2] who said to him, "Verily thy fortune is in Cairo; go thither and seek it." So he set out for Cairo; but when he arrived there, evening overtook him and he lay down to sleep in a mosque. Presently, by decree of Allah Almighty, a band of bandits entered the mosque and made their way thence into an adjoining house; but the owners, being aroused by the noise of the thieves, awoke and cried out; whereupon the Chief of Police came to their aid with his officers. The robbers made off; but the Wali entered the mosque and, finding the man from Baghdad asleep there, laid hold of him and beat him with palm-rods so grievous a beating that he was well-nigh dead. Then they cast him into jail, where he abode three days; after which the Chief of Police sent for him and asked him, "Whence art thou?"; and he answered, "From Baghdad." Quoth the Wali, "And what brought thee to Cairo?"; and quoth the Baghdadi, "I saw in a dream One

who said to me, Thy fortune is in Cairo; go thither to it.
But when I came to Cairo the fortune which he promised
me proved to be the palm-rods thou so generously gavest
to me." The Wali laughed till he showed his wisdom-teeth
and said, "O man of little wit, thrice have I seen in a dream
one who said to me:—There is in Baghdad a house in such
a district and of such a fashion and its courtyard is laid out
garden-wise, at the lower end whereof is a jetting-fountain
and under the same a great sum of money lieth buried. Go
thither and take it. Yet I went not; but thou, of the briefness
of thy wit, hast journeyed from place to place, on the faith
of a dream, which was but an idle galimatias of sleep."
Then he gave him money saying, "Help thee back herewith to thine own country;" and he took the money and set
out upon his homewards march. Now the house the Wali
had described was the man's own house in Baghdad; so the
wayfarer returned thither and, digging underneath the
fountain in his garden, discovered a great treasure. And
thus Allah gave him abundant fortune; and a marvellous
coincidence occurred. And a story is also current of

THE EBONY HORSE.[1]

There was once in times of yore and ages long gone before, a great and puissant King, of the Kings of the Persians, Sabur by name, who was the richest of all the Kings in store of wealth and dominion and surpassed each and every in wit and wisdom. He was generous, open handed and beneficent, and he gave to those who sought him and repelled not those who resorted to him; and he comforted the broken-hearted and honourably entreated those who fled to him for refuge. Moreover, he loved the poor and was hospitable to strangers and did the oppressed justice upon the oppressor. He had three daughters, like full moons of shining light or flower-gardens blooming bright; and a son as he were the moon; and it was his wont to keep two festivals in the twelvemonth, those of the Nau-Roz, or New Year, and Mihrgan the Autumnal Equinox,[2] on which occasions he threw open his palaces and gave largesse and made proclamation of safety and security and promoted his chamberlains and viceroys; and the people of his realm came in to him and saluted him and gave him joy of the holy day, bringing him gifts and servants and eunuchs. Now he loved science and geometry, and one festival-day as he sat on his kingly throne there came in to him three wise men, cunning artificers and past masters in all manner of craft and inventions, skilled in making things curious and rare, such as confound the wit; and versed in the knowledge of occult truths and perfect in mysteries and subtleties. And they were of three different tongues and countries, the first a Hindi or Indian,[3] the second a Roumi or Greek and the third a Farsi or Persian. The Indian came forwards and, prostrating himself before the King, wished him joy of the festival and laid before him a present befitting his dignity; that is to say, a man of gold, set with precious gems and jewels of price and hending in hand a golden trumpet. When Sabur[4] saw this, he asked, "O sage, what is the virtue of this figure?"; and the Indian answered, "O my lord, if this figure be set at the gate of thy city, it will be a guardian over it; for, if an enemy enter the place, it will blow this clarion against him and he will be seized with a palsy and drop down dead." Much the King marvelled at this and cried, "By Allah, O sage, an this thy word be true, I will grant thee thy wish and thy desire." Then came forward the Greek and, prostrating himself before the King, presented him with a basin of silver, in whose midst was a peacock of gold, surrounded by four-and-twenty chicks of the same metal. Sabur looked at them and turning to the Greek, said to him, "O sage, what is the virtue of this peacock?" "O my lord," answered he, "as often as an hour of the day or night passeth, it pecketh one of its young and crieth out and flappeth its wings, till the four-and-twenty hours are accomplished; and when the month cometh to an end, it will open its mouth and thou shalt see the crescent therein." And the King said, "An thou speak sooth, I will bring thee to thy wish and thy desire." Then came forward the Persian sage and, prostrating himself before the King, presented him with a horse[5] of the blackest ebony-wood inlaid with gold and jewels, and ready harnessed with saddle, bridle and stirrups such as befit Kings; which when Sabur saw, he marvelled with exceeding marvel and was confounded at the beauty of its

form and the ingenuity of its fashion. So he asked, "What is
the use of this horse of wood, and what is its virtue and
what the secret of its movement?"; and the Persian answered, "O my lord, the virtue of this horse is that, if one
mount him, it will carry him whither he will and fare with
its rider through the air and cover the space of a year in a
single day." The King marvelled and was amazed at these
three wonders, following thus hard upon one another on
the same day, and turning to the sage, said to him, "By
Allah the Omnipotent, and our Lord the Beneficent, who
created all creatures and feedeth them with meat and
drink, an thy speech be veritable and the virtue of thy contrivance appear, I will assuredly give thee whatsoever thou
lustest for and will bring thee to thy desire and thy wish!"⁶
Then he entertained the sages three days, that he might
make trial of their gifts; after which they brought the
figures before him and each took the creature he had
wroughten and showed him the mystery of its movement.
The trumpeter blew the trump; the peacock pecked its
chicks and the Persian sage mounted the ebony horse,
whereupon it soared with him high in air and descended
again. When King Sabur saw all this, he was amazed and
perplexed and felt like to fly for joy and said to the three
sages, "Now I am certified of the truth of your words and
it behoveth me to quit me of my promise. Ask ye, therefore, what ye will, and I will give you that same." Now the
report of the King's daughters had reached the sages, so
they answered, "If the King be content with us and accept
of our gifts and allow us to prefer a request to him, we
crave of him that he give us his three daughters in marriage, that we may be his sons-in-law; for that the stability
of Kings may not be gainsaid." Quoth the King, "I grant
you that which you wish and you desire," and bade summon the Kazi forthright, that he might marry each of the
sages to one of his daughters. Now it fortuned that the
Princesses were behind a curtain, looking on; and when
they heard this, the youngest considered her husband to be
and behold, he was an old man,⁷ an hundred years of age,

with hair frosted, forehead drooping, eye-brows mangy, ears slitten, beard and mustachios stained and dyed; eyes red and goggle; cheeks bleached and hollow; flabby nose like a brinjall, or egg-plant;[8] face like a cobbler's apron, teeth overlapping and lips like camel's kidneys, loose and pendulous; in brief a terror, a horror, a monster, for he was of the folk of his time the unsightliest and of his age the frightfullest; sundry of his grinders had been knocked out and his eye-teeth were like the tusks of the Jinni who frighteneth poultry in hen-houses. Now the girl was the fairest and most graceful of her time, more elegant than the gazelle however tender, than the gentlest zephyr blander and brighter than the moon at her full; for amorous fray right suitable; confounding in graceful sway the waving bough and outdoing in swimming gait the pacing roe; in fine she was fairer and sweeter by far than all her sisters. So, when she saw her suitor, she went to her chamber and strewed dust on her head and tore her clothes and fell to buffeting her face and weeping and wailing. Now the Prince, her brother, Kamar al-Akmar, or the Moon of Moons hight, was then newly returned from a journey and, hearing her weeping and crying came in to her (for he loved her with fond affection, more than his other sisters) and asked her, "What aileth thee? What hath befallen thee? Tell me and conceal naught from me." So she smote her breast and answered, "O my brother and my dear one, I have nothing to hide. If the palace be straitened upon thy father, I will go out; and if he be resolved upon a foul thing, I will separate myself from him, though he consent not to make provision for me; and my Lord will provide." Quoth he, "Tell me what meaneth this talk and what hath straitened thy breast and troubled thy temper." "O my brother and my dear one," answered the Princess, "Know that my father hath promised me in marriage to a wicked magician who brought him, as a gift, a horse of black wood, and hath bewitched him with his craft and his egromancy; but, as for me, I will none of him, and would, because of him, I had never come into this world!" Her brother soothed her and solaced her, then fared to his sire and said, "What be this wizard to whom thou hast given my youngest sister in marriage, and what is this present which he hath brought thee, so that thou hast killed⁹ my sister with chagrin? It is not right that this should be." Now the Persian was standing by and, when he heard the Prince's words, he was mortified and filled with fury and the King said, "O my son, an thou sawest this horse, thy wit would be confounded and thou wouldst be amated with amazement." Then he bade the slaves bring the horse before him and they did so; and, when the Prince saw it, it pleased him. So (being an accomplished cavalier) he mounted it forthright and struck its sides with the shovel-shaped stirrup-irons; but it stirred not and the King said to the Sage, "Go show him its movement, that he also may help thee to win thy wish." Now the Persian bore the Prince a grudge because he willed not he should have his sister; so he showed him the pin of ascent on the right side of the horse and saying to him, "Trill this," left him. Thereupon the Prince trilled the pin and lo! the horse forthwith soared with him high in ether, as it were a bird, and gave not overflying till it disappeared from men's espying, whereat the King was troubled and perplexed about his case and said to the Persian, "O sage, look how thou mayst make him descend." But he replied, "O my lord, I can do nothing, and thou wilt never see him again till Resurrection-day, for he, of his ignorance and pride, asked me not of the pin of descent and I forgot to acquaint him therewith." When the King heard this, he was enraged with sore rage; and bade bastinado the sorcerer and clap him in jail, whilst he himself cast the crown from his head and beat his face and smote his breast. Moreover, he shut the doors of his palaces and gave himself up to weeping and keening, he and his wife and daughters and all the folk of the city; and thus their joy was turned to annoy and their gladness changed into sore affliction and sadness. Thus far concerning them; but as regards the Prince, the horse gave not over soaring with him till he drew near the sun, whereat he gave himself up for lost and saw death in the skies, and was confounded at his case, repenting him of having mounted the horse and saying to himself, "Verily, this was a device of the Sage to destroy me on account of my youngest sister; but there is no Majesty and there is no Might save in Allah, the Glorious, the Great! I am lost without recourse; but I wonder, did not he who made the ascent-pin make also a descent-pin?" Now he was a man of wit and knowledge and intelligence; so he fell to feeling all the parts of the horse, but saw nothing save a screw, like a cock's head, on its right shoulder and the like on the left, when quoth he to himself, "I see no sign save these things like button." Presently he turned the right-hand pin, whereupon the horse flew heavenwards with increased speed. So he left it and looking at the sinister shoulder and finding another pin, he wound it up and immediately the steed's upwards motion slowed and ceased and it began to descend, little by little, towards the face of the earth, while the rider became yet more cautious and careful of his life. And when he saw this and knew the uses of the horse, his heart was filled with joy and gladness and he thanked Almighty Allah for that He had deigned deliver him from destruction. Then he began to turn the horse's head withersoever he would, making it rise and fall at pleasure, till he had gotten complete mastery over its every movement. He ceased not to descend the whole of that day, for that the steed's ascending flight had borne him afar from the earth; and, as he descended, he diverted himself with viewing the various cities and countries over which he passed and which he knew not, never having seen them in his life. Amongst the rest, he descried a city ordered after the fairest fashion in the midst of a verdant and riant land, rich in trees and streams, with gazelles pacing daintily over the plains; whereat he fell a-musing and said to himself, "Would I knew the name of yon town and in what land it is!" And he took to circling about it and observing it right and left. By this time, the day began to decline and the sun drew near to its downing; and he said in his mind, "Verily I find no goodlier place to night in than this city; so

I will lodge here and early on the morrow I will return to my kith and kin and my kingdom; and tell my father and family what hath passed and acquaint him with what mine eyes have seen." Then he addressed himself to seeking a place wherein he might safely bestow himself and his horse and where none should descry him, and presently behold, he espied amiddlemost of the city a palace rising high in upper air surrounded by a great wall with lofty crenelles and battlements, guarded by forty black slaves, clad in complete mail and armed with spears and swords, bows and arrows. Quoth he, "This is a goodly place," and turned the descent-pin, whereupon the horse sank down with him like a weary bird, and alighted gently on the terrace-roof of the palace. So the Prince dismounted and ejaculating "Alhamdolillah"—praise be to Allah[10]—he began to go round about the horse and examine it, saying, "By Allah, he who fashioned thee with these perfections was a cunning craftsman, and if the Almighty extend the term of my life and restore me to my country and kinsfolk in safety and reunite me with my father, I will assuredly bestow upon him all manner bounties and benefit him with the utmost beneficence." By this time night had overtaken him and he sat on the roof till he was assured that all in the palace slept; and indeed hunger and thirst were sore upon him, for that he had not tasted food nor drunk water since he parted from his sire. So he said within himself, "Surely the like of this palace will not lack of victual;" and, leaving the horse above, went down in search of somewhat to eat. Presently, he came to a staircase and descending it to the bottom, found himself in a court paved with white marble and alabaster, which shone in the light of the moon. He marvelled at the place and the goodliness of its fashion, but sensed no sound of speaker and saw no living soul and stood in perplexed surprise, looking right and left and knowing not whither he should wend. Then said he to himself, "I may not do better than return to where I left my horse and pass the night by it; and as soon as day shall dawn I will mount and ride away." However, as he tarried talking to himself, he espied a light within the palace, and making towards it, found that it came from a candle that stood before a door of the Harim, at the head of a sleeping eunuch, as he were one of the Ifrits of Solomon or a tribesman of the Jinn, longer than lumber and broader than a bench. He lay before the door, with the pommel of his sword gleaming in the flame of the candle, and at his head was a bag of leather[11] hanging from a column of granite. When the Prince saw this, he was affrighted and said, "I crave help from Allah the Supreme! O mine Holy One, even as Thou hast already delivered me from destruction, so vouchsafe me strength to quit myself of the adventure of this palace!" So saying, he put out his hand to the budget and taking it, carried it aside and opened it and found in it food of the best. He ate his fill and refreshed himself and drank water, after which he hung up the provision-bag in its place and drawing the eunuch's sword from its sheath, took it, whilst the slave slept on, knowing not whence destiny should come to him. Then the Prince fared forwards into the palace and ceased not till he came to a second door, with a curtain drawn before it; so he raised the curtain and behold, on entering he saw a couch of the whitest ivory, inlaid with pearls and jacinths and jewels, and four slave-girls sleeping about it. He went up to the couch, to see what was thereon, and found a young lady lying asleep, chemised with her hair[12] as she were the full moon rising[13] over the Eastern horizon, with flower-white brow and shining hair parting and cheeks like blood-red anemones and dainty moles thereon. He was amazed at her as she lay in her beauty and loveliness, her symmetry and grace, and he recked no more of death. So he went up to her, trembling in every nerve and, shuddering with pleasure, kissed her on the right cheek; whereupon she awoke forthright and opened her eyes, and seeing the Prince standing at her head, said to him, "Who art thou and whence comest thou?" Quoth he, "I am thy slave and thy lover." Asked she, "And who brought thee hither?" and he answered, "My Lord and my fortune." Then said Shams al-Nahar[14] (for such was her name), "Haply thou art he who demanded me yesterday of my father in marriage and he rejected thee, pretending that thou wast foul of favour. By Allah, my sire lied in his throat when he spoke this thing, for thou art not other than beautiful." Now the son of the King of Hind had sought her in marriage, but her father had rejected him, for that he was ugly and uncouth, and she thought the Prince was he. So, when she saw his beauty and grace (for indeed he was like the radiant moon) the syntheism[15] of love gat hold of her heart as it were a flaming fire, and they fell to talk and converse. Suddenly, her waiting-women awoke and, seeing the Prince with their mistress, said to her, "Oh my lady, who is this with thee?" Quoth she, "I know not; I found him sitting by me, when I woke up: haply 'tis he who seeketh me in marriage of my sire." Quoth they, "O my lady, by Allah the All-Father, this is not he who seeketh thee in marriage, for he is hideous and this man is handsome and of high degree. Indeed, the other is not fit to be his servant."[16] Then the handmaidens went out to the eunuch, and finding him slumbering awoke him, and he started up in alarm. Said they, "How happeth it that thou art on guard at the palace and yet men come in to us, whilst we are asleep?" When the black heard this, he sprang in haste to his sword, but found it not; and fear took him and trembling. Then he went in, confounded, to his mistress and seeing the Prince sitting at talk with her, said to him, "O my lord, art thou man or Jinni?" Replied the Prince, "Woe to thee, O unluckiest of slaves: how darest thou even the sons of the royal Chosroes[17] with one of the unbelieving Satans?" And he was as a raging lion. Then he took the sword in his hand and said to the slave, "I am the King's son-in-law, and he hath married me to his daughter and bidden me go in to her." And when the eunuch heard these words he replied, "O my lord, if thou be indeed of kind a man as thou avouchest, she is fit for none but for thee, and thou art worthier of her than any other." Thereupon the eunuch ran to the King, shrieking loud and rending his raiment and heaving dust upon his head; and when the King heard his outcry, he said to him, "What hath befallen thee?: speak quickly and be brief; for thou hast fluttered my heart." Answered the eunuch, "O King, come to thy daughter's succour; for a devil of the Jinn, in the likeness of a King's son, hath got possession of her; so up and at him!" When the King heard this, he thought to kill him and said, "How camest thou to be careless of my daughter and let this demon come at her?" Then he betook himself to the Princess's palace, where he found her slave-women standing to await him and asked them, "What is come to my daughter?" "O King," answered they, "slumber overcame us and, when we awoke, we found a young man sitting upon her couch in talk with her, as he were the full moon; never saw we aught fairer of favour than he. So we questioned him of his case and he declared that thou hadst given him thy daughter in marriage. More than this we know not, nor do we know if he be a man or a Jinni; but he is modest and well bred, and doth nothing unseemly or which leadeth to disgrace." Now when the King heard these words, his wrath cooled and he raised the curtain little by little and looking in, saw sitting at talk with his daughter a Prince of the goodliest with a face like the full moon for sheen. At this sight he could not contain himself, of his jealousy for his daughter's honour; and, putting aside the curtain, rushed in upon them drawn sword in hand like a furious Ghul. Now when the Prince saw him he asked the Princess, "Is this thy sire?"; and she answered, "Yes." Whereupon he sprang to his feet and, seizing his sword, cried out at the King with so terrible a cry that he was confounded. Then the youth would have fallen on him with the sword; but the King seeing that the Prince was doughtier than he, sheathed his scymitar and stood till the young man came up to him, when he accosted him courteously and said to him, "O youth, art thou a man or a Jinni?" Quoth the Prince, "Did I not respect thy right as mine host and thy daughter's honour, I would spill thy blood! How darest thou fellow me with devils, me that am a Prince of the sons of the royal Chosroes who, had they wished to take thy kingdom, could shake thee like an earthquake from thy glory and thy dominions and spoil thee of all thy possessions?" Now when the King heard his words, he was confounded with awe and bodily fear of him and rejoined, "If thou indeed be of the sons of the Kings, as thou pretendest, how cometh it that thou enterest my palace without my permission, and smirchest mine honour, making thy way to my daughter and feigning that thou art her husband and claiming that I have given her to thee to wife, I that have slain Kings and King's sons, who sought her of me in marriage? And now who shall save thee from my might and majesty when, if I cried out to my slaves and servants and bade them put thee to the vilest of deaths they would slay thee forthright? Who shall deliver thee out of my hand?" When the Prince heard this speech of the King he answered, "Verily, I wonder at thee and at the shortness and denseness of thy wit! Say me, canst covet for thy daughter a mate comelier than myself, and hast ever seen a stouter hearted man or one better fitted for a Sultan or a more glorious in rank and dominion than I?" Rejoined the King, "Nay, by Allah! but I would have had thee, O youth, act after the custom of Kings and demand her from me to wife before witnesses, that I might have married her to thee publicly; and now, even were I to marry her to thee privily, yet hast thou dishonoured me in her person." Rejoined the Prince, "Thou sayest sooth, O King, but if thou summon thy slaves and thy soldiers and they fall upon me and slay me, as thou pretendest, thou wouldst but publish thine own disgrace, and the folk would be divided between belief in thee and disbelief in thee. Wherefore, O King, thou wilt do well, meseemeth, to turn from this thought to that which I shall counsel thee." Quoth the King, "Let me hear what thou hast to advise;" and quoth the Prince, "What I have to propose to thee is this: either do thou meet me in combat singular, I and thou; and he who slayeth his adversary shall be held the worthier and having a better title to the kingdom; or else, let me be this night and, whenas dawns the morn, draw out against me thy horsemen and footmen and servants; but first tell me their number." Said the King, "They are forty thousand horse, besides my own slaves and their followers,[18] who are the like of them in number." Thereupon said the Prince, "When the day shall break, do thou array them against me and say to them——This man is a suitor to me for my daughter's hand, on condition that he shall do battle singlehanded against you all; for he pretendeth that he will overcome you and put you to the rout, and indeed that ye cannot prevail against him. After which, leave me to do battle with them; if they slay me, then is thy secret the surer guarded and thine honour the better warded; and if I overcome them and see their backs, then is it the like of me a King should covet to his son-in-law." So the King approved of his opinion and accepted his proposition, despite his awe at the boldness of his speech and amaze at the pretensions of the Prince to meet in fight his whole host, such as he had described it to him, being at heart assured that he would perish in the fray and so he should be quit of him and freed from the fear of dishonour. Thereupon he called the eunuch and bade him go to his Wazir without stay and delay and command him to assemble the whole of the army and cause them don their arms and armour and mount their steeds. So the eunuch carried the King's order to the Minister, who straightway summoned the Captains of the host and the Lords of the realm and bade them don their harness of derring-do and mount horse and sally forth in battle array. Such was their case; but as regards the King, he sat a long while conversing with the young Prince, being pleased with his wise speech and good sense and fine breeding. And when it was day-break he returned to his palace and, seating himself on his throne, commanded his merry men to mount and bade them saddle one of the best of the royal steeds with handsome selle and housings and trappings and bring it to the Prince. But the youth said, "O King, I will not mount horse, till I come in view of the troops and review them." "Be it as thou wilt," replied the King. Then the two repaired to the parade-ground, where the troops were drawn up, and the young Prince looked upon them and noted their great number; after which the King cried out to them, saying, "Ho, all ye men, there is come to me a youth who seeketh my daughter in marriage; and in very sooth never have I seen a goodlier than he; no, nor a stouter of heart nor a doughtier of arm, for he pretendeth that he can overcome you, single-handed, and force you to flight and that, were ye an hundred thousand in number, yet for him would ye be but few. Now when he chargeth down on you, do ye receive him upon point of pike and sharp of sabre; for, indeed, he hath undertaken a mighty matter." Then quoth the King to the Prince, "Up, O my son, and do thy devoir on them." Answered he, "O King, thou dealest not justly and fairly by me: how shall I go forth against them, seeing that I am afoot and the men be mounted?" The King retorted, "I bade thee mount, and thou refusedst; but choose thou which of my horses thou wilt." Then he said, "Not one of thy horses pleaseth me, and I will ride none but that on which I came." Asked the King, "And where is thy horse?" "Atop of thy palace." "In what part of my palace?" "On the roof." Now when the King heard these words, he cried, "Out on thee! this is the first sign thou hast given of madness. How can the horse be on the roof? But we shall at once see if thou speak truth or lies." Then he turned to one of his chief officers and said to him, "Go to my palace and bring me what thou findest on the roof." So all the people marvelled at the young Prince's words, saying one to other, "How can a horse come down the steps from the roof? Verily this is a thing whose like we never heard." In the mean time the King's messenger repaired to the palace and mounting to the roof, found the horse standing there and never had he looked on a handsomer; but when he drew near and examined it, he saw that it was made of ebony and ivory. Now the officer was accompanied by other high officers, who also looked on and they laughed to one another, saying, "Was it of the like of this horse that the youth spake? We cannot deem him other than mad; however, we shall soon see the truth of his case. Peradventure herein is some mighty matter, and he is a man of high degree." Then they lifted up the horse bodily and, carrying it to the King, set it down before him, and all the lieges flocked round to look at it, marvelling at the beauty of its proportions and the richness of its saddle and bridle. The King also admired it and wondered at it with extreme wonder; and he asked the Prince, "O youth, is this thy horse?" He answered, "Yes, O King, this is my horse, and thou shalt soon see the marvel it showeth." Rejoined the King, "Then take and mount it," and the Prince retorted, "I will not mount till the troops withdraw afar from it." So the King bade them retire a bowshot from the horse; whereupon quoth its owner, "O King, see thou; I am about to mount my horse and charge upon thy host and scatter them right and left and split their hearts asunder." Said the King, "Do as thou wilt; and spare not their lives, for they will not spare thine." Then the Prince mounted, whilst the troops ranged themselves in ranks before him, and one said to another, "When the youth cometh between the ranks, we will take him on the points of our pikes and the sharps of our sabres." Quoth another, "By Allah, this is a mere misfortune: how shall we slay a youth so comely of face and shapely of form?" And a third continued, "Ye will have hard work to get the better of him; for the youth had not done this, but for what he knew of his own prowess and pre-eminence of valour." Meanwhile, having settled himself in his saddle, the Prince turned the pin of ascent; whilst all eyes were strained to see what he would do, whereupon the horse began to heave and rock and sway to and fro and make the strangest of movements steed ever made, till its belly was filled with air and it took flight with its rider and soared high into the sky. When the King saw this, he cried out to his men, saying, "Woe to you! catch him, catch him, ere he 'scape you!" But his Wazirs and Viceroys said to him, "O King, can a man overtake the flying bird? This is surely none but some mighty magician or Marid of the Jinn or devil, and Allah save thee from him. So praise thou the Almighty for deliverance of thee and of all thy host from his hand." Then the King returned to his palace after seeing the feat of the Prince and, going in to his daughter, acquainted her with what had befallen them both on the parade-ground. He found her grievously afflicted for the Prince and bewailing her separation from him; wherefore she fell sick with violent sickness and took to her pillow. Now when her father saw her on this wise, he pressed her to his breast and kissing her between the eyes, said to her, "O my daughter, praise Allah Almighty and thank Him for that He hath delivered us from this crafty enchanter, this villain, this low fellow, this thief who thought only of seducing thee!" And he repeated to her the story of the Prince and how he had disappeared in the firmament; and he abused him and cursed him knowing not how dearly his daughter loved him. But she paid no heed to his words and did but redouble in her tears and wails, saying to herself, "By Allah, I will neither eat meat nor drain drink, till Allah reunite me with him!" Her father was greatly concerned for her case and mourned much over her plight; but, for all he could do to soothe her, love-longing only increased on her. Thus far concerning the King and Princess Shams al-Nahar; but as regards Prince Kamar al-Akmar, when he had risen high in air, he turned his horse's head towards his native land, and being alone mused upon the beauty of the Princess and her loveliness. Now he had enquired of the King's people the name of the city and of its King and his daughter; and men had told him that it was the city of Sana'a.[19] So he journeyed with all speed, till he drew near his father's capital and, making an airy circuit about the city, alighted on the roof of the King's palace, where he left his horse, whilst he descended into the palace and seeing its threshold strewn with ashes, thought that one of his family was dead. Then he entered, as of wont, and found his father and mother and sisters clad in mourning raiment of black, all pale of faces and lean of frames. When his sire descried him and was assured that it was indeed his son, he cried out with a great cry and fell down in a fit, but after a time coming to himself, threw himself upon him and embraced him, clipping him to his bosom and rejoicing in him with exceeding joy and extreme gladness. His mother and sisters heard this; so they came in and seeing the Prince, fell upon him, kissing him and weeping, and joying with exceeding joyance. Then they questioned him of his case; so he told them all that had past from first to last, and his father said to him, "Praised be Allah for thy safety, O coolth of my eyes and core of my heart!" Then the King bade hold high festival, and the glad tidings flew through the city. So they beat drums and cymbals and, doffing the weed of mourning, they donned the gay garb of gladness and decorated the streets and markets; whilst the folk vied with one another who should be the first to give the King joy, and the King proclaimed a general pardon and opening the prisons, released those who were therein prisoned. Moreover, he made banquets for the people, with great abundance of eating and drinking, for seven days and nights and all creatures were gladsomest; and he took horse with his son and rode out with him, that the folk might see him and rejoice. After awhile the Prince asked about the maker of the horse, saying, "O my father, what hath fortune done with him?"; and the King answered, "Allah never bless him nor the hour wherein I set eyes on him! For he was the cause of thy separation from us, O my son, and he hath lain in jail since the day of thy disappearance." Then the King bade release him from prison and, sending for him, invested him in a dress of satisfaction and entreated him with the utmost favour and munificence, save that he would not give him his daughter to wife; whereat the Sage raged with sore rage and repented of that which he had done, knowing that the Prince had secured the secret of the steed and the manner of its motion. Moreover, the King said to his son, "I reck thou wilt do well not to go near the horse henceforth and more especially not to mount it after this day; for thou knowest not its properties, and belike thou art in error about it." Now the Prince had told his father of his adventure with the King of Sana'a and his daughter and he said, "Had the King intended to kill thee, he had done so; but thine hour was not yet come." When the rejoicings were at an end, the people returned to their places and the King and his son to the palace, where they sat down and fell to eating, drinking and making merry. Now the King had a handsome hand maiden who was skilled in playing the lute; so she took it and began to sweep the strings and sing thereto before the King and his son of separation of lovers, and she chanted the following verses:—

Deem not that absence breeds in me aught of forgetfulness;
　What should remember I did you fro' my remembrance
　　wane?
Time dies but never dies the fondest love for you we bear;
　And in your love I'll die and in your love I'll arise again.[20]

When the Prince heard these verses, the fires of longing flamed up in his heart and pine and passion redoubled upon him. Grief and regret were sore upon him and his bowels yearned in him for love of the King's daughter of Sana'a; so he rose forthright and, escaping his father's notice, went forth the palace to the horse and mounting it, turned the pin of ascent, whereupon bird-like it flew with him high in air and soared towards the upper regions of the sky. In early morning his father missed him and, going up to the pinnacle of the palace, in great concern, saw his son rising into the firmament; whereat he was sore afflicted and repented in all penitence that he had not taken the horse and hidden it; and he said to himself, "By Allah, if but my son return to me, I will destroy the horse, that my heart may be at rest concerning my son." And he fell again to weeping and bewailing himself. Such was his case; but as regards the Prince, he ceased not flying on through air till he came to the city of Sana'a and alighted on the roof as before. Then he crept down stealthily and, finding the eunuch asleep, as of wont, raised the curtain and went on little by little, till he came to the door of the Princess's alcove-[21]chamber and stopped to listen; when lo! he heard her shedding plenteous tears and reciting verses, whilst her women slept round her. Presently, overhearing her weeping and wailing quoth they, "O our mistress, why wilt thou mourn for one who mourneth not for thee?" Quoth she, "O ye little of wit, is he for whom I mourn of those who forget or who are forgotten?" And she fell again to wailing and weeping, till sleep overcame her. Hereat the Prince's heart melted for her and his gall-bladder was like to burst, so he entered and, seeing her lying asleep without covering,[22] touched her with his hand; whereupon she opened her eyes and espied him standing by her. Said he, "Why all this crying and mourning?" And when she knew him, she threw herself upon him, and took him around the neck and kissed him and answered, "For thy sake and because of my separation from thee." Said he, "O my lady, I have been made desolate by thee all this long time!" But she replied, "'Tis thou who hast desolated *me;* and hadst thou tarried longer, I had surely died!" Rejoined he, "O my lady, what thinkest thou of my case with thy father and how he dealt with me? Were it not for my love of thee, O temptation and seduction of the Three Worlds, I had certainly slain him and made him a warning to all beholders; but, even as I love thee, so I love him for thy sake." Quoth she, "How couldst thou leave me: can my life be sweet to me after thee?" Quoth he, "Let what hath happened suffice: I am now hungry, and thirsty." So she bade her maidens make ready meat and drink, and they sat eating and drinking and conversing till night was well-nigh ended; and when day broke he rose to take leave of her and depart, ere the eunuch should awake. Shams al-Nahar asked him, "Whither goest thou?"; and he answered, "To my father's house, and I plight thee my troth that I will come to thee once in every week." But she wept and said, "I conjure thee, by Allah the Almighty, take me with thee whereso thou wendest and make me not taste anew the bitter-gourd[23] of separation from thee." Quoth he, "Wilt thou indeed go with me?" and quoth she, "Yes." "Then," said he, "arise that we depart." So she rose forthright and going to a chest, arrayed herself in what was richest and dearest to her of her trinkets of gold and jewels of price, and she fared forth her handmaids recking naught. So he carried her up to the roof of the palace and, mounting the ebony horse, took her up behind him and made her fast to himself, binding her with strong bonds; after which he turned the shoulder-pin of ascent, and the horse rose with him high in air. When her slave-women saw this, they shrieked aloud and told her father and mother, who in hot haste ran to the palace-roof and looking up, saw the magical horse flying away with the Prince and Princess. At this the King was troubled with ever-increasing trouble and cried out, saying, "O King's son, I conjure thee, by Allah, have ruth on me and my wife and bereave us not of our daughter!" The Prince made him no reply; but, thinking in himself that the maiden repented of leaving father and mother, asked her, "O ravishment of the age, say me, wilt thou that I restore thee to thy mother and father?": whereupon she answered, "By Allah, O my lord, that is not my desire: my only wish is to be with thee, wherever thou art; for I am distracted by the love of thee from all else, even from my father and mother." Hearing these words the Prince joyed with great joy, and made the horse fly and fare softly with them, so as not to disquiet her; nor did they stay their flight till they came in sight of a green meadow, wherein was a spring of running water. Here they alighted and ate and drank; after which the Prince took horse again and set her behind him, binding her in his fear for her safety; after which they fared on till they came in sight of his father's capital. At this, the Prince was filled with joy and bethought himself to show his beloved the seat of his dominion and his father's power and dignity and give her to know that it was greater than that of her sire. So he set her down in one of his father's gardens without the city where his parent was wont to take his pleasure; and, carrying her into a domed summer-house prepared there for the King, left the ebony horse at the door and charged the damsel keep watch over it, saying, "Sit here, till my messenger come to thee; for I go now to my father, to make ready a palace for thee and show thee my royal estate." She was delighted when she heard these words and said to him, "Do as thou wilt;" for she thereby understood that she should not enter the city but with due honour and worship, as became her rank. Then the Prince left her and betook himself to the palace of the King his father, who rejoiced in his return and met him and welcomed him; and the Prince said to him, "Know that I have brought with me the King's daughter of whom I told thee; and have left her without the city in such a garden and come to tell thee, that thou mayest make ready the procession of estate and go forth to meet her and show her the royal dignity and troops and guards." Answered the King, "With joy and gladness"; and straightway bade decorate the town with the goodliest adornment. Then he took horse and rode out in all magnificence and majesty, he and his host, high officers and household, with drums and kettle-drums, fifes and clarions and all manner instruments; whilst the Prince drew forth of his treasuries jewellery and apparel and what else of the things which Kings hoard and made a rare display of wealth and splendour: moreover he got ready for the Princess a canopied litter of brocades, green, red and yellow, wherein he set Indian and Greek and Abyssinian slave-girls. Then he left the litter and those who were therein and preceded them to the pavilion where he had set her down; and searched but found naught, neither Princess nor horse. When he saw this, he beat his face and rent his raiment and began to wander round about the garden, as he had lost his wits; after which he came to his senses and said to himself, "How could she have come at the secret of this horse, seeing I told her nothing of it? Maybe the Persian sage who made the horse hath chanced upon her and stolen her away, in revenge for my father's treatment of him." Then he sought the guardians of the garden and asked them if they had seen any pass the precincts; and said, "Hath any one come in here? Tell me the truth and the whole truth or I will at once strike off your heads." They were terrified by his threats; but they answered with one voice, "We have seen no man enter save the Persian sage, who came to gather healing herbs." So the Prince was certified that it was indeed he that had taken away the maiden and abode confounded and perplexed concerning his case. And he was abashed before the folk and, turning to his sire, told him what had happened and said to him, "Take the troops and march them back to the city. As for me, I will never return till I have cleared up this affair." When the King heard this, he wept and beat his breast and said to him, "O my son, calm thy choler and master thy chagrin and come home with us and look what King's daughter thou wouldst fain have, that I may marry thee to her." But the Prince paid no heed to his words and farewelling him departed, whilst the King returned to the city and their joy was changed into sore annoy. Now, as Destiny issued her decree, when the Prince left the Princess in the garden-house and betook himself to his father's palace, for the ordering of his affair, the Persian entered the garden to pluck certain simples and, scenting the sweet savour of musk and perfumes that exhaled from the Princess and impregnated the whole place, followed it till he came to the pavilion and saw standing at the door the horse which he had made with his own hands. His heart was filled with joy and gladness, for he had bemourned its loss much since it had gone out of his hand: so he went up to it and, examining its every part, found it whole and sound; whereupon he was about to mount and ride away, when he bethought himself and said, "Needs must I first look what the Prince hath brought and left here with the horse." So he entered the pavilion and, seeing the Princess sitting there, as she were the sun shining sheen in the sky serene, knew her at the first glance to be some high-born lady and doubted not but the Prince had brought her thither on the horse and left her in the pavilion, whilst he went to the city, to make ready for her entry in state procession with all splendour. Then he went up to her and kissed the earth between her hands, whereupon she raised her eyes to him and, finding him exceedingly foul of face and favour, asked, "Who art thou?"; and he answered, "O my lady, I am a messenger sent by the Prince who hath bidden me bring thee to another pleasance nearer the city; for that my lady the Queen cannot walk so far and is unwilling, of her joy in thee, that another should forestall her with thee." Quoth she, "Where is the Prince?"; and quoth the Persian, "He is in the city, with his sire and forthwith he shall come for thee in great state." Said she, "O thou! say me, could he find none handsomer to send to me?"; whereat loud laughed the Sage and said, "Yea verily, he hath not a Mameluke as ugly as I am; but, O my lady, let not the ill-favour of my face and the foulness of my form deceive thee. Hadst thou profited of me as hath the Prince, verily thou wouldst praise my affair. Indeed, he chose me as his messenger to thee, because of my uncomeliness and loathsomeness in his jealous love of thee: else hath he Mamelukes and negro slaves, pages, enunchs and attendants out of number, each goodlier than other." Whenas she heard this, it commended itself to her reason and she believed him; so she rose forthright; and, putting her hand in his, said, "O my father, what hast thou brought me to ride?" He replied, "O my lady, thou shalt ride the horse thou camest on;" and she, "I cannot ride it by myself." Whereupon he smiled and knew that he was her master and said, "I will ride with thee myself." So he mounted and, taking her up behind him bound her to himself with firm bonds, while she knew not what he would with her. Then he turned the ascent-pin, whereupon the belly of the horse became full of wind and it swayed to and fro like a wave of the sea, and rose with them high in air nor slackened in its flight, till it was out of sight of the city. Now when Shams al-Nahar saw this, she asked him, "Ho thou! what is become of that thou toldest me of my Prince, making me believe that he sent thee to me?" Answered the Persian, "Allah damn the Prince! he is a mean and skin-flint knave." She cried, "Woe to thee! How darest thou disobey thy lord's commandment?" Whereto the Persian replied, "He is no lord of mine: knowest thou who I am?" Rejoined the Princess, "I know nothing of thee save what thou toldest me;" and retorted he, "What I told thee was a trick of mine against thee and the King's son: I have long lamented the loss of this horse which is under us; for I constructed it and made myself master of it. But now I have gotten firm hold of it and of thee too, and I will burn his heart even as he hath burnt mine; nor shall he ever have the horse again; no, never! So be of good cheer and keep thine eyes cool and clear; for I can be of more use to thee than he; and I am generous as I am wealthy; my servants and slaves shall obey thee as their mistress; I will robe thee in finest raiment and thine every wish shall be at thy will." When she heard this, she buffeted her face and cried out, saying, "Ah, well-away! I have not won my beloved and I have lost my father and mother!" And she wept bitter tears over what had befallen her, whilst the Sage fared on with her, without ceasing, till he came to the land of the Greeks[24] and alighted in a verdant mead, abounding in streams and trees. Now this meadow lay near a city wherein was a King of high puissance, and it chanced that he went forth that day to hunt and divert himself. As he passed by the meadow, he saw the Persian standing there, with the damsel and the horse by his side; and, before the Sage was ware, the King's slaves fell upon him and carried him and the lady and the horse to their master who, noting the foulness of the man's favour and his loathsomeness and the beauty of the girl and her loveliness, said, "O my lady, what kin is this oldster to thee?" The Persian made haste to reply, saying, "She is my wife and the daughter of my father's brother." But the lady at once gave him the lie and said, "O King, by Allah, I know him not, nor is he my husband; nay, he is a wicked magician who hath stolen me away by force and fraud." Thereupon the King bade bastinado the Persian and they beat him till he was well-nigh dead; after which the King commanded to carry him to the city and cast him into jail; and, taking from him the damsel and the ebony horse (though he knew not its properties nor the secret of its motion), set the girl in his serraglio and the horse amongst his hoards. Such was the case with the Sage and the lady; but as regards Prince Kamar al-Akmar, he garbed himself in travelling gear and taking what he needed of money, set out tracking their trail in very sorry plight; and journeyed from country to country and city to city seeking the Princess and enquiring after the ebony horse, whilst all who heard him marvelled at him and deemed his talk extravagant. Thus he continued doing a long while; but, for all his enquiry and quest, he could hit on no news of her. At last he came to her father's city of Sana'a and there asked for her, but could get no tidings of her and found her father mourning her loss. So he turned back and made for the land of the Greeks, continuing to enquire concerning the twain as he went till, as chance would have it, he alighted at a certain Khan and saw a company of merchants sitting at talk. So he sat down near them and heard one say, "O my friends, I lately witnessed a wonder of wonders." They asked, "What was that?" and he answered, "I was visiting such a district in such a city (naming the city wherein was the Princess), and I heard its people chatting of a strange thing which had lately befallen. It was that their King went out one day hunting and coursing with a company of his courtiers and the lords of his realm; and, issuing from the city, they came to a green meadow where they espied an old man standing, with a woman sitting hard by a horse of ebony. The man was foulest-foul of face and loathly of form, but the woman was a marvel of beauty and loveliness and elegance and perfect grace; and as for the wooden horse, it was a miracle, never saw eyes aught goodlier than it nor more gracious than its make." Asked the others, "And what did the King with them?"; and the merchant answered, "As for the man, the King seized him and questioned him of the damsel and he pretended that she was his wife and the daughter of his paternal uncle; but she gave him the lie forthright and declared that he was a sorcerer and a villain. So the King took her from the old man and bade beat him and cast him into the trunk-house. As for the ebony horse, I know not what became of it." When the Prince heard these words, he drew near to the merchant and began questioning him discreetly and courteously touching the name of the city and of its King; which when he knew, he passed the night full of joy. And as soon as dawned the day he set out and travelled sans surcease till he reached that city; but, when he would have entered, the gate-keepers laid hands on him, that they might bring him before the King to question him of his condition and the craft in which he skilled and the cause of his coming thither—such being the usage and custom of their ruler. Now it was supper-time when he entered the city, and it was then impossible to go in to the King or take counsel with him respecting the stranger. So the guards carried him to the jail, thinking to lay him by the heels there for the night; but, when the warders saw his beauty and loveliness, they could not find it in their hearts to imprison him: they made him sit with them without the walls; and, when food came to them, he ate with them what sufficed him. As soon as they had made an end of eating, they turned to the Prince and said, "What countryman art thou?" "I come from Fars," answered he, "the land of the Chosroes." When they heard this they laughed and one of them said, "O Chosroan,²⁵ I have heard the talk of men and their histories and I have looked into their conditions; but never saw I or heard I a bigger liar than the Chosroan which is with us in the jail." Quoth another, "And never did I see aught fouler than his favour or more hideous than his visnomy." Asked the Prince, "What have ye seen of his lying?"; and they answered, "He pretendeth that he is one of the wise! Now the King came upon him, as he went a-hunting, and found with him a most beautiful woman and a horse of the blackest ebony, never saw I a handsomer. As for the damsel, she is with the King, who is enamoured of her and would fain marry her; but she is mad, and were this man a leach as he claimeth to be, he would have healed her, for the King doth his utmost to discover a cure for her case and a remedy for her disease, and this whole year past hath he spent treasures upon physicians and astrologers, on her account; but none can avail to cure her. As for the horse, it is in the royal hoard-house, and the ugly man is here with us in prison; and as soon as night falleth, he weepeth and bemoaneth himself and will not let us sleep." When the warders had recounted the case of the Persian egromancer they held in prison and his weeping and wailing, the Prince at once devised a device whereby he might compass his desire; and presently the guards of the gate, being minded to sleep, led him into the jail and locked the door. So he overheard the Persian weeping and bemoaning himself, in his own tongue, and saying, "Alack, and alas for my sin, that I sinned against myself and against the King's son, in that which I did with the damsel; for I neither left her nor won my will of her! All this cometh of my lack of sense, in that I sought for myself that which I deserved not and which befitted not the like of me; for whoso seeketh what suiteth him not at all, falleth with the like of my fall." Now when the King's son heard this, he accosted him in Persian, saying, "How long will this weeping and wailing last? Say me, thinkest thou that hath befallen thee that which never befel other than thou?" Now when the Persian heard this, he made friends with him and began to complain to him of his case and misfortunes. And as soon as the morning morrowed, the warders took the Prince and carried him before their King, informing him that he had entered the city on the previous night, at a time when audience was impossible. Quoth the King to the Prince, "Whence comest thou and what is thy name and trade and why hast thou travelled hither?" He replied, "As to my name I am called in Persian Harjah;[26] as to my country I come from the land of Fars; and I am of the men of art and especially of the art of medicine and healing the sick and those whom the Jinns drive mad. For this I go round about all countries and cities, to profit by adding knowledge to my knowledge, and whenever I see a patient I heal him and this is my craft."[27] Now when the King heard this, he rejoiced with exceeding joy and said, "O excellent Sage, thou hast indeed come to us at a time when we need thee." Then he acquainted him with the case of the Princess, adding, "If thou cure her and recover her from her madness, thou shalt have of me everything thou seekest." Replied the Prince, "Allah save and favour the King: describe to me all thou hast seen of her insanity and tell me how long it is since the access attacked her; also how thou camest by her and the horse and the Sage." So the King told him the whole story, from first to last, adding, "The Sage is in jail." Quoth the Prince, "O auspicious King, and what hast thou done with the horse?" Quoth the King, "O youth, it is with me yet, laid up in one of my treasure-chambers," whereupon said the Prince within himself, "The best thing I can do is first to see the horse and assure myself of its condition. If it be whole and sound, all will be well and end well; but, if its motor-works be destroyed, I must find some other way of delivering my beloved." Thereupon he turned to the King and said to him, "O King, I must see the horse in question: haply I may find in it somewhat that will serve me for the recovery of the damsel." "With all my heart," replied the King, and taking him by the hand, showed him into the place where the horse was. The Prince went round about it, examining its condition, and found it whole and sound, whereat he rejoiced greatly and said to the King, "Allah save and exalt the King! I would fain go in to the damsel, that I may see how it is with her; for I hope in Allah to heal her by my healing hand through means of the horse." Then he bade them take care of the horse and the King carried him to the Princess's apartment, where her lover found her wringing her hands and writhing and beating herself against the ground, and tearing her garments to tatters as was her wont; but there was no madness of Jinn in her, and she did this but that none might approach her. When the Prince saw her thus, he said to her, "No harm shall betide thee, O ravishment of the three worlds:" and went on to soothe her and speak her fair, till he managed to whisper, "I am Kamar al-Akmar;" whereupon she cried out with a loud cry and fell down fainting for excess of joy; but the King thought this was epilepsy[28] brought on by her fear of him, and by her suddenly being startled. Then the Prince put his mouth to her ear and said to her, "O Shams al-Nahar, O seduction of the universe, have a care for thy life and mine and be patient and constant; for this our position needeth sufferance and skilful contrivance to make shift for our delivery from this tyrannical King. My first move will be now to go out to him and tell him that thou art possessed of a Jinn and hence thy madness; but that I will engage to heal thee and drive away the evil spirit, if he will at once unbind thy bonds. So when he cometh in to thee, do thou speak him smooth words, that he may think I have cured thee, and all will be done for us as we desire." Quoth she, "Hearkening and obedience;" and he went out to the King in joy and gladness, and said to him, "O august King, I have, by thy good fortune, discovered her disease and its remedy, and have cured her for thee. So now do thou go in to her and speak her softly and treat her kindly, and promise her what may please her; so shall all thou desirest of her be accomplished to thee." Thereupon the King went in to her and when she saw him, she rose and kissing the ground before him, bade him welcome and said, "I admire how thou hast come to visit thy handmaid this day;" whereat he was ready to fly for joy and bade the waiting-women and the eunuchs attend her and carry her to the Hammam and make ready for her dresses and adornment. So they went in to her and saluted her, and she returned their salams with the goodliest language and after the pleasantest fashion; whereupon they clad her in royal apparel and, clasping a collar of jewels about her neck, carried her to the bath and served her there. Then they brought her forth, as she were the full moon; and, when she came into the King's presence, she saluted him and kissed ground before him; whereupon he joyed in her with joy exceeding and said to the Prince, "O Sage, O philosopher, all this is of thy blessing. Allah increase to us the benefit of thy healing breath!"[29] The Prince replied, "O King, for the

completion of her cure it behoveth that thou go forth, thou
and all thy troops and guards, to the place where thou
foundest her, not forgetting the beast of black wood which
was with her; for therein is a devil; and, unless I exorcise
him, he will return to her and afflict her at the head of
every month." "With love and gladness," cried the King, "O
thou Prince of all philosophers and most learned of all
who see the light of day." Then he brought out the ebony
horse to the meadow in question and rode thither with
all his troops and the Princess, little weeting the purpose
of the Prince. Now when they came to the appointed
place, the Prince still habited as a leach, bade them set the
Princess and the steed as far as eye could reach from the
King and his troops, and said to him, "With thy leave, and
at thy word, I will now proceed to the fumigations and
conjurations, and here imprison the adversary of mankind,
that he may never more return to her. After this, I shall
mount this wooden horse which seemeth to be made of
ebony, and take the damsel up behind me; whereupon it
will shake and sway to and fro and fare forwards, till it
come to thee, when the affair will be at an end; and after
this thou mayest do with her as thou wilt." When the King
heard his words, he rejoiced with extreme joy; so the
Prince mounted the horse, and, taking the damsel up behind him, whilst the King and his troops watched him,
bound her fast to him. Then he turned the ascending-pin
and the horse took flight and soared with them high in air,
till they disappeared from every eye. After this the King
abode half the day, expecting their return; but they returned not. So when he despaired of them, repenting him
greatly of that which he had done and grieving sore for the
loss of the damsel, he went back to the city with his troops.
He then sent for the Persian who was in prison and said to
him, "O thou traitor, O thou villain, why didst thou hide
from me the mystery of the ebony horse? And now a
sharper hath come to me and hath carried it off, together
with a slave-girl whose ornaments are worth a mint of
money, and I shall never see anyone or anything of them

again!" So the Persian related to him all his past, first and last, and the King was seized with a fit of fury which well-nigh ended his life. He shut himself up in his palace for a while, mourning and afflicted; but at last his Wazirs came in to him and applied themselves to comfort him, saying, "Verily, he who took the damsel is an enchanter, and praised be Allah who hath delivered thee from his craft and sorcery!" And they ceased not from him, till he was comforted for her loss. Thus far concerning the King; but as for the Prince, he continued his career towards his father's capital in joy and cheer, and stayed not till he alighted on his own palace, where he set the lady in safety; after which he went in to his father and mother and saluted them and acquainted them with her coming, whereat they were filled with solace and gladness. Then he spread great banquets for the townsfolk and they held high festival a whole month, at the end of which time he went in to the Princess and they took their joy of each other with exceeding joy. But his father brake the ebony horse in pieces and destroyed its mechanism for flight; moreover the Prince wrote a letter to the Princess's father, advising him of all that had befallen her and informing him how she was now married to him and in all health and happiness, and sent it by a messenger, together with costly presents and curious rarities. And when the messenger arrived at the city which was Sana'a and delivered the letter and the presents to the King, he read the missive and rejoiced greatly thereat and accepted the presents, honouring and rewarding the bearer handsomely. Moreover, he forwarded rich gifts to his son-in-law by the same messenger, who returned to his master and acquainted him with what had passed; whereat he was much cheered. And after this the Prince wrote a letter every year to his father-in-law and sent him presents till, in course of time, his sire King Sabur deceased and he reigned in his stead, ruling justly over his lieges and conducting himself well and righteously towards them, so that the land submitted to him and his subjects did him loyal service; and Kamar al-Akmar and his wife Shams al-Nahar abode in the enjoyment of all satisfaction and solace of life, till there came to them the Destroyer of delights and Sunderer of societies; the Plunderer of palaces, the Caterer for cemeteries and the Garnerer of graves. And now glory be to the Living One who dieth not and in whose hand is the dominion of the worlds visible and invisible! Moreover I have heard tell the tale of

How Abu Hasan Brake Wind.

They recount that in the City Kaukaban of Al-Yaman there was a man of the Fazli tribe who had left Badawi life, and become a townsman for many years and was a merchant of the most opulent merchants. His wife had deceased when both were young; and his friends were instant with him to marry again, ever quoting to him the words of the poet:—

> Go, gossip! re-wed thee, for Prime draweth near:
> A wife is an almanac—good for the year.

So being weary of contention, Abu Hasan entered into negotiations with the old women who procure matches, and married a maid like Canopus when he hangeth over the seas of Al-Hind. He made high festival therefor, bidding to the wedding-banquet kith and kin, Olema and Fakirs; friends and foes and all his acquaintances of that countryside. The whole house was thrown open to feasting: there were rices of five several colours, and sherbets of as many more; and kids stuffed with walnuts and almonds and pistachios and a camel-colt[1] roasted whole. So they ate and drank and made mirth and merriment; and the bride was displayed in her seven dresses and one more, to the women, who could not take their eyes off her. At last, the bridegroom was summoned to the chamber where she sat enthroned; and he rose slowly and with dignity from his divan; but in so doing, for that he was over full of meat and drink, lo and behold! he let fly a fart, great and terrible. Thereupon each guest turned to his neighbour and talked aloud and made as though he had heard nothing, fearing for his life. But a consuming fire was lit in Abu Hasan's heart; so he pretended a call of nature; and, in lieu of seeking the bride-chamber, he went down to the housecourt and saddled his mare and rode off, weeping bitterly, through the shadow of the night. In time he reached Lahej where he found a ship ready to sail for India; so he shipped on board and made Calicut of Malabar. Here he met with many Arabs, especially Hazramis,[2] who recommended him to the King; and this King (who was a Kafir) trusted him and advanced him to the captainship of his bodyguard. He remained ten years in all solace and delight of life; at the end of which time he was seized with homesickness; and the longing to behold his native land was that of a lover pining for his beloved; and he came near to die of yearning desire. But his appointed day had not dawned; so, after taking the first bath of health, he left the King without leave, and in due course landed at Makalla of Hazramut. Here he donned the rags of a religious; and, keeping his name and case secret, fared for Kaukaban a-foot; enduring a thousand hardships of hunger, thirst and fatigue; and braving a thousand dangers from the lion, the snake and the Ghul. But when he drew near his old home, he looked down upon it from the hills with brimming eyes, and said in himself, "Haply they might know thee; so I will wander about the outskirts, and hearken to the folk. Allah grant that my case be not remembered by them!" He listened carefully for seven nights and seven days, till it so chanced that, as he was sitting at the door of a hut, he heard the voice of a young girl saying, "O my mother, tell me the day when I was born; for such an one of my companions is about to take an omen[3] for me." And the mother answered, "Thou wast born, O my daughter, on the very night when Abu Hasan farted." Now the listener no sooner heard these words than he rose up from the bench, and fled away saying to himself, "Verily thy fart hath become a date, which shall last for ever and ever; even as the poet said:—

> As long as palms shall shift the flower;
> As long as palms shall sift the flour.[4]

And he ceased not travelling and voyaging and returned to India; and there abode in self-exile till he died; and the mercy of Allah be upon him![5] And they tell another story of

THE ANGEL OF DEATH
WITH THE PROUD KING
AND THE DEVOUT MAN.

It is related, O auspicious King, that one of the olden monarchs was once minded to ride out in state with the officers of his realm and the Grandees of his retinue and display to the folk the marvels of his magnificence. So he ordered his Lords and Emirs equip them therefor and commanded his keeper of the wardrobe to bring him of the richest of raiment, such as befitted the King in his state; and he bade them bring his steeds[1] of the finest breeds and pedigrees every man heeds; which being done, he chose out of the raiment what rejoiced him most and of the horses that which he deemed best; and, donning the clothes, together with a collar set with margarites and rubies and all manner jewels, mounted and set forth in state, making his destrier prance and curvet among his troops and glorying in his pride and despotic power. And Iblis came to him and, laying his hand upon his nose, blew into his nostrils the breath of hauteur and conceit, so that he magnified and glorified himself and said in his heart, "Who among men is like unto me?" And he became so puffed up with arrogance and self-sufficiency, and so taken up with the thought of his own splendour and magnificence, that he would not vouchsafe a glance to any man. Presently, there stood before him one clad in tattered clothes and saluted him, but he returned not his salam; whereupon the stranger laid hold of his horse's bridle. "Lift thy hand," cried the King, "thou knowest not whose bridle-rein it is whereof thou takest hold." Quoth the other, "I have a need of thee." Quoth the King, "Wait till I alight and then name thy need." Rejoined the stranger, "It is a secret and I will not tell it but in thine ear." So the King bowed his head to him and he said, "I am the Angel of Death and I purpose to take thy soul." Replied the King, "Have patience with me a little, whilst I return to my house and take leave of my people and children and neighbours and wife." "By no means so," answered the Angel; "thou shalt never return nor look on them again, for the fated term of thy life is past." So saying, he took the soul of the King (who fell off his horse's back dead) and departed thence. Presently the Death Angel met a devout man, of whom Almighty Allah had accepted, and saluted him. He returned the salute, and the Angel said to him, "O pious man, I have a need of thee which must be kept secret." "Tell it in my ear," quoth the devotee; and quoth the other, "I am the Angel of Death." Replied the man, "Welcome to thee! and praised be Allah for thy coming! I am aweary of awaiting thine arrival; for indeed long hath been thine absence from the lover which longeth for thee." Said the Angel, "If thou have any business, make an end of it;" but the other answered, saying, "There is nothing so urgent to me as the meeting with my Lord, to whom be honour and glory!" And the Angel said, "How wouldst thou fain have me take thy soul? I am bidden to take it as thou willest and choosest." He replied, "Tarry till I make the Wuzu-ablution and pray; and, when I prostrate myself, then take my soul while my body is on the ground."[2] Quoth the Angel, "Verily, my Lord (be He extolled and exalted!) commanded me not to take thy soul but with thy consent and as thou shouldst wish; so I will do thy will." Then the devout man made the minor ablution[3] and prayed: and the Angel of Death took his soul in the act of prostration and Almighty Allah transported it to the place of mercy and acceptance and forgiveness. And they tell another tale of the adventures of

Sindbad the Seaman[1] and Sindbad the Landsman.

There lived in the city of Baghdad, during the reign of the Commander of the Faithful, Harun al-Rashid, a man named Sindbad the Hammal,[2] one in poor case who bore burdens on his head for hire. It happened to him one day of great heat that whilst he was carrying a heavy load, he became exceeding weary and sweated profusely, the heat and the weight alike oppressing him. Presently, as he was passing the gate of a merchant's house, before which the ground was swept and watered, and there the air was temperate, he sighted a broad bench beside the door; so he set his load thereon, to take rest and smell the air. He sat down on the edge of the bench, and at once heard from within the melodious sound of lutes and other stringed instruments, and mirth-exciting voices singing and reciting, together with the song of birds warbling and glorifying Almighty Allah in various tunes and tongues; turtles, mocking-birds, merles, nightingales, cushats and stone-curlews,[3] whereat he marvelled in himself and was moved to mighty joy and solace. Then he went up to the gate and saw within a great flower-garden wherein were pages and black slaves and such a train of servants and attendants and so forth as is found only with Kings and Sultans; and his nostrils were greeted with the savoury odours of all manner meats rich and delicate, and delicious and generous wines. So he raised his eyes heavenwards and said, "Glory to Thee, O Lord, O Creator and Provider, who providest whomso Thou wilt without count or stint! O mine Holy One, I cry Thee pardon for all sins and turn to Thee repenting of all offences

> How many by my labours, that evermore endure,
> All goods of life enjoy and in cooly shade recline?
> Each morn that dawns I wake in travail and in woe,
> And strange is my condition and my burden gars me pine:
> Many others are in luck and from miseries are free,
> And Fortune never load them with loads the like o'mine:
> They live their happy days in all solace and delight;
> Eat, drink and dwell in honour 'mid the noble and the digne:
> All living things were made of a little drop of sperm,
> Thine origin is mine and my provenance is thine;
> Yet the difference and distance 'twixt the twain of us are far
> As the difference of savour 'twixt vinegar and wine:
> But at Thee, O God All-wise! I venture not to rail
> Whose ordinance is just and whose justice cannot fail."

When Sindbad the Porter had made an end of reciting his verses, he bore up his burden and was about to fare on, when there came forth to him from the gate a little foot-page, fair of face and shapely of shape and dainty of dress who caught him by the hand saying, "Come in and speak with my lord, for he calleth for thee." The Porter would have excused himself to the page but the lad would take no refusal; so he left his load with the doorkeeper in the vestibule and followed the boy into the house, which he found to be a goodly mansion, radiant and full of majesty, till he brought him to a grand sitting-room wherein he saw a company of nobles and great lords, seated at tables garnished with all manner of flowers and sweet-scented herbs, besides great plenty of dainty viands and fruits dried and fresh and confections and wines of the choicest vintages. There also were instruments of music and mirth and lovely slave-girls playing and singing. All the company was ranged according to rank; and in the highest place sat a man of worshipful and noble aspect whose beard-sides hoariness had stricken; and he was stately of stature and fair of favour, agreeable of aspect and full of gravity and dignity and majesty. So Sindbad the Porter was confounded at that which he beheld and said in himself, "By Allah, this must be either a piece of Paradise or some King's palace!" Then he saluted the company with much respect praying for their prosperity, and kissing the ground before them, stood with his head bowed down in humble attitude. The master of the house bade him draw near and be seated and bespoke him kindly, bidding him welcome. Then he set before him various kinds of viands, rich and delicate and delicious, and the Porter, after saying his Bismillah, fell to and ate his fill, after which he exclaimed, "Praised be Allah whatso be our case!"[4] and, washing his hands, returned thanks to the company for his entertainment. Quoth the host, "Thou art welcome and thy day is a blessed. But what is thy name and calling?" Quoth the other, "O my lord, my name is Sindbad the Hammal, and I carry folk's goods on my head for hire." The house-master smiled and rejoined, "Know, O Porter, that thy name is even as mine, for I am Sindbad the Seaman; and now, O Porter, I would have thee let me hear the couplets thou recitedst at the gate anon." The Porter was abashed and replied, "Allah upon thee! Excuse me, for toil and travail and lack of luck when the hand is empty, teach a man ill manners and boorish ways." Said the host, "Be not ashamed; thou art become my brother; but repeat to me the verses, for they pleased me whenas I heard thee recite them at the gate." Hereupon the Porter repeated the couplets and they delighted the merchant, who said to him:—Know, O Hammal, that my story is a wonderful one, and thou shalt hear all that befel me and all I underwent ere I rose to this state of prosperity and became the lord of this place wherein thou seest me; for I came not to this high estate save after travail sore and perils galore, and how much toil and trouble have I not suffered in days of yore! I have made seven voyages, by each of which hangeth a marvellous tale, such as confoundeth the reason, and all this came to pass by doom of fortune and fate; for from what destiny doth write there is neither refuge nor flight. Know, then, good my lords (continued he), that I am about to relate

THE FIRST VOYAGE OF SINDBAD HIGHT THE SEAMAN.[5]

My father was a merchant, one of the notables of my native place, a monied man and ample of means, who died whilst I was yet a child, leaving me much wealth in money and lands and farmhouses. When I grew up, I laid hands on the whole and ate of the best and drank freely and wore rich clothes and lived lavishly, companioning and consorting with youths of my own age, and considering that this course of life would continue for ever and ken no change. Thus did I for a long time, but at last I awoke from my heedlessness and, returning to my senses, I found my wealth had become unwealth and my condition ill-conditioned and all I once hent had left my hand. And recovering my reason I was stricken with dismay and confusion and bethought me of a saying of our lord Solomon, son of David (on whom be peace!), which I had heard aforetime from my father, "Three things are better than other three; the day of death is better than the day of birth, a live dog is better than a dead lion and the grave is better than want."[6] Then I got together my remains of estates and property and sold all, even my clothes, for three thousand dirhams, with which I resolved to travel to foreign parts, remembering the saying of the poet:—

By means of toil man shall scale the height;
Who to fame aspires mustn't sleep o'night:
Who seeketh pearl in the deep must dive,
Winning weal and wealth by his main and might:
And who seeketh Fame without toil and strife
Th' impossible seeketh and wasteth life.

So taking heart I bought me goods, merchandise and all needed for a voyage and, impatient to be at sea, I embarked, with a company of merchants, on board a ship bound for Bassorah. There we again embarked and sailed many days and nights, and we passed from isle to isle and sea to sea and shore to shore, buying and selling and bartering everywhere the ship touched, and continued our course till we came to an island as it were a garth of the gardens of Paradise. Here the captain cast anchor and making fast to the shore, put out the landing planks. So all on board landed and made furnaces[7] and lighting fires therein, busied themselves in various ways, some cooking and some washing, whilst other some walked about the island for solace, and the crew fell to eating and drinking and playing and sporting. I was one of the walkers but, as we were thus engaged, behold the master who was standing on the gunwale cried out to us at the top of his voice, saying, "Ho there! passengers, run for your lives and hasten back to the ship and leave your gear and save yourselves from destruction, Allah preserve you! For this island whereon ye stand is no true island, but a great fish stationary a-middlemost of the sea, whereon the sand hath settled and trees have sprung up of old time, so that it is become like unto an island;[8] but, when ye lighted fires on it, it felt the heat and moved; and in a moment it will sink with you into the sea and ye will all be drowned. So leave your gear and seek your safety ere ye die!" All who heard him left gear and goods, clothes washed and unwashed, fire pots and brass cooking-pots, and fled back to the ship for their lives, and some reached it while others (amongst whom was I) did not, for suddenly the island shook and sank into the abysses of the deep, with all that were thereon, and the dashing sea surged over it with clashing waves. I sank with the others down, down into the deep, but Almighty Allah preserved me from drowning and threw in my way a great wooden tub of those that had served the ship's company for tubbing. I gripped it for the sweetness of life and, bestriding it like one riding, paddled with my feet like oars, whilst the waves tossed me as in sport right and left. Meanwhile the captain made sail and departed with those who had reached the ship, regardless of the drowning and the drowned; and I ceased not following the vessel with my eyes, till she was hid from sight and I made sure of death. Darkness closed in upon me while in this plight and the winds and waves bore me on all that night and the next day, till the tub brought to with me under the lee of a lofty island, with trees overhanging the tide. I caught hold of a branch and by its aid clambered up on to the land, after coming nigh upon death; but when I reached the shore, I found my legs cramped and numbed and my feet bore traces of the nibbling of fish upon their soles; withal I had felt nothing for excess of anguish and fatigue. I threw myself down on the island ground, like a dead man, and drowned in desolation swooned away, nor did I return to my senses till next morning, when the sun rose and revived me. But I found my feet swollen, so made shift to move by shuffling on my breech and crawling on my knees, for in that island were found store of fruits and springs of sweet water. I ate of the fruits which strengthened me: and thus I abode days and nights, till my life seemed to return and my spirits began to revive and I was better able to move about. So, after due consideration, I fell to exploring the island and diverting myself with gazing upon all things that Allah Almighty had created there; and rested under the trees from one of which I cut me a staff to lean upon. One day as I walked along the marge, I caught sight of some object in the distance and thought it a wild beast or one of the monster-creatures of the sea; but, as I drew near it, looking hard the while, I saw that it was a noble mare, tethered on the beach. Presently I went up to her, but she cried out against me with a great cry, so that I trembled for fear and turned to go away, when there came forth a man from under the earth and followed me, crying out and saying, "Who and whence art thou, and what caused thee to come hither?" "O my lord," answered I, "I am in very sooth, a waif, a stranger, and was left to drown with sundry others by the ship we voyaged in;[9] but Allah graciously sent me a wooden tub; so I saved myself thereon and it floated with me, till the waves cast me up on this island." When he heard this, he took my hand and saying, "Come with me," carried me into a great Sardab, or underground chamber, which was spacious as a saloon. He made me sit down at its upper end; then he brought me somewhat of food and, being anhungered, I ate till I was satisfied and refreshed; and when he had put me at mine ease he questioned me of myself, and I told him all that had befallen me from first to last; and, as he wondered at my adventure, I said, "By Allah, O my lord, excuse me; I have told thee the truth of my case and the accident which betided me; and now I desire that thou tell me who thou art and why thou abidest here under the earth and why thou hast tethered yonder mare on the brink of the sea." Answered he, "Know, that I am one of the several who are stationed in different parts of this island, and we are of the grooms of King Mihrjan[10] and under our hand are all his horses. Every month, about new-moon tide we bring hither our best mares which have never been covered, and picket them on the sea-shore and hide ourselves in this place under the ground, so that none may espy us. Presently, the stallions of the sea scent the mares and come up out of the water and seeing no one, leap the mares and do their will of them. When they have covered them, they try to drag them away with them, but cannot, by reason of the leg-ropes; so they cry out at them and butt at them and kick them, which we hearing, know that the stallions have dismounted; so we run out and shout at them, whereupon they are startled and return in fear to the sea. Then the mares conceive by them and bear colts and fillies worth a mint of money, nor is their like to be found on earth's face. This is the time of the coming forth of the sea-stallions; and Inshallah! I will bear thee to King Mihrjan and show thee our country. And know that hadst thou not happened on us thou hadst perished miserably and none had known of thee: but I will be the means of the saving of thy life and of thy return to thine own land." I called down blessings on him and thanked him for his kindness and courtesy; and, while we were yet talking, behold, the stallion came up out of the sea; and, giving a great cry, sprang upon the mare and covered her. When he had done his will of her, he dismounted and would have carried her away with him, but could not by reason of the tether. She kicked and cried out at him, whereupon the groom took a sword and target[11] and ran out of the underground saloon, smiting the buckler with the blade and calling to his company, who came up shouting and brandishing spears; and the stallion took fright at them and plunging into the sea, like a buffalo, disappeared under the waves.[12] After this we sat awhile, till the rest of the grooms came up, each leading a mare, and seeing me with their fellow-Syce, questioned me of my case and I repeated my story to them. Thereupon they drew near me and spreading the table, ate and invited me to eat; so I ate with them, after which they took horse and mounting me on one of the mares, set out with me and fared on without ceasing, till we came to the capital city of King Mihrjan, and going in to him acquainted him with my story. Then he sent for me, and when they set me before him and salams had been exchanged, he gave me a cordial welcome and wishing me long life bade me tell him my tale. So I related to him all that I had seen and all that had befallen me from first to last, whereat he marvelled and said to me, "By Allah, O my son, thou hast indeed been miraculously preserved! Were not the term of thy life a long one, thou hadst not escaped from these straits; but praised be Allah for safety!" Then he spoke cheerily to me and entreated me with kindness and consideration: moreover, he made me his agent for the port and registrar of all ships that entered the harbour. I attended him regularly, to receive his commandments, and he favoured me and did me all manner of kindness and invested me with costly and splendid robes. Indeed, I was high in credit with him, as an intercessor for the folk and an intermediary between them and him, when they wanted aught of him. I abode thus a great while and, as often as I passed through the city to the port, I questioned the merchants and travellers and sailors of the city of Baghdad; so haply I might hear of an occasion to return to my native land, but could find none who knew it or knew any who resorted thither. At this I was chagrined, for I was weary of long strangerhood; and my disappointment endured for a time till one day, going in to King Mihrjan, I found with him a company of Indians. I saluted them and they returned my salam; and politely welcomed me and asked me of my country. When they asked me of my country I questioned them of theirs and they told me that they were of various castes, some being called Shakiriyah[13] who are the noblest of their castes and neither oppress nor offer violence to any, and others Brahmans, a folk who abstain from wine, but live in delight and solace and merriment and own camels and horses and cattle. Moreover, they told me that the people of India are divided into two-and-seventy castes, and I marvelled at this with exceeding marvel. Amongst other things that I saw in King Mihrjan's dominions was an island called Kasil,[14] wherein all night is heard the beating of drums and tabrets; but we were told by the neighbouring islanders and by travellers that the inhabitants are people of diligence and judgment.[15] In this sea I saw also a fish two hundred cubits long and the fishermen fear it; so they strike together pieces of wood and put it to flight.[16] I also saw another fish, with a head like that of an owl, besides many other wonders and rarities, which it would be tedious to recount. I occupied myself thus in visiting the islands till, one day, as I stood in the port, with a staff in my hand, according to my custom, behold, a great ship, wherein were many merchants, came sailing for the harbour. When it reached the small inner port where ships anchor under the city, the master furled his sails and making fast to the shore, put out the landing-planks, whereupon the crew fell to breaking bulk and landing cargo whilst I stood by, taking written note of them. They were long in bringing the goods ashore so I asked the master, "Is there aught left in thy ship?"; and he answered, "O my lord, there are divers bales of merchandise in the hold, whose owner was drowned from amongst us at one of the islands on our course; so his goods remained in our charge by way of trust and we purpose to sell them and note their price, that we may convey it to his people in the city of Baghdad, the Home of Peace." "What was the merchant's name?" quoth I, and quoth he, "Sindbad the Seaman;" whereupon I straitly considered him and knowing him, cried out to him with a great cry, saying, "O captain, I am that Sindbad the Seaman who travelled with other merchants; and when the fish heaved and thou calledst to us some saved themselves and others sank, I being one of them. But Allah Almighty threw in my way a great tub of wood, of those the crew had used to wash withal, and the winds and waves carried me to this island, where by Allah's grace, I fell in with King Mihrjan's grooms and they brought me hither to the King their master. When I told him my story, he entreated me with favour and made me his harbour-master, and I have prospered in his service and found acceptance with him. These bales, therefore are mine, the goods which God hath given me." The other exclaimed, "There is no Majesty and there is no Might save in Allah, the Glorious, the Great! Verily, there is neither conscience nor good faith left among men!" Said I, "O Rais,[17] what mean these words, seeing that I have told thee my case?" And he answered, "Because thou heardest me say that I had with me goods whose owner was drowned, thou thinkest to take them without right; but this is forbidden by law to thee, for we saw him drown before our eyes, together with many other passengers, nor was one of them saved. So how canst thou pretend that thou art the owner of the goods?" "O

captain," said I, "Listen to my story and give heed to my
words, and my truth will be manifest to thee; for lying and
leasing are the letter-marks of the hypocrites." Then I recounted to him all that had befallen me since I sailed from
Baghdad with him to the time when we came to the fish-
island where we were nearly drowned; and I reminded him
of certain matters which had passed between us; whereupon both he and the merchants were certified of the truth
of my story and recognised me and gave me joy of my deliverance, saying, "By Allah, we thought not that thou
hadst escaped drowning! But the Lord hath granted thee
new life." Then they delivered my bales to me, and I found
my name written thereon, nor was aught thereof lacking.
So I opened them and making up a present for King Mihrjan of the finest and costliest of the contents, caused the
sailors carry it up to the palace, where I went in to the King
and laid my present at his feet, acquainting him with what
had happened, especially concerning the ship and my
goods; whereat he wondered with exceeding wonder and
the truth of all that I had told him was made manifest to
him. His affection for me redoubled after that and he
showed me exceeding honour and bestowed on me a great
present in return for mine. Then I sold my bales and what
other matters I owned making a great profit on them, and
bought me other goods and gear of the growth and fashion
of the island-city. When the merchants were about to
start on their homeward voyage, I embarked on board the
ship all that I possessed, and going in to the King, thanked
him for all his favours and friendship and craved his leave
to return to my own land and friends. He farewelled me
and bestowed on me great store of the country-stuffs and
produce; and I took leave of him and embarked. Then we
set sail and fared on nights and days, by the permission of
Allah Almighty; and Fortune served us and Fate favoured
us, so that we arrived in safety at Bassorah-city where I
landed rejoiced at my safe return to my natal soil. After a
short stay, I set out for Baghdad, the House of Peace, with
store of goods and commodities of great price. Reaching

the city in due time, I went straight to my own quarter and entered my house where all my friends and kinsfolk came to greet me. Then I bought me eunuchs and concubines, servants and negro slaves till I had a large establishment, and I bought me houses, and lands and gardens, till I was richer and in better case than before, and returned to enjoy the society of my friends and familiars more assiduously than ever, forgetting all I had suffered of fatigue and hardship and strangerhood and every peril of travel; and I applied myself to all manner joys and solaces and delights, eating the daintiest viands and drinking the deliciousest wines; and my wealth allowed this state of things to endure. This, then, is the story of my first voyage, and to-morrow, Inshallah! I will tell you the tale of the second of my seven voyages. (Saith he who telleth the tale), Then Sindbad the Seaman made Sindbad the Landsman sup with him and bade give him an hundred gold pieces, saying, "Thou hast cheered us with thy company this day."[18] The Porter thanked him and, taking the gift, went his way, pondering that which he had heard and marvelling mightily at what things betide mankind. He passed the night in his own place and with early morning repaired to the abode of Sindbad the Seaman, who received him with honour and seated him by his side. As soon as the rest of the company was assembled, he set meat and drink before them and, when they had well eaten and drunken and were merry and in cheerful case, he took up his discourse and recounted to them in these words the narrative of

THE SECOND VOYAGE OF SINDBAD THE SEAMAN.

Know, O my brother, that I was living a most comfortable and enjoyable life, in all solace and delight, as I told you yesterday, until one day my mind became possessed with the thought of travelling about the world of men and seeing their cities and islands; and a longing seized me to traffic and to make money by trade. Upon this resolve I took a great store of cash and, buying goods and gear fit for travel, bound them up in bales. Then I went down to the river-bank, where I found a noble ship and brand-new about to sail, equipped with sails of fine cloth and well manned and provided; so I took passage in her, with a number of other merchants, and after embarking our goods we weighed anchor the same day. Right fair was our voyage and we sailed from place to place and from isle to isle; and whenever we anchored we met a crowd of merchants and notables and customers, and we took to buying and selling and bartering. At last Destiny brought us to an island, fair and verdant, in trees abundant, with yellow-ripe fruits luxuriant, and flowers fragrant and birds warbling soft descant; and streams crystalline and radiant; but no sign of man showed to the descrier, no, not a blower of the fire.[19] The captain made fast with us to this island, and the merchants and sailors landed and walked about, enjoying the shade of the trees and the song of the birds, that chanted the praises of the One, the Victorious, and marvelling at the works of the Omnipotent King.[20] I landed with the rest; and, sitting down by a spring of sweet water that welled up among the trees, took out some vivers I had with me and ate of that which Allah Almighty had allotted unto me. And so sweet was the zephyr and so fragrant were the flowers, that presently I waxed drowsy and, lying down in that place, was soon drowned in sleep. When I awoke, I found myself alone, for the ship had sailed and left me behind, nor had one of the merchants or sailors bethought himself of me. I searched the island right and left, but found neither man nor Jinn, whereat I was beyond measure troubled and my gall was like to burst for stress of chagrin and anguish and concern, because I was left quite alone, without aught of worldly gear or meat or drink, weary and heart-broken. So I gave myself up for lost and said, "Not always doth the crock escape the shock. I was saved the first time by finding one who brought me from the desert island to an inhabited place, but now there is no hope for me." Then I fell to weeping and wailing and gave myself up to an access

of rage, blaming myself for having again ventured upon
the perils and hardships of voyage, whenas I was at my ease
in mine own house in mine own land, taking my pleasure
with good meat and good drink and good clothes and lacking nothing, neither money nor goods. And I repented me
of having left Baghdad, and this the more after all the travails and dangers I had undergone in my first voyage,
wherein I had so narrowly escaped destruction, and exclaimed "Verily we are Allah's and unto Him we are returning!" I was indeed even as one mad and Jinn-struck
and presently I rose and walked about the island, right and
left and every whither, unable for trouble to sit or tarry
in any one place. Then I climbed a tall tree and looked in
all directions, but saw nothing save sky and sea and trees
and birds and isles and sands. However, after a while my
eager glances fell upon some great white thing, afar off in
the interior of the island; so I came down from the tree
and made for that which I had seen; and behold, it was a
huge white dome rising high in air and of vast compass. I
walked all around it, but found no door thereto, nor could
I muster strength or nimbleness by reason of its exceeding
smoothness and slipperiness. So I marked the spot where I
stood and went round about the dome to measure its cir-
cumference which I found fifty good paces. And as I stood,
casting about how to gain an entrance the day being near
its fall and the sun being near the horizon, behold, the sun
was suddenly hidden from me and the air became dull
and dark. Methought a cloud had come over the sun, but
it was the season of summer; so I marvelled at this and lifting my head looked steadfastly at the sky, when I saw that
the cloud was none other than an enormous bird, of gigantic girth and inordinately wide of wing which, as it flew
through the air, veiled the sun and hid it from the island. At
this sight my wonder redoubled and I remembered a story
I had heard aforetime of pilgrims and travellers, how in a
certain island dwelleth a huge bird, called the "Rukh"[21]
which feedeth its young on elephants; and I was certified
that the dome which caught my sight was none other than

a Rukh's egg. As I looked and wondered at the marvellous works of the Almighty, the bird alighted on the dome and brooded over it with its wings covering it and its legs stretched out behind it on the ground, and in this posture it fell asleep, glory be to Him who sleepeth not! When I saw this, I arose and, unwinding my turband from my head, doubled it and twisted it into a rope, with which I girt my middle and bound my waist fast to the legs of the Rukh, saying in myself, "Peradventure, this bird may carry me to a land of cities and inhabitants, and that will be better than abiding in this desert island." I passed the night watching and fearing to sleep, lest the bird should fly away with me unawares; and, as soon as the dawn broke and morn shone, the Rukh rose off its egg and spreading its wings with a great cry flew up into the air dragging me with it; nor ceased it to soar and to tower till I thought it had reached the limit of the firmament; after which it descended, earthwards, little by little, till it lighted on the top of a high hill. As soon as I found myself on the hard ground, I made haste to unbind myself, quaking for fear of the bird, though it took no heed of me nor even felt me; and, loosing my turband from its feet, I made off with my best speed. Presently, I saw it catch up in its huge claws something from the earth and rise with it high in air, and observing it narrowly I saw it to be a serpent big of bulk and gigantic of girth, wherewith it flew away clean out of sight. I marvelled at this and faring forwards found myself on a peak overlooking a valley, exceeding great and wide and deep, and bounded by vast mountains that spired high in air: none could descry their summits, for the excess of their height, nor was any able to climb up thereto. When I saw this, I blamed myself for that which I had done and said, "Would Heaven I had tarried in the island! It was better than this wild desert; for there I had at least fruits to eat and water to drink, and here are neither trees nor fruits nor streams. But there is no Majesty and there is no Might save in Allah, the Glorious, the Great! Verily, as often as I am quit of one peril, I fall into a worse danger and a more grievous." However, I took courage and walking along the Wady found that its soil was of diamond, the stone wherewith they pierce minerals and precious stones and porcelain and the onyx, for that it is a dense stone and a dure, whereon neither iron nor hardhead hath effect, neither can we cut off aught therefrom nor break it, save by means of leadstone.[22] Moreover, the valley swarmed with snakes and vipers, each big as a palm tree, that would have made but one gulp of an elephant; and they came out by night, hiding during the day, lest the Rukhs and eagles pounce on them and tear them to pieces, as was their wont, why I wot not. And I repented of what I had done and said, "By Allah, I have made haste to bring destruction upon myself!" The day began to wane as I went along and I looked about for a place where I might pass the night, being in fear of the serpents; and I took no thought of meat and drink in my concern for my life. Presently, I caught sight of a cave nearhand, with a narrow doorway; so I entered and seeing a great stone close to the mouth, I rolled it up and stopped the entrance, saying to myself, "I am safe here for the night; and as soon as it is day, I will go forth and see what destiny will do." Then I looked within the cave and saw at the upper end a great serpent brooding on her eggs, at which my flesh quaked and my hair stood on end; but I raised my eyes to Heaven and, committing my case to fate and lot, abode all that night without sleep till daybreak, when I rolled back the stone from the mouth of the cave and went forth, staggering like a drunken man and giddy with watching and fear and hunger. As in this sore case I walked along the valley, behold, there fell down before me a slaughtered beast; but I saw no one, whereat I marvelled with great marvel and presently remembered a story I had heard aforetime of traders and pilgrims and travellers; how the mountains where are the diamonds are full of perils and terrors, nor can any fare through them; but the merchants who traffic in diamonds have a device by which they obtain them, that is to say, they take a sheep and slaughter and skin it and cut it in pieces and cast them down from the mountain-tops into the valley-sole, where the meat being fresh and sticky with blood, some of the gems cleave to it. There they leave it till mid-day, when the eagles and vultures swoop down upon it and carry it in their claws to the mountain-summits, whereupon the merchants come and shout at them and scare them away from the meat. Then they come and, taking the diamonds which they find sticking to it, go their ways with them and leave the meat to the birds and beasts; nor can any come at the diamonds but by this device. So, when I saw the slaughtered beast fall (he pursued) and bethought me of the story, I went up to it and filled my pockets and shawlgirdle and turband and the folds of my clothes with the choicest diamonds; and, as I was thus engaged, down fell before me another great piece of meat. Then with my unrolled turband and lying on my back, I set the bit on my breast so that I was hidden by the meat, which was thus raised above the ground. Hardly had I gripped it, when an eagle swooped down upon the flesh and, seizing it with his talons, flew up with it high in air and me clinging thereto, and ceased not its flight till it alighted on the head of one of the mountains where, dropping the carcass he fell to rending it; but, behold, there arose behind him a great noise of shouting and clattering of wood, whereat the bird took fright and flew away. Then I loosed off myself the meat, with clothes daubed with blood therefrom, and stood up by its side; whereupon up came the merchant, who had cried out at the eagle, and seeing me standing there, bespoke me not, but was affrighted at me and shook with fear. However, he went up to the carcass and turning it over, found no diamonds sticking to it, whereat he gave a great cry and exclaimed, "Harrow, my disappointment! There is no Majesty and there is no Might save in Allah with whom we seek refuge from Satan the stoned!" And he bemoaned himself and beat hand upon hand, saying, "Alas, the pity of it! How cometh this?" Then I went up to him and he said to me, "Who art thou and what causeth thee to come hither?" And I, "Fear not, I am a man and a good man and a merchant. My story is a wondrous and my adventures marvellous and the manner of my coming hither is prodigious. So be of good cheer, thou shalt receive of me what shall rejoice thee, for I have with me great plenty of diamonds and I will give thee thereof what shall suffice thee; for each is better than aught thou couldst get otherwise. So fear nothing." The man rejoiced thereat and thanked and blessed me; then we talked together till the other merchants, hearing me in discourse with their fellow, came up and saluted me; for each of them had thrown down his piece of meat. And as I went off with them and told them my whole story, how I had suffered hardships at sea and the fashion of my reaching the valley. But I gave the owner of the meat a number of the stones I had by me, so they all wished me joy of my escape, saying, "By Allah a new life hath been decreed to thee, for none ever reached yonder valley and came off thence alive before thee; but praised be Allah for thy safety!" We passed the night together in a safe and pleasant place, beyond measure rejoiced at my deliverance from the Valley of Serpents and my arrival in an inhabited land; and on the morrow we set out and journeyed over the mighty range of mountains, seeing many serpents in the valley, till we came to a fair great island, wherein was a garden of huge camphor trees under each of which an hundred men might take shelter. When the folk have a mind to get camphor, they bore into the upper part of the bole with a long iron; whereupon the liquid camphor, which is the sap of the tree, floweth out and they catch it in vessels, where it concreteth like gum; but, after this, the tree dieth and becometh firewood.[23] Moreover, there is in this island a kind of wild beast, called "Rhinoceros,"[24] that pastureth as do steers and buffaloes with us; but it is a huge brute, bigger of body than the camel and like it feedeth upon the leaves and twigs of trees. It is a remarkable animal with a great and thick horn, ten cubits long, amiddleward its head; wherein, when cleft in twain, is the likeness of a man. Voyagers and pilgrims and travellers declare that this beast called "Karkadan" will carry off a great elephant on its horn and graze about the island and the sea-coast therewith and take no heed of it, till the elephant dieth and its fat, melting in the sun, runneth down into the rhinoceros's eyes and blindeth him, so that he lieth down on the shore. Then comes the bird Rukh and carrieth off both the rhinoceros and that which is on its horn to feed its young withal. Moreover, I saw in this island many kinds of oxen and buffaloes, whose like are not found in our country. Here I sold some of the diamonds which I had by me for gold dinars and silver dirhams and bartered others for the produce of the country; and, loading them upon beasts of burden, fared on with the merchants from valley to valley and town to town, buying and selling and viewing foreign countries and the works and creatures of Allah, till we came to Bassorah-city, where we abode a few days, after which I continued my journey to Baghdad. I arrived at home with great store of diamonds and money and goods, and foregathered with my friends and relations and gave alms and largesse and bestowed curious gifts and made presents to all my friends and companions. Then I betook myself to eating well and drinking well and wearing fine clothes and making merry with my fellows, and forgot all my sufferings in the pleasures of return to the solace and delight of life, with light heart and broadened breast. And every one who heard of my return came and questioned me of my adventures and of foreign countries, and I related to them all that had befallen me, and the much I had suffered, whereat they wondered and gave me joy of my safe return. This, then, is the end of the story of my second voyage; and to-morrow, Inshallah! I will tell you what befel me in my third voyage. The company marvelled at his story and supped with him; after which he ordered an hundred dinars of gold to be given to the Porter, who took the sum with many thanks and blessings (which he stinted not even when he reached home) and went his way, wondering at what he had heard. Next morning as soon as day came in its sheen and shone, he rose and praying the dawn-prayer, repaired to the house of Sindbad the Seaman, even as he had bidden him, and went in and gave him good-morrow. The merchant welcomed him and made him sit with him, till the rest of the company arrived; and when they had well eaten and drunken and were merry with joy and jollity, their host began by saying:—Hearken, O my brothers, to what I am about to tell you; for it is even more wondrous than what you have already heard; but Allah alone kenneth what things His Omniscience concealed from man! And listen to

THE THIRD VOYAGE OF SINDBAD THE SEAMAN.

As I told you yesterday, I returned from my second voyage overjoyed at my safety and with great increase of wealth, Allah having requited me all that I had wasted and lost, and I abode awhile in Baghdad-city savouring the utmost ease and prosperity and comfort and happiness, till the carnal man was once more seized with longing for travel and diversion and adventure, and yearned after traffic and lucre and emolument, for that the human heart is naturally prone to evil. So making up my mind I laid in great plenty of goods suitable for a sea-voyage and repairing to Bassorah, went down to the shore and found there a fine ship ready to sail, with a full crew and a numerous company of merchants, men of worth and substance; faith, piety and consideration. I embarked with them and we set sail on the blessing of Allah Almighty and on His aidance and His favour to bring our voyage to a safe and prosperous issue and already we congratulated one another on our good fortune and boon voyage. We fared on from sea to sea and from island to island and city to city, in all delight and contentment, buying and selling wherever we touched, and taking our solace and our pleasure, till one day when, as we sailed athwart the dashing sea, swollen with clashing billows, behold, the master (who stood on the gunwale examining the ocean in all directions) cried out with a great cry, and buffeted his face and pluckt out his beard and rent his raiment, and bade furl the sail and cast the anchors. So we said to him, "O Rais, what is the matter?" "Know, O my brethren (Allah preserve you!), that the wind hath gotten the better of us and hath driven us out of our course into mid-ocean, and destiny, for our ill luck, hath brought us to the Mountain of the Zughb, a hairy folk like apes,[25] among whom no man ever fell and came forth alive; and my heart presageth that we all be dead men." Hardly had the master made an end of his speech when the apes were upon us. They surrounded the ship on all sides swarming like locusts and crowding the shore. They were the most frightful of wild creatures, covered with black hair like felt, foul of favour and small of stature, being but four spans high, yellow-eyed and blackfaced; none knoweth their language nor what they are, and they shun the company of men. We feared to slay them or strike them or drive them away, because of their inconceivable multitude; lest, if we hurt one, the rest fall on us and slay us, for numbers prevail over courage; so we let them do their will, albeit we feared they would plunder our goods and gear. They swarmed up the cables and gnawed them asunder, and on like wise they did with all the ropes of the ship, so that it fell off from the wind and stranded upon their mountainous coast. Then they laid hands on all the merchants and crew, and landing us on the island, made off with the ship and its cargo and went their ways, we wot not whither. We were thus left on the island, eating of its fruits and pot-herbs and drinking of its streams till, one day, we espied in its midst what seemed an inhabited house. So we made for it as fast as our feet could carry us and behold, it was a castle strong and tall, compassed about with a lofty wall, and having a two-leaved gate of ebony-wood both of which leaves open stood. We entered and found within a space wide and bare like a great square, round which stood many high doors open thrown, and at the farther end a long bench of stone and brasiers, with cooking gear hanging thereon and about it great plenty of bones; but we saw no one and marvelled thereat with exceeding wonder. Then we sat down in the courtyard a little while and presently falling asleep, slept from the forenoon till sundown, when lo! the earth trembled under our feet and the air rumbled with a terrible tone. Then there came down upon us, from the top of the castle, a huge creature in the likeness of a man, black of colour, tall and big of bulk, as he were a great date-tree, with eyes like coals of fire and eye-teeth like boar's tusks and a vast big gape like the mouth of a well. Moreover, he had long loose lips like camel's, hanging down upon his breast, and ears like two Jarms[26] falling over his shoulder-blades and the nails of his hands were like the claws of a lion.[27] When we saw this frightful giant, we were like to faint and every moment increased our fear and terror; and we became as dead men for excess of horror and affright. And after trampling upon the earth, he sat awhile on the bench; then he arose and coming to us seized me by the arm choosing me out from among my comrades the merchants. He took me up in his hand and turning me over felt me, as a butcher feeleth a sheep he is about to slaughter, and I but a little mouthful in his hands; but finding me lean and fleshless for stress of toil and trouble and weariness, let me go and took up another, whom in like manner he turned over and felt and let go; nor did he cease to feel and turn over the rest of us, one after another, till he came to the master of the ship. Now he was a sturdy, stout, broad-shouldered wight, fat and in full vigour; so he pleased the giant, who seized him, as a butcher seizeth a beast, and throwing him down, set his foot on his neck and brake it; after which he fetched a long spit and thrusting it up his backside, brought it forth of the crown of his head. Then, lighting a fierce fire, he set over it the spit with the Rais thereon, and turned it over the coals, till the flesh was roasted, when he took the spit off the fire and set it like a Kabab-stick before him. Then he tare the body, limb from limb, as one jointeth a chicken and, rending the flesh with his nails, fell to eating of it and gnawing the bones, till there was nothing left but some of these, which he threw on one side of the wall. This done, he sat for a while; then he lay down on the stone-bench and fell asleep, snarking and snoring like the gurgling of a lamb or a cow with its throat cut; nor did he awake till morning, when he rose and fared forth and went his ways. As soon as we were certified that he was gone, we began to talk with one another, weeping and bemoaning ourselves for the risk we ran, and saying, "Would Heaven we had been drowned in the sea or that the apes had eaten us! That were better than to be roasted over the coals; by Allah, this is a vile, foul death! But whatso the Lord willeth must come to pass and there is no Majesty and there is no Might, save in Him, the Glorious, the Great! We shall assuredly perish miserably and none will know of us; as there is no escape for us from this place." Then we arose and roamed about the island, hoping that haply we might find a place to hide us in or a means of flight, for indeed death was a light matter to us, provided we were not roasted over the fire[28] and eaten. However, we could find no hiding-place and the evening overtook us; so, of the excess of our terror, we returned to the castle and sat down awhile. Presently, the earth trembled under our feet and the black ogre came up to us and turning us over, felt one after other, till he found a man to his liking, whom he took and served as he had done the captain, killing and roasting and eating him: after which he lay down on the bench[29] and slept all night, snarking and snoring like a beast with its throat cut, till daybreak, when he arose and went out as before. Then we drew together and conversed and said one to other, "By Allah, we had better throw ourselves into the sea and be drowned than die roasted; for this is an abominable death!" Quoth one of us, "Hear ye my words! let us cast about to kill him, and be at peace from the grief of him and rid the Moslems of his barbarity and tyranny." Then said I, "Hear me, O my brothers; if there is nothing for it but to slay him, let us carry some of this firewood and planks down to the seashore and make us a boat wherein, if we succeed in slaughtering him, we may either embark and let the waters carry us whither Allah willeth, or else abide here till some ship pass, when we will take passage in it. If we fail to kill him, we will embark in the boat and put out to sea; and if we be drowned, we shall at least escape being roasted over a kitchen fire with sliced weasands; whilst, if we escape, we escape, and if we be drowned, we die martyrs." "By Allah," said they all, "this rede is a right;" and we agreed upon this, and set about carrying it out. So we haled down to the beach the pieces of wood which lay about the bench; and, making a boat, moored it to the strand, after which we stowed therein somewhat of victual and returned to the castle. As soon as evening fell the earth trembled under our feet and in came the blackamoor upon us, snarling like a dog about to bite. He came up to us and feeling us and turning us over one by one, took one of us and did with him as he had done before and ate him, after which he lay down on the bench and snored and snorted like thunder. As soon as we were assured that he slept, we arose and taking two iron spits of those standing there, heated them in the fiercest of the fire, till they were red-hot, like burning coals, when we gripped fast hold of them and going up to the giant, as he lay snoring on the bench, thrust them into his eyes and pressed upon them, all of us, with our united might, so that his eyeballs burst and he became stone blind. Thereupon he cried with a great cry, whereat our hearts trembled, and springing up from the bench, he fell a-groping after us, blind-fold. We fled from him right and left and he saw us not, for his sight was altogether blent; but we were in terrible fear of him and made sure we were dead men despairing of escape. Then he found the door, feeling for it with his hands and went out roaring aloud; and behold, the earth shook under us, for the noise of his roaring, and we quaked for fear. As he quitted the castle we followed him and betook ourselves to the place where we had moored our boat, saying to one another, "If this accursed abide absent till the going down of the sun and come not to the castle, we shall know that he is dead; and if he come back, we will embark in the boat and paddle till we escape, committing our affair to Allah." But, as we spoke, behold, up came the blackamoor with other two as they were Ghuls, fouler and more frightful than he, with eyes like red-hot coals; which when we saw, we hurried into the boat and casting off the moorings paddled away and pushed out to sea. As soon as the ogres caught sight of us, they cried out at us and running down to the sea-shore, fell a-pelting us with rocks, whereof some fell amongst us and others fell into the sea.[30] We paddled with all our might till we were beyond their reach, but the most part of us were slain by the rock-throwing, and the winds and waves sported with us and carried us into the midst of the dashing sea, swollen with billows clashing. We knew not whither we went and my fellows died one after another, till there remained but three, myself and two others, for, as often as one died, we threw him into the sea. We were sore exhausted for stress of hunger, but we took courage and heartened one another and worked for dear life and paddled with main and might, till the winds cast us upon an island, as we were dead men for fatigue and fear and famine. We landed on the island and walked about it for a while, finding that it abounded in trees and streams and birds; and we ate of the fruits and re-joiced in our escape from the black and our deliverance from the perils of the sea; and thus we did till nightfall, when we lay down and fell asleep for excess of fatigue. But we had hardly closed our eyes before we were aroused by a hissing sound, like the sough of wind, and awakening, saw a serpent like a dragon, a seld-seen sight, of monstrous make and belly of enormous bulk which lay in a circle around us. Presently it reared its head and, seizing one of my companions, swallowed him up to his shoulders; then it gulped down the rest of him, and we heard his ribs crack in its belly. Presently it went its way, and we abode in sore amazement and grief for our comrade and mortal fear for ourselves, saying, "By Allah, this is a marvellous thing! Each kind of death that threateneth us is more terrible than the last. We were rejoicing in our escape from the black ogre and our deliverance from the perils of the sea; but now we have fallen into that which is worse. There is no Majesty and there is no Might save in Allah! By the Almighty, we have escaped from the blackamoor and from drowning: but how shall we escape from this abominable and viperish monster?" Then we walked about the island, eating of its fruits and drinking of its streams till dusk, when we climbed up into a high tree and went to sleep there, I being on the topmost bough. As soon as it was dark night, up came the serpent, looking right and left; and, making for the tree whereon we were, climbed up to my comrade and swallowed him down to his shoulders. Then it coiled about the bole[31] with him, whilst I, who could not take my eyes off the sight, heard his bones crack in its belly, and it swallowed him whole, after which it slid down from the tree. When the day broke and the light showed me that the serpent was gone, I came down, as I were a dead man for stress of fear and anguish, and thought to cast myself into the sea and be at rest from the woes of the world; but could not bring myself to this, for verily life is dear. So I took five pieces of wood, broad and long, and bound one crosswise to the soles of my feet and others in like fashion on my right and left sides and over my breast; and the broadest and largest I bound across my head and made them fast with ropes. Then I lay down on the ground on my back, so that I was completely fenced in by the pieces of wood, which enclosed me like a bier.[32] So as soon as it was dark, up came the serpent, as usual, and made towards me, but could not get at me to swallow me for the wood that fenced me in. So it wriggled round me on every side, whilst I looked on, like one dead by reason of my terror; and every now and then it would glide away and come back; but as often as it tried to come at me, it was hindered by the pieces of wood wherewith I had bound myself on every side. It ceased not to beset me thus from sundown till dawn, but when the light of day shone upon the beast it made off, in the utmost fury and extreme disappointment. Then I put out my hand and unbound myself, well-nigh down among the dead men for fear and suffering; and went down to the island-shore, whence a ship afar off in the midst of the waves suddenly struck my sight. So I tore off a great branch of a tree and made signs with it to the crew, shouting out the while; which when the ship's company saw they said to one another, "We must stand in and see what this is; peradventure 'tis a man." So they made for the island and presently heard my cries, whereupon they took me on board and questioned me of my case. I told them all my adventures from first to last, whereat they marvelled mightily and covered my shame[33] with some of their clothes. Moreover, they set before me somewhat of food and I ate my fill and I drank cold sweet water and was mightily refreshed; and Allah Almighty quickened me after I was virtually dead. So I praised the Most Highest and thanked Him for His favours and exceeding mercies, and my heart revived in me after utter despair, till meseemed as if all I had suffered were but a dream I had dreamed. We sailed on with a fair wind the Almighty sent us till we came to an island, called Al-Salahitah,[34] which aboundeth in sandal-wood when the captain cast anchor. And when we had cast anchor, the merchants and the sailors landed with their goods to sell and to buy. Then the captain turned to me and said, "Hark'ee, thou art a stranger and a pauper and tellest us that thou hast undergone frightful hardships; wherefore I have a mind to benefit thee with somewhat that may further thee to thy native land, so thou wilt ever bless me and pray for me." "So be it," answered I; "thou shalt have my prayers." Quoth he, "Know then that there was with us a man, a traveller, whom we lost, and we know not if he be alive or dead, for we had no news of him; so I purpose to commit his bales of goods to thy charge, that thou mayst sell them in this island. A part of the proceeds we will give thee as an equivalent for thy pains and service, and the rest we will keep till we return to Baghdad, where we will enquire for his family and deliver it to them, together with the unsold goods. Say me then, wilt thou undertake the charge and land and sell them as other merchants do?" I replied, "Hearkening and obedience to thee, O my lord; and great is thy kindness to me," and thanked him; whereupon he bade the sailors and porters bear the bales in question ashore and commit them to my charge. The ship's scribe asked him, "O master, what bales are these and what merchant's name shall I write upon them?"; and he answered, "Write on them the name of Sindbad the Seaman, him who was with us in the ship and whom we lost at the Rukh's island, and of whom we have no tidings; for we mean this stranger to sell them; and we will give him a part of the price for his pains and keep the rest till we return to Baghdad where, if we find the owner we will make it over to him, and if not, to his family." And the clerk said, "Thy words are apposite and thy rede is right." Now when I heard the captain give orders for the bales to be inscribed with my name, I said to myself, "By Allah, I am Sindbad the Seaman!" So I armed myself with courage and patience and waited till all the merchants had landed and were gathered together, talking and chaffering about buying and selling; then I went up to the captain and asked him, "O my lord, knowest thou what manner of man was this Sindbad, whose goods thou hast committed to me for sale?"; and he answered, "I know of him naught save that he was a man from Baghdad-city, Sindbad hight the Seaman, who was drowned with many others when we lay anchored at such an island and I have heard nothing of him since then." At this I cried out with a great cry and said, "O captain, whom Allah keep! know that I am that Sindbad the Seaman and that I was not drowned, but when thou castest anchor at the island, I landed with the rest of the merchants and crew; and I sat down in a pleasant place by myself and ate somewhat of food I had with me and enjoyed myself till I became drowsy and was drowned in sleep; and when I awoke, I found no ship and none near me. These goods are my goods and these bales are my bales; and all the merchants who fetch jewels from the Valley of Diamonds saw me there and will bear me witness that I am the very Sindbad the Seaman; for I related to them everything that had befallen me and told them how you forgot me and left me sleeping on the island, and that betided me which betided me." When the passengers and crew heard my words, they gathered about me and some of them believed me and others disbelieved; but presently, behold, one of the merchants, hearing me mention the Valley of Diamonds, came up to me and said to them, "Hear what I say, good people! When I related to you the most wonderful thing in my travels, and I told you that, at the time we cast down our slaughtered animals into the Valley of Serpents (I casting with the rest as was my wont), there came up a man hanging to mine, ye believed me not and gave me the lie." "Yes," quoth they, "thou didst tell us some such tale, but we had no call to credit thee." He resumed, "Now this is the very man, by token that he gave me diamonds of great value, and high price whose like are not to be found, requiting me more than would have come up sticking to my quarter of meat; and I companied with him to Bassorah-city, where he took leave of us and went on to his native stead, whilst we returned to our own land. This is he; and he told us his name, Sindbad the Seaman, and how the ship left him on the desert island. And know ye that Allah hath sent him hither, so might the truth of my story be made manifest to you. Moreover, these are his goods for, when he first foregathered with us, he told us of them; and the truth of his words is patent." Hearing the merchant's speech the captain came up to me and considered me straitly awhile, after which he said, "What was the mark on thy bales?" "Thus and thus," answered I, and reminded him of somewhat that had passed between him and me, when I shipped with him from Bassorah. Thereupon he was convinced that I was indeed Sindbad the Seaman and took me round the neck and gave me joy of my safety, saying, "By Allah, O my lord, thy case is indeed wondrous and thy tale marvellous; but lauded be Allah who hath brought thee and me together again, and who hath restored to thee thy goods and gear!" Then I disposed of my merchandise to the best of my skill, and profited largely on them whereat I rejoiced with exceeding joy and congratulated myself on my safety and the recovery of

my goods. We ceased not to buy and sell at the several islands till we came to the land of Hind, where we bought
cloves and ginger and all manner spices; and thence we
fared on to the land of Sind, where also we bought and
sold. In these Indian seas, I saw wonders without number
or count, amongst others a fish like a cow which bringeth
forth its young and suckleth them like human beings; and
of its skin bucklers are made.[35] There were eke fishes like
asses and camels[36] and tortoises twenty cubits wide.[37] And
I saw also a bird that cometh out of a sea-shell[38] and layeth
eggs and hatcheth her chicks on the surface of the water,
never coming up from the sea to the land. Then we set sail
again with a fair wind and the blessing of Almighty Allah;
and, after a prosperous voyage, arrived safe and sound at
Bassorah. Here I abode a few days and presently returned
to Baghdad where I went at once to my quarter and my
house and saluted my family and familiars and friends. I
had gained on this voyage what was beyond count and
reckoning, so I gave alms and largesse and clad the widow
and the orphan, by way of thanksgiving for my happy return, and fell to feasting and making merry with my companions and intimates and forgot, while eating well and
drinking well and dressing well, everything that had befallen me and all the perils and hardships I had suffered.
These, then, are the most admirable things I sighted on my
third voyage, and to-morrow, an it be the will of Allah, you
shall come to me and I will relate the adventures of my
fourth voyage, which is still more wonderful than those
you have already heard. (Saith he who telleth the tale),
Then Sindbad the Seaman bade give Sindbad the Landsman an hundred golden dinars as of wont and called for
food. So they spread the tables and the company ate the
night-meal and went their ways, marvelling at the tale they
had heard. The Porter after taking his gold passed the
night in his own house, also wondering at what his namesake the Seaman had told him, and as soon as day broke
and the morning showed with its sheen and shone, he rose
and praying the dawn-prayer betook himself to Sindbad

the Seaman, who returned his salute and received him with an open breast and cheerful favour and made him sit with him till the rest of the company arrived, when he caused set on food and they ate and drank and made merry. Then Sindbad the Seaman bespake them and related to them the narrative of

THE FOURTH VOYAGE OF SINDBAD THE SEAMAN.

Know, O my brethren that after my return from my third voyage and foregathering with my friends, and forgetting all my perils and hardships in the enjoyment of ease and comfort and repose, I was visited one day by a company of merchants who sat down with me and talked of foreign travel and traffic, till the old bad man within me yearned to go with them and enjoy the sight of strange countries, and I longed for the society of the various races of mankind and for traffic and profit. So I resolved to travel with them and buying the necessaries for a long voyage, and great store of costly goods, more than ever before, transported them from Baghdad to Bassorah where I took ship with the merchants in question, who were of the chief of the town. We set out, trusting in the blessing of Almighty Allah; and with a favouring breeze and the best conditions we sailed from island to island and sea to sea, till one day, there arose against us a contrary wind and the captain cast out his anchors and brought the ship to a standstill, fearing lest she should founder in mid-ocean. Then we all fell to prayer and humbling ourselves before the Most High; but, as we were thus engaged there smote us a furious squall which tore the sails to rags and tatters: the anchor-cable parted and, the ship foundering, we were cast into the sea, goods and all. I kept myself afloat by swimming half the day, till, when I had given myself up for lost, the Almighty threw in my way one of the planks of the ship, whereon I and some others of the merchants scrambled, and, mounting it as we would a horse, paddled with our feet in the sea. We abode thus a day and a night, the wind and waves helping us on, and on the second day shortly before the mid-time between sunrise and noon[39] the breeze freshened and the sea wrought and the rising waves cast us upon an island, well-nigh dead bodies for weariness and want of sleep, cold and hunger and fear and thirst. We walked about the shore and found abundance of herbs, whereof we ate enough to keep breath in body and to stay our failing spirits, then lay down and slept till morning hard by the sea. And when morning came with its sheen and shone, we arose and walked about the island to the right and left, till we came in sight of an inhabited house afar off. So we made towards it, and ceased not walking till we reached the door thereof when lo! a number of naked men issued from it and without saluting us or a word said, laid hold of us masterfully and carried us to their king, who signed us to sit. So we sat down and they set food before us such as we knew not[40] and whose like we had never seen in all our lives. My companions ate of it, for stress of hunger, but my stomach revolted from it and I would not eat; and my refraining from it was, by Allah's favour, the cause of my being alive till now: for no sooner had my comrades tasted of it than their reason fled and their condition changed and they began to devour it like madmen possessed of an evil spirit. Then the savages gave them to drink of cocoa-nut oil and anointed them therewith; and straightway after drinking thereof, their eyes turned into their heads and they fell to eating greedily, against their wont. When I saw this, I was confounded and concerned for them, nor was I less anxious about myself, for fear of the naked folk. So I watched them narrowly, and it was not long before I discovered them to be a tribe of Magian cannibals whose King was a Ghul.[41] All who came to their country or whoso they caught in their valleys or on their roads they brought to this King and fed them upon that food and anointed them with that oil, whereupon their stomachs dilated that they might eat largely, whilst their reason fled and they lost the power of thought and became idiots. Then they stuffed them with cocoa-nut oil and the aforesaid food, till they became fat and gross, when they slaughtered them by cutting their throats and roasted them for the King's eating; but, as for the savages themselves, they ate human flesh raw.[42] When I saw this, I was sore dismayed for myself and my comrades, who were now become so stupefied that they knew not what was done with them and the naked folk committed them to one who used every day to lead them out and pasture them on the island like cattle. And they wandered amongst the trees and rested at will, thus waxing very fat. As for me, I wasted away and became sickly for fear and hunger and my flesh shrivelled on my bones; which when the savages saw, they left me alone and took no thought of me and so far forgot me that one day I gave them the slip and walking out of their place made for the beach which was distant and there espied a very old man seated on a high place, girt by the waters. I looked at him and knew him for the herdsman, who had charge of pasturing my fellows, and with him were many others in like case. As soon as he saw me, he knew me to be in possession of my reason and not afflicted like the rest whom he was pasturing; so signed to me from afar, as who should say, "Turn back and take the right-hand road, for that will lead thee into the King's highway." So I turned back, as he bade me, and followed the right-hand road, now running for fear and then walking leisurely to rest me, till I was out of the old man's sight. By this time, the sun had gone down and the darkness set in; so I sat down to rest and would have slept, but sleep came not to me that night, for stress of fear and famine and fatigue. When the night was half spent, I rose and walked on, till the day broke in all its beauty and the sun rose over the heads of the lofty hills and athwart the low gravelly plains. Now I was weary and hungry and thirsty; so I ate my fill of herbs and grasses that grew in the island and kept life in body and stayed my stomach, after which I set out again and fared on all that day and the next night, staying my greed with roots and herbs; nor did I cease walking for seven days and their nights, till the morn of the eighth day, when I caught sight of a faint object in the distance. So I made towards it, though my heart quaked for all I had suffered first and last, and behold it was a company of men gathering pepper-grains.[43] As soon as they saw me, they hastened up to me and surrounding me on all sides, said to me, "Who art thou and whence come?" I replied, "Know, O folk, that I am a poor stranger," and acquainted them with my case and all the hardships and perils I had suffered, whereat they marvelled and gave me joy of my safety, saying, "By Allah, this is wonderful! But how didst thou escape from these blacks who swarm in the island and devour all who fall in with them; nor is any safe from them, nor can any get out of their clutches?" And after I had told them the fate of my companions, they made me sit by them, till they got quit of their work; and fetched me somewhat of good food, which I ate, for I was hungry, and rested awhile, after which they took ship with me and carrying me to their island-home brought me before their King, who returned my salute and received me honourably and questioned me of my case. I told him all that had befallen me, from the day of my leaving Baghdad-city, whereupon he wondered with great wonder at my adventures, he and his courtiers, and bade me sit by him; then he called for food and I ate with him what sufficed me and washed my hands and returned thanks to Almighty Allah for all His favours praising Him and glorifying Him. Then I left the King and walked for solace about the city, which I found wealthy and populous, abounding in market-streets well stocked with food and merchandise and full of buyers and sellers. So I rejoiced at having reached so pleasant a place and took my ease there after my fatigues; and I made friends with the townsfolk, nor was it long before I became more in honour and favour with them and their King than any of the chief men of the realm. Now I saw that all the citizens, great and small, rode fine horses, high-priced and thoroughbred, without saddles or housings, whereat I wondered and said to the King, "Wherefore, O my lord, dost thou not ride with a saddle?

Therein is ease for the rider and increase of power." "What is a saddle?" asked he: "I never saw nor used such a thing in all my life;" and I answered, "With thy permission I will make thee a saddle, that thou mayest ride on it and see the comfort thereof." And quoth he, "Do so." So quoth I to him, "Furnish me with some wood," which being brought, I sought me a clever carpenter and sitting by him showed him how to make the saddle-tree, portraying for him the fashion thereof in ink on the wood. Then I took wool and teased it and made felt of it, and, covering the saddle-tree with leather, stuffed it and polished it and attached the girth and stirrup leathers; after which I fetched a black-smith and described to him the fashion of the stirrups and bridle-bit. So he forged a fine pair of stirrups and a bit, and filed them smooth and tinned them.[44] Moreover, I made fast to them fringes of silk and fitted bridle-leathers to the bit. Then I fetched one of the best of the royal horses and saddling and bridling him, hung the stirrups to the saddle and led him to the King. The thing took his fancy and he thanked me; then he mounted and rejoiced greatly in the saddle and rewarded me handsomely for my work. When the King's Wazir saw the saddle, he asked of me one like it and I made it for him. Furthermore, all the grandees and officers of state came for saddles to me; so I fell to making saddles (having taught the craft to the carpenter and black-smith), and selling them to all who sought, till I amassed great wealth and became in high honour and great favour with the King and his household and grandees. I abode thus till, one day, as I was sitting with the King in all respect and contentment, he said to me, "Know thou, O such an one, thou art become one of us, dear as a brother, and we hold thee in such regard and affection that we cannot part with thee nor suffer thee to leave our city; wherefore I desire of thee obedience in a certain matter, and I will not have thee gainsay me." Answered I, "O King, what is it thou desirest of me? Far be it from me to gainsay thee in aught, for I am indebted to thee for many favours and bounties and much kindness, and (praised be Allah!) I am become one of thy servants." Quoth he, "I have a mind to marry thee to a fair, clever and agreeable wife who is wealthy as she is beautiful; so thou mayst be naturalised and domiciled with us: I will lodge thee with me in my palace; wherefore oppose me not neither cross me in this." When I heard these words I was ashamed and held my peace nor could make him any answer,[45] by reason of my much bashfulness before him. Asked he, "Why dost thou not reply to me, O my son?"; and I answered, saying, "O my master, it is thine to command, O king of the age!" So he summoned the Kazi and the witnesses and married me straightway to a lady of a noble tree and high pedigree; wealthy in moneys and means; the flower of an ancient race; of surpassing beauty and grace, and the owner of farms and estates and many a dwelling-place. Now after the King my master had married me to this choice wife, he also gave me a great and goodly house standing alone, together with slaves and officers, and assigned me pay and allowances. So I became in all ease and contentment and delight and forgot everything which had befallen me of weariness and trouble and hardship; for I loved my wife with fondest love and she loved me no less, and we were as one and abode in the utmost comfort of life and in its happiness. And I said in myself, "When I return to my native land, I will carry her with me." But whatso is predestined to a man, that needs must be, and none knoweth what shall befal him. We lived thus a great while, till Almighty Allah bereft one of my neighbours of his wife. Now he was a gossip of mine; so hearing the cry of the keeners I went in to condole him on his loss and found him in very ill plight, full of trouble and weary of soul and mind. I condoled with him and comforted him, saying, "Mourn not for thy wife who hath now found the mercy of Allah; the Lord will surely give thee a better in her stead and thy name shall be great and thy life shall be long in the land, Inshallah!"[46] But he wept bitter tears and replied, "O my friend, how can I marry another wife and how shall Allah replace her to me with a better than she, whenas I have but one day left to live?" "O my brother," said I, "return to thy senses and announce not the glad tidings of thine own death, for thou art well, sound and in good case." "By thy life, O my friend," rejoined he, "to-morrow thou wilt lose me and wilt never see me again till the Day of Resurrection." I asked, "How so?" and he answered, "This very day they bury my wife, and they bury me with her in one tomb; for it is the custom with us, if the wife die first, to bury the husband alive with her and in like manner the wife, if the husband die first; so that neither may enjoy life after losing his or her mate." "By Allah," cried I, "this is a most vile, lewd custom and not to be endured of any!" Meanwhile, behold, the most part of the townsfolk came in and fell to condoling with my gossip for his wife and for himself. Presently they laid the dead woman out, as was their wont; and, setting her on a bier, carried her and her husband without the city, till they came to a place in the side of a mountain at the end of the island by the sea; and here they raised a great rock and discovered the mouth of a stone-rivetted pit or well,[47] leading down into a vast underground cavern that ran beneath the mountain. Into this pit they threw the corpse, then tying a rope of palm-fibres under the husband's armpits, they let him down into the cavern, and with him a great pitcher of fresh water and seven scones by way of viaticum.[48] When he came to the bottom, he loosed himself from the rope and they drew it up; and, stopping the mouth of the pit with the great stone, they returned to the city, leaving my friend in the cavern with his dead wife. When I saw this, I said to myself, "By Allah, this fashion of death is more grievous than the first!" And I went in to the King and said to him, "O my lord, why do ye bury the quick with the dead?" Quoth he, "It hath been the custom, thou must know, of our forebears and our olden Kings from time immemorial, if the husband die first, to bury his wife with him, and the like with the wife, so we may not sever them, alive or dead." I asked, "O King of the age, if the wife of a foreigner like myself die among you, deal ye with him as with yonder man?"; and he answered, "Assuredly, we do with him even as thou hast seen." When I heard this, my gall-bladder was like to burst, for the violence of my dismay and concern for myself: my wit became dazed; I felt as if in a vile dungeon; and hated their society; for I went about in fear lest my wife should die before me and they bury me alive with her. However, after a while, I comforted myself, saying, "Haply I shall predecease her, or shall have returned to my own land before she die, for none knoweth which shall go first and which shall go last." Then I applied myself to diverting my mind from this thought with various occupations; but it was not long before my wife sickened and complained and took to her pillow and fared after a few days to the mercy of Allah; and the King and the rest of the folk came, as was their wont, to condole with me and her family and to console us for her loss and not less to condole with me for myself. Then the women washed her and arraying her in her richest raiment and golden ornaments, necklaces and jewellery, laid her on the bier and bore her to the mountain aforesaid, where they lifted the cover of the pit and cast her in; after which all my intimates and acquaintances and my wife's kith and kin came round me, to farewell me in my lifetime and console me for my own death, whilst I cried out among them, saying, "Almighty Allah never made it lawful to bury the quick with the dead! I am a stranger, not one of your kind; and I cannot abear your custom, and had I known it I never would have wedded among you!" They heard me not and paid no heed to my words, but laying hold of me, bound me by force and let me down into the cavern, with a large gugglet of sweet water and seven cakes of bread, according to their custom. When I came to the bottom, they called out to me to cast myself loose from the cords, but I refused to do so; so they threw them down on me and, closing the mouth of the pit with the stones aforesaid, went their ways. I looked about me and found myself in a vast cave full of dead bodies, that exhaled a fulsome and loathsome smell and the air was heavy with the groans of the dying. Thereupon I fell to blaming myself for what I had done, saying,

"By Allah, I deserve all that hath befallen me and all that shall befall me! What curse was upon me to take a wife in this city? There is no Majesty and there is no Might save in Allah, the Glorious, the Great! As often as I say, I have escaped from one calamity, I fall into a worse. By Allah, this is an abominable death to die! Would Heaven I had died a decent death and been washed and shrouded like a man and a Moslem. Would I had been drowned at sea or perished in the mountains! It were better than to die this miserable death!" And on such wise I kept blaming my own folly and greed of gain in that black hole, knowing not night from day; and I ceased not to ban the Foul Fiend and to bless the Almighty Friend. Then I threw myself down on the bones of the dead and lay there, imploring Allah's help and in the violence of my despair, invoking death which came not to me, till the fire of hunger burned my stomach and thirst set my throat aflame when I sat up and feeling for the bread, ate a morsel and upon it swallowed a mouthful of water. After this, the worst night I ever knew, I arose, and exploring the cavern, found that it extended a long way with hollows in its sides; and its floor was strewn with dead bodies and rotten bones, that had lain there from olden time. So I made myself a place in a cavity of the cavern, afar from the corpses lately thrown down and there slept. I abode thus a long while, till my provision was like to give out; and yet I ate not save once every day or second day; nor did I drink more than an occasional draught, for fear my victual should fail me before my death; and I said to myself, "Eat little and drink little; belike the Lord shall vouchsafe deliverance to thee!" One day, as I sat thus, pondering my case and bethinking me how I should do, when my bread and water should be exhausted, behold, the stone that covered the opening was suddenly rolled away and the light streamed down upon me; Quoth I, "I wonder what is the matter: haply they have brought another corpse." Then I espied folk standing about the mouth of the pit, who presently let down a dead man and a live woman, weeping and bemoaning herself, and with her an ampler supply of bread and water than usual.[49] I saw her and she was a beautiful woman; but she saw me not; and they closed up the opening and went away. Then I took the leg-bone of a dead man and, going up to the woman, smote her on the crown of the head; and she cried one cry and fell down in a swoon. I smote her a second and a third time, till she was dead, when I laid hands on her bread and water and found on her great plenty of ornaments and rich apparel, necklaces, jewels and gold trinkets;[50] for it was their custom to bury women in all their finery. I carried the vivers to my sleeping place in the cavern-side and ate and drank of them sparingly, no more than sufficed to keep the life in me, lest the provaunt come speedily to an end and I perish of hunger and thirst. Yet did I never wholly lose hope in Almighty Allah. I abode thus a great while, killing all the live folk they let down into the cavern and taking their provisions of meat and drink; till one day, as I slept, I was awakened by something scratching and burrowing among the bodies in a corner of the cave and said, "What can this be?" fearing wolves or hyænas. So I sprang up and seizing the leg-bone aforesaid, made for the noise. As soon as the thing was ware of me, it fled from me into the inward of the cavern, and lo! it was a wild beast. However, I followed it to the further end, till I saw afar off a point of light not bigger than a star, now appearing and then disappearing. So I made for it, and as I drew near, it grew larger and brighter, till I was certified that it was a crevice in the rock, leading to the open country; and I said to myself, "There must be some reason for this opening: either it is the mouth of a second pit, such as they by which they let me down, or else it is a natural fissure in the stonery." So I bethought me awhile and nearing the light, found that it came from a breach in the back side of the mountain, which the wild beasts had enlarged by burrowing, that they might enter and devour the dead and freely go to and fro. When I saw this, my spirits revived and hope came back to me and I made sure of life, after having died a death. So I went on, as in a dream, and making shift to scramble through the breach found myself on the slope of a high mountain, overlooking the salt sea and cutting off all access thereto from the island, so that none could come at that part of the beach from the city.[51] I praised my Lord and thanked Him, rejoicing greatly and heartening myself with the prospect of deliverance; then I returned through the crack to the cavern and brought out all the food and water I had saved up and donned some of the dead folk's clothes over my own; after which I gathered together all the collars and necklaces of pearls and jewels and trinkets of gold and silver set with precious stones and other ornaments and valuables I could find upon the corpses; and, making them into bundles with the grave clothes and raiment of the dead, carried them out to the back of the mountain facing the sea-shore, where I established myself, purposing to wait there till it should please Almighty Allah to send me relief by means of some passing ship. I visited the cavern daily and as often as I found folk buried alive there, I killed them all indifferently, men and women, and took their victual and valuables and transported them to my seat on the sea-shore. Thus I abode a long while till one day I caught sight of a ship passing in the midst of the clashing sea, swollen with dashing billows. So I took a piece of a white shroud I had with me and, tying it to a staff, ran along the sea-shore, making signals therewith and calling to the people in the ship, till they espied me and hearing my shouts, sent a boat to fetch me off. When it drew near, the crew called out to me, saying, "Who art thou and how camest thou to be on this mountain, whereon never saw we any in our born days?" I answered, "I am a gentleman[52] and a merchant, who hath been wrecked and saved myself on one of the planks of the ship, with some of my goods; and by the blessing of the Almighty and the decrees of Destiny and my own strength and skill, after much toil and moil I have landed with my gear in this place where I awaited some passing ship to take me off." So they took me in their boat together with the bundles I had made of the jewels and valuables from the cavern, tied up in clothes and shrouds, and rowed back with me to the ship, where the captain said to me, "How camest thou, O man, to yonder place on yonder mountain behind which lieth a great city? All my life I have sailed these seas and passed to and fro hard by these heights; yet never saw I here any living thing save wild beasts and birds." I repeated to him the story I had told the sailors,[53] but acquainted him with nothing of that which had befallen me in the city and the cavern, lest there should be any of the islandry in the ship. Then I took out some of the best pearls I had with me and offered them to the captain, saying, "O my lord, thou hast been the means of saving me off this mountain. I have no ready money; but take this from me in requital of thy kindness and good offices." But he refused to accept it of me, saying, "When we find a shipwrecked man on the seashore or on an island, we take him up and give him meat and drink, and if he be naked we clothe him; nor take we aught from him; nay, when we reach a port of safety, we set him ashore with a present of our own money and entreat him kindly and charitably, for the love of Allah the Most High." So I prayed that his life be long in the land and rejoiced in my escape, trusting to be delivered from my stress and to forget my past mishaps; for every time I remembered being let down into the cave with my dead wife I shuddered in horror. Then we pursued our voyage and sailed from island to island and sea to sea, till we arrived at the Island of the Bell, which containeth a city two days' journey in extent whence after a six days' run we reached the Island Kala, hard by the land of Hind.[54] This place is governed by a potent and puissant King and it produceth excellent camphor and an abundance of the Indian rattan: here also is a lead mine. At last by the decree of Allah, we arrived in safety at Bassorah-town where I tarried a few days, then went on to Baghdad-city, and, finding my quarter, entered my house with lively pleasure. There I foregathered with my family and friends, who rejoiced in my happy return and gave me joy of my safety. I laid up in my storehouses all the goods I had brought with me, and gave

alms and largesse to Fakirs and beggars and clothed the
widow and the orphan. Then I gave myself up to pleasure
and enjoyment, returning to my old merry mode of life.
Such, then, be the most marvellous adventures of my
fourth voyage, but to-morrow if you will kindly come to
me, I will tell you that which befel me in my fifth voyage,
which was yet rarer and more marvellous than those which
forewent it. And thou, O my brother Sindbad the Landsman, shalt sup with me as thou art wont. (Saith he who telleth the tale), When Sindbad the Seaman had made an end
of his story, he called for supper; so they spread the table
and the guests ate the evening meal; after which he gave
the Porter an hundred dinars as usual, and he and the rest
of the company went their ways, glad at heart and marvelling at the tales they had heard, for that each story was
more extraordinary than that which forewent it. The
porter Sindbad passed the night in his own house, in all joy
and cheer and wonderment; and, as soon as morning came
with its sheen and shone, he prayed the dawn-prayer and
repaired to the house of Sindbad the Seaman, who welcomed him and bade him sit with him till the rest of the
company arrived, when they ate and drank and made
merry and the talk went round amongst them. Presently,
their host began the narrative of

THE FIFTH VOYAGE OF SINDBAD THE SEAMAN.

Know, O my brothers, that when I had been awhile on
shore after my fourth voyage; and when, in my comfort and
pleasures and merry-makings and in my rejoicing over my
large gains and profits, I had forgotten all I had endured of
perils and sufferings, the carnal man was again seized with
the longing to travel and to see foreign countries and islands.[55] Accordingly I bought costly merchandise suited to
my purpose and, making it up into bales, repaired to Bassorah, where I walked about the river-quay till I found a
fine tall ship, newly builded with gear unused and fitted

ready for sea. She pleased me; so I bought her and, embarking my goods in her, hired a master and crew, over whom I set certain of my slaves and servants as inspectors. A number of merchants also brought their outfits and paid me freight and passage-money; then, after reciting the Fatihah we set sail over Allah's pool in all joy and cheer, promising ourselves a prosperous voyage and much profit. We sailed from city to city and from island to island and from sea to sea viewing the cities and countries by which we passed, and selling and buying in not a few till one day we came to a great uninhabited island, deserted and desolate, whereon was a white dome of biggest bulk half buried in the sands. The merchants landed to examine this dome, leaving me in the ship; and when they drew near, behold, it was a huge Rukh's egg. They fell a-beating it with stones, knowing not what it was, and presently broke it open, whereupon much water ran out of it and the young Rukh appeared within. So they pulled it forth of the shell and cut its throat and took of it great store of meat. Now I was in the ship and knew not what they did; but presently one of the passengers came up to me and said, "O my lord, come and look at the egg that we thought to be a dome." So I looked and seeing the merchants beating it with stones, called out to them, "Stop, stop! do not meddle with that egg, or the bird Rukh will come out and break our ship and destroy us."[56] But they paid no heed to me and gave not over smiting upon the egg, when behold, the day grew dark and dun and the sun was hidden from us, as if some great cloud had passed over the firmament.[57] So we raised our eyes and saw that what we took for a cloud was the Rukh poised between us and the sun, and it was his wings that darkened the day. When he came and saw his egg broken, he cried a loud cry, whereupon his mate came flying up and they both began circling about the ship crying out at us with voices louder than thunder. I called to the Rais and crew, "Put out to sea and seek safety in flight, before we be all destroyed." So the merchants came on board and we cast off and made haste from the island to gain the open sea. When the Rukhs saw this, they flew off and we crowded all sail on the ship, thinking to get out of their country; but presently the two re-appeared and flew after us and stood over us, each carrying in its claws a huge boulder which it had brought from the mountains. As soon as the he-Rukh came up with us, he let fall upon us the rock he held in his pounces; but the master put about ship, so that the rock missed her by some small matter and plunged into the waves with such violence, that the ship pitched high and then sank into the trough of the sea and the bottom of the ocean appeared to us. Then the she-Rukh let fall her rock, which was bigger than that of her mate, and as Destiny had decreed, it fell on the poop of the ship and crushed it, the rudder flying into twenty pieces; whereupon the vessel foundered and all and everything on board were cast into the main.[58] As for me I struggled for sweet life, till Almighty Allah threw in my way one of the planks of the ship, to which I clung and bestriding it, fell a-paddling with my feet. Now the ship had gone down hard by an island in the midst of the main and the winds and waves bore me on till, by permission of the Most High, they cast me up on the shore of the island, at the last gasp for toil and distress and half dead with hunger and thirst. So I landed more like a corpse than a live man and throwing myself down on the beach, lay there awhile, till I began to revive and recover spirits, when I walked about the island and found it as it were one of the garths and gardens of Paradise. Its trees, in abundance dight, bore ripe-yellow fruit for freight; its streams ran clear and bright; its flowers were fair to scent and to sight and its birds warbled with delight the praises of Him to whom belong permanence and all-might. So I ate my fill of the fruits and slaked my thirst with the water of the streams till I could no more and I returned thanks to the Most High and glorified Him; after which I sat till nightfall, hearing no voice and seeing none inhabitant. Then I lay down, well-nigh dead for travail and trouble and terror, and slept without surcease till morning, when I arose and walked about under the trees, till I came to the channel of a draw-well fed by a spring of running water, by which well sat an old man of venerable aspect, girt about with a waist-cloth[59] made of the fibre of palm-fronds.[60] Quoth I to myself, "Haply this Shaykh is of those who were wrecked in the ship and hath made his way to this island." So I drew near to him and saluted him, and he returned my salam by signs, but spoke not; and I said to him, "O nuncle mine, what causeth thee to sit here?" He shook his head and moaned and signed to me with his hand as who should say, "Take me on thy shoulders and carry me to the other side of the well-channel." And quoth I in my mind, "I will deal kindly with him and do what he desireth; it may be I shall win me a reward in Heaven for he may be a paralytic." So I took him on my back and carrying him to the place whereat he pointed, said to him, "Dismount at thy leisure." But he would not get off my back and wound his legs about my neck. I looked at them and seeing that they were like a buffalo's hide for blackness and roughness,[61] was affrighted and would have cast him off; but he clung to me and gripped my neck with his legs, till I was well-nigh choked, the world grew black in my sight and I fell senseless to the ground like one dead. But he still kept his seat and raising his legs drummed with his heels and beat harder than palm-rods my back and shoulders, till he forced me to rise for excess of pain. Then he signed to me with his hand to carry him hither and thither among the trees which bore the best fruits; and if ever I refused to do his bidding or loitered or took my leisure he beat me with his feet more grievously than if I had been beaten with whips. He ceased not to signal with his hand wherever he was minded to go; so I carried him about the island, like a captive slave, and he dismounted not night or day; and whenas he wished to sleep he wound his legs about my neck and leaned back and slept awhile, then arose and beat me; whereupon I sprang up in haste, unable to gainsay him because of the pain he inflicted on me. And indeed I blamed myself and sore repented me of having taken compassion on him and continued in this condition, suffering fatigue not to be described, till I said to myself, "I wrought him a weal and he requited me with my ill; by Allah, never more will I do any man a service so long as I live!" And again and again I besought the Most High that I might die, for stress of weariness and misery; and thus I abode a long while till, one day, I came with him to a place wherein was abundance of gourds, many of them dry. So I took a great dry gourd and, cutting open the head, scooped out the inside and cleaned it; after which I gathered grapes from a vine which grew hard by and squeezed them into the gourd, till it was full of the juice. Then I stopped up the mouth and set it in the sun, where I left it for some days, until it became strong wine; and every day I used to drink of it, to comfort and sustain me under my fatigues with that froward and obstinate fiend; and as often as I drank myself drunk, I forgot my troubles and took new heart. One day he saw me drinking and signed to me with his hand, as who should say, "What is that?" Quoth I, "It is an excellent cordial, which cheereth the heart and reviveth the spirits." Then, being heated with wine, I ran and danced with him among the trees, clapping my hands and singing and making merry; and I staggered under him by design. When he saw this, he signed to me to give him the gourd that he might drink, and I feared him and gave it him. So he took it and, draining it to the dregs, cast it on the ground, whereupon he grew frolicsome and began to clap hands and jig to and fro on my shoulders and he made water upon me so copiously that all my dress was drenched. But presently the fumes of the wine rising to his head, he became helplessly drunk and his side-muscles and limbs relaxed and he swayed to and fro on my back. When I saw that he had lost his senses for drunkenness, I put my hand to his legs and, loosing them from my neck, stooped down well-nigh to the ground and threw him at full length. Then I took up a great stone from among the trees and coming up to him smote him therewith on the head with all my might and crushed in his skull as he lay dead drunk. Thereupon his flesh and fat and blood being in a pulp, he died and went to his deserts, The Fire, no mercy of Allah be upon him! I then returned, with a heart at ease, to my former station on the sea-shore and abode in that island many days, eating of its fruits and drinking of its waters and keeping a look-out for passing ships; till one day, as I sat on the beach, recalling all that had befallen me and saying, "I wonder if Allah will save me alive and restore me to my home and family and friends!" behold, a ship was making for the island through the dashing sea and clashing waves. Presently, it cast anchor and the passengers landed; so I made for them, and when they saw me all hastened up to me and gathering round me questioned me of my case and how I came thither. I told them all that had betided me, whereat they marvelled with exceeding marvel and said, "He who rode on thy shoulder is called the 'Shaykh al-Bahr' or Old Man of the Sea,[62] and none ever felt his legs on neck and came off alive but thou; and those who die under him he eateth: so praised be Allah for thy safety!" Then they set somewhat of food before me, whereof I ate my fill, and gave me somewhat of clothes wherewith I clad myself anew and covered my nakedness; after which they took me up into the ship, and we sailed days and nights, till fate brought us to a place called the City of Apes, builded with lofty houses, all of which gave upon the sea and it had a single gate studded and strengthened with iron nails. Now every night, as soon as it is dusk the dwellers in this city use to come forth of the gates and, putting out to sea in boats and ships, pass the night upon the waters in their fear lest the apes should come down on them from the mountains. Hearing this I was sore troubled remembering what I had before suffered from the ape-kind. Presently I landed to solace myself in the city, but meanwhile the ship set sail without me and I repented of having gone ashore, and calling to mind my companions and what had befallen me with the apes, first and after, sat down and fell a-weeping and lamenting. Presently one of the townsfolk accosted me and said to me, "O my lord, meseemeth thou art a stranger to these parts?" "Yes," answered I, "I am indeed a stranger and a poor one, who came hither in a ship which cast anchor here, and I landed to visit the town; but when I would have gone on board again, I found they had sailed without me." Quoth he, "Come and embark with us, for if thou lie the night in the city, the apes will destroy thee." "Hearkening and obedience," replied I, and rising, straightway embarked with him in one of the boats, whereupon they pushed off from shore and anchoring a mile or so from the land, there passed the night. At daybreak, they rowed back to the city and landing, went each about his business. Thus they did every night, for if any tarried in the town by night the apes came down on him and slew him. As soon as it was day, the apes left the place and ate of the fruits of the gardens, then went back to the mountains and slept there till nightfall, when they again came down upon the city.[63] Now this place was in the farthest part of the country of the blacks, and one of the strangest things that befel me during my sojourn in the city was on this wise. One of the company with whom I passed the night in the boat asked me, "O my lord, thou art apparently a stranger in these parts; hast thou any craft whereat thou canst work?"; and I answered, "By Allah, O my brother, I have no trade nor know I any handicraft, for I was a merchant and a man of money and substance and had a ship of my own, laden with great store of goods and merchandise; but it foundered at sea and all were drowned excepting me who saved myself on a piece of plank which Allah vouchsafed to me of His favour." Upon this he brought me a cotton bag and giving it to me, said, "Take this bag and fill it with pebbles from the beach and go forth with a company of the townsfolk to whom I will give a charge respecting thee. Do as they do and belike thou shalt gain what may further thy return voyage to thy native land." Then he carried me to the beach, where I filled my bag with pebbles large and small, and presently we saw a company of folk issue from the town, each bearing a bag like mine, filled with pebbles. To these he committed me, commending me to their care, and saying, "This man is a stranger, so take him with you and teach him how to gather, that he may get his daily bread, and you will earn your reward and recompense in Heaven." "On our head and eyes be it!" answered they and bidding me welcome, fared on with me till we came to a spacious Wady, full of lofty trees with trunks so smooth that none might climb them. Now sleeping under these trees were many apes, which when they saw us rose and fled from us and swarmed up among the branches; whereupon my companions began to pelt them with what they had in their bags, and the apes fell to plucking of the fruit of the trees and casting them at the folk. I looked at the fruits they cast at us and found them to be Indian or cocoa nuts;[64] so I chose out a great tree, full of apes, and going up to it, began to pelt them with stones, and they in return pelted me with nuts, which I collected, as did the rest; so that even before I had made an end of my bagful of pebbles, I had gotten great plenty of nuts; and as soon as my companions had in like manner gotten as many nuts as they could carry, we returned to the city, where we arrived at the fag-end of day. Then I went in to the kindly man who had brought me in company with the nut-gatherers and gave him all I had gotten, thanking him for his kindness; but he would not accept them, saying, "Sell them and make profit by the price;" and presently he added (giving me the key of a closet in his house) "Store thy nuts in this safe place and go thou forth every morning and gather them as thou hast done today, and choose out the worst for sale and supplying thyself; but lay up the rest here, so haply thou mayst collect enough to serve thee for thy return home." "Allah requite thee!" answered I and did as he advised me, going out daily with the cocoa-nut gatherers, who commended me to one another and showed me the best-stocked trees.[65] Thus did I for some time, till I had laid up great store of excellent nuts, besides a large sum of money, the price of those I had sold. I became thus at my ease and bought all I saw and had a mind to, and passed my time pleasantly greatly enjoying my stay in the city, till, as I stood on the beach, one day, a great ship steering through the heart of the sea presently cast anchor by the shore and landed a company of merchants, who proceeded to sell and buy and barter their goods for cocoa-nuts and other commodities. Then I went to my friend and told him of the coming of the ship and how I had a mind to return to my own country; and he said, " 'Tis for thee to decide." So I thanked him for his bounties and took leave of him; then, going to the captain of the ship, I agreed with him for my passage and embarked my cocoa-nuts and what else I possessed. We weighed anchor the same day and sailed from island to island and sea to sea; and whenever we stopped, I sold and traded with my cocoa-nuts, and the Lord requited me more than I erst had and lost. Amongst other places, we came to an island abounding in cloves and cinnamon[66] and pepper; and the country people told me that by the side of each pepper-bunch groweth a great leaf which shadeth it from the sun and casteth the water off it in the wet season; but, when the rain ceaseth the leaf turneth over and droopeth down by the side of the bunch.[67] Here I took in great store of pepper and cloves and cinnamon, in exchange for cocoa-nuts, and we passed thence to the Island of Al-Usirat,[68] whence cometh the Comorin aloes-wood and thence to another island, five days' journey in length, where grows the Chinese lign-aloes, which is better than the Comorin; but the people of this island[69] are fouler of condition and religion than those of the other, for that they love fornication and wine-bibbing, and know not prayer nor call to prayer. Thence we came to the pearl-fisheries, and I gave the divers some of my cocoa-nuts and said to them, "Dive for my luck and lot!" They did so and brought up from the deep bight[70] great store of large and priceless pearls; and they said to me, "By Allah, O my master, thy luck is a lucky!" Then we sailed on, with the blessing of Allah (whose name be exalted!); and ceased not sailing till we arrived safely at Bassorah. There I abode a little and then went on to Baghdad, where I entered my quarter and found my house and foregathered with my family and saluted my friends who gave me joy of my safe return, and

I laid up all my goods and valuables in my storehouses. Then I distributed alms and largesse and clothed the widow and the orphan and made presents to my relations and comrades; for the Lord had requited me fourfold that I had lost. After which I returned to my old merry way of life and forgot all I had suffered in the great profit and gain I had made. Such, then, is the history of my fifth voyage and its wonderments, and now to supper; and to-morrow, come again and I will tell you what befel me in my sixth voyage; for it was still more wonderful than this. (Saith he who telleth the tale), Then he called for food; and the servants spread the table, and when they had eaten the evening-meal, he bade give Sindbad the porter an hundred golden dinars and the Landsman returned home and lay him down to sleep, much marvelling at all he had heard. Next morning, as soon as it was light, he prayed the dawn-prayer; and, after blessing Mohammed the Cream of all creatures, betook himself to the house of Sindbad the Sea-man and wished him a good day. The merchant bade him sit and talked with him, till the rest of the company arrived. Then the servants spread the table and when they had well eaten and drunken and were mirthful and merry, Sindbad the Seaman began in these words the narrative of

THE SIXTH VOYAGE OF SINDBAD THE SEAMAN.

Know, O my brothers and friends and companions all, that I abode some time, after my return from my fifth voyage, in great solace and satisfaction and mirth and merriment, joyance and enjoyment; and I forgot what I had suffered, seeing the great gain and profit I had made till, one day, as I sat making merry and enjoying myself with my friends, there came in to me a company of merchants whose case told tales of travel, and talked with me of voyage and adventure and greatness of pelf and lucre. Hereupon I remembered the days of my return from abroad, and my joy at once more seeing my native land and foregathering with my family and friends; and my soul yearned for travel and traffic. So compelled by Fate and Fortune I resolved to undertake another voyage; and, buying me fine and costly merchandise meet for foreign trade, made it up into bales, with which I journeyed from Baghdad to Bassorah. Here I found a great ship ready for sea and full of merchants and notables, who had with them goods of price; so I embarked my bales therein. And we left Bassorah in safety and good spirits under the safeguard of the King, the Preserver and continued our voyage from place to place and from city to city, buying and selling and profiting and diverting ourselves with the sight of countries where strange folk dwell. And Fortune and the voyage smiled upon us, till one day, as we went along, behold, the captain suddenly cried with a great cry and cast his turband on the deck. Then he buffeted his face like a woman and plucked out his beard and fell down in the waist of the ship well nigh fainting for stress of grief and rage, and crying, "Oh and alas for the ruin of my house and the orphanship of my poor children!" So all the merchants and sailors came round about him and asked him, "O master, what is the matter?"; for the light had become night before their sight. And he answered, saying, "Know, O folk, that we have wandered from our course and left the sea whose ways we wot, and come into a sea whose ways I know not; and unless Allah vouchsafe us a means of escape, we are all dead men; wherefore pray ye to the Most High, that He deliver us from this strait. Haply amongst you is one righteous whose prayers the Lord will accept." Then he arose and clomb the mast to see an there were any escape from that strait; and he would have loosed the sails; but the wind redoubled upon the ship and whirled her round thrice and drave her backwards; whereupon her rudder brake and she fell off towards a high mountain. With this the captain came down from the mast, saying, "There is no Majesty and there is no Might save in Allah, the Glorious, the Great; nor can man prevent that which is fore-ordained of fate! By Allah, we are fallen on a place of sure destruction, and there is no way of escape for us, nor can any of us be saved!" Then we all fell a-weeping over ourselves and bidding one another farewell for that our days were come to an end, and we had lost all hopes of life. Presently the ship struck the mountain and broke up, and all and everything on board of her were plunged into the sea. Some of the merchants were drowned and others made shift to reach the shore and save themselves upon the mountain; I amongst the number, and when we got ashore, we found a great island, or rather peninsula[71] whose base was strewn with wreckage of crafts and goods and gear cast up by the sea from broken ships whose passengers had been drowned; and the quantity confounded compt and calculation. So I climbed the cliffs into the inward of the isle and walked on inland, till I came to a stream of sweet water, that welled up at the nearest foot of the mountains and disappeared in the earth under the range of hills on the opposite side. But all the other passengers went over the mountains to the inner tracts; and, dispersing hither and thither, were confounded at what they saw and became like madmen at the sight of the wealth and treasures wherewith the shores were strewn. As for me I looked into the bed of the stream aforesaid and saw therein great plenty of rubies, and great royal pearls[72] and all kinds of jewels and precious stones which were as gravel in the bed of the rivulets that ran through the fields, and the sands sparkled and glittered with gems and precious ores. Moreover we found in the island abundance of the finest lign-aloes, both Chinese and Comorin; and there also is a spring of crude ambergris[73] which floweth like wax or gum over the stream-banks, for the great heat of the sun, and runneth down to the sea-shore, where the monsters of the deep come up and swallowing it, return into the sea. But it burneth in their bellies; so they cast it up again and it congealeth on the surface of the water, whereby its colour and quantities are changed; and at last, the waves cast it ashore, and the travellers and merchants who know it, collect it and sell it. But as to the raw amber-gris which is not swallowed, it floweth over the channel and congealeth on the banks and when the sun shineth on it, it melteth and scenteth the whole valley with a musk-like fragrance: then, when the sun ceaseth from it, it congealeth again. But none can get to this place where is the crude ambergris, because of the mountains which enclose the is-land on all sides and which foot of man cannot ascend.[74] We continued thus to explore the island, marvelling at the wonderful works of Allah and the riches we found there, but sore troubled for our own case, and dismayed at our prospects. Now we had picked up on the beach some small matter of victual from the wreck and husbanded it care-fully, eating but once every day or two, in our fear lest it should fail us and we die miserably of famine and affright. Moreover, we were weak for colic brought on by sea-sickness and low diet, and my companions deceased, one after other, till there was but a small company of us left. Each that died we washed and shrouded in some of the clothes and linen cast ashore by the tides; and after a little, the rest of my fellows perished, one by one, till I had buried the last of the party and abode alone on the island, with but a little provision left, I who was wont to have so much. And I wept over myself, saying, "Would Heaven I had died before my companions and they had washed me and buried me! It had been better than I should perish and none wash me and shroud me and bury me. But there is no Majesty and there is no Might save in Allah, the Glorious, the Great!" Now after I had buried the last of my party and abode alone on the island, I arose and dug me a deep grave on the sea-shore, saying to myself, "Whenas I grow weak and know that death cometh to me, I will cast myself into the grave and die there, so the wind may drift the sand over me and cover me and I be buried therein."[75] Then I fell to reproaching myself for my little wit in leaving my native land and betaking me again to travel, after all I had suf-fered during my first five voyages, and when I had not made a single one without suffering more horrible perils and more terrible hardships than in its forerunner and having no hope of escape from my present stress; and I repented me of my folly and bemoaned myself, especially as I had no need of money, seeing that I had enough and more than enough and could not spend what I had, no, nor a half of it in all my life. However, after a while Allah sent me a thought and I said to myself, "By God, needs must this stream have an end as well as a beginning; ergo an issue somewhere, and belike its course may lead to some inhabited place; so my best plan is to make me a little boat[76] big enough to sit in, and carry it and launching it on the river, embark therein and drop down the stream. If I escape, I escape, by God's leave; and if I perish, better die in the river than here." Then, sighing for myself, I set to work collecting a number of pieces of Chinese and Comorin aloes-wood and I bound them together with ropes from the wreckage; then I chose out from the broken up ships straight planks of even size and fixed them firmly upon the aloes-wood, making me a boat-raft a little narrower than the channel of the stream; and I tied it tightly and firmly as though it were nailed. Then I loaded it with the goods, precious ores and jewels: and the union pearls which were like gravel and the best of the ambergris crude and pure, together with what I had collected on the island and what was left me of victual and wild herbs. Lastly I lashed a piece of wood on either side, to serve me as oars; and launched it, and embarking, did according to the saying of the poet:—

> Fly, fly with life whenas evils threat;
> Leave the house to tell of its builder's fate!
> Land after land shalt thou seek and find
> But no other life on thy wish shall wait:
> Fret not thy soul in thy thoughts o' night;
> All woes shall end or sooner or late.
> Whoso is born in one land to die,
> There and only there shall gang his gait:
> Nor trust great things to another wight,
> Soul hath only soul for confederate.

My boat-raft drifted with the stream, I pondering the issue of my affair; and the drifting ceased not till I came to the place where it disappeared beneath the mountain. I rowed my conveyance into the place which was intensely dark; and the current carried the raft with it down the underground channel.[77] The thin stream bore me on through a narrow tunnel where the raft touched either side and my head rubbed against the roof, return therefrom being impossible. Then I blamed myself for having thus risked my life, and said, "If this passage grow any straiter, the raft will hardly pass, and I cannot turn back; so I shall inevitably perish miserably in this place." And I threw myself down upon my face on the raft, by reason of the narrowness of the channel, whilst the stream ceased not to carry me along, knowing not night from day, for the excess of the gloom which encompassed me about and my terror and concern for myself lest I should perish. And in such condition my course continued down the channel which now grew wider and then straiter till, sore aweary by reason of the darkness which could be felt, I fell asleep, as I lay prone on the craft, and I slept knowing not an the time were long or short. When I awoke at last, I found myself in the light of Heaven and opening my eyes I saw myself in a broad of the stream and the raft moored to an island in the midst of a number of Indians and Abyssinians. As soon as these black-amoors[78] saw that I was awake, they came up to me and bespoke me in their speech; but I understood not what they said and thought that this was a dream and a vision which had betided me for stress of concern and chagrin. But I was delighted at my escape from the river. When they saw I understood them not and made them no answer, one of them came forward and said to me in Arabic, "Peace be with thee, O my brother! Who art thou and whence faredst thou hither? How camest thou into this river and what manner of land lies behind yonder mountains, for never knew we any one make his way thence to us?" Quoth I, "And upon thee be peace and the ruth of Allah and His blessing! Who are ye and what country is this?" "O my brother," answered he, "we are husband-men and tillers of the soil, who came out to water our fields and plantations; and, finding thee asleep on this raft, laid hold of it and made it fast by us, against thou shouldst awake at thy leisure. So tell us how thou camest hither?" I answered, "For Allah's sake, O my lord, ere I speak give me somewhat to eat, for I am starving, and after ask me what thou wilt." So he hastened to fetch me food and I ate my fill, till I was refreshed and my fear was calmed by a good belly-full and my life returned to me. Then I rendered thanks to the Most High for mercies great and small, glad to be out of the river and rejoicing to be amongst them, and I told them all my adventures from first to last, especially my troubles in the narrow channel. They consulted among themselves and said to one another, "There is no help for it but we carry him with us and present him to our King, that he may acquaint him with his adventures." So they took me, together with the raft-boat and its lading of monies and merchandise; jewels, minerals and golden gear, and brought me to their King, who was King of Sarandib,[79] telling him what had happened; whereupon he saluted me and bade me welcome. Then he questioned me of my condition and adventures through the man who had spoken Arabic and I repeated to him my story from beginning to end, whereat he marvelled exceedingly and gave me joy of my deliverance; after which I arose and fetched from the raft great store of precious ores and jewels and ambergris and lign-aloes and presented them to the King, who accepted them and entreated me with the utmost honour, appointing me a lodging in his own palace. So I consorted with the chief of the islanders, and they paid me the utmost respect. And I quitted not the royal palace. Now the Island Sarandib lieth under the equinoctial line, its night and day both numbering twelve hours. It measureth eighty leagues long by a breadth of thirty and its width is bounded by a lofty mountain[80] and a deep valley. The mountain is conspicuous from a distance of three days and it containeth many kinds of rubies and other minerals, and spice-trees of all sorts. The surface is covered with emery wherewith gems are cut and fashioned; diamonds are in its rivers and pearls are in its valleys. I ascended that mountain and solaced myself with a view of its marvels which are indescribable and afterwards I returned to the King.[81] Thereupon, all the travellers and merchants who came to the place questioned me of the affairs of my native land and of the Caliph Harun al-Rashid and his rule and I told them of him and of that wherefor he was renowned, and they praised him because of this; whilst I in turn questioned them of the manners and customs of their own countries and got the knowledge I desired. One day, the King himself asked me of the fashions and form of government of my country, and I acquainted him with the circumstance of the Caliph's sway in the city of Baghdad and the justice of his rule. The King marvelled at my account of his appointments and said, "By Allah, the Caliph's ordinances are indeed wise and his fashions of praiseworthy guise and thou hast made me love him by what thou tellest me; wherefore I have a mind to make him a present and send it by thee." Quoth I, "Hearkening and obedience, O my lord; I will bear thy gift to him and inform him that thou art his sincere lover and true friend." Then I abode with the King in great honour and regard and consideration for a long while till, one day, as I sat in his palace, I heard news of a company of merchants, that were fitting out a ship for Bassorah, and said to myself, "I cannot do better than voyage with these men." So I rose without stay or delay and kissed the King's hand and acquainted him with my longing to set out with the merchants, for that I pined after my people and mine own land. Quoth he, "Thou art thine own master; yet, if it be thy will to abide with us, on our head and eyes be it, for thou gladdenest us with thy company." "By Allah, O my lord," answered I, "thou hast indeed overwhelmed me with thy favours and well-doings; but I weary for a sight of my friends and family and native country." When he heard this, he summoned the merchants in question and commended me to their care, paying my freight and passage-money. Then he bestowed on me great riches from his treasuries and charged me with a magnificent present for the Caliph Harun al-Rashid. Moreover he gave me a sealed letter, saying, "Carry this with thine own hand to the Commander of the Faithful and give him many salutations from us!" "Hearing and obedience," I replied. The missive was written on the skin of the Khawi[82] (which is finer than lamb-parchment and of yellow colour), with ink of ultramarine and the contents were as follows. "Peace be with thee from the King of Al-Hind, before whom are a thousand elephants and upon whose palace-crenelles are a thousand jewels. But after (laud to the Lord and praises to His Prophet!): we send thee a trifling gift which be thou pleased to accept. Thou art to us a brother and a sincere friend; and great is the love we bear for thee in heart; favour us therefore with a reply. The gift besitteth not thy dignity: but we beg of thee, O our brother, graciously to accept it and peace be with thee." And the present was a cup of ruby a span high[83] the inside of which was adorned with precious pearls; and a bed covered with the skin of the serpent which swalloweth the elephant, which skin hath spots each like a dinar and whoso sitteth upon it never sickeneth;[84] and an hundred thousand miskals of Indian lign-aloes and a slave-girl like a shining moon. Then I took leave of him and of all my intimates and acquaintances in the island and embarked with the merchants aforesaid. We sailed with a fair wind, committing ourselves to the care of Allah (be He extolled and exalted!) and by His permission arrived at Bassorah, where I passed a few days and nights equipping myself and packing up my bales. Then I went on to Baghdad-city, the House of Peace, where I sought an audience of the Caliph and laid the King's presents before him. He asked me whence they came and I said to him, "By Allah, O Commander of the Faithful, I know not the name of the city nor the way thither!" He then asked me, "O Sindbad, is this true which the King writeth?"; and I answered, after kissing the ground, "O my lord, I saw in his kingdom much more than he hath written in his letter. For state processions a throne is set for him upon a huge elephant, eleven cubits high: and upon this he sitteth having his great lords and officers and guests standing in two ranks, on his right hand and on his left. At his head is a man hending in hand a golden javelin and behind him another with a great mace of gold whose head is an emerald[85] a span long and as thick as a man's thumb. And when he mounteth horse there mount with him a thousand horsemen clad in gold brocade and silk; and as the King proceedeth a man precedeth him, crying, This is the King of great dignity, of high authority! And he continueth to repeat his praises in words I remember not, saying at the end of his panegyric, This is the King owning the crown whose like nor Solomon nor the Mihraj[86] ever possessed. Then he is silent and one behind him proclaimeth, saying, He will die! Again I say he will die!; and the other addeth, Extolled be the perfection of the Living who dieth not![87] Moreover by reason of his justice and ordinance and intelligence, there is no Kazi in his city, and all his lieges distinguish between Truth and Falsehood." Quoth the Caliph, "How great is this King! His letter hath shown me this; and as for the mightiness of his dominion thou hast told us what thou hast eye-witnessed. By Allah, he hath been endowed with wisdom as with wide rule." Then I related to the Commander of the Faithful all that had befallen me in my last voyage; at which he wondered exceedingly and bade his historians record my story and store it up in his treasuries, for the edification of all who might see it. Then he conferred on me exceeding great favours, and I repaired to my quarter and entered my home, where I warehoused all my goods and possessions. Presently, my friends came to me and I distributed presents among my family and gave alms and largesse; after which I yielded myself to joyance and enjoyment, mirth and merry-making, and forgot all that I had suffered. Such, then, O my brothers, is the history of what befel me in my sixth voyage, and to-morrow, Inshallah! I will tell you the story of my seventh and last voyage, which is still more wondrous and marvellous than that of the first six. (Saith he who telleth the tale), Then he bade lay the table, and the company supped with him; after which he gave the Porter an hundred dinars, as of wont, and they all went their ways, marvelling beyond measure at that which they had heard. Sindbad the Landsman went home and slept as of wont. Next day he rose and prayed the dawn-prayer and repaired to his namesake's house where, after the company was all assembled, the host began to relate

THE SEVENTH VOYAGE OF SINDBAD THE SEAMAN.

Know, O company, that after my return from my sixth voyage, which brought me abundant profit, I resumed my former life in all possible joyance and enjoyment and mirth and making merry day and night; and I tarried some time in this solace and satisfaction till my soul began once more to long to sail the seas and see foreign countries and company with merchants and hear new things. So having made up my mind, I packed up in bales a quantity of precious stuffs suited for sea-trade and repaired with them from Baghdad-city to Bassorah-town, where I found a ship ready for sea, and in her a company of considerable merchants. I shipped with them and becoming friends, we set forth on our venture, in health and safety; and sailed with a fair wind, till we came to a city called Madinat-al-Sin; but after we had left it, as we fared on in all cheer and confidence, devising of traffic and travel, behold, there sprang up a violent head-wind and a tempest of rain fell on us and drenched us and our goods. So we covered the bales with our cloaks and garments and drugget and canvas, lest they be spoiled by the rain, and betook ourselves to prayer and supplication to Almighty Allah and humbled ourselves before Him for deliverance from the peril that was upon us. But the captain arose and tightening his girdle tucked up his skirts and, after taking refuge with Allah from Satan the

Stoned, clomb to the mast-head, whence he looked out right and left and gazing at the passengers and crew fell to buffeting his face and plucking out his beard. So we cried to him, "O Rais, what is the matter?"; and he replied saying, "Seek ye deliverance of the Most High from the strait into which we have fallen and bemoan yourselves and take leave of one another; for know that the wind hath gotten the mastery of us and hath driven us into the uttermost of the seas of the world." Then he came down from the mast-head and opening his sea-chest, pulled out a bag of blue cotton, from which he took a powder like ashes. This he set in a saucer wetted with a little water and, after waiting a short time, smelt and tasted it; and then he took out of the chest a booklet, wherein he read awhile and said weeping, "Know, O ye passengers, that in this book is a marvellous matter, denoting that whoso cometh hither shall surely die, without hope of escape; for that this ocean is called the Sea of the Clime of the King, wherein is the sepulchre of our lord Solomon, son of David (on both be peace!) and therein are serpents of vast bulk and fearsome aspect: and what ship soever cometh to these climes there riseth to her a great fish[88] out of the sea and swalloweth her up with all and everything on board her." Hearing these words from the captain great was our wonder, but hardly had he made an end of speaking, when the ship was lifted out of the water and let fall again and we applied to praying the death-prayer[89] and committing our souls to Allah. Presently we heard a terrible great cry like the loud-pealing thunder, whereat we were terror-struck and became as dead men, giving ourselves up for lost. Then behold, there came up to us a huge fish, as big as a tall mountain, at whose sight we became wild for affright and, weeping sore, made ready for death, marvelling at its vast size and gruesome semblance; when lo! a second fish made its appearance than which we had seen naught more monstrous. So we bemoaned ourselves of our lives and farewelled one another; but suddenly up came a third fish bigger than the two first; whereupon we lost the power of thought and reason and were stupefied for the excess of our fear and horror. Then the three fish began circling round about the ship and the third and biggest opened his mouth to swallow it, and we looked into its mouth and behold, it was wider than the gate of a city and its throat was like a long valley. So we besought the Almighty and called for succour upon His Apostle (on whom be blessing and peace!), when suddenly a violent squall of wind arose and smote the ship, which rose out of the water and settled upon a great reef, the haunt of sea-monsters, where it broke up and fell asunder into planks and all and everything on board were plunged into the sea. As for me, I tore off all my clothes but my gown and swam a little way, till I happened upon one of the ship's planks whereto I clung and bestrode it like a horse, whilst the winds and the waters sported with me and the waves carried me up and cast me down; and I was in most piteous plight for fear and distress and hunger and thirst. Then I reproached myself for what I had done and my soul was weary after a life of ease and comfort; and I said to myself, "O Sindbad, O Seaman, thou repentest not and yet thou art ever suffering hardships and travails; yet wilt thou not renounce sea-travel; or, an thou say, 'I renounce,' thou liest in thy renouncement. Endure then with patience that which thou sufferest, for verily thou deservest all that betideth thee!" And I ceased not to humble myself before Almighty Allah and weep and bewail myself, recalling my former estate of solace and satisfaction and mirth and merriment and joyance; and thus I abode two days, at the end of which time I came to a great island abounding in trees and streams. There I landed and ate of the fruits of the island and drank of its waters, till I was refreshed and my life returned to me and my strength and spirits were restored and I recited:—

> Oft when thy case shows knotty and tangled skein,
> Fate downs from Heaven and straightens every ply:
> In patience keep thy soul till clear thy lot
> For He who ties the knot can eke untie.

Then I walked about, till I found on the further side, a great river of sweet water, running with a strong current; whereupon I called to mind the boat-raft I had made aforetime and said to myself, "Needs must I make another; haply I may free me from this strait. If I escape, I have my desire and I vow to Allah Almighty to forswear travel; and if I perish I shall be at peace and shall rest from toil and moil." So I rose up and gathered together great store of pieces of wood from the trees (which were all of the finest sanders-wood, whose like is not albe I knew it not), and made shift to twist creepers and tree-twigs into a kind of rope, with which I bound the billets together and so contrived a raft. Then saying, "An I be saved, 'tis of God's grace," I embarked thereon and committed myself to the current, and it bore me on for the first day and the second and the third after leaving the island; whilst I lay in the raft, eating not and drinking, when I was athirst, of the water of the river, till I was weak and giddy as a chicken, for stress of fatigue and famine and fear. At the end of this time I came to a high mountain, whereunder ran the river; which when I saw, I feared for my life by reason of the straitness I had suffered in my former journey, and I would fain have stayed the raft and landed on the mountainside; but the current overpowered me and drew it into the subterranean passage like an archway; whereupon I gave myself up for lost and said, "There is no Majesty and there is no Might save in Allah, the Glorious, the Great!" However, after a little, the raft glided into open air and I saw before me a wide valley, whereinto the river fell with a noise like the rolling of thunder and a swiftness as the rushing of the wind. I held on to the raft, for fear of falling off it, whilst the waves tossed me right and left; and the craft continued to descend with the current nor could I avail to stop it nor turn it shorewards, till it stopped with me at a great and goodly city, grandly edified and containing much people. And when the townsfolk saw me on the raft, dropping down with the current, they threw me out ropes which I had not strength enough to hold; then they tossed a net over the craft and drew it ashore with me, whereupon I fell to the ground amidst them, as I were a dead man, for stress of fear and hunger and lack of sleep. After a while, there came up to me out of the crowd an old man of reverend aspect, well stricken in years, who welcomed me and threw over me abundance of handsome clothes, wherewith I covered my nakedness. Then he carried me to the Hammam-bath and brought me cordial sherbets and delicious perfumes; moreover, when I came out, he bore me to his house, where his people made much of me and, seating me in a pleasant place, set rich food before me, whereof I ate my fill and returned thanks to God the Most High for my deliverance. Thereupon his pages fetched me hot water, and I washed my hands, and his handmaids brought me silken napkins, with which I dried them and wiped my mouth. Also the Shaykh set apart for me an apartment in a part of his house and charged his pages and slave-girls to wait upon me and do my will and supply my wants. They were assiduous in my service, and I abode with him in the guest-chamber three days, taking my ease of good eating and good drinking and good scents till life returned to me and my terrors subsided and my heart was calmed and my mind was eased. On the fourth day the Shaykh, my host, came in to me and said, "Thou cheerest us with thy company, O my son, and praised be Allah for thy safety! Say: wilt thou now come down with me to the beach and the bazar and sell thy goods and take their price? Belike thou mayest buy thee wherewithal to traffic. I have ordered my servants to remove thy stock-in-trade from the sea and they have piled it on the shore." I was silent awhile and said to myself, "What mean these words and what goods have I?" Then said he, "O my son, be not troubled nor careful, but come with me to the market and if any offer for thy goods what price contenteth thee, take it; but, an thou be not satisfied, I will lay them up for thee in my warehouse, against a fitting occasion for sale." So I bethought me of my case and said to myself, "Do his bidding and see what are these goods!"; and I said to him, "O my nuncle the Shaykh,

I hear and I obey; I may not gainsay thee in aught for Allah's blessing is on all thou dost." Accordingly he guided me to the market-street, where I found that he had taken in pieces the raft which carried me and which was of sandal-wood and I heard the broker crying it for sale. Then the merchants came and opened the gate of bidding for the wood and bid against one another till its price reached a thousand dinars, when they left bidding and my host said to me, "Hear, O my son, this is the current price of thy goods in hard times like these: wilt thou sell them for this or shall I lay them up for thee in my storehouses, till such time as prices rise?" "O my lord," answered I, "the business is in thy hands: do as thou wilt." Then asked he, "Wilt thou sell the wood to me, O my son, for an hundred gold pieces over and above what the merchants have bidden for it?" and I answered, "Yes: I have sold it to thee for monies received."[90] So he bade his servants transport the wood to his storehouses and, carrying me back to his house, seated me and counted out to me the purchase money; after which he laid it in bags and setting them in a privy place, locked them up with an iron padlock and gave me its key. Some days after this, the Shaykh said to me, "O my son, I have somewhat to propose to thee, wherein I trust thou wilt do my bidding." Quoth I, "What is it?" Quoth he, "I am a very old man and have no son; but I have a daughter who is young in years and fair of favour and endowed with abounding wealth and beauty. Now I have a mind to marry her to thee, that thou mayest abide with her in this our country, and I will make thee master of all I have in hand for I am an old man and thou shalt stand in my stead." I was silent for shame and made him no answer, whereupon he continued, "Do my desire in this, O my son, for I wish but thy weal; and if thou wilt but do as I say, thou shalt have her at once and be as my son; and all that is under my hand or that cometh to me shall be thine. If thou have a mind to traffic and travel to thy native land, none shall hinder thee, and thy property will be at thy sole disposal; so do as thou wilt." "By Allah, O my uncle," replied I, "thou art become to me even as my father, and I am a stranger and have undergone many hardships: while for stress of that which I have suffered naught of judgment or knowledge is left to me. It is for thee, therefore, to decide what I shall do." Hereupon he sent his servants for the Kazi and the witnesses and married me to his daughter making for us a noble marriage-feast[91] and high festival. When I went in to her, I found her perfect in beauty and loveliness and symmetry and grace, clad in rich raiment and covered with a profusion of ornaments and necklaces and other trinkets of gold and silver and precious stones, worth a mint of money, a price none could pay. She pleased me and we loved each other; and I abode with her in all solace and delight of life, till her father was taken to the mercy of Allah Almighty. So we shrouded him and buried him, and I laid hands on the whole of his property and all his servants and slaves became mine. Moreover, the merchants installed me in his office, for he was their Shaykh and their Chief; and none of them purchased aught but with his knowledge and by his leave. And now his rank passed on to me. When I became acquainted with the townsfolk, I found that at the beginning of each month they were transformed, in that their faces changed and they became like unto birds and they put forth wings wherewith they flew unto the upper regions of the firmament and none remained in the city save the women and children; and I said in my mind, "When the first of the month cometh, I will ask one of them to carry me with them, whither they go." So when the time came and their complexion changed and their forms altered, I went in to one of the townsfolk and said to him, "Allah upon thee! carry me with thee, that I might divert myself with the rest and return with you." "This may not be," answered he; but I ceased not to solicit him and I importuned him till he consented. Then I went out in his company, without telling any of my family[92] or servants or friends, and he took me on his back and flew up with me so high in air, that I heard the angels glorifying God in the heavenly dome, whereat I wondered and exclaimed, "Praised be Allah! Extolled be the perfection of Allah!" Hardly had I made an end of pronouncing the Tasbih—praised be Allah!—when there came out a fire from heaven and all but consumed the company; whereupon they fled from it and descended with curses upon me and, casting me down on a high mountain, went away, exceeding wroth with me, and left me there alone. As I found myself in this plight, I repented of what I had done and reproached myself for having undertaken that for which I was unable, saying, "There is no Majesty and there is no Might, save in Allah, the Glorious, the Great! No sooner am I delivered from one affliction than I fall into a worse." And I continued in this case knowing not whither I should go, when lo! there came up two young men, as they were moons, each using as a staff a rod of red gold. So I approached them and saluted them; and when they returned my salam, I said to them, "Allah upon you twain; who are ye and what are ye?" Quoth they, "We are of the servants of the Most High Allah, abiding in this mountain;" and, giving me a rod of red gold they had with them, went their ways and left me. I walked on along the mountain-ridge staying my steps with the staff and pondering the case of the two youths, when behold, a serpent came forth from under the mountain, with a man in her[93] jaws, whom she had swallowed even to below his navel, and he was crying out and saying, "Whoso delivereth me, Allah will deliver him from all adversity!" So I went up to the serpent and smote her on the head with the golden staff, whereupon she cast the man forth of her mouth. Then I smote her a second time, and she turned and fled; whereupon he came up to me and said, "Since my deliverance from yonder serpent hath been at thy hands I will never leave thee, and thou shalt be my comrade on this mountain." "And welcome," answered I; so we fared on along the mountain, till we fell in with a company of folk, and I looked and saw amongst them the very man who had carried me and cast me down there. I went up to him and spake him fair, excusing myself to him and saying, "O my comrade, it is not thus that friend should deal with friend." Quoth he, "It was thou who well-nigh destroyed us by thy Tasbih and thy glorifying God on my back." Quoth I, "Pardon me, for I had no knowledge of this matter; but, if thou wilt take me with thee, I swear not to say a word." So he relented and consented to carry me with him, but he made an express condition that, so long as I abode on his back, I should abstain from pronouncing the Tasbih or otherwise glorifying God. Then I gave the wand of gold to him whom I had delivered from the serpent and bade him farewell, and my friend took me on his back and flew with me as before, till he brought me to the city and set me down in my own house. My wife came to meet me and saluting me gave me joy of my safety and then said, "Beware of going forth hereafter with yonder folk, neither consort with them, for they are brethren of the devils, and know not how to mention the name of Allah Almighty; neither worship they Him." "And how did thy father with them?" asked I; and she answered, "My father was not of them, neither did he as they; and as now he is dead methinks thou hadst better sell all we have and with the price buy merchandise and journey to thine own country and people, and I with thee; for I care not to tarry in this city, my father and my mother being dead." So I sold all the Shaykh's property piecemeal, and looked for one who should be journeying thence to Bassorah that I might join myself to him. And while thus doing I heard of a company of townsfolk who had a mind to make the voyage, but could not find them a ship; so they bought wood and built them a great ship wherein I took passage with them, and paid them all the hire. Then we embarked, I and my wife, with all our moveables, leaving our houses and domains and so forth, and set sail, and ceased not sailing from island to island and from sea to sea, with a fair wind and a favouring, till we arrived at Bassorah safe and sound. I made no stay there, but freighted another vessel and, transferring my goods to her, set out forthright for Baghdad-city, where I arrived in safety, and entering my quarter and repairing to my house, foregathered with my family and friends and familiars and laid up my goods in my warehouses. When my people who, reckoning the period of my absence on this my seventh voyage, had found it to be seven and twenty years, and had given up all hope of me, heard of my return, they came to welcome me and to give me joy of my safety; and I related to them all that had befallen me; whereat they marvelled with exceeding marvel. Then I foreswore travel and vowed to Allah the Most High I would venture no more by land or sea, for that this seventh and last voyage had surfeited me of travel and adventure; and I thanked the Lord (be He praised and glorified!), and blessed Him for having restored me to my kith and kin and country and home. "Consider, therefore, O Sindbad, O Landsman," continued Sindbad the Seaman, "what sufferings I have undergone and what perils and hardships I have endured before coming to my present state." "Allah upon thee, O my Lord!" answered Sindbad the Landsman, "pardon me the wrong I did thee."[94] And they ceased not from friendship and fellowship, abiding in all cheer and pleasures and solace of life, till there came to them the Destroyer of delights and the Sunderer of Societies and the Shatterer of palaces and the Caterer for Cemeteries to wit, the Cup of Death, and glory be to the Living One who dieth not![95] And there is a tale touching

THE CITY OF BRASS.[1]

It is related that there was, in tide of yore and in times and years long gone before, at Damascus of Syria, a Caliph known as Abd al-Malik bin Marwan, the fifth of the Ommiade house. As this Commander of the Faithful was seated one day in his palace, conversing with his Sultans and Kings and the Grandees of his empire, the talk turned upon the legends of past peoples and the traditions of our Lord Solomon, David's son (on the twain be peace!), and on that which Allah Almighty had bestowed on him of lordship and dominion over men and Jinn and birds and beasts and reptiles and the wind and other created things; and quoth the Caliph, "Of a truth we hear from those who forewent us that the Lord (extolled and exalted be He!) vouchsafed unto none the like of that which He vouchsafed unto our lord Solomon and that he attained unto that whereto never attained other than he, in that he was wont to imprison Jinns and Marids and Satans in cucurbites of copper and to stop them with lead and seal[2] them with his ring." Then said Talib bin Sahl (who was a seeker after treasures and had books that discovered to him hoards and wealth hidden under the earth), "O Commander of the

Faithful,—Allah make thy dominion to endure and exalt thy dignity here and hereafter!—my father told me of my grandfather, that he once took ship with a company, intending for the island of Sikiliyah or Sicily, and sailed until there arose against them a contrary wind, which drove them from their course and brought them, after a month, to a great mountain in one of the lands of Allah the Most High, but where that land was they wot not. Quoth my grandfather:—This was in the darkness of the night and as soon as it was day, there came forth to us, from the caves of the mountain, folk black of colour and naked of body, as they were wild beasts, understanding not one word of what was addressed to them; nor was there any of them who knew Arabic, save their King who was of their own kind. When he saw the ship, he came down to it with a company of his followers and saluting us, bade us welcome and questioned us of our case and our faith. We told him all concerning ourselves and he said, Be of good cheer for no harm shall befal you. And when we, in turn, asked them of their faith, we found that each was of one of the many creeds prevailing before the preaching of Al-Islam and the mission of Mohammed, whom may Allah bless and keep! So my shipmates remarked, We wot not what thou sayest. Then quoth the King, No Adam-son hath ever come to our land before you: but fear not, and rejoice in the assurance of safety and of return to your own country. Then he entertained us three days, feeding us on the flesh of birds and wild beasts and fishes, than which they had no other meat; and, on the fourth day, he carried us down to the beach, that we might divert ourselves by looking upon the fisher-folk. There we saw a man casting his net to catch fish, and presently he pulled them up and behold, in them was a cucurbite of copper, stopped with lead and sealed with the signet of Solomon, son of David, on whom be peace! He brought the vessel to land and broke it open, when there came forth a smoke, which rose a-twisting blue to the zenith, and we heard a horrible voice, saying, I repent! I repent! Pardon, O Prophet of Allah! I will never return to that which I did aforetime. Then the smoke became a terrible Giant frightful of form, whose head was level with the mountain-tops, and he vanished from our sight, whilst our hearts were well-nigh torn out for terror; but the blacks thought nothing of it. Then we returned to the King and questioned him of the matter; whereupon quoth he, Know that this was one of the Jinns whom Solomon, son of David, being wroth with them, shut up in these vessels and cast into the sea, after stopping the mouths with melted lead. Our fishermen ofttimes, in casting their nets, bring up such bottles, which being broken open, there come forth of them Jinnis who, deeming that Solomon is still alive and can pardon them, make their submission to him and say, I repent, O Prophet of Allah!" The Caliph marvelled at Talib's story and said, "Glory be to God! Verily, to Solomon was given a mighty dominion." Now Al-Nabighah al-Zubyani[3] was present, and he said, "Talib hath spoken soothly as is proven by the saying of the All-wise, the Primæval One:—

> And Solomon, when Allah to him said,
> 'Rise, be thou Caliph, rule with righteous sway:
> Honour obedience for obeying thee;
> And who rebels imprison him for aye.'

Wherefore he used to put them in copper-bottles and cast them into the sea." The poet's words seemed good to the Caliph, and he said, "By Allah, I long to look upon some of these Solomonic vessels, which must be a warning to whoso will be warned." "O Commander of the Faithful," replied Talib, "it is in thy power to do so, without stirring abroad. Send to thy brother Abd al-Aziz bin Marwan, so he may write to Musa bin Nusayr,[4] governor of the Maghrib or Morocco, bidding him take horse thence to the mountains whereof I spoke and fetch thee therefrom as many of such cucurbites as thou hast a mind to; for those mountains adjoin the frontiers of his province." The Caliph approved his counsel and said "Thou hast spoken sooth, O Talib, and

I desire that, touching this matter, thou be my messenger to Musa bin Nusayr; wherefore thou shalt have the White Flag[5] and all thou hast a mind to of monies and honour and so forth; and I will care for thy family during thine absence." "With love and gladness, O Commander of the Faithful!" answered Talib. "Go, with the blessing of Allah and His aid," quoth the Caliph, and bade write a letter to his brother, Abd al-Aziz, his viceroy in Egypt, and another to Musa bin Nusayr, his viceroy in North-Western Africa, bidding him go himself in quest of the Solomonic bottles, leaving his son to govern in his stead. Moreover, he charged him to engage guides and to spare neither men nor money, nor to be remiss in the matter as he would take no excuse. Then he sealed the two letters and committed them to Talib bin Sahl, bidding him advance the royal ensigns before him and make his utmost speed; and he gave him treasure and horsemen and footmen, to further him on his way, and make provision for the wants of his household during his absence. So Talib set out and arrived in due course at Cairo,[6] where the Governor came out to meet him and entreated him and his company with high honour whilst they tarried with him. Then he gave them a guide to bring them to the Sa'id or Upper Egypt, where the Emir Musa had his abiding-place; and when the son of Nusayr heard of Talib's coming, he went forth to meet him and rejoiced in him. Talib gave him the Caliph's letter, and he took it reverently and, laying it on his head, cried, "I hear and I obey the Prince of the Faithful." Then he deemed it best to assemble his chief officers and when all were present he acquainted them with the contents of the Caliph's letter and sought counsel of them how he should act. "O Emir," answered they, "if thou seek one who shall guide thee to the place summon the Shaykh 'Abd al-Samad, ibn 'Abd al-Kuddus, al-Samudi;[7] for he is a man of varied knowledge, who hath travelled much and knoweth by experience all the seas and wastes and wolds and countries of the world and the inhabitants and wonders thereof; wherefore send thou for him and he will surely guide thee to thy desire." So Musa sent for him, and behold, he was a very ancient man shot in years and broken down with lapse of days. The Emir saluted him and said, "O Shaykh Abd al-Samad, our lord the Commander of the Faithful, Abd al-Malik bin Marwan, hath commanded me thus and thus. I have small knowledge of the land wherein is that which the Caliph desireth; but it is told me that thou knowest it well and the ways thither. Wilt thou, therefore, go with me and help me to accomplish the Caliph's need? So it please Allah the Most High, thy trouble and travail shall not go waste." Replied the Shaykh, "I hear and obey the bidding of the Commander of the Faithful; but know, O Emir, that the road thither is long and difficult and the ways few." "How far is it?" asked Musa, and the Shaykh answered, "It is a journey of two years and some months going and the like returning; and the way is full of hardships and terrors and things wondrous and marvellous. Now thou art a champion of the Faith[8] and our country is hard by that of the enemy; and peradventure the Nazarenes may come out upon us in thine absence; wherefore it behoveth thee to leave one to rule thy government in thy stead." "It is well," answered the Emir and appointed his son Harun Governor during his absence, requiring the troops to take the oath of fealty to him and bidding them obey him in all he should command. And they heard his words and promised obedience. Now this Harun was a man of great prowess and a renowned warrior and a doughty knight, and the Shaykh Abd al-Samad feigned to him that the place they sought was distant but four months' journey along the shore of the sea, with camping-places all the way, adjoining one another, and grass and springs, adding, "Allah will assuredly make the matter easy to us through thy blessing, O Lieutenant of the Commander of the Faithful!" Quoth the Emir Musa, "Knowest thou if any of the Kings have trodden this land before us?"; and quoth the Shaykh, "Yes, it belonged aforetime to Darius the Greek, King of Alexandria." But he said to Musa privily, "O Emir, take with thee a thousand camels laden with victual and store of gugglets."[9] The Emir asked, "And what shall we do with these?"; and the Shaykh answered, "On our way is the desert of Kayrawan or Cyrene, the which is a vast wold four days' journey long, and lacketh water; nor therein doth sound of voice ever sound nor is soul at any time to be seen. Moreover, there bloweth the Simoon[10] and other hot winds called Al-Juwayb, which dry up the water-skins; but if the water be in gugglets, no harm can come to it." "Right," said Musa and sending to Alexandria, let bring thence great plenty of gugglets. Then he took with him his Wazir and two thousand cavalry, clad in mail cap-à-pie and set out, without other to guide them but Abd al-Samad who forewent them, riding on his hackney. The party fared on diligently, now passing through inhabited lands, then ruins and anon traversing frightful wolds and thirsty wastes and then mountains which spired high in air; nor did they leave journeying a whole year's space till, one morning, when the day broke, after they had travelled all night, behold, the Shaykh found himself in a land he knew not and said, "There is no Majesty and there is no Might save in Allah, the Glorious, the Great!" Quoth the Emir, "What is to do, O Shaykh?"; and he answered, saying, "By the Lord of the Ka'abah, we have wandered from our road!" "How cometh that?" asked Musa, and Abd al-Samad replied, "The stars were overclouded and I could not guide myself by them." "Where on God's earth are we now?" asked the Emir, and the Shaykh answered, "I know not; for I never set eyes on this land till this moment." Said Musa, "Guide us back to the place where we went astray"; but the other, "I know it no more." Then Musa, "Let us push on; haply Allah will guide us to it or direct us aright of His power." So they fared on till the hour of noon-prayer, when they came to a fair champaign, and wide and level and smooth as it were the sea when calm, and presently there appeared to them, on the horizon some great thing, high and black, in whose midst was as it were smoke rising to the confines of the sky. They made for this, and stayed not in their course till they drew near thereto, when, lo!

it was a high castle, firm of foundations and great and gruesome, as it were a towering mountain, builded all of black stone, with frowning crenelles and a door of gleaming China steel, that dazzled the eyes and dazed the wits. Round about it were a thousand steps and that which appeared afar off as it were smoke was a central dome of lead an hundred cubits high. When the Emir saw this, he marvelled thereat with exceeding marvel and how this place was void of inhabitants; and the Shaykh, after he had certified himself thereof, said, "There is no god but *the* God and Mohammed is the Apostle of God!" Quoth Musa, "I hear thee praise the Lord and hallow Him, and meseemeth thou rejoicest." "O Emir," answered Abd al-Samad, "Rejoice, for Allah (extolled and exalted be He!) hath delivered us from the frightful wolds and thirsty wastes." "How knowest thou that?" said Musa, and the other, "I know it for that my father told me of my grandfather that he said:— We were once journeying in this land and, straying from the road, we came to this palace and thence to the City of Brass; between which and the place thou seekest is two full months' travel; but thou must take to the sea-shore and leave it not, for there be watering-places and wells and camping-grounds established by King Zu al-Karnayn Iskandar who, when he went to the conquest of Mauritania, found by the way thirsty deserts and wastes and wilds and dug therein water-pits and built cisterns." Quoth Musa, "Allah rejoice thee with good news!" and quoth the Shaykh, "Come, let us go look upon yonder palace and its marvels, for it is an admonition to whoso will be admonished." So the Emir went up to the palace, with the Shaykh and his officers, and coming to the gate, found it open. Now this gate was built with lofty columns and porticoes whose walls and ceilings were inlaid with gold and silver and precious stones; and there led up to it flights of steps, among which were two wide stairs of coloured marble, never was seen their like; and over the doorway was a tablet whereon were graven letters of gold in the old ancient Ionian character. "O Emir," asked the Shaykh, "shall I read?"; and Musa answered, "Read and God bless thee!; for all that betideth us in this journey dependeth upon thy blessing." So the Shaykh, who was a very learned man and versed in all tongues and characters, went up to the tablet and read whatso was thereon and it was verse like this:—

> The signs that here their mighty works portray
> Warn us that all must tread the self-same way:
> O thou who standest in this stead to hear
> Tidings of folk, whose power hath passed for aye,
> Enter this palace-gate and ask the news
> Of greatness fallen into dust and clay:
> Death has destroyed them and dispersed their might
> And in the dust they lost their rich display;
> As had they only set their burdens down
> To rest awhile, and then had rode away.

When the Emir Musa heard these couplets, he wept till he lost his senses and said, "There is no god but *the* God, the Living, the Eternal, who ceaseth not!" Then he entered the palace and was confounded at its beauty and the goodliness of its construction. He diverted himself awhile by viewing the pictures and images therein, till he came to another door, over which also were written verses, and said to the Shaykh, "Come read me these!" So he advanced and read as follows:—

> Under these domes how many a company
> Halted of old and fared withouten stay:
> See thou what might displays on other wights
> Time with his shifts which could such lords waylay:
> They shared together what they gathered
> And left their joys and fared to Death-decay:
> What joys they joyed! what food they ate! and now
> In dust they're eaten, for the worm a prey.

When Musa heard these verses, he wept with such weeping that he swooned away; then, coming to himself, he entered a pavilion and saw therein a long tomb, awesome to look upon, whereon was a tablet of China steel and Shakyh Abd al-Samad drew near it and read this inscription: In the name of Everlasting Allah, the Never-beginning, the Never-ending; in the name of Allah who begetteth not nor is He begot and unto whom the like is not; in the name of Allah the Lord of Majesty and Might; in the name of the Living One who to death is never dight! O thou who comest to this place, take warning by that which thou seest of the accidents of Time and the vicissitudes of Fortune and be not deluded by the world and its pomps and vanities and fallacies and falsehoods and vain allurements, for that it is flattering, deceitful and treacherous, and the things thereof are but a loan to us which it will borrow back from all borrowers. It is like unto the dreams of the dreamer and the sleep-visions of the sleeper or as the mirage of the desert, which the thirsty take for water;[11] and Satan maketh it fair for men even unto death. These are the ways of the world; wherefore put not thou thy trust therein neither incline thereto, for it bewrayeth him who leaneth upon it and who committeth himself thereunto in his affairs. Fall not thou into its snares neither take hold upon its skirts, but be warned by my example. I possessed four thousand bay horses and a haughty palace, and I had to wife a thousand daughters of kings, high-bosomed maids, as they were moons: I was blessed with a thousand sons as they were fierce lions, and I abode a thousand years, glad of heart and mind, and I amassed treasures beyond the competence of all the Kings of the regions of the earth, deeming that delight would still endure to me. But there fell on me unawares the Destroyer of delights and the Sunderer of societies, the Desolator of domiciles and the Spoiler of inhabited spots, the Murtherer of great and small, babes and children and mothers, he who hath no ruth on the poor for his poverty, or feareth the King for all his bidding or forbidding. Verily, we abode safe and secure in this palace, till there descended upon us the judgment of the Lord of the Three Worlds, Lord of the Heavens, and Lord of the Earths, the vengeance of the Manifest Truth[12] overtook us, when there died of us every day two, till a great company of us had perished. When I saw that destruction had entered our dwellings and had homed with us and in the sea of deaths had drowned us, I summoned a writer and bade him indite these verses and instances and admonitions, the which I let grave, with rule and compass, on these doors and tablets and tombs. Now I had an army of a thousand thousand bridles, men of warrior mien with forearms strong and keen, armed with spears and mail-coats sheen and swords that gleam; so I bade them don their long-hanging hauberks and gird on their biting blades and mount their high-mettled steeds and level their dreadful lances; and whenas there fell on us the doom of the Lord of heaven and earth, I said to them, "Ho, all ye soldiers and troopers, can ye avail to ward off that which is fallen on me from the Omnipotent King?" But troopers and soldiers availed not unto this and said, "How shall we battle with Him to whom no chamberlain barreth access, the Lord of the door which hath no doorkeeper?" Then quoth I to them, "Bring me my treasures." Now I had in my treasuries a thousand cisterns in each of which were a thousand quintals[13] of red gold and the like of white silver, besides pearls and jewels of all kinds and other things of price, beyond the attainment of the kings of the earth. So they did that and when they had laid all the treasure in my presence, I said to them, "Can ye ransom me with all this treasure or buy me one day of life therewith?" But they could not! So they resigned themselves to fore-ordained Fate and fortune and I submitted to the judgment of Allah, enduring patiently that which he decreed unto me of affliction, till He took my soul and made me to dwell in my grave. And if thou ask of my name, I am Kush, the son of Shaddad son of Ad the Greater. And upon the tablets were engraved these lines:—

An thou wouldst know my name, whose day is done
With shifts of time and changes 'neath the sun,
Know I am Shaddad's son, who ruled mankind
And o'er all earth upheld dominion!
All stubborn peoples abject were to me;
And Sham to Cairo and to Adnanwone;[14]
I reigned in glory conquering many kings;
And peoples feared my mischief every one.
Yea, tribes and armies in my hand I saw;
The world all dreaded me, both friends and fone.
When I took horse, I viewed my numbered troops,
Bridles on neighing steeds a million.
And I had wealth that none could tell or count,
Against misfortune treasuring all I won;
Fain had I bought my life with all my wealth,
And for a moment's space my death to shun;
But God would naught save what His purpose willed;
So from my brethren cut I 'bode alone:
And Death, that sunders man, exchanged my lot
To pauper hut from grandeur's mansion,
When found I all mine actions gone and past
Wherefor I'm pledged[15] and by my sin undone.
Then fear, O man, who by a brink dost range,
The turns of Fortune and the chance of Change.

The Emir Musa was hurt to his heart and loathed his life
for what he saw of the slaughtering-places of the folk; and,
as they went about the highways and byeways of the palace,
viewing its sitting-chambers and pleasaunces, behold they
came upon a table of yellow onyx, upborne on four feet
of juniper-wood,[16] and thereon these words graven:—"At
this table have eaten a thousand kings blind of the right eye
and a thousand blind of the left and yet other thousand
sound of both eyes, all of whom have departed the world
and have taken up their sojourn in the tombs and the cata-
combs." All this the Emir wrote down and left the palace,
carrying off with him naught save the table aforesaid. Then
he fared on with his host three days' space, under the guid-

ance of the Shaykh Abd al-Samad, till they came to a high hill, whereon stood a horseman of brass. In his hand he held a lance with a broad head, in brightness like blinding leven, whereon was graven:—"O thou that comest unto me, if thou know not the way to the City of Brass, rub the hand of this rider and he will turn round and presently stop. Then take the direction whereto he faceth and fare fearless, for it will bring thee, without hardship, to the city aforesaid." When the Emir Musa rubbed the horseman's hand he revolved like the dazzling lightning, and stopped facing in a direction other than that wherein they were journeying. So they took the road to which he pointed (which was the right way) and, finding it a beaten track, fared on through their days and nights till they had covered a wide tract of country. Then they came upon a pillar of black stone like a furnace-chimney wherein was one sunken up to his armpits. He had two great wings and four arms, two of them like the arms of the sons of Adam and other two as they were lion's paws, with claws of iron, and he was black and tall and frightful of aspect, with hair like horses' tails and eyes like blazing coals, slit upright in his face. Moreover, he had in the middle of his forehead a third eye, as it were that of a lynx, from which flew sparks of fire, and he cried out saying, "Glory to my Lord, who hath adjudged unto me this grievous torment and sore punishment until the Day of Doom!" When the folk saw him, they lost their reason for affright and turned to flee; so the Emir Musa asked the Shaykh Abd al-Samad, "What is this?"; and he answered, "I know not." Whereupon quoth Musa, "Draw near and question him of his condition; haply he will discover to thee his case." "Allah assain thee, Emir! Indeed, I am afraid of him;" replied the Shaykh; but the Emir rejoined, saying, "Fear not; he is hindered from thee and from all others by that wherein he is." So Abd al-Samad drew near to the pillar and said to him which was therein, "O creature, what is thy name and what art thou and how camest thou here in this fashion?" "I am an Ifrit of the Jinn," replied he, "by name Dahish, son of Al-A'amash,[17] and am confined here by the

All-might, prisoned here by the Providence and punished by the judgment of Allah, till it pleases Him, to whom belong Might and Majesty, to release me." Then said Musa, "Ask him why he is in durance of this column?" So the Shaykh asked him of this, and the Ifrit replied, saying:— Verily my tale is wondrous and my case marvellous, and it is this. One of the sons of Iblis had an idol of red carnelian, whereof I was guardian, and there served it a King of the Kings of the sea, a Prince of puissant power and prow of prowess, over-ruling a thousand thousand warriors of the Jann who smote with swords before him and answered his summons in time of need. All these were under my commandment and obeyed my behest, being each and every rebels against Solomon, son of David, on whom be peace! And I used to enter the belly of the idol and thence bid and forbid them. Now this King's daughter loved the idol and was frequent in prostration to it and assiduous in its service; and she was the fairest woman of her day, accomplished in beauty and loveliness, elegance and grace. She was described unto Solomon and he sent to her father, saying, "Give me thy daughter to wife and break thine idol of carnelian and testify saying, There is no god but *the* God and Solomon is the Prophet of Allah!, an thou do this, our due shall be thy due and thy debt shall be our debt but, if thou refuse, make ready to answer the summons of the Lord and don thy grave-gear, for I will come upon thee with an irresistible host, which shall fill the waste places of earth and make thee as yesterday that is passed away and hath no return for aye." When this message reached the King, he waxed insolent and rebellious, pride-full and contumacious and he cried to his Wazirs, "What say ye of this? Know ye that Solomon son of David hath sent requiring me to give him my daughter to wife, and break my idol of carnelian and enter his faith!" And they replied, "O mighty King, how shall Solomon do thus with thee? Even could he come at thee in the midst of this vast ocean, he could not prevail against thee, for the Marids of the Jann will fight on thy side and thou wilt ask succour of thine idol whom thou servest, and he will help thee and give thee victory over him. So thou wouldst do well to consult on this matter thy Lord," (meaning the idol aforesaid) "and hear what he saith. If he say, Fight him, fight him, and if not, not." So the King went in without stay or delay to his idol and offered up sacrifices and slaughtered victims; after which he fell down before him, prostrate and weeping, and repeated these verses:—

> "O my Lord, well I weet thy puissant hand:
> Sulayman would break thee and see thee bann'd.
> O my Lord, to crave succour here I stand
> Command and I bow to thy high command!"

Then I (continued the Ifrit addressing the Shaykh and those about him), of my ignorance and want of wit and recklessness of the commandment of Solomon and lack of knowledge anent his power, entered the belly of the idol and made answer as follows:—

> "As for me, of him I feel naught affright;
> For my lore and my wisdom are infinite:
> If he wish for warfare I'll show him fight
> And out of his body I'll tear his sprite!"

When the King heard my boastful reply, he hardened his heart and resolved to wage war upon the Prophet and to offer him battle; whereas he beat the messenger with a grievous beating and returned a foul answer to Solomon, threatening him and saying, "Of a truth, thy soul hath suggested to thee a vain thing; dost thou menace me with mendacious words? But gird thyself for battle; for, an thou come not to me, I will assuredly come to thee." So the messenger returned to Solomon and told him all that had passed and whatso had befallen him, which when the Prophet heard, he raged like Doomsday and addressed himself to the fray and levied armies of men and Jann and birds and reptiles. He commanded his Wazir Al-Dimiryat, King of the Jann, to gather together the Marids of the Jinn from all parts, and he collected for him six hundred thousand thousand of devils.[18] Moreover, by his order, his Wazir Asaf bin Barkhiya levied him an army of men, to the number of a thousand thousand or more. These all he furnished with arms and armour and mounting, with his host, upon his carpet, took flight through the air, while the beasts fared under him and the birds flew overhead, till he lighted down on the island of the refractory King and encompassed it about, filling earth with his hosts. Then he sent to our King, saying, "Behold, I am come: defend thy life against that which is fallen upon thee, or else make thy submission to me and confess my apostleship and give me thy daughter to lawful wife and break thine idol and worship the one God, the alone Worshipful; and testify, thou and thine, and say, There is no God but *the* God, and Solomon is the Apostle of Allah![19] This if thou do, thou shalt have pardon and peace; but if not, it will avail thee nothing to fortify thyself in this island, for Allah (extolled and exalted be He!) hath bidden the Wind obey me; so I will bid it bear me to thee on my carpet and make thee a warning and an example to deter others." But the King made answer to his messenger, saying, "It may not on any wise be as he requireth of me; so tell him I come forth to him." With this reply the messenger returned to Solomon, who thereupon gathered together all the Jinn that were under his hand, to the number of a thousand thousand, and added to them other than they of Marids and Satans from the islands of the sea and the tops of the mountains and, drawing them up on parade, opened his armouries and distributed to them arms and armour. Then the Prophet drew out his host in battle array, dividing the beasts into two bodies, one on the right wing of the men and the other on the left, and bidding them tear the enemies' horses in sunder. Furthermore, he ordered the birds which were in the island to hover over their heads and, whenas the assault should be made, that they should swoop down and tear out the foe's eyes with their beaks and buffet their faces with their wings; and they answered, saying, "We hear and we obey Allah and thee, O Prophet of Allah!" Then Solomon seated himself on a throne of alabaster, studded with precious stones and plated with red gold; and, commanding the wind to bear him aloft, set his Wazir Asaf bin Barkhiya[20] and the kings of mankind on his right and his Wazir Al-Dimiryat and the kings of the Jinn on his left, arraying the beasts and vipers and serpents in the van. Thereupon they all set on us together, and we gave them battle two days over a vast plain; but, on the third day, disaster befel us, and the judgment of Allah the Most High was executed upon us. Now the first to charge upon them were I and my troops, and I said to my companions, "Abide in your places, whilst I sally forth to them and provoke Al-Dimiryat to combat singular." And behold, he came forth to the duello as he were a vast mountain, with his fires flaming and his smoke spireing, and shot at me a falling star of fire; but I swerved from it and it missed me. Then I cast at him in my turn, a flame of fire, and it smote him; but his shaft[21] overcame my fire and he cried out at me so terrible a cry that meseemed the skies were fallen flat upon me, and the mountains trembled at his voice. Then he commanded his hosts to charge; accordingly they rushed on us and we rushed on them, each crying out upon other, and battle reared its crest rising in volumes and smoke ascending in columns and hearts well-nigh cleaving. The birds and the flying Jinn fought in the air and the beasts and men and the foot-faring Jann in the dust and I fought with Al-Dimiryat, till I was aweary and he not less so. At last, I grew weak and turned to flee from him, whereupon my companions and tribesmen likewise took to flight and my hosts were put to the rout, and Solomon cried out, saying, "Take yonder furious tyrant, the accursed, the infamous!" Then man fell upon man and Jinn upon Jinn and the armies of the Prophet charged down upon us, with the wild beasts and lions on their right hand and on their left, rending our horses and tearing our men; whilst the birds hovered overhead in air pecking out our eyes with their claws and beaks and beating our faces with their wings, and the serpents struck us with their fangs, till the most of our folk lay prone upon the face of the earth, like the trunks of datetrees. Thus defeat befel our King and we became a spoil unto Solomon. As to me, I fled from before Al-Dimiryat; but he followed me three months' journey, till I fell down for weariness and he overtook me, and pouncing upon me, made me prisoner. Quoth I, "By the virtue of Him who hath exalted thee and abased me, spare me and bring me into the presence of Solomon, on whom be peace!" So he carried me before Solomon, who received me after the foulest fashion and bade bring this pillar and hollow it out. Then he set me herein and chained me and sealed me with his signet-ring, and Al-Dimiryat bore me to this place wherein thou seest me. Moreover, he charged a great angel to guard me, and this pillar is my prison until Judgmentday. When the Jinni who was prisoned in the pillar had told them his tale, from first to last, the folk marvelled at his story and at the frightfulness of his favour, and the Emir Musa said, "There is no God but *the* God! Soothly was Solomon gifted with a mighty dominion." Then said the Shaykh Abd al-Samad to the Jinni, "Ho there! I would fain ask thee of a thing, whereof do thou inform us." "Ask what thou wilt," answered the Ifrit Dahish and the Shaykh said, "Are there hereabouts any of the Ifrits imprisoned in bottles of brass from the time of Solomon (on whom be peace!)?" "Yes," replied the Jinni; "there be such in the sea of Al-Karkar[22] on the shores whereof dwell a people of the lineage of Noah (on whom be peace!); for their country was not reached by the Deluge and they are cut off there from the other sons of Adam." Quoth Abd al-Samad, "And which is the way to the City of Brass and the place wherein are the cucurbites of Solomon, and what distance lieth between us and it?" Quoth the Ifrit, "It is near at hand," and directed them in the way thither. So they left him and fared forward till there appeared to them afar off a great blackness and therein two fires facing each other, and the Emir Musa asked the Shaykh, "What is yonder vast blackness and its twin fires?"; and the guide answered, "Rejoice, O Emir, for this is the City of Brass, as it is described in the Book of Hidden Treasures which I have by me. Its walls are of black stone and it hath two towers of Andalusian brass,[23] which appear to the beholder in the distance as they were twin fires, and hence is it named the City of Brass." Then they fared on without ceasing till they drew near the city and behold, it was as it were a piece of a mountain or a mass of iron cast in a mould and impenetrable for the height of its walls and bulwarks; while nothing could be more beautiful than its buildings and its ordinance. So they dismounted down and sought for an entrance, but saw none neither found any trace of opening in the walls, albeit there were five-and-twenty portals to the city, but none of them was visible from without. Then quoth the Emir, "O Shaykh, I see to this city no sign of any gate;" and quoth he, "O Emir, thus is it described in my Book of Hidden Treasures; it hath five-and-twenty portals; but none thereof may be opened save from within the city." Asked Musa, "And how shall we do to enter the city and view its wonders?" and Talib son of Sahl, his Wazir, answered, "Allah assain the Emir! let us rest here two or three days and, God willing, we will make shift to come within the walls." Then said Musa to one of his men, "Mount thy camel and ride round about the city, so haply thou may light upon a gate or a place somewhat lower than this fronting us, or Inshallah! a breach whereby we can enter." Accordingly he mounted his beast, taking water and victuals with him, and rode round the city two days and two nights, without drawing rein to rest, but found the wall thereof as it were one block, without reach or way of ingress; and on the third day, he came again in sight of his companions, dazed and amazed at what he had seen of the extent and loftiness of the place, and said, "O

Emir, the easiest place of access is this where you have alighted." Then Musa took Talib and Abd al-Samad and ascended the highest hill which overlooked the city. When they reached the top, they beheld beneath them a city, never saw eyes a greater or a goodlier, with dwelling-places and mansions of towering height, and palaces and pavilions and domes gleaming gloriously bright and scones and bulwarks of strength infinite; and its streams were a-flowing and flowers a-blowing and fruits a-glowing. It was a city with gates impregnable; but void and still, without a voice or a cheering inhabitant. The owl hooted in its quarters; the bird skimmed circling over its squares and the raven croaked in its great thoroughfares weeping and bewailing the dwellers who erst made it their dwelling.[24] The Emir stood awhile, marvelling and sorrowing for the desolation of the city and saying, "Glory to Him whom nor ages nor changes nor times can blight, Him who created all things of His Might!" Presently, he chanced to look aside and caught sight of seven tablets of white marble afar off. So he drew near them and finding inscriptions graven thereon, called the Shaykh and bade him read these. Accordingly he came forward and, examining the inscriptions, found that they contained matter of admonition and warning and instances and restraint to those of understanding. On the first tablet was inscribed, in the ancient Greek character: "O son of Adam, how heedless art thou of that which is before thee! Verily, thy years and months and days have diverted thee therefrom. Knowest thou not that the cup of death is filled for thy bane which in a little while to the dregs thou shalt drain? Look to thy doom ere thou enter thy tomb. Where be the Kings who held dominion over the lands and abased Allah's servants and built these palaces and had armies under their commands? By Allah, the Destroyer of delights and the Severer of societies and the Devastator of dwelling-places came down upon them and transported them from the spaciousness of their palaces to the straitness of their burial-places." And at the foot of the tablet were written the following verses:—

"Where are the Kings earth-peopling, where are they?
The built and peopled left they e'er and aye!
They're tombed yet pledged to actions past away
And after death upon them came decay.
Where are their troops? They failed to ward and guard!
Where are the wealth and hoards in treasuries lay?
Th' Empyrean's Lord surprised them with one word,
Nor wealth nor refuge could their doom delay!"

When the Emir heard this, he cried out and the tears ran down his cheeks and he exclaimed, "By Allah, from the world abstaining is the wisest course and the sole assaining!" And he called for pen-case and paper and wrote down what was graven on the first tablet. Then he drew near the second tablet and found these words graven thereon, "O son of Adam, what hath seduced thee from the service of the Ancient of Days and made thee forget that one day thou must defray the debt of death? Wottest thou not that it is a transient dwelling wherein for none there is abiding; and yet thou takest thought unto the world and cleavest fast thereto? Where be the kings who Irak peopled and the four quarters of the globe possessed? Where be they who abode in Ispahan and the land of Khorasan? The voice of the Summoner of Death summoned them and they answered him, and the Herald of Destruction hailed them and they replied, Here are we! Verily, that which they builded and fortified profited them naught; neither did what they had gathered and provided avail for their defence." And at the foot of the tablet were graven the following verses:—

Where be the men who built and fortified
High places never man their like espied?
In fear of Fate they levied troops and hosts,
Availing naught when came the time and tide,
Where be the Kisras homed in strongest walls?
As though they ne'er had been from home they hied!

The Emir Musa wept and exclaimed, "By Allah, we are indeed created for a grave matter!" Then he copied the inscription and passed on to the third tablet, whereon was written, "O son of Adam, the things of this world thou lovest and prizest and the hest of thy Lord thou spurnest and despisest. All the days of thy life pass by and thou art content thus to aby. Make ready thy viaticum against the day appointed for thee to see and prepare to answer the Lord of every creature that be!" And at the foot were written these verses:—

> Where is the wight who peopled in the past
> Hind-land and Sind; and there the tyrant played?
> Who Zanj[25] and Habash bound beneath his yoke,
> And Nubia curbed and low its puissance laid.
> Look not for news of what is in his grave.
> Ah, he is far who can thy vision aid!
> The stroke of death fell on him sharp and sure;
> Nor saved him palace, nor the lands he swayed.

At this Musa wept with sore weeping and, going on to the fourth tablet, he read inscribed thereon, "O son of Adam, how long shall thy Lord bear with thee and thou every day sunken in the sea of thy folly? Hath it then been stablished unto thee that some day thou shalt not die? O son of Adam, let not the deceits of thy days and nights and times and hours delude thee with their delights; but remember that death lieth ready for thee ambushing, fain on thy shoulders to spring, nor doth a day pass but he morneth with thee in the morning and nighteth with thee by night. Beware, then, of his onslaught and make provision thereagainst. As was with me, so it is with thee; thou wastest thy whole life and squanderest the joys in which thy days are rife. Hearken, therefore, to my words and put thy trust in the Lord of Lords; for in the world there is no stability; it is but as a spider's web to thee." And at the foot of the tablet were written these couplets:—

Where is the man who did those labours ply
And based and built and reared these walls on high?
Where be the castles' lords? Who therein dwelt
Fared forth and left them in decay to lie.
All are entombed, in pledge against the day
When every sin shall show to every eye.
None but the Lord Most High endurance hath,
Whose Might and Majesty shall never die.

When the Emir read this, he swooned away and presently
coming to himself marvelled exceedingly and wrote it
down. Then he drew near the fifth tablet and behold,
thereon was graven, "O son of Adam, what is it that dis-
tracteth thee from obedience of thy Creator and the
Author of thy being, Him who reared thee whenas thou
wast a little one, and fed thee whenas thou wast full-
grown? Thou art ungrateful for His bounty, albeit He
watcheth over thee with His favours, letting down the curtain of His protection over thee. Needs must there be for
thee an hour bitterer than aloes and hotter than live coals.
Provide thee, therefore, against it; for who shall sweeten its
gall or quench its fires? Bethink thee who forewent thee
of peoples and heroes and take warning by them, ere thou
perish." And at the foot of the tablet were graven these
couplets:—

Where be the Earth-kings who from where they 'bode,
Sped and to graveyards with their hoardings yode:
Erst on their mounting-days there hadst beheld
Hosts that concealed the ground whereon they rode:
How many a king they humbled in their day!
How many a host they led and laid on load!
But from th'Empyrean's Lord in haste there came
One word, and joy waxed grief ere morning glowed.

The Emir marvelled at this and wrote it down; after which
he passed on to the sixth tablet and behold, was inscribed

thereon, "O son of Adam, think not that safety will endure for ever and aye, seeing that death is sealed to thy head alway. Where be thy fathers, where be thy brethren, where thy friends and dear ones? They have all gone to the dust of the tombs and presented themselves before the Glorious, the Forgiving, as if they had never eaten nor drunken, and they are a pledge for that which they have earned. So look to thyself, ere thy tomb come upon thee." And at the foot of the tablet were these couplets:—

> Where be the Kings who ruled the Franks of old?
> Where be the King who peopled Tingis-wold?[26]
> Their works are written in a book which He,
> The One, th' All-father shall as witness hold.

At this the Emir Musa marvelled and wrote it down, saying, "There is no god but *the* God! Indeed, how goodly were these folks!" Then he went up to the seventh tablet and behold, thereon was written, "Glory to Him who foreordaineth death to all He createth, the Living One, who dieth not! O son of Adam, let not thy days and their delights delude thee, neither thine hours and the delices of their time, and know that death to thee cometh and upon thy shoulder sitteth. Beware, then, of his assault and make ready for his onslaught. As it was with me, so it is with thee; thou wastest the sweet of thy life and the joyance of thine hours. Give ear, then, to my rede and put thy trust in the Lord of Lords and know that in the world is no stability, but it is as it were a spider's web to thee and all that is therein shall die and cease to be. Where is he who laid the foundation of Amid[27] and builded it and builded Farikin[28] and exalted it? Where be the peoples of the strong places? Whenas them they had inhabited, after their might into the tombs they descended. They have been carried off by death and we shall in like manner be afflicted by doom. None abideth save Allah the Most High, for He is Allah the Forgiving One." The Emir Musa wept and copied all this, and indeed the world was belittled in his eyes. Then he descended the hill and rejoined his host, with whom he passed the rest of the day, casting about for a means of access to the city. And he said to his Wazir Talib bin Sahl and to the chief officers about him, "How shall we contrive to enter this city and view its marvels?: haply we shall find therein wherewithal to win the favour of the Commander of the Faithful." "Allah prolong the Emir's fortune!" replied Talib, "let us make a ladder and mount the wall therewith, so peradventure we may come at the gate from within." Quoth the Emir, "This is what occurred to my thought also, and admirable is the advice!" Then he called for carpenters and blacksmiths and bade them fashion wood and build a ladder plated and banded with iron. So they made a strong ladder and many men wrought at it a whole month. Then all the company laid hold of it and set it up against the wall, and it reached the top as truly as if it had been built for it before that time. The Emir marvelled and said, "The blessing of Allah be upon you. It seems as though ye had taken the measure of the mure, so excellent is your work." Then said he to his men, "Which of you will mount the ladder and walk along the wall and cast about for a way of descending into the city, so to see how the case stands and let us know how we may open the gate?" Whereupon quoth one of them, "I will go up, O Emir, and descend and open to you"; and Musa answered, saying, "Go and the blessing of Allah go with thee!" So the man mounted the ladder; but, when he came to the top of the wall, he stood up and gazed fixedly down into the city, then clapped his hands and crying out, at the top of his voice, "By Allah, thou art fair!" cast himself down into the place, and Musa cried, "By Allah, he is a dead man!" But another came up to him and said, "O Emir, this was a madman and doubtless his madness got the better of him and destroyed him. I will go up and open the gate to you, if it be the will of Allah the Most High." "Go up," replied Musa, "and Allah be with thee! But beware lest thou lose thy head, even as did thy comrade." Then the man mounted the ladder, but no sooner had he reached the top of the wall than he laughed aloud, saying, "Well done! well done!"; and clapping palms cast himself down into the city and died forthright. When the Emir saw this, he said "An such be the action of a reasonable man, what is that of the madman? If all our men do on this wise, we shall have none left and shall fail of our errand and that of the Commander of the Faithful. Get ye ready for the march: verily we have no concern with this city." But a third one of the company said, "Haply another may be steadier than they." So a third mounted the wall and a fourth and a fifth and all cried out and cast themselves down, even as did the first; nor did they leave to do thus, till a dozen had perished in like fashion. Then the Shaykh Abd al-Samad came forward and heartened himself and said, "This affair is reserved to none other than myself; for the experienced is not like the inexperienced." Quoth the Emir, "Indeed thou shalt not do that nor will I have thee go up: an thou perish, we shall all be cut off to the last man since thou art our guide." But he answered, saying, "Peradventure, that which we seek may be accomplished at my hands, by the grace of God Most High!" So the folk all agreed to let him mount the ladder, and he arose and heartening himself, said, "In the name of Allah, the Compassionating, the Compassionate!" and mounted the ladder, calling on the name of the Lord and reciting the Verses of Safety.[29] When he reached the top of the wall, he clapped his hands and gazed fixedly down into the city; whereupon the folk below cried out to him with one accord, saying, "O Shaykh Abd al-Samad, for the Lord's sake, cast not thyself down!"; and they added, "Verily we are Allah's and unto Him we are returning! If the Shaykh fall, we are dead men one and all." Then he laughed beyond all measure and sat a long hour, reciting the names of Allah Almighty and repeating the Verses of Safety; then he rose and cried out at the top of his voice, saying, "O Emir, have no fear; no hurt shall betide you, for Allah (to whom belong Might and Majesty!) hath averted from me the wiles and malice of Satan, by the blessing of the words, 'In the name of Allah, the Compassionating, the Compassionate!' " Asked Musa, "What didst thou see, O Shaykh?"; and Abd al-Samad answered, "I saw ten maidens like Houris of Heaven,[30] and they calling and signing:[31]—Come hither to us; and meseemed there was below me a lake of water. So I thought to throw myself down, when behold, I espied my twelve companions lying dead; so I restrained myself and recited somewhat of Allah's Book, whereupon He dispelled from me the damsels' witchlike wiles and malicious guiles and they disappeared. And doubtless this was an enchantment devised by the people of the city, to repel any who should seek to gaze upon or to enter the place. And it hath succeeded in slaying our companions." Then he walked on along the wall, till he came to the two towers of brass aforesaid and saw therein two gates of gold, without padlocks or visible means of opening. Hereat he paused as long as Allah pleased[32] and gazed about him awhile, till he espied in the middle of one of the gates, a horseman of brass with hand outstretched as if pointing, and in his palm was somewhat written. So he went up to it and read these words, "O thou who comest to this place, an thou wouldst enter turn the pin in my navel twelve times and the gate will open." Accordingly, he examined the horseman and finding in his navel a pin of gold, firm-set and fast fixed, he turned it twelve times, whereupon the horseman revolved like the blinding lightning and the gate swung open with a noise like thunder. He entered and found himself in a long passage,[33] which brought him down some steps into a guard-room furnished with goodly wooden benches, whereon sat men dead, over whose heads hung fine shields and keen blades and bent bows and shafts ready notched. Thence, he came to the main gate of the city; and, finding it secured with iron bars and curiously wrought locks and bolts and chains and other fastenings of wood and metal, said to himself, "Belike the keys are with yonder dead folk." So he turned back to the guard-room and seeing amongst the dead an old man seated upon a high wooden bench, who seemed the chiefest of them, said in his mind, "Who knows but they are with this Shaykh? Doubtless he was the warder of the city, and these others were under his hand." So he went up to him and lifting his gown, behold, the keys were hanging to his girdle; whereat he joyed with exceeding joy and was like to fly for gladness. Then he took them and going up to the portal, undid the padlocks and drew back the bolts and bars, whereupon the great leaves flew open with a crash like the pealing thunder by reason of its greatness and terribleness. At this he cried out, saying, "Allaho Akbar—God is most great!" And the folk without answered him with the same words, rejoicing and thanking him for his deed. The Emir Musa also was delighted at the Shaykh's safety and the opening of the city-gate, and the troops all pressed forward to enter; but Musa cried out to them, saying, "O folk, if we all go in at once we shall not be safe from some ill-chance which may betide us. Let half enter and other half tarry without." So he pushed forwards with half his men, bearing their weapons of war, and finding their comrades lying dead, they buried them; and they saw the doorkeepers and eunuchs and chamberlains and officers reclining on couches of silk and all were corpses. Then they fared on till they came to the chief market-place, full of lofty buildings whereof none overpassed the others, and found all its shops open, with the scales hung out and the brazen vessels ordered and the caravanserais full of all manner goods; and they beheld the merchants sitting on the shop-boards dead, with shrivelled skin and rotted bones, a warning to those who can take warning; and here they saw four separate markets all replete with wealth. Then they left the great bazar and went on till they came to the silk market, where they found silks and brocades, orfrayed with red gold and diapered with white silver upon all manner of colours, and the owners lying dead upon mats of scented goats' leather, and looking as if they would speak; after which they traversed the market-street of pearls and rubies and other jewels and

came to that of the schroffs and money-changers, whom
they saw sitting dead upon carpets of raw silk and dyed
stuffs in shops full of gold and silver. Thence they passed
to the perfumers' bazar where they found the shops filled
with drugs of all kinds and bladders of musk and ambergis
and Nadd-scent and camphor and other perfumes, in vessels of ivory and ebony and Khalanj-wood and Andalusian
copper, the which is equal in value to gold; and various
kinds of rattan and Indian cane; but the shopkeepers all
lay dead nor was there with them aught of food. And hard
by this drug-market they came upon a palace, imposingly
edified and magnificently decorated; so they entered and
found therein banners displayed and drawn sword-blades
and strung bows and bucklers hanging by chains of gold
and silver and helmets gilded with red gold. In the vestibules stood benches of ivory, plated with glittering gold
and covered with silken stuffs, whereon lay men, whose
skin had dried up on their bones; the fool had deemed
them sleeping; but, for lack of food, they had perished and
tasted the cup of death. Now when the Emir Musa saw
this, he stood still, glorifying Allah the Most High and hal-
lowing Him and contemplating the beauty of the palace
and the massiveness of its masonry and fair perfection of
its ordinance, for it was builded after the goodliest and sta-
blest fashion and the most part of its adornment was of
green[34] lapis-lazuli; and on the inner door, which stood
open, were written in characters of gold and ultramarine,
these couplets:—

Consider thou, O man, what these places to thee showed
And be upon thy guard ere thou travel the same road:
And prepare thee good provision some day may serve thy
   turn
For each dweller in the house needs must yede wi' those
   who yode
Consider how this people their palaces adorned
And in dust have been pledged for the seed of acts they
   sowed:

They built but their building availed them not, and hoards
Nor saved their lives nor day of Destiny forslowed:
How often did they hope for what things were undecreed.
And passed unto their tombs before Hope the bounty
    showed:
And from high and awful state all a-sudden they were sent
To the straitness of the grave and oh! base is their abode:
Then came to them a Crier after burial and cried,
What booted thrones or crowns or the gold to you bestowed:
Where now are gone the faces hid by curtain and by veil,
Whose charms were told in proverbs, those beauties
    à-la-mode?
The tombs aloud reply to the questioners and cry,
"Death's canker and decay those rosy cheeks corrode!"
Long time they ate and drank, but their joyaunce had a term;
And the eater eke was eaten, and was eaten by the worm.

When the Emir read this, he wept, till he was like to swoon away, and bade write down the verses, after which he passed on into the inner palace and came to a vast hall, at each of whose four corners stood a pavilion lofty and spacious, washed with gold and silver and painted in various colours. In the heart of the hall was a great jetting-fountain of alabaster, surmounted by a canopy of brocade, and in each pavilion was a sitting-place and each place had its richly-wrought fountain and tank paved with marble and streams flowing in channels along the floor and meeting in a great and grand cistern of many-coloured marbles. Quoth the Emir to the Shaykh Abd al-Samad, "Come, let us visit yonder pavilion!" So they entered the first and found it full of gold and silver and pearls and jacinths and other precious stones and metals, besides chests filled with brocades, red and yellow and white. Then they repaired to the second pavilion, and, opening a closet there, found it full of arms and armour, such as gilded helmets and Davidean[35] hauberks and Hindi swords and Arabian spears and Chorasmian[36] maces and other gear of fight and fray. Thence they passed to the third pavilion, wherein they saw

closets padlocked and covered with curtains wrought with
all manner of embroidery. They opened one of these and
found it full of weapons curiously adorned with open work
and with gold and silver damascene and jewels. Then they
entered the fourth pavilion, and opening one of the closets
there, beheld in it great store of eating and drinking vessels
of gold and silver, with platters of crystal and goblets set
with fine pearls and cups of carnelian and so forth. So they
all fell to taking that which suited their tastes and each of
the soldiers carried off what he could. When they left the
pavilions, they saw in the midst of the palace a door of
teak-wood marquetried with ivory and ebony and plated
with glittering gold, over which hung a silken curtain purfled with all manner of embroideries; and on this door
were locks of white silver, that opened by artifice without a key. The Shaykh Abd al-Samad went valiantly up
thereto and by the aid of his knowledge and skill opened
the locks, whereupon the door admitted them into a corri-
dor paved with marble and hung with veil-like[37] tapestries
embroidered with figures of all manner beasts and birds,
whose bodies were of red gold and white silver and their
eyes of pearls and rubies, amazing all who looked upon
them. Passing onwards they came to a saloon builded all of
polished marble, inlaid with jewels, which seemed to the
beholder as though the floor were flowing water[38] and
whoso walked thereon slipped. The Emir bade the Shaykh
strew somewhat upon it, that they might walk over it;
which being done, they made shift to fare forwards till they
came to a great domed pavilion of stone, gilded with red
gold and crowned with a cupola of alabaster, about which
were set lattice-windows carved and jewelled with rods of
emerald,[39] beyond the competence of any King. Under this
dome was a canopy of brocade, reposing upon pillars of
red gold and wrought with figures of birds whose feet were
of smaragd, and beneath each bird was a network of fresh-
hued pearls. The canopy was spread above a jetting fountain of ivory and carnelian, plated with glittering gold and
thereby stood a couch set with pearls and rubies and other

jewels and beside the couch a pillar of gold. On the capital of the column stood a bird fashioned of red rubies and holding in his bill a pearl which shone like a star; and on the couch lay a damsel, as she were the lucident sun, eyes never saw a fairer. She wore a tight-fitting body-robe of fine pearls, with a crown of red gold on her head, filleted with gems, and on her forehead were two great jewels, whose light was as the light of the sun. On her breast she wore a jewelled amulet, filled with musk and ambergris and worth the empire of the Cæsars; and around her neck hung a collar of rubies and great pearls, hollowed and filled with odoriferous musk. And it seemed as if she gazed on them to the right and to the left. The Emir Musa marvelled at her exceeding beauty and was confounded at the blackness of her hair and the redness of her cheeks, which made the beholder deem her alive and not dead, and said to her, "Peace be with thee, O damsel!" But Talib ibn Sahl said to him, "Allah preserve thee, O Emir, verily this damsel is dead and there is no life in her; so how shall she return thy salam?"; adding, "Indeed, she is but a corpse embalmed with exceeding art; her eyes were taken out after her death and quicksilver set under them, after which they were restored to their sockets. Wherefore they glisten and when the air moveth the lashes, she seemeth to wink and it appeareth to the beholder as though she looked at him, for all she is dead." At this the Emir marvelled beyond measure and said, "Glory be to God who subjugateth His creatures to the dominion of Death!" Now the couch on which the damsel lay, had steps, and thereon stood two statues of Andalusian copper representing slaves, one white and the other black. The first held a mace of steel[40] and the second a sword of watered steel which dazzled the eye; and between them, on one of the steps of the couch, lay a golden tablet, whereon were written, in characters of white silver, the following words: "In the name of God, the Compassionating, the Compassionate! Praise be to Allah, the Creator of mankind; and He is the Lord of Lords, the Causer of Causes! In the name of Allah, the Never-beginning, the

Everlasting, the Ordainer of Fate and Fortune! O son of Adam! what hath befooled thee in this long esperance? What hath unminded thee of the Death-day's mischance? Knowest thou not that Death calleth for thee and hasteneth to seize upon the soul of thee? Be ready, therefore, for the way and provide thee for thy departure from the world; for, assuredly, thou shalt leave it without delay. Where is Adam, first of humanity? Where is Noah with his progeny? Where be the Kings of Hind and Irak-plain and they who over earth's widest regions reign? Where do the Amalekites abide and the giants and tyrants of olden tide? Indeed, the dwelling-places are void of them and they have departed from kindred and home. Where be the Kings of Arab and Ajem? They are dead, all of them, and gone and are become rotten bones. Where be the lords so high in stead? They are all done dead. Where are Kora and Haman? Where is Shaddad son of Ad? Where be Canaan and Zu'l-Autad,[41] Lord of the Stakes? By Allah, the Reaper of lives hath reaped them and made void the lands of them. Did they provide them against the Day of Resurrection or make ready to answer the Lord of men? O thou, if thou know me not, I will acquaint thee with my name: I am Tadmurah,[42] daughter of the Kings of the Amalekites, of those who held dominion over the lands in equity and brought low the necks of humanity. I possessed that which never King possessed and was righteous in my rule and did justice among my lieges; yea, I gave gifts and largesse and freed bondsmen and bondswomen. Thus lived I many years in all ease and delight of life, till Death knocked at my door and to me and to my folk befel calamities galore; and it was on this wise. There betided us seven successive years of drought, wherein no drop of rain fell on us from the skies and no green thing sprouted for us on the face of earth.[43] So we ate what was with us of victual, then we fell upon the cattle and devoured them, until nothing was left. Thereupon I let bring my treasures and meted them with measures and sent out trusty men to buy food. They circuited all the lands in quest thereof and left no city unsought, but found it not to be bought and returned to us with the treasure after a long absence; and gave us to know that they could not succeed in bartering fine pearls for poor wheat, bushel for bushel, weight for weight. So, when we despaired of succour, we displayed all our riches and things of price and, shutting the gates of the city and its strong places, resigned ourselves to the deme of our Lord and committed our case to our King. Then we all died,[44] as thou seest us, and left what we had builded and all we had hoarded. This, then, is our story, and after the substance naught abideth but the trace." When the Emir Musa read this, he wept with exceeding weeping till he swooned away and presently coming to himself, wrote down all he had seen and was admonished by all he had witnessed. Then he said to his men, "Fetch the camels and load them with these treasures and vases and jewels." "O Emir," asked Talib, "shall we leave our damsel with what is upon her, things which have no equal and whose like is not to be found and more perfect than aught else thou takest; nor couldst thou find a goodlier offering wherewithal to propitiate the favour of the Commander of the Faithful?" But Musa answered, "O man, heardest thou not what the Lady saith on this tablet? More by token that she giveth it in trust to us who are no traitors." "And shall we," rejoined the Wazir Talib, "because of these words, leave all these riches and jewels, seeing that she is dead? What should she do with these that are the adornments of the world and the ornament of the worldling, seeing that one garment of cotton would suffice for her covering? We have more right to them than she." So saying he mounted the steps of the couch between the pillars, but when he came within reach of the two slaves, lo! the mace-bearer smote him on the back and the other struck him with the sword he held in his hand and lopped off his head, and he dropped down dead. Quoth the Emir, "Allah have no mercy on thy resting-place! Indeed there was enough in these treasures; and greed of gain assuredly degradeth a man." Then he bade admit the troops; so they entered and loaded the camels with those treasures and precious ores; after which they went forth and the emir commanded them to shut the gate as before. They fared on along the sea-shore a whole month, till they came in sight of a high mountain over-looking the sea and full of caves, wherein dwelt a tribe of blacks, clad in hides, with burnooses also of hide and speaking an unknown tongue. When they saw the troops they were startled like shying steeds and fled into the caverns, whilst their women and children stood at the cave-doors, looking on the strangers. "Oh Shaykh Abd al-Samad," asked the Emir, "what are these folk?" and he answered, "They are those whom we seek for the Commander of the Faithful." So they dismounted and setting down their loads, pitched their tents; whereupon, almost before they had done, down came the King of the blacks from the mountain and drew near the camp. Now he understood the Arabic tongue; so, when he came to the Emir he saluted him with the salam and Musa returned his greeting and entreated him with honour. Then quoth he to the Emir, "Are ye men or Jinn?" "Well, we are men," quoth Musa; "but doubtless ye are Jinn, to judge by your dwelling apart in this mountain which is cut off from mankind, and by your inordinate bulk." "Nay," rejoined the black; "we also are children of Adam, of the lineage of Ham, son of Noah (with whom be peace!), and this sea is known as Al-Karkar." Asked Musa, "O King, what is your religion and what worship ye?"; and he answered, saying, "We worship the God of the heavens and our religion is that of Mohammed, whom Allah bless and preserve!" "And how came ye by the knowledge of this," questioned the Emir, "seeing that no prophet was inspired to visit this country?" "Know, Emir," replied the King, "that there appeared to us whilere from out the sea a man, from whom issued a light that illumined the horizons and he cried out, in a voice which was heard of men far and near, saying:—O children of Ham, reverence to Him who seeth and is not seen and say ye, There is no god but *the* God, and Mohammed is the messenger of God! And he added:—I am Abu al-Abbas al-

Khizr. Before this we were wont to worship one another, but he summoned us to the service of the Lord of all creatures; and he taught us to repeat these words, There is no god save *the* God alone, who hath for partner none, and His is the kingdom and His is the praise. He giveth life and death and He over all things is Almighty. Nor do we draw near unto Allah (be He exalted and extolled!) except with these words, for we know none other; but every eve before Friday[45] we see a light upon the face of earth and we hear a voice saying, Holy and glorious, Lord of the Angels and the Spirit! What He willeth is, and what He willeth not, is not. Every boon is of His grace and there is neither Majesty nor is there Might save in Allah, the Glorious, the Great! But ye," quoth the King, "who and what are ye and what bringeth you to this land?" Quoth Musa, "We are officers of the Sovereign of Al-Islam, the Commander of the Faithful, Abd al-Malik bin Marwan, who hath heard tell of the lord Solomon, son of David (on whom be peace!) and of that which the Most High bestowed upon him of supreme dominion; how he held sway over Jinn and beast and bird and was wont when he was wroth with one of the Marids, to shut him in a cucurbite of brass and, stopping its mouth on him with lead, whereon he impressed his seal-ring, to cast him into the sea of Al-Karkar. Now we have heard tell that this sea is nigh your land; so the Commander of the Faithful hath sent us hither, to bring him some of these cucurbites, that he may look thereon and solace himself with their sight. Such, then, is our case and what we seek of thee, O King, and we desire that thou further us in the accomplishment of our errand commanded by the Commander of the Faithful." "With love and gladness," replied the black King, and carrying them to the guest-house, entreated them with the utmost honour and furnished them with all they needed, feeding them upon fish. They abode thus three days, when he bade his divers fetch from out the sea some of the vessels of Solomon. So they dived and brought up twelve cucurbites, whereat the Emir and the Shaykh and all the company rejoiced in the accomplishment of the Caliph's need. Then Musa gave the King of the blacks many and great gifts; and he, in turn, made him a present of the wonders of the deep, being fishes in human form,[46] saying "Your entertainment these three days hath been of the meat of these fish." Quoth the Emir, "Needs must we carry some of these to the Caliph, for the sight of them will please him more than the cucurbites of Solomon." Then they took leave of the black King and, setting out on their homeward journey, travelled till they came to Damascus, where Musa went in to the Commander of the Faithful and told him all that he had sighted and heard of verses and legends and instances, together with the manner of the death of Talib bin Sahl; and the Caliph said, "Would I had been with you, that I might have seen what you saw!" Then he took the brazen vessels and opened them, cucurbite after cucurbite, whereupon the devils came forth of them, saying, "We repent, O Prophet of Allah! Never again will we return to the like of this thing; no never!" And the Caliph marvelled at this. As for the daughters of the deep presented to them by the black King, they made them cisterns of planks, full of water, and laid them therein; but they died of the great heat. Then the Caliph sent for the spoils of the Brazen City and divided them among the Faithful, saying, "Never gave Allah unto any the like of that which he bestowed upon Solomon David-son!" Thereupon the Emir Musa sought leave of him to appoint his son Governor of the Province in his stead, that he might betake himself to the Holy City of Jerusalem, there to worship Allah. So the Commander of the Faithful invested his son Harun with the government and Musa repaired to the Glorious and Holy City, where he died. This, then, is all that hath come down to us of the story of the City of Brass, and God is All-knowing!—Now (continued Shahrazad) I have another tale to tell anent

THE LADY AND
HER FIVE SUITORS.[1]

A woman of the daughters of the merchants was married to a man who was a great traveller. It chanced once that he set out for a far country and was absent so long that his wife, for pure ennui, fell in love with a handsome young man of the sons of the merchants, and they loved each other with exceeding love. One day, the youth quarrelled with another man, who lodged a complaint against him with the Chief of Police, and he cast him into prison. When the news came to the merchant's wife his mistress, she well-nigh lost her wits; then she arose and donning her richest clothes repaired to the house of the Chief of Police. She saluted him and presented a written petition to this purport:—"He thou hast clapped in jail is my brother, such and such, who fell out with such an one; and those who testified against him bore false witness. He hath been wrongfully imprisoned, and I have none other to come in to me nor to provide for my support; therefore I beseech thee of thy grace to release him." When the magistrate had read the paper, he cast his eyes on her and fell in love with her forthright; so he said to her, "Go into the houses till I bring him before me; then I will send for thee and thou shalt take him." "O my lord," replied she, "I have none to protect me save Almighty Allah!: I am a stranger and may not enter any man's abode." Quoth the Wali, "I will not let him go, except thou come to my home and I take my will of thee." Rejoined she, "If it must be so, thou must needs come to my lodging and sit and sleep the siesta and rest the whole day there." "And where is thy abode?" asked he; and she answered, "In such a place," and appointed him for such a time. Then she went out from him, leaving his heart taken with love of her, and she repaired to the Kazi of the city, to whom she said, "O our lord the Kazi!" He exclaimed, "Yes!" and she continued, "Look into my case, and thy reward be with Allah the Most High!" Quoth he, "Who hath wronged thee?" and quoth she, "O my lord, I have a brother and I have none but that one, and it is on his account that I come to thee; because the Wali hath imprisoned him for a criminal and men have borne false witness against him that he is a wrong-doer; and I beseech thee to intercede for him with the Chief of Police." When the Kazi looked on her, he fell in love with her forthright and said to her, "Enter the house and rest awhile with my handmaids whilst I send to the Wali to release thy brother. If I knew the money-fine which is upon him, I would pay it out of my own purse, so I may have my desire of thee, for thou pleasest me with thy sweet speech." Quoth she, "If thou, O my lord, do thus, we must not blame others." Quoth he, "An thou wilt not come in, wend thy ways." Then said she, "An thou wilt have it so, O our lord, it will be privier and better in my place than in thine, for here are slave-girls and eunuchs and goers-in and comers-out, and indeed I am a woman who wotteth naught of this fashion; but need compelleth." Asked the Kazi, "And where is thy house?"; and she answered, "In such a place," and appointed him for the same day and time as the Chief of Police. Then she went out from him to the Wazir, to whom she preferred her petition for the release from prison of her brother who was absolutely necessary to her: but he also required her of herself, saying, "Suffer me to have my will of thee and I will set thy brother free." Quoth she, "An thou wilt have it so, be it in my house, for there it will be privier both for me and for thee. It is not far distant and thou knowest that which behoveth us women of cleanliness and adornment." Asked he, "Where is thy house?" "In such a place," answered she and appointed him for the same time as the two others. Then she went out from him to the King of the city and told him her story and sought of him her brother's release. "Who imprisoned him?" enquired he; and she replied, " 'Twas thy Chief of Police." When the King heard her speech, it transpierced his heart with the arrows of love and he bade her enter the palace with him, that he might send to the Kazi and release her brother. Quoth she, "O King, this thing is easy to thee, whether I will or nill; and if the King will indeed have this of me, it is of my good fortune; but, if he come to my house, he will do me the more honour by setting step therein, even as saith the poet:—

> O my friends, have ye seen or have ye heard
> Of his visit whose virtues I hold so high?"

Quoth the King, "We will not cross thee in this." So she appointed him for the same time as the three others, and told him where her house was. Then she left him and betaking herself to a man which was a carpenter, said to him, "I would have thee make me a cabinet with four compartments one above other, each with its door for locking up. Let me know thy hire and I will give it thee." Replied he, "My price will be four dinars; but, O noble lady and well-protected, if thou wilt vouchsafe me thy favours, I will ask nothing of thee." Rejoined she, "An there be no help but that thou have it so, then make thou five compartments with their padlocks;" and she appointed him to bring it exactly on the day required. Said he, "It is well; sit down, O my lady, and I will make it for thee forthright, and after I will come to thee at my leisure." So she sat down by him, whilst he fell to work on the cabinet, and when he had made an end of it she chose to see it at once carried home and set up in the sitting-chamber. Then she took four gowns and carried them to the dyer, who dyed them each of a different colour; after which she applied herself to making ready meat and drink; fruits, flowers and perfumes. Now when the appointed trysting day came, she donned her costliest dress and adorned herself and scented herself, then spread the sitting-room with various kinds of rich carpets and sat down to await who should come. And behold, the Kazi was the first to appear, devancing the rest, and when she saw him, she rose to her feet and kissed the ground before him; then, taking him by the hand, made him sit down by her on the couch and lay with him and fell to jesting and toying with him. By and by, he would have her do his desire, but she said, "O my lord, doff thy clothes and turband and assume this yellow cassock and this head-kerchief,[2] whilst I bring thee meat and drink; and after thou shalt win thy will." So saying, she took his clothes and turband and clad him in the cassock and the kerchief; but hardly had she done this, when lo! there came a knocking at the door. Asked he, "Who is that rapping at the door?" and she answered, "My husband." Quoth the Kazi, "What is to be done, and where shall I go?" Quoth she, "Fear nothing, I will hide thee in this cabinet;" and he, "Do as seemeth good to thee." So she took him by the hand and pushing him into the lowest compartment, locked the door upon him. Then she went to the house-door, where she found the Wali; so she bussed ground before him and taking his hand brought him into the saloon, where she made him sit down and said to him, "O my lord, this house is thy house; this place is thy place, and I am thy handmaid: thou shalt pass all this day with me; wherefore do thou doff thy clothes and don this red gown, for it is a sleeping gown." So she took away his clothes and made him assume the red gown and set on his head an old patched rag she had by her; after which she sat by him on the divan and she sported with him while he toyed with her awhile, till he put out his hand to her. Whereupon she said to him, "O our lord, this day is thy day and none shall share in it with thee; but first, of thy favour and benevolence, write me an order for my brother's release from gaol that my heart may be at ease." Quoth he, "Hearkening and obedience: on my head and eyes be it!"; and wrote a letter to his treasurer, saying:—"As soon as this communication shall reach thee, do thou set such an one free, without stay or delay; neither answer the bearer a word." Then he sealed it and she took it from him, after which she began to toy again with him on the divan when, behold, some one knocked at the door. He asked, "Who is that?" and she answered, "My husband." "What shall I do?" said he, and she, "Enter this cabinet, till I send him away and return to thee." So she clapped him into the second compartment from the bottom and pad-locked the door on him; and meanwhile the Kazi heard all they said. Then she went to the house-door and opened it, whereupon lo! the Wazir entered. She bussed the ground before him and received him with all honour and worship, saying, "O my lord, thou exaltest us by thy com-ing to our house; Allah never deprive us of the light of thy countenance!" Then she seated him on the divan and said to him, "O my lord, doff thy heavy dress and turband and don these lighter vestments." So he put off his clothes and turband and she clad him in a blue cassock and a tall red bonnet, and said to him, "Erst thy garb was that of the Wazirate; so leave it to its own time and don this light gown, which is better fitted for carousing and making merry and sleep." Thereupon she began to play with him and he with her, and he would have done his desire of her; but she put him off, saying, "O my lord, this shall not fail us." As they were talking there came a knocking at the door, and the Wazir asked her, "Who is that?": to which she answered, "My husband." Quoth he, "What is to be done?" Quoth she, "Enter this cabinet, till I get rid of him and come back to thee and fear thou nothing." So she put him in the third compartment and locked the door on him, after which she went out and opened the house-door when lo and behold! in came the King. As soon as she saw him she kissed ground before him, and taking him by the hand, led him into the saloon and seated him on the divan at the upper end. Then said she to him, "Verily, O King, thou dost us high honour, and if we brought thee to gift the world and all that therein is, it would not be worth a single one of thy steps us-wards." And when he had taken his seat upon the divan she said, "Give me leave to speak one word." "Say what thou wilt," answered he, and she said, "O my lord, take thine ease and doff thy dress and turband." Now his clothes were worth a thousand dinars; and when he put them off she clad him in a patched gown, worth at the very most ten dirhams, and fell to talking and jesting with him; all this while the folk in the cabinet hearing everything that passed, but not daring to say a word. Presently, the King put his hand to her neck and sought to do his desire of her; when she said, "This thing shall not fail us, but I had first promised myself to entertain thee in this sitting-chamber, and I have that which shall content thee." Now as they were speaking, some one knocked at the door and he asked her, "Who is that?" "My husband," answered she, and he, "Make him go away of his own good will, or I will fare forth to him and send him away perforce." Replied she, "Nay, O my lord, have patience till I send him away by my skilful contrivance." "And I, how shall I do!" enquired the King; whereupon she took him by the hand and making him enter the fourth compartment of the cabinet, locked it upon him. Then she went out and opened the house door when behold, the carpenter entered and saluted her. Quoth she, "What manner of thing is this cabinet thou hast made me?" "What aileth it, O my lady?" asked he, and she answered, "The top compartment is too strait." Rejoined he, "Not so;" and she, "Go in thyself and see; it is not wide enough for thee." Quoth he, "It is wide enough for four," and entered the fifth compartment, whereupon she locked the door on him. Then she took the letter of the Chief of Police and carried it to the treasurer who, having read and understood it, kissed it and delivered her lover to her. She told him all she had done and he said, "And how shall we act now?" She answered, "We will remove hence to another city, for after this work there is no tarrying for us here." So the twain packed up what goods they had and, loading them on camels, set out forthright for another city. Meanwhile, the five abode each in his compartment of the cabinet without eating or drinking three whole days, during which time they held their water until at last the carpenter could retain his no longer; so he staled on the King's head, and the King urined on the Wazir's head, and the Wazir piddled on the Wali and the Wali pissed on the head of the Kazi; whereupon the Judge cried out and said, "What nastiness[3] is this? Doth not what strait we are in suffice us, but you must make water upon us?" The Chief of Police recognised the Kazi's voice and answered, saying aloud, "Allah increase thy reward, O Kazi!" And when the Kazi heard him, he knew him for the Wali. Then the Chief of Police lifted up his voice and said, "What means this nastiness?" and the Wazir answered, saying, "Allah increase thy reward, O Wali!" whereupon he knew him to be the Minister. Then the Wazir lifted up his voice and said, "What means this nastiness?" But when the King heard and recognised his Minister's voice, he held his peace and concealed his affair. Then said the Wazir, "May Allah damn[4] this woman for her dealing with us! She hath brought hither all the Chief Officers of the state, except the King." Quoth the King, "Hold your peace, for I was the first to fall into the toils of this lewd strumpet." Whereat cried the carpenter, "And I, what have I done? I made her a cabinet for four gold pieces, and when I came to seek my hire, she tricked me into entering this compartment and locked the door on me." And they fell to talking with one another, diverting the King and doing away his chagrin. Presently the neighbours came up to the house and, seeing it deserted, said one to other, "But yesterday our neighbour, the wife of such an one, was in it; but now no sound is to be heard therein nor is soul to be seen. Let us break open the doors and see how the case stands, lest it come to the ears of the Wali or the King and we be cast into prison and regret not doing this thing before." So they broke open the doors and entered the saloon, where they saw a large wooden cabinet and heard men within groaning for hunger and thirst. Then said one of them, "Is there a Jinni in this cabinet?" and his fellow, "Let us heap fuel about it and burn it with fire." When the Kazi heard this, he bawled out to them, "Do it not!" And they said to one another, "Verily the Jinn make believe to be mortals and speak with men's voices." Thereupon the Kazi repeated somewhat of the Sublime Koran and said to the neighbours, "Draw near to the cabinet wherein we are." So they drew near, and he said, "I am so and so the Kazi, and ye are such an one and such an one, and we are here a company." Quoth the neighbours, "Who brought you here?" And he told them the whole case from beginning to end. Then they fetched a carpenter, who opened the five doors and let out Kazi, Wazir, Wali, King and carpenter in their queer disguises; and each, when he saw how the others were accoutred, fell a-laughing at them. Now she had taken away all their clothes; so every one of them sent to his people for fresh clothes and put them on and went out, covering himself therewith from the sight of the folk. Consider, therefore, what a trick this woman played off upon the folk! And I have heard tell also a tale of

Judar[1] and His Brethren.

There was once a man and a merchant named Omar and he had for issue three sons, the eldest called Sálim, the youngest Judar, and the cadet Salím. He reared them all till they came to man's estate, but the youngest he loved more than his brothers, who, seeing this, waxed jealous of Judar and hated him. Now when their father, who was a man shotten in years, saw that his two eldest sons hated their brother, he feared lest after his death trouble should befal him from them. So he assembled a company of his kinsfolk, together with divers men of learning and property-distributors of the Kazi's court, and bidding bring all his monies and cloth, said to them, "O folk, divide ye this money and stuff into four portions according to the law." They did so, and he gave one part to each of his sons and kept the fourth himself, saying, "This was my good and I have divided it among them in my lifetime; and this that I have kept shall be for my wife, their mother, wherewithal to provide for her subsistence whenas she shall be a widow." A little while after this he died, and neither of the two elder brothers was content with his share,[2] but sought more of Judar, saying, "Our father's wealth is in thy hands." So he appealed to the judges; and the Moslems who had been present at the partition came and bore witness of that which they knew, wherefore the judge forbade them from one another; but Judar and his brothers wasted much money in bribes to him. After this, the twain left him awhile; presently, however, they began again to plot against him and he appealed a second time to the magistrate, who once more decided in his favour; but all three lost much money which went to the judges. Nevertheless Sálim and Salím forbore not to seek his hurt and to carry the case from court to court,[3] he and they losing till they had given all their good for food to the oppressors and they became poor, all three. Then the two elder brothers went to their mother and flouted her and beat her, and seizing her money drave her away. So she betook herself to her son Judar and told him how his brothers had dealt with her and fell to cursing the twain. Said he, "O my mother, do not curse them, for Allah will requite each of them according to his deed. But, O mother mine, see, I am become poor, and so are my brethren, for strife occasioneth loss ruin-rife, and we have striven amain, and fought, I and they, before the judges, and it hath profited us naught: nay, we have wasted all our father left us and are disgraced among the folk by reason of our testimony one against other. Shall I then contend with them anew on thine account and shall we appeal to the judges? This may not be! Rather do thou take up thine abode with me, and the scone I eat I will share with thee. Do thou pray for me and Allah will give me the means of thine alimony. Leave them to receive of the Almighty the recompense of their deed, and console thyself with the saying of the poet who said:—

> If a fool oppress thee bear patiently;
> And from Time expect thy revenge to see:
> Shun tyranny; for if mount oppressed
> A mount, 'twould be shattered by tyranny."

And he soothed and comforted her till she consented and took up her dwelling with him. Then he gat him a net and went a-fishing every day in the river or the banks about Bulak and old Cairo or some other place in which there was water; and one day he would earn ten coppers,⁴ another twenty and another thirty, which he spent upon his mother and himself, and they ate well and drank well. But, as for his brothers, they plied no craft and neither sold nor bought; misery and ruin and overwhelming calamity entered their houses and they wasted that which they had taken from their mother and became of the wretched naked beggars. So at times they would come to their mother, humbling themselves before her exceedingly and complaining to her of hunger; and she (a mother's heart being pitiful) would give them some mouldy, sour-smelling bread or, if there were any meat cooked the day before, she would say to them, "Eat it quick and go ere your brother come; for 'twould be grievous to him and he would harden his heart against me, and ye would disgrace me with him." So they would eat in haste and go. One day among days they came in to their mother, and she set cooked meat and bread before them. As they were eating, behold, in came their brother Judar, at whose sight the parent was put to shame and confusion, fearing lest he should be wroth with her; and she bowed her face earthwards abashed before her son. But he smiled in their faces, saying, "Welcome, O my brothers! A blessed day!⁵ How comes it that ye visit me this blessed day?" Then he embraced them both and entreated them lovingly, saying to them, "I thought not that ye would have left me desolate by your absence nor that ye would have forborne to come and visit me and your mother." Said they, "By Allah, O our brother, we longed sore for thee and naught withheld us but abashment because of what befel between us and thee; but indeed we have repented much. 'Twas Satan's doing, the curse of Allah the Most High be upon him! And now we have no blessing but thyself and our mother." And

his mother exclaimed, "Allah whiten thy face, and increase
thy prosperity, for thou art the most generous of us all, O
my son!" Then he said "Welcome to you both! Abide with
me; for the Lord is bountiful and good aboundeth with
me." So he made peace with them, and they supped and
nighted with him; and next morning, after they had broken
their fast, Judar shouldered his net and went out, trusting in The Opener[6] whilst the two others also went forth
and were absent till midday, when they returned and their
mother set the noon-meal before them. At nightfall Judar
came home, bearing meat and greens, and they abode on
this wise a month's space, Judar catching fish and selling it
and spending their price on his mother and his brothers,
and these eating and frolicking till, one day, it chanced he
went down to the riverbank and throwing his net, brought
it up empty. He cast it a second time, but again it came up
empty and he said to himself, "No fish in this place!" So he
removed to another and threw the net there, but without
avail. And he ceased not to remove from place to place till
nightfall, but caught not a single sprat[7] and said to himself,
"Wonderful! Hath the fish fled the river or what?" Then he
shouldered the net and made for home, chagrined, concerned, feeling for his mother and brothers and knowing
not how he should feed them that night. Presently, he came
to a baker's oven and saw the folk crowding for bread, with
silver in their hands, whilst the baker took no note of them.
So he stood there sighing, and the baker said to him, "Welcome to thee, O Judar! Dost thou want bread?" But he was
silent and the baker continued, "An thou have no dirhams,
take thy sufficiency and thou shalt get credit." So Judar
said, "Give me ten coppers' worth of bread and take this
net in pledge." Rejoined the baker, "Nay, my poor fellow,
the net is thy gate of earning thy livelihood, and if I take it
from thee, I shall close up against thee the door of thy subsistence. Take thee ten Nusfs' worth of bread and take
these other ten, and to-morrow bring me fish for the
twenty." "On my head and eyes be it!" quoth Judar and took
the bread and money saying, "To-morrow the Lord will

dispel the trouble of my case and will provide me the means of acquittance." Then he bought meat and vegetables and carried them home to his mother, who cooked them and they supped and went to bed. Next morning he arose at daybreak and took the net, and his mother said to him, "Sit down and break thy fast." But he said, "Do thou and my brothers breakfast," and went down to the river about Bulak where he ceased not to cast once, twice, thrice; and to shift about all day, without aught falling to him, till the hour of mid-afternoon prayer, when he shouldered his net and went away sore dejected. His way led him perforce by the booth of the baker who when he saw him, counted out to him the loaves and the money, saying, "Come, take it and go; an it be not today, 'twill be tomorrow." Judar would have excused himself, but the baker said to him, "Go! There needeth no excuse; an thou had netted aught, it would be with thee; so seeing thee empty-handed, I knew thou hadst gotten naught; and if tomorrow thou have no better luck, come and take bread and be not abashed, for I will give thee credit." So Judar took the bread and money and went home. On the third day also he sallied forth and fished from tank to tank until the time of afternoon-prayer, but caught nothing; so he went to the baker and took the bread and silver as usual. On this wise he did seven days running, till he became disheartened and said in himself, "To-day I go to the Lake Karun."[8] So he went thither and was about to cast his net, when there came up to him unawares a Maghribi, a Moor, clad in splendid attire and riding a she-mule with a pair of gold-embroidered saddle-bags on her back and all her trappings also orfrayed. The Moor alighted and said to him, "Peace be upon thee, O Judar, O son of Omar!" "And on thee likewise be peace, O my lord the pilgrim!" replied the fisherman. Quoth the Maghribi, "O Judar, I have need of thee and, given thou obey me, thou shalt get great good and shalt be my companion and manage my affairs for me." Quoth Judar, "O my lord, tell me what is in thy mind and I will obey thee, without demur." Said the Moor, "Repeat

the Fatihah, the Opening Chapter of the Koran."[9] So he recited it with him and the Moor bringing out a silken cord,
said to Judar, "Pinion my elbows behind me with this cord,
as fast as fast can be, and cast me into the lake; then wait a
little while; and, if thou see me put forth my hands above
the water, raising them high ere my body show, cast thy net
over me and drag me out in haste; but if thou see me come
up feet foremost, then know that I am dead; in which case
do thou leave me and take the mule and saddle-bags and
carry them to the merchants' bazar, where thou wilt find a
Jew by name Shamayah. Give him the mule and he will
give thee an hundred dinars, which do thou take and go thy
ways and keep the matter secret with all secrecy." So Judar
tied his arms tightly behind his back and he kept saying,
"Tie tighter." Then said he, "Push me till I fall into the
lake:" so he pushed him in and he sank. Judar stood waiting
some time till, behold, the Moor's feet appeared above the
water, whereupon he knew that he was dead. So he left him
and drove the mule to the bazar, where seated on a stool at
the door of his storehouse he saw the Jew who spying the
mule, cried, "In very sooth the man hath perished," adding,
"and naught undid him but covetise." Then he took the
mule from Judar and gave him an hundred dinars, charging
him to keep the matter secret. So Judar went and bought
what bread he needed, saying to the baker, "Take this
gold piece!"; and the man summed up what was due to him
and said, "I still owe thee two days bread." Judar replied,
"Good," and went on to the butcher, to whom he gave a
gold piece and took meat, saying, "Keep the rest of the
dinar on account." Then he bought vegetables and going
home, found his brothers importuning their mother for
victual, whilst she cried, "Have patience till your brother
come home, for I have naught." So he went in to them and
said, "Take and eat;" and they fell on the food like cannibals. Then he gave his mother the rest of his gold saying,
"If my brothers come to thee, give them wherewithal to
buy food and eat in my absence." He slept well that night
and next morning he took his net and going down to Lake

Karun stood there and was about to cast his net, when behold, there came up to him a second Maghribi, riding on a she-mule more handsomely accoutred than he of the day before and having with him a pair of saddle-bags of which each pocket contained a casket. "Peace be with thee, O Judar!" said the Moor: "And with thee be peace, O my lord the pilgrim!" replied Judar. Asked the Moor, "Did there come to thee yesterday a Moor riding on a mule like this of mine?" Hereat Judar was alarmed and answered, "I saw none," fearing lest the other say, "Whither went he?" and if he replied, "He was drowned in the lake," that haply he should charge him with having drowned him; wherefore he could not but deny. Rejoined the Moor, "Hark-ye, O unhappy![10] this was my brother, who is gone before me." Judar persisted, "I know naught of him." Then the Moor enquired, "Didst thou not bind his arms behind him and throw him into the lake, and did he not say to thee:—If my hands appear above the water first, cast thy net over me and drag me out in haste; but, if my feet show first, know that I am dead and carry the mule to the Jew Shamayah, who shall give thee an hundred dinars." Quoth Judar, "Since thou knowest all this why and wherefore dost thou question me?"; and quoth the Moor, "I would have thee do with me as thou didst with my brother." Then he gave him a silken cord, saying, "Bind my hands behind me and throw me in, and if I fare as did my brother, take the mule to the Jew and he will give thee other hundred dinars." Said Judar, "Come on;" so he came and he bound him and pushed him into the lake, where he sank. Then Judar sat watching and after awhile, his feet appeared above the water and the fisher said, "He is dead and damned! Inshallah, may Maghribis come to me every day, and I will pinion them and push them in and they shall die; and I will content me with an hundred dinars for each dead man." Then he took the mule to the Jew, who seeing him asked, "The other is dead?" Answered Judar, "May thy head live!"; and the Jew said, "This is the reward of the covetous!" Then he took the mule and gave Judar an hundred dinars, with which he returned to his mother. "O my son," said she, "whence hast thou this?" So he told her, and she said, "Go not again to Lake Karun, indeed I fear for thee from the Moors." Said he, "O my mother, I do but cast them in by their own wish, and what am I to do? This craft bringeth me an hundred dinars a day and I return speedily; wherefore, by Allah, I will not leave going to Lake Karun, till the trace of the Magharibah[11] is cut off and not one of them is left." So, on the morrow which was the third day, he went down to the lake and stood there, till there came up a third Moor, riding on a mule with saddle-bags and still more richly accoutred than the first two, who said to him, "Peace be with thee, O Judar, O son of Omar!" And the fisherman saying in himself, "How comes it that they all know me?" returned his salute. Asked the Maghribi, "Have any Moors passed by here?" "Two," answered Judar. "Whither went they?" enquired the Moor, and Judar replied, "I pinioned their hands behind them and cast them into the lake, where they were drowned, and the same fate is in store for thee." The Moor laughed and rejoined, saying, "O unhappy! every life hath its term appointed." Then he alighted and gave the fisherman the silken cord, saying, "Do with me, O Judar, as thou didst with them." Said Judar, "Put thy hands behind thy back, that I may pinion thee, for I am in haste, and time flies." So he put his hands behind him and Judar tied him up and cast him in. Then he waited awhile; presently the Moor thrust both hands forth of the water and called out to him, saying, "Ho, good fellow, cast out thy net!" So Judar threw the net over him and drew him ashore, and lo! in each hand he held a fish as red as coral. Quoth the Moor, "Bring me the two caskets that are in the saddlebags." So Judar brought them and opened them to him, and he laid in each casket a fish and shut them up. Then he pressed Judar to his bosom and kissed him on the right cheek and the left, saying, "Allah save thee from all stress! By the Almighty, hadst thou not cast the net over me and pulled me out, I should have kept hold of these two fishes till I sank and was drowned, for I could not get ashore of myself." Quoth Judar, "O my lord the pilgrim, Allah upon thee, tell me the true history of the two drowned men and the truth anent these two fishes and the Jew." The Maghribi answered:—Know, O Judar, that these drowned men were my two brothers, by name Abd al-Salam and Abd al-Ahad. My own name is Abd al-Samad, and the Jew also is our brother; his name is Abd al-Rahim and he is no Jew, but a true believer of the Maliki school. Our father, whose name was Abd al-Wadud,¹² taught us magic and the art of solving mysteries and bringing hoards to light, and we applied ourselves thereto, till we compelled the Ifrits and Marids of the Jinn to do us service. By-and-by, our sire died and left us much wealth, and we divided amongst us his treasures and talismans, till we came to the books, when we fell out over a volume called "The Fables of the Ancients," whose like is not in the world, nor can its price be paid of any, nor is its value to be evened with gold and jewels; for in it are particulars of all the hidden hoards of the earth and the solution of every secret. Our father was wont to make use of this book, of which we had some small matter by heart, and each of us desired to possess it, that he might acquaint himself with what was therein. Now when we fell out there was in our company an old man by name Cohen Al-Abtan,¹³ who had reared our sire and taught him divination and gramarye, and he said to us, "Bring me the book." So we gave it to him and he continued:—Ye are my son's sons, and it may not be that I should wrong any of you. So whoso is minded to have the volume, let him address himself to achieve the treasure of Al-Shamardal¹⁴ and bring me the celestial planisphere and the Kohl-phial and the seal-ring and the sword. For the ring hath a Marid that serveth it called Al-Ra'ad al-Kasif;¹⁵ and whoso hath possession thereof, neither King nor Sultan may prevail against him; and if he will, he may therewith make himself master of the earth, in all the length and breadth thereof. As for the brand, if its bearer draw it and brandish it against an army, the army will be put to the rout; and if he say the while,

"Slay yonder host," there will come forth of that sword lightning and fire, that will kill the whole many. As for the planisphere, its possessor hath only to turn its face toward any country, east or west, with whose sight he hath a mind to solace himself, and therein he will see that country and its people, as they were between his hands and he sitting in his place; and if he be wroth with a city and have a mind to burn it, he hath but to face the planisphere towards the sun's disc, saying, "Let such a city be burnt," and that city will be consumed with fire. As for the Kohl-phial, whoso pencilleth his eyes therefrom, he shall espy all the treasures of the earth. And I make this condition with you which is that whoso faileth to hit upon the boards shall forfeit his right; and that none save he who shall achieve the treasure and bring me the four precious things which be therein shall have any claim to take this book. So we all agreed to this condition, and he continued, "O my sons, know that the treasure of Al-Shamardal is under the commandment of the sons of the Red King, and your father told me that he had himself essayed to open the treasure, but could not; for the sons of the Red King fled from him into the land of Egypt and took refuge in a lake there, called Lake Karun, whither he pursued them, but could not prevail over them, by reason of their stealing into that lake, which was guarded by a spell. So your father returned empty-handed and unable to win to his wish; and after failing he complained to me of his ill-success, whereupon I drew him an astrological figure and found that the treasure could be achieved only by means of a young fisherman of Cairo, hight Judar bin Omar, the place of foregathering with whom was at Lake Karun, for that he should be the means of capturing the sons of the Red King and that the charm would not be dissolved, save if he should bind the hands of the treasure-seeker behind him and cast him into the lake, there to do battle with the sons of the Red King. And he whose lot it was to succeed would lay hands upon them; but, if it were not destined to him he should perish and his feet appear above water. As for him who was

successful, his hands would show first, whereupon it behoved that Judar should cast the net over him and draw
him ashore." Now quoth my brothers Abd al-Salam and
Abd al-Ahad, "We will wend and make trial, although we
perish;" and quoth I, "And I also will go;" but my brother
Abd al-Rahim (he whom thou sawest in the habit of a Jew)
said, "I have no mind to this." Thereupon we agreed with
him that he should repair to Cairo in the disguise of a Jewish merchant, so that if one of us perished in the lake, he
might take his mule and saddle-bags and give the bearer
an hundred dinars. The first that came to thee the sons
of the Red King slew, and so did they with my second
brother; but against me they could not prevail and I laid
hands on them. Cried Judar, "And where is thy catch?"
Asked the Moor, "Didst thou not see me shut them in the
caskets?" "Those were fishes," said Judar. "Nay," answered
the Maghribi, "they are Ifrits in the guise of fish. But, O
Judar," continued he, "thou must know that the treasure
can be opened only by thy means: so say, wilt thou do my
bidding and go with me to the city Fez and Mequinez[16]
where we will open the treasure?; and after I will give thee
what thou wilt and thou shalt ever be my brother in the
bond of Allah and return to thy family with a joyful heart."
Said Judar, "O my lord the pilgrim, I have on my neck a
mother and two brothers, whose provider I am; and if I
go with thee, who shall give them bread to eat?" Replied
the Moor, "This is an idle excuse! if it be but a matter of
expenditure, I will give thee a thousand ducats for thy
mother, wherewith she may provide herself till thou come
back; and indeed thou shalt return before the end of four
months." So when Judar heard mention of the thousand
dinars, he said, "Here with them, O Pilgrim, and I am thy
man," and the Moor, pulling out the money, gave it to him,
whereupon he carried it to his mother and told her what
had passed between them, saying, "Take these thousand
dinars and expend of them upon thyself and my brothers,
whilst I journey to Marocco with the Moor, for I shall
be absent four months, and great good will betide me; so

bless me, O my mother!" Answered she, "O my son, thou desolatest me and I fear for thee." "O my mother," rejoined he, "no harm can befal him who is in Allah's keeping, and the Maghribi is a man of worth;" and he went on to praise his condition to her. Quoth she, "Allah incline his heart to thee! Go with him, O my son; peradventure, he will give thee somewhat." So he took leave of his mother and rejoined the Moor Abd al-Samad, who asked him, "Hast thou consulted thy mother?" "Yes," answered Judar; "and she blessed me." "Then mount behind me," said the Maghribi. So Judar mounted the mule's crupper and they rode on from noon till the time of mid-afternoon prayer, when the fisherman was an-hungered; but seeing no victual with the Moor, said to him, "O my lord the pilgrim, belike thou hast forgotten to bring us aught to eat by the way?" Asked the Moor, "Art thou hungry?" and Judar answered, "Yes." So Abd al-Samad alighted and made Judar alight and take down the saddle-bags;[17] then he said to him, "What wilt thou have, O my brother?" "Anything." "Allah upon thee, tell me what thou hast a mind to." "Bread and cheese." "O my poor fellow! bread and cheese besit thee not; wish for something good." "Just now everything is good to me." "Dost thou like nice browned chicken?" "Yes!" "Dost thou like rice and honey?" "Yes!" And the Moor went on to ask him if he liked this dish and that dish till he had named four-and-twenty kinds of meats; and Judar thought to himself, "He must be daft! Where are all these dainties to come from, seeing he hath neither cook nor kitchen? But I'll say to him, 'Tis enough!" So he cried, "That will do: thou makest me long for all these meats, and I see nothing." Quoth the Moor, "Thou art welcome, O Judar!" and, putting his hand into the saddle-bags, pulled out a golden dish containing two hot browned chickens. Then he thrust his hand a second time and drew out a golden dish, full of kabobs;[18] nor did he stint taking out dishes from saddle-bags, till he had brought forth the whole of the four-and-twenty kinds he had named, whilst Judar looked on. Then said the Moor, "Fall to, poor fellow!", and Judar said to him,

"O my lord, thou carriest in yonder saddle-bags kitchen and kitcheners!" The Moor laughed and replied, "These are magical saddle-bags and have a servant, who would bring us a thousand dishes an hour, if we called for them." Quoth Judar, "By Allah, a meet thing in saddle-bags!" Then they ate their fill and threw away what was left; after which the Moor replaced the empty dishes in the saddle-bags and putting in his hand, drew out an ewer. They drank and making the Wuzu-ablution, prayed the mid-afternoon prayer; after which Abd al-Samad replaced the ewer and the two caskets in the saddle-bags and throwing them over the mule's back, mounted and cried, "Up with thee and let us be off," presently adding, "O Judar, knowest thou how far we have come since we left Cairo?" "Not I, by Allah," replied he, and Abd al-Samad, "We have come a whole month's journey." Asked Judar, "And how is that?"; and the Moor answered, "Know, O Judar, that this mule under us is a Marid of the Jinn who every day performeth a year's journey; but, for thy sake, she hath gone an easier pace." Then they set out again and fared on westwards till night-fall, when they halted and the Maghribi brought out supper from the saddle-bags, and in like manner, in the morning, he took forth wherewithal to break their fast. So they rode on four days, journeying till midnight and then alighting and sleeping until morning, when they fared on again; and all that Judar had a mind to, he sought of the Moor, who brought it out of the saddle-bags. On the fifth day, they arrived at Fez and Mequinez and entered the city, where all who met the Maghribi saluted him and kissed his hands; and he continued riding through the streets, till he came to a certain door, at which he knocked, whereupon it opened and out came a girl like the moon, to whom said he, "O my daughter, O Rahmah,[19] open us the upper chamber." "On my head and eyes, O my papa!" replied she and went in, swaying her hips to and fro with a graceful and swimming gait like a thirsting gazelle, movements that ravished Judar's reason, and he said, "This is none other than a King's daughter." So she opened the upper chamber, and the Moor, taking the saddle-bags from the mule's back, said, "Go, and God bless thee!" when lo! the earth clove asunder and swallowing the mule, closed up again as before. And Judar said, "O Protector! praised be Allah, who hath kept us in safety on her back!" Quoth the Maghribi, "Marvel not, O Judar. I told thee that the mule was an Ifrit; but come with us into the upper chamber." So they went up into it, and Judar was amazed at the profusion of rich furniture and pendants of gold and silver and jewels and other rare and precious things which he saw there. As soon as they were seated, the Moor bade Rahmah bring him a certain bundle[20] and opening it, drew out a dress worth a thousand dinars, which he gave to Judar, saying, "Don this dress, O Judar, and welcome to thee!" So Judar put it on and became a fair ensample of the Kings of the West. Then the Maghribi laid the saddle-bags before him, and, putting in his hand, pulled out dish after dish, till they had before them a tray of forty kinds of meat, when he said to Judar, "Come near, O my master! eat and excuse us for that we know not what meats thou desirest; but tell us what thou hast a mind to, and we will set it before thee without delay." Replied Judar, "By Allah, O my lord the pilgrim, I love all kinds of meat and unlove none; so ask me not of aught, but bring all that cometh to thy thought, for save eating to do I have nought." After this he tarried twenty days with the Moor, who clad him in new clothes every day, and all this time they ate from the saddle-bags; for the Maghribi bought neither meat nor bread nor aught else, nor cooked, but brought everything out of the bags, even to various sorts of fruit. On the twenty-first day, he said, "O Judar, up with thee; this is the day appointed for opening the hoard of Al-Shamardal." So he rose and they went afoot[21] without the city, where they found two slaves, each holding a she-mule. The Moor mounted one beast and Judar the other, and they ceased not riding till noon, when they came to a stream of running water, on whose banks Abd al-Samad alighted saying, "Dismount, O Judar!" Then he signed with his hand to the slaves and said, "To it!" So they took the mules and going each his own way, were absent awhile, after which they returned, one bearing a tent, which he pitched, and the other carpets, which he spread in the tent and laid mattresses, pillows and cushions there-around. Then one of them brought the caskets containing the two fishes; and another fetched the saddle-bags; whereupon the Maghribi arose and said, "Come, O Judar!" So Judar followed him into the tent and sat down beside him; and he brought out dishes of meat from the saddle-bags and they ate the undurn meal. Then the Moor took the two caskets and conjured over them both, whereupon there came from within voices that said, "Adsumus, at thy service, O diviner of the world! Have mercy upon us!" and called aloud for aid. But he ceased not to repeat conjurations and they to call for help, till the two caskets flew in sunder, the fragments flying about, and there came forth two men, with pinioned hands saying, "Quarter, O diviner of the world! What wilt thou with us?" Quoth he, "My will is to burn you both with fire, except ye make a covenant with me, to open to me the treasure of Al-Shamardal." Quoth they, "We promise this to thee, and we will open the treasure to thee, so thou produce to us Judar bin Omar, the fisherman, for the hoard may not be opened but by his means, nor can any enter therein save Judar." Cried the Maghribi, "Him of whom ye speak, I have brought, and he is here, listening to you and looking at you." Thereupon they covenanted with him to open the treasure to him, and he released them. Then he brought out a hollow wand and tablets of red carnelian which he laid on the rod; and after this he took a chafing-dish and setting charcoal thereon, blew one breath into it and it kindled forthwith. Presently he brought incense and said, "O Judar, I am now about to begin the necessary conjurations and fumigations, and when I have once begun, I may not speak, or the charm will be naught; so I will teach thee first what thou must do to win thy wish." "Teach me," quoth Judar. "Know," quoth the Moor, "that when I have recited the spell and thrown on the incense, the water will dry up from the river's bed and discover to thee, a golden door, the bigness of the city-gate, with two rings of metal thereon; whereupon do thou go down to the door and knock a light knock and wait awhile; then knock a second time a knock louder than the first and wait another while; after which give three knocks in rapid succession, and thou wilt hear a voice ask:—Who knocketh at the door of the treasure, unknowing how to solve the secrets? Do thou answer:—I am Judar the fisher-man son of Omar; and the door will open and there will come forth a figure with a brand in hand who will say to thee: If thou be that man, stretch forth thy neck, that I may strike off thy head. Then do thou stretch forth thy neck and fear not; for, when he lifts his hand and smites thee with the sword,[22] he will fall down before thee, and in a lit-tle thou wilt see him a body sans soul; and the stroke shall not hurt thee nor shall any harm befal thee; but, if thou gainsay him, he will slay thee. When thou hast undone his enchantment by obedience, enter and go on till thou see another door, at which do thou knock, and there will come forth to thee a horseman riding a mare with a lance on his shoulder and say to thee:—What bringeth thee hither, where none may enter ne man ne Jinni? And he will shake his lance at thee. Bare thy breast to him and he will smite thee and fall down forthright and thou shalt see him a body without a soul; but if thou cross him he will kill thee. Then go on to the third door, whence there will come forth to thee a man with a bow and arrows in his hand and take aim at thee. Bare thy breast to him and he will shoot at thee and fall down before thee, a body without a soul; but if thou oppose him, he will kill thee. Then go on to the fourth door and knock and it shall be opened to thee, when there will come forth to thee a lion huge of bulk which will rush upon thee, opening his mouth and showing he hath a mind to devour thee. Have no fear of him, neither flee from him: but when he cometh to thee, give him thy hand and he will bite at it and fall straightway, nor shall aught of hurt betide thee. Then enter the fifth door, where thou shalt find a black slave, who will say to thee, Who art thou? Say, I am

Judar! and he will answer, If thou be that man, open the sixth door. Then do thou go up to the door and say, O Isa, tell Musa to open the door; whereupon the door will fly open and thou wilt see two dragons, one on the left hand and another on the right, which will open their mouths and fly at thee, both at once. Do thou put forth to them both hands and they will bite each a hand and fall down dead; but an thou resist them, they will slay thee. Then go on to the seventh door and knock, whereupon there will come forth to thee thy mother and say:—Welcome, O my son! Come, that I may greet thee! But do thou reply, Hold off from me and doff thy dress. And she will make answer:— O my son, I am thy mother and I have a claim upon thee for suckling thee and for rearing thee: how then wouldst thou strip me naked? Then do thou say, Except thou put off thy clothes, I will kill thee! and look to thy right where thou wilt see a sword hanging up. Take it and draw it upon her, saying, Strip! whereupon she will wheedle thee and humble herself to thee; but have thou no ruth on her nor be beguiled, and as often as she putteth off aught, say to her, Off with the lave; nor do thou cease to threaten her with death, till she doff all that is upon her and fall down, whereupon the enchantment will be dissolved and the charms undone, and thou wilt be safe as to thy life. Then enter the hall of the treasure, where thou wilt see the gold lying in heaps; but pay no heed to aught thereof, but look to a closet at the upper end of the hall, where thou wilt see a curtain drawn. Draw back the curtain and thou wilt descry the enchanter, Al-Shamardal, lying upon a couch of gold, with something at his head round and shining like the moon, which is the celestial planisphere. He is baldrick'd with the sword; on his finger is the ring and about his neck hangs a chain, to which hangs the Kohl-phial. Bring me the four talismans, and beware lest thou forget aught of that which I have told thee, or thou wilt repent and there will be fear for thee." And he repeated his directions a second and a third and a fourth time, till Judar said, "I have them by heart: but who may face all these enchantments

that thou namest and endure against these mighty terrors?"
Replied the Moor, "O Judar, fear not, for they are semblances without life;" and he went on to hearten him, till
he said, "I put my trust in Allah." Then Abd al-Samad
threw perfumes on the chafing-dish, and addressed himself
to reciting conjurations for a time when, behold, the water
disappeared and uncovered the river-bed and discovered
the door of the treasure, whereupon Judar went down to
the door and knocked. Therewith he heard a voice saying,
"Who knocketh at the door of the treasure, unknowing
how to solve the secrets?" Quoth he, "I am Judar son of
Omar;" whereupon the door opened and there came forth
a figure with a drawn sword, who said to him, "Stretch
forth thy neck." So he stretched forth his neck and the
species smote him and fell down, lifeless. Then he went on
to the second door and did the like, nor did he cease to do
thus, till he had undone the enchantments of the first six
doors and came to the seventh door, whence there issued
forth to him his mother, saying, "I salute thee, O my son!"
He asked, "What art thou?", and she answered, "O my son,
I am thy mother who bare thee nine months and suckled
thee and reared thee." Quoth he, "Put off thy clothes."
Quoth she, "Thou art my son, how wouldst thou strip me
naked?" But he said "Strip, or I will strike off thy head with
this sword;" and he stretched out his hand to the brand and
drew it upon her saying, "Except thou strip, I will slay
thee." Then the strife became long between them and as
often as he redoubled on her his threats, she put off somewhat of her clothes and he said to her, "Doff the rest," with
many menaces; while she removed each article slowly and
kept saying, "O my son, thou hast disappointed my fosterage of thee," till she had nothing left but her petticoat-
trousers. Then said she, "O my son, is thy heart stone? Wilt
thou dishonour me by discovering my shame? Indeed, this
is unlawful, O my son!" And he answered, "Thou sayest
sooth; put not off thy trousers." At once, as he uttered
these words, she cried out, "He hath made default; beat
him!" Whereupon there fell upon him blows like rain-

drops and the servants of the treasure flocked to him and dealt him a tunding which he forgot not in all his days; after which they thrust him forth and threw him down without the treasure and the hoard-doors closed of themselves, whilst the waters of the river returned to their bed. Abd al-Samad the Maghribi took Judar up in haste and repeated conjurations over him, till he came to his senses but still dazed as with drink, when he asked him, "What hast thou done, O wretch?" Answered Judar, "O my brother, I undid all the opposing enchantments, till I came to my mother and there befel between her and myself a long contention. But I made her doff her clothes, O my brother, till but her trousers remained upon her and she said to me, Do not dishonour me; for to discover one's shame is forbidden. So I left her her trousers out of pity, and behold, she cried out and said, He hath made default; beat him! Whereupon there came out upon me folk, whence I know not, and tunding me with a belabouring which was a Sister of Death, thrust me forth; nor do I know what befel me after this." Quoth the Moor, "Did I not warn thee not to swerve from my directions? Verily, thou hast injured me and hast injured thyself: for if thou hadst made her take off her petticoat-trousers, we had won to our wish; but now thou must abide with me till this day next year." Then he cried out to the two slaves, who struck the tent forthright and loaded it on the beasts; then they were absent awhile and presently returned with the two mules; and the twain mounted and rode back to the city of Fez, where Judar tarried with the Maghribi, eating well and drinking well and donning a grand dress every day, till the year was ended and the anniversary day dawned. Then the Moor said to him, "Come with me, for this is the appointed day." And Judar said, "'Tis well." So the Maghribi carried him without the city, where they found the two slaves with the mules, and rode on till they reached the river. Here the slaves pitched the tent and furnished it; and the Moor brought forth the tray of food and they ate the morning meal; after which Abd al-Samad brought out

the wand and the tablets as before and, kindling the fire
in the chafing-dish, made ready the incense. Then said he,
"O Judar, I wish to renew my charge to thee." "O my lord
the pilgrim," replied he, "if I have forgotten the bastinado,
I have forgotten the injunctions."[23] Asked the Moor, "Dost
thou indeed remember them?" and he answered, "Yes."
Quoth the Moor, "Keep thy wits, and think not that the
woman is thy very mother; nay, she is but an enchantment
in her semblance, whose purpose is to find thee default-
ing. Thou camest off alive the first time; but, an thou trip
this time, they will slay thee." Quoth Judar, "If I slip this
time, I deserve to be burnt of them." Then Abd al-Samad
cast the perfumes into the fire and recited the conjurations,
till the river dried up; whereupon Judar descended and
knocked. The door opened and he entered and undid the
several enchantments, till he came to the seventh door and
the semblance of his mother appeared before him, saying,
"Welcome,[24] O my son!" But he said to her, "How am I thy
son, O accursed? Strip!" And she began to wheedle him and
put off garment after garment, till only her trousers remained; and he said to her, "Strip, O accursed!" So she put
off her trousers and became a body without a soul. Then
he entered the hall of the treasures, where he saw gold
lying in heaps, but paid no heed to it and passed on to the
closet at the upper end, where he saw the enchanter Al-
Shamardal lying on a couch of gold, baldrick'd with the
sword, with the ring on his finger, the Kohl-phial on his
breast and the celestial planisphere hanging over his head.
So he loosed the sword and taking the ring, the Kohl-phial
and the planisphere, went forth, when behold, a band of
music sounded for him and the servants of the treasure
cried out, saying, "Mayest thou be assained with that thou
hast gained, O Judar!" Nor did the music leave sounding, till he came forth of the treasure to the Maghribi,
who gave up his conjurations and fumigations and rose
up and embraced him and saluted him. Then Judar made
over to him the four hoarded talismans, and he took them
and cried out to the slaves, who carried away the tent and

brought the mules. So they mounted and returned to Fez-city, where the Moor fetched the saddle-bags and brought forth dish after dish of meat, till the tray was full, and said, "O my brother, O Judar, eat!" So he ate till he was satisfied, when the Moor emptied what remained of the meats and other dishes and returned the empty platters to the saddle-bags. Then quoth he, "O Judar, thou hast left home and native land on our account and thou hast accomplished our dearest desire; wherefore thou hast a right to require a reward of us. Ask, therefore, what thou wilt, it is Almighty Allah who giveth unto thee by our means.[25] Ask thy will and be not ashamed, for thou art deserving." "O my lord," quoth Judar, "I ask first of Allah the Most High and then of thee, that thou give me yonder saddle-bags." So the Maghribi called for them and gave them to him, saying, "Take them, for they are thy due; and, if thou hadst asked of me aught else instead, I had given it to thee. Eat from them, thou and thy family; but, my poor fellow, these will not profit thee, save by way of provaunt, and thou hast wearied thyself with us and we promised to send thee home rejoicing. So we join to these other saddle-bags, full of gold and gems, and forward thee back to thy native land, where thou shalt become a gentleman and a merchant and clothe thyself and thy family; nor shalt thou want ready money for thine expenditure. And know that the manner of using our gift is on this wise. Put thy hand therein and say:—O servant of these saddle-bags, I conjure thee by the virtue of the Mighty Names which have power over thee, bring me such a dish! And he will bring thee whatsoever thou askest, though thou shouldst call for a thousand different dishes a day." So saying, he filled him a second pair of saddle-bags half with gold and half with gems and precious stones; and, sending for a slave and a mule, said to him, "Mount this mule, and the slave shall go before thee and show thee the way, till thou come to the door of thy house, where do thou take the two pairs of saddle-bags and give him the mule, that he may bring it back. But admit none into thy secret; and so we commend thee to Allah!"

"May the Almighty increase thy good!" replied Judar and, laying the two pairs of saddle-bags on the mule's back, mounted and set forth. The slave went on before him and the mule followed him all that day and night, and on the morrow he entered Cairo by the Gate of Victory,[26] where he saw his mother seated, saying, "Alms, for the love of Allah!" At this sight he well-nigh lost his wits and alighting, threw himself upon her: and when she saw him she wept. Then he mounted her on the mule and walked by her stirrup,[27] till they came to the house, where he set her down and, taking the saddle-bags, left the she-mule to the slave, who led her away and returned with her to his master, for that both slave and mule were devils. As for Judar, it was grievous to him that his mother should beg; so, when they were in the house, he asked her, "O my mother, are my brothers well?"; and she answered, "They are both well." Quoth he, "Why dost thou beg by the wayside?" Quoth she, "Because I am hungry, O my son," and he, "Before I went away, I gave thee an hundred dinars one day, the like the next and a thousand on the day of my departure." "O my son, they cheated me and took the money from me, saying:—We will buy goods with it. Then they drove me away, and I fell to begging by the wayside, for stress of hunger." "O my mother, no harm shall befal thee, now I am come; so have no concern, for these saddle-bags are full of gold and gems, and good aboundeth with me." "Verily, thou art blessed, O my son! Allah accept of thee and increase thee of His bounties! Go, O my son, fetch us some victual, for I slept not last night for excess of hunger, having gone to bed supperless." "Welcome to thee, O my mother! Call for what thou wilt to eat, and I will set it before thee this moment; for I have no occasion to buy from the market, nor need I any to cook." "Oh my son, I see naught with thee." "I have with me in these saddle-bags all manner of meats." "O my son, whatever is ready will serve to stay hunger." "True, when there is no choice, men are content with the smallest thing; but where there is plenty, they like to eat what is good: and I have abundance; so call for what thou hast a mind to." "O my son, give me some hot bread and a slice of cheese." "O my mother, this befitteth not thy condition." "Then give me to eat of that which befitteth my case, for thou knowest it." "O my mother," rejoined he, "what suit thine estate are browned meat and roast chicken and peppered rice and it becometh thy rank to eat of sausages and stuffed cucumbers and stuffed lamb and stuffed ribs of mutton and vermicelli with broken almonds and nuts and honey and sugar and fritters and almond cakes." But she thought he was laughing at her and making mock of her; so she said to him, "Yauh! Yauh![28] what is come to thee? Dost thou dream or art thou daft?" Asked he, "Why deemest thou that I am mad?" and she answered, "Because thou namest to me all manner rich dishes. Who can avail unto their price, and who knoweth how to dress them?" Quoth he, "By my life! thou shalt eat of all that I have named to thee, and that at once;" and quoth she, "I see nothing;" and he, "Bring me the saddle-bags." So she fetched them and feeling them, found them empty. However, she laid them before him and he thrust in his hand and pulled out dish after dish, till he had set before her all he had named. Whereupon asked she, "O my son, the saddle-bags are small and moreover they were empty; yet hast thou taken thereout all these dishes. Where then were they all?"; and he answered, "O my mother, know that these saddle-bags, which the Moor gave me, are enchanted and they have a servant whom, if one desire aught, he hath but to adjure by the Names which command him, saying, O servant of these saddle-bags, bring me such a dish! and he will bring it." Quoth his mother, "And may I put out my hand and ask of him?" Quoth he, "Do so." So she stretched out her hand and said, "O servant of the saddle-bags, by the virtue of the Names which command thee, bring me stuffed ribs." Then she thrust in her hand and found a dish containing delicate stuffed ribs of lamb. So she took it out, and called for bread and what else she had a mind to: after which Judar said to her, "O my mother, when thou hast made an end of eating, empty what is left

of the food into dishes other than these, and restore the
empty platters to the saddle-bags carefully." So she arose
and laid them up in a safe place. "And look, O mother
mine, that thou keep this secret," added he; "and whenever
thou hast a mind to aught, take it forth of the saddle-bags
and give alms and feed my brothers, whether I be present
or absent." Then he fell to eating with her and behold,
while they were thus occupied, in came his two brothers,
whom a son of the quarter[29] had apprised of his return,
saying, "Your brother is come back, riding on a she-mule,
with a slave before him, and wearing a dress that hath not
its like." So they said to each other, "Would to Heaven we
had not evilly entreated our mother! There is no hope but
that she will surely tell him how we did by her, and then,
oh our disgrace with him!" But one of the twain said, "Our
mother is soft-hearted, and if she tell him, our brother is
yet tenderer over us than she; and, given we excuse ourselves to him, he will accept our excuse." So they went in
to him and he rose to them and saluting them with the
friendliest salutation, bade them sit down and eat. So they
ate till they were satisfied, for they were weak with hunger;
after which Judar said to them, "O my brothers, take what
is left and distribute it to the poor and needy." "O brother,"
replied they, "let us keep it to sup withal." But he answered, "When supper-time cometh, ye shall have more
than this." So they took the rest of the victual and going
out, gave it to every poor man who passed by them, saying,
"Take and eat," till nothing was left. Then they brought
back the dishes and Judar said to his mother, "Put them in
the saddle-bags." And when it was eventide, he entered the
saloon and took forth of the saddle-bags a table of forty
dishes; after which he went up to the upper room and, sitting down between his brothers, said to his mother, "Bring
the supper."[30] So she went down to the saloon and, finding
there the dishes ready, laid the tray and brought up the
forty dishes, one after other. Then they ate the evening
meal, and when they had done, Judar said to his brothers,
"Take and feed the poor and needy." So they took what was

left and gave alms thereof, and presently he brought forth to them sweetmeats, whereof they ate, and what was left he bade them give to the neighbours. On the morrow, they brake their fast after the same fashion, and thus they fared ten days, at the end of which time quoth Sálim to Salím, "How cometh it that our brother setteth before us a banquet in the morning, a banquet at noon, and a banquet at sundown, besides sweetmeats late at night, and all that is left he giveth to the poor? Verily, this is the fashion of Sultans. Yet we never see him buy aught, and he hath neither kitchener nor kitchen, nor doth he light a fire. Whence hath he this great plenty? Hast thou not a mind to discover the cause of all this?" Quoth Salím, "By Allah, I know not: but knowest thou any who will tell us the truth of the case?" Quoth Sálim, "None will tell us save our mother." So they laid a plot and repairing to their mother one day, in their brother's absence, said to her, "O our mother, we are hungry." Replied she, "Rejoice, for ye shall presently be satisfied;" and going into the saloon, sought of the servant of the saddle-bags hot meats, which she took out and set before her sons. "O our mother," cried they, "this meat is hot; yet hast thou not cooked, neither kindled a fire." Quoth she, "It cometh from the saddle-bags;" and quoth they, "What manner of thing be these saddle-bags?" She answered, "They are enchanted; and the required is produced by the charm:" she then told her sons their virtue, enjoining them to secrecy. Said they, "The secret shall be kept, O our mother, but teach us the manner of this." So she taught them the fashion thereof and they fell to putting their hands into the saddle-bags and taking forth whatever they had a mind to. But Judar knew naught of this. Then quoth Sálim privily to Salím, "O my brother, how long shall we abide with Judar servant-wise and eat of his alms? Shall we not contrive to get the saddle-bags from him and make off with them?" "And how shall we make shift to do this?" "We will sell him to the galleys." "How shall we do that?" "We two will go to the Rais, the Chief Captain of the Sea of Suez and bid him to an entertainment, with two of his company. What I say to Judar do thou confirm, and at the end of the night I will show thee what I will do." So they agreed upon the sale of their brother and going to the Captain's quarters said to him, "O Rais, we have come to thee on an errand that will please thee." "Good," answered he; and they continued, "We are two brethren, and we have a third brother, a lewd fellow and good-for-nothing. When our father died, he left us some money, which we shared amongst us, and he took his part of the inheritance and wasted it in frowardness and debauchery, till he was reduced to poverty, when he came upon us and cited us before the magistrates, avouching that we had taken his good and that of his father, and we disputed the matter before the judges and lost the money. Then he waited awhile and attacked us a second time, until he brought us to beggary; nor will he desist from us, and we are utterly weary of him; wherefore we would have thee buy him of us." Quoth the Captain, "Can ye cast about with him and bring him to me here? If so, I will pack him off to sea forthright." Quoth they, "We cannot manage to bring him here; but be thou our guest this night and bring with thee two of thy men, not one more; and when he is asleep, we will aid one another to fall upon him, we five, and seize and gag him. Then shalt thou carry him forth the house, under cover of the night, and after do thou with him as thou wilt." Rejoined the Captain, "With all my heart! Will ye sell him for forty dinars?" and they, "Yes, come after nightfall to such a street, by such a mosque, and thou shalt find one of us awaiting thee." And he replied, "Now be off." Then they repaired to Judar and waited awhile, after which Sálim went up to him and kissed his hand. Quoth Judar, "What ails thee, O my brother?" And he made answer, saying, "Know that I have a friend, who hath many a time bidden me to his house in thine absence and hath ever hospitably entreated me, and I owe him a thousand kindnesses, as my brother here wotteth. I met him to-day and he invited me to his house, but I said to him:—I cannot leave my brother Judar. Quoth he, Bring him with thee; and quoth I:—He will not consent to that; but if ye will be my guests, thou and thy brothers[31] (for his brothers were sitting with him); and I invited them thinking that they would refuse. But he accepted my invitation for all of them, saying, Look for me at the gate of the little mosque,[32] and I will come to thee, I and my brothers. And now I fear they will come and am ashamed before thee. So wilt thou hearten my heart and entertain them this night, for thy good is abundant, O my brother? Or if thou consent not, give me leave to take them into the neighbours' houses." Replied Judar, "Why shouldst thou carry them into the neighbours' houses? Is our house then so strait or have we not wherewith to give them supper? Shame on thee to consult me! Thou hast but to call for what thou needest and have rich viands and sweetmeats and to spare. Whenever thou bringest home folk in my absence, ask thy mother, and she will set before thee victual more than enough. Go and fetch them; blessings have descended upon us through such guests." So Sálim kissed his hand and going forth, sat at the gate of the little mosque till after sundown, when the Captain and his men came up to him, and he carried them to the house. When Judar saw them he bade them welcome and seated them and made friends of them, knowing not what the future had in store for him at their hands. Then he called to his mother for supper, and she fell to taking dishes out of the saddle-bags, whilst he said, "Bring such and such meats," till she had set forty different dishes before them. They ate their sufficiency and the tray was taken away, the sailors thinking the while that this liberal entertainment came from Sálim. When a third part of the night was past, Judar set sweetmeats before them and Sálim served them, whilst his two brothers sat with the guests, till they sought to sleep. Accordingly Judar lay down and the others with him, who waited till he was asleep, when they fell upon him together and gagging and pinioning him, before he was awake, carried him forth of the house,[33] under cover of the night, and at once packed him off to Suez, where they shackled him and set him to work as a galley-slave; and he ceased not to serve thus in silence a whole year.³⁴ So far concerning Judar; but as for his brothers, they went in next morning to his mother and said to her, "O our mother, our brother Judar is not awake." Said she, "Do ye wake him." Asked they, "Where lieth he?" and she answered, "With the guests." They rejoined, "Haply he went away with them whilst we slept, O mother. It would seem that he had tasted of strangerhood and yearned to get at hidden boards; for we heard him at talk with the Moors, and they said to him, We will take thee with us and open the treasure to thee." She enquired, "Hath he then been in company with Moors?"; and they replied, saying, "Were they not our guests yesternight?" And she, "Most like he hath gone with them, but Allah will direct him on the right way; for there is a blessing upon him and he will surely come back with great good." But she wept, for it was grievous to her to be parted from her son. Then said they to her, "O accursed woman, dost thou love Judar with all this love, whilst as for us, whether we be absent or present, thou neither joyest in us nor sorrowest for us? Are we not thy sons, even as Judar is thy son?" She said, "Ye are indeed my sons: but ye are reprobates who deserve no favour of me, for since your father's death I have never seen any good in you; whilst as for Judar, I have had abundant good of him and he hath heartened my heart and entreated me with honour; wherefore it behoveth me to weep for him, because of his kindness to me and to you." When they heard this, they abused her and beat her; after which they sought for the saddle-bags, till they found the two pairs and took the enchanted one and all the gold from one pouch and jewels from the other of the unenchanted, saying, "This was our father's good." Said their mother, "Not so, by Allah!; it belongeth to your brother Judar, who brought it from the land of the Magharibah." Said they, "Thou liest, it was our father's property; and we will dispose of it, as we please." Then they divided the gold and jewels between them; but a brabble arose between them concerning the enchanted saddle-bags, Sálim saying, "I will have them;" and Salím, saying, "I will take them;" and they came to high words. Then said she, "O my sons, ye have divided the gold and the jewels, but this may not be divided, nor can its value be made up in money; and if it be cut in twain, its spell will be voided; so leave it with me and I will give you to eat from it at all times and be content to take a morsel with you. If ye allow me aught to clothe me, 'twill be of your bounty, and each of you shall traffic with the folk for himself. Ye are my sons and I am your mother; wherefore let us abide as we are, lest your brother come back and we be disgraced." But they accepted not her words and passed the night, wrangling with each other. Now it chanced that a Janissary[35] of the King's guards was a guest in the house adjoining Judar's and heard them through the open window. So he looked out and listening, heard all the angry words that passed between them and saw the division of the spoil. Next morning he presented himself before the King of Egypt, whose name was Shams al-Daulah,[36] and told him all he had heard, whereupon he sent for Judar's brothers and put them to the question, till they confessed; and he took the two pairs of saddle-bags from them and clapped them in prison, appointing a sufficient daily allowance to their mother. Now as regards Judar, he abode a whole year in service at Suez, till one day, being in a ship bound on a voyage over the sea, a wind arose against them and cast the vessel upon a rock projecting from a mountain, where she broke up and all on board were drowned and none gat ashore save Judar. As soon as he landed he fared on inland, till he reached an encampment of Badawi, who questioned him of his case, and he told them he had been a sailor.[37] Now there was in camp a merchant, a native of Jiddah, who took pity on him and said to him, "Wilt thou take service with me, O Egyptian, and I will clothe thee and carry thee with me to Jiddah?" So Judar took service with him and companied him to Jiddah, where he showed him much favour. After awhile, his master the merchant set out on a pilgrimage to Meccah, taking Judar with him, and when they reached the city, the

Cairene repaired to the Haram temple, to circumambulate the Ka'abah. As he was making the prescribed circuits,[38] he suddenly saw his friend Abd al-Samad the Moor doing the like; and when the Maghribi caught sight of him, he saluted him and asked him of his state; whereupon Judar wept and told him all that had befallen him. So the Moor carried him to his lodging and entreated him with honour, clothing him in a dress of which the like was not, and saying to him, "Thou hast seen the end of thine ills, O Judar." Then he drew out for him a geomantic figure, which showed what had befallen Sálim and Salím and said to Judar, "Such and such things have befallen thy brothers and they are now in the King of Egypt's prison; but thou art right welcome to abide with me and accomplish thine ordinances of pilgrimage and all shall be well." Replied Judar, "O my lord, let me go and take leave of the merchant with whom I am and after I will come back to thee." "Dost thou owe money?" asked the Moor, and he answered, "No." Said Abd al-Samad, "Go thou and take leave of him and come back forthright, for bread hath claims of its own from the ingenuous." So Judar returned to the merchant and farewelled him, saying, "I have fallen in with my brother."[39] "Go bring him here," said the merchant, "and we will make him an entertainment." But Judar answered, saying, "He hath no need of that; for he is a man of wealth and hath many servants." Then the merchant gave Judar twenty dinars, saying, "Acquit me of responsibility;"[40] and he bade him adieu and went forth from him. Presently, he saw a poor man, so he gave him the twenty ducats and returned to the Moor, with whom he abode till they had accomplished the pilgrimage-rites when Abd al-Samad gave him the seal-ring, that he had taken from the treasure of Al-Shamardal, saying, "This ring will win thee thy wish, for it enchanteth and hath a servant, by name Al-Ra'ad al-Kasif; so whatever thou hast a mind to of the wants of this world, rub this ring and its servant will appear and do all thou biddest him." Then he rubbed the ring before him, whereupon the Jinni appeared, saying, "Adsum, O my lord! Ask what thou wilt and it shall be given thee. Hast thou a mind to people a ruined city or ruin a populous one? to slay a king or to rout a host?" "O Ra'ad," said Abd al-Samad, "this is become thy lord; do thou serve him faithfully." Then he dismissed him and said to Judar, "Rub the ring and the servant will appear; and do thou command him to do whatever thou desirest, for he will not gainsay thee. Now go to thine own country and take care of the ring, for by means of it thou wilt battle thine enemies; and be not ignorant of its puissance." "O my lord," quoth Judar, "with thy leave, I will set out homewards." Quoth the Maghribi, "Summon the Jinni and mount upon his back; and if thou say to him:—Bring me to my native city this very day, he will not disobey thy commandment." So he took leave of Moor Abd al-Samad and rubbed the ring, whereupon Al-Ra'ad presented himself, saying, "Adsum; ask and it shall be given to thee." Said Judar, "Carry me to Cairo this day"; and he replied, "Thy will be done;" and, taking him on his back, flew with him from noon till midnight, when he set him down in the courtyard of his mother's house and disappeared. Judar went in to his mother, who rose weeping, and greeted him fondly, and told him how the King had beaten his brothers and cast them into gaol and taken the two pairs of saddle-bags; which when he heard, it was no light matter to him and he said to her, "Grieve not for the past; I will show thee what I can do and bring my brothers hither forthright." So he rubbed the ring, whereupon its servant appeared, saying, "Here am I! Ask and thou shalt have." Quoth Judar, "I bid thee bring me my two brothers from the prison of the King." So the Jinni sank into the earth and came not up but in the midst of the gaol where Sálim and Salím lay in piteous plight and sore sorrow for the plagues of prison,[41] so that they wished for death, and one of them said to the other, "By Allah, O my brother, affliction is longsome upon us! How long shall we abide in this prison? Death would be relief." As he spoke, behold, the earth clove in sunder and out came Al-Ra'ad, who took both up and plunged with them into the earth.

They swooned away for excess of fear, and when they recovered, they found themselves in their mother's house and saw Judar seated by her side. Quoth he, "I salute you, O my brothers! you have cheered me by your presence." And they bowed their heads and burst into tears. Then said he, "Weep not, for it was Satan and covetise that led you to do thus. How could you sell me? But I comfort myself with the thought of Joseph, whose brothers did with him even more than ye did with me, because they cast him into the pit. Repent unto Allah and crave pardon of Him, and He will forgive you both, for He is the Most Forgiving, the Merciful. As for me, I pardon you and welcome you: no harm shall befal you." Then he comforted them and set their hearts at ease and related to them all he had suffered, till he fell in with Shaykh Abd al-Samad, and told them also of the seal-ring. They replied, "O our brother, forgive us this time; and, if we return to our old ways, do with us as thou wilt." Quoth he, "No harm shall befal you; but tell me what the King did with you." Quoth they, "He beat us and threatened us with death and took the two pairs of saddle-bags from us." "Will he not care?"[42] said Judar, and rubbed the ring, whereupon Al-Ra'ad appeared. When his brothers saw him, they were affrighted and thought Judar would bid him slay them; so they fled to their mother, crying, "O our mother, we throw ourselves on thy generosity; do thou intercede for us, O our mother!" And she said to them, "O my sons, fear nothing!" Then said Judar to the servant, "I command thee to bring me all that is in the King's treasury of goods and such; let nothing remain and fetch the two pairs of saddle-bags he took from my brothers." "I hear and I obey," replied Al-Ra'ad; and, disappearing straightway gathered together all he found in the treasury and returned with the two pairs of saddle-bags and the deposits therein and laid them before Judar, saying, "O my lord, I have left nothing in the treasury." Judar gave the treasure to his mother bidding her keep it and laying the enchanted saddle-bags before him, said to the Jinni, "I command thee to build me this night a lofty palace and overlay it with liquid gold and furnish it with magnificent furniture: and let not the day dawn, ere thou be quit of the whole work." Replied he, "Thy bidding shall be obeyed;" and sank into the earth. Then Judar brought forth food and they ate and took their ease and lay down to sleep. Meanwhile, Al-Ra'ad summoned his attendant Jinn and bade them build the palace. So some of them fell to hewing stones and some to building, whilst others plastered and painted and furnished; nor did the day dawn ere the ordinance of the palace was complete; whereupon Al-Ra'ad came to Judar and said to him, "O my lord, the palace is finished and in best order, an it please thee to come and look on it." So Judar went forth with his mother and brothers and saw a palace, whose like there was not in the whole world; and it confounded all minds with the goodliness of its ordinance. Judar was delighted with it while he was passing along the highway and withal it had cost him nothing. Then he asked his mother, "Say me, wilt thou take up thine abode in this palace?" and she answered, "I will, O my son," and called down blessings upon him. Then he rubbed the ring and bade the Jinni fetch him forty handsome white hand-maids and forty black damsels and as many Mamelukes and negro slaves. "Thy will be done," answered Al-Ra'ad and betaking himself, with forty of his attendant Genii to Hind and Sind and Persia, snatched up every beautiful girl and boy they saw, till they had made up the required number. Moreover, he sent other fourscore, who fetched comely black girls, and forty others brought male chattels and carried them all to Judar's house, which they filled. Then he showed them to Judar, who was pleased with them and said, "Bring for each a dress of the finest." "Ready!" replied the servant. Then quoth he, "Bring a dress for my mother and another for myself, and also for my brothers." So the Jinni fetched all that was needed and clad the female slaves, saying to them, "This is your mistress: kiss her hands and cross her not, but serve her, white and black." The Mamelukes also dressed themselves and kissed Judar's hands; and he and his brothers arrayed themselves in the robes the Jinni had brought them and Judar became like unto a King and his brothers as Wazirs. Now his house was spacious; so he lodged Sálim and his slave-girls in one part thereof and Salím and his slave-girls in another, whilst he and his mother took up their abode in the new palace; and each in his own palace was like a Sultan. So far concerning them; but as regards the King's Treasurer, thinking to take something from the treasury, he went in and found it altogether empty, even as saith the poet:—

> 'Twas as a hive of bees that greatly thrived;
> But, when the bee-swarm fled, 'twas clean unhived.[43]

So he gave a great cry and fell down in a fit. When he came to himself, he left the door open and going in to King Shams al-Daulah, said to him, "O Commander of the Faithful,[44] I have to inform thee that the treasury hath become empty during the night." Quoth the King, "What hast thou done with my monies which were therein?" Quoth he, "By Allah, I have not done aught with them nor know I what is come of them! I visited the place yesterday and saw it full; but to-day when I went in, I found it clean empty, albeit the doors were locked, the walls were unpierced and the bolts are unbroken; nor hath a thief entered it." Asked the King, "Are the two pairs of saddle-bags gone?" "Yes," replied the Treasurer; whereupon the King's reason flew from his head and he rose to his feet, saying, "Go thou before me." Then he followed the Treasurer to the treasury and he found nothing there, whereat he was wroth with him; and he said to them, "O soldiers! know that my treasury hath been plundered during the night, and I know not who did this deed and dared thus to outrage me, without fear of me." Said they, "How so?"; and he replied, "Ask the Treasurer." So they questioned him, and he answered, saying, "Yesterday I visited the treasury and it was full, but this morning when I entered it I found it empty, though the walls were unpierced[45] and the doors[46] unbroken." They all marvelled at this and could make the

King no answer, when in came the Janissary, who had denounced Sálim and Salím, and said to Shams al-Daulah, "O King of the age, all this night I have not slept for that which I saw." And the King asked, "And what didst thou see?" "Know, O King of the age," answered the Kawwas, "that all night long I have been amusing myself with watching builders at work; and, when it was day, I saw a palace ready edified, whose like is not in the world. So I asked about it and was told that Judar had come back with great wealth and Mamelukes and slaves and that he had freed his two brothers from prison, and built this palace, wherein he is as a Sultan." Quoth the King, "Go, look in the prison." So they went thither and not finding Sálim and Salím, returned and told the King, who said, "It is plain now who be the thief; he who took Sálim and Salím out of prison it is who hath stolen my monies." Quoth the Wazir, "O my lord, and who is he?"; and quoth the King, "Their brother Judar, and he hath taken the two pairs of saddle-bags; but, O Wazir, do thou send him an Emir with fifty men to seal up his goods and lay hands on him and his brothers and bring them to me, that I may hang them." And he was sore enraged and said, "Ho, off with the Emir at once, and fetch them, that I may put them to death." But the Wazir said to him, "Be thou merciful, for Allah is merciful and hasteth not to punish His servants, whenas they sin against Him. Moreover, he who can build a palace in a single night, as these say, none in the world can vie with him; and verily I fear lest the Emir fall into difficulty for Judar. Have patience, therefore, whilst I devise for thee some device of getting at the truth of the case, and so shalt thou win thy wish, O King of the age." Quoth the King, "Counsel me how I shall do, O Wazir." And the Minister said, "Send him an Emir with an invitation; and I will make much of him for thee and make a show of love for him and ask him of his estate; after which we will see. If we find him stout of heart, we will use sleight with him, and if weak of will, then do thou seize him and do with him thy desire." The King agreed to this and despatched one of his Emirs, Othman hight, to go and invite Judar and say to him, "The King biddeth thee to a banquet;" and the King said to him, "Return not, except with him." Now this Othman was a fool, proud and conceited; so he went forth upon his errand, and when he came to the gate of Judar's palace, he saw before the door an eunuch seated upon a chair of gold, who at his approach rose not, but sat as if none came near, though there were with the Emir fifty footmen. Now this eunuch was none other than Al-Ra'ad al-Kasif, the servant of the ring, whom Judar had commanded to put on the guise of an eunuch and sit at the palace-gate. So the Emir rode up to him and asked him, "O slave, where is thy lord?"; whereto he answered, "In the palace;" but he stirred not from his leaning posture; whereupon the Emir Othman waxed wroth and said to him, "O pestilent slave, art thou not ashamed, when I speak to thee, to answer me, sprawling at thy length, like a gallows-bird?" Replied the eunuch, "Off and multiply not words." Hardly had Othman heard this, when he was filled with rage and drawing his mace[47] would have smitten the eunuch, knowing not that he was a devil; but Al-Ra'ad leapt upon him and taking the mace from him, dealt him four blows with it. Now when the fifty men saw their lord beaten, it was grievous to them; so they drew their swords and ran to slay the slave; but he said, "Do ye draw on us, O dogs?" and rose at them with the mace, and every one whom he smote, he broke his bones and drowned him in his blood. So they fell back before him and fled, whilst he followed them, beating them, till he had driven them far from the palace-gate; after which he returned and sat down on his chair at the door, caring for none. But as for the Emir and his company, they returned, discomfited and tunded, to King Shams al-Daulah, and Othman said, "O King of the age, when I came to the palace gate, I espied an eunuch seated there in a chair of gold and he was passing proud for, when he saw me approach, he stretched himself at full length albeit he had been sitting in his chair and entreated me contumeliously, neither offered to rise to me. So I began to speak to him and he answered without stirring, whereat wrath got hold of me and I drew the mace upon him, thinking to smite him. But he snatched it from me and beat me and my men therewith and overthrew us. So we fled from before him and could not prevail against him." At this, the King was wroth and said, "Let an hundred men go down to him." Accordingly, the hundred men went down to attack him; but he arose and fell upon them with the mace and ceased not smiting them till he had put them to the rout; when he regained his chair; upon which they returned to the King and told him what had passed, saying, "O King of the age, he beat us and we fled for fear of him." Then the King sent two hundred men against him, but these also he put to the rout, and Shams al-Daulah said to his Minister, "I charge thee, O Wazir, take five hundred men and bring this eunuch in haste, and with him his master Judar and his brothers." Replied the Wazir, "O King of the age, I need no soldiers, but will go down to him alone and unarmed." "Go," quoth the King, "and do as thou seest suitable." So the Wazir laid down his arms and donning a white habit,[48] took a rosary in his hand and set out afoot alone and unattended. When he came to Judar's gate, he saw the slave sitting there; so he went up to him and seating himself by his side courteously, said to him, "Peace be with thee!"; whereto he replied, "And on thee be peace, O mortal! What wilt thou?" When the Wazir heard him say "O mortal," he knew him to be of the Jinn and quaked for fear; then he asked him, "O my lord, tell me, is thy master Judar here?" Answered the eunuch, "Yes, he is in the palace." Quoth the Minister, "O my lord, go thou to him and say to him:— King Shams al-Daulah saluteth thee and biddeth thee honour his dwelling with thy presence and eat of a banquet he hath made for thee." Quoth the eunuch, "Tarry thou here, whilst I consult him." So the Wazir stood in a respectful attitude, whilst the Marid went up to the palace and said to Judar, "Know, O my lord, that the King sent to thee an Emir and fifty men, and I beat them and drove them away. Then he sent an hundred men and I beat them also; then two hundred, and these also I put to the rout. And now he hath sent thee his Wazir unarmed, bidding thee visit him and eat of his banquet. What sayst thou?" Said Judar, "Go, bring the Wazir hither." So the Marid went down and said to him, "O Wazir, come speak with my lord." "On my head be it," replied he and going in to Judar, found him seated, in greater state than the King, upon a carpet, whose like the King could not spread, and was dazed and amazed at the goodliness of the palace and its decoration and appointments, which made him seem as he were a beggar in comparison. So he kissed the ground before Judar and called down blessings on him; and Judar said to him, "What is thy business, O Wazir?" Replied he, "O my lord, thy friend King Shams al-Daulah saluteth thee with the salam and longeth to look upon thy face; wherefore he hath made thee an entertainment. So say, wilt thou heal his heart and eat of his banquet?" Quoth Judar, "If he be indeed my friend, salute him and bid him come to me." "On my head be it," quoth the Minister. Then Judar bringing out the ring rubbed it and bade the Jinni fetch him a dress of the best, which he gave to the Wazir, saying, "Don this dress and go tell the King what I say." So the Wazir donned the dress, the like whereof he had never donned, and returning to the King told him what had passed and praised the palace and that which was therein, saying, "Judar biddeth thee to him." So the King called out, "Up, ye men; mount your horses and bring me my steed, that we may go to Judar!" Then he and his suite rode off for the Cairene palace. Meanwhile Judar summoned the Marid and said to him, "It is my will that thou bring me some of the Ifrits at thy command in the guise of guards and station them in the open square before the palace, that the King may see them and be awed by them; so shall his heart tremble and he shall know that my power and majesty be greater than his." Thereupon Al-Ra'ad brought him two hundred Ifrits of great stature and strength, in the guise of guards, magnificently armed and equipped, and when the King came and saw these tall burly fellows his heart feared them. Then he entered the palace, and found Judar sitting in such state as nor King nor Sultan could even. So he saluted him and made his obeisance to him; yet Judar rose not to him nor did him honour nor said "Be seated," but left him standing,[49] so that fear entered into him and he could neither sit nor go away and said to himself, "If he feared me, he would not leave me thus unheeded; peradventure he will do me a mischief, because of that which I did with his brothers." Then said Judar, "O King of the age, it beseemeth not the like of thee to wrong the folk and take away their good." Replied the King, "O my lord, deign excuse me, for greed impelled me to this and fate was thereby fulfilled; and, were there no offending, there would be no forgiving." And he went on to excuse himself for the past and pray to him for pardon and indulgence. And he ceased not to humble himself before him, till he said, "Allah pardon thee!" and bade him be seated. So he sat down and Judar invested him with garments of pardon and immunity and ordered his brothers spread the table. When they had eaten, he clad the whole of the King's company in robes of honour and gave them largesse; after which he bade the King depart. So he went forth and thereafter came every day to visit Judar and held not his Divan save in his house: wherefore friendship and familiarity waxed great between them, and they abode thus awhile, till one day the King, being alone with his Minister, said to him, "O Wazir, I fear lest Judar slay me and take the kingdom away from me." Replied the Wazir, "O King of the age, as for his taking the kingdom from thee, have no fear of that, for Judar's present estate is greater than that of the King, and to take the kingdom would be a lowering of his dignity; but, if thou fear that he kill thee, thou hast a daughter: give her to him to wife and thou and he will be of one condition." Quoth the King, "O Wazir, be thou intermediary between us and him"; and quoth the Minister, "Do thou invite him to an entertainment and pass the night with him in one of thy saloons. Then bid thy daughter don her richest dress and orna-

ments and pass by the door of the saloon. When he seeth
her, he will assuredly fall in love with her, and when we
know this, I will turn to him and tell him that she is thy
daughter and engage him in converse and lead him on, so
that thou shalt seem to know nothing of the matter, till he
ask her of thee to wife. When thou hast married him to the
Princess, thou and he will be as one thing and thou wilt be
safe from him; and if he die, thou wilt inherit all he hath,
both great and small." Replied the King, "Thou sayst sooth,
O my Wazir," and made a banquet and invited thereto
Judar who came to the Sultan's palace and they sat in the
saloon in great good cheer till the end of the day. Now the
King had commanded his wife to array the maiden in her
richest raiment and ornaments and carry her by the door
of the saloon. She did as he told her, and when Judar saw
the Princess, who had not her match for beauty and grace,
he looked fixedly at her and said, "Ah!"; and his limbs were
loosened; for love and longing and passion and pine were
sore upon him; desire and transport gat hold upon him and
he turned pale. Quoth the Wazir, "May no harm befal thee,
O my lord! Why do I see thee change colour and in suffering?" Asked Judar, "O Wazir, whose daughter is this
damsel? Verily she hath enthralled me and ravished my
reason." Replied the Wazir, "She is the daughter of thy
friend the King; and if she please thee, I will speak to him
that he marry thee to her." Quoth Judar, "Do so, O Wazir,
and as I live, I will bestow on thee what thou wilt and will
give the King whatsoever he shall ask to her dowry; and we
will become friends and kinsfolk." Quoth the Minister,
"It shall go hard but thy desire be accomplished." Then
he turned to the King and said in his ear, "O King of the
age, thy friend Judar seeketh alliance with thee and will
have me ask of thee for him the hand of thy daughter, the
Princess Asiyah; so disappoint me not, but accept my intercession, and what dowry soever thou askest he will give
thee." Said the King, "The dowry I have already received,
and as for the girl, she is his handmaid; I give her to him to
wife and he will do me honour by accepting her." So they

spent the rest of that night together and on the morrow the King held a court, to which he summoned great and small, together with the Shaykh al-Islam.⁵⁰ Then Judar demanded the Princess in marriage and the King said, "The dowry I have received." Thereupon they drew up the marriage-contract and Judar sent for the saddle-bags containing the jewels and gave them to the King as settlement upon his daughter. The drums beat and the pipes sounded and they held high festival, whilst Judar went in unto the girl. Thenceforward he and the King were as one flesh and they abode thus for many days, till Shams al-Daulah died; whereupon the troops proclaimed Judar Sultan, and he refused; but they importuned him, till he consented and they made him King in his father-in-law's stead. Then he bade build a cathedral-mosque over the late King's tomb in the Bundukaniyah⁵¹ quarter and endowed it. Now the quarter of Judar's house was called Yamaniyah; but, when he became Sultan he built therein a congregational mosque and other buildings, wherefore the quarter was named after him and was called the Judariyah⁵² quarter. Moreover, he made his brother Sálim his Wazir of the right and his brother Salím his Wazir of the left hand; and thus they abode a year and no more; for, at the end of that time, Sálim said to Salím, "O my brother, how long is this state to last? Shall we pass our whole lives in slavery to our brother Judar? We shall never enjoy luck or lordship whilst he lives," adding, "so how shall we do to kill him and take the ring and the saddle-bags?" Replied Salím, "Thou art craftier than I; do thou device, whereby we may kill him." "If I effect this," asked Sálim, "wilt thou agree that I be Sultan and keep the ring and that thou be my right-hand Wazir and have the saddle-bags?" Salím answered, "I consent to this;" and they agreed to slay Judar their brother for love of the world and of dominion. So they laid a snare for Judar and said to him, "O our brother, verily we have a mind to glory in thee and would fain have thee enter our houses and eat of our entertainment and solace our hearts." Replied Judar, "So be it, in whose house shall the banquet be?" "In mine," said Sálim, "and after thou hast eaten of my victual, thou shalt be the guest of my brother." Said Judar, "'Tis well," and went with him to his house, where he set before him poisoned food, of which when he had eaten, his flesh rotted from his bones and he died.[53] Then Sálim came up to him and would have drawn the ring from his finger, but it resisted him; so he cut off the finger with a knife. Then he rubbed the ring and the Marid presented himself, saying, "Adsum! Ask what thou wilt." Quoth Sálim, "Take my brother Salím and put him to death and carry forth the two bodies, the poisoned and the slaughtered, and cast them down before the troops." So the Marid took Salím and slew him; then, carrying the two corpses forth, he cast them down before the chief officers of the army, who were sitting at table in the parlour of the house. When they saw Judar and Salím slain, they raised their hands from the food and fear gat hold of them and they said to the Marid, "Who hath dealt thus with the Sultan and the Wazir?" Replied the Jinni, "Their brother Sálim." And behold, Sálim came up to them and said, "O soldiers, eat and make merry, for Judar is dead and I have taken to me the seal-ring, whereof the Marid before you is the servant; and I bade him slay my brother Salím lest he dispute the kingdom with me, for he was a traitor and I feared lest he should betray me. So now I am become Sultan over you; will ye accept of me? If not, I will rub the ring and bid the Marid slay you all, great and small." They replied, "We accept thee to King and Sultan." Then he bade bury his brothers and summoned the Divan; and some of the folk followed the funeral, whilst others forewent him in state procession to the audience-hall of the palace, where he sat down on the throne and they did homage to him as King; after which he said, "It is my will to marry my brother Judar's wife." Quoth they, "Wait till the days of widowhood are accomplished."[54] Quoth he, "I know not days of widowhood nor aught else. As my head liveth, I needs must go in unto her this very night." So they drew up the marriage-contract and sent to tell the Princess Asiyah, who replied, "Bid him enter." Accordingly, he went in to her and she received him with a show of joy and welcome; but by and by she gave him poison in water and made an end of him. Then she took the ring and broke it, that none might possess it thenceforward, and tore up the saddle-bags; after which she sent to the Shaykh al-Islam and other great Officers of state, telling them what had passed and saying to them, "Choose you out a King to rule over you." And this is all that hath come down to us of the story of Judar and his brethren.[55] But there is also told, O King, the tale of

JULNAR THE SEA-BORN
AND HER SON
KING BADR BASIM OF PERSIA.

There was once in days of yore and in ages and times long
gone before, in Ajam-land, a King Shahriman hight,[1] whose
abiding place was Khorasan. He owned an hundred concubines, but by none of them had he been blessed with boon
of child, male or female, all the days of his life. One day,
among the days, he bethought him of this and fell lamenting for that the most part of his existence was past and he
had not been vouchsafed a son, to inherit the kingdom
after him, even as he had inherited it from his fathers
and forebears; by reason whereof there betided him sore
cark and care and chagrin exceeding. As he sat thus one of
his Mamelukes came in to him and said, "O my lord, at the
door is a slave-girl with her merchant, and fairer than she
eye hath never seen." Quoth the King, "Hither to me
with merchant and maid!"; and both came in to him. Now
when Shahriman beheld the girl, he saw that she was like a
Rudaynian lance,[2] and she was wrapped in a veil of gold-
purfled silk. The merchant uncovered her face, whereupon
the place was illumined by her beauty and her seven
tresses hung down to her anklets like horses' tails. She had
Nature-kohl'd eyes, heavy hips and thighs and waist of slen-

derest guise; her sight healed all maladies and quenched
the fire of sighs, for she was even as the poet cries:—

> I love her madly for she is perfect fair,
> Complete in gravity and gracious way;
> Nor overtall nor overshort, the while
> Too full for trousers are those hips that sway:
> Her shape is midmost 'twixt o'er small and tall;
> Nor long to blame nor little to gainsay:
> O'erfall her anklets tresses black as night
> Yet in her face resplends eternal day.

The King seeing her marvelled at her beauty and loveliness, her symmetry and perfect grace and said to the merchant, "O Shaykh, how much for this maiden?" Replied the
merchant, "O my lord, I bought her for two thousand dinars of the merchant who owned her before myself, since
when I have travelled with her three years and she hath
cost me, up to the time of my coming hither, other three
thousand gold pieces; but she is a gift from me to thee."
The King robed him with a splendid robe of honour and
ordered him ten thousand ducats, whereupon he kissed his
hands, thanking him for his bounty and beneficence, and
went his ways. Then the King committed the damsel to
the tirewomen, saying, "Amend ye the case of this maiden[3]
and adorn her and furnish her a bower and set her therein."
And he bade his chamberlains carry her everything she
needed and shut all the doors upon her. Now his capital
wherein he dwelt, was called the White City and was seated
on the sea-shore; so they lodged her in a chamber, whose
latticed casements overlooked the main. Then Shahriman
went in to her; but she spake not to him neither took any
note of him.[4] Quoth he, " 'Twould seem she hath been with
folk who have not taught her manners." Then he looked at
the damsel and saw her surpassing beauty and loveliness
and symmetry and perfect grace, with a face like the rondure of the moon at its full or the sun shining in the sheeny
sky. So he marvelled at her charms of favour and figure and

he praised Allah the Creator (magnified be His might!),
after which he walked up to her and sat him down by her
side; then he pressed her to his bosom and seating her on
his thighs, sucked the dew of her lips, which he found
sweeter than honey. Presently he called for trays spread
with richest viands of all kinds and ate and fed her by
mouthfuls, till she had enough; yet she spoke not one word.
The King began to talk to her and asked her of her name;
but she abode still silent and uttered not a syllable nor
made him any answer, neither ceased to hang down her
head groundwards; and it was but the excess of her beauty
and loveliness and the amorous grace that saved her from
the royal wrath. Quoth he to himself, "Glory be to God,
the Creator of this girl! How charming she is, save that she
speaketh not! But perfection belongeth only to Allah the
Most High." And he asked the slave-girls whether she had
spoken, and they said, "From the time of her coming until
now she hath not uttered a word nor have we heard her
address us." Then he summoned some of his women and
concubines and bade them sing to her and make merry
with her, so haply she might speak. Accordingly they
played before her all manner instruments of music and
sports and what not and sang, till the whole company was
moved to mirth, except the damsel, who looked at them in
silence, but neither laughed nor spoke. The King's breast
was straitened; thereupon he dismissed the women and
abode alone with that damsel: after which he doffed his
clothes and disrobing her with his own hand, looked upon
her body and saw it as it were a silvern ingot. So he loved
her with exceeding love and falling upon her, took her
maidenhead and found her a pure virgin; whereat he rejoiced with excessive joy and said in himself, "By Allah, 'tis
a wonder that a girl so fair of form and face should have
been left by the merchants a clean maid as she is!"[5] Then
he devoted himself altogether to her, heeding none other
and forsaking all his concubines and favourites, and tarried
with her a whole year as it were a single day. Still she spoke
not till, one morning he said to her (and indeed the love of

livery is at hand and my family needs must be present, that they may tend me; for the women of the land know not the manner of childbearing of the women of the sea, nor do the daughters of the ocean know the manner of the daughters of the earth; and when my people come, I shall be reconciled to them and they will be reconciled to me." Quoth the King, "How do the people of the sea walk therein, without being wetted?"; and quoth she, "O King of the Age, we walk in the waters with our eyes open, as do ye on the ground, by the blessing of the names graven upon the seal-ring of Solomon David-son (on whom be peace!). But, O King, when my kith and kin come, I will tell them how thou boughtest me with thy gold, and hast entreated me with kindness and benevolence. It behoveth that thou confirm my words to them and that they witness thine estate with their own eyes and they learn that thou art a King, son of a King." He rejoined, "O my lady, do what seemeth good to thee and what pleaseth thee; and I will consent to thee in all thou wouldst do." The damsel continued, "Yes, we walk in the sea and see what is therein and behold the sun, moon, stars and sky, as it were on the surface of earth; and this irketh us naught. Know also that there be many peoples in the main and various forms and creatures of all kinds that are on the land, and that all that is on the land compared with that which is in the main is but a very small matter." And the King marvelled at her words. Then she pulled out from her bosom two bits of Comorin lign-aloes and, kindling fire in a chafing-dish, chose somewhat of them and threw it in, then she whistled a loud whistle and spake words none understood. Thereupon arose a great smoke and she said to the King, who was looking on, "O my lord, arise and hide thyself in a closet that I may show thee my brother and mother and family, whilst they see thee not; for I design to bring them hither, and thou shalt presently espy a wondrous thing and shalt marvel at the several creatures and strange shapes which Almighty Allah hath created." So he arose without stay or delay and entering a closet, fell awatching what she should do. She continued her fumigations and conjurations till the sea foamed and frothed turbid and there rose from it a handsome young man of a bright favour, as he were the moon at its full, with brow flower-white, cheeks of ruddy light and teeth like the marguerite. He was the likest of all creatures to his sister and after him there came forth of the sea an ancient dame with hair speckled gray and five maidens, as they were moons, bearing a likeness to the damsel hight Julnar. The King looked upon them as they all walked upon the face of the water, till they drew near the window and saw Julnar, whereupon they knew her and went in to her. She rose to them and met them with joy and gladness, and they embraced her and wept with sore weeping. Then said they to her, "O Julnar, how couldst thou leave us four years, and we unknowing of thine abiding place? By Allah the world hath been straitened upon us for stress of severance from thee, and we have had no delight of food or drink; no, not for one day, but have wept with sore weeping night and day for the excess of our longing after thee!" Then she fell to kissing the hands of the youth her brother and her mother and cousins, and they sat with her awhile, questioning her of her case and of what had betided her, as well as of her present estate. "Know," replied she, "that, when I left you, I issued from the sea and sat down on the shore of an island, where a man found me and sold me to a merchant, who brought me to this city and sold me for ten thousand dinars to the King of the country, who entreated me with honour and forsook all his concubines and women and favourites for my sake and was distracted by me from all he had and all that was in his city." Quoth her brother, "Praised be Allah, who hath reunited us with thee! But now, O my sister, 'tis my purpose that thou arise and go with us to our country and people." When the King heard these words, his wits fled him for fear lest the damsel accept her brother's words and he himself avail not to stay her, albeit he loved her passionately, and he became distracted with fear of losing her. But Julnar answered, "By Allah, O my brother, the mortal who bought me is lord of this city and he is a mighty King and a wise man, good and generous with extreme generosity. Moreover, he is a personage of great worth and wealth and hath neither son nor daughter. He hath entreated me with honour and done me all manner of favour and kindness; nor, from the day of his buying me to this time have I heard from him an ill word to hurt my heart; but he hath never ceased to use me courteously; doing nothing save with my counsel, and I am in the best of case with him and in the perfection of fair fortune. Furthermore, were I to leave him, he would perish; for he cannot endure to be parted from me an hour; and if I left him, I also should die, for the excess of the love I bear him, by reason of his great goodness to me during the time of my sojourn with him; for, were my father alive, my estate with him would not be like my estate with this great and glorious and puissant potentate. And verily, ye see me with child by him and praise be to Allah, who hath made me a daughter of the Kings of the sea, and my husband the mightest of the Kings of the land, and Allah, in very sooth, he hath compensated me for whatso I lost. Now this King hath no issue, male or female, so I pray the Almighty to vouchsafe me a son who shall inherit of this mighty sovran that which the Lord hath bestowed upon him of lands and palaces and possessions." Now when her brother and the daughters of her uncle heard this her speech, their eyes were cooled thereby and they said, "O Julnar, thou knowest thy value with us and thou wottest the affection we bear thee and thou art certified that thou art to us the dearest of all creatures and thou art assured that we seek but ease for thee, without travail or trouble. Wherefore, an thou be in unease, arise and go with us to our land and our folk; but, an thou be at thine ease here, in honour and happiness, this is our wish and our will; for we desire naught save thy welfare in any case."[9] Quoth she, "By Allah, I am here in the utmost ease and solace and honour and grace!" When the King heard what she said, he joyed with a heart set at rest and thanked her silently for this; the love of her redoubled on him and entered his heartcore and he knew that she loved him as he loved her and that she desired to abide with him, that she might see his child by her. Then Julnar bade her women lay the tables and set on all sorts of viands, which had been cooked in kitchen under her own eyes, and fruits and sweetmeats, whereof she ate, she and her kinsfolk. But, presently, they said to her, "O Julnar, thy lord is a stranger to us, and we have entered his house, without his leave or weeting. Thou hast extolled to us his excellence and eke thou hast set before us of his victual whereof we have eaten; yet have we not companied with him nor seen him, neither hath he seen us nor come to our presence and eaten with us, so there might be between us bread and salt." And they all left eating and were wroth with her, and fire issued from their mouths, as from cressets; which when the King saw, his wits fled for excess of fear of them. But Julnar arose and soothed them and going to the closet where was the King her lord, said to him, "O my lord, hast thou seen and heard how I praised thee and extolled thee to my people and hast thou noted what they said to me of their desire to carry me away with them?" Quoth he, "I both heard and saw: May the Almighty abundantly requite thee for me! By Allah, I knew not the full measure of thy fondness until this blessed hour, and now I doubt not of thy love to me!" Quoth she, "O my lord, is the reward of kindness aught but kindness? Verily, thou hast dealt generously with me and hast entreated me with worship and I have seen that thou lovest me with the utmost love, and thou hast done me all manner of honour and kindness and preferred me above all thou lovest and desirest. So how should my heart be content to leave thee and depart from thee, and how should I do thus after all thy goodness to me? But now I desire of thy courtesy that thou come and salute my family, so thou mayst see them and they thee and pure love and friendship may be between you; for know, O King of the Age, that my brother and mother and cousins love thee with exceeding love, by reason of my praises of thee to them, and they say:—We will not depart from thee nor go to our homes till we have foregathered with the King and saluted him. For indeed they desire to see thee and make acquaintance with thee." The King replied, "To hear is to obey, for this is my very own wish." So saying, he rose and went in to them and saluted them with the goodliest salutation; and they sprang up to him and received him with the utmost worship, after which he sat down in the palace and ate with them; and he entertained them thus for the space of thirty days. Then, being desirous of returning home, they took leave of the King and Queen and departed with due permission to their own land, after he had done them all possible honour. Awhile after this, Julnar completed the days of her pregnancy and the time of her delivery being come, she bore a boy, as he were the moon at its full; whereat the utmost joy betided the King, for that he had never in his life been vouchsafed son or daughter. So they held high festival and decorated the city seven days, in the extreme of joy and jollity: and on the seventh day came Queen Julnar's mother, Farashah[10] hight, and brother and cousins, whenas they knew of her delivery. The King received them with joy at their coming and said to them, "I said that I would not give my son a name till you should come and name him of your knowledge." So they named him Badr Basim,[11] and all agreed upon this name. Then they showed the child to his uncle Salih, who took him in his arms and arising began to walk about the chamber with him in all directions right and left. Presently he carried him forth of the palace and going down to the salt sea, fared on with him, till he was hidden from the King's sight. Now when Shahriman saw him take his son and disappear with him in the depth of the sea, he gave the child up for lost and fell to weeping and wailing; but Julnar said to him, "O King of the Age, fear not, neither grieve for thy son, for I love my child more than thou and he is with my brother; so reck thou not of the sea neither fear for him drowning. Had my brother known that aught of harm would betide the little one, he had not done this deed; and he will presently bring thee thy son safe, Inshallah—an it please the Almighty." Nor was an hour past before the sea became turbid and troubled and King Salih came forth and flew from the sea till he came up to them with the child lying quiet and showing a face like the moon on the night of fulness. Then, looking at the King he said, "Haply thou fearedest harm for thy son, whenas I plunged into the sea with him?" Replied the father, "Yes, O my lord, I did indeed fear for him and thought he would never be saved therefrom." Rejoined Salih, "O King of the land, we pencilled his eyes with an eye-powder we know of and recited over him the names graven upon the seal-ring of Solomon David-son (on whom be the Peace!), for this is what we use to do with children newly born among us; and now thou needst not fear for him drowning or suffocation in all the oceans of the world, if he should go down into them; for, even as ye walk on the land, so walk we in the sea." Then he pulled out of his pocket a casket, graven and sealed and, breaking open the seals, emptied it; whereupon there fell from it strings of all manner jacinths and other jewels, besides three hundred bugles of emerald and other three hundred hollow gems, as big as ostrich eggs, whose light dimmed that of sun and moon. Quoth Salih, "O King of the Age, these jewels and jacinths are a present from me to thee. We never yet brought thee a gift, for that we knew not Julnar's abiding-place neither had we of her any tidings or trace; but now that we see thee to be united with her and we are all become one thing, we have brought thee this present; and every little while we will bring thee the like thereof, Inshallah! for that these jewels and jacinths are more plentiful with us than pebbles on the beach and we know the good and the bad of them and their whereabouts and the way to them, and they are easy to us." When the King saw the jewels, his wits were bewildered and his sense was astounded and he said, "By Allah, one single gem of these jewels is worth my realm!" Then he thanked for his bounty Salih the Sea-born and, looking towards Queen Julnar, said, "I am abashed before thy brother, for that he hath dealt munificently by me and bestowed on me this splendid gift, which the folk of the land were unable to present." So she thanked her brother for his deed and he said, "O King of the Age, thou hast the prior claim on us and it behoves us to thank thee, for thou hast entreated our sister with kindness and we have entered thy dwelling and eaten of thy victual. And if we stood on our faces in thy service, O King of the Age, a thousand years, yet had we not the might to requite thee, and this were but a scantling of thy due." The King thanked him with heartiest thanks and the Merman and Merwomen abode with him forty days' space, at the end of which Salih arose and kissed the ground before his brother-in-law, who asked "What wantest thou, O Salih?" He answered, "O King of the Age, indeed thou hast done us overabundant favours, and we crave of thy bounties that thou deal charitably with us and grant us permission to depart; for we yearn after our people and country and kinsfolk and our homes; so will we never forsake thy service nor that of my sister and my nephew; and by Allah, O King of the Age, 'tis not pleasant to my heart to part from thee; but how shall we do, seeing that we have been reared in the sea and that the sojourn of the shore liketh us not?" When the King heard these words he rose to his feet and farewelled Salih the Sea-born and his mother and his cousins, and all wept together, because of parting and presently they said to him, "Anon we will be with thee again, nor will we forsake thee, but will visit thee every few days." Then they flew off and descending into the sea, disappeared from sight. After this King Shahriman showed the more kindness to Julnar and honoured her with increase of honour; and the little one grew up and flourished, whilst his maternal uncle and grandam and cousins visited the King every few days and abode with him a month or two months at a time. The boy ceased not to increase in beauty and loveliness with increase of years, till he attained the age of fifteen and was unique in his perfection and symmetry. He learnt writing and Koran-reading; history, syntax and lexicography; archery, spear-play and horsemanship and what not else behoveth the sons of Kings; nor was there one of the children of the folk of the city, men or women, but would talk of the youth's charms, for he was of surpassing beauty and perfection, even such an one as is praised in the saying of the poet:[12]—

> The whiskers write upon his cheek, with ambergris on
> pearl,
> Two lines, as 'twere with jet upon an apple, line for
> line.
> Death harbours in his languid eye and slays with every
> glance,
> And in his cheek is drunkenness, and not in any wine.

And indeed the King loved him with exceeding love, and summoning his Wazir and Emirs and the Chief Officers of state and Grandees of his realm, required of them a binding oath that they would make Badr Basim King over them after his sire; and they sware the oath gladly, for the sovran was liberal to the lieges pleasant in parley and a very compend of goodness, saying naught but that wherein was advantage for the people. On the morrow Shahriman mounted, with all his troops and Emirs and Lords, and went forth into the city and returned. When they drew near the palace, the King dismounted, to wait upon his son who abode on horseback, and he and all the Emirs and Grandees bore the saddle-cloth of honour before him, each and every of them bearing it in his turn, till they came to the vestibule of the palace, where the Prince alighted and his father and the Emirs embraced him and seated him on the throne of Kingship, whilst they (including his sire) stood before him. Then Badr Basim judged the people, deposing the unjust and promoting the just and continued so doing till near upon noon, when he descended from the throne and went in to his mother, Julnar the Sea-born, with the crown upon his head, as he were the moon. When she saw him, with the King standing before him, she rose and kissing him, gave him joy of the Sultanate and wished him and his sire length of life and victory over their foes. He sat with her and rested till the hour of mid-afternoon prayer, when he took horse and repaired, with the Emirs before him, to the Maydan-plain, where he played at arms with his father and his lords, till night-fall, when he returned to the palace, preceded by all the folk. He rode forth thus every day to the tilting-ground, returning to sit and judge the people and do justice between carl and churl; and thus he continued doing a whole year, at the end of which he began to ride out a-hunting and a-chasing and to go round about in the cities and countries under his rule, proclaiming security and satisfaction and doing after the fashion of Kings; and he was unique among the people of his day for glory and valour and just dealing among the subjects. And it chanced that one day the old King fell sick and his fluttering heart forbode him of translation to the Mansion of Eternity. His sickness grew upon him till he was nigh upon death, when he called his son and commended his mother and subjects to his care and caused all the Emirs and Grandees once more swear allegiance to the Prince and assured himself of them by strongest oaths; after which he lingered a few days and departed to the mercy of Almighty Allah. His son and widow and all the Emirs and Wazirs and Lords mourned over him, and they built him a tomb and buried him therein. They ceased not ceremonially to mourn for him a whole month, till Salih and his mother and cousins arrived and condoled with their grieving for the King and said, "O Julnar, though the King be dead, yet hath he left this noble and peerless youth, and not dead is whoso leaveth the like of him, the rending lion and the shining moon." Thereupon the Grandees and notables of the Empire went in to King Badr Basim and said to him, "O King, there is no harm in mourning for the late sovran: but over-mourning beseemeth none save women; wherefore occupy thou not thy heart and our hearts with mourning for thy sire; inasmuch as he hath left thee behind him, and whoso leaveth the like of thee is not dead." Then they comforted him and diverted him and lastly carried him to the bath. When he came out of the Hammam, he donned a rich robe, purfled with gold and embroidered with jewels and jacinths; and, setting the royal crown on his head, sat down on his throne of kingship and ordered the affairs of the folk, doing equal justice between strong and weak, and exacting from the prince the dues of the pauper; wherefore the people loved him with exceeding love. Thus he continued doing for a full year, whilst, every now and then, his kinsfolk of the sea visited him, and his life was pleasant and his eye was cooled. Now it came to pass that his uncle Salih went in one night of the nights to Julnar and saluted her; whereupon she rose and embracing him seated him by her side and asked him, "O my brother, how art thou and my mother and my cousins." He answered, "O my sister, they are well and glad and in good case, lacking naught save a sight of thy face." Then she set somewhat of food before him and he ate, after which talk ensued between the twain and they spake of King Badr Basim and his beauty and loveliness, his symmetry and skill in cavalarice and cleverness and good breeding. Now Badr was propped upon his elbow hard by them; and, hearing his mother and uncle speak of him, he feigned sleep and listened to their talk.[13] Presently Salih said to his sister, "Thy son is now seventeen years old and is unmarried, and I fear lest mishap befal him and he have no son; wherefore it is my desire to marry him to a Princess of the princesses of the sea, who shall be a match for him in beauty and loveliness." Quoth Julnar, "Name them to me for I know them all." So Salih proceeded to enumerate them to her, one by one, but to each she said, "I like not this one for my son; I will not marry him but to one who is his equal in beauty and loveliness and wit and piety and good breeding and magnanimity and dominion and rank and lineage."[14] Quoth Salih, "I know none other of the daughters of the Kings of the sea, for I have numbered to thee more than an hundred girls and not one of them pleaseth thee: but see, O my sister, whether thy son be asleep or no." So she felt Badr and finding on him the signs of slumber said to Salih, "He is asleep; what hast thou to say and what is thine object in making sure his sleeping?" Replied he, "O my sister, know that I have bethought me of a Mermaid of the mermaids who befitteth thy son; but I fear to name her, lest he be awake and his heart be taken with her love and maybe we shall be unable to win to her; so should he and we and the Grandees of the realm be wearied in vain and trouble betide us through this; for, as saith the poet:—

> Love, at first sight, is a spurt of spray;[15]
> But a spreading sea when it gaineth sway."

When she heard these words, she cried, "Tell me the condition of this girl, and her name for I know all the damsels of the sea, Kings' daughters and others; and, if I judge her worthy of him, I will demand her in marriage for him of her father, though I spend on her whatso my hand possesseth. So recount to me all anent her and fear naught, for my son sleepeth." Quoth Salih, "I fear lest he be awake; and the poet saith:—

> I loved him, soon as his praise I heard;
> For ear oft loveth ere eye survey."

But Julnar said, "Speak out and be brief and fear not, O my brother." So he said, "By Allah, O my sister, none is worthy of thy son save the Princess Jauharah, daughter of King Al-Samandal,[16] for that she is like unto him in beauty and loveliness and brilliancy and perfection; nor is there found, in sea or on land, a sweeter or pleasanter of gifts than she; for she is prime in comeliness and seemlihead of face and symmetrical shape of perfect grace; her cheek is ruddy dight, her brow flower white, her teeth gem-bright, her eyes blackest black and whitest white, her hips of heavy weight, her waist slight and her favour exquisite. When she turneth she shameth the wild cattle[17] and the gazelles and when she walketh, she breedeth envy in the willow branch: when she unveileth her face outshineth sun and moon and all who look upon her she enslaveth soon: sweet-lipped and soft-sided indeed is she." Now when Julnar heard what Salih said, she replied, "Thou sayest sooth, O my brother! By Allah, I have seen her many and many a time and she was my companion, when we were little ones; but now we have no knowledge of each other, for constraint of distance; nor have I set eyes on her for eighteen years. By Allah, none is worthy of my son but she!" Now Badr heard all they said and mastered what had passed, first and last, of these praises bestowed on Jauharah daughter of King Al-Samandal; so he fell in love with her on hearsay, pretending sleep the while, wherefore fire was kindled in his heart on her account full sore and he was drowned in a sea without bottom or shore. Then Salih, looking at his sister, exclaimed, "By Allah, O my sister, there is no greater fool among the Kings of the sea than her father nor one more violent of temper than he! So name thou not the girl to thy son, till we demand her in marriage of her father. If he favour us with his assent, we will praise Allah Almighty; and if he refuse us and will not give her to thy son to wife, we will say no more about it and seek another match." Answered Julnar, "Right is thy rede"; and they parleyed no more; but Badr passed the night with a heart on fire with passion for Princess Jauharah. However he concealed his case and spake not of her to his mother or his uncle, albeit he was on coals of fire for love of her. Now when it was morning, the King and his uncle went to the Hammam-bath and washed, after which they came forth and drank wine and the servants set food before them, whereof they and Julnar ate their sufficiency, and washed their hands. Then Salih rose and said to his nephew and sister, "With your leave, I would fain go to my mother and my folk for I have been with you some days and their hearts are troubled with awaiting me." But Badr Basim said to him, "Tarry with us this day;" and he consented. Then quoth the King, "Come, O my uncle, let us go forth to the garden." So they sallied forth and promenaded about the pastures and took their solace awhile, after which King Badr lay down under a shady tree, thinking to rest and sleep; but he remembered his uncle's description of the maiden and her beauty and loveliness and shed railing tears, reciting these two couplets:[18]—

> Were it said to me while the flame is burning within me,
> And the fire blazing in my heart and bowels,
> Wouldst thou rather that thou shouldest behold them
> Or a draught of pure water?—I would answer, Them.

When Salih heard what his nephew said, he smote hand upon hand and said, "There is no god but *the* God! Mohammed is the Apostle of God and there is no Majesty and there is no Might save in Allah, the Glorious, the Great!" adding, "O my son, heardest thou what passed between me and thy mother respecting Princess Jauharah?" Replied Badr Basim, "Yes, O my uncle, and I fell in love with her by hearsay through what I heard you say. Indeed, my heart cleaveth to her and I cannot live without her." Rejoined his uncle, "O King, let us return to thy mother and tell her how the case standeth and crave her leave that I may take thee with me and seek the Princess in marriage of her sire; after which we will farewell her and I and thou will return. Indeed, I fear to take thee and go without her leave, lest she be wroth with me; and verily the right would be on her side, for I should be the cause of her separation from us. Moreover, the city would be left without king and there would be none to govern the citizens and look to their affairs; so should the realm be disordered against thee and the kingship depart from thy hands." But Badr Basim, hearing these words, cried, "O my uncle, if I return to my mother and consult her on such matter, she will not suffer me to do this; wherefore I will not return to my mother nor consult her." And he wept before him and presently added, "I will go with thee and tell her not and after will return." When Salih heard what his nephew said, he was confused anent his case and said, "I crave help of the Almighty in any event." Then, seeing that Badr Basim was resolved to go with him, whether his mother would let him or no, he drew from his finger a seal-ring, whereon were graven certain of the names of Allah the Most High, and gave it to him, saying, "Put this on thy finger, and thou shalt be safe from drowning and other perils and from the mischief of sea-beasts and great fishes." So King Badr Basim took the ring and set it on his finger. Then they dove into the deep, and fared on till they came to Salih's palace, where they found Badr Basim's grandmother, the mother of his mother, seated with her kinsfolk; and, going in to them, kissed their hands. When the old Queen saw Badr, she rose to him and embracing him, kissed him between the eyes and said to him, "A blessed coming, O my son! How didst thou leave thy mother Julnar?" He replied, "She is well in health and fortune, and saluteth thee and her uncle's daughters." Then Salih related to his mother what had occurred between him and his sister and how King Badr Basim had fallen in love with the Princess Jauharah daughter of Al-Samandal by report and told her the whole tale from beginning to end adding, "He hath not come save to demand her in wedlock of her sire;" which when the old Queen heard, she was wroth against her son with exceeding wrath and sore troubled and concerned and said, "O Salih, O my son, in very sooth thou diddest wrong to name the Princess before thy nephew, knowing, as thou dost, that her father is stupid and violent, little of wit and tyrannical of temper, grudging his daughter to every suitor; for all the Monarchs of the Main have sought her hand, but he rejected them all; nay, he would none of them, saying:—Ye are no match for her in beauty or in loveliness or in aught else. Wherefore we fear to demand her in wedlock of him, lest he reject us, even as he hath rejected others; and we are a folk of high spirit and should return broken-hearted." Hearing these words Salih answered, "O my mother, what is to do? For King Badr Basim saith:—There is no help but that I seek her in marriage of her sire, though I expend my whole kingdom; and he avoucheth that, an he take her not to wife, he will die of love for her and longing." And Salih continued, "He is handsomer and goodlier than she; his father was King of all the Persians, whose King he now is, and none is worthy of Jauharah save Badr Basim. Wherefore I purpose to carry her father a gift of jacinths and jewels befitting his dignity, and demand her of him in marriage. An he object to us that he is a King, behold, our man also is a King and the son of a King; or, if he object to us her beauty, behold our man is more beautiful than she; or, again, if he object to us the vastness of his dominion, behold our man's dominion is vaster than hers and her father's and numbereth more troops and guards, for that his kingdom is greater than that of Al-Samandal. Needs must I do my endeavour to further the desire of my sister's son, though it relieve me of my life; because I was the cause of whatso hath betided; and, even as I plunged him into the ocean of her love, so will I go about to marry him to her, and may Almighty Allah help me thereto!" Rejoined his mother, "Do as thou wilt, but beware of giving her father rough words, whenas thou speakest with him; for thou knowest his stupidity and violence and I fear lest he do thee a mischief, for he knoweth not respect for any." And Salih answered, "Hearkening and obedience." Then he sprang up and taking two bags full of gems such as rubies and bugles of emerald, noble ores and all manner jewels gave them to his servants to carry and set out with his nephew for the palace of Al-Samandal. When they came thither, he sought audience of the King and being admitted to his presence, kissed ground before him and saluted him with the goodliest Salam. The King rose to him and honouring him with the utmost honour, bade him be seated. So he sat down and presently the King said to him, "A blessed coming: indeed thou hast desolated us, O Salih! But what bringeth thee to us? Tell me thine errand that we may fulfil it to thee." Whereupon Salih arose and, kissing the ground a second time, said, "O King of the age, my errand is to Allah and the magnanimous liege lord and the valiant lion, the report of whose good qualities the caravans far and near have dispread and whose renown for benefits and beneficence and clemency and graciousness and liberality to all climes and countries hath sped." Thereupon he opened the two bags and, displaying their contents before Al-Samandal, said to him, "O King of the Age, haply wilt thou accept my gift and by showing favour to me heal my heart." King Al-Samandal asked, "With what object dost thou gift me with this gift? Tell me thy tale and acquaint me with thy requirement. An its accomplishment be in my power I will straightway accomplish it to thee and and spare thee toil and trouble; and if I be unable thereunto, Allah compelleth not any soul aught beyond its power."[19] So Salih rose and kissing ground three times, said, "O King of the Age, that which I desire thou art indeed able to do; it is in thy power and thou art master thereof; and I impose not on the King a difficulty, nor am I Jinn-demented, that I should crave of the King a thing whereto he availeth not; for one of the sages saith:—An thou wouldst be complied with ask that which can be readily supplied. Wherefore, that of which I am come in quest, the King (whom Allah preserve!) is able to grant." The King replied, "Ask what thou wouldst have, and state thy case and seek thy need." Then said Salih,[20] "O King of the Age, know that I come as a suitor, seeking the unique pearl and the hoarded jewel, the Princess Jauharah, daughter of our lord the King; wherefore, O King, disappoint thou not thy suitor." Now when the King heard this, he laughed till he fell backwards, in mockery of him and said, "O Salih, I had thought thee a man of worth and a youth of sense, seeking naught save what was reasonable and speaking not save advisedly. What then hath befallen thy reason and urged thee to this monstrous matter and mighty hazard, that thou seekest in marriage daughters of Kings, lords of cities and climates? Say me, art thou of a rank to aspire to this great eminence and hath thy wit failed thee to this extreme pass that thou affrontest me with this demand?" Replied Salih, "Allah amend the King! I seek her not for myself (albeit, an I did, I am her match and more than her match, for thou knowest that my father was King of the Kings of the sea, for all thou art this day our King), but I seek her for King Badr Basim, lord of the lands of the Persians and son of King

Shahriman, whose puissance thou knowest. An thou object that thou art a mighty great King, King Badr is a greater; and if thou object thy daughter's beauty, King Badr is more beautiful than she and fairer of form and more excellent of rank and lineage; and he is the champion of the people of his day. Wherefore, if thou grant my request, O King of the Age, thou wilt have set the thing in its stead; but, if thou deal arrogantly with us, thou wilt not use us justly nor travel with us the 'road which is straight.'[21] Moreover, O King, thou knowest that the Princess Jauharah, the daughter of our lord the King, must needs be wedded and bedded, for the sage saith, a girl's lot is either grace of marriage or the grave.[22] Wherefore, an thou mean to marry her, my sister's son is worthier of her than any other man." Now when Al-Samandal heard Salih's words, he was wroth with exceeding wrath; his reason well nigh fled and his soul was like to depart his body for rage, and he cried, "O dog, shall the like of thee dare to bespeak me thus and name my daughter in the assemblies,[23] saying that the son of thy sister Julnar is a match for her? Who art thou and who is this sister of thine and who is her son and who was his father,[24] that thou durst say to me such say and address me with such address? What are ye all, in comparison with my daughter, but dogs?" And he cried out to his pages, saying, "Take yonder gallows-bird's head!" So they drew their swords and made for Salih, but he fled and for the palace-gate sped; and reaching the entrance, he found of his cousin and kinsfolk and servants, more than a thousand horse armed cap-à-pie in iron and close knitted mail-coats, hending in hand spears and naked swords glittering white. And these when they saw Salih come running out of the palace (they having been sent by his mother to his succour,) questioned him and he told them what was to do; whereupon they knew that the King was a fool and violent-tempered to boot. So they dismounted and baring their blades, went in to the King Al-Samandal, whom they found seated upon the throne of his Kingship, unaware of their coming and enraged against Salih with furious rage; and they beheld his eunuchs and pages and officers unprepared. When the King saw them enter, drawn brand in hand, he cried out to his people, saying "Woe to you! Take me the heads of these hounds!" But ere an hour had sped Al-Samandal's party were put to the rout and relied upon flight, and Salih and his kinsfolk seized upon the King and pinioned him. Princess Jauharah awoke and knew that her father was a captive and his guards slain. So she fled forth the palace to a certain island, and climbing up into a high tree, hid herself in its summit. Now when the two parties came to blows, some of King Al-Samandal's pages fled and Badr Basim meeting them, questioned them of their case and they told him what had happened. But when he heard that the King was a prisoner, Badr feared for himself and fled, saying in his heart, "Verily, all this turmoil is on my account and none is wanted but I." So he sought safety in flight, security to sight, knowing not whither he went; but destiny from Eternity fore-ordained drave him to the very island where the Princess had taken refuge, and he came to the very tree whereon she sat and threw himself down, like a dead man, thinking to lie and repose himself and knowing not there is no rest for the pursued, for none knoweth what Fate hideth for him in the future. As he lay down, he raised his eyes to the tree and they met the eyes of the Princess. So he looked at her and seeing her to be like the moon rising in the East, cried, "Glory to Him who fashioned yonder perfect form, Him who is the Creator of all things and who over all things is Almighty! Glory to the Great God, the Maker, the Shaper and Fashioner! By Allah, if my presentiments be true, this is Jauharah, daughter of King Al-Samandal! Methinks that, when she heard of our coming to blows with her father, she fled to this island and, happening upon this tree, hid herself on its head; but, if this be not the Princess herself, 'tis one yet goodlier than she." Then he bethought himself of her case and said in himself, "I will arise and lay hands on her and question her of her condition; and, if she be indeed the she, I will demand her in wedlock of herself and so win my wish." So he stood up and said to her, "O end of all desire, who art thou and who brought thee hither?" She looked at Badr Basim and seeing him to be as the full moon,[25] when it shineth from under the black cloud, slender of shape and sweet of smile, answered, "O fair of fashion, I am Princess Jauharah, daughter of King Al-Samandal, and I took refuge in this place, because Salih and his host came to blows with my sire and slew his troops and took him prisoner, with some of his men; wherefore I fled, fearing for my very life," presently adding, "And I weet not what fortune hath done with my father." When King Badr Basim heard these words he marvelled with exceeding marvel at this strange chance and thought, "Doubtless I have won my wish by the capture of her sire." Then he looked at Jauharah and said to her, "Come down, O my lady; for I am slain for love of thee and thine eyes have captivated me. On my account and thine are all these broils and battles; for thou must know that I am King Badr Basim, Lord of the Persians, and Salih is my mother's brother and he it is who came to thy sire to demand thee of him in marriage. As for me, I have quitted my kingdom for thy sake, and our meeting here is the rarest coincidence. So come down to me and let us twain fare for thy father's palace, that I may beseech uncle Salih to release him and I may make thee my lawful wife." When Jauharah heard his words, she said in herself, " 'Twas on this miserable gallows-bird's account, then, that all this hath befallen and that my father hath fallen prisoner and his chamberlains and suite have been slain and I have been departed from my palace, a miserable exile and have fled for refuge to this island. But, an I devise not against him some device to defend myself from him, he will possess himself of me and take his will of me; for he is in love and for aught that he doeth a lover is not blamed." Then she beguiled him with winning words and soft speeches, whilst he knew not the perfidy against him she purposed, and asked him, "O my lord and light of my eyes, say me, art thou indeed King Badr Basim, son of Queen Julnar?" And he answered, "Yes, O my lady." Then she, "May Allah cut off my father and gar his kingdom cease from him and heal not his heart neither avert from him strangerhood, if he could desire a comelier than thou or aught goodlier than these fair qualities of thine! By Allah, he is of little wit and judgment!" presently adding, "But, O King of the Age, punish him not for that he hath done; more by token that an thou love me a span, verily I love thee a cubit. Indeed, I have fallen into the net of thy love and am become of the number of thy slain. The love that was with thee hath transferred itself to me and there is left thereof with thee but a tithe of that which is with me." So saying, she came down from the tree and drawing near him strained him to her bosom and fell to kissing him; whereat passion and desire for her redoubled on him and doubting not but she loved him, he trusted in her, and returned her kisses and caresses. Presently he said to her, "By Allah, O Princess, my uncle Salih set forth to me not a fortieth part of thy charms; no, nor a quarter-carat[26] of the four-and-twenty." Then Jauharah pressed him to her bosom and pronounced some unintelligible words; then spat on his face, saying, "Quit this form of man and take shape of bird, the handsomest of birds, white of robe, with red bill and legs." Hardly had she spoken, when King Badr Basim found himself transformed into a bird, the handsomest of birds, who shook himself and stood looking at her. Now Jauharah had with her one of her slave-girls, by name Marsinah;[27] so she called her and said to her, "By Allah, but that I fear for the life of my father, who is his uncle's prisoner, I would kill him! Allah never requite him with good! How unlucky was his coming to us; for all this trouble is due to his hardheadedness! But do thou, O slave-girl, bear him to the Thirsty Island and leave him there to die of thirst." So Marsinah carried him to the island in question and would have returned and left him there; but she said in herself, "By Allah, the lord of such beauty and loveliness deserveth not to die of thirst!" So she went forth from that island and brought him to another abounding in trees and fruits and rills and, setting him down there, returned to her mistress

and told her, "I have left him on the Thirsty Island." Such
was the case with Badr Basim; but as regards King Salih, he
sought for Jauharah after capturing the King and killing his
folk; but, finding her not, returned to his palace and said to
his mother, "Where is my sister's son, King Badr Basim?"
"By Allah, O my son," replied she, "I know nothing of him!
For when it reached him that you and King Al-Samandal
had come to blows and that strife and slaughter had betided between you, he was affrighted and fled." When Salih
heard this, he grieved for his nephew and said, "O my
mother, by Allah, we have dealt negligently by King Badr
and I fear lest he perish or lest one of King Al-Samandal's
soldiers or his daughter Jauharah fall in with him. So
should we come to shame with his mother and no good
betide us from her, for that I took him without her leave."
Then he despatched guards and scouts throughout the sea
and elsewhere to seek for Badr; but they could learn no
tidings of him; so they returned and told King Salih,
wherefore cark and care redoubled on him and his breast
was straitened for King Badr Basim. So far concerning
nephew and uncle, but as for Julnar the Sea-born, after
their departure she abode in expectation of them, but her
son returned not and she heard no report of him. So when
many days of fruitless waiting had gone by, she arose and
going down into the sea, repaired to her mother, who
sighting her rose to her and kissed her and embraced her,
as did the Mermaids her cousins. Then she questioned her
mother of King Badr Basim, and she answered, saying, "O
my daughter, of a truth he came hither with his uncle, who
took jacinths and jewels and carrying them to King Al-
Samandal, demanded his daughter in marriage for thy son;
but he consented not and was violent against thy brother in
words. Now I had sent Salih nigh upon a thousand horse
and a battle befel between him and King Al-Samandal; but
Allah aided thy brother against him, and he slew his guards
and troops and took himself prisoner. Meanwhile, tidings
of this reached thy son, and it would seem as if he feared
for himself; wherefore he fled forth from us, without our

will, and returned not to us, nor have we heard any news of him." Then Julnar enquired for King Salih, and his mother said, "He is seated on the throne of his kingship, in the stead of King Al-Samandal, and hath sent in all directions to seek thy son and Princess Jauharah." When Julnar heard the maternal words, she mourned for her son with sad mourning and was highly incensed against her brother Salih for that he had taken him and gone down with him into the sea without her leave; and she said, "O my mother, I fear for our realm; as I came to thee without letting any know; and I dread tarrying with thee, lest the state fall into disorder and the kingdom pass from our hands. Wherefore I deem best to return and govern the reign till it please Allah to order our son's affair for us. But look ye forget him not neither neglect his case; for should he come to any harm, it would infallibly kill me, since I see not the world save in him and delight but in his life." She replied, "With love and gladness, O my daughter. Ask not what we suffer by reason of his loss and absence." Then she sent to seek for her grandson, whilst Julnar returned to her kingdom, weeping-eyed and heavy-hearted, and indeed the gladness of the world was straitened upon her. So fared it with her; but as regards King Badr Basim, after Princess Jauharah had ensorcelled him and had sent him with her handmaid to the Thirsty Island, saying, "Leave him there to die of thirst," and Marsinah had set him down in a green islet, he abode days and nights in the semblance of a bird eating of its fruits and drinking of its waters and knowing not whither to go nor how to fly; till, one day, there came a certain fowler to the island to catch somewhat wherewithal to get his living. He espied King Badr Basim in his form of a white-robed bird, with red bill and legs, captivating the sight and bewildering the thought; and, looking thereat, said in himself, "Verily, yonder is a beautiful bird: never saw I its like in fairness or form." So he cast his net over Badr and taking him, carried him to the town, mentally resolved to sell him for a high price. On his way one of the townsfolk accosted him and said, "For how much this fowl, O fowler?" Quoth the fowler, "What wilt thou do with him an thou buy him?" Answered the other, "I will cut his throat and eat him;" whereupon said the birder, "Who could have the heart to kill this bird and eat him? Verily, I mean to present him to our King, who will give me more than thou wouldest give me and will not kill him, but will divert himself by gazing upon his beauty and grace, for in all my life, since I have been a fowler, I never saw his like among land game or water fowl. The utmost thou wouldst give me for him, however much thou covet him, would be a dirham, and, by Allah Almighty, I will not sell him!" Then he carried the bird up to the King's palace and when the King saw it, its beauty and grace pleased him and the red colour of its beak and legs. So he sent an eunuch to buy it, who accosted the fowler and said to him, "Wilt thou sell this bird?" Answered he, "Nay, 'tis a gift from me to the King."[28] So the eunuch carried the bird to the King and told him what the man had said; and he took it and gave the fowler ten dinars, whereupon he kissed ground and fared forth. Then the eunuch carried the bird to the palace and placing him in a fine cage, hung him up after setting meat and drink by him. When the King came down from the Divan, he said to the eunuch, "Where is the bird? Bring it to me, that I may look upon it; for, by Allah, 'tis beautiful!" So the eunuch brought the cage and set it between the hands of the King, who looked and seeing the food untouched, said, "By Allah, I wis not what it will eat, that I may nourish it!" Then he called for food and they laid the tables and the King ate. Now when the bird saw the flesh and meats and sweet-meats, he ate of all that was upon the trays before the King, whereat the Sovran and all the bystanders marvelled and the King said to his attendants, eunuchs and Mamelukes, "In all my life I never saw a bird eat as doth this bird!" Then he sent an eunuch to fetch his wife that she might enjoy looking upon the bird, and he went in to summon her and said, "O my lady, the King desireth thy presence, that thou mayst divert thyself with the sight of a bird he hath bought. When we set on the food, it flew down from its cage and perching on the table, ate of all that was thereon. So arise, O my lady, and solace thee with the sight for it is goodly of aspect and is a wonder of the wonders of the age." Hearing these words she came in haste; but, when she noted the bird, she veiled her face and turned to fare away. The King rose up and looking at her, asked, "Why dost thou veil thy face when there is none in presence save the women and eunuchs who wait on thee and thy husband?" Answered she, "O King, this bird is no bird, but a man like thyself." He rejoined, "Thou liest, this is too much of a jest. How should he be other than a bird?"; and she, "O King, by Allah, I do not jest with thee nor do I tell thee aught but the truth; for verily this bird is King Badr Basim, son of King Shahriman, Lord of the land of the Persians, and his mother is Julnar the Sea-born." Quoth the King, "And how came he in this shape?"; and quoth she, "Princess Jauharah, daughter of King Al-Samandal, hath enchanted him:" and told him all that had passed with King Badr Basim from first to last.[29] The King marvelled exceedingly at his wife's words and conjured her, on his life, to free Badr from his enchantment (for she was the no-tablest enchantress of her age), and not leave him in tor-ment, saying, "May Almighty Allah cut off Jauharah's hand, for a foul witch as she is! How little is her faith and how great her craft and perfidy!" Said the Queen, "Do thou say to him:—O Badr Basim, enter yonder closet!" So the King bade him enter the closet and he went in obediently. Then the Queen veiled her face and taking in her hand a cup of water,[30] entered the closet, where she pronounced over the water certain incomprehensible words ending with, "By the virtue of these mighty names and holy verses and by the majesty of Allah Almighty, Creator of heaven and earth, the Quickener of the dead and Appointer of the means of daily bread and the terms determined, quit this thy form wherein thou art and return to the shape in which the Lord created thee!" Hardly had she made an end of her words, when the bird trembled once and became a man; and the King saw before him a handsome youth, than

whom on earth's face was none goodlier. But when King
Badr Basim found himself thus restored to his own form he
cried, "There is no god but *the* God and Mohammed is the
Apostle of God! Glory be to the Creator of all creatures
and Provider of their provision, and Ordainer of their life-
terms preordained!" Then he kissed the King's hand and
wished him long life, and the King kissed his head and said
to him, "O Badr Basim, tell me thy history from commencement to conclusion." So he told him his whole tale, concealing naught; and the King marvelled thereat and said to
him, "O Badr Basim, Allah hath saved thee from the spell:
but what hath thy judgment decided and what thinkest
thou to do?" Replied he, "O King of the Age, I desire of
thy bounty that thou equip me a ship with a company
of thy servants and all that is needful; for 'tis long since I
have been absent and I dread lest the kingdom depart from
me. And I misdoubt me my mother is dead of grief for my
loss; and this doubt is the stronger for that she knoweth
not what is come of me nor whether I am alive or dead.
Wherefore, I beseech thee, O King, to crown thy favours to
me by granting me what I seek." The King, after beholding
the beauty and grace of Badr Basim and listening to his
sweet speech, said, "I hear and obey." So he fitted him out
a ship, to which he transported all that was needful and
which he manned with a company of his servants; and
Badr Basim set sail in it, after having taken leave of the
King. They sailed over the sea ten successive days with a
favouring wind; but, on the eleventh day, the ocean became troubled with exceeding trouble, the ship rose and
fell and the sailors were powerless to govern her. So they
drifted at the mercy of the waves, till the craft neared a
rock in mid-sea which fell upon her[31] and broke her up
and all on board were drowned, save King Badr Basim who
got astride one of the planks of the vessel, after having
been nigh upon destruction. The plank ceased not to be
borne by the set of the sea, whilst he knew not whither
he went and had no means of directing its motion, as the
wind and waves wrought for three whole days. But on

the fourth the plank grounded with him on the seashore where he sighted a white city, as it were a dove passing white, builded upon a tongue of land that jutted out into the deep and it was goodly of ordinance, with high towers and lofty walls against which the waves beat. When Badr Basim saw this, he rejoiced with exceeding joy, for he was well-nigh dead of hunger and thirst, and dismounting from the plank, would have gone up the beach to the city; but there came down to him mules and asses and horses, in number as the sea-sands and fell to striking at him and staying him from landing. So he swam round to the back of the city, where he waded to shore and entering the place, found none therein and marvelled at this, saying, "Would I knew to whom doth this city belong, wherein is no lord nor any liege, and whence came these mules and asses and horses that hindered me from landing?" And he mused over his case. Then he walked on at hazard till he espied an old man, a grocer.[32] So he saluted him and the other returned his salam and seeing him to be a handsome young man, said to him, "O youth, whence comest thou and what brought thee to this city?" Badr told him his story; at which the old man marvelled and said, "O my son, didst thou see any on thy way?" He replied, "Indeed, O my father, I wondered in good sooth to sight a city void of folk." Quoth the Shaykh, "O my son, come up into the shop, lest thou perish." So Badr Basim went up into the shop and sat down; whereupon the old man set before him somewhat of food, saying, "O my son, enter the inner shop; glory be to Him who hath preserved thee from yonder she-Sathanas!" King Badr Basim was sore affrighted at the grocer's words; but he ate his fill and washed his hands; then glanced at his host and said to him, "O my lord, what is the meaning of these words? Verily thou hast made me fearful of the city and its folk." Replied the old man, "Know, O my son, that this is the City of the Magicians and its Queen is as she were a she-Satan, a sorceress and a mighty enchantress, passing crafty and perfidious exceedingly. All thou sawest of horses and mules and asses were once sons of Adam like thee and me; they were also strangers, for whoever entereth this city, being a young man like thyself, this miscreant witch taketh him and hometh him for forty days, after which she enchanteth him, and he becometh a mule or a horse or an ass, of those animals thou sawest on the sea-shore. All these people hath she spelled; and, when it was thy intent to land they feared lest thou be transmewed like themselves; so they counselled thee by signs that said:—Land not, of their solicitude for thee, fearing that haply she should do with thee like as she had done with them. She possessed herself of this city and seized it from its citizens by sorcery and her name is Queen Lab, which being interpreted, meaneth in Arabic 'Almanac of the Sun.' "[33] When Badr Basim heard what the old man said, he was affrighted with sore affright and trembled like reed in wind saying in himself, "Hardly do I feel me free from the affliction wherein I was by reason of sorcery, when Destiny casteth me into yet sorrier case!" And he fell a-musing over his condition and that which had betided him. When the Shaykh looked at him and saw the violence of his terror, he said to him, "O my son, come, sit at the threshold of the shop and look upon yonder creatures and upon their dress and complexion and that wherein they are by reason of gramarye and dread not; for the Queen and all in the city love and tender me and will not vex my heart or trouble my mind." So King Badr Basim came out and sat at the shop-door, looking out upon the folk; and there passed by him a world of creatures without number. But when the people saw him, they accosted the grocer and said to him, "O elder, is this thy captive and thy prey gotten in these days?" The old man replied, "He is my brother's son, I heard that his father was dead; so I sent for him and brought him here that I might quench with him the fire of my home-sickness." Quoth they, "Verily, he is a comely youth; but we fear for him from Queen Lab, lest she turn on thee with treachery and take him from thee, for she loveth handsome young men." Quoth the Shaykh, "The Queen will not gainsay my commandment, for she loveth and tendereth me; and when she shall know that he is my brother's son, she will not molest him or afflict me in him neither trouble my heart on his account." Then King Badr Basim abode some months with the grocer, eating and drinking, and the old man loved him with exceeding love. One day, as he sat in the shop according to his custom, behold, there came up a thousand eunuchs, with drawn swords and clad in various kinds of raiment and girt with jewelled girdles: all rode Arabian steeds and bore in baldrick Indian blades. They saluted the grocer, as they passed his shop and were followed by a thousand damsels like moons, clad in various raiments of silks and satins fringed with gold and embroidered with jewels of sorts, and spears were slung to their shoulders. In their midst rode a damsel mounted on a Rabite mare, saddled with a saddle of gold set with various kinds of jewels and jacinths; and they reached in a body the Shaykh's shop. The damsel saluted him and passed on, till, lo and behold! up came Queen Lab, in great stride, and seeing King Badr Basim sitting in the shop, as he were the moon at its full, was amazed at his beauty and loveliness and became passionately enamoured of him, and distraught with desire of him. So she alighted and sitting down by King Badr Basim said to the old man, "Whence hadst thou this handsome one?"; and the Shaykh replied, "He is my brother's son, and is lately come to me." Quoth Lab, "Let him be with me this night, that I may talk with him;" and quoth the old man, "Wilt thou take him from me and not enchant him?" Said she, "Yes," and said he, "Swear to me." So she sware to him that she would not do him any hurt or ensorcell him, and bidding bring him a fine horse, saddled and bridled with a golden bridle and decked with trappings all of gold set with jewels, gave the old man a thousand dinars, saying, "Use this."[34] Then she took Badr Basim and carried him off, as he were the full moon on its fourteenth night, whilst all the folk, seeing his beauty, were grieved for him and said, "By Allah, verily, this youth deserveth not to be bewitched by yonder sorceress, the accursed!" Now King Badr Basim heard all they said, but was silent, committing

his case to Allah Almighty, till they came to her palace-
gate, where the Emirs and eunuchs and Lords of the realm
took foot and she bade the Chamberlains dismiss her Officers and Grandees, who kissed ground and went away,
whilst she entered the palace with Badr Basim and her eunuchs and women. Here he found a place, whose like he
had never seen at all, for it was builded of gold and in its
midst was a great basin brimful of water midmost a vast
flower-garden. He looked at the garden and saw it abounding in birds of various kinds and colours, warbling in all
manner tongues and voices, pleasurable and plaintive. And
everywhere he beheld great state and dominion and said,
"Glory be to God, who of His bounty and long-suffering
provideth those who serve other than Himself!" The Queen
sat down at a latticed window overlooking the garden
on a couch of ivory, whereon was a high bed, and King
Badr Basim seated himself by her side. She kissed him and
pressing him to her breast, bade her women bring a tray
of food. So they brought a tray of red gold, inlaid with
pearls and jewels and spread with all manner of viands and
he and she ate, till they were satisfied, and washed their
hands; after which the waiting-women set on flagons of
gold and silver and glass, together with all kinds of flowers
and dishes of dried fruits. Then the Queen summoned the
singing-women and there came ten maidens, as they were
moons, hending all manner of musical instruments. Queen
Lab crowned a cup and drinking it off, filled another and
passed it to King Badr Basim, who took it and drank; and
they ceased not to drink till they had their sufficiency.
Then she bade the damsels sing, and they sang all manner
modes till it seemed to Badr Basim as if the palace danced
with him for joy. His sense was ecstasied and his breast
broadened, and he forgot his strangerhood and said in
himself, "Verily, this Queen is young and beautiful[35] and
I will never leave her; for her kingdom is vaster than my
kingdom and she is fairer than Princess Jauharah." So he
ceased not to drink with her till even-tide came, when they
lighted the lamps and waxen candles and diffused censer-

perfumes; nor did they leave drinking, till they were both drunken, and the singing-women sang the while. Then Queen Lab, being in liquor, rose from her seat and lay down on a bed and dismissing her women called to Badr Basim to come and sleep by her side. So he lay with her, in all delight of life till the morning. When the Queen awoke she repaired to the Hammam-bath in the palace, King Badr Basim being with her, and they bathed and were purified; after which she clad him in the finest of raiment and called for the service of wine. So the waiting women brought the drinking-gear and they drank. Presently, the Queen arose and taking Badr Basim by the hand, sat down with him on chairs and bade bring food, whereof they ate, and washed their hands. Then the damsels fetched the drinking-gear and fruits and flowers and confections, and they ceased not to eat and drink,[36] whilst the singing-girls sang various airs till the evening. They gave not over eating and drinking and merry-making for a space of forty days, when the Queen said to him, "O Badr Basim, say me whether is the more pleasant, this place or the shop of thine uncle the grocer?" He replied. "By Allah, O Queen, this is the pleasanter, for my uncle is but a beggarly man, who vendeth pot-herbs." She laughed at his words and the twain lay together in the pleasantest of case till the morning, when King Badr Basim awoke from sleep and found not Queen Lab by his side, so he said, "Would Heaven I knew where can she have gone!" And indeed he was troubled at her absence and perplexed about the case, for she stayed away from him a great while and did not return; so he donned his dress and went seeking her but not finding her, and he said to himself, "Haply, she is gone to the flower-garden." Thereupon he went out into the garden and came to a running rill beside which he saw a white she-bird and on the stream-bank a tree full of birds of various colours, and he stood and watched the birds without their seeing him. And behold, a black bird flew down upon that white she-bird and fell to billing her pigeon-fashion, then he leapt on her and trod her three consecutive times, after which the bird changed and became a woman. Badr looked at her and lo! it was Queen Lab. So he knew that the black bird was a man transmewed and that she was enamoured of him and had transformed herself into a bird, that he might enjoy her; wherefore jealousy got hold upon him and he was wroth with the Queen because of the black bird. Then he returned to his place and lay down on the carpet-bed and after an hour or so she came back to him and fell to kissing him and jesting with him; but being sore incensed against her he answered her not a word. She saw what was to do with him and was assured that he had witnessed what befel her when she was a white bird and was trodden by the black bird; yet she discovered naught to him but concealed what ailed her. When he had done her need, he said to her, "O Queen, I would have thee give me leave to go to my uncle's shop, for I long after him and have not seen him these forty days." She replied, "Go to him but tarry not from me, for I cannot brook to be parted from thee, nor can I endure without thee an hour." He said, "I hear and I obey," and mounting, rode to the shop of the Shaykh, the grocer, who welcomed him and rose to him and embracing him said to him, "How hast thou fared with yonder idolatress?" He replied, "I was well in health and happiness till this last night," and told him what had passed in the garden with the black bird.[37] Now when the old man heard his words, he said, "Beware of her, for know that the birds upon the trees were all young men and strangers, whom she loved and enchanted and turned into birds. That black bird thou sawest was one of her Mamelukes whom she loved with exceeding love, till he cast his eyes upon one of her women, wherefore she changed him into a black bird. And," continued the Shaykh, "whenas she lusteth after him she transformeth herself into a she-bird that he may enjoy her, for she still loveth him with passionate love. When she found that thou knewest of her case, she plotted evil against thee, for she loveth thee not wholly. But no harm shall betide thee from her, so long as I protect thee; therefore fear nothing; for I am a Moslem, by name Abdallah, and there is none in my day more magical than I; yet I do not make use of gramarye save upon constraint. Many a time have I put to naught the sorceries of yonder accursed and delivered folk from her, and I care not for her, because she can do me no hurt: nay, she feareth me with exceeding fear, as do all in the city who, like her, are magicians and serve the fire, not the Omnipotent Sire. So tomorrow, come thou to me and tell me what she doth with thee; for this very night she will cast about to destroy thee, and I will tell thee how thou shalt do with her, that thou mayst save thyself from her malice." Then King Badr Basim farewelled the Shaykh and returned to the Queen whom he found awaiting him. When she saw him, she rose and seating him and welcoming him brought him meat and drink and the two ate till they had enough and washed their hands; after which she called for wine and they drank till the night was well nigh half spent, when she plied him with cup after cup till he was drunken and lost sense[38] and wit. When she saw him thus, she said to him, "I conjure thee by Allah and by whatso thou worshippest, if I ask thee a question wilt thou inform me rightly and answer me truly?" And he being drunken, answered, "Yes, O my lady." Quoth she, "O my lord and light of mine eyes, when thou awokest last night and foundest me not, thou soughtest me, till thou sawest me in the garden, under the guise of a white she-bird, and also thou sawest the black bird leap on me and tread me. Now I will tell the truth of this matter. That black bird was one of my Mamelukes, whom I loved with exceeding love; but one day he cast his eyes upon a certain of my slave-girls, wherefore jealousy gat hold upon me and I transformed him by my spells into a black bird and her I slew. But now I cannot endure without him a single hour; so, whenever I lust after him, I change myself into a she-bird and go to him, that he may leap me and enjoy me, even as thou hast seen. Art thou not therefore incensed against me, because of this, albeit, by the virtue of Fire and Light, Shade and Heat, I love thee more than ever and have made thee my portion of the world?" He answered (being drunken), "Thy conjecture of the cause of my rage is correct, and it had no reason other than this." With this she embraced him and kissed him and made great show of love to him; then she lay down to sleep and he by her side. Presently, about midnight she rose from the carpet-bed and King Badr Basim was awake; but he feigned sleep and watched stealthily to see what she would do. She took out of a red bag a something red, which she planted a-middlemost the chamber, and it became a stream, running like the sea; after which she took a handful of barley and strewing it on the ground, watered it with water from the river; whereupon it became wheat in the ear, and she gathered it and ground it into flour. Then she set it aside and returning to bed, lay down by Badr Basim till morning when he arose and washed his face and asked her leave to visit the Shaykh his uncle. She gave him permission and he repaired to Abdallah and told him what had passed. The old man laughed and said, "By Allah, this miscreant witch plotteth mischief against thee; but reck thou not of her ever!" Then he gave him a pound of parched corn[39] and said to him, "Take this with thee and know that, when she seeth it, she will ask thee:—What is this and what wilt thou do with it? Do thou answer:—Abundance of good things is good; and eat of it. Then will she bring forth to thee parched grain of her own and say to thee:—Eat of this Sawik; and do thou feign to her that thou eatest thereof, but eat of this instead, and beware and have a care lest thou eat of hers even a grain; for, an thou eat so much as a grain thereof, her spells will have power over thee and she will enchant thee and say to thee:—Leave this form of a man. Whereupon thou wilt quit thine own shape for what shape she will. But, an thou eat not thereof, her enchantments will be null and void and no harm will betide thee therefrom; whereat she will be shamed with shame exceeding and say to thee:—I did but jest with thee! Then will she make a show of love and fondness to thee; but this will all be but hypocrisy in her and craft. And do thou also make a show of love to her and say to her:—O my lady and light of mine eyes, eat of this parched barley and see how delicious it is. And if she eat thereof, though it be but a grain, take water in thy hand and throw it in her face, saying:—Quit this human form (for what form soever thou wilt have her take). Then leave her and come to me and I will counsel thee what to do." So Badr Basim took leave of him and returning to the palace, went in to the Queen, who said to him, "Welcome and well come and good cheer to thee!" And she rose and kissed him, saying, "Thou hast tarried long from me, O my lord." He replied, "I have been with my uncle, and he gave me to eat of this Sawik." Quoth she, "We have better than that." Then she laid his parched Sawik in one plate and hers in another and said to him, "Eat of this, for 'tis better than thine." So he feigned to eat of it and when she thought he had done so, she took water in her hand and sprinkled him therewith saying, "Quit this form, O thou gallows-bird, thou miserable, and take that of a mule one-eyed and foul of favour." But he changed not; which when she saw, she arose and went up to him and kissed him between the eyes, saying, "O my beloved, I did but jest with thee; bear me no malice because of this." Quoth he, "O my lady, I bear thee no whit of malice; nay, I am assured that thou lovest me: but eat of this my parched barley." So she eat a mouthful of Abdallah's Sawik; but no sooner had it settled in her stomach than she was convulsed; and King Badr Basim took water in his palm and threw it in her face, saying, "Quit this human form and take that of a dapple mule." No sooner had he spoken than she found herself changed into a she-mule, whereupon the tears rolled down her cheeks and she fell to rubbing her muzzle against his feet. Then he would have bridled her, but she would not take the bit; so he left her and, going to the grocer, told him what had passed. Abdallah brought out for him a bridle and bade him rein her forthwith. So he took it to the palace, and when she saw him, she came up to him and he set the bit in her mouth and mounting her, rode forth to find the Shaykh. But when the old man saw her, he rose and said to her, "Almighty Allah confound thee, O accursed woman!" Then quoth he to Badr, "O my son, there is no more tarrying for thee in this city; so ride her and fare with her whither thou wilt and beware lest thou commit the bridle[40] to any." King Badr thanked him and farewelling him, fared on three days, without ceasing, till he drew near another city and there met him an old man, gray-headed and comely, who said to him, "Whence comest thou, O my son?" Badr replied, "From the city of this witch;" and the old man said, "Thou art my guest to-night." He consented and went with him; but by the way behold, they met an old woman, who wept when she saw the mule, and said, "There is no god but *the* God! Verily, this mule resembleth my son's she-mule, which is dead, and my heart acheth for her; so Allah upon thee, O my lord, do thou sell her to me!" He replied, "By Allah, O my mother, I cannot sell her." But she cried, "Allah upon thee, do not refuse my request, for my son will surely be a dead man except I buy him this mule." And she importuned him, till he exclaimed, "I will not sell her save for a thousand dinars," saying in himself, "Whence should this old woman get a thousand gold pieces?" Thereupon she brought out from her girdle a purse containing a thousand ducats, which when King Badr Basim saw, he said, "O my mother, I did but jest with thee; I cannot sell her." But the old man looked at him and said, "O my son, in this city none may lie, for whoso lieth they put to death." So King Badr Basim lighted down from the mule, and delivered her to the old woman, who drew the bit from her mouth and, taking water in her hand, sprinkled the mule therewith, saying, "O my daughter, quit this shape for that form wherein thou wast aforetime!" Upon this she was straightway restored to her original semblance and the two women embraced and kissed each other. So King Badr Basim knew that the old woman was Queen Lab's mother and that he had been tricked and would have fled; when, lo! the old woman whistled a loud whistle and her call was obeyed by an Ifrit as he were a great mountain, whereat Badr was affrighted and stood still. Then the old woman mounted on the Ifrit's back, taking her daughter behind her and King Badr Basim before her, and the Ifrit flew off with them; nor was it a full hour ere they were in the palace of Queen Lab, who sat down on the throne of kingship and said to Badr, "Gallows-bird that thou art, now am I come hither and have attained to that I desired and soon will I show thee how I will do with thee and with yonder old man the grocer! How many favours have I shown him! Yet he doth me frowardness; for thou hast not attained thine end but by means of him." Then she took water and sprinkled him therewith, saying, "Quit the shape wherein thou art for the form of a foul-favoured fowl, the foulest of all fowls;" and she set him in a cage and cut off from him meat and drink; but one of her women seeing this cruelty, took compassion on him and gave him food and water without her knowledge. One day, the damsel took her mistress at unawares and going forth the palace, repaired to the old grocer, to whom she told the whole case, saying, "Queen Lab is minded to make an end of thy brother's son." The Shaykh thanked her and said, "There is no help but that I take the city from her and make thee Queen thereof in her stead." Then he whistled a loud whistle and there came forth to him an Ifrit with four wings to whom he said, "Take up this damsel and carry her to the city of Julnar the Sea-born and her mother Farashah[41] for they twain are the most powerful magicians on face of earth." And he said to the damsel, "When thou comest thither, tell them that King Badr Basim is Queen Lab's captive." Then the Ifrit took up his load and, flying off with her, in a little while set her down upon the terrace roof of Queen Julnar's palace. So she descended and going in to the Queen, kissed the earth and told her what had passed to her son, first and last, whereupon Julnar rose to her and entreated her with honour and thanked her. Then she let beat the drums in the city and acquainted her lieges and the lords of her realm with the good news that King Badr Basim was found; after which she and her mother Farashah and her brother Salih assembled all the tribes of the Jinn and the troops of the main;

for the Kings of the Jinn obeyed them since the taking of
King Al-Samandal. Presently they all flew up into the air
and lighting down on the city of the sorceress, sacked the
town and the palace and slew all the Unbelievers therein
in the twinkling of an eye. Then said Julnar to the damsel,
"Where is my son?" And the slave-girl brought her the
cage and signing to the bird within, cried, "This is thy son."
So Julnar took him forth of the cage and sprinkled him
with water, saying "Quit this shape for the form wherein
thou wast aforetime;" nor had she made an end of her
speech ere he shook and became a man as before: whereupon his mother, seeing him restored to human shape, embraced him and he wept with sore weeping. On like wise
did his uncle Salih and his grandmother and the daughters
of his uncle and fell to kissing his hands and feet. Then
Julnar sent for Shaykh Abdallah and thanking him for his
kind dealing with her son, married him to the damsel, whom
he had despatched to her with news of him, and made him
King of the city. Moreover, she summoned those who survived of the citizens (and they were Moslems), and made
them swear fealty to him and take the oath of loyalty,
whereto they replied, "Hearkening and obedience!" Then
she and her company farewelled him and returned to their
own capital. The townsfolk came out to meet them, with
drums beating, and decorated the place three days and
held high festival, of the greatness of their joy for the return of their King Badr Basim. After this Badr said to his
mother, "O my mother, naught remains but that I marry
and we be all united." She replied, "Right is thy rede, O my
son, but wait till we ask who befitteth thee among the
daughters of the Kings." And his grandmother Farashah,
and the daughters of both his uncles said, "O Badr Basim,
we will help thee to win thy wish forthright." Then each of
them arose and fared forth questing in the lands, whilst
Julnar sent out her waiting women on the necks of Ifrits,
bidding them leave not a city nor a King's palace without
noting all the handsome girls that were therein. But, when
King Badr Basim saw the trouble they were taking in this

matter, he said to Julnar, "O my mother, leave this thing, for none will content me save Jauharah, daughter of King Al-Samandal; for that she is indeed a jewel,[42] according to her name." Replied Julnar, "I know that which thou seekest;" and bade forthright bring Al-Samandal the King. As soon as he was present, she sent for Badr Basim and acquainted him with the King's coming, whereupon he went in to him. Now when Al-Samandal was aware of his presence, he rose to him and saluted him and bade him welcome; and King Badr Basim demanded of him his daughter Jauharah in marriage. Quoth he, "She is thine handmaid and at thy service and disposition," and despatched some of his suite bidding them seek her abode and, after telling her that her sire was in the hands of King Badr Basim, to bring her forthright. So they flew up into the air and disappeared and they returned after a while, with the Princess who, as soon as she saw her father, went up to him and threw her arms round his neck. Then looking at her he said, "O my daughter, know that I have given thee in wedlock to this magnanimous Sovran, and valiant lion King Badr Basim, son of Queen Julnar the Sea-born, for that he is the goodliest of the folk of his day and most powerful and the most exalted of them in degree and the noblest in rank; he befitteth none but thee and thou none but him." Answered she, "I may not gainsay thee, O my sire; do as thou wilt, for indeed chagrin and despite are at an end, and I am one of his handmaids." So they summoned the Kazi and the witnesses who drew up the marriage-contract between King Badr Basim and the Princess Jauharah, and the citizens decorated the city and beat the drums of rejoicing, and they released all who were in the jails, whilst the King clothed the widows and the orphans and bestowed robes of honour upon the Lords of the Realm and Emirs and Grandees: and they made bride-feasts and held high festival night and morn ten days, at the end of which time they displayed the bride, in nine different dresses, before King Badr Basim who bestowed an honourable robe upon King Al-Samandal and sent him back to his country and people and kinsfolk. And they ceased not from living the most delectable of life and the most solaceful of days, eating and drinking and enjoying every luxury, till there came to them the Destroyer of delights and the Sunderer of Societies; and this is the end of their story,[43] may Allah have mercy on them all! Moreover, O auspicious King, a tale is also told anent

KHALIFAH THE FISHERMAN
OF BAGHDAD.

There was once in tides of yore and in ages and times long gone before in the city of Baghdad a fisherman, Khalifah hight, a pauper wight, who had never once been married in all his days.¹ It chanced one morning, that he took his net and went with it to the river, as was his wont with the view of fishing before the others came. When he reached the bank, he girt himself and tucked up his skirts; then stepping into the water, he spread his net and cast it a first cast and a second but it brought up naught. He ceased not to throw it, till he had made ten casts, and still naught came up therein; wherefore his breast was straitened and his mind perplexed concerning his case and he said, "I crave pardon of God the Great, there is no god but He, the Living, the Eternal, and unto Him I repent. There is no Majesty and there is no Might save in Allah, the Glorious, the Great! Whatso He willeth is and whatso He nilleth is not! Upon Allah (to whom belong Honour and Glory!) dependeth daily bread! Whenas He giveth to His servant, none denieth him; and whenas He denieth a servant, none giveth to him." And of the excess of his distress, he recited these two couplets:—

An Fate afflict thee, with grief manifest,
Prepare thy patience and make broad thy breast;
For of His grace the Lord of all the worlds
Shall send to wait upon unrest sweet Rest.

Then he said in his mind, "I will make this one more cast,
trusting in Allah, so haply He may not disappoint my
hope;" and he rose and casting into the river the net as far
as his arm availed, gathered the cords in his hands and
waited a full hour, after which he pulled at it and, finding
it heavy, handled it gently and drew it in, little by little,
till he got it ashore, when lo and behold! he saw in it a one-
eyed, lame-legged ape. Seeing this quoth Khalifah, "There
is no Majesty and there is no Might save in Allah! Verily,
we are Allah's and to Him we are returning! What meaneth
this heart-breaking, miserable ill-luck and hapless fortune? What is come to me this blessed day? But all this
is of the destinies of Almighty Allah!" Then he took the
ape and tied him with a cord to a tree which grew on the
river-bank, and grasping a whip he had with him, raised
his arm in the air, thinking to bring down the scourge upon
the quarry, when Allah made the ape speak with a fluent
tongue, saying, "O Khalifah, hold thy hand and beat me
not, but leave me bounden to this tree and go down to the
river and cast thy net, confiding in Allah; for He will give
thee thy daily bread." Hearing this Khalifah went down to
the river and casting his net, let the cords run out. Then he
pulled it in and found it heavier than before; so he ceased
not to tug at it, till he brought it to land, when, behold,
there was another ape in it, with front teeth wide apart,[2]
Kohl-darkened eyes and hands stained with Henna-dyes;
and he was laughing and wore a tattered waistcloth about
his middle. Quoth Khalifah, "Praised be Allah who hath
changed the fish of the river into apes!"[3] Then, going up to
the first ape, who was still tied to the tree, he said to him,
"See, O unlucky, how fulsome was the counsel thou gavest
me! None but thou made me light on this second ape: and
for that thou gavest me good-morrow with thy one eye and

thy lameness,[4] I am become distressed and weary, without dirham or dinar." So saying, he hent in hand a stick[5] and flourishing it thrice in the air, was about to come down with it upon the lame ape, when the creature cried out for mercy and said to him, "I conjure thee, by Allah, spare me for the sake of this my fellow and seek of him thy need; for he will guide thee to thy desire!" So he held his hand from him and throwing down the stick, went up to and stood by the second ape, who said to him, "O Khalifah, this my speech[6] will profit thee naught, except thou hearken to what I say to thee; but, an thou do my bidding and cross me not, I will be the cause of thine enrichment." Asked Khalifah, "And what hast thou to say to me that I may obey thee therein?" The Ape answered, "Leave me bound on the bank and hie thee down to the river; then cast thy net a third time, and after I will tell thee what to do." So he took his net and going down to the river, cast it once more and waited awhile. Then he drew it in and finding it heavy, laboured at it and ceased not his travail till he got it ashore, when he found in it yet another ape; but this one was red, with a blue waistcloth about his middle; his hands and feet were stained with Henna and his eyes blackened with Kohl. When Khalifah saw this, he exclaimed, "Glory to God the Great! Extolled be the perfection of the Lord of Dominion! Verily, this is a blessed day from first to last: its ascendant was fortunate in the countenance of the first ape, and the scroll[7] is known by its superscription! Verily, to-day is a day of apes: there is not a single fish left in the river, and we are come out to-day but to catch monkeys!" Then he turned to the third ape and said, "And what thing art thou also, O unlucky?" Quoth the ape, "Dost thou not know me, O Khalifah!"; and quoth he, "Not I!" The ape cried, "I am the ape of Abu al-Sa'adat[8] the Jew, the shroff." Asked Khalifah, "And what dost thou for him?"; and the ape answered, "I give him good-morrow at the first of the day, and he gaineth five ducats; and again at the end of the day, I give him good-even and he gaineth other five ducats." Whereupon Khalifah turned to the first ape and said to him, "See, O unlucky, what fine apes other folk have! As for thee, thou givest me good-morrow with thy one eye and thy lameness and thy ill-omened phiz and I become poor and bankrupt and hungry!" So saying, he took the cattle-stick and flourishing it thrice in the air, was about to come down with it on the first ape, when Abu al-Sa'adat's ape said to him, "Let him be, O Khalifah, hold thy hand and come hither to me, that I may tell thee what to do." So Khalifah threw down the stick and walking up to him cried, "And what hast thou to say to me, O monarch of all monkeys?" Replied the ape, "Leave me and the other two apes here, and take thy net and cast it into the river; and whatever cometh up, bring it to me, and I will tell thee what shall gladden thee." He replied, "I hear and obey," and took the net and gathered it on his shoulder, reciting these couplets:—

When straitened is my breast I will of my Creator pray,
Who may and can the heaviest weight lighten in easiest way;
For ere man's glance can turn or close his eye by God His grace
Waxeth the broken whole and yieldeth jail its prison-prey.
Therefore with Allah one and all of thy concerns commit
Whose grace and favour men of wit shall nevermore gainsay.

Now when Khalifah had made an end of his verse, he went down to the river and casting his net, waited awhile; after which he drew it up and found therein a fine young fish,[9] with a big head, a tail like a ladle and eyes like two gold pieces. When Khalifah saw this fish, he rejoiced, for he had never in his life caught its like, so he took it, marvelling, and carried it to the ape of Abu al-Sa'adat the Jew, as 'twere he had gotten possession of the universal world. Quoth the ape, "O Khalifah, what wilt thou do with this and with thine ape?"; and quoth the Fisherman, "I will tell thee, O monarch of monkeys, all I am about to do. Know then that first, I will cast about to make away with yonder accursed, my ape, and take thee in his stead and give thee every day to eat of whatso thou wilt." Rejoined the ape, "Since thou hast made choice of me, I will tell thee how thou shalt do wherein, if it please Allah Almighty, shall be the mending of thy fortune. Lend thy mind, then, to what I say to thee and 'tis this! Take another cord and tie me also to a tree, where leave me and go to the midst of The Dyke[10] and cast thy net into the Tigris.[11] Then after waiting awhile, draw it up and thou shalt find therein a fish, than which thou never sawest a finer in thy whole life. Bring it to me and I will tell thee how thou shalt do after this." So Khalifah rose forthright and casting his net into the Tigris, drew up a great cat-fish[12] the bigness of a lamb; never had he set eyes on its like, for it was larger than the first fish. He carried it to the ape, who said to him, "Gather thee some green grass and set half of it in a basket; lay the fish therein and cover it with the other moiety. Then, leaving us here tied, shoulder the basket and betake thee to Baghdad. If any bespeak thee or question thee by the way, answer him not, but fare on till thou comest to the market-street of the money-changers, at the upper end whereof thou wilt find the shop of Master Abu al-Sa'adat[13] the Jew, Shaykh of the shroffs, and wilt see him sitting on a mattress, with a cushion behind him and two coffers, one for gold and one for silver, before him, while around him stand his Mamelukes and negro-slaves and servant-lads. Go up to him and set the basket before him, saying:—O Abu al-Sa'adat, verily I went out to-day to fish and cast my net in thy name, and Allah Almighty sent me this fish. He will ask, Hast thou shown it to any but me?; and do thou answer, No, by Allah! Then will he take it of thee and give thee a dinar. Give it him back and he will give thee two dinars; but do thou return them also and so do with everything he may offer thee; and take naught from him, though he give thee the fish's weight in gold. Then will he say to thee, Tell me what thou wouldst have; and do thou reply, By Allah, I will not sell the fish save for two words! He will ask, What are they? And do thou answer, Stand up and say, Bear witness, O ye who are present in the market, that I give Khalifah the fisherman my ape in exchange for his ape, and that I barter for his lot my lot and luck for his luck. This is the price of the fish, and I have no need of gold. If he do this, I will every day give thee good-morrow and good-even, and every day thou shalt gain ten dinars of good gold; whilst this one-eyed, lame-legged ape shall daily give the Jew good-morrow, and Allah shall afflict him every day with an avanie[14] which he must needs pay, nor will he cease to be thus afflicted till he is reduced to beggary and hath naught. Hearken then to my words; so shalt thou prosper and be guided aright." Quoth Khalifah, "I accept thy counsel, O monarch of all the monkeys! But, as for this unlucky, may Allah never bless him! I know not what to do with him." Quoth the ape, "Let him go[15] into the water, and let me go also." "I hear and obey," answered Khalifah and unbound the three apes, and they went down into the river. Then he took up the cat-fish[16] which he washed then laid it in the basket upon some green grass, and covered it with other; and lastly shouldering his load, set out with the basket upon his shoulder and ceased not faring till he entered the city of Baghdad. And as he threaded the streets the folk knew him and cried out to him, saying, "What hast thou there, O Khalifah?" But he paid no heed to them and passed on till he came to the market-street of the money-changers and fared between the shops, as the ape had charged him, till he found the Jew seated at the upper end, with his servants in attendance upon him, as he were a King of the Kings of Khorasan. He knew him at first sight; so he went up to him and stood before him, whereupon Abu al-Sa'adat raised his eyes and recognising him, said, "Welcome, O Khalifah! What wantest thou and what is thy need? If any have missaid thee or spited thee, tell me and I will go with thee to the Chief of Police, who shall do thee justice on him." Replied Khalifah, "Nay, as thy head liveth, O chief of the Jews, none hath missaid me. But I went forth this morning to the river and, casting my net into the Tigris on thy luck, brought up this fish." Therewith he opened the basket and threw the fish before the Jew who admired it and said, "By the Pentateuch and the Ten Commandments,[17] I dreamt last night that the Virgin came to me and said:—Know, O Abu al-Sa'adat, that I have sent thee a pretty present! And doubtless 'tis this fish." Then he turned to Khalifah and said to him, "By thy faith, hath any seen it but I?" Khalifah replied, "No, by Allah, and by Abu Bakr the Viridical,[18] none hath seen it save thou, O chief of the Jews!" Whereupon the Jew turned to one of his lads and said to him, "Come, carry this fish to my house and bid Sa'adah[19] dress it and fry and broil it, against I make an end of my business and hie me home." And Khalifah said, "Go, O my lad; let the master's wife fry some of it and broil the rest." Answered the boy, "I hear and I obey, O my lord" and, taking the fish, went away with it to the house. Then the Jew put out his hand and gave Khalifah the fisherman a dinar, saying, "Take this for thyself, O Khalifah, and spend it on thy family." When Khalifah saw the dinar on his palm, he took it, saying, "Laud to the Lord of Dominion!" as if he had never seen aught of gold in his life, and went somewhat away; but, before he had gone far, he was minded of the ape's charge and turning back threw down the ducat, saying, "Take thy gold and give folk back their fish! Dost thou make a laughing stock of folk?" The Jew hearing this thought he was jesting and offered him two dinars upon the other, but Khalifah said, "Give me the fish and no nonsense. How knewest thou I would sell it at this price?" Whereupon the Jew gave him two more dinars and said, "Take these five ducats for thy fish and leave greed." So Khalifah hent the five dinars in hand and went away, rejoicing, and gazing and marvelling at the gold and saying, "Glory be to God! There is not with the Caliph of Baghdad what is with me this day!" Then he ceased not faring on till he came to the end of the market-street, when he remembered the words of the ape and his charge and returning to the Jew, threw him back the gold. Quoth he, "What aileth thee, O Khalifah? Dost thou want

silver in exchange for gold?" Khalifah replied, "I want nor
dirhams nor dinars. I only want thee to give me back folk's
fish." With this the Jew waxed wroth and shouted out at
him, saying, "O fisherman, thou bringest me a fish not
worth a sequin and I give thee five for it; yet art thou not
content! Art thou Jinn-mad? Tell me for how much thou
wilt sell it." Answered Khalifah, "I will not sell it for silver
nor for gold, only for two sayings[20] thou shalt say me."
When the Jew heard speak of the "Two Sayings," his eyes
sank into his head, he breathed hard and ground his teeth
for rage and said to him, "O nail-paring of the Moslems,
wilt thou have me throw off my faith for the sake of thy
fish, and wilt thou debauch me from my religion and stul-
tify my belief and my conviction which I inherited of old
from my forebears?" Then he cried out to the servants who
were in waiting and said, "Out on you! Bash me this unlucky rogue's neck and bastinado him soundly!" So they
came down upon him with blows and ceased not beating him till he fell beneath the shop, and the Jew said to
them, "Leave him and let him rise." Whereupon Khalifah
jumped up, as if naught ailed him, and the Jew said to him,
"Tell me what price thou asketh for this fish and I will give
it thee: for thou hast gotten but scant good of us this day."
Answered the Fisherman, "Have no fear for me, O master,
because of the beating; for I can eat ten donkeys' rations of
stick." The Jew laughed at his words and said, "Allah upon
thee, tell me what thou wilt have and by the right of my
Faith, I will give it thee!" The Fisherman replied, "Naught
from thee will remunerate me for this fish save the two
words whereof I spake." And the Jew said, "Meseemeth
thou wouldst have me become a Moslem?"[21] Khalifah rejoined, "By Allah, O Jew, an thou islamise 'twill nor advantage the Moslems nor damage the Jews; and in like manner,
an thou hold to thy misbelief 'twill nor damage the
Moslems nor advantage the Jews. But what I desire of thee
is that thou rise to thy feet and say:—Bear witness against
me, O people of the market, that I barter my ape for the
ape of Khalifah the Fisherman and my lot in the world for

his lot and my luck for his luck." Quoth the Jew, "If this be all thou desirest 'twill sit lightly upon me." So he rose without stay or delay and standing on his feet, repeated the required words; after which he turned to the Fisherman and asked him, "Hast thou aught else to ask of me?" "No," answered he, and the Jew said, "Go in peace!" Hearing this Khalifah sprung to his feet forthright; took up his basket and net and returned straight to the Tigris, where he threw his net and pulled it in. He found it heavy and brought it not ashore but with travail, when he found it full of fish of all kinds. Presently, up came a woman with a dish, who gave him a dinar, and he gave her fish for it; and after her an eunuch, who also bought a dinar's worth of fish, and so forth till he had sold ten dinars' worth. And he continued to sell ten dinars' worth of fish daily for ten days, till he had gotten an hundred dinars. Now Khalifah the Fisherman had quarters in the Passage of the Merchants,[22] and, as he lay one night in his lodging much bemused with Hashish, he said to himself, "O Khalifah, the folk all know thee for a poor fisherman, and now thou hast gotten an hundred golden dinars. Needs must the Commander of the Faithful, Harun al-Rashid, hear of this from some one, and haply he will be wanting money and will send for thee and say to thee:—I need a sum of money and it hath reached me that thou hast an hundred dinars: so do thou lend them to me those same." I shall answer, "O Commander of the Faithful, I am a poor man, and whoso told thee that I had an hundred dinars lied against me; for I have naught of this." Thereupon he will commit me to the Chief of Police, saying:—Strip him of his clothes and torment him with the bastinado till he confess and give up the hundred dinars in his possession. Wherefore, meseemeth to provide against this predicament, the best thing I can do, is to rise forthright and bash myself with the whip, so to use myself to beating." And his Hashish[23] said to him, "Rise, doff thy dress." So he stood up and putting off his clothes, took a whip he had by him and set handy a leather pillow; then he fell to lashing himself, laying every other blow upon the pillow and roaring out the while, "Alas! Alas! By Allah, 'tis a false saying, O my lord, and they have lied against me; for I am a poor fisherman and have naught of the goods of the world!" The noise of the whip falling on the pillow and on his person resounded in the still of night and the folk heard it, and amongst others the merchants, and they said, "Whatever can ail the poor fellow, that he crieth and we hear the noise of blows falling on him? 'Twould seem robbers have broken in upon him and are tormenting him." Presently they all came forth of their lodgings, at the noise of the blows and the crying, and repaired to Khalifah's room, but they found the door locked and said one to other, "Belike the robbers have come in upon him from the back of the adjoining saloon. It behoveth us to climb over by the roofs." So they clomb over the roofs and coming down through the sky-light,[24] saw him naked and flogging himself and asked him, "What aileth thee, O Khalifah?" He answered, "Know, O folk, that I have gained some dinars and fear lest my case be carried up to the Prince of True Believers, Harun al-Rashid, and he send for me and demand of me those same gold pieces; whereupon I should deny, and I fear that, if I deny, he will torture me, so I am torturing myself, by way of accustoming me to what may come." The merchants laughed at him and said, "Leave this fooling, may Allah not bless thee and the dinars thou hast gotten! Verily thou hast disturbed us this night and hast troubled our hearts." So Khalifah left flogging himself and slept till the morning, when he rose and would have gone about his business, but bethought him of his hundred dinars and said in his mind, "An I leave them at home, thieves will steal them, and if I put them in a belt[25] about my waist, peradventure some one will see me and lay in wait for me till he come upon me in some lonely place and slay me and take the money: but I have a device that should serve me well, right well." So he jumped up forthright and made him a pocket in the collar of his gaberdine and tying the hundred dinars up in a purse, laid them in the collar-pocket. Then he took his net and basket and staff and went down to the Tigris, where he made a cast but brought up naught. So he removed from that place to another and threw again, but once more the net came up empty; and he went on removing from place to place till he had gone half a day's journey from the city, ever casting the net which kept bringing up naught. So he said to himself, "By Allah, I will throw my net a-stream but this once more, whether ill come of it or weal!"²⁶ Then he hurled the net with all his force, of the excess of his wrath and the purse with the hundred dinars flew out of his collar-pocket and, lighting in mid-stream, was carried away by the strong current; whereupon he threw down the net and doffing his clothes, left them on the bank and plunged into the water after the purse. He dived for it nigh a hundred times, till his strength was exhausted and he came up for sheer fatigue without chancing on it. When he despaired of finding the purse, he returned to the shore, where he saw nothing but staff, net and basket and sought for his clothes, but could light on no trace of them: so he said in himself, "O vilest of those wherefor was made the byword:—The pilgrimage is not perfected save by copulation with the camel!"²⁷ Then he wrapped the net about him and taking staff in one hand and basket in other, went trotting about like a camel in rut, running right and left and backwards and forwards, dishevelled and dusty, as he were a rebel Marid let loose from Solomon's prison.²⁸ So far for what concerns the Fisherman Khalifah; but as regards the Caliph Harun al-Rashid, he had a friend, a jeweller called Ibn al-Kirnas,²⁹ and all the traders, brokers and middle-men knew him for the Caliph's merchant; wherefore there was naught sold in Baghdad, by way of rarities and things of price or Mamelukes or handmaidens, but was first shown to him. As he sat one day in his shop, behold, there came up to him the Shaykh of the brokers, with a slave-girl, whose like seers never saw, for she was of passing beauty and loveliness, symmetry and perfect grace, and among her gifts was that she knew all arts and sciences and could make verses and play upon all manner musical instruments. So Ibn al-Kirnas bought her for five thousand golden dinars and clothed her with other thousand; after which he carried her to the Prince of True Believers, with whom she lay the night and who made trial of her in every kind of knowledge and accomplishment and found her versed in all sorts of arts and sciences, having no equal in her time. Her name was Kut al-Kulub[30] and she was even as saith the poet:—

> I fix my glance on her, whene'er she wends;
> And non-acceptance of my glance breeds pain:
> She favours graceful-necked gazelle at gaze;
> And "Graceful as gazelle" to say we're fain.

On the morrow the Caliph sent for Ibn al-Kirnas the Jeweller, and bade him receive ten thousand dinars to her price. And his heart was taken up with the slave-girl Kut al-Kulub and he forsook the Lady Zubaydah bint al-Kasim, for all she was the daughter of his father's brother[31] and he abandoned all his favourite concubines and abode a whole month without stirring from Kut al-Kulub's side save to go to the Friday prayers and return to her all in haste. This was grievous to the Lords of the Realm and they complained thereof to the Wazir Ja'afar the Barmecide, who bore with the Commander of the Faithful and waited till the next Friday, when he entered the cathedral-mosque and, foregathering with the Caliph, related to him all that occurred to him of extraordinary stories anent seld-seen love and lovers with intent to draw out what was in his mind. Quoth the Caliph, "By Allah, O Ja'afar, this is not of my choice; but my heart is caught in the snare of love and wot I not what is to be done!" The Wazir Ja'afar replied, "O Commander of the Faithful, thou knowest how this girl Kut al-Kulub is become at thy disposal and of the number of thy servants, ánd that which hand possesseth soul coveteth not. Moreover, I will tell thee another thing which is that the highest boast of Kings and Princes is in hunting and the pursuit of sport and victory; and if thou apply thyself to this, perchance it will divert thee from her, and it may be thou wilt forget her." Rejoined the Caliph, "Thou sayest well, O Ja'afar; come let us go a-hunting forthright, without stay or delay." So soon as Friday prayers were prayed, they left the mosque and at once mounting their she-mules rode forth to the chase, occupied with talk, and their attendants outwent them. Presently the heat became overhot and Al-Rashid said to his Wazir, "O Ja'afar, I am sore athirst." Then he looked around and espying a figure in the distance on a high mound, asked Ja'afar, "Seest thou what I see?" Answered the Wazir, "Yes, O Commander of the Faithful; I see a dim figure on a high mound; belike he is the keeper of a garden or of a cucumber-plot, and in whatso wise water will not be lacking in his neighbourhood;" presently adding, "I will go to him and fetch thee some." But Al-Rashid said, "My mule is swifter than thy mule; so do thou abide here, on account of the troops, whilst I go myself to him and get of this person[32] drink and return." So saying, he urged his she-mule, which started off like racing wind or railing-water and, in the twinkling of an eye, made the mound, where he found the figure he had seen to be none other than Khalifah the Fisherman, naked and wrapped in the net; and indeed he was horrible to behold, as to and fro he rolled with eyes for very redness like cresset-gleam and dusty hair in dishevelled trim, as he were an Ifrit or a lion grim. Al-Rashid saluted him and he returned his salutation; but he was wroth and fires might have been lit at his breath. Quoth the Caliph, "O man, hast thou any water?"; and quoth Khalifah, "Ho thou, art thou blind, or Jinn-mad? Get thee to the river Tigris, for 'tis behind this mound." So Al-Rashid went around the mound and going down to the river, drank and watered his mule: then without a moment's delay he returned to Khalifah and said to him, "What aileth thee, O man, to stand here, and what is thy calling?" The Fisherman cried, "This is a

stranger and sillier question than that about the water!
Seest thou not the gear of my craft on my shoulder?" Said
the Caliph, "Belike thou art a fisherman?"; and he replied,
"Yes." Asked Al-Rashid, "Where is thy gaberdine,³³ and
where are thy waistcloth and girdle and where be the rest
of thy raiment?" Now these were the very things which
had been taken from Khalifah, like for like; so, when he
heard the Caliph name them, he got into his head that it
was he who had stolen his clothes from the river-bank and
coming down from the top of the mound, swiftlier than
the blinding leven, laid hold of the mule's bridle, saying,
"Hark-ye, man, bring me back my things and leave jesting
and joking." Al-Rashid replied, "By Allah, I have not seen
thy clothes, nor know aught of them!" Now the Caliph had
large cheeks and a small mouth;³⁴ so Khalifah said to him,
"Belike, thou art by trade a singer or a piper on pipes? But
bring me back my clothes fairly and without more ado, or
I will bash thee with this my staff till thou bepiss thyself
and befoul thy clothes." When Al-Rashid saw the staff in
the Fisherman's hand and that he had the vantage of him,
he said to himself, "By Allah, I cannot brook from this mad
beggar half a blow of that staff!" Now he had on a satin
gown; so he pulled it off and gave it to Khalifah, saying, "O
man, take this in place of thy clothes." The Fisherman took
it and turned it about and said, "My clothes are worth ten
of this painted 'Aba-cloak;" and rejoined the Caliph, "Put
it on till I bring thee thy gear." So Khalifah donned the
gown, but finding it too long for him, took a knife he had
with him, tied to the handle of his basket,³⁵ and cut off
nigh a third of the skirt, so that it fell only beneath his
knees. Then he turned to Al-Rashid and said to him, "Allah
upon thee, O piper, tell me what wage thou gettest every
month from thy master, for thy craft of piping." Replied
the Caliph, "My wage is ten dinars a month," and Khalifah
continued, "By Allah, my poor fellow, thou makest me sorry
for thee! Why, I make thy ten dinars every day! Hast thou a
mind to take service with me and I will teach thee the art
of fishing and share my gain with thee? So shalt thou make

five dinars a day and be my slavey and I will protect thee against thy master with this staff." Quoth Al-Rashid, "I will well"; and quoth Khalifah, "Then get off thy she-ass and tie her up, so she may serve us to carry the fish hereafter, and come hither, that I may teach thee to fish forthright." So Al-Rashid alighted and hobbling his mule, tucked his skirts into his girdle, and Khalifah said to him, "O piper, lay hold of the net thus and put it over thy forearm thus and cast it into the Tigris thus." Accordingly, the Caliph took heart of grace and, doing as the fisherman showed him, threw the net and pulled at it, but could not draw it up. So Khalifah came to his aid and tugged at it with him; but the two together could not hale it up: whereupon said the fisherman, "O piper of ill-omen, for the first time I took thy gown in place of my clothes; but this second time I will have thine ass and will beat thee to boot, till thou bepiss and beskite thyself! An I find my net torn." Quoth Al-Rashid, "Let the twain of us pull at once." So they both pulled together and succeeded with difficulty in hauling that net ashore, when they found it full of fish of all kinds and colours; and Khalifah said to Al-Rashid, "By Allah, O piper, thou art foul of favour but, an thou apply thyself to fishing, thou wilt make a mighty fine fisherman. But now 'twere best thou bestraddle thine ass and make for the market and fetch me a pair of frails,[36] and I will look after the fish till thou return, when I and thou will load it on thine ass's back. I have scales and weights and all we want, so we can take them with us and thou wilt have nothing to do but to hold the scales and pouch the price; for here we have fish worth twenty dinars. So be fast with the frails and loiter not." Answered the Caliph, "I hear and obey" and mounting, left him with his fish, and spurred his mule, in high good humour, and ceased not laughing over his adventure with the Fisherman, till he came up to Ja'afar, who said to him, "O Commander of the Faithful, belike, when thou wentest down to drink, thou foundest a pleasant flower-garden and enteredst and tookest thy pleasure therein alone?" At this Al-Rashid fell a-laughing again and all the Barmecides rose and kissed the ground before him, saying, "O Commander of the Faithful, Allah make joy to endure for thee and do away annoy from thee! What was the cause of thy delaying when thou faredst to drink and what hath befallen thee?" Quoth the Caliph, "Verily, a right wondrous tale and a joyous adventure and a wondrous hath befallen me." And he repeated to them what had passed between himself and the Fisherman and his words, "Thou stolest my clothes!" and how he had given him his gown and how he had cut off a part of it, finding it too long for him. Said Ja'afar, "By Allah, O Commander of the Faithful, I had it in mind to beg the gown of thee: but now I will go straight to the Fisherman and buy it of him." The Caliph replied, "By Allah, he hath cut off a third part of the skirt and spoilt it! But, O Ja'afar, I am tired with fishing in the river, for I have caught great store of fish which I left on the bank with my master Khalifah, and he is watching them and waiting for me to return to him with a couple of frails and a matchet.[37] Then we are to go, I and he, to the market and sell the fish and share the price." Ja'afar rejoined, "O Commander of the Faithful, I will bring you a purchaser for your fish." And Al-Rashid retorted, "O Ja'afar, by the virtue of my holy forefathers, whoso bringeth me one of the fish that are before Khalifah, who taught me angling, I will give him for it a gold dinar!" So the crier proclaimed among the troops that they should go forth and buy fish for the Caliph, and they all arose and made for the river-side. Now, while Khalifah was expecting the Caliph's return with the two frails, behold, the Mamelukes swooped down upon him like vultures and took the fish and wrapped them in gold-embroidered kerchiefs, beating one another in their eagerness to get at the Fisherman. Whereupon quoth Khalifah, "Doubtless these are of the fish of Paradise!"[38] and hending two fish in right hand and left, plunged into the water up to his neck and fell a-saying, "O Allah, by the virtue of these fish, let Thy servant the piper, my partner, come to me at this very moment." And suddenly up to him came a black slave which was the chief of the Caliph's negro eunuchs. He had tarried behind the rest, by reason of his horse having stopped to make water by the way, and finding that naught remained of the fish, little or much, looked right and left, till he espied Khalifah standing in the stream, with a fish in either hand, and said to him, "Come hither, O Fisherman!" But Khalifah replied, "Begone and none of your impudence!"[39] So the eunuch went up to him and said, "Give me the fish and I will pay thee their price." Replied the Fisherman, "Art thou little of wit? I will not sell them." Therewith the eunuch drew his mace upon him, and Khalifah cried out, saying, "Strike not, O loon! Better largesse than the mace."[40] So saying, he threw the two fishes to the eunuch, who took them and laid them in his kerchief. Then he put hand in pouch, but found not a single dirham and said to Khalifah, "O Fisherman, verily thou art out of luck for, by Allah, I have not a silver about me! But come to-morrow to the Palace of the Caliphate and ask for the eunuch Sandal; whereupon the castratos will direct thee to me and by coming thither thou shalt get what falleth to thy lot and therewith wend thy ways." Quoth Khalifah, "Indeed, this is a blessed day and its blessedness was manifest from the first of it!"[41] Then he shouldered his net and returned to Baghdad; and as he passed through the streets, the folk saw the Caliph's gown on him and stared at him till he came to the gate of his quarter, by which was the shop of the Caliph's tailor. When the man saw him wearing a dress of the apparel of the Caliph, worth a thousand dinars, he said to him, "O Khalifah, whence hadst thou that gown?" Replied the Fisherman, "What aileth thee to be impudent? I had it of one whom I taught to fish and who is become my apprentice. I forgave him the cutting off of his hand[42] for that he stole my clothes and gave me this cape in their place." So the tailor knew that the Caliph had come upon him as he was fishing and jested with him and given him the gown. Such was his case; but as regards Harun al-Rashid, he had gone out a-hunting and a-fishing only to divert his thoughts from the damsel, Kut al-Kulub. But when Zubaydah heard of her and of the Caliph's devotion to her, the Lady was fired with the jealousy which the more especially fireth women, so that she refused meat and drink and rejected the delights of sleep and awaited the Caliph's going forth on a journey or what not, that she might set a snare for the damsel. So when she learnt that he was gone hunting and fishing, she bade her women furnish the Palace fairly and decorate it splendidly and serve up viands and confections; and amongst the rest she made a China dish of the daintiest sweetmeats that can be made wherein she had put Bhang. Then she ordered one of her eunuchs go to the damsel Kut al-Kulub and bid her to the banquet, saying, "The Lady Zubaydah bint Al-Kasim, the wife of the Commander of the Faithful, hath drunken medicine to-day and, having heard tell of the sweetness of thy singing, longeth to divert herself with somewhat of thine art." Kut al-Kulub replied, "Hearing and obedience are due to Allah and the Lady Zubaydah," and rose without stay or delay, unknowing what was hidden for her in the Secret Purpose. Then she took with her what instruments she needed and, accompanying the eunuch, ceased not faring till she stood in the presence of the Princess. When she entered she kissed the ground before her again and again, then rising to her feet, said, "Peace be on the Lady of the exalted seat and the presence whereto none may avail, daughter of the house Abbasi and scion of the Prophet's family! May Allah fulfil thee of peace and prosperity in the days and the years!"[43] Then she stood with the rest of the women and eunuchs, and presently the Lady Zubaydah raised her eyes and considered her beauty and loveliness. She saw a damsel with cheeks smooth as rose and breasts like granado, a face moon-bright, a brow flower-white and great eyes black as night; her eyelids were languor-dight and her face beamed with light, as if the sun from her forehead arose and the murks of the night from the locks of her brow; and the fragrance of musk from her breath strayed and flowers bloomed in her lovely face inlaid; the moon beamed from her forehead and in her slender shape the branches swayed. She was like the full moon shining in the nightly shade; her eyes wantoned, her eyebrows were like a bow arched and her lips of coral moulded. Her beauty amazed all who espied her and her glances amated all who eyed her. Glory be to Him who formed her and fashioned her and perfected her! Quoth the Lady Zubaydah, "Well come, and welcome and fair cheer to thee, O Kut al-Kulub! Sit and divert us with thine art and the goodliness of thine accomplishments." Quoth the damsel, "I hear and I obey"; and rose and exhibited tricks of sleight of hand and legerdemain and all manner pleasing arts, till the Princess came near to fall in love with her and said to herself, "Verily, my cousin Al-Rashid is not to blame for loving her!" Then the damsel kissed ground before Zubaydah and sat down, whereupon they set food before her. Presently they brought her the drugged dish of sweetmeats and she ate thereof; and hardly had it settled in her stomach when her head fell backward and she sank on the ground sleeping. With this, the Lady said to her women, "Carry her up to one of the chambers, till I summon her"; and they replied, "We hear and we obey." Then said she to one of her eunuchs, "Fashion me a chest and bring it hitherto to me!", and shortly afterwards she bade make the semblance of a tomb and spread the report that Kut al-Kulub had choked and died, threatening her familiars that she would smite the neck of whoever should say, "She is alive." Now, behold, the Caliph suddenly returned from the chase, and the first enquiry he made was for the damsel. So there came to him one of his eunuchs, whom the Lady Zubaydah had charged to declare she was dead, if the Caliph should ask for her and, kissing ground before him, said, "May thy head live, O my lord! Be certified that Kut al-Kulub choked in eating and is dead." Whereupon cried Al-Rashid, "God never gladden thee with good news, O thou bad slave!" and entered the Palace, where he heard of her death from every one and asked, "Where is her tomb?" So they brought him to the sepulchre and showed him the pretended tomb, saying, "This is her burial-place." The Caliph, weeping sore for her, abode by the tomb a full hour, after which he arose and went away, in the utmost distress and the deepest melancholy. So the Lady Zubaydah saw that her plot had succeeded and forthright sent for the eunuch and said, "Hither with the chest!" He set it before her when she bade bring the damsel and locking her up therein, said to the Eunuch, "Take all pains to sell this chest and make it a condition with the purchaser that he buy it locked; then give alms with its price."[44] So he took it and went forth, to do her bidding. Thus fared it with these; but as for Khalifah the Fisherman, when morning morrowed and shone with its light and sheen, he said to himself, "I cannot do aught better to-day than visit the Eunuch who bought the fish of me, for he appointed me to come to him in the Palace of the Caliphate." So he went forth of his lodging, intending for the palace, and when he came thither, he found Mamelukes, negro-slaves and eunuchs standing and sitting; and looking at them, behold, seated amongst them was the Eunuch who had taken the fish of him, with the white slaves waiting on him. Presently, one of the Mameluke-lads called out to him; whereupon the Eunuch turned to see who he was and lo! it was the Fisherman. Now when Khalifah was ware that he saw him and recognised him, he said to him, "I have not failed thee, O my little Tulip![45] On this wise are men of their word." Hearing his address Sandal the Eunuch[46] laughed and replied, "By Allah, thou art right, O Fisherman," and put his hand to his pouch, to give him somewhat; but at that moment there arose a great clamour. So he raised his head to see what was to do and finding that it was the Wazir Ja'afar the Barmecide coming forth from the Caliph's presence, he rose to him and forewent him, and they walked about, conversing for a longsome time. Khalifah the fisherman waited awhile; then, growing weary of standing and finding that the Eunuch took no heed of him, he set himself in his way and beckoned to him from afar, saying, "O my lord Tulip, give me my due and let me go!" The Eunuch heard him, but was ashamed to answer him because of the Minister's presence; so he went on talking with Ja'afar and took no notice whatever of the Fisherman. Whereupon quoth Khalifah, "O Slow o' Pay![47] May Allah put to shame all churls and all who take folk's goods and are niggardly with them! I put myself under thy protection, O my lord Bran-belly,[48] to give me my due and let me go!" The Eunuch heard him, but was ashamed to answer him before Ja'afar; and the Minister saw the Fisherman beckoning and talking to him, though he knew not what he was saying; so he said to Sandal, misliking his behaviour, "O Eunuch, what would yonder beggar with thee?" Sandal replied, "Dost thou not know him, O my lord the Wazir?"; and Ja'afar answered, "By Allah, I know him not! How should I know a man I have never seen but at this moment?" Rejoined the Eunuch, "O my lord, this is the Fisherman whose fish we seized on the banks of the Tigris. I came too late to get any and was ashamed to return to the Prince of True Believers, empty-handed, when all the Mamelukes had some. Presently I espied the Fisherman standing in mid-stream, calling on Allah, with four fishes in his hands, and said to him:—Give me what thou hast there and take their worth. He handed me the fish and I put my hand into my pocket, purposing to gift him with somewhat, but found naught therein and said:—Come to me in the Palace, and I will give thee wherewithal to aid thee in thy poverty. So he came to me to-day and I was putting hand to pouch, that I might give him somewhat, when thou camest forth and I rose to wait on thee and was diverted with thee from him, till he grew tired of waiting; and this is the whole story, how he cometh to be standing here." The Wazir, hearing this account, smiled and said, "O Eunuch, how is it that this Fisherman cometh in his hour of need and thou satisfiest him not? Dost thou not know him, O Chief of the Eunuchs?" "No," answered Sandal and Ja'afar said, "This is the Master of the Commander of the

Faithful, and his partner and our lord the Caliph hath arisen this morning, strait of breast, heavy of heart and troubled in thought, nor is there aught will broaden his breast save this fisherman. So let him not go, till I crave the Caliph's pleasure concerning him and bring him before him; perchance Allah will relieve him of his oppression and console him for the loss of Kut al-Kulub, by means of the Fisherman's presence, and he will give him wherewithal to better himself; and thou wilt be the cause of this." Replied Sandal, "O my lord, do as thou wilt and may Allah Almighty long continue thee a pillar of the dynasty of the Commander of the Faithful, whose shadow Allah perpetuate[49] and prosper it, root and branch!" Then the Wazir Ja'afar rose up and went in to the Caliph and Sandal ordered the Mamelukes not to leave the Fisherman; whereupon Khalifah cried, "How goodly is thy bounty, O Tulip! The seeker is become the sought. I come to seek my due, and they imprison me for debts in arrears!"[50] When Ja'afar came in to the presence of the Caliph, he found him sitting with his head bowed earthwards, breast straitened and mind melancholy, humming the verses of the poet:—

My blamers instant bid that I for her become consoled;
But I, what can I do, whose heart declines to be controlled?
And how can I in patience bear the loss of lovely maid,
When fails me patience for a love that holds with firmest
   hold!
Ne'er I'll forget her nor the bowl that 'twixt us both went
   round
And wine of glances maddened me with drunkenness
   ensoul'd.

Whenas Ja'afar stood in the presence, he said, "Peace be upon thee, O Commander of the Faithful, Defender of the honour of the Faith and descendant of the uncle of the Prince of the Apostles, Allah assain him and save him and his family one and all!" The Caliph raised his head and answered, "And on thee be peace and the mercy of Allah and

His blessings!" Quoth Ja'afar; "With leave of the Prince of True Believers, his servant would speak without restraint." Asked the Caliph, "And when was restraint put upon thee in speech and thou the Prince of Wazirs? Say what thou wilt." Answered Ja'afar, "When I went out, O my lord, from before thee, intending for my house, I saw standing at the door thy master and teacher and partner, Khalifah the Fisherman, who was aggrieved at thee and complained of thee saying:—Glory be to God! I taught him to fish and he went away to fetch me a pair of frails, but never came back: and this is not the way of a good partner or of a good apprentice. So, if thou hast a mind to partnership, well and good; and if not, tell him, that he may take to partner another." Now when the Caliph heard these words he smiled and his straitness of breast was done away with and he said, "My life on thee, is this the truth thou sayest, that the Fisherman standeth at the door?" and Ja'afar replied, "By thy life, O Commander of the Faithful, he standeth at the door." Quoth the Caliph, "O Ja'afar, by Allah, I will assuredly do my best to give him his due! If Allah at my hands send him misery, he shall have it; and if prosperity he shall have it." Then he took a piece of paper and cutting it in pieces, said to the Wazir, "O Ja'afar, write down with thine own hand twenty sums of money, from one dinar to a thousand, and the names of all kinds of offices and dignities from the least appointment to the Caliphate; also twenty kinds of punishment from the lightest beating to death."[51] "I hear and I obey, O Commander of the Faithful," answered Ja'afar and did as he was bidden. Then said the Caliph, "O Ja'afar, I swear by my holy forefathers and by my kinship to Hamzah[52] and Akil,[53] that I mean to summon the fisherman and bid him take one of these papers, whose contents none knoweth save thou and I; and whatsoever is written in the paper which he shall choose, I will give it to him; though it be the Caliphate I will divest myself thereof and invest him therewith and grudge it not to him; and, on the other hand, if there be written therein hanging or mutilation or death, I will execute it upon him.

Now go and fetch him to me." When Ja'afar heard this, he said to himself, "There is no Majesty and there is no Might save in Allah, the Glorious, the Great! It may be somewhat will fall to this poor wretch's lot that will bring about his destruction, and I shall be the cause. But the Caliph hath sworn; so nothing remains now but to bring him in, and naught will happen save whatso Allah willeth." Accordingly he went out to Khalifah the Fisherman and laid hold of his hand, to carry him in to the Caliph, whereupon his reason fled and he said in himself, "What a stupid I was to come after yonder ill-omened slave, Tulip, whereby he hath brought me in company with Bran-belly!" Ja'afar fared on with him, with Mamelukes before and behind, whilst he said, "Doth not arrest suffice, but these must go behind and before me, to hinder my making off?" till they had traversed seven vestibules, when the Wazir said to him, "Mark my words, O Fisherman! Thou standest before the Commander of the Faithful and Defender of the Faith!" Then he raised the great curtain and Khalifah's eyes fell on the Caliph, who was seated on his couch, with the Lords of the realm standing in attendance upon him. As soon as he knew him, he went up to him and said, "Well come, and welcome to thee, O piper! 'Twas not right of thee to make thyself a Fisherman and go away, leaving me sitting to guard the fish, and never to return! For, before I was aware, there came up Mamelukes on beasts of all manner colours, and snatched away the fish from me, I standing alone, and this was all of thy fault; for, hadst thou returned with the frails forthright, we had sold an hundred dinars' worth of fish. And now I come to seek my due, and they have arrested me. But thou, who hath imprisoned thee also in this place?" The Caliph smiled and raising a corner of the curtain, put forth his head and said to the Fisherman, "Come hither and take thee one of these papers." Quoth Khalifah the Fisherman, "Yesterday thou wast a fisherman, and to-day thou hast become an astrologer; but the more trades a man hath, the poorer he waxeth." Thereupon Ja'afar said, "Take the paper at once, and do as the Commander of the Faithful biddeth thee without prating." So he came forward and put forth his hand saying, "Far be it from me that this piper should ever again be my knave and fish with me!" Then taking the paper he handed it to the Caliph, saying, "O piper, what hath come out for me therein? Hide naught thereof." So Al-Rashid received it and passed it on to Ja'afar and said to him, "Read what is therein." He looked at it and said, "There is no Majesty there is no Might save in Allah, the Glorious, the Great!" Said the Caliph, "Good news,⁵⁴ O Ja'afar? What seest thou therein?" Answered the Wazir, "O Commander of the Faithful, there came up from the paper:——Let the Fisherman receive an hundred blows with a stick." So the Caliph commanded to beat the Fisherman and they gave him an hundred sticks: after which he rose, saying, "Allah damn this, O Bran-belly! Are jail and sticks part of the game?" Then said Ja'afar, "O Commander of the Faithful, this poor devil is come to the river, and how shall he go away thirsting? We hope that among the alms-deeds of the Commander of the Faithful, he may have leave to take another paper, so haply somewhat may come out wherewithal he may succour his poverty." Said the Caliph, "By Allah, O Ja'afar, if he take another paper and death be written therein, I will assuredly kill him, and thou wilt be the cause." Answered Ja'afar, "If he die he will be at rest." But Khalifah the Fisherman said to him, "Allah ne'er gladden thee with good news! Have I made Baghdad strait upon you, that ye seek to slay me?" Quoth Ja'afar, "Take thee a paper and crave the blessing of Allah Almighty!" So he put out his hand and taking a paper, gave it to Ja'afar, who read it and was silent. The Caliph asked, "Why art thou silent, O son of Yahya?"; and he answered, "O Commander of the Faithful, there hath come out on this paper:——Naught shall be given to the Fisherman." Then said the Caliph, "His daily bread will not come from us: bid him fare forth from before our face." Quoth Ja'afar, "By the claims of thy pious forefathers, let him take a third paper, it may be it will bring him alimony;" and quoth the Caliph, "Let him take one and no more." So he put out his hand and took a third paper, and behold, therein was written, "Let the Fisherman be given one dinar." Ja'afar cried to him, "I sought good fortune for thee, but Allah willed not to thee aught save this dinar." And Khalifah answered, "Verily, a dinar for every hundred sticks were rare good luck, may Allah not send thy body health!" The Caliph laughed at him and Ja'afar took him by the hand and led him out. When he reached the door, Sandal the eunuch saw him and said to him, "Hither, O Fisherman! Give us portion of that which the Commander of the Faithful hath bestowed on thee, whilst jesting with thee." Replied Khalifah, "By Allah, O Tulip, thou art right! Wilt thou share with me, O nigger? Indeed, I have eaten stick to the tune of an hundred blows and have earned one dinar, and thou art but too welcome to it." So saying, he threw him the dinar and went out, with the tears flowing down the plain of his cheeks. When the Eunuch saw him in this plight, he knew that he had spoken sooth and called to the lads to fetch him back: so they brought him back and Sandal, putting his hand to his pouch, pulled out a red purse, whence he emptied an hundred golden dinars into the Fisherman's hand, saying, "Take this gold in payment of thy fish and wend thy ways." So Khalifah, in high good humour, took the hundred ducats and the Caliph's one dinar and went his way, and forgot the beating. Now, as Allah willed it for the furthering of that which He had decreed, he passed by the mart of the hand-maidens and seeing there a mighty ring where many folks were foregathering, said to himself, "What is this crowd?" So he brake through the merchants and others, who said, "Make wide the way for Skipper Rapscallion,[55] and let him pass." Then he looked and behold, he saw a chest, with an eunuch seated thereon and an old man standing by it, and the Shaykh was crying, "O merchants, O men of money, who will hasten and hazard his coin for this chest of unknown contents from the Palace of the Lady Zubaydah bint al-Kasim, wife of the Commander of the Faithful? How much shall I say for you, Allah bless you all!" Quoth one of the merchants, "By

Allah, this is a risk! But I will say one word and no blame to
me. Be it mine for twenty dinars." Quoth another, "Fifty,"
and they went on bidding, one against other, till the price
reached an hundred ducats. Then said the crier, "Will any
of you bid more, O merchants?" And Khalifah the Fisherman said, "Be it mine for an hundred dinars and one dinar."
The merchants, hearing these words, thought he was jesting and laughed at him, saying, "O eunuch, sell it to Khalifah for an hundred dinars and one dinar!" Quoth the eunuch, "By Allah, I will sell it to none but him! Take it, O
Fisherman, the Lord bless thee in it, and here with thy
gold." So Khalifah pulled out the ducats and gave them to
the eunuch, who, the bargain being duly made, delivered
to him the chest and bestowed the price in alms on the
spot; after which he returned to the Palace and acquainted
the Lady Zubaydah with what he had done, whereat she
rejoiced. Meanwhile the Fisherman hove the chest on
shoulder, but could not carry it on this wise for the excess
of its weight; so he lifted it on to his head and thus bore it
to the quarter where he lived. Here he set it down and
being weary, sat awhile, bemusing what had befallen him
and saying in himself, "Would Heaven I knew what is in
this chest!" Then he opened the door of his lodging and
haled the chest till he got it into his closet; after which he
strove to open it, but failed. Quoth he, "What folly possessed me to buy this chest? There is no help for it but to
break it open and see what is herein." So he applied himself to the lock, but could not open it, and said to himself,
"I will leave it till to-morrow." Then he would have
stretched him out to sleep, but could find no room; for the
chest filled the whole closet. So he got upon it and lay him
down; but, when he had lain awhile, behold, he felt something stir under him whereat sleep forsook him and his
reason fled. So he arose and cried, "Meseems there be Jinns
in the chest. Praise to Allah who suffered me not to open it!
For, had I done so, they had risen against me in the dark
and slain me, and from them would have befallen me
naught of good." Then he lay down again when, lo! the

chest moved a second time, more than before; whereupon he sprang to his feet and said, "There it goes again: but this is terrible!" And he hastened to look for the lamp, but could not find it and had not the wherewithal to buy another. So he went forth and cried out, "Ho people of the quarter!" Now the most part of the folk were asleep; but they awoke at his crying and asked, "What aileth thee, O Khalifah?" He answered, "Bring me a lamp, for the Jinn are upon me." They laughed at him and gave him a lamp, wherewith he returned to his closet. Then he smote the lock of the chest with a stone and broke it and opening it, saw a damsel like a Houri lying asleep within. Now she had been drugged with Bhang, but at that moment she threw up the stuff and awoke; then she opened her eyes and feeling herself confined and cramped, moved. At this sight quoth Khalifah, "By Allah, O my lady, whence art thou?"; and quoth she, "Bring me Jessamine, and Narcissus."[56] And Khalifah answered, "There is naught here but Henna-flowers."[57] Thereupon she came to herself and considering Khalifah, said to him, "What art thou?" presently adding, "And where am I?" He said, "Thou art in my lodging." Asked she, "Am I not in the Palace of the Caliph Harun al-Rashid?" And quoth he, "What manner of thing is Al-Rashid?[58] O madwoman, Thou art naught but my slave-girl: I bought thee this very day for an hundred dinars and one dinar, and brought thee home, and thou wast asleep in this here chest." When she heard these words she said to him, "What is thy name?" Said he, "My name is Khalifah. How comes my star to have grown propitious, when I know my ascendant to have been otherwise?" She laughed and cried, "Spare me this talk! Hast thou anything to eat?" Replied he, "No, by Allah, nor yet to drink! I have not eaten these two days and am now in want of a morsel." She asked, "Hast thou no money?"; and he said, "Allah keep this chest which hath beggared me: I gave all I had for it and am become bankrupt." The damsel laughed at him and said, "Up with thee and seek of thy neighbours somewhat for me to eat, for I am hungry." So he went forth and cried out, "Ho, people of the quarter!" Now the folk were asleep; but they awoke and asked, "What aileth thee, O Khalifah?" Answered he, "O my neighbours, I am hungry and have nothing to eat." So one came down to him with a bannock and another with broken meats and a third with a bittock of cheese and a fourth with a cucumber; and so on till his lap was full and he returned to his closet and laid the whole between her hands, saying, "Eat." But she laughed at him, saying, "How can I eat of this, when I have not a mug of water whereof to drink? I fear to choke with a mouthful and die." Quoth he, "I will fill thee this pitcher."[59] So he took the pitcher and going forth, stood in the midst of the street and cried out, saying, "Ho, people of the quarter!" Quoth they, "What calamity is upon thee to-night,[60] O Khalifah!" And he said, "Ye gave me food and I ate; but now I am a-thirst; so give me to drink." Thereupon one came down to him with a mug and another with an ewer and a third with a gugglet; and he filled his pitcher and, bearing it back, said to the damsel, "O my lady, thou lackest nothing now." Answered she, "True, I want nothing more at this present." Quoth he, "Speak to me and say me thy story." And quoth she, "Fie upon thee! An thou knowest me not, I will tell thee who I am. I am Kut al-Kulub, the Caliph's hand-maiden, and the Lady Zubaydah was jealous of me; so she drugged me with Bhang and set me in this chest," presently adding "Alhamdolillah—praised be God—for that the matter hath come to easy issue and no worse! But this befel me not save for thy good luck, for thou wilt certainly get of the Caliph Al-Rashid money galore, that will be the means of thine enrichment." Quoth Khalifah, "Is not Al-Rashid he in whose Palace I was imprisoned?" "Yes," answered she; and he said, "By Allah, never saw I more niggardly wight than he, that piper little of good and wit! He gave me an hundred blows with a stick yesterday and but one dinar, for all I taught him to fish and made him my partner; but he played me false." Replied she, "Leave this unseemly talk, and open thine eyes and look thou bear thyself respectfully, whenas thou seest him after this, and thou shalt win thy wish." When he heard her words, it was if he had been asleep and awoke; and Allah removed the veil from his judgment, because of his good luck,[61] and he answered, "On my head and eyes!" Then said he to her, "Sleep, in the name of Allah."[62] So she lay down and fell asleep (and he afar from her) till the morning, when she sought of him ink-case[63] and paper and, when they were brought wrote to Ibn al-Kirnas, the Caliph's friend, acquainting him with her case and how at the end of all that had befallen her she was with Khalifah the Fisherman, who had bought her. Then she gave him the scroll, saying, "Take this and hie thee to the jewel-market and ask for the shop of Ibn al-Kirnas the Jeweller and give him this paper and speak not." "I hear and I obey," answered Khalifah and going with the scroll to the market, enquired for the shop of Ibn al-Kirnas. They directed him thither and on entering it he saluted the merchant, who returned his salam with contempt and said to him, "What dost thou want?" Thereupon he gave him the letter and he took it, but read it not, thinking the Fisherman a beggar, who sought an alms of him, and said to one of his lads, "Give him half a dirham." Quoth Khalifah, "I want no alms; read the paper." So Ibn al-Kirnas took the letter and read it; and no sooner knew its import than he kissed it and laid it on his head; then he arose and said to Khalifah, "O my brother, where is thy house?" Asked Khalifah, "What wantest thou with my house? Wilt thou go thither and steal my slave-girl?" Then Ibn al-Kirnas answered, "Not so: on the contrary, I will buy thee somewhat whereof you may eat, thou and she." So he said, "My house is in such a quarter;" and the merchant rejoined, "Thou hast done well. May Allah not give thee health, O unlucky one!"[64] Then he called out to two of his slaves and said to them, "Carry this man to the shop of Mohsin the Shroff and say to him, 'O Mohsin, give this man a thousand dinars of gold; then bring him back to me in haste.'" So they carried him to the money-changer, who paid him the money, and returned with him to their master, whom they found mounted on a dapple she-mule worth a thousand dinars, with Mamelukes and pages about him, and by his side another mule like his own, saddled and bridled. Quoth the jeweller to Khalifah, "Bismillah, mount this mule." Replied he, "I won't; for by Allah, I fear she throw me;" and quoth Ibn al-Kirnas, "By God, needs must thou mount." So he came up and mounting her, face to crupper, caught hold of her tail and cried out; whereupon she threw him on the ground and they laughed at him; but he rose and said, "Did I not tell thee I would not mount this great jenny-ass?" Thereupon Ibn al-Kirnas left him in the market and repairing to the Caliph, told him of the damsel; after which he returned and removed her to his own house. Meanwhile Khalifah went home to look after the handmaid and found the people of the quarter foregathering and saying, "Verily, Khalifah is to-day in a terrible pickle!⁶⁵ Would we knew whence he can have gotten this damsel?" Quoth one of them, "He is a mad pimp: haply he found her lying on the road drunken, and carried her to his own house, and his absence showeth that he knoweth his offence." As they were talking, behold, up came Khalifah, and they said to him, "What a plight is thine, O unhappy! knowest thou not what is come to thee?" He replied, "No, by Allah!" and they said, "But just now there came Mamelukes and took away thy slave-girl whom thou stolest, and sought for thee, but found thee not." Asked Khalifah, "And how came they to take my slave-girl?"; and quoth one, "Had he fallen in their way, they had slain him." But he, so far from heeding them, returned running to the shop of Ibn al-Kirnas, whom he met riding, and said to him, "By Allah, 'twas not right of thee to wheedle me and meanwhile send thy Mamelukes to take my slave-girl!" Replied the jeweller, "O idiot, come with me and hold thy tongue." So he took him and carried him into a house handsomely builded, where he found the damsel seated on a couch of gold, with ten slave-girls like moons round her. Sighting her Ibn al-Kirnas kissed ground before her and she said, "What hast thou done with my new master, who bought me with all he owned?" He replied, "O my lady, I gave him a thousand golden dinars;" and related to her Khalifah's history from first to last, whereat she laughed and said, "Blame him not; for he is but a common wight. These other thousand dinars are a gift from me to him and Almighty Allah willing, he shall win of the Caliph what shall enrich him." As they were talking, there came an eunuch from the Commander of the Faithful, in quest of Kut al-Kulub for, when he knew that she was in the house of Ibn al-Kirnas, he could not endure the severance, but bade bring her forthwith. So she repaired to the Palace, taking Khalifah with her, and going into the presence, kissed ground before the Caliph, who rose to her, saluting and welcoming her, and asked her how she had fared with him who had brought her. She replied, "He is a man, Khalifah the Fisherman hight, and there he standeth at the door. He telleth me that he hath an account to settle with the Commander of the Faithful, by reason of a partnership between him and the Caliph in fishing." Asked Al-Rashid, "Is he at the door?" and she answered, "Yes." So the Caliph sent for him and he kissed ground before him and wished him endurance of glory and prosperity. The Caliph marvelled at him and laughed at him and said to him, "O Fisherman, wast thou in very deed my partner[66] yesterday?" Khalifah took his meaning and heartening his heart and summoning spirit replied, "By Him who bestowed upon thee the succession to thy cousin,[67] I know her not in anywise and have had no commerce with her save by way of sight and speech!" Then he repeated to him all that had befallen him, since he last saw him,[68] whereat the Caliph laughed and his breast broadened and he said to Khalifah, "Ask of us what thou wilt, O thou who bringest to owners their own!" But he was silent; so the Caliph ordered him fifty thousand dinars of gold and a costly dress of honour such as great Sovrans don, and a she-mule, and gave him black slaves of the Sudan to serve him, so that he became as he were one of the Kings of that time. The Caliph was rejoiced at the recovery of his favourite and knew that all this was the doing of his cousin-wife, the Lady Zubaydah; wherefore he was sore enraged against her and held aloof from her a great while, visiting her not neither inclining to pardon her. When she was certified of this, she was sore concerned for his wrath and her face, that was wont to be rosy, waxed pale and wan till, when her patience was exhausted, she sent a letter to her cousin, the Commander of the Faithful, making her excuses to him and confessing her offences, and ending with these verses:—

I long once more the love that was between us to regain,
That I may quench the fire of grief and bate the force of
    bane.
O lords of me, have ruth upon the stress my passion deals
Enough to me is what you doled of sorrow and of pain.
'Tis life to me an deign you keep the troth you deigned to
    plight
'Tis death to me an troth you break and fondest vows
    profane:
Given I've sinned a sorry sin, yet grant me ruth, for naught
By Allah, sweeter is than friend who is of pardon fain.

When the Lady Zubaydah's letter reached the Caliph, and reading it he saw that she confessed her offence and sent her excuses to him therefor, he said to himself, "Verily, all sins doth Allah forgive; aye, Gracious, Merciful is He!"[69] And he returned her an answer, expressing satisfaction and pardon and forgiveness for what was past, whereat she rejoiced greatly. As for Khalifah, the Fisherman, the Caliph assigned him a monthly solde of fifty dinars, and took him into especial favour, which would lead to rank and dignity, honour and worship. Then he kissed ground before the Commander of the Faithful and went forth with stately gait. When he came to the door, the Eunuch Sandal, who had given him the hundred dinars, saw him and knowing him, said to him, "O Fisherman, whence all this?" So he told him all that had befallen him, first and last, whereat Sandal rejoiced, because he had been the cause of his enrichment, and said to him, "Wilt thou not give me largesse of this wealth which is now become thine?" So Khalifah put hand to pouch and taking out a purse containing a thousand dinars, gave it to the Eunuch, who said, "Keep thy coins and Allah bless thee therein!" and marvelled at his manliness and at the liberality of his soul, for all his late poverty.[70] Then leaving the eunuch, Khalifah mounted his she-mule and rode, with the slaves' hands on her crupper, till he came to his lodging at the Khan, whilst the folk stared at him in surprise for that which had betided him of advancement. When he alighted from his beast they accosted him and enquired the cause of his change from poverty to prosperity, and he told them all that had happened to him from incept to conclusion. Then he bought a fine mansion and laid out thereon much money, till it was perfect in all points. And he took up his abode therein and was wont to recite thereon these two couplets:—

Behold a house that's like the Dwelling of Delight;[71]
Its aspect heals the sick and banishes despite.
Its sojourn for the great and wise appointed is,
And Fortune fair therein abideth day and night.

Then, as soon as he was settled in his house, he sought him in marriage the daughter of one of the chief men of the city, a handsome girl, and went in unto her and led a life of solace and satisfaction, joyaunce and enjoyment; and he rose to passing affluence and exceeding prosperity. So, when he found himself in this fortunate condition, he offered up thanks to Allah (extolled and excelled be He!) for what He had bestowed on him of wealth exceeding and of favours ever succeeding, praising his Lord with the praise of the grateful. And thereafter Khalifah continued to pay frequent visits to the Caliph Harun al-Rashid, with whom he found acceptance and who ceased not to overwhelm him with boons and bounty: and he abode in the enjoyment of the utmost honour and happiness and joy and gladness and in riches more than sufficing and in rank ever rising; brief, a sweet life and a savoury, pure as pleasurable, till there came to him the Destroyer of delights and the Sunderer of societies; and extolled be the perfection of Him to whom belong glory and permanence and He is the Living, the Eternal, who shall never die! And amongst the tales they tell is one of

ABU KIR THE DYER AND

ABU SIR THE BARBER.

There dwelt once, in Alexander city, two men, of whom one was a dyer, by name Abu Kir, and the other a barber Abu Sir,[1] and they were neighbours in the market-street where their shops stood side by side. The dyer was a swindler and a liar, an exceeding wicked wight, as if indeed his head-temples were hewn out of a boulder rock or fashioned of the threshold of a Jewish synagogue, nor was he ashamed of any shameful work he wrought amongst the folk. It was his wont, when any brought him cloth for staining, first to require of him payment under pretence of buying dyestuffs therewith. So the customer would give him the wage in advance and wend his ways, and the dyer would spend all he received on meat and drink; after which he would sell the cloth itself as soon as ever its owner turned his back and waste its worth in eating and drinking and what not else, for he ate not but of the daintiest and most delicate viands nor drank but of the best of that which doth away the wit of man. And when the owner of the cloth came to him, he would say to him, "Return to me to-morrow before sunrise and thou shalt find thy stuff dyed." So the customer would go away, saying to himself,

"One day is near another day," and return next day at the appointed time, when the dyer would say to him, "Come to-morrow; yesterday I was not at work, for I had with me guests and was occupied with doing what their wants required till they went: but to-morrow before sunrise come and take thy cloth dyed." So he would fare forth and return on the third day, when Abu Kir would say to him, "Indeed yesterday I was excusable, for my wife was brought to bed in the night and all day I was busy with manifold matters; but to-morrow, without fail, come and take thy cloth dyed." When the man came again at the appointed time, he would put him off with some other pretence,[2] it mattered little what, and would swear to him, as often as he came, till the customer lost patience and said, "How often wilt thou say to me, 'To-morrow?' Give me my stuff: I will not have it dyed." Whereupon the dyer would make answer, "By Allah, O my brother, I am abashed at thee; but I must tell the truth and may Allah harm all who harm folk in their goods!" The other would exclaim, "Tell me what hath happened;" and Abu Kir would reply, "As for thy stuff I dyed that same on matchless wise and hung it on the drying rope but 'twas stolen and I know not who stole it." If the owner of the stuff were of the kindly he would say, "Allah will compensate me;" and if he were of the ill-conditioned, he would haunt him with exposure and insult, but would get nothing of him, though he complained of him to the judge. He ceased not doing thus till his report was noised abroad among the folk and each used to warn other against Abu Kir who became a byword amongst them. So they all held aloof from him and none would be entrapped by him save those who were ignorant of his character; but, for all this, he failed not daily to suffer insult and exposure from Allah's creatures. By reason of this his trade became slack and he used to go to the shop of his neighbour the barber Abu Sir and sit there, facing the dyery and with his eyes on the door. Whenever he espied any one who knew him not standing at the dyery-door, with a piece of stuff in his hand, he would leave the barber's booth and go up to him saying, "What seekest thou, O thou?"; and the man would reply, "Take and dye me this thing." So the dyer would ask, "What colour wilt thou have it?" For, with all his knavish tricks his hand was in all manner of dyes; but he was never true to any one; wherefore poverty had gotten the better of him. Then he would take the stuff and say, "Give me my wage in advance and come to-morrow and take the stuff." So the stranger would advance him the money and wend his way; whereupon Abu Kir would carry the cloth to the market-street and sell it and with its price buy meat and vegetables and tobacco[3] and fruit and what not else he needed; but, whenever he saw any one who had given him stuff to dye standing at the door of his shop, he would not come forth to him or even show himself to him. On this wise he abode years and years, till it fortuned one day that he received cloth to dye from a man of wrath and sold it and spent the proceeds. The owner came to him every day, but found him not in his shop; for, whenever he espied any one who had claim against him, he would flee from him into the shop of the barber Abu Sir. At last, that angry man finding that he was not to be seen and growing weary of such work, repaired to the Kazi and bringing one of his serjeants to the shop, nailed up the door, in presence of a number of Moslems, and sealed it, for that he saw therein naught save some broken pans of earthenware to stand him instead of his stuff; after which the serjeant took the key, saying to the neighbours, "Tell him to bring back this man's cloth then come to me[4] and take his shop key;" and went his way, he and the man. Then said Abu Sir to Abu Kir, "What ill business is this?[5] Whoever bringeth thee aught thou losest it for him. What hath become of this angry man's stuff?" Answered the dyer, "O my neighbour, 'twas stolen from me." "Prodigious!" exclaimed the barber. "Whenever any one giveth thee aught, a thief stealeth it from thee! Art thou then the meeting-place of every rogue upon town? But I doubt me thou liest: so tell me the truth." Replied Abu Kir, "O my neighbour, none hath stolen aught from me." Asked Abu

Sir, "What then dost thou with the people's property?" and the dyer answered, "Whenever any one giveth me aught to dye, I sell it and spend the price." Quoth Abu Sir, "Is this permitted thee of Allah?" and quoth Abu Kir, "I do this only out of poverty, because business is slack with me and I am poor and have nothing."[6] And he went on to complain to him of the dulness of his trade and his lack of means. Abu Sir in like manner lamented the little profit of his own calling, saying, "I am a master of my craft and have not my equal in this city; but no one cometh to me to be polled, because I am a pauper; and I loathe this art and mystery, O my brother." Abu Kir replied, "And I also loathe my own craft, by reason of its slackness; but, O my brother, what call is there for our abiding in this town? Let us depart from it, I and thou, and solace ourselves in the lands of mankind, carrying in our hands our crafts which are in demand all the world over; so shall we breathe the air and rest from this grievous trouble." And he ceased not to command travel to Abu Sir, till the barber became wishful to set out; so they agreed upon their route. When they agreed to travel together Abu Kir said to Abu Sir, "O my neighbour, we are become brethren and there is no difference between us, so it behoveth us to recite the Fatihah[7] that he of us who gets work shall of his gain feed him who is out of work, and whatever is left, we will lay in a chest; and when we return to Alexandria, we will divide it fairly and equally." "So be it," replied Abu Sir, and they repeated the Opening Chapter of the Koran on this understanding. Then Abu Sir locked up his shop and gave the key to its owner, whilst Abu Kir left his door locked and sealed and let the key lie with the Kazi's serjeant; after which they took their baggage and embarked on the morrow in a galleon[8] upon the salt sea. They set sail the same day and fortune attended them, for, of Abu Sir's great good luck, there was not a barber in the ship albeit it carried an hundred and twenty men, besides captain and crew. So, when they loosed the sails, the barber said to the dyer, "O my brother, this is the sea and we shall need meat and drink;

we have but little provaunt with us and haply the voyage will be long upon us; wherefore methinks I will shoulder my budget and pass among the passengers, and may be some one will say to me:—Come hither, O barber, and shave me, and I will shave him for a scone or a silver bit or a draught of water: so shall we profit by this, I and thou too." "There's no harm in that," replied the dyer and laid down his head and slept, whilst the barber took his gear and water-tasse[9] and throwing over his shoulder a rag, to serve as napkin (because he was poor), passed among the passengers. Quoth one of them, "Ho, master, come and shave me." So he shaved him, and the man gave him a half-dirham;[10] whereupon quoth Abu Sir, "O my brother, I have no use for this bit; hadst thou given me a scone 'twere more blessed to me in this sea, for I have a shipmate and we are short of provision." So he gave him a loaf and a slice of cheese and filled him the tasse with sweet water. The barber carried all this to Abu Kir and said, "Eat the bread and cheese and drink the water." Accordingly he ate and drank, whilst Abu Sir again took up his shaving gear and, tasse in hand and rag on shoulder, went round about the deck among the passengers. One man he shaved for two scones and another for a bittock of cheese, and he was in demand, because there was no other barber on board. Also he bargained with every one who said to him, "Ho, master, shave me!" for two loaves and a half dirham, and they gave him whatever he sought, so that, by sundown, he had collected thirty loaves and thirty silvers with store of cheese and olives and botargoes.[11] And besides these he got from the passengers whatever he asked for and was soon in possession of things galore. Amongst the rest he shaved the Captain,[12] to whom he complained of his lack of victual for the voyage, and the skipper said to him, "Thou art welcome to bring thy comrade every night and sup with me and have no care for that so long as ye sail with us." Then he returned to the dyer, whom he found asleep; so he roused him; and when Abu Kir awoke, he saw at his head an abundance of bread and cheese and olives and botargoes and

said, "Whence gottest thou all this?" "From the bounty of
Allah Almighty," replied Abu Sir. Then Abu Kir would
have fallen to, but the barber said to him, "Eat not of this,
O my brother; but leave it to serve us another time; for
know that I shaved the Captain and complained to him of
our lack of victual: whereupon quoth he:——Welcome to
thee! Bring thy comrade and sup both of ye with me every
night. And this night we sup with him for the first time."
But Abu Kir replied, "My head goeth round with sea-
sickness and I cannot rise from my stead; so let me sup off
these things and fare thou alone to the Captain." Abu Sir
replied, "There is no harm in that;" and sat looking at the
other as he ate, and saw him hew off gobbets, as the quar-
ryman heweth stone from the hill-quarries and gulp them
down with the gulp of an elephant which hath not eaten
for days, bolting another mouthful ere he had swallowed
the previous one and glaring the while at that which was
before him with the glowering of a Ghul and blowing as
bloweth the hungry bull over his beans and bruised straw.
Presently up came a sailor and said to the barber, "O
craftsmaster, the Captain biddeth thee come to supper and
bring thy comrade." Quoth the barber to the dyer, "Wilt
thou come with us?"; but quoth he, "I cannot walk." So the
barber went by himself and found the Captain sitting before a tray whereon were a score or more of dishes and all
the company were awaiting him and his mate. When the
Captain saw him he asked, "Where is thy friend?"; and Abu
Sir answered, "O my lord, he is sea-sick." Said the skipper,
"That will do him no harm; his sickness will soon pass off;
but do thou carry him his supper and come back, for we
tarry for thee." Then he set apart a porringer of Kababs
and putting therein some of each dish, till there was
enough for ten, gave it to Abu Sir, saying, "Take this to thy
chum." He took it and carried it to the dyer, whom he
found grinding away with his dog-teeth[13] at the food which
was before him, as he were a camel, and heaping mouthful
on mouthful in his hurry. Quoth Abu Sir, "Did I not say to
thee:——Eat not of this? Indeed the Captain is a kindly man.

See what he hath sent thee, for that I told him thou wast sea-sick." "Give it here," cried the dyer. So the barber gave him the platter, and he snatched it from him and fell upon his food, ravening for it and resembling a grinning dog or a raging lion or a Rukh pouncing on a pigeon or one well-nigh dead for hunger who seeing meat falls ravenously to eat. Then Abu Sir left him and going back to the Captain, supped and enjoyed himself and drank coffee[14] with him; after which he returned to Abu Kir and found that he had eaten all that was in the porringer and thrown it aside, empty. So he took it up and gave it to one of the Captain's servants, then went back to Abu Kir and slept till the morning. On the morrow he continued to shave, and all he got by way of meat and drink he gave to his shipmate, who ate and drank and sat still, rising not save to do what none could do for him, and every night the barber brought him a full porringer from the Captain's table. They fared thus twenty days until the galleon cast anchor in the harbour of a city; whereupon they took leave of the skipper and landing, entered the town and hired them a closet in a Khan. Abu Sir furnished it and buying a cooking pot and a platter and spoons[15] and what else they needed, fetched meat and cooked it; but Abu Kir fell asleep the moment he entered the Caravanserai and awoke not till Abu Sir aroused him and set the tray of food[16] before him. When he awoke, he ate and saying to Abu Sir, "Blame me not, for I am giddy," fell asleep again. Thus he did forty days, whilst, every day, the barber took his gear and making the round of the city, wrought for that which fell to his lot,[17] and returning, found the dyer asleep and aroused him. The moment he awoke he fell ravenously upon the food, eating as one who cannot have his fill nor be satisfied; after which he went asleep again. On this wise he passed other forty days and whenever the barber said to him, "Sit up and be comfortable[18] and go forth and take an airing in the city, for 'tis a gay place and a pleasant and hath not its equal among the cities," he would reply, "Blame me not, for I am giddy." Abu Sir cared not to hurt his feelings nor give him hard words; but, on the forty-first day, he himself fell sick and could not go abroad; so he engaged the porter of the Khan to serve them both, and he did the needful for them and brought them meat and drink whilst Abu Kir would do nothing but eat and sleep. The man ceased not to wait upon them on this wise for four days, at the end of which time the barber's malady redoubled on him, till he lost his senses for stress of sickness; and Abu Kir, feeling the sharp pangs of hunger, arose and sought in his comrade's clothes, where he found a thousand silver bits. He took them and, shutting the door of the closet upon Abu Sir, fared forth without telling any; and the door-keeper was then at market and thus saw him not go out. Presently Abu Kir betook himself to the bazar and clad himself in costly clothes, at a price of five hundred half-dirhams; then he proceeded to walk about the streets and divert himself by viewing the city which he found to be one whose like was not among cities; but he noted that all its citizens were clad in clothes of white and blue, without other colour. Presently he came to a dyer's and seeing naught but blue in his shop, pulled out to him a kerchief and said, "O master, take this and dye it and win thy wage." Quoth the dyer, "The cost of dyeing this will be twenty dirhams;" and quoth Abu Kir, "In our country we dye it for two." "Then go and dye it in your own country! As for me, my price is twenty dirhams and I will not bate a little thereof." "What colour wilt thou dye it?" "I will dye it blue." "But I want it dyed red." "I know not how to dye red." "Then dye it green." "I know not how to dye it green." "Yellow." "Nor yet yellow." Thereupon Abu Kir went on to name the different tints to him, one after other, till the dyer said, "We are here in this city forty master-dyers, not one more nor one less; and when one of us dieth, we teach his son the craft. If he leave no son, we abide lacking one, and if he leave two sons, we teach one of them the craft, and if he die, we teach his brother. This our craft is strictly ordered, and we know how to dye but blue and no other tint whatsoever." Then said Abu Kir, "Know that I too am a dyer and wot how to

dye all colours; and I would have thee take me into thy service on hire, and I will teach thee everything of my art, so
thou mayst glory therein over all the company of dyers."
But the dyer answered, "We never admit a stranger into
our craft." Asked Abu Kir, "And what if I open a dyery for
myself?"; whereto the other answered, "We will not suffer
thee to do that on any wise;" whereupon he left him and
going to a second dyer, made him the like proposal; but he
returned him the same answer as the first; and he ceased
not to go from one to other, till he had made the round of
the whole forty masters; but they would not accept him either to master or apprentice. Then he repaired to the
Shaykh of the Dyers and told what had passed, and he said,
"We admit no strangers into our craft." Hereupon Abu Kir
became exceeding wroth and going up to the King of that
city, made complaint to him, saying, "O King of the age, I
am a stranger and a dyer by trade"; and he told him whatso
had passed between himself and the dyers of the town,
adding, "I can dye various kinds of red, such as rose-colour
and jujubel-colour[19] and various kinds of green, such as
grass-green and pistachio-green and olive and parrot's wing,
and various kinds of black, such as coal-black and Kohl-
black, and various shades of yellow, such as orange and
lemon-colour," and went on to name to him the rest of the
colours. Then said he, "O King of the age, all the dyers in
thy city can not turn out of hand any one of these tincts,
for they know not how to dye aught but blue; yet they will
not admit me amongst them, either to master or apprentice." Answered the King, "Thou sayst sooth for that matter, but I will open to thee a dyery and give thee capital and
have thou no care anent them; for whoso offereth to do
thee let or hindrance, I will hang him over his shop-door."
Then he sent for builders and said to them, "Go round
about the city with this master-dyer, and whatsoever place
pleaseth him, be it shop or Khan or what not, turn out its
occupier and build him a dyery after his wish. Whatsoever
he biddeth you, that do ye and oppose him not in aught."
And he clad him in a handsome suit and gave him two

white slaves to serve him, and a horse with housings of brocade and a thousand dinars, saying, "Expend this upon thyself against the building be completed." Accordingly Abu Kir donned the dress and mounting the horse, became as he were an Emir. Moreover the King assigned him a house and bade furnish it; so they furnished it for him and he took up his abode therein. On the morrow he mounted and rode through the city, whilst the architects went before him; and he looked about him till he saw a place which pleased him and said, "This stead is seemly;" whereupon they turned out the owner and carried him to the King, who gave him as the price of his holding, what contented him and more. Then the builders fell to work, whilst Abu Kir said to them, "Build thus and thus and do this and that," till they built him a dyery that had not its like; whereupon he presented himself before the King and informed him that they had done building the dyery and that there needed but the price of the dye-stuffs and gear to set it going. Quoth the King, "Take these four thousand dinars to thy capital and let me see the first fruits of thy dyery." So he took the money and went to the market where, finding dye-stuffs[20] plentiful and well-nigh worthless, he bought all he needed of materials for dyeing; and the King sent him five hundred pieces of stuff, which he set himself to dye of all colours and then he spread them before the door of his dyery. When the folk passed by the shop, they saw a wonder-sight whose like they had never in their lives seen; so they crowded about the entrance, enjoying the spectacle and questioning the dyer and saying, "O master, what are the names of these colours?" Quoth he, "This is red and that yellow and the other green" and so on, naming the rest of the colours. And they fell to bringing him longcloth and saying to him, "Dye it for us like this and that and take what hire thou seekest." When he had made an end of dyeing the King's stuffs, he took them and went up with them to the Divan; and when the King saw them he rejoiced in them and bestowed abundant bounty on the dyer. Furthermore, all the troops brought him stuffs, saying, "Dye for us thus and thus;" and he dyed for them to their liking, and they threw him gold and silver. After this his fame spread abroad and his shop was called the Sultan's Dyery. Good came in to him at every door and none of the other dyers could say a word to him, but they used to come to him kissing his hands and excusing themselves to him for past affronts they had offered him and saying, "Take us to thine apprentices." But he would none of them for he had become the owner of black slaves and handmaids and had amassed store of wealth. On this wise fared it with Abu Kir; but as regards Abu Sir, after closet door had been locked on him and his money had been stolen, he abode prostrate and unconscious for three successive days, at the end of which the Concierge of the Khan, chancing to look at the door, observed that it was locked and bethought himself that he had not seen and heard aught of the two companions for some time. So he said in his mind, "Haply they have made off, without paying rent,[21] or perhaps they are dead, or what is to do with them?" And he waited till sunset, when he went up to the door and heard the barber groaning within. He saw the key in the lock; so he opened the door and entering, found Abu Sir lying, groaning, and said to him, "No harm to thee: where is thy friend?" Replied Abu Sir, "By Allah, I came to my senses only this day and called out; but none answered my call. Allah upon thee, O my brother, look for the purse under my head and take from it five half-dirhams and buy me somewhat nourishing, for I am sore anhungered." The porter put out his hand and taking the purse, found it empty and said to the barber, "The purse is empty; there is nothing in it." Whereupon Abu Sir knew that Abu Kir had taken that which was therein and had fled and he asked the porter, "Hast thou not seen my friend?" Answered the door-keeper, "I have not seen him for these three days; and indeed methought you had departed, thou and he." The barber cried, "Not so; but he coveted my money and took it and fled seeing me sick." Then he fell a-weeping and a-wailing but the door-keeper said to him, "No harm shall befal thee, and Allah will requite him his deed." So he went away and cooked him some broth, whereof he ladled out a plateful and brought it to him; nor did he cease to tend him and maintain him with his own monies for two months' space, when the barber sweated[22] and the Almighty made him whole of his sickness. Then he stood up and said to the porter, "An ever the Most High Lord enable me, I will surely requite thee thy kindness to me; but none requiteth save the Lord of His bounty!" Answered the porter, "Praised be He for thy recovery! I dealt not thus with thee but of desire for the face of Allah the Bountiful." Then the barber went forth of the Khan and threaded the market-streets of the town, till Destiny brought him to the bazar wherein was Abu Kir's dyery, and he saw the vari-coloured stuffs dispread before the shop and a jostle of folk crowding to look upon them. So he questioned one of the townsmen and asked him. "What place is this and how cometh it that I see the folk crowding together?"; whereto the man answered, saying, "This is the Sultan's Dyery, which he set up for a foreigner Abu Kir hight; and whenever he dyeth new stuff, we all flock to him and divert ourselves by gazing upon his handiwork, for we have no dyers in our land who know how to stain with these colours; and indeed there befel him with the dyers who are in the city that which befel."[23] And he went on to tell him all that had passed between Abu Kir and the master-dyers and how he had complained of them to the Sultan who took him by the hand and built him that dyery and gave him this and that: brief, he recounted to him all that had occurred. At this the barber rejoiced and said in himself, "Praised be Allah who hath prospered him, so that he is become a master of his craft! And the man is excusable, for of a surety he hath been diverted from thee by his work and hath forgotten thee; but thou actedst kindly by him and entreatedst him generously, what time he was out of work; so, when he seeth thee, he will rejoice in thee and entreat thee generously, even as thou entreatedst him." According he made for the door of the dyery and saw Abu Kir seated on a high mattress spread upon a bench beside the doorway, clad in royal apparel and attended by four blackamoor slaves and four white Mamelukes all robed in the richest of raiment. Moreover, he saw the workmen, ten negro slaves, standing at work; for, when Abu Kir bought them, he taught them the craft of dyeing, and he himself sat amongst his cushions, as he were a Grand Wazir or a mighty Monarch putting his hand to naught, but only saying to the men, "Do this and do that." So the barber went up to him and stood before him, deeming he would rejoice in him when he saw him and salute him and entreat him with honour and make much of him; but, when eye fell upon eye, the dyer said to him, "O scoundrel, how many a time have I bidden thee stand not at the door of the workshop? Hast thou a mind to disgrace me with the folk, thief[24] that thou art? Seize him." So the blackamoors ran at him and laid hold of him; and the dyer rose up from his seat and said, "Throw him." Accordingly they threw him down and Abu Kir took a stick and dealt him an hundred strokes on the back; after which they turned him over and he beat him other hundred blows on his belly. Then he said to him, "O scoundrel, O villain, if ever again I see thee standing at the door of this dyery, I will forthwith send thee to the King, and he will commit thee to the Chief of Police, that he may strike thy neck. Begone, may Allah not bless thee!" So Abu Sir departed from him, broken-hearted by reason of the beating and shame that had betided him; whilst the bystanders asked Abu Kir, "What hath this man done?" He answered, "The fellow is a thief, who stealeth the stuffs of folk; he hath robbed me of cloth, how many a time! and I still said to myself:—Allah forgive him! He is a poor man; and I cared not to deal roughly with him; so I used to give my customers the worth of their goods and forbid him gently; but he would not be forbidden: and if he come again, I will send him to the King, who will put him to death and rid the people of his mischief." And the bystanders fell to abusing the barber after his back was turned. Such was the behaviour of Abu Kir; but as regards

Abu Sir, he returned to the Khan, where he sat pondering that which the dyer had done by him and he remained seated till the burning of the beating subsided, when he went out and walked about the markets of the city. Presently, he bethought him to go to the Hammambath; so he said to one of the townsfolk, "O my brother, which is the way to the Baths?" Quoth the man, "And what manner of thing may the Baths be?" and quoth Abu Sir, "'Tis a place where people wash themselves and do away their dirt and defilements, and it is of the best of the good things of the world." Replied the townsman, "Get thee to the sea," but the barber rejoined, "I want the Hammambaths." Cried the other, "We know not what manner of thing is the Hammam, for we all resort to the sea; even the King, when he would wash, betaketh himself to the sea." When Abu Sir was assured that there was no bath in the city and that the folk knew not the Baths nor the fashion thereof, he betook himself to the King's Divan and kissing ground between his hands called down blessings on him and said, "I am a stranger and a Bath-man by trade, and I entered thy city and thought to go to the Hammam; but found not one therein. How cometh a city of this comely quality to lack a Hammam, seeing that the bath is of the highest of the delights of this world?" Quoth the King, "What manner of thing is the Hammam?" So Abu Sir proceeded to set forth to him the quality of the bath, saying, "Thy capital will not be a perfect city till there be a Hammam therein." "Welcome to thee!" said the King and clad him in a dress that had not its like and gave him a horse and two blackamoor slaves, presently adding four handmaids and as many white Mamelukes: he also appointed him a furnished house and honoured him yet more abundantly than he had honoured the dyer. After this he sent builders with him saying to them, "Build him a Hammam in what place soever shall please him." So he took them and went with them through the midst of the city, till he saw a stead that suited him. He pointed it out to the builders and they set to work, whilst he directed them, and they wrought till they builded him a Hammam that had not its like. Then he bade them paint it, and they painted it rarely, so that it was a delight to the beholders; after which Abu Sir went up to the King and told him that they had made an end of building and decorating the Hammam, adding, "There lacketh naught save the furniture." The King gave him ten thousand dinars wherewith he furnished the Bath and ranged the napkins on the ropes; and all who passed by the door stared at it and their mind was confounded at its decorations. So the people crowded to this spectacle, whose like they had never in their lives seen, and solaced themselves by staring at it and saying, "What is this thing?" To which Abu Sir replied, "This is a Hammam;" and they marvelled thereat. Then he heated water and set the bath a-working,[25] and he made a jetting fountain in the great basin, which ravished the wit of all who saw it of the people of the city. Furthermore, he sought of the King ten Mamelukes not yet come to manhood, and he gave him ten boys like moons; whereupon Abu Sir proceeded to shampoo them, saying, "Do in this wise with the bathers." Then he burnt perfumes and sent out a crier to cry aloud in the city, saying, "O creatures of Allah, get ye to the Baths which be called the Sultan's Hammam!" So the lieges came thither and Abu Sir bade the slave-boys wash their bodies. The folk went down into the tank and coming forth, seated themselves on the raised pavement, whilst the boys shampooed them, even as Abu Sir had taught them; and they continued to enter the Hammam and do their need therein gratis and go out, without paying, for the space of three days. On the fourth day the barber invited the King, who took horse with his Grandees and rode to the Baths, where he put off his clothes and entered; then Abu Sir came in to him and rubbed his body with the bag-gloves, peeling from his skin dirt-rolls like lamp-wicks and showing them to the King, who rejoiced therein, and clapping his hand upon his limbs heard them ring again for very smoothness and cleanliness;[26] after which thorough washing Abu Sir mingled rose-water with the water of the tank and the King went down therein. When he came forth, his body was refreshed and he felt a lightness and liveliness such as he had never known in his life. Then the barber made him sit on the daïs and the boys proceeded to shampoo him, whilst the censers fumed with the finest lign-aloes.[27] Then said the King, "O master, is this the Hammam?"; and Abu Sir said, "Yes." Quoth the King, "As my head liveth, my city is not become a city indeed but by this Bath," presently adding, "But what pay takest thou for each person?" Quoth Abu Sir, "That which thou biddest will I take;" whereupon the King cried, "Take a thousand gold pieces for every one who washeth in thy Hammam." Abu Sir, however, said, "Pardon, O King of the age! All men are not alike, but there are amongst them rich and poor, and if I take of each a thousand dinars, the Hammam will stand empty, for the poor man cannot pay this price." Asked the King, "How then wilt thou do for the price!"; and the barber answered, "I will leave it to their generosity.[28] Each who can afford aught shall pay that which his soul grudgeth not to give, and we will take from every man after the measure of his means. On this wise will the folk come to us and he who is wealthy shall give according to his station and he who is wealth-less shall give what he can afford. Under such condition the Hammam will still be at work and prosper exceedingly; but a thousand dinars is a Monarch's gift, and not every man can avail to this." The Lords of the Realm confirmed Abu Sir's words, saying, "This is the truth, O King of the age! Thinkest thou that all folk are like unto thee, O glorious King?"[29] The King replied, "Ye say sooth; but this man is a stranger and poor and 'tis incumbent on us to deal generously with him, for that he hath made in our city this Hammam whose like we have never in our lives seen and without which our city were not adorned nor hath gotten importance; wherefore, an we favour him with increase of fee 'twill not be much." But the Grandees said, "An thou wilt guerdon him be generous with thine own monies, and let the King's bounty be extended to the poor by means of the low price of the Hammam, so the lieges may bless thee; but, as for the thousand dinars, we are the Lords of thy Land, yet do our souls grudge to pay it; and how then should the poor be pleased to afford it?" Quoth the King, "O my Grandees, for this time let each of you give him an hundred dinars and a Mameluke, a slave-girl and a blackamoor;" and quoth they, " 'Tis well; we will give it; but after to-day whoso entereth shall give him only what he can afford, without grudging." "No harm in that," said the King; and they gave him the thousand gold pieces and three chattels. Now the number of the Nobles who were washed with the King that day was four hundred souls; so that the total of that which they gave him was forty thousand dinars, besides four hundred Mamelukes and a like number of negroes and slave-girls.[30] Moreover the King gave him ten thousand dinars, besides ten white slaves and ten hand-maidens and a like number of black-amoors; whereupon coming forward Abu Sir kissed the ground before him and said, "O auspicious Sovereign, lord of justice, what place will contain me all these women and slaves?" Quoth the King, "O weak o' wit, I bade not my no-bles deal thus with thee but that we might gather together unto thee wealth galore; for may be thou wilt bethink thee of thy country and family and repine for them and be minded to return to thy mother-land; so shalt thou take from our country muchel of money to maintain thyself withal, what while thou livest in thine own country." And quoth Abu Sir, "O King of the age, (Allah advance thee!) these white slaves and women and negroes befit only Kings and hadst thou ordered me ready money, it were more profitable to me than this army; for they must eat and drink and dress, and whatever betideth me of wealth, it will not suffice for their support." The King laughed and said, "By Allah thou speakest sooth! They are indeed a mighty host, and thou hast not the wherewithal to maintain them; but wilt thou sell them to me for an hundred dinars a head?" Said Abu Sir, "I sell them to thee at that price." So the King

sent to his treasurer for the coin and he brought it and gave
Abu Sir the whole of the price without abatement[31] and in
full tale; after which the King restored the slaves to their
owners, saying, "Let each of you who knoweth his slaves
take them; for they are a gift from me to you." So they
obeyed his bidding and took each what belonged to him;
whilst Abu Sir said to the King, "Allah ease thee, O King of
the age, even as thou hast eased me of these Ghuls, whose
bellies none may fill save Allah!"[32] The King laughed, and
said he spake sooth; then taking the Grandees of his Realm
from the Hammam returned to his palace; but the barber
passed the night in counting out his gold and laying it up
in bags and sealing them; and he had with him twenty
black slaves and a like number of Mamelukes and four
slave-girls to serve him. Now when morning morrowed, he
opened the Hammam and sent out a crier to cry, saying,
"Whoso entereth the Baths and washeth shall give that
which he can afford and which his generosity requireth
him to give." Then he seated himself by the pay-chest[33]
and customers flocked in upon him, each putting down
that which was easy to him, nor had eventide evened ere
the chest was full of the good gifts of Allah the Most High.
Presently the Queen desired to go to the Hammam, and
when this came to Abu Sir's knowledge, he divided the day
on her account into two parts, appointing that between
dawn and noon to men and that between midday and sundown to women.[34] As soon as the Queen came, he stationed
a handmaid behind the pay-chest; for he had taught four
slave-girls the service of the Hammam, so that they were
become expert bath-women and tire-women. When the
Queen entered, this pleased her and her breast waxed
broad and she laid down a thousand dinars. Thus his report was noised abroad in the city, and all who entered
the bath he entreated with honour, were they rich or poor;
good came in upon him at every door and he made acquaintance with the royal guards and got him friends and
intimates. The King himself used to come to him one day

in every week, leaving with him a thousand dinars and the other days were for rich and poor alike; and he was wont to deal courteously with the folk and use them with the utmost respect. It chanced that the King's sea-captain came in to him one day in the bath; so Abu Sir did off his dress and going in with him, proceeded to shampoo him and entreated him with exceeding courtesy. When he came forth, he made him sherbet and coffee; and when he would have given him somewhat, he swore that he would not accept from him aught. So the captain was under obligation to him, by reason of his exceeding kindness and courtesy and was perplexed how to requite the bath-man his generous dealing. Thus fared it with Abu Sir: but as regards Abu Kir, hearing all the people recounting wonders of the Baths and saying, "Verily, this Hammam is the Paradise of this world! Inshallah, O such an one, thou shalt go with us tomorrow to this delightful bath," he said to himself, "Needs must I fare like the rest of the world, and see this bath that hath taken folk's wits." So he donned his richest dress and mounting a she-mule and bidding the attendance of four white slaves and four blacks, walking before and behind him, he rode to the Hammam. When he alighted at the door, he smelt the scent of burning aloes-wood and found people going in and out and the benches full of great and small. So he entered the vestibule and saw Abu Sir, who rose to him and rejoiced in him: but the dyer said to him, "Is this the way of well-born men? I have opened me a dyery and am become master-dyer of the city and acquainted with the King and have risen to prosperity and authority: yet camest thou not to me nor askest of me nor saidst, Where's my comrade? For my part I sought thee in vain and sent my slaves and servants to make search for thee in all the Khans and other places; but they knew not whither thou hadst gone, nor could any one give me tidings of thee." Said Abu Sir, "Did I not come to thee and didst thou not make me out a thief and bastinado me and dishonour me before the world?" At this Abu Kir made a show of concern and asked, "What manner of talk is this? Was it thou whom I beat?"; and Abu Sir answered, "Yes, 'twas I." Whereupon Abu Kir swore to him a thousand oaths that he knew him not and said, "There was a fellow like thee, who used to come every day and steal the people's stuff, and I took thee for him." And he went on to pretend penitence, beating hand upon hand and saying, "There is no Majesty and there is no Might save in Allah, the Glorious, the Great! Indeed we have sinned against thee; but would that thou hadst discovered thyself to me and said, I am such an one! Indeed the fault is with thee, for that thou madest not thyself known unto me, more especially seeing that I was distracted for much business." Replied Abu Sir, "Allah pardon thee,[35] O my comrade! This was foreordained in the Secret Purpose, and reparation is with Allah. Enter and put off thy clothes and bathe at thine ease." Said the dyer, "I conjure thee, by Allah, O my brother, forgive me!"; and said Abu Sir, "Allah acquit thee of blame and forgive thee! Indeed this thing was decreed to me from all eternity." Then asked Abu Kir, "Whence gottest thou this high degree?"; and answered Abu Sir, "He who prospered thee prospered me; for I went up to the King and described to him the fashion of the Hammam and he bade me build one." And the dyer said, "Even as thou art beknown of the King, so also am I; and, Inshallah,—God willing—I will make him love and favour thee more than ever, for my sake, he knoweth not that thou art my comrade, but I will acquaint him of this and commend thee to him." But Abu Sir said, "There needeth no commendation; for He who moveth man's heart to love still liveth; and indeed the King and all his court affect me and have given me this and that." And he told him the whole tale and said to him, "Put off thy clothes behind the chest and enter the Hammam, and I will go in with thee and rub thee down with the glove." So he doffed his dress and Abu Sir, entering the bath with him, soaped him and gloved him and then dressed him and busied himself with his service till he came forth, when he brought him dinner and sherbets, whilst all the folk marvelled at the honour he did him. Then Abu Kir would have given him somewhat; but he swore that he would not accept aught from him and said to him, "Shame upon such doings! Thou art my comrade, and there is no difference between us." Then Abu Kir observed, "By Allah, O my comrade, this is a mighty fine Hammam of thine, but there lacketh somewhat in its ordinance." Asked Abu Sir, "And what is that?" and Abu Kir answered, "It is the depilatory,[36] to wit, the paste compounded of yellow arsenic and quick-lime which removeth the hair with comfort. Do thou prepare it and next time the King cometh, present it to him, teaching him how he shall cause the hair to fall off by such means, and he will love thee with exceeding love and honour thee." Quoth Abu Sir, "Thou speakest sooth, and Inshallah, I will at once make it." Then Abu Kir left him and mounted his mule and going to the King said to him, "I have a warning to give thee, O King of the age!" "And what is thy warning?" asked the King; and Abu Kir answered, "I hear that thou hast built a Hammam." Quoth the King, "Yes: there came to me a stranger and I builded the Baths for him, even as I builded the dyery for thee; and indeed 'tis a mighty fine Hammam and an ornament to my city;" and he went on to describe to him the virtues of the bath. Quoth the dyer, "Hast thou entered therein?"; and quoth the King, "Yes." Thereupon cried Abu Kir, "Alhamdolillah—praised be God,—who saved thee from the mischief of yonder villain and foe of the Faith, I mean the bath-keeper!" The King enquired, "And what of him?"; and Abu Kir replied, "Know, O King of the age that, an thou enter the Hammam again, after this day, thou wilt surely perish." "How so?" said the King; and the dyer said, "This bath-keeper is thy foe and the foe of the Faith, and he induced thee not to stablish this Bath but because he designed therein to poison thee. He hath made for thee somewhat and he will present it to thee when thou enterest the Hammam, saying:—This is a drug which, if one apply to his parts below the waist, will remove the hair with comfort. Now it is no drug, but a drastic dreg and a deadly poison; for the Sultan of the Christians hath promised this obscene fellow to release to him his wife and children, an he will kill thee; for they are prisoners in the hands of that Sultan. I myself was captive with him in their land, but I opened a dyery and dyed for them various colours, so that they conciliated the King's heart to me and he bade me ask a boon of him. I sought of him freedom and he set me at liberty, whereupon I made my way to this city and seeing yonder man in the Hammam, said to him, "How didst thou effect thine escape and win free with thy wife and children?" Quoth he, "We ceased not to be in captivity, I and my wife and children, till one day the King of the Nazarenes held a court whereat I was present, amongst a number of others; and as I stood amongst the folk, I heard them open out on the Kings and name them, one after other, till they came to the name of the King of this city, whereupon the King of the Christians cried out Alas! and said, 'None vexeth me[37] in the world, but the King of such a city![38] Whosoever will contrive me his slaughter I will give him all he shall ask.' So I went up to him and said, 'An I compass for thee his slaughter, wilt thou set me free, me and my wife and my children?' The King replied 'Yes; and I will give thee to boot whatso thou shalt desire.' So we agreed upon this and he sent me in a galleon to this city, where I presented myself to the King and he built me this Hammam. Now, therefore, I have nought to do but to slay him and return to the King of the Nazarenes, that I may redeem my children and my wife and ask a boon of him." Quoth I:—And how wilt thou go about to kill him?; and quoth he:—By the simplest of all devices; for I have compounded him somewhat wherein is poison; so, when he cometh to the bath, I shall say to him:—Take this paste and anoint therewith thy parts below the waist for it will cause the hair to drop off.[39] So he will take it and apply it to himself and the poison will work in him a day and a night, till it reacheth his heart and destroyeth him; and meanwhile I shall have made off and none will know that it was I slew him. "When I heard this," added Abu Kir, "I feared for thee, my benefactor, wherefore I have told thee of what is doing." As soon as the King heard the dyer's story, he was wroth with exceeding wrath and said to him, "Keep this secret." Then he resolved to visit the Hammam, that he might dispel doubt by supplying certainty; and when he entered, Abu Sir doffed his dress and betaking himself as of wont to the service of the King, proceeded to glove him; after which he said to him, "O King of the age, I have made a drug which assisteth in plucking out the lower hair." Cried the King, "Bring it to me"; so the barber brought it to him and the King, finding it nauseous of smell, was assured that it was poison; wherefore he was incensed and called out to his guards, saying, "Seize him!" Accordingly they seized him and the King donned his dress and returned to his palace, boiling with fury, whilst none knew the cause of his indignation; for, of the excess of his wrath he had acquainted no one therewith and none dared ask him. Then he repaired to the audience-chamber and causing Abu Sir to be brought before him, with his elbows pinioned, sent for his Sea-captain and said to him, "Take this villain and set him in a sack with two quintals of lime unslacked and tie its mouth over his head. Then lay him in a cock-boat and row out with him in front of my palace, where thou wilt see me sitting at the lattice. Do thou say to me:—Shall I cast him in? and if I answer, Cast him! throw the sack into the sea, so the quick-lime may be slaked on him to the intent that he shall die drowned and burnt."[40] "Hearkening and obeying;" quoth the Captain and taking Abu Sir from the presence carried him to an island facing the King's palace, where he said to him, "Ho thou, I once visited thy Hammam and thou entreatedst me with honour and accomplishedst all my needs and I had great pleasure of thee: moreover, thou swarest that thou wouldst take no pay of me, and I love thee with a great love. So tell me how the case standeth between thee and the King and what abominable deed thou hast done with him that he is wroth with thee and hath commanded me that thou shouldst die this foul death." Answered Abu Sir, "I have done nothing, nor weet I of any crime I have committed against him which merited this!" Rejoined the Captain, "Verily, thou wast high in rank with the King, such as none ever won before thee, and all who are prosperous are envied. Haply some one was jealous of thy good fortune and threw out certain hints concerning thee to the King, by reason whereof he is become enraged against thee with rage so violent: but be of good cheer; no harm shall befal thee; for, even as thou entreatedst me generously, without acquaintanceship between me and thee, so now I will deliver thee. But, an if I release thee, thou must abide with me on this island till some galleon sail from our city to thy native land, when I will send thee thither therein." Abu Sir kissed his hand and thanked him for that; after which the Captain fetched the quick-lime and set it in a sack, together with a great stone, the size of a man, saying, "I put my trust in Allah!"[41] Then he gave the barber a net, saying, "Cast this net into the sea, so haply thou mayest take somewhat of fish. For I am bound to supply the King's kitchen with fish every day; but to-day I have been distracted from fishing by this calamity which hath befallen thee, and I fear lest the cook's boys come to me in quest of fish and find none. So, an thou take aught, they will find it and thou wilt veil my face,[42] whilst I go and play off my practice in front of the palace and feign to cast thee into the sea." Answered Abu Sir, "I will fish the while; go thou and God help thee!" So the Captain set the sack in the boat and paddled till it came under the palace, where he saw the King seated at the lattice and said to him, "O King of the age, shall I cast him in?" "Cast him!" cried the King, and signed to him with his hand, when lo and behold!; something flashed like leven and fell into the sea. Now that which had fallen into the water was the King's seal-ring; and the same was enchanted in such way that, when the King was wroth with any one and was minded to slay him, he had but to sign to him with his right hand, whereon was the signet-ring, and therefrom issued a flash of lightning, which smote the object, and thereupon his head fell from between his shoulders; and the troops obeyed him not, nor did he overcome the men of might save by means of the ring. So, when it dropped from his finger, he concealed the matter and kept silence, for that he dared not say, "My ring is fallen into the sea," for fear of the troops, lest they rise against him and slay him. On this wise it befel the King; but as regards Abu Sir, after the Captain had left him on the island he took the net and casting it into the sea presently drew it up full of fish; nor did he cease to throw it and pull it up full, till there was a great mound of fish before him. So he said in himself, "By Allah, this long while I have not eaten fish!"; and chose himself a large fat fish, saying, "When the Captain cometh back, I will bid him fry it for me, so I may dine on it." Then he cut its throat with a knife he had with him; but the knife stuck in its gills and there he saw the King's signet-ring; for the fish had swallowed it and Destiny had driven it to that island, where it had fallen into the net. He took the ring and drew it on his little finger,[43] not knowing its peculiar properties. Presently, up came two of the cook's boys in quest of fish and seeing Abu Sir, said to him, "O man, whither is the Captain gone?" "I know not," said he and signed to them with his right hand; when, behold, the heads of both underlings dropped off from between their shoulders. At this Abu Sir was amazed and said, "Would I wot who slew them!" And their case was grievous to him and he was still pondering it, when the Captain suddenly returned and seeing the mound of fishes and two men lying dead and the seal-ring on Abu Sir's finger, said to him, "O my brother, move not thy hand whereon is the signet-ring; else thou wilt kill me." Abu Sir wondered at this speech and kept his hand motionless; whereupon the Captain came up to him and said, "Who slew these two men?" "By Allah, O my brother, I wot not!" "Thou sayest sooth; but tell me whence hadst thou that ring?" "I found it in this fish's gills." "True,"

said the Captain, "for I saw it fall flashing from the King's
palace and disappear in the sea, what time he signed towards
thee,[44] saying, Cast him in. So I cast the sack into the water,
and it was then that the ring slipped from his finger and fell
into the sea, where this fish swallowed it, and Allah drave it
to thee, so that thou madest it thy prey, for this ring was thy
lot; but kennest thou its property?" Said Abu Sir, "I knew
not that it had any properties peculiar to it;" and the Captain said, "Learn, then, that the King's troops obey him not
save for fear of this signet-ring, because it is spelled, and
when he was wroth with any one and had a mind to kill
him, he would sign at him therewith and his head would
drop from between his shoulders; for there issued a flash
of lightning from the ring and its ray smote the object of
his wrath, who died forthright." At this, Abu Sir rejoiced
with exceeding joy and said to the Captain, "Carry me
back to the city;" and he said, "That will I, now that I no
longer fear for thee from the King; for, wert thou to sign at
him with thy hand, purposing to kill him, his head would
fall down between thy hands; and if thou be minded to slay
him and all his host, thou mayst slaughter them without let
or hindrance." So saying, he embarked him in the boat and
bore him back to the city; so Abu Sir landed and going up
to the palace, entered the council-chamber, where he
found the King seated facing his officers, in sore cark and
care by reason of the seal-ring and daring not tell any of
his folk anent its loss. When he saw Abu Sir, he said to him,
"Did we not cast thee into the sea? How hast thou contrived to come forth of it?" Abu Sir replied, "O King of the
age, whenas thou badest throw me into the sea, thy Captain carried me to an island and asked me of the cause
of thy wrath against me, saying:——What hast thou done
with the King, that he should decree thy death? I answered,
By Allah, I know not that I have wrought him any wrong!
Quoth he:——Thou wast high in rank with the King, and
haply some one envied thee and threw out certain hints
concerning thee to him, so that he is become incensed
against thee. But when I visited thee in thy Hammam, thou

entreatedst me honourably, and I will requite thee thy hospitality to me by setting thee free and sending thee back to thine own land. Then he set a great stone in the sack in my stead and cast it into the sea; but, when thou signedst to him to throw me in, thy seal-ring dropped from thy finger into the main, and a fish swallowed it. Now I was on the island a-fishing, and this fish came up in the net with others; whereupon I took it, intending to broil it; but, when I opened its belly, I found the signet-ring therein; so I took it and put it on my finger. Presently, up came two of the servants of the kitchen, questing fish, and I signed to them with my hand, knowing not the property of the seal-ring, and their heads fell off. Then the Captain came back, and seeing the ring on my finger, acquainted me with its spell; and behold, I have brought it back to thee, for that thou dealtest kindly by me and entreatedst me with the utmost honour, nor is that which thou hast done me of kindness lost upon me. Here is thy ring; take it! But an I have done with thee aught deserving of death, tell me my crime and slay me and thou shalt be absolved of sin in shedding my blood." So saying, he pulled the ring from his finger and gave it to the King who, seeing Abu Sir's noble conduct, took the ring and put it on and felt life return to him afresh. Then he rose to his feet and embracing the barber, said to him, "O man, thou art indeed of the flower of the well-born! Blame me not, but forgive me the wrong I have done thee. Had any but thou gotten hold of this ring, he had never restored it to me." Answered Abu Sir, "O King of the age, an thou wouldst have me forgive thee, tell me what was my fault which drew down thine anger upon me, so that thou commandedst to do me die." Rejoined the King, "By Allah, 'tis clear to me that thou art free and guiltless in all things of offence since thou hast done this good deed; only the dyer denounced thee to me in such and such words;" and he told him all that Abu Kir had said. Abu Sir replied, "By Allah, O King of the age, I know no King of the Nazarenes nor during my days have ever journeyed to a Christian country, nor did it ever come into my mind to kill thee. But this dyer was my comrade and neighbour in the city of Alexandria where life was straitened upon us; therefore we departed thence, to seek our fortunes, by reason of the narrowness of our means at home, after we had recited the Opening Chapter of the Koran together, pledging ourselves that he who got work should feed him who lacked work; and there befel me with him such and such things." Then he went on to relate to the King all that had betided him with Abu Kir the dyer; how he had robbed him of his dirhams and had left him alone and sick in the Khan-closet and how the door-keeper had fed him of his own monies till Allah recovered him of his sickness, when he went forth and walked about the city with his budget, as was his wont, till he espied a dyery, about which the folk were crowding; so he looked at the door and seeing Abu Kir seated on a bench there, went in to salute him, whereupon he accused him of being a thief and beat him a grievous beating; brief, he told him his whole tale, from first to last, and added, "O King of the age, 'twas he who counselled me to make the depilatory and present it to thee, saying:—The Hammam is perfect in all things but that it lacketh this; and know, O King of the age, that this drug is harmless and we use it in our land where 'tis one of the requisites of the bath; but I had forgotten it: so, when the dyer visited the Hammam I entreated him with honour and he reminded me of it, and enjoined me to make it forthwith. But do thou send after the porter of such a Khan and the workmen of the dyery and question them all of that which I have told thee." Accordingly the King sent for them and questioned them one and all and they acquainted him with the truth of the matter. Then he summoned the dyer, saying, "Bring him barefooted, bareheaded and with elbows pinioned!" Now he was sitting in his house, rejoicing in Abu Sir's death; but ere he could be ware, the King's guards rushed in upon him and cuffed him on the nape, after which they bound him and bore him into the presence, where he saw Abu Sir seated by the King's side and the door-keeper of the Khan and workmen of the dyery standing before him. Quoth the door-keeper to him, "Is not this thy comrade whom thou robbedst of his silvers and leftest with me sick in the closet doing such and such by him?" And the workmen said to him, "Is not this he whom thou badest us seize and beat?" Therewith Abu Kir's baseness was made manifest to the King and he was certified that he merited torture yet sorer than the torments of Munkar and Nakir.[45] So he said to his guards, "Take him and parade him about the city and the markets; then set him in a sack and cast him into the sea." Whereupon quoth Abu Sir, "O King of the age, accept my intercession for him, for I pardon him all he hath done with me." But quoth the King, "An thou pardon him all his offences against thee, I cannot pardon him his offences against me." And he cried out, saying, "Take him." So they took him and paraded him about the city, after which they set him in a sack with quick-lime and cast him into the sea, and he died, drowned and burnt. Then said the King to the barber, "O Abu Sir, ask of me what thou wilt and it shall be given thee." And he answered, saying, "I ask of thee to send me back to my own country, for I care no longer to tarry here." Then the King gifted him great store of gifts, over and above that which he had whilome bestowed on him; and amongst the rest a galleon freighted with goods; and the crew of this galleon were Mamelukes; so he gave him these also, after offering to make him his Wazir whereto the barber consented not. Presently he farewelled the King and set sail in his own ship manned by his own crew; nor did he cast anchor till he reached Alexandria and made fast to the shore there. Then they landed and one of his Mamelukes, seeing a sack on the beach, said to Abu Sir, "O my lord, there is a great heavy sack on the sea-shore, with the mouth tied up and I know not what therein." So Abu Sir came up and opening the sack, found therein the remains of Abu Kir, which the sea had borne thither. He took it forth and burying it near Alexandria, built over the grave a place of visitation. After this Abu Sir abode awhile, till Allah took him to Himself, and they buried him hard by the tomb of his comrade Abu Kir; wherefore that place was called Abu Kir and Abu Sir; but it is now known as Abu Kir only. This, then, is that which hath reached us of their history, and glory be to Him who endureth for ever and aye and by whose will interchange the night and the day. And of the stories they tell is one anent

THE SLEEPER AND THE WAKER.[1]

It hath reached me, O auspicious King, that there was once at Baghdad, in the Caliphate of Harun al-Rashid, a man and a merchant, who had a son Abu al-Hasan-al-Khali'a by name.[2] The merchant died leaving great store of wealth to his heir who divided it into two equal parts, whereof he laid up one and spent of the other half; and he fell to companying with Persians[3] and with the sons of the merchants and he gave himself up to good drinking and good eating, till all the wealth[4] he had with him was wasted and wantoned; whereupon he betook himself to his friends and comrades and cup-companions and expounded to them his case, discovering to them the failure of that which was in his hand of wealth. But not one of them took heed of him or even deigned answer him. So he returned to his mother (and indeed his spirit was broken) and related to her that which had happened to him and what had befallen him from his friends, how they had neither shared with him nor requited him with speech. Quoth she, "O Abu al-Hasan, on this wise are the sons[5] of this time: an thou have aught, they draw thee near to them,[6] and if thou have naught, they put thee away from them." And she went on to condole with him, what while he bewailed himself and his tears flowed and he repeated these lines:—

> An wane my wealth, no man will succour me,
> When my wealth waxeth all men friendly show:
> How many a friend, for wealth showed friendliness
> Who, when my wealth departed, turned to foe!

Then he sprang up and going to the place wherein was the other half of his good, took it and lived with it well; and he sware that he would never again consort with a single one of those he had known, but would company only with the stranger nor entertain even him but one night and that, when it morrowed, he would never know him more. Accordingly he fell to sitting every eventide on the bridge over Tigris and looking at each one who passed by him; and if he saw him to be a stranger, he made friends with him and carried him to his house, where he conversed and caroused with him all night till morning. Then he dismissed him and would never more salute him with the Salam nor ever more drew near unto him neither invited him again. Thus he continued to do for the space of a full year, till, one day, while he sat on the bridge, as was his wont, expecting who should come to him so he might take him and pass the night with him, behold, up came the Caliph and Masrur, the Sworder of his vengeance,[7] disguised in merchants' dress, according to their custom. So Abu al-Hasan looked at them and rising, because he knew them not, asked them, "What say ye? Will ye go with me to my dwelling-place, so ye may eat what is ready and drink what is at hand, to wit, platter-bread[8] and meat cooked and wine strained?" The Caliph refused this, but he conjured him and said to him, "Allah upon thee, O my lord, go with me, for thou art my guest this night, and baulk not my hopes of thee!" And he ceased not to press him till he consented; whereat Abu al-Hasan rejoiced and walking on before him, gave not over talking with him till they came to his house and he carried the Caliph into the saloon. Al-Rashid entered a hall such as an thou sawest it and gazedst upon its walls, thou hadst beheld marvels; and hadst thou looked narrowly at its water-conduits thou wouldst have seen a fountain cased with gold. The Caliph made his man abide at the door; and, as soon as he was seated, the host brought him somewhat to eat; so he ate, and Abu al-Hasan ate with him that eating might be grateful to him. Then he removed the tray and they washed their hands and the Commander of the Faithful sat down again; whereupon Abu al-Hasan set on the drinking vessels and seating himself by his side, fell to filling and giving him to drink[9] and entertaining him with discourse. And when they had drunk their sufficiency the host called for a slave-girl like a branch of Ban who took a lute and sang to it these two couplets:—

> O thou aye dwelling in my heart,
> Whileas thy form is far from sight,
> Thou art my sprite by me unseen,
> Yet nearest near art thou, my sprite.

His hospitality pleased the Caliph and the goodliness of his manners, and he said to him, "O youth, who art thou? Make me acquainted with thyself, so I may requite thee thy kindness." But Abu al-Hasan smiled and said, "O my lord, far be it, alas! that what is past should again come to pass and that I company with thee at other time than this time!" The Prince of True Believers asked, "Why so? and why wilt thou not acquaint me with thy case?" and Abu al-Hasan answered, "Know, O my lord, that my story is strange and that there is a cause for this affair." Quoth Al-Rashid, "And what is the cause?" and quoth he, "The cause hath a tail." The Caliph[10] laughed at his words and Abu al-Hasan said, "I will explain to thee this saying by the tale of the Larrikin and the Cook. So hear thou, O my lord, the

STORY OF THE LARRIKIN[11]
AND THE COOK."

One of the ne'er-do-wells found himself one fine morning without aught and the world was straitened upon him and patience failed him; so he lay down to sleep and ceased not slumbering till the sun stang him and the foam came out upon his mouth, whereupon he arose, and he was penniless and had not even so much as a single dirham. Presently he arrived at the shop of a Cook, who had set his pots and pans over the fire and washed his saucers and wiped his scales and swept his shop and sprinkled it; and indeed his fats and oils were clear and clarified and his spices fragrant and he himself stood behind his cooking-pots ready to serve customers. So the Larrikin, whose wits had been sharpened by hunger, went in to him and saluting him, said to him, "Weigh me half a dirham's worth of meat and a quarter of a dirham's worth of boiled grain[12] and the like of bread." So the Kitchener weighed it out to him and the good-for-naught entered the shop, whereupon the man set the food before him and he ate till he had gobbled up the whole and licked the saucers and sat perplexed, knowing not how he should do with the Cook concerning the price of that he had eaten, and turning his eyes about upon everything in the shop; and as he looked, behold, he caught sight of an earthen pan lying arsy-versy upon its mouth; so he raised it from the ground and found under it a horse's tail, freshly cut off and the blood oozing from it; whereby he knew that the Cook adulterated his meat with horseflesh. When he discovered this default, he rejoiced therein and washing his hands, bowed his head and went out; and when the Kitchener saw that he went and gave him naught, he cried out, saying, "Stay, O pest, O burglar!" So the Larrikin stopped and said to him, "Dost thou cry out upon me and call to me with these words, O cornute?" Whereat the Cook was angry and coming down from the shop, cried, "What meanest thou by thy speech, O low fellow, thou that devourest meat and millet and bread and kitchen and goest forth with 'the Peace[13] be on thee!' as it were the thing had not been, and payest down naught for it?" Quoth the Lackpenny, "Thou liest, O accursed son of a cuckold!" Whereupon the Cook cried out and laying hold of his debtor's collar, said, "O Moslems, this fellow is my first customer[14] this day and he hath eaten my food and given me naught." So the folk gathered about them and blamed the Ne'er-do-well and said to him, "Give him the price of that which thou hast eaten." Quoth he, "I gave him a dirham before I entered the shop;" and quoth the Cook, "Be everything I sell this day forbidden to me, if he gave me so much as the name of a coin! By Allah, he gave me naught, but ate my food and went out and would have made off, without aught said." Answered the Larrikin, "I gave thee a dirham," and he reviled the Kitchener, who returned his abuse; whereupon he dealt him a buffet and they gripped and grappled and throttled each other. When the folk saw them fighting, they came up to them and asked them, "What is this strife between you, and no cause for it?" and the Lackpenny answered, "Ay, by Allah, but there is a cause for it, and the cause hath a tail!" Whereupon, cried the Cook, "Yea, by Allah, now thou mindest me of thyself and thy dirham! Yes, he gave me a dirham and but a quarter of the coin is spent. Come back and take the rest of the price of thy dirham." For he understood what was to do, at the mention of the tail; "and I, O my brother" (added Abu al-Hassan), "my story hath a cause, which I will tell thee." The Caliph laughed at his speech and said, "By Allah, this is none other than a pleasant tale! Tell me thy story and the cause." Replied the host, "With love and goodly gree! Know, O my lord, that my name is Abu al-Hasan al-Khali'a and that my father died and left me abundant wealth, of which I made two parts. One I laid up and with the other I betook myself to enjoying the pleasures of friendship and conviviality and consorting with intimates and boon-companions and the sons of the merchants, nor did I leave one but I caroused with him and he with me, and I lavished all my money on comrades and good cheer, till there remained with me naught;[15] whereupon I betook myself to the friends and fellow-topers upon whom I had wasted my wealth, so perhaps they might provide for my case; but, when I visited them and went round about to them all, I found no vantage in one of them, nor would any so much as break a bittock of bread in my face. So I wept for myself and repairing to my mother, complained to her of my case. Quoth she:—Such are friends; an thou have aught, they frequent thee and devour thee, but, an thou have naught, they cast thee off and chase thee away. Then I brought out the other half of my money and bound myself by an oath that I would never more entertain any save one single night, after which I would never again salute him nor notice him; hence my saying to thee:—Far be it, alas! that what is past should again come to pass, for I will never again company with thee after this night." When the Commander of the Faithful heard this, he laughed a loud laugh and said, "By Allah, O my brother, thou art indeed excused in this matter, now that I know the cause and that the cause hath a tail. Nevertheless, Inshallah, I will not sever myself from thee." Replied Abu al-Hasan, "O my guest, did I not say to thee, Far be it, alas! that what is past should again come to pass? For indeed I will never again foregather with any!" Then the Caliph rose and the host set before him a dish of roast goose and a bannock of first-bread[16] and sitting down, fell to cutting off morsels and morselling the Caliph therewith. They gave not over eating till they were filled, when Abu al-Hasan brought basin and ewer and potash[17] and they washed their hands. Then he lighted three wax-candles and three lamps, and spreading the drinking-cloth, brought strained wine, clear, old and fragrant, whose scent was as that of virgin musk. He filled the first cup and saying, "O my boon-companion, be ceremony laid aside between us by thy leave! Thy slave is by thee; may I not be afflicted with thy loss!" drank it off and filled a second cup, which he handed to the Caliph with due reverence. His fashion pleased the Commander of the Faithful, and the goodliness of his speech and he said to himself, "By Allah, I will assuredly requite him for this!" Then Abu al-Hasan filled the cup again and handed it to the Caliph, reciting these two couplets:[18]—

> Had we thy coming known, we would for sacrifice
> Have poured thee out heart's blood or blackness of
>   the eyes;
> Ay, and we would have spread our bosoms in thy way,
> That so thy feet might fare on eyelids, carpet-wise.

When the Caliph heard his verses, he took the cup from his hand and kissed it and drank it off and returned it to Abu al-Hasan, who made him an obeisance and filled and drank. Then he filled again and kissing the cup thrice, recited these lines:—

> Your presence honoureth the base,
> And we confess the deed of grace;
> An you absent yourself from us,
> No freke we find to fill your place.

Then he gave the cup to the Caliph, saying, "Drink it in health and soundness! It doeth away malady and bringeth remedy and setteth the runnels of health to flow free." So they ceased not carousing and conversing till middle-night, when the Caliph said to his host, "O my brother, hast thou in thy heart a concupiscence thou wouldst have accomplished or a contingency thou wouldst avert?" said he, "By Allah, there is no regret in my heart save that I am not empowered with bidding and forbidding, so I might manage what is in my mind!" Quoth the Commander of the Faithful, "By Allah, and again by Allah,[19] O my brother, tell me what is in thy mind!" And quoth Abu al-Hasan, "Would Heaven I might be Caliph for one day and avenge myself on my neighbours, for that in my vicinity is a mosque and therein four shaykhs, who hold it a grievance when there cometh a guest to me, and they trouble me with talk and worry me in words and menace me that they will complain of me to the Prince of True Believers, and indeed they oppress me exceedingly, and I crave of Allah the Most High power for one day, that I may beat each and every of them with four hundred lashes, as well as the Imam of the mosque, and parade them round about the city of Baghdad and bid cry before them:—This is the reward and the least of the reward of whoso exceedeth in talk and vexeth the folk and turneth their joy to annoy. This is what I wish, and no more." Said the Caliph, "Allah grant thee that thou seekest! Let us crack one last cup and rise ere the dawn draw near, and to-morrow night I will be with thee again." Said Abu al-Hasan, "Far be it!" Then the Caliph crowned a cup, and putting therein a piece of Cretan Bhang,[20] gave it to his host and said to him, "My life on thee, O my brother, drink this cup from my hand!" and Abu al-Hasan answered, "Ay, by thy life, I will drink it from thy hand." So he took it and drank it off; but hardly had it settled in his stomach, when his head forewent his heels and he fell to the ground like one slain; whereupon the Caliph went out and said to his slave Masrur, "Go in to yonder young man, the house master, and take him up and bring him to me at the palace; and when thou goest out, shut the door." So saying, he went away, whilst Masrur entered, and taking up Abu al-Hasan, shut the door behind him, and made after his master, till he reached with him the palace what while the night drew to an end and the cocks began crowing,[21] and set him down before the Commander of the Faithful, who laughed at him.[22] Then he sent for Ja'afar the Barmecide and when he came before him, said to him, "Note thou yonder young man" (pointing to Abu al-Hasan), "and when thou shalt see him to-morrow seated in my place of estate and on the throne[23] of my Caliphate and clad in my royal clothing, stand thou in attendance upon him and enjoin the Emirs and Grandees and the folk of my household and the officers of my realm to be upon their feet, as in his service and obey him in whatso he shall bid them do; and thou, if he speak to thee of aught, do it and hearken unto his say and gainsay him not in anything during this coming day." Ja'afar acknowledged the order with "Hearkening and obedience" and withdrew, whilst the Prince of True Believers went in to the palace women, who came up to him, and he said to them, "When this sleeper shall awake to-morrow, kiss ye the ground between his hands, and do ye wait upon him and gather round about him and clothe him in the royal clothing and serve him with the service of the Caliphate and deny not aught of his estate, but say to him, Thou art the Caliph." Then he taught them what they should say to him and how they should do with him and withdrawing to a retired room,[24] let down a curtain before himself and slept. Thus fared it with the Caliph; but as regards Abu al-Hasan, he gave not over snoring in his sleep till the day brake clear, and the rising of the sun drew near, when a woman in waiting came up to him and said to him, "O our lord, the morning prayer!" Hearing these words he laughed and opening his eyes, turned them about the palace and found himself in an apartment whose walls were painted with gold and lapis lazuli and its ceiling dotted and starred with red gold. Around it were sleeping chambers, with curtains of gold-embroidered silk let down over their doors, and all about vessels of gold and porcelain and crystal and furniture and carpets dispread and lamps burning before the niche wherein men prayed, and slave-girls and eunuchs and Mamelukes and black slaves and boys and pages and attendants. When he saw this he was bewildered in his wit and said, "By Allah, either I am dreaming a dream, or this is Paradise and the Abode of Peace!"[25] And he shut his eyes and would have slept again. Quoth one of the eunuchs, "O my lord, this is not of thy wont, O Commander of the Faithful!" Then the rest of the handmaids of the palace came up to him and lifted him into a sitting posture, when he found himself upon a mat-

trass, raised a cubit's height from the ground and all stuffed
with floss silk. So they seated him upon it and propped his
elbow with a pillow, and he looked at the apartment and
its vastness and saw those eunuchs and slave-girls in attendance upon him and standing about his head, whereupon
he laughed at himself and said, "By Allah, 'tis not as I were
on wake, yet I am not asleep!" And in his perplexity he
bowed his chin upon his bosom and then opened his eyes,
little by little, smiling and saying, "What is this state
wherein I find myself?" Then he arose and sat up, whilst
the damsels laughed at him privily; and he was bewildered
in his wit, and bit his finger; and as the bite pained him, he
cried "Oh!" and was vexed; and the Caliph watched him,
whence he saw him not, and laughed. Presently Abu al-
Hasan turned to a damsel and called to her; whereupon
she answered, "At thy service, O Prince of True Believers!"
Quoth he, "What is thy name?" and quoth she, "Shajarat al-
Durr."[26] Then he said to her, "By the protection of Allah, O
damsel, am I Commander of the Faithful?" She replied,
"Yes, indeed, by the protection of Allah thou in this time
art Commander of the Faithful." Quoth he, "By Allah,
thou liest, O thousandfold whore!"[27] Then he glanced at
the Chief Eunuch and called to him, whereupon he came
to him and kissing the ground before him, said, "Yes, O
Commander of the Faithful." Asked Abu al-Hasan, "Who
is Commander of the Faithful?" and the Eunuch answered
"Thou." And Abu al-Hasan said, "Thou liest, thousandfold
he-whore that thou art!" Then he turned to another eunuch and said to him, "O my chief,[28] by the protection
of Allah, am I Prince of the True Believers?" Said he, "Ay,
by Allah, O my lord, thou art in this time Commander
of the Faithful and Viceregent of the Lord of the three
Worlds." Abu al-Hasan laughed at himself and doubted
of his reason and was bewildered at what he beheld, and
said, "In one night do I become Caliph? Yes-terday I was
Abu al-Hasan the Wag, and to-day I am Commander of
the Faithful." Then the Chief Eunuch came up to him and

said, "O Prince of True Believers, (the name of Allah encompass thee!) thou art indeed Commander of the Faithful and Viceregent of the Lord of the three Worlds!" And the slave-girls and eunuchs flocked round about him, till he arose and abode wondering at his case. Hereupon the Eunuch brought him a pair of sandals wrought with raw silk and green silk and purfled with red gold, and he took them and after examining them set them in his sleeve; whereat the Castrato cried out and said, "Allah! Allah! O my lord, these are sandals for the treading of thy feet, so thou mayst wend to the wardrobe." Abu al-Hasan was confounded, and shaking the sandals from his sleeve, put them on his feet, whilst the Caliph died[29] of laughter at him. The slave forewent him to the chapel of ease, where he entered and doing his job,[30] came out into the chamber, whereupon the slave-girls brought him a basin of gold and an ewer of silver and poured water on his hands[31] and he made the Wuzu-ablution. Then they spread him a prayer-carpet and he prayed. Now he knew not how to pray[32] and gave not over bowing and prostrating for twenty inclinations,[33] pondering in himself the while and saying, "By Allah, I am none other than the Commander of the Faithful in very truth! This is assuredly no dream, for all these things happen not in a dream." And he was convinced and determined in himself that he was Prince of True Believers; so he pronounced the Salam[34] and finished his prayers; whereupon the Mamelukes and slave-girls came round about him with bundled suits of silken and linen stuffs and clad him in the costume of the Caliphate and gave the royal dagger in his hand. Then the Chief Eunuch came in and said, "O Prince of True Believers, the Chamberlain is at the door craving permission to enter." Said he, "Let him enter!" whereupon he came in and after kissing ground offered the salutation, "Peace be upon thee, O Commander of the Faithful!" At this Abu al-Hasan rose and descended from the couch to the floor; whereupon the official exclaimed "Allah! Allah! O Prince of True Believers, wottest thou not that all men are thy lieges and under thy rule and that it is not meet for the Caliph to rise to any man?" Presently the Eunuch went out before him and the little white slaves behind him, and they ceased not going till they raised the curtain and brought him into the hall of judgment and the throne-room of the Caliphate. There he saw the curtains and the forty doors and Al-'Ijli and Al-Rakashi the poet, and 'Ibdan and Jadim and Abu Ishak[35] the cup-companion and beheld swords drawn and the lions[36] compassing the throne as the white of the eye encircleth the black, and gilded glaives and death-dealing bows and Ajams and Arabs and Turks and Daylamites and folk and peoples and Emirs and Wazirs and Captains and Grandees and Lords of the land and men of war in band, and in very sooth there appeared the might of the house of Abbas[37] and the majesty of the Prophet's family. So he sat down upon the throne of the Caliphate and set the dagger[38] on his lap, whereupon all present came up to kiss ground between his hands and called down on him length of life and continuance of weal. Then came forward Ja'afar the Barmecide and kissing the ground, said, "Be the wide world of Allah the treading of thy feet and may Paradise be thy dwelling-place and the fire the home of thy foes! Never may neighbour defy thee nor the lights of fire die out for thee,[39] O Caliph of all cities and ruler of all countries!" Therewithal Abu al-Hasan cried out at him and said, "O dog of the sons of Barmak, go down forthright, thou and the chief of the city police, to such a place in such a street and deliver an hundred dinars of gold to the mother of Abu al-Hasan the Wag and bear her my salutation. Then, go to such a mosque and take the four Shaykhs and the Imam and scourge each of them with a thousand lashes[40] and mount them on beasts, face to tail, and parade them round about all the city and banish them to a place other than this city; and bid the crier make cry before them, saying:—This is the reward and the least of the reward of whoso multiplieth words and molesteth his neighbours and damageth their delights and stinteth their eating and drinking!" Ja'afar received the command and answered "With obedience"; after which he went down from before Abu al-Hasan to the city and did all he had ordered him to do. Meanwhile, Abu al-Hasan abode in the Caliphate, taking and giving, bidding and forbidding and carrying out his command till the end of the day, when he gave leave and permission to withdraw, and the Emirs and Officers of state departed to their several occupations and he looked towards the Chamberlain and the rest of the attendants and said, "Begone!" Then the Eunuchs came to him and calling down on him length of life and continuance of weal, walked in attendance upon him and raised the curtain, and he entered the pavilion of the Harem, where he found candles lighted and lamps burning and singing-women smiting on instruments, and ten slave-girls, high-bosomed maids. When he saw this, he was confounded in his wit and said to himself, "By Allah, I am in truth Commander of the Faithful!" presently adding, "or haply these are of the Jann and he who was my guest yesternight was one of their kings who saw no way to requite my favours save by commanding his Ifrits to address me as Prince of True Believers. But an these be of the Jann may Allah deliver me in safety from their mischief!" As soon as he appeared, the slave-girls rose to him and carrying him up on to the daïs,[41] brought him a great tray, bespread with the richest viands. So he ate thereof with all his might and main, till he had gotten his fill, when he called one of the handmaids and said to her, "What is thy name?" Replied she, "My name is Miskah,"[42] and he said to another, "What is thy name?" Quoth she, "My name is Tarkah."[43] Then he asked a third, "What is thy name?" who answered, "My name is Tohfah;"[44] and he went on to question the damsels of their names, one after other, till he had learned the ten, when he rose from that place and removed to the wine-chamber. He found it every way complete and saw therein ten great trays, covered with all fruits and cates and every sort of sweetmeats. So he sat down and ate thereof after the measure of his competency, and finding there three

troops of singing-girls, was amazed and made the girls eat.
Then he sat and the singers also seated themselves, whilst
the black slaves and the white slaves and the eunuchs and
pages and boys stood, and of the slave-girls some sat and
others stood. The damsels sang and warbled all varieties of
melodies and the place rang with the sweetness of the
songs, whilst the pipes cried out and the lutes with them
wailed, till it seemed to Abu al-Hasan that he was in Paradise and his heart was heartened and his breast broadened.
So he sported and joyance grew on him and he bestowed
robes of honour on the damsels and gave and bestowed,
challenging this girl and kissing that and toying with a
third, plying one with wine and morselling another with
meat, till nightfall. All this while the Commander of the
Faithful was diverting himself with watching him and
laughing, and when night fell he bade one of the slave-girls
drop a piece of Bhang in the cup and give it to Abu al-
Hasan to drink. So she did his bidding and gave him the
cup, which no sooner had he drunk than his head forewent
his feet.[45] Therewith the Caliph came forth from behind
the curtain, laughing, and calling to the attendant who had
brought Abu al-Hasan to the palace, said to him, "Carry[46]
this man to his own place." So Masrur took him up, and
carrying him to his own house, set him down in the saloon.
Then he went forth from him, and shutting the saloon-
door upon him, returned to the Caliph, who slept till the
morrow. As for Abu al-Hasan, he gave not over slumbering till Almighty Allah brought on the morning, when he
recovered from the drug and awoke, crying out and saying, "Ho, Tuffahah! Ho, Rahat al-Kulub! Ho, Miskah! Ho,
Tohfah!"[47] And he ceased not calling upon the palace
handmaids till his mother heard him summoning strange
damsels, and rising, came to him and said, "Allah's name
encompass thee! Up with thee, O my son, O Abu al-Hasan!
Thou dreamest." So he opened his eyes, and finding an
old woman at his head, raised his eyes and said to her,
"Who art thou?" Quoth she, "I am thy mother;" and quoth

he, "Thou liest! I am the Commander of the Faithful, the Viceregent of Allah." Whereupon his mother shrieked aloud and said to him, "Heaven preserve thy reason! Be silent, O my son, and cause not the loss of our lives and the wasting of thy wealth, which will assuredly befal us if any hear this talk and carry it to the Caliph." So he rose from his sleep, and finding himself in his own saloon and his mother by him, had doubts of his wit, and said to her, "By Allah, O my mother, I saw myself in a dream in a palace, with slave-girls and Mamelukes about me and in attendance upon me, and I sat upon the throne of the Caliphate and ruled. By Allah, O my mother, this is what I saw, and in very sooth it was no dream!" Then he bethought himself awhile and said, "Assuredly,[48] I am Abu al-Hasan al-Khali'a, and this that I saw was only a dream when I was made Caliph and bade and forbade." Then he bethought himself again and said, "Nay, but 'twas not a dream, and I am none other than the Caliph, and indeed I gave gifts and bestowed honour-robes." Quoth his mother to him, "O my son, thou sportest with thy reason: thou wilt go to the madhouse[49] and become a gazing-stock. Indeed, that which thou hast seen is only from the foul Fiend, and it was an imbroglio of dreams, for at times Satan sporteth with men's wits in all manner of ways." Then said she to him, "O my son, was there any one with thee yesternight?" And he reflected and said, "Yes; one lay the night with me and I acquainted him with my case and told him my tale. Doubtless, he was of the Devils, and I, O my mother, even as thou sayst truly, am Abu al-Hasan al-Khali'a." She rejoined, "O my son, rejoice in tidings of all good, for yesterday's record is that there came the Wazir Ja'afar the Barmecide and his many, and beat the Shaykhs of the mosque and the Imam, each a thousand lashes; after which they paraded them round about the city, making proclamation before them and saying:—This is the reward and the least of the reward of whoso faileth in goodwill to his neighbours and troubleth on them their lives! And he banished them from

Baghdad. Moreover, the Caliph sent me an hundred dinars and sent to salute me." Whereupon Abu al-Hasan cried out and said to her, "O ill-omened crone, wilt thou contradict me and tell me that I am not the Prince of True Believers? 'Twas I who commanded Ja'afar the Barmecide to beat the Shaykhs and parade them about the city and make proclamation before them and 'twas I, very I, who sent thee the hundred dinars and sent to salute thee, and I, O beldam of ill-luck, am in very deed the Commander of the Faithful, and thou art a liar, who would make me out an idiot." So saying, he rose up and fell upon her and beat her with a staff of almond-wood, till she cried out, "Help, O Moslems!" and he increased the beating upon her, till the folk heard her cries and coming to her, found Abu al-Hasan bashing his mother and saying to her, "Old woman of ill-omen, am I not the Commander of the Faithful? Thou hast ensorcelled me!" When the folk heard his words, they said, "This man raveth," and doubted not of his madness. So they came in upon him, and seizing him, pinioned his elbows, and bore him to the Bedlam. Quoth the Superintendant, "What aileth this youth?" and quoth they, "This is a madman, afflicted of the Jinn." "By Allah," cried Abu al-Hasan, "they lie against me! I am no madman, but the Commander of the Faithful." And the Superintendant answered him, saying, "None lieth but thou, O foulest of the Jinn-maddened!" Then he stripped him of his clothes, and clapping on his neck a heavy chain,[50] bound him to a high lattice and fell to beating him two bouts a day and two anights; and he ceased not abiding on this wise the space of ten days. Then his mother came to him and said, "O my son, O Abu al-Hasan, return to thy right reason, for this is the Devil's doing." Quoth he, "Thou sayst sooth, O my mother, and bear thou witness of me that I repent me of that talk and turn me from my madness. So do thou deliver me, for I am nigh upon death." Accordingly his mother went out to the Superintendant[51] and procured his release and he returned to his own house. Now this was at the beginning of the month, and when it ended, Abu al-Hasan longed to drink liquor and, returning to his former habit, furnished his saloon and made ready food and bade bring wine; then, going forth to the bridge, he sat there, expecting one whom he should converse and carouse with, according to his custom. As he sat thus, behold, up came the Caliph and Masrur to him; but Abu al-Hasan saluted them not and said to Al-Rashid, "No friendly welcome to thee, O King of the Jann!" Quoth Al-Rashid, "What have I done to thee?" and quoth Abu al-Hasan, "What more couldst thou do than what thou hast done to me, O foulest of the Jann? I have been beaten and thrown into Bedlam, where all said I was Jinn-mad and this was caused by none save thyself. I brought thee to my house and fed thee with my best; after which thou didst empower thy Satans and Marids to disport themselves with my wits from morning to evening. So avaunt and aroynt thee and wend thy ways!" The Caliph smiled and, seating himself by his side said to him, "O my brother, did I not tell thee that I would return to thee?" Quoth Abu al-Hasan, "I have no need of thee; and as the byword sayeth in verse:—

> Fro' my friend, 'twere meeter and wiser to part,
> For what eye sees not born shall ne'er sorrow heart.

And indeed, O my brother, the night thou camest to me and we conversed and caroused together, I and thou, 'twas as if the Devil came to me and troubled me that night." Asked the Caliph, "And who is he, the Devil?" and answered Abu al-Hasan, "He is none other than thou;" whereat the Caliph laughed and coaxed him and spake him fair, saying, "O my brother, when I went out from thee, I forgot the door and left it open and perhaps Satan came in to thee."[52] Quoth Abu al-Hasan, "Ask me not of that which hath betided me. What possessed thee to leave the door open, so that the Devil came in to me and there befel me with him this and that?" And he related to him all that had betided him,

first and last (and in repetition is no fruition); what while
the Caliph laughed and hid his laughter. Then said he to
Abu al-Hasan, "Praised be Allah who hath done away from
thee whatso irked thee and that I see thee once more
in weal!" And Abu al-Hasan said, "Never again will I take
thee to cup-companion or sitting-comrade; for the proverb
saith:—Whoso stumbleth on a stone and thereto returneth,
upon him be blame and reproach. And thou, O my brother,
nevermore will I entertain thee nor company with thee, for
that I have not found thy heel propitious to me."[53] But the
Caliph coaxed him and said, "I have been the means of thy
winning to thy wish anent the Imam and the Shaykhs."
Abu al-Hasan replied, "Thou hast;" and Al-Rashid continued, "And haply somewhat may betide which shall gladden
thy heart yet more." Abu al-Hasan asked, "What dost thou
require of me?" and the Commander of the Faithful answered, "Verily, I am thy guest; reject not the guest." Quoth
Abu al-Hasan, "On condition that thou swear to me by the
characts on the seal of Solomon David's son (on the twain
be the Peace!) that thou wilt not suffer thine Ifrits to make
fun of me." He replied, "To hear is to obey!" Whereupon
the Wag took him and brought him into the saloon and set
food before him and entreated him with friendly speech.
Then he told him all that had befallen him, whilst the
Caliph was like to die of stifled laughter; after which Abu
al-Hasan removed the tray of food and bringing the wine-
service, filled a cup and cracked it three times, then gave it
to the Caliph, saying, "O boon-companion mine, I am thy
slave and let not that which I am about to say offend thee,
and be thou not vexed, neither do thou vex me." And he
recited these verses:—

> Hear one that wills thee well! Lips none shall bless
> Save those who drink for drunk and all transgress.
> Ne'er will I cease to swill while night falls dark
> Till lout my forehead low upon my tasse:
> In wine like liquid sun is my delight
> Which clears all care and gladdens allegresse.

When the Caliph heard these his verses and saw how apt he was at couplets, he was delighted with exceeding delight and taking the cup, drank it off, and the twain ceased not to converse and carouse till the wine rose to their heads. Then quoth Abu al-Hasan to the Caliph, "O boon-companion mine, of a truth I am perplexed concerning my affair, for meseemed I was Commander of the Faithful and ruled and gave gifts and largesse, and in very deed, O my brother, it was not a dream." Quoth the Caliph, "These were the imbroglios of sleep," and crumbling a bit of Bhang into the cup, said to him, "By my life, do thou drink this cup;" and said Abu al-Hasan, "Surely I will drink it from thy hand." Then he took the cup and drank it off, and no sooner had it settled in his stomach than his head fell to the ground before his feet. Now his manners and fashions pleased the Caliph and the excellence of his composition and his frankness, and he said in himself, "I will assuredly make him my cup-companion and sitting-comrade." So he rose forthright and saying to Masrur, "Take him up," returned to the palace. Accordingly, the Eunuch took up Abu al-Hasan and carrying him to the palace of the Caliphate, set him down before Al-Rashid, who bade the slaves and slave-girls compass him about, whilst he himself hid in a place where Abu al-Hasan could not see him. Then he commanded one of the handmaidens to take the lute and strike it over the Wag's head, whilst the rest smote upon their instruments. So they played and sang, till Abu al-Hasan awoke at the last of the night and heard the symphony of lutes and tambourines and the sound of the flutes and the singing of the slave-girls, whereupon he opened his eyes and finding himself in the palace, with the handmaids and eunuchs about him, exclaimed, "There is no Majesty and there is no Might save in Allah, the Glorious, the Great! Come to my help this night which meseems more unlucky than the former! Verily, I am fearful of the Madhouse and of that which I suffered therein the first time, and I doubt not but the Devil is come to me again, as before. O Allah, my Lord, put thou Satan to shame!" Then he shut his eyes and laid his head in his sleeve, and fell to laughing softly and raising his head bytimes, but still found the apartment lighted and the girls singing. Presently, one of the eunuchs sat down at his head and said to him, "Sit up, O Prince of True Believers, and look on thy palace and thy slave-girls." Said Abu al-Hasan, "Under the veil of Allah, am I in truth Commander of the Faithful, and dost thou not lie? Yesterday I rode not forth neither ruled, but drank and slept, and this eunuch cometh to make me rise." Then he sat up and recalled to thought that which had betided him with his mother and how he had beaten her and entered the Bedlam, and he saw the marks of the beating, wherewith the Superintendant had beaten him, and was perplexed concerning his affair and pondered in himself, saying, "By Allah, I know not how my case is nor what is this that betideth me!" Then, gazing at the scene around him, he said privily, "All these are of the Jann in human shape, and I commit my case to Allah." Presently he turned to one of the damsels and said to her, "Who am I?" Quoth she, "Thou art the Commander of the Faithful;" and quoth he, "Thou liest, O calamity![54] If I be indeed the Commander of the Faithful, bite my finger." So she came to him and bit it with all her might, and he said to her, "It doth suffice." Then he asked the Chief Eunuch, "Who am I?" and he answered, "Thou art the Commander of the Faithful." So he left him and returned to his wonderment: then, turning to a little white slave, said to him, "Bite my ear;" and he bent his head low down to him and put his ear to his mouth. Now the Mameluke was young and lacked sense; so he closed his teeth upon Abu al-Hasan's ear with all his might, till he came near to sever it; and he knew not Arabic, so, as often as the Wag said to him, "It doth suffice," he concluded that he said, "Bite like a vice," and redoubled his bite and made his teeth meet in the ear, whilst the damsels were diverted from him with hearkening to the singing-girls, and Abu al-Hasan cried out for succour from the boy and the Caliph lost his senses for laughter. Then he dealt the boy a cuff, and he let go his ear, whereupon all present fell down with laughter and said to the little Mameluke, "Art mad that thou bitest the Caliph's ear on this wise?" And Abu al-Hasan cried to them, "Sufficeth ye not, O ye wretched Jinns, that which hath befallen me? But the fault is not yours: the fault is of your Chief who transmewed you from Jinn shape to mortal shape. I seek refuge against you this night by the Throne-verse and the Chapter of Sincerity[55] and the Two Preventives!" So saying the Wag put off his clothes till he was naked, with prickle and breech exposed, and danced among the slave-girls. They bound his hands and he wantoned among them, while they died of laughing at him and the Caliph swooned away for excess of laughter. Then he came to himself and going forth the curtain to Abu al-Hasan, said to him, "Out on thee, O Abu al-Hasan! Thou slayest me with laughter." So he turned to him and knowing him, said to him, "By Allah, 'tis thou slayest me and slayest my mother and slewest the Shaykhs and the Imam of the Mosque!" After which he kissed ground before him and prayed for the permanence of his prosperity and the endurance of his days. The Caliph at once robed him in a rich robe and gave him a thousand dinars; and presently he took the Wag into especial favour and married him and bestowed largesse on him and lodged him with himself in the palace and made him of the chief of his cup-companions, and indeed he was preferred with him above them and the Caliph advanced him over them all, so that he sat with him and the Lady Zubaydah bint al-Kasim, whose treasuress Nuzhat al-Fuad[56] hight, was given to him in marriage. After this Abu al-Hasan the Wag abode with his wife in eating and drinking and all delight of life, till whatso was with them went the way of money, when he said to her, "Harkye, O Nuzhat al-Fuad!" Said she, "At thy service;" and he continued, "I have it in mind to play a trick on the Caliph[57] and thou shalt do the like with the Lady Zubaydah, and we will take of them at once, to begin with, two hundred dinars and two pieces of silk." She rejoined, "As thou willest, but what thinkest thou to do?" And he said, "We will feign ourselves dead and this is the trick. I will die before thee and lay myself out, and do thou spread over me a silken napkin and loose my turban over me and tie my toes and lay on my stomach a knife and a little salt.[58] Then let down thy hair and betake thyself to thy mistress Zubaydah, tearing thy dress and slapping thy face and crying out. She will ask thee, What aileth thee? and do thou answer her, May thy head outlive Abu al-Hasan the Wag; for he is dead. She will mourn for me and weep and bid her new treasuress give thee an hundred dinars and a piece of silk and will say to thee:—Go, lay him out and carry him forth. So do thou take of her the hundred dinars and the piece of silk[59] and come back, and when thou returnest to me, I will rise up and thou shalt lie down in my place, and I will go to the Caliph and say to him, May thy head outlive Nuzhat al-Fuad, and rend my raiment and pluck out my beard. He will mourn for thee and say to his treasurer, Give Abu al-Hasan an hundred dinars and a piece of silk. Then he will say to me, Go; lay her out and carry her forth; and I will come back to thee." Therewith Nuzhat al-Fuad rejoiced and said, "Indeed, this is an excellent device." Then Abu al-Hasan stretched himself out forthright and she shut his eyes and tied his feet and covered him with the napkin and did whatso her lord had bidden her; after which she tare her gear and bared her head and letting down her hair, went in to the Lady Zubaydah, crying out and weeping. When the Princess saw her in this state, she cried, "What plight is this? What is thy story and what maketh thee weep?" And Nuzhat al-Fuad answered, weeping and loud-wailing the while, "O my lady, may thy head live and mayst thou survive Abu al-Hasan al Khali'a; for he is dead!" The Lady Zubaydah mourned for him and said, "Alas, poor Abu al-Hasan the Wag!" and she shed tears for him awhile. Then she bade her treasuress give Nuzhat al-Fuad an hundred dinars and a piece of silk and said to her, "O Nuzhat al-Fuad, go, lay him out and carry him forth." So she took the hundred dinars and the piece of silk and returned to her dwelling, rejoicing, and went in to her spouse and acquainted him what had befallen, whereupon he arose and rejoiced and girdled his middle and danced and took the hundred dinars and the piece of silk and laid them up. Then he laid out Nuzhat al-Fuad and did with her as she had done with him; after which he rent his raiment and plucked out his beard and disordered his turban and ran out nor ceased running till he came in to the Caliph, who was sitting in the judgment-hall, and he in this plight, beating his breast. The Caliph asked him, "What aileth thee, O Abu al-Hasan?" and he wept and answered, "Would heaven thy cup-companion had never been and would his hour had never come!"[60] Quoth the Caliph, "Tell me thy case:" and quoth Abu al-Hasan, "O my lord, may thy head outlive Nuzhat al-Fuad!" The Caliph exclaimed, "There is no god but God;" and smote hand upon hand. Then he comforted Abu al-Hasan and said to him, "Grieve not, for we will bestow upon thee a bed-fellow other than she." And he ordered the treasurer to give him an hundred dinars and a piece of silk. Accordingly the treasurer did what the Caliph bade him, and Al-Rashid said to him, "Go, lay her out and carry her forth and make her a handsome funeral." So Abu al-Hasan took that which he had given him and returning to his house, rejoicing, went in to Nuzhat al-Fuad and said to her, "Arise, for our wish is won." Hereat she arose and he laid before her the hundred ducats and the piece of silk, whereat she rejoiced, and they added the gold to the gold and the silk to the silk and sat talking and laughing each to other. Meanwhile, when Abu al-Hasan fared forth the presence of the Caliph and went to lay out Nuzhat al-Fuad, the Commander of the Faithful mourned for her and dismissing the divan, arose and betook himself, leaning upon Masrur, the Sworder of his vengeance, to the Lady Zubaydah, that he might condole with her for her handmaid. He found her sitting weeping and awaiting his coming, so she might condole with him for his boon-companion Abu al-Hasan the Wag. So he said to her, "May thy head outlive thy slave-girl Nuzhat al-Fuad!" and said she, "O my lord, Allah preserve my slave-girl! Mayst thou live and long survive thy boon-companion Abu al-Hasan al-Khali'a; for he is dead." The Caliph smiled and said to his eunuch, "O Masrur, verily women are little of wit. Allah upon thee, say, was not Abu al-Hasan with me but now?"[61] Quoth the Lady Zubaydah, laughing from a heart full of wrath, "Wilt thou not leave thy jesting? Sufficeth thee not that Abu al-Hasan is dead, but thou must put to death my slave-girl also and bereave us of the twain, and style me little of wit?" The Caliph answered, "Indeed, 'tis Nuzhat al-Fuad who is dead." And the Lady Zubaydah said, "Indeed he hath not been with thee, nor hast thou seen him, and none was with me but now save Nuzhat al-Fuad, and she sorrowful, weeping, with her clothes torn to tatters. I exhorted her to patience and gave her an hundred dinars and a piece of silk; and indeed I was awaiting thy coming, so I might console thee for thy cup-companion Abu al-Hasan al-Khali'a, and was about to send for thee."[62] The Caliph laughed and said, "None is dead save Nuzhat al-Fuad;" and she, "No, no, good my lord; none is dead but Abu al-Hasan the Wag." With this the Caliph waxed wroth, and the Hashimi vein[63] started out from between his eyes and throbbed: and he cried out to Masrur and said to him, "Fare thee forth to the house of Abu al-Hasan the Wag, and see which of them is dead." So Masrur went out, running, and the Caliph said to the Lady Zubaydah, "Wilt thou lay me a wager?" And said she, "Yes, I will wager, and I say that Abu al-Hasan is dead." Rejoined the Caliph, "'And I wager and say that none is dead save Nuzhat al-Fuad; and the stake between me and thee shall be the Garden of Pleasance[64] against thy palace and the Pavilion of Pictures."[65] So they agreed upon this and sat awaiting Masrur's return with the news. As for the Eunuch, he ceased not running till he came to the by-street, wherein was the stead of Abu al-Hasan al-Khali'a. Now the Wag was comfortably seated and leaning back against the lattice,[66] and chancing to look round, saw Masrur running along the street and said to Nuzhat al-Fuad, "Meseemeth the Caliph, when I went forth from him dismissed the Divan and went in to the Lady Zubaydah, to condole with her; whereupon she arose and condoled with him, saying, Allah increase thy recompense for the loss of Abu al-Hasan al-Khali'a! And he said to her, None is dead save Nuzhat al-Fuad, may thy head outlive her! Quoth she, 'Tis not she who is dead, but Abu al-Hasan al-Khali'a, thy boon-companion. And quoth he, None is dead save Nuzhat al-Fuad. And they waxed so obstinate that the Caliph became wroth and they laid a wager, and he hath sent Masrur the Sworder to see who is dead. Now, therefore, 'twere best that thou lie down, so he may sight thee and go and acquaint the Caliph and confirm my saying."[67] So Nuzhat al-Fuad stretched herself out and Abu al-Hasan covered her with her mantilla and sat weeping at her head. Presently, Masrur the eunuch suddenly came in to him and saluted him, and seeing Nuzhat al-Fuad stretched out, uncovered her face and said, "There is no god but God! Our sister Nuzhat al-Fuad is dead indeed. How sudden was the stroke of Destiny! Allah have ruth on thee and acquit thee of all charge!" Then he returned and related what had passed before the Caliph and the Lady Zubaydah, and he laughing as he spoke. "O accursed one," cried the Caliph, "this is no time for laughter! Tell us which is dead of them." Masrur replied, "By Allah, O my lord, Abu al-Hasan is well, and none is dead but Nuzhat al-Fuad." Quoth the Caliph to Zubaydah, "Thou hast lost thy pavilion in thy play," and he jeered at her and said, "O Masrur, tell her what thou sawest." Quoth the Eunuch, "Verily, O my lady, I ran without ceasing till I came in to Abu al-Hasan in his house and found Nuzhat al-Fuad lying dead and Abu al-Hasan sitting tearful at her head. I saluted him and condoled with him and sat down by his side and uncovered the face of Nuzhat al-Fuad and saw her dead and her face swollen.[68] So I said to him:—Carry her out forthwith, so we may pray over her. He replied:—'Tis well; and I left him to lay her out and came hither, that I might tell you the news." The Prince of True Believers laughed and said, "Tell it again and again to thy lady Littlewits." When the Lady Zubaydah heard Masrur's words and those of the Caliph she was wroth and said, "None is little of wit save he who believeth a black slave." And she abused Masrur, whilst the Commander of the Faithful laughed: and the Eunuch, vexed at this, said to the Caliph, "He spake sooth who said:—Women are little of wits and lack religion."[69] Then said the Lady Zubaydah to the Caliph, "O Commander of the Faithful, thou sportest and jestest with me, and this slave hoodwinketh me, the better to please thee; but I will send and see which of them be dead." And he answered, saying, "Send one who shall see which of them is dead." So the Lady Zubaydah cried out to an old duenna, and said to her, "Hie thee to the house of Nuzhat al-Fuad in haste and see who is dead and loiter not." And she used hard words to her.[70] So the old woman went out running, whilst the Prince of True Believers and Masrur laughed, and she ceased not running till she came into the street. Abu al-Hasan saw her, and knowing her, said to his wife, "O Nuzhat al-Fuad, meseemeth the Lady Zubaydah hath sent to us to see who is dead and hath not given credit to Masrur's report of thy death: accordingly, she hath despatched the old crone, her duenna, to discover the truth. So it behoveth me to be dead in my turn for the sake of thy credit with the Lady Zubaydah." Hereat he lay down and stretched himself out, and she covered him and bound his eyes and feet and sat in tears at his head. Presently the old woman came in to her and saw her sitting at Abu al-Hasan's head, weeping and recounting his fine qualities; and when she saw the old trot, she cried out and said to her, "See what hath befallen me! Indeed Abu al-Hasan is dead and hath left me lone and lorn!" Then she shrieked out and rent her raiment and said to the crone, "O my mother, how very good he was to me!"[71] Quoth the other, "Indeed thou art excused, for thou wast used to him and he to thee." Then she considered what Masrur had reported to the Caliph and the Lady Zubaydah and said to her, "Indeed, Masrur goeth about to cast discord between the Caliph and the Lady Zubaydah." Asked Nuzhat al-Fuad, "And what is the cause of discord, O my mother?" and the other replied, "O my daughter, Masrur came to the Caliph and the Lady Zubaydah and gave them news of thee that thou wast dead and that Abu al-Hasan was well." Nuzhat al-Fuad said to her, "O naunty mine,[72] I was with my lady just now and she gave me an hundred dinars and a piece of silk; and now see my case and that which hath befallen me! Indeed, I am bewildered, and how shall I do, and I lone, and lorn? Would heaven I had died and he had lived!" Then she wept and with her wept the old woman, who, going up to Abu al-Hasan and uncovering his face, saw his eyes bound and swollen for the swathing. So she covered him again and said, "Indeed, O Nuzhat al-Fuad, thou art afflicted in Abu al-Hasan!" Then she condoled with her and going out from her, ran along the street till she came into the Lady Zubaydah and related to her the story; and the Princess said to her, laughing, "Tell it over again to the Caliph, who maketh me out little of wit, and lacking of religion, and who made this ill-omened liar of a slave presume to contradict me." Quoth Masrur, "This old woman lieth; for I saw Abu al-Hasan well and Nuzhat al-Fuad it was who lay dead." Quoth the duenna, " 'Tis thou that liest, and wouldst fain cast discord between the Caliph and the Lady Zubaydah." And Masrur cried, "None lieth but thou, O old woman of ill-omen, and thy lady believeth thee and she must be in her dotage." Whereupon the Lady Zubaydah cried out at him, and in very sooth she was enraged with him and with his speech and shed tears. Then said the Caliph to her, "I lie and my eunuch lieth, and thou liest and thy waiting-woman lieth; so 'tis my rede we go, all four of us together, that we may see which of us telleth the truth." Masrur said, "Come, let us go, that I may do to this ill-omened old woman evil deeds[73] and deal her a sound drubbing for her lying." And the duenna answered him, "O dotard, is thy wit like unto my wit? Indeed, thy wit is as the hen's wit." Masrur was incensed at her words and would have laid violent hands on her, but the Lady Zubaydah pushed him away from her and said to him, "Her truth-speaking will presently be distinguished from thy truth-speaking and her leasing from thy leasing." Then they all four arose, laying wagers one with other, and went forth a-foot from the palace-gate and hied on till they came in at the gate of the street where Abu al-Hasan al-Khali'a dwelt. He saw them and said to his wife Nuzhat al-Fuad, "Verily, all that is sticky is not a pancake[74] they cook nor every time shall the crock escape the shock. It seemeth the old woman hath gone and told her lady and acquainted her with our case and she hath disputed with Masrur the Eunuch and they have laid wagers each with other about our death and are come to us, all four, the Caliph and the Eunuch and the Lady Zubaydah and the old trot." When Nuzhat al-Fuad heard this, she started up from her outstretched posture and asked, "How shall we do?" whereto he answered, "We will both feign ourselves dead together and stretch ourselves out and hold our breath." So she hearkened unto him and they both lay down on the place where they usually slept the siesta[75] and bound their feet and shut their eyes and covered themselves with the veil and held their breath. Presently, up came the Caliph, Zubaydah, Masrur and the old woman and entering, found Abu al-Hasan the Wag and wife both stretched out as dead; which when the Lady saw, she wept and said, "They ceased not to bring ill-news of my slave-girl till she died,[76] methinketh Abu al-Hasan's death was grievous to her and that she died after him."[77] Quoth the Caliph, "Thou shalt not prevent me with thy prattle and prate. She certainly died before Abu al-Hasan, for he came to me with his raiment rent and his beard plucked out, beating his breast with two bits of un-baked brick,[78] and I gave him an hundred dinars and a piece of silk and said to him, Go, bear her forth and I will give thee a bedfellow other than she and handsomer, and she shall be in stead of her. But it would appear that her death was no light matter to him and he died after her;[79] so it is I who have beaten thee and gotten thy stake." The Lady Zubaydah answered him in words galore and the dispute between them waxed sore. At last the Caliph sat down at the heads of the pair and said, "By the tomb of the Apostle of Allah (whom may He save and assain!) and the sepulchres of my fathers and forefathers, whoso will tell me which of them died before the other, I will willingly give him a thousand dinars!" When Abu al-Hasan heard the Caliph's words, he sprang up in haste and said, "I died first, O Commander of the Faithful! Here with the thousand dinars and acquit thee of thine oath and the swear thou sworest." Nuzhat al-Fuad rose also and stood up before the Caliph and the Lady Zubaydah, who both rejoiced in this and in their safety, and the Princess chid her slave-girl. Then the Caliph and Zubaydah gave them joy of their well-being and knew that this death was a trick to get the gold; and the Lady said to Nuzhat al-Fuad, "Thou shouldst have sought of me that which thou needest, without this fashion, and not have burned[80] my heart for thee." And she, "Verily, I was ashamed, O my lady." As for the Caliph, he swooned away for laughing and said, "O Abu al-Hasan, thou wilt never cease to be a wag and do peregrine things and prodigious!" Quoth he, "O Commander of the Faithful, this trick I played off for that the money which thou gavest me was exhausted, and I was ashamed to ask of thee again. When I was single, I could never keep money in hand; but since thou marriedst me to this damsel, if I possessed even thy wealth, I should lay it waste. Wherefore when all that was in my hand was spent, I wrought this sleight, so I might get of thee the hundred dinars and the piece of silk; and all this is an alms from our lord. But now make haste to give me the thousand dinars and acquit thee of thine oath." The Caliph and the Lady Zubaydah laughed and returned to the palace; and he gave Abu al-Hasan the thousand dinars saying, "Take them as a *douceur*[81] for thy preservation from death," whilst her mistress did the like with Nuzhat al-Fuad, honouring her with the same words. Moreover, the Caliph increased the Wag in his solde and supplies, and he and his wife ceased not to live in joy and contentment, till there came to them the Destroyer of delights and Severer of societies, the Plunderer of palaces, and the Garnerer of graves. And among tales they tell is one touching.

ALAEDDIN; OR,

THE WONDERFUL LAMP.

It hath reached me, O King of the Age, that there dwelt in a city of the cities of China a man which was a tailor, withal a pauper, and he had one son, Alaeddin hight. Now this boy had been from his babyhood a ne'er-do-well, a scapegrace; and, when he reached his tenth year, his father inclined to teach him his own trade; and, for that he was over indigent to expend money upon his learning other work or craft or apprenticeship, he took the lad into his shop that he might be taught tailoring. But, as Alaeddin was a scapegrace and a ne'er-do-well and wont to play at all times with the gutter boys of the quarter, he would not sit in the shop for a single day; nay, he would await his father's leaving it for some purpose, such as to meet a creditor, when he would run off at once and fare forth to the gardens with the other scapegraces and low companions, his fellows. Such was his case; counsel and castigation were of no avail, nor would he obey either parent in aught or learn any trade; and presently, for his sadness and sorrowing because of his son's vicious indolence, the tailor sickened and died. Alaeddin continued in his former ill courses and, when his mother saw that her spouse had deceased, and that her son was a scapegrace and good for nothing at all[1] she sold the shop and whatso was to be found therein and fell to spinning cotton yarn. By this toilsome industry she fed herself and found food for her son Alaeddin the scapegrace who, seeing himself freed from bearing the severities of his sire, increased in idleness and low habits; nor would he ever stay at home save at mealhours while his miserable wretched mother lived only by what her hands could spin until the youth had reached his fifteenth year. It befel, one day of the days, that as he was sitting about the quarter at play with the vagabond boys behold, a Darwaysh from the Maghrib, the Land of the Setting Sun, came up and stood gazing for solace upon the lads and he looked hard at Alaeddin and carefully considered his semblance, scarcely noticing his companions the while. Now this Darwaysh was a Moorman from Inner Marocco and he was a magician who could upheap by his magic hill upon hill, and he was also an adept in astrology. So after narrowly considering Alaeddin he said in himself, "Verily, this is the lad I need and to find whom I have left my natal land." Presently he led one of the children apart and questioned him anent the scapegrace saying, "Whose[2] son is he?" And he sought all information concerning his condition and whatso related to him. After this he walked up to Alaeddin and drawing him aside asked, "O my son, haply thou art the child of Such-an-one the tailor?" and the lad answered, "Yes, O my lord, but 'tis long since he died." The Maghrabi,[3] the Magician, hearing these words threw himself upon Alaeddin and wound his arms around his neck and fell to bussing him, weeping the while with tears trickling adown his cheeks. But when the lad saw the Moorman's case he was seized with surprise thereat and questioned him, saying, "What causeth thee weep, O my lord; and how camest thou to know my father?" "How canst thou, O my son," replied the Moorman, in a soft voice saddened by emotion, "question me with such query after informing me that thy father and my brother is deceased; for that he was my brother-german and now I come from my adopted country and after long exile I rejoiced with exceeding joy in the hope of looking upon him once more and condoling with him over the past; and now thou hast announced to me his demise. But blood hideth not from blood[4] and it hath revealed to me that thou art my nephew, son of my brother, and I knew thee amongst all the lads, albeit thy father, when I parted from him, was yet unmarried." Then he again clasped Alaeddin to his bosom crying, "O my son, I have none to condole with now save thyself; and thou standest in stead of thy sire, thou being his issue and representative and 'whoso leaveth issue dieth not,'[5] O my child!" So saying, the Magician put hand to purse and pulling out ten gold pieces gave them to the lad asking, "O my son, where is your house and where dwelleth she, thy mother, and my brother's widow?" Presently Alaeddin arose with him and showed him the way to their home and meanwhile quoth the Wizard, "O my son, take these moneys and give them to thy mother, greeting her from me, and let her know that thine uncle, thy father's brother, hath reappeared from his exile and that Inshallah—God willing—on the morrow I will visit her to salute her with the salam and see the house wherein my brother was homed and look upon the place where he lieth buried." Thereupon Alaeddin kissed the Maghrabi's hand, and, after running in his joy at fullest speed to his mother's dwelling, entered to her clean contrariwise to his custom, inasmuch as he never came near her save at meal-times only. And when he found her, the lad exclaimed in his delight, "O my mother, I give thee glad tidings of mine uncle who hath returned from his exile and who now sendeth me to salute thee." "O my son," she replied, "meseemeth thou mockest me! Who is this uncle and how canst thou have an uncle in the bonds of life?" He rejoined, "How sayest thou, O my mother, that I have nor living uncles nor kinsmen, when this man is my father's own brother? Indeed he embraced me and bussed me, shedding tears the while, and bade me acquaint thee herewith." She retorted, "O my son, well I wot thou haddest an uncle, but he is now dead nor am I ware that thou hast other eme." The Maroccan Magician fared forth next morning and fell to finding out Alaeddin, for his heart no longer permitted him to part from the lad; and, as he was to-ing and fro-ing about the city-highways, he came face to face with him disporting himself, as was his wont, amongst the vagabonds and the scapegraces. So he drew near to him and, taking his hand, embraced him and bussed him; then pulled out of his poke two dinars and said, "Hie thee to thy mother and give her these couple of ducats and tell her that thine uncle would eat the evening-meal with you; so do thou take these two gold pieces and prepare for us a succulent supper. But before all things show me once more the way to your home." "On my head and mine eyes be it, O my uncle," replied the lad and forewent him, pointing out the street leading to the house. Then the Moorman left him and went his ways and Alaeddin ran home and, giving the news and the two sequins to his parent, said, "My uncle would sup with us." So she arose straightway and going to the market-street bought all she required; then, returning to her dwelling she borrowed from the neighbours whatever was needed of pans and platters and so forth and when the meal was cooked and suppertime came she said to Alaeddin, "O my child, the meat is ready but peradventure thine uncle wotteth not the way to our dwelling; so do thou fare forth and meet him on the road." He replied, "To hear is to obey," and before the twain ended talking a knock was heard at the door. Alaeddin went out and opened when, behold, the Maghrabi, the Magician, together with an eunuch carrying the wine and the dessert-fruits; so the lad led them in and the slave went about his business. The Moorman on entering saluted his sister-in-law with the salam; then began to shed tears and to question her saying, "Where be the place whereon my brother went to sit?" She showed it to him, whereat he went up to it and prostrated himself in prayer[6] and kissed the floor crying, "Ah, how scant is my satisfaction and how luckless is my lot, for that I have lost thee, O my brother, O vein of my eye!" And after such fashion he continued weeping and wailing till he swooned away for excess of sobbing and lamentation; wherefor Alaeddin's mother was certified of his soothfastness. So coming up to him she raised him from the floor and said, "What gain is there in slaying thyself?" As soon as he was seated at his ease and before the food-trays were served up, he fell to talking with her and saying, "O wife of my brother, it must be a wonder to thee how in all thy days thou never sawest me nor learnedst thou aught of me during the life-time of my brother who hath found mercy.[7] Now the reason is that forty years ago I left this town and exiled myself from my birthplace and wandereth forth over all the lands of Al-Hind and Al-Sind and entered Egypt and settled for a long time in its magnificent city,[8] which is one of the world-wonders, till at last I fared to the regions of the Setting Sun and abode for a space of thirty years in the Maroccan interior. Now one day of the days, O wife of my brother, as I was sitting alone at home, I fell to thinking of mine own country and of my birthplace and of my brother (who hath found mercy); and my yearning to see him waxed excessive and I bewept and bewailed my strangerhood and distance from him. And at last my longings drave me homewards until I resolved upon travelling to the region which was the falling-place of my head[9] and my homestead, to the end that I might again see my brother. Then quoth I to myself:—O man,[10] how long wilt thou wander like a wild Arab from thy place of birth and native stead? Moreover, thou hast one brother and no more; so up with thee and travel and look upon him[11] ere thou die; for who wotteth the woes of the world and the changes of the days? 'Twould be saddest regret an thou lie down to die without beholding thy brother and Allah (laud be to the Lord!) hath vouchsafed thee ample wealth; and belike he may be straitened and in poor case, when thou wilt aid thy brother as well as see him. So I arose at once and equipped me for wayfare and recited the Fatihah; then, whenas Friday prayers ended, I mounted and travelled to this town, after suffering manifold toils and travails which I patiently endured whilst the Lord (to whom be honour and glory!) veiled me with the veil of His protection. So I entered and whilst wandering about the streets, the day before yesterday, I beheld my brother's son Alaeddin disporting himself with the boys and, by God the Great, O wife of my brother, the moment I saw him this heart of mine went forth to him (for blood yearneth unto blood!), and my soul felt and informed me that he was my very nephew. So I forgot all my travails and troubles at once on sighting him and I was like to fly for joy; but, when he told me of the dear one's departure to the ruth of Allah Almighty, I fainted for stress of distress and disappointment. Perchance, however, my nephew hath informed thee of the pains which prevailed upon me; but after a fashion I am consoled by the sight of Alaeddin, the legacy bequeathed to us by him who hath found mercy for that 'whoso leaveth issue is not wholly dead.' "[12] And when he looked at his sister-in-law she wept at these his words; so he turned to the lad that he might cause her to forget the mention of her mate, as a means of comforting her and also of completing his deceit, and asked him, saying, "O my son Alaeddin, what hast thou learned in the way of work and what is thy business? Say me, hast thou mastered any craft whereby to earn a livelihood for thyself and for thy mother?" The lad was abashed and put to shame and he hung down his head and bowed his brow groundwards; but his parent spake out, "How, forsooth? By Allah, he knoweth nothing at all, a child so ungracious as this I never yet saw; no, never! All the day long he idleth away his time with the sons of the quarter, vagabonds like himself, and his father (O regret of me!) died not save of dolour for him. And I also am now in piteous plight: I spin cotton and toil at my distaff, night and day, that I may earn me a couple of scones of bread which we eat together. This is his condition, O my brother-in-law; and, by the life of thee, he cometh not near me save at meal-times and none other. Indeed, I am thinking to lock the house-door nor ever open to him again but leave him to go and seek a livelihood whereby he can live, for that I am now grown a woman in years and have no longer strength to toil and go about for a maintenance after this fashion. O Allah, I am compelled to provide him with daily bread when I require to be provided!" Hereat the Moorman turned to Alaeddin and said, "Why is this, O son of my brother, thou goest about in such ungraciousness? 'Tis a disgrace to thee and unsuitable for men like thyself. Thou art a youth of sense, O my son, and the child of honest folk, so 'tis for thee a shame that thy mother, a woman in years, should struggle to support thee. And now that thou hast grown to man's estate it becometh thee to devise thee some device whereby thou canst live, O my child. Look around thee and Alhamdolillah—praise be to Allah—in this our town are many teachers of all manner of crafts and nowhere are they more numerous; so choose thee some calling which may please thee to the end that I stablish thee therein; and, when thou growest up, O my son, thou shalt have some business whereby to live. Haply thy father's industry may not be to thy liking; and, if so it be, choose thee some other handicraft which suiteth thy fancy; then let me know and I will aid thee with all I can, O my son." But when the Maghrabi saw that Alaeddin kept silence and made him no reply, he knew that the lad wanted none other occupation than a scapegrace-life, so he said to him, "O son of my brother, let not my words seem hard and harsh to thee, for, if despite all I say, thou still dislike to learn a craft, I will open thee a merchant's store[13] furnished with costliest stuffs and thou shalt become famous amongst the folk and take and give and buy and sell and be well known in the city." Now when Alaeddin heard the words of his uncle the Moorman, and the design of making him a Khwajah[14]—merchant and gentleman,—he joyed exceedingly knowing that such folk dress handsomely and fare delicately. So he looked at the Maghrabi smiling and drooping his head groundwards and saying with the tongue of the case that he was content. The Maghrabi, the Magician, looked at Alaeddin and saw him smiling, whereby he understood that the lad was satisfied to become a trader. So he said to him, "Since thou art content that I open thee a merchant's store and make thee a gentleman, do thou, O son of my brother, prove thyself a man and Inshallah—God willing—to-morrow I will take thee to the Bazar in the first place and will have a fine suit of clothes cut out for thee, such gear as merchants wear; and, secondly, I will look after a store for thee and keep my word." Now Alaeddin's mother had somewhat doubted the Maroccan being her brother-in-law; but as soon as she heard his promise of opening a merchant's store for her son and setting him up with stuffs and capital and so forth, the woman decided and determined in her mind that this Maghrabi was in very sooth her husband's brother, seeing that no stranger man would do such goodly deed by her son. So she began directing the lad to the right road and teaching him to cast ignorance from out his head and to prove himself a man; moreover she bade him ever obey his excellent uncle as though he were his son and to make up for the time he had wasted in frowardness with his fellows. After this she arose and spread the table, then served up supper; so all sat down and fell to eating and drinking, while the Maghrabi conversed with Alaeddin upon matters of business and the like, rejoicing him to such degree that he enjoyed no sleep that night. But when the Moorman saw that the dark hours were passing by, and the wine was drunken, he arose and sped to his own stead; but, ere going, he agreed to return next morning and take Alaeddin and look to his suit of merchant's clothes being cut out for him. And as soon as it was dawn, behold, the Maghrabi rapped at the door which was opened by Alaeddin's mother: the Moorman, however, would not enter, but asked to take the lad with him to the market-street. Accordingly Alaeddin went forth to his uncle and, wishing him good morning, kissed his hand; and the Maroccan took him by the hand and fared with him to the Bazar. There he entered a clothier's shop containing all kinds of clothes and called for a suit of the most sumptuous; whereat the merchant brought him out his need, all wholly fashioned and ready sewn; and the Moorman said to the lad, "Choose, O my child, whatso pleaseth thee." Alaeddin rejoiced exceedingly seeing that his uncle had given him his choice, so he picked out the suit most to his own liking and the Maroccan paid to the merchant the price thereof in ready money. Presently he led the lad to the Hammam-baths where they bathed; then they came out and drank sherbets, after which Alaeddin arose and, donning his new dress in huge joy and delight, went up to his uncle and kissed his hand and thanked him for his favours. The Maghrabi, the Magician, after leaving the Hammam with Alaeddin, took him and trudged with him to the Merchant's bazar; and, having diverted him by showing the market and its sellings and buyings, said to him, "O my son, it besitteth thee to become familiar with the folk, especially with the merchants, so thou mayest learn of them merchant-craft, seeing that the same hath now become thy calling." Then he led him forth and showed him the city and its cathedral-mosques together with all the pleasant sights therein; and, lastly, made him enter a cook's shop. Here dinner was served to them on platters of silver and they dined well and ate and drank their sufficiency, after which they went their ways. Presently the Moorman pointed out to Alaeddin the pleasances and noble buildings, and went in with him to the Sultan's Palace and diverted him with displaying all the apartments which were mighty fine and grand; and led him finally to the Khan of stranger merchants where he himself had his abode. Then the Maroccan invited sundry traders which were in the Caravanserai; and they came and sat down to supper, when he notified to them that the youth was his nephew, Alaeddin by name. And after they had eaten and drunken and night had fallen, he rose up and taking the lad with him led him back to his mother, who no sooner saw her boy as he were one of the merchants[15] than her wits took flight and she waxed sad for very gladness. Then she fell to thanking her false connection, the Moorman, for all his benefits and said to him, "O my brother-in-

law, I can never say enough though I expressed my gratitude to thee during the rest of thy days and praised thee
for the good deeds thou hast done by this my child."
Thereupon quoth the Maroccan, "O wife of my brother,
deem this not mere kindness of me, for that the lad is mine
own son and 'tis incumbent on me to stand in the stead of
my brother, his sire. So be thou fully satisfied!" And quoth
she, "I pray Allah by the honour of the Hallows, the ancients and the moderns, that He preserve thee and cause
thee continue, O my brother-in-law, and prolong for me
thy life; so shalt thou be a wing overshadowing this orphan
lad; and he shall ever be obedient to thine orders nor shall
he do aught save whatso thou biddest him thereunto." The
Maghrabi replied, "O wife of my brother, Alaeddin is now
a man of sense and the son of goodly folk, and I hope to
Allah that he will follow in the footsteps of his sire and
cool thine eyes. But I regret that, to-morrow being Friday,
I shall not be able to open his shop, as 'tis meeting-day
when all the merchants, after congregational prayer, go
forth to the gardens and pleasances. On the Sabbath,[16]
however, Inshallah!—an it please the Creator—we will do
our business. Meanwhile tomorrow I will come to thee betimes and take Alaeddin for a pleasant stroll to the gardens
and pleasances without the city which haply he may hitherto not have beheld. There also he shall see the merchants
and notables who go forth to amuse themselves, so shall
he become acquainted with them and they with him." The
Maghrabi went away and lay that night in his quarters; and
early next morning he came to the tailor's house and
rapped at the door. Now Alaeddin (for stress of his delight
in the new dress he had donned and for the past day's enjoyment in the Hammam and in eating and drinking and
gazing at the folk; expecting furthermore his uncle to
come at dawn and carry him off on pleasuring to the gardens) had not slept a wink that night, nor closed his eyelids, and would hardly believe it when day broke. But
hearing the knock at the door he went out at once in hot
haste, like a spark of fire, and opened and saw his uncle, the

Magician, who embraced him and kissed him. Then, taking his hand, the Moorman said to him as they fared forth together, "O son of my brother, this day will I show thee a sight thou never sawest in all they life," and he began to make the lad laugh and cheer him with pleasant talk. So doing they left the city gate, and the Maroccan took to promenading with Alaeddin amongst the gardens and to pointing out for his pleasure the mighty fine pleasances and the marvellous high-builded pavilions. And whenever they stood to stare at a garth or a mansion or a palace the Maghrabi would say to his companion, "Doth this please thee, O son of my brother?" Alaeddin was nigh to fly with delight at seeing sights he had never seen in all his born days; and they ceased not[17] to stroll about and solace themselves until they waxed aweary, when they entered a mighty grand garden which was nearhand, a place that the heart delighted and the sight belighted; for that its swift-running rills flowed amidst the flowers and the waters jetted from the jaws of lions moulded in yellow brass like unto gold. So they took seat over against a lakelet and rested a little while, and Alaeddin enjoyed himself with joy exceeding and fell to jesting with his uncle and making merry with him as though the Magician were really his father's brother. Presently the Maghrabi arose and loosing his girdle drew forth from thereunder a bag full of victual, dried fruits and so forth, saying to Alaeddin, "O my nephew, haply thou art become anhungered; so come forward and eat what thou needest." Accordingly the lad fell upon the food and the Moorman ate with him and they were gladdened and cheered by rest and good cheer. Then quoth the Magician, "Arise, O son of my brother, an thou be reposed and let us stroll onwards a little and reach the end of our walk." Thereupon Alaeddin arose and the Maroccan paced with him from garden to garden until they left all behind them and reached the base of a high and naked hill; when the lad who, during all his days, had never issued from the city-gate and never in his life had walked such a walk as this, said to the Maghrabi, "O uncle mine, whither are we wending? We have left the gardens behind us one and all and have reached the barren hill-country;[18] and, if the way be still long, I have no strength left for walking: indeed I am ready to fall with fatigue. There are no gardens before us, so let us hark back and return to town." Said the Magician, "No, O my son; this is the right road, nor are the gardens ended for we are going to look at one which hath ne'er its like amongst those of the Kings and all thou hast beheld are naught in comparison therewith. Then gird thy courage to walk; thou art now a man, Alhamdolillah—praise be to Allah!" Then the Maghrabi fell to soothing Alaeddin with soft words and telling him wondrous tales, lies as well as truth, until they reached the site intended by the African Magician who had travelled from the Sunset-land to the regions of China for the sake thereof. And when they made the place, the Moorman said to Alaeddin, "O son of my brother, sit thee down and take thy rest, for this is the spot we are now seeking and, Inshallah, soon will I divert thee by displaying marvel-matters whose like not one in the world ever saw; nor hath any solaced himself with gazing upon that which thou art about to behold. But when thou art rested, arise and seek some wood-chips and fuel sticks[19] which be small and dry, wherewith we may kindle a fire: then will I show thee, O son of my brother, matters beyond the range of matter."[20] Now, when the lad heard these words, he longed to look upon what his uncle was about to do and, forgetting his fatigue, he rose forthright and fell to gathering small wood-chips and dry sticks, and continued until the Moorman cried to him, "Enough, O son of my brother!" Presently the Magician brought out from his breast-pocket a casket which he opened, and drew from it all he needed of incense; then he fumigated and conjured and adjured, muttering words none might understand. And the ground straightway clave asunder after thick gloom and quake of earth and bellowings of thunder. Hereat Alaeddin was startled and so affrighted that he tried to fly; but, when the African Magician saw his design, he waxed wroth with exceeding wrath, for that without the lad his work would profit him naught, the hidden hoard which he sought to open being not to be opened save by means of Alaeddin. So noting this attempt to run away, the Magician arose and raising his hand smote Alaeddin on the head a buffet so sore that well-nigh his back-teeth were knocked out, and he fell swooning to the ground. But after a time he revived by the magic of the Magician, and cried, weeping the while, "O my uncle, what have I done that deserveth from thee such a blow as this?" Hereat the Maghrabi fell to soothing him, and said, "O my son, 'tis my intent to make thee a man; therefore, do thou not gainsay me, for that I am thine uncle and like unto thy father. Obey me, therefore, in all I bid thee, and shortly thou shalt forget all this travail and toil whenas thou shalt look upon the marvel-matters I am about to show thee." And soon after the ground had cloven asunder before the Maroccan it displayed a marble slab wherein was fixed a copper ring. The Maghrabi, striking a geomantic table,[21] turned to Alaeddin, and said to him, "An thou do all I shall bid thee, indeed thou shalt become wealthier than any of the kings, and for this reason, O my son, I struck thee, because here lieth a hoard which is stored in thy name; and yet thou designedst to leave it and to levant. But now collect thy thoughts, and behold how I opened earth by my spells and adjurations. Under yon stone wherein the ring is set lieth the treasure wherewith I acquainted thee: so set thy hand upon the ring and raise the slab, for that none other amongst the folk, thyself excepted, hath power to open it, nor may any of mortal birth, save thyself, set foot within this Enchanted Treasury which hath been kept for thee. But 'tis needful that thou learn of me all wherewith I would charge thee; nor gainsay e'en a single syllable of my words. All this, O my child, is for thy good; the hoard being of immense value, whose like the kings of the world never accumulated, and do thou remember that 'tis for thee and me." So poor Alaeddin forgot his fatigue and buffet and tear-shedding, and he was dumbed and dazed at the Maghrabi's words and rejoiced that he was fated to become rich in such measure that not even the Sultans would be richer than himself. Accordingly, he cried, "O my uncle, bid me do all thou pleasest, for I will be obedient unto thy bidding." The Maghrabi replied, "O my nephew, thou art to me as my own child and even dearer, for being my brother's son and for my having none other kith and kin except thyself; and thou, O my child, art my heir and successor." So saying, he went up to Alaeddin and kissed him and said, "For whom do I intend these my labours? Indeed, each and every are for thy sake, O my son, to the end that I may leave thee a rich man and one of the very greatest. So gainsay me not in all I shall say to thee, and now go up to yonder ring and uplift it as I bade thee." Alaeddin answered, "O uncle mine, this ring is over heavy for me: I cannot raise it single-handed, so do thou also come forward and lend me strength and aidance towards uplifting it, for indeed I am young in years." The Moorman replied, "O son of my brother, we shall find it impossible to do aught if I assist thee, and all our efforts would be in vain. But do thou set thy hand upon the ring and pull it up, and thou shalt raise the slab forthright, and in very sooth I told thee that none can touch it save thyself. But whilst haling at it cease not to pronounce thy name and the names of thy father and mother, so 'twill rise at once to thee nor shalt thou feel its weight." Thereupon the lad mustered up strength and girt the loins of resolution and did as the Maroccan had bidden him, and hove up the slab with all ease when he pronounced his name and the names of his parents, even as the Magician had bidden him. And as soon as the stone was raised he threw it aside and there appeared before him a Sardab, a souterrain, whereunto led a case of some twelve stairs and the Maghrabi said, "O Alaeddin, collect thy thoughts and do whatso I bid thee to the minutest detail nor fail in aught thereof. Go down with all care into yonder vault until thou reach the bottom and there shalt thou find a space divided into four halls,[22] and in each of these thou shalt see four golden jars[23] and others of virgin or and silver. Beware, however, lest thou take aught therefrom or touch them, nor allow thy gown or its skirts even to brush the jars or the walls. Leave them and fare forwards until thou reach the fourth hall without lingering for a single moment on the way; and, if thou do aught contrary thereto thou wilt at once be transformed and become a black stone. When reaching the fourth hall thou wilt find therein a door which do thou open, and pronouncing the names thou spakest over the slab, enter therethrough into a garden adorned everywhere with fruit-bearing trees. This thou must traverse by a path thou wilt see in front of thee measuring some fifty cubits long, beyond which thou wilt come upon an open saloon[24] and therein a ladder of some thirty rungs. Thou shalt there find a Lamp hanging from its ceiling; so mount the ladder and take that Lamp and place it in thy breast-pocket after pouring out its contents; nor fear evil from it for thy clothes because its contents are not common oil.[25] And on return thou art allowed to pluck from the trees whatso thou pleasest, for all is thine so long as the Lamp is in thy hand." Now when the Moorman ended his charge to Alaeddin, he drew off a seal-ring[26] and put it upon the lad's forefinger saying, "O my son, verily this signet shall free thee from all hurt and fear which may threaten thee, but only on condition that thou bear in mind all I have told thee.[27] So arise straightway and go down the stairs, strengthening thy purpose and girding the loins of resolution: moreover fear not for thou art now a man and no longer a child. And in shortest time, O my son, thou shalt win thee immense riches and thou shalt become the wealthiest of the world." Accordingly, Alaeddin arose and descended into the souterrain, where he found the four halls, each containing four jars of gold and these he passed by, as the Maroccan had bidden him, with the utmost care and caution. Thence he fared into the garden and walked along its length until he entered the saloon, where he mounted the ladder and took the Lamp which he extinguished, pouring out the oil which was therein, and placed it in his breast-pocket. Presently, descending the ladder he returned to the garden where he fell to gazing at the trees whereupon sat birds glorifying with loud voices their Great Creator. Now he had not observed them as he went in, but all these trees bare for fruitage costly gems; moreover each had its own kind of growth and jewels of its peculiar sort; and these were of every colour, green and white; yellow, red and other such brilliant hues and the radiance flashing from these gems paled the rays of the sun in forenoon sheen. Furthermore the size of each stone so far surpassed description that no King of the Kings of the world owned a single gem equal to the larger sort nor could boast of even one half the size of the smaller kind of them. Alaeddin walked amongst the trees and gazed upon them and other things which surprised the sight and bewildered the wits; and, as he considered them, he saw that in lieu of common fruits the produce was of mighty fine jewels and precious stones,[28] such as emeralds and diamonds; rubies, spinels and balasses, pearls and similar gems astounding the mental vision of man. And forasmuch as the lad had never beheld things like these during his born days nor had reached those years of discretion which would teach him the worth of such valuables (he being still but a little lad), he fancied that all these jewels were of glass or crystal. So he collected them until he had filled his breast-pockets and began to certify himself if they were or were not common fruits, such as grapes, figs and such like edibles. But seeing them of glassy substance, he, in his ignorance of precious stones and their prices, gathered into his breast-pockets every kind of growth the trees afforded; and, having failed of his purpose in finding them food, he said in his mind, "I will collect a portion of these glass fruits for playthings at home." So he fell to plucking them in quantities and cramming them in his pokes and breast-pockets till these were stuffed full; after which he picked others which he placed in his waist-shawl and then, girding himself therewith, carried off all he availed to, purposing to place them in the house by way of ornaments and, as hath been mentioned, never imagining that they were other than glass. Then he hurried his pace in fear of his uncle, the Maghrabi, until he had passed through the four halls and lastly on his return reached the souterrain where he cast not a look at the jars of gold, albeit he was able and allowed to take of the contents on his way back. But when he came to the souterrain-stairs²⁹ and climb the steps till naught remained but the last; and, finding this higher than all the others, he was unable alone and unassisted, burthened moreover as he was, to mount it. So he said to the Maghrabi, "O my uncle, lend me thy hand and aid me to climb;" but the Moorman answered, "O my son, give me the Lamp and lighten thy load; belike 'tis that weigheth thee down." The lad rejoined, "O my uncle, 'tis not the Lamp downweigheth me at all; but do thou lend me a hand and as soon as I reach ground I will give it to thee." Hereat the Maroccan, the Magician, whose only object was the Lamp and none other, began to insist upon Alaeddin giving it to him at once; but the lad (forasmuch as he had placed it at the bottom of his breast-pocket and his other pouches being full of gems bulged outwards)³⁰ could not reach it with his fingers to hand it over, so the wizard after much vain persistency in requiring what his nephew was unable to give, fell to raging with furious rage and to demanding the Lamp whilst Alaeddin could not get at it. Yet had the lad promised truthfully that he would give it up as soon as he might reach ground, without lying thought or ill-intent. But when the Moorman saw that he would not hand it over, he waxed wroth with wrath exceeding and cut off all his hopes of winning it; so he conjured and adjured and cast incense amiddlemost the fire, when forthright the slab made a cover of itself, and by the might of magic lidded the entrance; the earth buried the stone as it was aforetime and Alaeddin, unable to issue forth, remained underground. Now the Sorcerer was a stranger, and, as we have mentioned, no uncle of Alaeddin's, and he had misrepresented himself and preferred a lying claim, to the end that he might obtain the Lamp by means of the lad for whom this Hoard had been upstored. So the Accursed heaped the earth over him and left him to die of hunger. For this Maghrabi was an African of Afrikiyah proper, born in the Inner Sunset-land, and from his earliest age upwards he had been addicted to witchcraft and had studied and practised every manner of occult science, for which unholy lore the city of Africa[31] is notorious. And he ceased not to read and hear lectures until he had become a past-master in all such knowledge. And of the abounding skill in spells and conjurations which he had acquired by the perusing and the lessoning of forty years, one day of the days he discovered by devilish inspiration that there lay in an extreme city of the cities of China, named Al-Kal'as,[32] an immense Hoard, the like whereof none of the Kings in this world had ever accumulated: moreover, that the most marvellous article in this Enchanted Treasure was a wonderful Lamp which, whoso possessed, could not possibly be surpassed by any man upon earth, either in high degree or in wealth and opulence; nor could the mightiest monarch of the universe attain to the all-sufficiency of this Lamp with its might of magical means. When the Maghrabi assured himself by his science and saw that this Hoard could be opened only by the presence of a lad named Alaeddin, of pauper family and abiding in that very city, and learnt how taking it would be easy and without hardships, he straightway and without stay or delay equipped himself for a voyage to China (as we have already told), and he did what he did with Alaeddin fancying that he would become Lord of the Lamp. But his attempt and his hopes were baffled and his work was clean wasted; whereupon, determining to do the lad die, he heaped up the earth over him by gramarye to the end that the unfortunate might perish, reflecting that "The live man hath no murtherer."[33] Secondly, he did so with the design that, as Alaeddin could not come forth from underground, he would also be impotent to bring out the Lamp from the souterrain. So presently he wended his ways and retired to his own land, Africa, a sadder man and disappointed of all his expectations. Such was the case with the Wizard; but as regards Alaeddin when the earth was heaped over him, he began shouting to the Moorman whom he believed to be his uncle, and praying him to lend a hand that he might issue from the souterrain and return to earth's surface; but, however loudly he cried, none was found to reply. At that moment he comprehended the sleight which the Maroccan had played upon him, and that the man was no uncle but a liar and a wizard. Then the unhappy despaired of life, and learned to his sorrow that there was no escape for him; so he fell to beweeping with sore weeping the calamity had befallen him; and after a little while he stood up and descended the stairs to see if Allah Almighty had lightened his grief-load by leaving a door of issue. So he turned him to the right and to the left but he saw naught save darkness and four walls closed upon him, for that the Magician had by his magic locked all the doors and had shut up even the garden, where through the lad erst had passed, lest it offer him the means of issuing out upon earth's surface, and that he might surely die. Then Alaeddin's weeping waxed sorer, and his wailing louder whenas he found all the doors fast shut, for he had thought to solace himself awhile in the garden. But when he felt that all were locked, he fell to shedding tears and lamenting like unto one who hath lost his every hope, and he returned to sit upon the stairs of the flight whereby he had entered the souterrain. But it is a light matter for Allah (be He exalted and extolled!) whenas He designeth aught to say, "Be" and it becometh; for that He createth joy in the midst of annoy; and on this wise it was with Alaeddin. Whilst the Maghrabi, the Magician, was sending him down into the souterrain he set upon his finger by way of gift, a seal-ring and said, "Verily this signet shall save thee from every strait an thou fall into calamity and ill shifts of time; and it shall remove from thee all hurt and harm, and aid thee with a strong arm whereso thou mayest be set."[34] Now this was by destiny of God the Great, that it might be the means of Alaeddin's escape; for whilst he sat wailing and weeping over his case and cast away all hope of life, and utter misery overwhelmed him, he rubbed his hands together for excess of sorrow, as is the wont of the woeful; then, raising them in supplication to Allah, he cried, "I testify that there is no God save Thou alone, The Most Great, the Omnipotent, the All-conquering, Quickener of the dead, Creator of man's need and Granter thereof, Resolver of his difficulties and duresse and Bringer of joy not of annoy. Thou art my sufficiency and Thou art the Truest of Trustees. And I bear my witness that Mohammed is Thy servant and Thine Apostle and I supplicate Thee, O my God, by his favour with Thee to free me from this my foul plight." And whilst he implored the Lord and was chafing his hands in the soreness of his sorrow for that had befallen him of calamity, his fingers chanced to rub the Ring when, lo and behold! forthright its Familiar rose upright before him and cried, "Adsum; thy slave between thy hands is come! Ask whatso thou wantest, for that I am the thrall of him on whose hand is the Ring, the Signet of my lord and master." Hereat the lad looked at him and saw standing before him a Marid like unto an Ifrit[35] of our lord Solomon's Jinns. He trembled at the terrible sight; but, hearing the Slave of the Ring say, "Ask whatso thou wantest, verily, I am thy thrall, seeing that the signet of my lord be upon thy finger," he recovered his spirits and remembered the Moorman's saying when giving him the Ring. So he rejoiced exceedingly and became brave and cried, "Ho thou, Slave of the Lord of the Ring, I desire thee to set me upon the face of earth." And hardly had he spoken this speech when suddenly the ground clave asunder and he found himself at the door of the Hoard and outside it in full view of the world. Now for three whole days he had been sitting in the darkness of the Treasury underground and when the sheen of day and the shine of sun smote his face he found himself unable to keep his eyes open; so he began to unclose the lids a little and to close them a little until his eyeballs regained force and got used to the light and were purged of the noisome murk. Withal he was astounded at finding himself without the Hoard-door whereby he had passed in when it was opened by the Maghrabi, the Magician; especially as the adit had been lidded and the ground had been smoothed, showing no sign whatever of entrance. Thereat his surprise increased until he fancied himself in another place, nor was his mind convinced that the stead was the same until he saw the spot whereupon they had kindled the fire of wood-chips and dried sticks, and where the African Wizard had conjured over the incense. Then he turned him rightwards and leftwards and sighted the gardens from afar and his eyes recognised the road whereby he had come. So he returned thanks to Allah Almighty who had restored him to the face of earth and had freed him from death after he had cut off all hopes of life. Presently he arose and walked along the way to the town, which now he knew well, until he entered the streets and passed on to his own home. Then he went in to his mother and on seeing her, of the overwhelming stress of joy at his escape and the memory of past affright and the hardships he had borne and the pangs of hunger, he fell to the ground before his parent in a fainting-fit. Now his mother had been passing sad since the time of his leaving her and he found her moaning and crying about him; however on sighting him enter the house she joyed with exceeding joy, but soon was overwhelmed with woe when he sank upon the ground swooning before her eyes. Still,[36] she did not neglect the matter or treat it lightly, but at once hastened to sprinkle water upon his face and after she asked of the neighbours some scents which she made him snuff up. And when he came round a little, he prayed her to bring him somewhat of food saying, "O my mother, 'tis now three days since I ate anything at all." Thereupon she arose and brought him what she had by her; then, setting it before him, said, "Come forward, O my son; eat and be cheered[37] and, when thou shalt have rested, tell me what hath betided and affected thee, O my child; at this present I will not question thee for thou art aweary in very deed." Alaeddin ate and drank and was cheered and after he had rested and had recovered spirits he cried, "Ah, O my mother, I have a sore grievance against thee for leaving me to that accursed wight who strave to compass my destruction and designed to take my life.[38] Know thou that I beheld Death with mine own eyes at the hand of this damned wretch, whom thou didst certify to be my uncle; and, had not Almighty Allah rescued me from him, I and thou, O my mother, had been cozened by the excess of this Accursed's promises to work my welfare, and by the great show of affection which he manifested to us. Learn, O my mother, that this fellow is a sorcerer, a Moorman, an accursed, a liar, traitor, a hypocrite;[39] nor deem I that the devils under the earth are damnable as he. Allah abase him in his every book! Hear then, O my mother, what this abominable one did, and all that I shall tell thee will be soothfast and certain. See how the damned villain brake every promise he made, certifying that he would soon work all good with me; and do thou consider the fondness which he displayed to me and the deeds which he did by me; and all this only to win his wish, for his design was to destroy me; and Alhamdolillah—laud to the Lord—for my deliverance. Listen and learn, O my mother, how this Accursed entreated me." Then Alaeddin informed his mother of all that had befallen him (weeping the while for stress of gladness); how the Maghrabi had led him to a hill wherein was hidden the Hoard and how he had conjured and fumigated, adding,[40] "After which, O my mother, mighty fear gat hold of me when the hill split and the earth gaped before me by his wizardry; and I trembled with terror at the rolling of thunder in mine ears and the murk which fell upon us when he fumigated and muttered spells. Seeing these horrors I in mine affright designed to fly; but, when he understood mine intent he reviled me and smote me a buffet so sore that it caused me swoon. However, inasmuch as the Treasury was to be opened only by means of me, O my mother, he could not descend therein himself, it being in my name and not in his; and, for that he is an ill-omened magician, he understood that I was necessary to him and this was his need of me." Alaeddin acquainted his mother with all that had befallen him from the Maghrabi, the Magician, and said, "After he had buffeted me, he judged it advisable to soothe me in order that he might send me down into the Enchanted Treasury; and first he drew from his finger a Ring which he placed upon mine. So I descended and found four halls all full of gold and silver which counted as naught, and the Accursed had charged me not to touch aught thereof. Then I entered a mighty fine flower-garden every where bedecked with tall trees whose foliage and fruitage bewildered the wits, for all, O my mother, were of vari-coloured glass, and lastly I reached the Hall wherein hung this Lamp. So I took it straightway and put it out and poured forth its contents."[41] And so saying, Alaeddin drew the Lamp from his breast-pocket and showed it to his mother, together with the gems and jewels which he had brought from the garden; and there were two large bag-pockets full of precious stones, whereof not one was to be found amongst the kings of the world. But the lad knew naught anent their worth deeming them glass or crystal; and presently he resumed, "After this, O mother mine, I reached the Hoard-door carrying the Lamp and shouted to the accursed Sorcerer, which called himself my uncle, to lend me a hand and hale me up, I being unable to mount of myself the last step for the over-weight of my burthen. But he would not and said only:—First hand me the Lamp! As, however, I had placed it at the bottom of my breast-pocket and the other pouches bulged out beyond it, I was unable to get at it and said:—O my uncle, I cannot reach thee the Lamp, but I will give it to thee when outside the Treasury. His only need was the Lamp and he designed, O my mother, to snatch it from me and after that slay me, as indeed he did his best to do by heaping the earth over my head. Such then is what befel me from this foul Sorcerer." Hereupon Alaeddin fell to abusing the Magician in hot wrath and with a burning heart and crying, "Well-away! I take refuge from this damned wight, the ill-omened, the wrong-doer, the forswearer, the lost to all humanity, the arch-traitor, the hypocrite, the annihilator of ruth and mercy." When Alaeddin's mother heard his words and what had befallen him from the Maghrabi, the Magician, she said, "Yea, verily, O my son, he is a miscreant, a hypocrite who murthereth the folk by his magic; but 'twas the grace of Allah Almighty, O my child, that saved thee from the tricks and the treachery of this accursed Sorcerer whom I deemed to be truly thine uncle."[42] Then, as the lad had not slept a wink for three days and found himself nodding, he sought his natural rest, his mother doing on like wise; nor did he awake till about noon on the second day. As soon as he shook off slumber he called for somewhat of food being sore anhungered, but said his mother, "O my son, I have no victual for thee inasmuch as yesterday thou atest all that was in the house. But wait patiently a while: I have spun a trifle of yarn which I will carry to the market-street and sell it and buy with what it may be worth some victual for thee." "O my mother," said he, "keep your yarn and sell it not; but fetch me the Lamp I brought hither that I may go vend it and with its price purchase provaunt, for that I deem 'twill bring more money than the spinnings." So Alaeddin's mother arose and fetched the Lamp for her son; but, while so doing, she saw that it was dirty exceedingly; so she said, "O my son, here is the Lamp, but 'tis very foul: after we shall have washed it and polished it 'twill sell better." Then, taking a handful of sand she began to rub therewith, but she had only begun when appeared to her one of the Jann whose favour was frightful and whose bulk was horrible big, and he was gigantic as one of the Jababirah.[43] And forthright he cried to her, "Say whatso thou wantest of me? Here am I, thy Slave and Slave to whoso holdeth the Lamp; and not I alone, but all the Slaves of the Wonderful Lamp which thou hendest in hand." She quaked and terror was sore upon her when she looked at that frightful form and her tongue being tied she could not return aught reply, never having been accustomed to espy similar semblances. Now her son was standing afar off and he had already seen the Jinni of the Ring which he had rubbed within the

Treasury; so when he heard the Slave speaking to his parent, he hastened forwards and snatching the Lamp from her hand, said, "O Slave of the Lamp, I am anhungered and 'tis my desire that thou fetch me somewhat to eat and let it be something toothsome beyond our means." The Jinni disappeared for an eye-twinkle and returned with a mighty fine tray and precious of price, for that 'twas all in virginal silver and upon it stood twelve golden platters of meats manifold and dainties delicate, with bread snowier than snow; also two silvern cups and as many black jacks⁴⁴ full of wine clear-strained and long-stored. And after setting all these before Alaeddin, he evanished from vision. Thereupon the lad went and sprinkled rose water upon his mother's face and caused her snuff up perfumes pure and pungent and said to her when she revived, "Rise, O mother mine, and let us eat of these meats wherewith Almighty Allah hath eased our poverty." But when she saw that mighty fine silvern tray she fell to marvelling at the matter and quoth she, "O my son, who be this generous, this beneficent one who hath abated our hunger-pains and our penury? We are indeed under obligation to him and, meseemeth, 'tis the Sultan who, hearing of our mean condition and our misery, hath sent us this food-tray." Quoth he, "O my mother, this be no time for questioning: arouse thee and let us eat for we are both a-famished." Accordingly, they sat down to the tray and fell to feeding when Alaeddin's mother tasted meats whose like in all her time she had never touched; so they devoured them with sharpened appetites and all the capacity engendered by stress of hunger; and, secondly, the food was such that marked the tables of the Kings. But neither of them knew whether the tray was or was not valuable, for never in their born days had they looked upon aught like it. As soon as they had finished the meal (withal leaving victual enough for supper and eke for the next day), they arose and washed their hands and sat at chat, when the mother turned to her son and said, "Tell me, O my child, what befel thee from the Slave, the Jinni, now that Alhamdolillah—laud to the

Lord!—we have eaten our full of the good things wherewith He hath favoured us and thou hast no pretext for saying to me, 'I am anhungered.'" So Alaeddin related to her all that took place between him and the Slave what while she had sunk upon the ground aswoon for sore terror; and at this she, being seized with mighty great surprise, said, "'Tis true; for the Jinns do present themselves before the Sons of Adam[45] but I, O my son, never saw them in all my life and meseemeth that this be the same who saved thee when thou wast within the Enchanted Hoard." "This is not he, O my mother: this who appeared before thee is the Slave of the Lamp!" "Who may this be, O my son?" "This be a Slave of sort and shape other than he; that was the Familiar of the Ring and this his fellow thou sawest was the Slave of the Lamp thou hendest in hand." And when his parent heard these words she cried, "There! there![46] so this Accursed, who showed himself to me and went nigh unto killing me with affright, is attached to the Lamp." "Yes," he replied, and she rejoined, "Now I conjure thee, O my son, by the milk wherewith I suckled thee, to throw away from thee this Lamp and this Ring; because they can cause us only extreme terror and I especially can never abear a second glance at them. Moreover all intercourse with them is unlawful, for that the Prophet (whom Allah save and assain!) warned us against them with threats." He replied, "Thy commands, O my mother, be upon my head[47] and mine eyes; but, as regards this saying thou saidest, 'tis impossible that I part or with Lamp or with Ring. Thou thyself hast seen what good the Slave wrought us whenas we were famishing; and know, O my mother, that the Maghrabi, the liar, the Magician, when sending me down into the Hoard, sought nor the silver nor the gold wherewith the four halls were fulfilled, but charged me to bring him only the Lamp (naught else), because in very deed he had learned its priceless value; and, had he not been certified of it, he had never endured such toil and trouble nor had he travelled from his own land to our land in search thereof; neither had he shut me up in the Treasury when

he despaired of the Lamp which I would not hand to him.
Therefore it befitteth us, O my mother, to keep this Lamp
and take all care thereof nor disclose its mysteries to any;
for this is now our means of livelihood and this it is shall
enrich us. And likewise as regards the Ring, I will never
withdraw it from my finger, inasmuch as but for this thou
hadst nevermore seen me on life; nay I should have died
within the Hoard underground. How then can I possibly
remove it from my finger? And who wotteth that which
may betide me by the lapse of Time, what trippings or
calamities or injurious mishaps wherefrom this Ring may
deliver me? However, for regard to thy feelings I will stow
away the Lamp nor ever suffer it to be seen of thee hereafter." Now when his mother heard his words and pondered them she knew they were true and said to him, "Do,
O my son, whatso thou willest; for my part I wish never to
see them nor ever sight that frightful spectacle I erst saw."
Alaeddin and his mother continued eating of the meats
brought them by the Jinni for two full told days till they
were finished; but when he learned that nothing of food
remained for them, he arose and took a platter of the platters which the Slave had brought upon the tray. Now they
were all of the finest gold but the lad knew naught thereof;
so he bore it to the Bazar and there, seeing a man which
was a peddler, a viler than the Satans,[48] offered it to him for
sale. When the peddler espied it he took the lad aside that
none might see him, and he looked at the platter and considered it till he was certified that it was of gold refined.
But he knew not whether Alaeddin was acquainted with
its value or he was in such matters a raw laddie;[49] so he
asked him, "For how much, O my lord, this platter?" and
the other answered, "Thou wottest what be its worth." The
peddler debated with himself as to how much he should
offer, because Alaeddin had returned him a craftsman-like
reply; and he thought of the smallest valuation; at the same
time he feared lest the lad haply knowing its worth, should
expect a considerable sum. So he said in his mind, "Belike
the fellow is an ignoramus in such matters nor is ware of

the price of the platter." Whereupon he pulled out of his pocket a dinar, and Alaeddin eyed the gold piece lying in his palm and hastily taking it went his way; whereby the peddler was certified of his customer's innocence of all such knowledge, and repented with entire repentance that he had given him a golden dinar in lieu of a copper carat,[50] a bright-polished groat. However, Alaeddin made no delay but went at once to the baker's where he bought him bread and changed the ducat; then, going to his mother, he gave her the scones and the remaining small coin and said, "O my mother, hie thee and buy thee all we require." So she arose and walked to the Bazar and laid in the necessary stock; after which they ate and were cheered. And whenever the price of the platter was expended, Alaeddin would take another and carry it to the accursed peddler who bought each and every at a pitiful price; and even this he would have minished but, seeing how he had paid a dinar for the first, he feared to offer a lesser sum, lest the lad go and sell to some rival in trade and thus he lose his usurious gains. Now when all the golden platters were sold, there remained only the silver tray whereupon they stood; and, for that it was large and weighty, Alaeddin brought the peddler to his house and produced the article, when the buyer, seeing its size gave him ten dinars and these being accepted went his ways. Alaeddin and his mother lived upon the sequins until they were spent; then he brought out the Lamp and rubbed it and straightway appeared the Slave who had shown himself aforetime. And said the lad, "I desire that thou bring me a tray of food like unto that thou broughtest me erewhiles, for indeed I am famisht." Accordingly, in the glance of an eye the Slave produced a similar tray supporting twelve platters of the most sumptuous, furnished with requisite cates; and thereon stood clean bread and sundry glass bottles[51] of strained wine. Now Alaeddin's mother had gone out when she knew he was about to rub the Lamp that she might not again look upon the Jinni; but after a while she returned and, when she sighted the tray covered with silvern platters[52] and smelt the savour of the rich meats diffused over the house, she marvelled and rejoiced. Thereupon quoth he, "Look, O my mother! Thou badest me throw away the Lamp, see now its virtues;" and quoth she, "O my son, Allah increase his[53] weal, but I would not look upon him." Then the lad sat down with his parent to the tray and they ate and drank until they were satisfied; after which they removed what remained for use on the morrow. As soon as the meats had been consumed, Alaeddin arose and stowed away under his clothes a platter of the platters and went forth to find the Jew, purposing to sell it to him; but by fiat of Fate he passed by the shop of an ancient jeweller, an honest man and a pious who feared Allah. When the Shaykh saw the lad, he asked him saying, "O my son, what dost thou want? for that times manifold have I seen thee passing hereby and having dealings with a Jewish man; and I have espied thee handing over to him sundry articles; now also I fancy thou hast somewhat for sale and thou seekest him as a buyer thereof. But thou wottest not, O my child, that the Jews ever hold lawful to them the good of Moslems,[54] the Confessors of Allah Almighty's unity, and always defraud them; especially this accursed Jew with whom thou hast relations and into whose hands thou hast fallen. If then, O my son, thou have aught thou wouldest sell show the same to me and never fear, for I will give thee its full price by the truth of Almighty Allah." Thereupon Alaeddin brought out the platter which when the ancient goldsmith saw, he took and weighed it in his scales and asked the lad saying, "Was it the fellow of this thou soldest to the Jew?" "Yes, its fellow and its brother," he answered, and quoth the old man, "What price did he pay thee?" Quoth the lad, "One dinar." The ancient goldsmith, hearing from Alaeddin how the Jew used to give only one dinar as the price of the platter, cried, "Ah! I take refuge from this Accursed who cozeneth the servants of Allah Almighty!" Then, looking at the lad, he exclaimed, "O my son, verily yon tricksy Jew hath cheated thee and laughed at thee, this platter being pure silver and virginal. I have weighed it and found it worth seventy dinars; and, if thou please to take its value, take it." Thereupon the Shaykh counted out to him seventy gold pieces, which he accepted and presently thanked him for his kindness in exposing the Jew's rascality. And after this, whenever the price of a platter was expended, he would bring another, and on such wise he and his mother were soon in better circumstances; yet they ceased not to live after their olden fashion as middle class folk[55] without spending on diet overmuch or squandering money. But Alaeddin had now thrown off the ungraciousness of his boyhood; he shunned the society of scapegraces and he began to frequent good men and true, repairing daily to the market-street of the merchants and there companying with the great and small of them, asking about matters of merchandise and learning the price of investments and so forth; he likewise frequented the Bazars of the Goldsmiths and the Jewellers[56] where he would sit and divert himself by inspecting their precious stones and by noting how jewels were sold and bought therein. Accordingly, he presently became ware that the tree-fruits, wherewith he had filled his pockets what time he entered the Enchanted Treasury, were neither glass nor crystal but gems rich and rare; and he understood that he had acquired immense wealth such as the Kings never can possess. He then considered all the precious stones which were in the Jewellers' Quarter, but found that their biggest was not worth his smallest. On this wise he ceased not every day repairing to the Bazar and making himself familiar with the folk and winning their loving will;[57] and enquiring anent selling and buying, giving and taking, the dear and the cheap, until one day of the days when, after rising at dawn and donning his dress he went forth, as was his wont, to the Jewellers' Bazar; and, as he passed along it he heard the crier crying as follows: "By command of our magnificent master, the King of the Time and the Lord of the Age and the Tide, let all the folk lock up their shops and stores and retire within their houses, for that the Lady Badr al-Budur,[58] daughter of the Sultan, designeth to visit

the Hammam; and whoso gainsayeth the order shall be
punished with death-penalty and be his blood upon his
own neck!" But when Alaeddin heard the proclamation, he
longed to look upon the King's daughter and said in his
mind, "Indeed all the lieges talk of her beauty and loveliness and the end of my desires is to see her." Then Alaeddin fell to contriving some means whereby he might look
upon the Princess Badr al-Budur and at last judged best to
take his station behind the Hammam-door whence he
might see her face as she entered.[59] Accordingly, without
stay or delay he repaired to the Baths before she was expected and stood a-rear of the entrance, a place whereat
none of the folk happened to be looking. Now when the
Sultan's daughter had gone the rounds of the city and its
main streets and had solaced herself by sight-seeing, she finally reached the Hammam and whilst entering she raised
her veil, and Alaeddin saw her favour he said, "In very
truth her fashion magnifieth her Almighty Fashioner and
glory be to Him who created her and adorned her with this
beauty and loveliness." His strength was struck down from
the moment he saw her and his thoughts were distraught;
his gaze was dazed, the love of her gat hold of the whole of
his heart; and, when he returned home to his mother, he
was as one in ecstasy. His parent addressed him, but he neither replied nor denied; and, when she set before him the
morning meal he continued in like case; so quoth she, "O
my son, what is't may have befallen thee? Say me, doth
aught ail thee? Let me know what ill hath betided thee for,
unlike thy custom, thou speakest not when I bespeak thee."
Thereupon Alaeddin (who used to think that all women
resembled his mother[60] and who, albeit he had heard of
the charms of Badr al-Budur, daughter of the Sultan, yet
knew not what "beauty" and "loveliness" might signify)
turned to his parent and exclaimed, "Let me be!" However,
she persisted in praying him to come forwards and eat, so
he did her bidding but hardly touched food; after which he
lay at full length on his bed all the night through in cogita-
tion deep until morning morrowed. The same was his con-

dition during the next day, when his mother was perplexed
for the case of her son and unable to learn what had happened to him. So, thinking that belike he might be ailing,
she drew near him and asked him saying, "O my son, an
thou sense aught of pain or such like, let me know that I
may fare forth and fetch thee the physician; and to-day
there be in this our city a leech from the Land of the Arabs
whom the Sultan hath sent to summon and the bruit
abroad reporteth him to be skilful exceedingly. So, an be
thou ill let me go and bring him to thee." Alaeddin, hearing his parent's offer to summon the mediciner, said, "O
my mother, I am well in body and on no wise ill. But I ever
thought that all women resembled thee until yesterday,
when I beheld the Lady Badr al-Budur, daughter of the
Sultan, as she was faring for the Baths." Then he related to
her all and everything that had happened to him adding,
"Haply thou also hast heard the crier a-crying:—Let no
man open shop or stand in street that the Lady Badr al-
Budur may repair to the Hammam without eye seeing her.
But I have looked upon her even as she is, for she raised her
veil at the door; and, when I viewed her favour and beheld
that noble work of the Creator, a sore fit of ecstasy, O my
mother, fell upon me for love of her and firm resolve to
win her hath opened its way into every limb of me, nor is
repose possible for me except I win her. Wherefor I purpose asking her to wife from the Sultan her sire in lawful
wedlock." When Alaeddin's mother heard her son's words,
she belittled his wits and cried, "O my child, the name of
Allah upon thee! meseemeth thou hast lost thy senses. But
be thou rightly guided, O my son, nor be thou as the men
Jinn-maddened!" He replied, "Nay, O mother of mine, I
am not out of my mind nor am I of the maniacs; nor shall
this thy saying alter one jot of what is in my thoughts, for
rest is impossible to me until I shall have won the dearling
of my heart's core, the beautiful Lady Badr al-Budur. And
now I am resolved to ask her of her sire the Sultan." She
rejoined, "O my son, by my life upon thee speak not such
speech, lest any overhear thee and say thou be insane: so

cast away from thee such nonsense! Who shall undertake a matter like this or make such request to the King? Indeed, I know not how, supposing thy speech to be soothfast, thou shalt manage to crave such grace of the Sultan or through whom thou desirest to propose it." He retorted, "Through whom shall I ask it, O my mother, when thou art present? And who is there fonder and more faithful to me than thyself? So my design is that thou thyself shalt proffer this my petition." Quoth she, "O my son, Allah remove me far therefrom! What! have I lost my wits like thyself? Cast the thought away and a long way from thy heart. Remember whose son thou art, O my child, the orphan boy of a tailor, the poorest and meanest of the tailors toiling in this city; and I, thy mother, am also come of pauper folk and indigent. How then durst thou ask to wife the daughter of the Sultan, whose sire would not deign marry her with the sons of the Kings and the Sovrans, except they were his peers in honour and grandeur and majesty; and, were they but one degree lower, he would refuse his daughter to them." Alaeddin took patience until his parent had said her say, when quoth he, "O my mother, everything thou hast called to mind is known to me; moreover 'tis thoroughly well known to me that I am the child of pauper parents; withal do not these words of thee divert me from my design at all, at all. Nor the less do I hope of thee, an I be thy son and thou truly love me, that thou grant me this favour, otherwise thou wilt destroy me; and present Death hovereth over my head except I win my will of heart's dearling; and I, O my mother, am in every case thy child." Hearing these words, his parent wept of her sorrow for him and said, "O my child! Yes, in very deed I am thy mother, nor have I any son or life's blood of my liver except thyself, and the end of my wishes is to give thee a wife and rejoice in thee. But suppose that I would seek a bride of our likes and equals, her people will at once ask an thou have any land or garden, merchandise or handicraft, wherewith thou canst support her; and what is the reply I can return? Then, if I cannot possibly answer the poor like ourselves, how shall I be bold enough, O my son, to ask for the daughter of the Sultan of China-land who hath no peer or behind or before him? Therefore do thou weigh this matter in thy mind. Also who shall ask her to wife for the son of a snip? Well indeed I wot that my saying aught of this kind will but increase our misfortunes; for that it may be the cause of our incurring mortal danger from the Sultan; peradventure even death for thee and me. And, as concerneth myself, how shall I venture upon such rash deed and perilous, O my son? and in what way shall I ask the Sultan for his daughter to be thy wife; and, indeed, how ever shall I even get access to him? And should I succeed therein, what is to be my answer an they ask me touching thy means? Haply the King will hold me to be a madwoman. And, lastly, suppose that I obtain audience of the Sultan, what offering is there I can submit to the King's majesty?[61] 'Tis true, O my child, that the Sultan is mild and merciful, never rejecting any who approach him to require justice or ruth or protection, nor any who pray him for a present; for he is liberal and lavisheth favour upon near and far. But he dealeth his boons to those deserving them, to men who have done some derring-do in battle under his eyes or have rendered as civilians great service to his estate. But thou! do thou tell me what feat thou hast performed in his presence or before the public that thou meritest from him such grace? And, secondly, this boon thou ambitionest is not for one of our condition, nor is it possible that the King grant to thee the bourne of thine aspiration; for whoso goeth to the Sultan and craveth of him a favour, him it besitteth to take in hand somewhat that suiteth the royal majesty, as indeed I warned thee aforetime. How, then, shalt thou risk thyself to stand before the Sultan and ask his daughter in marriage, when thou hast with thee naught to offer him of that which beseemeth his exalted station?" Hereto Alaeddin replied, "O my mother, thou speakest to the point and hast reminded me aright and 'tis meet that I revolve in mind the whole of thy remindings. But, O my mother, the love of Princess Badr al-

Budur hath entered into the core of my heart; nor can I rest without I win her. However, thou hast also recalled to me a matter which I forgot and 'tis this emboldeneth me to ask his daughter of the King. Albeit thou, O my mother, declarest that I have no gift which I can submit to the Sultan, as is the wont of the world, yet in very sooth I have an offering and a present whose equal, O my mother, I hold none of the Kings to possess; no, nor even aught like it. Because verily that which I deemed glass or crystal was nothing but precious stones and I hold that all the Kings of the World have never possessed any thing like one of the smallest thereof. For, by frequenting the jeweller-folk, I have learned that they are the costliest gems and these are what I brought in my pockets from the Hoard, whereupon, an thou please, compose thy mind. We have in our house a bowl of China porcelain; so arise thou and fetch it, that I may fill it with these jewels, which thou shalt carry as a gift to the King, and thou shalt stand in his presence and solicit him for my requirement. I am certified that by such means the matter will become easy to thee; and, if thou be unwilling, O my mother, to strive for the winning of my wish as regards the Lady Badr al-Budur, know thou that surely I shall die. Nor do thou imagine that this gift is of aught save the costliest of stones and be assured, O my mother, that in my many visits to the Jewellers' Bazar I have observed the merchants selling for sums man's judgment may not determine jewels whose beauty is not worth one quarter carat of what we possess; seeing which I was certified that ours are beyond all price. So arise, O my mother, as I bade thee and bring me the porcelain bowl aforesaid, that I may arrange therein some of these gems and we will see what semblance they show." So she brought him the China bowl saying in herself, "I shall know what to do when I find out if the words of my child concerning these jewels be soothfast or not;" and she set it before her son who pulled the stones out of his pockets and disposed them in the bowl and ceased not arranging therein gems of sorts till such time as he had filled it. And when it was brimful she could not fix her eyes firmly upon it; on the contrary, she winked and blinked for the dazzle of the stones and their radiance and excess of lightning-like glance; and her wits were bewildered thereat; only she was not certified of their value being really of the enormous extent she had been told. Withal she reflected that possibly her son might have spoken aright when he declared that their like was not to be found with the Kings. Then Alaeddin turned to her and said, "Thou hast seen, O my mother, that this present intended for the Sultan is magnificent, and I am certified that it will procure for thee high honour with him and that he will receive thee with all respect. And now, O my mother, thou hast no excuse; so compose thy thoughts and arise; take thou this bowl and away with it to the palace." His mother rejoined, "O my son, 'tis true that the present is high-priced exceedingly and the costliest of the costly; also that according to thy word none owneth its like. But who would have the boldness to go and ask the Sultan for his daughter, the Lady Badr al-Budur? I indeed dare not say to him:—I want thy daughter! when he shall ask me:—What is thy want? for know thou, O my son, that my tongue will be tied. And, granting that Allah assist me and I embolden myself to say to him:—My wish is to become a connection of thine through the marriage of thy daughter the Lady Badr al-Budur, to my son Alaeddin, they will surely decide at once that I am demented and will thrust me forth in disgrace and despised. I will not tell thee that I shall thereby fall into danger of death, for 'twill not be I only but thou likewise. However, O my son, of my regard for thine inclination, I needs must embolden myself and hie thither; yet, O my child, if the King receive me and honour me on account of the gift and enquire of me what thou desirest, and in reply I ask of him that which thou desirest in the matter of thy marriage with his daughter, how shall I answer him and he ask me, as is man's wont, What estates hast thou, and what income? And perchance, O my son, he will question me of this before questioning me of thee." Alaeddin replied, "'Tis not possible that the Sultan should make such demand what time he considereth the jewels and their magnificence; nor is it meet to think of such things as these which may never occur. Now do thou but arise and set before him this present of precious stones and ask of him his daughter for me, and sit not yonder making much of the difficulty in thy fancy. Ere this thou hast learned, O mother mine, that the Lamp which we possess hath become to us a stable income and that whatso I want of it the same is supplied to me; and my hope is that by means thereof I shall learn how to answer the Sultan should he ask me of that thou sayest."[62] Then Alaeddin and his mother fell to talking over the subject all that night long and when morning morrowed, the dame arose and heartened her heart, especially as her son had expounded to her some little of the powers of the Lamp and the virtues thereof; to wit, that it would supply all they required of it. Alaeddin, however, seeing his parent take courage when he explained to her the workings of the Lamp, feared lest she might tattle to the folk thereof;[63] so he said to her, "O my mother, beware how thou talk to any of the properties of the Lamp and its profit, as this is our one great good. Guard thy thoughts lest thou speak over much concerning it before others, whoso they be; haply we shall lose it and lose the boon fortune we possess and the benefits we expect, for that 'tis of him."[64] His mother replied, "Fear not therefor, O my son," and she arose and took the bowl full of jewels, which she wrapped up in a fine kerchief, and went forth betimes that she might reach the Divan ere it became crowded. When she passed into the Palace, the levée not being fully attended, she saw the Wazirs and sundry of the Lords of the land going into the presence-room and after a short time, when the Divan was made complete by the Ministers and high Officials and Chieftains and Emirs and Grandees, the Sultan appeared and the Wazirs made their obeisance and likewise did the Nobles and the Notables. The King seated himself upon the throne of his kingship, and all present at the levée stood before him with crossed arms awaiting his commandment to sit; and, when they received it, each took his place according to his degree; then the claimants came before the Sultan who delivered sentence, after his wonted way, until the Divan was ended, when the King arose and withdrew into the palace[65] and the others all went their ways. And when Alaeddin's mother saw the throne empty and the King passing into his Harem, she also wended her ways and returned home. But as soon as her son espied her, bowl in hand, he thought that haply something untoward had befallen her, but he would not ask of aught until such time as she had set down the bowl, when she acquainted him with that had occurred and ended by adding, "Alhamdolillah,—laud to the Lord!—O my child, that I found courage enough and secured for myself standing-place in the levée this day; and, albe I dreaded to bespeak the King yet (Inshallah!) on the morrow I will address him. Even to-day were many who, like myself, could not get audience of the Sultan. But be of good cheer, O my son, and to-morrow needs must I bespeak him for thy sake; and what happened not may happen." When Alaeddin heard his parent's words, he joyed with excessive joy; and, although he expected the matter to be managed hour by hour, for excess of his love and longing to the Lady Badr al-Budur yet he possessed his soul in patience. They slept well that night and betimes next morning the mother of Alaeddin arose and went with her bowl to the King's court which she found closed. So she asked the people and they told her that the Sultan did not hold a levée every day but only thrice in the se'nnight; wherefor she determined to return home; and, after this, whenever she saw the court open she would stand before the King until the reception ended and when it was shut she would go to make sure thereof; and this was the case for the whole month. The Sultan was wont to remark her presence at every levée, but, on the last day when she took her station, as was her wont, before the Council, she allowed it to close and lacked boldness to come forwards and speak even a syllable. Now as the King having risen was making for his

Harem accompanied by the Grand Wazir, he turned to him and said, "O Wazir, during the last six or seven levée days I see yonder old woman present herself at every reception and I also note that she always carrieth a something under her mantilla. Say me, hast thou, O Wazir, any knowledge of her and her intention?" "O my lord the Sultan," said the other, "verily women be weakly of wits, and haply this goodwife cometh hither to complain before thee[66] against her goodman or some of her people." But this reply was far from satisfying the Sultan; nay, he bade the Wazir, in case she should come again, set her before him; and forthright the Minister placed hand on head and exclaimed, "To hear is to obey, O our lord the Sultan!" Now one day of the days, when she did according to her custom, the Sultan cast his eyes upon her as she stood before him, and said to his Grand Wazir, "This be the very woman whereof I spake to thee yesterday, so do thou straightway bring her before me, that I may see what be her suit and fulfil her need." Accordingly, the Minister at once introduced her and when in the presence she saluted the King by kissing her finger tips and raising them to her brow;[67] and, praying for the Sultan's glory and continuance and the permanence of his prosperity, bussed ground before him. Thereupon, quoth he, "O woman,[68] for sundry days I have seen thee attend the levée sans a word said; so tell me an thou have any requirement I may grant." She kissed ground a second time and after blessing him, answered, "Yea, verily, as thy head liveth, O King of the Age, I have a want; but first of all, do thou deign grant me a promise of safety that I may prefer my suit to the ears of our lord the Sultan; for haply thy Highness[69] may find it a singular." The King, wishing to know her need, and being a man of unusual mildness and clemency, gave his word for her immunity and bade forthwith dismiss all about him, remaining without other but the Grand Wazir. Then he turned towards his suppliant and said, "Inform me of thy suit: thou hast the safeguard of Allah Almighty." "O King of the Age," replied she, "I also require of thee pardon;"

and quoth he, "Allah pardon thee even as I do." Then, quoth she, "O our lord the Sultan, I have a son, Alaeddin hight; and he, one day of the days, having heard the crier commanding all men to shut shop and shun the streets, for that the Lady Badr al-Budur, daughter of the Sultan, was going to the Hammam, felt an uncontrollable longing to look upon her, and hid himself in a stead whence he could sight her right well, and that place was behind the door of the Baths. When she entered he beheld her and considered her as he wished, and but too well; for, since the time he looked upon her, O King of the Age, unto this hour, life hath not been pleasant to him. And he hath required of me that I ask her to wife for him from thy Highness, nor could I drive this fancy from his mind because love of her hath mastered his vitals and to such degree that he said to me: Know thou, O mother mine, that an I win not my wish surely I shall die. Accordingly I hope that thy Highness will deign be mild and merciful and pardon this boldness on the part of me and my child and refrain to punish us therefor." When the Sultan heard her tale he regarded her with kindness and, laughing aloud, asked her, "What may be that thou carriest and what be in yonder kerchief?" And she seeing the Sultan laugh in lieu of waxing wroth at her words, forthright opened the wrapper and set before him the bowl of jewels, whereby the audience-hall was illumined as it were by lustres and candelabra;[70] and he was dazed and amazed at the radiance of the rare gems, and he fell to marvelling at their size and beauty and excellence and cried, "Never at all until this day saw I anything like these jewels for size and beauty and excellence: nor deem I that there be found in my treasury a single one like them." Then he turned to his Minister and asked, "What sayest thou, O Wazir? Tell me, hast thou seen in thy time such mighty fine jewels as these?" The other answered, "Never saw I such, O our lord the Sultan, nor do I think that there be in the treasures of my lord the Sultan the fellow of the least thereof." The King resumed, "Now indeed whoso hath presented to me such jewels meriteth to become bridegroom to my daughter, Badr al-Budur; because, as far as I see, none is more deserving of her than he." When the Wazir heard the Sultan's words he was tongue-tied with concern and he grieved with sore grief, for the King had promised to give the Princess in marriage to his son; so after a little while he said, "O King of the Age, thy Highness deigned promise me that the Lady Badr al-Budur should be spouse to my son; so 'tis but right that thine exalted Highness vouchsafe us a delay of three months, during which time, Inshallah! my child may obtain and present an offering yet costlier than this." Accordingly the King, albeit he knew that such a thing could not be done, or by the Wazir or by the greatest of his Grandees, yet of his grace and kindness granted him the required delay. Then he turned to the old woman, Alaeddin's mother, and said, "Go to thy son and tell him I have pledged my word that my daughter shall be in his name;[71] only 'tis needful that I make the requisite preparations of nuptial furniture for her use; and 'tis only meet that he take patience for the next three months." Receiving this reply, Alaeddin's mother thanked the Sultan and blessed him; then, going forth in hottest haste, as one flying for joy, she went home; and when her son saw her entering with a smiling face, he was gladdened at the sign of good news, especially because she had returned without delay as on the past days, and had not brought back the bowl. Presently he asked her saying, "Inshallah, thou bearest me, O my mother, glad tidings; and peradventure the jewels and their value have wrought their work and belike thou hast been kindly received by the King and he hath shown thee grace and hath given ear to thy request?" So she told him the whole tale, how the Sultan had entreated her well and had marvelled at the extraordinary size of the gems and their surpassing water as did also the Wazir, adding, "And he promised that his daughter should be thine. Only, O my child, the Wazir spake of a secret contract made with him by the Sultan before he pledged himself to me and, after speaking privily, the King put me off to the end of three months: therefore I have become fearful lest the Wazir be evilly disposed to thee and perchance he may attempt to change the Sultan's mind." When Alaeddin heard his mother's words and how the Sultan had promised him his daughter, deferring, however, the wedding until after the third month, his mind was gladdened and he rejoiced exceedingly and said, "Inasmuch as the King hath given his word after three months (well, it *is* a long time!), at all events my gladness is mighty great." Then he thanked his parent, showing her how her good work had exceeded her toil and travail; and said to her, "By Allah, O my mother, hitherto I was as 'twere in my grave and therefrom thou hast withdrawn me; and I praise Allah Almighty because I am at this moment certified that no man in the world is happier than I or more fortunate." Then he took patience until two of the three months had gone by. Now one day of the days his mother fared forth about sundown to the Bazar that she might buy somewhat of oil; and she found all the market shops fast shut and the whole city decorated, and the folk placing waxen tapers and flowers at their casements; and she beheld the soldiers and household troops and Aghas[72] riding in procession and flambeaux and lustres flaming and flaring, and she wondered at the marvellous sight and the glamour of the scene. So she went in to an oilman's store which stood open still and bought her need of him and said, "By thy life, O uncle, tell me what be the tidings in town this day, that people have made all these decorations and every house and market-street are adorned and the troops all stand on guard?" The oilman asked her, "O woman, I suppose thou art a stranger and not one of this city?" and she answered, "Nay, I am thy townswoman." He rejoined, "Thou a townswoman, and yet wottest not that this very night the son of the Grand Wazir goeth in to the Lady Badr al-Budur, daughter of the Sultan! He is now in the Hammam and all this power of soldiery is on guard and standing under arms to await his coming forth, when they will bear him in bridal procession to the palace where the Princess expecteth him." As the mother of Alaeddin

summation of her nuptials with the Wazir's son. On the other hand the Lady Badr al-Budur passed a night the evillest of all nights; nor in her born days had she seen a worse; and the same was the case with the Minister's son who lay in the chapel of ease and who dared not stir for the fear of the Jinni which overwhelmed him. As soon as it was morning the Slave appeared before Alaeddin, without the Lamp being rubbed, and said to him, "O my lord, an thou require aught, command me therefor, that I may do it upon my head and mine eyes." Said the other, "Go, take up and carry the bride and bridegroom to their own apartment;" so the Servitor did his bidding in an eye-glance and bore away the pair, and placed them in the palace as whilome they were and without their seeing any one; but both died of affright when they found themselves being transported from stead to stead.[78] And the Marid had barely time to set them down and wend his ways ere the Sultan came on a visit of congratulation to his daughter; and, when the Wazir's son heard the doors thrown open, he sprang straightway from his couch and donned his dress[79] for he knew that none save the King could enter at that hour. Yet it was exceedingly hard for him to leave his bed wherein he wished to warm himself a trifle after his cold night in the water-closet which he had lately left. The Sultan went in to his daughter Badr al-Budur and kissing her between the eyes gave her good morning and asked her of her bride-groom and whether she was pleased and satisfied with him. But she returned no reply whatever and looked at him with the eye of anger and, although he repeated his words again and again, she held her peace nor bespake him with a single syllable. So the King quitted her and, going to the Queen, informed her of what had taken place between him and his daughter; and the mother, unwilling to leave the Sultan angered with their child, said to him, "O King of the Age, this be the custom of most newly-married couples at least during their first days of marriage, for that they are bashful and somewhat coy. So deign thou excuse her and after a little while she will again become herself and

speak with the folk as before, whereas now her shame, O
King of the Age, keepeth her silent. However 'tis my wish
to fare forth and see her." Thereupon the Queen arose and
donned her dress; then, going to her daughter, wished her
good morning and kissed her between the eyes. Yet would
the Princess make no answer at all, whereat quoth the
Queen to herself, "Doubtless some strange matter hath occurred to trouble her with such trouble as this." So she
asked her saying, "O my daughter, what hath caused this
thy case? Let me know what hath betided thee that, when I
come and give thee good morning, thou hast not a word to
say to me?" Thereat the Lady Badr al-Budur raised her
head and said, "Pardon me, O my mother, 'twas my duty to
meet thee with all respect and worship, seeing that thou
hast honoured me by this visit. However, I pray thee to
hear the cause of this my condition and see how the night
I have just spent hath been to me the evillest of the nights.
Hardly had we lain down, O my mother, than one whose
form I wot not uplifted our bed and transported it to a
darksome place, fulsome and mean." Then the Princess related to the Queen-mother all that had befallen her that
night; how they had taken away her bridegroom, leaving
her lone and lonesome, and how after a while came another youth who lay beside her, in lieu of her bridegroom,
after placing his scymitar between her and himself; "and in
the morning" (she continued) "he who carried us off returned and bore us straight back to our own stead. But at
once when he arrived hither he left us and suddenly my
sire the Sultan entered at the hour and moment of our
coming and I had nor heart nor tongue to speak him
withal, for the stress of the terror and trembling which
came upon me. Haply such lack of duty may have proved
sore to him, so I hope, O my mother, that thou wilt acquaint him with the cause of this my condition and that he
will pardon me for not answering him and blame me not,
but rather accept my excuses." When the Queen heard
these words of Princess Badr al-Budur, she said to her, "O
my child, compose thy thoughts. An thou tell such tale be-

fore any, haply shall he say:—Verily, the Sultan's daughter hath lost her wits. And thou hast done right well in not choosing to recount thine adventure to thy father; and beware and again I say beware, O my daughter, lest thou inform him thereof." The Princess replied, "O my mother, I have spoken to thee like one sound in senses nor have I lost my wits: this be what befel me and, if thou believe it not because coming from me, ask my bridegroom." To which the Queen replied, "Rise up straightway, O my daughter, and banish from thy thoughts such fancies as these; and robe thyself and come forth to glance at the bridal feasts and festivities they are making in the city for the sake of thee and thy nuptials; and listen to the drumming and the singing and look at the decorations all intended to honour thy marriage, O my daughter." So saying, the Queen at once summoned the tirewomen who dressed and prepared the Lady Badr al-Budur; and presently she went in to the Sultan and assured him that their daughter had suffered during all her wedding-night from swevens and nightmare and said to him, "Be not severe with her for not answering thee." Then the Queen sent privily for the Wazir's son and asked of the matter, saying, "Tell me, are these words of the Lady Badr al-Budur soothfast or not?" But he, in his fear of losing his bride out of hand, answered, "O my lady, I have no knowledge of that whereof thou speakest." Accordingly the mother made sure that her daughter had seen visions and dreams. The marriage-feasts lasted throughout that day with Almahs[80] and singers and the smiting of all manner instruments of mirth and merriment, while the Queen and the Wazir and his son strave right strenuously to enhance the festivities that the Princess might enjoy herself; and that day they left nothing of what exciteth to pleasure unrepresented in her presence, to the end that she might forget what was in her thoughts and derive increase of joyance. Yet did naught of this take any effect upon her; nay, she sat in silence, sad of thought, sore perplexed at what had befallen her during the last night. It is true that the Wazir's son had suffered even more because he had passed his sleeping hours lying in the water-closet: he, however, had falsed the story and had cast out remembrance of the night; in the first place for his fear of losing his bride and with her the honour of a connection which brought him such excess of consideration and for which men envied him so much; and, secondly, on account of the wondrous loveliness of the Lady Badr al-Budur and her marvellous beauty. Alaeddin also went forth that day and looked at the merry-makings which extended throughout the city as well as the palace and he fell a-laughing, especially when he heard the folk prating of the high honour which had accrued to the son of the Wazir and the prosperity of his fortunes in having become son-in-law to the Sultan and the high consideration shown by the wedding fêtes. And he said in his mind, "Indeed ye wot not, O ye miserables, what befel him last night that ye envy him!" But after darkness fell and it was time for sleep, Alaeddin arose and, retiring to his chamber, rubbed the Lamp, whereupon the Slave incontinently appeared and was bidden to bring him the Sultan's daughter together with her bridegroom as on the past night ere the Wazir's son could abate her maidenhead. So the Marid without stay or delay evanished for a little while until the appointed time, when he returned carrying the bed whereon lay the Lady Badr al-Budur and the Wazir's son; and he did with the bridegroom as he had done before, to wit, he took him and lay him at full length in the jakes and there left him dried up for excess of fear and trembling. Then Alaeddin arose, and placing the scymitar between himself and the Princess, lay down beside her; and when day broke the Slave restored the pair to their own place, leaving Alaeddin filled with delight at the state of the Minister's son. Now when the Sultan woke up amorn he resolved to visit his daughter and see if she would treat him as on the past day; so shaking off his sleep he sprang up and arrayed himself in his raiment and, going to the apartment of the Princess bade open the door. Thereat the son of the Wazir arose forthright and came down from his bed and began donning his dress whilst his ribs were wrung with cold; for when the King entered the Slave had but just brought him back. The Sultan, raising the arras,[81] drew near his daughter as she lay abed and gave her good morning; then kissing her between the eyes, he asked her of her case. But he saw her looking sour and sad and she answered him not at all, only glowering at him as one in anger and her plight was pitiable. Hereat the Sultan waxed wroth with her for that she would not reply and he suspected that something evil had befallen her,[82] whereupon he bared his blade and cried to her, brand in hand, saying, "What be this hath betided thee? Either acquaint me with what happened or this very moment I will take thy life! Is such conduct the token of honour and respect I expect of thee, that I address thee and thou answerest me not a word?" When the Lady Badr al-Budur saw her sire in high dudgeon and the naked glaive in his grip, she was freed from her fear of the past, so she raised her head and said to him, "O my beloved father, be not wroth with me nor be hasty in thy hot passion, for I am excusable in what thou shalt see of my case. So do thou lend an ear to what occurred to me and well I wot that after hearing my account of what befel to me during these two last nights, thou wilt pardon me and thy Highness will be softened to pitying me even as I claim of thee affection for thy child." Then the Princess informed her father of all that had betided her adding, "O my sire, an thou believe me not, ask my bridegroom and he will recount to thy Highness the whole adventure; nor did I know either what they would do with him when they bore him away from my side or where they would place him." When the Sultan heard his daughter's words, he was saddened and his eyes brimmed with tears; then he sheathed his sabre and kissed her saying, "O my daughter, wherefore[83] didst thou not tell me what happened on the past night that I might have guarded thee from this torture and terror which visited thee a second time? But now 'tis no matter. Rise and cast out all such care and to-night I will set a watch to ward thee nor shall any mishap again make thee miserable."

Then the Sultan returned to his palace and straightway bade summon the Grand Wazir and asked him, as he stood before him in his service, "O Wazir, how dost thou look upon this matter? Haply thy son hath informed thee of what occurred to him and to my daughter." The Minister replied, "O King of the Age, I have not seen my son or yesterday or to-day." Hereat the Sultan told him all that had afflicted the Princess, adding, "'Tis my desire that thou at once seek tidings of thy son concerning the facts of the case: peradventure of her fear my daughter may not be fully aware of what really befel her; withal I hold all her words to be truthful." So the Grand Wazir arose and, going forth, bade summon his son and asked him anent all his lord had told him whether it be true or untrue. The youth replied, "O my father the Wazir, Heaven forbid that the Lady Badr al-Budur speak falsely: indeed all she said was sooth and these two nights proved to us the evillest of our nights instead of being nights of pleasure and marriage-joys. But what befel me was the greater evil because, instead of sleeping abed with my bride, I lay in the wardrobe, a black hole, frightful, noisome of stench, truly damnable; and my ribs were bursten with cold." In fine, the young man told his father the whole tale, adding as he ended it, "O dear father mine, I implore thee to speak with the Sultan that he may set me free from this marriage. Yes, indeed 'tis a high honour for me to be the Sultan's son-in-law and especially the love of the Princess hath gotten hold of my vitals; but I have no strength left to endure a single night like unto these two last." The Wazir, hearing the words of his son, was saddened and sorrowful exceedingly, for it was his design to advance and promote his child by making him son-in-law to the Sultan. So he became thoughtful and perplexed about the affair and the device whereby to manage it, and it was sore grievous for him to break off the marriage, it having been a rare enjoyment to him that he had fallen upon such high good fortune. Accordingly he said, "Take patience, O my son, until we see what may happen this night, when we will set watchmen to ward you;

nor do thou give up the exalted distinction which hath fallen to none save to thyself." Then the Wazir left him and, returning to the sovran, reported that all told to him by the Lady Badr al-Budur was a true tale; whereupon quoth the Sultan, "Since the affair is on this wise, we require no delay," and he at once ordered all the rejoicings to cease and the marriage to be broken off. This caused the folk and the citizens to marvel at the matter, especially when they saw the Grand Wazir and his son leaving the palace in pitiable plight for grief and stress of passion; and the people fell to asking, "What hath happened and what is the cause of the wedding being made null and void?" Nor did any know aught of the truth save Alaeddin the lover who claimed the Princess's hand, and he laughed in his sleeve. But even after the marriage was dissolved, the Sultan forgot nor even recalled to mind his promise made to Alaeddin's mother; and the same was the case with the Grand Wazir, while neither had any inkling of whence befel them that which had befallen. So Alaeddin patiently awaited the lapse of the three months after which the Sultan had pledged himself to give him to wife his daughter; but, soon as ever the term came, he sent his mother to the Sultan for the purpose of requiring him to keep his covenant. So she went to the palace and when the King appeared in the Divan and saw the old woman standing before him, he remembered his promise to her concerning the marriage after a term of three months, and he turned to the Minister and said "O Wazir, this be the ancient dame who presented me with the jewels and to whom we pledged our word that when the three months had elapsed we would summon her to our presence before all others." So the Minister went forth and fetched her[84] and when she went in to the Sultan's presence she saluted him and prayed for his glory and permanence of prosperity. Hereat the King asked her if she needed aught, and she answered, "O King of the Age, the three months' term thou assignedst to me is finished, and this is thy time to marry my son Alaeddin with thy daughter, the Lady Badr al-

Budur." The Sultan was distraught at this demand, especially when he saw the old woman's pauper condition, one of the meanest of her kind; and yet the offering she had brought to him was of the most magnificent, far beyond his power to pay the price. Accordingly, he turned to the Grand Wazir and said, "What device is there with thee? In very sooth I did pass my word, yet meseemeth that they be pauper folk and not persons of high condition." The Grand Wazir, who was dying of envy and who was especially saddened by what had befallen his son, said to himself, "How shall one like this wed the King's daughter and my son lose this highmost honour?" Accordingly, he answered his Sovran speaking privily, "O my lord, 'tis an easy matter[85] to keep off a poor devil such as this, for he is not worthy that thy Highness give his daughter to a fellow whom none knoweth what he may be?" "By what means," enquired the Sultan, "shall we put off the man when I pledged my promise; and the word of the Kings is their bond?" Replied the Wazir, "O my lord, my rede is that thou demand of him forty platters made of pure sand-gold[86] and full of gems (such as the woman brought thee aforetime), with forty white slave-girls to carry the platters and forty black eunuch-slaves." The King rejoined, "By Allah, O Wazir, thou hast spoken to the purpose, seeing that such thing is not possible and by this way we shall be freed." Then quoth he to Alaeddin's mother, "Do thou go and tell thy son that I am a man of my word even as I plighted it to him, but on condition that he have power to pay the dower of my daughter; and that which I require of him is a settlement consisting of two score platters of virgin gold, all brimming with gems the like of those thou broughtest to me, and as many white handmaids to carry them and two score black eunuch-slaves to serve and escort the bearers. An thy son avail hereto I will marry him with my daughter." Thereupon she returned home wagging her head and saying in her mind, "Whence can my poor boy procure these platters and such jewels? And granted that he return to the Enchanted Treasury and pluck them from the trees which, however, I hold impossible; yet given that he bring them whence shall he come by the girls and the blacks?" Nor did she leave communing with herself till she reached her home, where she found Alaeddin awaiting her, and she lost no time in saying, "O my son, did I not tell thee never to fancy that thy power would extend to the Lady Badr al-Budur, and that such a matter is not possible to folk like ourselves?" "Recount to me the news," quoth he; so quoth she, "O my child, verily the Sultan received me with all honour according to his custom and, meseemeth his intentions towards us be friendly. But thine enemy is that accursed Wazir; for, after I addressed the King in thy name as thou badest me say:—In very sooth the promised term is past, adding:—'Twere well an thy Highness would deign issue commandment for the espousals of thy daughter the Lady Badr al-Budur to my son Alaeddin, he turned to and addressed the Minister who answered privily, after which the Sultan gave me his reply." Then she enumerated the King's demand and said, "O my son, he indeed expecteth of thee an instant reply; but I fancy that we have no answer for him." When Alaeddin heard these words he laughed and said, "O my mother, thou affirmest that we have no answer and thou deemest the case difficult exceedingly; but compose thy thoughts and arise and bring me somewhat we may eat; and, after we have dined, an the Compassionate be willing, thou shalt see my reply. Also the Sultan thinketh like thyself that he hath demanded a prodigious dower in order to divert me from his daughter, whereas the fact is that he hath required of me a matter far less than I expected. But do thou fare forth at once and purchase the provision and leave me to procure thee a reply." So she went out to fetch her needful from the Bazar and Alaeddin retired to his chamber and taking the Lamp rubbed it, when forthright appeared to him its Slave and said, "Ask, O my lord, whatso thou wantest." The other replied, "I have demanded of the Sultan his daughter to wife and he hath required of me forty bowls of purest gold each weighing ten pounds[87] and all to be filled with gems such as we find in the Gardens of the Hoard; furthermore, that they be borne on the heads of as many white handmaids, each attended by her black eunuch-slave, also forty in full rate; so I desire that thou bring all these into my presence." "Hearkening and obeying, O my lord," quoth the Slave and, disappearing for the space of an hour or so, presently returned bringing the platters and jewels, handmaids and eunuchs; then, setting them before him the Marid cried, "This be what thou demandedst of me: declare now an thou want any matter or service other than this." Alaeddin rejoined, "I have need of naught else; but, an I do, I will summon thee and let thee know." The Slave now disappeared and, after a little while, Alaeddin's mother returned home and, on entering the house, saw the blacks and the handmaids.[88] Hereat she wondered and exclaimed, "All this proceedeth from the Lamp which Allah perpetuate to my son!" But ere she doffed her mantilla Alaeddin said to her, "O my mother, this be thy time before the Sultan enter his Serraglio-palace[89] do thou carry to him what he required and wend thou with it at once, so may he know that I avail to supply all he wanteth and yet more; also that he is beguiled by his Grand Wazir and the twain imagined vainly that they would baffle me." Then he arose forthright and opened the house-door, when the handmaids and blackamoors paced forth in pairs, each girl with her eunuch beside her, until they crowded the quarter, Alaeddin's mother foregoing them. And when the folk of that ward sighted such mighty fine sight and marvellous spectacle, all stood at gaze and they considered the forms and figures of the handmaids marvelling at their beauty and loveliness, for each and every wore robes inwrought with gold and studded with jewels, no dress being worth less than a thousand dinars.[90] They stared as intently at the bowls and albeit these were covered with pieces of brocade, also orfrayed and dubbed with precious stones, yet the sheen outshot from them dulled the shine of sun. Then Alaeddin's mother walked forwards and all the handmaids and eunuchs paced behind her in the best of ordinance and disposition, and the citizens gathered to gaze at the beauty of the damsels, glorifying God the Most Great, until the train reached the palace and entered it accompanied by the tailor's widow. Now when the Aghas and Chamberlains and Army-officers beheld them, all were seized with surprise, notably by seeing the handmaids who each and every would ravish the reason of an anchorite. And albeit the royal Chamberlains and Officials were men of family, the sons of Grandees and Emirs, yet they could not but especially wonder at the costly dresses of the girls and the platters borne upon their heads; nor could they gaze at them open-eyed by reason of the exceeding brilliance and radiance. Then the Nabobs went in and reported to the King who forthright bade admit them to the presence-chamber, and Alaeddin's mother went in with them. When they stood before the Sultan, all saluted him with every sign of respect and worship and prayed for his glory and prosperity; then they set down from their heads the bowls at his feet and, having removed the brocade covers, rested with arms crossed behind them. The Sultan wondered with exceeding wonder and was distraught by the beauty of the handmaids and their loveliness which passed praise; and his wits were wildered when he considered the golden bowls brimful of gems which captured man's vision, and he was perplexed at the marvel until he became, like the dumb, unable to utter a syllable for the excess of his wonder. Also his sense was stupefied the more when he bethought him that within an hour or so all these treasures had been collected. Presently he commanded the slave-girls to enter, with what loads they bore, the dower of the Princess; and, when they had done his bidding Alaeddin's mother came forward and said to the Sultan, "O my lord, this be not much wherewith to honour the Lady Badr al-Budur, for that she meriteth these things multiplied times manifold." Hereat the Sovran turned to the Minister and asked, "What sayest thou, O Wazir? is not he who could produce such wealth in a time so brief, is he not, I say, worthy to become the Sultan's son-in-law and take the King's daughter to wife?" Then the Minister (although he marvelled at these riches even more than did the Sultan), whose envy was killing him and growing greater hour by hour, seeing his liege lord satisfied with the moneys and the dower and yet being unable to fight against fact, made answer, " 'Tis not worthy of her." Withal he fell to devising a device against the King that he might withhold the Lady Badr al-Budur from Alaeddin and accordingly he continued, "O my liege, the treasures of the universe all of them are not worth a nail-paring of thy daughter: indeed thy Highness hath prized these things overmuch in comparison with her." When the King heard the words of his Grand Wazir, he knew that the speech was prompted by excess of envy, so turning to the mother of Alaeddin he said, "O woman, go to thy son and tell him that I have accepted of him the dower and stand to my bargain, and that my daughter be his bride and he my son-in-law: furthermore, bid him at once make act of presence that I may become familiar with him: he shall see naught from me save all honour and consideration, and this night shall be the beginning of the marriage-festivities. Only, as I said to thee, let him come to me and tarry not." Thereupon Alaeddin's mother returned home with the speed of the stormwinds that she might hasten her utmost to congratulate her son; and she flew with joy at the thought that her boy was about to become[91] son-in-law to the Sultan. After her departure the King dismissed the Divan and, entering the palace of the Princess, bade them bring the bowls and the handmaids before him and before her, that she also might inspect them. But when the Lady Badr al-Budur considered the jewels, she waxed distraught and cried, "Meseemeth that in the treasuries of the world there be not found one jewel rivalling these jewels." Then she looked at the handmaids and marvelled at their beauty and loveliness, and knew that all this came from her new bridegroom who had sent them in her service. So she was gladdened, albeit she had been grieved and saddened on account of her former husband, the Wazir's son, and she rejoiced with exceeding joy when she gazed upon the damsels and their charms; nor was her sire, the Sultan, less pleased and inspirited when he saw his daughter relieved of all her mourning and melancholy and his own vanished at the sight of her enjoyment. Then he asked her, "O my daughter, do these things divert thee? Indeed I deem that this suitor of thine be more suitable to thee than the son of the Wazir; and right soon, (Inshallah!) O my daughter, thou shalt have fuller joy with him." Such was the case with the King; but as regards Alaeddin, as soon as he saw his mother entering the house with face laughing for stress of joy he rejoiced at the sign of glad tidings and cried, "To Allah alone be lauds! Perfected is all I desired." Rejoined his mother, "Be gladdened at my good news, O my son, and hearten thy heart and cool thine eyes for the winning of thy wish. The Sultan hath accepted thine offering, I mean the moneys and the dower of the Lady Badr al-Budur, who is now thine affianced bride; and, this very night, O my child, is your marriage and thy first visit to her; for the King, that he might assure me of his word, hath proclaimed to the world thou art his son-in-law and promised this night to be the night of going in. But he also said to me:—Let thy son come hither forthright that I may become familiar with him and receive him with all honour and worship. And now here am I, O my son, at the end of my labours: happen whatso may happen the rest is upon thy shoulders." Thereupon Alaeddin arose and kissed his mother's hand and thanked her, enhancing her kindly service: then he left her and entering his chamber took the Lamp and rubbed it when, lo and behold! its Slave appeared and cried, "Adsum! Ask whatso thou wantest." The young man replied, "'Tis my desire that thou take me to a Hammam whose like is not in the world; then, fetch me a dress so costly and kingly that no royalty ever owned its fellow." The Marid replied, "I hear and I obey," and carried him to Baths such as were never seen by the Kings of the Chosroes, for the building was all of alabaster and carnelian and it contained marvellous limnings which captured the sight; and the great hall[92] was studded with precious stones. Not a soul was therein but, when Alaeddin entered, one of the Jann in human shape washed him and bathed[93] him to the best of his desire. Alaeddin, after having been washed and bathed, left the Baths and went into the great hall where he found that his old dress had been removed and replaced by a suit of the most precious and princely. Then he was served with sherbets and ambergris'd coffee[94] and, after drinking, he arose and a party of black slaves came forwards and clad him in the costliest of clothing, then perfumed and fumigated him. It is known that Alaeddin was the son of a tailor, a pauper, yet now would none deem him to be such; nay, all would say, "This be the greatest that is of the progeny of the Kings: praise be to Him who changeth and who is not changed!" Presently came the Jinni and lifting him up bore him to his home and asked, "O my lord, tell me hast thou aught of need?" He answered, "Yes, 'tis my desire that thou bring me eight and forty Mamelukes, of whom two dozen shall forego me and the rest follow me, the whole number with their warchargers and clothing and accoutrements; and all upon them and their steeds must be of naught save of highest worth and the costliest, such as may not be found in treasuries of the Kings. Then fetch me a stallion fit for the riding of the Chosroes and let his furniture, all thereof, be of gold crusted with the finest gems:[95] fetch me also eight and forty thousand dinars that each white slave may carry a thousand gold pieces. 'Tis now my intent to fare to the Sultan, so delay thou not, for that without all these requisites whereof I bespake thee I may not visit him. Moreover set before me a dozen slave-girls unique in beauty and dight with the most magnificent dresses, that they wend with my mother to the royal palace; and let every handmaid be robed in raiment that befitteth Queen's wearing." The Slave replied, "To hear is to obey;" and, disappearing for an eye-twinkling, brought all he was bidden bring and led by hand a stallion whose rival was not amongst the Arabian Arabs, and its saddle cloth was of splendid brocade gold-inwrought. Thereupon, without stay or delay, Alaeddin sent for his mother and gave her the garments she should wear and committed to her charge the twelve slave-girls forming her suite to the palace. Then he sent one of the Mamelukes, whom the Jinni had brought, to see if the Sultan had left the Serraglio or not. The white slave went forth lighter than the lightning and returning in like haste, said, "O my lord, the Sultan awaiteth thee!" Hereat Alaeddin arose and took horse, his Mamelukes riding a-van and arear of him, and they were such that all must cry, "Laud to the Lord who created them and clothed them with such beauty and loveliness." And they scattered gold amongst the crowd in front of their master who surpassed them all in comeliness and seemlihead nor needest thou ask concerning the sons of the Kings,—praise be to the Bountiful, the Eternal! All this was of the virtues of the Wonderful Lamp,[96] which, whoso possessed, him it gifted with fairest favour and finest figure, with wealth and with wisdom. The folk admired Alaeddin's liberality and exceeding generosity and all were distraught seeing his charms and elegance, his gravity and his good manners, they glorified the Creator for this noble creation, they blessed him each and every and, albeit they knew him for the son of Such-an-one, the tailor, yet no man envied him; nay, all owned that he deserved his great good fortune. Now the Sultan had assembled the Lords of the land and, informing them of the promise he had passed to Alaeddin, touching the marriage of his daughter, had bidden them await his approach and then go forth, one and all, to meet him and greet him. Hereupon the Emirs and Wazirs, the Chamberlains, the Nabobs and the Army-officers took their stations expecting him at the palace gate. Alaeddin would fain have dismounted at the outer entrance; but one of the Nobles, whom the King had deputed for such duty, approached him and said, "O my lord, 'tis the Royal Command that thou enter riding thy steed nor dismount except at the Divan-door."[97] Then they all forewent him in a body and conducted him to the appointed place where they crowded about him, these to hold his stirrup and those supporting him on either side whilst others took him by the hands and helped him dismount; after which all the Emirs and Nobles preceded him into the Divan and led him close up to the royal throne. Thereupon the Sultan came down forthright from his seat of estate and, forbidding him to buss the carpet, embraced and kissed and seated him to the right[98] of and beside himself. Alaeddin did whatso is suitable, in the case of the Kings, of salutation and offering of blessings, and said, "O our lord the Sultan, indeed the generosity of thy Highness demanded that thou deign vouchsafe to me the hand of thy daughter, the Lady Badr al-Budur, albeit I undeserve the greatness of such gift, I being but the humblest of thy slaves. I pray Allah grant thee prosperity and perpetuance; but in very sooth, O King, my tongue is helpless to thank thee for the fullness of the favour, passing all measure, which thou hast bestowed upon me. And I hope of thy Highness that thou wilt give me a piece of ground fitted for a pavilion which shall besit thy daughter, the Lady Badr al-Budur." The Sultan was struck with admiration when he saw Alaeddin in his princely suit and looked upon him and considered his beauty and loveliness, and noted the Mamelukes standing to serve him in their comeliness and seemlihead; and still his marvel grew when the mother of Alaeddin approached him in costly raiment and sumptuous, clad as though she were a Queen, and when he gazed upon the twelve handmaids standing before her with crossed arms and with all worship and reverence doing her service. He also considered the eloquence of Alaeddin and his delicacy of speech and he was astounded thereat, he and all his who were present at the levée. Thereupon fire was kindled in the Grand Wazir's heart for envy of Alaeddin until he was like to die: and it was worse when the Sultan, after hearing the youth's succession of prayers and seeing his high dignity of demeanour, respectful withal, and his eloquence and elegance of language, clasped him to his bosom and kissed him and cried, "Alas, O my son, that I have not enjoyed thy converse before this day!" He rejoiced in him with mighty great joy and straightway bade the music[99] and the bands strike up; then he arose and, taking the youth led him into the palace where supper had been prepared and the Eunuchs at once laid the tables. So the Sovran sat down and seated his son-in-law on his right side and the Wazirs and high officials and Lords of the land took places each according to his degree, whereupon the bands played and a mighty fine marriage-feast was dispread in the palace. The King now applied himself to making friendship with Alaeddin and conversed with the youth, who answered him with all courtesy and eloquence, as though he had been bred in the palaces of the kings or he had lived with them his daily life. And the more the talk was prolonged between them, the more did the Sultan's pleasure and delight increase, hearing his son-in-law's readiness of reply and his sweet flow of language. But after they had eaten and drunken and the trays were removed, the King bade summon the Kazis and witnesses who presently attended and knitted the knot and wrote out the contract-writ between Alaeddin and the Lady Badr al-Budur. And presently the bridegroom arose and would have fared forth, when his father-in-law withheld him and asked, "Whither away, O my child? The bride-fêtes have begun and the marriage is made and the tie is tied and the writ is written." He replied, "O my lord the King, 'tis my desire to edify, for the Lady Badr al-Budur, a pavilion befitting her station and high degree, nor can I visit her before so doing. But, Inshallah! the building shall be finished within the shortest time, by the utmost endeavour of thy slave and by the kindly regard of thy Highness; and, although I do (yes indeed!) long to enjoy the society of the Lady Badr al-Budur, yet 'tis incumbent on me first to serve her and it becometh me to set about the work forthright." "Look around thee, O my son," replied the Sultan, "for what ground thou deemest suitable to thy design and do thou take all things into thy hands; but I deem the best for thee will be yonder broad plain facing my palace; and, if it please thee, build thy pavilion thereupon." "And this," answered Alaeddin, "is the sum of my wishes that I may be nearhand to thy Highness." So saying he farewelled the King and took horse, with his Mamelukes riding before him and behind him, and all the world blessed him and cried, "By Allah he is deserving," until such time as he reached his home. Then he alighted from his stallion and repairing to his chamber, rubbed the Lamp and behold, the Slave stood before him and said, "Ask, O my lord, whatso thou wantest;" and Alaeddin rejoined, "I require of thee a service grave and important which thou must do for me, and 'tis that thou build me with all urgency a pavilion fronting the palace of the Sultan; and it must be a marvel for it shall be provided with every requisite, such as royal furniture and so forth." The Slave replied, "To hear is to obey" and evanished and, before the next dawn brake, returned to Alaeddin and said, "O my lord, the pavilion is finished to the fullest of thy fancy; and, if thou wouldst inspect it, arise forthright and fare with me." Accordingly, he rose up and the Slave carried him in the space of an eye-glance to the pavilion which, when Alaeddin looked upon it, struck him with surprise at such building, all its stones being of jasper and alabaster, Sumaki[100]-marble and mosaic-work. Then the Slave led him into the treasury which was full of all manner of gold and silver and costly gems, not to be counted or computed, priced or estimated. Thence to another place, where Alaeddin saw all requisites for the table, plates and dishes, spoons and ladles, basins and covers, cups and tasses, the whole of precious metal: thence to the kitchen, where they found the kitcheners provided with their needs and cooking batteries, likewise golden and silvern; thence to a warehouse piled up with chests full-packed of royal raiment, stuffs that captured the reason, such as gold-wrought brocades from India and China and kimcobs[101] or orfrayed cloths; thence to many apartments replete with appointments which beggar description; thence to the stables containing coursers whose like was not to be met with amongst the kings of the universe; and, lastly, they went to the harness-rooms all hung with housings, costly saddles and other furniture, everywhere studded with pearls and precious stones. And all this was the work of one night. Alaeddin was wonder-struck and astounded by that magnificent display of wealth which not even the mightiest monarch on earth could produce; and more so to see his pavilion fully provided with eunuchs and handmaids whose beauty would seduce a saint. Yet the prime marvel of the pavilion was an upper kiosque or belvedere of four-and-twenty windows all made of emeralds and rubies and other gems;[102] and one window remained unfinished at the requirement of Alaeddin that the Sultan might prove him impotent to complete it. When the youth had inspected the whole edifice, he was pleased and gladdened exceedingly: then, turning to the Slave he said, "I require of thee still one thing which is yet wanting and whereof I had forgotten to tell thee." "Ask, O my lord, thy want," quoth the Servitor; and quoth the other, "I demand of thee a carpet of the primest brocade all gold-inwrought which, when unrolled and outstretched, shall extend hence to the Sultan's palace in order that the Lady Badr al-Budur may, when coming hither, pace upon it[103] and not tread common earth." The Slave departed for a short while and said on his return, "O my lord, verily that which thou demandest is here." Then he took him and showed him a carpet which wildered the wits, and it extended from palace to pavilion; and after this the Servitor bore off Alaeddin and set him down in his own home. Now day was brightening so the Sultan rose from his sleep and throwing open the casement looked out[104] and espied, opposite his palace, a palatial pavilion ready edified. Thereupon he fell to rubbing his eyes and opening them their widest and considering the scene, and he soon was certified that the new edifice was mighty fine and grand enough to bewilder the wits. Moreover, with amazement as great he saw the carpet dispread between palace and pavilion: like their lord also the royal doorkeepers and the household, one and all, were dazed and amazed at the spectacle.

Meanwhile[105] the Wazir came in and, as he entered, espied
the newly-builded pavilion and the carpet, whereat he also
wondered; and, when he went in to the Sultan the twain
fell to talking on this marvellous matter with great surprise
at a sight which distracted the gazer and attracted the
heart. They said finally, "In very truth, of this pavilion we
deem that none of the royalties could build its fellow;" and
the King, turning to the Minister, asked him, "Hast thou
seen now that Alaeddin is worthy to be the husband of the
Princess my daughter? Hast thou looked upon and considered this right royal building, this magnificence of opulence, which thought of man can not contain?" But the
Wazir in his envy of Alaeddin replied, "O King of the Age,
indeed this foundation and this building and this opulence
may not be save by means of magic nor can any man in the
world, be he the richest in good or the greatest in governance, avail to found and finish in a single night such edifice as this." The Sultan rejoined, "I am surprised to see
in thee how thou dost continually harp on evil opinion
of Alaeddin; but I hold that 'tis caused by thine envy and
jealousy. Thou wast present when I gave him the ground at
his own prayer for a place whereon he might build a pavilion wherein to lodge my daughter, and I myself favoured
him with a site for the same and that too before thy very
face. But however that be, shall one who could send me as
dower for the Princess such store of such stones whereof
the kings never obtained even a few, shall he, I say, be unable to edify an edifice like this?" When the Wazir heard
the Sultan's words, he knew that his lord loved Alaeddin
exceedingly; so his envy and malice increased; only, as
he could do nothing against the youth, he sat silent and impotent to return a reply. But Alaeddin seeing that it was
broad day, and the appointed time had come for his repairing to the palace (where his wedding was being celebrated
and the Emirs and Wazirs and Grandees were gathered together about the Sultan to be present at the ceremony),
arose and rubbed the Lamp, and when its Slave appeared
and said, "O my lord, ask whatso thou wantest, for I stand

before thee and at thy service," said he, "I mean forthright to seek the palace, this day being my wedding-festival
and I want thee to supply me with ten thousand dinars."
The Slave evanished for an eye-twinkling and returned
bringing the moneys, when Alaeddin took horse with his
Mamelukes a-van and arear and passed on his way, scattering as he went gold pieces upon the lieges until all were
fondly affected towards him and his dignity was enhanced.
But when he drew near the palace, and the Emirs and
Aghas and Army-officers who were standing to await him
noted his approach, they hastened straightway to the King
and gave him the tidings thereof; whereupon the Sultan
rose and met his son-in-law and, after embracing and kissing him, led him still holding his hand into his own apartment where he sat down and seated him by his right side.
The city was all decorated and music rang through the
palace and the singers sang until the King bade bring the
noon-meal, when the eunuchs and Mamelukes hastened to
spread the tables and trays which are such as are served to
the kings. Then the Sultan and Alaeddin and the Lords of
the land and the Grandees of the realm took their seats
and ate and drank until they were satisfied. And it was a
mighty fine wedding in city and palace and the high nobles
all rejoiced therein and the commons of the kingdom were
equally gladdened, while the Governors of provinces and
Nabobs of districts flocked from far regions to witness
Alaeddin's marriage and its processions and festivities. The
Sultan also marvelled in his mind to look at Alaeddin's
mother[106] and recall to mind how she was wont to visit
him in pauper plight, while her son could command all
this opulence and magnificence. And when the spectators,
who crowded the royal palace to enjoy the wedding-feasts,
looked upon Alaeddin's pavilion and the beauties of the
building, they were seized with an immense surprise that
so vast an edifice as this could be reared on high during a
single night; and they blessed the youth and cried, "Allah
gladden him! By Allah, he deserveth all this! Allah bless
his days!" When dinner was done, Alaeddin rose and, fare-

welling the Sultan, took horse with his Mamelukes and rode to his own pavilion that he might prepare to receive therein his bride, the Lady Badr al-Budur. And as he passed, all the folk shouted their good wishes with one voice and their words were, "Allah gladden thee! Allah increase thy glory. Allah grant thee length of life!" while immense crowds of people gathered to swell the marriage procession and they conducted him to his new home, he showering gold upon them during the whole time. When he reached his pavilion, he dismounted and walked in and sat him down on the divan, whilst his Mamelukes stood before him with arms afolded; also after a short delay they brought him sherbets and, when these were drunk, he ordered his white slaves and handmaids and eunuchs and all who were in the pavilion to make ready for meeting the Lady Badr al-Budur. Moreover, as soon as mid-afternoon came and the air had cooled and the great heat of the sun was abated, the Sultan bade his Army-officers and Emirs and Wazirs go down into the Maydan-plain[107] whither he likewise rode. And Alaeddin also took horse with his Mamelukes, he mounting a stallion whose like was not among the steeds of the Arab al-Arba,[108] and he showed his horsemanship in the hippodrome and so played with the Jarid[109] that none could withstand him, while his bride sat gazing upon him from the latticed balcony of her bower and, seeing in him such beauty and cavalarice, she fell headlong in love of him and was like to fly for joy. And after they had ringed their horses on the Maydan and each had displayed whatso he could of horsemanship, Alaeddin proving himself the best man of all, they rode in a body to the Sultan's palace and the youth also returned to his own pavilion. But when it was evening, the Wazirs and Nobles took the bridegroom and, falling in, escorted him to the royal Hammam (known as the Sultani), when he was bathed and perfumed. As soon as he came out he donned a dress more magnificent than the former and took horse with the Emirs and the soldier-officers riding before him and forming a grand cortège, wherein four of the Wazirs

bore naked swords round about him.[110] All the citizens and
the strangers and the troops marched before him in ordered throng carrying wax candles and kettle drums and
pipes and other instruments of mirth and merriment, until
they conducted him to his pavilion. Here he alighted and
walking in took his seat and seated the Wazirs and Emirs
who had escorted him, and the Mamelukes brought sherbets and sugared drinks, which they also passed to the people who had followed in his train. It was a world of folk
whose tale might not be told; withal Alaeddin bade his
Mamelukes stand without the pavilion-doors and shower
gold upon the crowd. When the Sultan returned from the
Maydan-plain to his palace he ordered the household,
men as well as women, straightway to form a cavalcade
for his daughter, with all ceremony, and bear her to her
bridegroom's pavilion. So the nobles and soldier-officers,
who had followed and escorted the bridegroom, at once
mounted, and the handmaids and eunuchs went forth with
wax candles and made a mighty fine procession for the
Lady Badr al-Budur and they paced on preceding her till
they entered the pavilion of Alaeddin whose mother walked
beside the bride. In front of the Princess also fared the
wives of the Wazirs and Emirs, Grandees and Notables,
and in attendance on her were the eight and forty slave-
girls presented to her aforetime by her bridegroom, each
hending in hand a huge cierge scented with camphor and
ambergris and set in a candlestick of gem-studded gold.
And reaching Alaeddin's pavilion they led her to her bower
in the upper storey and changed her robes and enthroned
her; then, as soon as the displaying was ended, they accompanied her to Alaeddin's apartments and presently he
paid her the first visit. Now his mother was with the bride
and, when the bridegroom came up and did off her veil,
the ancient dame fell to considering the beauty of the
Princess and her loveliness; and she looked around at the
pavilion which was all litten up by gold and gems besides
the manifold candelabra of precious metals encrusted with
emeralds and jacinths; so she said in her mind, "Once upon

a time I thought the Sultan's palace mighty fine, but this pavilion is a thing apart; nor do I deem that any of the greatest Kings or Chosroes attained in his day to aught like thereof; also am I certified that all the world could not build anything evening it." Nor less did the Lady Badr al-Budur fall to gazing at the pavilion and marvelling for its magnificence. Then the tables were spread and they all ate and drank and were gladdened; after which fourscore damsels came before them each holding in hand an instrument of mirth and merriment; then they deftly moved their fingertips and touched the strings smiting them into song, most musical, most melancholy, till they rent the hearts of the hearers. Hereat the Princess increased in marvel and quoth she to herself, "In all my life ne'er heard I songs like these,"[111] till she forsook food, the better to listen. And at last Alaeddin poured out for her wine and passed it to her with his own hand; so great joy and jubilee went round amongst them and it was a notable night, such an one as Iskandar, Lord of the Two Horns,[112] had never spent in his time. When they had finished eating and drinking and the tables were removed from before them, Alaeddin arose and went in to his bride.[113] As soon as morning morrowed he left his bed and the treasurer brought him a costly suit and a mighty fine, of the most sumptuous robes worn by the kings. Then, after drinking coffee flavoured with ambergris, he ordered the horses be saddled and, mounting with his Mamelukes before and behind him, rode to the Sultan's palace and on his entering its court the eunuchs went in and reported his coming to their lord. When the Sultan heard of Alaeddin's approach, he rose up forthright to receive him and embraced and kissed him as though he were his own son: then, seating him on his right, he blessed and prayed for him, as did the Wazirs and Emirs, the Lords of the land and the Grandees of the realm. Presently, the King commanded bring the morning-meal which the attendants served up and all broke their fast together, and when they had eaten and drunken their sufficiency and the tables were removed by the eunuchs, Alaeddin turned to the Sultan and said, "O my lord, would thy Highness deign honour me this day at dinner, in the house of the Lady Badr al-Budur thy beloved daughter, and come accompanied by all thy Ministers and Grandees of the reign?" The King replied (and he was delighted with his son-in-law,) "Thou art surpassing in liberality, O my son!" Then he gave orders to all invited and rode forth with them (Alaeddin also riding beside him) till they reached the pavilion and as he entered it and considered its construction, its architecture and its stonery, all jasper and carnelian, his sight was dazed and his wits were amazed at such grandeur and magnificence of opulence. Then turning to the Minister he thus addressed him, "What sayest thou? Tell me hast thou seen in all thy time aught like this amongst the mightiest of earth's monarchs for the abundance of gold and gems we are now beholding?" The Grand Wazir replied, "O my lord the King, this be a feat which cannot be accomplished by might of monarch amongst Adam's sons;[114] nor could the collected peoples of the universal world build a palace like unto this; nay, even builders could not be found to make aught resembling it, save (as I said to thy Highness) by force of sorcery." These words certified the King that his Minister spake not except in envy and jealousy of Alaeddin, and would stablish in the royal mind that all this splendour was not made of man but by means of magic and with the aid of the Black Art. So quoth he to him, "Suffice thee so much, O Wazir: thou hast none other word to speak and well I know what cause urgeth thee to say this say." Then Alaeddin preceded the Sultan till he conducted him to the upper Kiosque where he saw its skylights, windows and latticed casements and jalousies wholly made of emeralds and rubies and other costly gems; whereat his mind was perplexed and his wits were bewildered and his thoughts were distraught. Presently he took to strolling round the Kiosque and solacing himself with these sights which captured the vision, till he chanced to cast a glance at the window which Alaeddin by design had left unwrought and not finished like the rest; and, when he noted its lack of completion, he cried, "Woe and well-away for thee, O window, because of thine imperfection;"[115] and, turning to his Minister he asked, "Knowest thou the reason of leaving incomplete this window and its framework?" The Wazir said, "O my lord, I conceive that the want of finish in this window resulteth from thy Highness having pushed on Alaeddin's marriage and he lacked the leisure to complete it." Now at that time, Alaeddin had gone in to his bride, the Lady Badr al-Budur, to inform her of her father's presence; and, when he returned, the King asked him, "O my son what is the reason why the window of this Kiosque was not made perfect?" "O King of the Age, seeing the suddenness of my wedding," answered he, "I failed to find artists for finishing it." Quoth the Sultan, "I have a mind to complete it myself;" and quoth Alaeddin, "Allah perpetuate thy glory, O thou the King; so shall thy memory endure in thy daughter's pavilion." The Sultan forthright bade summon jewellers and goldsmiths and ordered them be supplied from the treasury with all their needs of gold and gems and noble ores; and, when they were gathered together he commanded them to complete the work still wanting in the Kiosque-window. Meanwhile the Princess came forth to meet her sire the Sultan who noticed, as she drew near, her smiling face; so he embraced her and kissed her, then led her to the pavilion and all entered in a body. Now this was the time of the noon-day meal and one table had been spread for the Sovran, his daughter and his son-in-law and a second for the Wazirs, the Lords of the land, the Grandees of the realm, the Chief Officers of the host, the Chamberlains and the Nabobs. The King took seat between the Princess and her husband; and, when he put forth his hand to the food and tasted it, he was struck with surprise by the flavour of the dishes and their savoury and sumptuous cooking. Moreover, there stood before him the fourscore damsels each and every saying to the full moon, "Rise that I may seat myself in thy stead!"[116] All held instruments of mirth and merriment and they tuned the same and deftly moved their finger-tips and smote the strings into song, most musical, most melodious, which expanded the mourner's heart. Hereby the Sultan was gladdened and time was good to him and for high enjoyment he exclaimed, "In very sooth the thing is beyond the compass of King and Kaysar." Then they fell to eating and drinking; and the cup went round until they had drunken enough, when sweetmeats and fruits of sorts and other such edibles were served, the dessert being laid out in a different salon whither they removed and enjoyed of these pleasures their sufficiency. Presently the Sultan arose that he might see if the produce of his jewellers and goldsmiths favoured that of the pavilion; so he went upstairs to them and inspected their work and how they had wrought; but he noted a mighty great difference and his men were far from being able to make anything like the rest of Alaeddin's pavilion. They informed him how all the gems stored in the Lesser Treasury had been brought to them and used by them but that the whole had proved insufficient; wherefor he bade open the Greater Treasury and gave the workmen all they wanted of him. Moreover he allowed them, an it sufficed not, to take the jewels wherewith Alaeddin had gifted him. They carried off the whole and pushed on their labours but they found the gems fail them, albeit had they not finished half the part wanting to the Kiosque-window. Herewith the King commanded them to seize all the precious stones owned by the Wazirs and Grandees of the realm; but, although they did his bidding, the supply still fell short of their requirements. Next morning Alaeddin arose to look at the jewellers' work and remarked that they had not finished a moiety of what was wanting to the Kiosque-window: so he at once ordered them to undo all they had done and restore the jewels to their owners. Accordingly, they pulled out the precious stones and sent the Sultan's to the Sultan and the Wazirs' to the Wazirs. Then the jewellers went to the King and told him of what Alaeddin had bidden; so he asked them, "What said he to you, and what was his reason and wherefore was he not content that the window be finished and why did he undo the work ye wrought?" They answered, "O our lord, we know not at all, but he bade us deface whatso we had done." Hereupon the Sultan at once called for his horse, and mounting, took the way pavilionwards, when Alaeddin, after dismissing the goldsmiths and jewellers had retired into his closet and had rubbed the Lamp. Hereat straightway its Servitor appeared to him and said, "Ask whatso thou wantest: thy Slave is between thy hands;" and said Alaeddin, "'Tis my desire that thou finish the window which was left unfinished." The Marid replied, "On my head be it and also upon mine eyes!" then he vanished and after a little while returned saying, "O my lord, verily that thou commandedst me do is completed." So Alaeddin went upstairs to the Kiosque and found the whole window in wholly finished state; and, whilst he was still considering it, behold, a castrato came in to him and said, "O my lord, the Sultan hath ridden forth to visit thee and is passing through the pavilion-gate." So Alaeddin at once went down and received his father-in-law. The Sultan, on sighting his son-in-law, cried to him, "Wherefore, O my child, hast thou wrought on this wise and sufferedst not the jewellers to complete the Kiosque-window leaving in the pavilion an unfinished place?" Alaeddin replied, "O King of the Age, I left it not imperfect save for a design of mine own; nor was I incapable of perfecting it nor could I purpose that thy Highness should honour me with visiting a pavilion wherein was aught of deficiency. And, that thou mayest know I am not unable to make it perfect, let thy Highness deign walk upstairs with me and see if anything remain to be done therewith or not." So the Sultan went up with him and, entering the Kiosque, fell to looking right and left, but he saw no default at all in any of the windows; nay, he noted that all were perfect. So he marvelled at the sight and embraced Alaeddin and kissed him, saying, "O my son, what be this singular feat? Thou canst work in a single night what in months the jewellers could not do. By

Allah, I deem thou hast nor brother nor rival in this world."
Quoth Alaeddin, "Allah prolong thy life and preserve thee
to perpetuity! thy slave deserveth not this encomium;" and
quoth the King, "By Allah, O my child, thou meritest all
praise for a feat whereof all the artists of the world were
incapable." Then the Sultan came down and entered the
apartments of his daughter, the Lady Badr al-Budur, to take
rest beside her, and he saw her joyous exceedingly at the
glory and grandeur wherein she was; then, after reposing
awhile he returned to his palace. Now Alaeddin was wont
every day to thread the city-streets with his Mamelukes
riding a-van and arear of him showering rightwards and
leftwards gold upon the folk; and all the world, stranger
and neighbour, far and near, were fulfilled of his love for
the excess of his liberality and generosity. Moreover he increased the pensions of the poor Religious and the paupers
and he would distribute alms to them with his own hand;
by which good deed, he won high renown throughout the
realm and most of the Lords of the land and Emirs would
eat at his table; and men swore not at all save by his precious life. Nor did he leave faring to the chase and the
Maydan-plain and the riding of horses and playing at
javelin-play[117] in presence of the Sultan; and, whenever
the Lady Badr al-Budur beheld him disporting himself
on the backs of steeds, she loved him much the more, and
thought to herself that Allah had wrought her abundant
good by causing to happen whatso happened with the son
of the Wazir and by preserving her virginity intact for her
true bridegroom, Alaeddin. Alaeddin won for himself day
by day a fairer fame and a rarer report, while affection for
him increased in the hearts of all the lieges and he waxed
greater in the eyes of men. Moreover it chanced that in
those days certain enemies took horse and attacked the
Sultan, who armed and accounted an army to repel them
and made Alaeddin commander thereof. So he marched
with his men nor ceased marching until he drew near the
foe whose forces were exceeding many; and, presently,

when the action began he bared his brand and charged home upon the enemy. Then battle and slaughter befel and violent was the hurly-burly, but at last Alaeddin broke the hostile host and put all to flight, slaying the best part of them and pillaging their coin and cattle, property and possessions; and he despoiled them of spoils that could not be counted nor computed. Then he returned victorious after a noble victory and entered the capital which had decorated herself in his honour, of her delight in him; and the Sultan went forth to meet him and giving him joy embraced him and kissed him; and throughout the kingdom was held high festival with great joy and gladness. Presently, the Sovran and his son-in-law repaired to the pavilion where they were met by the Princess Badr al-Budur who rejoiced in her husband and, after kissing him between the eyes, led him to her apartments. After a time the Sultan also came and they sat down while the slave-girls brought them sherbets and confections which they ate and drank. Then the Sultan commanded that the whole kingdom be decorated for the triumph of his son-in-law and his victory over the invader: and the subjects and soldiery and all the people knew only Allah in heaven and Alaeddin on earth; for that their love, won by his liberality, was increased by his noble horsemanship and his successful battling for the country and putting to flight the foe. Such then was the high fortune of Alaeddin; but as regards the Maghrabi, the Magician, after returning to his native country, he passed all this space of time in bewailing what he had borne of toil and travail to win the Lamp and mostly that his trouble had gone vain and that the morsel when almost touching his lips had flown from his grasp. He pondered all this and mourned and reviled Alaeddin for the excess of his rage against him and at times he would exclaim, "For this bastard's death underground I am well satisfied and hope only that some time or other I may obtain the Lamp, seeing how 'tis yet safe." Now one day of the days he struck a table of sand and dotted down the figures and carefully considered their consequence; then he transferred them to paper that he might study them and make sure of Alaeddin's destruction and the safety of the Lamp preserved beneath the earth. Presently, he firmly stablished the sequence of the figures, mothers as well as daughters,[118] but still he saw not the Lamp. Thereupon rage overrode him and he made another trial to be assured of Alaeddin's death; but he saw him not in the Enchanted Treasure. Hereat his wrath still grew, and it waxed greater when he ascertained that the youth had issued from underground and was now upon earth's surface alive and alert: furthermore, that he had become owner of the Lamp, for which he had himself endured such toil and travail and troubles as man may not bear save for so great an object. Accordingly quoth he to himself, "I have suffered sore pains and penalties which none else could have endured for the Lamp's sake in order that other than I may carry it off; and this Accursed hath taken it without difficulty. And who knoweth an he wot the virtues of the Lamp, than whose owner none in the world should be wealthier? There is no help but that I work for his destruction." He then struck another geomantic table and examining the figures saw that the lad had won for himself unmeasurable riches and had wedded the daughter of his King; so of his envy and jealousy he was fired with the flame of wrath; and, rising without let or stay, he equipped himself and set forth for China-land, where he arrived in due season. Now when he had reached the King's capital wherein was Alaeddin, he alighted at one of the Khans; and, when he had rested from the weariness of wayfare, he donned his dress and went down to wander about the streets, where he never passed a group without hearing them prate about the pavilion and its grandeur and vaunt the beauty of Alaeddin and his lovesomeness, his liberality and generosity, his fine manners and his good morals. Presently he entered an establishment wherein men were drinking a certain warm beverage;[119] and going up to one of those who were loud in their lauds, he said to him, "O

fair youth, who may be the man ye describe and commend?"
"Apparently thou art a foreigner, O man," answered the
other, "and thou comest from a far country; but, even this
granted, how happeneth it thou hast not heard of the Emir
Alaeddin whose renown, I fancy, hath filled the universe
and whose pavilion, known by report to far and near, is one
of the Wonders of the World? How, then, never came to
thine ears aught of this or the name of Alaeddin (whose
glory and enjoyment our Lord increase!) and his fame?"
The Moorman replied, "The sum of my wishes is to look
upon this pavilion and, if thou wouldest do me a favour,
prithee guide me thereunto, for I am a foreigner." The man
rejoined, "To hear is to obey;" and, foregoing him, pointed
out Alaeddin's pavilion whereupon the Maroccan fell to
considering it and at once understood that it was the work
of the Lamp. So he cried, "Ah! Ah! needs must I dig a pit for
this Accursed, this son of a snip, who could not earn for
himself even an evening meal: and, if the Fates abet me, I
will assuredly destroy his life and send his mother back to
spinning at her wheel, e'en as she was wont erewhiles to
do." So saying, he returned to his caravanserai in a sore
state of grief and melancholy and regret bred by his envy
and hate of Alaeddin. He took his astrological gear[120] and
geomantic table to discover where might be the Lamp; and
he found that it was in the pavilion and not upon Alaeddin's person. So he rejoiced thereat with joy exceeding and
exclaimed, "Now indeed 'twill be an easy task to take the
life of this Accursed and I see my way to getting the Lamp."
Then he went to a coppersmith and said to him, "Do thou
make me a set of lamps and take from me their full price
and more; only I would have thee hasten to finish them."
Replied the smith, "Hearing and obeying," and fell awork-
ing to keep his word; and when they were ready the Moorman paid him what price he required; then taking them
he carried them to the Khan and set them in a basket.
Presently he began wandering about the highways and
market-streets of the capital crying aloud, "Ho! who will
exchange old lamps for new lamps?"[121] But when the folk

heard him cry on this wise, they derided him and said, "Doubtless this man is Jinn-mad, for that he goeth about offering new for old;" and a world followed him and the children of the quarter caught him up from place to place, laughing at him the while, nor did he forbid them or care for their maltreatment. And he ceased not strolling about the streets till he came under Alaeddin's pavilion,[122] where he shouted with his loudest voice and the boys screamed at him, "A madman! A madman!" Now Destiny had decreed that the Lady Badr al-Budur be sitting in her Kiosque whence she heard one crying like a crier, and the children bawling at him; only she understood not what was going on; so she gave orders to one of her slave-girls saying,[123] "Go thou and see who 'tis that crieth and what be his cry?" The girl fared forth and looked on when she beheld a man crying, "Ho! who will exchange old lamps for new lamps?" and the little ones pursuing and laughing at him; and as loudly laughed the Princess when this strange case was told to her. Now Alaeddin had carelessly left the lamp in his pavilion without hiding it and locking it up in his strong box;[124] and one of the slave-girls who had seen it said, "O my lady, I think to have noticed, in the apartment of my lord Alaeddin, an old lamp: so let us give it in change for a new lamp to this man, and see if his cry be truth or lie." Whereupon the Princess said to the slave-girl, "Bring the old lamp which thou saidst to have seen in thy lord's apartment." Now the Lady Badr al-Budur knew naught of the Lamp and of the specialities thereof which had raised Alaeddin her spouse to such high degree and grandeur; and her only end and aim was to understand by experiment the mind of a man who would give in exchange the new for the old. So the handmaid fared forth and went up to Alaeddin's apartment and returned with the Lamp to her lady who, like all the others, knew nothing of the Maghrabi's cunning tricks and his crafty device. Then the Princess bade an Agha of the eunuchry go down and barter the old Lamp for a new lamp. So he obeyed her bidding and, after taking a new lamp from the man, he returned and laid it before his lady who looking at it and seeing that it was brand-new, fell to laughing at the Moorman's wits. But the Maroccan, when he held the article in hand and recognised it for the Lamp of the Enchanted Treasury,[125] at once placed it in his breast-pocket and left all the other lamps to the folk who were bartering of him. Then he went forth running till he was clear of the city, when he walked leisurely over the level grounds and he took patience until night fell on him in desert ground where was none other but himself. There he brought out the Lamp when suddenly appeared to him the Marid who said "Adsum! thy slave between thy hands is come: ask of me what so thou wantest." " 'Tis my desire," the Moorman replied, "that thou upraise from its present place Alaeddin's pavilion with its inmates and all that be therein, not forgetting myself, and set it down upon my own land, Africa. Thou knowest my town and I want the building placed in the gardens hard by it." The Marid-slave replied, "Hearkening and obedience: close thine eyes and open thine eyes whenas thou shalt find thyself together with the pavilion in thine own country." This was done; and, in an eye-twinkling, the Maroccan and the pavilion with all therein were transported to the African land. Such then was the work of the Maghrabi, the Magician; but now let us return to the Sultan and his son-in-law. It was the custom of the King, because of his attachment to and his affection for his daughter, every morning when he had shaken off sleep, to open the latticed casement and look out therefrom that he might catch sight of her abode. So that day he arose and did as he was wont. But when he drew near the latticed casement of his palace and looked out at Alaeddin's pavilion he saw naught; nay, the site was smooth as a well-trodden highway and like unto what it had been aforetime; and he could find nor edifice nor offices. So astonishment clothed him as with a garment, and his wits were wildered and he began to rub his eyes, lest they be dimmed or darkened, and to gaze intently; but at last he was certified that no trace of the pavilion remained nor sign of its being; nor wist he the why and the wherefore of its disappearance. So his surprise increased and he smote hand upon hand and the tears trickled down his cheeks over his beard, for that he knew not what had become of his daughter. Then he sent out officials forthright and summoned the Grand Wazir who at once attended; and, seeing him in this piteous plight said, "Pardon, O King of the Age, may Allah avert from thee every ill! Wherefore art thou in such sorrow?" Exclaimed the Sovran, "Methinketh thou wottest not my case?" and quoth the Minister, "On no wise, O our lord: by Allah, I know of it nothing at all." "Then," resumed the Sultan, "'tis manifest thou hast not looked this day in the direction of Alaeddin's pavilion." "True, O my lord," quoth the Wazir, "it must still be locked and fast shut;" and quoth the King, "Forasmuch as thou hast no inkling of aught,[126] arise and look out at the window and see Alaeddin's pavilion whereof thou sayest 'tis locked and fast shut." The Minister obeyed his bidding but could not see anything, or pavilion or other place; so with mind and thoughts sore perplexed he returned to his liege lord who asked him, "Hast now learned the reason of my distress and noted yon locked-up palace and fast shut?" Answered the Wazir, "O King of the Age, erewhile I represented to thy Highness that this pavilion and these matters be all magical." Hereat the Sultan, fired with wrath, cried, "Where be Alaeddin?" and the Minister replied, "He hath gone a-hunting," when the King commanded without stay or delay sundry of his Aghas and Army-officers to go and bring to him his son-in-law chained and with pinioned elbows. So they fared forth until they found Alaeddin when they said to him, "O our lord Alaeddin, excuse us nor be thou wroth with us; for the King hath commanded that we carry thee before him pinioned and fettered, and we hope pardon from thee because we are under the royal orders which we cannot gainsay." Alaeddin, hearing these words, was seized with surprise and not knowing the reason of this remained tongue-tied for a time, after which he turned to them and asked, "O assembly, have you naught of knowledge concerning the motive of the royal mandate? Well I wot my soul to be innocent and that I never sinned against king or against kingdom." "O our lord," answered they, "we have no inkling whatever." So Alaeddin alighted from his horse and said to them, "Do ye whatso the Sultan bade you do, for that the King's command is upon the head and the eyes."[127] The Aghas, having bound Alaeddin in bonds and pinioned his elbows behind his back, haled him in chains and carried him into the city. But when the lieges saw him pinioned and ironed, they understood that the Sultan purposed to strike off his head; and, forasmuch as he was loved of them exceedingly, all gathered together and seized their weapons; then, swarming out of their houses, followed the soldiery to see what was to do. And when the troops arrived with Alaeddin at the palace, they went in and informed the Sultan of this, whereat he forthright commanded the Sworder to cut off the head of his son-in-law. Now as soon as the subjects were aware of this order, they barricaded the gates and closed the doors of the palace and sent a message to the King saying, "At this very moment we will level thine abode over the heads of all it containeth and over thine own,[128] if the least hurt or harm befal Alaeddin." So the Wazir went in and reported to the Sultan, "O King of the Age, thy commandment is about to seal the roll of our lives; and 'twere more suitable that thou pardon thy son-in-law lest there chance to us a sore mischance; for that the lieges do love him far more than they love us." Now the Sworder had already dispread the carpet of blood and, having seated Alaeddin thereon, had bandaged his eyes; moreover he had walked round him three several times awaiting the last orders of his lord, when the King looked out of the window and saw his subjects, who had suddenly attacked him, swarming up the walls intending to tear them down. So forthright he bade the Sworder stay his hand from Alaeddin and commanded the crier fare forth to the crowd and cry aloud that he had pardoned his son-in-law and received him back into favour. But when Alaeddin found himself free and saw the Sultan seated on his throne, he went up to him and said, "O my lord, inasmuch as thy Highness hath favoured me throughout my life, so of thy grace now deign let me know the how and the wherein I have sinned against thee?" "O traitor," cried the King, "unto this present I knew not any sin of thine;" then, turning to the Wazir he said, "Take him and make him look out at the window and after let him tell us where be his pavilion." And when the royal order was obeyed Alaeddin saw the place level as a well-trodden road, even as it had been ere the base of the building was laid, nor was there the faintest trace of edifice. Hereat he was astonished and perplexed knowing not what had occurred; but, when he returned to the presence, the King asked him, "What is it thou hast seen? Where is thy pavilion and where is my daughter, the core of my heart, my only child, than whom I have none other?" Alaeddin answered, "O King of the Age, I wot naught thereof nor aught of what hath befallen," and the Sultan rejoined, "Thou must know, O Alaeddin, I have pardoned thee only that thou go forth and look into this affair and enquire for me concerning my daughter; nor do thou ever show thyself in my presence except she be with thee; and, if thou bring her not, by the life of my head I will cut off the head of thee." The other replied, "To hear is to obey: only vouchsafe me a delay and respite of some forty days; after which, an I produce her not, strike off my head[129] and do with me whatso thou wishest." The Sultan said to Alaeddin, "Verily I have granted thee thy request, a delay of forty days; but think not thou canst fly from my hand, for I would bring thee back even if thou wert above the clouds instead of being only upon earth's surface." Replied Alaeddin, "O my lord the Sultan, as I said to thy Highness, an I fail to bring her within the term appointed, I will present myself for my head to be stricken off." Now when the folk and the lieges all saw Alaeddin at liberty, they rejoiced with joy exceeding and were delighted for his release; but the shame of his treatment and bashfulness before his friends and the envious exultation of his foes had bowed down Alaeddin's head; so he went forth a-wandering through the city ways and he was perplexed concerning his case and knew not what had befallen him. He lingered about the capital for two days, in saddest state, wotting not what to do in order to find his wife and his pavilion, and during this time sundry of the folk privily brought him meat and drink. When the two days were done he left the city to stray about the waste and open lands outlying the walls, without a notion as to whither he should wend; and he walked on aimlessly until the path led him beside a river where, of the stress of sorrow that overwhelmed him, he abandoned himself to despair and thought of casting himself into the water. Being, however, a good Moslem who professed the unity of the Godhead, he feared Allah in his soul; and, standing upon the margin he prepared to perform the Wuzu-ablution. But as he was baling up the water in his right hand and rubbing his fingers,[130] it so chanced that he also rubbed the Ring. Hereat its Marid appeared and said to him, "Adsum! thy thrall between thy hands is come: ask of me whatso thou wantest." Seeing the Marid, Alaeddin rejoiced with exceeding joy and cried,[131] "O Slave, I desire of thee that thou bring before me my pavilion and therein my wife, the Lady Badr al-Budur, together with all and everything it containeth." "O my lord," replied the Marid, "'tis right hard upon me that thou demandest a service whereto I may not avail: this matter dependeth upon the Slave of the Lamp nor dare I even attempt it." Alaeddin rejoined, "Forasmuch as the matter is beyond thy competence, I require it not of thee, but at least do thou take me up and set me down beside my pavilion in what land soever that may be." The Slave exclaimed, "Hearing and obeying, O my lord;" and, uplifting him high in air, within the space of an eye-glance set him down beside his pavilion in the land of Africa and upon a spot facing his wife's apartment. Now this was at fall of night yet one look enabled him to recognise his home; whereby his

cark and care were cleared away and he recovered trust in
Allah after cutting off all his hope to look upon his wife
once more. Then he fell to pondering the secret and mysterious favours of the Lord (glorified be His omnipotence!);
and how, after despair had mastered him the Ring had come
to gladden him, and how, when all his hopes were cut off,
Allah had deigned bless him with the services of its Slave.
So he rejoiced and his melancholy left him; then, as he
had passed four days without sleep for the excess of his
cark and care and sorrow and stress of thought, he drew
near his pavilion and slept under a tree hard by the building which (as we mentioned) had been set down amongst
the gardens outlying the city of Africa. He slumbered till
Morning showed her face and, when awakened by the warbling of the small birds, he arose and went down to the
bank of the river which flowed thereby into the city; and
here he again washed hands and face and after finished his
Wuzu-ablution. Then he prayed the dawn-prayer, and
when he had ended his orisons he returned and sat down
under the windows of the Princess's bower. Now the Lady
Badr al-Budur, of her exceeding sorrow for severance from
her husband and her sire the Sultan, and for the great
mishap which had happened to her from the Maghrabi, the
Magician, the Accursed, was wont to rise during the murk
preceding dawn and to sit in tears inasmuch as she could
not sleep o' nights, and had forsworn meat and drink. Her
favourite slave-girl would enter her chamber at the hour of
prayer-salutation in order to dress her; and this time, by
decree of Destiny, when she threw open the window to let
her lady comfort and console herself by looking upon the
trees and rills, and she herself peered out of the lattice,
she caught sight of her master sitting below, and informed
the Princess of this, saying, "O my lady! O my lady! here's
my lord Alaeddin seated at the foot of the wall." So her
mistress arose hurriedly and gazing from the casement saw
him; and her husband raising his head saw her; so she
saluted him and he saluted her, both being like to fly for
joy. Presently quoth she, "Up and come in to me by the pri-

vate postern, for now the Accursed is not here;" and she gave orders to the slave-girl who went down and opened for him. Then Alaeddin passed through it and was met by his wife, when they embraced and exchanged kisses with all delight until they wept for overjoy. After this they sat down and Alaeddin said to her, "O my lady, before all things 'tis my desire to ask thee a question. 'Twas my wont to place an old copper lamp in such a part of my pavilion, what became of that same?" When the Princess heard these words she sighed and cried, "O my dearling, 'twas that very Lamp which garred us fall into this calamity!" Alaeddin asked her, "How befel the affair?" and she answered by recounting to him all that passed, first and last, especially how they had given in exchange an old lamp for a new lamp, adding, "And next day we hardly saw one another at dawn before we found ourselves in this land, and he who deceived us and took the lamp by way of barter informed me that he had done the deed by might of his magic and by means of the Lamp; that he is a Moorman from Africa, and that we are now in his native country." When the Lady Badr al-Budur ceased speaking, Alaeddin resumed, "Tell me the intent of this Accursed in thy respect, also what he sayeth to thee and what be his will of thee?" She replied, "Every day he cometh to visit me once and no more: he would woo me to his love and he sueth that I take him to spouse in lieu of thee and that I forget thee and be consoled for the loss of thee. And he telleth me that the Sultan my sire hath cut off my husband's head, adding that thou, the son of pauper parents, wast by him enriched. And he sootheth me with talk, but he never seeth aught from me save weeping and wailing; nor hath he heard from me one sugar-sweet word." Quoth Alaeddin, "Tell me where he hath placed the Lamp an thou know anything thereof;" and quoth she, "He beareth it about on his body alway, nor is it possible that he leave it for a single hour; moreover once when he related what I have now recounted to thee, he brought it out of his breast-pocket and allowed me to look upon it." When Alaeddin heard these words, he joyed with exceeding joy and said, "O my lady, do thou lend ear to me. 'Tis my design to go from thee forthright and to return only after doffing this my dress; so wonder not when thou see me changed, but direct one of thy women to stand by the private postern alway and, whenever she espy me coming, at once to open. And now I will devise a device whereby to slay this damned loon." Herewith he arose and, issuing from the pavilion-door, walked till he met on the way a Fellah to whom he said, "O man, take my attire and give me thy garments." But the peasant refused so Alaeddin stripped him of his dress per-force[132] and donned it, leaving to the man his own rich gear by way of gift. Then he followed the highway leading to the neighbouring city and entering it went to the Per-fumers' Bazar where he bought of one some rarely potent Bhang,[133] the son of a minute, paying two dinars for two drachms thereof and he returned in disguise by the same road till he reached the pavilion. Here the slave-girl opened to him the private postern wherethrough he went in to the Lady Badr al-Budur. And said, "Hear me! I desire of thee that thou dress and dight thyself in thy best and thou cast off all outer show and semblance of care; also when the Accursed, the Maghrabi, shall visit thee, do thou receive him with a 'Welcome and fair welcome,' and meet him with smiling face and invite him to come and sup with thee. Moreover, let him note that thou hast forgotten Alaeddin thy beloved, likewise thy father; and that thou hast learned to love him with exceeding love, displaying to him all manner joy and pleasure. Then ask him for wine which must be red and pledge him to his secret in a signifi-cant draught; and, when thou hast given him two or three cups full and hast made him wax careless, then drop these drops into his cup and fill it up with wine: no sooner shall he drink of it than he will fall upon his back senseless as one dead." Hearing these words, the Princess exclaimed, " 'Tis exceedingly sore to me that I do such deed;[134] withal must I do it that we escape the defilement of this Accursed who tortured me by severance from thee and from my sire. Lawful and right therefore is the slaughter of this Accursed." Then Alaeddin ate and drank with his wife what hindered his hunger; then, rising without stay or delay, fared forth the pavilion. So the Lady Badr al-Budur summoned the tirewoman who robed and arrayed her in her finest raiment and adorned her and perfumed her; and, as she was thus, behold, the accursed Maghrabi entered. He joyed much seeing her in such case and yet more when she confronted him, contrary to her custom, with a laughing face; and his love-longing increased and his desire to have her. Then she took him and, seating him beside her, said, "O my dearling, do thou (an thou be willing) come to me this night and let us sup together. Sufficient to me hath been my sorrow for, were I to sit mourning through a thousand years or even two thousand, Alaeddin would not return to me from the tomb; and I depend upon thy say of yesterday, to wit, that my sire the Sultan slew him in his stress of sorrow for severance from me. Nor wonder thou an I have changed this day from what I was yesterday; and the reason thereof is I have determined upon taking thee to friend and playfellow in lieu of and succession to Alaeddin, for that now I have none other man but thyself. So I hope for thy presence this night, that we may sup together and we may carouse and drink somewhat of wine each with other; and especially 'tis my desire that thou cause me taste the wine of thy natal soil, the African land, because belike 'tis better than aught of the wine of China we drink: I have with me some wine but 'tis the growth of my country and I vehemently wish to taste the wine produced by thine." When the Maghrabi saw the love lavisht upon him by the Lady Badr al-Budur, and noted her change from the sorrowful, melancholy woman she was wont to be, he thought that she had cut off her hope of Alaeddin and he joyed exceedingly and said to her, "I hear and obey, O my lady, whatso thou wishest and all thou biddest. I have at home a jar of our country wine, which I have carefully kept and stored deep in earth for a space of eight years; and I will now fare and fill from it our need and will return to thee in all haste." But the Princess, that she might wheedle him the more and yet more, replied, "O my darling, go not thou, leaving me alone, but send one of the eunuchs to fill for us thereof and do thou remain sitting beside me, that I may find in thee my consolation." He rejoined, "O my lady, none wotteth where the jar be buried save myself nor will I tarry from thee." So saying, the Moorman went out and after a short time he brought back as much wine as they wanted; whereupon quoth the Princess to him, "Thou hast been at pains and trouble to serve me and I have suffered for thy sake, O my beloved." Quoth he, "On no wise, O eyes of me; I hold myself enhonoured by thy service." Then the Lady Badr al-Budur sat with him at table, and the twain fell to eating and presently the Princess expressed a wish to drink, when the handmaid filled her a cup forthright and then crowned another for the Maroccan. So she drank to his long life and his secret wishes and he also drank to her life; then the Princess, who was unique in eloquence and delicacy of speech, fell to making a cup-companion of him and beguiled him by addressing him in the sweetest terms of hidden meaning. This was done only that he might become more madly enamoured of her, but the Maghrabi thought that it resulted from her true inclination for him; nor knew that it was a snare set up to slay him. So his longing for her increased, and he was dying of love for her when he saw her address him in such tenderness of words and thoughts, and his head began to swim and all the world seemed as nothing in his eyes. But when they came to the last of the supper and the wine had mastered his brains and the Princess saw this in him, she said, "With us there be a custom throughout our country, but I know not an it be the usage of yours or not." The Moorman replied, "And what may that be?" So she said to him, "At the end of supper each lover in turn taketh the cup of the beloved and drinketh it off;" and at once she crowned one with wine and bade the handmaid carry to him her cup wherein the drink was blended with the Bhang. Now she had taught the slave-girl what to do and all the hand-maids and eunuchs in the pavilion longed for the Sorcerer's slaughter and in that matter were one with the Princess. Accordingly the damsel handed him the cup and he, when he heard her words and saw her drinking from his cup and passing hers to him and noted all that show of love, fancied himself Iskandar, Lord of the Two Horns. Then said she to him, the while swaying gracefully to either side and putting her hand within his hand, "O my life, here is thy cup with me and my cup with thee, and on this wise[135] do lovers drink from each other's cups." Then she bussed the brim and drained it to the dregs and again she kissed its lip and offered it to him. Thereat he flew for joy and meaning to do the like, raised her cup to his mouth and drank off the whole contents, without considering whether there was therein aught harmful or not. And forthright he rolled upon his back in death-like condition and the cup dropped from his grasp, whereupon the Lady Badr al-Budur and the slave-girls ran hurriedly and opened the pavilion door to their lord Alaeddin who, disguised as a Fellah, entered therein. He went up to the apartment of his wife, whom he found still sitting at table; and facing her lay the Maghrabi as one slaughtered; so he at once drew near to her and kissed her and thanked her for this. Then rejoicing with joy exceeding he turned to her and said, "Do thou with thy handmaids betake thyself to the inner-rooms and leave me alone for the present that I may take counsel touching mine affair." The Princess hesitated not but went away at once, she and her women; then Alaeddin arose and, after locking the door upon them, walked up to the Moorman and put forth his hand to his breast-pocket and thence drew the Lamp; after which he unsheathed his sword and slew the villain.[136] Presently he rubbed the Lamp and the Marid-slave appeared and said, "Adsum, O my lord, what is it thou wantest?" "I desire of thee," said Alaeddin, "that thou take up my pavilion from this country and transport it to the land of China and there set it down upon the site

where it was whilome, fronting the palace of the Sultan."
The Marid replied, "Hearing and obeying, O my lord." Then
Alaeddin went and sat down with his wife and throwing his
arms round her neck kissed her and she kissed him, and
they sat in converse, what while the Jinni transported the
pavilion and all therein to the place appointed. Presently
Alaeddin bade the handmaids spread the table before him
and he and the Lady Badr al-Budur took seat thereat and
fell to eating and drinking, in all joy and gladness, till they
had their sufficiency when, removing to the chamber of
wine and cup-converse, they sat there and caroused in fair
companionship and each kissed other with all love-liesse.
The time had been long and longsome since they enjoyed
aught of pleasure; so they ceased not doing thus until the
wine-sun arose in their heads and sleep gat hold of them,
at which time they went to their bed in all ease and comfort. Early on the next morning Alaeddin woke and awoke
his wife, and the slave-girls came in and donned her dress
and prepared her and adorned her whilst her husband arrayed himself in his costliest raiment and the twain were
ready to fly for joy at reunion after parting. Moreover the
Princess was especially joyous and gladsome because on
that day she expected to see her beloved father. Such was
the case of Alaeddin and the Lady Badr al-Budur; but as
regards the Sultan, after he drove away his son-in-law he
never ceased to sorrow for the loss of his daughter; and
every hour of every day he would sit and weep for her as
women weep, because she was his only child and he had
none other to take to heart. And as he shook off sleep,
morning after morning, he would hasten to the window
and throw it open and peer in the direction where formerly stood Alaeddin's pavilion and pour forth tears until
his eyes were dried up and their lids were ulcered. Now on
that day he arose at dawn and, according to his custom,
looked out when, lo and behold! he saw before him an edifice; so he rubbed his eyes and considered it curiously
when he became certified that it was the pavilion of his
son-in-law. So he called for a horse[137] without let or delay;

and as soon as his beast was saddled, he mounted and made for the place; and Alaeddin, when he saw his father-in-law approaching, went down and met him half way: then, taking his hand, aided him to step upstairs to the apartment of his daughter. And the Princess, being as earnestly desirous to see her sire, descended and greeted him at the door of the staircase fronting the ground-floor hall. Thereupon the King folded her in his arms and kissed her, shedding tears of joy; and she did likewise till at last Alaeddin led them to the upper saloon where they took seats and the Sultan fell to asking her case and what had betided her. The Lady Badr al-Budur began to inform the Sultan of all which had befallen her, saying, "O my father, I recovered not life save yesterday when I saw my husband, and he it was who freed me from the thraldom of that Maghrabi, that Magician, that Accursed, than whom I believe there be none viler on the face of earth; and, but for my beloved, I had never escaped him nor hadst thou seen me during the rest of my days. But mighty sadness and sorrow gat about me, O my father, not only for losing thee but also for the loss of a husband, under whose kindness I shall be all the length of my life, seeing that he freed me from that fulsome sorcerer." Then the Princess began repeating to her sire every thing that happened to her, and relating to him how the Moorman had tricked her in the guise of a lamp-seller who offered in exchange new for old; how she had given him the Lamp whose worth she knew not, and how she had bartered it away only to laugh at the lampman's folly. "And next morning, O my father," she continued, "we found ourselves and whatso the pavilion contained in Africa-land, till such time as my husband came to us and devised a device whereby we escaped: and, had it not been for Alaeddin's hastening to our aid, the Accursed was determined to enjoy me perforce." Then she told him of the Bhang-drops administered in wine to the African and concluded, "Then my husband returned to me and how I know not, but we were shifted from Africa-land to this place." Alaeddin in his turn recounted how, finding the wizard dead drunken, he had sent away his wife and her women from the polluted place into the inner apartments; how he had taken the Lamp from the Sorcerer's breast-pocket whereto he was directed by his wife; how he had slaughtered the villain and, finally how, making use of the Lamp, he had summoned its Slave and ordered him to transport the pavilion back to its proper site, ending his tale with, "And, if thy Highness have any doubt anent my words, arise with me and look upon the accursed Magician." The King did accordingly and, having considered the Moorman, bade the carcase be carried away forthright and burned and its ashes scattered in air. Then he took to embracing Alaeddin and kissing him said, "Pardon me, O my son, for that I was about to destroy thy life through the foul deeds of this damned enchanter, who cast thee into such pit of peril; and I may be excused, O my child, for what I did by thee, because I found myself forlorn of my daughter; my only one, who to me is dearer than my very kingdom. Thou knowest how the hearts of parents yearn unto their offspring, especially when like myself they have but one and none other to love." And on this wise the Sultan took to excusing himself and kissing his son-in-law. Alaeddin said to the Sultan, "O King of the Time, thou didst naught to me contrary to Holy Law, and I also sinned not against thee; but all the trouble came from that Maghrabi, the impure, the Magician." Thereupon the Sultan bade the city be decorated and they obeyed him and held high feast and festivities. He also commanded the crier to cry about the streets saying, "This day is a mighty great fête, wherein public rejoicings must be held throughout the realm, for a full month of thirty days, in honour of the Lady Badr al-Budur and her husband Alaeddin's return to their home." On this wise befel it with Alaeddin and the Maghrabi; but withal the King's son-in-law escaped not wholly from the Accursed, albeit the body had been burnt and the ashes scattered in air. For the villain had a brother yet more villainous than himself, and a greater adept in necromancy, geomancy and astromancy; and, even as the old saw saith "A bean and 'twas split;"[138] so each one dwelt in his own quarter of the globe that he might fill it with his sorcery, his fraud and his treason.[139] Now, one day of the days it fortuned that the Moorman's brother would learn how it fared with him, so he brought out his sandboard and dotted it and produced the figures which, when he had considered and carefully studied them, gave him to know that the man he sought was dead and housed in the tomb. So he grieved and was certified of his decease, but he dotted a second time seeking to learn the manner of the death and where it had taken place; so he found that the site was the China-land and that the mode was the foulest of slaughter; furthermore, that he who did him die was a young man Alaeddin hight. Seeing this he straightway arose and equipped himself for wayfare; then he set out and cut across the wilds and wolds and heights for the space of many a month until he reached China and the capital of the Sultan wherein was the slayer of his brother. He alighted at the so-called Strangers' Khan and, hiring himself a cell, took rest therein for a while; then he fared forth and wandered about the highways that he might discern some path which would aid him unto the winning of his ill-minded wish, to wit, of wreaking upon Alaeddin blood-revenge[140] for his brother. Presently he entered a coffee-house, a fine building which stood in the market-place and which collected a throng of folk to play, some at the Mankalah,[141] others at the backgammon[142] and others at the chess and what not else. There he sat down and listened to those seated beside him and they chanced to be conversing about an ancient dame and a holy, by name Fatimah, who dwelt alway at her devotions in a hermitage without the town, and this she never entered save only two days each month. They mentioned also that she had performed many saintly miracles which, when the Maghrabi, the Necromancer, heard he said in himself, "Now have I found that which I sought: Inshallah—God willing—by means of this crone will I win to my wish."

The Necromancer went up to the folk who were talking of the miracles performed by the devout old woman and said to one of them, "O my uncle, I heard you all chatting about the prodigies of a certain saintess named Fatimah: who is she and where may be her abode?" "Marvellous!" exclaimed the man: "How canst thou be in our city and yet never have heard about the miracles of the Lady Fatimah? Evidently, O thou poor fellow, thou art a foreigner, since the fastings of this devotee and her asceticism in worldly matters and the beauties of her piety never came to thine ears." The Moorman rejoined, " 'Tis true, O my lord: yes, I am a stranger and came to this your city only yesternight; and I hope thou wilt inform me concerning the saintly miracles of this virtuous woman and where may be her wone, for that I have fallen into a calamity, and 'tis my wish to visit her and crave her prayers, so haply Allah (to whom be honour and glory!) will, through her blessings, deliver me from mine evil." Hereat the man recounted to him the marvels of Fatimah the Devotee and her piety and the beauties of her worship; then, taking him by the hand went with him without the city and showed him the way to her abode, a cavern upon a hillock's head. The Necromancer acknowledged his kindness in many words and, thanking him for his good offices, returned to his cell in the caravanserai. Now by the fiat of Fate on the very next day Fatimah came down to the city, and the Maghrabi, the Necromancer, happened to leave his hostelry a-morn, when he saw the folk swarming and crowding; wherefore he went up to discover what was to do and found the Devotee standing amiddlemost the throng, and all who suffered from pain or sickness flocked to her soliciting a blessing and praying for her prayers; and each and every she touched became whole of his illness.[143] The Maroccan, the Necromancer, followed her about until she returned to her antre; then, awaiting till the evening evened, he arose and repaired to a vintner's store where he drank a cup of wine. After this he fared forth the city and finding the Devotee's cavern, entered it and saw her lying prostrate[144] with her back

upon a strip of matting. So he came forward and mounted
upon her belly; then he drew his dagger and shouted at
her; and, when she awoke and opened her eyes, she espied
a Moorish man with an unsheathed poniard sitting upon
her middle as though about to kill her. She was troubled
and sore terrified, but he said to her, "Hearken! an thou cry
out or utter a word I will slay thee at this very moment:
arise now and do all I bid thee." Then he sware to her an
oath that if she obeyed his orders, whatever they might be,
he would not do her die. So saying, he rose up from off her
and Fatimah also arose, when he said to her, "Give me thy
gear and take thou my habit;" whereupon she gave him her
clothing and head-fillets, her face-kerchief and her mantilla. Then quoth he, " 'Tis also requisite that thou anoint
me with somewhat shall make the colour of my face like
unto thine." Accordingly she went into the inner cavern
and, bringing out a gallipot of ointment, spread somewhat
thereof upon her palm and with it besmeared his face until
its hue favoured her own; then she gave him her staff[145]
and, showing him how to walk and what to do when he entered the city, hung her rosary around his neck. Lastly she
handed to him a mirror and said, "Now look! Thou differest
from me in naught;" and he saw himself Fatimah's counterpart as though she had never gone or come.[146] But after
obtaining his every object he falsed his oath and asked for
a cord which she brought to him; then he seized her and
strangled her in the cavern; and presently, when she was
dead, haled the corpse outside and threw it into a pit hard
by and went back to sleep in her cavern; and, when broke
the day, he rose and repairing to the town took his stand
under the walls of Alaeddin's pavilion. Hereupon flocked
the folk about him, all being certified that he was Fatimah
the Devotee and he fell to doing whatso she was wont to
do: he laid hands on these in pain and recited for those a
chapter of the Koran and made orisons for a third. Presently
the thronging of the folk and the clamouring of the crowd
were heard by the Lady Badr al-Budur, who said to her

handmaidens, "Look what is to do and what be the cause of this turmoil!" Thereupon the Agha of the eunuchry fared forth to see what might be the matter and presently returning said, "O my lady, this clamour is caused by the Lady Fatimah, and if thou be pleased to command, I will bring her to thee; so shalt thou gain through her a blessing." The Princess answered, "Go bring her, for since many a day I am always hearing of her miracles and her virtues, and I do long to see her and get a blessing by her intervention, for the folk recount her manifestations in many cases of difficulty." The Agha went forth and brought in the Maroccan, the Necromancer, habited in Fatimah's clothing; and, when the wizard stood before the Lady Badr al-Budur, he began at first sight to bless her with a string of prayers; nor did any one of those present doubt at all but that he was the Devotee herself. The Princess arose and salam'd to him; then seating him beside her, said, "O my Lady Fatimah, 'tis my desire that thou abide with me alway, so might I be blessed through thee, and also learn of thee the paths[147] of worship and piety and follow thine example making for salvation." Now all this was a foul deceit of the accursed African and he designed furthermore to complete his guile, so he continued, "O my Lady, I am a poor woman and a religious that dwelleth in the desert; and the like of me deserveth not to abide in the palaces of the kings." But the Princess replied, "Have no care whatever, O my Lady Fatimah; I will set apart for thee an apartment of my pavilion, that thou mayest worship therein and none shall ever come to trouble thee; also thou shalt avail to worship Allah in my place better than in thy cavern." The Maroccan rejoined, "Hearkening and obedience, O my lady; I will not oppose thine order for that the commands of the children of the kings may not be gainsaid nor renounced. Only I hope of thee that my eating and my drinking and sitting may be within my own chamber which shall be kept wholly private; nor do I require or desire the delicacies of diet, but do thou favour me by sending thy handmaid every day with a bit of bread and a sup of water;[148] and, when I feel fain of food, let me eat by myself in my own room." Now the Accursed hereby purposed to avert the danger of haply raising his face-kerchief at meal times, when his intent might be baffled by his beard and mustachios discovering him to be a man. The Princess replied, "O my Lady Fatimah, be of good heart; naught shall happen save what thou wishest. But now arise and let me show thee the apartment in the palace which I would prepare for thy sojourn with us." The Lady Badr al-Budur arose and taking the Necromancer who had disguised himself as the Devotee, ushered him in to the place which she had kindly promised him for a home and said, "O my Lady Fatimah, here thou shalt dwell with every comfort about thee and in all privacy and repose; and the place shall be named after thy name;" whereupon the Maghrabi acknowledged her kindness and prayed for her. Then the Princess showed him the jalousies and the jewelled Kiosque with its four and twenty windows[149] and said to him, "What thinkest thou, O my Lady Fatimah, of this marvellous pavilion?" The Moorman replied, "By Allah, O my daughter, 'tis indeed passing fine and wondrous exceedingly; nor do I deem that its fellow is to be found in the whole universe; but alas for the lack of one thing which would enhance its beauty and decoration!" The Princess asked her, "O my Lady Fatimah, what lacketh it and what be this thing would add to its adornment? Tell me thereof, inasmuch as I was wont to believe it wholly perfect." The Maroccan answered, "O my lady, all it wanteth is that there be hanging from the middle of the dome the egg of a fowl called the Rukh; and, were this done, the pavilion would lack its peer all the world over." The Princess asked, "What be this bird and where can we find her egg?" and the Maroccan answered, "O my lady, the Rukh[150] is indeed a giant fowl which carrieth off camels and elephants in her pounces and flieth away with them, such is her stature and strength; also this fowl is mostly found in Mount Kaf; and the architect who built this pavilion is able to bring thee one of her eggs." They then left such talk as it was the hour for the noon-day meal and, when the handmaid had spread the table, the Lady Badr al-Budur sent down to invite the Accursed African to eat with her. But he accepted not and for a reason he would on no wise consent; nay, he rose and retired to the room which the Princess had assigned to him and whither the slave-girls carried his dinner. Now when evening evened, Alaeddin returned from the chase and met his wife who salam'd to him and he clasped her to his bosom and kissed her. Presently, looking at her face he saw thereon a shade of sadness and he noted that contrary to her custom, she did not laugh; so he asked her, "What hath betided thee, O my dearling? tell me, hath aught happened to trouble thy thoughts?" "Nothing whatever," answered she, "but, O my beloved, I fancied that our pavilion lacked naught at all; however, O eyes of me, Alaeddin, were the dome of the upper story hung with an egg of the fowl called Rukh, there would be naught like it in the universe." Her husband rejoined, "And for this trifle thou art saddened when 'tis the easiest of all matters to me! So cheer thyself; and, whatever thou wantest, 'tis enough thou inform me thereof, and I will bring it from the abysses of the earth in the quickest time and at the earliest hour." Alaeddin, after refreshing the spirits of his Princess by promising her all she could desire, repaired straightway to his chamber and taking the Lamp[151] rubbed it, when the Marid appeared without let or delay saying, "Ask whatso thou wantest." Said the other, "I desire thee to fetch me an egg of the bird Rukh and do thou hang it to the dome-crown of this my pavilion." But when the Marid heard these words, his face waxed fierce and he shouted with a mighty loud voice and a frightful, and cried, "O denier of kindly deeds, sufficeth it not for thee that I and all the Slaves of the Lamp are ever at thy service, but thou must also require me to bring thee our Liege Lady[152] for thy pleasure, and hang her up at thy pavilion-dome for the enjoyment of thee and thy wife! Now by Allah, ye deserve, thou and she, that I reduce you to ashes this very moment and scatter you upon the air; but, inasmuch as ye twain be ignorant of this matter, unknowing its inner from its outer significance, I will pardon you for indeed ye are but innocents. The offence cometh from that accursed Necromancer, brother to the Maghrabi, the Magician, who abideth here representing himself to be Fatimah, the Devotee, after assuming her dress and belongings and murthering her in the cavern: indeed he came hither seeking to slay thee by way of blood-revenge for his brother; and 'tis he who taught thy wife to require this matter of me."[153] So saying the Marid evanished. But when Alaeddin heard these words, his wits fled his head and his joints trembled at the Marid's terrible shout; but he empowered his purpose and, arising forthright issued from his chamber and went into his wife's. There he affected an ache of head, for that he knew how famous was Fatimah for the art and mystery of healing all such pains; and, when the Lady Badr al-Budur saw him sitting hand to head and complaining of unease, she asked him the cause and he answered, "I know of none other save that my head acheth exceedingly." Hereupon she straightway bade summon Fatimah that the Devotee might impose her hand upon his head;[154] and Alaeddin asked her, "Who may this Fatimah be?" So she informed him that it was Fatimah the Devotee to whom she had given a home in the pavilion. Meanwhile the slave-girls had fared forth and summoned the Maghrabi, and when the Accursed made act of presence, Alaeddin rose up to him, and, acting like one who knew naught of his purpose, salam'd to him as though he had been the real Fatimah and, kissing the hem of his sleeve, welcomed him and entreated him with honour and said, "O my Lady Fatimah, I hope thou wilt bless me with a boon, for well I wot thy practice in the healing of pains: I have gotten a mighty ache in my head." The Moorman, the Accursed, could hardly believe that he heard such words, this being all that he desired. The Necromancer, habited as Fatimah the Devotee, came up to Alaeddin that he might place hand upon his head and heal his ache; so he imposed one hand and, putting forth the other under his gown, drew a dagger wherewith to slay him. But Alaeddin watched him and, taking patience till he had wholly unsheathed the weapon, seized him with a forceful grip; and, wrenching the dagger from his grasp plunged it deep into his heart. When the Lady Badr al-Budur saw him do on this wise, she shrieked and cried out, "What hath this virtuous and holy woman done that thou hast charged thy neck with the heavy burthen of her blood shed wrongfully? Hast thou no fear of Allah that thou killest Fatimah, this saintly woman, whose miracles are far-famed?" "No," replied Alaeddin, "I have not killed Fatimah. I have slain only Fatimah's slayer, he that is the brother of the Maghrabi, the Accursed, the Magician, who carried thee off by his black art and transported my pavilion to the Africaland; and this damnable brother of his came to our city and wrought these wiles, murthering Fatimah and assuming her habit, only that he might avenge upon me his brother's blood; and he also 'twas who taught thee to require of me a Rukh's egg, that my death might result from such requirement. But, an thou doubt my speech, come forwards and consider the person I have slain." Thereupon Alaeddin drew aside the Moorman's face-kerchief and the Lady Badr al-Budur saw the semblance of a man with a full beard that well-nigh covered his features. She at once knew the truth and said to her husband, "O my beloved, twice have I cast thee into death-risk!" but he rejoined, "No harm in that, O my lady, by the blessing of your loving eyes: I accept with all joy all things thou bringest me." The Princess, hearing these words, hastened to fold him in her arms and kissed him saying, "O my dearling, all this is for my love to thee and I knew naught thereof; but indeed I do not deem lightly of thine affection." So Alaeddin kissed her and strained her to his breast; and the love between them waxed but greater. At that moment the Sultan appeared and they told him all that had happened, showing him the corpse of the Maghrabi, the Necromancer, when the King commanded the body to be burned and the ashes scattered on air, even as had befallen the Wizard's brother. And Alaeddin abode with his wife, the Lady Badr al-Budur, in all pleasure and joyance of life and thenceforward escaped every danger; and, after a while, when the Sultan deceased, his son-in-law was seated upon the throne of the Kingdom; and he commanded and dealt justice to the lieges so that all the folk loved him and he lived with his wife in all solace and happiness until there came to him the Destroyer of delights and the Severer of societies.[155] And a tale is also told about

ALI BABA AND THE

FORTY THIEVES. [1]

In days of yore and in times and tides long gone before
there dwelt in a certain town of Persia two brothers one
named Kasim and the other 'Ali Baba, who at their father's
demise had divided the little wealth he had left to them
with equitable division, and had lost no time in wasting
and spending it all. The elder, however, presently took
to himself a wife, the daughter of an opulent merchant;
so that when his father-in-law fared to the mercy of Almighty Allah, he became owner of a large shop filled with
rare goods and costly wares and of a storehouse stocked
with precious stuffs; likewise of much gold that was buried
in the ground. Thus was he known throughout the city as a
substantial man. But the woman whom Ali Baba had married was poor and needy; they lived, therefore, in a mean
hovel and Ali Baba eked out a scanty livelihood by the sale
of fuel which he daily collected in the jungle[2] and carried
about the town to the Bazar upon his three asses. Now it
chanced one day that Ali Baba had cut dead branches and
dry fuel sufficient for his need, and had placed the load
upon his beasts when suddenly he espied a dust-cloud
spireing high in air to his right and moving rapidly towards

him; and when he closely considered it he descried a troop of horsemen riding on amain and about to reach him. At this sight he was sore alarmed, and fearing lest perchance they were a band of bandits who would slay him and drive off his donkeys, in his affright he began to run; but forasmuch as they were near hand and he could not escape from out the forest, he drove his animals laden with the fuel into a bye-way of the bushes and swarmed up a thick trunk of a huge tree to hide himself therein; and he sat upon a branch whence he could descry everything beneath him whilst none below could catch a glimpse of him above; and that tree grew close beside a rock which towered high abovehead. The horsemen, young, active, and doughty riders, came close up to the rock-face and all dismounted; whereat Ali Baba took good note of them and soon he was fully persuaded by their mien and demeanour that they were a troop of highwaymen who, having fallen upon a caravan had despoiled it and carried off the spoil and brought their booty to this place with intent of concealing it safely in some cache. Moreover he observed that they were forty in number. Ali Baba saw the robbers, as soon as they came under the tree, each unbridle his horse and hobble it; then all took off their saddle-bags which proved to be full of gold and silver. The man who seemed to be the captain presently pushed forwards, load on shoulder, through thorns and thickets, till he came up to a certain spot where he uttered these strange words, "Open, O Simsim!"[3] and forthwith appeared a wide doorway in the face of the rock. The robbers went in and last of all their Chief and then the portal shut of itself. Long while they stayed within the cave whilst Ali Baba was constrained to abide perched upon the tree, reflecting that if he came down peradventure the band might issue forth that very moment and seize him and slay him. At last he had determined to mount one of the horses and driving on his asses to return townwards, when suddenly the portal flew open. The robber-chief was first to issue forth; then, standing at the entrance, he saw and counted his men as they came out, and lastly he spake the magical words, "Shut, O Simsim!" whereat the door closed of itself. When all had passed muster and review, each slung on his saddle-bags and bridled his own horse and as soon as ready they rode off, led by the leader, in the direction whence they came. Ali Baba remained still perched on the tree and watched their departure; nor would he descend until what time they were clean gone out of sight, lest perchance one of them return and look around and descry him. Then he thought within himself, "I too will try the virtue of those magical words and see if at my bidding the door will open and close." So he called out aloud, "Open, O Simsim!" And no sooner had he spoken than straightway the portal flew open and he entered within. He saw a large cavern and a vaulted, in height equalling the stature of a full-grown man and it was hewn in the live stone and lighted up with light that came through air-holes and bulls-eyes in the upper surface of the rock which formed the roof. He had expected to find naught save outer gloom in this robbers' den, and he was surprised to see the whole room filled with bales of all manner stuffs, and heaped up from sole to ceiling with camel-loads of silks and brocades and embroidered cloths and mounds on mounds of vari-coloured carpetings; besides which he espied coins golden and silvern without measure or account, some piled upon the ground and others bound in leathern bags and sacks. Seeing these goods and moneys in such abundance, Ali Baba determined in his mind that not during a few years only but for many generations thieves must have stored their gains and spoils in this place. When he stood within the cave, its door had closed upon him, yet he was not dismayed since he had kept in memory the magical words; and he took no heed of the precious stuffs around him, but applied himself only and wholly to the sacks of Ashrafis. Of these he carried out as many as he judged sufficient burthen for the beasts; then he loaded them upon his animals, and covered his plunder with sticks and fuel, so none might discern the bags, but might think that he was carrying home his usual ware.

Lastly he called out, "Shut, O Simsim!" and forthwith the door closed, for the spell so wrought that whensoever any entered the cave, its portal shut of itself behind him; and, as he issued therefrom, the same would neither open nor close again till he had pronounced the words, "Shut, O Simsim!" Presently, having laden his asses Ali Baba urged them before him with all speed to the city and reaching home he drove them into the yard; and, shutting close the outer door, took down first the sticks and fuel and after the bags of gold which he carried in to his wife. She felt them and finding them full of coin suspected that Ali Baba had been robbing and fell to berating and blaming him for that he should do so ill a thing. Quoth Ali Baba to his wife:— "Indeed I am no robber and rather do thou rejoice with me at our good fortune." Hereupon he told her of his adventure and began to pour the gold from the bags in heaps before her, and her sight was dazzled by the sheen and her heart delighted at his recital and adventures. Then she began counting the gold, whereat quoth Ali Baba, "O silly woman, how long wilt thou continue turning over the coin? now let me dig a hole wherein to hide this treasure that none may know its secret." Quoth she, "Right is thy rede! still would I weigh the moneys and have some inkling of their amount;" and he replied, "As thou pleasest, but see thou tell no man." So she went off in haste to Kasim's home to borrow weights and scales wherewith she might balance the Ashrafis and make some reckoning of their value; and when she could not find Kasim she said to his wife, "Lend me, I pray thee, thy scales for a moment." Replied her sister-in-law,[4] "Hast thou need of the bigger balance or the smaller?" and the other rejoined, "I need not the large scales, give me the little;" and her sister-in-law cried, "Stay here a moment whilst I look about and find thy want." With this pretext Kasim's wife went aside and secretly smeared wax and suet over the pan of the balance, that she might know what thing it was Ali Baba's wife would weigh, for she made sure that whatso it be some bit thereof would stick to the wax and fat. So the woman took this opportunity to satisfy her curiosity, and Ali Baba's wife suspecting naught thereof carried home the scales and began to weigh the gold, whilst Ali Baba ceased not digging; and, when the money was weighed, they twain stowed it into the hole which they carefully filled up with earth. Then the good wife took back the scales to her kinswoman, all unknowing that an Ashrafi had adhered to the cup of the scales; but when Kasim's wife espied the gold coin she fumed with envy and wrath, saying to herself, "So ho! they borrowed my balance to weigh out Ashrafis?" and she marvelled greatly whence so poor a man as Ali Baba had gotten such store of wealth that he should be obliged to weigh it with a pair of scales. Now after long pondering the matter, when her husband returned home at eventide, she said to him, "O man, thou deemest thyself a wight of wealth and substance, but lo, thy brother Ali Baba is an Emir by the side of thee and richer far than thou art. He hath such heaps of gold that he must needs weigh his moneys with scales, whilst thou, forsooth, art satisfied to count thy coin." "Whence knowest thou this?" asked Kasim, and in answer his wife related all anent the pair of scales and how she found an Ashrafi stuck to them, and shewed him the gold coin which bore the mark and superscription of some ancient king. No sleep had Kasim all that night by reason of his envy and jealousy and covetise; and next morning he rose betimes and going to Ali Baba said, "O my brother, to all appearance thou art poor and needy; but in effect thou hast a store of wealth so abundant that perforce thou must weigh thy gold with scales." Quoth Ali Baba, "What is this thou sayest? I understand thee not; make clear thy purport;" and quoth Kasim with ready rage, "Feign not that thou art ignorant of what I say and think not to deceive me." Then showing him the Ashrafi he cried, "Thousands of gold coins such as these thou hast put by; and meanwhile my wife found this one stuck to the cup of the scales." Then Ali Baba understood how both Kasim and his wife knew that he had store of Ashrafis, and said in his mind that it would not avail him to keep the matter hidden, but would rather cause ill-will and mischief; and thus he was induced to tell his brother every whit concerning the bandits[5] and also of the treasure trove in the cave. When he had heard the story, Kasim exclaimed, "I would fain learn of thee the certainty of the place where thou foundest the moneys; also the magical words whereby the door opened and closed; and I forewarn thee an thou tell me not the whole truth, I will give notice of those Ashrafis to the Wali;[6] then shalt thou forfeit all thy wealth and be disgraced and thrown into gaol." Thereupon Ali Baba told him his tale not forgetting the magical words; and Kasim who kept careful heed of all these matters next day set out, driving ten mules he had hired, and readily found the place which Ali Baba had described to him. And when he came to the aforesaid rock and to the tree whereon Ali Baba had hidden himself, and he had made sure of the door he cried in great joy, "Open, O Simsim!" The portal yawned wide at once and Kasim went within and saw the piles of jewels and treasures lying ranged all around; and, as soon as he stood amongst them the door shut after him as wont to do. He walked about in ecstasy marvelling at the treasures, and when weary of admiration he gathered together bags of Ashrafis, a sufficient load for his ten mules, and placed them by the entrance in readiness to be carried outside and set upon the beasts. But by the will of Allah Almighty he had clean forgotten the cabalistic words and cried out, "Open, O Barley!" whereat the door refused to move. Astonished and confused beyond measure he named the names of all manner of grains save sesame, which had slipped from his memory as though he had never heard the word; whereat in his dire distress he heeded not the Ashrafis that lay heaped at the entrance and paced to and fro, backwards and forwards, within the cave sorely puzzled and perplexed. The wealth whose sight had erewhile filled his heart with joy and gladness was now the cause of bitter grief and sadness. It came to pass that at noontide the robbers, returning by that way, saw from afar some mules standing beside the entrance and much they marvelled at what had brought the beasts to that place; for, inasmuch as Kasim by mischance had failed to tether or hobble them, they had strayed about the jungle and were browsing hither and thither. However, the thieves paid scant regard to the estrays nor cared they to secure them, but only wondered by what means they had wandered so far from the town. Then, reaching the cave the Captain and his troop dismounted and going up to the door repeated the formula and at once it flew open. Now Kasim had heard from within the cave the horse-hooves drawing nigh and yet nigher; and he fell down to the ground in a fit of fear never doubting that it was the clatter of the banditti who would slaughter him without fail. Howbeit he presently took heart of grace and at the moment when the door flew open he rushed out hoping to make good his escape. But the unhappy ran full tilt against the Captain who stood in front of the band, and felled him to the ground; whereupon a robber standing near his chief at once bared his brand and with one cut clave Kasim clean in twain. Thereupon the robbers rushed into the cavern, and put back as they were before the bags of Ashrafis which Kasim had heaped up at the doorway ready for taking away; nor recked they aught of those which Ali Baba had removed, so dazed and amazed were they to discover by what means the strange man had effected an entrance. All knew that it was not possible for any to drop through the skylights so tall and steep was the rock's face, withal slippery of ascent; and also that none could enter by the portal unless he knew the magical words whereby to open it. However they presently quartered the dead body of Kasim and hung it to the door within the cavern, two parts to the right jamb and as many to the left[7] that the sight might be a warning of approaching doom for all who dared enter the cave. Then coming out they closed the hoard door and rode away upon their wonted work. Now when night fell and Kasim came not home, his wife waxed uneasy in mind and running round to Ali Baba said, "O my brother, Kasim hath not returned: thou knowest whither he went, and sore I fear me some misfortune hath betided him." Ali Baba also divined that a mishap had happened to prevent his return; not the less, however, he strove to comfort his sister-in-law with words of cheer and said, "O wife of my brother, Kasim haply exerciseth discretion and, avoiding the city, cometh by a roundabout road and will be here anon. This, I do believe, is the reason why he tarrieth." Thereupon comforted in spirit Kasim's wife fared homewards and sat awaiting her husband's return; but when half the night was spent and still he came not, she was as one distraught. She feared to cry aloud for her grief, lest haply the neighbours hearing her should come and learn the secret; so she wept in silence and upbraiding herself fell to thinking, "Wherefore did I disclose this secret to him and beget envy and jealousy of Ali Baba? this be the fruit thereof and hence the disaster that hath come down upon me." She spent the rest of the night in bitter tears and early on the morrow hied in hottest hurry to Ali Baba and prayed that he would go forth in quest of his brother; so he strove to console her and straightway set out with his asses for the forest. Presently, reaching the rock he wondered to see stains of blood freshly shed and not finding his brother or the ten mules he forefelt a calamity from so evil a sign. He then went to the door and saying, "Open, O Simsim!" he pushed in and saw the dead body of Kasim, two parts hanging to the right, and the rest to the left of the entrance. Albeit he was affrighted beyond measure of affright he wrapped the quarters in two cloths and laid them upon one of his asses, hiding them carefully with sticks and fuel that none might see them. Then he placed the bags of gold upon the two other animals and likewise covered them most carefully; and, when all was made ready he closed the cave-door with the magical words, and set him forth wending homewards with all ward and watchfulness. The asses with the load of Ashrafis he made over to his wife and bade her bury the bags with diligence; but he told her not the condition in which he had come upon his brother Kasim. Then he went with the other ass, to wit, the beast whereon was laid the corpse to the widow's house and knocked gently at the door. Now Kasim had a slave-girl shrewd and sharp-witted, Morgiana hight. She as softly undid the bolt and admitted Ali Baba and the ass into the courtyard of the house, when he let down the body from the beast's back and said, "O Morgiana,[8] haste thee and make thee ready to perform the rites for the burial of thy lord: I now go to tell the tidings to thy mistress and I will quickly return to help thee in this matter." At that instant Kasim's widow seeing her brother-in-law, exclaimed, "O Ali Baba, what news bringest thou of my spouse? Alas, I see grief tokens written upon thy countenance. Say quickly what hath happened." Then he recounted to her how it had fared with her husband and how he had been slain by the robbers and in what wise he had brought home the dead body. Ali Baba pursued:—"O my lady, what was to happen hath happened, but it behoveth us to keep this matter secret, for that our lives depend upon privacy." She wept with sore weeping and made answer, "It hath fared with my husband according to the fiat of Fate; and now for thy safety's sake I give thee my word to keep the affair concealed." He replied, "Naught can avail when Allah hath decreed. Rest thee in patience; until the days of thy widowhood[9] be accomplisht; after which time I will take thee to wife, and thou shalt live in comfort and happiness; and fear not lest my first spouse vex thee or show aught of jealousy, for that she is kindly and tender of heart." The widow lamenting her loss noisily, cried, "Be it as e'en thou please." Then Ali Baba farewelled her, weeping and wailing for her husband; and joining Morgiana took counsel with her how to manage the burial of his brother. So, after much consultation and many warnings, he left the slave-girl and departed home driving his ass before him. As soon as Ali Baba had fared forth Morgiana went quickly to a druggist's shop; and, that she might the better dissemble with him and not make known the matter, she asked of him a drug often administered to men when diseased with dangerous distemper. He gave it saying, "Who is there in thy house that lieth so ill as to require this medicine?" and said she, "My Master Kasim is sick well nigh unto death: for many days he hath nor spoken nor tasted aught of food, so that almost we despair of his life." Next day Morgiana went again and asked the druggist for more of medicine and essences such as are adhibited to the sick when at door of death, that the moribund may haply rally before the last breath. The man gave the potion and she taking it sighed aloud and wept, saying, "I fear me he may not have strength to drink this draught: methinks all will be over with him ere I return to the house." Meanwhile Ali Baba was anxiously awaiting to hear sounds of wailing and lamentation in Kasim's home that he might at such signal hasten thither and take part in the ceremonies of the funeral. Early on the second day Morgiana went with veiled face to one Baba Mustafa,[10] a tailor well shotten in years whose craft was to make shrouds and cerecloths; and as soon as she saw him open his shop she gave him a gold piece and said, "Do thou bind a bandage over thine eyes and come along with me." Mustafa made as though he would not go, whereat Morgiana placed a second gold coin in his palm and entreated him to accompany her. The tailor presently consented for greed of gain, so tying a kerchief tightly over his eyes she led him by the hand to the house wherein lay the dead body of her master. Then, taking off the bandage in the darkened room she bade him sew together the quarters of the corpse, limb to its limb; and, casting a cloth upon the body, said to the tailor, "Make haste and sew a shroud according to the size of this dead man and I will give thee therefor yet another ducat." Baba Mustafa quickly made the cerecloth of fitting length and breadth, and Morgiana paid him the promised Ashrafi; then once more bandaging his eyes led him back to the place whence she had brought him. After this she returned hurriedly home and with the help of Ali Baba washed the body in warm water and donning the shroud lay the corpse upon a clean place ready for burial. This done Morgiana went to the mosque and gave notice to an Imam[11] that a funeral was awaiting the mourners in a certain household, and prayed that he would come to read the prayers for the dead; and the Imam went back with her. Then four neighbours took up the bier[12] and bore it on their shoulders and fared forth with the Imam and others who were wont to give assistance at such obsequies. After the funeral prayers were ended four other men carried off the coffin; and Morgiana walked before it bare of head, striking her breast and weeping and wailing with exceeding loud lament, whilst Ali Baba and the neighbours came behind. In such order they entered the cemetery and buried him; then, leaving him to Munkar and Nakir—the Questioners of the Dead—all wended their ways. Presently the women of the quarter, according to the custom of the city, gathered together in the house of mourning and sat an hour with Kasim's widow comforting and condoling, presently leaving her somewhat resigned and cheered. Ali Baba stayed forty days at home in ceremonial lamentation for the loss of his brother; so none within the town save himself and his wife (Kasim's widow) and Morgiana knew aught the secret. And when the forty days of mourning were ended Ali Baba removed to his own quarters all the property belonging to the deceased and openly married the widow; then he appointed his nephew, his brother's eldest son, who had lived a long time with a wealthy merchant and was perfect of knowledge in all matters of trade, such as selling and buying, to take charge of the defunct's shop and to carry on the business. It so chanced one day when the robbers, as was their wont, came to the treasure-cave that they marvelled exceedingly to find nor sign nor trace of Kasim's body whilst they observed that much of gold had been carried off. Quoth the Captain, "Now it behoveth us to make enquiry in this matter; else shall we suffer much of loss and this our treasure, which we and our forefathers have amassed during the course of many years, will little by little be wasted and spoiled." Hereto all assented and with single mind agreed that he whom they had slain had knowledge of the magical words whereby the door was made to open; moreover that some one beside him had cognizance of the spell and had carried off the body, and also much of gold; wherefore they needs must make diligent research and find out who the man ever might be. They then took counsel and determined that one amongst them, who should be sagacious and deft of wit, must don the dress of some merchant from foreign parts; then, repairing to the city he must go about from quarter to quarter and from street to street, and learn if any townsman had lately died and if so where he wont to dwell, that with this clue they might be enabled to find the wight they sought. Hereat said one of the robbers, "Grant me leave that I fare and find out such tidings in the town and bring thee word anon; and if I fail of my purpose I hold my life in forfeit." Accordingly that bandit, after disguising himself by dress, pushed at night into the town and next morning early he repaired to the market-square and saw that none of the shops had yet been opened, save only that of Baba Mustafa the tailor, who thread and needle in hand sat upon his working-stool. The thief bade him good day and said, "'Tis yet dark: how canst thou see to sew?" Said the tailor, "I perceive thou art a stranger. Despite my years my eyesight is so keen that only yesterday I sewed together a dead body whilst sitting in a room quite darkened." Quoth the bandit thereupon to himself, "I shall get somewhat of my want from this snip;" and to secure a further clue he asked, "Meseemeth thou wouldst jest with me and thou meanest that a cerecloth for a corpse was stitched by thee and that thy business is to sew shrouds." Answered the tailor, "It mattereth not to thee: question me no more questions." Thereupon the robber placed an Ashrafi in his hand and continued, "I desire not to discover aught thou hidest, albeit my breast like every honest man's is the grave of secrets; and this only would I learn of thee, in what house didst thou do that job? Canst thou direct me thither, or thyself conduct me thereto?" The tailor took the gold with greed and cried, "I have not seen with my own eyes the way to that house. A certain bondswoman led me to a place which I know right well and there she bandaged my eyes and guided me to some tenement and lastly carried me into a darkened room where lay the dead body dismembered. Then she unbound the kerchief and bade me sew together first the corpse and then the shroud, which having done she again blindfolded me and led me back to the stead whence she had brought me and left me there. Thou seest then I am not able to tell thee where thou shalt find the house." Quoth the robber, "Albeit thou knowest not the dwelling whereof thou speakest, still canst thou take me to the place where thou wast blindfolded; then I will bind a kerchief over thine eyes and lead thee as thou wast led: on this wise perchance thou mayest hit upon the site. An thou wilt do this favour by me, see here another golden ducat is thine." Thereupon the bandit slipped a second Ashrafi into the tailor's palm, and Baba Mustafa thrust it with the first into his pocket; then, leaving his shop as it was, he walked to the place where Morgiana had tied the kerchief around his eyes, and with him went the robber who, after binding on the bandage, led him by the hand. Baba Mustafa, who was clever and keen-witted, presently striking the street whereby he had fared with the handmaid, walked on counting step by step; then, halting suddenly, he said, "Thus far I came with her;" and the twain stopped in front of Kasim's house wherein now dwelt his brother Ali Baba. The robber then made marks with white chalk upon the door to the end that he might readily find it at some future time, and removing the bandage from the tailor's eyes said, "O Baba Mustafa, I thank thee for this favour: and Almighty Allah guerdon thee for thy goodness. Tell me now, I pray thee, who dwelleth in yonder house?" Quoth he, "In very sooth I wot not, for I have little knowledge concerning this quarter of the city;" and the bandit, understanding that he could find no further clue from the tailor, dismissed him to his shop with abundant thanks, and hastened back to the tryst-place in the jungle where the band awaited his coming. Not long after it so fortuned that Morgiana, going out upon some errand, marvelled exceedingly at seeing the chalk-marks showing white in the door; she stood awhile deep in thought and presently divined that some enemy had made the signs that he might recognise the house and play some sleight upon her lord. She therefore chalked the doors of all her neighbours in like manner and kept the matter secret, never entrusting it or to master or to mistress. Meanwhile the robber told his comrades his tale of adventure and how he had found the clue; so the Captain and with him all the band went one after other by different ways till they entered the city; and he who had placed the mark on Ali Baba's door accompanied the Chief to point out the place. He conducted him straightway to the house and shewing the sign exclaimed, "Here dwelleth he of whom we are in search!" But when the Captain looked around him he saw that all the dwellings bore chalk-marks after like fashion and he wondered saying, "By what manner of means knowest thou which house of all these houses that bear similar signs is that whereof thou spakest?" Hereat the robber-guide was confounded beyond measure of confusion, and could make no answer; then with an oath he cried, "I did assuredly set a sign upon a door, but I know not whence came all the marks upon the other entrances; nor can I say for a surety which it was I chalked." Thereupon the Captain returned to the marketplace and said to his men, "We have toiled and laboured in vain, nor have we found the house we went forth to seek. Return we now to the forest our rendezvous: I also will fare thither." Then all trooped off and assembled together within the treasure-cave; and, when the robbers had all met, the Captain judged him worthy of punishment who had spoken falsely and had led them through the city to no purpose. So he imprisoned him in presence of them all;[13] and then said he, "To him amongst you will I show special favour who shall go to town and bring me intelligence whereby we may lay hands upon the plunderer of our property." Hereat another of the company came forward and said, "I am ready to go and enquire into the case, and 'tis I who will bring thee to thy wish." The Captain after giving him presents and promises despatched him upon his errand; and by the decree of Destiny which none may gainsay, this second robber went first to the house of Baba Mustafa the tailor, as had done the thief who had foregone him. In like manner he also persuaded the snip with gifts of golden coin that he be led hoodwinked and thus too he was guided to Ali Baba's door. Here noting the work of his predecessor, he affixed to the jamb a mark with red chalk the better to distinguish it from the others whereon still showed the white. Then hied he back in stealth to his company; but Morgiana on her part also descried the red sign on the entrance and with subtle forethought marked all the others after the same fashion; nor told she any what she had done. Meanwhile the bandit rejoined his band and vauntingly said, "O our Captain, I have found the house and thereon put a mark whereby I shall distinguish it clearly from all its neighbours." But, as aforetime, when the troop repaired thither they saw each and every house marked with signs of red chalk. So they returned disappointed and the Captain, waxing displeased exceedingly and distraught, clapped also this spy into gaol. Then said the chief to himself, "Two men have failed in their endeavour and have met their rightful meed of punishment; and I trow that none other of my band will essay to follow up their research; so I myself will go and find the house of this wight." Accordingly he fared along and aided by the tailor Baba Mustafa, who had gained much gain of golden pieces in this matter, he hit upon the house of Ali Baba; and here he made no outward show or sign, but marked it on the tablet[14] of his heart and impressed the picture upon the page of his memory. Then returning to the jungle he said to his men, "I have full cognizance of the place and have limned it clearly in my mind; so now there will be no difficulty in finding it. Go forth straightways and buy me and bring hither nineteen mules together with one large leathern jar of mustard oil and seven and thirty vessels of the same kind clean empty. Without me and the two locked up in gaol ye number thirty-seven souls; so I will stow you away armed and accoutred each within his jar and will load two upon each mule, and upon the nineteenth mule there shall be a man in an empty jar on one side, and on the other the jar full of oil. I for my part, in guise of an oil-merchant, will drive the mules into the town, arriving at the house by night, and will ask permission of its master to tarry there until morning. After this we shall seek occasion during the dark hours to rise up and fall upon him and slay him." Furthermore the Captain spake saying, "When we have made an end of him we shall recover the gold and treasure whereof he robbed us and bring it back upon the mules." This counsel pleased the robbers who went forthwith and purchased mules and huge leathern jars, and did as the Captain had bidden them. And after a delay of three days shortly before nightfall they arose; and over-smearing all the jars with oil of mustard, each hid him inside an empty vessel. The Chief then disguised himself in trader's gear and placed the jars upon the nineteen mules; to wit, the thirty-seven vessels in each of which lay a robber armed and accoutred, and the one that was full of oil. This done, he drove the beasts before him and presently he reached Ali Baba's place at nightfall; when it chanced that the housemaster was strolling after supper to and fro in front of his home. The Captain saluted him with the salam and said, "I come from such and such a village with oil; and ofttimes have I been here a-selling oil, but now to my grief I have arrived too late and I am sore troubled and perplexed as to where I shall spend the night. An thou have pity on me I pray thee grant that I tarry here in thy courtyard and ease the mules by taking down the jars and giving the beasts somewhat of fodder." Albeit Ali Baba had heard the Captain's voice when perched upon the tree and had seen him enter the cave, yet by reason of the disguise he knew him not for the leader of the thieves, and granted his request with hearty welcome and gave him full license to halt there for the night. He then pointed out an empty shed wherein to tether the mules, and bade one of the slave-boys go fetch grain and water. He also gave orders to the slave-girl Morgiana saying, "A guest hath come hither and tarrieth here to-night. Do thou busy thyself with all speed about his supper and make ready the guest-bed for him." Presently, when the Captain had let down all the jars and had fed and watered his mules, Ali Baba received him with all courtesy and kindness, and summoning Morgiana said in his presence, "See thou fail not in service of this our stranger nor suffer him to lack for aught. Tomorrow early I would fare to the Hammam and bathe; so do thou give my slave-boy Abdullah a suit of clean white clothes which I may put on after washing; moreover make thee ready a somewhat of broth overnight that I may drink it after my return home." Replied she, "I will have all in readiness as thou hast bidden." So Ali Baba retired to his rest, and the Captain, having supped, repaired to the shed and saw that all the mules had their food and drink for the night. And finding utter privacy, whispered to his men who were in ambush, "This night at midnight when ye hear my voice, do you quickly open with your sharp knives the leathern jars from top to bottom and issue forth without delay." Then passing through the kitchen he reached the chamber wherein a bed had been dispread for him, Morgiana showing the way with a lamp. Quoth she, "An thou need aught beside I pray thee command this thy slave who is ever ready to obey thy say!" He made answer, "Naught else need I;" then, putting out the light, he lay down on the bed to sleep awhile ere the time came to rouse his men and finish off the work. Meanwhile Morgiana did as her master had bidden her: she first took out a suit of clean white clothes and made it over to Abdullah who had not yet gone to rest; then she placed the pipkin upon the hearth to boil the broth and blew the fire till it burnt briskly. After a short delay she needs must see an the broth be boiling, but by that time all the lamps had gone out and she found that the oil was spent and that nowhere could she get a light. The slave boy Abdullah observed that she was troubled and perplexed hereat, and quoth he to her, "Why make so much ado? In yonder shed are many jars of oil: go now and take as much soever as thou listest." Morgiana gave thanks to him for his suggestion; and Abdullah, who was lying at his ease in the hall, went off to sleep so that he might wake betimes and serve Ali Baba in the bath. So the handmaiden rose[15] and with oil-can in hand walked to the shed where stood the leathern jars all ragged in rows. Now, as she drew nigh unto one of the vessels, the thief who was hidden therein hearing the tread of footsteps bethought him that it was of his Captain whose summons he awaited; so he whispered, "Is it now time for us to sally forth?" Morgiana started back affrighted at the sound of human accents; but, inasmuch as she was bold and ready of wit, she replied, "The time is not yet come," and said to herself, "These jars are not full of oil and herein I perceive a manner of mystery. Haply the oil merchant hatcheth some treacherous plot against my lord; so Allah, the Compassionating, the Compassionate, protect us from his snares!" Wherefore she answered in a voice made like to the Captain's, "Not yet, the time is not come." Then she went to the next jar and returned the same reply to him who was within, and so on to all the vessels one by one. Then said she in herself, "Laud to the Lord! my master took this fellow in believing him to be an oil-merchant, but lo, he hath admitted a band of robbers, who only await the signal to fall upon him and plunder the place and do him die." Then passed she on to the furthest jar and finding it brimming with oil, filled her can, and returning to the kitchen, trimmed the lamp and lit the wicks; then, bringing forth a large cauldron, she set it upon the fire, and filling it with oil from out the jar heaped wood upon the hearth and fanned it to a fierce flame the readier to boil its contents. When this was done she baled it out in potfuls and poured it seething hot into the leathern vessels one by one while the thieves unable to escape were scalded to death and every jar contained a corpse.[16] Thus did this slave-girl by her subtle wit make a clean end of all noiselessly and unknown even to the dwellers in the house. Now when she had satisfied herself that each and every of the men had been slain, she went back to the kitchen and shutting to the door sat brewing Ali Baba's broth. Scarce had an hour passed before the Captain woke from sleep; and, opening wide his window, saw that all was dark and silent; so he clapped his hands as a signal for his men to come forth but not a sound was heard in return. After awhile he clapped again and called aloud but got no answer; and when he cried out a third time without reply he was perplexed and went out to the shed wherein stood the jars. He thought to himself, "Perchance all are fallen asleep whenas the time for action is now at hand, so I must e'en awaken them without stay or delay." Then approaching the nearest jar he was startled by a smell of oil and seething flesh; and touching it outside he felt it reeking hot; then going to the others one by one, he found all in like condition. Hereat he knew for a surety the fate which had betided his band and, fearing for his own safety, he clomb on to the wall, and thence dropping into a garden made his escape in high dudgeon and sore disappointment. Morgiana awaited awhile to see the Captain return from the shed but he came not; whereat she knew that he had scaled the wall and had taken to flight, for that the street-door was double-locked; and the thieves being all disposed of on this wise Morgiana laid her down to sleep in perfect solace and ease of mind. When two hours of darkness yet remained, Ali Baba awoke and went to the Hammam knowing naught of the night-adventure, for the gallant slave-girl had not aroused him, nor indeed had she deemed such action expedient, because had she sought an opportunity of reporting to him her plan, she might haply have lost her chance and spoiled the project. The sun was high over the horizon when Ali Baba walked back from the Baths; and he marvelled exceedingly to see the jars still standing under the shed and said, "How cometh it that he, the oil-merchant my guest, hath not carried to the market his mules and jars of oil?" She answered, "Allah Almighty vouchsafe to thee six score years and ten of safety! I will tell thee in privacy of this merchant." So Ali Baba went apart with his slave-girl, who taking him without the house first locked the court-door; then showing him a jar she said, "Prithee look into this and see if within there be oil or aught else." Thereupon peering inside it he perceived a man at which sight he cried aloud and fain would have fled in his fright. Quoth Morgiana, "Fear him not, this man hath no longer the force to work thee harm, he lieth dead and stone-dead." Hearing such words of comfort and reassurance Ali Baba asked, "O Morgiana, what evils have we escaped and by what means hath this wretch become the quarry of Fate?" She answered "Alhamdolillah—Praise be to Almighty Allah!—I will inform thee fully of the case; but hush thee, speak not aloud, lest haply the neighbours learn the secret and it end in our confusion. Look now into all the jars, one by one from first to last." So Ali Baba examined them severally and found in each a man fully armed and accoutred and all lay scalded to death. Hereat speechless for sheer amazement he stared at the jars, but presently recovering himself he asked, "And where is he, the oil-merchant?" Answered she, "Of him also I will inform thee. The villain was no trader but a traitorous assassin whose honied words would have ensnared thee to thy doom; and now I will tell thee what he was and what hath happened; but, meanwhile thou art fresh from the Hammam and thou shouldst first drink somewhat of this broth for thy stomach's and thy health's sake." So Ali Baba went within and Morgiana served up the mess; after which quoth her master, "I fain would hear this wondrous story: prithee tell it to me and set my heart at ease." Hereat the handmaid fell to relating whatso had betided in these words, "O my master, when thou badest me boil the broth and retiredst to rest, thy slave in obedience to thy command took out a suit of clean white clothes and gave it to the boy Abdullah; then kindled the fire and set on the broth. As soon as it was ready I had need to light a lamp so that I might see to skim it, but all the oil was spent, and, learning this I told my want to the slave-boy Abdullah, who advised me to draw somewhat from the jars which stood under the shed. Accordingly, I took a can and went to the first vessel when suddenly I heard a voice within whisper with all caution, 'Is it now time for us to sally forth?' I was amazed thereat and judged that the pretended merchant had laid some plot to slay thee; so I replied, 'The time is not yet come.' Then I went to the second jar and heard another voice to which I made the like answer, and so on with all of them. I now was certified that these men awaited only some signal from their Chief whom thou didst take to guest within thy walls supposing him to be a merchant in oil; and that after thou receivedst him hospitably the miscreant had brought these men to murther thee and to plunder thy good and spoil thy house. But I gave him no opportunity to win his wish. The last jar I found full of oil and taking somewhat therefrom I lit the lamp; then, putting a large cauldron upon the fire, I filled it up with oil which I brought from the jar and made a fierce blaze under it; and, when the contents were seething hot, I took out sundry cansful with intent to scald them all to death, and going to each jar in due order, I poured within them one by one boiling oil. On this wise having destroyed them utterly, I returned to the kitchen and having extinguished the lamps stood by the window watching what might happen, and how that false merchant would act next. Not long after I had taken my station, the robber-captain awoke and ofttimes signalled to his thieves. Then getting no reply he came downstairs and went out to the jars, and finding that all his men were slain he fled through the darkness I know not whither. So when he had clean disappeared I was assured that, the door being double-locked, he had scaled the wall and dropped into the garden and made his escape. Then with my heart at rest I slept." And Morgiana, after telling her story to her master, presently added, "This is the whole truth I have related to thee. For some days indeed have I had inkling of such matter, but withheld it from thee deeming it inexpedient to risk the chance of its meeting the neighbours' ears; now, however, there is no help but to tell thee thereof. One day as I came to the house-door I espied thereon a white chalk-mark, and on the next day a red sign beside the white. I knew not the intent wherewith the marks were made, nevertheless I set others upon the entrances of sundry neighbours, judging that some enemy had done this deed whereby to encompass my master's destruction. Therefore I made the marks on all the other doors in such perfect conformity with those I found, that it would be hard to distinguish amongst them. Judge now and see if these signs and all this villainy be not the work of the bandits of the forest, who marked our house that on such wise they might know it again. Of these forty thieves there yet remain two others concerning whose case I know naught; so beware of them, but chiefly of the third remaining robber, their Captain, who fled hence alive. Take good heed and be thou cautious of him, for, shouldst thou fall into his hands, he will in no wise spare thee but will surely murther thee. I will do all that lieth in me to save from hurt and harm thy life and property, nor shall thy slave be found wanting in any service to my lord." Hearing these words Ali Baba rejoiced with exceeding joyance and said to her, "I am well pleased with thee for this thy conduct; and say me what wouldst thou have me do in thy behalf; I shall not fail to remember thy brave deed so long as breath in me remaineth." Quoth she, "It behoveth us before all things forthright to bury these bodies in the ground, that so the secret be not known to any one." Hereupon Ali Baba took with him his slave-boy Abdullah into the garden and there under a tree they dug for the corpses of the thieves a deep pit in size proportionate to its contents, and they dragged the bodies (having carried off their weapons) to the fosse and threw them in; then, covering up the remains of the seven and thirty robbers they made the ground appear level and clean as it wont to be. They also hid the leathern jars and the gear and arms and presently Ali Baba sent the mules by ones and twos to the bazar and sold them all with the able aid of his slave-boy Abdullah. Thus the matter was hushed up nor did it reach the ears of any; however, Ali Baba ceased not to be ill at ease lest haply the Captain or the surviving two robbers should wreak their vengeance on his head. He kept himself private with all caution and took heed that none learn a word of what had happened and of the wealth which he had carried off from the bandits' cave. Meanwhile the Captain of the thieves having escaped with his life, fled to the forest in hot wrath and sore irk of mind; and his senses were scattered and the colour of his visage vanished like ascending smoke. Then he thought the matter over again and again, and at last he firmly resolved that he needs must take the life of Ali Baba, else he would lose all the treasure which his enemy, by knowledge of the magical words, would take away and turn to his own use. Furthermore, he determined that he would undertake the business single-handed; and, that after getting rid of Ali Baba, he would gather together another band of banditti and would pursue his career of brigandage, as indeed his forebears had done for many generations. So he lay down to rest that night, and rising early in the morning donned a dress of suitable appearance; then going to the city alighted at a caravanserai, thinking to himself, "Doubtless the murther of so many men hath reached the Wali's ears, and Ali Baba hath been seized and brought to justice, and his house is levelled and his good is confiscated. The townfolk must surely have heard tidings of these matters." So he straightway asked of the keeper of the khan, "What strange things have happened in the city during the last few days?" and the other told him all that he had seen and heard, but the Captain could not learn a whit of that which most concerned him. Hereby he understood that Ali Baba was ware and wise, and that he had not only carried away such store of treasure but he had also destroyed so many lives and withal had come off scatheless; furthermore, that he himself must needs have all his wits alert not to fall into the hands of his foe and perish. With this resolve the Captain hired a shop in the Bazar, whither he bore whole bales of the finest stuffs and goodly merchandise from his forest treasure-house; and presently he took his seat within the store and fell to doing merchant's business. By chance his place fronted the booth of the defunct Kasim where his son, Ali Baba's nephew, now traded; and the Captain, who called himself Khwajah Hasan, soon formed acquaintance and friendship with the shop keepers around about him and treated all with profuse civilities, but he was especially gracious and cordial to the son of Kasim, a handsome youth and a well-dressed, and ofttimes he would sit and chat with him for a long while. A few days after it chanced that Ali Baba, as he was sometimes wont to do, came to see his nephew, whom he found sitting in his shop. The Captain saw and recognised him at sight and one morning he asked the young man, saying, "Prithee tell me, who is he that ever and anon cometh to thee at thy place of sale?" whereto the youth made answer, "He is my uncle, the brother of my father." Whereupon the Captain showed him yet greater favour and affection the better to deceive him for his own devices, and gave him presents and made him sit at meat with him and fed him with the daintiest of dishes. Presently Ali Baba's nephew bethought him it was only right and proper that he also should invite the merchant to supper, but whereas his own house was small, and he was straitened for room and could not make a show of splendour, as did Khwajah Hasan, he took counsel with his uncle on the matter. Ali Baba replied to his nephew:—"Thou sayest well: it behoveth thee to entreat thy friend in fairest fashion even as he hath entreated thee. On the morrow, which is Friday, shut thy shop as do all merchants of repute; then, after the early meal, take Khwajah Hasan to smell the air,[17] and as thou walkest lead him hither unawares; meanwhile I will give orders that Morgiana shall make ready for his coming the best of viands and all necessaries for a feast. Trouble not thyself on any wise, but leave the matter in my hands." Accordingly on the next day, to wit, Friday, the nephew of Ali Baba took Khwajah Hasan to walk about the garden; and, as they were returning he led him by the street wherein his uncle dwelt. When they came to the house, the youth stopped at the door and knocking said, "O my lord, this is my second home: my uncle hath heard much of thee and of thy goodness mewards and desireth with exceeding desire to see thee; so, shouldst thou consent to enter and visit him, I shall be truly glad and thankful to thee." Albeit Khwajah Hasan rejoiced in heart that he had thus found means whereby he might have access to his enemy's house and household, and although he hoped soon to attain his end by treachery, yet he hesitated to enter in and stood to make his excuses and walk away. But when the door was opened by the slave-porter, Ali Baba's nephew seized his companion's hand and after abundant persuasion led him in, whereat he entered with great show of cheerfulness as though much pleased and honoured. The housemaster received him with all favour and worship and asked him of his welfare, and said to him, "O my lord, I am obliged and thankful to thee for that thou hast shewn favour to the son of my brother and I perceive that thou regardest him with an affection even fonder than my own." Khwajah Hasan replied with pleasant words and said, "Thy nephew vastly taketh my fancy and in him I am well pleased, for that although young in years yet he hath been endued by Allah with much of wisdom." Thus they twain conversed with friendly conversation and presently the guest rose to depart and said, "O my lord, thy slave must now farewell thee; but on some future day—Inshallah—he will again wait upon thee." Ali Baba, however, would not let him leave and asked, "Whither wendest thou, O my friend? I would invite thee to my table and I pray thee sit at meat with us and after hie thee home in peace. Perchance the dishes are not as delicate as those whereof thou art wont to eat, still deign grant me this request I pray thee and refresh thyself with my victual." Quoth Khwajah Hasan, "O lord, I am beholden to thee for thy gracious invitation, and with pleasure would I sit at meat with thee, but for a special reason must I needs excuse myself; suffer me therefore to depart for I may not tarry longer nor accept thy gracious offer." Hereto the host made reply, "I pray thee, O my lord, tell me what may be the reason so urgent and weighty?" And Khwajah Hasan answered, "The cause is this: I must not, by order of the physician, who cured me lately of my complaint, eat aught of food pre-

pared with salt." Quoth Ali Baba, "An this be all, deprive
me not, I pray thee, of the honour thy company will confer upon me: as the meats are not yet cooked, I will forbid
the kitchener to make use of any salt. Tarry here awhile
and I will return anon to thee." So saying Ali Baba went in
to Morgiana and bade her not put salt into any one of the
dishes; and she, while busied with her cooking, fell to marvelling greatly at such order and asked her master, "Who is
he that eateth meat wherein is no salt?" He answered,
"What to thee mattereth it who he may be? only do thou
my bidding." She rejoined, "'Tis well: all shall be as thou
wishest;" but in mind she wondered at the man who made
such strange request and desired much to look upon him.
Wherefore, when all the meats were ready for serving up,
she helped the slave-boy Abdullah to spread the table and
set on the meal; and no sooner did she see Khwajah Hasan
than she knew who he was, albeit he had disguised himself in the dress of a stranger merchant; furthermore, when
she eyed him attentively she espied a dagger hidden under
his robe. "So ho!" quoth she to herself, "this is the cause
why the villain eateth not of salt, for that he seeketh an opportunity to slay my master whose mortal enemy he is;
howbeit I will be beforehand with him and despatch him
ere he find a chance to harm my lord." Now when Ali Baba
and Khwajah Hasan had eaten their sufficiency, the slave-
boy Abdullah brought Morgiana word to serve the dessert,
and she cleared the table and set on fruit fresh and dried in
salvers, then she placed by the side of Ali Baba a small tri-
pod for three cups with a flagon of wine, and lastly she
went off with the slave-boy Abdullah into another room,
as though she would herself eat supper. Then Khwajah
Hasan, that is, the Captain of the robbers, perceiving that
the coast was clear, exulted mightily saying to himself,
"The time hath come for me to take full vengeance; with
one thrust of my dagger I will despatch this fellow, then escape across the garden and wend my ways. His nephew
will not aventure to stay my hand, for an he do but move a
finger or toe with that intent another stab will settle his

earthly account. Still must I wait awhile until the slave-boy and the cook-maid shall have eaten and lain down to rest them in the kitchen." Morgiana, however, watched him wistfully and divining his purpose said in her mind, "I must not allow this villain advantage over my lord, but by some means I must make void his project and at once put an end to the life of him." Accordingly, the trusty slave-girl changed her dress with all haste and donned such clothes as dancers wear; she veiled her face with a costly kerchief; around her head she bound a fine turband, and about her middle she tied a waist-cloth worked with gold and silver wherein she stuck a dagger, whose hilt was rich in filigree and jewellery. Thus disguised she said to the slave-boy Abdullah, "Take now thy tambourine that we may play and sing and dance in honour of our master's guest." So he did her bidding and the twain went into the room, the lad playing and the lass following. Then, making a low congée, they asked leave to perform and disport and play; and Ali Baba gave permission, saying "Dance now and do your best that this our guest may be mirthful and merry." Quoth Khwajah Hasan, "O my lord, thou dost indeed provide much pleasant entertainment." Then the slave-boy Abdullah standing by began to strike the tambourine whilst Morgiana rose up and showed her perfect art and pleased them vastly with graceful steps and sportive motion; and suddenly drawing the poniard from her belt she brandished it and paced from side to side, a spectacle which pleased them most of all. At times also she stood before them, now clapping the sharp-edged dagger under her armpit and then setting it against her breast. Lastly she took the tambourine from the slave-boy Abdullah, and still holding the poniard in her right she went round for largesse as is the custom amongst merry-makers. First she stood before Ali Baba who threw a gold coin into the tambourine, and his nephew likewise put in an Ashrafi; then Khwajah Hasan, seeing her about to approach him, fell to pulling out his purse, when she heartened her heart and quick as the blinding leven she plunged the dagger into his vitals, and forthwith the miscreant fell back stone-dead. Ali Baba was dismayed and cried in his wrath, "O unhappy, what is this deed thou hast done to bring about my ruin!" But she replied, "Nay, O my lord, rather to save thee and not to cause thee harm have I slain this man: loosen his garments and see what thou wilt discover thereunder." So Ali Baba searched the dead man's dress and found concealed therein a dagger. Then said Morgiana, "This wretch was thy deadly enemy. Consider him well: he is none other than the oil merchant, the Captain of the band of robbers. Whenas he came hither with intent to take thy life, he would not eat thy salt; and when thou toldest me that he wished not any in the meat I suspected him and at first sight I was assured that he would surely do thee die; Almighty Allah be praised 'tis even as I thought." Then Ali Baba lavished upon her thanks and expressions of gratitude, saying, "Lo, these two times hast thou saved me from his hand," and falling upon her neck he cried, "See thou art free, and as reward for this thy fealty I have wedded thee to my nephew." Then turning to the youth he said, "Do as I bid thee and thou shalt prosper. I would that thou marry Morgiana, who is a model of duty and loyalty: thou seest now yon Khwajah Hasan sought thy friendship only that he might find opportunity to take my life, but this maiden with her good sense and her wisdom hath slain him and saved us." Ali Baba's nephew straightway consented to marry Morgiana. After which the three, raising the dead body bore it forth with all heed and vigilance and privily buried it in the garden, and for many years no one knew aught thereof. In due time Ali Baba married his brother's son to Morgiana with great pomp, and spread a bride-feast in most sumptuous fashion for his friends and neighbours, and made merry with them and enjoyed singing and all manner of dancing and amusements. He prospered in every undertaking and Time smiled upon him and a new source of wealth was opened to him. For fear of the thieves he had not once visited the jungle-cave wherein lay the treasure, since the day he had carried forth the corpse of his brother Kasim. But some time after, he mounted his hackney one morning and journeyed thither, with all care and caution, till finding no signs of man or horse, and reassured in his mind he ventured to draw near the door. Then alighting from his beast he tied it up to a tree, and going to the entrance pronounced the words which he had not forgotten, "Open, O Simsim!" Hereat, as was its wont, the door flew open, and entering thereby he saw the goods and hoard of gold and silver untouched and lying as he had left them. So he felt assured that not one of all the thieves remained alive, and, that save himself there was not a soul who knew the secret of the place. At once he bound in his saddle-cloth a load of Ashrafis such as his horse could bear and brought it home; and in after days he showed the hoard to his sons and sons' sons and taught them how the door could be caused to open and shut. Thus Ali Baba and his household lived all their lives in wealth and joyance in that city where erst he had been a pauper, and by the blessing of that secret treasure he rose to high degree and dignities. Furthermore they relate a tale anent

Ma'aruf the Cobbler and
His Wife Fatimah.

There dwelt once upon a time in the God-guarded city of Cairo a cobbler who lived by patching old shoes.[1] His name was Ma'aruf[2] and he had a wife called Fatimah, whom the folk had nicknamed "The Dung;"[3] for that she was a whorish, worthless wretch, scanty of shame and mickle of mischief. She ruled her spouse and used to abuse him and curse him a thousand times a day; and he feared her malice and dreaded her misdoings; for that he was a sensible man and careful of his repute, but poor-conditioned. When he earned much, he spent it on her, and when he gained little, she revenged herself on his body that night, leaving him no peace and making his night black as her book;[4] for she was even as of one like her saith the poet:—

> How manifold nights have I passed with my wife
> In the saddest plight with all misery rife:
> Would Heaven when first I went in to her
> With a cup of cold poison I'd ta'en her life.

Amongst other afflictions which befel him from her one day she said to him, "O Ma'aruf, I wish thee to bring me this night a vermicelli-cake dressed with bees' honey."[5] He replied, "So Allah Almighty aid me to its price, I will bring it thee. By Allah, I have no dirhams to-day, but our Lord will make things easy."[6] She rejoined, "I wot naught of these words; whether He aid thee or aid thee not, look thou come not to me save with the vermicelli and bees' honey; and if thou come without it I will make thy night black as thy fortune whenas thou marriedst me and fellest into my hand." Quoth he, "Allah is bountiful!" and going out with grief scattering itself from his body, prayed the dawn-prayer and opened his shop, saying, "I beseech thee, O Lord, to vouchsafe me the price of the Kunafah and ward off from me the mischief of yonder wicked woman this night!" After which he sat in the shop till noon, but no work came to him and his fear of his wife redoubled. Then he arose and locking his shop, went out perplexed as to how he should do in the matter of the vermicelli-cake, seeing he had not even the wherewithal to buy bread. Presently he came up to the shop of the Kunafah-seller and stood before it distraught, whilst his eyes brimmed with tears. The pastry-cook glanced at him and said, "O Master Ma'aruf, why dost thou weep? Tell me what hath befallen thee." So he acquainted him with his case, saying, "My wife is a shrew, a virago who would have me bring her a Kunafah; but I have sat in my shop till past mid-day and have not gained even the price of bread; wherefore I am in fear of her." The cook laughed and said, "No harm shall come to thee. How many pounds wilt thou have?" "Five pounds," answered Ma'aruf. So the man weighed him out five pounds of vermicelli-cake and said to him, "I have clarified butter, but no bees' honey. Here is drip-honey,[7] however, which is better than bees' honey; and what harm will there be, if it be with drip-honey?" Ma'aruf was ashamed to object, because the pastry-cook was to have patience with him for the price, and said, "Give it me with drip-honey." So he fried a vermicelli-cake for him with butter and drenched it with drip-honey, till it was fit to present to Kings. Then he asked him, "Dost thou want bread and cheese?"; and Ma'aruf answered, "Yes." So he gave him four half dirhams worth of bread[8] and one of cheese, and the vermicelli was ten nusfs. Then said he, "Know, O Ma'aruf, that thou owest me fifteen nusfs; so go to thy wife and make merry and take this nusf for the Hammam;[9] and thou shalt have credit for a day or two or three till Allah provide thee with thy daily bread. And straiten not thy wife, for I will have patience with thee till such time as thou shalt have dirhams to spare." So Ma'aruf took the vermicelli-cake and bread and cheese and went away, with a heart at ease, blessing the pastry-cook and saying, "Extolled be Thy perfection, O my Lord! How bountiful art Thou!" When he came home, his wife enquired of him, "Hast thou brought the vermicelli-cake?"; and, replying "Yes," he set it before her. She looked at it and seeing it was dressed with cane-honey,[10] said to him, "Did I not bid thee bring it with bees' honey? Wilt thou contrary my wish and have it dressed with cane-honey?" He excused himself to her, saying, "I brought it not save on credit;" but said she, "This talk is idle; I will not eat Kunafah save with bees' honey." And she was wroth with it and threw it in his face, saying, "Begone, thou pimp, and bring me other than this!" Then she dealt him a buffet on the cheek and knocked out one of his teeth. The blood ran down upon his breast and for stress of anger he smote her on the head a single blow and a slight; whereupon she clutched his beard and fell to shouting out and saying, "Help, O Moslems!" So the neighbours came in and freed his beard from her grip; then they reproved and reproached her, saying, "We are all content to eat Kunafah with cane-honey. Why, then, wilt thou oppress this poor man thus? Verily, this is disgraceful in thee!" And they went on to soothe her till they made peace between her and him. But, when the folk were gone, she sware that she would not eat of the vermicelli, and Ma'aruf, burning with hunger, said in himself, "She sweareth that she will not eat; so I will e'en eat." Then he ate, and when she saw him eating, she said, "Inshallah, may the eating of it be poison to destroy the far one's body."[11] Quoth he, "It shall not be at thy bidding," and went on eating, laughing and saying, "Thou swarest that thou wouldst not eat of this; but Allah is bountiful, and to-morrow night, an the Lord decree, I will bring thee Kunafah dressed with bees' honey, and thou shalt eat it alone." And he applied himself to appeasing her, whilst she called down curses upon him; and she ceased not to rail at him and revile him with gross abuse till the morning, when she bared her forearm to beat him. Quoth he, "Give me time and I will bring thee other vermicelli-cake." Then he went out to the mosque and prayed, after which he betook himself to his shop and opening it, sat down; but hardly had he done this when up came two runners from the Kazi's court and said to him, "Up with thee, speak with the Kazi, for thy wife hath complained of thee to him and her favour is thus and thus." He recognised her by their description; and saying, "May Allah Almighty torment her!" walked with them till he came to the Kazi's presence, where he found Fatimah standing with her arm bound up and her face-veil besmeared with blood; and she was weeping and wiping away her tears. Quoth the Kazi, "Ho man, hast thou no fear of Allah the Most High? Why hast thou beaten this good woman and broken her forearm and knocked out her tooth and entreated her thus?" And quoth Ma'aruf, "If I beat her or put out her tooth, sentence me to what thou wilt; but in truth the case was thus and thus and the neighbours made peace between me and her." And he told him the story from first to last. Now this Kazi was a benevolent man; so he brought out to him a quarter dinar, saying, "O man, take this and get her Kunafah with bees' honey and do ye make peace, thou and she." Quoth Ma'aruf, "Give it to her." So she took it and the Kazi made peace between them, saying, "O wife, obey thy husband; and thou, O man, deal kindly with her."[12] Then they left the court, reconciled at the Kazi's hands, and the woman went one way, whilst her husband returned by another way to his shop and sat there, when, behold, the runners came up to him and said, "Give us our fee." Quoth he, "The Kazi took not of me aught; on the contrary, he gave me a quarter dinar." But quoth they, "'Tis no concern of ours whether the Kazi took of thee or gave to thee, and if thou give us not our fee, we will exact it in despite of thee." And they fell to dragging him about the market; so he sold his tools and gave them half a dinar, whereupon they let him go and went away, whilst he put his hand to his cheek and sat sorrowful, for that he had no tools wherewith to work. Presently, up came two ill-favoured fellows and said to them, "Come, O man, and speak with the Kazi; for thy wife hath complained of thee to him." Said he, "He made peace between us just now." But said they, "We come from another Kazi, and thy wife hath complained of thee to our Kazi." So he arose and went with them to their Kazi, calling on Allah for aid against her; and when he saw her, he said to her, "Did we not make peace, good woman?" Whereupon she cried, "There abideth no peace between me and thee." Accordingly he came forward and told the Kazi his story, adding, "And indeed the Kazi Such-an-one made peace between us this very hour." Whereupon the Kazi said to her, "O strumpet, since ye two have made peace with each other, why comest thou to me complaining?" Quoth she, "He beat me after that;" but quoth the Kazi, "Make peace each with other, and beat her not again, and she will cross thee no more." So they made peace and the Kazi said to Ma'aruf, "Give the runners their fee." So he gave them their fee and going back to his shop, opened it and sat down, as he were a drunken man for excess of the chagrin which befel him. Presently, while he was still sitting, behold, a man came up to him and said, "O Ma'aruf, rise and hide thyself, for thy wife hath complained of thee to the High Court[13] and Abu Tabak[14] is after thee." So he shut his shop and fled towards the Gate of Victory.[15] He had five Nusfs of silver left of the price of the lasts and gear; and therewith he bought four worth of bread and one of cheese, as he fled from her. Now it was the winter season and the hour of mid-afternoon prayer; so, when he came out among the rubbish-mounds the rain descended upon him, like water from the mouths of water-skins, and his clothes were drenched. He therefore entered the 'Adiliyah,[16] where he saw a ruined place and therein a deserted cell without a door; and in it he took refuge and found shelter from the rain. The tears streamed from his eyelids, and he fell to complaining of what had betided him and saying, "Whither shall I flee from this whore? I beseech Thee, O Lord, to vouchsafe me one who shall conduct me to a far country, where she shall not know the way to me!" Now while he sat weeping, behold, the wall clave and there came forth to him therefrom one of tall stature, whose aspect caused his body-pile to bristle and his flesh to creep, and said to him, "O man, what aileth thee that thou disturbest me this night? These two hundred years have I dwelt here and have never seen any enter this place and do as thou dost. Tell me what thou wishest and I will accomplish thy need, as ruth for thee hath got hold upon my heart." Quoth Ma'aruf, "Who and what art thou?"; and quoth he, "I am the Haunter[17] of this place." So Ma'aruf told him all that had befallen him with his wife and he said, "Wilt thou have me convey thee to a country, where thy wife shall know no way to thee?" "Yes," said Ma'aruf; and the other, "Then mount my back." So he mounted on his back and he flew with him from after supper-tide till daybreak, when he set him down on the top of a high mountain and said to him, "O mortal, descend this mountain and thou wilt see the gate of a city. Enter it, for therein thy wife cannot come at thee." He then left him and went his way, whilst Ma'aruf abode in amazement and perplexity till the sun rose, when he said to himself, "I will up with me and go down into the city: indeed there is no profit in my abiding upon this highland." So he descended to the mountain-foot and saw a city girt by towering walls, full of lofty palaces and gold-adorned buildings which was a delight to beholders. He entered in at the gate and found it a place such as lightened the grieving heart; but, as he walked through the streets the townsfolk stared at him as a curiosity and gathered about him, marvelling at his dress, for it was unlike theirs. Presently, one of them said to him, "O man, art thou a stranger?" "Yes." "What countryman art thou?" "I am from the city of Cairo the Auspicious." "And when didst thou leave Cairo?" "I left it yesterday, at the hour of afternoon-prayer." Whereupon the man laughed at him and cried out, saying, "Come look, O folk, at this man and hear what he saith!" Quoth they, "What doth he say?"; and quoth the townsman, "He pretendeth that he cometh from Cairo and left it yesterday at the hour of afternoon-prayer!" At this they all laughed and gathering round Ma'aruf, said to him, "O man, art thou mad to talk thus? How canst thou pretend that thou leftest Cairo at mid-afternoon yesterday and foundest thyself this morning here, when the truth is that between our city and Cairo lieth a full year's journey?" Quoth he, "None is mad but you. As for me, I speak sooth, for here is bread which I brought with me from Cairo, and see, 'tis yet new." Then he showed them the bread and they stared at it, for it was unlike their country bread. So the crowd increased about him and they said one to another, "This is Cairo bread: look at it;" and he became a gazing-stock in the city and some believed him, whilst others gave him the lie and made mock of him. Whilst this was going on, behold, up came a merchant riding on a she-mule and followed by two black slaves, and brake a way through the people, saying, "O folk, are ye not ashamed to mob this stranger and make mock of him and scoff at him?" And he went on to rate them, till he drave them away from Ma'aruf, and none could make him any answer. Then he said to the stranger, "Come, O my brother, no harm shall betide thee from these folk. Verily they have no shame."[18] So he took him and carrying him to a spacious and richly-adorned house, seated him in a speak-room fit for a King, whilst he gave an order to his slaves, who opened a chest and brought out to him a dress such as might be worn by a merchant worth a thousand.[19] He clad him therewith and Ma'aruf, being a seemly man, became as he were consul to the merchants. Then his host called for food and they set before them a tray full of all manner exquisite viands. The twain ate and drank and the merchant said to Ma'aruf, "O my brother, what is thy name?" "My name is Ma'aruf and I'm a cobbler by trade and patch old shoes." "What country-man art thou?" "I am from Cairo." "What quarter? Dost thou know Cairo?" "I am of its children.[20] I come from the Red Street."[21] "And whom dost thou know in the Red Street?" "I know such an one and such an one," answered Ma'aruf and named several people to him. Quoth the other, "Knowest thou Shaykh Ahmad the druggist?"[22] "He was my next neighbour, wall to wall." "Is he well?" "Yes." "How many sons hath he?" "Three, Mustafa, Mohammed and Ali." "And what hath Allah done with them?" "As for Mustafa, he is well and he is a learned man, a professor:[23] Mohammed is a druggist and opened him a shop beside that of his father, after he had married, and his wife hath borne him a son named Hasan." "Allah gladden thee with good news!" said the merchant; and Ma'aruf continued, "As for Ali, he was my friend, when we were boys, and we always played together, I and he. We used to go in the guise of the children of the Nazarenes and enter the church and steal the books of the Christians and sell them and buy food with the price. It chanced once that the Nazarenes caught us with a book, whereupon they complained of us to our folk and said to Ali's father:—An thou hinder not thy son from troubling us, we will complain of thee to the King. So he appeased them and gave Ali a thrashing; wherefore he ran away none knew whither and he hath now been absent twenty years and no man hath brought news of him." Quoth the host, "I am that very Ali, son of Shaykh Ahmad the druggist, and thou art my playmate Ma'aruf."[24] So they saluted each other and after the salam Ali said, "Tell me why, O Ma'aruf, thou camest from Cairo to this city." Then he told him all that had befallen him of ill-doing with his wife Fatimah the Dung and said, "So, when her annoy waxed on me, I fled from her towards the Gate of Victory and went forth the city. Presently, the rain fell heavy on me; so I entered a ruined cell in the Adiliyah and sat there, weeping; whereupon there came forth to me the Haunter of the place, which was an Ifrit of the Jinn, and questioned me. I acquainted him with my case and he took me on his back and flew with me all night between heaven and earth, till he set me down on yonder mountain and gave me to know of this city. So I came down from the mountain and entered the city, when the people crowded about me and questioned me. I told them that I had left Cairo yesterday, but they believed me not, and presently thou camest up and driving the folk away from me, carriedst me to this house. Such, then, is the cause of my quitting Cairo; and thou, what object brought thee hither?" Quoth Ali, "The giddiness[25] of folly turned my head when I was seven years old, from which time I wandered from land to land and city to city, till I came to this city, the name whereof is Ikhtiyan al-Khatan.[26] I found its people an hospitable folk and a kindly, compassionate for the poor man and selling to him on credit and believing all he said. So quoth I to them:—I am a merchant and have preceded my packs and I need a place wherein to bestow my baggage. And they believed me and assigned me a lodging. Then quoth I to them:—Is there any of you will lend me a thousand dinars, till my loads arrive, when I will repay it to him; for I am in want of certain things before my goods come?" They gave me what I asked and I went to the merchants' bazar, where, seeing goods, I bought them and sold them next day at a profit of fifty gold pieces and bought others.[27] And I consorted with the folk and treated them liberally, so that they loved me, and I continued to sell and buy, till I grew rich. Know, O my brother, that the proverb saith, The world is show and trickery: and the land where none wotteth thee, there do whatso liketh thee. Thou too, an thou say to all who ask thee, I'm a cobbler by trade and poor withal, and I fled from my wife and left Cairo yesterday, they will not believe thee and thou wilt be a laughingstock among them as long as thou abidest in the city; whilst, an thou tell them, An Ifrit brought me hither, they will take fright at thee and none will come near thee; for they will say, This man is possessed of an Ifrit and harm will betide whoso approacheth him. And such public report will be dishonouring both to thee and to me, because they ken I come from Cairo." Ma'aruf asked:—"How then shall I do?"; and Ali answered, "I will tell thee how thou shalt do, Inshallah! To-morrow I will give thee a thousand dinars and a she-mule to ride and a black slave, who shall walk before thee and guide thee to the gate of the merchants' bazar; and do thou go in to them. I will be there sitting amongst them, and when I see thee, I will rise to thee and salute thee with the salam and kiss thy hand and make a great man of thee. Whenever I ask thee of any kind of stuff, saying, Hast thou brought with thee aught of such a kind? do thou answer, Plenty.[28] And if they question me of thee, I will praise thee and magnify thee in their eyes and say to them, Get him a store-house and a shop. I also will give thee out for a man of great wealth and generosity; and if a beggar come to thee, bestow upon him what thou mayst; so will they put faith in what I say and believe in thy greatness and generosity and love thee. Then will I invite thee to my house and invite all the merchants on thy account and bring together thee and them, so that all may know thee and thou know them, whereby thou shalt sell and buy and take and give with them; nor will it be long ere thou become a man of money." Accordingly, on the morrow he gave him a thousand dinars and a suit of clothes and a black slave and mounting him on a she-mule, said to him, "Allah give thee quittance of responsibility for all this,[29] inasmuch as thou art my friend and it behoveth me to deal generously with thee. Have no care; but put away from thee the thought of thy wife's misways and name her not to any." "Allah requite thee with good!" replied Ma'aruf and rode on, preceded by his blackamoor till the slave brought him to the gate of the merchants' bazar, where they were all seated, and amongst them Ali, who when he saw him, rose and threw himself upon him, crying, "A blessed day, O Merchant Ma'aruf, O man of good works and kindness!"[30] And he kissed his hand before the merchants and said to them, "Our brothers, ye are honoured by knowing[31] the merchant Ma'aruf." So they saluted him, and Ali signed to them to make much of him, wherefore he was magnified in their eyes. Then Ali helped him to dismount from his she-mule and saluted him with the salam; after which he took the merchants apart, one after other, and vaunted Ma'aruf to them. They asked, "Is this man a merchant?"; and he answered, "Yes; and indeed he is the chiefest of merchants, there liveth not a wealthier than he; for his wealth and the riches of his father and forefathers are famous among the merchants of Cairo. He hath partners in Hind and Sind and Al-Yaman and is high in repute for generosity. So know ye his rank and exalt ye his degree and do him service, and wot also that his coming to your city is not for the sake of traffic, and none other save to divert himself with the sight of folk's countries: indeed, he hath no need of strangerhood for the sake of gain and profit, having wealth that fires cannot consume, and I am one of his servants." And he ceased not to extol him, till they set him above their heads and began to tell one another of his qualities. Then they gathered round him and offered him junkets[32] and sherbets, and even the Consul of the Merchants came to him and saluted him; whilst Ali proceeded to ask him, in the presence of the traders, "O my lord, haply thou hast brought with thee somewhat of such and such a stuff?"; and Ma'aruf answered, "Plenty." Now Ali had that day shown him various kinds of costly cloths and had taught him the names of the different stuffs, dear and cheap. Then said one of the merchants, "O my lord, hast thou brought with thee yellow broad cloth?"; and Ma'aruf said, "Plenty"! Quoth another, "And gazelles' blood red?";[33] and quoth the Cobbler, "Plenty"; and as often as he asked him of aught, he made him the same answer. So the other said, "O Merchant Ali, had thy countryman a mind to transport a thousand loads of costly stuffs, he could do so"; and Ali said, "He would take them from a single one of his store-houses, and miss naught thereof." Now whilst they were sitting, behold, up came a beggar and went the round of the merchants. One gave him a half dirham and another a copper,[34] but most of them gave him nothing, till he came to Ma'aruf who pulled out a handful of gold and gave it to him, whereupon he blessed him and went his ways. The merchants marvelled at this and said, "Verily, this is a King's bestowal for he gave the beggar gold without count, and were he not a man of vast wealth and money without end, he had not given a beggar a handful of gold." After a while, there came to him a poor woman and he gave her a handful of gold; whereupon she went away, blessing him, and told the other beggars, who came to him, one after other, and he gave them each a handful of gold, till he disbursed the thousand dinars. Then he struck hand upon hand and said, "Allah is our sufficient aid and excellent is the Agent!" Quoth the Consul, "What aileth thee, O Merchant Ma'aruf?"; and quoth he, "It seemeth that the most part of the people of this city are poor and needy; had I known their misery I would have brought with me a large sum of money in my saddle-bags and given largesse thereof to the poor. I fear me I may be long abroad[35] and 'tis not in my nature to baulk a beggar; and I have no gold left: so, if a pauper come to me, what shall I say to him?" Quoth the Consul, "Say, Allah will send thee thy daily bread!";[36] but Ma'aruf replied, "That is not my practice and I am care-ridden because of this. Would I had other thousand dinars, wherewith to give alms till my baggage come!" "Have no care for that," quoth the Consul and sending one of his dependents for a thousand dinars, handed them to Ma'aruf, who went on giving them to every beggar who passed till the call to noon-prayer. Then they entered the Cathedral-mosque and prayed the noon-prayers, and what was left him of the thousand gold pieces he scattered on the heads of the worshippers. This drew the people's attention to him and they blessed him, whilst the merchants marvelled at the abundance of his generosity and openhandedness. Then he turned to another trader and borrowing of him other thousand ducats, gave these also away, whilst Merchant Ali looked on at what he did, but could not speak. He ceased not to do this till the call to mid-afternoon prayer, when he entered the mosque and prayed and distributed the rest of the money. On this wise, by the time they locked the doors of the bazar,[37] he had borrowed five thousand sequins and given them away, saying to every one of whom he took aught, "Wait till my baggage come when, if thou desire gold I will give thee gold, and if thou desire stuffs, thou shalt have stuffs; for I have no end of them." At eventide Merchant Ali invited Ma'aruf and the rest of the traders to an entertainment and seated him in the upper end, the place of honour, where he talked of nothing but cloths and jewels, and whenever they made mention to him of aught, he said, "I have plenty of it." Next day, he again repaired to the market-street where he showed a friendly bias towards the merchants and borrowed of them more money, which he distributed to the poor: nor did he leave doing thus twenty days, till he had borrowed threescore thousand dinars, and still there came no baggage, no, nor a burning plague.[38] At last folk began to clamour for their money and say, "The merchant Ma'aruf's baggage cometh not. How long will he take people's monies and give them to the poor?" And quoth one of them, "My rede is that we speak to Merchant Ali." So they went to him and said, "O Merchant Ali, Merchant Ma'aruf's baggage cometh not." Said he, "Have patience, it cannot fail to come soon." Then he took Ma'aruf aside and said to him, "O Ma'aruf, what fashion is this? Did I bid thee brown[39] the bread or burn it? The merchants clamour for their coin and tell me that thou owest them sixty thousand dinars, which thou hast borrowed and given away to the poor. How wilt thou satisfy the folk, seeing that thou neither sellest nor buyest?" Said Ma'aruf, "What matters it;[40] and what are threescore thousand dinars? When my baggage shall come, I will pay them in stuffs or in gold and silver, as they will." Quoth Merchant Ali, "Allah is Most Great! Hast thou then any baggage?"; and he said, "Plenty." Cried the other, "Allah and the Hallows[41] requite thee thine impudence! Did I teach thee this saying, that thou shouldst repeat it to me?

But I will acquaint the folk with thee." Ma'aruf rejoined, "Begone and prate no more! Am I a poor man? I have end-less wealth in my baggage and as soon as it cometh, they shall have their money's worth, two for one. I have no need of them." At this Merchant Ali waxed wroth and said, "Un-mannerly wight that thou art, I will teach thee to lie to me and not be ashamed!" Said Ma'aruf, "E'en work the worst thy hand can do! They must wait till my baggage come, when they shall have their due and more." So Ali left him and went away, saying in himself, "I praised him whilome and if I blame him now, I make myself out a liar and become of those of whom it is said:—Whoso praiseth and then blameth lieth twice."⁴² And he knew not what to do. Presently, the traders came to him and said, "O Mer-chant Ali, hast thou spoken to him?" Said he, "O folk, I am ashamed and, though he owe me a thousand dinars, I cannot speak to him. When ye lent him your money ye consulted me not; so ye have no claim on me. Dun him yourselves, and if he pay you not, complain of him to the King of the city, saying:—He is an imposter who hath im-posed upon us. And he will deliver you from the plague of him." Accordingly, they repaired to the King and told him what had passed, saying, "O King of the age, we are per-plexed anent this merchant, whose generosity is excessive; for he doeth thus and thus, and all he borroweth, he giveth away to the poor by handful. Were he a man of naught, his sense would not suffer him to lavish gold on this wise; and were he a man of wealth, his good faith had been made manifest to us by the coming of his baggage; but we see none of his luggage, although he avoucheth that he hath a baggage-train and hath preceded it. Now some time hath past, but there appeareth no sign of his baggage-train, and he oweth us sixty thousand gold pieces, all of which he hath given away in alms." And they went on to praise him and extol his generosity. Now this King was a very cov-etous man, a more covetous than Ash'ab;⁴³ and when he heard tell of Ma'aruf's generosity and openhandedness, greed of gain got the better of him and he said to his Wazir,

"Were not this merchant a man of immense wealth, he had not shown all this munificence. His baggage-train will assuredly come, whereupon these merchants will flock to him and he will scatter amongst them riches galore. Now I have more right to this money than they; wherefore I have a mind to make friends with him and profess affection for him, so that, when his baggage cometh whatso the merchants would have had I shall get of him; and I will give him my daughter to wife and join his wealth to my wealth." Replied the Wazir, "O King of the age, methinks he is naught but an impostor, and 'tis the impostor who ruineth the house of the covetous." The King said, "O Wazir, I will prove him and soon know if he be an impostor or a true man and whether he be a rearling of Fortune or not." The Wazir asked, "And how wilt thou prove him?"; and the King answered, "I will send for him to the presence and entreat him with honour and give him a jewel which I have. An he know it and wot its price, he is a man of worth and wealth; but an he know it not, he is an impostor and an upstart and I will do him die by the foulest fashion of deaths." So he sent for Ma'aruf, who came and saluted him. The King returned his salam and seating him beside himself, said to him, "Art thou the merchant Ma'aruf?" and said he, "Yes." Quoth the King, "The merchants declare that thou owest them sixty thousand ducats. Is this true?" "Yes," quoth he. Asked the King, "Then why dost thou not give them their money?"; and he answered, "Let them wait till my baggage come and I will repay them twofold. An they wish for gold, they shall have gold; and should they wish for silver, they shall have silver; or an they prefer for merchandise, I will give them merchandise; and to whom I owe a thousand I will give two thousand in requital of that wherewith he hath veiled my face before the poor; for I have plenty." Then said the King, "O merchant, take this and look what is its kind and value." And he gave him a jewel the bigness of a hazel-nut, which he had bought for a thousand sequins and not having its fellow, prized it highly. Ma'aruf took it and pressing it between his thumb and forefinger brake it, for it was brittle and would not brook the squeeze. Quoth the King, "Why hast thou broken the jewel?"; and Ma'aruf laughed and said, "O King of the age, this is no jewel. This is but a bittock of mineral worth a thousand dinars; why dost thou style it a jewel? A jewel I call such as is worth threescore and ten thousand gold pieces and this is called but a piece of stone. A jewel that is not of the bigness of a walnut hath no worth in my eyes and I take no account thereof. How cometh it, then, that thou, who art King, stylest this thing a jewel, when 'tis but a bit of mineral worth a thousand dinars? But ye are excusable, for that ye are poor folk and have not in your possession things of price." The King asked, "O merchant, hast thou jewels such as those whereof thou speakest?"; and he answered, "Plenty." Whereupon avarice overcame the King and he said, "Wilt thou give me real jewels?" Said Ma'aruf, "When my baggage-train shall come, I will give thee no end of jewels; and all that thou canst desire I have in plenty and will give thee, without price." At this the King rejoiced and said to the traders, "Wend your ways and have patience with him, till his baggage arrive, when do ye come to me and receive your monies from me." So they fared forth and the King turned to his Wazir and said to him, "Pay court to Merchant Ma'aruf and take and give with him in talk and bespeak him of my daughter, Princess Dunya, that he may wed her and so we gain these riches he hath." Said the Wazir, "O King of the age, this man's fashion misliketh me and methinks he is an impostor and a liar: so leave this whereof thou speakest lest thou lose thy daughter for naught." Now this Minister had sued the King aforetime to give him his daughter to wife and he was willing to do so, but when she heard of it she consented not to marry him. Accordingly, the King said to him, "O traitor, thou desirest no good for me, because in past time thou soughtest my daughter in wedlock, but she would none of thee; so now thou wouldst cut off the way of her marriage and wouldst have the Princess lie fallow, that thou mayst take her; but hear from me one word. Thou hast no concern in this matter. How can he be an impostor and a liar, seeing that he knew the price of the jewel, even that for which I bought it, and brake it because it pleased him not? He hath jewels in plenty, and when he goeth in to my daughter and seeth her to be beautiful, she will captivate his reason and he will love her and give her jewels and things of price: but, as for thee, thou wouldst forbid my daughter and myself these good things." So the Minister was silent, for fear of the King's anger, and said to himself, "Set the curs on the cattle!"[44] Then with show of friendly bias he betook himself to Ma'aruf and said to him, "His highness the King loveth thee and hath a daughter, a winsome lady and a lovesome, to whom he is minded to marry thee. What sayst thou?" Said he, "No harm in that; but let him wait till my baggage come, for marriage-settlements on Kings' daughters are large and their rank demandeth that they be not endowed save with a dowry befitting their degree. At this present I have no money with me till the coming of my baggage, for I have wealth in plenty and needs must I make her marriage-portion five thousand purses. Then I shall need a thousand purses to distribute amongst the poor and needy on my wedding-night, and other thousand to give those who walk in the bridal procession and yet other thousand wherewith to provide provaunt for the troops and others;[45] and I shall want an hundred jewels to give to the Princess on the wedding-morning[46] and other hundred gems to distribute among the slave-girls and eunuchs, for I must give each of them a jewel in honour of the bride; and I need wherewithal to clothe a thousand naked paupers, and alms too needs must be given. All this cannot be done till my baggage come; but I have plenty and, once it is here, I shall make no account of all this outlay." The Wazir returned to the King and told him what Ma'aruf said, whereupon quoth he, "Since this is his wish, how canst thou style him impostor and liar?" Replied the Minister, "And I cease not to say this." But the King chid him angrily and threatened him, saying, "By the life of my head, an thou cease not this talk, I will slay thee! Go back to him and fetch him to me and I will manage matters with him myself." So the Wazir returned to Ma'aruf and said to him, "Come and speak with the King." "I hear and obey," said Ma'aruf and went in to the King, who said to him, "Thou shalt not put me off with these excuses, for my treasury is full; so take the keys and spend all thou needest and give what thou wilt and clothe the poor and do thy desire and have no care for the girl and the handmaids. When the baggage shall come, do what thou wilt with thy wife, by way of generosity, and we will have patience with thee anent the marriage-portion till then, for there is no manner of difference betwixt me and thee; none at all." Then he sent for the Shaykh Al-Islam[47] and bade him write out the marriage-contract between his daughter and Merchant Ma'aruf, and he did so; after which the King gave the signal for beginning the wedding festivities and bade decorate the city. The kettle drums beat and the tables were spread with meats of all kinds and there came performers who paraded their tricks. Merchant Ma'aruf sat upon a throne in a parlour and the players and gymnasts and effeminates[48] and dancing-men of wondrous movements and posture-makers of marvellous cunning came before him, whilst he called out to the treasurer and said to him, "Bring gold and silver." So he brought gold and silver and Ma'aruf went round among the spectators and largessed each performer by the handful; and he gave alms to the poor and needy and clothes to the naked and it was a clamorous festival and a right merry. The treasurer could not bring money fast enough from the treasury, and the Wazir's heart was like to burst for rage; but he dared not say a word, whilst Merchant Ali marvelled at this waste of wealth and said to Merchant Ma'aruf, "Allah and the Hallows visit this upon thy head-sides![49] Doth it not suffice thee to squander the traders' money, but thou must squander that of the King to boot?" Replied Ma'aruf, " 'Tis none of thy concern: whenas my baggage shall come, I will requite the King manifold." And he went on lavishing money and saying in himself, "A burning plague! What will happen will happen and there is no flying from that which is foreordained." The festivities ceased not for the space of forty days, and on the one-and-fortieth day, they made the bride's cortège and all the Emirs and troops walked before her. When they brought her in before Ma'aruf, he began scattering gold on the people's heads, and they made her a mighty fine procession, whilst Ma'aruf expended in her honour vast sums of money. Then they brought him in to Princess Dunya and he sat down on the high divan; after which they let fall the curtains and shut the doors and withdrew, leaving him alone with his bride; whereupon he smote hand upon hand and sat awhile sorrowful and saying, "There is no Majesty and there is no Might save in Allah, the Glorious, the Great!" Quoth the Princess, "O my lord, Allah preserve thee! What aileth thee that thou art troubled?" Quoth he, "And how should I be other than troubled, seeing that thy father hath embarrassed me and done with me a deed which is like the burning of green corn?" She asked, "And what hath my father done with thee? Tell me!"; and he answered, "He hath brought me in to thee before the coming of my baggage, and I want at very least an hundred jewels to distribute among thy handmaids, to each a jewel, so she might rejoice therein and say, My lord gave me a jewel on the night of his going in to my lady. This good deed would I have done in honour of thy station and for the increase of thy dignity; and I have no need to stint myself in lavishing jewels, for I have of them great plenty." Rejoined she, "Be not concerned for that. As for me, trouble not thyself about me, for I will have patience with thee till thy baggage shall come, and as for my women have no care for them. Rise, doff thy clothes and take thy pleasure; and when the baggage cometh we shall get the jewels and the rest." So he arose and putting off his clothes sat down on the bed and sought love-liesse and they fell to toying with each other. He laid his hand on her knee and she sat down in his lap and thrust her lip like a titbit of meat into his mouth, and that hour was such as maketh a man to forget his father and his mother. And merchant Ma'aruf abated her maidenhead and that night was one not to be counted among lives for that which it comprised of the enjoyment of the fair, till the dawn of day, when he arose and entered the Hammam whence, after donning a suit for sovrans suitable he betook himself to the King's Divan. All who were there rose to him and received him with honour and worship, giving him joy and invoking blessings upon him; and he sat down by the King's side and asked, "Where is the treasurer?" They answered, "Here he is, before thee," and he said to him, "Bring robes of honour for all the Wazirs and Emirs and dignitaries and clothe them therewith." The treasurer brought him all he sought and he sat giving to all who came to him and lavishing largesse upon every man according to his station. On this wise he abode twenty days, whilst no baggage appeared for him nor aught else, till the treasurer was straitened by him to the uttermost and going in to the King, as he sat alone with the Wazir in Ma'aruf's absence, kissed ground between his hands and said, "O King of the age, I must tell thee somewhat, lest haply thou blame me for not acquainting thee therewith. Know that the treasury is being exhausted; there is none but a little money left in it and in ten days more we shall shut it upon emptiness." Quoth the King, "O Wazir, verily my son-in-law's baggage-train tarrieth long and there appeareth no news thereof." The Minister laughed and said, "Allah be gracious to thee, O King of the age! Thou art none other but heedless with respect to this impostor, this liar. As thy head liveth, there is no baggage for him, no, nor a burning plague to rid us of him! Nay, he hath but imposed on thee without surcease, so that he hath wasted thy treasures and married thy daughter for naught. How long therefore wilt thou be heedless of this liar?" Then quoth the King, "O Wazir, how shall we do to learn the truth of his case?"; and quoth the Wazir, "O King of the age, none may come at a man's secret but his wife; so send for thy daughter and let her come behind the curtain, that I may question her of the truth of his estate, to the intent that she may make question of him and acquaint us with his case."

Cried the King, "There is no harm in that; and as my head liveth, if it be proved that he is a liar and an impostor, I will verily do him die by the foulest of deaths!" Then he carried the Wazir into the sitting-chamber and sent for his daughter, who came behind the curtain, her husband being absent, and said, "What wouldst thou, O my father?" Said he, "Speak with the Wazir." So she asked, "Ho thou, the Wazir, what is thy will?"; and he answered, "O my lady, thou must know that thy husband hath squandered thy father's substance and married thee without a dower; and he ceaseth not to promise us and break his promises, nor cometh there any tidings of his baggage; in short we would have thee inform us concerning him." Quoth she, "Indeed his words be many, and he still cometh and promiseth me jewels and treasures and costly stuffs; but I see nothing." Quoth the Wazir, "O my lady, canst thou this night take and give with him in talk and whisper to him:—Say me sooth and fear from me naught, for thou art become my husband and I will not transgress against thee. So tell me the truth of the matter and I will devise thee a device whereby thou shalt be set at rest. And do thou play near and far[50] with him in words and profess love to him and win him to confess and after tell us the facts of his case." And she answered, "O my papa, I know how I will make proof of him." Then she went away and after supper her husband came in to her, according to his wont, whereupon Princess Dunya rose to him and took him under the armpit and wheedled him with winsomest wheedling (and all-sufficient[51] are woman's wiles whenas she would aught of men); and she ceased not to caress him and beguile him with speech sweeter than the honey till she stole his reason; and when she saw that he altogether inclined to her, she said to him, "O my beloved, O coolth of my eyes and fruit of my vitals, Allah never desolate me by less of thee nor Time sunder us twain me and thee! Indeed, the love of thee hath homed in my heart and the fire of passion hath consumed my liver, nor will I ever forsake thee or transgress against thee. But I would have thee tell me the truth, for that the sleights of falsehood profit not, nor do they secure credit at all seasons. How long wilt thou impose upon my father and lie to him? I fear lest thine affair be discovered to him, ere we can devise some device and he lay violent hands upon thee? So acquaint me with the facts of the case for naught shall befal thee save that which shall begladden thee; and, when thou shalt have spoken sooth, fear not harm shall betide thee. How often wilt thou declare that thou art a merchant and a man of money and hast a luggage-train? This long while past thou sayest, My baggage! my baggage! but there appeareth no sign of thy baggage, and visible in thy face is anxiety on this account. So an there be no worth in thy words, tell me and I will contrive thee a contrivance whereby thou shalt come off safe, Inshallah!" He replied, "I will tell thee the truth, and do then thou whatso thou wilt." Rejoined she, "Speak and look thou speak soothly; for sooth is the ark of safety, and beware of lying, for it dishonoureth the liar." He said, "Know, then, O my lady, that I am no merchant and have no baggage, no, nor a burning plague; nay, I was but a cobbler in my own country and had a wife called Fatimah the Dung, with whom there befel me this and that." And he told her his story from beginning to end; whereat she laughed and said, "Verily, thou art clever in the practice of lying and imposture!" whereto he answered, "O my lady, may Allah Almighty preserve thee to veil sins and counterveil chagrins!" Rejoined she, "Know, that thou imposedst upon my sire and deceivedst him by dint of thy deluding vaunts, so that of his greed for gain he married me to thee. Then thou squanderedst his wealth and the Wazir beareth thee a grudge for this. How many a time hath he spoken against thee to my father, saying, Indeed, he is an impostor, a liar! But my sire hearkened not to his say, for that he had sought me in wedlock and I consented not that he be baron and I femme. However, the time grew longsome upon my sire and he became straitened and said to me, Make him confess. So I have made thee confess and that which was covered is discovered. Now my father purposeth thee a mischief because of this; but thou art become my husband and I will never transgress against thee. An I told my father what I have learnt from thee, he would be certified of thy falsehood and imposture and that thou imposest upon Kings' daughters and squanderest royal wealth: so would thine offence find with him no pardon and he would slay thee sans a doubt: wherefore it would be bruited among the folk that I married a man who was a liar, an impostor, and this would smirch mine honour. Furthermore an he kill thee, most like he will require me to wed another, and to such thing I will never consent; no, not though I die![52] So rise now and don a Mameluke's dress and take these fifty thousand dinars of my monies, and mount a swift steed, and get thee to a land whither the rule of my father does not reach. Then make thee a merchant and send me a letter by a courier who shall bring it privily to me, that I may know in what land thou art, so I may send thee all my hand can attain. Thus shall thy wealth wax great and if my father die, I will send for thee, and thou shalt return in respect and honour; and if we die, thou or I, and go to the mercy of God the Most Great, the Resurrection shall unite us. This, then, is the rede that is right: and while we both abide alive and well, I will not cease to send thee letters and monies. Arise ere the day wax bright and thou be in perplexed plight and perdition upon thy head alight!" Quoth he, "O my lady, I beseech thee of thy favour to bid me farewell with thine embracement;" and quoth she, "No harm in that."[53] So he embraced her and knew her carnally; after which he made the Ghusl-ablution; then, donning the dress of a white slave, he bade the syces saddle him a thoroughbred steed. Accordingly, they saddled him a courser and he mounted and farewelling his wife, rode forth the city at the last of the night, whilst all who saw him deemed him one of the Mamelukes of the Sultan going abroad on some business. Next morning, the King and his Wazir repaired to the sitting-chamber and sent for Princess Dunya who came behind the curtain; and her father said to her, "O my daughter, what sayst thou?" Said she, "I say, Allah blacken thy Wazir's face, because he would have blackened my face in my husband's eyes!" Asked the King, "How so?"; and she answered, "He came in to me yesterday; but, before I could name the matter to him, behold, in walked Faraj the Chief Eunuch, letter in hand, and said:—Ten white slaves stand under the palace window and have given me this letter, saying:—Kiss for us the hands of our lord, Merchant Ma'aruf, and give him this letter, for we are of his Mamelukes with the baggage, and it hath reached us that he hath wedded the King's daughter, so we are come to acquaint him with that which befel us by the way. Accordingly I took the letter and read as follows:—From the five hundred Mamelukes to his highness our lord Merchant Ma'aruf. But further. We give thee to know that, after thou quittedst us, the Arabs[54] came out upon us and attacked us. They were two thousand horse and we five hundred mounted slaves and there befel a mighty sore fight between us and them. They hindered us from the road thirty days doing battle with them and this is the cause of our tarrying from thee. They also took from us of the luggage two hundred loads of cloth and slew of us fifty Mamelukes. When the news reached my husband, he cried, Allah disappoint them! What ailed them to wage war with the Arabs for the sake of two hundred loads of merchandise? What are two hundred loads? It behoved them not to tarry on that account, for verily the value of the two hundred loads is only some seven thousand dinars. But needs must I go to them and hasten them. As for that which the Arabs have taken, 'twill not be missed from the baggage, nor doth it weigh with me a whit, for I reckon it as if I had given it to them by way of alms. Then he went down from me, laughing and taking no concern for the wastage of his wealth nor the slaughter of his slaves. As soon as he was gone, I looked out from the lattice and saw the ten Mamelukes who had brought him the letter, as they were moons, each clad in a suit of clothes worth two thousand dinars, there is not with my father a chattel to match one of them. He went forth with them to bring up his baggage and hallowed be Allah who hindered me from saying to him aught of that thou badest me, for he would have made mock of me and thee, and haply he would have eyed me with the eye of disparagement and hated me. But the fault is all with thy Wazir,[55] who speaketh against my husband words that besit him not." Replied the King, "O my daughter, thy husband's wealth is indeed endless and he recketh not of it; for, from the day he entered our city, he hath done naught but give alms to the poor. Inshallah, he will speedily return with the baggage, and good in plenty shall betide us from him." And he went on to appease her and menace the Wazir, being duped by her device. So fared it with the King; but as regards Merchant Ma'aruf he rode on into waste lands, perplexed and knowing not to what quarter he should betake him; and for the anguish of parting he lamented and wept with sore weeping, for indeed the ways were walled up before his face and death seemed to him better than dreeing life, and he walked on like a drunken man for stress of distraction, and stayed not till noontide, when he came to a little town and saw a plougher hard by, ploughing with a yoke of bulls. Now hunger was sore upon him; and he went up to the ploughman and said to him, "Peace be with thee!"; and he returned his salam and said to him, "Welcome, O my lord! Art thou one of the Sultan's Mamelukes?" Quoth Ma'aruf, "Yes;" and the other said, "Alight with me for a guest-meal." Whereupon Ma'aruf knew him to be of the liberal and said to him, "O my brother, I see with thee naught with which thou mayst feed me: how is it, then, that thou invitest me?" Answered the husbandman, "O my lord, weal is well nigh.[56] Dismount thee here: the town is near hand and I will go and fetch thee dinner and fodder for thy stallion." Rejoined Ma'aruf, "Since the town is near at hand, I can go thither as quickly as thou canst and buy me what I have a mind to in the bazar and eat." The peasant replied, "O my lord, the place is but a little village[57] and there is no bazar there, neither selling nor buying. So I conjure thee by Allah, alight here with me and hearten my heart, and I will run thither and return to thee in haste."

Accordingly he dismounted and the Fellah left him and went off to the village, to fetch dinner for him whilst Ma'aruf sat awaiting him. Presently he said in himself, "I have taken this poor man away from his work;[58] but I will arise and plough in his stead, till he come back, to make up for having hindered him from his work." Then he took the plough and started the bulls, ploughed a little, till the share struck against something and the beasts stopped. He goaded them on, but they could not move the plough; so he looked at the share and finding it caught in a ring of gold, cleared away the soil and saw that it was set centre-most a slab of alabaster, the size of the nether millstone. He strave at the stone till he pulled it from its place, when there appeared beneath it a souterrain with a stair. Presently he descended the flight of steps and came to a place like a Hammam, with four daïses, the first full of gold, from floor to roof, the second full of emeralds and pearls and coral also from ground to ceiling; the third of jacinths and rubies and turquoises and the fourth of diamonds and all manner other preciousest stones. At the upper end of the place stood a coffer of clearest crystal, full of union-gems each the size of a walnut, and upon the coffer lay a casket of gold, the bigness of a lemon. When he saw this, he marvelled and rejoiced with joy exceeding and said to himself, "I wonder what is in this casket?" So he opened it and found therein a seal-ring of gold, whereon were graven names and talismans, as they were the cracks of creeping ants. He rubbed the ring and behold, a voice said, "Adsum! Here am I, at thy service, O my lord! Ask and it shall be given unto thee. Wilt thou raise a city or ruin a capital or kill a king or dig a river-channel or aught of the kind? Whatso thou seekest, it shall come to pass, by leave of the King of Allmight, Creator of day and night." Ma'aruf asked, "O creature of my lord, who and what art thou?"; and the other answered, "I am the slave of this seal-ring standing in the service of him who possesseth it. Whatsoever he seeketh, that I accomplish for him, and I have no excuse in neglecting that he biddeth me do; because I am Sultan over two-

and-seventy tribes of the Jinn, each two-and-seventy thousand in number every one of which thousand ruleth over a thousand Marids, each Marid over a thousand Ifrits, each Ifrit over a thousand Satans and each Satan over a thousand Jinn: and they are all under command of me and may not gainsay me. As for me, I am spelled to this seal-ring and may not thwart whoso holdeth it. Lo! thou hast gotten hold of it and I am become thy slave; so ask what thou wilt, for I hearken to thy word and obey thy bidding; and if thou have need of me at any time, by land or by sea, rub the signet-ring and thou wilt find me with thee. But beware of rubbing it twice in succession, or thou wilt consume me with the fire of the names graven thereon; and thus wouldst thou lose me and after regret me. Now I have acquainted thee with my case and—the Peace!" The Merchant asked him, "What is thy name?" and the Jinni answered, "My name is Abu al-Sa'adat."[59] Quoth Ma'aruf, "O Abu al-Sa'adat what is this place and who enchanted thee in this casket?"; and quoth he, "O my lord, this is a treasure called the Hoard of Shaddad son of Ad, him who the base of 'Many-columned Iram laid, the like of which in the lands was never made.'[60] I was his slave in his lifetime and this is his Seal-ring, which he laid up in his treasure; but it hath fallen to thy lot." Ma'aruf enquired, "Canst thou transport that which is in this hoard to the surface of the earth?"; and the Jinni replied, "Yes! Nothing were easier." Said Ma'aruf, "Bring it forth and leave naught." So the Jinni signed with his hand to the ground, which clave asunder, and he sank and was absent a little while. Presently, there came forth young boys full of grace, and fair of face bearing golden baskets filled with gold which they emptied out and going away, returned with more; nor did they cease to transport the gold and jewels, till ere an hour had sped they said, "Naught is left in the hoard." Thereupon out came Abu al-Sa'adat and said to Ma'aruf, "O my lord, thou seest that we have brought forth all that was in the hoard." Ma'aruf asked, "Who be these beautiful boys?" and the Jinni answered, "They are my sons. This matter merited not that

I should muster for it the Marids, wherefore my sons have done thy desire and are honoured by such service. So ask what thou wilt beside this." Quoth Ma'aruf, "Canst thou bring me he-mules and chests and fill the chests with the treasure and load them on the mules?" Quoth Abu al-Sa'adat, "Nothing easier," and cried a great cry; whereupon his sons presented themselves before him, to the number of eight hundred, and he said to them, "Let some of you take the semblance of he-mules and others of muleteers and handsome Mamelukes, the like of the least of whom is not found with any of the Kings; and others of you be transmewed to muleteers, and the rest to menials." So seven hundred of them changed themselves into bat-mules and other hundred took the shape of slaves. Then Abu al-Sa'adat called upon his Marids, who presented themselves between his hands and he commanded some of them to assume the aspect of horses saddled with saddles of gold crusted with jewels. And when Ma'aruf saw them do as he bade he cried, "Where be the chests?" They brought them before him and he said, "Pack the gold and the stones, each sort by itself." So they packed them and loaded three hundred he-mules with them. Then asked Ma'aruf, "O Abu al-Sa'adat, canst thou bring me some loads of costly stuffs?"; and the Jinni answered, "Wilt thou have Egyptian stuffs or Syrian or Persian or Indian or Greek?" Ma'aruf said, "Bring me an hundred loads of each kind, on five hundred mules;" and Abu al-Sa'adat, "O my lord, accord me delay that I may dispose my Marids for this and send a company of them to each country to fetch an hundred loads of its stuffs and then take the form of he-mules and return, carrying the stuffs." Ma'aruf enquired, "What time dost thou want?"; and Abu al-Sa'adat replied, "The time of the blackness of the night, and day shall not dawn ere thou have all thou desirest." Said Ma'aruf, "I grant thee this time," and bade them pitch him a pavilion. So they pitched it and he sat down therein and they brought him a table of food. Then said Abu al-Sa'adat to him, "O my lord, tarry thou in this tent and these my sons shall guard thee: so fear thou nothing; for I go to muster my Marids and despatch them to do thy desire." So saying, he departed, leaving Ma'aruf seated in the pavilion, with the table before him and the Jinni's sons attending upon him, in the guise of slaves and servants and suite. And while he sat in this state behold, up came the husbandman, with a great porringer of lentils[61] and a nose-bag full of barley and seeing the pavilion pitched and the Mamelukes standing, hands upon breasts, thought that the Sultan was come and had halted on that stead. So he stood open-mouthed and said in himself, "Would I had killed a couple of chickens and fried them red with clarified cow-butter for the Sultan!" And he would have turned back to kill the chickens as a regale for the Sultan; but Ma'aruf saw him and cried out to him and said to the Mamelukes, "Bring him hither." So they brought him and his porringer of lentils before Ma'aruf, who said to him, "What is this?" Said the peasant, "This is thy dinner and thy horse's fodder! Excuse me, for I thought not that the Sultan would come hither; and, had I known that, I would have killed a couple of chickens and entertained him in goodly guise." Quoth Ma'aruf, "The Sultan is not come. I am his son-in-law and I was vexed with him. However he hath sent his officers to make his peace with me, and now I am minded to return to city. But thou hast made me this guest-meal without knowing me, and I accept it from thee, lentils though it be, and will not eat save of thy cheer." Accordingly he bade him set the porringer amiddlemost the table and ate of it his sufficiency, whilst the Fellah filled his belly with those rich meats. Then Ma'aruf washed his hands and gave the Mamelukes leave to eat; so they fell upon the remains of the meal and ate; and, when the porringer was empty, he filled it with gold and gave it to the peasant, saying, "Carry this to thy dwelling and come to me in the city, and I will entreat thee with honour." Thereupon the peasant took the porringer full of gold and returned to the village, driving the bulls before him and deeming himself akin to the King. Meanwhile, they brought Ma'aruf girls of the Brides of the Treasure,[62] who smote on instruments of music and danced before him, and he passed that night in joyance and delight, a night not to be reckoned among lives. Hardly had dawned the day when there arose a great cloud of dust which presently lifting, discovered seven hundred mules laden with stuffs and attended by muleteers and baggage-tenders and cresset-bearers. With them came Abu al-Sa'adat, riding on a she-mule, in the guise of a caravan-leader, and before him was a travelling-litter, with four corner-terminals[63] of glittering red gold, set with gems. When Abu al-Sa'adat came up to the tent, he dismounted and kissing the earth, said to Ma'aruf, "O my lord, thy desire hath been done to the uttermost and in the litter is a treasure-suit which hath not its match among Kings' raiment: so don it and mount the litter and bid us do what thou wilt." Quoth Ma'aruf, "O Abu al-Sa'adat, I wish thee to go to the city of Ikhtiyan al-Khutan and present thyself to my father-in-law the King; and go thou not in to him but in the guise of a mortal courier;" and quoth he, "To hear is to obey." So Ma'aruf wrote a letter to the Sultan and sealed it and Abu al-Sa'adat took it and set out with it; and when he arrived, he found the King saying, "O Wazir, indeed my heart is concerned for my son-in-law and I fear lest the Arabs slay him. Would Heaven I wot whither he was bound, that I might have followed him with the troops! Would he had told me his destination!" Said the Wazir, "Allah be merciful to thee for this thy heedlessness! As thy head liveth, the wight saw that we were awake to him and feared dishonour and fled, for he is nothing but an impostor, a liar." And behold, at this moment in came the courier and kissing ground before the King, wished him permanent glory and prosperity and length of life. Asked the King, "Who art thou and what is thy business?" "I am a courier," answered the Jinni, "and thy son-in-law who is come with the baggage sendeth me to thee with a letter, and here it is!" So he took the letter and read therein these words, "After salutations galore to our uncle[64] the glorious King! Know that I am at hand with the baggage-train: so come thou forth to meet me with the troops." Cried the King, "Allah blacken thy brow, O Wazir! How often wilt thou defame my son-in-law's name and call him liar and impostor? Behold, he is come with the baggage-train and thou art naught but a traitor." The Minister hung his head groundwards in shame and confusion and replied, "O King of the age, I said not this save because of the long delay of the baggage and because I feared the loss of the wealth he hath wasted." The King exclaimed, "O traitor, what are my riches! Now that his baggage is come he will give me great plenty in their stead." Then he bade decorate the city and going in to his daughter, said to her, "Good news for thee! Thy husband will be here anon with his baggage; for he hath sent me a letter to that effect and here am I now going forth to meet him." The Princess Dunya marvelled at this and said in herself, "This is a wondrous thing! Was he laughing at me and making mock of me, or had he a mind to try me, when he told me that he was a pauper? But Alhamdolillah, Glory to God, for that I failed not of my duty to him!" On this wise fared it in the Palace; but as regards Merchant Ali, the Cairene, when he saw the decoration of the city and asked the cause thereof, they said to him, "The baggage-train of Merchant Ma'aruf, the King's son-in-law, is come." Said he, "Allah is Almighty! What a calamity is this man![65] He came to me, fleeing from his wife, and he was a poor man. Whence then should he get a baggage-train? But haply this is a device which the King's daughter hath contrived for him, fearing his disgrace, and Kings are not unable to do anything. May Allah the Most High veil his fame and not bring him to public shame!" And all the merchants rejoiced and were glad for that they would get their monies. Then the King assembled his troops and rode forth, whilst Abu al-Sa'adat returned to Ma'aruf and acquainted him with the delivering of the letter. Quoth Ma'aruf, "Bind on the loads;" and when they had done so, he donned the treasure-suit and mounting the litter became a thousand times greater and more majestic than the King. Then he set forward; but, when he had gone half-way, behold, the King met him with the troops, and seeing him riding in the Takhtrawan and clad in the dress aforesaid, threw himself upon him and saluted him, and giving him joy of his safety, greeted him with the greeting of peace. Then all the Lords of the land saluted him and it was made manifest that he had spoken the truth and that in him there was no lie. Presently he entered the city in such state procession as would have caused the gall-bladder of the lion to burst[66] for envy and the traders pressed up to him and kissed his hands, whilst Merchant Ali said to him, "Thou hast played off this trick and it hath prospered to thy hand, O Shaykh of Impostors! But thou deservest it and may Allah the Most High increase thee of His bounty!"; whereupon Ma'aruf laughed. Then he entered the palace and sitting down on the throne said, "Carry the loads of gold into the treasury of my uncle the King and bring me the bales of cloth." So they brought them to him and opened them before him, bale after bale, till they had unpacked the seven hundred loads, whereof he chose out the best and said, "Bear these to Princess Dunya that she may distribute them among her slave-girls; and carry her also this coffer of jewels, that she may divide them among her handmaids and eunuchs." Then he proceeded to make over the merchants in whose debt he was stuffs by way of payment for their arrears, giving him whose due was a thousand, stuffs worth two thousand or more; after which he fell to distributing to the poor and needy, whilst the King looked on with greedy eyes and could not hinder him; nor did he cease largesse till he had made an end of the seven hundred loads, when he turned to the troops and proceeded to apportion amongst them emeralds and rubies and pearls and coral and other jewels by handsful, without count, till the King said to him, "Enough of this giving, O my son! There is but little left of the baggage." But he said, "I have plenty." Then indeed, his good faith was become manifest and none could give him the lie; and he had come to reck not of giving, for that the Slave of the Seal-ring brought him whatsoever he sought. Presently, the treasurer came in to the King and said, "O King of the age, the treasury is full indeed and will not hold the rest of the loads. Where shall we lay that which is left of the gold and jewels?" And he assigned to him another place. As for the Princess Dunya when she saw this, her joy redoubled and she marvelled and said in herself, "Would I wot how came he by all this wealth!" In like manner the traders rejoiced in that which he had given them and blessed him; whilst Merchant Ali marvelled and said to himself, "I wonder how he hath lied and swindled that he hath gotten him all these treasures?[67] Had they come from the King's daughter, he had not wasted them on this wise! But how excellent is his saying who said:—

> When the Kings' King giveth, in reverence pause
> And venture not to enquire the cause:
> Allah gives His gifts unto whom He will,
> So respect and abide by His Holy Laws!"

So far concerning him; but as regards the King, he also marvelled with passing marvel at that which he saw of Ma'aruf's generosity and open-handedness in the largesse of wealth. Then the Merchant went in to his wife, who met him, smiling and laughing-lipped and kissed his hand, saying, "Didst thou mock me or hadst thou a mind to prove me with thy saying:—I am a poor man and a fugitive from my wife? Praised be Allah for that I failed not of my duty to thee! For thou art my beloved and there is none dearer to me than thou, whether thou be rich or poor. But I would have thee tell me what didst thou design by these words." Said Ma'aruf, "I wished to prove thee and see whether thy love were sincere or for the sake of wealth and the greed of worldly good. But now 'tis become manifest to me that thine affection is sincere and as thou art a true woman, so welcome to thee! I know thy worth." Then he went apart into a place by himself and rubbed the seal-ring, whereupon Abu al-Sa'adat presented himself and said to him, "Adsum at thy service! Ask what thou wilt." Quoth Ma'aruf, "I want a treasure-suit and treasure-trinkets for my wife, including a necklace of forty unique jewels." Quoth the Jinni, "To hear is to obey," and brought him what he sought, whereupon Ma'aruf dismissed him and carrying the dress and ornaments in to his wife, laid them before her and said, "Take these and put them on and welcome!" When she saw this, her wits fled for joy, and she found among the ornaments a pair of anklets of gold set with jewels of the handiwork of the magicians, and bracelets and earrings and a belt[68] such as no money could buy. So she donned the dress and ornaments and said to Ma'aruf, "O my lord, I will treasure these up for holidays and festivals." But he answered, "Wear them always, for I have others in plenty." And when she put them on and her women beheld her, they rejoiced and bussed his hands. Then he left them and going apart by himself, rubbed the seal-ring whereupon its slave appeared and he said to him, "Bring me an hundred suits of apparel, with their ornaments of gold." "Hearing and obeying," answered Abu al-Sa'adat and brought him the hundred suits, each with its ornaments wrapped up within it. Ma'aruf took them and called aloud to the slave-girls, who came to him and he gave them each a suit: so they donned them and became like the black-eyed girls of Paradise, whilst the Princess Dunya shone amongst them as the moon among the stars. One of the handmaids told the King of this and he came in to his daughter and saw her and her women dazzling all who beheld them; whereat he wondered with passing wonderment. Then he went out and calling his Wazir, said to him, "O Wazir, such and such things have happened; what sayst thou now of this affair?" Said he, "O King of the age, this be no merchant's fashion; for a merchant keepeth a piece of linen by him for years and selleth it not but at a profit. How should a merchant have generosity such as this generosity, and whence should he get the like of these monies and jewels, of which but a slight matter is found with the Kings? So how should loads thereof be found with merchants? Needs must there be a cause for this; but, an thou wilt hearken to me, I will make the truth of the case manifest to thee." Answered the King,

"O Wazir, I will do thy bidding." Rejoined the Minister, "Do thou foregather with thy son-in-law and make a show of affect to him and talk with him and say:—O my son-in-law, I have a mind to go, I and thou and the Wazir but no more, to a flower-garden that we may take our pleasure there. When we come to the garden, we will set on the table wine, and I will ply him therewith and compel him to drink; for, when he shall have drunken, he will lose his reason and his judgment will forsake him. Then we will question him of the truth of his case and he will discover to us his secrets, for wine is a traitor and Allah-gifted is he who said:—

> When we drank the wine, and it crept its way
> To the place of Secrets, I cried, 'O stay!'
> In my fear lest its influence stint my wits
> And my friends spy matters that hidden lay.

When he hath told us the truth we shall ken his case and may deal with him as we will; because I fear for thee the consequences of this his present fashion: haply he will covet the kingship and win over the troops by generosity and lavishing money and so depose thee and take the kingdom from thee." The King said to him, "Thou hast spoken sooth!"; and they passed the night on this agreement. And when morning morrowed the King went forth and sat in the guest-chamber, when lo, and behold! the grooms and serving-men came in to him in dismay. Quoth he, "What hath befallen you?"; and quoth they, "O King of the age, the Syces curried the horses and foddered them and the hemules which brought the baggage; but, when we arose in the morning, we found that thy son-in-law's Mamelukes had stolen the horses and mules. We searched the stables, but found neither horse nor mule; so we entered the lodging of the Mamelukes and found none there, nor know we how they fled." The King marvelled at this, unknowing that the horses and Mamelukes were all Ifrits, the subjects of the Slave of the Spell, and asked the grooms, "O accursed, how could a thousand beasts and five hundred slaves and servants flee without your knowledge?" Answered they, "We know not how it happened," and he cried, "Go, and when your lord cometh forth of the Harim, tell him the case." So they went out from before the King and sat down bewildered, till Ma'aruf came out and, seeing them chagrined enquired of them, "What may be the matter?" They told him all that had happened and he said, "What is their worth that ye should be concerned for them? Wend your ways." And he sat laughing and was neither angry nor grieved concerning the case; whereupon the King looked in the Wazir's face and said to him, "What manner of man is this, with whom wealth is of no worth? Needs must there be a reason for this?" Then they talked with him awhile and the King said to him, "O my son-in-law, I have a mind to go, I, thou and the Wazir, to a garden, where we may divert ourselves." "No harm in that," said Ma'aruf. So they went forth to a flower-garden, wherein every sort of fruit was of kinds twain and its waters were flowing and its trees towering and its birds carolling. There they entered a pavilion, whose sight did away sorrow from the soul, and sat talking, whilst the Minister entertained them with rare tales and quoted merry quips and mirth-provoking sayings and Ma'aruf attentively listened, till the time of dinner came, when they set on a tray of meats and a flagon of wine. When they had eaten and washed hands, the Wazir filled the cup and gave it to the King, who drank it off; then he filled a second and handed it to Ma'aruf, saying, "Take the cup of the drink to which Reason boweth neck in reverence." Quoth Ma'aruf, "What is this, O Wazir?"; and quoth he, "This is the grizzled[69] virgin and the old maid long kept at home,[70] the giver of joy to hearts, whereof said the poet:—

The feet of sturdy Miscreants[71] went trampling heavy tread,
And she hath ta'en a vengeance dire on every Arab's head.
A Kafir youth like fullest moon in darkness hands her round

Whose eyne are strongest cause of sin by him
    inspiritèd.

And Allah-gifted is he who said:—

> 'Tis as if wine and he who bears the bowl,
> Rising to show her charms for man to see,[72]
> Were dancing undurn-Sun whose face the moon
> Of night adorned with stars of Gemini
> So subtle is her essence it would seem
> Through every limb like course of soul runs she.

And yet another;—

> Wine-cup and ruby-wine high worship claim;
> Dishonour 'twere to see their honour waste:
> Bury me, when I'm dead, by side of vine
> Whose veins shall moisten bones in clay misplaced;
> Nor bury me in wold and wild, for I
> Dread only after death no wine to taste."[73]

And he ceased not to egg him on to the drink, naming to
him such of the virtues of wine as he thought well and
reciting to him what occurred to him of poetry and pleasantries on the subject, till Ma'aruf addressed himself to
sucking the cup-lips and cared no longer for aught else.
The Wazir ceased not to fill for him and he to drink and
enjoy himself and make merry, till his wits wandered and
he could not distinguish right from wrong. When the Minister saw that drunkenness had attained in him to the utterest and the bounds transgressed, he said to him, "By
Allah, O Merchant Ma'aruf, I admire whence thou gottest
these jewels whose like the Kings of the Chosroes possess not! In all our lives never saw we a merchant that had
heaped up riches like unto thine or more generous than
thou, for thy doings are the doings of Kings and not merchants' doings. Wherefore, Allah upon thee, do thou acquaint
me with this, that I may know thy rank and condition."
And he went on to test him with questions and cajole him,

till Ma'aruf, being reft of reason, said to him, "I'm neither merchant nor King," and told him his whole story from first to last. Then said the Wazir, "I conjure thee by Allah, O my lord Ma'aruf, show us the ring, that we may see its make." So, in his drunkenness, he pulled off the ring and said, "Take it and look upon it." The Minister took it and turning it over, said, "If I rub it, will its slave appear?" Replied Ma'aruf, "Yes. Rub it and he will appear to thee, and do thou divert thyself with the sight of him." Thereupon the Wazir rubbed the ring and behold forthright appeared the Jinni and said, "Adsum, at thy service, O my lord! Ask and it shall be given to thee. Wilt thou ruin a city or raise a capital or kill a king? Whatso thou seekest, I will do for thee, sans fail." The Wazir pointed to Ma'aruf and said, "Take up yonder wretch and cast him down in the most desolate of desert lands, where he shall find nothing to eat nor drink, so he may die of hunger and perish miserably, and none know of him." Accordingly, the Jinni snatched him up and flew with him betwixt heaven and earth, which when Ma'aruf saw, he made sure of destruction and wept and said, "O Abu al-Sa'adat, whither goest thou with me?" Replied the Jinni, "I go to cast thee down in the Desert Quarter,[74] O ill-bred wight of gross wits. Shall one have the like of this talisman and give it to the folk to gaze at? Verily, thou deservest that which hath befallen thee; and but that I fear Allah, I would let thee fall from a height of a thousand fathoms, nor shouldst thou reach the earth, till the winds had torn thee to shreds." Ma'aruf was silent[75] and did not again bespeak him till he reached the Desert Quarter and casting him down there went away and left him in that horrible place. So much concerning him; but returning to the Wazir who was now in possession of the talisman, he said to the King, "How deemest thou now? Did I not tell thee that this fellow was a liar, an impostor, but thou wouldst not credit me?" Replied the King, "Thou wast in the right, O my Wazir, Allah grant thee weal! But give me the ring, that I may solace myself with the sight." The Minister looked at him angrily and spat in his face, saying, "O lackwits, how shall I give it to thee and abide thy servant, after I am become thy master? But I will spare thee no more on life." Then he rubbed the seal-ring and said to the Slave, "Take up this ill-mannered churl and cast him down by his son-in-law the swindlerman." So the Jinni took him up and flew off with him, whereupon quoth the King to him, "O creature of my Lord, what is my crime?" Abu al-Sa'adat replied, "That wot I not, but my master hath commanded me and I cannot cross whoso hath compassed the enchanted ring." Then he flew on with him, till he came to the Desert Quarter and, casting him down where he had cast Ma'aruf left him and returned. The King hearing Ma'aruf weeping, went up to him and acquainted him with his case; and they sat weeping over that which had befallen them and found neither meat nor drink. Meanwhile the Minister, after driving father-in-law and son-in-law from the country, went forth from the garden and summoning all the troops held a Divan, and told them what he had done with the King and Ma'aruf and acquainted them with the affair of the talisman, adding, "Unless ye make me Sultan over you, I will bid the Slave of the Seal-ring take you up one and all and cast you down in the Desert Quarter where you shall die of hunger and thirst." They replied, "Do us no damage, for we accept thee as Sultan over us and will not anywise gainsay thy bidding." So they agreed, in their own despite, to his being Sultan over them, and he bestowed on them robes of honour, seeking all he had a mind to of Abu al-Sa'adat, who brought it to him forthwith. Then he sat down on the throne and the troops did homage to him; and he sent to Princess Dunya, the King's daughter, saying, "Make thee ready, for I mean to come in unto thee this night, because I long for thee with love." When she heard this, she wept, for the case of her husband and father was grievous to her, and sent to him saying, "Have patience with me till my period of widowhood[76] be ended: then draw up thy contract of marriage with me and go in to me according to law." But he sent back to say to her, "I know neither period of widowhood nor to delay have I a mood; and I need not a contract nor know I lawful from unlawful; but needs must I go unto thee this night." She answered him saying, "So be it, then, and welcome to thee!"; but this was a trick on her part. When the answer reached the Wazir, he rejoiced and his breast was broadened, for that he was passionately in love with her. He bade set food before all the folk, saying, "Eat; this is my bride-feast; for I purpose to go in to the Princess Dunya this night." Quoth the Shaykh al-Islam, "It is not lawful for thee to go in unto her till her days of widowhood be ended and thou have drawn up thy contract of marriage with her." But he answered, "I know neither days of widowhood nor other period; so multiply not words on me." The Shaykh al-Islam was silent,[77] fearing his mischief, and said to the troops, "Verily, this man is a Kafir, a Miscreant, and hath neither creed nor religious conduct." As soon as it was evenfall, he went in to her and found her robed in her richest raiment and decked with her goodliest adornments. When she saw him, she came to meet him, laughing and said, "A blessed night! But hadst thou slain my father and my husband, it had been more to my mind." And he said, "There is no help but I slay them." Then she made him sit down and began to jest with him and make show of love caressing him and smiling in his face so that his reason fled; but she cajoled him with her coaxing and cunning only that she might get possession of the ring and change his joy into calamity on the mother of his forehead:[78] nor did she deal thus with him but after the rede of him who said:[79]—

> I attained by my wits
> What no sword had obtained,
> And return wi' the spoils
> Whose sweet pluckings I gained.

When he saw her caress him and smile upon him, desire surged up in him and he besought her of carnal knowledge; but, when he approached her, she drew away from him and burst into tears, saying, "O my lord, seest thou not the man looking at us? I conjure thee by Allah, screen me from his eyes! How canst thou know me what while he looketh on us?" When he heard this, he was angry and asked, "Where is the man?"; and answered she, "There he is, in the bezel of the ring! putting out his head and staring at us." He thought that the Jinni was looking at them and said laughing, "Fear not; this is the Slave of the Seal-ring, and he is subject to me." Quoth she, "I am afraid of Ifrits; pull it off and throw it afar from me." So he plucked it off and laying it on the cushion, drew near to her, but she dealt him a kick, her foot striking him full in the stomach,[80] and he fell over on his back senseless; whereupon she cried out to her attendants, who came to her in haste, and said to them, "Seize him!" So forty slave-girls laid hold on him, whilst she hurriedly snatched up the ring from the cushion and rubbed it; whereupon Abu al-Sa'adat presented himself, saying, "Adsum, at thy service, O my mistress." Cried she, "Take up yonder Infidel and clap him in jail and shackle him heavily." So he took him and throwing him into the Prison of Wrath[81] returned and reported, "I have laid him in limbo." Quoth she, "Whither wentest thou with my father and my husband?"; and quoth he, "I cast them down in the Desert Quarter." Then cried she, "I command thee to fetch them to me forthwith." He replied, "I hear and I obey," and taking flight at once, stayed not till he reached the Desert Quarter, where he lighted down upon them and found them sitting weeping and complaining each to other. Quoth he, "Fear not, for relief is come to you"; and he told them what the Wazir had done, adding, "Indeed I imprisoned him with my own hands in obedience to her, and she hath bidden me bear you back." And they rejoiced in his news. Then he took them both up and flew home with them; nor was it more than an hour before he brought them in to Princess Dunya, who rose and saluted sire and spouse. Then she made them sit down and brought them food and sweetmeats, and they passed the rest of the night with her. On the next day she clad them in rich clothing and said to the King, "O my papa, sit thou upon thy throne and be King as before and make my husband thy Wazir of the Right and tell thy troops that which hath happened. Then send for the Minister out of prison and do him die, and after burn him, for that he is a Miscreant, and would have gone in unto me in the way of lewdness, without the rites of wedlock and he hath testified against himself that he is an Infidel and believeth in no religion. And do tenderly by thy son-in-law, whom thou makest thy Wazir of the Right." He replied, "Hearing and obeying, O my daughter. But do thou give me the ring or give it to thy husband." Quoth she, "It behoveth not that either thou or he have the ring. I will keep the ring myself, and belike I shall be more careful of it than you. Whatso ye wish seek it of me and I will demand it for you of the Slave of the Seal-ring. So fear no harm so long as I live and after my death, do what ye twain will with the ring." Quoth the King, "This is the right rede, O my daughter," and taking his son-in-law went forth to the Divan. Now the troops had passed the night in sore chagrin for Princess Dunya and that which the Wazir had done with her, in going to her after the way of lewdness, without marriage-rites, and for his ill-usuage of the King and Ma'aruf, and they feared lest the law of Al-Islam be dishonoured, because it was manifest to them that he was a Kafir. So they assembled in the Divan and fell to reproaching the Shaykh al-Islam, saying "Why didst thou not forbid him from going in to the Princess in the way of lewdness?" Said he, "O folk, the man is a Miscreant and hath gotten possession of the ring and I and you may not prevail against him. But Almighty Allah will requite him his deed, and be ye silent, lest he slay you." And as the host was thus engaged in talk, behold the King and Ma'aruf entered the Divan. Then the King bade decorate the city and sent to fetch the Wazir from the place of duresse. So they brought him, and as he passed by the troops, they cursed him and abused him and menaced him, till he came to the King, who commanded to do him dead by the vilest of deaths. Accordingly, they slew him and after burned his body, and he went to Hell after the foulest of plights. The King made Ma'aruf his Wazir of the Right and the times were pleasant to them and their joys were untroubled. They abode thus five years till, in the sixth year, the King died and Princess Dunya made Ma'aruf Sultan in her father's stead, but she gave him not the seal-ring. During this time she had conceived by him and borne him a boy of passing loveliness, excelling in beauty and perfection, who ceased not to be reared in the laps of nurses till he reached the age of five, when his mother fell sick of a deadly sickness and calling her husband to her, said to him, "I am ill." Quoth he, "Allah preserve thee, O dearling of my heart!" But quoth she, "Haply I shall die and thou needst not that I commend to thy care thy son: wherefore I charge thee but be careful of the ring, for thine own sake and for the sake of this thy boy." And he answered, "No harm shall befal him whom Allah preserveth!" Then she pulled off the ring and gave it to him, and on the morrow she was admitted to the mercy of Allah the Most High,[82] whilst Ma'aruf abode in possession of the kingship and applied himself to the business of governing. Now it chanced that one day, as he shook the handkerchief[83] and the troops withdrew to their places that he betook himself to the sitting-chamber, where he sat till the day departed and the night advanced with murks bedight. Then came in to him his cup-companions of the notables according to their custom, and sat with by way of solace and diversion, till midnight, when they craved permission to withdraw. He gave them leave and they retired to their houses; after which there came in to him a slave-girl affected to the service of his bed, who spread him the mattress and doffing his apparel, clad him in his sleeping-gown. Then he lay down and she kneaded his feet, till sleep overpowered him; whereupon she withdrew to her own chamber and slept. But suddenly he felt something beside him in the bed and awaking started up in alarm and cried, "I seek refuge with Allah from Satan the stoned!" Then he opened his eyes and seeing by his side a woman foul of favour, said to her, "Who art thou?" Said she, "Fear not, I am thy wife Fatimah al-Urrah." Whereupon he looked in her face and knew her by her loathly form and the length of her dog-teeth: so he asked her, "Whence camest thou in to me and who brought thee to this country?" "In what country art thou at this present?" "In the city of Ikhtiyan al-Khutan. But thou, when didst thou leave Cairo?" "But now." "How can that be?" "Know," said she, "that, when I fell out with thee and Satan prompted me to do thee a damage, I complained of thee to the magistrates, who sought for thee and the Kazis enquired of thee, but found thee not. When two days were past, repentance gat hold upon me and I knew that the fault was with me; but penitence availed me not, and I abode for some days weeping for thy loss, till what was in my hand failed and I was obliged to beg my bread. So I fell to begging of all, from the courted rich to the contemned poor, and since thou leftest me, I have eaten of the bitterness of beggary and have been in the sorriest of conditions. Every night I sat beweeping our separation and that which I suffered, since thy departure, of humiliation and ignominy, of abjection and misery." And she went on to tell him what had befallen her whilst he stared at her in amazement, till she said, "Yesterday, I went about begging all day but none gave me aught; and as often as I accosted any one and craved of him a crust of bread, he reviled me and gave me naught. When night came, I went to bed supperless, and hunger burned me and sore on me was that which I suffered: and I sat weeping when, behold, one appeared to me and said, O woman why weepest thou? Said I, erst I had a husband who used to provide for me and fulfil my wishes; but he is lost to me and I know not whither he went and have been in sore straits since he left me. Asked he, What is thy husband's name? and I answered, His name is Ma'aruf. Quoth he, I ken him. Know that thy husband is now Sultan in a certain city, and if thou wilt, I will carry thee to him. Cried I, I am under thy protection: of thy bounty bring me to him! So he took me up and flew with me between heaven and earth, till he brought me to this pavilion and said to me:—Enter yonder chamber, and thou shalt see thy husband asleep on the couch. Accordingly I entered and found thee in this state of lordship. Indeed I had not thought thou wouldst forsake me, who am thy mate, and praised be Allah who hath united thee with me!" Quoth Ma'aruf, "Did I forsake thee or thou me? Thou complainedst of me from Kazi to Kazi and endedst by denouncing me to the High Court and bringing down on me Abu Tabak from the Citadel: so I fled in mine own despite." And he went on to tell her all that had befallen him and how he was become Sultan and had married the King's daughter and how his beloved Dunya had died, leaving him a son who was then seven years old. She rejoined, "That which happened was fore-ordained of Allah; but I repent me and I place myself under thy protection beseeching thee not to abandon me, but suffer me eat bread, with thee by way of an alms." And she ceased not to humble herself to him and to supplicate him till his heart relented towards her and he said, "Repent from mischief and abide with me, and naught shall betide thee save what shall pleasure thee: but, an thou work any wickedness, I will slay thee nor fear any one. And fancy not that thou canst complain of me to the High Court and that Abu Tabak will come down on me from the Citadel; for I am become Sultan and the folk dread me: but I fear none save Allah Almighty, because I have a talismanic ring which when I rub, the Slave of the Signet appeareth to me. His name is Abu al-Sa'adat, and whatsoever I demand of him he bringeth to me. So, an thou desire to return to thine own country, I will give thee what shall suffice thee all thy life long and will send thee thither speedily; but, an thou desire to abide with me, I will clear for thee a palace and furnish it with the choicest of silks and appoint thee twenty slave-girls to serve thee and provide thee with dainty dishes and sumptuous suits, and thou shalt be a Queen and live in all delight till thou die or I die. What sayest thou of this?" "I wish to abide with thee," she answered and kissed his hand and vowed repentance from frowardness. Accordingly he set apart a palace for her sole use and gave her slave-girls and eunuchs, and she became a Queen. The young Prince used to visit her as he visited his sire; but she hated him for that he was not her son; and when the boy saw that she looked on him with the eye of aversion and anger, he shunned her and took a dislike to her. As for Ma'aruf, he occupied himself with the love of fair handmaidens and bethought him not of his wife Fatimah the Dung, for that she was grown a grizzled old fright, foul-favoured to the sight, a bald-headed blight, loathlier than the snake speckled black and white; the more that she had beyond measure evil entreated him aforetime; and as saith the adage, "Ill-usage the root of desire disparts and sows hate in the soil of hearts;" and God-gifted is he who saith:—

Beware of losing hearts of men by thine injurious deed;
For when Aversion takes his place none may dear Love
    restore:
Hearts, when affection flies from them, are likest unto glass
Which broken, cannot whole be made,—'tis breached for
    evermore.

And indeed Ma'aruf had not given her shelter by reason of any praiseworthy quality in her, but he dealt with her thus generously only of desire for the approval of Allah Almighty.—Here Dunyazad interrupted her sister Shahrazad, saying, "How winsome are these words of thine which win hold of the heart more forcibly than enchanters' eyne; and how beautiful are these wondrous books thou hast cited and the marvellous and singular tales thou hast recited!" Quoth Shahrazad, "And where is all this compared with what I shall relate to thee on the coming night, an I live and the King deign spare my days?" So when morning morrowed and the day brake in its sheen and shone, the King arose from his couch with breast broadened and in high expectation for the rest of the tale and saying, "By Allah, I will not slay her till I hear the last of her story;" repaired to his Durbar while the Wazir, as was his wont, presented himself at the Palace, shroud under arm. Shahriyar tarried abroad all the day, bidding and forbidding between man and man; after which he returned to his Harim and, according to his custom, went in to his wife Shahrazad.[84]

NOW WHEN IT WAS THE
THOUSAND AND FIRST NIGHT,

Dunyazad said to her sister, "Do thou finish for us the History of Ma'aruf!" She replied, "With love and goodly gree, an my lord deign permit me recount it." Quoth the King, "I permit thee; for that I am fain of hearing it." So she said:—It hath reached me, O auspicious King, that Ma'aruf would have naught to do with his wife by way of conjugal duty. Now when she saw that he held aloof from her bed and occupied himself with other women, she hated him and jealously gat the mastery of her and Iblis prompted her to take the seal-ring from him and slay him and make herself Queen in his stead. So she went forth one night from her pavilion, intending for that in which was her husband King Ma'aruf; and it chanced by decree of the Decreer and His written destiny, that Ma'aruf lay that night with one of his concubines; a damsel endowed with beauty and loveliness, symmetry and a stature all grace. And it was his wont, of the excellence of his piety, that, when he was minded to have to lie with a woman, he would doff the enchanted seal-ring from his finger, in reverence to the Holy Names graven thereon, and lay it on the pillow, nor would he don it again till he had purified himself by the Ghusl-ablution. Moreover, when he had lain with a woman, he was used to order her go forth from him before daybreak, of his fear for the seal-ring; and when he went to the Hammam he locked the door of the pavilion till his return, when he put on the ring, and after this, all were free to enter according to custom. His wife Fatimah the Dung knew of all this and went not forth from her place till she had certified herself of the case. So she sallied out, when the night was dark, purposing to go in to him, whilst he was drowned in sleep, and steal the ring, unseen of him. Now it chanced at this time that the King's son had gone out, without light, to the Chapel of Ease for an occasion, and sat down over the marble slab[85] of the jakes in the dark, leaving the door open. Presently, he saw Fatimah come forth of her pavilion and make stealthily for that of his father and said in himself, "What aileth this witch to leave her lodging in the dead of the night and make for my father's pavilion? Needs must there be some reason for this:" so he went out after her and followed in her steps unseen of her. Now he had a short sword of watered steel, which he held so dear that he went not to his father's Divan, except he were girt therewith; and his father used to laugh at him and exclaim, "Mahallah![86] This is a mighty fine sword of thine, O my son! But thou hast not gone down with it to battle nor cut off a head therewith." Whereupon the boy would reply, "I will not fail to cut off with it some head which deserveth[87] cutting." And Ma'aruf would laugh at his words. Now when treading in her track, he drew the sword from its sheath and he followed her till she came to his father's pavilion and entered, whilst he stood and watched her from the door. He saw her searching about and heard her say to herself, "Where hath he laid the seal-ring?"; whereby he knew that she was looking for the ring and he waited till she found it and said, "Here it is." Then she picked it up and turned to go out; but he hid behind the door. As she came forth, she looked at the ring and turned it about in her grasp. But when she was about to rub it, he raised his hand with the sword and smote her on the neck; and she cried a single cry and fell down dead. With this Ma'aruf awoke and seeing his wife strown on the ground, with her blood flowing, and his son standing with the drawn sword in his hand, said to him, "What is this, O my son?" He replied, "O my father, how often hast thou said to me, Thou hast a mighty fine sword; but thou hast not gone down with it to battle nor cut off a head. And I have answered thee, saying, I will not fail to cut off with it a head which deserveth cutting. And now, behold, I have therewith cut off for thee a head well worth the cutting!" And he told him what had passed. Ma'aruf sought for the Seal-ring, but found it not; so he searched the dead woman's body till he saw her hand closed upon it; whereupon he took it from her grasp and said to the boy, "Thou art indeed my very son, without doubt or dispute; Allah ease thee in this world and the next, even as thou hast eased me of this vile woman! Her attempt led only to her own destruction, and Allah-gifted is he who said:—

> When forwards Allah's aid a man's intent,
> His wish in every case shall find consent:
> But an that aid of Allah be refused,
> His first attempt shall do him damagement."

Then King Ma'aruf called aloud to some of his attendants, who came in haste, and he told them what his wife Fatimah the Dung had done and bade them to take her and lay her in a place till the morning. They did his bidding, and next day he gave her in charge to a number of eunuchs, who washed her and shrouded her and made her a tomb[88] and buried her. Thus her coming from Cairo was but to her grave, and Allah-gifted is he who said:[89]—

> We trod the steps appointed for us: and he whose steps are appointed must tread them.
> He whose death is decreed to take place in our land shall not die in any land but that.

After this, King Ma'aruf sent for the husbandman, whose guest he had been, when he was a fugitive, and made him his Wazir of the Right and his Chief Counsellor.[90] Then, learning that he had a daughter of passing beauty and loveliness, of qualities nature-ennobled at birth and exalted of worth, he took her to wife; and in due time he married his son. So they abode awhile in all solace of life and its delight and their days were serene and their joys untroubled, till there came to them the Destroyer of delights and the Sunderer of societies, the Depopulator of populous places and the Orphaner of sons and daughters. And glory be to the Living who dieth not and in whose hand are the Keys of the Seen and the Unseen!

CONCLUSION.

Now, during this time, Shahrazad had borne the King three boy children: so, when she had made an end of the story of Ma'aruf, she rose to her feet and kissing ground before him, said, "O King of the time and unique one[1] of the age and the tide, I am thine handmaid and these thousand nights and a night have I entertained thee with stories of folk gone before and admonitory instances of the men of yore. May I then make bold to crave a boon of Thy Highness?" He replied, "Ask, O Shahrazad, and it shall be granted to thee."[2] Whereupon she cried out to the nurses and the eunuchs, saying, "Bring me my children." So they brought them to her in haste, and they were three boy children, one walking, one crawling and one suckling. She took them and setting them before the King, again kissed the ground and said, "O King of the age, these are thy children and I crave that thou release me from the doom of death, as a dole to these infants; for, an thou kill me, they will become motherless and will find none among women to rear them as they should be reared." When the King heard this, he wept and straining the boys to his bosom, said, "By Allah, O Shahrazad, I pardoned thee before the coming of these children, for that I found thee chaste, pure, ingenuous and pious! Allah bless thee and thy father and thy mother and thy root and thy branch! I take the Almighty to witness against me that I exempt thee from aught that can harm thee." So she kissed his hands and feet and rejoiced with exceeding joy, saying, "The Lord make thy life long and increase thee in dignity and majesty!";[3] presently adding, "Thou marvelledst at that which befel thee on the part of women; yet there betided the Kings of the Chosroes before thee greater mishaps and more grievous than that which hath befallen thee, and indeed I have set forth unto thee that which happened to Caliphs and Kings and others with their women, but the relation is longsome and hearkening groweth tedious, and in this is all-sufficient warning for the man of wits and admonishment for the wise." Then she ceased to speak, and when King Shahriyar heard her speech and profited by that which she said, he summoned up his reasoning powers and cleansed his heart and caused his understanding revert and turned to Allah Almighty and said to himself, "Since there befel the Kings of the Chosroes more than that which hath befallen me, never, whilst I live, shall I cease to blame myself for the past. As for this Shahrazad, her like is not found in the lands; so praise be to Him who appointed her a means for delivering His creatures from oppression and slaughter!" Then he arose from his seance and kissed her head, whereat she rejoiced, she and her sister Dunyazad, with exceeding joy. When the morning morrowed, the King went forth and sitting down on the throne of the Kingship, summoned the Lords of his land; whereupon the Chamberlains and Nabobs and Captains of the host went in to him and kissed ground before him. He distinguished the Wazir, Shahrazad's sire, with special favour and bestowed on him a costly and splendid robe of honour and entreated him with the utmost kindness, and said to him, "Allah protect thee for that thou gavest me to wife thy noble daughter, who hath been the means of my repentance from slaying the daughters of folk. Indeed I have found her pure and pious, chaste and ingenuous, and Allah hath vouchsafed me by her three boy children; wherefore praised be He for his passing favour." Then he bestowed robes of honour upon his Wazirs, and Emirs and Chief Officers and he set forth to them briefly that which had betided him with Shahrazad and how he had turned from his former ways and repented him of what he had done and purposed to take the Wazir's daughter, Shahrazad, to wife and let draw up the marriage-contract with her. When those who were present heard this, they kissed the ground before him and blessed him and his betrothed[4] Shahrazad, and the Wazir thanked her. Then Shahriyar made an end of his sitting in all weal, whereupon the folk dispersed to their dwelling-places and the news was bruited abroad that the King purposed to marry the Wazir's daughter, Shahrazad. Then he proceeded to make ready the wedding gear, and presently he sent after his brother, King Shah Zaman, who came, and King Shahriyar went forth to meet him with the troops. Furthermore, they decorated the city after the goodliest fashion and diffused scents from censers and burnt aloes-wood and other perfumes in all the markets and thoroughfares and rubbed themselves with saffron,[5] what while the drums beat and the flutes and pipes sounded and mimes and mountebanks played and plied their arts and the King lavished on them gifts and largesse; and in very deed it was a notable day. When they came to the palace, King Shahriyar commanded to spread the tables with beasts roasted whole and sweetmeats and all manner of viands and bade the crier cry to the folk that they should come up to the Divan and eat and drink and that this should be a means of reconciliation between him and them. So, high and low, great and small came up unto him and they abode on that wise, eating and drinking, seven days with their nights. Then the King shut himself up with his brother and related to him that which had betided him with the Wazir's daughter, Shahrazad, during the past three years and told him what he had heard from her of proverbs and parables, chronicles and pleasantries, quips and jests, stories and anecdotes, dialogues and histories and elegies and other verses; whereat King Shah Zaman marvelled with the uttermost marvel and said, "Fain would I take her younger sister to wife, so we may be two brothers-german to two sisters-german, and they on like wise be sisters to us; for that the calamity which befel me was the cause of our discovering that which befel thee and all this time of three years past I have taken no delight in woman, save that I lie each night with a damsel of my kingdom, and every morning I do her to death; but now I desire to marry thy wife's sister Dunyazad." When King Shahriyar heard his brother's words, he rejoiced with joy exceeding and arising forthright, went in to his wife Shahrazad and acquainted her with that which his brother purposed, namely that he sought her sister Dunyazad in wedlock; whereupon she answered, "O King of the age, we seek of him one condition, to wit, that he take up his abode with us, for that I cannot brook to be parted from my sister an hour, because we were brought up together and may not endure separation each from other.[6] If he accept this pact, she is his handmaid." King Shahriyar returned to his brother and acquainted him with that which Shahrazad had said; and he replied, "Indeed, this is what was in my mind, for that I desire nevermore to be parted from thee one hour. As for the kingdom, Allah the Most High shall send to it whomso He chooseth, for that I have no longer a desire for the kingship." When King Shahriyar heard his brother's words, he rejoiced exceedingly and said, "Verily, this is what I wished, O my brother. So Alhamdolillah—Praised be Allah—who hath brought about union between us." Then he sent after the Kazis and Olema, Captains and Notables, and they married the two brothers to the two sisters. The contracts were written out and the two Kings bestowed robes of honour of silk and satin on those who were present, whilst the city was decorated and the rejoicings were renewed. The King commanded each Emir and Wazir and Chamberlain and Nabob to decorate his palace and the folk of the city were gladdened by the presage of happiness and contentment. King Shahriyar also bade slaughter sheep and set up kitchens and made bride-feasts and fed all comers, high and low; and he gave alms to the poor and needy and extended his bounty to great and small. Then the eunuchs went forth, that they might perfume the Hammam for the brides; so they scented it with rose-water and willow-flower-water and pods of musk and fumigated it with Kakili[7] eagle-wood and ambergris. Then Shahrazad entered, she and her sister Dunyazad, and they cleansed their heads and clipped their hair. When they came forth of the Hammam-bath, they donned raiment and ornaments; such as men were wont prepare for the Kings of the Chosroes; and among Shahrazad's apparel was a dress purfled with red gold and wrought with counterfeit presentments of birds and beasts. And the two sisters encircled their necks with necklaces of jewels of price, in the like whereof Iskander[8] rejoiced not, for therein were great jewels such as amazed the wit and dazzled the eye; and the imagination was bewildered at their charms, for indeed each of them was brighter than the sun and the moon. Before them they lighted brilliant flambeaux of wax in candelabra of gold, but their faces outshone the flambeaux, for that they had eyes sharper than unsheathed swords and the lashes of their eyelids bewitched all hearts. Their cheeks were rosy red and their necks and shapes gracefully swayed and their eyes wantoned like the gazelle's; and the slave-girls came to meet them with instruments of music. Then the two Kings entered the Hammam-bath, and when they came forth, they sat down on a couch set with pearls and gems, whereupon the two sisters came up to them and stood between their hands, as they were moons, bending and leaning from side to side in their beauty and loveliness. Presently they brought forward Shahrazad and displayed her, for the first dress, in a red suit; whereupon

King Shahriyar rose to look upon her and the wits of all present, men and women, were bewitched for that she was even as saith of her one of her describers:—

> A sun on wand in knoll of sand she showed,
> Clad in her cramoisy-hued chemisette:
> Of her lips' honey-dew she gave me drink
> And with her rosy cheeks quencht fire she set.

Then they attired Dunyazad in a dress of blue brocade and she became as she were the full moon when it shineth forth. So they displayed her in this, for the first dress, before King Shah Zaman, who rejoiced in her and well-nigh swooned away for love-longing and amorous desire; yea, he was distraught with passion for her, whenas he saw her, because she was as saith of her one of her describers in these couplets:—

> She comes apparelled in an azure vest
> Ultramarine as skies are deckt and dight:
> I view'd th' unparallel'd sight, which showed my eyes
> A Summer-moon upon a Winter-night.

Then they returned to Shahrazad and displayed her in the second dress, a suit of surpassing goodliness, and veiled her face with her hair like a chin-veil.[9] Moreover, they let down her side-locks and she was even as saith of her one of her describers in these couplets:—

> O hail to him whose locks his cheeks o'ershade,
> Who slew my life by cruel hard despight:
> Said I, "Hast veiled the Morn in Night?" He said,
> "Nay I but veil Moon in hue of Night."

Then they displayed Dunyazad in a second and a third and a fourth dress and she paced forward like the rising sun, and swayed to and fro in the insolence of beauty; and she was even as saith the poet of her in these couplets:—

The sun of beauty she to all appears
And, lovely coy she mocks all loveliness:
And when he fronts her favour and her smile
A-morn, the sun of day in clouds must dress.

Then they displayed Shahrazad in the third dress and the fourth and the fifth and she became as she were a Ban-branch snell or a thirsting gazelle, lovely of face and perfect in attributes of grace, even as saith of her one in these couplets:—

She comes like fullest moon on happy night,
Taper of waist with shape of magic might:
She hath an eye whose glances quell mankind,
And ruby on her cheeks reflects his light:
Enveils her hips the blackness of her hair;
Beware of curls that bite with viper-bite!
Her sides are silken-soft, that while the heart
Mere rock behind that surface 'scapes our sight:
From the fringed curtains of her eyne she shoots
Shafts that at furthest range on mark alight.

Then they returned to Dunyazad and displayed her in the fifth dress and in the sixth, which was green, when she surpassed with her loveliness the fair of the four quarters of the world and outvied, with the brightness of her countenance, the full moon at rising tide; for she was even as saith of her the poet in these couplets:—

A damsel 'twas the tirer's art had decked with snare and
    sleight,
And robed with rays as though the sun from her had
    borrowed light:
She came before us wondrous clad in chemisette of green,
As veilèd by his leafy screen Pomegranate hides from sight:
And when he said, "How callest thou the fashion of thy
    dress?"
She answered us in pleasant way with double meaning
    dight,

"We call this garment *crève-cœur;* and rightly is it hight,
   For many a heart wi' this we brake and harried many a
     sprite."

Then they displayed Shahrazad in the sixth and seventh dresses and clad her in youth's clothing, whereupon she came forward swaying from side to side and coquettishly moving and indeed she ravished wits and hearts and ensorcelled all eyes with her glances. She shook her sides and swayed her haunches, then put her hair on sword-hilt and went up to King Shahriyar, who embraced her as hospitable host embraceth guest, and threatened her in her ear with the taking of the sword; and she was even as saith of her the poet in these words:—

Were not the Murk[10] of gender male,
   Than feminines surpassing fair,
Tirewomen they had grudged the bride,
   Who made her beard and whiskers wear!

Thus also they did with her sister Dunyazad, and when they had made an end of the display the King bestowed robes of honour on all who were present and sent the brides to their own apartments. Then Shahrazad went in to King Shahriyar and Dunyazad to King Shah Zaman and each of them solaced himself with the company of his beloved consort and the hearts of the folk were comforted. When morning morrowed, the Wazir came in to the two Kings and kissed ground before them; wherefore they thanked him and were large of bounty to him. Presently they went forth and sat down upon couches of Kingship, whilst all the Wazirs and Emirs and Grandees and Lords of the land presented themselves and kissed ground. King Shahriyar ordered them dresses of honour and largesse and they prayed for the permanence and prosperity of the King and his brother. Then the two Sovrans appointed their sire-in-law the Wazir to be Viceroy in Samarcand and assigned him five of the Chief Emirs to accompany him, charging them attend him and do him service. The Minister kissed the ground and prayed that they might be vouchsafed length of life: then he went in to his daughters, whilst the Eunuchs and Ushers walked before him, and saluted them and farewelled them. They kissed his hands and gave him joy of the Kingship and bestowed on him immense treasures; after which he took leave of them and setting out, fared days and nights, till he came near Samarcand, where the townspeople met him at a distance of three marches and rejoiced in him with exceeding joy. So he entered the city and they decorated the houses and it was a notable day. He sat down on the throne of his kingship and the Wazirs did him homage and the Grandees and Emirs of Samarcand and all prayed that he might be vouchsafed justice and victory and length of continuance. So he bestowed on them robes of honour and entreated them with distinction and they made him Sultan over them. As soon as his father-in-law had departed for Samarcand, King Shahriyah summoned the Grandees of his realm and made them a stupendous banquet of all manner of delicious meats and exquisite sweetmeats. He also bestowed on them robes of honour and guerdoned them and divided the kingdoms between himself and his brother in their presence, whereat the folk rejoiced. Then the two Kings abode, each ruling a day in turn, and they were ever in harmony each with other while on similar wise their wives continued in the love of Allah Almighty and in thanksgiving to Him; and the peoples and the provinces were at peace and the preachers prayed for them from the pulpits, and their report was bruited abroad and the travellers bore tidings of them to all lands. In due time King Shahriyah summoned chroniclers and copyists and bade them write all that had betided him with his wife, first and last; so they wrote this and named it *The Stories of the Thousand Nights and A Night*. The book came to thirty volumes and these the King laid up in his treasury. And the two brothers abode with their wives in all pleasance and solace of life and its delights, for that indeed Allah the Most High had changed their annoy into joy; and on this wise they continued till there took them the Destroyer of delights and the Severer of societies, the Desolator of dwelling-places and Garnerer of graveyards, and they were translated to the ruth of Almighty Allah; their houses fell waste and their palaces lay in ruins[11] and the Kings inherited their riches. Then there reigned after them a wise ruler, who was just, keen-witted and accomplished and loved tales and legends, especially those which chronicle the doings of Sovrans and Sultans, and he found in the treasury these marvellous stories and wondrous histories, contained in the thirty volumes aforesaid. So he read in them a first book and a second and a third and so on to the last of them, and each book astounded and delighted him more than that which preceded it, till he came to the end of them. Then he admired whatso he had read therein of description and discourse and rare traits and anecdotes and moral instances and reminiscences and bade the folk copy them and dispread them over all lands and climes; wherefore their report was bruited abroad and the people named them *The marvels and wonders of the Thousand Nights and A Night.* This is all that hath come down to us of the origin of this book, and Allah is All-knowing.[12] So Glory be to Him whom the shifts of Time waste not away, nor doth aught of chance or change affect His sway: whom one case diverteth not from other case and Who is sole in the attributes of perfect grace. And prayer and peace be upon the Lord's Pontiff and Chosen One among His creatures, our lord MOHAMMED the Prince of mankind through whom we supplicate Him for a goodly and a godly

FINIS.

NOTES

Sir Richard F. Burton

STORY OF KING SHAHRYAR AND HIS BROTHER

1. Allaho A'alam, a deprecatory formula, used because the writer is going to indulge in a series of what may possibly be untruths.

2. The "Sons of Sásán" are the famous Sassanides whose dynasty ended with the Arabian Conquest (A.D. 641). "Island" (Jazírah) in Arabic also means "Peninsula," and causes much confusion in geographical matters.

3. Shahryár not Shahriyar (Persian) = "City-friend." The Bulak edition corrupts it to Shahrbáz (City-hawk), and the Breslau to Shahrbán or "Defender of the City," like Marzban = Warden of the Marshes. Shah Zamán (Persian) = "King of the Age": Galland prefers Shah Zenan, or "King of women," and the Bul. edit. changes it to Shah Rummán, "Pomegranate King." Al-Ajam denotes all regions not Arab (Gentiles opposed to Jews, Mlechchhas to Hindus, Tajiks to Turks, etc., etc.), and especially Persia; Ajami (a man of Ajam) being an equivalent of the Gr. Βάρβαρος.

4. Galland writes "Vizier," a wretched frenchification of a mincing Turkish mispronunciation; Torrens, "Wuzeer" (Anglo-Indian and Gilchristian); Lane, "Wezeer"; (Egyptian

or rather Cairene); Payne, "Vizier," according to his system; Burckhardt (*Proverbs*), "Vizír"; and Mr. Keith-Falconer, "Vizir." The root is popularly supposed to be "wizr" (burden) and the meaning "Minister"; Wazir al-Wuzará being "Premier." In the Koran (chap. xx., 30) Moses says, "Give me a Wazir of my family, Harun (Aaron) my brother." Sale, followed by the excellent version of the Rev. J. M. Rodwell, translates a "Counsellor," and explains by "One who has the chief administration of affairs under a prince." But both learned Koranists learnt their Orientalism in London, and, like such students generally, fail only upon the easiest points, familiar to all old dwellers in the East.

5. This three-days term (rest-day, drest-day and departure day) seems to be an instinct-made rule in hospitality. Among Moslems it is a Sunnat or practice of the Prophet.

6. *i.e.,* I am sick at heart.

7. Debauched women prefer negroes on account of the size of their parts. I measured one man in Somali-land who, when quiescent, numbered nearly six inches. This is a characteristic of the negro race and of African animals; *e.g.* the horse; whereas the pure Arab, man and beast, is below the average of Europe; one of the best proofs by the by, that the Egyptian is not an Asiatic, but a negro partially white-washed. Moreover, these imposing parts do not increase proportionally during erection; consequently, the "deed of kind" takes a much longer time and adds greatly to the woman's enjoyment. In my time no honest Hindi Moslem would take his women-folk to Zanzibar on account of the huge attractions and enormous temptations there and thereby offered to them. Upon the subject of Imsák = retention of semen and "prolongation of pleasure," I shall find it necessary to say more.

8. The very same words were lately spoken in England proving the eternal truth of The Nights which the ignorant call "downright lies."

9. The Arab's *Tue la!*

10. Arab. "Sayd wa kanas": the former usually applied to fishing; hence Sayda (Sidon) = fish-town. But noble Arabs (except the Caliph Al-Amin) do not fish; so here it means simply "sport," chasing, coursing, birding (oiseler), and so forth.

11. In the Mac. Edit. the negro is called "Mas'úd"; here he utters a kind of war-cry and plays upon the name, "Sa'ád, Sa'íd, Sa'úd," and "Mas'ud," all being derived from one root, "Sa'ad" = auspiciousness, prosperity.

12. The Arab. singular (whence the French "génie"); fem. Jinniyah; the Div and Rakshah of old Guebre-land and the "Rakshasa," or "Yaksha," of Hinduism. It would be interesting to trace the evident connection, by no means "accidental," of "Jinn" with the "Genius" who came to the Romans through the Asiatic Etruscans, and whose name I cannot derive from "gignomai" or "genitus." He was unknown to the Greeks, who had the Daimon (δαίμων), a family which separated, like the Jinn and the Genius, into two categories, the good (Agatho-dæmons) and the bad (Kako-dæmons). We know nothing concerning the status of the Jinn amongst the pre-Moslemitic or pagan Arabs: the Moslems made him a supernatural anthropoid being, created of subtile fire (*Koran*, chaps. xv. 27; lv. 14), not of earth like man, propagating his kind, ruled by mighty kings, the last being Ján bin Ján, missionarized by Prophets and subject to death and Judgment. From the same root are "Junún" = madness (*i.e.*, possession or obsession by the Jinn) and "Majnún" = a madman. According to R. Jeremiah bin Eliazar in Psalm xli. 5, Adam was excommunicated for one hundred and thirty years, during which he begat children in his own image (Gen. v. 3) and these were Mazikeen or Shedeem—Jinns. Further details anent the Jinn will presently occur.

13. Arab. "Amsár" (cities): in Bul. Edit. "Amtár" (rains), as in Mac. Edit. So Mr. Payne (I., 5) translates:—

> And when she flashes forth the lightning of her glance,
> She maketh eyes to rain, like showers, with many a tear.

I would render it, "She makes whole cities shed tears"; and prefer it for a reason which will generally influence me—its superior exaggeration and impossibility.

14. Not "A-frit," pronounced Aye-frit, as our poets have it. This variety of the Jinn, who, as will be shown, are divided into two races like mankind, is generally, but not always, a malignant being, hostile and injurious to mankind (*Koran*, xxvii., 39).

15. *i.e.*, "I conjure thee by Allah"; the formula is technically called "Inshád."

16. This introducing the name of Allah into an indecent tale is essentially Egyptian and Cairene. But see Boccaccio, ii. 6; and vii. 9.

17. So in the Mac. Edit.; in others "ninety." I prefer the greater number as exaggeration is a part of the humour. In the Hindu *Kathá Sárit Ságara* (Sea of the Streams of Story), the rings are one hundred and the catastrophe is more moral; the good youth Yashodhara rejects the wicked one's advances; she awakes the water-sprite, who is about to slay him, but the rings are brought as testimony and the improper young person's nose is duly cut off. (Chap. lxiii.; p. 80, of the excellent translation by Prof. C. H. Tawney: for the Bibliotheca Indica: Calcutta, 1881.) The Kathá, etc., by Somadeva (century xi), is a poetical version of the prose compendium, the *Vrihat Kathá* (Great Story) by Gunadhya (cent. vi).

18. The Joseph of the Koran, very different from him of Genesis. We shall meet him often enough in The Nights.

19. "Iblis," vulgarly written "Eblis," from a root meaning The Despairer, with a suspicious likeness to Diabolos; possibly from "Balas," a profligate. Some translate it The Calumniator, as Satan is the Hater. Iblis (who appears in the Arab. version of the N. Testament) succeeded another revolting angel Al-Haris; and his story of pride, refusing to worship Adam, is told four times in the Koran from the Talmud (Sanhedrin 29). He caused Adam and Eve to lose Paradise (ii. 34); he still betrays mankind (xxv. 31), and at the end of time he, with the other devils, will be "gathered together on their knees round Hell" (xix. 69). He has evidently had the worst of the game, and we wonder, with Origen, Tillotson, Burns and many others, that he does not throw up the cards.

20. A similar tale is still told at Akká (St. John d'Acre) concerning the terrible "butcher"—Jazzár (Djezzar) Pasha. One can hardly pity women who are fools enough to run such risks. According to Frizzi, Niccolò, Marquis of Este, after beheading Parisina, ordered all the faithless wives of Ferrara to be treated in like manner.

21. "Shahrázád" (Persian)=City-freer; in the older version

Scheherazade (probably both from Shirzád=lion-born). "Dunyázád"=World-freer. The Bres. Edit. corrupts the former to Sháhrzád or Sháhrazád; and the Mac. and Calc. to Shahrzád or Shehrzád. I have ventured to restore the name as it should be. Galland for the second prefers Dinarzade (?) and Richardson Dinazade (Dinázád=Religion-freer): here I have followed Lane and Payne; though in *First Footsteps* I was misled by Galland.

22. Probably she proposed to "Judith" the King. These learned and clever young ladies are very dangerous in the East.

23. In Egypt, etc., the bull takes the place of the Western ox. The Arab. word is "Taur" (Thaur, Saur); in old Persian "Tora" and Lat. "Taurus," a venerable remnant of the days before the "Semitic" and "Aryan" families of speech had split into two distinct growths. "Taur" ends in the Saxon "Steor" and the English "Steer."

24. Arab. "Abú Yakzán"=the Wakener, because the ass brays at dawn.

25. Arab. "Tibn"; straw crushed under the sledge: the hay of Egypt, Arabia, Syria, etc. The old country custom is to pull up the corn by handfuls from the roots, leaving the land perfectly bare: hence the "plucking up" of Hebrew Holy Writ. The object is to preserve every atom of "Tibn."

26. Arab. "Yá Aftah": Al-Aftah is an epithet of the bull, also of the chameleon.

27. Arab. "Balíd," a favourite Egyptianism often pleasantly confounded with "Wali" (a Santon); hence the latter comes to mean "an innocent," a "ninny."

28. From the Calc. Edit., vol. 1, p. 29.

29. Arab. "Abu Yakzán" is hardly equivalent with "Père l'Eveillé."

30. In Arab. the wa (´,) is the sign of parenthesis.

31. In the nearer East the light little plough is carried afield by the bull or ass.

32. Arab. "Kat'a" (bit of leather): some read "Nat'a"; a leather used by way of table-cloth, and forming a bag for victuals; but it is never made of bull's hide.

33. The older "Cadi," a judge in religious matters. The Shuhúd, or Assessors, are officers of the Mahkamah or Kazi's Court.

34. He thus purified himself ceremonially before death.

35. This is Christian rather than Moslem: a favourite Maltese curse is "Yahrak Kiddisak man rabba-k!"=burn the Saint who brought thee up!

36. A popular Egyptian phrase: the dog and the cock speak like Fellahs.

37. *i.e.,* between the last sleep and dawn when they would rise to wash and pray.

THE FISHERMAN AND THE JINNI

1. Here, as in other places, I have not preserved the monorhyme, but have ended like the English sonnet with a couplet; as a rule the last two lines contain a "Husn makta' " or climax.

2. Arab. "Allahumma"=Yá Allah (O Allah) but with emphasis; the Fath being a substitute for the voc. part. Some connect it with the Heb. "Alihím," but that fancy is not Arab. In Al-Hariri and the rhetoricians it sometimes means to be sure; of course; unless indeed; unless possibly.

3. Probably in consequence of a vow. These superstitious practices, which have many a parallel amongst ourselves, are not confined to the lower orders in the East.

4. *i.e.,* saying "Bismillah!" the pious ejaculation which should precede every act. In Boccaccio (viii., 9) it is "remembering Iddio e' Santi."

5. Arab. Nahás asfar=brass, opposed to "Nahás" and "Nahás ahmar," = copper.

6. This alludes to the legend of Sakhr al-Jinni, a famous fiend cast by Solomon Davidson into Lake Tiberias whose storms make it a suitable place. Hence the "Bottle imp," a world-wide fiction of folk-lore: we shall find it in the *Book of Sindibad,* and I need hardly remind the reader of Le Sage's *Diable Boiteux,* borrowed from *El Diablo Cojuelo,* the Spanish novel by Luiz Velez de Guevara.

7. Márid (lit. "contumacious" from the Heb. root Marad to rebel, whence "Nimrod" in late Semitic) is one of the tribes of the Jinn, generally but not always hostile to man. His female is "Máridah."

8. As Solomon began to reign (according to vulgar chronometry) in 1015 B.C., the text would place the tale circ. A.D. 785,=A.H. 169. But we can lay no stress on this date which

may be merely fanciful. Professor Tawney very justly compares this Moslem Solomon with the Hindu King, Vikramáditya, who ruled over the seven divisions of the world and who had as many devils to serve him as he wanted.

9. Arab. "Yá Ba'íd"; a euphemism here adopted to prevent using grossly abusive language. Others will occur in the course of these pages.

10. *i.e.,* about to fly out; "My heart is in my mouth." The Fisherman speaks with the dry humour of a Fellah.

11. "Sulayman," when going out to ease himself, entrusted his seal-ring upon which his kingdom depended to a concubine "Amínah" (the "Faithful"), when Sakhr, transformed to the King's likeness, came in and took it. The prophet was reduced to beggary, but after forty days the demon fled throwing into the sea the ring which was swallowed by a fish and eventually returned to Sulayman. This Talmudic fable is hinted at in the Koran (chap. xxxviii.), and commentators have extensively embroidered it. Asaf, son of Barkhiya, was Wazir to Sulayman and is supposed to be the "one with whom was the knowledge of the Scriptures" (*Koran,* chap. xxxvii.), *i.e.* who knew the Ineffable Name of Allah. See the manifest descendant of the Talmudic-Koranic fiction in the *Tale of the Emperor Jovinian* (No. lix.) of the Gesta Romanorum, the most popular book of mediæval Europe composed in England (or Germany) about the end of the thirteenth century.

12. Arab. "Kumkum," a gourd-shaped bottle of metal, china or glass, still used for sprinkling scents. Lane gives an illustration (chap. viii., *Mod. Egypt*).

13. Arab. meaning "the Mother of Amir," a nickname for the hyena, which bites the hand that feeds it.

14. The intellect of man is stronger than that of the Jinni; the Ifrit, however, enters the jar because he has been adjured by the Most Great Name and not from mere stupidity. The seal-ring of Solomon according to the Rabbis contained a chased stone which told him everything he wanted to know.

15. The Mesmerist will notice this shudder which is familiar to him as preceding the "magnetic" trance.

16. Arab. "Bahr" which means a sea, a large river, a sheet of water, etc., lit. water cut or trenched in the earth. Bahri in

Egypt means Northern; so Yamm (Sea, Mediterranean) in
Hebrew is West.

17. The tale of these two women is now forgotten.

18. Arab. "Atadakhkhal." When danger threatens it is customary
to seize a man's skirt and cry "Dakhíl-ak!" (= under thy protection). Among noble tribes the Badawi thus invoked will
defend the stranger with his life. Foreigners have brought
themselves into contempt by thus applying to women or to
mere youths.

19. The formula of quoting from the Koran.

20. Lit. "Allah not desolate me" (by thine absence). This is still a
popular phrase—Lá tawáhishná = Do not make me desolate,
i.e. by staying away too long; and friends meeting after a term
of days exclaim "Auhashtani!" = thou hast made me desolate,
Je suis désolé.

21. Charming simplicity of manners when the Prime Minister
carries the fish (shade of Vattel!) to the cookmaid. The
"Gesta Romanorum" is nowhere more naïve.

22. Arab. "Kahílat al-taraf" = lit. eyelids lined with Kohl; and
figuratively "with black lashes and languorous look." This is
a phrase which frequently occurs in The Nights and which,
as will appear, applies to the "lower animals" as well as to
men. Moslems in Central Africa apply Kohl not to the thick-
ness of the eyelid but upon both outer lids, fixing it with
some greasy substance. The peculiar Egyptian (and Syrian)
eye with its thick fringes of jet-black lashes, looking like
lines of black drawn with soot, easily suggests the simile. In
England I have seen the same appearance amongst miners
fresh from the colliery.

23. Of course applying to her own case.

24. Prehistoric Arabs who measured from 60 to 100 cubits high:
Koran, chap. xxvi., etc. They will often be mentioned in The
Nights.

25. Arab. "Dastúr" (from Persian) = leave, permission. The word
has two meanings (see Burckhardt, Arab. Prov. No. 609) and
is much used, *e.g.* before walking up stairs or entering a room
where strange women might be met. So "Tarík" = Clear the
way (*Pilgrimage,* iii., 319). The old Persian occupation of
Egypt, not to speak of the Persian-speaking Circassians and
other rulers has left many such traces in popular language.
One of them is that horror of travellers—"Bakhshísh" pron.

Bakhsheesh and shortened to shísh from the Pers. "bakhshish." Our "Christmas *box*" has been most unnecessarily derived from the same, despite our reading:—

Gladly the boy, with Christmas box in hand.

And, as will be seen, Persians have bequeathed to the outer world worse things than bad language, *e.g.* heresy and sodomy.

26. He speaks of his wife, but euphemistically in the masculine.

27. A popular saying throughout Al-Islam.

28. Arab. "Fata": lit. = a youth; a generous man, one of noble mind (as youth-tide should be). It corresponds with the Lat. "vir," and has much the meaning of the Ital. "Giovane," the Germ. "Junker" and our "gentleman."

29. From the Bul. Edit.

30. The vagueness of his statement is euphemistic.

31. This readiness of shedding tears contrasts strongly with the external stoicism of modern civilization; but it is true to Arab character; and Easterns, like the heroes of Homer and Italians of Boccaccio, are not ashamed of what we look upon as the result of feminine hysteria—"a good cry."

32. The formula (constantly used by Moslems) here denotes displeasure, doubt how to act and so forth. Pronounce, "Lá haula wa lá kuwwata illá bi 'lláhi 'l-Aliyyi 'l-Azim." As a rule mistakes are marvellous: Mandeville (chap. xii.) for "Lá iláha illa 'lláhu wa Muhammadun Rasúlu 'llah" writes "La ellec sila, Machomete rores alla." The former (lá haula, etc.), on account of the four peculiar Arabic letters, is everywhere pronounced differently; and the exclamation is called "Haulak" or "Haukal."

33. An Arab holds that he has a right to marry his first cousin, the daughter of his father's brother, and if any win her from him a death and a blood-feud may result. It was the same in a modified form amongst the Jews and in both races the consanguineous marriage was not attended by the evil results (idiocy, congenital deafness, etc.) observed in mixed races like the English and the Anglo-American. When a Badawi speaks of "the daughter of my uncle" he means wife; and the former is the dearer title, as a wife can be divorced, but blood is thicker than water.

34. Arab. "Kahbah"; the coarsest possible term. Hence the unhappy "Cava" of Don Roderick the Goth, which simply means The Whore.

35. The Arab "Banj" and Hindú "Bhang" (which I use as most familiar) both derive from the old Coptic "Nibanj" meaning a preparation of hemp (*Cannabis sativa* seu *Indica*); and here it is easy to recognize the Homeric "Nepenthe." Al-Kazwini explains the term of "garden hemp (Kinnab bostáni or Sháhdánaj). On the other hand not a few apply the word to the henbane (*hyoscyamus niger*) so much used in mediæval Europe. The Kámús evidently means henbane distinguishing it from "Hashish al Haráfísh"=rascals' grass, *i.e.* the herb Pantagruelion. The "Alfáz Adwiya" (French translation) explains "Tabannuj" by "Endormir quelqu'un en lui faisant avaler de la jusquiame." In modern parlance Tabannuj is=our anæsthetic administered before an operation, a deadener of pain like myrrh and a number of other drugs. For this purpose hemp is always used (at least I never heard of henbane); and various preparations of the drug are sold at an especial bazar in Cairo. See the "powder of marvellous virtue" in Boccaccio, iii., 8; and iv., 10. Of these intoxicants, properly so termed, I shall have something to say in a future page.

The use of Bhang doubtless dates from the dawn of civilization, whose earliest social pleasures would be inebriants. Herodotus (iv. c. 75) show the Scythians burning the seeds (leaves and capsules) in worship and becoming drunken with the fumes, as do the S. African Bushmen of the present day. This would be the earliest form of smoking: it is still doubtful whether the pipe was used or not. Galen also mentions intoxication by hemp. Amongst Moslems, the Persians adopted the drink as an ecstatic, and about our thirteenth century Egypt, which began the practice, introduced a number of preparations to be noticed in the course of The Nights.

36. The rubbish heaps which outlie Eastern cities, some (near Cairo) are over a hundred feet high.

37. Arab. "Kurrat al-ayn"; coolness of eyes as opposed to a hot eye ("sakhin") *i.e.* one red with tears. The term is true and picturesque so I translate it literally. All coolness is pleasant to dwellers in burning lands: thus in Al-Hariri Abu Zayd

says of Bassorah, "I found there whatever could fill the eye with coolness." And a "cool booty" (or prize) is one which has been secured without plunging into the flames of war, or simply a pleasant prize.

38. Popularly rendered Caucasus: it corresponds so far with the Hindu "Udaya" that the sun rises behind it; and the "false dawn" is caused by a hole or gap. It is also the Persian Alborz, the Indian Meru (Sumeru), the Greek Olympus, and the Rhiphæan Range (Veliki Camenypoys) or great starry girdle of the world, etc.

39. Arab. "Mizr" or "Mizar"; vulg. Búzah; hence the medical Lat. Buza, the Russian Buza (millet beer), our "booze," the O. Dutch "buyzen" and the German "busen." This is the old ποτὸς θεῖος of negro and negroid Africa; the beer of Osiris, of which dried remains have been found in jars amongst Egyptian tombs. In Equatorial Africa it is known as "Pombe"; on the Upper Nile "Merissa" or "Mirisi" and amongst the Kafirs (Caffers) "Tshuala," "Oala" or "Boyala": I have also heard of "Buswa" in Central Africa which may be the origin of "Buzah." In the West it became ζῦθος (Romaic πίρρα), Xythum and cerevisia or cervisia, the humor ex hordeo, long before the days of King Gambrinus. Central Africans drink it in immense quantities: in Unyamwezi the standing bedsteads, covered with bark-slabs, are all made sloping so as to drain off the liquor. A chief lives wholly on beef and Pombe which is thick as gruel below. Hops are unknown: the grain, mostly Holcus, is made to germinate, then pounded, boiled and left to ferment. In Egypt the drink is affected chiefly by Berbers, Nubians and slaves from the Upper Nile; but it is a superior article and more like that of Europe than the "Pombe." I have given an account of the manufacture in *The Lake Regions of Central Africa*, vol. ii., p. 286. There are other preparations, Umm-bulbul (mother nightingale), Dinzáyah and Súbiyah, for which I must refer to the Shaykh El-Tounsy.

40. There is a terrible truth in this satire, which reminds us of the noble dame who preferred to her handsome husband the palefrenier laid, ord et infâme of Queen Margaret of Navarre (Heptameron No. xx.). We have all known women who sacrificed everything despite themselves, as it were, for the most worthless of men. The world stares and scoffs and

blames and understands nothing. There is for every woman one man and one only in whose slavery she is "ready to sweep the floor." Fate is mostly opposed to her meeting him but, when she does, adieu husband and children, honour and religion, life and "soul." Moreover Nature (human) commands the union of contrasts, such as fair and foul, dark and light, tall and short; otherwise mankind would be like the canines, a race of extremes, dwarf as toy-terriers, giants like mastiffs, bald as Chinese "remedy dogs," or hairy as New-foundlands. The famous Wilkes said only a half-truth when he backed himself, with an hour's start, against the hand-somest man in England; his uncommon and remarkable ugliness (he was, as the Italians say, *un bel brutto*) was the highest recommendation in the eyes of very beautiful women.

41. Every Moslem burial-ground has a place of the kind where honourable women may sit and weep unseen by the multitude. These visits are enjoined by the Apostle:—Frequent the cemetery, 'twill make you think of futurity! Also:—Whoever visiteth the graves of his parents (or one of them) every Friday, he shall be written a pious son, even though he might have been in the world, before that, a disobedient. (*Pilgrimage*, ii., 71.) The buildings resemble our European "mortuary chapels." Said, Pasha of Egypt, was kind enough to erect one on the island off Suez, for the "use of English ladies who would like shelter whilst weeping and wailing for their dead." But I never heard that any of the ladies went there.

42. Arab. "Ajal" = the period of life, the appointed time of death: the word is of constant recurrence and is also applied to sudden death. See Lane's Dictionary, s.v.

43. The words are the very lowest and coarsest; but the scene is true to Arab life.

44. Arab. "Hayhát": the word, written in a variety of ways is onomatopoetic, like our "heigh-ho!" it sometimes means "far from me (or you) be it!" but in popular usage it is simply "Alas."

45. Lane (i., 134) finds a date for the book in this passage. The Soldan of Egypt, Mohammed ibn Kala'ún, in the early eighth century (Hijrah = our fourteenth), issued a sumptuary law compelling Christians and Jews to wear indigo-blue and saffron-yellow turbans, the white being reserved for

Moslems. But the custom was much older and Mandeville (chap. ix.) describes it in A.D. 1322 when it had become the rule. And it still endures; although abolished in the cities it is the rule for Christians, at least in the country parts of Egypt and Syria. I may here remark that such detached passages as these are absolutely useless for chronology: they may be simply the additions of editors or mere copyists.

46. The ancient "Mustapha" = the Chosen (prophet, *i.e.* Mohammed), also titled Al-Mujtabá, the Accepted (*Pilgrimage,* ii., 309). "Murtazá" = the Elect, *i.e.* the Caliph Ali is the older "Mortada" or "Mortadi" of Ockley and his day, meaning "one pleasing to (or acceptable to) Allah." Still older writers corrupted it to "Mortis Ali" and readers supposed this to be the Caliph's name.

47. The gleam (zodiacal light) preceding the true dawn; the Persians call the former Subh-i-kázib (false or lying dawn) opposed to Subh-i-sádik (true dawn) and suppose that it is caused by the sun shining through a hole in the world-encircling Mount Kaf.

48. So the Heb. "Arún" = naked, means wearing the lower robe only; = our "in his shirt."

49. Here we have the vulgar Egyptian colloquialism "Aysh" (= Ayyu shayyin) for the classical "Má" = what.

50. "In the name of Allah!" here said before taking action.

51. Arab. "Mamlúk" (plur. Mamálik) lit. a chattel; and in The Nights a white slave trained to arms. The "Mameluke Beys" of Egypt were locally called the "Ghuzz." I use the convenient word in its old popular sense;

> 'Tis sung, there's a valiant Mameluke
> In foreign lands ycleped (Sir Luke)—
> > HUDIBRAS.

And hence, probably, Molière's "Mamamouchi"; and the modern French use "Mamaluc." See Savary's Letters, No. xl.

THE PORTER AND THE THREE LADIES OF BAGHDAD

1. The name of this celebrated successor of Nineveh, where some suppose The Nights were written, is orig. Μεσοπύλαι (middle-gates) because it stood on the way where four great

highways meet. The Arab. form "Mausil" (the vulgar "Mosul") is also significant, alluding to the "junction" of Assyria and Babylonia. Hence our "muslin."

2. This is Mr. Thackeray's "nose-bag." I translate by "walking-shoes" the Arab "Khuff" which are a manner of loose boot covering the ankle; they are not usually embroidered, the ornament being reserved for the inner shoe.

3. *i.e.* Syria (says Abulfeda) the "land on the left" (of one facing the east) as opposed to Al-Yaman the "land on the right." Osmani would mean Turkish, Ottoman. When Bernard the Wise (Bohn, p. 24) speaks of "Bagada and Axiam" (Mabillon's text) or "Axinarri" (still worse), he means Baghdad and Ash-Shám (Syria, Damascus), the latter word puzzling his Editor. Richardson (*Dissert.* lxxii.) seems to support a hideous attempt to derive Shám from Shámat, a mole or wart, because the country is studded with hillocks! Al-Shám is often applied to Damascus-city whose proper name Dimishk belongs to books: this term is generally derived from Dimáshik b. Káli b. Málik b. Sham (Shem). Lee (Ibn Batútah, 29) denies that ha-Dimishki means "Eliezer of Damascus."

4. From Oman = Eastern Arabia.

5. Arab. "Tamar Hanná" lit. date of Henna, but applied to the flower of the eastern privet (*Lawsonia inermis*) which has the sweet scent of freshly mown hay. The use of Henna as a dye is known even in England. The "myrtle" alluded to may either have been for a perfume (as it is held an anti-intoxicant) or for eating, the bitter aromatic berries of the "As" being supposed to flavour wine and especially Raki (raw brandy).

6. Lane (i. 211) pleasantly remarks, "A list of these sweets is given in my original, but I have thought it better to omit the names" (!) Dozy does not shirk his duty, but he is not much more satisfactory in explaining words interesting to students because they are unfound in dictionaries and forgotten by the people. "Akrás (cakes) Laymunìyah (of limes) wa Maymunìyah" appears in the Bresl. Edit. as "Ma'amuniyah" which may mean "Ma'amun's cakes" or "delectable cakes." "Amshát" = (combs) perhaps refers to a fine kind of Kunáfah (vermicelli) known in Egypt and Syria as "Ghazl al-banát" = girl's spinning.

7. The new moon carefully looked for by all Moslems because it begins the Ramazán-fast.

8. Solomon's signet ring has before been noticed.

9. The "high-bosomed" damsel, with breasts firm as a cube, is a favourite with Arab tale-tellers. *Fanno baruffa* is the Italian term for hard breasts pointing outwards.

10. A large hollow navel is looked upon not only as a beauty, but in children it is held a promise of good growth.

11. Arab. "Ka'ah," a high hall opening upon the central court: we shall find the word used for a mansion, barrack, men's quarters, etc.

12. Babel = Gate of God (El), or Gate of Ilu (p. n. of God), which the Jews ironically interpreted "Confusion." The tradition of Babylonia being the very centre of witchcraft and enchantment by means of its Seven Deadly Spirits, has survived in Al-Islam; the two fallen angels (whose names will occur) being confined in a well; Nimrod attempting to reach Heaven from the Tower in a magical car drawn by monstrous birds and so forth. (p. 114, Francois Lenormant's *Chaldean Magic,* London, Bagsters.)

13. Arab. "Kámat Alfiyyah" = like the letter Alif, a straight perpendicular stroke. In the Egyptian hieroglyphs, the origin of every alphabet (not syllabarium) known to man, one form was a flag or leaf of water-plant standing upright. Hence probably the Arabic Alif-shape; while other nations preferred other modifications of the letter (ox's head, etc.), which in Egyptian number some thirty-six varieties, simple and compound.

14. I have not attempted to order this marvellous confusion of metaphors so characteristic of The Nights and the exigencies of Al-Saj'a = rhymed prose.

15. Here and elsewhere I omit the "kála (*dice Turpino*)" of the original: Torrens preserves "Thus goes the tale" (which it only interrupts). This is simply letter-wise and sense-foolish.

16. *i.e.,* sealed with the Kazi or legal authority's seal of office.

17. "Nothing for nothing" is a fixed idea with the Eastern woman: not so much for greed as for a sexual *point d'honneur* when dealing with the adversary—man.

18. She drinks first, the custom of the universal East, to show that the wine she had bought was unpoisoned. Easterns, who

utterly ignore the "social glass" of Western civilization, drink honestly to get drunk; and, when far gone are addicted to horse-play (in Pers. "Badmasti" = *le vin mauvais*) which leads to quarrels and bloodshed. Hence it is held highly ir-reverent to assert of patriarchs, prophets and saints that they "drank wine"; and Moslems agree with our "Teatotallers" in denying that, except in the case of Noah, inebriatives are anywhere mentioned in Holy Writ.

19. Arab. "Húr al-Ayn," lit. (maids) with eyes of lively white and black, applied to the virgins of Paradise who will wive with the happy Faithful. I retain our vulgar "Houri," warning the reader that it is a masc. for a fem. ("Huríyah") in Arab, although accepted in Persian, a genderless speech.

20. "In the name of Allah," is here a civil form of dismissal.

21. Lane (i. 124) is scandalized and naturally enough by this scene, which is the only blot in an admirable tale admirably told. Yet even here the grossness is but little more pro-nounced than what we find in our old drama (*e.g.*, Shake-speare's King Henry V.) written for the stage, whereas tales like The Nights are not read or recited before both sexes. Lastly "nothing follows all this palming work"; in Europe the orgy would end very differently. These "nuns of Theleme" are physically pure: their debauchery is of the mind, not the body. Galland makes them five, including the two doggesses.

22. So Sir Francis Walsingham's "They which do that they should not, should hear that they would not."

23. The old "Calendar," pleasantly associated with that form of almanac. The Mac. Edit. has "Karandaliyah," a vile corrup-tion, like Ibn Batutah's "Karandar" and Torrens' "Kurundul": so in English we have the accepted vulgarism of "Kernel" for Colonel. The Bul. Edit. uses for synonym "Su'ulúk" = an asker, a beggar. Of these mendicant monks, for such they are, much like the Sarabaites of mediæval Europe, I have treated, and of their institutions and its founder, Shaykh Sharif Bu Ali Kalandar (ob. A.H. 724 = 1323–24), at some length in my *History of Sindh*, chap. viii. See also the Dabistan (i. 136) where the good Kalandar exclaims:—

If the thorn break in my body, how trifling the pain!
But how sorely I feel for the poor broken thorn!

D'Herbelot is right when he says that the Kalandar is not generally approved by Moslems: he labours to win free from every form and observance and he approaches the Malámati who conceals all his good deeds and boasts of his evil doings—our "Devil's hypocrite."

24. The "Kalandar" disfigures himself in this manner to show "mortification."

25. Arab. "Gharíb": the porter is offended because the word implies "poor devil"; especially one out of his own country.

26. A religious mendicant generally.

27. Very scandalous to Moslem "respectability": Mohammed said the house was accursed when the voices of women could be heard out of doors. Moreover the neighbours have a right to interfere and abate the scandal.

28. I need hardly say that these are both historical personages; they will often be mentioned.

29. Arab. "Sama 'an wa tá'atan"; a popular phrase of assent generally translated "to hear is to obey"; but this formula may be and must be greatly varied. In places it means "Hearing (the word of Allah) and obeying" (His prophet, viceregent, etc.)

30. Arab. "Sawáb" = reward in Heaven. This word for which we have no equivalent has been naturalized in all tongues (*e.g.* Hindostani) spoken by Moslems.

31. Wine-drinking, at all times forbidden to Moslems, vitiates the Pilgrimage-rite: the Pilgrim is vowed to a strict observance of the ceremonial law and many men date their "reformation" from the "Hajj." *Pilgrimage*, iii., 126.

32. Here some change has been necessary; as the original text confuses the three "ladies."

33. In Arab. the plural masc. is used by way of modesty when a girl addresses her lover; and for the same reason she speaks of herself as a man.

34. Arab. "Al-Na'ím"; in full "Jannat-al-Na'ím" = the Garden of Delights, *i.e.* the fifth Heaven made of white silver. The generic name of Heaven (the place of reward) is "Jannat," lit. a garden; "Firdaus" being evidently derived from the Persian through the Greek παράδεισος, and meaning a chase, a hunting park. Writers on this subject should bear in mind Mandeville's modesty, "Of Paradise I cannot speak properly, for I was not there."

35. Arab. "Mikra'ah," the dried mid-rib of a date-frond used for many purposes, especially the bastinado.

36. According to Lane (i., 229) these and the immediately following verses are from an ode by Ibn Sahl al-Ishbili. They are in the Bul. Edit. not the Mac. Edit.

37. The original is full of conceits and plays on words which in many cases are not easily rendered in English.

38. Arab. "Tarjumán," same root as Chald. Targum (= a translation), the old "Truchman," and through the Ital. "tergomano" our "Dragoman"; here a messenger.

39. Lit. the "person of the eyes," our "babe of the eyes," a favourite poetical conceit in all tongues; much used by the Elizabethans, but now neglected as a silly kind of conceit.

40. Arab. "Sár" (Thár) the revenge-right recognized by law and custom (*Pilgrimage*, iii., 69).

41. That is "We all swim in the same boat."

42. Ja'afar ever acts, on such occasions, the part of a wise and sensible man compelled to join in a foolish frolic. He contrasts strongly with the Caliph, a headstrong despot who will not be gainsaid, whatever be the whim of the moment. But Easterns would look upon this as a proof of his "kingliness."

43. Arab. "Wa'l-Salám" (pronounced Was-Salám); meaning "and here ends the matter." In our slang we say, "All right, and the child's name is Antony."

44. This is a favourite jingle; the play being upon "ibrat" (a needle-graver) and " 'ibrat" (an example, a warning).

45. That is "make his bow"; as the English peasant pulls his forelock. Lane (i., 249) suggests, as an afterthought, that it means:—"Recover thy senses; in allusion to a person's drawing his hand over his head after sleep or a fit." But it occurs elsewhere in the sense of "cut thy stick."

46. This would be a separate building like our family tomb and probably domed, resembling that mentioned in "The King of the Black Islands." Europeans usually call it "a little Wali"; or, as they write it, "Wely"; the contained for the container; the "Santon" for the "Santon's tomb." I have noticed this curious confusion (which begins with Robinson, i. 322) in *Unexplored Syria*, i. 161.

47. Arab. "Wiswás"=diabolical temptation or suggestion. The

"Wiswási" is a man with scruples (scrupulus, a pebble in the shoe), *e.g.* one who fears that his ablutions were deficient, etc.

48. Arab. "Katf" = pinioning by tying the arms behind the back and shoulders (Kitf), a dire disgrace to free-born men.

49. Arab. "Nafs." = Hebr. Nephesh (Nafash) = soul, life, as opposed to "Ruach" = spirit and breath. In these places it is equivalent to "I said to myself." Another form of the root is "Nafas," breath, with an idea of inspiration: so "Sáhib Nafas" (= master of breath) is a minor saint who heals by expiration, a matter familiar to mesmerists (*Pilgrimage*, i., 86).

50. Arab. "Kaus al-Banduk"; the "pellet-bow" of modern India; with two strings joined by a bit of cloth which supports a ball of dry clay or stone. It is chiefly used for birding.

51. In the East blinding was a common practice, especially in the case of junior princes not required as heirs. A deep perpendicular incision was made down each corner of the eyes; the lids were lifted and the balls removed by cutting the optic nerve and the muscles. The later Caliphs blinded their victims by passing a red-hot sword blade close to the orbit or a needle over the eye-ball. About the same time in Europe the operation was performed with a heated metal basin—the well-known *bacinare* (used by Ariosto), as happened to Pier delle Vigne (Petrus de Vineâ), the "godfather of modern Italian."

52. Arab. "Khinzír" (by Europeans pronounced "Hanzír"), prop. a wild-boar; but popularly used like our "you pig!"

53. Incest is now abominable everywhere except amongst the overcrowded poor of great and civilized cities. Yet such unions were common and lawful amongst ancient and highly cultivated peoples, as the Egyptians (Isis and Osiris), Assyrians and ancient Persians. Physiologically they are injurious only when the parents have constitutional defects: if both are sound, the issue, as amongst the so-called "lower animals," is viable and healthy.

54. Dwellers in the Northern Temperates can hardly imagine what a dust-storm is in sun-parched tropical lands. In Sind we were often obliged to use candles at midday, while above the dust was a sun that would roast an egg.

55. Arab. " 'Urban," now always used of the wild people, whom the French have taught us to call *les Bedouins*; "Badw" being a

waste or desert; and Badawi (fem. Badawíyah, plur. Badáwi and Bidwán), a man of the waste. Europeans have also learnt to miscall the Egyptians "Arabs": the difference is as great as between an Englishman and a Spaniard. Arabs proper divide their race into sundry successive families. "The Arab al-Arabá" (or al-Aribah, or al-Urubíyat) are the autochthones, prehistoric, proto-historic and extinct tribes; for instance, a few of the Adites who being at Meccah escaped the destruction of their wicked nation, but mingled with other classes. The "Arab al-Muta'arribah," (Arabized Arabs) are the first advenæ represented by such noble strains as the Koraysh (Koreish), some still surviving. The "Arab al-Musta'aribah" (institious, naturalized or instituted Arabs, men who claim to be Arabs) are Arabs like the Sinaites, the Egyptians and the Maroccans descended by intermarriage with other races. Hence our "Mosarabians" and the "Marrabais" of Rabelais (not, "a word compounded of Maurus and Arabs"). Some genealogists, however, make the Muta'arribah descendants of Kahtan (possibly the Joktan of Genesis x., a comparatively modern document, 700 B.C.?); and the Musta'aribah those descended from Adnán the origin of Arab genealogy. And, lastly, are the "Arab al-Musta'ajimah," barbarized Arabs, like the present population of Meccah and Al-Medinah. Besides these there are other tribes whose origin is still unknown; such as the Mahrah tribes of Hazramaut, the "Akhdám" (=serviles) of Oman (Maskat); and the "Ebná" of Al-Yaman: Ibn Ishak supposes the latter to be descended from the Persian soldiers of Anushirwan who expelled the Abyssinian invader from Southern Arabia. (*Pilgrimage,* iii., 31, etc.)

56. Arab. "Amír al-Muuminín." The title was assumed by the Caliph Omar to obviate the inconvenience of calling himself "Khalífah" (successor) of the Khalífah of the Apostle of Allah (*i.e.* Abu Bakr); which after a few generations would become impossible. It means "Emir (chief or prince) of the Muumins"; men who hold to the (true Moslem) Faith, the "Imán" (theory, fundamental articles) as opposed to the "Dín," ordinance or practice of the religion. It once became a Wazirial time conferred by Sultan Malikshah (King King-king) on his Nizám al-Mulk. (Richardson's *Dissert.* lviii.)

57. This may also mean "according to the seven editions of the Koran," the old revisions and so forth (Sale, Sect. iii. and D'Herbelot *Alcoran*). The schools of the "Mukri," who teach the right pronunciation wherein a mistake might be sinful, are seven, Hamzah, Ibn Katír, Ya'akúb, Ibn Amir, Kisái, Asim and Hafs, the latter being the favourite with the Hanafis and the only one now generally known in Al-Islam.

58. Arab. "Sadd" = wall, dyke, etc. the "bund" or "band" of Anglo-India. Hence the "Sadd" on the Nile, the banks of grass and floating islands which "wall" the stream. There are few sights more appalling than a sandstorm in the desert, the "Zauba'ah" as the Arabs call it. Devils, or pillars of sand, vertical and inclined, measuring a thousand feet high, rush over the plain lashing the sand at their base like a sea surging under a furious whirlwind; shearing the grass clean away from the roots, tearing up trees, which are whirled like leaves and sticks in air and sweeping away tents and houses as if they were bits of paper. At last the columns join at the top and form, perhaps three thousand feet above the earth, a gigantic cloud of yellow sand which obliterates not only the horizon but even the midday sun. These sand-spouts are the terror of travellers. In Sind and the Punjab we have the dust-storm which for darkness, I have said, beats the blackest London fog.

59. Arab. Sár = the vendetta, before mentioned, as dreaded in Arabia as in Corsica.

60. Arab. "Ghútah," usually a place where irrigation is abundant. It especially applies (in books) to the Damascus-plain because "it abounds with water and fruit trees." The Ghutah is one of the four earthly paradises, the others being Basrah (Bassorah), Shiraz and Samarcand. Its peculiarity is the likeness to a seaport; the Desert which rolls up almost to its doors being the sea and its ships being the camels. The first Arab to whom we owe this admirable term for the "Companion of Job" is "Tarafah," one of the poets of the Suspended Poems: he likens (v. v. 3, 4) the camels which bore away his beloved to ships sailing from Aduli. But "ships of the desert" is doubtless a term of the highest antiquity.

61. The exigencies of the "Saj'a," or rhymed prose, disjoint this and many similar passages.

62. The "Ebony" Islands; Scott's *Isle of Ebene*, i., 217.

63. "Jarjarís" in the Bul. Edit.
64. Arab. "Takbís." Many Easterns can hardly sleep without this kneading of the muscles, this "rubbing" whose hygienic properties England is now learning.
65. The converse of the breast being broadened, the drooping, "draggle-tail" gait compared with the head held high and the chest inflated.
66. This penalty is mentioned in the Koran (chap. v.) as fit for those who fight against Allah and his Apostle; but commentators are not agreed if the sinners are first to be put to death or to hang on the cross till they die. Pharaoh (chap. xx.) threatens to crucify his magicians on palm-trees, and is held to be the first crucifier.
67. Arab. " 'Ajami" = foreigner, esp. a Persian: the latter in The Nights is mostly a villain. I must here remark that the contemptible condition of Persians in Al-Hijáz (which I noted in 1852, *Pilgrimage*, i., 327) has completely changed. They are no longer, "The slippers of Ali and hounds of Omar": they have learned the force of union and now, instead of being bullied, they bully.
68. The Calc. Edit. turns into Tailors (Khayyátín) and Torrens does not see the misprint.
69. *i.e.* Axe and sandals.
70. Lit. "Strike his neck."
71. A phrase which will frequently recur, whose significance is "the situation suggested such words as these."
72. The comparison is peculiarly apposite; the earth seen from above appears hollow with a raised rim.
73. A hundred years old.
74. "Bahr" in Arab. means sea, river, piece of water; hence the adjective is needed.
75. The Captain or Master of the ship (not the owner). In Al-Yaman the word also means a "barber," in virtue of the root, Rass, a head.
76. The text has "in the character Ruká'í," or Riká'í, the correspondence-hand.
77. A curved character supposed to be like the basil-leaf (rayhán). Richardson calls it "Rohani."
78. I need hardly say that Easterns use a reed, a Calamus (Kalam applied only to the cut reed) for our quills and steel pens.
79. Famous for being inscribed on the Kiswah (cover) of Mo-

hammed's tomb; a large and more formal hand still used for engrossing and for mural inscriptions. Only seventy-two varieties of it are known (*Pilgrimage,* ii., 82).

80. The copying and transcribing hand which is either Arabi or Ajami. A great discovery has been lately made which upsets all our old ideas of Cufic, etc. Mr. Löytved of Bayrut has found, amongst the Hauranic inscriptions, one in pure Naskhi, dating A.D. 568, or fifty years before the Hijrah; and it is accepted as authentic by my learned friend, M. Ch. Clermont-Ganneau (p. 193, Pal. Explor. Fund; July, 1884). In D'Herbelot and Sale's day the Koran was supposed to have been written in rude characters, like those subsequently called "Cufic," invented shortly before Mohammed's birth by Murámir ibn Murrah of Anbar in Irák, introduced into Meccah by Bashar the Kindian, and perfected by Ibn Muklah (Al-Wazir, ob. A.H. 328 = 940). We must now change all that. See *Catalogue of Oriental Caligraphs,* etc., by G. P. Badger, London: Whiteley, 1885.

81. Arab. "Baghlah"; the male (Baghl) is used only for loads. This is everywhere the rule: nothing is more unmanageable than a restive "Macho"; and he knows that he can always get you off his back when so minded. From "Baghlah" is derived the name of the native craft Anglo-Indicè, a "Buggalow."

82. In Heb. "Ben-Adam" is any map opp. to "Beni ish" (Psalm iv. 3) = *filii viri,* not *homines.*

83. This posture is terribly trying to European legs; and few white men (unless brought up to it) can squat for any time on their heels. The "tailor-fashion," with crossed legs, is held to be free and easy.

84. This is the *vinum coctum,* the boiled wine, still a favourite in Southern Italy and Greece.

85. The Caliph Al-Maamún, who was a bad player, used to say, "I have the administration of the world and am equal to it, whereas I am straitened in the ordering of a space of two spans by two spans." The "board" was then "a square field of well-dressed leather."

86. The Rabbis (after Matth. xix. 12) count three kinds of Eunuchs; (1) Seris chammah = of the sun, *i.e.* natural; (2) Seris Adam = manufactured *per homines;* and (3) Seris Chammayim = of God (*i.e.* religious abstainer). Seris (castrated) or Abd (slave) is the general Hebrew name.

87. The "Lady of Beauty."

88. "Káf" has been noticed as the mountain which surrounds earth as a ring does the finger: it is popularly used like our Alp and Alpine. The "circumambient Ocean" (Bahr al-muhit) is the Homeric Ocean-stream.

89. The pomegranate is probably chosen here because each fruit is supposed to contain one seed from Eden-garden. Hence a host of superstitions (*Pilgrimage*, iii., 104) possibly connected with the Chaldaic-Babylonian god Rimmon or Ramanu. Hence Persephone or Ishtar tasted the "rich pomegranate's seed." Lenormant, loc. cit. pp. 166, 182.

90. *i.e.* for the love of God—a favourite Moslem phrase.

91. Arab. "Báb," also meaning a chapter (of magic, of war, etc.), corresponding with the Persian "Dar" as in Sad-dar, the Hundred Doors. Here, however, it is figurative "I tried a new mode." This scene is in the Mabinogion.

92. I use this Irish term = crying for the dead; as English wants the word for the præfica or myrialogist. The practice is not encouraged in Al-Islam; and Caliph Abu Bakr said, "Verily a corpse is sprinkled with boiling water by reason of the lamentations of the living," *i.e.* punished for not having taken measures to prevent their profitless lamentations. But the practice is from Negroland whence it reached Egypt; and the people have there developed a curious system in the "weeping-song": I have noted this in *The Lake-Regions of Central Africa*. In Zoroastrianism (*Dabistan*, chap. xcvii.) tears shed for the dead form a river in hell, black and frigid.

93. Every city in the East has its specific title: this was given to Baghdad either on account of its superior police or simply because it was the Capital of the Caliphate. The Tigris was also called the "River of Peace (or Security)."

94. This is very characteristic: the passengers finding themselves in difficulties at once take command. See in my *Pilgrimage*, (i. chap. xi.) how we beat and otherwise maltreated the Captain of the "Golden Wire."

95. The fable is probably based on the currents which, as in Eastern Africa, will carry a ship fifty miles a day out of her course. We first find it in Ptolemy (vii. 2) whose Maniólai Islands, of India extra Gangem, cause iron nails to fly out of ships, the effect of the Lapis Herculeus (Loadstone). Ra-

belais (v. c. 37) alludes to it and to the vulgar idea of magnetism being counteracted by Skordon (*Scordon* or garlic). Hence too the Adamant (Loadstone) Mountains of Mandeville (chap. xxvii.) and the "Magnetic Rock" in Mr. Puttock's clever *Peter Wilkins*. I presume that the myth also arose from seeing craft built, as on the East African Coast, without iron nails. We shall meet with the legend again. The word Jabal ("Jebel" in Egypt) often occurs in these pages. The Arabs apply it to any rising ground or heap of rocks; so it is not always = our mountain. It has found its way to Europe *e.g.* Gibraltar and Monte Gibello (or Mongibel in poetry) = "Mt. Ethne then clepen Mounte Gybelle." Other special senses of Jabal will occur.

96. As we learn from the Nubian Geographer the Arabs in early ages explored the Fortunate Islands (Jazírát al-Khálidát = Eternal Isles), or Canaries, on one of which were reported a horse and horseman in bronze with his spear pointing west. Ibn al-Wardi notes "two images of hard stone, each an hundred cubits high, and upon the top of each a figure of copper pointing with its hand backwards, as though it would say:—Return for there is nothing behind me!" But this legend attaches to older doings. The 23rd Tobba (who succeeded Bilkis), Malik bin Sharhabíl, (or Sharabíl or Sharahíl) surnamed Náshir al-Ni'ám = scatterer of blessings, lost an army in attempting the Western sands and set up a statue of copper upon whose breast was inscribed in antique characters:—

> There is no access behind me,
> Nothing beyond,
> (Saith) The Son of Sharabíl.

97. *i.e.* I exclaimed "Bismillah!"
98. The lesser ablution of hands, face and feet; a kind of "washing the points."
99. Arab. "Ruka'tayn"; the number of these bows which are followed by the prostrations distinguishes the five daily prayers.
100. The "Beth Kol" of the Hebrews; also called by the Moslems "Hátif"; for which ask the Spiritualists. It is the Hindu "voice divine" or "voice from heaven."

101. These formulæ are technically called Tasmiyah, Tahlíl (before noted) and Takbír: the "testifying" is Tashhíd.

102. Arab. "Samn," (Pers. "Raughan" Hind. "Ghi") the "single sauce" of the East; fresh butter set upon the fire, skimmed and kept (for a century if required) in leather bottles and demijohns. Then it becomes a hard black mass, considered a panacea for wounds and diseases. It is very "filling": you say jocosely to an Eastern threatened with a sudden inroad of guests, "Go, swamp thy rice with Raughan." I once tried training, like a Hindu Pahlawan or athlete, on Gur (raw sugar), milk and Ghi; and the result was being blinded by bile before the week ended.

103. These handsome youths are always described in the terms we should apply to women.

104. The Bul. Edit. (i. 43) reads otherwise:—"I found a garden and a second and a third and so on till they numbered thirty and nine; and, in each garden, I saw what praise will not express, of trees and rills and fruits and treasures. At the end of the last I sighted a door and said to myself, 'What may be in this place? needs must I open it and look in!' I did so accordingly and saw a courser ready saddled and bridled and picketed; so I loosed and mounted him; and he flew with me like a bird till he set me down on a terrace-roof; and, having landed me, he struck me a whisk with his tail and put out mine eye and fled from me. Thereupon I descended from the roof and found ten youths all blind of one eye who, when they saw me exclaimed, 'No welcome to thee, and no good cheer!' I asked them, 'Do ye admit me to your home and society?' and they answered, 'No, by Allah, thou shalt not live amongst us.' So I went forth with weeping eyes and grieving heart, but Allah had written my safety on the Guarded Tablet so I reached Baghdad in safety," etc. This is a fair specimen of how the work has been curtailed in that issue.

105. Arabs date pregnancy from the stopping of the menses, upon which the fœtus is supposed to feed. Kalilah wa Dimnah says, "The child's navel adheres to that of his mother and thereby he sucks" (i. 263).

106. This is contrary to the commands of Al-Islam; Mohammed expressly said "The Astrologers are liars, by the Lord of the Ka'abah!" and his saying is known to almost all Moslems, let-

tered or unlettered. Yet, the further we go East (Indiawards) the more we find these practices held in honour. Turning westwards we have:

> Iuridicis, Erebo, Fisco, fas vivere rapto:
> Militibus, Medicis, Tortori occidere ludo est;
> Mentiri Astronomis, Pictoribus atque Poetis.

107. He does not perform the Wuzu or lesser ablution because he neglects his dawn prayers.

108. For this game see Lane (*M. E.*, chap. xvii.). It is usually played on a checked cloth, not on a board like our draughts; and Easterns are fond of eating, drinking and smoking between and even during the games. Torrens (p. 142) translates "I made up some dessert," confounding "Mankalah" with "Nukl" (dried fruit, quatre-mendiants).

109. Quoted from Mohammed whose saying has been given.

110. We should say "the night of the thirty-ninth."

111. The bath first taken after sickness.

112. Arab. "Dikák" used by way of soap or rather to soften the skin: the meal is usually of lupins, "Adas" = *"Revalenta Arabica,"* which costs a penny in Egypt and half-a-crown in England.

113. Arab. "Sukkar-nabát." During my day (1842–49) we had no other sugar in the Bombay Presidency.

114. This is one of the myriad Arab instances that the decrees of "Anagké," Fate, Destiny, Weird, are inevitable. The situation is highly dramatic; and indeed The Nights . . . have already suggested a national drama.

115. Having lately moved by Ajib.

116. Mr. Payne (i. 131) omits these lines which appear out of place; but this mode of inappropriate quotation is a characteristic of Eastern tales.

117. This march of the tribe is a *lieu commun* of Arab verse *e.g.* the poet Labid's noble elegy on the *Deserted Camp*. We shall find scores of instances in The Nights.

118. I have heard of such sands in the Desert east of Damascus which can be crossed only on boards or camel furniture; and the same is reported of the infamous Region "Al-Ahkláf" (*Unexplored Syria*).

119. Hence the Arab. saying "The bark of a dog and not the

gleam of a fire"; the tired traveller knows from the former that the camp is near, whereas the latter shows from great distances.

120. Dark blue is the colour of mourning in Egypt as it was of the Roman Republic. The Persians hold that this tint was introduced by Kay Kawús (600 B.C.) when mourning for his son Siyáwush. It was continued till the death of Husayn on the 10th of Muharram (the first month, then representing the vernal equinox) when it was changed for black. As a rule Moslems do not adopt this symbol of sorrow (called "Hidád"), looking upon the practice as somewhat idolatrous and foreign to Arab manners. In Egypt and especially on the Upper Nile women dye their hands with indigo and stain their faces black or blacker.

121. The older Roc, of which more in the Tale of Sindbad. Meanwhile the reader curious about the Persian Símurgh (thirty bird) will consult the *Dabistan*, i., 55, 191 and iii., 237, and Richardson's *Diss.*; p. xlviii. For the Anka (Enka or Unka = long-necked bird) see *Dab.* iii., 249, and for the Humá (bird of Paradise) Richardson lxix. We still lack details concerning the Ben or Bennu (nycticorax) of Egypt which with the Article pi gave rise to the Greek "phœnix."

122. Probably the *Haledj* of Forskal (p. xcvi. *Flor. Ægypt. Arab.*), "lignum tenax, durum, obscuri generis." The Bres. Edit. has "ákúl"=teak wood, vulg. "Sáj."

123. The knocker ring is an invention well known to the Romans.

124. Arab. "Sadr"; denotes the place of honour; hence the "Sudder Adawlut" (Supreme Court) in the Anglo-Indian jargon.

125. Arab. "Ahlan wa sahlan wa marhabá," the words still popularly addressed to a guest.

126. This may mean "liquid black eyes"; but also, as I have noticed, that the lashes were long and thick enough to make the eyelids appear as if Kohl-powder had been applied to the inner rims.

127. A slight parting between the two front incisors, the upper only, is considered a beauty by Arabs; why it is hard to say except for the racial love of variety. "Sughr" (Thugr) in the text means, primarily, the opening of the mouth, the gape: hence the front teeth.

128. *i.e.* makes me taste the bitterness of death, "bursting the gall-bladder" (Marárah) being our "breaking the heart."

129. Almost needless to say that forbidden doors and rooms form a *lieu commun* in Fairie: they are found in the Hindu Katha Sarit Sagara and became familiar to our childhood by "Bluebeard."

130. Lit. "apply Kohl to my eyes," even as Jezebel "painted her face," in Heb. put her eyes in painting (2 Kings ix. 30).

131. Arab. "Al-Barkúk," whence our older "Apricock." Classically it is "Burkúk" and Pers. for Arab. "Mishmish," and it also denotes a small plum or damson. In Syria the "side next the sun" shows a glowing red flush.

132. Arab. "Hazár" (in Persian, a thousand)=a kind of mocking bird.

133. Some Edits. make the doors number a hundred, but the Princesses were forty and these coincidences, which seem to have significance and have none save for Arab symmetromania, are common in Arab stories.

134. Arab. "Májúr": hence possibly our "mazer," which is popularly derived from Masarn, a maple.

135. A compound scent of ambergris, musk and aloes.

136. The ends of the bridle-reins forming the whip.

137. The flying horse is Pegasus which is a Greek travesty of an Egyptian myth developed in India.

138. The Bres. Edit. wrongly says "the seventh."

139. Arab. "Sharmutah" (plur. Sharámít) from the root Sharmat, to shred, a favourite Egyptian word also applied in vulgar speech to a strumpet, a punk, a piece. It is also the popular term for strips of jerked or boucaned meat hung up in the sun to dry, and classically called "Kadíd."

140. Arab. "Izár," the man's waistcloth opposed to the Ridá or shoulder-cloth, is also the sheet of white calico worn by the poorer Egyptian women out of doors and covering head and hands. See Lane (*M. E.,* chap. i.). The rich prefer a "Habárah" of black silk, and the poor, when they have nothing else, use a bed-sheet.

141. *i.e.* "My dears."

142. Arab. "Lá tawákhizná": lit. "do not chastise (or blame) us"; the pop. expression for "excuse (or pardon) us."

143. Arab. "Maskhút," mostly applied to change of shape as man enchanted to monkey, and in vulgar parlance applied to a statue (of stone, etc.). The list of metamorphoses in Al-Islam is longer than that known to Ovid. Those who have

seen Petra, the Greek town of the Haurán and the Roman ruins in Northern Africa will readily detect the basis upon which these stories are built. I shall return to this subject in The City of Iram and The City of Brass.

144. A picturesque phrase enough to express a deserted site, a spectacle familiar to the Nomades and always abounding in pathos to the citizens.

145. The olden "Harem" (or gynæceum, Pers. Zenanah, Serraglio): Harím is also used by synecdoche for the inmates; especially the wife.

146. The pearl is supposed in the East to lose 1% per ann. of its splendour and value.

147. Arab. "Fass," properly the bezel of a ring; also a gem cut *en cabochon* and generally the *contenant* for the *contenu*.

148. Arab. "Mihráb" = the arch-headed niche in the Mosque-wall facing Meccah-wards. Here, with his back to the people and fronting the Ka'abah or Square House of Meccah (hence called the "Kiblah" = direction of prayer), stations himself the Imám, antistes or fugleman, lit. "one who stands *before* others"; and his bows and prostrations give the time to the congregation. I have derived the Mihrab from the niche in which the Egyptian God was shrined: the Jews ignored it, but the Christians preserved it for their statues and altars. Maundrell suggests that the empty niche denotes an invisible God. As the niche (symbol of Venus) and the minaret (symbol of Priapus) date only from the days of the tenth Caliph, Al-Walid (A.H. 86–96 = 705–715), the Hindus charge the Moslems with having borrowed the two from their favourite idols—The Linga-Yoni or Cunnusphallus (*Pilgrimage*, ii. 140), and plainly call the Mihrab a Bhaga = Cunnus (*Dabistan*, ii. 152). The Guebres further term Meccah "Mahgah," locus Lunæ, and Al-Medinah, "Mahdinah," = Moon of religion. See *Dabistan*, i., 49, etc.

149. Arab. "Kursi," a stool of palm-fronds, etc., X-shaped (see Lane's illustration, *Nights*, i., 197), before which the reader sits. Good Moslems will not hold the Holy Volume below the waist nor open it except when ceremonially pure. Englishmen in the East should remember this, for to neglect the "Adab al-Kúran" (respect due to Holy Writ) gives great scandal.

150. This is regular formula when speaking of Guebres.
151. Arab. "Faráiz"; the orders expressly given in the Koran which the reader will remember, is Uncreate and Eternal. In India "Farz" is applied to injunctions thrice repeated; and "Wájib" to those given twice over. Elsewhere scanty difference is made between them.
152. Arab. "Kufr" = rejecting the True Religion, *i.e.* Al-Islam, such rejection being "Tughyán" or rebellion against the Lord. The "terrible sound" is taken from the legend of the prophet Sálih and the proto-historic tribe of Thámúd which for its impiety was struck dead by an earthquake and a noise from heaven. The latter, according to some commentators, was the voice of the Archangel Gabriel crying "Die all of you" (*Koran*, chap. vii., xviii., etc.). We shall hear more of it in the "City of many-columned Iram." According to some, Salih, a mysterious Badawi prophet, is buried in the Wady al-Shaykh of the so-called Sinaitic Peninsula.
153. Yet they kept the semblance of man, showing that the idea arose from the basaltic statues found in Hauranic ruins. Mohammed in his various marches to Syria must have seen remnants of Greek and Roman settlements; and as has been noticed "Sesostris" left his mark near Meccah. (*Pilgrimage*, iii. 137.)
154. Arab. "Shuhadá"; highly respected by Moslems as by other religionists; although their principal if not only merit seems as a rule to have been intense obstinacy and devotion to one idea for which they were ready to sacrifice even life. The Martyrs-category is extensive including those killed by falling walls; victims to the plague, pleurisy and pregnancy; travellers drowned or otherwise lost when journeying honestly, and chaste lovers who die of "broken hearts" *i.e.* impaired digestion. Their souls are at once stowed away in the crops of green birds where they remain till Resurrection Day, "eating of the fruits and drinking of the streams of Paradise," a place however, whose topography is wholly uncertain. Thus the young Prince was rewarded with a manner of anti-Purgatory, a preparatory heaven.
155. Arab. "Su'ubán": the Badawin give the name to a variety of serpents all held to be venomous; but in tales the word, like "Tannín," expresses our "dragon" or "cockatrice."

156. She was ashamed to see the lady doing servile duty by rubbing her feet. This *massage*, which B. de la Brocquière describes in 1452 as "kneading and pinching," has already been noticed. The French term is apparently derived from the Arab. "Mas-h."

157. Alluding to the Most High Name, the hundredth name of God, the Heb. Shem hamphorash, unknown save to a favoured few who by using it were enabled to perform all manner of miracles.

158. *i.e.* the Mediterranean and the Indian Ocean.

159. *i.e.* Settled by the Koran.

160. The uglier the old woman the better procuress she is supposed to make. See the Santa Verdiana in Boccaccio v., 10. In Arab. "Ajuz" (old woman) is highly insulting and if addressed to an Egyptian, whatever be her age, she will turn fiercely and resent it. The polite term is Shaybah (*Pilgrimage*, iii., 200).

161. Arab. "Jilá" (the Hindostani Julwa)=the displaying of the bride before the bridegroom for the first time, in different dresses, to the number of seven which are often borrowed for the occasion. The happy man must pay a fee called "the tax of face-unveiling" before he can see her features. Amongst Syrian Christians he sometimes tries to lift the veil by a sharp movement of the sword which is parried by the women present, and the blade remains entangled in the cloth. At last he succeeds, the bride sinks to the ground covering her face with her hands and the robes of her friends: presently she is raised up, her veil is readjusted and her face is left bare.

162. Arab. "Ishá"=the first watch of the night, twilight, suppertime, supper. Moslems have borrowed the four watches of the Romans from 6 (a.m. or p.m.) to 6; and ignore the three original watches of the Jews, even, midnight and cockcrow (Sam. ii. 19, Judges vii. 19, and Exodus xiv. 24).

163. A popular Arab hyperbole.

164. Arab. "Shakáik al-Nu'mán," lit. the fissures of Nu'man, the beautiful anemone, which a tyrannical King of Hirah, Nu'uman Al-Munzir, a contemporary of Mohammed, attempted to monopolize.

165. I need hardly say that in the East, where bells are unused, clapping the hands summons the servants. In India men cry

"Quy hye" (Koi hái?) and in Brazil whistle "Pst!" after the fashion of Spain and Portugal.

166. Arab. "Simát" (prop. "Sumát"); the "dinner-table," composed of a round wooden stool supporting a large metal tray, the two being called "Sufrah" (or "Simat"): thus "Sufrah házirah!" means dinner is on the table. After the meal they are at once removed.

167. In the text "Dastúr," the Persian word before noticed; "Izn" would be the proper Arabic equivalent.

168. In the Moslem East a young woman, single or married, is not allowed to appear alone in the streets; and the police have a right to arrest delinquents. As a preventive of intrigues the precaution is excellent. During the Crimean war hundreds of officers, English, French and Italian, became familiar with Constantinople; and not a few flattered themselves on their success with Turkish women. I do not believe that a single *bona fide* case occurred: the "conquests" were all Greeks, Wallachians, Armenians or Jewesses.

169. Arab. "Azím": translators do not seem to know that this word in The Nights often bears its Egyptian and slang sense, somewhat equivalent to our "deuced" or "mighty" or "awfully fine."

170. This is a very serious thing amongst Moslems and scrupulous men often make great sacrifices to avoid taking an oath.

171. We should say "into the noose."

172. The man had fallen in love with her and determined to mark her so that she might be his.

173. Arab. "Dajlah," in which we find the Heb. Hid-dekel.

174. When a woman is bastinadoed in the East they leave her some portion of dress and pour over her sundry buckets of water for a delicate consideration. When the hands are beaten they are passed through holes in the curtain separating the sufferer from mankind, and made fast to a "falakah" or pole.

175. Arab. "Khalifah," Caliph. The word is also used for the successor of a Santon or holy man.

176. Arab. "Sár"; here the Koranic word for carrying out the venerable and undying *lex talionis*, the original basis of all criminal jurisprudence. Its main fault is that justice repeats the offence.

177. Both these sons of Harun became Caliphs, as we shall see in The Nights.

THE TALE OF THE THREE APPLES

1. "Dog" and "hog" are still highly popular terms of abuse. The Rabbis will not defile their lips with "pig"; but say "Dabhar akhir" = "another thing."

2. The "hero eponymus" of the Abbaside dynasty, Abbas having been the brother of Abdullah, the father of Mohammed. He is a famous personage in Al-Islam (D'Herbelot).

3. Europe translates the word "Barmecides." It is Persian from *bar* (up) and *makidan* (to suck). The vulgar legend is that Ja'afar, the first of the name, appeared before the Caliph Abd al-Malik with a ring poisoned for his own need; and that the Caliph, warned of it by the clapping of two stones which he wore *ad hoc*, charged the visitor with intention to murder him. He excused himself and in his speech occurred the Persian word "Barmakam," which may mean "I shall sup it up," or "I am a Barmak," that is, a high priest among the Guebres. See D'Herbelot s.v.

4. Arab. "Zulm," the deadliest of monarch's sins. One of the sayings of Mohammed, popularly quoted, is, "Kingdom endureth with Kufr or infidelity (*i.e.* without accepting Al-Islam) but endureth not with Zulm or injustice." Hence the good Moslem will not complain of the rule of Kafirs or Unbelievers, like the English, so long as they rule him righteously and according to his own law.

5. All this aggravates his crime: had she been a widow she would not have had upon him "the claims of maidenhead," the premio della verginita of Boccaccio, x. 10.

6. It is supposed that slaves cannot help telling these fatal lies. Arab story-books are full of ancient and modern instances and some have become "Joe Millers." Moreover it is held unworthy of a free-born man to take over-notice of these servile villainies; hence the scoundrel in the story escapes unpunished. I have already noticed the predilection of debauched women for these "skunks of the human race"; and the young man in the text evidently suspected that his wife had passed herself this "little caprice." The excuse which

the Caliph would find for him is the *pundonor* shown in killing one he loved so fondly.

7. The Arab equivalent of our pitcher and well.

8. *i.e.* Where the dress sits loosely about the bust.

9. He had trusted in Allah and his trust was justified.

TALE OF NUR AL-DIN ALI AND HIS SON BADR AL-DIN HASAN

1. Arab. "Khila'ah" prop. what a man strips from his person: gen. an honorary gift. It is something more than the "robe of honour" of our chivalrous romances, as it includes a horse, a sword (often gold-hilted), a black turban (amongst the Abbasides) embroidered with gold, a violet-coloured mantle, a waist-shawl and a gold neck-chain and shoe-buckles.

2. Arab. "Izá," *i.e.* the visits of condolence and so forth which are long and terribly wearisome in the Moslem East.

3. Arab. "Mahr," the money settled by the man before marriage on the woman and without which the contract is not valid. Usually half of it is paid down on the marriage-day and the other half when the husband dies or divorces his wife. But if she take a divorce she forfeits her right to it, and obscene fellows, especially Persians, often compel her to demand divorce by unnatural and preposterous use of her person.

4. Bismillah here means "Thou art welcome to it."

5. Arab. "Bassak," half Pers. (bas = enough) and -ak = thou; for thee. "Bas" sounds like our "buss" (to kiss) and there are sundry good old Anglo-Indian jokes of feminine mistakes on the subject.

6. This saving clause makes the threat worse. The scene between the two brothers is written with characteristic Arab humour; and it is true to nature. In England we have heard of a man who separated from his wife because he wished to dine at six and she preferred half-past six.

7. Arab. "Misr." (vulg. Masr). The word, which comes of a very ancient house, was applied to the present Capital about the time of its conquest by the Osmanli Turks A.H. 923 = 1517.

8. The Arab "Jízah" = skirt, edge; the modern village is the site of an ancient Egyptian city, as the "Ghizah inscription" proves (Brugsch, *History of Egypt*, ii. 415).

9. Arab. "Watan" literally meaning "birthplace," but also used

for "patria, native country"; thus "Hubb al-Watan" = patriotism. The Turks pronounce it "Vatan," which the French have turned into Va-t'en!

10. Arab. "Zarzariyah" = the colour of a stare or starling (Zurzúr).

11. Now a railway station on the Alexandria-Cairo line.

12. Even as late as 1852, when I first saw Cairo, the city was girt by waste lands and the climate was excellent. Now cultivation comes up to the house walls; while the Mahmudiyah Canal, the planting the streets with avenues and over-watering have seriously injured it; those who want the air of former Cairo must go to Thebes. Gout, rheumatism and hydrophobia (before unknown) have become common of late years.

13. This is the popular pronunciation: Yákút calls it "Bilbís."

14. An outlying village on the "Long Desert," between Cairo and Palestine.

15. Arab. "Al-Kuds" = holiness. There are few cities which in our day have less claim to this title than Jerusalem; and, curious to say, the "Holy Land" shows Jews, Christians and Moslems all in their worst form. The only religion (if it can be called one) which produces men in Syria is the Druse. "Heiligen-landes Jüden" are proverbial and nothing can be meaner than the Christians while the Moslems are famed for treachery.

16. Arab. "Shamm al-hawá." In vulgar parlance to "smell the air" is to take a walk, especially out of town. There is a peculiar Egyptian festival called "Shamm al-Nasím (smelling the Zephyr) which begins on Easter-Monday (O.S.), thus corresponding with the Persian Nau-roz, vernal equinox and introducing the fifty days of "Khammasín" or "Mirísi" (hot desert winds). On awakening, the people smell and bathe their temples with vinegar in which an onion has been soaked and break their fast with a "fisikh" or dried "búri" = mullet from Lake Menzalah: the late Hekekiyan Bey had the fish-heads counted in one public garden and found 70,000. The rest of the day is spent out of doors "Gypsying," and families greatly enjoy themselves on these occasions. For a longer description see a paper by my excellent friend Yacoub Artin Pasha, in the Bulletin de l'Institut Égyptien, 2nd series, No. 4, Cairo, 1884. I have noticed the Mirísi (south-wester) and other winds in the *Land of Midian*, i., 23.

17. So in the days of the "Mameluke Beys" in Egypt a man of rank would not cross the street on foot.

18. Basrah. The city now in decay and not to flourish again till the advent of the Euphrates Valley R.R., is a modern place, founded in A.H. 15, by the Caliph Omar upon the Aylah, a feeder of the Tigris. Here, according to Al-Haríri, the "whales and the lizards meet"; and, as the tide affects the river,

> Its stream shows prodigy, ebbing and flowing.

In its far-famed market-place, Al-Marbad, poems used to be recited; and the city was famous for its mosques and Saint-shrines, fair women and school of Grammar which rivalled that of Kúfah. But already in Al-Hariri's day (nat. A.H. 446=A.D. 1030) Baghdad had drawn off much of its population.

19. This fumigation (Bukhúr) is still used. A little incense or perfumed wood is burnt upon an open censer (Mibkharah) of earthenware or metal, and passed round, each guest holding it for a few moments under his beard. In the Somali Country, the very home of incense, both sexes fumigate the whole person after carnal intercourse. Lane (*Mod. Egypt*, chap. viii) gives an illustration of the Mibkharah.

20. The reader of The Nights will remark that the merchant is often a merchant-prince, consorting and mating with the highest dignitaries. Even amongst the Romans, a race of soldiers, statesmen and lawyers, "mercatura" on a large scale was "not to be vituperated." In Boccaccio (x. 19) they are netti e delicati uomini. England is perhaps the only country which has made her fortune by trade, and much of it illicit trade, like that in slaves which built Liverpool and Bristol, and which yet disdains or affects to disdain the trader. But the unworthy prejudice is disappearing with the last generation, and men who formerly would have half starved as curates and ensigns, barristers and *carabins* are now only too glad to become merchants.

21. These lines in the Calc. and Bul. Edits. have already occurred (page 36), but such carelessness is characteristic despite the proverb, "In repetition is no fruition." I quote Torrens (p. 60) by way of variety. As regards the anemone

(here called a tulip) being named "Shakík" = fissure, I would conjecture that it derives from the flower often forming long lines of red like stripes of blood in the landscape. Travellers in Syria always observe this.

22. Such an address to a royalty (Eastern) even in the present day would be a passport to future favours.

23. In England the man marries and the woman is married: there is no such distinction in Arabia.

24. "Sultan" (and its corruption "Soldan") etymologically means lord, victorious, ruler, ruling over. In Arabia it is a not uncommon proper name; and as a title it is taken by a host of petty kinglets. The Abbaside Caliphs (as Al-Wásik who has been noticed) formally created these Sultans as their regents. Al-Tá'i bi'llah (regn. A.H. 363 = 974) invested the famous Sabuktagin with the office; and, as Alexander-Sikandar was wont to do, fashioned for him two flags, one of silver, after the fashion of nobles, and the other of gold, as Viceroy-designate. Sabuktagin's son, the famous Mahmúd of the Ghaznavite dynasty in A.H. 393 = 1002, was the first to adopt "Sultan" as an independent title some two hundred years after the death of Harun al-Rashid. In old writers we have the Soldan of Egypt, the Soudan of Persia, and the Sowdan of Babylon; three modifications of one word.

25. i.e. he was a "Háfiz," one who commits to memory the whole of the Koran. It is a serious task and must be begun early. I learnt by rote the last "Juzw" (or thirtieth part) and found that quite enough. This is the vulgar use of "Hafiz": technically and theologically it means the third order of Traditionists (the total being five) who know by heart 300,000 traditions of the Prophet with their ascriptions. A curious "spiritualist" book calls itself "Hafed, Prince of Persia," proving by the very title that the Spirits are equally ignorant of Arabic and Persian.

26. This naive admiration of beauty in either sex characterized our chivalrous times. Now it is mostly confined to "professional beauties" of what is conventionally called the "fair sex"; as if there could be any comparison between the beauty of man and the beauty of woman, the Apollo Belvidere with the Venus de Medici.

27. Arab. "Shásh" (in Pers. urine), a light turband generally of muslin.

28. This is a *lieu commun* of Eastern worldly wisdom. Quite true! Very unadvisable to dive below the surface of one's acquaintances, but such intimacy is like marriage of which Johnson said, "Without it there is no pleasure in life."

29. The lines are attributed to the famous Al-Mutanabbi = the claimant to "Prophecy," of whom I have given a few details in my *Pilgrimage*, iii. 60, 62. He led the life of a true poet, somewhat Chauvinistic withal; and, rather than run away, was killed in A.H. 354 = 965.

30. Arab. "Nabíz" = wine of raisins or dates; any fermented liquor; from a root to "press out" in Syriac, like the word "Talmiz" (or Tilmiz, says the Kashf al-Ghurrah), a pupil, student. Date-wine (fermented from the fruit, not the Tádi, or juice of the stem, our "toddy") is called Fazikh. Hence the Masjid al-Fazikh at Al-Medinah where the Ansar or Auxiliaries of that city were sitting cup in hand when they heard of the revelation forbidding inebriants and poured the liquor upon the ground (*Pilgrimage*, ii. 322).

31. Arab. "Huda" = direction (to the right way), salvation, a word occurring in the Opening Chapter of the Koran. Hence to a Kafir who offers the Salam-salutation many Moslems reply "Allah-yahdík" = Allah direct thee! (*i.e.* make thee a Moslem), instead of Allay yusallimak = Allah lead thee to salvation. It is the root word of the Mahdi and Mohdi.

32. I quote with permission Mr. Payne's version (i. 93).

33. Arab. "Farajíyah," a long-sleeved robe worn by the learned (Lane, *M. E.*, chap. i.).

34. Arab. "Sarráf" (vulg. Sayrafi), whence the Anglo-Indian "Shroff," a familiar corruption.

35. Arab. "Yahúdi" which is less polite than "Banú Isráíl" = Children of Israel. So in Christendom "Israelite" when in favour and "Jew" (with an adjective or a participle) when nothing is wanted of him.

36. Also called "Ghilmán" = the beautiful youths appointed to serve the True Believers in Paradise. The Koran says (chap. lvi. 9, etc.) "Youths, which shall continue in their bloom for ever, shall go round about to attend them, with goblets, and beakers, and a cup of flowing wine," etc. Mohammed was an Arab (not a Persian, a born pederast) and he was too fond of women to be charged with love of boys: even Tristram

Shandy (vol. vii., chap. 7; "No, quoth a third; the gentleman has been committing——") knew that the two tastes are incompatibles. But this and other passages in the Koran have given the Chevaliers de la Pallie a hint that the use of boys, like that of wine, here forbidden, will be permitted in Paradise.

37. Which, by the by, is the age of an oldish old maid in Egypt. I much doubt puberty being there earlier than in England where our grandmothers married at fourteen. But Orientals are aware that the period of especial feminine devilry is between the first menstruation and twenty when, according to some, every girl is a "possible murderess." So they wisely marry her and get rid of what is called the "lump of grief," the "domestic calamity"—a daughter. Amongst them we never hear of the abominable egotism and cruelty of the English mother, who disappoints her daughter's womanly cravings in order to keep her at home for her own comfort; and an "old maid" in the house, especially a stout, plump old maid, is considered not "respectable." The ancient virgin is known by being lean and scraggy; and perhaps this diagnosis is correct.

38. This prognostication of destiny by the stars and a host of follies that end in -mancy is an intricate and extensive subject. Those who would study it are referred to chap. xiv. of the *Qanoon-e-Islam, or the Customs of the Mussulmans of India; etc., etc., by Jaffur Shurreeff and translated by G. A. Herklots, M. D. of Madras.* This excellent work first appeared in 1832 (Allen and Co., London) and thus it showed the way to Lane's *Modern Egyptians* (1833–35). The name was unfortunate as "Kuzzilbash" (which rhymed to guzzle and hash), and kept the book back till a second edition appeared in 1863 (Madras: J. Higginbotham).

39. Arab. "Bárid," lit. cold: metaph. vain, foolish, insipid.

40. Not to "spite thee" but "in spite of thee." The phrase is still used by high and low.

41. Arab. "Ahdab," the common hunchback: in classical language the Gobbo in the text would be termed "Ak'as" from "Ka'as," one with protruding back and breast; sometimes used for hollow back and protruding breast.

42. This is the custom with such gentry, who, when they see a

likely man sitting, are allowed by custom to ride astraddle upon his knees with most suggestive movements, till he buys them off. These Ghawází are mostly Gypsies who pretend to be Moslems; and they have been confused with the Almahs or Moslem dancing-girls proper (Awálim, plur. of Alimah, a learned feminine) by a host of travellers. They call themselves Barámikah or Barmecides only to affect Persian origin. Under native rule they were perpetually being banished from and returning to Cairo (*Pilgrimage*, i., 202). Lane (*M. E.*, chaps. xviii. and xix.) discusses the subject, and would derive Al'mah, often so pronounced, from Heb. Almah, girl, virgin, singing-girl, hence he would translate Al-Alamoth shir (Psalm xlvi.) and Nebalim al-alamoth (1. Chron., xv. 20) by a "song for singing-girls" and "harps for singing-girls." He quotes also St. Jerome as authority that Alma in Punic (Phœnician) signified a virgin, not a common article, I may observe, amongst singing-girls. I shall notice in a future page Burckhardt's description of the Ghawazi, p. 173, *Arabic Proverbs;* etc., etc. Second Edition. London: Quaritch, 1875.

43. I need hardly describe the Tarbúsh, a corruption of the Pers. "Sar-púsh" (head-cover) also called "Fez," from its old home; and "Tarbrush" by the travelling Briton. In old days it was a calotte worn under the turban; and it was protected from scalp-perspiration by an "Arakiyah" (Pers. Arak-chin), a white skull-cap. Now it is worn without either and as a head-dress nothing can be worse (*Pilgrimage,* ii. 275).

44. Arab "Tár.": the custom still prevails. Lane (*M. E.*, chap. xviii.) describes and figures this hoop-drum.

45. The couch on which she sits while being displayed. It is her throne, for she is the Queen of the occasion, with all the Majesty of Virginity.

46. This is a solemn "chaff"; such liberties being permitted at weddings and festive occasions.

47. The pre-Islamític dynasty of Al-Yaman in Arabia Felix, a region formerly famed for wealth and luxury. Hence the mention of Yamani work. The caravans from Sana'á, the capital, used to carry patterns of vases to be made in China and bring back the porcelains at the end of the third year: these are the Arabic inscriptions which have puzzled so

many collectors. The Tobba, or Successors, were the old Himyarite Kings, a dynastic name like Pharaoh, Kisra (Persia), Negush (Abyssinia), Khakan or Khan (Tartary), etc., who claimed to have extended their conquests to Samarcand and made war on China. Any history of Arabia (as Crichton, I., chap. iv.) may be consulted for their names and annals. I have been told by Arabs that "Tobba" (or Tubba) is still used in the old Himyarland = the Great or the Chief.

48. Lane and Payne (as well as the Bres. Edit.) both render the word "to kiss her," but this would be clean contrary to Moslem usage.

49. *i.e.* he was full of rage which he concealed.

50. On such occasions Miss Modesty shuts her eyes and looks as if about to faint.

51. After either evacuation the Moslem is bound to wash or sand the part; first however he should apply three pebbles, or potsherds or clods of earth. Hence the allusion in the Koran (chap. ix.), "men who love to be purified." When the Prophet was questioning the men of Kuba, where he founded a mosque (*Pilgrimage,* ii., 215), he asked them about their legal ablutions, especially after evacuation; and they told him that they used three stones before washing. Moslems and Hindus (who prefer water mixed with earth) abhor the unclean and unhealthy use of paper without ablution; and the people of India call European draught-houses, by way of opprobrium, "Kághaz-khánah" = paper closets. Most old Anglo-Indians, however, learn to use water.

52. "Miao" or "Mau" is the generic name of the cat in the Egyptian of the hieroglyphs.

53. Arab. "Ya Mash'úm" addressed to an evil spirit.

54. "Heehaw!" as we should say. The Bresl. Edit. makes the cat cry "Nauh! Nauh!" and the ass-colt "Manu! Manu!" I leave these onomatopœics as they are in Arabic; they are curious, showing the unity in variety of hearing inarticulate sounds. The bird which is called "Whip poor Will" in the U.S. is known to the Brazilians as "Joam corta páo" (John cut wood); so differently do they hear the same notes.

55. It is usually a slab of marble with a long slit in front and a round hole behind. The text speaks of a Kursi (= stool); but this is now unknown to native houses which have not adopted European fashions.

56. This again is chaff as she addresses the Hunchback. The Bul. Edit. has "O Abu Shiháb" (Father of the shooting-star = evil spirit); the Bresl. Edit. "O son of a heap! O son of a Some-thing!" (al-Afsh, a vulgarism).

57. As the reader will see, Arab ideas of "fun" and practical jokes are of the largest, putting the Hibernian to utter rout, and comparing favourably with those recorded in Don Quixote.

58. Arab. "Saráwil," a corruption of the Pers. "Sharwál"; popu-larly called "libás" which, however, may also mean clothing in general and especially outer-clothing. I translate "bag-trousers" and "petticoat-trousers," the latter being the di-vided skirt of our future. In the East, where Common Sense, not Fashion, rules dress, men, who have a protuberance to be concealed, wear petticoats and women wear trousers. The feminine article is mostly baggy but sometimes, as in India, *collant*-tight. A quasi-sacred part of it is the inkle, tape or string, often a most magnificent affair, with tassels of pearl and precious stones; and "laxity in the trouser-string" is equivalent to the loosest conduct. Upon the subject of "libás," "sarwál" and its variants the curious reader will con-sult Dr. Dozy's *Dictionnaire Détaillé des Noms des Vêtements chez les Arabes,* a most valuable work.

59. The turban out of respect is not put upon the ground (Lane, *M. E.,* chap. i.).

60. In Arab. the "he" is a "she"; and Habíb ("friend") is the Attic φιλος, a euphemism for lover. This will occur throughout The Nights. So the Arabs use a phrase corresponding with the Stoic φιλεῖ, *i.e.* is wont, is fain.

61. Part of the Azán, or call to prayer.

62. Arab. "Shiháb," these meteors being the flying shafts shot at evil spirits who approach too near heaven. The idea doubt-less arose from the showers of August and November mete-ors (The Perseides and Taurides) which suggest a battle raging in upper air. Christendom also has its superstition concerning them and called those of August the "fiery tears of Saint Lawrence," whose festival was on August 10.

63. Arab. "Tákiyah" = Pers. Arak-chin; the calotte worn under the Fez. It is, I have said, now obsolete and the red woollen cap (mostly made in Europe) is worn over the hair; an un-clean practice.

64. Often the effect of cold air after a heated room.

65. *i.e.* He was not a Eunuch, as the people guessed.

66. Arab. "this night" for the reason before given.

67. Meaning especially the drink prepared of the young leaves and florets of Cannabis Sativa. The word literally means "day grass" or "herbage." This intoxicant was much used by magicians to produce ecstasy and thus to "deify themselves and receive the homage of the genii and spirits of nature."

68. Torrens, being an Irishman, translates "and woke in the morning sleeping at Damascus."

69. Arab. "Labbayka," the cry technically called "Talbiyah" and used by those entering Meccah (*Pilgrimage*, iii. 125–232). I shall also translate it by "Adsum." The full cry is:—

Here am I, O Allah, here am I!
No partner hast Thou, here am I:
Verily the praise and the grace and the kingdom are thine:
No partner hast Thou: here am I!

A single Talbiyah is a "Shart" or positive condition: and its repetition is a Sunnat or Custom of the Prophet.

70. The staple abuse of the vulgar is cursing parents and relatives, especially feminine, with specific allusions to their "shame." And when dames of high degree are angry, Nature, in the East as in the West, sometimes speaks out clearly enough, despite Mistress Chapone and all artificial restrictions.

71. A great beauty in Arabia and the reverse in Denmark, Germany and Slav-land, where it is a sign of being a were-wolf or a vampire. In Greece also it denotes a "Brukolak" or vampire.

72. This is not physiologically true: a bride rarely conceives the first night, and certainly would not know that she had conceived. Moreover the number of courses furnished by the bridegroom would be against conception. It is popularly said that a young couple often undoes in the morning what it has done during the night.

73. Torrens (Notes, xxiv.) quotes "Fleisher" upon the word "Ghamghama" (*Diss. Crit. de Glossis Habichtionis*), which he compares with "Dumduma" and "Humbuma," determining them to be onomatopœics, "an incomplete and an obscure

murmur of a sentence as it were lingering between the teeth and lips and therefore difficult to be understood." Of this family is "Taghúm"; not used in modern days. In my *Pilgrimage* (i. 313) I have noticed another, "Khyas', Khyas'!" occurring in a Hizb al-Bahr (Spell of the Sea). Herklots gives a host of them; and their sole characteristics are harshness and strangeness of sound, uniting consonants which are not joined in Arabic. The old Egyptians and Chaldeans had many such words composed at will for theurgic operations.

74. This may mean either "it is of Mosul fashion" or, it is of muslin.

75. In those days the Arabs and the Portuguese recorded everything which struck them, as the Chinese and Japanese do in our times. And yet we complain of the amount of our modern writing!

76. This is mentioned because it is the act preliminary to naming the babe.

77. Arab. "Kahramánát" from Kahramán, an old Persian hero who conversed with the Simurgh-Griffon. Usually the word is applied to women-at-arms who defend the Harem, like the Urdu-begani of India, whose services were lately offered to England (1885), or the "Amazons" of Dahome.

78. He grew as fast in one day as other children in a month.

79. Arab. Al-Aríf; the tutor, the assistant-master.

80. Arab. "Ibn harám," a common term of abuse; and not a factual reflection on the parent. I have heard a mother apply the term to her own son.

81. Arab. "Khanjar" from the Persian, a syn. with the Arab. "Jambiyah." It is noticed in my *Pilgrimage,* iii., pp. 72, 75. To "silver the dagger," means to become a rich man. From "Khanjar," not from its fringed loop or strap, I derive our silly word "hanger." Dr. Steingass would connect it with Germ. Fänger, *e.g.,* Hirschfänger.

82. Again we have "Dastur" for "Izn."

83. Arab. "Iklím"; the seven climates of Ptolemy.

84. The "Plain of Pebbles" still so termed at Damascus; an open space west of the city.

85. Every Guide-book, even the Reverend Porter's *Murray,* gives a long account of this Christian Church 'verted to a Mosque.

86. Arab. "Nabút"; *Pilgrimage,* i. 336.
87. The Bres. Edit. says, "would have knocked him into Al-Yaman" (Southern Arabia), something like our slang phrase "into the middle of next week."
88. Arab. "Khádim": lit. a servant, politely applied (like Aghá=master) to a castrato. These gentry wax furious if baldly called "Tawáshi"=Eunuch. A mauvais plaisant in Egypt used to call me The Agha because a friend had placed his wife under my charge.
89. This sounds absurd enough in English, but Easterns always put themselves first for respect.
90. In Arabic the World is feminine.
91. Arab. "Sáhib"=lit. a companion; also a friend and especially applied to the Companions of Mohammed. Hence the Sunnis claim for them the honour of "friendship" with the Apostle; but the Shia'hs reply that the Arab says "Sahaba-hu'l-himár" (the Ass was his Sahib or companion). In the text it is a Wazirial title, in modern India it is=gentleman, *e.g.* "Sahib log" (the Sahib people) means their white conquerors, who, by the by, mostly mispronounce the word "Sáb."
92. Arab. "Suwán," prop. Syenite, from Syene (Al-Suwan) but applied to flint and any hard stone.
93. It was famous in the middle ages, and even now it is, perhaps, the most interesting to travellers after that "Sentina Gentium," the "Bhendi Bazar" of unromantic Bombay.
94. "The Gate of the Gardens," in the northern wall, a Roman archway of the usual solid construction shaming not only our modern shams, but our finest masonry.
95. Arab. "Al-Asr," which may mean either the hour or the prayer. It is also the moment at which the Guardian Angels relieve each other (Sale's *Koran,* chap. v.).
96. Arab. "Ya házá"=O this (one)! a somewhat slighting address equivalent to "Heus tu! O thou, whoever thou art." Another form is "Yá hú"=O he! Can this have originated Swift's "Yahoo"?
97. The Moslem does not use the European basin because water which has touched an impure skin becomes impure. Hence it is poured out from a ewer ("ibrík" Pers. Abríz) upon the hands and falls into a basin ("tisht") with an open-worked cover.
98. Arab. "Wahsh," a word of many meanings; nasty, insipid,

savage, etc. The offside of a horse is called Wahshi opposed to Insi, the near side. The Amir Taymur ("Lord Iron") whom Europeans unwittingly call after his Persian enemies' nickname, "Tamerlane," *i.e.* Taymur-i-lang, or limping Taymur, is still known as "Al-Wahsh" (the wild beast) at Damascus, where his Tartars used to bury men up to their necks and play at bowls with their heads for ninepins.

99. For "grandson" as being more affectionate. Easterns have not yet learned that clever Western saying:—The enemies of our enemies are our friends.

100. This was a simple bastinado on the back, not the more ceremonious affair of beating the feet-soles. But it is surprising what the Egyptians can bear; some of the rods used in the time of the Mameluke Beys are nearly as thick as a man's wrist.

101. The woman-like spite of the eunuch intended to hurt the grandmother's feelings.

102. The usual Cairene "chaff."

103. A necessary precaution against poison (*Pilgrimage,* i. 84, and iii. 43).

104. The Bresl. Edit. (ii. 108) describes the scene at greater length.

105. The Bul. Edit. gives by mistake of diacritical points, "Zabdaniyah": Raydaniyah is or rather was a camping ground to the north of Cairo.

106. Arab. "La'abat" = a plaything, a puppet, a lay figure. Lane (i. 326) conjectures that the cross is so called because it resembles a man with arms extended. But Moslems never heard of the fanciful ideas of mediæval Christian divines who saw the cross everywhere and in everything. The former hold that Pharaoh invented the painful and ignominious punishment. (*Koran,* chap. vii.)

107. Here good blood, driven to bay, speaks out boldly. But, as a rule, the humblest and mildest Eastern when in despair turns round upon his oppressors like a wild cat. Some of the criminals whom Fath Ali Shah of Persia put to death by chopping down the fork, beginning at the scrotum, abused his mother till the knife reached their vitals and they could no longer speak.

108. These repeated "laughs" prove the trouble of his spirit. Noble Arabs "show their back-teeth" so rarely that their

laughter is held worthy of being recorded by their biographers.

109. A popular phrase, derived from the Koranic "Truth is come, and falsehood is vanished: for falsehood is of short continuance" (chap. xvii.). It is an equivalent of our adaptation from 1 Esdras iv. 41, "Magna est veritas et prævalebit." But the great question still remains, What is Truth?

110. This is always mentioned: the nearer the seat the higher the honour.

111. Alluding to the phrase "Al-safar zafar" = voyaging is victory (*Pilgrimage* i., 127).

112. Arab. "Habb"; alluding to the black drop in the human heart which the Archangel Gabriel removed from Mohammed by opening his breast.

113. This phrase, I have said, often occurs: it alludes to the horripilation (Arab. Kush'arírah), horror or gooseflesh which, in Arab as in Hindu fables, is a symptom of great joy. So Boccaccio's "pelo arriciato" v., 8: Germ. Gänsehaut.

114. Arab. "Hasanta ya Hasan" = Bene detto, Benedetto! the usual word-play vulgarly called "pun": Hasan (not Hassan, as we *will* write it) meaning "beautiful."

115. Arab. "Loghah" also = a vocabulary, a dictionary; the Arabs had them by camel-loads.

116. The seventh of the sixteen "Bahr" (metres) in Arabic prosody; the easiest because allowing the most licence and, consequently, a favourite for didactic, homiletic and gnomic themes. It means literally "agitated" and was originally applied to the rude song of the Cameleer. De Sacy calls this doggrel "the poet's ass" (Torrens, Notes xxvi.). It was the only metre in which Mohammed the Apostle ever spoke: he was no poet (*Koran*, xxxvi., 69) but he occasionally recited a verse and recited it wrongly (*Dabistan*, iii., 212). In Persian prosody Rajaz is the seventh of nineteen and has six distinct varieties (pp. 79–81, *Gladwin's Dissertations on Rhetoric*, etc. Calcutta, 1801).

117. "Her stature tall—I hate a dumpy woman" (Don Juan).

118. A worthy who was Kazi of Kufah (Cufa) in the seventh century. Al-Najaf, generally entitled "Najaf al-Ashraf" (the Venerand) is the place where Ali, the son-in-law of Mohammed, lies or is supposed to lie buried, and has ever been a holy place to the Shi'ahs. I am not certain whether to trans-

late "Sa'a-lab" by fox or jackal; the Arabs make scant distinction between them. "Abu Hosayn" (Father of the Fortlet) is certainly the fox, and as certainly "Sha'arhar" is the jackal from the Pehlevi Shagál or Shaghál.

119. Usually by all manner of extortions and robbery, corruption and bribery, the ruler's motto being

Fiat *in*justitia ruat Cœlum.

There is no more honest man than the Turkish peasant or the private soldier; but the process of deterioration begins when he is made a corporal and culminates in the Pasha. Moreover official dishonesty is permitted by public opinion, because it belongs to the condition of society. A man buys a place (as in England two centuries ago) and retains it by presents to the heads of offices. Consequently he must recoup himself in some way, and he mostly does so by grinding the faces of the poor and by spoiling the widow and the orphan. The radical cure is high pay; but that phase of society refuses to afford it.

120. Arab. "Malik" (King) and "Malak" (angel) the words being written the same when lacking vowels and justifying the jingle.

121. Arab. "Hurr"; the Latin "ingenuus," lit. freeborn; metaph. noble as opp. to a slave who is not expected to do great or good deeds. In pop. use it corresponds, like "Fatá," with our "gentleman."

TALE OF GHANIM BIN AYYUB, THE DISTRAUGHT, THE THRALL O' LOVE

1. Our "Job." The English translators of the Bible, who borrowed Luther's system of transliteration (of A.D. 1522), transferred into English the German "j" which has the sound of "i" or "y"; intending us to pronounce Yacob (or Yakob), Yericho, Yimnites, Yob (or Hiob) and Yudah. Tyndall, who copied Luther (A.D. 1525–26), preserved the true sound by writing Iacob, Ben Iamin, and Iudas. But his successors unfortunately returned to the German; the initial "I" having from the thirteenth century been ornamentally lengthened and bent leftwards became a consonant; the

public adopted the vernacular sound of "j" (dg) and hence
our language and our literature are disgraced by such barbarisms as "Jehovah" and "Jesus"—Dgehovah and Dgeesus
for Yehovah and Yesus. Future generations of school-
teachers may remedy the evil; meanwhile we are doomed
for the rest of our days to hear

Gee-rusalem! Gee-rusalem! *etc.*

Nor is there one word to be said in favour of the corruption
except that, like the Protestant mispronunciation of Latin
and the Erasmian ill-articulation of Greek, it has become
"English," and has lent its little aid in dividing the Britons
from the rest of the civilized world.

2. The moon, I repeat, is masculine in the so-called "Semitic"
tongues.

3. *i.e.,* camel-loads, about 300 lbs.; and for long journeys 250 lbs.

4. Arab. "Janázah," so called only when carrying a corpse; else
Na'ash, Sarír, or Tábút: Irán being the large hearse on which
chiefs are borne. It is made of plank or stick-work; but there
are several varieties. (Lane, *M. E.,* chap. xxviii.)

5. It is meritorious to accompany the funeral cortège of a
Moslem even for a few paces.

6. Otherwise he could not have joined in the prayers.

7. Arab. "Halwá" made of sugar, cream, almonds, etc. That of
Maskat is famous throughout the East.

8. *i.e.,* "Camphor" to a negro as we say "Snowball," by the figure
antiphrase.

9. "Little Good Luck," a dim. form of "bakht" = luck, a Persian
word naturalized in Egypt.

10. There are, as I have shown, not a few cannibal tribes in Central Africa and these at times find their way into the slave
market.

11. *i.e.,* after we bar the door.

12. Arab. "Jáwísh" from Turk. Cháwúsh, Chiaoosh, a sergeant,
poursuivant, royal messenger. I would suggest that this is the
word "Shálish" or "Jálish" in Al-Siyuti's *History of the Caliphs*
(p. 501) translated by Carlyle "milites," by Schultens "Sagit-
tarius," and by Jarett "picked troops."

13. This familiarity with blackamoor slave-boys is common in
Egypt and often ends as in the story: Egyptian blood is suffi-

ciently mixed with negro to breed inclination for misce-
genation. But here the girl was wickedly neglected by her
mother at such an age as ten.

14. This ancient and venerable practice of inspecting the
marriage-sheet is still religiously preserved in most parts of
the East; and in old-fashioned Moslem families it is publicly
exposed in the Harem to prove that the "domestic calamity"
(the daughter) went to her husband a clean maid. Also the
general idea is that no blood will impose upon the experts,
or jury of matrons, except that of a pigeon-poult which exactly resembles hymeneal blood—when not subjected to the
microscope. This belief is universal in Southern Europe and
I have heard of it in England.

15. "Agha" Turk.=sir, gentleman, is, I have said, politely addressed to a eunuch.

16. As Bukhayt tell us, he lost only his testes, consequently his
erectio et distensio penis was as that of a boy before puberty and
it would last as long as his heart and circulation kept sound.
Hence the eunuch who preserves his penis is much prized in
the Zenanah where some women prefer him to the entire
man, on account of his long performance of the deed of
kind. Of this more in a future page.

17. It is or rather was the custom in Egypt and Syria to range
long rows of fine China bowls along the shelves running
round the rooms at the height of six or seven feet, and they
formed a magnificent cornice. I bought many of them at Damascus till the people, learning their value, asked prohibi-
tive prices.

18. The usual hysterical laughter of this nervous race.

19. Here the slave refuses to be set free and starve. For a master
so to do without ample reason is held disgraceful. I well remember the weeping and wailing throughout Sind when an
order from Sir Charles Napier set free the negroes whom
British philanthropy thus doomed to endure if not to die of
hunger.

20. Manumission, which is founded upon Roman law, is an extensive subject discussed in the Hidáyah and other canonical
works. The slave here lays down the law incorrectly, but his
claim shows his truly "nigger" impudence.

21. This is quite true to nature. The most remarkable thing in
the wild central African is his enormous development of

"destructiveness." At Zanzibar I never saw a slave break a glass or plate without a grin or a chuckle of satisfaction.

22. Arab. "Khassá-ni"; Khusyatáni (vulg.) being the testicles, also called "bayzatán" (the two eggs) a *double entendre* which has given rise to many tales. For instance in the witty Persian book *Dozd o Kazi* (The Thief and the Judge) a footpad strips the man of learning and offers to return his clothes if he can ask him a puzzle in law or religion. The Kazi (in folk-lore mostly a fool) fails, and his wife bids him ask the man to supper for a trial of wits on the same condition. She begins with compliments and ends by producing five eggs which she would have him distribute equally amongst the three; and, when he is perplexed, she gives one to each of the men taking three for herself. Whereupon the "Dozd" wends his way, having lost his booty as his extreme stupidity deserved. In the text the eunuch, Kafur, is made a "Sandali" or smooth-shaven, so that he was of no use to women.

23. Arab. "Khara," the lowest possible word: Yá Khara! is the commonest of insults, used also by modest women. I have heard one say it to her son.

24. Arab. "Kámah," a measure of length, a fathom, also called "Bá'a." Both are omitted in that sadly superficial book, Lane's *Modern Egyptians,* App. B.

25. Names of her slave-girls which mean (in order), Garden-bloom, Dawn (or Beautiful), Tree o' Pearl (p.n. of Saladin's wife), Light of (right) Direction, Star o' the Morn, Lewdness (=Shahwah, I suppose this is a chaff), Delight, Sweetmeat, and Miss Pretty.

26. This mode of disposing of a rival was very common in Harems. But it had its difficulties and on the whole the river was (and is) preferred.

27. An Eastern dislikes nothing more than drinking in a dim dingy place: the brightest lights seem to add to his "drinki-tite."

28. He did not sleep with her because he suspected some palace-mystery which suggested prudence; she also had her reasons.

29. This is called in Egypt "Aslah." (Lane *M. E.;* chap. i.)

30. It would be a broad ribbon-like band upon which the letters could be worked.

31. Arab. "Maragha" lit. rubbed his face on them like a fawning dog. Ghanim is another "softy" lover, a favourite character in Arab tales; and by way of contrast, the girl is masterful enough.

32. Because the Abbaside Caliphs descend from Al-Abbas, paternal uncle of Mohammed. The text more explicitly translated means, "O descendant of the Prophet's uncle!"

33. The most terrible part of a *belle passion* in the East is that the beloved will not allow her lover leave of absence for an hour.

34. Apparently the writer forgets that the Abbaside banners and dress were black, originally a badge of mourning for the Imám Ibrahim bin Mohammed put to death by the Ommiade Caliph Al-Marwan. The modern Egyptian mourning, like the old Persian, is indigo-blue of the darkest; but, as before noted, the custom is by no means universal.

35. *Koran,* chap. iv. In the East as elsewhere the Devil quotes Scripture.

36. A servant returning from a journey shows his master due honour by appearing before him in travelling suit and uncleaned.

37. The first name means "Rattan"; the second "Willow-wand," from the "Bán" or "Khiláf," the Egyptian willow (*Salix Ægyptiaca* Linn.) vulgarly called "Safsáf." Forskal holds the "Bán" to be a different variety.

38. Arab. "Ta'ám," which has many meanings: in mod. parlance it would signify millet, holcus-seed.

39. *i.e.,* "I well know how to deal with him."

40. The Pen (title of the Koranic chap. lxviii.) and the Preserved Tablet (before explained).

41. These plunderings were sanctioned by custom. But a few years ago, when the Turkish soldiers mutinied about arrears of pay (often delayed for years), the governing Pasha would set fire to the town and allow the men to loot what they pleased during a stated time. Rochet (*soi-disant* D'Héricourt) amusingly describes this manœuvre of the Turkish Governor of Al-Hodaydah in the last generation. (*Pilgrimage,* iii. 381.)

42. Another cenotaph whose use was to enable women to indulge in their pet pastime of weeping and wailing in company.

43. The lodging of pauper travellers, as the chapel in Iceland is of the wealthy. I have often taken benefit of the mosque, but as a rule it is unpleasant, the matting being not only torn but over-populous. Juvenal seems to allude to the Jewish Synagogue similarly used:—"in quâ te quæro proseuchâ"? (iii. 296) and in Acts iii. we find the lame, blind, and impotent in the Temple-porch.

44. This foul sort of vermin is supposed to be bred by perspiration. It is an epoch in the civilized traveller's life when he catches his first louse.

45. The Moslem peasant is a kind-hearted man and will make many sacrifices for a sick stranger even of another creed. It is a manner of "pundonor" with the village.

46. Such treatment of innocent women was only too common under the Caliphate and in contemporary Europe.

47. This may also be translated as, "And Heaven will reward thee"; but camel-men do not usually accept any drafts upon futurity.

48. He felt that he was being treated like a corpse.

49. This hatred of the Hospital extends throughout Southern Europe, even in places where it is not justified.

50. The importance of the pillow (wisádah or makhaddah) to the sick man is often recognized in The Nights. "He took to his pillow" is = took to his bed.

51. *i.e.*, in order that the reverend men, who do not render such suit and service gratis, might pray for him.

52. The reader will notice in The Nights the frequent mention of these physical prognostications, with which mesmerists are familiar.

53. The Pers. name of the planet Saturn in the Seventh Heaven. Arab. "Zuhal"; the Kiun or Chiun of Amos vi. 26.

54. *i.e.*, "Pardon me if I injured thee"—a popular mode of expression.

55. A "seduction," a charmer. The *double entendre* has before been noticed.

THE TALE OF THE BIRDS AND BEASTS AND THE CARPENTER

1. In beast stories generally when man appears he shows to disadvantage.

2. Shakespeare's "stone bow" not Lane's "cross-bow" (ii. 53).

3. The goad still used by the rascally Egyptian donkey-boy is a sharp nail at the end of a stick; and claims the special attention of societies for the protection of animals.

4. "The most ungrateful of all voices surely is the voice of asses" (*Koran*, xxxi. 18); and hence the "braying of hell" (*Koran*, lxvii. 7). The vulgar still believe that the donkey brays when seeing the Devil. "The last animal which entered the Ark with Noah was the Ass to whose tail Iblis was clinging. At the threshold the ass seemed troubled and could enter no further when Noah said to him:—'Fie upon thee! come in.' But as the ass was still troubled and did not advance Noah cried:—'Come in, though the Devil be with thee!' so the ass entered and with him Iblis. Thereupon Noah asked:—'O enemy of Allah who brought thee into the Ark?' and Iblis answered:—'Thou art the man, for thou saidest to the ass, come in though the Devil be with thee!' " (*Kitáb al-Unwán fi Makáid al-Niswán* quoted by Lane ii. 54).

5. Arab. "Rihl," a wooden saddle stuffed with straw and matting. In Europe the ass might complain that his latter end is the sausage. In England they say no man sees a dead donkey: I have seen dozens, one among them, unfortunately, my own.

6. The English reader will not forget Sterne's old mare. Even Al-Hariri, the prince of Arab rhetoricians, does not disdain to use "pepedit," the effect being put for the cause—terror. But Mr. Preston (p. 285) and polite men translate by "fled in haste" the Arabic "farted for fear."

7. This is one of the lucky signs and adds to the value of the beast. There are some fifty of these marks, some of them (like a spiral of hair in the breast which denotes that the rider is a cuckold) so ill-omened that the animal can be bought for almost nothing. Of course great attention is paid to colours, the best being the dark rich bay ("red" of Arabs) with black points, or the flea-bitten grey (termed Azrak=blue or Akhzar=green) which whitens with age. The worst are dun, cream coloured, piebald and black, which last are very rare. Yet according to the Mishkát al-Masábih (Lane 2, 54) Mohammed said, "The best horses are black (dark brown?) with white blazes (Arab. 'Ghurrah') and upper lips; next, black with blaze and three white legs (bad, because white hoofs are brittle): next, bay with white blaze

and white fore and hind legs." He also said, "Prosperity is with sorrel horses"; and praised a sorrel with white forehead and legs; but he dispraised the "Shikál," which has white stockings (Arab. "Muhajjil") on alternate hoofs (*e.g.* right hind and left fore). The curious reader will consult Lady Anne Blunt's *Bedouin Tribes of the Euphrates, with some Account of the Arabs and their Horses* (1879); but he must remember that it treats of the frontier tribes. The late Major Upton also left a book, *Gleanings from the Desert of Arabia* (1881); but it is a marvellous production deriving, *e.g.* Khayl (a horse generically) from Kohl or antimony (p. 275). What the Editor was dreaming of I cannot imagine. I have given some details concerning the Arab horse especially in Al-Yaman, among the Zú Mohammed, the Zú Husayn and the Banu Yam in *Pilgrimage,* iii. 270. As late as Marco Polo's day they supplied the Indian market *vîa* Aden; but the "Eye of Al-Yaman" has totally lost the habit of exporting horses.

8. The shovel-iron which is the only form of spur.

9. Used for the dromedary: the baggage-camel is haltered.

10. Arab. "Harwalah," the *pas gymnastique* affected when circumambulating the Ka'abah (*Pilgrimage,* iii. 208).

11. "This night" would be our "last night": the Arabs, I repeat, say "night and day," not "day and night."

12. The vulgar belief is that man's fate is written upon his skull, the sutures being the writing.

13. *Koran,* ii. 191.

14. Arab. "Tasbíh" = saying, "Subhán' Allah." It also means a rosary (Egypt. Sebhah for Subhah) a string of 99 beads divided by a longer item into sets of three and much fingered by the would-appear pious. The professional devotee carries a string of wooden balls the size of pigeons' eggs.

THE HERMITS

1. The pigeon is usually made to say, "Wahhidú Rabba-kumu 'llazi khalaka-kum, yaghfiru lakum zamba-kum" = "Unify (Assert the Unity of) your Lord who created you; so shall He forgive your sin!" As might be expected this "language" is differently interpreted. Pigeon-superstitions are found in all religions and I have noted (*Pilgrimage,* iii. 218) how the Hindu deity of Destruction-reproduction, the third Person of their

Triad, Shiva and his Spouse (or active Energy), are supposed to have dwelt at Meccah under the titles of Kapoteshwara (Pigeon-god) and Kapoteshí (Pigeon-goddess).

2. I have seen this absolute horror of women amongst the Monks of the Coptic Convents.

3. After the Day of Doom, when men's actions are registered, that of mutual retaliation will follow and all creatures (brutes included) will take vengeance on one another.

THE TALE OF KAMAR AL-ZAMAN

1. Lane is in error (vol. ii. 78) when he corrects this to "Sháh Zemán"; the name is fanciful and intended to be old Persian, on the "weight" of Kahramán. The Bul. Edit. has by misprint "Shahramán."

2. The "topothesia" is worthy of Shakespeare's day. "Khálidán" is evidently a corruption of "Khálidatáni" (for Khálidát), the Eternal, as Ibn Wardi calls the Fortunate Islands, or Canaries, which owe both their modern names to the classics of Europe. Their present history dates from A.D. 1385, unless we accept the Dieppe-Rouen legend of Labat which would place the discovery in A.D. 1326. I for one thoroughly believe in the priority, on the West African Coast, of the gallant descendants of the Northmen.

3. Four wives are allowed by Moslem law and for this reason. If you marry one wife she holds herself your equal, answers you and "gives herself airs"; two are always quarrelling and making a hell of the house; three are "no company" and two of them always combine against the nicest to make her hours bitter. Four *are* company; they can quarrel and "make it up" amongst themselves, and the husband enjoys comparative peace. But the Moslem is bound by his law to deal equally with the four; each must have her dresses, her establishment and her night, like her sister wives. The number is taken from the Jews (Arbah Turim Ev. Hazaer, i.) "the wise men have given good advice that a man should not marry more than four wives." Europeans, knowing that Moslem women are cloistered and appear veiled in public, begin with believing them to be mere articles of luxury; and only after long residence they find out that nowhere has the sex so much real liberty and power as in the Moslem East. They

can possess property and will it away without the husband's leave: they can absent themselves from the house for a month without his having a right to complain; and they assist in all his counsels for the best of reasons: a man can rely only on his wives and children, being surrounded by rivals who hope to rise by his ruin. As regards political matters the Circassian women of Constantinople really rule the Sultanate and there *soignez la femme!* is the first lesson of getting on in the official world.

4. This two-bow prayer is common on the bride-night; and at all times when issue is desired.

5. The older Camaralzaman = "Moon of the age." Kamar is the moon between her third and twenty-sixth day: Hilál during the rest of the month: Badr (plur. Budúr, whence the name of the Princess) is the full moon.

6. Showing how long ago forts were armed with metal plates which we have applied to warships only of late.

7. Two fallen angels who taught men the art of magic. They are mentioned in the Koran (chap. ii); and the commentators have extensively embroidered the simple text. Popularly they are supposed to be hanging by their feet in a well in the territory of Babel, hence the frequent allusions to "Babylonian sorcery" in Moslem writings; and those who would study the black art at headquarters are supposed to go there. They are counterparts of the Egyptian Jamnes and Mambres, the Jannes and Jambres of St. Paul (2 Tim. iii. 8).

8. An idol or idols of the Arabs (Allat and Ozza) before Mohammed (*Koran,* chap. ii. 256). Etymologically the word means "error" and the termination is rather Hebraic than Arabic.

9. Arab. "Khayt hamayán" (wandering threads of vanity), or Mukhát al-Shaytan (Satan's snivel), = our "gossamer" = God's summer (Mutter-Gottes-Sommer) or God's cymar (?).

10. A posture of peculiar submission; contrasting strongly with the attitude afterwards assumed by Prince Charming.

11. A mere term of vulgar abuse not reflecting on either parent: I have heard a mother call her own son, "Child of adultery."

12. Arab. "Ghazá," the Artemisia (Euphorbia?) before noticed. If the word be a misprint for Ghadá it means a kind of Euphorbia which, with the Arák (wild caper-tree) and the

Daum-palm (Crucifera thebiaca), is one of the three normal growths of the Arabian desert (*Pilgrimage,* iii. 22).

13. Lane (ii. 222) first read "Múroozee" and referred it to the Murúz tribe near Herat: he afterwards (iii. 748) corrected it to "Marwazee," of the fabric of Marw (Margiana), the place now famed for "Mervousness." As a man of Rayy (Rhages) becomes Rází (*e.g.* Ibn Fáris al-Rází), so a man of Marw is Marázi, not Murúzi nor Márwazi. The "Mikna' " was a veil forming a kind of "respirator," defending from flies by day and from mosquitos, dews and draughts by night. Easterns are too sensible to sleep with bodies kept warm by bedding, and heads bared to catch every blast. Our grandfathers and grandmothers did well to wear bonnets-de-nuit, however ridiculous they may have looked.

14. Iblis, meaning the Despairer, is called in the Koran (chap. xviii. 48) "One of the genii (Jinn) who departed from the command of his Lord." Mr. Rodwell (*in loco*) notes that the Satans and Jinn represent in the Koran (ii. 32, etc.) the evil-principle and finds an admixture of the Semitic Satans and demons with the "Genii from the Persian (Babylonian?) and Indian (Egyptian?) mythologies."

15. Of course she could not see his eyes when they were shut; nor is this mere Eastern inconsequence. The writer means, "had she seen them, they would have showed," etc.

16. To keep off the evil eye.

17. Like Dahnash this is a fanciful p. n., fit only for a Jinni. As a rule the appellatives of Moslem "genii" end in-ús (oos), as Tarnús, Húliyánus; the Jewish in-nas, as Jattunas; those of the Tarsá (the "funkers" *i.e.* Christians) in-dús, as Sidús; and the Hindus in-tús, as Naktús (who entered the service of the Prophet Shays, or Seth, and was converted to the Faith). The King of the Genii is Malik Katshán who inhabits Mount Kaf; and to the west of him lives his son-in-law, Abd al-Rahman with 33,000 domestics: these names were given by the Apostle Mohammed. "Baktanús" is lord of three Moslem troops of the wandering Jinn, which number a total of twelve bands and extend from Sind to Europe. The Jinn, Divs, Peris ("fairies") and other pre-Adamitic creatures were governed by seventy-two Sultans all known as Sulayman, and the last, I have said, was Ján bin Ján. The angel Háris was sent from

Heaven to chastise him, but in the pride of victory he also revolted with his followers the Jinn whilst the Peris held aloof. When he refused to bow down before Adam he and his chiefs were eternally imprisoned but the other Jinn are allowed to range over earth as a security for man's obedience. The text gives the three orders, flyers, walkers and divers.

18. *i.e.* distracted (with love); the Lakab, or poetical name, of apparently a Spanish poet.

19. Nothing is more "anti-pathetic" to Easterns than lean hips and flat hinder-cheeks in women and they are right in insisting upon the characteristic difference of the male and female figure. Our modern sculptors and painters, whose study of the nude is usually most perfunctory, have often scandalized me by the lank and greyhound-like fining off of the frame, which thus becomes rather simian than human.

20. The small fine foot is a favourite with Easterns as well as Westerns. Ovid (A.A.) is not ashamed "ad teneros Oscula (not basia or suavia) ferre pedes." Ariosto ends the august person in

Il breve, asciutto, e ritondetto piede,
(The short-sized, clean-cut, roundly-moulded foot).

And all the world over it is a sign of "blood," *i.e.* the fine nervous temperament.

21. *i.e.* "full moons": the French have corrupted it to "Badoure"; we to "Badoura," which is worse.

22. As has been said, a single drop of urine renders the clothes ceremonially impure, hence a stone or a handful of earth must be used after the manner of the torche-cul. Scrupulous Moslems, when squatting to make water, will prod the ground before them with the point of stick or umbrella, so as to loosen it and prevent the spraying of the urine.

23. It is not generally known to Christians that Satan has a wife called Awwá ("Hawwá" being the Moslem Eve) and, as Adam had three sons, the Tempter has nine, viz., Zu 'l-baysun who rules in bazars; Wassin who prevails in times of trouble; Awan who counsels kings; Haffan patron of wine-bibbers; Marrah of musicians and dancers; Masbut of news-spreaders

(and newspapers?); Dulhán who frequents places of worship and interferes with devotion; Dasim, lord of mansions and dinner tables, who prevents the Faithful saying "Bismillah" and "Inshallah," as commanded in the Koran (xviii. 23), and Lakís, lord of Fire-worshippers (Herklots, chap. xxix. sect. 4).

24. Strong perfumes, such as musk (which we Europeans dislike and suspect), are always insisted upon in Eastern poetry; and Mohammed's predilection for them is well known. Moreover the young and the beautiful are held (justly enough) to exhale a natural fragrance which is compared with that of the blessed in Paradise. Hence in the Mu'allakah of Imr al-Kays:—

> Breathes the scent of musk when they rise to rove,
> As the Zephyr's breath with the flavour o' clove.

It is made evident by dogs and other fine-nosed animals that every human being has his, or her, peculiar scent which varies according to age and health. Hence animals often detect the approach of death.

25. Arab. "Kahlá." This has been explained. Mohammed is said to have been born with "Kohl'd eyes."

26. [Burton's note for this word appears in full for a tale not included in this edition. It reads:]
Mr. Payne (ii. 227) translates "Hawá al-'Uzrí" by "the love of the Beni Udhra, an Arabian tribe famous for the passion and devotion with which love was practised among them." I understand it as "excusable love" which, for want of a better term, is here translated "platonic." It is, however, more like the old "bundling" of Wales and Northern England; and allows all the pleasures but one, the toyings which the French call *les plaisirs de la petite oie;* a term my dear old friend Fred. Hankey derived from *la petite voie.* The Afghans know it as "Námzad-bází" or betrothed-play (*Pilgrimage,* ii. 56); the Abyssinians as eye-love; and the Kafirs as Slambuka a Shlabonka, for which see the traveller Delegorgue.

27. These lines, with the Názir (eye or steward), the Hájib (Groom of the Chambers or Chamberlain) and Joseph, are also repeated from the 114th night. [Notes from the 114th

night read:] Arab. "Názir," a steward or an eye (a "looker"). The idea is borrowed from Al-Hariri (*Assemblies,* xiii.), and,—Arab. "Hájib," a groom of the chambers, a chamberlain; also an eyebrow. See Al-Hariri, *ibid.* xiii. and xxii. For the Nazir see Al-Hariri (Nos. xiii. and xxii.).

28. The usual allusion to the Húr (Houris) from "Hawar," the white and black of the eye shining in contrast. The Persian Magi also placed in their Heaven (Bihisht or Minu) "Huran," or black-eyed nymphs, under the charge of the angel Zamiyád.

29. This is a peculiarity of the Jinn tribe when wearing hideous forms. It is also found in the Hindu Rakshasa.

30. Which, by the by, are small and beautifully shaped. The animal is very handy with them, as I learnt by experience when trying to "Rareyfy" one at Bayrut.

31. She being daughter of Al-Dimiryát, King of the Jinn. Mr. W. F. Kirby has made him the subject of a pretty poem.

32. The young man must have been a demon of chastity.

33. Arab. "Kirát" from χεράτιον, *i.e.,* bean, the seed of the Abrus precatorius, in weight = two to three (English) grains; and in length = one finger-breadth here; 24 being the total. The Moslem system is evidently borrowed from the Roman "as" and "uncia."

34. Lit. "my liver"; which viscus, and not the heart, is held the seat of passion; a fancy dating from the oldest days. Theocritus says of Hercules, "In his liver Love had fixed a wound" (*Idyl.* xiii.). In the *Anthologia,* "Cease, Love, to wound my liver and my heart" (lib. vii.). So Horace (*Odes,* i. 2); his Latin Jecur and the Persian "Jigar" being evident congeners. The idea was long prevalent and we find in Shakespeare:—

> Alas, then Love may be called appetite,
> No motion of the liver but the palate.

35. A marvellous touch of nature, love ousting affection; the same trait will appear in the lover and both illustrate the deep Italian saying, "Amor discende, non ascende." The further it goes down the stronger it becomes, as of grandparent for grandchild and *vice versa.*

36. This tenet of the universal East is at once fact and unfact. As a generalism asserting that women's passion is ten times

greater than man's (*Pilgrimage,* ii. 282), it is unfact. The world shows that while women have more philoprogenitiveness, men have more amativeness; otherwise the latter would not propose and would nurse the doll and baby. Fact, however, in low-lying lands, like Persian Mazanderan versus the Plateau; Indian Malabar compared with Marátha-land; California as opposed to Utah and especially Egypt contrasted with Arabia. In these hot-damp climates the venereal requirements and reproductive powers of the female greatly exceed those of the male; and hence the dissoluteness of morals would be phenomenal, were it not obviated by seclusion, the sabre and the revolver. In cold-dry or hot-dry mountainous lands the reverse is the case; hence polygamy there prevails whilst the low countries require polyandry in either form, legal or illegal (*i.e.,* prostitution). I have discussed this curious point of "geographical morality" (for all morality is, like conscience, both geographical and chronological), a subject so interesting to the lawgiver, the student of ethics and the anthropologist, in *The City of the Saints.* But strange and unpleasant truths progress slowly, especially in England.

37. This morning evacuation is considered, in the East, a *sine quâ non* of health; and old Anglo-Indians are unanimous in their opinion of the "bari fajar" (as they mispronounce the dawn-clearance). The natives of India, Hindús (pagans) and Hindís (Moslems), unlike Europeans, accustom themselves to evacuate twice a day, evening as well as morning. This may, perhaps, partly account for their mildness and effeminacy; for:—

C'est la constipation qui rend l'homme rigoureux.

The English, since the first invasion of cholera, in October, 1831, are a different race from their costive grandparents who could not dine without a "dinner-pill." Curious to say the clyster is almost unknown to the people of Hindostan although the barbarous West Africans use it daily to "wash 'um belly," as the Bonney-men say. And, as Sonnini notes, to propose the process in Egypt under the Beys might have cost a Frankish medico his life.

38. The Egyptian author cannot refrain from this characteristic

polissonnerie; and reading it out is always followed by a roar of laughter. Even serious writers like Al-Hariri do not, as I have noted, despise the indecency.

39. "Long beard and little wits," is a saying throughout the East where the Kausaj (=man with thin, short beard) is looked upon as cunning and tricksy. There is a venerable Joe Miller about a schoolmaster who, wishing to singe his long beard short, burnt it off and his face to boot:—which reminded him of the saying. A thick beard is defined as one which wholly conceals the skin; and in ceremonial ablution it must be combed out with the fingers till the water reach the roots. The Sunnat, or practice of the Prophet, was to wear the beard not longer than one hand and two fingers' breadth. In Persian "Kúseh" (thin-beard) is an insulting term opposed to "Khush-rísh," a well-bearded man. The Iranian growth is perhaps the finest in the world, often extending to the waist; but it gives infinite trouble, requiring, for instance, a bag when travelling. The Arab beard is often composed of two tufts on the chin-sides and straggling hairs upon the cheeks; and this is a severe mortification, especially to Shaykhs and elders, who not only look upon the beard as one of man's characteristics, but attach a religious importance to the appendage. Hence the enormity of Kamar al-Zaman's behaviour. The Persian festival of the vernal equinox was called Kusehnishín (Thin-beard sitting). An old man with one eye paraded the streets on an ass with a crow in one hand and a scourge and fan in the other, cooling himself, flogging the bystanders and crying heat! heat! (garmá! garmá!). For other particulars see Richardson (*Dissertation,* p. lii.). This is the Italian Giorno delle Vecchie, Thursday in Mid-Lent, March 12 (1885), celebrating the death of Winter and the birth of Spring.

40. I quote Torrens (p. 400).

41. Moslems have only two names for week days, Friday, Al-Jum'ah or meeting-day, and Al-Sabt, Sabbath-day, that is Saturday. The others are known by numbers after Quaker fashion with us, the usage of Portugal and Scandinavia.

42. Our last night.

43. Arab. "Tayf" = phantom, the nearest approach to our "ghost," that queer remnant of Fetishism imbedded in Christianity;

the phantasma, the shade (not the soul) of the dead. Hence the accurate Niebuhr declares, "apparitions (*i.e.,* of the departed) are unknown in Arabia." Haunted houses are there tenanted by Ghuls, Jinn and a host of supernatural creatures; but not by ghosts proper; and a man may live years in Arabia before he ever hears of the "Tayf." With the Hindus it is otherwise (*Pilgrimage,* iii. 144). Yet the ghost, the embodied fear of the dead and of death is common, in a greater or lesser degree, to all peoples; and, as modern Spiritualism proves, that ghost is not yet laid.

44. Mr. Payne (iii. 133) omits the lines which are *à propos de rien* and read much like "nonsense verses." I retain them simply because they are in the text.

45. Arab. "Ar'ar," the Heb. "Aroer," which Luther and the A. V. translate "heath." The modern Aramaic name is "Lizzáb" (*Unexplored Syria,* i. 68).

46. In the old version and the Bresl. Edit. (iii. 220) the Princess beats the "Kahramánah," but does not kill her.

47. This is still the popular Eastern treatment of the insane.

48. Pers. "Marz-bán" = Warden of the Marches, Margrave. The foster-brother in the East is held dear as, and often dearer than, kith and kin.

49.   The moderns believe most in the dawn-dream.

                        —QUIRINUS

    Post mediam noctem visus, quum somnia vera.
                (*Horace,* Sat. i. 10, 33.)

50. The Bresl. Edit. (iii. 223) and Galland have "Torf": Lane (ii. 115) "El-Tarf."

51. Arab. "Maghzal"; a more favourite comparison is with a toothpick. Both are used by Nizami and Al-Hariri, the most "elegant" of Arab writers.

52. This symbolic action is repeatedly mentioned in The Nights.

53. Arab. "Shakhs"=a person, primarily a dark spot. So "Sawád"= blackness, in Al-Hariri means a group of people who darken the ground by their shade.

54. The first bath after sickness, I have said, is called "Ghusl al-Sihhah"—the Washing of Health.

55. The words "malady" and "disease" are mostly avoided during these dialogues as ill-omened words which may bring on a relapse.

56. Solomon's carpet of green silk which carried him and all his host through the air is a Talmudic legend generally accepted in Al-Islam though not countenanced by the Koran, chap. xxvii. When the "gnat's wing" is mentioned, the reference is to Nimrod who, for boasting that he was lord of all, was tortured during four hundred years by a gnat sent by Allah up his ear or nostril.

57. The absolute want of morality and filial affection in the chaste young man is supposed to be caused by the violence of his passion, and he would be pardoned because he "loved much."

58. I have noticed the geomantic process in my *History of Sindh* (chap. vii.). It is called "Zarb al-Raml" (strike the sand, the French say "frapper le sable") because the rudest form is to make on the ground dots at haphazard, usually in four lines one above the other: these are counted and, if even-numbered, two are taken (**); if odd one (*); and thus the four lines will form a scheme say

This is repeated three times, producing the same number of figures; and then the combination is sought in an explanatory table or, if the practitioner be expert, he pronounces off-hand. The Nights speak of a "Takht Raml" or a board, like a schoolboy's slate, upon which the dots are inked instead of points in sand. The moderns use a "Kura'h," or oblong die, upon whose sides the dots, odd and even, are marked; and these dice are hand-thrown to form the figure. By way of complication Geomancy is mixed up with astrology and then it becomes a most complicated kind of ariolation and an endless study. Napoleon's Book of Fate, a chap-book which appeared some years ago, was Geomancy in its simplest and most ignorant shape. For the rude African form see my Mission to Dahome, i. 332; and for that of Darfour, pp. 360–69 of Shaykh Mohammed's Voyage before quoted.

59. Translators understand this of writing marriage contracts; I take it in a more general sense.

60. These lines are repeated from the 75th night: with Mr. Payne's permission I give his rendering (iii. 153) by way of variety.

61. The comparison is characteristically Arab.

62. Not her "face": the head, and especially the back of the head, must always be kept covered, even before the father.

63. The "Mehari," of which the Algerine-French speak, are the dromedaries bred by the Mahrah tribe of Al-Yaman, the descendants of Mahrat ibn Haydán. They are covered by small wild camels (?) called Al-Húsh, found between Oman and Al-Shihr: others explain the word to mean "stallions of the Jinn," and term those savage and supernatural animals, "Najáib al-Mahriyah"—nobles of the Mahrah.

64. Arab. "Khaznah" = a thousand purses; now about £5000. It denotes a large sum of money, like the "Badrah," a purse containing 10,000 dirhams of silver (Al-Hariri), or 80,000 (Burckhardt, *Prov.* 380); whereas the "Nisáb" is a moderate sum of money, gen. 20 gold dinars = 200 silver dirhams.

65. As The Nights show, Arabs admire slender forms; but the hips and hinder cheeks must be highly developed and the stomach fleshy rather than lean. The reasons are obvious. The Persians who exaggerate everything say *e.g.* (Husayn Váiz in the Anvár-i-Suhayli):—

> How paint her hips and waist? Who saw
> A mountain (Koh) dangling to a straw (káh)?

In Antar his beloved Abla is a tamarisk (*T. Orientalis*). Others compare with the palm tree (Solomon), the Cypress (Persian, esp. Hafiz and Firdausi) and the Arák or wild Capparis (Arab.).

66. Ubi aves ibi angeli. All African travellers know that a few birds flying about the bush, and a few palm trees waving in the wind, denote the neighbourhood of a village or a camp (where angels are scarce). The reason is not any friendship for man but because food, animal and vegetable, is more plentiful. Hence Albatrosses, Mother Carey's (Mater Cara, the Virgin) chickens, and Cape pigeons follow ships.

67. Moslem port towns usually have (or had) only two gates. Such was the case with Bayrut, Tyre, Sidon and a host of others; the faubourg-growth of modern days has made these obsolete. The portals much resemble the entrances of old Norman castles—Arques for instance. (*Pilgrimage*, i. 185.)

68. Arab. "Lisám"; before explained.

69. *i.e.*, Life of Souls (persons, etc.).

70. Showing that there had been no consummation of the marriage which would have demanded "Ghusl," or total ablution, at home or in the Hammam.

71. The "situation" is admirable, solution appearing so difficult and catastrophe imminent.

72. This quatrain occurs in the 9th night: I have borrowed from Torrens (p. 79) by way of variety.

73. The belief that young pigeon's blood resembles the virginal discharge is universal; but the blood most resembling man's is that of the pig which in other points is so very human. In our day Arabs and Hindus rarely submit to inspection the nuptial sheet as practised by the Israelites and Persians. The bride takes to bed a white kerchief with which she staunches the blood and next morning the stains are displayed in the Harim. In Darfour this is done by the bridegroom. "Prima Venus debet esse cruenta," say the Easterns with much truth, and they have no faith in our complaisant creed which allows the hymen-membrane to disappear by any but one accident.

74. Not meaning the two central divisions commanded by the King and his Wazir.

75. Arab. "Rasy"=praising in a funeral sermon.

76. An allusion to a custom of the pagan Arabs in the days of ignorant Heathenism. The blood or brain, soul or personality of the murdered man formed a bird called Sady or Hámah (not the Humá or Humái, usually translated "phœnix") which sprang from the head, where four of the five senses have their seat, and haunted his tomb, crying continually, "Uskúni!"=Give me drink (of the slayer's blood)! and which disappeared only when the vendetta was accomplished. Mohammed forbade the belief. Amongst the Southern Slavs the cuckoo is supposed to be the sister of a murdered man ever calling for vengeance.

77. To obtain a blessing and show how he valued it.

78. Well-known tribes of proto-historic Arabs who flourished before the time of Abraham: see *Koran* (chap. xxvi. *et passim*). They will be repeatedly mentioned in The Nights and notes.

79. Arab. "Amtár"; plur. of "Matr," a large vessel of leather or wood for water, etc.

80. Arab. "Asáfírí," so called because they attract sparrows (asáfír), a bird very fond of the ripe oily fruit. In the Romance of "Antar" Asáfír camels are beasts that fly like birds in fleetness. The reader must not confound the olives of the text with the hard unripe berries ("little plums pickled in stale") which appear at English tables; nor wonder that bread and olives are the beef-steak and potatoes of many Mediterranean peoples. It is an excellent diet, the highly oleaginous fruit supplying the necessary carbon.

81. Arab. "Tamar al-Hindi"=the "Indian-date," whence our word "Tamarind." A sherbet of the pods, being slightly laxative, is much drunk during the great heats; and the dried fruit, made into small round cakes, is sold in the bazars. The traveller is advised not to sleep under the tamarind's shade, which is infamous for causing ague and fever. In Sind I derided the "native nonsense," passed the night under an "Indian date-tree" and awoke with a fine specimen of ague which lasted me a week.

82. Moslems are not agreed upon the length of the Day of Doom when all created things, marshalled by the angels, await final judgment; the different periods named are 40 years, 70, 300 and 50,000. Yet the trial itself will last no longer than while one may milk an ewe, or than "the space between two milkings of a she-camel." This is bringing down Heaven to Earth with a witness; but, after all, the Heaven of all faiths, including "Spiritualism," the latest development, is only an earth more or less glorified even as the Deity is humanity more or less perfected.

83. Arab. "Al-Kamaráni," lit. "the two moons." Arab rhetoric prefers it to "Shamsáni," or "two suns," because lighter (akhaff) to pronounce. So, albeit Omar was less worthy than Abu-Bakr, the two are called "Al-Omaráni," in vulgar parlance, Omarayn.

84. Alluding to the angels who appeared to the Sodomites in the shape of beautiful youths (*Koran*, xi.).

85. *Koran,* xxxiii. 38.
86. A prolepsis of Tommy Moore:—

> Your mother says, my little Venus,
> There's something not quite right between us,
>   And you're in fault as much as I,
> Now, on my soul, my little Venus,
> I swear 'twould not be right between us,
>   To let your mother tell a lie.

But the Arab is more moral than Mr. Little, as he proposes to repent.
87. This is a mere phrase for our "dying of laughter": the queen *was* on her back. And as Easterns sit on carpets, their falling back is very different from the same movement off a chair.
88. The Lady Budur shows her noble blood by not objecting to her friend becoming her Zarrat (sister-wife). This word is popularly derived from "Zarar" = injury; and is vulgarly pronounced in Egypt "Durrah" sounding like Durrah = a parrot (see Burckhardt's mistake in *Prov.* 314). The native proverb says, "Ayshat al-durrah murrah," the sister-wife hath a bitter life. We have no English equivalent; so I translate indifferently co-wife, co-consort, sister-wife or sister in wedlock.

HATIM OF THE TRIBE OF TAYY

1. A noble tribe of Badawin that migrated from Al-Yaman and settled in Al-Najd. Their Chief, who died a few years before Mohammed's birth, was Al-Hatim (the "black crow"), a model of Arab manliness and munificence; and although born in the Ignorance he will enter Heaven with the Moslems. Hatim was buried on the hill called Owárid: I have already noted this favourite practice of the wilder Arabs and the affecting idea that the Dead may still look upon his kith and kin. There is not an Arab book nor, indeed, a book upon Arabia which does not contain the name of Hatim: he is mentioned as unpleasantly often as Aristides.
2. Lord of "Cattle-feet," this King's name is unknown; but the Kámús mentions two Kings called Zu 'l Kalá'a, the

Greater and the Less. Lane's Shaykh (ii. 333) opined that the man who demanded Hatim's hospitality was one Abu 'l-Khaybari.

3. The camel's throat, I repeat, is not cut as in the case of other animals, the muscles being too strong: it is slaughtered by the "nahr," *i.e.*, thrusting a knife into the hollow at the commissure of the chest. (*Pilgrimage*, iii. 303.)

4. Adi became a Moslem and was one of the companions of the Prophet.

THE TALE OF MA'AN SON OF ZAIDAH AND THE BADAWI

1. Arab. "Shakhs" before noticed.

2. Arab. "Kussá'á" = the curling cucumber: the vegetable is of the cheapest and the poorer classes eat it as "kitchen" with bread.

3. Arab. "Haram-hu," a *double entendre*. Here the Badawi means his Harim, the inviolate part of the house; but afterwards he makes it mean the presence of His Honour.

THE CITY OF MANY-COLUMNED IRAM AND ABDULLAH SON OF ABI KILABAH

1. The Bresl. Edit. (vii. 171–174) entitles this tale, "Story of Shaddád bin Ad and the City of Iram the Columned"; but it relates chiefly to the building by the King of the First Adites who, being promised a future Paradise by Prophet Húd, impiously said that he would lay out one in this world. It also quotes Ka'ab al-Ahbár as an authority for declaring that the tale is in the "Pentateuch of Moses." Iram was in al-Yaman near Adan (our Aden), a square of ten parasangs (or leagues each = 18,000 feet) every way; the walls were of red (baked) brick 500 cubits high and 20 broad, with four gates of corresponding grandeur. It contained 300,000 Kasr (palaces) each with a thousand pillars of gold-bound jasper, etc. (whence its title). The whole was finished in five hundred years; and, when Shaddad prepared to enter it, the "Cry of Wrath" from the Angel of Death slew him and all his many. It is mentioned in the Koran (chap. lxxxix. 6–7) as

"Irem adorned with lofty buildings (or pillars)." But Ibn Khaldun declares that commentators have embroidered the passage; Iram being the name of a powerful clan of the ancient Adites and "imád" being a tent-pole: hence "Iram with the numerous tents or tent-poles." Al-Bayzawi tells the story of Abdullah ibn Kilabah (D'Herbelot's Colabah). At Aden I met an Arab who had seen the mysterious city on the borders of Al-Ahkáf, the waste of deep sands, west of Hadramaut; and probably he had, the mirage or sun-reek taking its place. Compare with this tale "The City of Brass."

2. The Biblical "Sheba," named from the great-grandson of Joctan, whence the Queen (Bilkis) visited Solomon. It was destroyed by the Flood of Márib.

3. The full title of the Holy City is "Madinat al-Nabi" = the City of the Prophet; of old, Yasrib (Yathrib) the Iatrippa of the Greeks (*Pilgrimage*, ii. 119). The reader will remember that there are two "Yasribs": that of lesser note being near Hujr in the Yamámah-province.

4. "Ka'ab of the Scribes," a well-known traditionist and religious poet who died (A.H. 32) in the Caliphate of Osman. He was a Jew who islamized; hence his name (Ahbár, plur. of Hibr, a Jewish scribe, doctor of science, etc., Jarrett's El-Siyuti, p. 123). He must not be confounded with another Ka'ab al-Ahbár the Poet of the (first) Cloak-poem or "Burdah," a noble Arab who was a distant cousin of Mohammed, and whose tomb at Hums (Emesa) is a place of pious visitation. According to the best authorities (no Christian being allowed to see them), the cloak traditionally given to the bard by Mohammed is still preserved together with the Khirkah or Sanjak Sherif ("Holy Coat" or Banner, the national oriflamme) at Stambul in the Upper Serraglio. (*Pilgrimage*, i. 213.) Many authors repeat this story of Mu'awiyah, the Caliph, and Ka'ab of the Burdah, but it is an evident anachronism, the poet having been dead nine years before the ruler's accession (A.H. 41).

5. *Koran*, lxxxix. 6–7.

6. In the text, Arabic "Kahramán," from the Persian, braves, heroes.

7. The Deity in the East is as whimsical a despot as any of his "shadows" or "vice-regents." According to the text Shaddád is killed for mere jealousy—a base passion utterly un-

worthy of a godhead; but one to which Allah was greatly addicted.

8. Some traditionist; but whether Sha'abi, Shi'abi or Shu'abi we cannot decide.

9. The Hazarmaveth of Genesis (x. 26) in South Eastern Arabia. Its people are the Adramitæ (mod. Hazrami) of Ptolemy who places in their land the Aribæ Emporium, as Pliny does his Massola. They border upon the Homeritæ or men of Himyar, often mentioned in The Nights. Hazramaut is still practically unknown to us, despite the excursions of many travellers; and the hard nature of the people, the Swiss of Arabia, offers peculiar obstacles to exploration.

10. *i.e.,* the prophet Hud generally identified (?) with Heber. He was commissioned (*Koran,* chap. vii.) to preach Al-Islam to his tribe the Adites who worshipped four goddesses, Sákiyah (the rain-giver), Rázikah (food-giver), Háfizah (the saviouress) and Sálimah (who healed sickness). As has been seen, he failed, so it was useless to send him.

THE SWEEP AND THE NOBLE LADY

1. I have described this scene, the wretch clinging to the curtain and sighing and crying as if his heart would break (*Pilgrimage,* iii. 216 and 220). The same is done at the place Al-Multazam, "the attached to" (*ibid.* 156) and various spots called Al-Mustajáb, "where prayer is granted" (*ibid.* 162). At Jerusalem the "Wailing place of the Jews" shows queer scenes; the worshippers embrace the wall with a peculiar wriggle, crying out in Hebrew, "O build Thy House, soon, without delay," etc.

2. *i.e.,* the wife. The scene in the text was common at Cairo twenty years ago; and no one complained of the stick. See *Pilgrimage,* i. 120.

3. Arab. "Udum, Udum" (plur. of Idám) = "relish," olives, cheese, pickled cucumbers, etc.

ALI THE PERSIAN

1. This "Cry of Haro" often occurs throughout The Nights. In real life it is sure to collect a crowd, especially if an Infidel (non-Moslem) be its cause.

2. In the East a cunning fellow always makes himself the claimant or complainant.

3. On the Euphrates some 40 miles west of Baghdad. The word is written "Anbár" and pronounced "Ambár" as is usual with the "n" before "b"; the case of the Greek double Gamma.

4. Syene on the Nile.

5. The tale is in the richest Rabelaisian humour; and the requisitions of the "Saj'a" (rhymed prose) in places explain the grotesque combinations. It is difficult to divine why Lane omits it: probably he held a hearty laugh not respectable.

THE MAN WHO STOLE THE DISH OF GOLD WHEREIN THE DOG ATE

1. In all hot-damp countries it is necessary to clothe dogs, morning and evening especially: otherwise they soon die of rheumatism and loin disease.

2. The Moslems borrowed the horrible idea of a "jealous God" from their kinsmen, the Jews. Every race creates its own Deity after the fashion of itself: Jehovah is distinctly a Hebrew; the Christian Theos is originally a Judæo-Greek and Allah a half-Badawi Arab. In this tale Allah, despotic and unjust, brings a generous and noble-minded man to beggary, simply because he fed his dogs off gold plate. Wisdom and morality have their infancy and youth: the great value of such tales as these is to show and enable us to measure man's development.

3. In Trébutien (Lane, ii. 501) the merchant says to ex-Dives, "Thou art wrong in charging Destiny with injustice. If thou art ignorant of the cause of thy ruin I will acquaint thee with it. Thou feddest the dogs in dishes of gold and leftest the poor to die of hunger." A superstition, but intelligible.

THE RUINED MAN WHO BECAME RICH AGAIN THROUGH A DREAM

1. The tale is told by Al-Isháki in the reign of Al-Maamun.

2. The speaker in dreams is the Heb. "Waggid," which the learned and angry Graetz (Geschichte, etc. vol. ix.) absurdly translates "Traum-souffleur."

THE EBONY HORSE

1. This tale (one of those translated by Galland) is best and fullest in the Bresl. Edit. iii. 329.

2. Europe has degraded this autumnal festival, the Sun-fête Mihrgán (which balanced the vernal Nau-roz) into Michaelmas and its goose-massacre. It was so called because it began on the 16th of Mihr, the seventh month; and lasted six days, with feasts, festivities and great rejoicings in honour of the Sun, who now begins his southing-course.

3. "Hindí" is an Indian Moslem as opposed to "Hindú," a pagan, or Gentoo.

4. The orig. Persian word is "Sháh-púr" = King's son: the Greeks (who had no *sh*) preferred Σαδώρ; the Romans turned it into Sapor and the Arabs (who lack the *p*) into Sábúr. See p. x. *Hamzæ ispahanensis Annalium Libri x.:* Gottwaldt, Lipsiæ, 1848.

5. The magic horse may have originated with the Hindu tale of a wooden Garuda (the bird of Vishnu) built by a youth as a vehicle. It came with the "Moors" to Spain and appears in "Le Cheval de Fust," a French poem of the 13th Cent. Thence it passed over to England as shown by Chaucer's "Half-told tale of Cambuscan (Janghíz Khan?) bold," as

> The wondrous steed of brass
> On which the Tartar King did ride.

And Leland (*Itinerary*) derives "Rutlandshire" from "a man named Rutter who rode round it on a wooden horse constructed by art magic." Lane (ii. 548) quotes the parallel story of Cleomades and Claremond which Mr. Keightley, *Tales and Popular Fictions,* chap. ii, dates from our thirteenth century. See vol. i., p. 181.

6. All Moslems, except those of the Máliki school, hold that the maker of an image representing anything of life will be commanded on the Judgment Day to animate it, and failing will be duly sent to the Fire. This severity arose apparently from the necessity of putting down idol-worship and, perhaps, for the same reason the Greek Church admits pictures but not statues. Of course the command has been honoured

with extensive breaching: for instance, all the Sultans of Stambul have had their portraits drawn and painted.

7. This description of ugly old age is written with true Arab *verve*.

8. "Badinján": Hind. Bengan: Pers. Bádingán or Badilján; the Mala insana (*Solanum pomiferum* or *S. Melongena*) of the Romans, well known in Southern Europe. It is of two kinds, the red (*Solanum lycopersicum*) and the black (*S. Melongena*). The Spaniards know it as "berengeria" and when Sancho Panza (Part ii. chap. 2) says, "The Moors are fond of egg-plants," he means more than appears. It is held to be exceedingly heating and thereby to breed melancholia and madness; hence one says to a man showing eccentricity, "Thou hast been eating brinjalls."

9. Again to be understood *Hibernicé* "kilt."

10. *i.e.*, for fear of the evil eye injuring the palace and, haply, himself.

11. The "Sufrah" before explained as acting provision-bag and table-cloth.

12. Eastern women, in hot weather, lie mother-nude under a sheet, here represented by the hair. The Greeks and Romans also slept stripped and in mediæval England the most modest women saw nothing indelicate in sleeping naked by their naked husbands. The "night-cap" and the "night-gown" are modern inventions.

13. Hindu fable turns this simile into better poetry, "She was like a second and a more wondrous moon made by the Creator."

14. "Sun of the Day."

15. Arab. "Shirk" = worshipping more than one God. A theological term here most appropriately used.

16. The Bul. Edit. as usual abridges (vol. i. 534). The Prince lands on the palace-roof where he leaves his horse, and finding no one in the building goes back to the terrace. Suddenly he sees a beautiful girl approaching him with a party of her women, suggesting to him these couplets,

> She came without tryst in the darkest hour,
> Like full moon lighting horizon's night:
> Slim-formed, there is not in the world her like
> For grace of form or for gifts of sprite:

"Praise him who made her from semen-drop,"
I cried, when her beauty first struck my sight:
I guard her from eyes, seeking refuge with
The Lord of mankind and of morning-light.

The two then made acquaintance and "follows what follows."

17. Arab. "Akásirah," (vol. i., 84) plur. of Kisrá.

18. The dearest ambition of a slave is not liberty but to have a slave of his own. This was systematized by the servile rulers known in history as the Mameluke Beys and to the Egyptians as the Ghuzz. Each had his household of servile pages and squires, who looked forward to filling the master's place as knight or baron.

19. The well-known capital of Al-Yaman, a true Arabia Felix, a Paradise inhabited by demons in the shape of Turkish soldiery and Arab caterans. According to Moslem writers Sana'a was founded by Shem son of Noah who, wandering southward with his posterity after his father's death, and finding the site delightful, dug a well and founded the citadel, Ghamdán, which afterwards contained a *Maison Carrée* rivalling (or attempting to rival) the Meccan Ka'abah. The builder was Surahbíl who, says M. C. de Perceval, coloured its four faces red, white, golden and green; the central quadrangle had seven stories (the planets) each forty cubits high, and the lowest was a marble hall ceiling'd with a single slab. At the four corners stood hollow lions through whose mouths the winds roared. This palatial citadel-temple was destroyed by order of Caliph Omar. The city's ancient name was Azal or Uzal whom some identify with one of the thirteen sons of Joktan (Genesis xi. 27): it took its present name from the Ethiopian conquerors (they say) who, seeing it for the first time, cried "Hazá Sana'ah!" meaning in their tongue, this is commodious, etc. I may note that the word is Kisawahili (Zanzibarian), *e.g.,* "Yámbo *sáná*—is the state *good?*" Sana'a was the capital of the Tabábi'ah or Tobba Kings who judaized; and the Abyssinians with their Negush made it Christian while the Persians under Anushirwán converted it to Guebrism. It is now easily visited but to little purpose; excursions in the neighbourhood being deadly dangerous. Moreover the Turkish garrison

would probably murder a stranger who sympathized with
the Arabs, and the Arabs kill one who took part with their
hated and hateful conquerors. The late Mr. Shapira of
Jerusalem declared that he had visited it and Jews have great
advantage in such travel. But his friends doubted him.

20. The Bresl. Edit. (iii. 347) prints three vile errors in four lines.

21. Alcove is a corruption of the Arab. Al-Kubbah (the dome)
through Span. and Port.

22. Easterns as a rule sleep with head and body covered by a
sheet or in cold weather a blanket. This practice is doubtless
hygienic, defending the body from draughts when the pores
are open; but Europeans find it hard to adopt; it seems to
stop their breathing. Another excellent practice in the East
and, indeed, amongst barbarians and savages generally, is
training children to sleep with mouths shut: in after life they
never snore and in malarious lands they do not require Out-
ram's "fever-guard," a swathe of muslin over the mouth. Mr.
Catlin thought so highly of the "shut mouth" that he made it
the subject of a book.

23. Arab. "Hanzal" = coloquintida, an article often mentioned
by Arabs in verse and prose; the bright coloured little gourd
attracts every eye by its golden glance when travelling
through the brown-yellow waste of sand and clay. A
favourite purgative (enough for a horse) is made by filling
the inside with sour milk which is drunk after a night's soak-
ing: it is as active as the croton-nut of the Gold Coast.

24. The Bresl. Edit. iii. 354, sends him to the "land of Sín"
(China).

25. Arab. "Yá Kisrawi!" = O subject of the Kisrá or Chosroë;
noted i., 84. "Fars" is the origin of "Persia"; and there is a
hint at the prodigious lying of the modern race, whose forefathers were so famous as truth-tellers. "I am a Persian, but I
am not lying now," is a phrase familiar to every traveller.

26. There is no such name: perhaps it is a clerical error for "Har
jáh" = (a man of) any place. I know an Englishman who in
Persian called himself "Mirza Abdullah-i-Híchmakáni" =
Master Abdullah of Nowhere.

27. The Bresl. Edit. (loc. cit.) gives a comical description of the
Prince assuming the dress of an astrologer-doctor, clapping
an old book under his arm, fumbling a rosary of beads, en-

larging his turband, lengthening his sleeves and blackening his eyelids with antimony. Here, it would be out of place. Very comical also is the way in which he pretends to cure the maniac by "muttering unknown words, blowing in her face, biting her ear," etc.

28. Arab. "Sar'a" = falling sickness. Here again we have in all its simplicity the old nursery idea of "possession" by evil spirits.

29. Arab. "Nafahát" = breathings, benefits, the Heb. Neshamah opp. to Nephesh (soul) and Ruach (spirit). Healing by the breath is a popular idea throughout the East and not unknown to Western Magnetists and Mesmerists. The miraculous cures of the Messiah were, according to Moslems, mostly performed by aspiration. They hold that in the days of Isa, physic had reached its highest development, and thus his miracles were mostly miracles of medicine; whereas, in Mohammed's time, eloquence had attained its climax and accordingly his miracles were those of eloquence, as shown in the Koran and Ahádís.

How Abu Hasan Brake Wind

1. This is a favourite Badawi dish, but too expensive unless some accident happen to the animal. Old camel is much like bull-beef, but the young meat is excellent, although not relished by Europeans because, like strange fish, it has no recognized flavour. I have noticed it in my *First Footsteps* (p. 68, etc.). There is an old idea in Europe that the maniacal vengeance of the Arab is increased by eating this flesh; the beast is certainly vindictive enough; but a furious and frantic vengefulness characterizes the North American Indian who never saw a camel. Mercy and pardon belong to the elect, not to the miserables who make up "humanity."

2. *i.e.*, of the Province Hazramaut, the Biblical Hazarmaveth (Gen. x. 26). The people are the Swiss of Arabia and noted for thrift and hard bargains; hence the saying, "If you meet a serpent and a Hazrami, slay the Hazrami." To prove how ubiquitous they are it is related that a man, flying from their society, reached the uttermost parts of China where he thought himself safe. But, as he was about to pass the night

in some ruin, he heard a voice hard by him exclaim, "O 'Imád al-Din!" (the name of the patron-saint of Hazramaut). Thereupon he arose and fled and he is, they say, flying still.

3. Arab. "Fál," alluding to the *Sortes Coranicae* and other silly practices known to the English servant-girl when curious about her future and her *futur*.

4. *i.e.,* in Arab-land (where they eat dates) and Ajam, or lands non-Arab (where bread is the staff of life); that is, all the world over.

5. This story is curious and ethnologically valuable. The Badawi who eructates as a civility has a mortal hatred to a *crepitus ventris;* and were a bystander to laugh at its accidental occurrence, he would at once be cut down as a "pundonor." The same is the custom amongst the Highlanders of Afghanistan, and its artificial nature suggests direct derivation; for the two regions are separated by a host of tribes, Persians and Baloch, Sindis and Panjábis who utterly ignore the point of honour and behave like Europeans. The raids of the pre-Islamitic Arabs over the lands lying to the northeast of them are almost forgotten; still, there are traces, and this may be one of them.

THE ANGEL OF DEATH WITH THE PROUD KING AND THE DEVOUT MAN

1. The popular English idea of the Arab horse is founded upon utter unfact. Book after book tells us, "There are three distinct breeds of Arabians—the *Attechi,* a very superior breed; the *Kadishi,* mixed with these and of little value; and the *Kochlani,* highly prized and very difficult to procure." "Attechi" may be At-Tázi (the Arab horse, or hound) or some confusion with "At" (Turk.), a horse. "Kadish" (Gadish or Kidish) is a nag, a gelding, a hackney, a "pacer" (generally called "Rahwán"). "Kochlani" is evidently "Kohláni," the Kohl-eyed, because the skin round the orbits is dark as if powdered. This is the true blue blood; and the bluest of all is "Kohláni al-Ajúz" (of the old woman), a name thus accounted for: an Arab mare dropped a filly when in flight; her rider perforce galloped on and presently saw the foal appear in camp, when it was given to an old woman for nursing and grew up to be famous. The home of the Arab horse is the

vast plateau of Al-Najd: the Tahámah or lower maritime regions of Arabia, like Malabar, will not breed good beasts. The pure blood all descends from five collateral lines called Al-Khamsah (the Cinque). Literary and pedantic Arabs derive them from the mares of Mohammed, a native of the dry and rocky region, Al-Hijaz, whither horses are all imported. Others go back (with the Koran, chap. xxviii) to Solomon, possibly Salmán, a patriarch fourth in descent from Ishmael and some 600 years older than the Hebrew King. The Badawi derive the five from Rabí'at al-Faras (R. of the mare) fourth in descent from Adnán, the fount of Arab genealogy. But they differ about the names: those generally given are Kahilan (Kohaylat), Sakláwi (which the Badawin pronounce Sagláwi), Abayán, and Hamdáni; others substitute Manákhi (the long-maned), Tanís and Jalfún. These require no certificate amongst Arabs; for strangers a simple statement is considered enough. The Badawin despise all half-breeds (Arab sires and country mares), Syrian, Turkish, Kurdish and Egyptian. They call these (first mentioned in the reign of Ahmes, 1600 B.C.) the "sons of horses"; as opposed to "sons of mares," or thoroughbreds. Nor do they believe in city-bred animals. I have great doubts concerning our old English sires, such as the Darley Arabian which looks like a Kurdish half-bred, the descendant of those Cappadocians so much prized by the Romans: in Syria I rode a "Harfúshí" (Kurd) the very image of it. There is no difficulty in buying Arab stallions except the price. Of course the tribe does not like to part with what may benefit the members generally; but offers of £500 to £1,000 would overcome men's scruples. It is different with mares, which are almost always the joint property of several owners. The people too dislike to see a hat on a thoroughbred mare: "What hast thou done that thou art ridden by that ill-omened Kafir?" the Badawin used to mutter when they saw a highly respectable missionary at Damascus mounting a fine Ruwalá mare. The feeling easily explains the many wars about horses occurring in Arab annals, *e.g.*, about Dáhis and Ghabrá. (C. de Perceval, *Essais*, vol. ii.)

2. The stricter kind of Eastern Jew prefers to die on the floor, not in bed, as was the case with the late Mr. Emmanuel Deutsch, who in his well-known article on the Talmud had

the courage to speak of "Our Saviour." But as a rule the Israelite, though he mostly appears as a Deist, a Unitarian, has a fund of fanatical feelings which crop up in old age and near death. The "converts" in Syria and elsewhere, whose Judaism is intensified by "conversion," when offers are made to them by the missionaries repair to the Khákhám (scribe) and, after abundant wrangling determine upon a *modus vivendi*. They are to pay a proportion of their wages, to keep careful watch in the cause of Israel and to die orthodox. In Istria there is a legend of a Jew Prior in a convent who was not discovered till he announced himself most unpleasantly on his death-bed. For a contrary reason to Jewish humility, the Roman Emperors preferred to die standing.

3. He wished to die in a state of ceremonial purity; as has before been mentioned.

SINDBAD THE SEAMAN AND SINDBAD THE LANDSMAN

1. Lane (vol. iii. 1) calls our old friend "Es-Sindibád of the Sea," and Benfey derives the name from the Sanskrit "Siddhapati"=lord of sages. The etymology (in Heb. Sandabar and in Greek Syntipas) is still uncertain, although the term often occurs in Arab stories; and some look upon it as a mere corruption of "Bidpai" (Bidyápati). The derivation offered by Hole (*Remarks on the Arabian Nights' Entertainments*, by Richard Hole, LL.D. London, Cadell, 1797) from the Persian ábád (a region) is impossible. It is, however, not a little curious that this purely Persian word (=a "habitation") should be found in Indian names as early as Alexander's day, *e.g.*, the "Dachina bades" of the Periplus is "Dakhshin-ábád," the Sanskr. being "Dakshinapatha."

2. A porter like the famous Armenians of Constantinople. Some edits call him "Al-Hindibád."

3. Arab. "Karawán" (Charadrius œdicnemus, Linn.): its shrill note is admired by Egyptians and hated by sportsmen.

4. This ejaculation, still popular, averts the evil eye. In describing Sindbad the Seaman the Arab writer seems to repeat what one reads of Marco Polo returned to Venice.

5. Our old friend must not be confounded with the eponym of the "Sindibád-námah," the Persian book of Sindbad the Sage.

6. The first and second are from *Eccles*. chaps. vii. 1, and ix. 4. The Bul. Edit. reads for the third, "The grave is better than the palace." None are from Solomon, but Easterns do not "verify quotations."

7. Arab. "Kánún"; a furnace, a brasier; here a pot full of charcoal sunk in the ground, or a little hearth of clay shaped like a horseshoe and opening down wind.

8. These fish-islands are common in the Classics, *e.g.*, the Pristis of Pliny (xvii. 4), which Olaus Magnus transfers to the Baltic (xxi. 6) and makes timid as the whales of Nearchus. C. J. Solinus (*Plinii Simia*) says, "Indica maria balænas habent ultra spatia quatuor jugerum." See also Bochart's *Hierozoicon* (i. 50) for Job's Leviathan (xli. 16–17). Hence Boiardo (Orl. Innam, lib. iv.) borrowed his magical whale and Milton (P.L. i.) his Leviathan deemed an island. A basking whale would readily suggest the Kraken and Cetus of Olaus Magnus (xxi. 25). Al-Kazwíni's famous treatise on the *Wonders of the World* (Ajáib al-Makhlúkát) tells the same tale of the "Sulahfah" tortoise, the colossochelys, for which see the Third Voyage of Sindbad.

9. Sindbad does not say that he was a shipwrecked man, being a model in the matter of "travellers' tales," *i.e.*, he always tells the truth when an untruth would not serve his purpose.

10. Lane (iii. 83) would make this a corruption of the Hindu "Maharáj"=great Rajah: but it is the name of the great autumnal fête of the Guebres; a term composed of two good old Persian words "Mihr" (the sun, whence "Mithras") and "ján"=life. As will presently appear, in the days of the Just King Anushirwán, the Persians possessed Southern Arabia and East Africa south of Cape Guardafui (Jird Háfún). On the other hand, supposing the word to be a corruption of Maharaj, Sindbad may allude to the famous Narsinga kingdom in Mid-south India whose capital was Vijaya-nagar; or to any great Indian Rajah even he of Kachch (Cutch), famous in Moslem story as the Balhará (Ballaba Rais, who founded the Ballabhi era; or the Zamorin of Camoens, the Samdry Rajah of Malabar). For Mahrage, or Mihrage, see Renaudot's *Two Mohammedan Travellers of the Ninth Century*. In the account of Ceylon by Wolf (English Transl. p. 168) it adjoins the "Ilhas de Cavalos" (of wild horses) to which the Dutch merchants sent their brood-mares. Sir W. Jones (*De-*

scription of Asia, chap. ii.) makes the Arabian island Soborma or Mahráj=Borneo.

11. Arab. "Darakah"; whence our word.

12. The myth of mares being impregnated by the wind was known to the Classics of Europe; and the "sea-stallion" may have arisen from the Arab practice of picketing mare asses to be covered by the wild ass. Colonel J. D. Watson of the Bombay Army suggests to me that Sindbad was wrecked at the mouth of the Ran of Kachch (Cutch) and was carried in a boat to one of the Islands there formed during the rains and where the wild ass (*Equus Onager*, Khar-gadh, in Pers. Gor-khar) still breeds. This would explain the "stallions of the sea" and we find traces of the ass blood in the true Kathi-awár horse, with his dun colour, barred legs and dorsal stripe.

13. The second or warrior caste (Kshatriya), popularly sup-posed to have been annihilated by Battle-axe Ráma (Parashu Ráma); but several tribes of Rajputs and other races claim the honourable genealogy. Colonel Watson would explain the word by "Shakháyát" or noble Káthis (Kathiawar-men), or by "Shikári," the professional hunter here acting as stable-groom.

14. In Bul. Edit. "Kábil." Lane (iii. 88) supposes it to be the "Bar-tail" of Al-Kazwini near Borneo and quotes the Spaniard B. L. de Argensola (History of the Moluccas), who places near Banda a desert island, Poelsatton, infamous for cries, whistlings, roarings and dreadful apparitions, suggesting that it was peopled by devils (Stevens, vol. i., p. 168).

15. Some texts substitute for this last phrase, "And the sailors say that Al-Dajjál is there." He is a manner of Moslem An-tichrist, the Man of Sin *per excellentiam*, who will come in the latter days and lay waste the earth, leading 70,000 Jews, till encountered and slain by Jesus at the gate of Lud. (Sale's Essay, sect. 4.)

16. Also from Al-Kazwini: it is an exaggerated description of the whale still common off the East African Coast. My crew was dreadfully frightened by one between Berberah and Aden. Nearchus scared away the whales in the Persian Gulf by trumpets (Strabo, lib. xv.). The owl-faced fish is unknown to me: it may perhaps be a seal or a manatee. Hole says that Fa-

ther Martini, the Jesuit (seventeenth century), placed in the Canton Seas, an "animal with the head of a bird and the tail of a fish,"—a parrot-beak?

17. The captain or master (not owner) of a ship.

18. The kindly Moslem feeling, shown to a namesake, however humble.

19. A popular phrase to express utter desolation.

20. The literature of all peoples contains this physiological perversion. Birds do not sing hymns; the song of the male is simply to call the female and when the pairing-season ends all are dumb.

21. The older "roc." The word is Persian, with many meanings, *e.g.*, a cheek (Lalla "Rookh"); a "rook" (hero) at chess; a rhinoceros, etc. The fable world-wide of the *Wundervogel* is, as usual, founded upon fact: man remembers and combines but does not create. The Egyptian Bennu (Ti-bennu=phœnix) may have been a reminiscence of gigantic pterodactyls and other winged monsters. From the Nile the legend fabled by these Oriental "putters out of five for one" overspread the world and gave birth to the Eorosh of the Zend, whence the Pers. "Símurgh" (=the "thirty-fowl-like"), the "Bar Yuchre" of the Rabbis, the "Garuda" of the Hindus; the "Anká" ("long-neck") of the Arabs; the "Hathilinga bird," of Buddhagosha's Parables, which had the strength of five elephants; the "Kerkes" of the Turks; the "Gryps" of the Greeks; the Russian "Norka"; the sacred dragon of the Chinese; the Japanese "Pheng" and "Kirni"; the "wise and ancient Bird" which sits upon the ash-tree yggdrasil, and the dragons, griffins, basilisks, etc. of the Middle Ages. A second basis wanting only a superstructure of exaggeration (M. Polo's Ruch had wing-feathers twelve paces long) would be the huge birds but lately killed out. Sindbad may allude to the Æpyornus of Madagascar, a gigantic ostrich whose egg contains 2.35 gallons. The late Herr Hildebrand discovered on the African coast, facing Madagascar, traces of another huge bird. Bochart (*Hierozoicon* ii. 854) notices the Avium Avis Ruch and taking the *pulli* was followed by lapidation on the part of the parent bird. A Persian illustration in Lane (iii. 90) shows the Rukh carrying off three elephants in beak and pounces with the proportions of a hawk and field mice: and

the Rukh hawking at an elephant is a favourite Persian subject. It is possible that the "Twelve Knights of the Round Table" were the twelve Rukhs of Persian story. We need not go, with Faber, to the Cherubim which guarded the Paradise-gate. The curious reader will consult Dr. H. H. Wilson's Essays, edited by my learned correspondent, Dr. Rost, Librarian of the India House (vol. i. pp. 192–3).

22. It is not easy to explain this passage unless it be a garbled allusion to the steel-plate of the diamond-cutter. Nor can we account for the wide diffusion of this tale of perils unless to enhance the value of the gem. Diamonds occur in alluvial lands mostly open and comparatively level, as in India, the Brazil and the Cape. Archbishop Epiphanius of Salamis (ob. A.D. 403) tells this story about the jacinth or ruby (Epiphanii Opera, a Petaio, Coloniæ 1682); and it was transferred to the diamond by Marco Polo (iii. 29, "of Eagles bring up diamonds") and Nicolò de Conti, whose "mountain Albenigaras" must be Vijayanagar in the kingdom of Golconda. Major Rennel places the famous mines of Pauna or Purna in a mountain tract of more than 200 miles square to the south-west of the Jumna. Al-Kazwini locates the "Chaos" in the "Valley of the Moon amongst the mountains of Serendib" (Ceylon); the Chinese tell the same tale in the campaigns of Hulaku; and it is known in Armenia. Col. Yule (M. P. ii. 349) suggests that all these are ramifications of the legend told by Herodotus concerning the Arabs and their cinnamon (iii. 3). But whence did Herodotus borrow the tale?

23. Sindbad correctly describes the primitive way of extracting camphor, a drug unknown to the Greeks and Romans, introduced by the Arabs and ruined in reputation by M. Raspail. The best Laurus Camphora grows in the Malay Peninsula, Sumatra and Borneo: although Marsden (Marco Polo) declares that the tree is not found South of the Equator. In the Calc. Edit. of two hundred Nights the camphor-island (or peninsula) is called "Al-Ríhah" which is the Arab name for Jericho-town.

24. In Bul. Edit. Kazkazan: Calc. Karkaddan and others Karkand and Karkadan; the word being Persian, Karg or Kargadan; the χαρτάζυνον of Ælian (*Hist. Anim.* xvi. 21). The length of the horn (greatly exaggerated) shows that the white species is meant; and it supplies only walking-sticks. Cups are made

of the black horn (a bundle of fibres) which, like Venetian glass, sweat at the touch of poison. A section of the horn is supposed to show white lines in the figure of a man, and sundry likenesses of birds; but these I never saw. The rhinoceros gives splendid sport and the African is perhaps the most dangerous of noble game. It has served to explain away and abolish the unicorn among the scientists of Europe. But Central Africa with one voice assures us that a horse-like animal with a single erectile horn on the forehead exists. The late Dr. Baikic, of Niger fame, thoroughly believed in it and those curious on the subject will read about Abu Karn (Father of a Horn) in Preface (pp. xvi.–xviii.) of the *Voyage au Darfour,* by Mohammed ibn Omar al-Tounsy (Al-Tunisi), Paris: Duprat, 1845.

25. Ibn al-Wardi mentions an "Isle of Apes" in the Sea of China and Al-Idrísi places it two days' sail from Sukutra (Dwipa Sukhatra, Socotra). It is a popular error to explain the Homeric and Herodotean legend of the Pygmies by anthropoid apes. The Pygmy fable (Pygmæi Spithamai=1 cubit=3 spans) was, as usual, based upon fact, as the explorations of late years have proved: the dwarfs are homunculi of various tribes, the Akka, Doko, Tiki-Tiki, Wambilikimo ("two-cubit men"), the stunted race that share the central regions of Intertropical Africa with the abnormally tall peoples who speak dialects of the Great South African tongue, miscalled the "Bantu." Hole makes the Pygmies "monkeys," a word we have borrowed from the Italians (monichio à mono=ape) and quotes Ptolemy, Νῆσοι τῶν Σατυρῶν (Ape-islands) East of Sunda.

26. A kind of barge (Arab. Bárijah, plur. Bawárij) used on the Nile of sub-pyriform shape when seen in bird's eye. Lane translates "ears like two mortars" from the Calc. Edit.

27. This giant is distinctly Polyphemus; but the East had giants and cyclopes of her own (*Hierozoicon* ii. 845). The Ajáib al-Hind (chap. cxxii.) makes Polyphemus copulate with the sheep. Sir John Mandeville (if such person ever existed) mentions men fifty feet high in the Indian Islands; and Al-Kazwini and Al-Idrisi transfer them to the Sea of China, a Botany Bay for monsters in general.

28. Fire is forbidden as a punishment amongst Moslems, the idea being that it should be reserved for the next world.

Hence the sailors fear the roasting more than the eating:
with ours it would probably be the reverse. The Persian insult "Pidar-sokhtah"=(son of a) burnt father, is well known.
I have noted the advisability of burning the Moslem's corpse
under certain circumstances: otherwise the murderer may
come to be canonized.

29. Arab. "Mastabah"=the bench or form of masonry before noticed. In olden Europe benches were much more used than
chairs, these being articles of luxury. So King Horne "sett
him abenche"; and hence our "King's Bench" (Court).

30. This is from the Bresl. Edit. vol. iv. 32: the Calc. Edit. gives
only an abstract and in the Bul. Edit. the Ogre returned "accompanied by a female, greater than he and more hideous."
We cannot accept Mistress Polyphemus.

31. This is from Al-Kazwini, who makes the serpent "wind itself
round a tree or a rock, and thus break to pieces the bones of
the beast in its belly."

32. "Like a closet," in the Calc. Edit. The serpent is an exaggeration of the python which grows to an enormous size.
Monstrous Ophidia are mentioned in sober history, *e.g.*, that
which delayed the army of Regulus. Dr. de Lacerda, a sober
and sensible Brazilian traveller, mentions his servants sitting
down upon a tree-trunk in the Captaincy of San Paulo
(Brazil), which began to move and proved to be a huge snake.
F. M. Pinto (the Sindbad of Portugal though not so respectable) when in Sumatra takes refuge in a tree from
"tigers, crocodiles, copped adders and serpents which slay
men with their breath." Father Lobo in Tigre (chap. x.) was
nearly killed by the poison-breath of a huge snake, and
healed himself with a bezoar carried *ad hoc*. Maffæus makes
the breath of crocodiles suavissimus, but that of the Malabar
serpents and vipers "adeo teter ac noxius ut afflatu ipso
necare perhibeantur."

33. Arab. "Aurat": the word has been borrowed by the Hindostani jargon, and means a woman, a wife.

34. So in Al-Idrísi and Langlès: the Bres. Edit. has "Al-
Kalásitah"; and Al-Kazwini "Al-Salámit." The latter notes in
it a petrifying spring which Camoens (*The Lus.* x. 104),
places in Sunda, *i.e.*, Java-Minor of M. Polo. Some read
Salabat-Timor, one of the Moluccas famed for sanders,
cloves, cinnamon, etc. (Purchas ii. 1784.)

35. Evidently the hippopotamus (*Pliny*, viii. 25; ix. 3 and xxiii. 11). It can hardly be the Mulaccan Tapir, as shields are not made of the hide. Hole suggests the buffalo which found its way to Egypt from India via Persia; but this would not be a speciosum miraculum.

36. The ass-headed fish is from Pliny (ix. cap. 3): all those tales are founded upon the manatee (whose dorsal protuberance may have suggested the camel), the seal and the dugong or sea-calf. I have noticed (*Zanzibar* i. 205) legends of ichthyological marvels current on the East African seaboard; and even the monsters of the Scottish waters are not all known: witness the mysterious "brigdie." See Bochart *De Cetis* i. 7; and Purchas iii..930.

37. The colossal tortoise is noticed by Ælian (*De Nat. Animal.* xvi. 17), by Strabo (Lib. xv.), by Pliny (ix. 10) and Diodorus Siculus (iv. 1) who had heard of a tribe of Chelonophagi. Ælian makes them 16 cubits long near Taprobane and serving as house-roofs; and others turn the shell into boats and coracles. A colossochelys was first found on the Scwalik Hills by Dr. Falconer and Major (afterwards Sir Proby) Cantley. In 1867 M. Emile Blanchard exhibited to the Académie des Sciences a monster crab from Japan 1.20 metres long (or 2.50 including legs); and other travellers have reported 4 metres. These crustacea seem never to cease growing and attain great dimensions under favourable circumstances, *i.e.*, when not troubled by man.

38. Lane suggests (iii. 97), and with some probability, that the "bird" was a nautilus; but the wild traditions concerning the barnacle-goose may perhaps have been the base of the fable. The albatross also was long supposed never to touch land. Possibly the barnacle, like the barometz or Tartarean lamb, may be a survivor of the day when the animal and vegetable kingdoms had not yet branched off into different directions.

39. Arab. "Zahwah," also meaning a luncheon. The five daily prayers made all Moslems take strict account of time, and their nomenclature of its division is extensive.

40. This is the "insane herb." Davis, who visited Sumatra in 1599 (*Purchas* i. 120) speaks "of a kind of seed, whereof a little being eaten, maketh a man to turn foole, all things seeming to him to be metamorphosed." Linschoten's "Dutroa" was a poppy-like bud containing small kernels like melons

which, stamped and administered as a drink, make a man "as if he were foolish, or out of his wits." This is Father Lobo's "Vanguini" of the Cafres, called by the Portuguese *dutro* (*Datura Stramonium*) still used by dishonest confectioners. It may be Dampier's Ganga (Ganjah) or Bang (Bhang) which he justly describes as acting differently "according to different constitutions; for some it stupefies, others it makes sleepy, others merry and some quite mad." (Harris, *Collect.* ii. 900.) Dr. Fryer also mentions Duty, Bung and Post, the Poust of Bernier, an infusion of poppyseed.

41. Arab. "Ghul," here an ogre, a cannibal. I cannot but regard the "Ghul of the waste" as an embodiment of the natural fear and horror which a man feels when he faces a really dangerous desert. As regards cannibalism, Al-Islam's religion of common sense freely allows it when necessary to save life, and unlike our mawkish modern sensibility, never blames those who

> Alimentis talibus usi
> Produxere animos.

42. For Cannibals, see the Massagetæ of Herod (i.), the Padæi of India (iii.), and the Essedones near Mæotis (iv.); Strabo (lib. iv.) of the Luci; Pomponius Mela (iii. 7) and St. Jerome (ad Jovinum) of Scoti. M. Polo locates them in Dragvia, a kingdom of Sumatra (iii. 17), and in Angaman (the Andamanian Isles?), possibly the ten Maniolai which Ptolemy (vii.), confusing with the Nicobars, places on the Eastern side of the Bay of Bengal; and thence derives the Heraklian stone (magnet) which attracts the iron of ships (See Serapion, *De Magnete*, fol. 6, Edit. of 1479, and Brown's *Vulgar Errors*, p. 74, 6th Edit.). Mandeville finds his cannibals in Lamaray (Sumatra) and Barthema in the "Isle of Gyava" (Java). Ibn Al-Wardi and Al-Kazwini notice them in the Isle Saksar, in the Sea of the Zanj (Zanzibar): the name is corrupted Persian "Sag-Sar" (Dogs'-heads) hence the dog-descended race of Camoens in Pegu (*The Lus.* x. 122). The Bresl. Edit. (iv. 52) calls them "Khawárij=certain sectarians in Eastern Arabia. Needless to say that cocoanut oil would have no stupefying effect unless mixed with opium or datura, hemp or henbane.

43. Black pepper is produced in the Goanese but we must go south to find the "Bilád al-Filfil" (home of pepper) *i.e.,* Malabar. The exorbitant prices demanded by Venice for this spice led directly to the discovery of the Cape route by the Portuguese; as the "Grains of Paradise" (Amomum Granum Paradisi) induced the English to explore the West African Coast.

44. Arabic "Kazdír." Sanskrit "Kastír." Greek "Kassiteron." Latin "Cassiteros," evidently derived from one root. The Hebrew form is "Badih," a substitute, an alloy. "Tanakah" is the vulgar Arabic word, a congener of the Assyrian "Anaku," and "Kala-i" is the corrupt Arabic term used in India.

45. Our Arabian Ulysses had probably left a Penelope or two at home and finds a Calypso in this Ogygia. His modesty at the mention of womankind is notable.

46. These are the commonplaces of Moslem consolation on such occasions: the artistic part is their contrast with the unfortunate widower's prospect.

47. Lit. "a margin of stone, like the curb-stone of a well."

48. I am not aware that this vivisepulture of the widower is the custom of any race, but the fable would be readily suggested by the Sati (Suttee) rite of the Hindus. Simple vivisepulture was and is practised by many people.

49. Because she was weaker than a man. The Bres. Edit. however, has "a gugglet of water and five scones."

50. The confession is made with true Eastern sang-froid and probably none of the hearers "disapproved" of the murders which saved the speaker's life.

51. This tale is evidently taken from the escape of Aristomenes the Messenian from the pit into which he had been thrown, a fox being his guide. The Arabs in an early day were eager students of Greek literature. Hole (p. 140) noted the coincidence.

52. Bresl. Edit. "Khwájah," our "Howajee," meaning a schoolmaster, a man of letters, a gentleman.

53. And he does repeat at full length what the hearers must have known right well. I abridge.

54. Island of the Bell (Arab. "Nákús"=a wooden gong used by Christians but forbidden to Moslems). "Kala" is written "Kela," "Kullah" and a variety of ways. Baron Walckenaer places it at Keydah in the Malay peninsula opposite Sumatra. Renaudot identifies it with Calabar, "somewhere about the point of Malabar."

55. Islands, because Arab cosmographers love to place their *speciosa miracula* in such places.

56. Like the companions of Ulysses who ate the sacred oxen (Od. xii.).

57. So the enormous kingfisher of Lucian's *True History* (lib. ii.).

58. This tale is borrowed from Ibn Al-Wardi, who adds that the greybeards awoke in the morning after eating the young Rukh with black hair which never turned white. The same legend is recounted by Al-Dimiri (ob. A.H. 808=1405–6) who was translated into Latin by Bochart (*Hierozoicon,* ii. p. 854) and quoted by Hole and Lane (iii. 103). An excellent study of Marco Polo's Rukh was made by my learned friend the late Prof. G. G. Bianconi of Bologna, *Dell'Uccello Ruc,* Bologna, Gamberini, 1868. Prof. Bianconi predicted that other giant birds would be found in Madagascar on the East African Coast opposite; but he died before hearing of Hildebrand's discovery.

59. Arab. "Izár," the earliest garb of Eastern man; and, as such preserved in the Meccan pilgrimage. The "waist-cloth" is either tucked in or kept in place by a girdle.

60. Arab. "Líf," a succedaneum for the unclean sponge, not unknown in the "Turkish Baths" of London.

61. The Persians have a Plinian monster called "Tasmeh-pá"= Strap-legs without bones. The "Old Man" is not an ourang-outang nor an Ifrít, but a jocose exaggeration of a custom prevailing in parts of Asia and especially in the African interior where the Tsetse-fly prevents the breeding of burden-beasts. Ibn Batútah tells us that in Malabar everything was borne upon men's backs. In Central Africa the kinglet rides a slave, and on ceremonious occasions mounts his Prime Minister. I have often been reduced to this style of conveyance and found man the worst imaginable riding: there is no hold and the sharpness of the shoulder-ridge soon makes the legs ache intolerably. The classicists of course find the Shaykh of the Sea in the Tritons and Nereus, and Bochart (*Hiero.* ii. 858, 880) notices the homo aquaticus, Senex Judæus and Senex Marinus. Hole (p. 151) suggests the inevitable ourang-outang (man o' wood), one of "our humiliating copyists," and quotes "Destiny" in Scarron's comical romance (Part ii. chap. 1) and "Jealousy" enfolding Rinaldo. (*O.F.* lib. 42.)

62. More literally "The Chief of the Sea (-Coast)," Shaykh being here a chief rather than an elder (eoldermann, alderman). So the "Old Man of the Mountain," famous in crusading days, was the Chief who lived on the Nusayriyah or Ansári range, a northern prolongation of the Libanus. Our "old man" of the text may have been suggested by the Koranic commentators on chap. vi. When an Infidel rises from the grave, a hideous figure meets him and says, "Why wonderest thou at my loathsomeness? I am thine Evil Deeds: thou didst ride upon me in the world and now I will ride upon thee." (Suiting the action to the words.)

63. In parts of West Africa and especially in Gorilla-land there are many stories of women and children being carried off by apes, and all believe that the former bear issue to them. It is certain that the anthropoid ape is lustfully excited by the presence of women and I have related how at Cairo (1856) a huge cynocephalus would have raped a girl had it not been bayonetted. Young ladies who visited the Demidoff Gardens and menagerie at Florence were often scandalized by the vicious exposure of the baboons' parti-coloured persons. The female monkey equally solicits the attentions of man and I heard in India from my late friend, Mirza Ali Akbar of Bombay, that to his knowledge connection had taken place. Whether there would be issue and whether such issue would be viable are still disputed points: the produce would add another difficulty to the pseudo-science called psychology, as such a mule would have only half a soul and issue by a congener would have a quarter-soul. A traveller well known to me once proposed to breed pithecoid men who might be useful as hewers of wood and drawers of water: his idea was to put the highest races of apes to the lowest of humanity. I never heard what became of his "breeding stables."

64. Arab. "Jauz al-Hindi": our word cocoa is from the Port. "Coco," meaning a "bug" (bugbear) in allusion to its caricature of the human face, hair, eyes and mouth. I may here note that a cocoa-tree is easily climbed with a bit of rope or a handkerchief.

65. Tomb-pictures in Egypt show tame monkeys gathering fruits and Grossier (*Description of China*, quoted by Hole and Lane) mentions a similar mode of harvesting tea by irritating the monkeys of the Middle Kingdom.

66. Bresl. Edit. Cloves and cinnamon in those days grew in widely distant places.

67. In pepper-plantations it is usual to set bananas (*Musa Paradisiaca*) for shading the young shrubs which bear bunches like ivy-fruit, not pods.

68. The Bresl. Edit. has "Al-Ma'arat." Langlès calls it the Island of Al-Kamárí. See Lane, iii. 86.

69. Insula, pro. peninsula. "Comorin" is a corrupt. of "Kanyá" (=Virgo, the goddess Durgá) and "Kumárí" (a maid, a princess); from a temple of Shiva's wife: hence Ptolemy's Κῶρυ ἄχρον and near it to the N. East Κομαρὶα ἄχρον χαὶ πόλις, "Promontorium Cori quod Comorini caput insulæ vocant," says Maffæus (*Hist. Indic.* i. p. 16). In the text "Al 'úd" refers to the eagle-wood (Aloekylon Agallochum) so called because spotted like the bird's plume. That of Champa (Cochin-China, mentioned by Camoens, *The Lus.* x. 129) is still famous.

70. Arab. "Birkat"=tank, pool, reach, bight. Hence Birkat Far'aun in the Suez Gulf. (*Pilgrimage,* i. 297.)

71. Probably Cape Comorin; to judge from the river, but the text names Sarandib (Ceylon Island) famous for gems. This was noticed by Marco Polo, iii. chap. 19; and ancient authors relate the same of "Taprobane."

72. I need hardly trouble the reader with a note on pearl-fisheries: the descriptions of travellers are continuous from the days of Pliny (ix. 35), Solinus (chap. 56) and Marco Polo (iii. 23). Maximilian of Transylvania, in his narrative of Magellan's voyage (*Novus Orbis,* p. 532) says that the Celebes produce pearls big as turtle-doves' eggs; and the King of Porne (Borneo) had two unions as great as goose's eggs. Pigafetta (in *Purchas*) reduces this to hen's eggs and Sir Thomas Herbert to dove's eggs.

73. Arab. "Anbar" pronounced "Ambar"; wherein I would derive "Ambrosia." Ambergris was long supposed to be a fossil, a vegetable which grew upon the sea-bottom or rose in springs; or a "substance produced in the water like naphtha or bitumen" (!): now it is known to be the egesta of a whale. It is found in lumps weighing several pounds upon the Zanzibar Coast and is sold at a high price, being held a potent aphrodisiac. A small hollow is drilled in the bottom of the cup and the coffee is poured upon the bit of ambergris it

contains; when the oleaginous matter shows in dots amidst the "Kaymagh" (coffee-cream), the bubbly froth which floats upon the surface and which an expert "coffee servant" distributes equally among the guests. Argensola mentions in Ceylon, "springs of liquid bitumen thicker than our oil and some of pure balsam."

74. The tale-teller forgets that Sindbad and his companions have just ascended it; but this *inconséquence* is a characteristic of the Eastern Saga. I may note that the description of ambergris in the text tells us admirably well what it is not.

75. This custom is alluded to by Lane (*Mod. Egypt*, ch. xv.): it is the rule of pilgrims to Meccah when too ill to walk or ride (*Pilgrimage,* i. 180). Hence all men carry their shrouds: mine, after being dipped in the Holy Water of Zemzem, was stolen from me by the rascally Somal of Berberah.

76. Arab. "Fulk"; some Edits. read "Kalak" and "Ramaz" (=a raft).

77. These underground rivers (which Dr. Livingstone derided) are familiar to every geographer from Spenser's "Mole" to the Poika of Adelberg and the Timavo near Trieste. Hence "Peter Wilkins" borrowed his cavern which led him to Grande-volet. I have some experience of Sindbad's sorrows, having once attempted to descend the Poika on foot. The Classics had the Alpheus (*Pliny* v. 31; and Seneca, *Nat. Quae.* vi.), and the Tigris-Euphrates supposed to flow underground: and the Mediævals knew the Abana of Damascus and the Zenderúd of Isfahan.

78. Abyssinians can hardly be called "blackamoors," but the arrogance of the white skin shows itself in Easterns (*e.g.*, Turks and Brahmans) as much as, if not more than, amongst Europeans. Southern India at the time it was explored by Vasco da Gama was crowded with Abyssinian slaves imported by the Arabs.

79. "Sarandib" and "Ceylon" (the Taprobane of Ptolemy and Diodorus Siculus) derive from the Pali "Sihalam" (not the Sansk. "Sinhala") shortened to Silam and Ilam in old Tamul. Van der Tunk would find it in the Malay "Pulo Selam"=Isle of Gems (the Ratna-dwípa or Jewel Isle of the Hindus and the Jazirat al-Yakút or Ruby-Island of the Arabs); and the learned Colonel Yule (*Marco Polo*, ii. 296) remarks that we have adopted many Malayan names, *e.g.*, Pegu, China and

Japan. Sarandib is clearly "Selan-dwípa," which Mandeville reduced to "Silha."

80. This is the well-known Adam's Peak, the Jabal al-Ramun of the Arabs where Adam fell when cast out of Eden in the lowest or lunar sphere. Eve fell at Jeddah (a modern myth) and the unhappy pair met at Mount Arafat (*i.e.*, recognition) near Mecca. Thus their fall was a fall indeed. (*Pilgrimage*, iii. 259.)

81. He is the Alcinous of our Arabian Odyssey.

82. This word is not in the dictionaries; Hole (p. 192) and Lane understand it to mean the hog-deer; but why, one cannot imagine. The animal is neither "beautiful" nor "uncommon" and most men of my day have shot dozens of them in the Sind-Shikárgáhs.

83. M. Polo speaks of a ruby in Seilan (Ceylon) a palm long and three fingers thick: William of Tyre mentions a ruby weighing twelve Egyptian drams (*Gibbon* ii. 123), and Mandeville makes the King of Mammera wear about his neck a "rubye orient" one foot long by five fingers large.

84. The fable is from Al-Kazwini and Ibn Al-Wardi who place the serpent (an animal sacred to Æsculapius, *Pliny*, xxix. 4) "in the sea of Zanj" (*i.e.*, Zanzibar). In the "garrow hills" of N. Eastern Bengal the skin of the snake Burrawar (?) is held to cure pain. (*Asiat. Res.* vol. iii.)

85. For "Emerald," Hole (p. 177) would read emery or adamantine spar.

86. Evidently Maháráj=Great Rajah, Rajah in Chief, an Hindu title common to the three potentates before alluded to, the Narsinga, Balhara or Samiry.

87. This is probably classical. So the page said to Philip of Macedon every morning, "Remember, Philip, thou art mortal"; also the slave in the Roman Triumph,

Respice poste te: hominem te esse memento!

And the dying Severus, "Urnlet, soon shalt thou enclose what hardly a whole world could contain." But the custom may also have been Indian: the contrast of external pomp with the real vanity of human life suggests itself to all.

88. Arab. "Hút"; a term applied to Jonah's whale and to monsters of the deep, "Samak" being the common fishes.

89. Usually a two-bow prayer.

90. This is the recognized formula of Moslem sales.

91. Arab. "Walímah"; similar to our wedding breakfast but a much more ceremonious and important affair.

92. *i.e.*, his wife (euphemistically). I remember an Italian lady being much hurt when a Maltese said to her "Mia moglie—con rispetto parlando" (my wife, saving your presence). "What," she cried, "he speaks of his wife as he would of the sweepings!"

93. The serpent in Arabic is mostly feminine.

94. *i.e.*, in envying his wealth, with the risk of the evil eye.

95. I subjoin a translation of the Seventh Voyage from the Calc. Edit. of the two hundred Nights which differs in essential points from the above. All respecting Sindbad the Seaman has an especial interest. In one point this world-famous tale is badly ordered. The most exciting adventures are the earliest and the falling off of the interest has a somewhat depressing effect. The Rukh, the Ogre and the Old Man o' the Sea should be last in order.

THE CITY OF BRASS

1. This is a true "City of Brass." (Nuhás asfar=yellow copper). It is situated in the "Maghrib" (Mauritania), the region of magic and mystery; and the idea was probably suggested by the grand Roman ruins which rise abruptly from what has become a sandy waste. In Egypt Nuhás is vulg. pronounced Nihás.

2. The Bresl. Edit. adds that the seal-ring was of stamped stone and iron, copper and lead. I have borrowed copiously from its vol. vi. pp. 343, *et seq.*

3. As this was a well-known pre-Islamitic bard, his appearance here is decidedly anachronistic, probably by intention.

4. The first Moslem conqueror of Spain whose lieutenant, Tárik, the gallant and unfortunate, named Gibraltar (Jabal al-Tarik).

5. The colours of the Banú Umayyah (Ommiade) Caliphs were white; of the Banú Abbás (Abbasides) black, and of the Fatimites green. Carrying the royal flag denoted the generalissimo or plenipotentiary.

6. *i.e.*, Old Cairo, or Fustat: the present Cairo was then a Cop-

tic village founded on an old Egyptian settlement called Lui-Tkeshroma, to which belonged the tanks on the hill and the great well, Bir Yusuf, absurdly attributed to Joseph the Patriarch. Lui is evidently the origin of Levi and means a high priest (Brugsh ii. 130) and his son's name was Roma.

7. I cannot but suspect that this is a clerical error for "Al-Samanhúdi," a native of Samanhúd (Wilkinson's "Semenood") in the Delta on the Damietta branch, the old Sebennytus (in Coptic Jem-nuti=Jem the God), a town which has produced many distinguished men in Moslem times. But there is also a Samhúd lying a few miles down stream from Denderah and, as investigation of its mounds proves, it is an ancient site.

8. Egypt had not then been conquered from the Christians.

9. Arab. "Kízán fukká'a," *i.e.,* thin and slightly porous earthenware jars used for Fukká'a, a fermented drink, made of barley or raisins.

10. I retain this venerable blunder: the right form is Samúm, from Samm, the poison-wind.

11. *Koran,* xxiv. 39. The word "Saráb" (mirage) is found in Isaiah (xxxv. 7) where the passage should be rendered "And the mirage (sharab) shall become a lake" (not, "and the parched ground shall become a pool"). The Hindus prettily call it "Mrigatrishná"=the thirst of the deer.

12. A name of Allah.

13. Arab. "Kintár"=a hundredweight (*i.e.,* 100 lbs.), about 98¾ lbs. avoir. Hence the French *quintal* and its congeners (Littré).

14. *i.e.,* "from Shám (Syria) to (the land of) Adnan," ancestor of the Naturalized Arabs, that is to say, to Arabia.

15. *Koran,* lii. 21. "Every man is given in pledge for that which he shall have wrought."

16. There is a constant clerical confusion in the texts between "Arar" (Juniperus Oxycedrus used by the Greeks for the images of their gods) and "Marmar" marble or alabaster, in the Talmud "Marmora"=marble, evidently from μάρμαρος= brilliant, the brilliant stone.

17. These Ifritical names are chosen for their *bizarrerie.* "Al-Dáhish"=the Amazed; and "Al-A'amash"=one with weak eyes always watering.

18. The Arabs have no word for million; so Messer Marco Miglione could not have learned it from them. On the other hand the Hindus have more quadrillions than modern Europe.

19. This formula, according to Moslems, would begin with the beginning "There is no iláh but Allah and Adam is the Apostle (rasúl=one sent, a messenger; not nabí=prophet) of Allah." And so on with Noah, Moses, David (not Solomon as a rule) and Jesus, to Mohammed.

20. This son of Barachia has been noticed in previous instances. The text embroiders the Koranic chapter xxvii.

21. The Bresl. Edit. (vi. 371) reads "Samm-hu"=his poison, prob. a clerical error for "Sahmhu"=his shaft. It was a duel with the "Shiháb" or falling stars, the meteors which are popularly supposed, I have said, to be the arrows shot by the angels against devils and evil spirits when they approach too near Heaven in order to overhear divine secrets.

22. A fanciful name for a sea, from the Latin "Carcer" (?).

23. Andalusian=Spanish, the Vandal-land, a term accepted by the Moslem invader.

24. This fine description will remind the traveller of the old Haurani towns deserted since the sixth century, which a silly writer miscalled the "Giant Cities of Bashan." I have never seen anything weirder than a moonlight night in one of these strong places whose masonry is perfect as when first built, the snowy light pouring on the jet-black basalt and the breeze sighing and the jackal wailing in the desert around.

25. "Zanj," I have said, is the Arab. form of the Persian "Zangbar" (=Black-land), our Zanzibar. Those who would know more of the etymology will consult my *Zanzibar*, etc., chap. i.

26. Arab. "Tanjah"=Strabo Τίγγις (derivation uncertain), Tingitania, Tangiers. But why the terminal *s*?

27. Or Amidah, by the Turks called "Kara (black) Amid" from the colour of the stones; and the Arabs "Diyar-bakr" (Diarbekir), a name which they also give to the whole province—Mesopotamia.

28. Mayyáfárikín, an episcopal city in Diyar-bakr: the natives are called Fárikí; hence the abbreviation in the text.

29. Arab. "Ayát al-Naját," certain Koranic verses which act as talismans, such as, "And wherefore should we not put our

trust in Allah?" (xiv. 15); "Say thou, 'Naught shall befall us save what Allah hath decreed for us,' " (ix. 51), and sundry others.

30. These were the "Brides of the Treasure," alluded to in the story of Hasan of Bassorah and elsewhere.

31. Arab. "Ishárah," which may also mean beckoning. Easterns reverse our process: we wave hand or finger towards ourselves; they towards the object; and our fashion represents to them, Go away!

32. *i.e.*, musing a long time and a longsome.

33. Arab. "Dihlíz" from the Persian. This is the long dark passage which leads to the inner or main gate of an Eastern city, and which is built up before a siege. It is usually furnished with Mastabah-benches of wood and masonry, and forms a favourite lounge in hot weather. Hence Lot and Moses sat and stood in the gate, and here man speaks with his enemies.

34. The names of colours are as loosely used by the Arabs as by the Classics of Europe; for instance, a light grey is called a "blue or a green horse." Much nonsense has been written upon the colours in Homer by men who imagine that the semi-civilized determine tints as we do. They see them but they do not name them, having no occasion for the words. As I have noticed, however, the Arabs have a complete terminology for the varieties of horse-hues. In our day we have witnessed the birth of colours, named by the dozen, because of the requirements of women's dress.

35. [In a note explaining "Davidean" in a tale not included in this edition Burton wrote:] All Prophets had some manual trade and that of David was making coats of mail, which he invented, for before his day men used plate-armour. So "Allah softened the iron for him" and in his hands it became like wax (*Koran,* xxi., xxxiv., etc.). Hence a good coat of mail is called "Davidean." I have noticed (*First Footsteps,* p. 33 and elsewhere) the homage paid to the blacksmith on the principle which made Mulciber (Malik Kabir) a god. The myth of David inventing mail possibly arose from his peculiarly fighting career. Moslems venerate Dáúd on account of his extraordinary devotion; nor has this view of his character ceased: a modern divine preferred him to "all characters in history."

36. Arab. "Khwárazm," the land of the Chorasmioi, who are

mentioned by Herodotus (iii. 93) and a host of classical ge-
ographers. They place it in Sogdiana (hod. Sughd) and it
corresponds with the Khiva country.

37. Arab. "Burka'," usually applied to a woman's face-veil and
hence to the covering of the Ka'abah, which is the "Bride of
Meccah."

38. Alluding to the trick played upon Bilkís by Solomon who
had heard that her legs were hairy like those of an ass: he
laid down a pavement of glass over flowing water in which
fish were swimming and thus she raised her skirts as she approached him and he saw that the report was true. Hence, as
I have said, the depilatory. (*Koran*, xxvii.)

39. I understand the curiously carved windows cut in ara-
besque-work of marble (India) or basalt (the Haurán) and
provided with small panes of glass set in emeralds where
tinfoil would be used by the vulgar.

40. Arab. "Bulád" from the Pers. "Pulád." Hence the name of the
famous Druze family "Jumblat," a corruption of "Ján-pulád"=
Life o' Steel.

41. Pharaoh, so called in Koran (xxxviii. 11) because he tortured
men by fastening them to four stakes driven into the ground.
Sale translates "the contriver of the stakes" and adds, "Some
understand the word figuratively, of the firm establishment
of Pharaoh's kingdom, because the Arabs fix their tents with
stakes; but they may possibly intend that prince's obstinacy
and hardness of heart." I may note that in "Tasawwuf," or
Moslem Gnosticism, Pharaoh represents, like Prometheus
and Job, the typical creature who upholds his own dignity
and rights in presence and despight of the Creator. Sáhib the
Súfí declares that the secret of man's soul (*i.e.*, its emanation)
was first revealed when Pharaoh declared himself god; and
Al-Ghazálí sees in his claim the most noble aspiration to the
divine, innate in the human spirit. (*Dabistan*, vol. iii.)

42. In the Calc. Edit. "Tarmuz, son of the daughter," etc. According to the Arabs, Tadmur (Palmyra) was built by Queen
Tadmurah, daughter of Hassán bin Uzaynah.

43. It is only by some such drought that I can account for the
survival of those marvellous Haurani cities in the great valley S. E. of Damascus.

44. So Moses described his own death and burial.

45. Arab. "Jum'ah" (=the assembly) so called because the Gen-

eral Resurrection will take place on that day and it witnessed the creation of Adam. Both these reasons are evidently after-thoughts; as the Jews received a divine order to keep Saturday, and the Christians, at their own sweet will, transferred the weekly rest-day to Sunday, wherefore the Moslem preferred Friday. Sabbatarianism, however, is unknown to Al-Islam and business is interrupted, by Koranic order (lxii. 9–10), only during congregational prayers in the Mosque. The most a Mohammedan does is not to work or travel till after public service. But the Moslem hardly wants a "day of rest"; whereas a Christian, especially in the desperately dull routine of daily life and toil, without a gleam of light to break the darkness of his civilized and most unhappy existence, distinctly requires it.

46. Mankind, which sees itself everywhere and in everything, must create its own analogues in all the elements, air (Sylphs), fire (Jinn), water (Mermen and Mermaids) and earth (Kobolds). These merwomen were of course seals or manatees, as the wild women of Hanno were gorillas.

The Lady and Her Five Suitors

1. This witty tale, ending somewhat grossly here, has overwandered the world. First we find it in the *Kathá S. S.* where Upakoshá, the merry wife of Vararuchi, disrobes her suitors, a family priest, a commander of the guard and the prince's tutor, under plea of the bath and stows them away in baskets which suggest Falstaff's "buck-basket." In Miss Stokes' *Indian Fairy Tales* the fair wife of an absent merchant plays a similar notable prank upon the Kotwal, the Wazir, the Kazi and the King; and akin to this is the exploit of Temal Rámákistnan, the Madrasi Tyl Eulenspiegel and Scogin who by means of a lady saves his life from the Rajah and the High Priest. Mr. G. H. Damant (pp. 357–360 of the *Indian Antiquary* of 1873) relates the "Tale of the Touchstone," a legend of Dinahpur, wherein a woman "sells" her four admirers. In the Persian Tales ascribed to the Dervish "Mokles" (Mukhlis) of Isfahan, the lady Aruyá tricks and exposes a Kazi, a doctor and a governor. Boccaccio (viii. 1) has the story of a lady who shut up her gallant in a chest with her husband's sanction; and a similar tale (ix. 1) of Rinuccio and Alexander

with the corpse of Scannadeo (Throkh-god). Hence a Lydgate (circ. A.D. 1430) derived the plot of his metrical tale of "The Lady Prioress and her Three Sisters"; which was modified in the Netherlandish version by the introduction of the Long Wapper, a Flemish Robin Goodfellow. Followed in English the metrical tale of "The Wright's Chaste Wife," by Adam of Cobham (edited by Mr. Furnivall from a MS. of circ. A.D. 1460) where the victims are a lord, a steward and a proctor. See also "The Master-Maid" in Dr. (now Sir George) Dasent's *Popular Tales from the Norse.* Mr. Clouston, who gives these details more fully, mentions a similar Scottish story concerning a lascivious monk and the chaste wife of a miller.

2. When Easterns sit down to a drinking bout, which means to get drunk as speedily and pleasantly as possible, they put off dresses of dull colours and robe themselves in clothes supplied by the host, of the brightest he may have, especially yellow, green and red of different shades. So the lady's proceeding was not likely to breed suspicion: although her tastes were somewhat fantastic and like Miss Julia's—peculiar.

3. Arab. "Najásah," meaning anything unclean which requires ablution before prayer. Unfortunately mucus is not of the number, so the common Moslem is very offensive in the matter of nose.

4. Here the word "la'an" is used which most Moslems express by some euphemism. The vulgar Egyptian says "Na'al" (*Sapré* and *Sapristi* for *Sacré* and *Sacristie*); the Hindostani use the expression "I send him the three letters"—lám, ayn and nún.

JUDAR AND HIS BRETHREN

1. The name is old and classical Arabic: in Antar the young Amazon Jaydá was called Judar in public (Story of Jaydá and Khálid). It is also, as will be seen, the name of a quarter in Cairo, and men are often called after such places, *e.g.*, Al-Jubní from the Súk al-Jubn in Damascus. The story is exceedingly Egyptian and the style abounds in Cairene vulgarisms; especially in the Bresl. Edit. (ix. 311).

2. Had the merchant left his property to be divided after his

death and not made a will the widow would have had only one-eighth instead of a fourth.

3. Lit. "from tyrant to tyrant," *i.e.,* from official to official, Al-Zalamah, the "tyranny" of popular parlance.

4. The coin is omitted in the text but it is evidently the "Nusf" or half-dirham. Lane (iii. 235), noting that the dinar is worth 170 "nusfs" in this tale, thinks that it was written (or copied?) after the Osmanli Conquest of Egypt. Unfortunately he cannot tell the precise period when the value of the small change fell so low.

5. Arab. "Yaum mubárak!" still a popular exclamation.

6. *i.e.,* of the door of daily bread.

7. Arab. "Sírah," a small fish differently described (De Sacy, *Relation de l'Egypte par Abd-allatif,* pp. 278–288: Lane, *Nights,* iii. 234). It is not found in Sonnini's list.

8. A tank or lakelet in the southern part of Cairo, long ago filled up; Von Hammer believes it inherited the name of the old Charon's Lake of Memphis, over which corpses were ferried.

9. Thus making the agreement a kind of religious covenant; as Catholics would recite a Pater or an Ave Maria.

10. Arab. "Yá miskín"=O poor devil; mesquin, meschino, words evidently derived from the East.

11. Plur. of Maghribí, a Western man, a Moor. I have already derived the word through the Lat. "Maurus" from Maghribiyún. Europeans being unable to pronounce the Ghayn (or gh like the modern Cairenes) would turn it into "Ma'ariyún." They are mostly of the Maliki school (for which see Sale) and are famous as magicians and treasure-finders. Amongst the suite of the late Amir Abd al-Kadir, who lived many years and died in Damascus, I found several men profoundly versed in Eastern spiritualism and occultism.

12. The names are respectively, Slave of the Salvation; of the One (God); of the Eternal; of the Compassionate; and of the Loving.

13. *i.e.,* "the most profound"; the root is that of "Bátiní," a gnostic, a reprobate.

14. *i.e.,* the Tall One.

15. The loud-pealing or (ear-) breaking Thunder.

16. Arab. "Fás and Miknás" which the writer evidently regards as one city. "Fás" means a hatchet, from the tradition of one

having been found, says Ibn Sa'íd, when digging the base, under the founder Idrís bin Idrís (A.D. 808). His sword was placed on the pinnacle of the minaret built by the Imám Abu Ahmad bin Abi Bakr enclosed in a golden étui studded with pearls and precious stones. From the local pronunciation "Fes" is derived the name of the red cap of the nearer Moslem East (see Ibn Batutah, p. 230).

17. Arab. "Al-Khurj," whence the Span. Las Alforjas.

18. Arab. "Kabáb," mutton or lamb cut into small squares and grilled upon skewers: it is the roast meat of the nearer East where, as in the West, men have not learned to cook meat so as to preserve all its flavour. This is found in the "Asa'o" of the Argentine Gaucho who broils the flesh while still quivering and before the fibre has time to set. Hence it is perfectly tender, if the animal be young, and has a "meaty" taste that is usually half lost by keeping.

19. This is the equivalent of our puritanical "Mercy."

20. Arab. "Bukjah," from the Persian Bukcheh: a favourite way of keeping fine clothes in the East is to lay them folded in a piece of rough long-cloth with pepper and spices to drive away moths.

21. This is always specified, for respectable men go out of town on horseback, never on "foot-back," as our friends the Boers say. I have seen a Syrian put to sore shame when compelled by politeness to walk with me, and every acquaintance he met addressed him, "Anta Zalamah!"—What! afoot?

22. This tale, including the Enchanted Sword which slays whole armies, was adopted in Europe as we see in Straparola (iv. 3), and the "Water of Life" which the Grimms found in Hesse, etc., *Gammer Grethel's German Popular Stories,* Edgar Taylor, Bells, 1878; and now published in fuller form as *Grimm's Household Tales,* by Mrs. Hunt, with Introduction by A. Lang, 2 vols. 8vo, 1884. It is curious that so biting and carping a critic, who will condescend to notice a misprint in another's book, should lay himself open to general animadversion by such a rambling farrago of half-digested knowledge as that which composes Mr. Andrew Lang's Introduction.

23. These retorts of Judar are exactly what a sharp Egyptian Fellah would say on such occasions.

24. Arab. "Salámát," plur. of Salam, a favourite Egyptian welcome.

25. This sentence expresses a Moslem idea which greatly puzzles strangers. Arabic has no equivalent of our "Thank you" (Kassara 'llah Khayr-ak being a mere blessing—Allah increase thy weal!), nor can Al-Islam express gratitude save by a periphrasis. The Moslem acknowledges a favour by blessing the donor and by wishing him increase of prosperity. "May thy shadow never be less!" means, Mayest thou always extend to me thy shelter and protection. I have noticed this before but it merits repetition. Strangers, and especially Englishmen, are very positive and very much mistaken upon a point, which all who have to do with Egyptians and Arabs ought thoroughly to understand. Old dwellers in the East know that the theory of ingratitude in no way interferes with the sense of gratitude innate in man (and beast) and that the "lively sense of favours to come," is as quick in Orient land as in Europe.

26. Outside this noble gate, the Bab al-Nasr, there is a great cemetery wherein, by the by, lies Burckhardt, my predecessor as a Hájj to Meccah and Al-Medinah. Hence many beggars are always found squatting in its neighbourhood.

27. Friends sometimes walk alongside the rider holding the stirrup in sign of affection and respect, especially to the returning pilgrim.

28. Equivalent to our Alas! It is a woman's word never used by men; and foreigners must be most careful of this distinction under pain of incurring something worse than ridicule. I remember an officer in the Bombay Army who, having learned Hindostani from women, always spoke of himself in the feminine and hugely scandalized the Sepoys.

29. *i.e.,* a neighbour. The "quarters" of a town in the East are often on the worst of terms. See my *Pilgrimage*.

30. In the patriarchal stage of society the mother waits upon her adult sons. Even in Dalmatia I found, in many old-fashioned houses, the ladies of the family waiting upon the guests. Very pleasant, but somewhat startling at first.

31. Here the apodosis would be "We can all sup together."

32. Arab. "Záwiyah" (=oratory), which is to a Masjid what a chapel is to a church.

33. Arab. "Kasr," prop. a palace: so the Tuscan peasant speaks of his "palazzo."

34. This sale of a free-born Moslem was mere felony. But many centuries later Englishmen used to be sold and sent to the plantations in America.

35. Arab. "Kawwás," lit. an archer, suggesting *les archers de la Sainte Hermandade*. In former days it denoted a serjeant, an apparitor, an officer who executed magisterial orders. In modern Egypt he became a policeman (*Pilgrimage*, i. 29). As "Cavass" he appears in gorgeous uniform and sword, an orderly attached to public offices and Consulates.

36. A purely imaginary King.

37. The Bresl. Edit. (ix. 370) here and elsewhere uses the word "Nútiyá"=Nautá, for the common Bahríyah or Malláh.

38. Arab. "Tawáf," the name given to the sets (Ashwát) of seven circuits with the left shoulder presented to the Holy House; that is walking "widdershins" or "against the sun" ("with the sun" being like the movement of a watch). For the requisites of this rite see *Pilgrimage*, iii. 234.

39. Arab. "Akh"; brother has a wide signification amongst Moslems and may be used in addressing or referring to any of the Saving Faith.

40. Said by the master when dismissing a servant and meaning, "I have not failed in my duty to thee!" The answer is, "Allah acquit thee thereof!"

41. A Moslem prison is like those of Europe a century ago; to think of it gives gooseflesh. Easterns laugh at our idea of penitentiary and the Arabs of Bombay call it "Al-Bistán" (the Garden) because the court contains a few trees and shrubs. And with them a garden always suggests an idea of Paradise. There are indeed only two efficacious forms of punishment all the world over, corporal for the poor and fines for the rich, the latter being the severer form.

42. *i.e.*, he shall answer for this.

43. A pun upon "Khalíyah" (bee-hive) and "Khaliyah" (empty). Khalíyah is properly a hive of bees with a honey-comb in the hollow of a tree-trunk, opposed to Kawwárah, hive made of clay or earth (Al-Hariri; Ass. of Tiflis). There are many other terms, for Arabs are curious about honey. *Pilgrimage*, iii. 110.

44. Lane (iii. 237) supposes by this title that the author referred his tale to the days of the Caliphate. "Commander of the

Faithful" was, I have said, the style adopted by Omar in order to avoid the clumsiness of "Caliph" (successor) of the Caliph (Abu Bakr) of the Apostle of Allah.

45. Eastern thieves count four modes of housebreaking; (1) picking out burnt bricks; (2) cutting through unbaked bricks; (3) wetting a mud wall and (4) boring through a wooden wall (Vikram and the Vampire p. 172).

46. Arab. "Zabbat," literally a lizard (fem.), also a wooden lock, the only one used throughout Egypt. An illustration of its curious mechanism is given in Lane (*Modern Egypt.*, Introduc.).

47. Arab. "Dabbús." The Eastern mace is well known to English collectors; it is always of metal, and mostly of steel, with a short handle like our facetiously called "life-preserver." The head is in various forms, the simplest a ball, smooth and round, or broken into sundry high and angular ridges like a melon, and in select weapons shaped like the head of some animal, bull, etc.

48. The red habit is a sign of wrath and vengeance and the Persian Kings like Fath Al Shah, used to wear it when about to order some horrid punishment, such as the "Shakk"; in this a man was hung up by his heels and cut into two from the fork downwards to the neck, when a turn of the chopper left that untouched. White robes denoted peace and mercy as well as joy. The "white" hand and "black" hand have been explained. A "white death" is quiet and natural, with forgiveness of sins. A "black death" is violent and dreadful, as by strangulation; a "green death" is robing in rags and patches like a dervish; and a "red death" is by war or bloodshed (A. P., ii. 670). Among the mystics it is the resistance of man to his passions.

49. This in the East is the way *"pour se faire valoir"*; whilst Europeans would hold it a mere "bit of impudence," aping dignity.

50. The Chief Mufti or Doctor of the Law, an appointment first made by the Osmanli Mohammed II., when he captured Constantinople in A.D. 1453. Before that time the functions were discharged by the Kázi al-Kuzát (Kazi-in-Chief), the Chancellor.

51. So called because here lived the makers of crossbows (Arab. Bunduk now meaning a fire-piece, musket, etc.). It is the modern district about the well-known Khan al-Hamzawi.

52. Pronounced "Goodareeyyah," and so called after one of the troops of the Fatimite Caliphs. The name "Yamániyah" is probably due to the story-teller's inventiveness.

53. I have noted that as a rule in The Nights poetical justice is administered with much rigour and exactitude. Here, however, the tale-teller allows the good brother to be slain by the two wicked brothers as he permitted the adulterous queens to escape the sword of Kamar al-Zaman. Dr. Steingass brings to my notice that I have failed to do justice to the story of Sharrkán, where I note that the interest is injured by the gratuitous incest. But this has a deeper meaning and a grander artistic effect. Sharrkán begins with most unbrotherly feelings towards his father's children by a second wife. But Allah's decree forces him to love his half-sister despite himself, and awe and repentance convert the savage, who joys at the news of his brother's reported death, to a loyal and devoted subject of the same brother. But Judar with all his goodness proved himself an arrant softy and was no match for two atrocious villains. And there may be overmuch of forgiveness as of every other good thing.

54. In such case the " 'iddah" would be four months and ten days.

55. Not quite true. Weil's German version, from a MS. in the Ducal Library of Gotha, gives the "Story of Judar of Cairo and Mahmud of Tunis" in a very different form. It has been pleasantly "translated (from the German) and edited" by Mr. W. F. Kirby, of the British Museum, under the title of *The New Arabian Nights* (London: W. Swan Sonnenschein & Co.), and the author kindly sent me a copy. *New Arabian Nights* seems now to have become a fashionable title applied without any signification: such at least is the case with the pleasant collection of Nineteenth Century Novelettes, published under that designation by Mr. Robert Louis Stevenson, Chatto and Windus, Piccadilly, 1884.

JULNAR THE SEA-BORN AND HER SON KING BADR BASIM OF PERSIA

1. In the Macnaghten Edition "Shahzamán," a corruption of Sháh Zamán=King of the Age.

2. [In a note to a tale not included in this edition Burton

wrote:] Antar notes the "Spears of Khatt" and "Rudaynian lances." Rudaynah is said to have been the wife of one Samhár, the Ferrara of lances; others make her the wife of Al-Ka'azab and hold Samhár to be a town in Abyssinia where the best weapons were manufactured.

3. *i.e.*, bathe her and apply cosmetics to remove all traces of travel.

4. These pretentious and curious displays of coquetry are not uncommon in handsome slave-girls when newly bought; and it is a kind of pundonor to humour them. They may also refuse their favours and a master who took possession of their persons by brute force would be blamed by his friends, men and women. Even the most despotic of despots, Fath Ali Shah of Persia, put up with refusals from his slave-girls and did not, as would the mean-minded, give them in marriage to the grooms or cooks of the palace.

5. Such continence is rarely shown by the young Jallabs or slave-traders; when older they learn how much money is lost with the chattel's virginity.

6. Midwives in the East, as in the less civilized parts of the West, have many nostrums for divining the sex of the unborn child.

7. Arabic (which has no written "g") from Pers. Gulnár (Gul-i-anár), pomegranate-flower, the "Gulnare" of Byron who learnt his Orientalism at the Mekhitarist (Armenian) Convent, Venice. I regret to see the little honour now paid to the gallant poet in the land where he should be honoured the most. The systematic depreciation was begun by the late Mr. Thackeray, perhaps the last man to value the noble independence of Byron's spirit; and it has been perpetuated, I regret to see, by better judges. These critics seem wholly to ignore the fact that Byron founded a school which covered Europe from Russia to Spain, from Norway to Sicily, and which from England passed over to the two Americas. This exceptional success, which has not yet fallen even to Shakespeare's lot, was due to genius only, for the poet almost ignored study and poetic art. His great misfortune was being born in England under the Georgium Sidus. Any Continental people would have regarded him as one of the prime glories of his race.

8. Arab. "Fí al-Kamar," which Lane renders "in the moonlight." It seems to me that the allusion is to the Comorin Islands; but the sequel speaks simply of an island.

9. Arab. " 'Alà Kulli hál," a popular phrase, like the Anglo-American "anyhow."

10. In the text the name does not appear till near the end of the tale.

11. *i.e.*, Full moon smiling.

12. I quote Mr. Payne.

13. This manner of listening is not held dishonourable amongst Arabs or Easterns generally; who, however, hear as little good of themselves as Westerns declare in proverb.

14. Arab. "Hasab wa nasab," before explained as inherited degree and acquired dignity. Arab. "Hasab" (=quantity), the honour a man acquires for himself; opposed to "Nasab" (genealogy), honours inherited from ancestry: the Arabic well expresses my old motto (adopted by Chinese Gordon),

Honour, not Honours.

15. Arab. "Mujájat"=spittle running from the mouth: hence Lane, "is like running saliva," which, in poetry is not pretty.

16. Arab. and Heb. "Salmandra" from Pers. Samandal (—dar—duk—dun, etc.), a Salamander, a mouse which lives in fire, some say a bird in India and China and others confuse with the chameleon (Bochart, *Hierozoicon,* Part ii. chap. vi).

17. Arab. "Mahá" one of the four kinds of wild cows or bovine antelopes, bubalus, Antelope defassa, A. leucoryx, etc.

18. I quote Lane (iii. 274) by way of variety; although I do not like his "bowels."

19. The last verse (286) of chap. ii. The Cow: "compelleth" in the sense of "burdeneth."

20. Salih's speeches are euphuistic.

21. From the Fatihah.

22. A truly Eastern saying, which ignores the "old maids" of the West.

23. *i.e.*, naming her before the lieges as if the speaker were her and his superior. It would have been more polite not to have gone beyond "the unique pearl and the hoarded jewel": the offensive part of the speech was using the girl's name.

24. Meaning emphatically that one and all were nobodies.
25. Arab. Badr, the usual pun.
26. Arab. "Kirát" (χεράτιον), the bean of the *Abrus precatorius,* used as a weight in Arabia and India and as a bead for decoration in Africa. It is equal to four Kamhahs or wheat-grains and about 3 grs. avoir.; and being the twenty-fourth of a miskal, it is applied to that proportion of everything. Thus the Arabs say of a perfect man, "He is of four-and-twenty Kirat" *i.e.,* pure gold.
27. The (she) myrtle: Kazimirski (A. de Biberstein) *Dictionnaire Arabe-Français* (Paris, Maisonneuve, 1867) gives Marsín=Rose de Jericho: myrtle.
28. Needless to note that the fowler had a right to expect a return present worth double or treble the price of his gift. Such is the universal practice of the East: in the West the extortioner says, "I leave it to you, sir!"
29. And she does tell him all that the reader well knows.
30. This was for sprinkling him, but the texts omit that operation. Arabic has distinct terms for various forms of metamorphosis. "Naskh" is change from a lower to a higher, as beast to man; "Maskh" (the common expression) is the reverse; "Raskh" is from animate to inanimate (man to stone) and "Faskh" is absolute wasting away to corruption.
31. I render this improbable detail literally: its only significance can be that the ship was dashed against a rock.
32. Who was probably squatting on his shop-counter. The "Bakkál" (who must not be confounded with the *épicier*), lit. "vender of herbs"=greengrocer, and according to Richardson used incorrectly for Baddál (?) vendor of provisions. Popularly it is applied to a seller of oil, honey, butter and fruit, like the Ital. "Pizzicagnolo"=Salsamentarius, and in North-West Africa to an inn-keeper.
33. Here the Shaykh is mistaken: he should have said, "The Sun in old Persian." "Almanac" simply makes nonsense of the Arabian Circe's name. In Arab. it is "Takwím," whence the Span. and Port. "Tacuino": in Heb. Hakamathá-Takunah= sapientia dispositionis astrorum (*Asiat. Research,* iii. 120).
34. *i.e.,* for thy daily expenses.
35. *Un adolescent aime toutes les femmes.* Man is by nature polygamic whereas woman as a rule is monogamic and polyandrous only when tired of her lover. For the man, as has been truly

said, loves the woman, but the love of the woman is for the love of the man.

36. I have already noted that the heroes and heroines of Eastern love-tales are always *bonnes fourchettes:* they eat and drink hard enough to scandalize the sentimental amourist of the West; but it is understood that this abundant diet is necessary to qualify them for the Herculean labours of the love night.

37. Here again a little excision is necessary; the reader already knows all about it.

38. Arab. "Hiss," prop. speaking a perception (as of sound or motion) as opposed to "Hadas," a surmise or opinion without proof.

39. Arab. "Sawík," the old and modern name for native frumenty, green grain (mostly barley) toasted, pounded, mixed with dates or sugar and eaten on journeys when cooking is impracticable. M. C. de Perceval (iii. 54), gives it a different and now unknown name; and Mr. Lane also applies it to "ptisane." It named the "Day of Sawaykah" (for which see *Pilgrimage,* ii. 19), called by our popular authors the "War of the Meal-sacks."

40. Mr. Keightley (H. 122–24 *Tales and Popular Fictions,* a book now somewhat obsolete) remarks, "There is nothing said about the bridle in the account of the sale (*infra*), but I am sure that in the original tale, Badr's misfortunes must have been owing to his having parted with it. In Chaucer's *Squier's Tale* the bridle would also appear to have been of some importance." He quotes a story from the *Notti Piacevoli* of Straparola, the Milanese, published at Venice in 1550. And there is a popular story of the kind in Germany.

41. Here, for the first time we find the name of the mother who has often been mentioned in the story. Faráshah is the fem. or singular form of "Farásh," a butterfly, a moth. Lane notes that his Shaykh gives it the very unusual sense of "a locust."

42. Punning upon Jauharah="a jewel," a name which has an Hibernian smack.

43. In the old version "All the lovers of the Magic Queen resumed their pristine forms as soon as she ceased to live"; moreover, they were all sons of kings, princes, or persons of high degree.

KHALIFAH THE FISHERMAN OF BAGHDAD

1. This is so rare, even amongst the poorest classes in the East, that it is mentioned with some emphasis.

2. A beauty amongst the Egyptians, not the Arabs.

3. True Fellah "chaff."

4. Alluding to the well-known superstition, which has often appeared in The Nights, that the first object seen in the morning, such as a crow, a cripple, or a cyclops, determines the fortunes of the day. Notices in Eastern literature are as old as the days of the Hitopadesa; and there is a something instinctive in the idea to a race of early risers. At an hour when the senses are most impressionable the aspect of unpleasant spectacles has double effect.

5. Arab. "Masúkah," the stick used for driving cattle, *bâton gourdin* (Dozy). Lane applies the word to a wooden plank used for levelling the ground.

6. *i.e.,* the words I am about to speak to thee.

7. Arab. "Sahífah," which may mean "page" (Lane) or "book" (Payne).

8. Pronounce, "Abussa'ádát"=Father of Prosperities: Lane imagines that it came from the Jew's daughter being called "Sa'adat." But the latter is the Jew's wife and the word in the text is plural.

9. Arab. "Furkh samak," lit. a fish-chick, an Egyptian vulgarism.

10. Arab. "Al-Rasíf"; usually a river quay, levée, an embankment. Here it refers to the great dyke which distributed the Tigris water.

11. Arab. "Dajlah." It is evidently the origin of the biblical "Hiddekel," "Hid"=fierceness, swiftness.

12. Arab. "Bayáz," a kind of Silurus (*S. Bajad,* Forsk.) which Sonnini calls Bayatto, Saksatt and Hébedé; also Bogar (Bakar, an ox). The skin is lubricous, the flesh is soft and insipid and the fish often grows to the size of a man. Captain Speke and I found huge specimens in the Tanganyika Lake.

13. Arab. "Mu'allim," vulg. "M'allim," prop.=teacher, master, esp. of a trade, a craft. In Egypt and Syria it is a civil address to a Jew or a Christian, as Hájj is to a Moslem.

14. Arab. "Gharámah," an exaction, usually on the part of government like a corvée, etc. The Europeo-Egyptian term is *avania* (Ital.) or *avanie* (French).

15. Arab. "Sayyib-hu," an Egyptian vulgarism found also in Syria. Hence Sáibah, a woman who lets herself go (a-whoring), etc. It is syn. with "Dashar," which Dozy believes to be a softening of Jashar; as Jashsh became Dashsh.

16. The Silurus is generally so called in English on account of the length of its feeler-acting mustachios.

17. This extraordinary confusion of two distinct religious mythologies cannot be the result of ignorance. Educated Moslems know at least as much as Christians do, on these subjects, but the Ráwi or story-teller speaks to the "Gallery." In fact it becomes a mere "chaff" and The Nights give some neat specimens of our modern linguistics.

18. "Al-Siddíkah" (fem.) is a title of Ayishah, who, however, does not appear to have deserved it.

19. The Jew's wife.

20. Here is a *double entendre*. The fisherman meant a word or two. The Jew understood the Shibboleth of the Moslem Creed, popularly known as the "Two Words"—I testify that there is no Ilah (god) but Allah (the God) and I testify that Mohammed is the Messenger of Allah. Pronouncing this formula would make the Jew a Moslem. Some writers are surprised to see a Jew ordering a Moslem to be flogged; but the former was rich and the latter was poor. Even during the worst days of Jewish persecutions their money-bags were heavy enough to lighten the greater part, if not the whole, of their disabilities. And the Moslem saying is, "The Jew is never your (Moslem or Christian) equal: he must be either above you or below you." This is high, because unintentional, praise of the (self-) Chosen People.

21. He understands by the "two words" (Kalmatáni) the Moslem's double profession of belief; and Khalifah's reply embodies the popular idea that the number of Moslems (who will be saved) is preordained and that no art of man can add to it or take from it.

22. Arab. "Mamarr al-Tujjár" (passing-place of the traders) which Lane renders "A chamber within the place through which the merchants passed." At the end of the tale (the 845th night) we find him living in a Khan and the Bresl. Edit. makes him dwell in a magazine (*i.e.*, ground-floor storeroom) of a ruined Khan.

23. The text is somewhat too concise and the meaning is that

the fumes of the Hashish he had eaten ("his mind under the influence of hasheesh," says Lane) suggested to him, etc.

24. Arab. "Mamrak," either a simple aperture in ceiling or roof for light and air or a more complicated affair of lattice-work and plaster; it is often octagonal and crowned with a little dome. Lane calls it "Memrak," after the debased Cairene pronunciation, and shows its base in his sketch of a Ka'áh (*M.E.*, Introduction).

25. Arab. "Kamar." This is a practice especially amongst pilgrims. In Hindostan the girdle, usually a waist-shawl, is called Kammar-band, our old "Cummerbund." Easterns are too sensible not to protect the pit of the stomach, that great ganglionic centre, against sun, rain and wind, and now our soldiers in India wear flannel-belts on the march.

26. Arab. "Fa-immá 'alayhá wa-immá bihá," *i.e.*, whether (luck go) against it or (luck go) with it.

27. "O vilest of sinners!" alludes to the thief. "A general plunge into worldly pursuits and pleasures announced the end of the pilgrimage ceremonies. All the devotees were now 'white-washed'—the book of their sins was a *tabula rasa:* too many of them lost no time in making a new departure down South and in opening a fresh account" (*Pilgrimage*, iii. 365). I have noticed that my servant at Jeddah would carry a bottle of Raki, uncovered by a napkin, through the main streets.

28. The copper cucurbits in which Solomon imprisoned the rebellious Jinn, often alluded to in The Nights.

29. *i.e.*, Son of the Chase: it is prob. a corruption of the Persian "Kurnas," a pimp, a cuckold, and introduced by way of chaff, intelligible only to a select few "fast" men.

30. For the name see note 32, in the Tale of Ghánim bin 'Ayyúb where the Caliph's concubine is also drugged by the Lady Zubaydah.

31. Zubaydah, I have said, was the daughter of Ja'afar, son of the Caliph al-Mansur, second Abbaside. The story-teller persistently calls her the daughter of Al-Kásim for some reason of his own.

32. Arab. "Shakhs," a word which has travelled as far as Hindostan.

33. Arab. "Shamlah," described in dictionaries as a cloak cover-

ing the whole body. For Hizám (girdle) the Bresl. Edit. reads "Hirám," vulg. "Ehrám," the waist-cloth, the Pilgrim's attire.

34. He is described by Al-Siyúti (p. 309) as "very fair, tall, handsome and of captivating appearance."

35. Arab. "Uzn al-Kuffah," lit. "Ear of the basket," which vulgar Egyptians pronounce "Wizn," so "Wajh" (face) becomes "Wishsh" and so forth.

36. Arab. "Bi-fardayn"=with two baskets, lit. "two singles," but the context shows what is meant. English *Frail* and French *Fraile* are from Arab. "Farsalah," a parcel (now esp. of coffee beans) evidently derived from the low Lat. "Parcella" (Du Cange, Paris: Firmin Didot, 1845).

37. Arab. "Sátúr," a kind of chopper which here would be used for the purpose of splitting and cleaning and scaling the fish.

38. And, consequently, that the prayer he is about to make will find ready acceptance.

39. Arab. "Ruh bilá Fuzúl" (lit. excess, exceedingly), still a popular phrase.

40. *i.e.*, better give the fish than have my head broken.

41. Said ironicé, a favourite figure of speech with the Fellah: the day began badly and threatened to end unluckily.

42. The penalty of theft.

43. This is the model of a courtly compliment; and it would still be admired wherever Arabs are not "frankified."

44. The instinctive way of juggling with Heaven like our sanding the sugar and going to church.

45. Arab. "Yá Shukayr," from Shakar, being red (clay, etc.): Shukár is an anemone or a tulip and Shukayr is its dim. form. Lane's Shaykh made it a dim. of "Ashkar"=tawny, ruddy (of complexion), so the former writes, "O Shukeyr." Mr. Payne prefers "O Rosy cheeks."

46. For "Sandal," see note 16 for The Tale of Ghanim. Sandalí properly means an Eunuch clean *rasé*, but here Sandal is a p.n.=Sandalwood.

47. Arab. "Yá mumátil," one who retards payment.

48. Arab. "Kirsh al-Nukhál"=Guts of bran, a term little fitted for the handsome and distinguished Persian. But Khalifah is a Fellah-*grazioso* of normal assurance, shrewd withal; he blunders like an Irishman of the last generation and uses the first epithet that comes to his tongue.

49. So the Persian "May your shadow never be less" means, I have said, the shadow which you throw over your servant. Shade, cold water and fresh breezes are the joys of life in arid Arabia.

50. When a Fellah demanded money due to him by the Government of Egypt, he was at once imprisoned for arrears of taxes and thus prevented from being troublesome. I am told that matters have improved under English rule, but I "doubt the fact."

51. This freak is, of course, not historical. The tale-teller introduces it to enhance the grandeur and majesty of Harun al-Rashid, and the vulgar would regard it as a right kingly diversion. Westerns only wonder that such things could be.

52. Uncle of the Prophet: for his death see *Pilgrimage*, ii. 248.

53. First cousin of the Prophet, son of Abú Tálib, a brother of Al-Abbas from whom the Abbasides claimed descent.

54. *i.e.,* I hope thou hast or Allah grant thou have good tidings to tell me.

55. Arab. "Nákhúzah Zulayt." The former, from the Persian Nákhodá or ship-captain which is also used in a playful sense, "a godless wight," one owning no (ná) God (Khudá). Zulayt=a low fellow, blackguard.

56. Yásamín and Narjis, names of slave-girls or eunuchs.

57. Arab. Tamar-hanná, the cheapest of dyes used by the poorest classes. Its smell, I have said, is that of newly mown hay, and is prized like that of the tea-rose.

58. The formula (meaning, "What has he to do here?") is by no means complimentary.

59. Arab. "Jarrah" (pron. "Garrah"), a "jar." See Lane (*M. E.,* chap. v.) who was deservedly reproached by Baron von Hammer for his superficial notices. The "Jarrah" is of pottery, whereas the "Dist" is a large copper cauldron and the Khalkínah one of lesser size.

60. *i.e.,* What a bother thou art, etc.

61. This sudden transformation, which to us seems exaggerated and unnatural, appears in many Eastern stories and in the biographies of their distinguished men, especially by students. A youth cannot master his lessons; he sees a spider climbing a slippery wall and, after repeated falls, succeeding. Allah opens the eyes of his mind, his studies become

easy to him, and he ends with being an Allámah (doctis-simus).

62. Arab. "Bismillah, Námí!" here it is not a blessing but a simple invitation, "Now please go to sleep."

63. The modern ink-case of the Universal East is a lineal descendant of the wooden palette with writing reeds. See an illustration of that of "Amásis, the good god and lord of the two lands" (circ. 1350 b.c.) in British Museum (p. 41, *The Dwellers on the Nile,* by E. A. Wallis Budge, London: 56, Paternoster Row, 1885).

64. Not ironical, as Lane and Payne suppose, but a specimen of inverted speech—Thou art in luck this time!

65. Arab. "Marhúb"=terrible: Lane reads "Mar'úb"=terrified. But the former may also mean, threatened with something terrible.

66. *i.e.,* in Kut al-Kulúb.

67. Lit. to the son of thy paternal uncle, *i.e.,* Mohammed.

68. In the text he tells the whole story beginning with the eunuch and the hundred dinars, the chest, etc.: but—"of no avail is a twice-told tale."

69. *Koran,* xxxix. 54. I have quoted Mr. Rodwell who affects the Arabic formula, omitting the normal copulatives.

70. Easterns find it far easier to "get the chill of poverty out of their bones" than Westerns.

71. Arab. "Dar al-Na'ím." Name of one of the seven stages of the Moslem heaven. This style of inscription dates from the days of the hieroglyphs. A papyrus describing the happy town of Raamses ends with these lines:—

> Daily is there a supply of food:
> Within it gladness doth ever brood
>
>   *   *   *   *
>
> Prolonged, increased; abides there Joy, etc. etc.

ABU KIR THE DYER AND ABU SIR THE BARBER

1. Abu Sír is a manifest corruption of the old Egyptian Pousiri, the Busiris of our classics, and it gives a name to sundry villages in modern Egypt where it is usually pronounced "Búsír." Abu Kír lit.=the Father of Pitch, is also corrupted to

Abou Kir (Bay); and the townlet now marks the site of jolly old Canopus, the Chosen Land of Egyptian debauchery.

2. It is interesting to note the superior gusto with which the Eastern, as well as the Western, tale-teller describes his scoundrels and villains whilst his good men and women are mostly colourless and unpicturesque. So Satan is the true hero of Paradise Lost and by his side God and man are very ordinary; and Mephistopheles is much better society than Faust and Margaret.

3. Arab. "Dukhán," lit.=smoke, here tobacco for the Chibouk, "Timbák" or "Tumbák" being the stronger (Persian and other) variety which must be washed before smoking in the Shíhah or water pipe. Tobacco is mentioned here only and is evidently inserted by some scribe: the "weed" was not introduced into the East before the end of the sixteenth century (about a hundred years after coffee), when it radically changed the manners of society.

4. Which meant that the serjeant, after the manner of such officials, would make him pay dearly before giving up the key. Hence a very severe punishment in the East is to "call in a policeman" who carefully fleeces all those who do not bribe him to leave them in freedom.

5. Arab. "Má Dáhiyatak?" lit. "What is thy misfortune?" The phrase is slighting if not insulting.

6. Amongst Moslems the plea of robbing to keep life and body together would be accepted by a good man like Abu Sir, who still consorted with a self-confessed thief.

7. To make their agreement religiously binding. [Burton here cross-references a note to a tale not included in this edition that reads:] The opening chapter is known as the "Mother of the Book" (as opposed to Yá Sín, the "heart of the Koran"), the "Surat (chapter) of Praise," and the "Surat of repetition" (because twice revealed?) or thanksgiving, or laudation (Al-Masáni) and by a host of other names for which see Mr. Rodwell who, however, should not write "Fatthah" (p. xxv.) nor "Fathah" (xxvii.). The Fátihah, which is to Al-Islam much what the "Paternoster" is to Christendom, consists of seven verses, in the usual Saj'a or rhymed prose, and I have rendered it as follows:—

In the name of the Compassionating, the Compassionate! * Praise be to Allah who all the Worlds made * The Compas-

sionating, the Compassionate * King of the Day of Faith! *
Thee only do we adore and of Thee only do we crave aid *
Guide us to the path which is straight * The path of those for
whom Thy love is great, not those on whom is hate, nor they
that deviate * Amen! O Lord of the Worlds trine.

8. Arab. "Ghaliyún"; many of our names for craft seem connected with Arabic: I have already noted "Carrack"=harrák:
to which add Uskuf, in Morocco pronounced 'Skuff=skiff;
Katírah=a cutter; Bárijah=a barge; etc. etc.

9. The patient is usually lathered in a big basin of tinned brass,
a "Mambrino's helmet" with a break in the rim to fit the
throat; but the poorer classes carry only a small cup with
water instead of soap and water, ignoring the Italian proverb,
"Barba ben saponata mezza fatta"=well lathered is half
shaved. A napkin fringed at either end is usually thrown over
the Figaro's shoulder and used to wipe the razor.

10. Arab. "Nusf." [Burton here cross-references a note to a tale
not included in this edition that reads:] Arab. "Nusf"=half
(a dirham): vulgarly pronounced "nuss," and synonymous
with the Egypt. "Faddah" (=silver), the Greek "Asper," and
the Turkish "paráh." It is the smallest Egyptian coin, made
of very base metal and, there being forty to the piastre, it is
worth nearly a quarter of a farthing.

11. Arab. "Batárikh," the roe (sperm or spawn) of the salted
Fasíkh (fish) and the Búrí (*mugil cephalus*), a salt-water fish
caught in the Nile and considered fair eating. Some write
Butárghá from the old Egyptian town Burát, now a ruin between Tinnis and Damietta (Sonnini).

12. Arab. "Kaptán." [Burton here cross-references a note to a
tale not included in this edition that reads:] From the Ital.
"Capitano."

13. Arab. "Anyáb," plur. of Náb, applied to the grinder teeth but
mostly to the canines or eye teeth, tusks of animals, etc.: opp.
to Saniyah, one of the four central incisors, a camel in the
sixth year and horse, cow, sheep and goat in the fourth year.

14. The coffee like the tobacco is probably due to the scribe; but
the tale appears to be comparatively modern. In The Nights
men eat, drink and wash their hands but do not smoke and
sip coffee like the moderns.

15. Arab. "Mi'lakah" (Bresl. Edit. x. 456). The fork is modern
even in the East and the Moors borrow their term for it from

fourchette. But the spoon, which may have begun with a cockle-shell, dates from the remotest antiquity.

16. Arab. "Sufrah," properly the cloth or leather upon which food is placed. See also note 166 to "The Porter and the Three Ladies of Baghdad."

17. *i.e.*, gaining much one day and little another.

18. Lit. "Rest thyself," *i.e.*, by changing posture.

19. Arab. " 'Unnábi"=between dark yellow and red.

20. Arab. "Nílah," lit.=indigo, but here applied to all the materials for dyeing. The word is Sanskrit, and the growth probably came from India, although during the Crusaders' occupation of Jerusalem it was cultivated in the valley of the lower Jordan. I need hardly say that it has nothing to do with the word "Nile" whose origin is still *sub judice*. And yet I lately met a sciolist who pompously announced to me this philological absurdity as a discovery of his own.

21. Still popular form of "bilking" in the Wakálahs or Caravanserais of Cairo: but as a rule the Bawwáb (porter or doorkeeper) keeps a sharp eye on those he suspects. The evil is increased when women are admitted into these places; so periodical orders for their exclusion are given to the police.

22. Natives of Egypt always hold this diaphoresis a sign that the disease has abated and they regard it rightly in the case of bilious remittents to which they are subject, especially after the hardships and sufferings of a sea-voyage with its alternations of fasting and over-eating.

23. Not simply, "such and such events happened to him" (Lane); but, "a curious chance befel him."

24. Arab. "Harámi," lit.=one who lives on unlawful gains; popularly a thief.

25. Meaning he turned on the water, hot and cold.

26. Men are often seen doing this in the Hammam. The idea is that the skin when free from sebaceous exudation sounds louder under the clapping. Easterns judge much by the taste of the perspiration, especially in horse-training, which consists of hand-gallops for many successive miles. The sweat must not taste over salt and when held between thumb and forefinger and the two drawn apart must not adhere in filaments.

27. Lit. "Aloes for making Nadd"; see vol. i. 364. "Eagle-wood" (the Malay Aigla and Agallochum, the Sansk. Agura) gave

rise to many corruptions as lignum aloes, the Portuguese Páo d' Aguila, etc. "Calamba" or "Calambak" was the finest kind. See Colonel Yule in the *Voyage of Linschoten* (vol. i. 120 and 150) edited for the Hakluyt Soc. (1885) by my learned and most amiable friend, the late Arthur Coke Burnell.

28. The Hammam is one of those unpleasant things which are left "Alà júdi-k"=to thy generosity; and the higher the bather's rank the more he or she is expected to pay. See *Pilgrimage*, i. 103. In 1853 I paid at Cairo 3 piastres and twenty paras, something more than sixpence, but now five shillings would be asked.

29. This is something like the mythical duchess in England who could not believe that the poor were starving when sponge-cakes were so cheap.

30. This magnificent "Bakhshish" must bring water into the mouths of all the bath-men in the coffee-house assembly.

31. *i.e.,* the treasurer did not, as is the custom of such gentry, demand and receive a large "Bakhshish" on the occasion.

32. A fair specimen of clever Fellah chaff.

33. In the first room of the Hammam, called the Maslakh or stripping-place, the keeper sits by a large chest in which he deposits the purses and valuables of his customers and also makes it the *caisse* for the pay. Something of the kind is now done in the absurdly called "Turkish baths" of London.

34. This is the rule in Egypt and Syria and a clout hung over the door shows that women are bathing. I have heard, but only heard, that in times and places when eunuchs went in with the women youths managed by long practice to retract the testicles so as to pass for castratos. It is hard to say what perseverance may not effect in this line; witness Orsini and his abnormal development of hearing, by exercising muscles which are usually left idle.

35. This reference to Allah shows that Abu Sir did not believe his dyer-friend.

36. Arab. "Dawá" (lit. remedy, medicine) the vulgar term: [Burton here cross-references a note to a tale not included in this edition that reads:] This is the popular idea of a bushy "veil of nature" in women: it is always removed by depilatories and vellication. When Bilkis Queen of Sheba discovered her legs by lifting her robe (*Koran*, xxvii.), Solomon was minded to marry her, but would not do so till the devils had by a de-

pilatory removed the hair. The popular preparation (called Núrah) consists of quicklime, 7 parts, and Zirník or orpiment, 3 parts: it is applied in the Hammam to a perspiring skin, and it must be washed off immediately the hair is loosened or it burns and discolours. The rest of the body-pile (Sha'arat opp. to Sha'ar=hair) is eradicated by applying a mixture of boiled honey with turpentine or other gum, and rolling it with the hand till the hair comes off. Men, I have said, remove the pubes by shaving, and pluck the hair of the arm-pits, one of the vestiges of pre-Adamite man. A good depilatory is still a desideratum, the best perfumers of London and Paris have none which they can recommend. The reason is plain: the hair-bulb can be eradicated only by destroying the skin.

37. Arab. "Má Kahara-ní"=or none hath overcome me.

38. Bresl. Edit. "The King of Isbániya." For the "Ishbán" (Spaniards) an ancient people descended from Japhet, son of Noah, and who now are no more, see Al-Mas'udi (Fr. Transl. i. 361). The "Herodotus of the Arabs" recognizes only the "Jalálikah" or Gallicians, thus bearing witness to the antiquity and importance of the Gallego race.

39. Arab. "Sha'r," properly, hair of body, pile, especially the pecten. See Burckhardt (*Prov.* No. 202), "grieving for lack of a cow she made a whip of her bush," said of those who console themselves by building castles in Spain. The "parts below the waist" is the decent Turkish term for the privities.

40. The drowning is a martyr's death, the burning is a foretaste of Hell-fire.

41. Meaning that if the trick had been discovered the Captain would have taken the barber's place. We have seen the Prime Minister superintending the royal kitchen and here the Admiral fishes for the King's table. It is even more naïve than the Court of Alcinöus.

42. Bresl. Edit. xi. 32: *i.e.,* save me from disgrace.

43. Arab. "Khinsir" or "Khinsar," the little finger or the middle finger. In Arabic each has its own name or names which is also that of the corresponding toe, *e.g.,* Ibhám (thumb); Sabbábah, Musabbah or Da'áah (forefinger); Wastá (medius); Binsir (annularis, ring-finger) and Khinsar (minimus). There are also names for the several spaces between the fingers. See the *English Arabic Dictionary* (London: Kegan Paul and

Co., 1881) by the Rev. Dr. Badger, a work of immense labour and research, but which, I fear, has been to the learned author a labour of love not of profit.

44. Meaning of course that the King signed towards the sack in which he supposed the victim to be, but the ring fell off before it could take effect. The Eastern story-teller often balances his multiplicity of words and needless details by a conciseness and an elliptical style which make his meaning a matter of divination.

45. [Burton here cross-references a note to a tale not included in this edition that reads:] Alluding to the Fishár or "Squeeze of the tomb." This is the Jewish Hibbut hakkeber which all must endure, save those who lived in the Holy Land or died on the Sabbath-eve (Friday night). Then comes the questioning by the Angels Munkar and Nakir (vulgarly called Nákir and Nakír) for which see Lane (*M. E.* chap. xviii.). In Egypt a "Mulakkin" (intelligencer) is hired to prompt and instruct the dead. Moslems are beginning to question these facts of their faith: a Persian acquaintance of mine filled his dead father's mouth with flour and finding it *in loco* on opening the grave, publicly derided the belief. But the Mullahs had him on the hip, after the fashion of reverends, declaring that the answers were made through the whole body, not only by the mouth. At last the Voltairean had to quit Shiraz.

THE SLEEPER AND THE WAKER

1. Arab. "Al-Náim wa al-Yakzán." This excellent story is not in the Mac. or Bresl. Edits.; but is given in the Breslau Text, iv. 134–189. It is familiar to readers of the old "Arabian Nights Entertainments" as "Abou-Hassan or the Sleeper Awakened"; and as yet it is the only one of the eleven added by Galland whose original has been discovered in Arabic: the learned Frenchman, however, supplied it with embellishments *more suo*, and seems to have taken it from an original fuller than our text as is shown by sundry poetical and other passages which he apparently did not invent. Lane (vol. ii. chap. 12), noting that its chief and best portion is an historical anecdote related as a fact, is inclined to think that it is not a genuine tale of The Nights. He finds it in Al-Isháki who finished his history about the close of Sultan Mustafá

the Osmanli's reign, circa A.H. 1032 (=1623) and he avails himself of this version as it is "narrated in a simple and agreeable manner." Mr. Payne remarks, ("The above title (Asleep and Awake) is of course intended to mark the contrast between the everyday (or waking) hours of Aboul-husn and his fantastic life in the Khalif's palace, supposed by him to have passed in a dream"; I may add that amongst frolicsome Eastern despots the adventure might often have happened and that it might have given a hint to Cervantes.

2. *i.e.* The Wag. The old version calls him "the Debauchee."

3. Arab. "Al-Fárs"; a people famed for cleverness and debauchery. I cannot see why Lane omitted the Persians, unless he had Persian friends at Cairo.

4. *i.e.* the half he intended for spending-money.

5. *i.e.* "men," a characteristic Arab idiom: here it applies to the sons of all time.

6. *i.e.* make much of thee.

7. In Lane the Caliph is accompanied by "certain of his domestics."

8. Arab. "Khubz Mutabbak,"=bread baked in a platter, instead of in an oven, an earthen jar previously heated, to the sides of which the scones or bannocks of dough are applied: "it is lighter than oven-bread, especially if it be made thin and leavened." See Al-Shakúrí, a medical writer quoted by Dozy.

9. In other parts of The Nights Harun al-Rashid declines wine-drinking.

10. The 'Allámah (doctissimus) Sayce (p. 212, *Comparative Philology*, London, Trübner, 1885) goes far back for Khalifah= a deputy, a successor. He begins with the Semitic (Hebrew?) root "Khaliph"=to change, exchange: hence "Khaleph"= agio. From this the Greeks got their κόλλυβος and Cicero his "Collybus," a money-lender.

11. Arab. "Harfúsh," (in Bresl. Edit. iv. 138, "Kharfúsh"), in popular parlance a "blackguard." I have to thank Mr. Alexander J. Cotheal, of New York, for sending me a MS. copy of this tale.

12. Arab. "Ta'ám," in Egypt and Somaliland=millet seed (*Holcus Sorghum*) cooked in various ways. In Barbary it is applied to the local staff of life, Kuskusú, wheaten or other flour damped and granulated by hand to the size of peppercorns,

and lastly steamed (as we steam potatoes), the cullender-pot being placed over a long-necked jar full of boiling water. It is served with clarified butter, shredded onions and meat; and it represents the Risotto of Northern Italy. Europeans generally find it too greasy for digestion. This Barbary staff of life is of old date and is thus mentioned by Leo Africanus in early sixth century. "It is made of a lump of Dow, first set upon the fire, in a vessel full of holes and afterwards tempered with Butter and Pottage." So says good Master John Pory, *A Geographical Historie of Africa, by John Leo, a Moor,* London, 1600, impensis George Bishop.

13. Arab. "Bi al-Salám" (pron. "Bissalám")=in the Peace (of Allah).

14. And would bring him bad luck if allowed to go without paying.

15. *i.e.* of the first half, as has been shown.

16. Arab. "Kumájah" from the Persian Kumásh=bread unleavened and baked in ashes. Egyptians use the word for bannocks of fine flour.

17. Arab. "Kalí," our "alcali."

18. These lines have occurred twice; I quote Mr. Payne.

19. Arab. "Yá 'llah, yá 'lláh"; vulg. used for "Look sharp!" *e.g.* "Yá 'llah jári, yá walad"="Be off at once, boy."

20. Arab. "Banj akrítashí," a term which has occurred before.

21. A natural clock, called by West Africans Cokkerapeek= Cock-speak. All the world over it is the subject of superstition: see Giles's "Strange Stories from a Chinese Studio" (i. 177), where Miss Li, who is a devil, hears the cock crow and vanishes.

22. In Lane Al-Rashid "found at the door his young men waiting for him and ordered them to convey Abu-l-Hasan upon a mule and returned to the palace; Abu-l-Hasan being intoxicated and insensible. And when the Khaleefeh had rested himself in the palace, he called for," etc.

23. Arab. "Kursi," Assyrian "Kussú"=throne; and "Korsái" in Aramaic (or Nabathean as Al-Mas'udi calls it), the second growth-period of the "Semitic" family, which supplanted Assyrian and Babylonian, and became, as Arabic now is, the common speech of the "Semitic" world.

24. Arab. "Makán mahjúb," which Lane renders by "a private closet," and Payne by a "privy place," suggesting that the Caliph slept in a numéro cent. So, when starting for the "Trakki Campaign," Sir Charles Napier (of Sind), in his zeal

for lightening officers' baggage, inadvertently chose a water-closet tent for his head-quarters—*magno cum risu* not of the staff, who had a strange fear of him, but of the multitude who had not.

25. Arab. "Dar al-Salam," one of the seven "Gardens" into which the Mohammedan Paradise is divided. Man's fabled happiness began in a Garden (Eden) and the suggestion came naturally that it would continue there.

26. Branch of Pearl.

27. Arab. "Kahbah," the lowest word, effectively used in contrast with the speaker's surroundings.

28. Arab. "Yá kabírí,"=mon brave, my good man.

29. This exaggeration has now become familiar to English speech.

30. Like an Eastern he goes to the water-closet the first thing in the morning, or rather dawn, and then washes ceremonially before saying the first prayer. In Europe he would probably wait till after breakfast.

31. I have explained why an Eastern does not wash in the basin as Europeans do in note 97 for "Tale of Nur al-Din and His Son."

32. *i.e.* He was so confused that he forgot. All Moslems know how to pray, whether they pray or not.

33. The dawn-prayer consists of only four inclinations (*raka'át*); two "Farz" (divinely appointed), and two Sunnah (the custom of the Apostle). For the Raka'áh see Lane, M.E. chapt. iii.; it cannot be explained without illustrations.

34. After both sets of prayers, Farz and Sunnah, the Moslem looks over his right shoulder and says "The Peace (of Allah) be upon you and the ruth of Allah," and repeats the words over the left shoulder. The salutation is addressed to the Guardian Angels or to the bystanders (Moslems) who, however, do not return it.

35. *i.e.* Ibrahim of Mosul the musician.

36. Arab. "Líyúth" plur. of "Layth," a lion: here warriors are meant.

37. The Abbasides traced their descent from Al-Abbas, Mohammed's uncle, and justly held themselves as belonging to the family of the Prophet.

38. Arab. "Nímshah"="half-sword."

39. *i.e.* May thy dwelling-place never fall into ruin. The prayer has, strange to say, been granted. "The present city on the

Eastern bank of the Tigris was built by Haroun al-Rashid, and his house still stands there and is an object of reverent curiosity." So says my friend Mr. Grattan Geary (vol. i. p. 212, *Through Asiatic Turkey*, London: Low, 1878). He also gives a sketch of Zubaydah's tomb on the western bank of the Tigris near the suburb which represents old Baghdad: it is a pineapple dome springing from an octagon, both of brick once revetted with white stucco.

40. In the Bresl. Edit. four hundred. I prefer the exaggerated total.

41. *i.e.* the raised recess at the upper end of an Oriental saloon, and the place of honour, which Lane calls by its Egyptian name "Líwán." See his vol. i. 312 and his M.E. chapt. i.

42. "Bit o'Musk."

43. "A gin," a snare.

44. "A gift," a present. It is instructive to compare Abu al-Hasan with Sancho Panza, sprightly Arab wit with grave Spanish humour.

45. *i.e.* he fell down senseless. The old version has "his head knocked against his knees."

46. Arab. "Waddí" vulg. Egyptian and Syrian for the classical "Addí" (ii. of Adú=preparing to do). No wonder that Lane complains (iii. 376) of the "vulgar style, abounding in errors."

47. O Apple, O Repose o' Hearts, O Musk, O Choice Gift.

48. Arab. "Doghrí," a pure Turkish word, in Egypt meaning "truly, with truth," straightforwardly; in Syria=straight (going), directly.

49. Arab. "Máristán."

50. Arab. "Janzir," another atrocious vulgarism for "Zanjír," which, however, has occurred before.

51. Arab. "Arafshah."

52. In the "Mishkát al-Masábih" (ii. 341), quoted by Lane, occurs the Hadis, "Shut your doors anights and when so doing repeat the Basmalah; for the Devil may not open a door shut in Allah's name." A pious Moslem in Egypt always ejaculates, "In the name of Allah, the Compassionating," etc., when he locks a door, covers up bread, doffs his clothes, etc., to keep off devils and dæmons.

53. An Arab idiom meaning, "I have not found thy good fortune (Ka'b=heel, glory, prosperity) do me any good."

54. Arab. "Yá Nakbah"=a calamity to those who have to do with thee!

55. Koran cxii., the "Chapter of Unity."

56. *i.e.* "Delight of the vitals" (or heart).

57. The trick is a rechauffé of the trick played on Al-Rashid and Zubaydah.

58. "Kalb" here is not heart, but stomach. The big toes of the Moslem corpse are still tied in most countries, and in some a sword is placed upon the body; but I am not aware that a knife and salt (both believed to repel evil spirits) are so used in Cairo.

59. The Moslem, who may not wear unmixed silk during his lifetime, may be shrouded in it. I have noted that the "Shukkah," or piece, averages six feet in length.

60. A vulgar ejaculation; the "hour" referring either to birth or to his being made one of the Caliph's equerries.

61. Here the story-teller omits to say that Masrúr bore witness to the Caliph's statement.

62. Arab. "Wa kuntu ráihah ursil warák," the regular Fellah language.

63. Arab. " 'Irk al-Háshimi." Lane remarks, "Whether it was so in Hashim himself (or only in his descendants), I do not find; but it is mentioned amongst the characteristics of his great-grandson, the Prophet."

64. Arab. "Bostán al-Nuzhah," whose name made the stake appropriate.

65. Arab. "Tamásíl"=generally carved images, which, amongst Moslems, always suggest idols and idolatry.

66. The "Shubbák" here would be the "Mashrabiyah," or latticed balcony, projecting from the saloon-wall, and containing room for three or more sitters. It is Lane's "Meshrebeeyeh," sketched in M.E. (Introduction) and now has become familiar to Englishmen.

67. This is to show the cleverness of Abu al-Hasan, who had calculated upon the difference between Al-Rashid and Zubaydah. Such marvels of perspicacity are frequent enough in the folk-lore of the Arabs.

68. An artful touch, showing how a tale grows by repetition. In Abu al-Hasan's case (*infra*) the eyes are swollen by the swathes.

69. A Hadis attributed to the Prophet, and very useful to Moslem husbands when wives differ overmuch with them in opinion.

70. Arab. "Masarat fí-há," which Lane renders, "And she threw money to her."
71. A saying common throughout the world, especially when the afflicted widow intends to marry again at the first opportunity.
72. Arab. "Yá Khálati"=O my mother's sister; addressed by a woman to an elderly dame.
73. *i.e.* That I may put her to shame.
74. Arab. "Zalábiyah."
75. Arab. " 'Alà al-Kaylah," which Mr. Payne renders by "Siesta-carpet." Lane reads "Kiblah" ("in the direction of the Kiblah") and notes that some Moslems turn the corpse's head towards Meccah and others the right side, including the face. So the old version reads "feet towards Mecca." But the preposition "Alà" requires the former sig.
76. Many places in this text are so faulty that translation is mere guess-work; *e.g.* "Bashárah" can hardly be applied to ill-news.
77. *i.e.* of grief for his loss.
78. Arab. "Tobáni" which Lane renders "two clods." I have noted that the Tob (Span. Adobe=At Tob) is a sunbaked brick. Beating the bosom with such material is still common amongst Moslem mourners of the lower class and the hardness of the blow gives the measure of the grief.
79. *i.e.* of grief for her loss.
80. Arab. "Ihtirák" often used in the metaphorical sense of consuming, torturing.
81. Arab. "Haláwat," lit.=a sweetmeat, a gratuity, a thank-offering.

ALAEDDIN; OR, THE WONDERFUL LAMP

1. Arab. " 'Abadan," a term much used in this MS. and used correctly. It refers always and only to future time, past being denoted by "Kattu" from Katta=he cut (in breadth, as opposed to Kadda=he cut lengthwise). See De Sacy, *Chrestom.* ii. 443.
2. In the text "Ibn mín," a vulgarism for "man." Galland adds that the tailor's name was Mustapha—*il y avait un tailleur nommé Mustafa.*
3. In classical Arabic the word is "Maghribi," the local form of the root Gharaba=he went far away, (the sun) set, etc.,

whence "Maghribi"=a dweller in the Sunset-land. The vulgar, however, prefer "Maghrab" and "Maghrabi," of which foreigners made "Mogrebin." The "Moormen" are famed as magicians; so we find a Maghrabi Sahhár=wizard, who by the by takes part in a transformation scene like that of the Second Kalandar, in p. 10 of Spitta Bey's *Contes Arabes Modernes,* etc. I may note that "Sihr," according to Jauhari and Firozábádi=anything one can hold by a thin or subtle place, *i.e.,* easy to handle. Hence it was applied to all sciences, "Sahhár" being=to 'Álim (or sage): and the older Arabs called poetry "Sihr al-halál"—lawful magic.

4. *i.e.* blood is thicker than water, as the Highlanders say.

5. A popular saying amongst Moslems which has repeatedly occurred in The Nights. The son is the "lamp of a dark house."

6. Out of respect to his brother, who was probably the senior: the H.V. expressly says so.

7. Al-Marhúm=my late brother.

8. This must refer to Cairo not to Al-Medinah whose title is "Al-Munawwarah"=the Illumined.

9. A picturesque term for birth-place.

10. In text "Yá Rájul" (for Rajul)=O man, an Egypto-Syrian form, broad as any Doric.

11. Arab. Shúf-hu, the colloquial form of Shuf-hu.

12. For the same sentiment see "Julnar the Sea-born," p. 556.

13. "I will hire thee a shop in the Chauk"—Carfax or market street says the H.V.

14. The MS. writes the word Khwájá for Khwájah. Here we are at once interested in the scapegrace who looked Excelsior. In fact the tale begins with a strong inducement to boyish vagabondage and scampish indolence; but the Moslem would see in it the hand of Destiny bringing good out of evil. Amongst other meanings of "Khwájah" it is a honorific title given by Khorásánis to their notables. In Arab, the similarity of the word to "Khuwáj"=hunger, has given rise to a host of conceits, more or less frigid (Ibn Khallikán, iii. 45).

15. Arab. "Wáhid min al-Tujjár," the very vulgar style.

16. *i.e.* the Saturday established as a God's rest by the so-called "Mosaic" commandment No. 4. How it gradually passed out of observance, after so many centuries of most stringent application, I cannot discover: certainly the text in Cor. ii.

16–17 is insufficient to abolish or supersede an order given with such singular majesty and impressiveness by God and so strictly obeyed by man. The popular idea is that the Jewish Sabbath was done away with in Christ; and that sundry of the 1604 councils, *e.g.* Laodicea, anathematized those who kept it holy after such fashion. With the day the aim and object changed; and the early Fathers made it the "Feast of the Resurrection" which could not be kept too joyously. The "Sabbatismus" of our Sabbatarians, who return to the Israelitic practice and yet honour the wrong day, is heretical and vastly illogical; and the Sunday is better kept in France, Italy and other "Catholic" countries than in England and Scotland.

17. All these words sárú, dakhalú, jalasú, &c. are in the plur. for the dual—popular and vulgar speech. It is so throughout the MS.

18. The Persians apply the Arab word "Sahrá"=desert, to the waste grounds about a town.

19. Arab. Kashákísh from kashkasha=he gathered fuel.

20. In text "Shayy bi-lásh" which would mean lit. a thing gratis or in vain.

21. In the text "Sabba raml"=cast in sand. It may be a clerical error for "Zaraba raml"=he struck sand *i.e.* made geomantic figures.

22. Arab. Mauza'=a place, an apartment, a saloon.

23. Galland makes each contain *quatre vases de bronze, grands comme des cuves.*

24. The Arab. is "Líwán." Galland translates it by a "terrace" and "niche."

25. The idea is borrowed from the *lume eterno* of the Rosicrucians. It is still prevalent throughout Syria where the little sepulchral lamps buried by the Hebrews, Greeks and Romans are so called. Many tales are told of their being found burning after the lapse of centuries: but the traveller will never see the marvel.

26. The first notice of the signet-ring and its adventures is by Herodotus in the Legend of the Samian Polycrates; and here it may be observed that the accident is probably founded on fact; every fisherman knows that fish will seize and swallow spoon-bait and other objects that glitter. The text is the Talmudic version of Solomon's seal-ring. The king of the

demons, after becoming a "Bottle-imp," prayed to be set free upon condition of teaching a priceless secret, and after cajoling the Wise One flung his signet into the sea and cast the owner into a land four hundred miles distant. Here David's son begged his bread till he was made head cook to the King of Ammon at Mash Kernín. After a while, he eloped with Na'úzah, the daughter of his master, and presently when broiling a fish found therein his missing property. In the Moslem version, Solomon had taken prisoner Amínah, the daughter of a pagan prince, and had homed her in his Harem, where she taught him idolatry. One day before going to the Hammam he entrusted to her his signet-ring presented to him by the four angelic Guardians of sky, air, water and earth when the mighty Jinni Al-Sakhr, who was hovering about unseen, snatching away the ring, assumed the king's shape, whereby Solomon's form became so changed that his courtiers drove him from his own doors. Thereupon Al-Sakhr, taking seat upon the throne, began to work all manner of iniquity, till one of the Wazirs, suspecting the transformation, read aloud from a scroll of the law: this caused the demon to fly shrieking and to drop the signet into the sea. Presently Solomon, who had taken service with a fisherman, and received for wages two fishes a day, found his ring and made Al-Sakhr a "Bottle-imp." The legend of St. Kentigern or Mungo of Glasgow, who recovered the Queen's ring from the stomach of a salmon, is a palpable imitation of the Biblical incident which paid tribute to Cæsar.

27. The Magician evidently had mistaken the powers of the Ring. This is against all probability and possibility, but on such abnormal traits are tales and novels founded.

28. These are the Gardens of the Hesperides and of King Isope (Tale of Beryn Supplem. *Canterbury Tales,* Chaucer Soc. p. 84):—

> In mydward of this gardyn stant a feirè tre
> Of alle manner levis that under sky be,
> I-forgit and i-fourmyd, eche in his degre
> Of sylver, and of golde fyne, that lusty been to see.

So in the Kathá (S. S.) there are trees with trunks of gold, branches of pearls, and buds and flowers of clear white pearls.

29. The text causes some confusion by applying "Sullam" to staircase and ladder, hence probably the latter is not mentioned by Galland and Co., who speak only of an *escalier de cinquante marches*. "Sullam" (plur. "Salálim") in modern Egyptian is popularly used for a flight of steps: see Spitta-Bey's *Contes Arabes Modernes*, p. 70. The H. V. places under the slab a hollow space measuring four paces (kadam=25 feet), and at one corner a wicket with a ladder. This leads to a vault of three rooms, one with the jars of gold; the second not to be swept by the skirts, and the third opening upon the garden of gems. "There thou shalt see a path, whereby do thou fare straight forwards to a lofty palace with a flight of fifty steps leading to a flat terrace; and here shalt thou find a niche wherein a lamp burneth."

30. In the H. V. he had thrust the lamp into the bosom of his dress, which, together with his sleeves, he had filled full of fruit, and had wound his girdle tightly around him lest any fall out.

31. Africa (Arab. Afrikíyah) here is used in its old and classical sense for the limited tract about Carthage (Tunis) *i.e.*, Africa Propria. But the scribe imagines it to be the P.N. of a city: so in Judar we find Fás and Miknás (Fez and Mequinez) converted into one settlement. The Maghribi, Mauritanian or Maroccan is famed for sorcery throughout the Moslem world. The Moslem "Kingdom of Afrikiyah" was composed of four provinces, Tunis, Tripoli, Constantina, and Bugia; and a considerable part of it was held by the Berber tribe of Sanhája or Sinhága, also called the Zenag, whence our modern "Senegal." Another noted tribe which held Bajaiyah (Bugia) in Afrikiyah proper was the "Zawáwah," the European "Zouaves." (Ibn Khall. iv. 84.)

32. Galland omits the name, which is outlandish enough.

33. Meaning that he had incurred no blood-guiltiness, as he had not killed the lad and only left him to die.

34. The H. V. explains away the improbability of the Magician forgetting his gift. "In this sore disquietude he bethought him not of the ring which, by the decree of Allah, was the means of Alaeddin's escape; and indeed not only he but oft times those who practice the Black Art are baulked of their designs by Divine Providence."

35. The word is mostly derived from " 'afar"=dust, and denotes,

according to some, a man coloured like the ground or one who "dusts" all his rivals. " 'Ifr" (fem. 'Ifrah) is a wicked and dangerous man. Al-Jannabi, I may here notice, is the chief authority for Afrikus son of Abraha and xviiith Tobba being the eponymus of "Africa."

36. Arab. "Ghayr an"=otherwise that, except that, a favourite form in this MS. The first word is the Syriac "Gheir"=for, a conjunction which is most unnecessarily derived by some from the Gr. γὰρ.

37. Galland and the H. V. make the mother deliver a little hy-gienic lecture about not feeding too fast after famine: ex-actly what an Eastern parent would not dream of doing.

38. The lad now turns the tables upon his mother and becomes her master, having "a crow to pick" with her.

39. Arab. "Munáfik" for whose true sense, "an infidel who pre-tendeth to believe in Al-Islam." Here the epithet comes last being the climax of abuse, because the lowest of the seven hells was created for "hypocrites," *i.e.* those who feign to be Moslems when they are Miscreants.

40. Here a little abbreviation has been found necessary to avoid the whole of a twice-told tale; but nothing material has been omitted.

41. Arab. "Taffaytu-hu." This is the correct term=to extinguish. They relate of the great scholar Firozábádí, author of the *Kámús* (ob. A.H. 817=A.D. 1414), that he married a Badawi wife in order to study the purest Arabic and once when going to bed said to her, "Uktuli's-siráj," the Persian "Chirágh-rá bi-kush"=Kill the lamp. "What," she cried, "Thou an 'Álim and talk of killing the lamp instead of putting it out!"

42. In the H. V. the mother takes the "fruits" and places them upon the ground; "but when darkness set in, a light shone from them like the rays of a lamp or the sheen of the sun."

43. D'Herbelot (s.v. Giabbar=Giant) connects "Jabábirah" with the Heb. Ghibbor, Ghibborim and the Pers. Div, Diván: of these were 'Ád and Shaddád, Kings of Syria: the Falastín (Philistines) 'Auj, Amálik and Banú Shayth or Seth's descen-dants, the sons of God (Benu-Elohim) of the Book of Gene-sis (vi. 2) who inhabited Mount Hermon and lived in purity and chastity.

44. Arab. Musawwadatayn=lit. two black things, rough copies, etc.

45. Arab. Banú Adam, as opposed to Banú Elohim (Sons of the Gods), B. al-Jánn etc. The Banú al-Asfar=sons of the yellow, are Esau's posterity in Edom, also a term applied by Arab historians to the Greeks and Romans whom Jewish fable derived from Idumæa: they are the people of the yellow or tawny faces. For the legend see Ibn Kkall. iii. 8, where the translator suggests that the by-name may be=the "sons of the Emperor" Flavius, confounded with "flavus," a title left by Vespasian to his successors. The Banú al-Khashkhash= sons of the (black) poppy are the Ethiopians.

46. Arab. Há! há! so Háka (fem. Háki)=Here for thee!

47. So in Mediæval Europe Papal bulls and Kings' letters were placed for respect on the head. See Duffield's *Don Quixote*, Part i. xxxi.

48. Galland makes the Juif only *rusé et adroit*.

49. Arab. "Ghashím"=a "Johnny Raw" from the root "Gha-shm"=inquity: Builders apply the word to an unhewn stone; addressed to a person it is considered slighting, if not insulting.

50. The carat (Kírát) being most often, but not always, one twenty-fourth of the dinar.

51. Kanání, plur. of Kinnínah.

52. Here and below silver is specified, when as the platters in [other tales] were of gold. This is one of the many changes, contradictions and confusions which are inherent in Arab stories. See Spitta-Bey's *Contes Arabes*, Preface.

53. *i.e.* the Slave of the Lamp.

54. This may be true, but my experience has taught me to prefer dealing with a Jew than with a Christian. The former will "jew" me perhaps, but his commercial cleverness will induce him to allow me some gain in order that I may not be quite disheartened: the latter will strip me of my skin and will grumble because he cannot gain more.

55. Arab. "Hálah mutawassitah," a phrase which has a European touch.

56. In the text "Jauharjíyyah," common enough in Egypt and Syria; an Arab. plur. of an Arabised Turkish sing,—ji for—chí=(crafts-) man.

57. We may suppose some years may have passed in this process and that Alaeddin from a lad of fifteen had reached the age of manhood. The H. V. declares that for many a twelve-

month the mother and son lived by cotton spinning and the sale of the plate.

58. *i.e.* Full moon of full moons. It is pronounced "Badroo'l-Budoor," hence Galland's "Badr-oul-boudour."

59. In the H. V. Alaeddin "bethought him of a room adjacent to the Baths where he might sit and see the Princess through the door-chinks, when she raised her veil before the handmaids and eunuchs."

60. Such a statement may read absurdly to the West but it is true in the East. "Selim" had seen no woman's face unveiled, save that of his sable mother Rosebud in Morier's Tale of Yeldoz, the wicked woman (*The Mirza*, vol. iii. 135). The H. V. adds that Alaeddin's mother was old and verily had little beauty even in her youth. So at the sight of the Princess he learnt that Allah had created women exquisite in loveliness and heart-ensnaring; and at first glance the shaft of love pierced his heart and he fell to the ground afaint. He loved her with a thousand lives and, when his mother questioned him, "his lips formed no friendship with his speech."

61. "There is not a present (Teshurah) to bring to the Man of God" (1 Sam. ix. 7), and Menachem explains Teshurah as a gift offered with the object of being admitted to the presence. See also the offering of oil to the King in Isaiah lvii. 9. Even in Maundriell's *Day Travels* (p. 26) it was counted uncivil to visit a dignitary without an offering in hand.

62. As we shall see further on, the magical effect of the Ring and the Lamp extend far and wide over the physique and morale of the owner: they turn a "raw laddie" into a finished courtier, warrior, statesman, etc.

63. In Eastern states the mere suspicion of having such an article would expose the suspected at least to torture. Their practical system of treating "treasure trove," as I saw when serving with my regiment in Gujarát (Guzerat), is at once to imprison and "molest" the finder, in order to make sure that he has not hidden any part of his find.

64. Here the MS. text is defective, the allusion is, I suppose, to the Slave of the Lamp.

65. In the H. V. the King retired into his private apartment; and, dismissing all save the Grand Wazir, "took cognisance of special matters" before withdrawing to the Harem.

66. The levée, Divan or Darbár being also a *lit de justice* and a Court of Cassation.

67. All this is expressed by the Arabic in one word "Tamanná." Galland adds *pour marquer qu'il etait prêt à la perdre s'il y man-quait;* and thus he conveys a wrong idea.

68. This would be still the popular address, nor is it considered rude or slighting. In John (ii. 4) "Atto," the Heb. Eshah, is similarly used, not complimentarily, but in popular speech.

69. This sounds ridiculous enough in English, but not in German; *e.g.* Deine Königliche Hoheit is the formula de rigueur when an Austrian officer, who always addresses brother-soldiers in the familiar second person, is speaking to a camarade who is also a royalty.

70. "Suráyyát (lit.=the Pleiades) and "Sham'ádín" a would-be Arabic plur. of the Persian "Sham'adán"=candlestick, chandelier, for which more correctly Sham'adánát is used.

71. *i.e.* betrothed to her—*j'agrée la proposition,* says Galland.

72. Here meaning Eunuch-officers and officials.

73. In the H. V. Alaeddin on hearing this became as if a thunderbolt had stricken him, and, losing consciousness, swooned away.

74. These calls for food at critical times, and oft-recurring allusions to eating are not yet wholly obsolete amongst the civilised of the nineteenth century. The ingenious M. Jules Verne often enlivens a tedious scene by *Dejeunons!* And French travellers, like English, are not unready to talk of food and drink, knowing that the subject is never displeasing to their readers.

75. The H. V. gives a sketch of the wedding. "And when the ceremonies ended at the palace with pomp and parade and pageant, and the night was far spent, the eunuchs led the Wazir's son into the bridal chamber. He was the first to seek his couch; then the Queen, his mother-in-law, came into him leading the bride, and followed by her suite. She did with her virgin daughter as parents are wont to do, removed her wedding-raiment, and donning a night-dress, placed her in her bridegroom's arms. Then, wishing her all joy, she with her ladies went away and shut the door. At that instant came the Jinni," etc.

76. The happy idea of the wedding night in the water-closet is

repeated from the tale of Nur-al-Din Ali Hasan, and the mishap of the Hunchback bridegroom.

77. For the old knightly practice of sleeping with a drawn sword separating man and maid, see Mr. Clouston's *Popular Tales and Fictions,* vol. i. 316. In Poland the intermediary who married by procuration slept alongside the bride in all his armour. The H. V. explains, "He (Alaeddin) also lay a naked sword between him and the Princess, so she might perceive that he was ready to die by that blade should he attempt to do aught of villainy by the bride."

78. Galland says: *Ils ne s'aperçurent que de l'ébranlement du lit et que de leur transport d'un lieu à l'autre: c'était bien assez pour leur donner une frayeur qu'il est aisé d'imaginer.*

79. Galland very unnecessarily makes the Wazir's son pass into the wardrobe (*garderobe*) to dress himself.

80. Professional singing and dancing girls: Properly the word is the fem. of 'Álim=a learned man; but it has been anglicised by Byron's

> "The long chibouque's dissolving cloud supply,
> Where dance the Almahs to wild minstrelsy."
> —(The Corsair, ii. 2.)

They go about the streets with unveiled faces and are seldom admitted into respectable Harems, although on festal occasions they perform in the court or in front of the house; but even this is objected to by the Mrs. Grundy of Egypt. Lane (*M. E.* chap. xviii) derives with Saint Jerome the word from the Heb. or Phœnician Almah=a virgin, a girl, a singing-girl; and thus explains "Alámoth" in Psalms xlvi, and I Chron. xv. 20. Parkhurst (s.v. 'Alamah=an undeflowered virgin), renders Job xxxix. 30, "the way of a man with a maid" (bi-álmah) "The way of a man in his virgin state, shunning youthful lust and keeping himself pure and unspotted."

81. The text reads "Rafa' " (he raised) "al-Bashkhánah" which is a hanging, a curtain. Apparently it is a corruption of the Pers. "Pashkhánah," mosquito-curtain.

82. The father suspected that she had not gone to bed a clean maid.

83. Arab. Aysh=Ayyu Shayyin and Laysh=li ayyi Shayyin. This vulgarism, or rather popular corruption, is of olden date

and was used by such a purist as Al-Mutanabbi in such a phrase as "Aysh Khabara-k?"=how art thou? See Ibn Khallikan, iii. 79.

84. In the H. V. the Minister sends the Chob-dár=rod-bearer, mace-bearer, usher, etc.

85. In the text Sáhal for Sahal, again the broad "Doric" of Syria.

86. Arab. Dahab ramli=gold dust washed out of the sand, *placer*-gold. I must excuse myself for using this Americanism, properly a diluvium or deposit of sand, and improperly (Bartlett) a find of drift gold. The word, like many mining terms in the Far West, is borrowed from the Spaniards; it is not therefore one of the many American vulgarisms which threaten hopelessly to defile the pure well of English speech.

87. Arab. "Ratl," by Europeans usually pronounced "Rotl" (Rotolo).

88. In the H. V. she returns from the bazar; and, "seeing the house filled with so many persons in goodliest attire, marvelled greatly. Then setting down the meat lately bought she would have taken off her veil, but Alaeddin prevented her and said," etc.

89. The word is popularly derived from Serai in Persian= a palace; but it comes from the Span. and Port. *Cerrar*=to shut up, and should be written with the reduplicated liquid.

90. In the H. V. the dresses and ornaments of the slaves were priced at ten millions (Karúr=a crore) of gold coins. I have noticed that Messer Marco "Milione" did not learn his high numerals in Arabia, but that India might easily have taught them to him.

91. Arab. "Ráih yasír," peasant's language.

92. Arab. Ká'ah, the apodyterium or undressing room upon which the vestibule of the Hammam opens. See the plan in Lane's *M. E.* chapt. xvi. The Kár'ah is now usually called "Maslakh"=stripping-room.

93. Arab. "Hammam-hu"=went through all the operations of the Hammam, scraping, kneading, soaping, wiping and so forth.

94. An aphrodisiac. The subject of aphrodisiacs in the East would fill a small library: almost every medical treatise ends in a long disquisition upon fortifiers, provocatives, etc. We may briefly divide them into three great classes. The first is the medicinal, which may be either external or internal. The

second is the mechanical, such as scarification, flagellation, and the application of insects as practised by certain savage races. There is a venerable Joe Miller of an old Brahmin whose young wife always insisted, each time before he possessed her, upon his being stung by a bee in certain parts. The third is magical, superstitious and so forth.

95. This may sound exaggerated to English ears, but a petty Indian Prince, such as the Gáikwár, or Rajah of Baroda, would be preceded in state processions by several led horses all whose housings and saddles were gold studded with diamonds. The sight made one's mouth water.

96. Arab. "Al-Kandíl al-'ajíb": here its magical virtues are specified and remove many apparent improbabilities from the tale.

97. This was the highest of honours. At Abyssinian Harar even the Grandees were compelled to dismount at the door of the royal "compound." See my *First Footsteps in East Africa*, p. 296.

98. "The right hand" seems to me a European touch in Galland's translation, *leur chef mit Aladdin a sa droite.* Amongst Moslems the great man sits in the sinistral corner of the Divan as seen from the door, so the place of honour is to his left.

99. Arab. "Músiká," classically "Musiki"=Μουσική: the Pers. form is "Músikár"; and the Arab. equivalent is Al-Lahn. In the H. V. the King "made a signal and straightway drums (*dhol*) and trumpets (*trafír*) and all manner wedding instruments struck up on every side."

100. Arab. "Marmar Sumáki"=porphyry of which ancient Egypt supplied the finest specimens. I found a vein of it in the Anti-Libanus. Strange to say, the quarries which produced the far-famed giallo antico, verd' antico (serpentine limestone) and rosso antico (mostly a porphyry) worked by the old Nilotes, are now unknown to us.

101. *i.e.* velvets with gold embroidery.

102. The Arabic says, "There was a kiosque with four-and-twenty alcoves (Líwán) all builded of emerald, etc., and one remained with the kiosque (kushk) unfinished." I adopt Galland's reading *salon à vingt-quatre croisées* which are mentioned in the Arab. text towards the end of the tale, and thus avoid the confusion between kiosque and window. In the H. V. there is a domed belvedere (bárah-dari-i-gumbaz-dár),

four-sided, with six doors on each front (*i.e.* twenty-four), and all studded with diamonds, etc.

103. In Persia this is called "Pá-andáz," and must be prepared for the Shah when he deigns to visit a subject. It is always of costly stuffs, and becomes the perquisite of the royal attendants.

104. Here the European hand again appears to me: the Sultan as a good Moslem should have made the Wuzú-ablution and prayed the dawn-prayers before doing anything worldly.

105. Arab. "Fi ghuzúni zálika," a peculiar phrase; Ghazn= a crease, a wrinkle.

106. In the H. V. the King "marvelled to see Alaeddin's mother without her veil and magnificently adorned with costly jewels and said in his mind, 'Methought she was a grey-haired crone, but I find her still in the prime of life and comely to look upon, somewhat after the fashion of Badr al-Budúr.' " This also was one of the miracles of the Lamp.

107. A Joe Miller is told in Western India of an old General Officer boasting his knowledge of Hindostani. "How do you say, Tell a plain story, General?" asked one of the hearers, and the answer was, "Maydán-kí bát bolo!"="speak a word about the plain" (or level space).

108. The prehistoric Arabs.

109. Popularly, Jeríd, the palm-frond used as javelin.

110. In order to keep off the evil eye, one of the functions of iron and steel.

111. The H. V. adds, "Little did the Princess know that the singers were fairies whom the Slave of the Lamp had brought together."

112. Alexander the Great. The H. V. adds, "Then only one man and one woman danced together, one with other, till midnight, when Alaeddin and the Princess stood up; for it was the wont of China in those days that bride and bridegroom perform together in presence of the wedding company."

113. The exceptional reserve of this and other descriptions makes M. H. Zotenberg suspect that the tale was written for one of the Mameluke Princesses: I own to its modesty but I doubt that such virtue would have recommended it to the dames in question. The H. V. adds a few details:—"Then, when the bride and bridegroom had glanced and gazed each at other's face, the Princess rejoiced with excessive joy to be-

hold his comeliness, and he exclaimed, in the courtesy of his gladness, 'O happy me, whom thou deignest, O Queen of the Fair, to honour despite mine unworth, seeing that in thee all charms and graces are perfected.' "

114. The term has not escaped ridicule amongst Moslems. A common fellow having stood in his way the famous wit Abú al-'Ayná asked "What is that?" "A man of the Sons of Adam" was the reply. "Welcome, welcome," cried the other, "Allah grant thee length of days! I deemed that all his sons were dead." See Ibn Khallikan iii. 57.

115. This address to an inanimate object (here a window) is highly idiomatic and must be cultivated by the practical Arabist. In the H. V. the unfinished part is the four-and-twentieth door of the fictitious (ja'alí) palace.

116. This is true Orientalism, a personification or incarnation which Galland did not think proper to translate.

117. Arab. "La'ab al-Andáb"; the latter word is from "Nadb"= brandishing or throwing the javelin.

118. The "mothers" are the prime figures, the daughters being the secondary. For the " 'Ilm al-Raml"=(Science of the sand) our geomancy see D'Herbelot's sub. *Raml* or *Reml.*

119. This is from Galland, whose *certaine boisson chaude* evidently means tea. It is preserved in the H. V.

120. *i.e.* his astrolabe, his "Zíj" or table of the stars, his almanack, etc. For a highly fanciful derivation of the "Arstable" see Ibn Khallikán (iii. 580). He makes it signify "balance or lines (Pers. 'Astur') of the sun," which is called "Láb" as in the case of wicked Queen Láb. According to him the Astrolabe was suggested to Ptolemy by an armillary sphere which had accidentally been flattened by the hoof of his beast: this is beginning late in the day, the instrument was known to the ancient Assyrians. Chardin (*Voyages* ii. 149) carefully describes the Persian variety of—

"The cunning man hight Sidrophil

(as Will. Lilly was called). Amongst other things he wore at his girdle an astrolabe not bigger than the hollow of a man's hand, often two to three inches in diameter and looking at a distance like a medal." These men practised both natural astrology=astronomy, as well as judicial astrology which foretells events and of which Kepler said that "she, albeit a fool, was the daughter of a wise mother, to whose support and life the silly maid was indispensable." Isidore of Seville (A.D. 600–636) was the first to distinguish between the two branches, and they flourished side by side till Newton's day. Hence the many astrological terms in our tongue, *e.g.* consider, contemplate, disaster, jovial, mercurial, saturnine, etc.

121. In the H. V. "New brass-lamps for old ones! who will exchange?" So in the story of the Fisherman's son, a Jew who had been tricked of a cock, offers to give new rings for old rings. See Jonathan Scott's excerpts from the Wortley-Montague MSS. vol. vi. pp. 210–12.

122. The H. V. adds that Alaeddin loved to ride out a-hunting and had left the city eight days whereof three had passed by.

123. Galland makes her say, *Hé bien, folle, veux-tu me dire pourquoi tu ris?* The H. V. renders "Cease, giddyhead, why laughest thou?" and the vulgate "Well, giggler," said the Princess, etc.

124. Nothing can be more improbable than this detail, but upon such abnormal situations almost all stories, even in our most modern "Society-novels," depend and the cause is clear—without them there would be no story. And the modern will, perhaps, suggest that "the truth was withheld for a higher purpose, for the working out of certain ends." In the H. V. Alaeddin, when about to go a-hunting, always placed the Lamp high up on the cornice with all care lest any touch it.

125. The H. V. adds, "The Magician, when he saw the Lamp, at once knew that it must be the one he sought; for he knew that all things, great and small, appertaining to the palace would be golden or silvern."

126. In truly Oriental countries the Wazir is expected to know everything, and if he fail in this easy duty he may find himself in sore trouble.

127. *i.e.*, must be obeyed.

128. We see that "China" was in those days the normal Oriental "despotism tempered by assassination."

129. In the H. V. Alaeddin promises, "if I fail to find and fetch the Princess, I will myself cut off my head and cast it before the throne." Hindus are adepts in suicide and this self-decapitation, which sounds absurd further West, is quite possible to them.

130. In Galland Alaeddin unconsciously rubbed the ring against

un petit roc, to which he clung in order to prevent falling into the stream. In the H. V. "The bank was high and difficult of descent and the youth would have rolled down headlong had he not struck upon a rock two paces from the bottom and remained hanging over the water. This mishap was of the happiest for during his fall he struck the stone and rubbed his ring against it," etc.

131. In the H. V. he said, "First save me that I fall not into the stream and then tell me where is the pavilion thou builtest for her and who hath removed it."

132. The Fellah had a natural fear of being seen in fine gear, which all would have supposed to be stolen goods; and Alaeddin was justified in taking it perforce, because *necessitas non habet legem.* See a similar exchange of dress in Spitta-Bey's *Contes Arabes Modernes,* p. 91. In Galland the peasant when pressed consents; and in the H. V. Alaeddin persuades him by a gift of money.

133. *i.e.* which would take effect in the shortest time.

134. Her modesty was startled by the idea of sitting at meat with a strange man and allowing him to make love to her.

135. In the text Kidí, pop. for Ka-zálika. In the H. V. the Magician replies to the honeyed speech of the Princess, "O my lady, we in Africa have not so gracious customs as the men of China. This day I have learned of thee a new courtesy which I shall ever keep in mind."

136. Galland makes the Princess poison the Maghrabi, which is not gallant. The H. V. follows suit and describes the powder as a mortal poison.

137. His dignity forbade him to walk even the length of a carpet. When Harun al-Rashid made his famous pilgrimage afoot from Baghdad to Meccah (and he was the last of the Caliphs who performed this rite), the whole way was spread with a "Pá-andáz" of carpets and costly cloths.

138. The proverb suggests our "par nobile fratrum," a pair resembling each other as two halves of a split bean.

139. In the H. V. "If the elder Magician was in the East the other was in the West; but once a year, by their skill in geomancy, they had tidings of each other."

140. The act was religiously laudable, but to the Eastern, as to the South European mind, fair play is *not* a jewel; moreover the story-teller may insinuate that vengeance would be taken

only by foul and unlawful means—the Black Art, perjury, murder and so forth.

141. For this game, a prime favourite in Egypt, see De Sacy (*Chrestomathie* i. 477) and his authorities Hyde, *Syntagma Dissert.* ii. 374; P. Labat, *Mémoires du Chev. d'Arvieux,* iii. 321; Thevenot, *Voyage du Levant,* p. 107; and Niebuhr, *Voyages,* 1, 139, Plate 25, fig. H.

142. Evidently "(jeu de) dames" (supposed to have been invented in Paris during the days of the Regency: see Littré); and, although in certain Eastern places now popular, a term of European origin. It is not in Galland. According to Ibn Khallikan (iii. 69) "Nard"=tables, arose with King Ardashír son of Babuk, and was therefore called Nardashír (Nard Ardashir?).

143. Evidently *la force de l'imagination,* of which a curious illustration was given in Paris during the debauched days of the Second Empire. Before a highly "fashionable" assembly of men appeared a youth in fleshings who sat down upon a stool, bared his pudenda and closed his eyes when, by "force of fancy," erection and emission took place. But presently it was suspected and proved that the stool was hollow and admitted from below a hand whose titillating fingers explained the phenomenon.

144. Moslems are curious about sleeping postures and the popular saying is:—Lying upon the right side is proper to Kings, upon the left to Sages; to sleep supine is the position of Allah's Saints and prone upon the belly is peculiar to the Devils.

145. This "'Asá," a staff five to six feet long, is one of the properties of Moslem Saints and reverends who, imitating that furious old Puritan, Caliph Omar, make and are allowed to make a pretty liberal distribution of its caresses.

146. *i.e.* as she was in her own home.

147. Arab. "Sulúk" a Sufistical expression, the road to salvation, &c.

148. In the H. V. her diet consisted of dry bread and fruits.

149. This is the first mention of the windows in the Arabic MS.

150. I may remind the reader that the O. Egyptian "Rokh," or "Rukh," by some written "Rekhit," whose ideograph is a monstrous bird with one claw raised, also denotes pure wise Spirits, the Magi, &c. I know a man who derives from it our "rook"=beak and parson.

151. In the H. V. he takes the Lamp from his bosom, where he had ever kept it since his misadventure with the African Magician.

152. Here the mythical Rukh is mixed up with the mysterious bird Símurgh.

153. The H. V. adds, "hoping thereby that thou and she and all the household should fall into perdition."

154. Rank mesmerism, which has been practised in the East from ages immemorial. In Christendom Santa Guglielma worshipped at Brunate, "works many miracles, chiefly healing aches of head." In the H. V. Alaeddin feigns that he is ill and fares to the Princess with his head tied up.

155. Mr. Morier in *The Mirza* (vol. i. 87) says, "Had the Arabian Nights' Entertainments, with all their singular fertility of invention and never-ending variety, appeared as a new book in the present day, translated literally and not adapted to European taste in the manner attempted in M. Galland's translation, I doubt whether they would have been tolerated, certainly not read with the avidity they are, even in the dress with which he has clothed them, however imperfect that dress may be." But in Morier's day the literal translation was so despised that an Eastern book was robbed of half its charms, both of style and idea.

ALI BABA AND THE FORTY THIEVES

1. Mr. Coote is unable to produce a *puramythe* containing all of "Ali Bába"; but, for the two leading incidents he quotes from Prof. Sakellarios two tales collected in Cyprus. One is Morgiana marking the village doors (p. 187), which has occurred doubtless a hundred times. The other, in the "Story of Drakos," is an ogre, hight "Three Eyes," who attempts the rescue of his wife with a party of blackamoors (μαύρους) packed in bales and these are all discovered and slain.

2. *Dans la forêt*, says Galland.

3. Or "Samsam," The grain=*Sesamum Orientale:* hence the French, *Sésame, ouvre-toi!* The term is cabalistical, like Súlem, Súlam or Shúlam in the *Directorium Vitæ Humanæ* of Johannes di Capuâ: Inquit vir: Ibam in nocte plenilunii et ascendebam super domum ubi furari intendebam, et accedens ad fenestram ubi radii lune ingrediebantur, et dicebam hanc coniu-

rationem, scilicet sulem sulem, septies, deinde amplecte-
bar lumen lune et sine lesione descendebam ad domum, etc.
(pp. 24–25) par Joseph Derenbourg, Membre de l'Institut 1re
Fascicule, Paris, F. Vieweg, 67, Rue de Richelieu, 1887.

4. In the text "Jatháni"=the wife of an elder brother. Hindostani, like other Eastern languages, is rich in terms for
kinship whereof English is so exceptionally poor. Mr. Francis Galtson, in his well-known work *Hereditary Genius,* a mis-
nomer by the by for "Hereditary Talent," felt this want
severely and was at pains to supply it.

5. In the text "Thag," our English "Thug," often pronounced
moreover by the Briton with the sibilant "th." It means
simply a cheat: you say to your servant "Tú bará Thag
hai"=thou art a precious rascal; but it has also the secondary
meaning of robber, assassin, and the tertiary of Bhawáni-
worshippers who offer indiscriminate human sacrifices to
the Deëss of Destruction. The word and the thing have been
made popular in England through the "Confessions of a
Thug" by my late friend Meadows Taylor; and I may record
my conviction that were the English driven out of India,
"Thuggee," like piracy in Cutch and in the Persian Gulf,
would revive at the shortest possible time.

6. *i.e.* the Civil Governor, who would want nothing better.

7. This is in Galland and it is followed by the H. V.; but it
would be more natural to suppose that of the quarters two
were hung up outside the door and the others within.

8. I am unwilling to alter the time honoured corruption: properly it is written Marjánah=the "Coralline," from Marján=
red coral.

9. *i.e.* the " 'Iddah," during which she could not marry.

10. In Galland he is a *savetier ... naturellement gai, et qui avait tou-
jours le mot pour rire:* the H. V. naturally changed him to a tailor as the Chámár or leather-worker would be inadmissible
to polite conversation.

11. *i.e.* a leader of prayer; the Pers. "Pish-namáz"=fore-prayer.
Galland has "imán," which can mean only faith, belief,
and in this blunder he is conscientiously followed by his
translators—servum pecus.

12. Galland nails down the corpse in the bier—a Christian
practice—and he certainly knew better. Moreover, prayers
for the dead are mostly recited over the bier when placed

upon the brink of the grave; nor is it usual for a woman to play so prominent a part in the ceremony.

13. Galland is less merciful, *"Aussitôt le conducteur fut déclaré digne de mort tout d'une voix, et il s'y condamna lui-même,"* etc. The criminal, indeed, condemns himself and firmly offers his neck to be stricken.

14. In the text "Lauh."

15. In Arab. "Káma"=he rose, which, in vulgar speech especially in Egypt,=he began. So in Spitta-Bey's *Contes Arabes Modernes* (p. 124) "Kámat al-Sibhah dhákat fí yad akhí-h"=the chaplet began (lit. arose) to wax tight in his brother's hand. This sense is shadowed forth in classical Arabic.

16. So in old Arabian history "Kasír" (the Little One), the Arab Zopyrus, stows away in huge camel-bags the 2,000 warriors intended to surprise masterful Queen Zebba. *Chronique de Tabari,* vol. ii. 26. Also the armed men in boxes by which Shamar, King of Al-Yaman, took Shamar-kand=Shamar's-town, now Samarkand. (*ibid.* ii. 158.)

17. *i.e.* for a walk, a "constitutional": the phrase is very common in Egypt, and has occurred before.

MA'ARUF THE COBBLER AND HIS WIFE FATIMAH

1. Arab. "Zarábín" (pl. of zarbún), lit. slaves' shoes or sandals, the chaussure worn by Mamelukes. Here the word is used in its modern sense of stout shoes or walking boots.

2. The popular word means goodness, etc.

3. Dozy translates " 'Urrah"=Une Mégère: Lane terms it a "vulgar word signifying a wicked, mischievous shrew." But it is the fem. form of 'Urr=dung; not a bad name for a daughter of Billingsgate.

4. *i.e.,* black like the book of her actions which would be shown to her on Doomsday.

5. The "Kunáfah" (vermicelli-cake) is a favourite dish of wheaten flour, worked somewhat finer than our vermicelli, fried with samn (butter melted and clarified) and sweetened with honey or sugar. Thus distinguishing it from "Asal-kasab," cane honey or sugar.

6. *i.e.,* will send us aid. The shrew's rejoinder is highly impious in Moslem opinion.

7. Arab. Asal Katr; "a fine kind of black honey, treacle," says

Lane; but it is afterwards called cane-honey ('Asal Kasab). I have never heard it applied to "the syrup which exudes from ripe dates, when hung up."

8. Arab. " 'Aysh," lit.=that on which man lives: "Khubz" being the more popular term. "Hubz and Joobn" is well known at Malta.

9. Insinuating that he had better make peace with his wife by knowing her carnally. It suggests the story of the Irishman who brought over to the holy Catholic Church three several Protestant wives, but failed with the fourth on account of the decline of his "Converter."

10. Arab. "Asal Kasab," *i.e.*, sugar, possibly made from sorgho-stalks, *Holcus sorghum,* of which I made syrup in Central Africa.

11. For this unpleasant euphemy see [here Burton cross-references to a note for a tale not included in this edition that reads:] The euphemism has before been noticed: the Moslem reader would not like to pronounce the words, "I am a Nazarene." The same formula occurs a little lower down to save the reciter or reader from saying, "Be *my* wife divorced," etc.

12. This is a true picture of the leniency with which women were treated in the Kazi's court at Cairo; and the effect was simply deplorable. I have noted that matters have grown even worse since the English occupation, for history repeats herself; and the same was the case in Afghanistan and in Sind. We govern too much in these matters, which should be directed, not changed, and too little in other things, especially in exacting respect for the conquerors from the conquered.

13. Arab. "Báb al-'Áli"=the high gate or Sublime Porte; here used of the Chief Kazi's court: the phrase is a descendant of the Coptic "Per-ao" whence "Pharaoh."

14. "Abú Tabak," in Cairene slang, is an officer who arrests by order of the Kazi and means "Father of whipping" (=tabaka, a low word for beating, thrashing, whopping) because he does his duty with all possible violence *in terrorem.*

15. Bab al-Nasr, the Eastern or Desert Gate: see note 26 to "Judar and His Brethren."

16. This is a mosque outside the great gate built by Al-Malik al-'Ádil Túmán Bey in A.H. 906 (=1501). The date is *not* wor-

thy of much remark for these names are often inserted by the scribe.

17. Arab. " 'Ámir," lit.=one who inhabiteth, a peopler; here used in technical sense. As has been seen, ruins and impure places such as privies and Hammám-baths are the favourite homes of the Jinn. The fire-drake in the text was summoned by the cobbler's exclamation and even Marids at times do a kindly action.

18. The style is modern Cairene jargon.

19. Purses or gold pieces; [here Burton cross-references a note to a tale not included in this edition that reads:] Arab. "Tájir Alfí" which may mean a thousand dinars (£500) or a thousand purses (=£5,000). "Alfí" is not an uncommon p.n., meaning that the bearer (Pasha or pauper) had been bought for a thousand left indefinite.

20. *i.e.*, I am a Cairene.

21. Arab. "Darb al-Ahmar," a street still existing near to and outside the noble Bab Zuwaylah, for which see [here Burton refers to a note to a tale not included in this edition that reads:] More correctly Bab Zawilah from the name of a tribe in Northern Africa. This gate dates from the same age as the Eastern or Desert gate, Bab al-Nasr (A.D. 1087) and is still much admired. M. Jomard describes it (*Description*, etc., ii. 670) and lately my good friend Yacoub Artin Pasha has drawn attention to it in Bulletin de l'Inst. Egypt., Deuxième Série, No. 4, 1883.

22. Arab. " 'Attár," perfume-seller and druggist; the word is connected with our "ottar" ('Atr).

23. Arab. "Mudarris," lit.=one who gives lessons or lectures (dars) and pop. applied to a professor in a collegiate mosque like Al-Azhar of Cairo.

24. This thoroughly dramatic scene is told with a charming naïveté. No wonder that The Nights has been made the basis of a national theatre amongst the Turks.

25. Arab. "Taysh," lit.=vertigo, swimming of head.

26. Here Trébutien (iii. 265) reads "la ville de Khaïtan (so the Mac. Edit. iv. 708) capital du royaume de Sohatan." "Ikhti-yán" Lane suggests to be fictitious: Khatan is a district of Tartary east of Káshgar, so called by Sádik al-Isfaháni, p. 24.

27. This is a true picture of the tact and *savoir faire* of the

Cairenes. It was a study to see how, under the late Khedive, they managed to take precedence of Europeans who found themselves in the background before they knew it. For instance, every Bey, whose degree is that of a Colonel, was made an "Excellency" and ranked accordingly at Court, whilst his father, some poor Fellah, was ploughing the ground. Tanfík Pasha began his ill-omened rule by always placing natives close to him in the place of honour, addressing them first and otherwise snubbing Europeans who, when English, were often too obtuse to notice the petty insults lavished upon them.

28. Arab. "Kathír" (pron. Katir)=much: here used in its slang sense, "no end."

29. *i.e.*, "May the Lord soon make thee able to repay me; but meanwhile I give it to thee for thy own free use."

30. Punning upon his name. Much might be written upon the significance of names as ominous of good and evil; but the subject is far too extensive for a footnote.

31. Lane translates "Ánisa-kum" by "he hath delighted you by his arrival"; Mr. Payne, "I commend him to you."

32. Arab. "Fatúrát,"=light food for the early breakfast of which the "Fatírah"-cake was a favourite item. See [here Burton cross-references a note to a tale not included in this edition that reads:] This "Futur" is the real "breakfast" of the East, the "Chhoti házri" (petit déjeuner) of India, a bit of bread, a cup of coffee or tea, and a pipe on rising. In the text, however, it is a ceremonious affair.

33. A dark red dye (Lane).

34. Arab. "Jadíd"; see [here Burton cross-references a note to a tale not included in this edition that reads:] Arab. "Judad," plur. of Jadíd, lit.=new coin, ergo applied to those old and obsolete; 10 Judad were=one nusf or half dirham.

35. Both the texts read thus, but the reading has little sense. Ma'aruf probably would say, "I fear that my loads will be long coming."

36. One of the many formulas of polite refusal.

37. Each bazar, in a large city like Damascus, has its tall and heavy wooden doors which are locked every evening and opened in the morning by the Ghafir or guard. The "silver key," however, always lets one in.

38. Arab. "Wa lá Kabbata hámiyah," a Cairene vulgarism mean-

ing, "There came nothing to profit him nor to rid the people
of him."

39. Arab. "Kammir," *i.e.*, brown it before the fire, toast it.

40. It is insinuated that he had lied till he himself believed
the lie to be truth—not an uncommon process, I may remark.

41. Arab. "Rijál"=the Men, equivalent to the Walis, Saints or
Santons; with perhaps an allusion to the Rijál al-Ghayb, the
Invisible Controls concerning whom I have quoted Herklots
in [here Burton refers to a note to a tale not included in this
edition that reads:] Arab. "Rijál al-Ghayb," somewhat like
the "Himalayan Brothers" of modern superstition. See
Herklots (Qanoon-e-Islam) for a long and careful description of these "Mardán-i-Ghayb" (Pers.), a "class of people
mounted on clouds," invisible, but moving in a circular orbit
round the world; and suggesting the Hindu "Lokapálas."
They should not be in front of the traveller nor on his right,
but either behind or on his left hand. Hence tables, memorial couplets and hemistichs are required to ascertain the
station, without which precaution journeys are apt to end
badly.

42. A saying attributed to Al-Hariri (Lane). It is good enough to
be his: the Persians say, "Cut not down the tree thou plant-
edst," and the idea is universal throughout the East.

43. A quotation from Al-Hariri (*Ass. of the Badawin*). Ash'ab (ob.
A.H. 54), a Medinite servant of Caliph Osman, was proverbial for greed and sanguine, Micawber-like expectation of
"windfalls." The Scholiast Al-Sharíshi (of Xeres) describes
him in Theophrastic style. He never saw a man put hand to
pocket without expecting a present, or a funeral go by without hoping for a legacy, or a bridal procession without
preparing his own house, hoping they might bring the bride
to him by mistake. . . . When asked if he knew aught greed-
ier than himself he said, "Yes; a sheep I once kept upon my
terrace-roof, seeing a rainbow, mistook it for a rope of hay
and jumping to seize it broke its neck!" Hence "Ash'ab's
sheep" became a byword (Preston tells the tale in full,
p. 288).

44. *i.e.*, "Show a miser money and hold him back, if you can."

45. He wants £40,000 to begin with.

46. Arab. "Sabíhat al-'urs," the morning after the wedding.

47. Another sign of modern composition as in Kamar al-Zaman II.

48. Arab. "Al-Jink" (from Turk.) are boys and youths, mostly Jews, Armenians, Greeks and Turks, who dress in woman's dress with long hair braided. Lane (*M. E.* chaps. xix. and xxv.) gives some account of the customs of the "Gink" (as the Egyptians call them) but cannot enter into details concerning these catamites. Respectable Moslems often employ them to dance at festivals in preference to the Ghawázi-women, a freak of Mohammedan decorum. When they grow old they often preserve their costume, and a glance at them makes a European's blood run cold.

49. Lane translates this, "May Allah and the Rijal retaliate upon thy temple!"

50. As we should say, "play fast and loose."

51. Arab. "Náhí-ka," lit.=thy prohibition, but idiomatically used=let it suffice thee!

52. A character-sketch like that of Princess Dunya makes ample amends for a book full of abuse of women. And yet the superficial say that none of the characters have much personal individuality.

53. This is indeed one of the touches of nature which makes all the world kin.

54. As we are in Tartary, "Arabs" here means plundering nomads, like the Persian "Iliyát" and other shepherd races.

55. The very cruelty of love which hates nothing so much as a rejected lover. The Princess, be it noted, is not supposed to be merely romancing, but speaking with the second sight, the clairvoyance, of perfect affection. Men seem to know very little upon this subject, though every one has at times been more or less startled by the abnormal introvision and divination of things hidden which are the property and prerogative of perfect love.

56. Euphemistic: "I will soon fetch thee food." To say this bluntly might have brought misfortune.

57. Arab. "Kafr"=a village in Egypt and Syria, *e.g.*, Capernaum (Kafr Nahum).

58. He has all the bonhomie of the Cairene and will do a kindness whenever he can.

59. *i.e.*, the Father of Prosperities: pron. Aboosa'ádát; as in the "Tale of Hasan of Bassorah."

60. *Koran,* lxxxix. "The Daybreak" which also mentions Thamud and Pharaoh.

61. In Egypt the cheapest and poorest of food, never seen at a hotel table d'hôte.

62. The beautiful girls who guard ensorcelled hoards; see note 30 for "The City of Brass."

63. Arab. "Asákir," the ornaments of litters, which are either plain balls of metal or tapering cones based on crescents or on balls and crescents. See in Lane (*M. E.* chap. xxiv.) the sketch of the Mahmal.

64. Arab. "Amm"=father's brother, courteously used for "father-in-law," which suggests having slept with his daughter, and which is indecent in writing. Thus by a pleasant fiction the husband represents himself as having married his first cousin.

65. *i.e.,* a calamity to the enemy: see [Burton here refers to a note for a tale that is not included in this edition. It reads:] "Dawáhí," plur. of Dáhiyah=a mishap.

66. Both texts read "Asad" (lion) and Lane accepts it: there is no reason to change it for "Hásid" (Envier), the Lion being the Sultan of the Beasts and the most majestic.

67. The Cairene knew his fellow Cairene and was not to be taken in by him.

68. Arab. "Hizám": Lane reads "Khizám"=a nose-ring for which see appendix to Lane's *M. E.* The untrained European eye dislikes these decorations and there is certainly no beauty in the hoops which Hindu women insert through the nostrils, camel-fashion, as if to receive the cord-acting bridle. But a drop-pearl hanging to the septum is at least as pretty as the heavy pendants by which some European women lengthen their ears.

69. Arab. "Shamtá," one of the many names of wine, the "speck-led" alluding to the bubbles which dance upon the freshly filled cup.

70. *i.e.,* in the cask. These "merry quips" strongly suggest the dismal toasts of our not remote ancestors.

71. Arab. "A'láj," plur. of " 'Ilj" and rendered by Lane "the stout foreign infidels." The next line alludes to the cupbearer who was generally a slave and a non-Moslem.

72. As if it were a bride. See [Burton here refers to a note to a tale not included in this edition. It reads:] Arab. "Ijtilá"=the

displaying of the bride on her wedding night so often alluded to in The Nights. The stars of Jauzá (Gemini) are the cupbearer's eyes.

73. Compare the charming song of Abu Miján translated from the German of Dr. Weil in Bohn's Edit. of Ockley (p. 149),

> When the Death-angel cometh mine eyes to close,
> Dig my grave 'mid the vines on the hill's fair side;
> For though deep in earth may my bones repose,
> The juice of the grape shall their food provide.
> Ah, bury me not in a barren land,
> Or Death will appear to me dread and drear!
> While fearless I'll wait what he hath in hand
> An the scent of the vineyard my spirit cheer.

> The glorious old drinker!

74. Arab. "Rub'a al-Kharáb," in Ibn al-Wardi Central Africa south of the Nile sources, one of the richest regions in the world. Here it prob. alludes to the Rub'a al-Khálí or Great Arabian Desert: for which see [Burton here refers to a note to a tale not included in this edition. It reads:] Arab. "Ruba'-al-Kharáb" or Ruba'al-Khálí (empty quarter), the great central wilderness of Arabia covering some 50,000 square miles and still left white on our maps. (*Pilgrimage*, i. 14.) In rhetoric it is opposed to the "Rub'a Maskún," or populated fourth of the world, the rest being held to be ocean.

75. This is the noble resignation of the Moslem. What a dialogue there would have been in a European book between man and devil!

76. Arab. "Al-'iddah," the period of four months and ten days which must elapse before she could legally marry again. But this was a palpable wile: she was not sure of her husband's death and he had not divorced her; so that although a "grass widow," a "Strohwitwe" as the Germans say, she could not wed again either with or without interval.

77. Here the silence is of cowardice and the passage is a fling at the "time-serving" of the Olema, a favourite theme, like "banging the bishops" amongst certain Westerns.

78. Arab. "Umm al-raas," the poll, crown of the head, here the place where a calamity coming down from heaven would first alight.

79. From Al-Hariri (Lane): the lines are excellent.

80. When the charming Princess is so ready at the *voie de faits,* the reader will understand how common is such energetic action among women of lower degree. The "fair sex" in Egypt has a horrible way of murdering men, especially husbands, by tying them down and tearing out the testicles. See Lane, *M. E.* chap. xiii.

81. Arab. "Sijn al-Ghazab," the dungeons appropriated to the worst of criminals where they suffer penalties far worse than hanging or guillotining.

82. Very simple and pathetic is this short sketch of the noble-minded Princess's death.

83. In sign of dismissal; I have noted that "throwing the kerchief" is not an Eastern practice: the idea probably arose from the Oriental practice of sending presents in richly embroidered napkins and kerchiefs. [After "noted," above, Burton refers to a note to a tale not included in this edition. It reads:] This shaking the kerchief is a signal to disperse and the action suggests its meaning. Thus it is used in an opposite sense to "throwing the kerchief," a pseudo-Oriental practice whose significance is generally understood in Europe.

84. Curious to say, both Lane and Payne omit this passage which appears in both texts (Mac. and Bul.). The object is evidently to prepare the reader for the ending by reverting to the beginning of the tale; and its prolixity has its effect as in the old romances of chivalry from Amadis of Gaul to the Seven Champions of Christendom. If it provoke impatience, it also heightens expectation; "it is like the long elm-avenues of our forefathers; we wish ourselves at the end; but we know that at the end there is something great."

85. Arab. "alà malákay bayti 'l-ráhah"; on the two slabs at whose union are the round hole and longitudinal slit. See note 51 to "Nur al-Din Ali and His Son."

86. Here the exclamation wards off the Evil Eye from the Sword and the wearer: Mr. Payne notes, "The old English exclamation, 'Cock's 'ill!' (*i.e.,* God's will, thus corrupted for the purpose of evading the statute of 3 Jac. I against profane swearing) exactly corresponds to the Arabic"—with a difference, I add.

87. Arab. "Mustahakk"=deserving (Lane) or worth (Payne) the cutting.

88. Arab. "Mashhad," the same as "Sháhid"=the upright stones at the head and foot of the grave. Lane mistranslates, "Made for her a funeral procession."

89. These lines have occurred before. I quote Lane.

90. There is nothing strange in such sudden elevations amongst Moslems and even in Europe we still see them occasionally. The family in the East, however humble, is a model and miniature of the state, and learning is not always necessary to wisdom.

CONCLUSION

1. Arab. "Fárid," which may also mean "union-pearl."

2. Trébutien (iii. 497) cannot deny himself the pleasure of a French touch, making the King reply, "C'est assez; qu'on lui coupe la tête, car ces dernières histoires surtout m'ont causé un ennui mortel." This reading is found in some of the MSS.

3. After this I borrow from the Bresl. Edit., inserting passages from the Mac. Edit.

4. *i.e.*, whom he intended to marry with regal ceremony.

5. The use of coloured powders in sign of holiday-making is not obsolete in India. See Herklots for the use of "Huldee" (Haldí) or turmeric-powder, pp. 64–65.

6. Many Moslem families insist upon this before giving their girls in marriage, and the practice is still popular amongst many Mediterranean peoples.

7. *i.e.*, Sumatran.

8. *i.e.*, Alexander, according to the Arabs; see [here Burton refers to a note to a tale not included in this edition. It reads:] the Koranic and our mediæval Alexander, Lord of the two Horns (East and West) much "Matagrobolized" and very different from him of Macedon. The title is variously explained, from two protuberances on his head or helm, from two long locks and, possibly, from the ram-horns of Jupiter Ammon. The anecdote in the text seems suggested by the famous interview (probably a *canard*) with Diogenes: see in the *Gesta*, Tale cxlvi., "The answer of Diomedes the Pirate to Alexander." Iskandar was originally called Marzbán (Lord of the Marches), son of Marzabah; and, though descended from Yunán, son of Japhet, the eponymus of the Greeks, was born obscure, the son of an old woman.

According to the Persians he was the son of the Elder Dáráb (Darius Codomannus of the Kayanian or Second dynasty), by a daughter of Philip of Macedon; and was brought up by his grandfather. When Abraham and Isaac had rebuilt the Ka'abah they foregathered with him and Allah sent him forth against the four quarters of the earth to convert men to the faith of the Friend or to cut their throats; thus he became one of the four world-conquerors with Nimrod, Solomon, Bukht al-Nasr (Nabochodonosor); and he lived down two generations of men. His Wazir was Aristú (the Greek Aristotle) and he carried a couple of flags, white and black, which made day and night for him and facilitated his conquests. At the end of Persia, where he was invited by the people, on account of the cruelty of his half brother Darab II, he came upon two huge mountains on the same line, behind which dwelt a host of abominable pygmies, two spans high, with curious eyes, ears which served as mattresses and coverlets, huge fanged mouths, lions' claws and hairy hind quarters. They ate men, destroyed everything, copulated in public and had swarms of children. These were Yájúj and Májúj (Gog and Magog) descendants of Japhet. Sikandar built against them the famous wall with stones cemented and riveted by iron and copper. The "Great Wall" of China, the famous bulwark against the Tartars, dates from 320 B.C. (Alexander of Macedon died 324 B.C.); and as the Arabs knew Canton well before Mohammed's day, they may have built their romance upon it. The Guebres consigned Sikandar to hell for burning the Nusks or sections of the Zendavesta.

9. All these coquetries require as much inventiveness as a cotillion; the text alludes to fastening the bride's tresses across her mouth giving her the semblance of beard and mustachios.

10. Arab. Sawád=the blackness of the hair.

11. Because Easterns build, but never repair.

12. *i.e.,* God only knows if it be true or not.

COMMENTARY

JOHN ADDINGTON SYMONDS

SIR RICHARD F. BURTON

THE NATION

ALGERNON CHARLES SWINBURNE

LADY ISABEL BURTON

Burton's translation of The Arabian Nights *was a much anticipated work which, when it was finally published, met a stormy and varied reception. While there were many critics who loved the work for its scholarly completeness and faithfulness to the original text, there were just as many who censured it for its unseemly content. The following quotes and extracts from various sources provide insight into the critical response elicited by Burton's frank and literal translation.*

JOHN ADDINGTON SYMONDS

John Addington Symonds was a well-known critic and historian in the nineteenth century who argues in the following excerpt that it is inconsistent to censor Burton's translation of The Arabian Nights *while allowing free access to complete texts of classical literature.*

There is an outcry in some quarters against Captain Burton's translation of the *Arabian Nights.* Only one volume of that work has reached me, and I have not as yet read the whole of it. Of the translator's notes I will not speak, the present sample being clearly insufficient to judge by; but I wish to record a protest against the hypocrisy which condemns his text. When we invite our youth to read an unexpurgated Bible (in Hebrew and Greek, or in the authorised version), an unexpurgated Aristophanes, an unexpurgated Juvenal, an unexpurgated Boccaccio, an unexpurgated Rabelais, an unexpurgated collection of Elizabethan dramatists, including Shakespeare, and an unexpurgated Plato (in Greek or in Prof. Jowett's English version), it is surely inconsistent to exclude the unexpurgated *Arabian Nights,* whether in the original or in any English version, from the studies of a nation who rule India and administer Egypt.

The qualities of Capt. Burton's translation are similar to those of his previous literary works, and the defects of those qualities are also similar. Commanding a vast and miscellaneous vocabulary, he takes such pleasure in the use of it that sometimes he transgresses the unwritten laws of artistic harmony. From the point of view of language, I hold that he is too eager to seize the *mot propre* of his author, and to render that by any equivalent which comes to hand from field or fallow, waste or warren, hill or hedgerow, in our vernacular. Therefore, as I think, we find some coarse passages of the *Arabian Nights* rendered with unnecessary crudity, and some poetic passages marred by archaisms or provincialisms. But I am at a loss to perceive how Burton's method of translation should be less applicable to the *Arabian Nights* than to the *Lusiad*. . . .

This, however, is a minor point. The real question is whether a word-for-word version of the *Arabian Nights*, executed with peculiar literary vigour, exact scholarship, and rare insight into Oriental modes of thought and feeling, can under any shadow of pretence be classed with "the garbage of the brothels." In the lack of lucidity, which is supposed to distinguish English folk, our middle-class censores morum strain at the gnat of a privately circulated translation of an Arabic classic, while they daily swallow the camel of higher education based upon minute study of Greek and Latin literature. When English versions of Theocritus and Ovid, of Plato's *Phaedrus* and the *Ecclesiazusae*, now within the reach of every schoolboy, have been suppressed, then and not till then can a "plain and literal" rendering of the *Arabian Nights* be denied with any colour of consistency to adult readers. I am far from saying that there are not valid reasons for thus dealing with Hellenic and Graeco-Roman and Oriental literature in its totality. But let folk reckon what Anglo-Saxon Puritanism logically involves. If they desire an Anglo-Saxon Index Librorum Prohibitorum, let them equitably and consistently apply their principles of inquisitorial scrutiny to every branch of human culture.

The Academy, 1885

SIR RICHARD F. BURTON

Expressing similar ideas to those of Symonds, Burton himself defends his translation of The Arabian Nights *by saying that, if his translation is to be justly censured, the bulk of great literature would have to come under heavy scrutiny. This well-known quote has appeared in many biographies of Burton, most notably in that written by Isabel Burton shortly after his death.*

I have not only preserved the spirit of the original, but the mécanique. I don't care a button about being prosecuted, and if the matter comes to a fight, I will walk into court with my Bible and my Shakespeare and my Rabelais under my arm, and prove to them that before they condemn me, they must cut half of them out, and not allow them to be circulated to the public.

THE NATION

Fairly rare among criticisms of The Arabian Nights, *this excerpt attacks Burton's writing style rather than the content of his translation. It appeared as the first of a series of critical essays dealing with the history of the translation of* The Arabian Nights *into European languages.*

To the English reader it gives no true idea of the original, and nothing could be further from being an English classic. No one will ever delight in it; many will study it. Perversities of style make it unreadable for its own sake. Such phrases as "a red cent," "belle and beldame," "a veritable beauty of a man," "O, my cuss," "thy hubby," "a Charley," may possibly have Arabic equivalents, but certainly cannot render those for us. No illusion can survive such barbarisms. The long, lumbering lope of its verses, too, is only a degree better than Lane's prose. Its futilities of annotation are a perpetual menace. The fate of the Household Edition brings all to a point: when deprived of unpublishable matter and relying solely on its English value, the book was a flat failure.

From "On Translating 'The Arabian Nights,' " 1890

ALGERNON CHARLES SWINBURNE

Swinburne was one of the greatest and most renowned poets of the nineteenth century and a friend of Burton. Shortly after the completion of the first volume of The Arabian Nights, *he composed this sonnet to commemorate the occasion and congratulate Burton for his achievement.*

TO RICHARD F. BURTON.
On his Translation of the Arabian Nights.

Westward the sun sinks, grave and glad; but far
    Eastward, with laughter and tempestuous tears,
    Cloud, rain, and splendour as of Orient spears,
Keen as the sea's thrill toward a kindling star
The sundawn breaks the barren twilight's bar
    And fires the mist and slays it. Years on years
Vanish, but he that hearkens eastward hears
Bright music from the world where shadows are.
Where shadows are not shadows. Hand-in-hand
A man's word bids them rise and smile and stand
    And triumph. All that glorious Orient glows
Defiant of the dusk. Our twilight land
    Trembles; but all the heaven is all one rose,
    Whence laughing love dissolves her frosts and snows.

From *The Athenaeum*, 1886

LADY ISABEL BURTON

The following passage is excerpted from Isabel Burton's biography of her husband, which was published shortly after his death and provides one of the few sources of information concerning Burton's personal life. Isabel Burton has come under a great deal of criticism for her unsympathetic attitude toward her husband's work. This statement dated to before her husband's death and concerns The Arabian Nights—*a work she was later to edit and reissue in a second edition shortly after he died.*

I have never read, nor do I intend to read, at his own request, and to be true to my promise to him, my husband's "Arabian Nights." But I have read the reviews, some with pride and some with pain, while all the private letters of congratulation have been a great source of gratification to me; and I have gathered all together, pro and con, which form an interesting book.

Out of a thousand picked scholars it is something to be able to assert that all the men whose good opinion is worth having, are loud in its praise. I think a man who gives years of study to a great work, purely with the motive that the rulers of his country may thoroughly understand the peoples they are governing by millions, and who gives that knowledge freely and unselfishly, and who while so doing runs the gauntlet of abuse from the vulgar, silly Philistine, who sees what the really pure and modest never see, deserves great commendation. To throw mud at him because the mediæval Arab lacks the varnish of our world of to-day, is as foolish as it would be not to look up because there are a few spots on the sun.

READING GROUP GUIDE

1. To the minds of a Western audience, *The Arabian Nights* is the most important work we have from medieval Arabic. Its influence can be seen throughout Western culture, from references in *Jane Eyre* to the plots of cartoons. What are some examples of the direct influence *The Arabian Nights* has had on Western literature or culture? Why did readers, then and now, enjoy it?

2. Burton has been quoted as having said, "The main difficulty, however, is to erase the popular impression that the 'Nights' is a book for babies, a 'classic for children'; whereas its lofty morality, its fine character-painting, its artful development of the story, and its original snatches of rare poetry, fit it for the reading of men and women, and these, too, of no puerile or vulgar wit. In fact, its prime default is that it flies too high." How does one account for the fact that, historically, *The Arabian Nights* has been seen as a children's book? Is it more appropriate for adults than for children given its content and depth? What are the main attributes that make it suitable for either audience?

3. The structure of *The Arabian Nights* is an entire study in itself. Debate has raged over the tales' relation to one another and to the overall structure of the work. Is the narrative structure effective? Are the tales related to one another or are they simply

a mixture of unrelated stories bound by a narrative created solely for that purpose? How important is the setting of *The Arabian Nights* to the interpretation of each individual tale?

4. One of the most important moral concepts in *The Arabian Nights* is that of fidelity. From the very beginning of the work, fidelity is the driving force that binds the brothers together and that provides the backdrop for the telling of the tales. Fidelity of all kinds is explored in *The Arabian Nights:* that between a husband and wife, between brothers, and between a lord and his servant. Describe different depictions of fidelity in specific tales and explain how they are central to the advancement of the plot and the characters. Why is such a high premium placed on fidelity throughout the book?

5. Morals and ethics are among the most important subjects dealt with throughout *The Arabian Nights*. Describe the moral system as it is depicted throughout the course of the book, giving examples of important moral concepts in specific tales. How do the morals serve to propel the plot of the tales? How can one reconcile the bawdiness of these tales with the serious moral and ethical messages conveyed? Does the overt sexuality and "inappropriate" content reduce in any way the impact or importance of these moral messages?

A NOTE ON THE TYPE

The principal text of this Modern Library edition
was set in a digitized version of Janson, a typeface that
dates from about 1690 and was cut by Nicholas Kis,
a Hungarian working in Amsterdam. The original matrices have
survived and are held by the Stempel foundry in Germany.
Hermann Zapf redesigned some of the weights and sizes for
Stempel, basing his revisions on the original design.

MODERN LIBRARY IS ONLINE AT WWW.MODERNLIBRARY.COM

MODERN LIBRARY ONLINE IS YOUR GUIDE
TO CLASSIC LITERATURE ON THE WEB

THE MODERN LIBRARY E-NEWSLETTER

Our free e-mail newsletter is sent to subscribers, and features sample chapters, interviews with and essays by our authors, upcoming books, special promotions, announcements, and news.

To subscribe to the Modern Library e-newsletter, send a blank e-mail to: sub_modernlibrary@info.randomhouse.com or visit www.modernlibrary.com

THE MODERN LIBRARY WEBSITE

Check out the Modern Library website at
www.modernlibrary.com for:

- The Modern Library e-newsletter
- A list of our current and upcoming titles and series
- Reading Group Guides and exclusive author spotlights
- Special features with information on the classics and other paperback series
- Excerpts from new releases and other titles
- A list of our e-books and information on where to buy them
- The Modern Library Editorial Board's 100 Best Novels and 100 Best Nonfiction Books of the Twentieth Century written in the English language
- News and announcements

Questions? E-mail us at modernlibrary@randomhouse.com
For questions about examination or desk copies, please visit
the Random House Academic Resources site at
www.randomhouse.com/academic